THE GOOD

CD
1992

GUIDE

THE GOOD

CD

1992

GUIDE

Published by

General Gramophone

Publications Ltd

177-179 Kenton Road

Harrow Middlesex HA3 0HA

Great Britain

in association with

Quad Electroacoustics Ltd

© General Gramophone Publications Ltd 1991
ISBN 0-902470-34-5

Recording companies reserve the right to
withdraw any Compact Disc without giving
previous notice, and although every effort is
made to obtain the latest information for inclusion
in this book, no guarantee can be given that all the
discs listed are immediately available. Any
difficulties should be referred to the issuing
company concerned. When ordering, purchasers
are advised to quote all the relevant information
in addition to the disc numbers. The publishers
cannot accept responsibility for the consequences
of any error.

The Good CD Guide is published by General Gramophone Publications Ltd in association with Quad Electroacoustics Ltd. The publishers gratefully acknowledge their help with this venture.

Editor   Christopher Pollard

Reviews Editor   Máire Taylor

Editorial Consultant   Robert Seeley

Production Editors   Dermot Jones, Ivor Humphreys

Contributors   Nicholas Anderson, Mary Berry, Alan Blyth, Joan Chissell, John Duarte, Jessica Duchen, David Fallows, David Fanning, Edward Greenfield, David Gutman, Douglas Hammond, Christopher Headington, Stephen Johnson, James Jolly, Lindsay Kemp, Michael Kennedy, Andrew Lamb, Robert Layton, Ivan March, John Milsom, Michael Oliver, Marc Rochester, Julie-Anne Sadie, Stanley Sadie, Alan Sanders, Edward Seckerson, John Steane, Michael Stewart, Jonathan Swain, Arnold Whittall and Richard Wigmore.

Designed by RSCG Conran Design Ltd., The Clove Building, 4 Maguire Street, London SE1 2NQ

GRAMOPHONE   Typeset on Acorn Archimedes computers using Impression II by Computer Concepts Ltd., Gaddesden Place, Hemel Hemptsead, Herts HP2 6EX

Printed in Great Britain by Pindar Graphics Plc, Thornburgh Road, Eastfield, Scarborough, YO11 3UY

Contents

THE GOOD CD 1992 GUIDE

Introduction

There are too many CDs in the market: the shops are full of expensive, unnecessary 'flops' yet there is no sign of the flood abating.

Harsh words perhaps, but the reality of the situation sees major record companies madly pandering to the whims of capricious artists by indulging their every recording desire. Another disposable Mahler cycle, another routine set of Mozart's Da Ponte operas and the umpteenth 'even more authentic' *Four Seasons*. The list is endless and can be added to each time another predictable record company release lands on the reviewer's doormat.

So much choice

Of course, it is not just routine repertoire that has been heard a thousand times before: sometimes it is that 'essential' world première which modern scholarship has finally brought to life. Generally this means that the record company in question has exhumed something that has been laid to rest for the perfectly good reason that it really isn't very good: alternatively, an artist has been coaxed out of his or her exclusive contract with another company with the offer of a recording which is so obscure and/or so expensive to make that nobody else would ever bother with it.

New recordings face tough competition: for about six weeks they are centre stage while the round of reviews, interviews and advertisements ensure that the public is enlightened. Then, well, then nothing very much: the record shuffles off the new release rack in the record store, dutifully making way for its replacement and taking its place in the A-Z browsers. After a while, if it still refuses to sell or if the pressure of more recent material becomes too great, it will appear in the 'bargain' department, becoming increasingly unrecognizable beneath the litter of price stickers which chart its long journey in search of a buyer. Later still it may re-appear on a mid- or budget-price line, spruced up and ready to try its luck once again.

Why the Good CD Guide?

For a book which sets out to encourage the purchasing of CDs these may seem unduly negative opinions; actually they are some of the reasons why it has found such a ready market. The sheer volume of CDs flooding the market makes it hard for collectors, particularly the less experienced ones, to identify what is really worth having. That the amount of recorded material is increasing in inverse proportion to the number of knowledgeable sales assistants is not in dispute either.

All of this leaves the collector either in the hands of the record companies' marketing departments or turning to a title such as this or its monthly parent publication *Gramophone*, for advice.

Despite the foregoing the CD collector is really in a fortunate position. Amongst the ever-lengthening release lists there are treasures to be found. This book is the means to their discovery.

How to use the Guide

Details are given of composer(s), work(s), instrument(s), voice range(s), record company or label (see Index of Labels/Manufacturers and Distributors), disc number (and previous number when the newcomer is a reissue) and review date(s) in *Gramophone*. Addresses of distributing companies are provided at the rear of this book.

On the musical staves following a heading, information is provided by a system of symbols as follows:

The symbols

Price	Quantity/ availability	Review date	Mode	Timing
	② ②	6/88	DDD	57'

Price

Full price: £10·00 and over   Medium price: £7·00–£9·99

Budget price: £5·00–£6·99   Super-budget price: below £4·99

Quantity/availability
If there is more than one disc, the number involved is shown here. The first type of circle indicates sets in which the individual discs are not available separately. The second type indicates that the discs are *only* available separately.

Review date
The month and year in which the recording was reviewed in *Gramophone*.

Mode
This three-letter code is now used by almost all manufacturers to indicate the type of processing employed during manufacture. The letters A or D are used to denote Analogue or Digital and the letter sequence represents chronological steps in the chain: the recording session itself; the editing and/or mixing routines; and finally the mastering or transcription used in preparation of the master tape which is sent to the factory.

Timing
Calculated to the nearest minute.

Bargains	Quality of performance	Quality of sound	Basic library	Discs worth exploring	Period performance

Bargains
Sometimes it is more than price alone which makes for a true bargain. A disc which involves some of the finest artists in a superlative performance and

recording, for example, or possibly the sheer length in terms of playing time, will occasionally emerge at mid or bargain price. This symbol is the key to these special releases.

Quality of performance
Recordings which really brook no argument—'musts' for the keen collector. Often the older recordings among these might well have won a *Gramophone* Record Award had the Awards existed when they first appeared.

Quality of sound
Those recordings which truly merit the epithet 'demonstration quality'.

Basic library
Recordings with which to begin building your CD collection.

Discs worth exploring
For the adventurous! Recordings which might easily be overlooked since they are not among the best-known works or by the better-known composers. But they could well provide some interesting surprises.

Period performance
Recordings in which some attempt is made at historical authenticity. Typically these involve the use of period instruments and/or original manuscript sources.

Two further symbols are used in the reviews:

Gramophone Award winners
The classical music world's most coveted accolades for recordings, these are awarded each year by our parent magazine in categories ranging from Orchestral to Operatic, Baroque to Contemporary. One recording is also chosen from the overall list to be given the Award of Record of the Year.

Artists of the Year
Four artists whose qualities of musicianship and overall interpretation have consistently brought them to our attention.
See also the artist profiles beginning on page 22.

Introduction

Le marché croule sous les disques compacts! Les magasins sont inondés de 'fiascos', des disques chers et inutiles dont le flot ne semble pourtant pas devoir se calmer.

Propos bien sévères, direz-vous. Peut-être. Mais telle est la réalité de la situation: les grandes maisons de disques se pliant désespérément aux moindre lubies d'artistes capricieux et cédant avec complaisance à leur moindre désir. Et voilà un autre cycle de Mahler dont on pourrait se passer, une autre collection banale des opéras de Mozart d'après les livrets de Da Ponte et le énième enregistrement 'encore plus authentique' des *Quatre Saisons*. La liste est interminable et s'allonge à chaque fois que le dernier disque d'une société dénuée d'originalité atterrit sur le bureau du critique musical.

Un tel choix...

Non pas qu'il s'agisse toujours du répertoire habituel mille fois entendu: quelquefois, c'set une première mondiale 'de la plus haute importance' que l'érudition moderne nous livre enfin. Il faut en général comprendre par là que la maison de disques en question à déniché une oeuvre qui avait sombré dans l'oubli, ce pour la bonne raison qu'elle ne valait pas vraiment la peine qu'on s'en souvienne. A moins qu'un artiste se soit laissé convaincre de rompre son contrat exclusif avec une autre société, avec la promesse d'un enregistrement tellement obscur et/ou tellement difficile à réaliser que personne d'autre n'y songerait.

Les nouveaux enregistrements doivent faire face à une rude concurrence: environ six semaines durant, les voici en vedette; critiques, interviews et publicité assurant l'édification du public. Et puis ... Eh bien, plus grand-chose. Le disque quitte le présentoir des nouveautés, laissant bien sagement la place à son successeur, et se retrouve au classement alphabétique. Le temps passe et s'il ne se vend toujours pas ou si la pression exercée par les nouveaux disques est trop forte, le voilà relégué au rayon des 'bonnes affaires', de plus en plus méconnaissable sous la couche d'étiquettes successives qui retracent son long intinéraire à la recherche d'un acheteur. Plus tard encore, peut-être réapparaîtra-t-il, à nouveau sur son trente et un, et prêt à tenter encore une fois sa chance aux rayons des prix moyens ou modiques.

Pourquoi le Good CD Guide?

Voilà des opinions qui peuvent sembler par trop négatives venant d'un livre dont le but est d'encourager l'achat de disques compacts; mais ce sont en fait là certaines des raisons qui expliquent la présence d'un marché tout trouvé pour cet ouvrage. Etant donné l'énorme volume de disques compacts inondant le marché, les collectionneurs, et particulièrement les moins expérimentés, ont bien du mal à décider de ce qui vaut la peine d'être acheté, d'autant plus que la quantité croissante d'enregistrements est indéniablement inversement proportionnelle au nombre de vendeurs bien informés.

Le collectionneur est alors livré aux mains des services de marketing des maisons de disques, à moins qu'il ne se tourne vers un ouvrage comme celui-ci ou vers la publication mensuelle dont il est issu, *Gramophone*, pour y puiser des conseils.

En dépit de tout ce qui vient d'être dit, le collectionneur de disques compacts de trouve en fait dans une position enviable. Ces listes sans cesse plus longues cachent des trésors. Ce livre est là pour vous aider à les découvrir.

Comment utiliser ce guide?

Compositeur(s), oeuvre(s), instrument(s), registre(s) de voix, maison de disques ou label (reportez-vous à l'index des labels/fabricants et sociétés de distribution), numéro de disque (et le numéro précédent lorsque le disque est ressorti) et date(s) de critique(s) dans *Gramophone* sont indiqués.

Les portées à la suite des titres vous fournissent des informations grâce au système de symboles suivant.

Les symboles

Prix	Quantité/ disponibilité	Date de la critique	Mode	Durée
	② ②	6/88	DDD	57'

Prix

Prix normal

Prix moyen

Prix modique

Prix très modique

Quantité/disponiblité

S'il y a plus d'un disque, le nombre est indiqué ici. Le premier type de cercle indique des séries dont les disques ne sont pas vendus séparément. Le second type indique que les disques ne sont disponibles *que* séparément.

Date de la critique

Le mois et l'année de publication de la critique de l'enregistrement dans *Gramophone*.

Mode

Ce code de trois lettres est maintenant utilisé par presque tous les fabricants pour indiquer le procédé utilisé lors de la fabrication. Les lettres A ou D signifient 'analogique' ou 'numérique' et l'ordre des lettres correspond aux étapes, par ordre chronologique, dans la chaîne: la séance d'enregistrement à proprement parler, le mixage et/ou le montage, et enfin la gravure pour la préparation de la bande maîtresse envoyée à l'usine.

Durée

Calculée à la minute près.

Bonnes affaires	Qualité du son	Disques à découvrir

Qualité de l'interprétation	Discothèque de base	Interprétation 'historique'

Bonnes affaires

Parfois, ce n'est pas le prix seul qui fait la bonne affaire. Un disque regroupant certains des meilleurs artistes dans une interprétation et un enregistrement excellents par exemple, ou peut-être même un enregistrement particulièrement long, est parfois vendu à un prix moyen ou très modique. Ce symbole indique ces disques spéciaux.

Qualité de l'interprétation

Des enregistrements dont la qualité est indiscutable—des 'musts' pour le collectionneur passionné. Les plus anciens parmi ceux-ci auraient souvent remporté le prix du disque *Gramophone* s'il avait existé à leur sortie.

Qualité du son

Des enregistrements dont on peut vraiment dire qu'ils sont de 'qualité démonstration'.

Discothèque de base

Des enregistrements qui constitueront les fondements de votre collection de disques compacts.

Disques à découvrir

Pour les touche-à-tout de la musique! Des enregistrements à côté desquels on aurait tendance à passer parce qu'on ne les doit pas aux compositeurs les plus célèbres, mais qui peuvent réserver de bien agréables surprises.

Interprétation 'historique'

Des enregistrements empreints de tentatives d'authenticité historique, généralement grâce à l'utilisation d'instruments d'époque et/ou de manuscrits d'origine.

Deux autres symboles sont utilisés dans les critiques:

Lauréats du prix Gramophone

La distinction la plus convoitée dans le monde de la musique classique, décernée chaque année par le magazine dont nous sommes issus, par catégories allant d'Orchestral à Opéra en passant par Baroque et Contemporain. Un enregistrement est également sélectionné sur toute la liste pour le prix du disque de l'année.

Artistes de l'année

Quatre artistes qui se sont distingués par leurs qualités de musiciens et d'interprètes. Voir aussi les profils page 22 et suivantes.

Einführung

Es gibt zu viele CDs auf dem Markt; die Läden sind voll von teuren, sinnlosen 'Flops', und ein Ende der Flut ist nicht abzusehen. Dies sind vielleicht harte Worte, doch die Situation stellt sich in der Realität so dar, daß große Plattenfirmen sich den verrückten Launen eigenwilliger Künstler allzu willig beugen, um deren Wünsche nach immer neuen Aufnahmen zu befriedigen. Und der Markt wird dann mit einem weiteren überflüssigen Mahler-Zyklus, noch einer Routinepressung von Mozarts Da-Ponte-Opern und der soundsovielten 'noch authentischeren' Aufnahme der *Vier Jahreszeiten* überschwemmt. Die Liste ist endlos und verlängert sich jedesmal, wenn, wie zu erwarten, eine weitere solche Veröffentlichung auf dem Schreibtisch des Rezensenten landet.

Zuviel Auswahl

Es sind natürlich nicht nur Routineaufnahmen, die man schon tausendmal gehört hat; zuweilen handelt es sich um eine 'sensationelle' Weltpremiere, die durch die moderne Wissenschaft endlich zu neuem Leben erweckt wurde. Gewöhnlich bedeutet dies, daß die betreffende Plattenfirma eine Aufnahme ausgegraben hat, die aus gutem Grund beerdigt wurde: sie verdiente es. Oder ein Künstler wurde dazu überredet, aus seinem Exklusivvertrag mit einer anderen Plattenfirma auszusteigen, um eine Aufnahme herzustellen, die so obskur und/oder so teuer in der Produktion ist, daß sich niemand sonst jemals damit abgeben würde.

Neue Aufnahmen sind einem harten Konkurrenzkampf ausgesetzt. Etwa sechs Wochen lang sorgt eine Serie von Besprechungen, Interviews und Anzeigen dafür, daß sie im Mittelpunkt der Öffentlichkeit stehen. Und dann—das war's dann auch schon: im Laden wird die betreffende Aufnahme nicht mehr unter Neuerscheinungen geführt, sondern macht dort für ihre Nachfolgerin Platz und verschwindet im normalen A-Z-Sortiment. Nach einer Weile, wenn sie sich immer noch nicht verkauft oder der Druck immer neuer Aufnahmen zu groß wird, ist sie dann bei den 'Sonderangeboten' zu finden und ist dort schließlich kaum wiederzuerkennen unter mehreren Lagen von Preisaufklebern, mit denen sie verzweifelt nach Käufern sucht. Später taucht sie dann vielleicht in der mittleren Preisschiene oder im Billigsortiment auf—neue Aufmachung, neues Glück.

Warum der Good CD Guide?

Für ein Buch, das den Kauf von CDs fördern will, scheint dies einer unangemessen negative Einstellung zu sein; doch liegen hier einige der Gründe dafür, daß diese Veröffentlichung eine solche Beliebtheit erlangte. Das schiere Volumen an CDs, die den Markt überfluten, macht es für den Sammler schwer, insbesondere wenn er weniger Erfahrung hat, diejenigen zu identifizieren, deren Anschaffung wirklich lohnt. Daß der Anstieg an Aufnahmen sich umgekehrt proportional zur Zahl sachkundiger Verkäufer entwickelt, ist ebenfalls unbestritten.

Durch all dies ist der Sammler entweder den Marketing-Abteilungen der Plattenfirmen ausgeliefert oder er hält sich an Veröffentlichungen wie diese oder ihre Mutterzeitschrift *Gramophone*.

Trotz der hier geäußerten Kritik ist der CD-Sammler insgesamt in einer glücklichen Lage. In den ständig länger werdenden Veröffentlichungslisten sind auch Schätze zu finden. Dieses Buch ist der Schlüssel zu ihrer Entdeckung.

Benutzungshinweise

Die angegebenen Einzelheiten betreffen Komponist(en), Werk(e), Instrument(e), Stimmumfang, Plattenfirma oder Label (siehe das Verzeichnis von Labels/ Herstellern und Händlern), CD-Nummer (plus alter Nummer, falls es sich um eine Wiederveröffentlichung handelt) und Besprechungsdatum in *Gramophone*. Auf den Notenlinien unter einer Überschrift werden folgende Informationen durch Symbole wiedergegeben:

Symbole

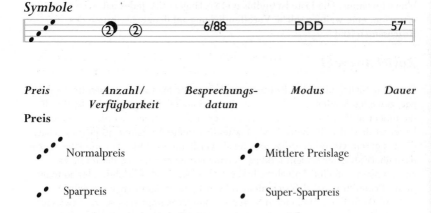

Preis	Anzahl/ Verfügbarkeit	Besprechungs- datum	Modus	Dauer

Preis

- ♪ Normalpreis
- ♪ Mittlere Preislage
- ♪ Sparpreis
- ♪ Super-Sparpreis

Anzahl/Verfügbarkeit
Falls es sich um mehr als eine CD handelt, wird die entsprechende Zahl hier angegeben. Der erste Kreistyp zeigt Sets an, bei denen individuelle CDs nicht separat verfügbar sind. Der zweite Kreistyp zeigt an, daß die CDs *nur* separat verfügbar sind.

Besprechungsdatum
Monat und Jahr, in dem die Aufnahme in *Gramophone* besprochen wurde.

Modus
Dieser Code aus drei Buchstaben wird heute von fast allen Herstellern verwendet, um Verfahren bei Aufnahme, Schnitt und Abmischung zu kennzeichnen. Die Buchstaben A und D stehen für Analog bzw Digital, und die Buchstabenfolge bezeichnet die chronologischen Schritte der Produktionskette: die Aufnahme selbst; das Schnitt- und/oder Abmischverfahren; und schließlich die Art der Überspielung oder Transkription, die zur Vorbereitung des Originalbandes verwendet wird, welches dann die Vorlage für die Pressung bildet.

Dauer
Auf volle Minuten ab- oder aufgerundet.

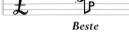

**Beste
Interpretationen**   **Grundstock**   **Historische
Authentizität**

Sonderangebote
Manchmal ist es nicht der Preis allein, der ein wahres Sonderangebot ausmacht. Eine CD, die die besten Künstler zu einer unübertrefflichen Aufnahme bei bester Aufnahmetechnik vereint, oder die sich vielleicht einfach durch die außergewöhnliche Länge der Spielzeit auszeichnet, wird gelegentlich in der mittleren oder Sonderpreislage auftauchen. Dieses Symbol ist der Schlüssel zu diesen speziellen Veröffentlichungen.

Beste Interpretationen
Aufnahmen, die über jede Kritik erhaben sind—ein 'Muß' für jeden Sammler. Viele der älteren Aufnahmen hätten *Gramophone*-Preise gewonnen, hätte es diese Auszeichnung bei ihrem ersten Erscheinen bereits gegeben.

Beste Klangqualität
Aufnahmen, die wirklich die Bezeichnung "Vorspielqualität" verdienen.

Grundstock
Aufnahmen, die die Basis für Ihre CD-Sammlung bilden sollten.

Lohnende Aufnahmen
Nur für musikalisch Vielseitige! Diese Aufnahmen könnten leicht übersehen werden, da sie von weniger bekannten Komponisten stammen, sind jedoch oft für eine angenehme Überraschung gut.

Historische Authentizität
Aufnahmen, bei denen der Versuch historischer Authentizität unternommen wurde, etwa durch Verwendung von zeitgenössischen Instrumenten und/oder Originalmanuskripten.

Zwei weitere Symbole werden in Besprechungen verwendet:

Gramophone-Preisträger
Die begehrtesten Auszeichnungen für Aufnahmen im Bereich der klassischen Musik. Sie werden jedes Jahr von unserer Mutterzeitschrift in verschiedenen Kategorien verliehen, die von Orchestermusik bis Oper, von Barock- bis zu zeitgenössischer Musik reichen. Aus dieser Liste wird ebenfalls eine Aufnahme ausgewählt, die den Titel Platte des Jahres erhält.

Musiker des Jahres
Vier Künstler, die uns regelmäßig aufgrund ihrer Fähigkeiten als Musiker und Interpreten aufgefallen sind. Siehe auch die Künstlerprofile auf Seite 22.

Introducción

Hay demasiados discos compactos en el mercado: los comersios están llenos de costosas grabaciones innecesarias que han fracasado, sin que haya señales de que su número disminuya.

Quizá resulte duro decirlo tan llanamente, pero la realidad de la situación es que hay grandes compañías grabadoras que se rinden sin dignidad ninguna a todos los caprichos de los artistas en sus grabaciones. Otro ciclo de Mahler de poca calidad, otro conjunto rutinario de las óperas de Mozart de Da Ponte y el infinitésimo número de unas *Cuatro Estaciones* 'cada vez más auténticas'. La lista es interminable y sigue alargándose cada vez que una compañía pone un nuevo disco en el escritorio del crítico.

¿Cómo se puede escoger?

Como es natural, no queda la cosa en un repertorio rutinario escuchado ya miles de veces: a veces se trata de algún obscuro estreno mundial 'absolutamente esencial' para el público, que la búsqueda de la moderna erudición ha puesto a su alcance. En general, esto significa que la compañía grabadora en cuestión ha exhumado material que había quedado enterrado por muy buenas razones, y por el que no merece la pena molestarse. También puede tratarse de un artista a quien han convencido para que rescinda su contrato en exclusiva con otra compañía para ofrecerle una grabación que es tan poco conocida y tan costosa, que nadie que estuviese en sus cabales se comprometería a hacerla.

Las nuevas grabaciones se enfrentan a un mercado de competencia muy dura: durante unas seis semanas están en ek candelero mientras la ronda de críticas, entrevistas y publicidad consigue que el público se entere de su existencia. A partir de entonces, nada más va a suceder. En los comersios musicales, el disco desaparece de la sección de música nueva, dejando su lugar al que le sucede para pasar a engrosar los títulos de los catálogos de actualidad. Con el transcurso del tiempo, si todavía no se vende o la presión de material más reciente continúa en aumento, aparecerá en el departamento de "gangas" cada vez más difícil de reconocer bajo las etiquetas acumuladas de los precios sucesivos que dan buena idea del camino recorrido en busca de comprador. Más tarde, puede reaparecer en la sección de precios medios o económicos, con aire remozado para volver a intentar suerte.

¿Cuál es el porqué de la Good CD Guide?

Para los creadores de un índice que se propone fomentar la compra de discos compactos, las anteriores opiniones pueden parecer excesivamente negativas; en realidad, éstas son varias de las razones por las que ha encontrado un mercado bien preparado para recibirlo. El ingente volumen de discos compactos que inundan el mercado hace muy difícil para los coleccionistas (especialmente los menos experimentados) el buscar los que merece la pena adquirir. Además, la cantidad de material grabado está en relación inversa al número de dependientes conocedores de lo que venden, cosa que nadie puede disputar.

Por todo esto, el coleccionista se vería obligado a depender de los departamentos de comercialización de las compañías grabadoras si no se le brindase una publicación como ésta o su matriz *Gramophone*, de aparición mensual, para asesorarse.

A pesar de lo antedicho, la posición del coleccionista de discos compactos es afortunada. Entre las listas de grabaciones, cada vez más largas, hay tesoros que encontrar. Este libro es el medio de conseguir tales descubrimientos.

Cómo valerse de esta Guía

Se ofrecen detalles de los compositores, obras, instrumentos, escala vocal, compañía o etiqueta productora de los discos (véase el índice de Etiquetas/Fabricantes y Distribuidores), número de disco (y número anterior cuando el nuevo es una reedición), así como la fecha o fechas de la revisión en *Gramophone*. En los pentagramas musicales que siguen el título se facilita un índice informativo con el sistema de símbolos siguiente:

Los símbolos

Precio	Cantidad/disponibilidad	Fecha revisión	Proceso	Duración

Precio

símbolo Precio completo   *símbolo* Precio intermedio

símbolo Precio asequible   *símbolo* Precio módico

Cantidad/Disponibilidad

Si hubiese más de un disco, el número de que se trate se mostrará aquí. El primer tipo de círculo indica los álbumes en que no están disponibles los discos por separado. El segundo tipo indica que los discos *solamente* están disponibles por separado.

Fecha de revisión

El mes y el año en qué se revisó la grabación en *Gramophone*.

Proceso

Este es un código formado por tres letras, que usan en la actualidad casi todos los fabricantes para indicar el tipo de proceso empleado en la manufactura. Las letras A ó D se emplean como denotadoras de Análogo o Digital, y la secuencia de las letras representa los pasos cronológicos en la cadena: la misma sesión de grabación, los procesos de edición y/o mezcla y, por último, la preparación del disco maestro de la transcripción, según el método de preparación de la cinta maestra que se envía a la fábrica.

Duración

Cálculo redondeado hasta el minuto más próximo.

Gangas	Calidad de sonido			Disco que merece la pena explorar

Calidad de ejecución		Biblioteca básica		Ejecución con instrumentos de la época

Gangas

A veces, hay otros elementos, aparte del precio, que hacen del disco una verdadera ganga. Un disco grabado por buenas artistas en una ejecución excepcional con una magnífica grabación, por ejemplo, o quizá la gran duración de la grabación, pueden a veces venderse a precios de ganga o intermedios. Este símbolo es el que denota tales ediciones.

Calidad de la Ejecución

Grabaciones indiscutibles—'obligatorias' para el buen coleccionista. A veces, las ediciones más antiguas hubieran merecido un Premio al Disco de *Gramophone* si dicho Premio hubiese existido cuando aparecieron.

Calidad de Sonido

Estas grabaciones merecen verdaderamente el epíteto de 'parangones de buena calidad'.

Colección Fundamental

Grabaciones con que comenzar a coleccionar discos compactos.

Discos que merece la pena explorar

¡Para el musicalmente promiscuo! Grabaciones que podrían pasarse por alto con facilidad puesto que no pertenecen a los compositores más conocidos. Pero quizá encierran agradables sorpresas.

Ejecución con instrumentos de la época

Grabaciones en que se ha intentado una autenticidad histórica. Habitualmente se han ejecutado con instrumentos de la época y/o empleando los manuscritos originales.

Dos símbolos más que se emplean en estas revisiones:

Ganadores de Premios Gramophone

Los más ambicionados en el mundo de la música clásica; se conceden todos los años por nuestra revista matriz en categorías desde Orquestal hasta Opera, Barroco y Contemporánea. Una grabación se escoge también en la lista general para recibir el Premio al Disco del Año.

Artistas del Año

Cuatro artistas, cuyas cualidades y maestría musical, junto con sus interpretaciones generales, les han dado, a nuestro juicio, la notoriedad. Véanse también las reseñas de los mismos, que comienzan en la página 22.

Common Abbreviations

alto	counter-tenor	*narr*	narrator
anon	anonymous	*ob*	oboe
arr	arranged	*Op*	opus/opera
attrib	attributed	*orig*	original
bar	baritone	*org*	organ
bass-bar	bass-baritone	*perc*	percussion
bn	bassoon	*pf*	piano
c.	circa (about)	*picc*	piccolo
cl	clarinet	*pub*	publisher/published
clav	clavichord	*rec*	recorder
cont	continuo	*rev*	revised
contr	contralto	*sax*	saxophone
cor ang	cor anglais	*sop*	soprano
cpte(d)	complete(d)	*spkr*	speaker
db	double-bass	*stg*	string
dig pf	digital piano	*synth*	synthesizer
dir	director	*tbn*	trombone
ed	edited (by)/edition	*ten*	tenor
exc	excerpt	*timp*	timpani
fl	flute	*tpt*	trumpet
fp	fortepiano	*trad*	traditional
gtr	guitar	*trans*	transcribed
harm	harmonium	*treb*	treble
hn	horn	*va*	viola
hp	harp	*va da gamba*	viola da gamba
hpd	harpsichord	*vars*	variations
keybd	keyboard	*vc*	cello
lte	lute	*vib*	vibraphone
mez	mezzo-soprano	*vn*	violin
mndl	mandolin	*voc*	vocal/vocalist

Chamber Music Forms

string trio	violin, viola, cello
piano trio	violin, cello, piano
horn trio	horn, piano, violin
clarinet trio	clarinet, piano, cello
wind trio	oboe, clarinet, basssoon
baryton trio	baryton, viola, bass instrument
string quartet	2 violins, viola, cello
piano quartet	piano, string trio
wind quartet	flute, clarinet, horn, bassoon
string quintet	2 violins, 2 violas, cello
piano quintet	piano, string quartet
clarinet quintet	clarinet, string quartet
flute quartet	flute, string quartet
wind quintet	flute, oboe, clarinet, basson, horn
string sextet	piano, violin, 2 violas, cello, double bass

Articles

Artists of the Year

John Eliot Gardiner

John Eliot Gardiner's work continues at an almost super-human rate. Hardly a month seems to pass without a major work from him on one or other of the four labels for which he records, and he spreads his interests ever wider. As the name of his own choir would imply Gardiner began his career in Monteverdi, and one of his first major recordings was of the *Vespers*[1], which he then committed to disc again in 1989 at St Mark's, Venice[2]. Very soon he moved forward a few decades in time to take in the masters of the baroque, renewing interest in Rameau, newly investigating rare and popular Handel and Bach, and reviving neglected Gluck. Whether dealing with the everlasting matters of Bach's *St Matthew Passion*[3] or the more earthly events described in Handel's *Saul*[4], the latest of his excellent Handel sets made in Göttingen, it seems he can breathe new life into the score in hand.

Next to come under the survey of his polymath mind and baton have been the operas of Mozart, which he is recording in turn for DG's Archiv label. So far issued is a probing, dramatic account of *Idomeneo*[5], the most exhaustively researched and complete version of the work as yet to appear on disc. At the time of writing he is doing the same service for *Entführung*. As with all his work, Gardiner refuses to accept any convention of the past until he has convinced himself it is fulfilling the wishes of the composer in hand. That attitude has applied as much to his advances into the nineteenth-century repertory as his recent CDs of Beethoven's *Missa solemnis*[6] and

[photo: DG / Dominic]

Brahms's *Ein deutsches Requiem*[7] have shown.

Finally there is the French wing of Gardiner's repertory. Always an ardent Francophile, he put thought into practice when he became music director of the Lyon Opera Orchestra. That led to a succession of recordings of repertory from Rameau through to Offenbach, taking in on the way, most significantly, recordings of Gluck's two *Iphigénie* operas[8] and of Berlioz's *L'enfance du Christ*[9] and, more recently, *Les nuits d'été*[10], with other of the composer's orchestral songs, for Erato. Those who treasure lighter things adore his accounts of Chabrier's neglected *L'étoile*[11] and Offenbach's uproarious *Les brigands*[12], not to forget his delicious performance of Rossini's French comedy *Le comte*

Ory[13]. It is an altogether formidable list from a protean artist.

[1] Monteverdi. Vespro della Beata Vergine. Decca 414 572-2DH2 (2/86).
[2] Monteverdi. Vespro della Beata Vergine. Archiv 429 565-2AH2 (1/91).
[3] Bach. St Matthew Passion. Archiv 427 648-2AH3 (10/89).
[4] Handel. Saul. Philips 426 265-2PH3 (8/91).
[5] Mozart. Idomeneo. Archiv 431 674-2AH3 (6/91).
[6] Beethoven. Mass in D major, "Missa solemnis". Archiv 429 779-2AH (3/91).
[7] Brahms. Ein deutsches Requiem. Philips 432 140-2PH (4/91).
[8] Gluck. Iphigénie en Aulide. Erato 2292-45003-2 (6/90).
Gluck. Iphigénie en Tauride. Philips 416 148-2PH2 (6/86).
[9] Berlioz. L'enfance du Christ, Erato 2292-45275-2 (1/88).
[10] Berlioz. Les nuits d'été. Erato 2292-45517-2 (2/91).
[11] Chabrier. L'étoile. EMI CDS7 47889-8 (8/88).
[12] Offenbach. Les brigands. EMI CDS7 49830-2 (2/90).
[13] Rossini. Le comte Ory. Philips 422 406-2PH2 (10/89).

The Chamber Orchestra of Europe

The Chamber Orchestra of Europe, founded in 1981 by a group of players from the European Community Youth Orchestra, has already established itself as one of the most dynamic and enthusiastic band of players on the classical music scene. Claudio Abbado, who encouraged its formation and who supported its enterprise during its first decade, has been instrumental in its tremendous success in the concert hall and on record. The *Gramophone* Award-winning DG sets of Schubert symphonies[1] and Rossini's *Il viaggio a Reims*[2] both featured him as conductor, and more recently the same combination put youthful enthusiasm and zest back into Prokofiev's *Peter and the wolf*[3] with Sting as an engaging narrator. But the COE also works regularly with other conductors. Alexander Schneider, long associated with the Malboro Festival in Vermont, has directed the orchestra regularly and has made a number of discs with them on their COE label that speak with an old-world elegance and a genuine feeling of chamber music-making. Recently Nikolaus Harnoncourt has directed them to thrilling effect and his much-vaunted cycle of the Beethoven symphonies[4] is sure to attract great critical attention.

The Chamber Orchestra of Europe, a collection of musicians from all the European states, has a quality that too many professional bands lack: they play with affection and a sense of really wanting to make music that communicates to its audiences. The ensemble is crisp and precise (listen to their Prokofiev and Schubert), the wind-playing quite magnificent (with Douglas Boyd an outstanding Principal Oboe) whilst their ability to switch from one period and style to another makes them one of today's most versatile orchestras.

[1] Schubert. Symphonies. DG 423 651-2GH5 (2/89).
[2] Rossini. Il viaggio a Reims. DG 415 498-2GH3 (1/86).
[3] Prokofiev. Peter and the wolf DG 429 396-2GH (4/91).
[4] Beethoven. Symphonies. Teldec 2292-46452-2 (11/91).

[photo: Teldec

[photo: DG / Holt]

Anthony Rolfe Johnson

Anthony Rolfe Johnson appears on everyone's list of favourite British tenors. A dairy farmer until he was 29, he made a comparatively late entry into the music profession, but quickly made up for lost time once he had discovered his voice. Apart from a major vocal problem that alarmed his admirers and nearly ended his career a few years back, his progress to his present pre-eminence has been steady and strong. His repertory is nothing if not wide in range, encompassing everything from Monteverdi to Britten. Of late he has been most in demand perhaps as a Mozartian, taking the title role in Gardiner's recently issued set of *Idomeneo*[1] and at the Salzburg Festival, Tamino in Norrington's *Die Zauberflöte*[2] and the title part in Gardiner's forthcoming *La clemenza di Tito*[3]. In the baroque and classical field other recent credits have been the Evangelist in the *St Matthew Passion*[4], also for Gardiner, and *Die Schöpfung*[5] for Hogwood.

Alongside his work in oratorio and opera, Rolfe Johnson has been a keen recitalist. He was one of the founder members of The Songmaker's Almanac and early in his career he gave memorable performances of *Die schöne Müllerin*. More recently he has made a much-admired CD for Hyperion's Schubert Edition[6], the brainchild of Graham Johnson, who has always been a close friend and colleague of the tenor. Also with Johnson, he has recorded a volume of Shakespeare settings for Hyperion, acknowledging his interest in British song. To follow are discs of songs by women composers and one of Houseman settings for the same company.

Rolfe Johnson was one of the natural successors to Sir Peter Pears in interpreting the music of Britten, so much of it for the tenor voice. He sang the *Serenade for tenor, horn and strings* for the first time when a student and has since sung that and all the other cycles with increasing frequency while being a regular soloist in the *War Requiem*[7], which he has recorded under Robert Shaw for Telarc. Forthcoming are a disc of the Canticles (Hyperion), a set of *Peter Grimes* with Haitink as conductor for EMI and *Gloriana* in which he is the Earl of Essex (Virgin Classics), a role he has also done on video from the ENO. To complete the picture, he sings Cassio in the new Solti/Decca set of *Otello*[8]. All this is typical of the versatility of this questing artist with the silvery tone, acute diction, and depth of insights into everything he approaches.

[1] Mozart. Idomeneo. Archiv 431 674-2AH3 (6/91).
[2] Mozart. Die Zauberflöte. EMI CDS7 54287-2.
[3] Mozart. La clemenza di Tito. Archiv 431 806-2AH2.
[4] Bach. St Matthew Passion. Archiv 427 648-2AH3 (10/89).
[5] Haydn. Die Schöpfung. L'Oiseau-Lyre 430 397-20H2 (3/91).
[6] Schubert. Hyperion CDJ33006 (6/90).
[7] Britten. War Requiem. Telarc CD80157 (11/89).
[8] Verdi. Otello. Decca 433 669-2DH2.

András Schiff

András Schiff has probably done more than any pianist since Glenn Gould to revive the performance of Bach on the modern grand piano. His repertoire, however, embraces a vast range of music; he has made more than 40 recordings and has an exclusive contract with Decca.

Schiff was born in Budapest, Hungary, on December 21st, 1953. His mother too had been a pianist, but her career was cut short by the onset of Nazism and the Second World War. Schiff's first piano lessons were with Elisabeth Vadasz; later he attended the Franz Liszt Academy where his teachers included the renowned pedagogues Pál Kadosa, György Kurtág and Ferenc Rados. He subsequently studied in England with George Malcolm, whose influence was vital.

In choosing his recital programmes Schiff likes, if playing music of several composers, to select works which are culturally or stylistically related rather than what he describes as "mixed-salad programmes"; he has a marked preference for giving recital series covering complete cycles such as Bach's *48*[1] or *Clavierübung*, Mozart's complete sonatas[2], and the Schubert sonatas. His repertoire eschews only those works which he feels place virtuoso display and volume before musical quality and spirituality. Of all forms of music-making, Schiff is most drawn to chamber music, and his partnerships with such musicians as the Takács Quartet with whom he has recorded the Dohnányi[3] and Brahms[4] piano quintets, Heinz Holliger, Sándor Végh (who is his partner, with the Salzburg Mozarteum Camerata Accademica, in the complete Mozart piano concertos[5]), Aurèle Nicolet, Gidon Kremer and Yuuko Shiokawa (now his wife) have won much acclaim. His work with singers has included recitals with Robert Holl, Peter Schreier[6] and Barbara Hendricks.

He makes regular appearances at festivals such as Hohenems, Salzburg, Vienna, Lucerne and Ansbach. In 1989 he founded his own festival, 'Musiktage Mondsee' in the Austrian countryside and he was director of a sell-out one-week Haydn Festival at London's Wigmore Hall in 1989. He continues to work with most of the major orchestras in Europe, North America, Japan and Israel. International awards he has received include the Premio della Accademia Chigiana, Siena (1987), the Wiener Flötenuhr Mozart Prize of the City of Vienna (1989) and the Bartók Prize (1991).

[1] Bach. Well-tempered Clavier. Decca 414 388-2DH2 (9/86), 417 236-2DH2 (3/87).
[2] Mozart. Sonatas. Decca 430 333-2DM5.
[3] Dohnányi. Decca 421 423-2DH (12/88).
[4] Brahms. Decca 430 529-2DH.
[5] Mozart. 417 886-2DH (12/89).
[6] Schubert. 425 612-2DH (12/89).

Authentic Performance

John Duarte on the composer's intentions

[photo: Sotheby's

Flemish Single Manual Harpsichord, Antwerp 1755

Just what is 'authenticity', and why does the word so often appear in reviews of recordings of early music? Quite simply, 'authenticity' implies that the music is presented, as closely as possible, in the way in which it might have been heard at the time when it was composed. Since we can never hear any contemporary performance that predated the invention of the gramophone we must depend on scholarly research to provide the answers, and, since new information keeps coming to light—and we can never know when there is no more to come, they can never finally be definitive. The best that performers can do is to put the available knowledge to practical use, and that is what the best performers do. We cannot of course turn the clock back all the way: even if we had benefit of a Tardis we would remain people of our own time, with our reflexes to some extent conditioned by our exposure to several centuries of later musics. If we can never become 'earlier' people we *can* nevertheless listen to what they heard (as nearly as we can recreate it) and let it speak to us in its own language. Every performance begins with a score, the notes themselves, and so too does authenticity — the text should be unpolluted by underinformed editing; unless the reviewer indicates otherwise, this may be assumed to be so. Where there is more than one manuscript source or contemporary printed version of a work, this too may be discussed in the review. Given that the text itself is in good order, the next question is, what instrument(s) should be used?

There is no instrument that has not changed significantly since 'pre-gramophonic' times, so we may safely assume that the instruments on which the music was played in those times were not those we use now. Broadly speaking, instruments have developed in order to keep pace with the demands of 'new' music and, in terms of volume and carrying power, the use of increasingly large auditoria. When music was in transition so too were instruments, and some doubts will probably always remain—harpsichord *versus* fortepiano, for instance, but in general it is true to say that the instruments and the music of any period were well matched. Composers conceived their music in terms of the instruments they knew, and if it is played on others of different character it may be distorted. To point the gun in the opposite direction, how might Bartók have felt if he had heard his *Concerto for orchestra* played on baroque instruments?

It is true to say that instruments have evolved over the centuries, but this does not mean that their earlier forms were necessarily 'primitive'—they were just *different* in sonority and tone-quality. The explosion of interest in early music following World War II triggered a return to 'period' instruments but there was an acute shortage of players who could use them with professional competence. Modern violinists, for instance, soon found that the earlier instruments were no pushover and that it was exceedingly difficult to master them when the bulk of their living came from 'general-purpose' chamber or orchestral work on the very different modern instruments. At the same time, many sought 'authenticity' through the strict observance of the known academic 'rules', with expressiveness taking a back seat, and the synergetic effect of low instrumental competence and grim-faced academicism was to give 'authenticity' a bad name with those listeners whose hearts monitored the messages received through their ears. That phase has happily passed: there is now no shortage of highly skilled players, there is now a good living to be made within the field of early music alone and, perhaps even more importantly, expressiveness has returned to early-musical performance—external fashions and appearances have changed, but human emotions and the desire to express them have not.

Modern and period instruments have different tones and in some cases the former cannot adequately replace the latter; the modern cello, for instance, cannot approach the viola da gamba in expressing the loneliness and desolation of Christ on the Cross in the aria "Es ist vollbracht" in Bach's *St John Passion,* and when cellos replace gambas in the Sixth *Brandenburg* Concerto they radically change the balance of sonorities. Modern instruments may often be used to the satisfaction of all but the most rabid purist if they are played appropriately; in the case of the strings this means, *inter alia,* the abatement of intense vibrato (reserved in earlier times for use as an ornament, to emphasize important notes) and the use of a more finely drawn tone than we are accustomed to hearing in twentieth-century music. The Guildhall String Ensemble accomplish this in their recording of Handel's *Concerti grossi,* Op. 6[1] —compare this with the one by The English Concert[2], who use period instruments. The recording of Vivaldi's *Concerto for two cellos and strings,* RV531, by Anner Bylsma and Anthony Pleeth with the Academy of Ancient Music[3]

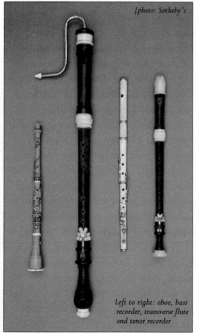

[photo: Sotheby's]

Left to right: oboe, bass recorder, transverse flute and tenor recorder

provides a fine illustration (especially in the *Largo*) of the use of pronounced vibrato as an expressive ornament. Bylsma and Pleeth use period instruments, which have a leaner sound than today's cello, but the latter may also be used to telling effect when played with a lighter touch, as may be heard in the recordings of Vivaldi's Cello Concertos by Ofra Harnoy.

The softer, warmer, and often more pitch-flexible sounds of the baroque woodwind instruments have more expressive intimacy than those of their modern counterparts: compare, for instance, the recordings of the Flute Sonatas of Bach by Stephen Preston[4] and Jean-Pierre Rampal[5]—both with Trevor Pinnock and both finely played. The term 'flute' meant different things to different people at different times: transverse flute or recorder. Some works are often played on whichever the performer believes to be appropriate—or perhaps specializes in playing; recordings of the flute/recorder Concertos of Vivaldi or the *Brandenburg* Concertos of Bach, for example, abound in examples. In such a case, providing that the instruments are of the appropriate period, no great offence against 'authenticity' is committed; composers of 'early' music tended to have liberal views of such matters. A common bone of contention is the use of the piano to play harpsichord music written at a time when the piano did not exist. The only thing the two have in common is, that they are both keyboard instruments, yet, though 'authenticity' cannot be claimed, much harpsichord music may be acceptably presented on the piano. For this to be the case it is necessary that the player should eschew overtly pianistic effects, such as the imposition of crescendos and diminuendos that, being impossible on a harpsichord, could not have been in the composer's mind. The exaggerated over-use of staccato by some pianists, whose mistaken notion it is that this is how the harpsichord sounds, cannot be taken seriously. As examples of the intelligent use of the piano as a medium for baroque music, recordings by Angela Hewitt[6] and Keith Jarrett[7] would be hard to better.

[photo: Sotheby's

Division Viol, London 1692

Numbers may too come into the reckoning: archival evidence often tells us how many players were available in specific places and at particular times, making nonsense of the performance of many orchestral works with large forces of modern instruments, with their louder and less transparent sounds. It may however leave room for debate, as in the case of the B minor Mass of Bach. Whether Joshua Rifkin is right in concluding that one voice per part is appropriate, or Andrew Parrott in using less minimal forces, the Victorian-traditional deployment of large choirs is *inauthentic*, no matter how impressive it may sound.

Whatever instruments are used, the style of the performance should, in line with current knowledge, be appropriate to the period of the music. It is, for instance, necessary to know how ornaments were played, and where it is 'in style' to add others that are not shown. Written music is an approximate guide to performance, to be interpreted in accordance with practices that are generally understood in the music's own time—and may not need to be 'spelt out'; nowhere is this more true than it is with pre-classical music. A case in point is that of the duration of notes: pairs of equal notes were not always played as such (*notes inégales*), and dotted rhythms were often played as though they were double-dotted. Performers were, too, expected to add something of their own by way of embellishment, especially in the repeats of dance movements—the late Robert Thurston Dart said that, in baroque times, anyone who played a repeat without changing anything "would have been considered a very dull dog". At the same time, embellishment was intended to be spontaneous, not prepared and repeated in every performance, whereas in a recording it remains the same—and may become a spurious part of the text. In the absence of a score it is desirable to have more than one recording of the same work—one well, the other minimally if at all embellished. Compare, for instance, the stylish performances of Vivaldi's *The Four Seasons* by Simon Standage[8] and Monica Huggett[9] with one another, and with those by more conservative (albeit high-class) non-specialist virtuosos, of which there are very many in *The Classical Catalogue*.

There are many other features of good style, such as articulation, which is often dictated by the 'tools' themselves, e.g. the short renaissance violin bow lends itself naturally to detaching rather than to slurring notes, and which may be identified by listening to good performances by period-specialized musicians.

'Authenticity' thus implies that the music is being re-created, as well as we know how, stripped of the layers of extraneous matter that have overlaid many performances in later centuries; there is a measure of arrogance in any notion that, with the benefit of modern implements, we can now do it 'better'. Any resistance to the sound of well played period instruments may well owe something to prejudice and later conditioning. However, acceptable performances may be given to using modern instruments—what, for want of a better term, we call 'middle-of-the-road' versions. Does 'authenticity' really matter? Yes, it does if you are really interested in hearing what we have good reason to believe is what the composer really wrote. Come to period performances with an open mind and goodwill, be guided by what the reviewers have to say, and reap the rich rewards.

[1] Handel. Concerti grossi, Op. 6. RCA Victor Red Seal RD87895, 87907, 87921 (2/90, 4/90).
[2] Handel. Concerti grossi, Op. 6. Archiv 410 897-2AH (6/85).
[3] Vivaldi. Concerto for two cellos, RV531. L'Oiseau-Lyre 414 588-20H (6/86).
[4] Bach. Flute Sonatas. CRD 3314/5 (1/90).
[5] Bach. Flute Sonatas. CBS CD39746 (12/85).
[5] Bach. Keyboard works. DG 429 975-2GDC.
[7] Bach. Wohltemperierte Klavier Book 1. ECM835 246-2 (10/88).
[8] Vivaldi. The Four Seasons. Archiv 400 045-2AH (3/83).
[9] Vivaldi. The Four Seasons. Virgin Classics Veritas VC7 91147-2.

Wolfgang Amadeus Mozart

Christopher Headington considers the treasures of the bicentenary year

A native of the Malaysian rain forest once told a group of tourists that he had no idea how old he was because the absence of seasons meant that he and his fellow villagers did not count years. And this reminds us that anniversaries, whether they are birthdays or bicentenaries, are basically artificial, even though they are useful for all sorts of reasons. Not the least of them is that of taking stock, and of course in the case of Mozart's bicentenary year we have been able to remind ourselves of the rich output of a composer who by common consent is among the greatest of all. Another factor in this last decade of the millennium is that skilful media work and marketing—not least of good hardware in the shape of discs and reasonably priced quality playing equipment to go with them—have made classical music popular as it never was before, and there is a whole new youngish audience ready to explore and enthuse. (Maybe the one odd thing about 1991 is that there was no well-publicized Nigel Kennedy 'Mozza' issue to reach out to this public.)

All this had to be good news, although there was always the danger in the bicentenary year that record company committees making commercial decisions about issues would sacrifice quality for quantity or simply mistake the latter for the former. In fact this did happen to some extent, as executives dug out material from their back catalogues (sometimes as far back as the 1950s) which was undistinguished in performance and/or recording quality, a fact which showed up especially when they placed it in the same package as something better played and recorded. Another kind of zeal was blamelessly non-commercial but arguably also misguided, that of the musicologist who, on being given a free hand, supervised performances of notional completions of Mozart fragments which are frankly the scrapings from the bottom of the barrel (admittedly a fine barrel). Thus the last of the three discs in a set of chamber music in the Mozart Complete Edition from Philips included no less than five fragmentary pieces from the fringes of his catalogue which were provided with completions by the series producer Erik Smith. Undoubtedly there is a case to be made out for completeness at all costs, and it is argued in this scholar's careful booklet essay. But what Mozart would have thought of this scholarly piety is hard to imagine—or on second thoughts, given his notoriously straight-from-the-shoulder directness, perhaps it isn't!

But one should not criticize the Philips Complete Mozart Edition for aiming to be precisely that, and its 45 volumes with their 180 discs in all are by now occupying over two metres of shelf space in the homes of those collectors who wanted (and could afford, even at medium price) to have the lot. Those who didn't could still choose well, for example the set of String Quartets (Volume 12)[1] with the Quartetto Italiano or the Piano Concertos (Volume 7)[2] with Alfred Brendel, Sir Neville Marriner and the Academy of St Martin in the Fields. In fact, Philips have offered a high overall standard of performance and recording, with some older material still sounding very well, for example the orchestral performances from the 1970s by Marriner and the ASMF standing alongside more recent ones with the same conductor and orchestra, the preferred orchestra for the series. These older and newer recordings accord well, and so does the stylish playing. I am thinking here of the Marriner/ASMF four volumes and 24 discs that include the symphonies (up to 52 because of the inclusion of rediscovered, reassigned and doubtful works), serenades, cassations, divertimentos, marches and miscellaneous orchestral pieces.

There is no question that the 12 discs of symphonies in Volumes 1[3] and 2[4], offering over 13 hours of music, represent a pretty good investment for a lifetime's listening pleasure, for Mozart's inspiration is often marvellous as well as being varied in moods and colours, and in Marriner's hands he receives consistently sure and sensitive performances. There is a natural balance, too, to the orchestra, which includes a harpsichord, and at the 'real' end of the series the *Jupiter* Symphony (which Grieg called "perfect, as if created by a god") crowns the series splendidly with its vision of Olympian sunlit heights. For the non-specialist collector, Volume 2 is the best here, containing as it does the symphonies Nos. 21-41. The other two volumes are more of a mixed bag, and the three discs in Volume 3[5] consisting entirely of music in D major face us with too much of a good thing, although the *Galimathias musicum* (a kind of compendium of popular themes in no less than 17 sections) and the exquisitely tongue-in-cheek *Musical Joke* are both wittily written and charmingly played. That most famous of serenades, *Eine kleine Nachtmusik*, is here (and in almost every other orchestral anthology!) and nicely done though with a biggish orchestra, as is the *Haffner* Serenade with Iona Brown as the violin soloist. While on the subject of the orchestral music, I was less

Sir Neville Marriner [photo: EMI/Morrison

impressed with the EMI set of four mid-price discs[6] with the symphonies from No. 26 to 41 which omits not only No. 37 (which is incomplete) but No. 28, which is definitely one of the canon. It draws heavily on elderly catalogue material (e.g. Nos. 38, 40 and 41 respectively done by Karajan, Klemperer and Beecham in the late 1950s) while also using much more recent performances, such as those of Jeffrey Tate and the English Chamber Orchestra and (as with Philips) Sir Marriner and his Academy of St Martin in the Fields. In omitting exposition repeats in the works just mentioned, Klemperer and Beecham immediately sound dated, and the septuagenarian Klemperer had a sluggish idea of *Molto allegro* in the first movement of No. 40. The large orchestral string bodies of the period also accord uncomfortably with the chamber forces rightly employed nowadays, as by Marriner, Tate and, for that matter, Daniel Barenboim in his accounts with the ECO of Nos. 30, 33 and 39, of which the last goes back to the late 1960s but is none the worse for that.

Another big EMI issue was an anthology of orchestral, chamber, vocal, choral and operatic works on 24 discs in their bargain-price Laser series. One advantage here was that all the discs were available separately, though there were no booklet notes. It is easy to find stylish and pleasing things, such as the fairly recent recordings of flute and oboe concertos[7] and *Eine kleine Nachtmusik*[8] with Barenboim and the Orchestre de Paris, but anyone buying the whole set might be put out to find that the latter work, good though it is, also turns up twice more in performances under Kubelik[9] and Marriner[10]. And again there were ancient performances that did not have quite the distinction to deserve reissue after three decades, such as Annie Fischer's of Piano Concertos Nos. 21 and 22 with the Philharmonia Orchestra under Sawallisch[11], which date from 1958. The same year is that of a famous account of the Clarinet Concerto with Jack Brymer and Sir Thomas Beecham conducting the Royal Philharmonic Orchestra[12], where there are some pretty stodgy tempos, and the same kind of heaviness occurs in the slightly later account of the celestial Flute and Harp Concerto under Menuhin[13]. But this was also an issue with some real bargains: the 1966 performance of the Requiem under Wolfgang Gönnenwein[14] has solid merit and character and so does the same conductor's account of the dramatic C minor Mass[15], while the 19 tracks of operatic arias and duets on another disc has some splendid things including Lucia Popp's personification of the Queen of Night in *The Magic Flute*[16]. The four horn concertos (buoyantly played by Alan Civil with Klemperer and the Philharmonia) make for another attractive disc[17]; so do three of the symphonies (Nos. 31, 39 and 40), alertly done by Barenboim and the ECO[18], and the nicely characterful *Haffner* Serenade and *Serenata notturna* with Menuhin and his Bath Festival Orchestra[19]. One only wishes that such a big anthology had found room for more than just three of the string quartets, and that the Heutling Quartet had been recorded less closely in them[20].

Other big compilations came from other companies, including Capriccio, but I will only discuss one more which had the virtue of being more interestingly planned. Decca made its bid for the attention of collectors seeking an anthology with their Mozart Almanac of 20 mid-price discs which were also available separately. (Few people want to lash out that much on Mozart unless they are already interested, and if that is so they no doubt already have a fair amount of the music.) It has a very wide-ranging mixture, and includes solo piano pieces with such artists as

Daniel Barenboim   [photo: Teldec]

Rogé[21], András Schiff[22] and Larrocha[23], unfamiliar chamber works like the Church Sonata in D major, K69[24], and the Violin Duo in G major (played by the Oistrakhs, father and son)[25] as well as the familiar and glorious Clarinet Quintet[26] and A major String Quintet[27], while on a bigger scale there are Schiff and Ashkenazy in piano concertos[28], sacred music from the beautiful *Ave verum corpus*[29] to the C minor Mass[30] and Requiem[31], and excerpts from the seven best known operas with star singers including Dame Kiri Te Kanawa and Pavarotti[32]. The order of the music is not by category but chronological, because that great scholar H.C. Robbins Landon has compiled the whole thing as a survey of Mozart's development with one disc allotted to each of the 16 years from 1775 to 1790 and two of the others devoted to the last year of all, 1791. Decca claim this to be "a diary of Mozart's life", an almanac in fact, and with Robbins Landon's hand on the proceedings it's emphatically not what someone called "an unthinking short cut to swelling one's collection". But be warned about just one thing: though many expected goodies are here (and *Eine kleine Nachtmusik*[33] is yet again played by the ubiquitous Marriner and the ASMF, this time culled from an Argo disc of 1971!), not all are, and you will look in vain for the *Jupiter* Symphony to follow No. 40 in G minor under Hogwood[34], and equally fruitlessly for one of the great series of six string quartets dedicated to Haydn. These are for the most part good or very good performances, but once again most are back-catalogue material, some of which goes back three decades.

For all the convenience of big, competitively priced compilations in which the record company chooses for the collector, individual taste is inevitably better served (if not so economically) by individual issues. This 1992 *Guide* lists mostly single discs or works but Daniel Barenboim's complete set of Piano Concertos is recommended as a major achievement[35]. There is no recommendation for a complete series of symphonies or sonatas: the nearest things to that are one for the string quintets with an ensemble led by Arthur Grumiaux[36] and another two for the horn concertos, one with Dennis Brain[37] being nearly 40 years old and the other one with Barry Tuckwell[38] dating from 1985. The serious collector is often also a connoisseur of performance style, and so we make no apology for listing in this *Guide* four discs coupling the last two symphonies[39], or three performances of *Don Giovanni*[40].

Talking of opera, here is another growth area in public taste, and Mozart's operas are masterpieces that come up new and fresh for every generation of singers, audiences - and producers too, though hopefully not *too* fresh in this profession where self-indulgence has overmuch sway.

The new *Don Giovanni* which comes from L'Oiseau-Lyre and uses period instruments is new in the right way because less artificial and more immediate than usual[41]. This Swedish production is conducted by Arnold Ostman and has Håkan Hagegård as a convincing Giovanni and Arleen Auger as Donna Anna: powerfully suave and stylish, it reveals this *opera buffa* with a serious moral line as one of intelligence and sophistication as well as gut feeling.

It is another male singer, British this time, who shines especially in a new Archiv account of *Idomeneo* under John Eliot Gardiner[42] in which the King is played by Anthony Rolfe Johnson. This was hailed in *Gramophone* by Alan Blyth as "the definitive recording"; it has tension as well as beauty and Rolfe Johnson brings warmth and dignity to the title role while his son Idamante (a role sung by the male soprano Vicenzo del Prato in the first production) is convincingly played by Anne Sofie von Otter. Both this performance and the Swedish *Don Giovanni* have found ways of handling the conversational recitatives (so stiff in many productions) skilfully so that they integrate naturally into the sequence of more formal arias, duets and ensembles. Indeed, they have that best kind of authenticity which simply sounds natural as well as being justifiable by musicologists and it may well be that in the 1990s the authentic performance movement will finally reach maturity and enlighten us afresh even in familiar pieces.

Roger Norrington   *[photo: EMI*

While on that subject, let us pay tribute to the conductor Christopher Hogwood who has been at the forefront of the period instrument movement. He has given us all the symphonies[43], a selection of the wind concertos[44] and the major choral works[45]. On a more controversial level—many would say excitingly so—is Roger Norrington; he has been one of the pioneers of the movement to strip away dead foliage from interpretative traditions and—when the result works well, as it often does—reveal something which should have been there all the time, the immediacy of fresh creation. His practice is thus the very opposite of innovation for innovation's sake and gives evidence of a deep sympathy with the past, and to more conventional people he might well say, as Stravinsky did about his re-composition of eighteenth-century Italian music, "you respect, but I love". Sometimes Norrington's enthusiasm goes a bit over the top—for example, some fast tempos tend to breathlessness and surprises can become shocks—but boldness inevitably exacts some price, and it's one worth paying. He first hit the headlines in the Beethoven symphonies, and it is only now that he and his London Classical Players (playing period instruments, of course) seem to be turning their attention to Mozart. His recent recording of Symphonies

Nos. 39 and 41 is in this *Guide*[46], but a *Gramophone* reviewer had his reservations about the slow introduction of No. 39: "The hard, dry thwacks of the period timpani cut ferociously through the opening orchestral chords, and the violins perform their octave-and-a-half descents not with the usual poise and grandeur but rapidly, almost precipitously. The slow introduction here is not the customary dignified prelude but an impassioned, hectic, near-violent piece of rhetoric".

Ferocious and precipitous Mozart? Not a performance for every day, doubtless, but it reminds us that this unique composer who died at 35 was neither a polite courtier nor any kind of conformist (which is why his life was so difficult) and that he wrote this music exactly one year before the French Revolution. It also reminds us that music, like drama, is a recreative art: performers must always bring something of their own vision to music, just as an actor who undertakes the role of Hamlet must also be himself. It would be nice to be around for Mozart's tercentenary and find out how artists not yet born will see his music.

[1] String Quartets. Philips 422 512-2PME8.
[2] Piano Concertos. Philips 422 507-2PME12 (5/91).
[3] Symphonies. Philips 422 501-2PME6 (12/90).
[4] Symphonies. Philips 422 502-2PME6 (12/90).
[5] Various. Philips 422 503-2PME7; 422 504-2PME5 (12/90).
[6] Symphonies. EMI CMS7 63585-2 (4/91).
[7] Flute Concerto No. 1. EMI Laser CDZ7 67008-2 (7/91).
[8] Serenade No. 13 ("Eine kleine Nachtmusik"). EMI Laser CDZ7 67008-2 (7/91).
[9] Serenade No. 13 ("Eine kleine Nachtmusik") CDZ7 67009-2 (7/91).
[10] Serenade No. 13 ("Eine kleine Nachtmusik") CDZ7 67017-2 (7/91).
[11] Piano Concertos. EMI Laser CDZ7 67002-2 (7/91).
[12] Clarinet Concertos. EMI Laser CDZ7 67007-2 (7/91).
[13] Flute and Harp Concerto. EMI Laser CDZ7 67007-2 (7/91).
[14] Mass No. 19, "Requiem". EMI Laser CDZ7 67014-2 (7/91).
[15] Mass No. 18 in C minor. EMI Laser CDZ7 67019-2 (7/91).
[16] Operatic Arias and Duets. EMI Laser CDZ7 67015-2 (7/91).
[17] Horn Concertos. EMI Laser CDZ7 67012-2 (7/91).
[18] Symphonies. EMI Laser CDZ7 67011-2 (7/91).
[19] Serenades. EMI Laser CDZ7 67013-2 (7/91).
[20] String Quartets. EMI Laser CDZ7 67018-2 (7/91).
[21] Menuets. Allegros. Decca 430 112-2DM (5/91).
[22] Piano Sonatas, K309/284b; K311/284c. Decca 430 116-2DM (5/91).
[23] Piano Sonata, K576. Decca 430 128-2DM (5/91).
[24] Church Sonata. Decca 430 116-2DM (5/91).
[25] Violin Duo. Decca 430 122-2DM (5/91).
[26] Clarinet Quintet. Decca 430 128-2DM (5/91).
[27] String Quintet. Decca 430 128-2DM (5/91).
[28] Piano Concertos—(Schiff) No. 9: Decca 430 116-2DM; Nos. 17 and 18: 430 123-2DM;
    No. 27: 430 130-2DM. (Ashkenazy) Nos. 20 and 21: 430 124-2DM; No. 23: 430 125-2DM (all 5/91).
[29] Ave verum corpus. Decca 430 130-2DM (5/91).
[30] Mass No. 18 in C minor. Decca 430 122-2DM (5/91).
[31] Mass No. 19, "Requiem". Decca 430 131-2DM (5/91).
[32] Idomeneo—Decca 430 120-2DM; Die Entführung aus dem Serail—430 121-2DM;
    Le Nozze di Figaro—430 125-2DM; Don Giovanni—430 126-2DM; Così fan tutte—430 129-2DM;
    La Clemenza di Tito, Die Zauberflöte—430 130-2DM (all 5/91).
[33] Eine kleine Nachtmusik. Decca 430 126-2DM (5/91).
[34] Symphony No. 40. Decca 430 127-2DM (5/91).
[35] Piano Concertos. EMI CZS7 62825-2 (6/90).
[36] String Quintets. Philips 416 486-2PH3 (7/86).
[37] Horn Concertos. EMI CDH7 61013-2 (2/88).
[38] Horn Concertos. Decca 410 284-2DH (11/84).
[39] Symphonies Nos. 40 and 41. EMI CDC7 47147-2 (7/85); CBS CD44649 (9/89); Telarc CD80139 (5/87);
    CBS CD42538 (5/90).
[40] Don Giovanni. EMI CDS7 47037-8 (12/84); EMI CDS7 47260-8 (12/87); L'Oiseau-Lyre
    425 943-20H3 (12/90).
[41] Don Giovanni. L'Oiseau-Lyre 425 943-2OH3 (6/91).
[42] Idomeneo. Archiv Produktion 431 674-2AH3 (6/91).
[43] Symphonies. L'Oiseau-Lyre 430 639-2OM19.
[44] Oboe and Clarinet Concertos. L'Oiseau-Lyre 414 339-2OH (5/89).
[45] Requiem. Clarinet Concerto. L'Oiseau-Lyre 430 131-2DM (5/91).
[46] Symphonies. EMI CDC7 54090-2 (6/91).

Figures in brackets refer to review date in *Gramophone*.

Contemporary music

Michael Stewart
argues the case for the music of today

The availability of contemporary music on CD has increased enormously in the last two years or so. Not only have the record companies made available once again some of the classic recordings of the last decade (the most notable reissues can be found in DG's 20th Century Classics and Decca's Enterprise series) but there has also been an increasing commitment to new recordings—and not just from the big companies either. Unicorn-Kanchana, Etcetera, Wergo, Hyperion and Continuum are just a few of the smaller companies who, though working with smaller budgets than some of their major competitors, have managed to bring us superb recordings of some of the finest contemporary music on offer.

If there's one thing to be learnt from this renewed commitment then it must surely be that it is as diverse and varied as any other category of music, perhaps even more so. Hopefully the following will provide a sample of the riches that lie in wait for the intrepid explorer, and prove that contemporary music need not mean unapproachable music. One need only sample the fresh, invigorating scores of the young composer Michael Torke, whose début album on Decca's Argo label is just one of several important issues of minimalist music to appear in recent years. Torke, an American composer of considerable talent, has successfully integrated into his style not only the influence of his classical training, and the minimalist workings of composers like Glass, Reich and Adams, but also the dynamic energy and zest of the pop and rock cultures[1].

Minimalism is now so well established within the musical world that it is difficult in retrospect to pin-point precisely where it began, though most agree that the ex-featherweight wrestler, cab driver, furniture mover and Nadia Boulanger pupil Philip Glass

Michael Torke   [photo: Decca/Robert

John Adams   [photo: O'Grady

Philip Glass   [photo: Sony Classical]

was one of the first to bring minimalism to a wider audience. One of his most influential works, and considered by many to be his finest, is his *Music in Twelve Parts*[2]—a vast series of kaleidoscopic pieces that should certainly not be overlooked by anyone exploring minimalist territory. His operas *Einstein on the Beach*[3], *Satyagraha*[4] and *Akhnaten*[5] are considered to be classics of the genre and have enjoyed considerable success in the major opera houses of the world. After the enormous success of his opera *Nixon in China*[6], John Adams offers us a chance to explore the two divergent sides of his creativity. *The Wound-dresser*[6]: a dark, sombre soliloquy for baritone and orchestra has been brilliantly contrasted with one of Adams's more humorous and immediately entertaining pieces, *Fearful symmetries*[7], a strange, dream-like construction that seems to feed off its own kinetic energy[7].

All the minimalists mentioned so far have been American. But what of the European variety? The two that immediately spring to mind are Michael Nyman and Louis Andriessen. Nyman is primarily known for his music soundtracks to Peter Greenaway's off-beat films. Those who have enjoyed his scores to *The Draughtsman's Contract*, *A Zed and two Noughts* and *Drowning by Numbers* may like to sample the less frequently heard, though equally compelling String Quartets[8], or his short one-act chamber opera *The Man who mistook his Wife for a Hat*[9]. Louis Andriessen has been scantily represented on disc outside his own country, but last year saw the release of one of his most well known works—*De Staat*[10]. This highly influential piece deserves to be heard more often, and it's to be hoped that more recordings of Andriessen's music will follow.

Back to America, but away from minimalism, the music of the American composer David Del Tredici has also had relatively little exposure on record, which is surprising considering the approachability of his style. His early works, written in a knotty, post-Schoenbergian style, were much admired by Aaron Copland, but in the 1970s Del Tredici's harmonic language became increasingly more melodic and tonally orientated. Since then his works have revolved almost exclusively around settings of Lewis Carroll. *Final Alice*, *Vintage Alice* and *In Memory of a summer Day* are just some of the rich, sumptuous scores that form part of his singular but always highly original output. Those with an ear for the unusual are directed to a New World disc containing *Haddock's Eyes* (a setting of the *White Knight's Song* from *Through the Looking Glass*) for soprano, narrator and chamber ensemble, and *Steps* (one of his few orchestral works not directly inspired by Carroll). Both are excellent introductions to this highly colourful and imaginative composer[11].

Another composer whose music has always been largely conventional in outlook is Sir Andrzej Panufnik. And although his methods of working involve careful attention to symmetry, number symbolism and a quasi-serial approach to melodic material, the end results are always immediately communicative and filled with a deep concern for humanity. The Violin Concerto of 1971 and the Bassoon Concerto[12] (written in memory of Father Jerzy Popieluszko) are an ideal starting place if you are approaching his music for the first time. His *Arbor cosmica* ("Cosmic tree") for 12 solo strings, considered by many to be his masterpiece, can be found on an Elektra-Nonesuch disc coupled with his early *Sinfonia sacra*[13].

Interest in the music of John Tavener grows apace once again, and rightly so. Tavener, now in his forties, first met critical acclaim at the early age of 19, when his dramatic cantata *The Whale* was first performed as part of the inaugural concert of the London Sinfonietta in 1968. That work, along with his *Celtic Requiem*, made an all too brief appearance on disc when it was taken up and recorded on The Beatles' Apple label. Since then, however, Tavener's music has undergone a considerable sea-change in style—partly due perhaps to his conversion to the Russian Orthodox faith in 1977. Although his music had always been orientated toward the spiritual rather than the intellectual, it was in the Russian Orthodox faith that Tavener found a rich source of inspiration in the powerful image of the ikon. An excellent example of his current style can be found in The Tallis Scholars recording of his *Ikon of Light*[14] and Hyperion's disc of choral music[15].

Sir Andrzej Panufnik   *[photo:Conifer*

A deep concern for things spiritual has also led the Estonian composer Arvo Pärt away from the more rigorously intellectual school of composition. His *St John Passion* (1982) and his haunting *Tabula rasa*[16] (literally 'clean slate') for two violins, prepared piano and strings, have become classics of our time and almost certainly played an important part in bringing his music to a wider audience. His more radical, avant-garde compositions from the mid 1960s to the early 1970s (including three symphonies)[17] reveal an altogether different but no less fascinating insight into the creative processes of this extraordinary artist.

In many ways the more hard line approach of composers like Sir Peter Maxwell Davies and Sir Harrison Birtwistle pose greater problems for the first time explorer, though their undoubted stature as two of Britain's greatest

Sir Peter Maxwell Davies   [photo: Unicorn-Kanchana

Sir Harrison Birtwistle   [photo: Royal Opera House/Barda

living composers should signal the worthiness of such an exploration. Maxwell Davies has been well represented on disc since the days of vinyl. An excellent starting place for investigation has been thoughtfully provided by Unicorn-Kanchana, on a disc entitled *A Celebration of Scotland*[18], featuring several of his more immediately accessible pieces. *An Orkney Wedding with Sunrise* combines Maxwell Davies's love of the Orkneys (his adopted home) with a desire to write music for people to enjoy on a purely non-intellectual level, without compromise to either his own artistic integrity or the integrity of his listeners. Those delving deeper into his music are urged to investigate the symphonies[19] and the marvellously atmospheric chamber works: *Ave Maris Stella* and *Image, Reflection, Shadow*[20]. Unfortunately, though, the First Symphony, by far the most immediately accessible of the four, still awaits transfer to CD. Harrison Birtwistle's natural inclination toward folk-lore and myth (especially the Greek variety) has inevitably led him to explore music orientated toward the theatre and opera. His first notable success in this area was his opera *Punch and Judy* (now reissued on CD by Etcetera)[21]. There followed several important compositions (among them *Down by the Greenwood Side, The Triumph of Time* and *Verse for Ensemble*) that placed Birtwistle firmly on the international scene and confirmed his stature as one of Britain's finest contemporary composers. His operas *The Mask of Orpheus* (1973-84) and *Gawain* (which took the musical world by storm in 1990) are without doubt two of the finest contemporary operas to emerge in the last decade, and deserve to be recorded as soon as possible. There are no easy ways into Birtwistle's music but those who take the plunge are rarely disappointed; try the orchestral pieces *Silbury Air, The Secret Theatre* and *Carmen Arcadiae Mechanicae Perpetuum* on the Etcetera label[22], or Håkan Hardenberger's stunning performance of *Endless Parade* (for trumpet, vibraphone and strings) on Philips[23].

Theatrical and operatic works are also a prominent feature in the output of Hans Werner Henze. Disenchanted by the radical stance of many of his fellow German composers he left Germany in 1953 and settled in Italy, where his music immediately took on the warmth and vibrancy of its Mediterranean surroundings. Typical examples include the operas *König Hirsch* "King Stag", *Elegy for Young Lovers* and *The Bassarids*[24], and Symphonies Nos. 4 and 5. The symphonies[25] offer an excellent insight into Henze's creative processes, as they often explore and comment upon material used in his operas and theatre pieces. At present the only opera available on disc is *The Bassarids* (though vigilant CD hunters might be lucky to track down a copy of *Boulevard Solitude*). Set in English and imaginatively and colourfully scored *The Bassarids* should pose no greater problems than the operas of Britten or Tippett.

Space does not allow a complete survey of all that is active in contemporary music; it would take a book of considerable volume to do that and there are many established composers such as Luciano Berio, György Ligeti, Krzysztof Penderecki and Witold Lutoslawski who have not been touched on either. But hopefully the above will give the listener some idea of the diversity and range on offer to anyone willing to lend an ear and an open mind. It's an oft-used saying but the contemporary music of today is the classical music of tomorrow, and sometimes our closeness to events can blind us to their importance or relevance. True, many of the more extreme pieces from the 1950s, 1960s and 1970s have not worn the test of time well and may seem dated, but it's arguable that without those years of radicalism we would not have such a rich pool to plunder now. Music, after all, requires a two-way effort, and that applies to a Mozart symphony just as much as it does to the latest offering from a Birtwistle or a Torke. Explore and enjoy!

[1] Torke. Chamber works. Argo 430 209-2ZH (12/90).
[2] Glass. Music in Twelve Parts. Virgin Venture CDVEBX32 (6/90).
[3] Glass. Einstein on the Beach. CBS CD38875 (9/86).
[4] Glass. Satyagraha. CBS CD39672 (9/86).
[5] Glass. Akhnaten. CBS CD42457 (2/88).
[6] Adams. Nixon in China. Elektra-Nonesuch 7559-79177-2 (10/88).
[7] Adams. The Wound-dresser; Fearful Symmetries. Elektra-Nonesuch 7559-79218-2 (6/90).
[8] Nyman. String Quartets Nos. 1-3. Argo 433 093-2ZH (8/91).
[9] Nyman. The Man who mistook his Wife for a Hat. CBS CD44669 (11/88).
[10] Andriessen. De Staat. Elektra-Nonesuch 7559-79251-2.
[11] Del Tredici. Steps; Haddock's Eyes. New World 80390-2.
[12] Panufnik. Violin Concerto; Bassoon Concerto, etc. Conifer CDCF182 (7/90).
[13] Panufnik. Arbor cosmica; Sinfonia sacra. Elektra-Nonesuch 7559-79228-2 (5/91).
[14] Tavener. Ikon of Light, etc. Gimell CDGIM 005 (5/91).
[15] Tavener. Choral music. Hyperion CDA66464.
[16] Pärt. Tabula rasa; Fratres, etc. ECM 817 764-2.
[17] Pärt. Three Symphonies; Cello Concerto, etc. BIS CD434 (9/89).
[18] Maxwell Davies. A Celebration of Scotland. Various. Unicorn-Kanchana DKPCD9070 (12/88).
[19] Maxwell Davies. Symphony No. 4. Trumpet Concerto. Collins Classics 1181-2 (6/91).
[20] Maxwell Davies. Ave Maris Stella; Image, Reflection, Shadow; Runes from a Holy Island. Unicorn-Kanchana UKCD2038 (3/91).
[21] Birtwistle. Punch and Judy. Etcetera KTC2014 (12/89).
[22] Birtwistle. Silbury Air; The Secret Theatre, etc. Etcetera KTC1052 (4/88).
[23] Birtwistle. Endless Parade (with works by Maxwell Davies and Blake Watkins). Philips 432 075-2PH (6/91).
[24] Werner Henze. The Bassarids. Schwann 314006 (10/91).
[25] Werner Henze. Six Symphonies. DG 429 854-2GC2 (12/90).

FURTHER RECOMMENDED LISTENING

Luciano Berio. Formazioni. Decca 425 832-2DH (8/90).
Berio. Voci Requies Corale. RCA RD87898.
Sofia Gubaidulina. Offertorium. DG 427 336-2GH (9/89).
Alexander Goehr. Metamorphosis Dance. Romanza. Unicorn-Kanchana UKCD2039 (6/91).
Oliver Knussen. Symphonies Nos. 2 and 3. Ophelia Dances, etc. Unicorn-Kanchana UKCD 2010 (9/88).
Ligeti. Choral Works. EMI CDC7 54096-2.
Ligeti. Le Grande Macabre. Wergo WER 6170-2.
Elizabeth Maconchy. String Quartets Nos. 5-8. Unicorn-Kanchana DKPCD 9081 (6/90).
Nicholas Maw. Odyssey. EMI CDS7 542772 (9/91).
Penderecki. St Luke Passion. Argo 430 328-2ZH (3/91).
Astor Piazzolla. Five Tango Sensations. Elektra-Nonesuch 7559-79253/5-2.
Steve Reich. The Four Sections, Music for Mallet Instruments, Voices and Organ. Elektra-Nonesuch 7559-79220-2 (5/91).
Reich. The Desert Music. Nonesuch 7559-79101-2 (6/86).
Toru Takemitsu. Quatrain; A Flock Descends into the Pentagonal Garden. DG 423 253-2GC.
Takemitsu. riverrun, etc. Virgin Classics VC7 91188-2 (9/91).
Alfred Schnittke. Symphony No. 5. BIS CD427 (8/90).
Simpson. Symphony No. 9. Hyperion CDA66299 (12/88).
Iannis Xenakis. Oresteïa. Salabert HM83 (9/91).
Xenakis. Palimpsest; Epeï; Dikhthas; Akanthos. Wergo WER6178-2.

The dates in brackets refer to the review date in *Gramophone*.

Herbert von Karajan

**Christopher Headington
on the anatomy of a musical giant**

[photo: DG

Human beings differ from other animals in our awareness of time, our ability to plan for or fear the future, and our occasional despair at the transience of our lives. For 1,500 years one of the chief aims of Asian and European alchemists was to discover the elixir of life, in other words to achieve immortality, and writers from Marlowe to Goethe and Mann (as well as Gounod and Busoni in their operas) have been drawn to the story of Faust, the restless Renaissance man who uses illicit magic to overcome the limitations of humanity. Though he and his works perish, they are transformed into spirit, which the world's great religions tell us is immortal. And poets too, for Shakespeare wrote in Sonnet 19, "Yet, do thy worst, old Time: despite thy wrong, My love shall in my verse live ever young".

What has tempted me into these not strictly musical musings is the thought that creative artists strive, consciously or otherwise, to bring into the world something which does not die with them. I have always felt that we know Beethoven better through his music than most people did who actually met him. But no one creates from nothing, not even a composer (Beethoven didn't invent the piano, the symphony orchestra or sonata form) and while a performer has not made the score from which he plays he creates the performance itself as sound, structure and expressive experience. We can argue, I think, that the conductor of the *Pastoral* Symphony or *La mer* stands in the same relation to the score as a painter does to a landscape or a flower arrangement and that both kinds of artists reveal their subjects to us through their personal and unique ways of seeing and hearing. Thus a conductor is a creator too, and while a composer has only his own psyche to express, this performer whose instrument is the orchestra must be able to see into, and then reveal, many human worlds.

One of Herbert von Karajan's favourite ways of praising a fellow musician was to say that he or she was "full of music". He himself spent 75 years in its service, having made his début at the age of five as a pianist and then worked right up to the end of his life at the age of 81. Auspiciously, his birthplace was the same as Mozart's, and he studied music in the Salzburg Mozarteum and Vienna before conducting *Le nozze di Figaro* at the Ulm City Theatre just before his twenty-first birthday. Such a background inevitably meant that his musical orientation was towards the German-Austrian tradition, but there was a considerable breadth to that tradition and, in any case, its chief composers had often been wide-ranging, with Handel composing Italian operas and English oratorios for British audiences and Mozart writing Italian operas for Vienna and Prague.

[photo: DG

This article is not meant to be a mere Karajan biography or obituary, for over two years after his death in July 1989 it is late to be writing one. Yet to understand his gifts and achievement it is useful to know that throughout his life he was a man of the theatre, or more specifically the opera house. His Berlin Staatsoper account of *Tristan und Isolde* in 1937 was a landmark in his career, and showed that he could bring an intense expressive force and sweep to such music as well as remarkable orchestral precision. The mention of Wagner's great Nordic love story is perhaps the cue to note Karajan's affiliation to the Nazi party in 1934, something that has since been much discussed. But according to his biographer Richard Osborne, he had to accept membership in order to become the Generalmusik-direktor at Aachen. In any case, it seems to have been nothing more to him than an unwanted necessity and after he married the partly Jewish Anita Gütermann during the war (in 1942) he made the stand of relinquishing it, although that did not save him from later opprobrium and even a brief post-war prohibition on work.

In his thirties, Karajan was Musical Director at the Berlin State Opera right through the terrible years of 1938-45. But after the war, his career faltered, and Richard Osborne maintains that it was largely "disrupted, diverted and blocked", not least by his Berlin-born older rival Furtwängler until that conductor's death in 1954. He went for the 1948-49 season to conduct at La Scala in Milan, and although he was already familiar with the Italian repertory this enlarged his experience of it and

[photo: DG

he became a master conductor of Verdi in particular while also learning to be at home in other repertory such as Puccini. It was also just after the war in 1947 that he made his début with the Philharmonia Orchestra in London, largely thanks to its founder Walter Legge, a Gramophone Company executive who discovered him and brought him to Britain to record Verdi's *Falstaff* and Strauss's *Der Rosenkavalier*. Karajan's long and successful career in the recording studio undoubtedly owes much to the discriminating and entrepreneurial Legge.

Thus, little by little, Karajan re-established himself among Europe's most wanted conductors. Outside opera, his reputation had also grown and in 1949 he was appointed conductor for life of the Vienna Gesellschaft der Musikfreunde (Music Society) and conducted the Vienna Symphony Orchestra or the Vienna Philharmonic for the Society's concerts. From 1950 onwards he recorded with the latter orchestra and with the Philharmonia, taking the British orchestra on a European tour in 1952. But as every collector knows, his longest and most rewarding association with an orchestra was with the Berlin Philharmonic, where in 1955 he asked for and obtained a life contract—though near the end of his life he did give up his post after tensions appeared among his players.

Karajan's masterly work with the Berlin Philharmonic Orchestra is now part of musical history. And to revert to the point with which I began this article, it is especially through his many recordings with them that his art as a performer has achieved the kind of permanence that was inconceivable for Bach as an organist, Liszt as a pianist, or (closer to our own time) Mahler as a conductor. He recorded the Beethoven symphonies at least three times, and there were cycles too of Brahms, Bruckner, Tchaikovsky and Mahler that were also based on long experience: indeed he recorded Tchaikovsky's Sixth Symphony for the first time in 1939 with the Berlin Philharmonic Orchestra and Brahms's First as early as 1943 with the Concertgebouw.

Of course, Karajan was at home, too, in the music of his fellow Salzburger Mozart. His début recording in 1939 was of the Overture to *Die Zauberflöte*, and his celebrated 1953 account with Dennis Brain and the Philharmonia Orchestra of the four horn concertos is in this *Guide*[1]. He was also skilful in Haydn, performing and recording some of the later symphonies and the oratorios *The Creation* and *The Seasons*. But (and I am thinking now of concert music rather than opera, where Mozart was among his great loves) broadly speaking we value him most in nineteenth-century and early twentieth-century repertory, for he was above all a musical narrator, dramatist and colourist.

From his student days in Vienna, Karajan understood the link between Mahler and the Second Viennese School, and although he never regularly programmed Schoenberg he made a thoughtful and persuasive recording of his sultrily late-romantic *Verklärte Nacht* and toughly terse Variations for Orchestra[2] as well as one of Webern that includes the enigmatic ten-minute Symphony[3]. Among more recent 'advanced' music, he conducted some Henze, Ligeti and Penderecki, but he was not always sympathetic to radically new styles, saying of some composers, "it is difficult if you get a score and you don't know what he is thinking ... I can only do it if I am convinced". Thus there was no Stockhausen or Boulez. With some older contemporaries he was also not fully at home, and his Bartók recordings are few[4]. Although he conducted Stravinsky he must have been wounded by that composer's remark that his first recorded BPO *Rite of Spring*[5] was "too polished, a pet savage rather than a real one...I doubt whether *The Rite* can be satisfactorily performed in terms of Herr von Karajan's traditions". But he did not apparently bear a grudge and when interviewed in March 1988 he talked about plans to perform Stravinsky's *Oedipus rex*.

For whatever reason, the music of the English-speaking world largely passed him by. We draw a blank on Copland, Gershwin and American music generally, and though he recorded Britten's *Variations on a theme of Frank Bridge*[6] and strong yet refined accounts of Holst's *The Planets*[7] he does not seem to have performed any Elgar, nor explored to any great extent the music of Vaughan Williams or Walton. However, his interests elsewhere were wide-ranging. More than most Austrian and German conductors, he had an affinity for Sibelius (he recorded the Fifth Symphony[8] four times and there is a memorably atmospheric Sixth)[9], Honegger (his recording of the sombre Third Symphony, the wartime *Symphonie liturgique*[10], is another modern classic) and Shostakovich, whose dramatic Tenth Symphony he recorded twice[11]. The Russian master was deeply impressed by his performance of this symphony in Moscow, but Karajan was no less admiring and said of him, "he was a very great composer". He was always ready to praise others who were in his view "full of music", and people who think of him as an egotist may be reminded that he refused to conduct Shostakovich's Sixth Symphony because the great Russian conductor, Evgeny Mravinsky, had already done it so well. Debussy's music was always special for him, but while he and his Berlin orchestra brought an exceptional sensuous refinement to *La mer* or the *Prélude à l'après-midi d'un faune*[12], his 1978 account of the French composer's operatic masterpiece *Pelléas et Mélisande*[13] was also powerful in its revelation of Golaud's agonising jealousy and the tender, doomed innocence of its young lovers.

Early in his career, Karajan recognized the importance of recording and ensured that he was in artistic charge when in the studio, taking a keen interest in the technical side as well. He appreciated the special (and spatial) problems involved in recording big choral works such as Beethoven's *Missa solemnis* and Brahm's *German Requiem*, and above all opera, a musical realm which was always central to his activities. He was appointed as conductor of the Vienna State Opera in 1957, and although he left that post in 1964 after opposition to his views on production (he thought some traditions outmoded), he returned to it in 1977. He had the vital gift of being able to get on musically and personally with opera singers who were themselves stars and expected to be treated

accordingly, saying of Maria Callas, with whom he recorded *Madama Butterfly*[14], that "if she was rightly handled she was very easy" and that her rhythm was "incredible—she heard so well and sang always with the orchestra". Often he singled out youngish and relatively untried singers for stage productions and the recordings which commonly followed, and his detractors said that he sometimes then dropped them, having made excessive demands which spoilt them vocally or interpretatively. Of course it was difficult to refuse an invitation from Karajan, and the soprano Helen Donath said, "if you tell him no, he feels almost personally rejected". But when she sang Eva for him in a Dresden *Die Meistersinger*[15] in 1970 she noticed how considerate he was for the strength of her voice, saying, "Every other conductor would have blown me off the record, but he tunes the orchestra down". Other singers have been equally impressed, and Josephine Barstow (his chosen Amelia for the Verdi *Un Ballo in maschera* which was almost his last recording)[16] says, "Music-making on this level is what I came into the profession for". Jon Vickers (who sang Florestan, Otello and Tristan for him) once declared in an interview, "Karajan stands head and shoulders above every conductor in the world today, he demands an incredible standard for music's sake, he believes I am much better than I believe I am".

It has been said that if Karajan sought power, it was only to achieve independence. Underneath his patent authority there was something idealistic about him, and it is significant that he admitted to being deeply touched by Don Quixote's remark in Cervantes's story, and then also by implication in Richard Strauss's tone poem: "I have battled, I have made mistakes, but I have lived my life as best I can according to the world as I see it". In other words, "I did it my way". Such a man, said Jon Vickers, "cannot help but produce enemies. It is one of the sad things about the heart of mankind. The jealousy and envy this man is a victim to absolutely horrifies me, for he is a great, great human being." In the obituaries in 1989, at a time when one wanted to give thanks for a life devoted to music that enriched us all, it was saddening to note the degree to which praise was grudged and the occasional splashes of what Osborne called "gratuitous vitriol", whether in references to his supposed support of Nazi Germany or to his 'megalomania'.

This was a great conductor, certainly: a man who liked to perform music ranging from Bach's *St Matthew Passion* (which he directed from the harpsichord)[17] to Lehár's operettas and the Johann Strauss waltzes and polkas that he conducted at New Year's Day concerts in Vienna. The sound and skill of the Berlin Philharmonic Orchestra was the fruit not only of the discipline that he imparted but also of an indefinable flair, and he once said that his aim was "to combine Toscanini's precision with Furtwängler's fantasy". He enjoyed life to the full, including skiing, piloting aircraft and sailing, and lived latterly with his second wife Eliette (a painter whose work has appeared on the sleeves and jewel-cases of his records) in a spacious but un-grandiose house not far from Salzburg which looked out towards the mountains that he knew from childhood expeditions. He was a dominant figure in Salzburg's annual music festival and in 1967 founded an additional Easter Festival there to produce opera in the new Festspielhaus with its enormous stage which he considered suitable for Wagner. In 1969 he set up a Herbert von Karajan Foundation that supported music therapy and scientific conferences. Towards the end of his life he suffered debilitating pain from spinal problems perhaps connected with the bad fall from a tree which he had as a bold and active boy of 12. But he hardly reduced his schedule at Salzburg, Berlin and Vienna, and filmed some 40 performances which he planned to release when videodisc or other superior video technology (i.e. with high quality sound) became more widely available domestically. In time, these will add to the already rich recorded legacy that he left us.

For once, it is a critic who deserves to have the last word, or nearly the last. Tim Page said to a student after an American concert that Karajan conducted not long before his death, "You may never again hear such playing, but now you know it can be done". But he was wrong: although Karajan has gone, for we *can* hear such playing again and again, recording does what no alchemy could do, preserving something that remains alive with an incomparable vitality.

[1] Mozart. Horn Concertos. EMI CDH7 61013-2 (2/88).
[2] Schoenberg. Verklärt Nacht. Variations. DG 415 326-2GH (3/86).
[3] Webern. Passacaglia. Pieces for strings and orchestra. Symphony, Op. 21. DG 423 254-2GC (7/88); DG 427 424-2GC3 (9/89).
[4] Bartók. Concerto for Orchestra (various works by Brahms, Dvořák, Schubert, Schumann, Sibelius and Wagner). EMI CMS7 63321-2; Concerto for Orchestra. Music for Strings, Percussion and Celesta. DG 415 322-2GH (10/85); Concerto for Orchestra. Music for Strings, Percussion and Celesta (various works by Britten, Debussy, Handel, Kodály, Sibelius and Vaughan Williams). EMI CMS7 63464-2.
[5] Stravinsky. The Rite of Spring. Apollo. DG 415 979-2GH (9/86); The Rite of Spring/Mussorgsky. Pictures at an Exhibition. DG 423 214-2GMW (4/88).
[6] Britten. Variations on a theme of Frank Bridge. EMI CMS7 63464-2.
[7] Holst. The Planets. DG 400 028-2GH (7/83); Decca 417 709-2DM (5/88).
[8] Sibelius. Symphonies Nos. 5 and 7. DG 415 107-2GH (6/85); Symphonies Nos. 4 and 5. EMI CDM7 69244-2 (4/88).
[9] Sibelius. Symphonies Nos. 4 and 6. DG 415 108-2GH (6/85).
[10] Honegger. Symphonies Nos. 2 and 3. DG 423 242-2GC (6/88).
[11] Shostakovich. Symphony No. 10. DG 413 361-2GH (8/84); DG 429 716-2GGA (8/90).
[12] Debussy. La mer. Prélude à l'après-midi d'un faune. EMI CDM7 69007-2; EMI CMS7 63464-2; DG 413 589-2GH (12/86); DG 423 217-2GMW (7/88); DG 427 250-2GGA (7/89).
[13] Debussy. Pelléas et Mélisande. EMI CDS7 49350-2 (2/88).
[14] Puccini. Madama Butterfly. EMI CDS7 47959-8 (10/87).
[15] Wagner. Die Meistersinger von Nürnberg. EMI CDS7 49683-2 (7/88).
[16] Verdi. Un Ballo in maschera. DG 427 635-2GH2 (11/89).
[17] Bach. St Matthew Passion. DG 419 789-2GH3 (3/88).

Figures in brackets refer to review date in *Gramophone*.

Leonard Bernstein

David Gutman remembers the irrepressible man of music

[photo: DG/Hunstein

For all that Leonard Bernstein dared to be versatile, a jack of all trades in an era of one-club specialization, he bequeathed a very particular legacy to the gramophone. On one level no doubt he embodied the optimism and can-do of the American way. As Tim Page pointed out, Bernstein's decision to make a career in the USA "had the same effect on our native musicians that Ralph Waldo Emerson's lecture *The American Scholar* did on nineteenth-century literati. It was a declaration of independence." Bernstein took his American mission seriously: single-handedly, he resurrected Charles Ives, pushed towards the re-evaluation of dozens of lesser talents, mesmerized the New York Philharmonic into playing like the world's best and pushed Broadway to its greatest heights. At the same time, many took him to be the last of the great maestros. He had no problem exercising a charismatic spell on audiences in the great Viennese classics, and, as the Vienna Philharmonic were quick to spot, was uniquely capable of stealing the limelight from Herbert von Karajan even in his native Salzburg.

For most of us, I suspect, Bernstein was indelibly associated with the music of Gustav Mahler. How characteristic it is that he felt he had to construct a philosophical justification for the Mahler boom rather than simply exulting in his personal role in helping it along. Bernstein put down the long years of neglect to the agonizing message contained in

Mahler's *oeuvre*, but found in it a new and appropriate paradox for our nuclear age: Mahler is death-obsessed, yet his music reanimates. The Ninth Symphony's concluding *Adagio* "takes the form of a prayer, Mahler's last chorale, his closing hymn, so to speak; and it prays for the restoration of life, of tonality, of faith". Here, too, is Bernstein's own world view, the source of that peculiar generosity of spirit which informs so much of his music-making. He is always reaching out beyond orthodox Judaism for some "ebullient, renewed will to survive the apocalyptic". His own compositions reflect personal, spiritual concerns ("me down here looking up to find Him") to such an extent that the Third Symphony, *Kaddish*, finds him literally haranguing the deity.

Bernstein was of course a controversial figure with a propaganda image at odds with conventional notions of artistic depth. No doubt, Lenny alive *was* ludicrously over the top. But if his personal life was lived not wisely but to excess, we might do well to remember that where Karajan wished to dominate, Bernstein wanted only to be loved. As Hermann Bahr said of Gustav Mahler, his personal impact was so strong that most people could not reach over it to his work. In his seventieth year, Bernstein put it like this: "As I grow older, I take more risks, whether in daily life, in execution or composition. Life becomes more chancy, more fun the less of it is left, and you have to take every opportunity there is to try everything." For Bernstein it was never enough to compose and play and teach and record music well. Always there was something more to say and write, or do on TV, film and video. Sadly, that chapter is closed now, but even as DG's posthumous release schedule passes its peak, so Sony Classical's ambitious programme of reissues will bring many unfamiliar recordings onto CD for a new audience of music lovers.

[photo: DG / Hunstein]

Bernstein's discography falls naturally into three broad phases. The first, virtually unrepresented in the current catalogues, precedes his appointment as sole Music Director of the New York Philharmonic in 1958. Bernstein the wunderkind recorded for a variety of labels as pianist and conductor. Starting with some of his own music, he specialized in what were then reckoned contemporary novelties (works by Copland, Milhaud, Stravinsky, and the like) before setting down his first Beethoven, Brahms, Schumann and Tchaikovsy in the mid-1950s. The Maestro Bernstein of phase two made over 200 records for American Columbia,

[photo: DG/Burton

dashing into the studio with the alacrity of a Neeme Järvi to galvanize an often ill-prepared New York Philharmonic into enthusiastic accounts of unusual repertoire and invigorating (if sometimes ill-received) renditions of the standard classics. Few of the more audacious issues were remade in Bernstein's third, 'European' phase, dominated at first by operatic projects and mainstream repertoire which reflected his long-running affair with the Vienna Philharmonic. Deutsche Grammophon ensured world-wide distribution for what, despite the vagaries of live recording, were generally better recorded, sometimes more polished, grander, slower, deliberately less vital performances, confirming the creeping Furtwänglerization of Bernstein's New World brashness. Some of these late releases preserve the sort of one-off interpretations which thrill in the concert hall; unfortunately, they can prove unsuitable for repeated listening at home. Bernstein himself backtracked on his idiosyncratic *Enigma* Variations, admitting that the funereal "Nimrod" didn't really work on disc[1]. This was a rare, pre-Nigel Kennedy, case of a classical issue provoking widespread critical outcry. Writing in the *New Yorker*, Andrew Porter gave high praise to the New York orchestra's "incandescent [concert] account, a blazing and beautiful dithyramb to love and friendship". Closer to home, Edward Pearce has described the (recorded) BBC performance as tantamount to deliberate sabotage: a misplaced attack on a British Imperialist tradition Bernstein found distasteful. DG's compact disc seems pretty inoffensive today: right or wrong, the performance never descends to the routine.

An overtly romantic interpreter regardless of tempo, Bernstein was never a conscious stylist. He was attracted by the drama of great music and found it in Haydn as in Tchaikovsky or Mahler. Therein, for many, lies his greatest gift as a conductor—that of "revivifying the old" as his brother, Burton Bernstein, described it. Bernstein exemplified a musical approach so different from that of today's predominantly literal conductors that his loss should give us pause for thought. After all, most of the great conductors of the past have been composers (however bad), for the act of creation means more to one who knows what it is to create.

At the very end of his life, Bernstein seems to have regretted not spending more time on his composing. Clearly, his recordings of his own music occupy a special place, even though the works themselves do not always escape accusations of well-crafted banality. What can distinguish his compositions is actually what distinguishes them from many of the contemporary trends he picked up, the better to throw his own meanings into relief. Shamelessly eclectic as it is, whether pop, pap or post-Schoenberg, even the worst of his music is recognizable as indubitably his own. The best of it? Possibly *West Side Story*[2], so memorably embalmed in the famous operatic version released by DG in 1985. But there are plenty of other works, all preserved on CD in 'authentic' performances, whose time is coming: *Prelude, Fugue And Riffs*[3] ('composed' jazz at its finest), the *Serenade on Plato's Symposium*[4] (if only he'd called it just plain Violin Concerto), *On the Waterfront*[5] (surely the best film score to come out of Hollywood) and the unclassifiable *Candide*[6]. Its perfect overture[7] is already a classic, while the new recording of the complete score, Bernstein's last in the recording studio, reveals it to be *musically* no less a masterpiece than *West Side Story*. The maestro's more extended serious pieces are not always up to this standard, faring best where they retain links with song. The *Songfest*[8], which he wrote to celebrate America's Bicentenary in 1976, and the recent *Arias and Barcarolles*[9] are underrated examples. And if the hip outrageousness of the *Mass*[10] fails to transcend its era, a work like the *Chichester Psalms*[11] is surprisingly, surpassingly modest.

Bernstein himself was many things but never exactly this. One report has Lenny going missing at his own party. Guests eventually find him sitting alone in a room, conducting one of his own recordings of Mahler. Through the tears he can be heard to murmur, "Wonderful, marvellous. Nobody conducts Mahler like that". It is interesting to speculate on how Bernstein's art will be received by a new generation who neither experienced him in the concert hall nor read about him in the gossip columns. Bernstein's insatiable capacity for wonder is not in doubt (all that leaping about on the podium) but the glorious subjectivity of his music-making has tended to preclude the formation of a critical consensus around individual readings. Perhaps he will always have his detractors, critics who reject exactly the qualities those well-disposed towards him find most impressive. Nevertheless, as the years pass we'll be able to view the recorded legacy with increasing objectivity and, many believe, increasing respect and admiration.

---

[1] Enigma Variations. DG 413 490-2GH (11/84).

[2] West Side Story. DG 415 253-2GH2 (4/85).

[3] Prelude, Fugue and Riffs. Columbia Jazz Combo/Bernstein—CBS CD42227 (4/87); London Sinfonietta/Rattle—EMI CDC7 47991-2 (12/87); London Symphony Orchestra/L. Smith. RCA RD87762 (4/89).

[4] Serenade for violin, strings, harp and percussion. Israel Philharmonic Orchestra/Bernstein—DG 423 583-2GH (1/89); Symphony of the Air/Bernstein—Sony Classical CD45956 (12/90).

[5] On the Waterfront. Israel Philharmonic Orchestra/Bernstein—DG 431 028-2GBE, DG 415 253-2GH2 (4/85), coupled with West Side Story; New York Philharmonic Orchestra/Bernstein—CBS CD44773 (2/91).

[6] Candide. DG 429 734-2GH2 (8/91).

[7] Candide—Overture. There are ten recordings currently listed in *The Classical Catalogue*. The most recent are with the New York Philharmonic Orchestra conducted by Bernstein—CBS CD44723 (11/88); CBS44773 (2/91).

[8] Songfest. Washington National Symphony Orchestra/Bernstein—DG 415 965-2GH (5/86); KOCH 37000-2 (6/90).

[9] Arias and Barcarolles—KOCH 37000-2 (6/90); Delos DE3078 (9/90).

[10] Mass. CBS CD44593.

[11] Chichester Psalms. There are seven recordings currently listed in *The Classical Catalogue*. The most recent are: Atlanta Symphony Orchestra/R. Shaw—Telarc CD80181 (3/90); New York Philharmonic Orchestra/Bernstein—CBS CD44710 (12/88).

Figures in brackets refer to review date in *Gramophone*.

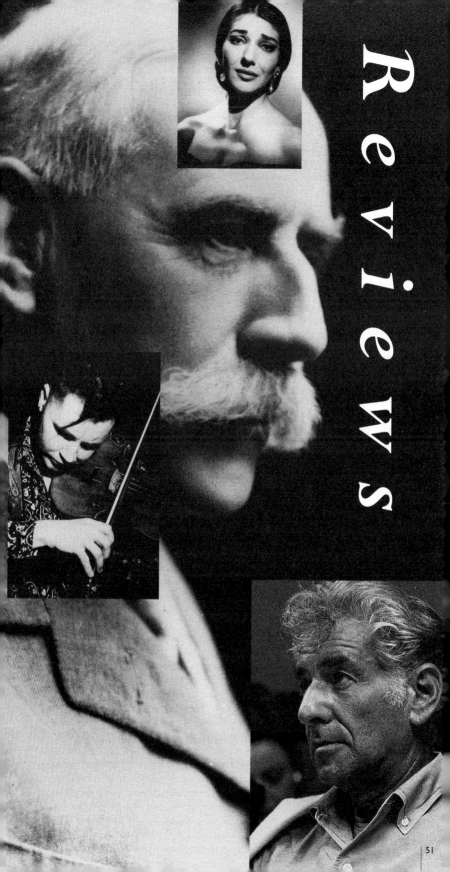

Reviews

Adolphe Adam

French 1803-1856

Adam. Giselle (abridged). **Vienna Philharmonic Orchestra/Herbert von Karajan.** Decca Ovation 417 738-2DM.

60' ADD

Adam's ballet *Giselle* is a typically romantic work and tells of the Wilis, affianced maidens who die before their wedding. Unable to rest they rise from their graves at night and enjoy the dancing that they were unable to indulge in whilst living. Anyone who comes across them as they dance is forced to join them until he drops dead. Set into this framework is the love between Giselle and Prince Albrecht. The music is lively, tuneful and evocative—in other words, excellent ballet music. Given a performance as recorded here which unites a top-class conductor, an outstanding orchestra and a superb recording (totally belying its 26 years) *Giselle* could wish for nothing more.

John Adams

American 1947

Adams. ORCHESTRAL WORKS. **San Francisco Symphony Orchestra/ Edo de Waart.** Elektra-Nonesuch 7559-79144-2.
The Chairman Dances—foxtrot for orchestra (1985). Christian Zeal and Activity (1973). Two Fanfares for Orchestra—Tromba Iontana (1986); Short Ride in a Fast Machine (1986). Common Tones in Simple Time (1980).

52' DDD 8/88

There is no better way of sampling the music of John Adams than through this attractive compilation. His descriptive scores combine pastiche or parody with glossy orchestration and also set out to shrewdly scrutinize his own nationality. Thus the earliest piece, *Christian Zeal and Activity*, is a variation on *Onward, Christian Soldiers*, not sung with upstanding confidence but rather played *pianissimo* by a small body of strings, naked and vulnerable. In similar but more flamboyant vein, *The Chairman Dances* enters the world of American politics, drawing on the same events as Adams's opera *Nixon in China*. It's a Hollywood-like fantasy, part slick, part sleazy, that evokes a bygone age of glamour and style. Even the works that have no obvious story to tell have a sensuality that makes them instantly alluring. Both orchestra and conductor have long-standing connections with Adams, and the performances are as full of life as they are authoritative.

Adams. The Wound-dresser[a]. Fearful symmetries. [a]**Sanford Sylvan** (bar); **St Luke's Orchestra/John Adams.** Elektra-Nonesuch 979 218-2. Text included.

47' DDD 6/90

This disc displays particularly well the two "opposing polarities" (the composer's words) of Adam's creativity. *The Wound-dresser* is a setting of Walt Whitman's poem of the same name, recounting Whitman's own experience of nursing the wounded and dying soldiers during the American Civil War. Though the poem is graphic in its description of the atrocities of war, it is also a profoundly moving testament of compassion and humanity. Adams's elegiac and atmospheric setting is one of his most accessible and luminously scored pieces—its strong triadic harmonies and lyrical, melodic beauty underpinning and elevating the compassionate overtones of the text. *Fearful symmetries* on the other hand is an example of what Adams calls his "trickster" pieces—irreverent and hugely entertaining. More overtly minimalist in its language, its relatively slender material sometimes comes close to outstaying it welcome. But the work's propulsive energy and its almost diabolic moto-perpetuam (one is reminded of the complex and comical inventions of Heath Robinson or even the paintings of Hieronymus Bosch) seem to keep the listener riveted and fascinated until the very last note. Performances and recording are excellent.

Adams. NIXON IN CHINA. **Sanford Sylvan** (bar) Chou en-Lai; **James Maddalena** (bar) Richard Nixon; **Thomas Hammons** (bar) Henry Kissinger; **Mari Opatz** (mez) Nancy T'ang (First Secretary to Mao); **Stephanie Friedman** (mez) Second Secretary to Mao; **Marion Dry** (mez) Third Secretary to Mao; **John Duykers** (ten) Mao Tse-Tung; **Carolann Page** (sop) Pat Nixon; **Trudy Ellen Craney** (sop) Chiang Ch'ing; **St Luke's Chorus and Orchestra/Edo de Waart.** Elektra-Nonesuch 7559-79177-2. Notes and text included.

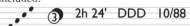 ③ 2h 24' DDD 10/88

If few operas deal with current affairs and even fewer address political issues, then *Nixon in China* takes the unusual risk of bordering on the documentary. But it is also a study in the psychology of its principal characters, and by peering into the personalities it goes well beyond fact alone, revealing instead a truly human drama. Alice Goodman's libretto is structured around the American presidential visit to Beijing in February 1972. At first all is a whirl of formalities, functions and fervent debate, but as the energy begins to flag so human vulnerabilities show through, and the opera ends in a state of lassitude, a strange super-imposition of bedroom scenes in which the protagonists share with one another their various reminiscences and dreams.

Adams's score is particularly strong when the action is fast-moving: he is a master of energetic, sonorous music, and his minimalist leanings serve him well in those parts of the story that require movement or depend upon quick-fire exchanges. Less dynamic moments—and Goodman's libretto is rich in poetical soliloquies and dialogues—he perhaps handles less elegantly, though in the long final act the mood of intimacy and soul-searching is cleverly caught. Best of all, however, is the music that captures the mood of the public scenes. Adams revels in evoking tawdry glamour, and a hint of fox-trot often hangs deliciously in the

[photo: Caldwell]

air. The cast is a strong one; James Maddalena in particular faces us with a life-like Richard Nixon, and Trudy Ellen Craney is memorable in Adams's most exaggerated character, the coloratura Madame Mao. So familiar are the faces behind the names that *Nixon in China* cannot be an easy work to watch on stage. On disc, with a few photographs provided in the insert booklet to jog the memory, it's perhaps easier to reconcile historical truth with the fantasy-world of this curious opera.

Richard Addinsell   *Refer to Index*   British 1904-1977

Jehan Alain

French 1911-1940

Alain. ORGAN WORKS. **Thomas Trotter.** Argo 430 838-2ZH. Played on the Het Van den Heuvel organ, Nieuwe Kerk te Katwijk aan Zee, Holland. Trois danses (1937-9). Fantasmagorie (1935). Première fantasie (1934). Deuxième fantasie (1936). Suite (1934-6). Deux danses à Agni Yavishta (1934). Trois pièces (1934-7).

76' DDD 7/91

No doubt Jehan Alain would have become one of the most significant composers of his generation had he not been killed in action during World War II. As it is, though, he left sufficient music of considerable genius and originality to earn him a lasting place among this century's major French composers of organ music. A strong impression left after listening through this generously-filled disc is of electrifying rhythmic intensity reaching a climax, as it were, with his most enduringly popular piece, "Litanies". The *Trois danses* and the two dances to the Hindu God of fire, Agni Yavishta, have an equally hypnotic effect which Thomas Trotter's compelling playing underlines superbly. This splendid Dutch organ helps matters immeasurably as does Argo's close recording. Particularly successful is the delightful set of ornate variations Alain based on a charming melody attributed to the sixteenth-century composer, Clément Jannequin. Perhaps in the few more reflective moments which this programme offers (such as the evocation of the Hanging Gardens of Babylon, "Le Jardin Suspendu") the very directness of the organ sound, not to mention some rather obvious action noise detracts from the atmosphere. But against this the organ possesses some magical colours and produces some captivating sounds which suit this somewhat other-worldly music.

Isaac Albéniz

Spanish 1860-1909

Albéniz (orch. Halffter). Rapsodia española, Op. 70.
Falla. Nights in the gardens of Spain (1915).
Turina. Rapsodia sinfónica, Op. 66. **Alicia de Larrocha** (pf); **London Philharmonic Orchestra/Rafael Frühbeck de Burgos.** Decca 410 289-2DH. From 410 289-1DH (6/84).

52' DDD 10/84

The three magically beautiful nocturnes which make up Falla's *Nights in the gardens of Spain* express the feelings and emotions evoked by contrasted surroundings, whilst Albéniz's enjoyably colourful *Rapsodia española* is a loosely assembled sequence of Spanish dances such as the *jota* and the *malagueña*. Like Falla's *Nights* the work was conceived as a piano solo, but this disc contains a version with orchestra arranged by Cristobal Halffter. The disc is completed by Turina's short, two-part work for piano and strings. All three pieces are excellently performed, but it is the Falla work which brings out the quality of Larrocha's artistry; her ability to evoke the colour of the Spanish atmosphere is remarkable. Frühbeck de Burgos supports her magnificently and persuades the LPO to some very Latin-sounding playing. The recording is suitably atmospheric.

Albéniz. Suite Iberia. Navarra (compl. de Séverac). Suite española, Op. 47. **Alicia de Larrocha** (pf). Decca 417 887-2DH2.

② 126' DDD 6/88

The *Iberia* suite is the greatest piano work in all Spanish musical literature and when played by Spain's leading pianist and recorded with warm but superlatively clean sound-quality is pure joy. A Catalan like Albéniz himself, Larrocha revels in the colour of these 12 highly picturesque and mostly Andalusian impressions, such as the quiet reverie of "Evocación", the lively bustle of "El puerto", the tense religious fervour of "El Corpus Christi en Sevilla", the swirling gaiety of "Triana", the brooding melancholy of "El Albaicín" and the exuberant bravura of *Navarra*. The Albéniz of 20 years earlier is illustrated by the 1886 *Suite española*, which Larrocha presents with winningly natural ease and charm.

Tomaso Albinoni *Italian 1671-1750*

Albinoni. WIND CONCERTOS.
Vivaldi. WIND CONCERTOS. **Paul Goodwin** (ob); **King's Consort/ Robert King.** Hyperion CDA66383.
Albinoni: Concertos, Op. 9—No. 2 in D minor; No. 6 in G major; No. 9 in C major. Concerto in C major. *Vivaldi:* Concertos—C major, RV560; F major, RV457; C major, RV559.

70' DDD 6/91

Few lovers of baroque concertos will be disappointed by this anthology. For the most part the programme has been well chosen both for the quality of the music and for the variety of instrumental colour which it affords. One piece, though, for trumpet, three oboes and a bassoon, for whom Albinoni's authorship is claimed is spurious and musically of a lower order than the remainder of the concertos. Albinoni was, if not the first, one of the first to write concertos for one and two solo oboes. They are without exception appealing for their warm colours and alluring conviviality. Happily, the disc includes one of Albinoni's most impressive compositions, the Oboe Concerto in D minor (Op. 9 No. 2) with its lyrical, aria-like *Adagio*; thankfully, not *the Adagio* but a genuine product from the composer's pen and an incomparably superior creation. The Vivaldi concertos are immediately engaging for their rhythmic energy and their varied colours. Two of the works are for pairs of oboes and clarinets, the latter very much in their infancy; the third is a piece for oboe and strings which the composer adapted from an earlier bassoon concerto. It has an especially effective opening movement, sensitively played by Paul Goodwin.

Albinoni. Concerti a cinque, Op. 7. **Heinz Holliger,** [a]**Hans Elhorst** (obs); **Berne Camerata.** Archiv Produktion Galleria 427 111-2AGA. From 2533 404 (11/79).
No. 2 in C major[a]; No. 3 in B flat major; No. 5 in C major[a]; No. 6 in D major; No. 8 in D major[a]; No. 9 in F major; No. 11 in C major[a]; No. 12 in C major.

57' ADD 4/89

Tomaso Albinoni, thanks to family money, was able to pursue his art without worrying overly about where the next ducat was coming from. He also had musical talent in abundance, writing 53 operas and over 150 instrumental works including the 12 *Concerti a cinque*, published in 1715. At that time concertos were customarily works for strings only, but those of Albinoni's Op. 7 were among the first (and his own first) to include wind instruments such as the oboe, and his use of the instrument displays the composer's remarkable gift of melody. It was however not only in their inclusion of wind instruments that these works were significant: in them Albinoni moved away from Corelli, in adopting a fast-slow-fast, three-movement format, and towards Vivaldi in sowing the seeds of *ritornello* form. Holliger and Elhorst are eloquent players, keeping a rounded edge on their sounds and they receive the most spruce and spirited of support from Berne Camerata. The recorded sound, acoustic and balance could hardly be bettered.

Gregorio Allegri

Allegri. Miserere[a].
W. Mundy. Vox patris caelestis.
Palestrina. Missa Papae Marcelli. [a]**Alison Stamp** (sop); **The Tallis Scholars/Peter Phillips.** Gimell CDGIM339. From Classics for Pleasure CFP40339 (10/80).

69' ADD 7/86

This is a favourite recording of Allegri's *Miserere*. Peter Phillips has used the natural acoustics of Merton College Chapel, adding a note of variety which relieves the repetitive nature of the long penitential psalm: what a simple idea it was to space the singers so that those with the low-lying verses were near the microphone and the others half-way down the chapel, with Alison Stamp's high C rising pure and clear above distant hushed voices! *Vox patris caelestis* is an imaginative and cleverly-designed motet for the Assumption of the Virgin, dating from the mid-sixteenth century-Catholic revival and based on texts from the *Song of Songs*. The music rises to an ecstatic climax at the words "Veni, veni ...", with two high trebles at the top of their range crowning the rich harmonies of the lower voices. In marked contrast to such exuberance, Palestrina's *Missa Papae Marcelli*, dating from the same period, represents a sober, lapidary style. The declamatory speech-rhythms are admirably rendered and the performance is not lacking in its moments of intense, if restrained, emotion. Highly recommended.

Thomas Arne

Arne. INSTRUMENTAL WORKS. **Le Nouveau Quatuor** (Utako Ikeda, fl; Catherine Weiss, vn; Mark Caudle, vc; [a]Paul Nicholson, hpd). Amon Ra CDSAR-42.
Favourite Concertos—No. 1 in C major (solo hpd version)[a]. Keyboard Sonatas (1756)—No. 1 in F major[a]. Trio Sonatas (1757)—No. 2 in G major; No. 5; No. 6 in B minor; No. 7 in E minor.

58' DDD 5/90

If the music history books offer little more than a passing reference to the slim repertoire of enchanting chamber music by Thomas Arne, the ordinary man in the street, who can at least whistle *Rule Britannia*, is unlikely even to have heard that any exists. This disc comes therefore as something of a revelation. The members of the Nouveau Quatuor perform on instruments dating from the composer's lifetime, tuned down a semitone. The trio sonatas, originally published for two violins and continuo, are played here by a mixed quartet: flute, violin, cello and harpsichord, which is believed to have been what the composer really intended. The introduction of the flute adds colour, brightness and definition to these charming pieces and gives the listener a chance to savour the admirable tone and phrasing of the flautist, Utako Ikeda. Paul Nicholson's harpsichord solos are distinguished as much by their elegance as by their extraordinary power and brilliance. A word, finally, in praise of Peter Holman's excellent sleeve-notes: they are both scholarly and extremely readable.

Malcolm Arnold

Arnold. CONCERTOS. [a]**Karen Jones** (fl); [b]**Michael Collins** (cl); [c]**Richard Watkins** (hn); [d]**Kenneth Sillito**, [d]**Lyn Fletcher** (vns); **London Musici/ Mark Stephenson.** Conifer CDCF172.
Concerto for two violins and orchestra, Op. 77[d]. Concerto No. 1 for clarinet and strings, Op. 20[b]. Concerto No. 1 for flute and strings, Op. 45[a]. Concerto No. 2 for horn and strings, Op. 58[c].

56' DDD 8/89

The four concertos presented on this disc provide an excellent opportunity to sample Arnold's wonderful gift for concertante writing. Each was written for or commissioned by an outstanding British virtuoso, which in turn reflects the admiration and respect with which Arnold is held by his musical colleagues. Listening to these concertos it's easy to see why he is so frequently commissioned by soloists for new works, as his ability to bring out the natural characteristics of each instrument as well as capture something of the style and personality for whom he writes is quite extraordinary. The Clarinet Concerto dates from 1948 and is a work full of contrast and contradictions,

Malcolm Arnold

sometimes introspective and serious (slow movement), sometimes humorous and light-hearted, but always extremely approachable and lyrical. The exuberant and extrovert outer movements of the Flute Concerto capture the mercurial qualities of the instrument very well, and these are contrasted by a slow movement of great beauty and simplicity. Not surprisingly the Horn Concerto reflects the considerable virtuosity of its dedicatee, Dennis Brain, who died so tragically only a few weeks after its first performance in 1957. The Double Violin Concerto of 1964 surprisingly finds its way on to disc for the first time, and a most welcome addition to the catalogue it is too. Though it has a rather more

serious, neo-classical approach than the other concertos its immediacy and charm are evident from the very beginning, and one is left wondering why this work is not heard or recorded more frequently. The superb performances from all concerned, not least the beautifully rich string tone of the London Musici, make this a highly recommendable introduction to Arnold's music.

Arnold. Guitar Concerto, Op. 67.
Brouwer. Retrats Catalans.
Chappell. Guitar Concerto No. 1, "Caribbean Concerto". **Eduardo Fernández** (gtr); **English Chamber Orchestra/Barry Wordsworth.** Decca 430 233-2DH.

60' DDD 4/91

In a world swamped by Rodrigo's *Concierto de Aranjuez*, Malcolm Arnold's Guitar Concerto has been heard much less often than it deserves. His musical roots spread in many directions, here toward lighter soil; the first movement's second subject might make a very popular song (if someone provided it with lyrics), the second movement, a lament for Django Reinhardt, breathes the late-night air of a jazz club, and the one-octave glissando that ends the third is the last of the many demands placed on the soloist in this joyous romp. Brouwer's *Retrats* (portraits) are of Federico Mompou and Antoni Gaudi, painted in fresh colours to which the guitar (and, unusually, the piano) contributes; the guitar here acts as an orchestral 'voice', rather than a concerto-status soloist, and, like Arnold, Brouwer is a master of the orchestral medium. Herbert Chappell, avoiding the cliché of 'Spanishry', enters the guitarist's domain via the Caribbean door; his Concerto is a stunning *tour de force*, a kaleidoscope of colour and movement, and no less a vehicle for the virtuosity of anyone bold enough to approach it. If *Aranjuez* is to have a successor, this could well be it; if so, this recording will along remain a touchstone. Fernández plays brilliantly—and stimulates the ECO to do likewise.

Arnold. DANCES. **London Philharmonic Orchestra / Malcolm Arnold.** Lyrita SRCD201. Item marked ª from SRCS109 (3/79).
Four Cornish Dances, Op. 91ª. English Dances, Op. 27; Op. 33ª. Irish Dances, Op. 126. Four Scottish Dances, Op. 59ª. Solitaire—Sarabande; Polka.

♪♫ 61' ADD/DDD 12/90

The arrival of Malcolm Arnold as a composer in the 1940s blew a gust of fresh air through English music, as William Walton's had some decades earlier. His training was as a composer and a trumpet player, in which latter capacity he first achieved prominence; his experience as a "rude mechanical" both gave him the insight that contributed to his remarkable skill in orchestration, and helped him to keep his aesthetic feet on the ground. Arnold has never lost faith in tonality, has never hesitated to write tunes that, despite their subtle craftsmanship, sound 'popular', and has not remained aloof from the influences of jazz and rock; he is in the best sense 'Everyman's composer'. The regional characters of his dances (1950-86) are as he perceives them to be, for he makes no use of folk material, and they are reinforced by the versatility of his orchestration. This is music that speaks directly, but does not talk down to the common man, and here it has the benefit of joyous performances conducted by the composer himself, and recorded sound that is as clear as Arnold's orchestral textures. One might describe it as 'Music for Pleasure'.

Arnold. Symphonies—No. 7, Op. 113; No. 8, Op. 124. **Royal Philharmonic Orchestra / Vernon Handley.** Conifer CDCF177.

♪♫ 64' DDD 3/91 ❓

When we consider the music of Malcolm Arnold we generally conjure up his marvellously ebullient and good humoured works such as his Suites of English and Scottish Dances, his Overtures *Tam o'Shanter* and *Beckus the Dandipratt* or one of his many brilliant and lyrical concertos. But there is a darker, more serious side too, to this versatile and much misunderstood composer. Here we are presented with two of his most fierce and dissonant works—the Seventh and Eighth Symphonies. The Seventh was written in 1973 and is one of his longest and darkest symphonic utterances. The Symphony is dedicated to Arnold's three children—Katherine, Robert and Edward, and the composer explains that each are loosely portrayed in one of the three movements. Quite why they should be linked with such bleak and ferocious music remains something of an enigma. However, what we do have is a fascinating and compelling work that gives us a deeper insight into Arnold's creative personality. The dissonance and savagery of the first movement is heightened by the movement's disturbing and restless spirit and builds to an impressive, well-calculated climax. The second movement is a dark and melancholy landscape that, as the sleeve-notes point out, is conceivably

an evocation of the world of Arnold's autistic Edward. The last movement
returns to the unsettled, restless nature of the first, and includes a folksy Irish
episode that imitates the style of the Irish folk band, The Chieftains—a particular
favourite of Arnold's son Robert. The Eighth Symphony shares with the Seventh
a quixotic and dissonant nature, if perhaps somewhat less pessimistic in its
overall mood. Arnold's fondness for Irish whimsy makes another appearance with
the inclusion in the first movement of a marching tune first used in his score to
the film *The Reckoning*. The final movement recalls the high spirits of Arnold's
earlier symphonies, though one is constantly aware of sobering and more
dramatic undercurrents at work. Vernon Handley's affection for and
commitment to these symphonies is evident from these powerful and persuasive
performances. Recordings are first-class. Well worth investigating.

Carl Philipp Emanuel Bach   *German 1714-1788*

C.P.E. Bach. Cello Concertos—A major, Wq172; A minor, Wq170; B flat
major, Wq171. **Anner Bylsma** (vc); **Orchestra of the Age of
Enlightenment/Gustav Leonhardt.** Virgin Classics Veritas VC7 90800-2.

70' DDD 2/90

During his many years at the court of Frederick the Great, C.P.E. Bach
composed these three cello concertos. The fact that they also exist in his
transcriptions for harpsichord and flute hardly suggests very idiomatic writing for
the cello and in a way the implied comment is true; nevertheless, they go very
well on the tenor instrument and Anner Bylsma brings out their quirky charm (a
quality never in short supply with this composer) while coping adequately with
some tricky figuration in the quicker movements; he's also eloquent in the highly
expressive slower ones that are especially characteristic of this Bach. This is
perhaps not a CD for a basic collection, even of cello music, but it should give
the pleasure which is itself audible in the music-making by players completely at
home in the idiom. The recording was made in the well-tried location of All
Saints' Church in Petersham in the UK; it places the cello rather far back, but
convincingly, and has an agreeably warm sound. The period pitch is about a
quarter of a tone lower than a modern one and the booklet gives the date and
maker's name of the orchestra's 23 instruments, though, oddly, not those of the
soloist's baroque cello.

C.P.E. Bach. Harpsichord Concertos—D minor, Wq23; C minor, Wq31; F
major, Wq33. **Miklós Spányi** (hpd); **Budapest Concerto Armonico.**
Hungaroton Antiqua HCD31159.

72' DDD 10/90

C.P.E. Bach, in keeping with family tradition, was both original composer and
skilful keyboard player. His legacy of music for harpsichord and clavichord is
large and varied and includes some 50 harpsichord concertos. This disc contains
three of them, well-chosen for their contrasting features, imaginatively played
and vividly recorded. These and indeed the majority of the others date from
Bach's long period of employment as court harpsichordist to Frederick the Great.
Each contains qualities which reflect the north German *empfindsamer Stil* or
'sensitive style' of which this member of the Bach family was a noted exponent.
Emotions are projected in a powerful musical language whose idiom resists
definition but has recognizable features; among these are short-winded phrases,
strong dynamic contrasts, abrupt rhythmic disturbances and an abstracted
intimacy. In short, temperamental unpredictability is of the essence. Miklós

Spányi and the period-instrument ensemble enter wholeheartedly into this world of turbulent emotions and passionate gestures with vigour, insight and, especially where slow movements are concerned, affecting sensibility. These are vivid accounts of three strong compositions and should make an impact on any listener.

C.P.E. Bach. Oboe Concerto in E flat major, H468.
Lebrun. Oboe Concerto No. 1 in D minor.
Mozart. Oboe Concerto in C major, K314/285d. **Paul Goodwin** (ob); **The English Concert/Trevor Pinnock.** Archiv Produktion 431 821-2AH.

· • 62' DDD 7/91

The oboe is supposed to have been Handel's favourite instrument, and with the move away from baroque to classical styles in the later eighteenth century, it still continued to attract composers, not least because there were fine players to inspire them. Of the three concertos here, Mozart's is the most familiar and arguably the finest, but the others are also well worth getting to know. Mozart

himself admired C.P.E. Bach for his originality and expressive force, and his individuality comes out at once here: the vigorous first movement of his concerto has an unusual opening theme with repeated notes, and the *Adagio* a depth of feeling that looks forward to Beethoven, while a bouncily *galant* finale in triple time rounds things off well. Paul Goodwin's cadenzas are imaginative and appropriate, and the tone of his two-keyed modern replica of an old instrument is entirely convincing as well as pleasingly rounded. Lebrun is an almost forgotten figure today, but on the evidence of this piece this oboist-composer had plenty to say and his Concerto in D minor has an

Trevor Pinnock   *[photo :Gramophone/Vallis*

urgently dramatic first movement with trumpets and timpani often to the fore; in fact, there seems to be an operatic influence here and the slow movement is like a graceful aria. A finely textured recording complements the skilful playing of the soloist and Trevor Pinnock's orchestra.

C.P.E. Bach. Symphonies, Wq 182. **The English Concert/Trevor Pinnock.** Archiv Produktion 415 300-2AH. From 2533 499 (10/80).
No. 1 in G major; No. 2 in B flat major; No. 3 in C major; No. 4 in A major; No. 5 in B minor; No. 6 in E major.

· • 65' ADD 5/86

Carl Philipp Emanuel worked for 28 years at the Potsdam Court of Frederick the Great and although the post provided secure employment, Frederick's dictatorial attitude did nothing to encourage Bach's aspirations to break new ground. His 'imprisonment' ended in 1756 when Frederick reluctantly released him to succeed Telemann, his godfather, as Music Director at Hamburg. Now he was able to give free rein to his imagination and the Symphonies are as remarkable as they are stimulating, with abrupt, even wild changes of mood, dynamics and key. They are required listening, not least when they are played with so much vitality and vivid response to their wayward changeability as they are here by The English Concert, using period instruments. The engineers use theirs, of a much later period, in securing the cleanest of recordings.

C.P.E. Bach. SINFONIAS, Wq183. **Amsterdam Baroque Orchestra/Ton Koopman.** Erato 2292-45361-2.
D major; E flat major; F major; G major.

43' DDD 8/89

Ton Koopman's Amsterdam Baroque Orchestra consists of rather less than half the number of players that would have performed these pieces originally, but this is of benefit rather than hindrance to the music's colourful textures. Each symphony is scored for pairs of horns, flutes and oboes, with bassoon, violins, viola, cello, bass and continuo. Emanuel Bach himself described these works as the most substantial works of the kind that he had written; "modesty forbids me to say more", he added. Certainly they are strikingly original if not, in the end, *entirely* satisfying. Wind instruments are freed from their hitherto supporting role and given a greater degree of independence, yet the music remains anchored to the basso continuo. Emanuel Bach's strongly personal idiom, darkly reflective at one moment, intense and agitated at another, is vividly captured in these lively performances and the orchestral playing maintains a high standard throughout. Flutes, oboes and horns emerge clearly from the full texture and careful thought has been given to sonority and internal balance. The recording is spacious yet allowing for detail and the character of period instruments is pleasingly captured.

C.P.E. Bach. SINFONIAS, Wq183. **Orchestra of the Age of Enlightenment/Gustav Leonhardt.** Virgin Classics Veritas VC7 90806-2. Sinfonias. D major; E flat major; F major; G major. Sinfonia in B minor, Wq182 No. 5.

54' DDD 8/90

C.P.E. Bach wrote two sets of symphonies during his period as Hamburg city's Music Director (1768-88). This disc contains all four works from the second set (*c.*1776) and one from the earlier collection (1773). At least in terms of orchestration the later set, with its parts for horns, flutes, oboes, bassoon and strings, is more ambitious than the other providing an excellent showcase for the wind players of the Orchestra of the Age of Enlightenment. Gustav Leonhardt enjoys a warm rapport both with the Orchestra and the repertory and his interpretation of these symphonies is perceptive and spirited. Rhythms are taut yet with an effective elasticity well-suited to Bach's individual, sometimes quirky temperament. Leonhardt prefers a somewhat larger band than some of his competitors and this too, has positive advantages in as much as it allows for more telling contrasts between strings and wind; it is recorded that Emanuel Bach himself fielded an ensemble of 40 instrumentalists, no less. Perhaps the performance of the remaining symphony on the disc does not quite match the others in vigour and finesse, but its phrases are beautifully shaped and well articulated. The recorded sound is bright, clear and ideally resonant.

Johann Christian Bach
German 1735-1782

J.C. Bach. CHAMBER WORKS. **The English Concert** (Lisa Beznosiuk, fl; David Reichenberg, ob; Anthony Halstead, David Cox, hns; Simon Standage, vn; Trevor Jones, va; Anthony Pleeth, vc; Trevor Pinnock, hpd, fp, square pf). Archiv Produktion 423 385-2AH.

Quintet in D major for flute, oboe, violin, cello and keyboard, Op. 22 No. 1.
Sextet in C major for oboe, two horns, violin, cello and keyboard. Quintets for
flute, oboe, violin, viola and continuo, Op. 11—No. 1 in C major; No. 6 in D
major.

69' DDD 5/88

Johann Christian Bach was the youngest of J.S. Bach's sons and the most widely
travelled of them. After studying with his father and with his half-brother C.P.E.
Bach, Johann Christian worked in Italy and in England where he settled in 1762.
For the remaining 20 years of his life J.C. Bach played a central role in London
musical circles composing, playing and teaching. As well as operas, sacred music,
symphonies and concertos the "London Bach" as he became affectionately known,
composed various types of chamber music. Among the most engaging of these
are the six Quintets, Op. 11, those of Op. 22 and the Sextet in C major once
thought to be the work of his elder brother J.C.F. Bach. Trevor Pinnock and
members of The English Concert give sparkling performances of music
conspicuous for its abundance of captivating melodies, transparent textures and
fine craftsmanship. Slow movements are especially beguiling and the subtly
shaded dynamics, delicately contrived instrumental sonorities and informed sense
of style with which these artists bring the music to life give the performances a
rare delicacy and refinement. Pinnock himself plays a variety of keyboard
instruments whose contrasting sound adds another pleasing dimension to the
interpretations. Each of the artists makes a strong contribution but special praise,
perhaps, should be given to the artistry of the late David Reichenberg, an oboist
with outstanding lyrical gifts. Good recorded sound.

Johann Sebastian Bach

German 1685-1750

Bach. Violin Concertos—No. 1 in A minor, BWV1041; No. 2 in E major,
BWV1042. Double Violin Concerto in D minor, BWV1043ᵃ. **Simon Standage,**
ᵃ**Elizabeth Wilcock** (vns); **The English Concert/Trevor Pinnock** (hpd).
Archiv Produktion 410 646-2AH. From 410 646-1AH (10/83).

46' DDD 8/84 Ⓑ

This is bright, fresh-faced playing of these three baroque concertos that brings
out all their tireless energy, crispness and intellectual force. They are a model of
baroque instrumental utterance: quintessentially Bachian in their superlative craft

and strength of purpose. The soloist Simon Standage is particularly good and sounds wholly authentic in appearing to be a first among equals in an ensemble instead of an artistically separate being. If the studied authenticity of the skilled English Concert may, for some collectors, leave an impression of impersonality and inflexibility, for those who like their Bach vigorous and without frills their performances can be recommended as a safe choice.

Bach. BRANDENBURG CONCERTOS[a]. Orchestral Suites, BWV1066-9[b]. **The English Concert/Trevor Pinnock.** Archiv Produktion 423 492-2AX3. Items marked [a] from 2742 003 (2/83), [b] 2533 410/1 (5/79).
No. 1 in F major, BWV1046; No. 2 in F major, BWV1047; No. 3 in G major, BWV1048; No. 4 in G major, BWV1049; No. 5 in D major, BWV1050; No. 6 in B flat major, BWV1051.

③ 2h 53' DDD/ADD 10/88

Bach. BRANDENBURG CONCERTOS. **English Chamber Orchestra/ Raymond Leppard** (hpd). Philips Silver Line 420 345/6-2PM. From 6747 166 (4/75).
420 345-2PM—No. 1 in F major, BWV1046; No. 2 in F major, BWV1047; No. 3 in G major, BWV1048. *420 346-2PM*—No. 4 in G major, BWV1049; No. 5 in D major, BWV1050; No. 6 in B flat major, BWV1051.

② 54' 46' ADD 6/87

These concertos, written in 1721, were Bach's response to a request from the Margrave of Brandenburg, whose name they now bear, but despite the dedication we do not know whether the Margrave acknowledged their receipt or ever heard them. Two, Concertos Nos. 3 and 6, are written for strings only, the latter without violins, but the others call for different combinations of other instrumental soloists. The music itself displays an amazing variety of form and use of instrumental colour, and since The English Concert use period instruments their performances must closely approach those which Bach may have heard, in both colour and balance—but he is unlikely to have heard them to greater advantage than we can through these excellent recordings.

As a modern instrument alternative to Pinnock's spirited readings, Raymond Leppard's 1974 recordings offer vigorous, rhythmically stylish performances with some fine individual contributions from the accomplished soloists. Leppard's alert harpsichord continuo lays the foundations for performances where the colour and energy of the music are finely observed. Particular joys are the late David Munrow's recorder, John Wilbraham's trumpet and Leppard's harpsichord playing. The recording is well focused and warm.

Bach. Keyboard Concertos, BWV1052-58. **Chamber Orchestra of Europe/ András Schiff** (pf). Decca 425 676-2DH2.

② 1h 48' DDD 11/90

Although Bach's duties in Leipzig centred on the church he also wrote secular music for a series of coffee-house concerts, at which his keyboard concertos were probably first performed. The *Brandenburgs* were *concerti grossi*, in which the keyboard shares the limelight with other instruments; BWV1052-58 were the first-ever true keyboard concertos, a genre of which Bach was the 'father'. Practically all the music of the concertos was adapted from existing works of various kinds—cantatas and concertos (mostly for the violin) and the Fourth *Brandenburg* Concerto, a time-saving expedient for a hard-pressed composer. The instrument for which they were written was of course the harpsichord, but only the most rabid purist would now object to their presentation on the piano—providing that it embodies no stylistic anachronism. Schiff, with the attentive support of both the COE and the recording engineers, comes the closest yet to achieving that elusive goal.

Bach. DOUBLE CONCERTOS. [a]**Jaap Schröder**, [a]**Christopher Hirons**, [b]**Catherine Mackintosh** (vns); [b]**Stephen Hammer** (ob); [c]**Christophe Rousset** (hpd); **Academy of Ancient Music/Christopher Hogwood** ([c]hpd). L'Oiseau-Lyre Florilegium 421 500-2OH. Item marked [a] from DSDL702 (8/82), [b] and [c] new to UK.
D minor for two violins, BWV1043[a]; C minor for violin and oboe, BWV1060[b]; C minor for two harpsichords, BWV1060[c]; C minor for two harpsichords, BWV1062[c].

58' DDD 9/89

The concept of a concerto with two or more soloists grew naturally out of the *concerto grosso*, and Bach was among those baroque composers who explored its possibilities. The Concerto in D minor, BWV1043, for two violins is perhaps the best known of his works in the *genre*, which Bach himself reworked as a Concerto for two harpsichords, BWV1062, in the key of C minor. No alternative version has survived in the case of the two-harpsichord Concerto BWV1060, also in C minor, but musicological evidence suggests that it was originally intended for two single-line instruments—two violins or one violin and an oboe. The work has thus been notionally reconstructed in the latter form and, unlike the other three concertos in this recording, it has at present no other version on CD; neither are these two revealing comparisons available on any other single disc. Baroque music never sounds better than when it is played on period instruments, in proper style, and by performers of the quality of those in this recording, not least the well matched soloists. The famous slow movement of BWV1043 is taken a little faster than usual, convincingly stripped of the specious sentimentality with which it is often invested. The recording is of suitably high quality.

Bach. OBOE CONCERTOS—F major, BWV1053; D minor, BWV1059; A major, BWV1055. **Chamber Orchestra of Europe/Douglas Boyd** (ob, ob d'amore). DG 429 225-2GH.

46' DDD 4/90

Although Bach is not known to have written any concerto for the oboe he did entrust it with some beautiful *obbligato* parts, so he clearly did not underrate its expressive capacities. He did however rearrange many of his works for different instrumental media and there is musicological evidence that original oboe concertos were the (lost) sources from which other works were derived. The Harpsichord Concerto in A major, BWV1055, is believed originally to have been written for the oboe d'amore, whilst the other two Oboe Concertos have been reassembled from movements found in various cantatas. Whatever the validity of the academic reasoning, the results sound very convincing. Douglas Boyd is a superb oboist, with a clear sound that is free from stridency, and a fluency that belies the instrument's technical difficulty. He plays the faster, outer movements with winsome lightness of tongue and spirit, and with alertness to dynamic nuance; the slow ones, the hearts of these works, are given with sensitivity but without sentimentality—which can easily invade that of BWV1059, taken from Cantata No. 156, *Ich steh mit einem Fuss im Grabe*. The Chamber Orchestra of Europe partners him to perfection in this crisp recording.

Bach. ORCHESTRAL SUITES, BWV1066-9. **Amsterdam Baroque Orchestra/Ton Koopman.** Deutsche Harmonia Mundi RD77864. No. 1 in C major; No. 2 in B minor (with Wilbert Hazelzet, fl); No. 3 in D major; No. 4 in D major.

② 79' DDD ⑧

There is no shortage of stylish performances on disc of Bach's four Orchestral Suites but the prospective buyer can be pointed towards this set with confidence. Ton Koopman and his Amsterdam Baroque Orchestra capture variously the ebullience, the courtly elegance and the subtle inflections of the music with unfailing charm. There are strongly contrasting colours in Bach's instrumentation and these are realized sensitively and with a degree of technical skill barely rivalled by other period instrument competitors. Oboes and bassoon play with assurance in the Suite No. 1 while in Suites Nos. 3 and 4, trumpets and drums make a thrilling contribution. The Suite No. 2 is a work of an altogether different character and here the solo flute playing of Wilbert Hazelzet deserves high praise. He is an artist of rare sensibility who reveals both a deep understanding of and warmth of affection towards music sometimes more elusive in character than that of the other three works. In short, there is little to disappoint the listener in playing that is stylistically informed, technically accomplished and altogether musicianly. Fine recorded sound.

Bach. The Art of Fugue, BWV1080[a]. A Musical Offering, BWV1079[b]. Canons, BWV1072-8; 1086-7[a]. **Cologne Musica Antiqua/Reinhard Goebel.** Archiv Produktion 413 642-2AH3. Booklet included. Items marked [a] from 413 728-1AH2 (4/85); [b] 2533 422 (11/79).

③ 2h 20' ADD 4/85

The great compilation of fugues, canons and a trio sonata which Bach dedicated to King Frederick the Great is one of the monuments of baroque instrumental music. Every contrapuntal device of canon at various intervals, augmentation, inversion, retrograde motion and so on is displayed here, and the performances are splendidly alive and authentic-sounding. It goes without saying that period instruments or modern replicas are used. The intellectually staggering *Art of Fugue* is a kind of testament to Bach's art and for this recording the instrumentation, unspecified by the composer, has been well chosen. The 14 miniature Canons which close this issue are for the most part a recent discovery and were written on a page of Bach's own copy of the *Goldberg Variations*; of curiosity value certainly but not much more than that. Excellent recording for these performances which have great authority.

Bach. VIOLIN SONATAS. **Monica Huggett** (vn); **Ton Koopman** (hpd). Philips 410 401-2PH2. From 410 401-1PH2 (8/84). B minor, BWV1014; A major, BWV1015; E major, BWV1016; C minor, BWV1017; F minor, BWV1018; G major, BWV1019. Cantabile, ma un poco adagio, BWV1019*a*/1. Adagio, BWV1019*a*/2.

② 1h 41' DDD 3/86

These six Sonatas were preserved only in the form of copies made by Bach's pupils and the date of their composition is unknown. Fortunately several copies were made and except in the case of the Sixth Sonata all the versions correspond. The works are of great importance in the historical development of the violin sonata. For the first time the keyboard instrument has a fully written out part and is treated as an equal and not merely as an obbligato instrument—indeed it is in many ways the senior partner.

Huggett and Koopman have worked together for several years, and this is apparent in their confident and secure performances. Sometimes Huggett inclines towards blandness of expression, and Koopman seems the livelier musical personality, but these two discs will give great pleasure to those who like Bach played on period instruments. The recording leaves nothing to be desired.

Bach. FLUTE SONATAS. **Stephen Preston** (fl); [a]**Trevor Pinnock** (hpd); [b]**Jordi Savall** (va da gamba). CRD CRD3314/15. From CRD1014/15 (8/75).
Sonatas—B minor, BWV1030[a]; E flat major, BWV1031[a]; A major, BWV1032[a]; C major, BWV1033[ab]; E minor, BWV1034[ab]; E major, BWV1035[ab]. Partita in A minor, BWV1013.

② 98' ADD 1/90

Eight Flute Sonatas have at various times been attributed to Bach. Five of these are certainly from his hand: BWV1030, 1032, 1034-5 and 1013. The first two are for flute and 'concertate' harpsichord (true duos in which the keyboard part is fully notated), the second are for flute and continuo (the keyboard player is left to fill out his part from the figured bass), and the last, a Partita, is for flute alone. The authenticity of two, BWV1031 and 1033 (both for flute and continuo), is questioned but their musical quality is sufficient to make the doubts almost irrelevant; the remaining Sonata, BWV1020, omitted from this recording, is now recognized to have been misattributed. These were not the earliest works of their kind but they are by far the most adventurous and substantial of their time, and the best of them have rightly been described as masterpieces; BWV1013 is a *tour de force* in which the single-line instrument clothes its melody with implied harmony—and even counterpoint. The baroque flute is a gentle instrument that caresses the sound and pitch of its notes, an art of which Preston is a master. Pinnock is the perfect partner, as also is Savall in the 'with-continuo' items, and the recording captures the warm intimacy of these wonderful works.

Bach (arr. Holliger). ORGAN SONATAS, BWV525-30. **Heinz Holliger** (ob); **Tabea Zimmermann** (va); **Thomas Demenga** (vc); **Christiane Jaccottet** (hpd). Philips 422 328-2PH.
No. 1 in E flat major; No. 2 in C minor; No. 3 in D minor; No. 4 in E minor; No. 5 in C major; No. 6 in G major.

63' DDD 6/89

These six works, though simply described as 'Sonatas', are in fact trio sonatas, i.e. their textures comprise two melodic lines, supported by a continuo. In this case the music was written for a keyboard instrument with manuals and pedals, but a line is a line and may thus be played on any suitable instrument, as Bach affirmed in leaving alternative versions of two of the movements. Holliger has followed Bach's example in adapting the rest, retaining the oboe d'amore in all three movements of No. 4, and adds the premise that in this form the lines may be more expressively delivered than through a keyboard instrument alone; his claim is fully borne out in these performances. The instruments used, save the harpsichord, appear to be modern ones but they are used with the degree of skill, sensitivity and regard for style that makes such information academic. Bach shared Scarlatti's capacity for writing music that can be happily listened to without thought of its didactic purpose and the good news extends equally to the sound-quality and internal balance of this fine recording.

Bach. Sonatas and Partitas for Solo Violin, BWV1001-06. **Oscar Shumsky** (vn). ASV CDDCD454.
Sonatas: No. 1 in G minor, BWV1001; No. 2 in A minor, BWV1003; No. 3 in C major, BWV1005. *Partitas:* No. 1 in B minor, BWV1002; No. 2 in D minor, BWV1004; No. 3 in E major, BWV1006.

② 2h 27' ADD 9/87

It was during his employment at the Court of Prince Leopold of Cöthen that Bach was able to devote himself to writing secular music. His six innovatory Suites for the cello and the six works for solo violin date from this period (*c*.1720) and could have been written only by someone with an intimate practical knowledge of the instrument. As the small fingerboard of the violin enables the player's left hand to encompass complex textures, Bach took full advantage of this. It remains difficult, even in the hi-tech state of today's violinistic art, simply to produce the notes with accurate intonation and without making heavy weather of the three- and four-note chords, but that is only the beginning. The player still has to realize the part-writing and to absorb and project the style and spirit of the immensely varied movements. All these parameters, and more, are admirably met by Oscar Shumsky; with this excellent recording one is able to fully appreciate the richness of the music, with little consciousness of the immense technical skill that makes the performances possible.

Bach. Solo Cello Suites, BWV1007-12. **Pierre Fournier.** DG 419 359-2GCM2. Items marked [a] from Archiv Produktion SAPM198 186 (11/62), [b] SAPM198 187 (3/63), [c] SAPM198 188 (6/63).
No. 1 in G major[a]; No. 2 in D minor[a]; No. 3 in C major[b]; No. 4 in E flat major[b]; No. 5 in C minor[c]; No. 6 in D major[c].

② 2h 19' ADD 3/89 £

Pierre Fournier made this fine recording during the early 1960s. His sense of style, unerring rhythmic intuition, polished technique and noble poise have lost none of their charm or potency during the intervening years. Fournier is outstandingly perceptive in his treatment of the Preludes with their improvisatory character. In his hands they unfold with a majestic grace whose grand gestures are nevertheless light of tread. Sarabandes are declaimed with a profound awareness of their poetic content while Allemandes, Courantes and the little 'galanteries' are full of nimble, dance-like gestures. Above all, Fournier's playing is richly endowed with eloquence and lyricism matched by a warm, resonant tone. He belonged to a generation which generally did not make concessions towards 'authenticity' where tuning and choice of instruments are concerned. Thus in the Fifth and Sixth Suites Fournier remains content with his standard cello with its conventional tuning and four strings. No matter, for in these works he is brilliantly communicative, placing an unsurpassed technique at the service of two of the most challenging works in the solo cello repertory. The recorded sound is excellent.

Bach. KEYBOARD WORKS. **Maggie Cole** (hpd). Virgin Classics Veritas VC7 90712-2.
Chromatic Fantasia and Fugue in D minor, BWV903. Partita No. 1 in B flat major, BWV825. Toccata, Adagio and Fugue in G major, BWV916. Prelude, Fugue and Allegro in E flat major, BWV998. Italian Concerto in F major, BWV971.

62' DDD 1/89

This recital includes three of Bach's best known solo harpsichord pieces: the Italian Concerto, the Chromatic Fantasia and Fugue in D minor, and the Partita

No. 1 in B flat. The other works will perhaps be less familiar, but together these pieces provide a fascinating example of the wide range of forms, disciplines and national traits which Bach assimilated into his keyboard writing. Maggie Cole's performances are carefully thought out and meticulously executed, with a nice sense of poise and easy gracefulness in her playing. There is no empty rhetoric here but rather a lucid exposition of the music which is almost always coherent in its articulation, elegant in its phrasing and unhurried in its measure. The instrument itself is a beauty—a Dutch harpsichord of 1612 by Ruckers—and the fine recording was made in the National Trust's Fenton House, Hampstead in north London. Helpful, informed presentation furthermore sets the seal on a splendid issue.

Bach. The Well-tempered Clavier, BWV846-93. **Kenneth Gilbert** (hpd). Archiv Produktion 413 439-2AH4. From 413 439-1AH5 (9/84).

④ 4h 16' DDD 2/87

Bach. The Well-tempered Clavier, Book 2, BWV870-93. **András Schiff** (pf). Decca 417 236-2DH2.

② 2h 24' DDD 3/87

There are currently several versions in the catalogue which shed light in a variety of different ways on this orderly yet entertaining anthology. Kenneth Gilbert's blend of scholarship and technique with sensitive artistry makes him superbly equipped to perform Bach's *48*, as these preludes and fugues are affectionately known. His vital rhythmic sense and love of refinement which so enhance his playing of French music are also a pre-requisite for performing Bach and nowhere more so, perhaps, than in Book 1, where the first group of 24 preludes and fugues have virtually no markings to assist the performer. Gilbert is lyrical, dazzlingly virtuosic and profound too, as he makes his way on the upward semitone journey in the course of which Bach set about exploring as many keys as was then practicable. The digitally-recorded LPs were first-rate and have been successfully transferred to CD with the harpsichord sounding pleasantly clear and resonant. The set comes with an informative and detailed booklet.

András Schiff, playing only Book 2, shows that he also possesses the technical assurance and exceptional mental clarity needed to play Bach's *48* well. He produces lucid textures, keeping contrapuntal strands always alive and particularly interesting is the way he varies phrasing or balance in the repeats of Prelude sections. Sensibly, he uses the piano as a piano and not an imitation harpsichord and manages to steer a middle course between coldly mechanical and overly romantic treatments. For the most part his rhythmic control is admirable; and after the excesses of some other noted Bach pianists his freedom from eccentricities is particularly welcome. The recorded quality is excellent, and to have satisfactorily contained 144 minutes of music on two discs is something of an achievement.

Bach. French Suites, BWV812-7. Suite in A minor, BWV818*a*. Suite in E flat major, BWV819*a*. **Davitt Moroney** (hpd). Virgin Classics Veritas VCD7 91201-2.

② 2h 24' DDD 4/91

Bach. French Suites, BWV812-17. **Gustav Leonhardt** (hpd). RCA Victor Seon GD71963. From Philips 6709 500 (10/77).

② 78' ADD 5/90

Bach compiled his *French Suites*, so-called—the composer himself did not give them this title—towards the end of his Cöthen period and at the beginning of

Davitt Moroney　　　*[photo: Virgin Classics*

his final appointment at Leipzig. As well as performing the customary six suites, five of which have survived in Bach's own hand, Davitt Moroney includes two further suites prepared by Bach's pupil, Heinrich Nikolaus Gerber, in 1725. These and extra movements to the well-known six suites belong to various surviving sources and though we can be sure that Bach himself had good reason to discard them from his final thoughts, so-to-speak, their presence in this album is nonetheless welcome. Moroney has given careful thought and preparation to the project and the results are often illuminating. His interpretations are relaxed, articulate and show a lively awareness of the music's poetic content. There is a clarity in these performances which stems from lucid punctuation highlighting the significance of every phrase. Shorter dance movements have poise and are allowed to breathe while longer ones, notably *allemandes,* have a taut rhythmic elasticity which enable the listener to savour their eloquent often pensive inflexions. Perhaps *sarabandes* are sometimes a little too weighty, but this is to some extent a matter of taste and few will be disappointed by Moroney's stylistically informed and technically fluent playing. The recording is excellent.

Over a period of some 25 years Gustav Leonhardt has recorded all the major Bach harpsichord repertory. Many of the releases have established themselves at the forefront of Bach interpretation, illuminating audiences and an inspiration to a younger generation of harpsichord players. One aspect of more recent recordings by Leonhardt which must disappoint listeners is his disdain for the conventional double-bar repeat. In this respect the French Suites fare better since many, though not all, repeats are observed. Allemandes and Gigues generally are not afforded repeats while Courantes, Sarabandes and the simpler galanteries such as Menuets, Gavottes and Bourrées usually qualify for some or all of them. The most beguiling features of Leonhardt's interpretation, however, lies in rhythmic suppleness, a graceful feeling for gesture, eloquence of phrase, clarity of articulation and a sure understanding of Bach's infinitely varied melodic patterns. These are performances full of energy yet retaining a courtly elegance which complements the spirit of the stylized dance. The character of the harpsichord, a Taskin copy, is faithfully conveyed, though the recorded sound may strike listeners as a shade too reverberant

Bach. Goldberg Variations, BWV988. **Trevor Pinnock** (hpd). Archiv Produktion 415 130-2AH. From 2533 425 (12/80).

61' ADD 8/85

Bach. Goldberg Variations, BWV988. **András Schiff** (pf). Decca 417 116-2DH. From D275D2 (1/84).

73' DDD 12/86

Insomniac Count Hermann Carl von Kayserling, in order that his harpsichordist might relieve the monotony of his sleepless hours, commissioned Bach to provide some quiet but cheerful music and as a result was rewarded with a golden goblet containing 100 Louis d'or, probably the largest single fee he ever received. The

Variations, virtually a compendium of contemporary keyboard techniques, become more difficult as the work progresses, but Pinnock meets their demands brilliantly. Indeed, you don't have to wrestle with the technicalities of the music itself—enjoy it for the ravishing sounds it makes. Pinnock uses a glowingly resonant Ruckers harpsichord of 1646, recorded with the utmost fidelity.

Of all Bach's keyboard works, the Variations are perhaps the most idiomatic to the harpsichord and thus the least suited to the modern piano. Almost one-third of the variations are marked clearly "on two keyboards", which pianos do not have and to play them on a single one calls for feats of balletic skill to keep the dancing hands from colliding. Schiff is not the only one to have mastered this choreography but he does it with better musical results than the others. Pianists are wont to introduce inappropriate elements of rubato, colour, embellishment and dynamics from later keyboard and musical styles—things that Bach could not have envisaged and occasionally to 'play at harpsichords' with exaggerated staccato and/or changes of register; Schiff does a little of these things, but not enough to deter one from hailing his recording as the most intelligent and stimulatingly imaginative of its kind. The *Goldberg* Variations should always sound at their best on the harpsichord but if you prefer to hear them on today's piano, this is the recording to have.

Bach. ORGAN PARTITAS. **Simon Preston.** DG 429 775-2GH. Played on the Lorentz organ of Sorø Abbey, Denmark.
Christ, der du bist der helle Tag, BWV766; O Gott, du frommer Gott, BWV767; Sei gegrüsset, Jesu gütig, BWV768; Ach, was soll ich Sünder machen?, BWV770.

54'   DDD   3/91

At the last count the number of chorale preludes for organ believed to be by Bach was 239. In addition there are six Chorale Preludes—more extended sets of variations on the Lutheran chorales. These continue a tradition some of the greatest masters of which were Bach's immediate predecessors Böhm, Buxtehude and Pachelbel. While Bach's magnificent set on *Vom Himmel hoch, da komm ich her* (not included on this disc) is generally regarded as the pinnacle of the genre, the other partitas are all early works and with the exception of that based on *Sei gegrüsset* do not call for pedals. It seems that these pieces could just as easily have been intended for domestic consumption by harpsichordists as for church use by organists. As such, they have perhaps been somewhat overlooked by present-day organists, yet as this captivating disc shows most convincingly, the music contains an abundant wealth of variety, interest and charm. Simon Preston is on excellent form, showing his customary formidable technical mastery. His performances bring this music vividly to life and he unearths an astonishing variety of tone colours from a famous and historic organ. All of this is recorded with outstanding clarity and the overall sound is simply delicious.

Bach. ORGAN WORKS. **Christopher Herrick.** Hyperion CDA66434. Played on the Metzler organ of the Stadtkirche, Zofingen, Switzerland.
Toccatas and Fugues—D minor, BWV565; F major, BWV540; D minor, BWV538, "Dorian". Toccata, Adagio and Fugue in C major, BWV564. Passacaglia and Fugue in C minor, BWV582.

64'   DDD   4/91

If you only have one disc of organ music in your collection, this must be it. It more than fulfils all the basic criteria which combine to make a 'Good CD'. First the music. Here are the five most important and impressive organ works by the indisputable king of organ music. Everyone knows Bach's *Toccata and Fugue* in D minor and such is its popularity that it is currently the most widely available piece of organ music on CD. Of the others, many would consider the *Passacaglia and Fugue* as the finest piece of organ music ever written while the *Adagio* from the *Toccata, Adagio and Fugue* is as beautiful a melody as can ever have been composed for the instrument. Second the performances. Christopher Herrick's playing is simply outstanding. He has just the right blend of dramatic flair, technical virtuosity and musical sensitivity. He avoids personal idiosyncrasies (rare indeed in such an old war-horse as the D minor) and maintains a bright, lively approach throughout the entire programme, giving it all a wonderful lift. Finally the recording. Hyperion have found the ideal organ set in the most magnificent of acoustics. Their recording has caught the finest detail with total clarity while the overall opulence of sound is a sheer aural delight.

Bach. ORGAN WORKS. Volume 3. **Peter Hurford.** Decca Ovation 421 617-2DM3.
Chorale Variations and Partitas, BWV766-71. The Schübler Chorale Preludes, BWV645-50. Chorale Preludes—Herr Jesu Christ, dich zu uns wend', BWV726; Herzlich tut mich verlangen, BWV727; Jesus, meine Zuversicht, BWV728; In dulci jubilo, BWV729; Liebster Jesu, wir sind hier, BWV730; Liebster Jesu, wir sind hier, BWV731; Lobt Gott, ihr Christen, allzugleich, BWV732; Meine Seele erhebt den Herrn, BWV733; Nun freut euch, lieben Christen g'mein, BWV734; Valet will ich dir geben, BWV735; Valet will ich dir geben, BWV736; Vater unser im Himmelreich, BWV737; Vom Himmel hoch, da komm'ich her, BWV738; Wie schön leuchtet der Morgenstern, BWV739; Wir glauben all' an einen Gott, BWV740. Concertos—No. 1 in G major, BWV592; No. 2 in A minor, BWV593; No. 3 in C major, BWV594; No. 4 in C major, BWV595; No. 5 in D minor, BWV596; No. 6 in E flat, BWV597.

③ 3h 31' ADD 6/90

Most record collectors will be familiar with Bach's great organ works; not least the ubiquitous *Toccata and Fugue* in D minor. While these are undeniably essential ingredients in any CD collection they represent only a tiny fraction of Bach's enormous output for the instrument. The majority of his organ music was based on Lutheran chorales: the equivalent of today's hymn-tune. Generally these are what are known as chorale preludes; miniature pieces reflecting both the chorale's melody and the character of its words. Here are some of Bach's most ingenious and personal creations. In more extended form are the six Chorale Partitas which provide variations for each of the verses of the original chorale. Unique among his organ works are the secular concertos, transcriptions of string concertos by Vivaldi and Ernst. While Bach made few changes to the original, his unique genius has turned typically Italianate violin writing (in the third even the violin cadenzas have been retained) into something utterly at ease on the organ. Here is some of the most charming

and effervescent music in the entire repertoire. Peter Hurford's playing, Decca's superlative recordings and a selection of top-rate organs from around the world provide the best realization imaginable of these works. If a three-disc set of lesser-known Bach organ works (even at mid-price) seems a tall order, rest assured you are buying some of the finest organ music, organ playing and organ recordings available. Here is a recording to be dipped into time and time again; it never loses its freshness or ability to captivate.

Peter Hurford [*photo: Decca/Holt*]

Bach. ORGAN WORKS. Volume 4. **Peter Hurford.** Decca Ovation 421 621-2DM3.

Chorales from the Neumeister Collection Nos. 1-35. Chorale Preludes, BWV651-668, The "Eighteen". Chorale Preludes—O Lamm Gottes unschuldig, NBA; Ach Gott und Herr, BWV714; Allein Gott in der Höh' sei Ehr', BWV715; Allein Gott in der Höh' sei Ehr', BWV716; Allein Gott in der Höh', BWV717; Christ lag in Todesbanden, BWV718; Der Tag, der ist so freudenrich, BWV719; Ein' feste Burg ist unser Gott, BWV720; Erbarm' dich mein, o Herre Gott, BWV721; Gelobet seist du, Jesu Christ, BWV722; Gelobet seist du, Jesu Christ, BWV723; Gottes Sohn ist kommen, BWV724; Herr Gott, dich loben wir, BWV725.

③ 3h 50' ADD/DDD 6/90

It's tantalizing to think that there is still music written by the great composers lying untouched and unrecognized by past generations just waiting to be discovered. That such major finds are still cropping up was evidenced in 1984, fortuitously timed for the tercentenary celebration of Bach's birth, when two scholars working independently in Yale University library came across a substantial manuscript put together in the early nineteenth century by J.G. Neumeister. Here they unearthed no less than 38 chorales for organ by Bach, most of which were not previously known to exist. Most experts accept them as genuine, although some doubts still exist. But for the CD collector such doubts should be irrelevant, for regardless of the music's origins, here is the fourth (and final) boxed set of Peter Hurford's landmark recordings of Bach's complete organ music; recordings no serious collector should be without. The music is wonderful; included here are, in addition to the 'Neumeister' chorales, some of Bach's greatest chorale-based organ works. Hurford's playing is a delight to behold. Every piece, no matter how small or simple, is treated as the gem it is; with loving care and an unerring sensitivity towards the finest detail. As with the other discs in the series, Decca have taken their microphones quite literally around the world to find the best instruments for the music—here organs from England, Germany, Austria, America and Australia are featured. The results from both a musical and technical point of view are superlative. Discs two and three were originally issued on LP and it goes almost without saying, given the emphasis on excellence with this entire venture, that the transfers to CD are magnificent.

Bach. ORGAN WORKS. Volume 3. **Ton Koopman.** Novalis 150036-2.

Played on the organ of the Great Church, Leeuwarden, Holland.

"Dorian" Toccata and Fugue in D minor, BWV538. Partita on "Sei gegrüsset, Jesu gutig", BWV768. Fantasia in G major, BWV572. Trio Sonata No. 6 in G major, BWV530. Chorale Preludes—"Vater Unser im Himmelreich", BWV682; "Jesu Christus unser Heiland", BWV688. Prelude and Fugue in A minor, BWV543.

70' DDD 8/89

The Young Bach. **Michael Murray.** Telarc CD80179. Played on the organ of the College of St Thomas, St Paul, Minnesota, USA.

Prelude and Fugues—C major, BWV531; G minor, BWV535; D minor, BWV539. Concerto No. 1 in G major, BWV592. Fantasia in G major, BWV572. Prelude in C major, BWV567. "Little" Fugue in G minor, BWV578. Canzona in D minor, BWV588. Chorale Prelude "In dulci jubilo", BWV751.

58' DDD 8/89

It is inconceivable that any self-respecting CD collection would not contain at least one disc of Bach's organ music and here are two which constitute 'Good CDs' from any standpoint. The playing is unwavering in its excellence, the instruments are well chosen, the combined programmes present a good cross-section of some of Bach's finest (if not exactly his best-known) organ compositions and the recordings are superlative (indeed Telarc's sound is nothing short of stunning). The one work common to both (the *Fantasia* in G) receives such utterly different interpretations that it is well worth having in both versions.

Ton Koopman (playing on an instrument built when Bach was 42) is an acknowledged Bach expert and whilst his performances undoubtedly show scholarship and a keen appreciation of style, they are also exceedingly enjoyable in their own right. In fact, Koopman's playing is so compelling and vivacious that he manages to make accessible works which in lesser hands come across as dull and academic.

Michael Murray uses a much more modern instrument. It has a bright, forthright tone which is ideally suited to this joyous and energetic music. Murray, too, plays with an infectious enthusiasm and allows the music to speak for itself, never allowing fussiness of detail or extravagant use of the organ to obscure the sheer ebullience of the writing.

Bach. ORGAN WORKS. **Nicholas Danby.** CBS Digital Masters CD45807. Played on the organ of Lübeck Cathedral, Germany.
Chorale Preludes—Wachet auf, ruft uns die stimme, BWV645; Nun komm' der Heiden Heiland, BWV659; Dies sind die Heil'gen zehn gebot', BWV678; Liebster Jesu, wir sind hier, BWV706; Herr Jesu Christ, dich zu uns wend', BWV709; Erbarm' dich mein, O Herre Gott, BWV721; Herzlich thut mich verlangen, BWV727; Vater unser im Himmelreich, BWV737; Aus der tiefe rufe ich, BWV745. Fantasia in G major, BWV572. Prelude and Fugues—A minor, BWV543; C minor, BWV546. Toccata and Fugue in D minor, BWV565.
71' DDD

This is an excellent CD on every count. The music is wonderful, Bach at his most varied and interesting. The playing is sympathetic, tasteful, elegant and persuasive, with the organ making a really sumptuous sound. And the recording is exemplary, perfectly realizing the cathedral's warm atmosphere and the organ's splendid array of charms, but without any disturbing background thuds or clatters. Add to all this a generous playing time (forget about the useless accompanying booklet) and here is a disc for everyone's collection. Nicholas Danby has planned his programme with commendable good sense. It begins and ends with quiet reflective Chorale Preludes and passes through the powerful, quasi-orchestral C minor Prelude and Fugue, the exciting A minor Prelude and Fugue, the colourful Fantasia (one of the best performances of all, this) and numerous Chorale Preludes of widely differing moods before launching into everybody's favourite, the Toccata and Fugue in D minor. It makes compelling listening. This is not a disc from which to pick out your favourites; sit down, press 'play' and enjoy an hour and ten minutes' worth of unfettered pleasure.

Bach (arr. Bylsma). Partita in E major, BWV1006. Sonata in A minor, BWV1013 (trans. G minor). Sonata in A minor, BWV1003. **Anner Bylsma** (vc piccolo). Deutsche Harmonia Mundi RD77998.
62' DDD 11/89

Anner Bylsma, one of Holland's leading string players, has produced here a recording of sheer delight, revealing with amazing insight, dexterity and musicianship the unexplored potential of the violoncello piccolo—in this instance a genuine child's instrument, tuned down a generous semitone and played with a Dutch Baroque bow. The three unaccompanied works are well calculated to demonstrate the unexpected qualities of the smaller cello, which, according to Bylsma, is the true bass of the violin family. In the *Partita* we are given a first taste of the delicacy, grace and lightness of touch appropriate to such a diminutive bass instrument. In the *Allemande* and the *Sarabande* of the G minor Sonata we experience the full palette of its varied sonorities, so different from those of the larger standard instrument; enjoy the speed and flow of the *Corrente* and the quiet humour of the *Bourrée Anglaise*. The *Grave*, which opens the A minor Sonata, is one of those pieces where composer, performer and instrument are totally at one and it was precisely such a coming together of all the elements that makes the 'rightness' of this unique recital convincing; indeed, it provides a degree of musical enjoyment rarely encountered.

Bach. TOCCATAS. **Bob van Asperen** (hpd). EMI Reflexe CDC7 54081-2. F sharp minor, BWV910; C minor, BWV911; D minor, BWV912; D minor, BWV913; E minor, BWV914; G minor, BWV915; G major, BWV916.

67' DDD 5/91

Bob van Asperen is a fine exponent of Bach's harpsichord music. His interpretations are considered, articulate and technically fluent if on occasion a shade severe. The latter reservation, however, would be entirely misplaced in the context of his recital of Bach's seven harpsichord Toccatas (BWV910-16). The music dates from the composer's Weimar period (1708-17) and its idiom is richly endowed with contrast and variety. A youthful energy infuses these pieces with flourishes, embellishments, exuberant passagework, engaging dance measures and a multitude of expressive gestures. Van Asperen conveys the markedly improvisatory character present in several of the movements with panache while at the same time never sacrificing clarity of thought or a firm rhythmic pulse in the interests of empty virtuosity. This is firmly disciplined playing with an underlying passion which perhaps might have been allowed to surface more prominently. These are, nevertheless, interpretations which enable us to marvel at Bach's fertile imagination and wide terms of reference; performances which in equal measure stem from intellectual and technical rigour. The recorded sound is ideal.

Bach. The Art of Fugue, BWV1080. **Davitt Moroney** (hpd). Harmonia Mundi HMC90 1169/70. From HMC1169/70 (2/86).

② 99' DDD 5/86

Bach died before the process of engraving his last great work had been completed, thus leaving a number of issues concerning performance in some doubt. However, Davitt Moroney is a performer-scholar who has a mature understanding of the complexity of Bach's work; in a lucid essay in the booklet, he discusses the problems of presenting *The Art of Fugue* whilst at the same time explaining his approach to performing it. Certain aspects of this version will be of particular importance to prospective buyers: Moroney, himself, has completed Contrapunctus 14 but he also plays the same Contrapunctus in its unfinished state as a fugue on three subjects. He omits Bach's own reworkings for two harpsichords of Contrapunctus 13 on the grounds that they do not play a part in the composer's logically-constructed fugue cycle; and he omits the Chorale Prelude in G major (BWV668*a*) which certainly had nothing to do with Bach's scheme but was added in the edition of 1751 so that the work should not end in an incomplete state. Moroney's performing technique is of a high order, placing emphasis on the beauty of the music which he reveals with passionate conviction. Exemplary presentation and an appropriate recorded sound enhance this fine achievement.

Bach. Cantatas—Nos. 5-8. **Paul Esswood** (alto); **Kurt Equiluz** (ten); **Max van Egmond** (bass); **Vienna Boys' Choir; Chorus Viennensis; Vienna Concentus Musicus/Nikolaus Harnoncourt; Regensburger Domspatzen; King's College Choir, Cambridge; Leonhardt Consort/ Gustav Leonhardt.** Teldec 2292-42498-2. Texts and translations included. From Telefunken SKW2 (2/72).
No. 5, Wo soll ich fliehen hin; No. 6, Bleib bei uns, denn ens will Abend werden; No. 7, Christ unser Herr zum Jordan kam; No. 8, Liebster Gott, wann werd' ich sterben.

② 87' ADD 9/85

It was during Bach's final period of employment as Cantor at the Leipzig Thomass that he wrote his great series of church cantatas. His powerful Lutheran beliefs here fuse with his musical genius to create a series of beautifully integrated works. *Wo soll ich fliehen hin* follows the typical pattern: opening chorale; bass recitative; tenor aria (with a lovely viola obbligato); alto recitative; bass aria (with a characterful rhythm); soprano recitative; final chorale (in a stately measured gait). The effect is to illustrate with the greatest possible variety the religious measure of the service. This set is an excellent introduction to Bach's cantata writing with four uniformly accomplished and varied works. Harnoncourt and Leonhardt's cantata series is one of the monuments of the recorded age, a magnificent achievement that still continues. The soloists are excellent and the orchestras and choirs perform with imagination.

Bach. Cantatas—No. 106, Gottes Zeit ist die allerbeste Zeit, "Actus tragicus"; No. 118, O Jesu Christ, meins Lebens Licht; No. 198, Lass, Fürstin, lass noch einen Strahl, "Trauer Ode". **Nancy Argenta** (sop); **Michael Chance** (alto); **Anthony Rolfe Johnson** (ten); **Stephen Varcoe** (bass); **Monteverdi Choir; English Baroque Soloists/John Eliot Gardiner.** Archiv Produktion 429 782-2AH. Texts and translations included.

59' DDD 5/91

The cantatas on this disc illustrate the astonishing range of effects with which Bach, at different periods in his life, treated the subject of death. Cantata No. 106 is one of the very earliest of Bach's surviving sacred cantatas and dates from 1707 when the composer was employed briefly at Mühlhausen. Cantata No. 198, by contrast, is a Leipzig piece written in 1727 and performed at a memorial service for Christiane Eberhardine, Queen of Poland, Electoral Princess of Saxony and wife of Augustus the Strong. The two works could hardly be more different from one another, the earlier with a strong biblical orientation, the later an elegy, an evocation of death by the German Enlightenment poet Gottsched. Gardiner's interpretations have all the technical refinement with which we associate his performances and his soloists by-and-large are first rate. The *Actus tragicus* comes over especially well with unhurried but effectively contrasted tempos; the other is perhaps more variable only intermittently capturing the deep pathos of Bach's music. The disc also includes a beautiful funeral motet, *O Jesu Christ, meins Lebens Licht* (BWV118), performed here in its later version dating from around 1740.

Bach. Cantatas—No. 140, Wachet auf! ruft uns die Stimme; No. 147, Herz und Mund und Tat und Leben. **Vienna Concentus Musicus/Nikolaus Harnoncourt.** Teldec 2292-43109-2.

60' ADD

This is another disc drawn from Teldec's pioneering Bach Cantata series shared by Harnoncourt and Leonhardt. Harnoncourt directs both cantatas here with a strong team of soloists, the Tölz Boys' Choir and the Vienna Concentus Musicus. Cantata No. 140 *Wachet auf!*, which includes the famous 'Sleepers wake', is variously charged with excitement, anticipation and tenderness. There are strong contributions from the solo treble, Allan Bergius, Kurt Equiluz, the oboist Jürg Schaeftlein and Alice Harnoncourt who gives a lyrical account of the violino piccolo solo in the first duet. Cantata No. 147 *Herz und Mund und Tat und Leben* includes the much loved chorale verses which conclude the first and second parts of the work, popularly known as "Jesu, joy of man's desiring", with a colourful assembly of instruments underlining the joyful nature of the Feast of the Visitation of Mary the Virgin. The four solo vocalists are impressive and the Vienna Concentus Musicus is on characteristically fine form in these brisk, joyful performances.

Bach. Cantatas—No. 211, Schweigt stille, plaudert nicht, "Coffee"; No. 212, Mer hahn en neue Oberkeet, "Peasant". **Emma Kirkby** (sop); **Rogers Covey-Crump** (ten); **David Thomas** (bass); **Academy of Ancient Music/ Christopher Hogwood.** L'Oiseau-Lyre 417 621-2OH.

52' DDD 10/89

These two most delightful of Bach's secular cantatas here receive sparkling performances fully alive to the humour and invention of the music. The *Coffee* Cantata illustrates a family altercation over a current enthusiasm, the drinking of coffee. A narrator tells the story whilst the soprano and bass soloists confront each other in a series of delightful arias. Thomas brings out the crabby dyspeptic side of Schlendrian's character imaginatively and Kirkby makes a charming minx-like Lieschen. Covey-Crump's sweet light tenor acts as a good foil. The *Peasant* Cantata also takes the form of a dialogue, here between a somewhat dull and simple young man and his sweetheart Mieke, a girl who intends to better herself. Through the 24 short movements Bach conjures up a wonderfully rustic picture with some vivid dance numbers and rumbustious ritornellos. The soloists' nicely rounded characterizations emerge with great humour and Hogwood directs with vitality and sprightly rhythmic control. The recording is excellent.

Bach. CANTATAS, Volumes 44 and 45. [ad]**Helmut Wittek,** [a]**Hans Stricker,** [b]**Stefan Gienger,** [cef]**Jan Patrick O'Farrell** (trebs); [g]**Barbara Bonney** (sop); [cef]**René Jacobs** (alto); [cf]**John Elwes,** [bd]**Kurt Equiluz** (tens); [abd]**Thomas Hampson,** [cef]**Harry van der Kamp** (basses); [abd]**Tölz Boys' Choir;** [cef]**Hanover Boys' Choir;** [cef]**Ghent Collegium Vocale;** [abdg]**Vienna Concentus Musicus/Nikolaus Harnoncourt;** [cef]**Leonhardt Consort/. Gustav Leonhardt.** Teldec Das Alte Werk 244 193/4-2.
244 193-1/2—No. 192, Nun danket alle Gott[a]; No. 194, Höchsterwünschtes Freudenfest[b]; No. 195, Dem Gerechten muss das Licht immer wieder aufgehen[c]. *214 194-1/2*—No. 196, Der Herr denket an uns[d]; No. 197, Gott ist unser Zuversicht[e]; No. 198, Lass, Fürstin, lass noch einen Strahl[f]; No. 199, Mein Herze schwimmt im Blut[g].

71' DDD ② 102' DDD 5/90

Almost inevitably, in Teldec's Bach Cantata series, the interpretations and performances have their ups and downs, but their finest qualities serve Bach's music well. In general, Harnoncourt's Vienna Concentus Musicus has the edge over the Leonhardt Consort but Harnoncourt can be stridently idiosyncratic on occasion and his inclination to over-stress strong beats is a feature of his direction which has found few adherents. Volumes 44 and 45 contain strengths and weaknesses characteristic of the series as a whole with strong solo contributions but less convincing choral ones. Much of the instrumental obbligato playing is first-rate and both directors give careful thought to phrasing and articulation. Two works only throughout the series introduce a female voice, Cantata No. 51 (Vol. 14) and Cantata No. 199 with which the project is concluded. Elsewhere, the solo soprano parts are sung by boys and the alto parts by counter-tenors in all but a handful of instances where boys' voices are preferred. Accompanying documentation is informative and translations of the German texts are included. Recorded sound is usually clear and effective in the later volumes of the series but is variable in the earlier ones which have been transferred from LP to CD.

Bach. SECULAR CANTATAS. [a]**Elly Ameling** (sop); [b]**Gerald English** (ten); [c]**Siegmund Nimsgern** (bass); **Collegium Aureum.** Deutsche Harmonia Mundi Editio Classica GD77151. Texts and translations included. From BASF BAC3052/3 (9/74).
No. 202, Weichet nur, betrübte Schatten, "Wedding Cantata"[a]. No. 209, Non sa che sia dolore[a]. No. 211, Schweigt stille, plaudert nicht, "Coffee Cantata"[abc]. No. 212, Mer hahn en neue Oberkeet, "Peasant Cantata"[abc].

⨀ ② 1h 46' ADD 10/90

Nowadays there is no shortage of recordings of Bach's best known secular cantatas; but the four contained in this double album, though now comparatively elderly—they were first issued on LPs in 1968—were among the most stylish of their day. Much has happened in the sphere of baroque playing and interpretation since then and not everything here is as polished and assured as listeners will have come to expect from today's finest ensembles. Nevertheless, the performances are anything but dull and much of the singing is first rate. It is the *Coffee* Cantata and the *Peasant* Cantata which come over with the greater conviction with Elly Ameling as a beguiling but wilful Lieschen in the former, and a spirited, coquettish Miecke in Bach's pastoral romp. In these works the two other singers, Gerald English as the narrator and Siegmund Nimsgern as the peppery Schlendrian (BWV211) and the country lad with little on his mind but opening time and a good roll in the hay (BWV212) are excellent. Much of the instrumental playing by members of the Collegium Aureum is enjoyable, too, with stylish harpsichord continuo. Good recorded sound and full texts in German, English and French for each cantata.

Bach. Mass in B minor, BWV232. **Emma Kirkby, Emily Van Evera** (sops); **Panito Iconomou, Christian Immler, Michael Kilian** (altos); **Rogers Covey-Crump** (ten); **David Thomas** (bass); **Taverner Consort; Taverner Players/Andrew Parrott.** EMI Reflexe CDS7 47293-8. Notes, text and translation included. From EX270239-3 (10/85).

⨀ ② 1h 43' DDD 8/86 ⑧

The richly contrasting styles and colours of the B minor Mass demonstrates Bach's prowess as a composer as well as his profound Christian faith. In this recording Andrew Parrott pursues a train of thought motivated by the American scholar/performer, Joshua Rifkin, who has argued in favour of one singer to each vocal part, although Parrott prefers to use a ripieno group of voices in addition to his soloists. In this and other respects, he has aimed in his own words "to adopt the conventions of a hypothetical performance by Bach himself at Leipzig, where the work was written". Voices and instrumentalists comprise a strong team and Parrott's direction is lively and authoritative, generating excitement and a vigorous sense of purpose. The recorded sound is clear and effectively resonant and the disc includes a booklet with full texts.

Bach. Magnificat in D major, BWV243[a]. Cantata No. 21, "Ich hatte viel Bekümmernis". **Greta de Reyghere** (sop); [a]**René Jacobs** (alto); **Christoph Prégardien** (ten); **Peter Lika** (bass); **Netherlands Chamber Choir; La Petite Bande/Sigiswald Kuijken.** Virgin Classics Veritas VC7 90779-2. Texts and translations included.

73' DDD 2/90   **ⓑ** 🖋

Bach. Magnificat in D major, BWV243. Cantata No. 51, Jauchzet Gott in allen Landen![a]. **Nancy Argenta, Patrizia Kwella,** [a]**Emma Kirkby** (sops); **Charles Brett** (alto); **Anthony Rolfe Johnson** (ten); **David Thomas** (bass); **English Baroque Soloists/John Eliot Gardiner.** Philips 411 458-2PH. Texts and translations included. From 411 458-1PH (4/85).

41' DDD 9/85   ⓟ ⓢ **ⓑ**

The profound and beautifully constructed cantata *Ich hatte viel Bekümmernis* is justifiably considered among the finest works from Bach's pen. It was performed at Weimar in 1714 but much of the music may well have been composed earlier. Subsequent performances included one in Leipzig in 1723 for which occasion Bach added four trombones to one of the choruses. It is this Leipzig version which is performed here. The *Magnificat*, too, is performed in its later D major version. Kuijken's interpretations are thoughtful, stylistically informed and sometimes profound. He chooses tempos discerningly, allowing the music to breathe and is often pleasingly at variance with current fashion in this respect. Not everything here is achieved with finesse, but the results are largely satisfying, both on account of Kuijken's assured direction and the strong team of soloists. Christoph Prégardien is excellent in the two strongly contrasting tenor arias of the cantata and Greta de Reyghere and Peter Lika ardently project the dialogue between Jesus (bass) and the Soul (soprano). Good recorded sound.

The *Magnificat*'s colourful textures are richly brought out in Gardiner's performance. His chorus sings with buoyancy and vigour, the orchestra have a clear, sharp, virtuoso style and the soloists are all first rate, so that with some racy tempos spirits remain high. The Italianate style of Cantata No. 51 also conveys a mood of celebration and rejoicing. Originally the solo part was taken by a boy treble and there is an important solo trumpet part (played by Crispian Steele-Perkins). Emma Kirkby's clear, rather white-toned soprano voice is not unsuited to the boy's part though it would be an exceptional young man who could reach her level of accomplishment and artistry. She is particularly successful in conveying a sense of joyful homage, and Gardiner supports her well. A bright, clear, and quite forward sound aids and abets the performances admirably.

Bach. St John Passion, BWV245. **Anthony Rolfe Johnson** (ten) Evangelist; **Stephen Varcoe** (bass) Jesus; **Nancy Argenta, Ruth Holton** (sops); **Michael Chance** (alto); **Neill Archer, Rufus Müller** (tens); **Cornelius Hauptmann** (bass); **Monteverdi Choir; English Baroque Soloists/John Eliot Gardiner.** Archiv Produktion 419 324-2AH2. Notes, text and translation included.

② Ih 47' DDD 2/87

Like most other oratorio passions of this period, the *St John Passion* is in two parts with the biblical text paragraphed by contemplative 'madrigal' numbers. This is glorious, timeless music and few who encounter numbers like the opening ("Lord, our master") and penultimate ("Lie in peace") choruses or the incomparable aria, "It is accomplished", can fail to respond and to be deeply moved. Gardiner gives a fresh appraisal of the work, with consistently fast tempos which suit his authentically-scaled forces. Superb solo singers and splendidly fresh and alert choral singing are features of this interpretation, which stresses above all else the continuity of the work. The recording is in every way sympathetic to this approach, with excellent detail and a fine overall balance.

Bach. St Matthew Passion. **Anthony Rolfe Johnson** (ten) Evangelist; **Andreas Schmidt** (bar) Jesus; **Barbara Bonney, Anne Monoyios** (sops); **Anne Sofie von Otter** (mez); **Michael Chance** (alto); **Howard Crook** (ten); **Olaf Bär** (bar); **Cornelius Hauptmann** (bass); **London Oratory Junior Choir; Monteverdi Choir; English Baroque Soloists/John Eliot Gardiner.** DG 427 648-2AH3. Notes, text and translation included.

③ 2h 47' DDD 10/89

What makes John Eliot Gardiner's *St Matthew Passion* stand out in the face of stiff competition is perhaps more than anything his vivid sense of theatre. Bach's score is, after all, a sacred drama and Gardiner interprets this aspect of the work with lively and colourful conviction. That in itself, of course, is not sufficient to ensure a fine performance but here we have a first-rate group of solo voices, immediately responsive choral groups in the Monteverdi Choir and the London Oratory Junior Choir—a distinctive element this—and refined obbligato and orchestral playing from the English Baroque Soloists. Anthony Rolfe Johnson declaims the Evangelist's role with clarity, authority and the subtle inflexion of an accomplished story-teller. Ann Monoyios, Howard Crook and Olaf Bär also make strong contributions but it is Michael Chance's "Erbarme dich", tenderly accompanied by the violin obbligato which sets the seal of distinction on the performance. Singing and playing of this calibre deserve to win many friends and Gardiner's deeply-felt account of Bach's great Passion does the music considerable justice. Clear recorded sound.

Bach. Christmas Oratorio, BWV248. **Anthony Rolfe Johnson** (ten) Evangelist; **Ruth Holton, Katie Pringle, Nancy Argenta** (sops); **Anne Sofie von Otter** (mez); **Hans-Peter Blochwitz** (ten); **Olaf Bär** (bar); **Monteverdi Choir; English Baroque Soloists/John Eliot Gardiner.** Archiv Produktion 423 232-2AH2. Notes, text and translation included.

② 2h 20' DDD 12/87

The *Christmas Oratorio* is a collection of six cantatas written to celebrate the whole of the Christmas festival and though deriving from earlier material is, nevertheless, a coherent, structured whole which has common threads running through it, not least in its settings of the chorales and in the use of an Evangelist who acts as narrator. John Eliot Gardiner and his impressive choral and orchestral forces are extremely well versed in this music and their disciplined approach is rewarding on many levels, not least in its precision of intonation and crisp, rhythmic drive. The English Baroque Soloists play on period instruments and the result is in every way thoroughly rewarding. The recording, though tending towards the analytical at the expense of an entirely plausible acoustic setting does, nevertheless, convey the thrust of the music very effectively.

Simon Bainbridge *British 1952*

Bainbridge. Viola Concerto (1976)[a]. Fantasia for Double Orchestra (1983-4)[b]. Concertante in Moto Perpetuo (1979, rev. 1983)[c]. [a]**Walter Trampler** (va); **London Symphony Orchestra / Michael Tilson Thomas;** [b]**BBC Symphony Orchestra;** [c]**The Composers Ensemble /** [bc]**Simon Bainbridge.** Continuum CCD1020. Item marked [a] from Unicorn RHD400 (2/82), [bc] new to UK.

54' DDD 5/91

When the recording of Simon Bainbridge's early Viola Concerto was first issued, it was rather overshadowed by the more outgoing, brightly-coloured music of Oliver Knussen with which it was coupled. Now the more outgoing, brightly-coloured coupling has been provided by Bainbridge himself, and the result is a disc as distinctive as it is distinguished. Bainbridge's music is modern in tone, romantic in temperament, and the most recent work on the disc, the *Fantasia for Double Orchestra*, presents a wide-ranging tapestry of moods and textures with an air of complete and justified confidence. There is a boldness, a directness that enables Bainbridge to evoke the opening of Wagner's *Das Rheingold* at the start without either irony or inappropriateness. His intention is evidently not to parody, but to build his own edifice on archetypically striking and substantial foundations. Structurally, the *Fantasia* works extremely well: expressively, it can be enjoyed even if the structure passes you by. The Viola Concerto is more introspective and more intense, but no less cogent. It may take longer to get the hang of than the *Fantasia*, but the results will be no less rewarding. The brief *Concertante in Moto Perpetuo* is an uncomplicated delight, and the whole disc has excellent sound and first-rate performance.

Mily Balakirev *Russian 1837-1910*

Balakirev. Symphony No. 1 in C major[a]. Tamara— symphonic poem[b]. **Royal Philharmonic Orchestra / Sir Thomas Beecham.** EMI Beecham Edition CDM7 63375-2. Item marked [a] from HMV SXLP30002 (6/62), [b] Philips mono ABL3047 (6/55).

61' ADD 7/90

Balakirev was a major figure of Russian nationalism and one of the group of composers called "The Five", and he also gave useful advice and encouragement to Tchaikovsky. In some ways the most intellectual of these artists, he was also highly self-critical and this meant that his output was all too small, though of high quality. The spacious and sombre beginning of the First Symphony tells us at once that this is a work of epic proportions, imbued with the kind of Russianness that is hard to describe but easy to recognize. Sir Thomas Beecham had a real affinity with this music, and his performance is one of power as well as ample colour, with good detail but holding the attention throughout the big structure. Both in this work and *Tamara*, which was inspired by a Lermontov poem depicting a kind of Lorelei figure, a siren whose beauty lures travellers to their doom, the Royal Philharmonic Orchestra plays with fervour and skill. Their stereo recording of the Symphony was made as long ago as December 1955, and that of the symphonic poem *Tamara* in mono early in 1954, but no apology need be made for the sound on the present digital transfers, which is vivid although with less definition than we would expect today; the slight background hiss in quieter passages is not obtrusive.

Granville Bantock

British 1868-1946

Bantock. The Pierrot of the Minute—comedy overture (1908).
Bridge. Suite for strings (1908). Summer (1914). There is a Willow Grows Aslant a Brook (1928).
Butterworth. The Banks of Green Willow (1913). **Bournemouth Sinfonietta/Norman Del Mar.** Chandos CHAN8373. From RCA Red Seal RL25184 (12/79).

> 58' ADD 8/85

All the works on this disc of English music were composed in the first three decades of this century, yet they inhabit very different sound-worlds. Granville Bantock's sparkling *The Pierrot of the Minute* Overture has its heart in the nineteenth century and has few undercurrents of disquiet. Butterworth's *The Banks of Green Willow,* with its folk-song base, already has signs of nostalgia for the passing of a whole way of life. Bridge's delightful *Suite* still retains the Edwardian glow of his earlier compositional style, with darkness only intruding, appropriately enough, in the third-movement Nocturne; even the shimmering textures of *Summer* intimate little of the cataclysm to come. With *There is a Willow Grows Aslant a Brook*, however, Bridge realized his bleakest misgivings —the security of pre-World War I England was never to be regained and could only be glimpsed fleetingly, in dream-like recollection. The diverse moods of all these works are splendidly captured by Del Mar and his Bournemouth players, and what the Sinfonietta lacks here in terms of solid ensemble and weight of string tone, it more than makes up for in zest and commitment to this music.

Samuel Barber

American 1910-1981

Barber. Violin Concerto, Op. 14[a].
Hanson. Symphony No. 2, Op. 30, "Romantic". [a]**Elmar Oliveira** (vn); **St Louis Symphony Orchestra/Leonard Slatkin.** EMI CDC7 47850-2.

> 55' DDD 10/87

This vividly recorded disc gives us two of the most cherishable of romantic American works. Hanson's lushly orchestrated Second Symphony has been well represented on LP but this version must take its place at the head of any list for the sheer breadth and excitement of the playing. The haunting opening motif coils its way beguilingly throughout the symphony's three movements, only standing aside for the glorious melody of the second movement. Elmar Oliveira handles the languorous cantilena of the opening two movements of Barber's Violin Concerto with just the right richness of tone, never forcing himself above the orchestra—it is a genuine dialogue of a particularly rapt nature. Slatkin and the orchestra capture the darker elements of the work nicely and allow their soloist full rein in the virtuoso *presto* finale—Oliviera shows us something of the quirky, spiky humour that underlies this brief movement. This is a fine disc for lovers of American music or for those taking the first tentative steps in that field.

Barber. Cello Concerto, Op. 22.
Britten. Symphony for cello and orchestra, Op. 68. **Yo-Yo Ma** (vc);
Baltimore Symphony Orchestra/David Zinman. CBS Masterworks
CD44900.

> 62' DDD 6/89

This recording is highly recommended. The acoustic is warm, balance ideal and
there is sufficient resonance. On this evidence, the Baltimore is a splendid
orchestra, responding alertly and intelligently to David Zinman's very positive

interpretation. How enterprising,
too, to record two works which
are not in the main repertoire of
cello concertos, excellent though
they are. Barber's dates from
1945 and has something of the
late-romanticism of the Violin
Concerto, but with a more
classical approach. It makes large
demands on the virtuosity of the
soloist, which are met with
apparent ease and relish by Yo-
Yo Ma. Britten's Cello
Symphony is more
problematical. Its predominantly
dark and brooding mood, with a
savage *scherzo* followed by an
almost jaunty finale, disconcerts
some listeners, but the clue lies
in the dedication to
Rostropovich, for the music
seems also to be an act of
homage to the composer's friend
Shostakovich and emulates the

Yo-Yo Ma   *[photo: Sony Classical/Friedman*

Russian master's ability to combine the tragic and the bizarre within one
framework. Once the listener has penetrated the rather forbidding outer shell of
this work, the rewards are great. Ma and Zinman obviously agree on the music's
stature, for this is a compelling performance.

Barber. Adagio for Strings.
Copland. Appalachian Spring—suite.
Gershwin. Rhapsody in Blue. **Los Angeles Philharmonic Orchestra/
Leonard Bernstein** (pf). DG 431 048-2GBE. Recorded at a performance in
Davies Symphony Hall, San Francisco in July 1982.

> 54' DDD

This disc shows Bernstein on home ground: American music played by an
American orchestra. It captures, too, the most enduring elements of his music-
making—the rythmic vitality and the sense of poise that he could so winningly
embrace in music with a strong melody. This is Bernstein at his most engaging,
his piano-playing as impressive as always, his feeling for the ebb and flow of this
most elusive music beautifully judged. The 'big-band' version of the piece is used
but with such a vital response from soloist and orchestra alike—the sense of real
interplay between the musicians is almost palpable. Copland's lyrical *Appalachian
Spring* is gloriously unfolded, the tempos are nicely judged and the Los Angeles
orchestra clearly revels in the melodic weave of the piece. Similarly, the serene
Adagio by Barber finds the strings rapt, unhurried and poised, the tempo

dangerously slow but carried along by the commitment of the inspirational conductor. The live recordings are well handled, with virtually no evidence of the audience to be heard.

Barber. SONGS. **Roberta Alexander** (sop); **Tan Crone** (pf). Etcetera KTC1055.
Three Songs, Op. 2. Three Songs, Op. 10. Four Songs, Op. 13. Two Songs, Op. 18. Nuvoletta, Op. 25. Hermit Songs, Op. 29. Despite and Still, Op. 41.

● 61' DDD 9/88

If Samuel Barber had not been a composer he could have had a very respectable career as a baritone; he made a beautiful recording of his own *Dover Beach* many years ago. He also confessed to having "sometimes thought that I'd rather write words than music". Good qualifications for writing songs, both of them; so is his individual and discriminating taste in poetry. The average length of the ten *Hermit Songs* (settings of medieval Irish texts) is less than two minutes, but they often distil big images from tiny ones: the ringing of a little bell amid silence evokes a longing for the solitary life and the tranquil solitude of death, the cry of a bird is the starting point for a pitying description of the crucified Christ and his mother, a lazy rocking in the piano serves as metaphor for the simple contentment of an old scholar-monk and the purring of his companionable cat.

Simplicity of imagery plus economy of means equals intensity of utterance is often Barber's equation, but there is humour here as well (lines from James Joyce's *Finnegan's Wake* are set as a brilliant, slightly dizzy waltz-song) and suave melodiousness ("Sure on this shining night") and bold, almost operatic declamation ("I hear an army"). There is scarcely a weak song among them. They need a singer with quite a range, and Roberta Alexander has it; her bright, vibrant but precise singing is as sensitive to words as Barber himself, and she never allows her expressiveness to break the poised elegance of his lines. Her pianist is excellent and the recording is clean, though rather close.

Béla Bartók

Hungarian 1881-1945

Bartók. ORCHESTRAL WORKS. ᵇᶜ**Géza Anda** (pf); **Berlin RIAS Symphony Orchestra/Ferenc Fricsay.** DG Dokumente 427 410-2GDO2.
Item marked ᵃ from DGM18377 (1/58), ᵇ SLPM138708 (1/62), ᶜ SLPM138111 (5/61).
Concerto for Orchestra, Sz116ᵃ. Rhapsody for piano and orchestra, Op. 1ᵇ.
Piano Concertos—No. 1, Sz83ᵇ; No. 2, Sz95ᶜ; No. 3, Sz119ᶜ.

② 2h 19' ADD 5/89   £ ?

This very useful compilation gathers together all of Bartók's *concertante* works for piano and orchestra as well as a simply magnificent account of the *Concerto for Orchestra*. Ferenc Fricsay was a pupil of Bartók in Hungary and the experience clearly gave him some very special insights into the composer's music. He discerns better than the majority of conductors the darker elements of the music, the subtle undertones. He phrases the music with great breadth which is perhaps his secret for capturing and sustaining a sense of atmosphere. Géza Anda, too, brings to the piano works a zest and unsophisticated directness that the music often fails to receive. Like Fricsay, Anda speaks the right language and the performances are the better for it. The Third Concerto, written as an insurance policy for his wife Ditta in the face of his inevitable death, is a very fine reading.

The recordings, 30 years old, sound well and the attractive price of these two well-filled discs makes this a set worth exploring.

Bartók. Piano Concertos—No. 1, Sz83; No. 2, Sz95. **Maurizio Pollini** (pf); **Chicago Symphony Orchestra/Claudio Abbado.** DG 415 371-2GH. From 2530 901 (7/79).

52' ADD 9/86

Bartók. Piano Concertos—No. 1, Sz83[a]; No. 2, Sz95[b]; No. 3, Sz119[a]. **Stephen Kovacevich** (pf); [a]**London Symphony Orchestra;** [b]**BBC Symphony Orchestra/Sir Colin Davis.** Philips 426 660-2PSL. Items marked [a] from 9500 043 (7/76), [b] SAL3779 (3/70).

77' ADD 5/91

The First Piano Concerto of 1926 was one of the first fruits of a new-found confidence in Bartók—a totally serious, uncompromisingly aggressive assertion that the future could be faced and shaped by human will-power. It is tough listening, and Bartók admitted as much, promising that the Second Concerto would be easier to play and to take in. Certainly the themes here tend to be a little more folk-like, but in no other respect could Bartók be said to have realized that aim. The pianist has to cope with one of the most fearsome cadenzas in the repertoire on top of an unrelenting complexity of argument which draws the orchestra into its maelstrom. Not surprisingly these concertos can sound dauntingly abstract and nothing more. Pollini's pianistic mastery is so complete, however, that he can find all sorts of shades and perspectives which turn apparently abstract geometry into a three-dimensional experience. Abbado and the Chicago orchestra are the perfect partners for his diamond-edged virtuosity, and the faithful recording provides an admirable vehicle for communication.

Kovacevich is also as intelligent a virtuoso as they come, and both the LSO and the BBC Symphony make first-rate contributions under Sir Colin Davis; together they achieve a winning blend of drive, fantasy and inner intensity. More recent recordings may have captured more orchestral detail, and the interplay between piano and orchestra is not always as clear here as it might be, but this disc is still an admirable mid-price alternative to Pollini's recording.

Bartók. Violin Concertos—No. 1, Sz36[a]; No. 2, Sz112[b]. **Kyung-Wha Chung** (vn); [a]**Chicago Symphony Orchestra;** [b]**London Philharmonic Orchestra/Sir Georg Solti.** Decca Ovation 425 015-2DM. Item marked [a] from 411 804-1DH (10/84), [b] SXL6212 (4/78).

59' ADD/DDD 2/91

Long gone are the times when Bartók was thought of as an arch-modernist incapable of writing a melody and the young Yehudi Menuhin was considered daring in championing his Violin Concerto. Today this work is listed as his second in this form, but four decades ago it stood alone because the composer had suppressed an earlier one dating from 1908, or more precisely reshaped it into another work called *Two Portraits*. When this earlier piece was finally published in its original form some 30 years ago, it became his First Concerto and the more familiar one of 1938 his Second. The First was inspired by a beloved woman friend, but it does not by any means wear its heart on its sleeve, being a complex and edgy work to which Kyung-Wha Chung brings a passionate lyricism. Her conductor Sir Georg Solti is the composer's compatriot and was actually his piano pupil as well, so that he too knows how to make this music breathe and sing. Chung and Solti are equally at home in the more obviously colourful and dramatic Second Concerto, giving it all the range, expressive force and occasional violence, driving momentum and sheer Hungarian charm that one could desire. The London Philharmonic Orchestra play as if inspired and the recordings (in two locations, seven years apart) are subtle yet lit with the right brilliance.

Bartók. Violin Concerto No. 2, Sz112[a].
Sibelius. Violin Concerto in D minor, Op. 47[b]. **Isaac Stern** (vn); [a]**New York Philharmonic Orchestra/Leonard Bernstein; ** [b]**Philadelphia Orchestra/Eugene Ormandy.** CBS Maestro CD44873. Item marked [a] from Fontana SCFL106 (10/59).

66' ADD 11/89

Stern's ability to cut through the technical difficulties of a work and dig deep into the heart of the music are nowhere more evident than in these performances. His lyrical and passionate playing bring great beauty to the Bartók where he captures the rhapsodic, almost dream-like, quality exceptionally well (the opening bars have rarely sounded as magical as this). Some may find the recording perhaps a little artificial, the soloist is forwardly placed and the inner orchestral details are revealed in a way that only a multi-mike recording can achieve. But in the end it is the performance that wins the day, with Bernstein's probing and sumptuous accompaniment every bit the equal of Stern's inspired playing. The Sibelius Concerto has been exceptionally well served on disc and although Stern's account might not quite make front running, it certainly has much to offer. There is a strong sense of organic development in the first movement, coupled with an urgency and heartfelt lyricism in Stern's playing that brings great poignancy to this movement. The slow movement is beautifully crafted, with some very intense and passionate playing. The exhilarating last movement is full of electricity and rhythmic drive, with Ormandy providing a positively volcanic accompaniment. At mid-price this CD offers excellent value.

Bartók. Two Portraits, Sz46[a].
Szymanowski. Symphonies—No. 2 in B flat major, Op. 19[b]; No. 3, Op. 27, "The song of the night"[c]. [c]**Ryszard Karczykowski** (ten); [c]**Kenneth Jewell Chorale; Detroit Symphony Orchestra/Antál Dorati.** Decca Enterprise 425 625-2DM. Text and translation included. Item marked [a] from SXL6897 (10/79), [bc]SXDL7524 (7/81).

70' [a]ADD /DDD 7/90

Szymanowski was the first major Polish composer after Chopin, and is a leading figure of a generation that also includes Bartók and Stravinsky. Although his music is less well known than theirs, it has a strong personality of its own, exotic and ecstatic by turns, with an extraordinary opulence. Though we may not want to hear such richness (and decadence maybe) every day, there are certain aspects of the human spirit that it expresses with an unashamed hedonism for which the nearest parallels are perhaps Scriabin and, in certain moods, Messaien. The opening of the Third Symphony is typical of him, with its mysterious sustained chord, faintly throbbing drums and luscious string melody conveying the mood of the Persian poem celebrating the beauty of night which is here set for tenor and chorus. The performance of this exotically scored music by the Detroit orchestra under Dorati is highly idiomatic, and so is the singing of the Polish soloist and the American choir. The Second, completed six years previously, is less extreme in mood and shows us that the composer had learned much from the music of Richard Strauss; but though more obviously melodious than the Third, it is still sumptuous and sensuous music. Bartók's *Two Pictures* are contemporary with this work, but while they also evoke nature in an impressionistic way they are sharper in feeling and the composer's compatriot Dorati directs them strongly. The recording is rich yet detailed.

Bartók. The Wooden Prince—ballet, Sz60[a]. Dance Suite, Sz77[b]. **New York Philharmonic Orchestra/Pierre Boulez.** CBS Masterworks CD44700. Item marked [a] from 76625 (10/77), [b] 73031 (1/73).

71' ADD 3/89

The Wooden Prince comes as a surprise if you associate Bartók exclusively with the grimness and violence of *Bluebeard's Castle* or *The Miraculous Mandarin*. It is a fairy story, and a fairly implausible one at that; a Princess finds a Prince's wooden staff more desirable than the Prince himself. In due course roles are reversed: the Princess changes her mind, but now the Prince resists her, and only when she cuts off her own hair does he relent and allow a happy ending. Fortunately Bartók clothes this farrago in some of his most opulent and warmly expressive music. Because of its length and the large forces demanded—even the celesta part requires two players—the complete score is seldom heard in theatre or concert hall, and has rarely been recorded: but Boulez is the ideal conductor, neither over-indulging its expansiveness nor seeking to play down its lusciousness. The *Dance Suite* is Bartók in more familiar guise, with its strong basis in folk-music (North African as well as East European) promoting a vitality and freshness that far transcend the limitations of mere arrangement. The rich orchestration and vibrant rhythms of both works are finely conveyed in this impressive, well-filled disc.

Bartók. The Miraculous Mandarin, Sz73—ballet[a]. Two portraits, Sz37[b]. **Prokofiev.** Scythian Suite, Op. 20[c]. [b]**Shlomo Mintz** (vn); [a]**Ambrosian Singers; [ab]London Symphony Orchestra, [c]Chicago Symphony Orchestra/Claudio Abbado.** DG 410 598-2GH. Items marked [a] and [b] from 410 589-1GH (9/83), [c] 2530 967 (11/78).

63' ADD/DDD 6/87

It is scarcely surprising that *The Miraculous Mandarin* failed to reach the stage for some years after it was composed, for the plot concerns three ruffians who force a girl into luring men from the street up to a shabby garret where they rob them. Bartók's music matches the savagery of the subject, with wild pounding rhythms and jagged outbursts: it is a marvellously imaginative and inventive score which Abbado realizes with enormous energy and knife-edge playing from the orchestra. No greater contrast could be provided than the first of the *Two Portraits*, where in the most tender and ethereal fashion Bartók expresses his love for the young violinist Steffi Geyer. Here Mintz plays most beautifully. The second *Portrait* is a brief, boisterous, transcription of a piano *Bagatelle*. An excellent disc is completed by Prokofiev's *Scythian Suite*. Here Prokofiev was very much influenced by Stravinsky's *Rite of Spring* in a scenario involving an ancient tribe who worship the sun god. Again it is a score with savage, pungent rhythms expressed through the medium of a very large orchestra; and again Abbado conducts with virtuoso control and vehemence. Though the recordings come from different sources they are all first class.

Bartók. Concerto for two pianos and orchestra, Sz115[a]. Sonata for two pianos and percussion, Sz110. **Katia and Marièlle Labèque** (pfs); **Sylvio Gualda, Jean-Pierre Drouet** (perc); [a]**City of Birmingham Symphony Orchestra/ Simon Rattle.** EMI CDC7 47446-2.

52' DDD 9/87

Amongst other things Bartók is famous for having acknowledged the 'true' status of the piano as a percussion instrument and his alliance of the instrument with an array of percussion in the Sonata of 1937 certainly indicates an attitude to the piano that no nineteenth-century composer could have envisaged. In fact it is not an especially violent or even astringent work, for all the calculated rigour of its construction. The three movements are dominated respectively by asymmetrical pulse, nocturnal atmospherics and folk-like exuberance, and the percussion adds colour, punctuation and dialogue, but hardly ever noise or harshness for its own sake. Successful performance depends on close understanding and an especially acute rhythmical sense from all four players. This is precisely what the Labèque sisters and their percussionists supply, plus an irresistible verve and interplay of accent. Recording quality is on the soft-focused side of ideal, and in the Concerto (a modest re-texturing of the same piece) the orchestra is surprisingly remote. Still, there are no finer performances of this exhilarating music currently available, the coupling is convenient (and unique) and minor reservations need not deter the interested listener.

Bartók. Music for strings, percussion and celesta, Sz116.
Hindemith. Mathis der Maler—symphony. **Berlin Philharmonic Orchestra/ Herbert von Karajan.** EMI Studio CDM7 69242-2. From Columbia SAX2432 (2/62).

56' ADD 4/88   Ⓑ

This is highly recommendable, even if Karajan's well-known preoccupation with beauty of sound somewhat softens asperities intended by the composers as in the final movement of the Hindemith. But the central movement is a deeply moving threnody, and in the first movement virtuoso playing by the Berlin Philharmonic

produces the utmost clarity of detail in Hindemith's busy textural web. The Bartók is both more demanding intellectually and more diverse in idiom: the sombre initial fugue provides the source for the ensuing vigorous neo-classical movement, an impressionistic piece of his characteristic night music, and an exuberant finale owing much to Hungarian folk style. Karajan is a little free over Bartók's meticulously marked nuances of pace, but the fast movements in particular generate a compulsive forward impulse. From the admirable recorded quality one would never guess that these performances date from 1962.

Herbert von Karajan   *[photo: DG/Lauterwasser]*

Bartók. Concerto for Orchestra, Sz116.
Mussorgsky. Pictures at an exhibition (orch. Ravel). **Chicago Symphony Orchestra/Sir Georg Solti.** Decca 417 754-2DM.

⏺ 69' DDD   Ⓑ

With its five contrasted movements Bartók's Concerto demands the highest orchestral virtuosity, but it has mystery too—the very opening is highly evocative—and charm, with the *Scherzo* offering the orchestral soloists in pairs, tripping along, like animals joining Noah on his Ark. The *Elegia* is a haunting nocturnal piece and the *Intermezzo* has a bizarre element, quoting irreverently from Shostakovich's *Leningrad* Symphony. Solti's is not a genial view but he brings a biting and compulsive intensity to his reading, matched by superlative playing—the finale is breathtaking in its physical excitement. Mussorgsky's famous conducted tour round an exhibition of his friend Victor Hartman's paintings and design-sketches is hardly less compelling in Solti's hands and the brilliantly clear Decca digital recording, which gives such a powerful projection to the Bartók, brings comparable vividness and great clarity of detail to Ravel's brilliant scoring. Each of the pictures springs to life in sharp focus and the closing "Great Gate of Kiev" is resplendently powerful.

Bartók. CHAMBER WORKS. [a]**Michael Collins** (cl); **Krysia Osostowicz** (vn); [b]**Susan Tomes** (pf). Hyperion CDA66415.
Contrasts, Sz111[ab]. Rhapsodies—No. 1, Sz86; No. 2, Sz89[b]. Romanian folk-dances, Sz56 (arr. Székely)[b]. Sonata for solo violin, Sz117.

⏺ 72' DDD 4/91

Unusually for a composer who wrote so much fine chamber music Bartók was not himself a string player. But he did enjoy close artistic understanding with a succession of prominent violin virtuosos, including the Hungarians Jelly d'Arányi, Joseph Szigeti and Zoltán Székely, and, towards the end of his life, Yehudi Menuhin. It was Menuhin who commissioned the Sonata for solo violin, but Bartók died before he could hear him play it—Menuhin was unhappy with the occasional passages in quarter-tones and the composer had reserved judgement on his proposal to omit them. It was Menuhin's edition which was later printed and which has been most often played and recorded; but Krysia Osostowicz returns to the original and, more importantly, plays the whole work with intelligence, imaginative flair and consummate skill. The Sonata is the most substantial work on this disc, but the rest of the programme is no less thoughtfully prepared or idiomatically delivered. There is the additional attraction of an extremely well balanced and natural-sounding recording. As a complement to the string quartets, which are at the very heart of Bartók's output, this is a most recommendable disc.

Bartók. STRING QUARTETS. **Emerson Quartet** (Eugene Drucker, Philip Setzer, vns; Lawrence Dutton, va; David Finckel, vc). DG 423 657-2GH2.
No. 1 in A minor; No. 2 in A minor; No. 3 in C sharp minor; No. 4 in C major; No. 5 in B flat major; No. 6 in D major.

⏺ ② 2h 29' DDD 12/88   𝄞ₛ

It has long been recognized that this series of string quartets written over three decades has been one of the major contributions to Western music. The Emerson Quartet does not play them all the same way, for as its first violinist Eugene Drucker rightly says, "each has its own style". The Quartet has a fine unanimity and is equally good in the tense melodic lines and harmony of slower movements and the infectious rhythmic drive of quicker ones; and it also copes extremely well with Bartók's frequent changes of dynamics, texture and tempo. Here is not only striking virtuosity—to be convinced, listen to the wildly exciting *Allegro molto* finale of No. 4—and yet great subtlety too. The recording is excellent, with good detail yet without harshness. Where most Bartók cycles take three discs, here 149 minutes are accommodated on two CDs. One readily concurs with the critic who called this "one of the most exciting chamber music recordings of recent years".

Bartók. Piano Sonata, Sz80.
Berg. Piano Sonata, Op. 1.
Liszt. Piano Sonata in B minor, S178. Bagatelle sans tonalité, S216a. **Peter Donohoe** (pf). EMI CDC7 49916-2.

59' DDD 3/90

Peter Donohoe is now well established as one of the finest British pianists of his generation, possessing a seemingly dauntless technique. If one at first wonders why he's coupled the Liszt Sonata with those by Berg and Bartók, the clue must lie in his additional choice of Liszt's terse late piece called *Bagatelle without tonality*, which lasts less than three minutes but manages in that brief time to point forward boldly to the twentieth century. The performance of the difficult and thrilling Bartók Sonata is arguably the finest thing here, not only because of the astonishing technical command but also partly because every marking of tempo, phrasing, dynamics and the like is scrupulously observed. Compared to this work the Berg is romantic, albeit in a slightly decadent way; it is an amazing 'Opus 1' completed when he was 23, and Donohoe gives it the right kind of spaciousness. The recital begins chronologically, however, with the biggest work: Liszt's Sonata resembles the Berg in having just a single movement but is over twice as long. Here there are places where the sheer romanticism of the music could have a still warmer affection, a more spacious delivery and richer sound, but perhaps the pianist has a valid point if he seems to reserve his sense of wonder for the beautiful, meditative F sharp major section marked *Quasi adagio* that comes relatively late in the work but is arguably its expressive heart. Overall, this recital is to be praised more for its intellectual strength than for its charm, but it is a fine achievement and the recording is sharply immediate.

Bartók. DUKE BLUEBEARD'S CASTLE. **Christa Ludwig** (mez) Judith; **Walter Berry** (bass) Bluebeard. **London Symphony Orchestra/István Kertész.** Decca 414 167-2DH. From SET311 (5/66).

60' ADD 1/89

Bartók's lucid but mysterious fable is ideally suited to recording. On CD in particular the mysterious arrival of the music from darkness and silence and its return to shadow at the end are as gripping as (and can be more disturbing than) any stage production. That is certainly true of this performance, which has had many rivals but still stands up well to comparison with the best of them. You will need to hunt out a copy of the libretto and a translation, alas (the opera is sung in Hungarian). Decca provides neither, and although a detailed synopsis is supplied, keyed to cueing bands at crucial points, it would be a pity to miss the detail of Berry's subtle colouring of words, the sense of urgent attack and defence, of fear and concern as Ludwig's Judith unlocks the secrets of Bluebeard's heart and her attempts to let light into his castle draw her inexorably towards endless dark. Kertész is outstandingly imaginative and the orchestral playing is both vivid and rich. The sound has dated little: even some very up-to-date versions have a less satisfying blaze of orchestra-plus-organ major chords when the fifth door opens on Bluebeard's dominions.

Arnold Bax   British 1883-1953

Bax. TONE-POEMS. **Ulster Orchestra/Bryden Thomson.** Chandos
CHAN8307. From ABRD1066 (4/83).
November Woods. The Happy Forest. The Garden of Fand. Summer Music.

57' DDD 1/84

In a well-balanced programme, here are four of the descriptive pieces Bax
composed before turning to symphonic writing. The least well known is *Summer
Music*, a short, serene, exquisite tone painting of a hot June midday in the woods
of southern England. In *The Happy Forest* a nimble-footed dance-like portrayal of
merry-making wood spirits flanks a slow, reflective and passionate middle
section, whilst *November Woods* is a darker, more complex evocation of woodland
nature. The best known and most sumptuous of the four, however, is *The Garden
of Fand*, an opulent piece inspired by the legends and heroes of western Eire.
Everywhere the orchestral playing is excellent and the recording has a marvellous
presence and depth of tone, so that every strand of Bax's complex orchestration
is reproduced clearly and tellingly.

Bax. Symphony No. 3. Four Orchestral Sketches—Dance of Wild Irravel.
Paean. **London Philharmonic Orchestra/Bryden Thomson.** Chandos
CHAN8454.

59' DDD 12/86

Bax's Third Symphony has a long and gravely beautiful epilogue, one of the most
magical things he ever wrote: a noble processional with a disturbing, motionless
glitter at its centre and, just before the very end, a sudden bitter chill. It is pure
Bax, and will haunt you for days. We may associate some of the Symphony with
the lonely sands and the shining sea of Morar in Inverness-shire (where the work
was written), the impassioned string music that rises from that sea in the centre
of the slow movement with deep emotion, the war-like dance of the finale with
conflict or war and the frequent violent intercuttings of lyricism and darkness
with what we know about Bax's temperament. But it is harder to explain in
programmatic terms why lyric can become dark or vigour become brooding
within startlingly few bars, why that epilogue seems so inevitable, why the
Symphony for all its wild juxtapositions does not sound like a random sequence
of vivid memories and passionate exclamations. That it is a real symphony after
all, powered by purely musical imperatives, is suggested by this finely paced and
tautly controlled performance, one of the finest in Thomson's Bax cycle. The
enjoyable racket of *Paean* and the glittering colour of *Irravel* respond no less
gratefully to the sumptuousness of the recording.

Bax. Symphony No. 4. Tintagel—tone-poem. **Ulster Orchestra/Bryden
Thomson.** Chandos CHAN8312. From ABRD1091 (1/84).

57' DDD 8/84

Bax's Fourth Symphony is less well regarded than most of his others, yet after
several hearings this reviewer finds it deeply affecting. The opening *Allegro
moderato* movement has a dark, brooding eloquence typical of the composer, but
it is well-argued and coherent in form. There follows a *Lento* movement, full of
sad passion and poetry, and then the mood lightens a little in the last movement
with a defiant *Allegro*, sub-titled *Tempo di marcia trionfale*. Thomson directs a
performance which is lucid, extremely well played by the orchestra, and
objective in style. The more familiar *Tintagel* is from an earlier, more rhapsodic
phase of Bax's development. It portrays not only the Cornish seascape but also

more intimate feelings arising from a romantic relationship. Here Thomson responds more to the ardent romanticism of the score. Both works are written for a very large orchestra and benefit from an outstanding recording which reproduces the heaviest passages with richness as well as clarity.

Bax. Oboe Quintet (1922).
Bliss. Oboe Quintet (1927).
Britten. Phantasy for oboe quartet, Op. 2. **Pamela Woods** (ob); **Audubon Quartet** (David Ehrlich, David Salness, vns; Doris Lederer, va; Thomas Shaw, vc). Telarc CD80205.

55' DDD 10/89

The wealth of British chamber music composed during the first half of this century is now enjoying a richly-deserved boom, with the release of a number of first-class discs that revitalize pieces neglected for over 60 years. This disc is a prime example, effectively coupling works from the 1920s and early 1930s in deliciously idiomatic performances from these American players. The three-movement Bax Quintet dates from the time of his First Symphony and finds him in fine humour, characteristically infiltrating his rhapsodic style with Irish idioms and ending up with a spirited jig. The Bliss, composed in response to a Coolidge commission, still has much of the flame of adventure and innovation that was a feature of his early music, but which tended to spark less frequently in his later career. The better-known *Phantasy* Quartet of Benjamin Britten, with its satisfying, one-movement arch shape, brilliantly shows a major composer at the outset of his career already displaying those main features of his genius that were to bear such marvellous fruit later. All these works are played with vibrant involvement, the rounded, open sounds of Pamela Wood's timbre set in balanced contrast with the more effulgent warmth of the Audubon Quartet. Only a touch of plumpness in the loudest sections mars an otherwise exemplary recording.

Bax. PIANO WORKS. **Eric Parkin** (pf). Chandos CHAN8732.
Two Russian Tone Pictures—Nocturne, "May Night in the Ukraine"; Gopak, "National Dance". The Maiden with the Daffodil—Idyll. The Princess's Rose Garden—Nocturne. Apple Blossom Time. On a May Evening. O Dame get up and bake your pies— Variations on a North Country Christmas carol. Nereid. Sleepy Head. A romance. Burlesque.

59' DDD 7/90

These are ideal performances of Bax's piano music, recorded by Chandos in the Snape Maltings in very true sound. It is the third volume of Eric Parkin's series and covers mainly the years 1912 to 1916, a crucial period in the composer's life. The works on this disc were inspired by his visit to Russia at the height of a love affair, then the beginning of his long association with the pianist Harriet Cohen, and the Easter Rising in Dublin. *May Night in the Ukraine* is a nocturnal tone-poem, evoking the heat of summer in languorous, shifting harmonies, and is perhaps the finest music in the selection. Bax's first meeting with Harriet Cohen is preserved in *The Maiden with the Daffodil*, a most touching piece. His gift for suggesting a wide range of colour on the keyboard rivals that displayed in his scoring for orchestra, while in these shorter forms his tendency to sprawl is curbed. In Parkin he has a sympathetic and persuasive interpreter.

Antonio Bazzini   *Refer to Index*   *Italian 1818-1897*

Ludwig van Beethoven

German 1770-1827

Beethoven. Violin Concerto in D major, Op. 61. **Itzhak Perlman** (vn); **Philharmonia Orchestra/Carlo Maria Giulini.** EMI CDC7 47002-2. From ASD4059 (9/81).

44' DDD 2/84

Beethoven. Violin Concerto in D major, Op. 61[a]. Two Romances—No. 1 in G major, Op. 40; No. 2 in F major, Op. 50. **Itzhak Perlman** (vn); **Berlin Philharmonic Orchestra/Daniel Barenboim.** EMI CDC7 49567-2. Item marked [a] recorded at a performance in the Philharmonie, Berlin in November 1986.

61' DDD 11/89

Beethoven. Violin Concerto in D major, Op. 61[a]. Two Romances—No. 1 in G major, Op. 40[b]; No. 2 in F major, Op. 50[b]. [a]**Wolfgang Schneiderhan,** [b]**David Oistrakh** (vns); [a]**Berlin Philharmonic Orchestra/Eugen Jochum;** [b]**Royal Philharmonic Orchestra/Sir Eugene Goossens.** DG Privilege 427 197-2GR. Item marked [a] from SLPM138999 (11/62), [b] SEPL121586 (12/61).

63' AAD 10/89

Perlman and Giulini fuse the classical and romantic elements of this work together skilfully. The first movement's opening tutti is beautifully managed by Giulini, for it has a blend of purpose and repose, the tempo unhurried yet with plenty of momentum. Perlman's clear-cut, delicately poised playing then takes the stage: his style is classical, but quietly expressive. He has a beautiful, elegant tone-quality and a rock-like technique, and it is interesting that in Kreisler's excellent but more overtly romantic cadenza his tone becomes a little more ripe. Not often does the shape of the first movement emerge so clearly as here. In the second movement Perlman and Giulini find a good balance of serenity and expressive warmth; the music is never allowed to dawdle or lose its way. The last has a well-defined rhythmic 'lift' at a good, steady tempo and never plods as it sometimes can. The sound-quality is luminous, clear and well balanced. This is one of the most satisfying accounts of a difficult and elusive concerto.

Nevertheless, Perlman's live recording has a spontaneity and yet also a depth that makes it a rather special experience. He and Barenboim both fully understand the music, yet although they are close colleagues each must do so in

terms of his own psychology and musical experience; here, the interaction of these factors makes for something altogether worthy of the repeated listening that Compact Disc affords us. The audience must have felt privileged; at any rate, they are quiet enough not to disturb the music and we can readily allow them, and the artists, the ovation at the end of the relaxed yet brilliant finale. The recording does justice to Perlman's beautiful tone and instrumental command, not least in the rapt phrases of the Larghetto, while Kreisler's beautiful cadenza to the enormous first movement can rarely have sounded more effective in its rare combination of lyrical sweetness and virtuoso display. The two *Romances* are much more than a fill-up to this outstanding performance, for although they were recorded in the studio, in this gentle music, too, the artists convey a feeling of occasion.

Although the DG recording is perhaps less than ideal compared with today's standards it, too, remains one of the finest accounts of Beethoven's Violin Concerto on disc. Schneiderhan and Jochum work well together, creating a well-structured performance that eschews the often romantic and sentimental approach taken by many performers. This is a performance of innate sensibility, where poetry takes precedence over virtuosity; although Schneiderhan is certainly not lacking in the latter. The slow movement has great serenity and beauty and the finale an infectious joyfulness that makes it hard to resist. It is also worth pointing out that Schneiderhan uses Beethoven's cadenzas for his transcription of the work for piano and orchestra. This disc is made all the more attractive with the inclusion of Oistrakh's outstanding performances of the two *Romances*. At bargain price, this CD is to be strongly recommended.

Beethoven. Triple Concerto in C major, Op. 56[a]. Choral Fantasia in C minor, Op. 80[b]. [a]**Christian Funke** (vn); [a]**Jürnjakob Timm** (vc); [a]**Peter Rösel**, [b]**Jörg-Peter Weigle** (pfs); [b]**Leipzig Radio Chorus; Dresden Philharmonic Orchestra/Herbert Kegel.** Capriccio 10 150.

·•˙ **54' DDD 9/87**

Beethoven. Triple Concerto in C major, Op. 56[a]. Piano Sonata in D minor, Op. 31 No. 2, "Tempest"[b]. **Sviatoslav Richter** (pf); [a]**David Oistrakh** (vn); [a]**Mstislav Rostropovich** (vc); [a]**Berlin Philharmonic Orchestra/Herbert von Karajan.** EMI Studio CDM7 69032-2. Item marked [a] from ASD2582 (9/70), [b] ASD450 (10/61).

·•˙ **60' ADD 4/88**

The two major works featured on the Capriccio disc were for a long time considered to some extent ugly ducklings among a group of much beloved swans. Part of the trouble is that they are difficult and expensive to programme in the concert hall. The Triple Concerto needs three good soloists who can also play together as a chamber trio and that is hard to arrange artistically; as for the *Choral Fantasia*, it includes a chorus that are only used near the end and a solo pianist who can cope convincingly with the lengthy and difficult opening cadenza and then play a more restricted role latterly without being overshadowed. Performances such as these unobtrusively musicianly ones from Kegel and his skilful Dresden soloists and orchestra do a great deal to make both of these works convincing and likeable. Each of the four soloists accomplishes his role well, while Kegel and his orchestral players are also well inside the style of the music, performing it with the kind of affection that is highly persuasive. The sound is unforced and agreeable, and the balance between soloists and orchestra well managed and natural.

It is hardly possible to imagine a more starry line-up than Richter, Oistrakh and Rostropovich with the Berlin Philharmonic under Karajan. With lesser men, the result could perhaps have been an undignified contest in limelight-hugging, but these great Soviet soloists have often played together in chamber music and although the cellist Rostropovich can and does make the most conventional figuration sound musically alive, what we hear from them is for the most part like the playing of a piano trio, a real ensemble which acts as a kind of composite soloist. Karajan and his orchestra play most sympathetically too and often delicately, holding the enormous first movement together gently but firmly so that it cannot sprawl, and the recorded balance is good too, although the piano could have been placed more forwardly. Warm, big-bodied sound is another plus, not least in the expansive slow movement. But while the D minor Piano Sonata used as a fill-up has dramatic and shapely playing, the 1961 recording for this work doesn't do justice to Richter's beautiful tonal palette and we hear some tape hiss.

Beethoven. Piano Concertos—No. 1 in C major, Op. 15[a]; No. 2 in B flat major, Op. 19[b]. **Wilhelm Kempff** (pf); **Berlin Philharmonic Orchestra/ Ferdinand Leitner.** DG Galleria 419 856-2GGA. Item marked [a] from SLPM138774 (6/62), [b] SLPM138775 (9/62).

65' ADD 9/88

The Second Piano Concerto was in fact written before the First, and recent research suggests that an initial version of the so-called Second Concerto dates back to Beethoven's teenage years. If the Second Concerto inevitably reflects eighteenth-century classical style, it has Beethoven's familiar drive and energy and a radical use of form and technique. The First Concerto pre-dates the revolutionary *Eroica* Symphony by some eight years and still shows classical influences, but it is on a larger scale than the Second Concerto, and has greater powers of invention. Kempff's recording of these two works dates from the early 1960s, but the sound quality is pleasingly open and full-bodied, so that the soloist's pearly, immaculate tone quality is heard to good effect. Kempff and Leitner enjoy what is obviously a close rapport and their aristocratic, Olympian but poetic music-making suits both works admirably well.

Beethoven. Piano Concertos—No. 3 in C minor, Op. 37; No. 4 in G major, Op. 58. **Murray Perahia** (pf); **Concertgebouw Orchestra, Amsterdam/ Bernard Haitink.** CBS Masterworks CD39814. From IM39814 (7/86).

70' DDD 10/86 **Ⓑ**

Beethoven. Piano Concertos—No. 3 in C minor, Op. 37; No. 4 in G major, Op. 58. **Vladimir Ashkenazy** (pf); **Chicago Symphony Orchestra/Sir Georg Solti.** Decca Ovation 417 740-2DM. From SXLG6594/7 (9/73).

71' ADD 5/88 *£*

The CBS issue is an outstanding disc, containing two of the finest Beethoven performances to appear in recent years. In both works one feels that there is no conscious striving to interpret the music, rather that Perahia is allowing it simply to flow through him—an illusion, of course, but one which he is able to sustain with almost miraculous consistency. But the honours do not belong solely to Perahia: the contributions of Haitink and the Concertgebouw cannot be praised too highly, and the extraordinary sense of rapport and shared purpose that exist between these two fine musical minds is perhaps the most impressive aspect of the performances. The recordings are unusually sensitive, both to the sound of the piano and to the need for an overall balance that is homogeneous and clearly detailed.

At medium price, Ashkenazy's compelling and brilliantly vital account of these two splendid piano concertos is a bargain, particularly when the length of the CD is over 71 minutes. It does not displace all others, but offers other kinds of truths about these works. Throughout the Third Ashkenazy goes for youthful strength and energy as well as the sense of exaltation that the possession of these qualities inspires, and Solti follows him with orchestral playing of great musical electricity. In the Fourth he offers a different approach which is more relaxed and consciously poetic, bringing a sense of spontaneity to a work which in its lyricism provided a model for the gentler kind of 'romantic' piano concerto. These 1972 recordings do not betray their age in any significant way, although some collectors may feel that their sheer impact demands that one turns both the treble and bass controls down a little from their normal setting: there is still more than enough power after doing so.

Beethoven. Piano Concerto No. 5 in E flat major, Op. 73, "Emperor"[a]. Piano Sonata No. 7 in D major, Op. 10 No. 3[b]. **Edwin Fischer** (pf); [a]**Philharmonia Orchestra/Wilhelm Furtwängler.** EMI Références mono CDH7 61005-2. Item marked [a] from ALP1051 (6/53), [b] ALP1271 (11/57).

| 60' ADD 3/88 | |

Beethoven. Piano Concerto No. 5 in E flat major, Op. 73, "Emperor". **Claudio Arrau** (pf); **Staatskapelle Dresden/Sir Colin Davis.** Philips 416 215-2PH. From 416 215-1PH (4/86).

| 41' DDD 8/86 | |

Beethoven. Piano Concerto No. 5 in E flat major, Op. 73, "Emperor"[a]. Piano Sonata in C minor, Op. 111[b]. **Wilhelm Kempff** (pf); [a]**Berlin Philharmonic Orchestra/Ferdinand Leitner.** DG Galleria 419 468-2GGA. Item marked [a] from SLPM138777 (5/62), [b] SLPM138945 (3/68).

| 63' ADD 12/87 | |

By the time he wrote his Fifth Concerto, Beethoven was too deaf to continue playing in public and though he was still only 39 years old he wrote no more concertos. So the *Emperor* has a particular heroic quality, as if the composer was making a final, defiant contribution to a medium in which he could no longer physically participate. The concerto is more symphonic and on a bigger scale in terms of length and emotional content than its predecessors; no contemporary pianist had yet come face to face with a score of such weight and energy. Furtwängler's recording was made in 1951, but on CD the sound has plenty of clarity and tonal depth, even if it obviously lacks modern refinement and tonal

Wilhelm Kempff   *[photo: DG*

bloom. But any recording deficiencies are as naught in the face of a performance which has seldom if ever been surpassed. Fischer and Furtwängler seem to inspire each other to greater and greater heights of inspiration, and with the vintage Philharmonia at full stretch the result is an interpretation of immense intellectual power, extraordinary energy and great vision. The early Sonata makes an attractive pendant here to the main work.

Arrau's is a highly personal and obviously deeply considered reading which appears to have gained in depth and insight over the years. The *Adagio* and *Rondo* come over particularly well: the slow movement sounds very relaxed, but there is actually considerable tension in Arrau's playing, as when he arrives at the astonishing transitional passage from which the finale suddenly erupts; it's as if a store of accumulated energy were suddenly translated into action, though once again there's a wonderful leisurely quality here, for all the purposefulness of the playing. Davis and the orchestra provide firm and dynamic support in a recording whose aural perspective is entirely plausible.

Wilhelm Kempff's recording dates from 1962, but the sound doesn't show its age and the performance takes on board the work's wartime background without descending to the jingoism that hovers dangerously near. Kempff and his sympathetic partners are spacious and dignified yet alert to details and are especially good in the poised central Adagio. The Piano Sonata is not an ideal partner for a concerto, but this performance too is a good one. Kempff keeps things in proportion and an evident crisp intelligence is at work; and though the piano sound is unyielding to say the least this reflects his consistent approach to what he himself calls the "rocklike and inflexible" mood of the first subject and the consoling descent "from azure heights" of the second.

Beethoven Symphonies—No. 1 in C major, Op. 21[a]; No. 4 in B flat major, Op. 60[b]. Egmont Overture, Op. 84[b]. **Berlin Philharmonic Orchestra/Herbert von Karajan.** DG Galleria 419 048-2GGA. Item marked [a] from 2740 172 (10/77), [b] 2707 046 (7/71).

64' ADD 4/88

Beethoven. Symphonies—No. 1 in C major, Op. 21; No. 5 in C minor, Op. 67. **Leipzig Gewandhaus Orchestra/Kurt Masur.** Philips 426 782-2PH.

63' DDD 7/90

The DG mid-price issue is taken from Karajan's third complete Beethoven symphony cycle made in 1977. Some collectors favoured his earlier DG cycle from the 1960s but there's no denying the sheer beauty and lustre of these performances. Conductor and orchestra give thoroughly committed readings of these two surprisingly rarely played symphonies. The First is light on its toes though the setting is undoubtedly large scale: the Berlin strings play with great crispness and precision. The Fourth Symphony, a work that has always drawn an interesting response from Karajan, is again carefully conceived; the weight and drama of the work are never underplayed but neither is the detail. Karajan always conducted the *Egmont* Overture fully aware of its dramatic intensity and colour. The recordings are good with a nice sense of space around the orchestra whilst detail is never blurred.

So many loud partisan claims are made about Beethoven performances these days—that you must use the instruments of the composer's own time, or that it's hopeless trying to equal past giants like Furtwängler, Toscanini or Klemperer that it's very refreshing indeed to discover a conductor who pursues his own course, and argues for it so convincingly. Kurt Masur always gives the impression of having gone back to the score and thought it all through afresh. He not only adopts the recent innovation of restoring the scherzo-trio repeat in No. 5, he shows deep understanding of how this affects the finale's thunderous self-assertion. And while he avoids the old-fashioned wallowing of a Leonard Bernstein, the *Andantes* of both symphonies show that classicism doesn't mean coldness—far from it—and the dancing energy of the First Symphony's *Scherzo* and finale make some revered older versions sound stodgy. There is a slight snag: the recording in the Fifth Symphony pushes the trumpets and drums back and the piccolo in the finale isn't the glittering presence it should be, but don't let that put you off buying these refreshing and authoritative Beethoven performances from Philips.

Beethoven Symphonies—No. 2 in D major, Op. 36; No. 4 in B flat major, Op. 60. **North German Radio Symphony Orchestra/Günter Wand.** RCA Victor Red Seal RD60058.

68' DDD 9/89

Beethoven Symphonies—No. 2 in D major, Op. 36; No. 8 in F major, Op. 93. **London Classical Players/Roger Norrington.** EMI CDC7 47698-2.

59' DDD 3/87

Seldom has Beethoven's Second Symphony sounded as fresh, dynamic or persuasive as this. The work occupies a transitional place in the symphonic line as begun by Mozart and Haydn; on the one hand it forms the climax of that line, on the other it looks forward to new beginnings. Gunter Wand's stance clearly leans towards those new beginnings, with a reading that is more 'Beethovian' in approach than most, highlighting the fingerprints of his future symphonic style. The Fourth Symphony has always tended to be eclipsed by the towering edifices of the Third and Fifth Symphonies, but the Fourth takes stock, and with the maturity gained in the writing of the Third, looks back once more in an act of hommage to the triumphs of the past. Wand's performances are inspired; he is a conductor who never imposes his own ego and never does anything for the sake of effect, resulting in performances that are honest, direct and unpretentious. His tempos are superbly judged; brisk, but not hurried, allowing the pristine articulation of the strings to come shining through (this needs to be heard to be believed; orchestral playing such as this is rare indeed). The orchestral balance is ideal, with woodwind textures nicely integrated into the orchestral sound, and this is supported by the excellent recorded sound which approaches demonstration quality. A very fine issue indeed.

The thrilling recording with which Roger Norrington launched his period-instrument Beethoven cycle has changed many people's conception of just what to expect from a Beethoven performance. Norrington brings all his experience as a conductor of opera to these two delightful works with outstanding results. His orchestra of 44 make a wonderful sound with crisp articulation the dominant feature. The strings have the bite and dexterity one has come to expect from period instruments, but it is the wind and percussion that are ultimately so thrilling. The 12 years that separate these two works is interestingly illuminated on this disc. The scale is not dissimilar but the individuality and innovation of the later work seem all the more remarkable when so clearly articulated as here. Beethoven on record will never be quite the same again.

Beethoven. Symphony No. 3 in E flat major, Op. 55, "Eroica". Grosse Fuge, Op. 133. **Philharmonia Orchestra/Otto Klemperer.** EMI Studio CDM7 63356-2. From CDC7 47186-2 (10/85) and ED290171-1 (5/85).

> 70' ADD — B

At the time of this Symphony's conception Beethoven was coming face to face with debilitating deafness. In 1802 he wrote the celebrated Heiligenstadt Testament in which he openly contemplates suicide and, in terms which remain awe-inspiring to this day, rejects it. Thus the fierce discords which cry out from the height of the *Eroica*'s first movement development, not to mention the symphony's defiant opening chords or Prometheus-based finale, speak of Beethoven's pain and his resolute response. No single conductor has ever had the symphony's complete measure in a single performance. None the less, Klemperer's 1961 stereo recording still stands out. His Funeral March is certainly awe-inspiring and elsewhere his reading is classical in its formal shaping, romantic in its sensing the huge issues that are being addressed by the composer. The performance is marked out by a certain deliberation of gait, a persistent steadiness of tempo; but it is as satisfying a reading as any before the public and there is a commanding account of the orchestral version of the *Grosse Fuge* with which to round off the disc. The recordings come up very well in the remasterings.

Beethoven. Symphony No. 5 in C minor, Op. 67. **Vienna Philharmonic Orchestra/Carlos Kleiber.** DG 415 861-2GH. From 2530 516 (6/75).

> 33' ADD 11/85 — B

Rarely, if ever, has the spirit of revolutionary turbulence been better expressed in music than in the first movement of the Fifth Symphony; and no musical transformation is more likely to lift the spirits than the transition from scherzo to finale over which Beethoven laboured so hard and pondered so long. Even if our century cannot always share Beethoven's unshakeable sense of optimism, the visionary goal he proposes is one which we abandon at our peril. The trouble with the Fifth Symphony is that it is, for all its apparent familiarity, a brute of a piece to conduct. The opening bars have unseated many a professional conductor, and it must be admitted that even Carlos Kleiber comes perilously close to allowing the famous motto to be played as a fast triplet. Thereafter, Kleiber barely puts a foot wrong. There have been a handful of distinguished interpreters of the symphony before Kleiber, but his reading has an electricity, a sense of urgency and fresh discovery which put it in a class of its own. The DG recording is rather dry and immediate, but the lean texturing is an aspect of Kleiber's radicalism without which the reading would not be the astounding thing it is.

Beethoven. Symphony No. 7 in A major, Op. 92[a]. Die Geschöpfe des Prometheus—Overture, Op. 43[b]. **Philharmonia Orchestra/Otto Klemperer.** EMI Studio CDM7 69183-2. Item marked [a] appears in stereo for the first time, [b] from Columbia SAX2331 (9/60).

44' ADD 4/88 £ P B

Beethoven. Symphony No. 7 in A major, Op. 92. **Vienna Philharmonic Orchestra/Carlos Kleiber.** DG 415 862-2GH. From 2530 706 (9/76).

39' ADD 2/86 S B

Beethoven. Symphonies—No. 7 in A major, Op. 92; No. 8 in F major, Op. 93. **London Symphony Orchestra/Wyn Morris.** Pickwick IMP Classics PCD918.

66' DDD 2/90 £ B

Klemperer may sometimes have been idiosyncratic in his approach, but he nearly always had something original and revelatory to say in his readings and here is probably the best of his recordings of Beethoven's No. 7. His tempos are especially apposite, not fast, but just right to lift the lightness of articulation and phrasing he draws from his players. Insistent melodic and accompaniment figures are always difficult to handle but Klemperer keeps the Philharmonia on its collective toes for the 'Amsterdam' rhythm of the first movement and throughout the following slow movement, with its characteristic rhythmic identity. The *Scherzo* and finale may seem a touch deliberate at first, but so vivacious is the playing and so persuasive the conductor's long-term view of the music, that few will find themselves unmoved. The recording itself has a fascinating history, being the result of a secret stereo taping made simultaneously with the mono recording. It is remarkably fine for its vintage and has been further refined in the digital remastering. The splendid coupled performance of the not-too-often-heard *Prometheus* Overture gives added weight to this recommendation.

DG's 39 minutes may seem short measure, but when the performance is of this revealing quality, the duration of the experience is of relatively little importance. Kleiber's performance fairly bristles with electricity, but at all times one is aware of a tight control which never lets the exuberance get out of hand; moreover, he shows a scrupulous regard for the composer's instructions: all repeats are observed (to thrilling effect in the scherzo and finale) and tempo relationships are carefully calculated. It is

Carlos Kleiber [*photo: Sony Classical/Vivanne-Rome*

Kleiber's feeling for the overall shape of each movement that is most impressive: how else could there be such a powerful sense of cumulative excitement in the finale? The recording is pre-digital, but it hardly seems to matter when given such a high-quality CD transfer.

However, don't be put off by the 'special offer' price of the Pickwick disc or the fact that you may not have heard of the conductor: these are among the finest recordings of these two symphonies to have appeared in a long time. Morris doesn't show any of the tendency to play around with tempo that keeps Furtwängler's Beethoven controversial; he takes Beethoven's markings very seriously (all the repeats are observed—and a good thing too!), but there's nothing rigid about the results. Rarely has Wagner's famous description of the Seventh Symphony, "the apotheosis of the dance", sounded more appropriate. If Morris's Eighth takes a little longer to show its true colours, it soon develops into a performance which, no less than the Seventh, is full of character and delight in movement. Those who don't know the works could have no better introduction; those who know them too well may find these performances the ideal restorative for the jaded palate.

Beethoven. Symphony No. 8 in F major, Op. 93. Overtures—Coriolan; Fidelio; Leonore No. 3. **Berlin Philharmonic Orchestra/Herbert von Karajan.** DG 415 507-2GH.

56' DDD 6/86

The Eighth, for all its apparent brevity, lean athleticism and snapping vitality is at times generously expansive. The Trio of the steadily treading scherzo is as leisurely and countrified as anything you will find in the *Pastoral*; and even the finale, full of joy and abrupt changes of direction and mood, was expanded by Beethoven from material that was too dry, too laconic even for his taste. Following in Toscanini's footsteps, Karajan has always been a gifted exponent of this symphony, treating it as a vibrant and witty successor to the great Seventh rather than a throwback to the style of the First. His 1962 Berlin performance was more careful and keener-eared than this later CD version, but the performance here is a distinguished one still and the overtures are played and recorded with a great deal of power.

Beethoven. Symphony No. 9 in D minor, Op. 125, "Choral". **Anna Tomowa-Sintow** (sop); **Agnes Baltsa** (mez); **Peter Schreier** (ten); **José van Dam** (bass-bar); **Vienna Singverein; Berlin Philharmonic Orchestra/ Herbert von Karajan.** DG Galleria 415 832-2GGA. Text and translation included. From 2740 172 (10/77).

67' ADD 4/87 £

Beethoven. Symphony No. 9 in D minor, Op. 125, "Choral". **Eileen Farrell** (sop); **Nan Merriman** (mez); **Jan Peerce** (ten); **Norman Scott** (bass); **Robert Shaw Chorale; NBC Symphony Orchestra/Arturo Toscanini.** RCA Gold Seal mono GD60256. From EMI ALP1039/40 (4/53).

65' ADD 3/88 Ⓑ

Beethoven. Symphony No. 9 in D minor, Op. 125, "Choral". **Heather Harper** (sop); **Helen Watts** (contr); **Alexander Young** (ten); **Donald McIntyre** (bass); **London Symphony Chorus and Orchestra/Leopold Stokowski.** Decca Weekend 421 636-2DC. From PFS4183 (10/70).

67' AAD 12/89 £ ⁹ₚ

All collections need Beethoven's *Choral* Symphony as one of the works at the very core of the nineteenth-century romantic movement. Within its remarkable span, Beethoven celebrates both the breadth and power of man's conception of his position in relation to the Universe; his sense of spirituality— especially in the great slow movement—and in the finale the essential life-enhancing optimism emerges, which makes human existence philosophically possible against all odds. There are many fine recordings of this work; among them may be counted the versions by Toscanini and Stokowski reviewed here, and also Böhm, Szell, Jochum, Solti and Bernstein, who celebrated the fall of the Berlin wall with an almost apocalyptic performance *in situ*, with multi-national participants. Yet it is not really surprising that first choice for many remains with Karajan. He lived alongside the Beethoven symphonies throughout his long and very distinguished recording career, and he recorded the Ninth three times in stereo. Sadly the most recent digital version, in spite of glorious playing in the *Adagio*, is flawed, but both analogue versions are very impressive indeed. Taken all-in-all it is his 1977 version which is the one to have. The slow movement has great intensity, and the finale brings a surge of incandescent energy and exuberance which is hard to resist. All four soloists are excellent individually and they also make a good team. The reading as a whole has the inevitability of greatness and the recording is vivid, full and clear. At mid-price this is very recommendable indeed.

One of the most poignant Beethoven stories concerns the first performance of the Ninth Symphony in 1824, when the profoundly deaf composer had to have his attention drawn to the audience's storms of applause. It was of course an extraordinary feat for the stricken Beethoven to have composed such a revolutionary work. Though there have been very many recordings of the Ninth Toscanini's 1952 performance remains one of the greatest ever committed to record. Seldom, if ever, has the urgency and the blazing conviction of Beethoven's vision been so completely captured in performance, and Toscanini's own drive and intensity of vision has an inspiring effect on his performers. Some feat for an 85-year-old conductor. The recording is a little coarse and confined, and one yearns for such a performance to be liberated from its sonic strait-jacket, but we can hear more than sufficient to appreciate Beethoven's and Toscanini's genius.

Too many recordings of the *Choral*, whether budget or not, may offer very adequate accounts of the Symphony, with tolerable sound, yet do not really set free the soaring spirit of the work, lacking the singleness of purpose that can recreate the intensity of Beethoven's vision as he first forged the piece. That is not a criticism that could reasonably be levelled at Stokowski's reading, for above all it presents a startlingly single-minded view that drives the music inexorably from start to finish. There may be the few odd moments when the conductor's interpretative idiosyncrasies make themselves felt, with not-altogether appropriate tempos; the recording now feels its age, and is not always consistent and perfectly natural. Yet, at the end of this performance, there could be few who would not be burning with the magnitude of Beethoven's euphoric and affirmative statement. The soloist line-up is strong, and the chorus is on top form in the taxing finale. For those jaded by the blandness of so much of today's Beethoven interpretation, this could be just the right alternative view to revitalize their enthusiasm.

Beethoven. OVERTURES. **Bavarian Radio Symphony Orchestra/Sir Colin Davis.** CBS Masterworks CD44790. From MK42103 (9/86).
The Ruins of Athens, Op. 113. Coriolan, Op. 62. Leonore Nos. 1 and 3. The Creatures of Prometheus, Op. 43. Egmont, Op. 84. Fidelio, Op. 72*b*.

63' DDD 9/89		♩P Ⓑ

A collection of overtures must offer more than just a series of good performances: the juxtaposition of the works must provide contrast and variety, and the whole should progress so that some sense of climax and finality is reached at the end of the CD. Of course, it is possible for the listener to program the items in any order, but that shouldn't be necessary. Sir Colin Davis has here ordered the overtures in a way that could hardly be bettered, with the programme building through light and shade until the exultant finale of the *Fidelio* Overture is reached. In a full-bodied recording that allows the bloom of the strings to develop their richness, each overture receives a thoughtful, well-prepared reading that might not outrank the best of the competition, but which fits exactly in place in this Beethoven concert. *Coriolan* and *Egmont* make the most substantial individual effect here, Davis obviously warming to their expressive weight and the power with which Beethoven moves inexorably to their dramatic conclusions, yet the lighter works, the *Ruins of Athens* and *Prometheus* for example, are done with no less commitment, and the smoothness of approach adds a new dimension to their interpretation. In all, then, probably the most convincing collection of its kind in the catalogue.

Beethoven. Quintet in E flat major for piano and wind, Op. 16.
Mozart. Quintet in E flat major for piano and wind, K452. **Murray Perahia** (pf); members of the **English Chamber Orchestra** (Neil Black, ob; Thea King, cl; Antony Halstead, hn; Graham Sheen, bn). CBS Masterworks CD42099. From IM42099 (8/86).

53' DDD 12/86

"I myself consider it to be the finest work I have ever composed", stated Mozart on his Piano Quintet in a letter to his father in April 1784. The Quintet had in fact been composed at great speed but, dating as it does from the beginning of the composer's most impressive creative period, there are no signs of hasty work—indeed, it is written on quite an ambitious scale. Beethoven obviously knew the Mozart work when he came to write a quintet for the same combination of instruments and in the same key of E flat some 12 years later. There is but one difference in style. Mozart wrote the piano part as an integral part of the ensemble, whereas Beethoven wrote a piano part which was more soloistic. It is a delight to hear such immaculate ensemble and understanding between the players in these recordings. The clean and clear tone of the wind players, particularly that of the oboist Neil Black, is also a source of pleasure, as is Perahia's elegant pianism. Tempos are predominantly expansive and occasionally both works could have benefited from a little more thrust and brio, but the performances are most accomplished. The recording is pure in tone and well balanced.

Murray Perahia   *[photo: Sony Classical]*

Beethoven. Septet in E flat major, Op. 20.[a]
Mendelssohn. Octet in E flat major, Op. 20.[b] Members of the **Vienna Octet.** Decca 421 093-2DM. Item marked [a] from SXL2157 (3/60), [b] SDD389 (12/73).

74' ADD 5/88

Beethoven's Septet is a happy, relaxed divertimento-like work in six movements, scored for string trio with double-bass, clarinet, horn and bassoon. After its highly successful first performance in 1800 the work became very popular, and was arranged for many different instrumental combinations. Mendelssohn's Octet was written when the composer was only 16 years old. Scored for double string quartet, it is his first work to show individuality of expression and mastery of form and its mood is outgoing and high-spirited. Though the recording of the Beethoven work dates from 1959 the sound is warm and attractive, to complement a delightfully unhurried, spontaneous yet relaxed performance which has a good deal of old-fashioned Viennese charm. The Octet performance dates from 1972, and has a less atmospheric, rather clean quality of sound. But the playing has just the right degree of delicacy and buoyancy, with textures very light and clear.

Beethoven. Serenades—D major, Op. 8[a]; D major, Op. 25[b]. [b]**Maxence Larrieu** (fl); **Grumiaux Trio** (Arthur Grumiaux, vn; Georges Janzer, va; [a]Eva Czako, vc). Philips Musica da Camera 426 090-2PC. From AX0071/3 (10/69).

51' ADD 6/90

These two well-known Trios, both in the multi-movement form of a Serenade, stand in stark contrast with one another; whilst Op. 8 has a substantial cello contribution, Op. 25 is focused much more in the upper register, with the viola providing the bass and the lighter flute timbre further emphasising the treble. Both, however, share Beethoven's half-serious approach to the genre, with some movements rivalling those from his early string quartets for intellectual and emotional meat, whilst others are like zabaglione, deliciously frothy concoctions that leave a warm afterglow. Although occasionally a touch heavy-handed, these performances adroitly capture that dichotomy of mood and impress with their full-blooded zest, exact ensemble, and impeccable intonation. Grumiaux's decisive lead leaves no doubt that these Serenades are much more than simple entertainment. Although it is doubtful that Beethoven would have wanted these pieces to have, in live performance, the immediacy that this recording provides, the benefits for home listening are clearly ones of intimacy and involvement. It is as though the listener is in amongst the Trio, playing along.

Beethoven. String Quartet in F major, Op. 59 No. 1, "Rasumovsky". **Lindsay Quartet** (Peter Cropper, Ronald Birks, vns; Roger Bigley, va; Bernard Gregor-Smith, vc). ASV CDDCA553. From ALHB307 (10/84).

44' DDD 4/87

Beethoven. String Quintet in C major, Op. 29[a]. String Quartet in F major, Op. 59 No. 1, "Rasumovsky". **Medici Quartet** (Paul Robertson, David Matthews, vns; Ivo-Jan van der Werff, va; Anthony Lewis, vc); [a]**Simon Rowland-Jones** (va). Nimbus NI5207.

74' DDD 3/90

In the few years that separate the Op. 18 from the Op. 59 quartets, Beethoven's world was shattered by the oncoming approach of deafness and the threat of growing isolation. The Op. 59 consequently inhabit a totally different plane, one in which the boundaries of sensibility had been extended in much the same way as the map of Europe was being redrawn. Each of the three quartets alludes to a Russian theme by way of compliment to Count Rasumovsky, who had commissioned the set. The immediate impression the F major Quartet conveys is of great space, breadth and vision; this is to the quartet what the *Eroica* is to the symphony. The Lindsays' performance is very impressive indeed, with the tempos sounding so completely right and ideally judged in relation to their overall conception of the work. In each movement the players make all the interpretative points they wish without our feeling hurried. Not only is theirs the most consistently illuminating reading but arguably the most inspired account of this wonderful quartet on record—and they are eminently well served by the engineers.

The neglect of Beethoven's C major Quintet is unaccountable for it is a rewarding and remarkable score, written only a year before the First Symphony. At one time the presto finale earned it the nickname "Der Sturm", doubtless on account of the similarity, or rather anticipation of the storm in the *Pastoral* Symphony. The Medici Quartet with Simon Rowland-Jones give an eminently faithful and musical reading, free from any egocentric posturing. Tempos are sensible and the performance has all the spontaneity of live music-making: nothing is glamorized, yet there is no lack of polish. The first *Rasumovsky*, on the other hand, is not quite as successful: it is well played and there are some felicitous touches of phrasing and colour. Their first movement is on the fast side—not unacceptably so, but the slow movement is far too brisk and this may pose problems for some collectors. All the same the String Quintet alone is worth the price of the disc.

Beethoven. String Quartets—F minor, Op. 95, "Serioso"[a]; A minor, Op. 132[b]. **Végh Quartet** (Sándor Végh, Sándor Zöldy, vns; Georges Janzer, va; Paul Szabó, vc). Auvidis Valois V4406. Item marked [a] from Telefunken EX6 35041 (8/76); [b] EX6 35040 (10/74).

> ♪ 68' ADD 4/88

Beethoven. String Quartets—A minor, Op. 132[a]; F major, Op. 135[b]. **Talich Quartet** (Petr Messiereur, Jan Kvapil, vns; Jan Talich, va; Evžen Rattai, vc). Calliope CAL9639. Item marked [a] from CAL1639, (6/80), [b] CAL1640 (6/80).

> ♪ 68' ADD 12/86

After the expansive canvas of the Op. 59 Quartets and the *Eroica*, Beethoven's F minor Quartet, Op. 95, displays musical thinking of the utmost compression. The first movement is a highly concentrated sonata design, which encompasses in its four minutes almost as much drama as a full-scale opera. With it comes one of the greatest masterpieces of his last years, the A minor, Op. 132. The isolation wrought first by his deafness and secondly, by the change in fashion of which he complained in the early 1820s, forced Beethoven in on himself. Op. 132 with its other-worldly *Heiliger Dankgesang*, written on his recovery from an illness, is music neither of the 1820s nor of Vienna, it belongs to that art which transcends time and place. Though other performances may be technically more perfect, these are interpretations that come closer to the spirit of this great music than any other on CD.

Talich Quartet   *[photo: EMI/Krob]*

Collectors need have no doubts as to the depth and intelligence of the Talich Quartet's readings for they bring a total dedication to this music: their performances are innocent of artifice and completely selfless. There is no attempt to impress the listener with their own virtuosity or to draw attention to themselves in any way. The recordings are eminently faithful and natural, not 'hi-fi' or overbright but the overall effect is thoroughly pleasing.

Beethoven. EARLY STRING QUARTETS. **Alban Berg Quartet** (Günter Pichler, Gerhard Schulz, vns; Thomas Kakuska, va; Valentin Erben, vc). EMI CDC7 47127/8/9-2. From SLS5217 (1/82).
CDC7 47127-2—Op. 18: F major, No. 1; G major, No. 2. *CDC7 47128-2*—Op. 18: D major, No. 3; C minor, No. 4. *CDC7 47129-2*—Op. 18: A major, No. 5; B flat major, No. 6.

③ 52' 48' 52' ADD/DDD 1/89

Beethoven was in his late twenties when he started work on the Op. 18 string quartets and he had reached 30 by the time they were complete. Even so, they are far more than a summation of the string quartet as it had developed in the hands of Haydn and Mozart, though they could not have been written without these masters. Beethoven is his own man right from the start and the F major with its Shakespearian inspiration explores depths that seem quite new. The formal symmetry and grace of Haydn can be found in the first movements of the G major and the D major but the sense of scale is different. The dramatic fire of the C minor has clear precedents in Haydn but the strange harmonies that haunt the Adagio opening of the finale of the B flat point to a new era. The Alban Berg Quartet is undoubtedly one of the greatest ensembles now before the public and they offer performances of enormous polish and finesse. The playing is immaculate and the sound has excellent definition, presence and body. Strongly recommended.

Beethoven. STRING QUARTETS. **Végh Quartet** (Sándor Végh, Sándor Zöldy, vns; Georges Janzer, va; Paul Szabó, vc). Auvidis Valois V4405, V4408. Items marked [a] from Telefunken EX6 35041 (8/76), [b] SKA25113T/1-4 (10/74).
V4405—E flat major, Op. 74, "Harp"[a]; E flat major, Op. 127[b]. *V4408*—C sharp minor, Op. 131[b]; F major, Op. 135[b].

② 71' 66' ADD 6/87   ♀P

Beethoven stepped both outside and beyond his period nowhere more so than in the late quartets and the last five piano sonatas. The Op. 127 has been called Beethoven's "crowning monument to lyricism", whilst the Op. 131 is more inward-looking. Every ensemble brings a different set of insights to this great music so that it is not possible to hail any single quartet as offering the whole truth—yet these are as near to the whole truth as we are ever likely to come. The Végh give us music-making that has a profundity and spirituality that completely outweigh any tiny blemish of intonation or ensemble. One does not get the feeling of four professional quartet players performing publicly for an audience but four thoughtful musicians sharing their thoughts about this music in the privacy of their home. They bring us closer to this music than do any of their high-powered rivals.

Beethoven. String Quartets—B flat major, Op. 130[a]; E minor, Op. 59 No. 2, "Rasumovsky"[b]. **Talich Quartet** (Petr Messiereur, Jan Kvapil, vns; Jan Talich, va; Evžen Rattai, vc). Calliope CAL9637. Item marked [a] from CAL1637/40, [b] CAL1634/6.

73' ADD 3/87

The Beethoven quartets are one of the greatest musical expressions of the human spirit and they must be represented in any collection. The advantage of this Talich recording is that it couples a masterpiece from Beethoven's middle period, the great E minor Quartet, with one of the greatest of his last years. The B flat was the third of the late quartets to be composed and at its first performance in 1826 its last movement, the *Grosse Fuge*, baffled his contemporaries.

Later that same year, he substituted the present finale, publishing the *Grosse Fuge* separately. The Talich Quartet have a no less impressive technical command than other ensembles but theirs are essentially private performances, which one is privileged to overhear rather than the over-projected 'public' accounts we so often hear on record nowadays. At 73 minutes this is marvellous value too.

Beethoven. 33 Variations on a Waltz by Diabelli, Op. 120. **Sviatoslav Richter** (pf). Philips 422 416-2PH. Recorded at a performance in the Grote Zaal, Concertgebouw, Amsterdam on June 17th, 1986.

> 52' DDD 12/88

Beethoven. 33 Variations on a Waltz by Diabelli, Op. 120. **Stephen Kovacevich** (pf). Philips Concert Classics 422 969-2PCC. From SAL3676 (1/69).

> 54' ADD 8/90

In 1819, when Anton Diabelli asked some 50 composers to contribute a variation on a waltz of his composition, he might have guessed that Beethoven would not take kindly to such a democratic proposal. Diabelli could hardly have dreamed, however, that four years later Beethoven would produce a set of no fewer than 32 variations, the most monumental work in the entire classical keyboard literature. The Variations is one of those supreme masterpieces for which performer and listener must gird their spiritual loins. It is not only a summing-up of Beethoven's keyboard writing, or a compendium of the resources of the classical style, but also a journey through inner realms—demanding courage and rewarding it with revelation. Richter sets out his intentions very clearly in the first variation—at exactly half the speed of Brendel and others, it immediately establishes a titanic scale and rock-like character entirely appropriate to the music. Not that the rest of the interpretation is in any way eccentric—it hardly needs to be when the playing is so totally commanding. But in following Beethoven's train of thought so closely it inevitably explores regions beyond the accustomed barriers of mere musicality. Connoisseurs of keyboard giants will know how often Richter's live performances have been inspirational. This is no exception—not ideal in recorded quality and surely not a single live take, but no less effective for that.

Few recordings of the *Diabelli* Variations fail to present new insights into some hitherto neglected corner of this enduringly fascinating work. Kovacevich does not quite bring off the final climactic build-up of the set, but he does manage to reach the heart of an abnormally high number of these variations; in some, such as Var. 6 with its brilliant, imitative trills and plummeting arpeggios, he is the only pianist on disc to come to grips fully with the implications of the score. His is clearly a first choice for a buyer unfamiliar with the work and yet the strengths of other readings of this masterpiece will be made all the more telling by a thorough acquaintance with his view. A further bonus of this issue is the clarity of the recording—already over 20 years old, it has been shone up like a new pin for CD issue. Detail abounds, and the sheer quality of the bright piano sound is deeply satisfying in itself.

Beethoven. PIANO SONATAS. **Wilhelm Kempff** (pf). DG Galleria 415 834-2GGA. From SKL901/11 (12/66).
C minor, Op. 13, "Pathétique"; C sharp minor, Op. 27 No. 2, "Moonlight"; D major, Op. 28, "Pastoral"; F sharp major, Op. 78.

> 60' ADD 8/87   **(B)**

The discography of the Beethoven piano sonatas has been dominated by two pianistic giants, Wilhelm Kempff and Emil Gilels who, alas, did not live to finish his planned complete cycle for DG. If Gilels's recordings are notable for their searching eloquence and intellectual strength, Kempff's performances are hardly less impressive for their combination of classical purity and lyrical individuality. They may at times be less imposing, but they are not less profound. Moreover Kempff had the supreme gift of achieving complete spontaneity, giving the impression to the listener that the music is being re-created for him at that moment. Kempff's timbre was essentially cool and clean, yet there is no lack of warmth or colour, so that the opening of the *Moonlight* Sonata with its serene simplicity and the crisply articulated *Allegretto* make a . perfect foil for the stormy finale. The *Adagio* of the *Pathétique* has a disarming direct eloquence, with the urgency of the outer movements in perfect perspective; the *Pastoral* too, again shows Kempff in his element. The two-movement F sharp Sonata makes a fitting bonus for a popular collection that is worthy of any collector's allegiance.

Beethoven. Piano Sonatas—C major, Op. 53, "Waldstein"; F minor, Op. 57, "Appassionata"; E flat major, Op. 81*a*, "Les adieux". **Melvyn Tan** (fp). EMI Reflexe CDC7 49330-2.

63' DDD 5/88

Here are three of Beethoven's most popular sonatas, played on the kind of instrument the composer himself would have used. Tan is a very brilliant player; the outer movements of the *Waldstein* are dazzlingly done, yet carefully too and with due attention to detail. But both here and in *Les adieux*, where the quick music again abounds in vitality, one sometimes wonders whether Tan is fully in command of the music's structure, for he does not always manage to convey just where it is going. A little more intellectual weight occasionally seems to be needed. It is more in evidence in the *Appassionata*, which is the most successful performance of the three works. Nevertheless, this is an impressive disc, with much brilliance and immediacy making the music seem just a little unnerving, which perhaps is what it should be.

Beethoven. Piano Sonatas—D minor, Op. 31 No. 2, "Tempest"; E flat major, Op. 31 No. 3; E flat major, Op. 81*a*, "Les Adieux". **Murray Perahia** (pf). CBS Masterworks CD42319.

61' DDD 2/88

"I am by no means satisfied with my works hitherto, and I intend to make a fresh start", so Beethoven is reputed to have remarked before embarking on the

three sonatas comprising his Op. 31 in 1802. Ominous symptoms of deafness were already overshadowing his private life, as the flanking movements of the D minor Sonata betray even if feeling runs too deep to ruffle the tranquil surface of the central *Adagio*. Perahia's texture is crystalline (with skilful half-pedalling in the problematical recitatives in the opening movement of the D minor work) and even amidst the *con fuoco* of the E flat Sonata's finale rhythm is held on a tautly controlled rein. Whereas these two sonatas were studio recordings, the venue for *Les Adieux* was a warmer, more reverberant concert hall. Here we rightly meet a more impressionably romantic Perahia making every passing innuendo wholly his own in response to Beethoven's overtly expressed sadness, yearning and joy at the departure from—and return to—Vienna at the time of the Napoleonic invasion. Ingratiating in tone throughout a wide dynamic range, perfectly proportioned and finally excitingly brilliant, this performance has with good reason been widely hailed as "one of the most complete realizations of this work that has appeared in recent years".

Beethoven. Piano Sonata No. 29 in B flat major, Op. 106, "Hammerklavier". **Emil Gilels** (pf). DG 410 527-2GH. From 410 527-1GH (12/83).

· · **49'   DDD   2/84**

The great Soviet pianist Emil Gilels died in 1986, not many months before his 70th birthday, and left behind him a major legacy of recorded performances. This account of the *Hammerklavier* is a fine memorial. The work is very long and exceedingly taxing technically and the pianist must plumb its often turbulent emotional depth, not least in the enormous 20-minute slow movement which requires deep concentration from player and listener alike. After the recording was made in 1983, the pianist told his producer: "I feel that the weight has been lifted, but I feel very empty." Gilels manages to give it more tonal beauty and warmth than most pianists, without any loss of strength or momentum. His is measured and beautiful playing, and finely recorded too.

Beethoven. LATE PIANO SONATAS. **Maurizio Pollini** (pf). DG 419 199-2GH2.
A major, Op. 101 (from 2740 166, 1/78); B flat major, Op. 106, "Hammerklavier" (2740 166, 1/78). E major, Op. 109 (2740 166, 1/78); A flat major, Op. 110 (2530 645, 5/76); C minor, Op. 111 (2530 645, 5/76).

· · ② **2h 6'   ADD   12/86**

If Beethoven's 32 piano sonatas may be likened to a range of foothills and mountains, then these five sonatas are the last lofty pinnacles, difficult of access but offering great rewards to both pianist and listener. No library is complete without them. Pollini made these recordings between 1975-7 and his playing must be praised for its interpretative mastery as well as its exemplary keyboard skill. This is a prizewinning issue which has been widely admired, not least for the magnificent last sonata of all, Op. 111, and the recording hardly shows its age.

Beethoven. Violin Sonatas—No. 5 in F major, Op. 24, "Spring"[a]; No. 9 in A major, Op. 47, "Kreutzer"[b]. **Itzhak Perlman** (vn); **Vladimir Ashkenazy** (pf). Decca 410 554-2DH. Item marked [a] from SXL6736 (7/76), [b] SXL6632 (2/75).

· · **62'   ADD   11/83**   Ⓑ

Under ideal conditions this is music which can give the listener the feeling that anything is possible, just as it seemed to be, artistically, for Beethoven. Perlman and Ashkenazy come remarkably close to that ideal. So complete is the identification between performers and music that to praise the one is in effect to praise the other. From the open-hearted ease of the *Spring* Sonata's first phrase, Perlman and Ashkenazy steer a delightful course. In the *Kreutzer* they each find remarkable reserves of strength, never underplaying the sense of struggle but always sufficiently in control to keep longer-term goals in view. The recording places the listener in the front row of the stalls, close enough to feel involved in the performance but without artificially jacking up the excitement. Neither Beethoven nor Perlman and Ashkenazy need it.

Beethoven. Piano Trios—B flat major, Op. 97, "Archduke"; B flat major, WoO39. **Itzhak Perlman** (vn); **Lynn Harrell** (vc); **Vladimir Ashkenazy** (pf). EMI CDC7 47010-2. From ASD4315 (3/83).

43' DDD 11/84   **Ⓑ**

The *Archduke* starts with a theme so self-evidently great as to dispel any notion that Beethoven was not an inspired melodist. It has the noble embracing quality of the cello opening of the First *Rasumovsky* Quartet or the striding theme in the first movement of the Violin Concerto, both masterpieces from Beethoven's middle period. The other movements are no less remarkable—an unstoppable *Scherzo*, a hymn-like *Andante* with variations, and an earthy finale, described by d'Indy as a "joyous meeting of the rude peasantry". That's exactly how Perlman, Harrell and Ashkenazy play the last movement, and it is a fitting conclusion to a performance which does full justice to the range of Beethoven's vision. The recording quality is on the dry side, but extremely clear and lifelike. In any case the players create such atmosphere with their tone and personality that no lack of warmth is registered. The single-movement Trio, WoO39 is a bonus of no mean substance.

Beethoven. Piano Trios—E flat major, Op. 1 No. 1; B flat major, Op. 97, "Archduke". **Trio Zingara** (Elizabeth Layton, vn; Felix Schmidt, vc; Annette Cole, pf). Collins Classics 1057-2.

73' DDD 5/90   **P**

The young Trio Zingara's performance of Beethoven's great *Archduke* Trio is one of the most impressive versions in the current catalogue. It's a performance that flows, sometimes slowly and thoughtfully, sometimes with elegant quickness. Despite a slightly hesitant start, the *Andante* third movement grows steadily in intensity, and its quietly rippling fourth variation is revealed as the heart of the work. Impressive too is the way Trio Zingara manage the transition to the genial finale: all too often this can seem like a let-down—not here. The early E flat Trio makes a fine foil for the *Archduke*, and Zingara wisely don't try to find intimations of later profundity here, but then neither is there any twee 'classicizing'—the tone seems just right throughout. Balancing a grand piano with two solo strings is a nightmare for any recording producer, but the Collins team seem to have got it about right: the strings are clearly audible, the piano doesn't sound over-restrained. One minor word of warning though: the insert note refers to the wrong E flat trio—Op. 70/2, instead of Op. 1/1.

Beethoven. CHORAL WORKS. **Ambrosian Singers; London Symphony Orchestra/Michael Tilson Thomas.** CBS Masterworks CD76404. Texts and translations included. From 76404 (11/75).
König Stephan—incidental music, Op. 117. Elegischer Gesang, Op. 118. Opferlied, Op. 121*b* (with Lorna Haywood, sop). Bundeslied, Op. 122. Meeresstille und glückliche Fahrt, Op. 112.

52' ADD 11/88

Astonishing as it may seem, none of the choral works here, with the exception of the imaginative setting of Goethe's *Calm sea and prosperous voyage*, appears to have been recorded before. This disc is therefore warmly to be welcomed because of its first-class orchestral playing (heard on its own in the curious but lively *King Stephan* overture) and splendid choral singing, with a recording quality to match. The tender orchestral introduction to the elegy for the wife of Beethoven's sympathetic landlord Baron Pasqualati is a real gem (and is beautifully played); and two of the other works are of particular interest for their unusual scoring. The light-hearted convivial *Bundeslied* was mulled over in the composer's mind for a quarter of a century before emerging in 1822; and Beethoven was so fascinated by the poem of the *Opferlied* that he made no fewer than three settings of it before this last one.

Beethoven. LIEDER.
Brahms. LIEDER. **Dietrich Fischer-Dieskau** (bar); **Jörg Demus** (pf). DG 415 189-2GH. Notes, text and translations included.
Beethoven: An die ferne Geliebte. Op 98. Adelaide, Op. 46. Zärtliche Liebe, WoO123. L'amante impaziente, Op. 82 Nos. 3 and 4. In questa tomba oscura, WoO133. Maigesang, Op. 52 No. 4. Es war einmal ein König, Op. 75 No. 3 (all from SLPM139216/18, 2/67). **Brahms:** Vier ernste Gesänge, Op. 121[a]. O wüsst' ich doch den Weg zurück, Op. 63 No. 8[b]. Auf dem Kirchhofe, Op. 105 No. 4[b]. Alte Liebe, Op. 72 No. 1[b]. Verzagen, Op. 72 No. 4.[b] Nachklang, Op. 59 No. 4[b]. Feldeinsamkeit, Op. 86 No. 2[b] ([a] from SLPM138644, 10/61; [b] SLPM138011 (5/59).

| 71' ADD 9/85 |

Beethoven's small oeuvre of songs is rich and varied. The six songs of *An die ferne Geliebte* follow the unrequited lover's reflections on his beloved, with the piano weaving its way between the individual songs setting the mood and gently assisting the narrative; indeed, it even has the last word. Fischer-Dieskau's intelligent and intense delivery are assisted by his warm tone and easy legato. He adds Beethoven's great song *Adelaide* and, among others, three Italian settings, lightening the tone and raising the spirits for the second half of the programme. Brahms's *Vier ernste Gesänge*, drawn from the image-laden texts of the Old Testament, reflect on man's fate in the great order of life and more particularly on death. The songs have a solemn character and settle in the lower register of the baritone's vocal range, a range that finds a particularly appropriate tone-colour in Fischer-Dieskau's expressive voice. The remainder of the recital draws on similarly severe songs, making for a well-devised programme with a consistent theme. Jörg Demus accompanies sensitively and the elderly recordings sound well.

Beethoven. Mass in D major, Op. 123, "Missa solemnis"[a]. Choral Fantasia in C major, Op. 80[b]. [a]**Elisabeth Söderström** (sop); [a]**Marga Höffgen** (contr); [a]**Waldemar Kmentt** (ten); [a]**Martti Talvela** (bass); [b]**Daniel Barenboim** (pf); [a]**New Philharmonia Chorus;** [b]**John Alldis Choir; New Philharmonia Orchestra/Otto Klemperer.** EMI CMS7 69538-2. Texts and translations included. Item marked [a] from SAN165/6 (7/66), [b] SLS5180 (4/69).

| ② 1h 40' ADD 12/88 |

Beethoven. Mass in D major, Op. 123, "Missa solemnis". **Charlotte Margiono** (sop); **Catherine Robbin** (mez); **William Kendall** (ten); **Alastair Miles** (bass); **Monteverdi Choir; English Baroque Soloists/John Eliot Gardiner.** Archiv Produktion 429 779-2AH. Text and translation included.

| 72' DDD 3/91 |

"Nothing shakes my conviction that Klemperer comes nearest to the heart of the matter, the grandeur and spiritual intensity of Beethoven's vision". That was Alec Robertson's 1966 view in *The Gramophone* whilst Trevor Harvey, reviewing a version under Solti in 1978, returned to Klemperer in the course of his listening

John Eliot Gardiner   [photo: Phlips/Holt]

and found, as he said, "unrivalled depth: of exultation, as in the *Gloria*, and of inward feeling as in the many slow and soft sections". These critics, despite their enthusiasm, were certainly not unaware of some shortcomings, especially in the soloists, who are not entirely satisfactory either individually or as a well-integrated quartet. Modern listeners may also find an almost plodding earnestness in the fugues which more recent practice has set free to dance their way to the life to come. But the sense of authority, of power and purpose, is there from the start and throughout the performance, with the New Philharmonia Orchestra playing magnificently; it is their Chorus that provides the special joy. Not only are they on top form but they are recorded so as to sound much more forward in the balance than would be likely nowadays. The choir is the true protagonist here, giving the Mass to the human voice and so coming through to the human heart as its composer in his famous *envoi* said he wished it to.

However, no modern recording goes further than Gardiner's towards catching the immense spirit of the work, and certainly none has been so well served by all the forces involved, including producer and technical staff. With a highly expert choir of 36 singers and the orchestra of 60 playing on period instruments, Gardiner aims in the first place at a "leaner and fitter" sound. There is still plenty of body to it, no feeling of miniaturism, but it does mean that the *allegro* passages can dance more fleet of foot and with more clarity of movement. A superb example is the "Et vitam venturi" section of the *Credo*: these fugues, so intricate and exhausting for the singers, have a joyful energy and sense of liberation about them. But again this is not achieved at the expense of depth and, at the right moments, stillness. The play of serenity and conflict in the "Dona nobis pacem" achieves exactly the right profundity of expression. The soloists, too, form an unusually homogeneous quartet, all of them doing fine work. They are recorded in due proportion with the choir and orchestra, and that is more exceptional still.

Beethoven. FIDELIO. **Gundula Janowitz** (sop) Leonore; **René Kollo** (ten) Florestan; **Lucia Popp** (sop) Marzelline; **Manfred Jungwirth** (bass) Rocco; **Hans Sotin** (bass) Don Pizarro; **Adolf Dallapozza** (ten) Jacquino; **Dietrich Fischer-Dieskau** (bar) Don Fernando; **Karl Terkal** (ten) First Prisoner; **Alfred Sramek** (bar) Second Prisoner; **Vienna State Opera Chorus; Vienna Philharmonic Orchestra/Leonard Bernstein.** DG 419 436-2GH2. Notes, text and translation included. From 2709 082 (10/78).

② 2h 15' ADD 6/87 Ⓑ

Beethoven. FIDELIO. **Christa Ludwig** (mez) Leonore; **Jon Vickers** (ten) Florestan; **Walter Berry** (bass) Pizarro; **Gottlob Frick** (bass) Rocco; **Ingeborg Hallstein** (sop) Marzelline; **Gerhard Unger** (ten) Jacquino; **Franz Crass** (bass) Don Fernando; **Kurt Wehofschitz** (ten) Prisoner I; **Raymond Wolansky** (bar) Prisoner II; **Philharmonia Chorus and Orchestra/Otto Klemperer.** EMI CMS7 69324-2. Notes, text and translation included. From Columbia SAX2451/3 (6/62).

② 2h 8' ADD 1/90 £ ⁹ₚ Ⓑ

Fidelio teems with emotional overtones and from the arresting nature of the Overture, through the eloquence of the quartet, through the mounting tension of the prison scene to the moment of release when the wrongly imprisoned Florestan is freed, Beethoven unerringly finds the right music for his subject. You can sense this theatrical excitement in Bernstein's ebbing and flowing interpretation, sometimes free with *ritardandos* and other of the conductor's quirks but at all times a reading that catches the listener by the throat. Bernstein obviously inspired Janowitz to give a performance as Leonore that projects all her sorrow and struggle against evil. Kollo is a properly agonized and pained Florestan, Sotin the incarnation of terror as Pizarro. Jungwirth's fatherly Rocco, Popp's charming Marzelline, Dallapozza's fresh Jacquino and Fischer-Dieskau's noble Don Fernando complete the excellent cast.

Klemperer's set has been a classic since it first appeared on LP way back in 1962. The performance draws its strength from Klemperer's conducting: he shapes the whole work with a granite-like strength and a sense of forward movement that is unerring, while paying very deliberate attention to instrumental detail, particularly as regards the contribution of the woodwind. With the authoritative help of producer Walter Legge, the balance between voices and orchestra is faultlessly managed. The cumulative effect of the whole reading is something to wonder at and shows great dedication on all sides. Most remarkable among the singers is the soul and intensity of Christa Ludwig's Leonore. In her dialogue as much as in her singing she conveys the single-minded conviction in her mission of rescuing her beleaguered and much-loved husband. Phrase after phrase is given a frisson that has the ring of truth to it. As her Florestan, Jon Vickers conveys the anguish of his predicament. One or two moments of exaggeration apart this is another memorable assumption. Walter Berry, as Pizarro, suggests a small man given too much power. Gottlob Frick is a warm, touching Rocco, Ingeborg Hallstein a fresh, eager Marzelline, Gerhard Unger a youthful Jacquino, Franz Crass a noble Don Fernando. This is a set that should be in any worthwhile collection of opera.

Vincenzo Bellini
Italian 1801-1835

Bellini. OPERATIC ARIAS.
Puccini. OPERATIC ARIAS. **Maria Callas** (sop); [a]**Philharmonia Orchestra;** [b]**Orchestra of La Scala, Milan / Tullio Serafin.** EMI mono CDC7 47966-2. Notes, texts and translations included. Items marked [a] from Columbia mono 33CX1204 (12/54), [b] HMV stereo ASD3535 (8/78).
Puccini: MANON LESCAUT[a]—In quelle trine morbide; Sola, perduta, abbandonata. MADAMA BUTTERFLY[a]—Un bel dì vedremo; Con onor muore. LA BOHEME[a]—Sì, mi chiamano Mimì; Donde lieta uscì. SUOR ANGELICA[a]—Senza mamma. GIANNI SCHICCHI[a]—O mio babbino caro. TURANDOT[a]—Signore, ascolta!; In questa reggia; Tu che di gel sei cinta. *Bellini:* LA SONNAMBULA[b]—Compagne, teneri amici ... Come per me sereno; Oh, se una volta sola ... Ah, non credea mirarti ... Ah, non giunge.

65' ADD 12/87

This coupling gives a fine insight into Maria Callas's unparalleled interpretative powers. The Puccini arias are all much-loved favourites. As Mimì, the heroine of *La bohème*, Callas softens the voice, seeking out the character's gloriously wide-eyed view of life as well as the vulnerability, whilst as Butterfly she displays a nobility and powerful optimism that holds our attention quite as powerfully as our obvious sympathy for her plight. Those two most beautiful melodies "Senza mamma" and "O mio babbino caro" are gently shaded and masterfully accompanied by Tullio Serafin, one of Callas's most sensitive accompanists. The sound dates from 1954-5 but is clear, well balanced and atmospheric. The two

Bellini arias elicit a different response from singer and conductor. The character is carried totally in the voice, the shaping of a line, the shading of a word. The great Sleepwalking scene with which the disc closes is one of Callas's greatest assumptions and shows an insight into the psychology of the opera's central character that has never been equalled.

Bellini. NORMA. **Maria Callas** (sop) Norma; **Ebe Stignani** (mez) Adalgisa; **Mario Filippeschi** (ten) Pollione; **Nicola Rossi-Lemeni** (bass) Orovesco; **Paolo Caroli** (ten) Flavio; **Rina Cavallari** (sop) Clotilde; **Chorus and Orchestra of La Scala, Milan/Tullio Serafin.** EMI mono CDS7 47304-8. Notes, text and translation included. From Columbia mono 33CX1179/80 (11/54).

③ 2h 40' ADD 3/86

Norma may be considered the most potent of Bellini's operas, both in terms of its subject—the secret love of a Druid priestess for a Roman general—and its musical content. It has some of the most eloquent music ever written for the soprano voice and two duets that show Bellini's gift for liquid melody. The title-role has always been coveted by dramatic sopranos, but there have been few in the history of the opera who have completely fulfilled its considerable vocal and histrionic demands: in recent times the leading exponent has been Maria Callas. The mono recording comes up sounding remarkably forward and immediate on CD, and it captures Callas's commanding and moving assumption of the title part, the vocal line etched with deep feeling, the treatment of the recitative enlivening the text. Stignani is a worthy partner whilst Filippeschi is rough but quite effective. Serafin knew better than anyone since how to mould a Bellinian line to best effect.

Bellini. I PURITANI. **Montserrat Caballé** (sop) Elvira; **Alfredo Kraus** (ten) Arturo; **Matteo Manuguerra** (bar) Riccardo; **Agostino Ferrin** (bass) Giorgio; **Júlia Hamari** (mez) Enrichetta; **Stefan Elenkov** (bass) Gualtiero; **Dennis O'Neill** (ten) Bruno; **Ambrosian Opera Chorus; Philharmonia Orchestra/Riccardo Muti.** EMI CMS7 69663-2. Notes, text and translation included. From SLS5201 (1/81).

③ 2h 52' ADD 4/89

Bellini's opera of the English Civil War is probably his most readily attractive score, for its moods encompass a gaiety unknown to *Norma* and the writing is much more robust than *La sonnambula*. As in all of his work, a great deal depends upon the singers and it is to them that one normally looks first. Here, however, Riccardo Muti is in charge, a conductor with strong ideas about what may be allowed the singers by way of traditional license: on the whole he keeps a tight rein but compensates by taking slow speeds so that the melodies may never pass by with their beauties unobserved. The refinement is notable in the introduction to the bass aria near the start of Act 2, and there is no lack of strength and rhythmic excitement in the surging melody of the Finale to Act 1. The performance also benefits from particularly alert choral work by the Ambrosians, and from imaginative production. The spotlight is on the singers even so. As the sorely tried heroine Caballé is ideal as long as nothing too strenuous arises to put pressure on her exceptionally lovely voice. Her ethereal tones have a fine effect in the off-stage prayer, and her "Qui la voce" is deeply felt as well as beautifully sung. Kraus is perhaps the best tenor of recent times in this repertoire and there is nearly always a personal character about his singing that gives it distinction. This is a quality somewhat lacking in the baritone,

Matteo Manuguerra; all the same there is some good solid tone and he makes an honest job of his cadenzas.

Bellini. LA SONNAMBULA. **Maria Callas** (sop) Amina; **Nicola Monti** (ten) Elvino; **Nicola Zaccaria** (bass) Count Rodolfo; **Fiorenza Cossotto** (Mez) Teresa; **Eugenia Ratti** (sop) Lisa; **Giuseppe Morresi** (bass) Alessio; **Franco Ricciardi** (ten) Notary. **Chorus and Orchestra of La Scala, Milan / Antonino Votto.** EMI mono CDS7 47378-8. Notes text and translation included. From EX290043-3 (6/86).

② 2h I' ADD 9/86

Maria Callas 　　　　　*[photo: EMI*

Dramatically this opera is a tepid little mix which might be subtitled *The mistakes of a night* if that did not suggest something more amusing than what actually takes place. Musically, the promise of a brilliant finale keeps most people in their seats until the end, and there are half-a-dozen charming, sometimes exquisite items on the way. But it is all a little insubstantial, and much depends upon the performance, especially that of the soprano. The name of Maria Callas is sufficient to guarantee that there will be a particular interest in the work of the heroine. As usual, her individuality is apparent from the moment of her arrival. Immediately a character is established, not an insipid little miss but a woman in whom lurks a potential for tragedy. This is the pattern throughout and much has exceptional beauty of voice and spirit. Nicola Monti has all the sweetness of the traditional lyric tenor; the pity is that what might have been a most elegant performance is marred by the intrusion of unwanted aspirates. Nicola Zaccaria sings the bass aria gracefully, and carrying off her small role with distinction is Fiorenza Cossotto, at the start of her career. The orchestral playing is neat, the conducting sensible and the recording clear.

George Benjamin
British 1960-

G. Benjamin. Antara.
Boulez. Dérive. Memoriale[a].
J. Harvey. Song Offerings[b]. [b]**Penelope Walmsley-Clark** (sop); [a]**Sebastian Bell** (fl); **London Sinfonietta / George Benjamin.** Nimbus NI5167. Text included.

50' DDD 10/89 　　　　　❓

Well before reaching his thirtieth birthday in 1990 George Benjamin achieved a high reputation as a promising young composer and conductor. This disc sees that promise abundantly fulfilled with a well-balanced, satisfying programme of modern music. Benjamin's own work takes its titles from the Inca word for the panpipe and *Antara*'s scoring includes two synthesizer keyboards, linked to a sophisticated computer system, which enrich and transform the music's fascinating exploration of panpipe sound. Jonathan Harvey's inspiration is Indian rather than South American. In *Song Offerings* he sets a group of mystical love poems by Rabindranath Tagore in English, the music lacking nothing in immediacy of mood and exotic variety of vocal and instrumental colour. The two short pieces by Pierre Boulez are characteristically refined tributes: *Dérive* for Sir William Glock, who brought Boulez to the BBC in the 1960s, *Memoriale* for the French flautist Lawrence Beauregard, who died in 1985. They complete an excellently performed, atmospherically recorded disc: a cross-section of contemporary European music at its best.

Alban Berg

Austrian 1885-1935

Berg. Violin Concerto (1935).
Stravinsky. Violin Concerto in D major (1931). **Itzhak Perlman** (vn); **Boston Symphony Orchestra/Seiji Ozawa.** DG 413 725-2GH. From 2531 110 (3/80).

| 48' ADD 12/84 |

Berg. Violin Concerto (1935)[a].
Stravinsky. Violin Concerto in D major (1931)[b]. **Arthur Grumiaux** (vn); **Concertgebouw Orchestra, Amsterdam/[a]Igor Markevitch, [b]Ernest Bour.** Philips Legendary Classics 422 136-2PLC. From SAL3650 (4/68).

| 45' ADD 10/88 |

The lifeblood of the nineteenth-century concerto was the self-assertion of the soloist, but since about 1910, with the general collapse of faith in individualism, most concertos have had to replace or redefine these qualities. Stravinsky's Violin Concerto redefines virtuosity in terms of "circusization" (a buzz-word of the Parisian theatrical circles in which he moved), whereas Berg redefines poetic eloquence in terms of heartbreak and protest. Perlman brings to each concerto his characteristically generous musicianship and clarity of execution. DG have obliged him in his liking for forward placement of the violin, but without serious loss of orchestral detail. Indeed the balance in the final pages of the Berg, where the Bach chorale *Es ist genug* ("It is enough") stands as a poignant symbol of loss, is exceptionally fine, thanks not least to the tonal refinement of the Boston Orchestra. In the Stravinsky the violin is cast in the role of acrobat, or maybe puppet, with the Devil from *The Soldier's Tale* pulling the strings. Meanwhile the orchestra introduces, whips up excitement, spotlights the soloist's tricks, and incites to applause. Perlman and Ozawa are in their element here and once again the recording is clear and lifelike.

Arthur Grumiaux's performances have rightly been acclaimed as classics and are also highly recommended. Some may prefer more weight and daemonism in the Berg, but Grumiaux's relatively restrained interpretation convinces on its own terms, and the Stravinsky is deliciously deft. The sound is never less than clear in detail and balance, and with such playing who could wish for more?

Berg. Lulu Suite (1935)[a]. Three Orchestral Pieces, Op. 6 (rev. 1929). Altenberg Lieder, Op. 4[a]. [a]**Margaret Price** (sop); **London Symphony Orchestra/Claudio Abbado.** DG 20th Century Classics 423 238-2GC. Texts and translations included. From 2530 146 (4/72).

| 67' ADD 8/88 | Ⓑ

For all its subtlety and calculation, this is music that constantly spills over into
raw, uninhibited aggressiveness, and Abbado's interpretations convey this quality

magnificently. Berg's destiny as an opera composer is already discernible in the poised, arching vocal lines of the *Altenberg Lieder*, whose intricate accompaniments seem extravagantly detailed, given the brevity of the structures. Here, and even more clearly in the Three Orchestral Pieces, we can hear the sound-world and thematic characteristics of Mahler's later works carried to a still higher power, the music veering from frozen calm to frenzy in an instant. Berg's last years were dominated by his two great operas *Wozzeck* and *Lulu*, complementary studies in the psychopathology of degradation and despair that work the aesthetic miracle of drawing sublime music from the most sordid subject-matter. Although *Lulu* can now be heard complete, there is still a place for this suite of extracts that draws together some of the opera's most gripping and poignant music. Here, as in the *Altenberg Lieder*, the young Margaret Price is ideally flexible and full-toned. Although the digital remastering has produced an almost harshly immediate sound, the glare is tameable to a degree and is not inappropriate, given performances that vividly convey the barely-controlled violence of Berg's emotions.

Berg. Lyric Suite—arr. string orchestra (1929).
Schoenberg. Pelleas und Melisande, Op. 5. **Berlin Philharmonic Orchestra/Herbert von Karajan.** DG 423 132-2GH. From 2711 014 (3/75).

61' ADD 5/88

If you thought Schoenberg's music was dominated by a singular distrust of harmony and other a-traditional beliefs then his vast tone-poem *Pelleas und Melisande* should restore the balance. Dating from 1903, *Pelleas* employs all the resources of the late-romantic symphony orchestra and the magnificent wash of colour Schoenberg conjures from these forces receives magnificent advocacy from Karajan and his Berliners. The music evocatively delineates the psychological contours of Maeterlinck's mysterious and emotionally-laden plot. Berg's *Lyric Suite* was composed as a six-movement chamber work but in 1927 his publisher suggested a string transcription. Berg chose the second, third and fourth movements as a suite for strings. Sparer and more advanced in sound than *Pelleas* these pieces have a shimmering beauty that is very intoxicating. Karajan obviously has great sympathy with this music and it receives a tender performance from him. The recordings are good if a trifle hazy.

Berg. Lulu Suite (1935)[a].
Schoenberg. Five Orchestral Pieces, Op. 16.
Webern. Six Pieces, Op. 6. [a]**Arleen Auger** (sop); **City of Birmingham Symphony Orchestra/Simon Rattle.** EMI CDC7 49857-2.

66' DDD 11/89

Simon Rattle doesn't go to ostentatious lengths to demonstrate the different sound worlds these three composers inhabit (Schoenberg equals sinewy and Brahmsian, Berg equals lusciously Mahleresque, Webern equals coolly crystalline, would be an over-simple set of equations anyway) but he is good at recognizing each composer's tone of voice and his particular preoccupations; Berg's for a sort of sumptuous but ordered complexity, for instance, or Schoenberg's for an urgent forward impulse. All three have a refined lyricism in common, but Rattle's is a lighter, somewhat cooler lyricism than the polished but rather heavy-featured manner offered by many conductors in this repertoire, and he reaches subtle or poignant areas of expression with greater ease. With the exception of a slight recessing of the soloist in the Berg, the recordings are excellent, their clarity revealing much beautifully moulded playing and precisely calculated internal balance.

Berg. WOZZECK. **Franz Grundheber** (bar) Wozzeck; **Hildegard Behrens** (sop) Marie; **Heinz Zednik** (ten) Captain; **Aage Haugland** (bass) Doctor; **Philip Langridge** (ten) Andres; **Walter Raffeiner** (ten) Drum-Major; **Anna Gonda** (mez) Margret; **Alfred Sramek** (bass) First Apprentice; **Alexander Maly** (bar) Second Apprentice; **Peter Jelosits** (ten) Idiot; **Vienna Boys' Choir; Vienna State Opera Chorus; Vienna Philharmonic Orchestra/ Claudio Abbado.** DG 423 587-2GH2. Notes, text and translation included. Recorded at performances at the Vienna State Opera during June 1987.

② 89' DDD 2/89

A live recording, in every sense of the word. The cast is uniformly excellent, with Grundheber, good both at the wretched pathos of Wozzeck's predicament and his helpless bitterness, and Behrens as an outstandingly intelligent and involving Marie, even the occasional touch of strain in her voice heightening her characterization. The Vienna Philharmonic respond superbly to Abbado's ferociously close-to-the-edge direction. It is a live recording with a bit of a difference, mark you: the perspectives are those of a theatre, not a recording studio. The orchestra is laid out as it would be in an opera house pit and the movement of singers on stage means that voices are occasionally overwhelmed. I like the effect very much: the crowded inn-scenes, the arrival and departure of the military band, the sense of characters actually reacting to each other, not to a microphone, makes for a grippingly theatrical experience. Audiences no longer think of *Wozzeck* as a 'difficult' work, but recordings have sometimes treated it as one, with a clinical precision either to the performance or the recorded perspective. This version has a raw urgency, a sense of bitter protest and angry pity that are quite compelling and uncomfortably eloquent.

Luciano Berio
Italian 1925-

Berio. Sinfonia (1969)[a]. Eindrücke (1973-4). [a]**Regis Pasquier** (vn); [a]**New Swingle Singers; French National Orchestra/Pierre Boulez.** Erato 2292-45228-2. From NUM75198 (2/86).

45' DDD 7/88

Berio. Formazioni. 11 Folk Songs[a]. Sinfonia[b]. [a]**Jard van Nes** (mez); [b]**Electric Phoenix; Royal Concertgebouw Orchestra/Riccardo Chailly.** Decca 425 832-2DH. Texts and translations included.

70' DDD 8/90

It's now far easier to distinguish avant garde pieces of lasting value from ones that stand rather as historical curiosities and without question the music of Berio lives on, and his audience grows rather than dwindles. It says much for Berio's craftsmanship that his works still have a freshness about them where others today sound impossibly dated. Even *Sinfonia*, with its reference to Lévi-Strauss, Samuel Beckett and the death of Martin Luther King, transcends its original context and challenges us with extraordinary riches. Especially striking is the third movement, a weird collage of quotations from all manner of composers from Bach to Berg and from Beethoven to Boulez, carried out in stream-of-consciousness fashion against the ever-present background of the scherzo from Mahler's second symphony. Nor is it easy to forget the haunting second movement, in which a cloud of isolated floating syllables gradually coalesce into the words "Martin Luther King". Even in the movements that lack such a neat framework, the sheer energy of Berio's sound-world and the logic of his invention is utterly fascinating. This Boulez recording is authoritative and supersedes Berio's own. It is nicely complemented by the short but imposing orchestral score *Eindrücke*.

Riccardo Chailly   *[photo: Decca*

Riccardo Chailly's performance offers an innovative though still valid perspective of the *Sinfonia*. This is particularly noticeable in the now famous 'Mahler' movement, where Chailly tends to favour a more veiled and recessed balancing of the voices. This may seem rather an odd preference at first but it should be remembered that Berio himself asks for the voices to be only half-heard throughout the orchestral web of sound—an approach that is intended to encourage the listener to re-explore the music on each successive hearing. Chailly's performance certainly reveals more of the orchestral detail, and whereas Boulez brings to the surface the more menacing aspects of the work, in this recording they become submerged into an uneasy, subterranean undercurrent. The inclusion of the splendid *Formazioni* (Formations) of 1987 make this disc all the more desirable. The title reflects Berio's fascination for unusual displacements and groupings of instruments; in this case the dramatic deployment of antiphonal brass sections seated on either side of the orchestra, with strings occupying centre stage (the spatial qualities of this work are particularly effective in this recording). The result is a marvellously compelling and sonically spectacular piece of music which surely ranks as one of his most cogently structured and impressive works. The Decca recording is excellent.

Berio. A-ronne. Cries of London—for eight voices (1975). **Swingle II** (Olive Simpson, Catherine Bott, sops; Carol Hall, Linda Hirst, mez; John Potter, Ward Swingle, tens; John Lubbock, David Beaven, basses)/**Luciano Berio.** Decca Enterprise 425 620-2DM. Texts included. From HEAD15 (1/77).

• • 45' ADD 7/90

Berio's *A-ronne* is considered by many to be one of the finest pieces of *avant-garde* choral writing to emerge from the seventies. The title is derived from an old Italian dictum "from A to ronne" (the equivalent to our saying "from A to Z"), and Berio calls the composition "a documentary on a poem by Edoardo Sanguinetti" and describes his approach to the text as "a text to be analysed and used as a generator of different vocal situations and expressions" (the poem itself is a collage built out of various sources as diverse as *The Communist Manifesto*, *The Bible* and a verse by Dante). The resulting musical collage is a brilliant *tour de force*, confronting the listener with a tirade of vocal techniques ranging from shouts, groans, sighs and whistling to conventional singing. The effect created is a superb piece of theatre for the imagination. The hauntingly beautiful *Cries of London* is a reworking of a piece originally written for The King's Singers, and its immediate, often humorous charm provides an excellent contrast to the more modernistic sounds of *A-ronne*. The texts are the same as those used by the Elizabethan madrigalists, though the musical techniques used by Berio are closer to those of the medieval composers. Swingle II are extremely persuasive advocates for these challenging and compelling works and the recording is of demonstration quality.

Lennox Berkeley   *Refer to Index*   *British 1903-1989*

Hector Berlioz

Berlioz. BEATRICE ET BENEDICT—Overture[a].
Franck. Symphony in D minor[b].
d'Indy. Symphonie sur un chant montagnard français (Symphonie cévenole)[c].
[c]**Nicole Henriot-Schweitzer** (pf); [ac]**Boston Symphony Orchestra/
Charles Munch;** [b]**Chicago Symphony Orchestra/ Pierre Monteux.** RCA
Victor Papillon GD86805. Item marked [a] from SB2125 (10/61), [b] SB6631 (10/
65), [c] SB2053 (1/60).

> 72' ADD 3/89

This exceptionally well-filled disc links three French favourites. Munch directs a
fine performance of the Berlioz overture, one which truly relishes the long-
breathed string writing. The Boston orchestra play superbly. A similar freshness
and idiomatic flair is brought to the rarely heard but delightful d'Indy work, in
essence a piano concerto of rhapsodic exuberance. Munch conducts with a great
deal of vigour and Gallic verve, and orchestra and soloist join in with high spirits
and evident pleasure. The piano tone in this 1958 recording is a trifle
clangy but not disagreeably so. Pierre Monteux, surely one of the great
conductors of the century, reminds us in his fine reading of the Franck
Symphony, that he was quite as adept at controlling the long line and regal
architecture of a work that has closer ties to the German symphonic tradition
than is sometimes granted, as he was as an equalled colourist in the great French
tradition. His performance is never lugubrious but has an appropriate weight and
scale whilst always being alive to the work's ardent moments. The 1961
recording still sounds remarkably well for its age.

Berlioz. Rêverie et caprice, Op. 8.
Lalo. Symphonie espagnole, Op. 21. **Itzhak Perlman** (vn); **Orchestre de
Paris/Daniel Barenboim.** DG 400 032-2GH. From 2532 011 (1/82).

> 41' DDD 3/83

Among the *concertante* works where the solo violin is invited to entertain the
listener by alternately seducing and dazzling the ear, Lalo's *Symphonie espagnole*
stands out. As well as the bravura excitement there are plenty of good tunes,
too, which Perlman plays with freshness and flair, yet without missing its
underlying sultry colour. He is greatly helped by the strong character of
Barenboim's accompaniment which provides a firm, supple base for the wizardry
of the solo fireworks. There has been no more enticing version than this.
Berlioz's *Rêverie et caprice* makes an imaginative coupling, a less memorable piece,
perhaps, but still ripely enjoyable when presented with such conviction. The DG
recording is brilliant and clear and even though the soloist is forwardly balanced
the orchestral focus is sharp enough to ensure that no detail is obscured. The
effect is undoubtedly exhilarating.

Berlioz. Harold in Italy, Op. 14[a]. Tristia, Op. 18[b]. Les troyens à
Carthage—Act 2, Prelude[c]. [a]**Nobuko Imai** (va); [b]**John Alldis Choir;
London Symphony Orchestra/Sir Colin Davis.** Philips 416 431-2PH.
Texts and translations included. Item marked [a] from 9500 026 (3/76), [b] 9500
944 (6/83), [c] SAL3788 (3/70).

> 70' ADD 12/86

Berlioz was much influenced by the British romantic poet, Byron, and his travels
in Italy—where he went in 1831 as the winner of the Prix de Rome—led him
to conceive a big orchestral work based on one of Byron's most popular works,

Childe Harold's Pilgrimage. Like Berlioz's earlier *Symphonie fantastique, Harold in Italy* was not only a programme work but brilliantly unconventional and imaginative in its structure and argument. A commission from the great virtuoso, Paganini, led him to conceive a big viola concerto, but the idea of a Byronic symphony got in the way of that. Though there is an important viola solo in the symphony as we know it—richly and warmly played on this recording by Nobuko Imai—it is far from being the vehicle for solo display that Paganini was wanting. Sir Colin Davis's 1975 performance, beautifully transferred to CD, emphasizes the symphonic strength of the writing without losing the bite of the story-telling. The shorter works are also all valuable in illustrating Berlioz's extraordinary imagination. Excellent sound on all the different vintage recordings.

Berlioz. Symphonie fantastique, Op. 14. **Orchestre National de France/ Leonard Bernstein.** EMI Studio CDM7 69002-2. From ASD3397 (11/77).

52' ADD 9/87

Berlioz. Symphonie fantastique, Op. 14. **London Classical Players/Roger Norrington.** EMI Reflexe CDC7 49541-2.

53' DDD 4/89

Berlioz. Symphonie fantastique, Op. 14. Le carnaval romain, Op. 9. Le corsaire, Op. 21. **Toulouse Capitole Orchestra/Michel Plasson.** EMI CDC7 54010-2.

68' DDD 9/90

No romantic composer was ever more highly charged and committed in his art (even sometimes to excess) than Berlioz, and no conductor can be said to generate more emotional electricity than Leonard Bernstein. Working with the French orchestra, Bernstein secures exciting yet precise playing of their compatriot's music, together with some ravishing sounds. The 1976 recording in the Salle Wagram in Paris is rich yet detailed, with some lovely string and harp sounds and thrilling brass and percussion, including bells, in the finale; and the analogue original has transferred well with little background noise. At full price this issue would be worth having; at medium price it is a real bargain.

The advances by the period instrument movement have often been startling in the way they force us to listen afresh to classic works of the repertoire, but none has been so remarkable as Norrington's recording of the *Symphonie*. For a work that was already advanced in its own time, and one conceived with great attention to colour and its pictorial detail, the 'new' sounds created by period instruments are even more extraordinary. Quite apart from the restoration of the ophicleide to the orchestral texture Norrington's attention to the detail of the score consistently re-awakens our perceptions of this remarkable work. Tempos are re-thought, the March is taken at a steady, menacing pace and the Ball dances at what is surely the perfect speed. The whole recording has an impulsive, trail-blazing quality that comes from the joining of scholarship and imagination and really demands to be heard, even by those sceptical of the period performance movement.

The later EMI performance by a French conductor and orchestra has drama and sensitivity in the right proportions, creating great atmosphere and excitement, not least in the terrifying "March to the Scaffold" that ends with the fall of the guillotine and the roar of the spectators as the severed head rolls away from the block, all portrayed with grisly force in the music. The two overtures, brimful of extrovert brilliance, are also done with panache and the recording is crisp and full-toned.

Berlioz. Roméo et Juliette—dramatic symphony, Op. 16. **Patricia Kern** (contr); **Robert Tear** (ten); **John Shirley-Quirk** (bar); **John Alldis Choir; London Symphony Chorus and Orchestra/Sir Colin Davis.** Philips 416 962-2PH2. Notes, text and translation included. From SAL3695/6 (12/68).

② 97' ADD 6/88

Berlioz's 'dramatic symphony' of 1839 is a prime example of early and full-blooded romanticism. The impulsive young composer adored Shakespeare and here he took the English playwright's celebrated love story and set it to music, not as an opera but a symphony with voices, partly because he felt that the language of instrumental music was "richer, more varied and free of limitations and … incomparably more powerful". This music is, nevertheless, sometimes inspired and sometimes simply naïve, but always spontaneous and Sir Colin Davis, a great Berlioz champion, plays it as if he believed passionately and urgently in every note. He is well supported by his three vocal soloists and the London Symphony Orchestra and Chorus plus the John Alldis Choir, and although the recording is now over 20 years old it does not show its age to any significant extent and indeed may be regarded as a classic Berlioz performance although the total length of 97 minutes for two discs is not generous by CD standards.

Berlioz. Grande messe des morts[a]. Symphonie funèbre et triomphale[b]. [a]**Ronald Dowd** (ten); [b]**Dennis Wick** (tb); [a]**Wandsworth School Boys' Choir;** [b]**John Alldis Choir; London Symphony Chorus**[a] **and Orchestra/ Sir Colin Davis.** Philips 416 283-2PH2. Notes, texts and translation included. Item marked [a] from 6700 019 (9/70), [b] SAL3788 (3/70).

② 2h 7' 4/86

Berlioz's Requiem is not a liturgical work, any more than the *Symphonie funèbre* is really for the concert hall; but both are pieces of high originality, composed as ceremonials for the fallen, and standing as two of the noblest musical monuments to the French ideal of a *gloire*. The Requiem is most famous for its apocalyptic moment when, after screwing the key up stage by stage, Berlioz's four brass bands blaze forth "at the round earth's imagin'd corners"; this has challenged the engineers of various companies, but the Philips recording for Colin Davis remains as fine as any, not least since Davis directs the bands with

such a strong sense of character. He also gives the troubled rhythms of the *Lacrymosa* a stronger, more disturbing emphasis than any other conductor, and time and again finds out the expressive counterpoint, the emphatic rhythm, the telling few notes within the texture, that reveal so much about Berlioz's intentions. The notorious flute and trombone chords of the *Hostias* work admirably. Ronald Dowd is a little strained in the *Sanctus*, but the whole performance continues to stand the test of time and of other competing versions. The same is true of the *Symphonie funèbre et triomphale*, which moves at a magisterial tread and is given a recording that does well by its difficult textures. A fine coupling of two remarkable works.

Sir Colin Davis   [photo: Philips

Berlioz. Les nuits d'été[a]. La mort de Cléopâtre[b]. Les troyens—Act 5, scenes 2 and 3[c]. **Dame Janet Baker** (mez); [c]**Bernadette Greevy** (contr); [c]**Keith Erwen** (ten); [c]**Gwynne Howell** (bass); [c]**Ambrosian Opera Chorus;** [a]**New Philharmonia Orchestra/Sir John Barbirolli;** [bc]**London Symphony Orchestra/Sir Alexander Gibson.** EMI Studio CDM7 69544-2. Item marked [a] from ASD2444 (2/69), [b] and [c] ASD2516 (12/69).

♪♪ 78' ADD 11/88 £ Ⓑ

These performances can be recommended without hesitation, but unfortunately the presentation provides no texts and little information about the music. This is all very well if the listener has access to scores or librettos, but except for the laziest kind of enjoyment there is a real need here to know what the soloist is singing about. The words of *Les nuits d'été* are not too difficult to find, but with the deaths of Cleopatra and Dido you need to have more than a broad knowledge of the general situation. In mitigation it might be said that if any singer can be relied on to convey the sense of the words purely by her expression, and if any composer has a power of communication so vivid that words can almost be dispensed with, these are surely Baker and Berlioz respectively. The yearning and desperation of Cleopatra live in the singer's tone, just as surely as her pulse weirdly beats and then dies in the music. Similarly, Dido's changes of mood, her passionate intensity, her tender farewell to Carthage, are all imaginatively realized and deeply felt. *Les nuits d'été,* too, is wonderfully well caught in the whole range of its moods, with Barbirolli handling the orchestral score with unsurpassed sensitivity and care for detail.

Berlioz. La damnation de Faust. **Nicolai Gedda** (ten) Faust; **Jules Bastin** (bass) Méphistophélès; **Josephine Veasey** (mez) Marguérite; **Richard Van Allan** (bass) Brander; **Gillian Knight** (mez) Celestial Voice; **Wandsworth School Boys' Choir; Ambrosian Singers; London Symphony Chorus and Orchestra/Sir Colin Davis.** Philips 416 395-2PH2. Notes, text and translation included. From 6703 042 (1/74).

♪♪ ② 2h 11' ADD 1/87

Sir Colin Davis's performance of *La damnation* reveals the colour and excitement of a work that has never found a true home in the opera house. No other of Berlioz's scores excels it in the subtle and telling use of detail, from the whole orchestra in full cry to the subtly judged chamber music combinations and to details of instrumental choice (as when the husky viola for Marguérite's touching little song about the bereft King of Thule yields to the mournful cor anglais for her abandonment by Faust). Davis's performance has the grandeur and excitement of Berlioz's vision of romantic man compassing his own damnation by being led to test and reject the consolations maliciously offered by Méphistophélès. No other conductor has made the Hungarian March turn so chillingly from its brave panoply to a menacing emptiness. The sylphs and will-o'-the-wisps flit and hover delicately. The transformation from the raucous boozers in Auerbach's cellar to Faust's dream of love on the banks of the Elbe is beautifully done, as the hurtling pace slows and the textures soften, Méphistophélès's sweet melodic line betrayed by the snarling brass accompaniment. The arrival of CD gave an extra edge to all this vivid and expressive detail. The singers are very much within this fine and faithful concept of the work. Gedda is an incomparably elegant, noble Faust, whose very gentleness is turned against him by the cold, sneering, ironic Méphistophélès of Jules Bastin. Josephine Veasey is a touching Marguérite who is not afraid to be simple; and Richard Van Allan knocks off a jovial Brander. Chorus and orchestra clearly enjoy the whole occasion, and rise to it.

Berlioz. SONGS. [a]**Brigitte Fournier** (sop); [b]**Diana Montague,** [c]**Catherine Robbin** (mezs); [d]**Howard Crook** (ten); [e]**Gilles Cachemaille** (bar); **Lyon Opéra Orchestra/John Eliot Gardiner.** Erato MusiFrance 2292-45517-2. Texts and translations included.

Le jeune pâtre breton, Op. 13 No. 4[d]. La captive, Op. 12[c]. Le chasseur danois, Op. 19 No. 6[e]. Zaïde, Op. 19 No. 1[a]. La belle voyageuse, Op. 2 No. 4[b]. Les nuits d'été, Op. 7—Villanelle[d]; Le spectre de la rose[c]; Sur les lagunnes[e]; Absence[b]; Au cimetière[d]; L'île inconnue[b]. Aubade[d]. Tristia, Op. 18—No. 2, La mort d'Ophélie[c].

65' DDD 2/91

Berlioz intended the songs in his cycle *Les nuits d'eté* to be assigned to different types of singers. This excellent issue fulfils his wishes, and each of the performers has been carefully chosen to fit his or her particular offering. In turn, Montague, Robbin, Crook and Cachemaille ideally catches the mood and feeling of his or her piece, and each has the kind of tone that seems perfectly suited to Berlioz's idiom. In support, Gardiner finds just the right tempo for each song, never indulging in the over-deliberate speed that can kill the slower songs with kindness. He and his orchestra play Berlioz's wonderfully atmospheric accompaniments with beauty and sensitivity. To add to one's pleasure there is a generous selection of Berlioz's other songs with orchestra, equally well interpreted. Robbin's account of the marvellous *La captive*, the very essence of this composer's brand of romanticism, is a particular joy.

Berlioz. L'enfance du Christ, Op. 25. **Robert Tear** (ten) Narrator; **David Wilson-Johnson** (bar) Herod; **Ann Murray** (mez) Mary; **Thomas Allen** (bar) Joseph; **Matthew Best** (bass) Ishmaelite Father; **Gerald Finley** (bar) Polydorus; **William Kendall** (ten) Centurion; **Choir of King's College, Cambridge; Royal Philharmonic Orchestra/Stephen Cleobury.** EMI CDS7 49935-2. Notes, text and translation included.

② 97' DDD 12/90

The Choir of King's College, Cambridge has made this splendid recording of *L'enfance du Christ* with a strong, well-chosen all-English cast. The important role of Narrator falls to Robert Tear, who assumes it with warmth and sympathy and a good sense of the drama as it unfolds. David Wilson-Johnson makes a superb Herod, tortured and anguished in his mind before delivering his half-demented

sentence of death upon the Holy Innocents. Ann Murray, as Mary, is tender and gentle, particularly in the quiet, idyllic stable scene. Thomas Allen portrays a convincing Joseph, firm and decisive in his singing, well able to face up to his responsibilities as head of the Holy Family. Matthew Best sings a rich and heart-warming welcome to them on their arrival in Egypt. The King's Choir, amply assisted by the chapel acoustics, are able to make the choir of angelic voices sound truly other-worldly, their repeated "Hosannas" fading gently upwards and away into the fan-vaulting—like clouds of incense—with magical effect. The acoustics also play an important part at the close of the oratorio, enabling the choir to bring it almost inevitably to its breathtaking conclusion of peace and quiet contemplation. Even if you've never heard any of this music before, except the famous "Shepherds' farewell" chorus, this really is compulsory Christmas listening!

Berlioz. LES TROYENS. **Jon Vickers** (ten) Aeneas; **Josephine Veasey** (mez) Dido; **Berit Lindholm** (sop) Cassandra; **Peter Glossop** (bar) Corebus, Ghost of Corebus; **Heather Begg** (sop) Anna; **Roger Soyer** (bar) Narbal, Spirit of Hector; **Anne Howells** (mez) Ascanius; **Anthony Raffell** (bass) Panthus; **Ian Partridge** (ten) Iopas; **Pierre Thau** (bass) Priam, Mercury, a Trojan soldier; **Elizabeth Bainbridge** (mez) Hecuba, Ghost of Cassandra; **Ryland Davies** (ten) Hylas; **David Lennox** (ten) Helenus; **Raimund Herincx** (bass) Ghost of Priam, First Sentry; **Dennis Wicks** (bar) Ghost of Hector, Second Sentry, Greek Chieftain; **Wandsworth School Boys' Choir; Royal Opera House, Covent Garden Chorus and Orchestra/Sir Colin Davis.** Philips 416 432-2PH4. Notes, text and translation included. From 6709 002 (5/70).

④   4h 1' ADD 12/86   ♩P   ♩S

One of the largest canvases in the whole genre of opera, *Les troyens* was for long considered unperformable. Yet it is no longer than some of Wagner's scores and certainly no more difficult to encompass in one evening. That has been proved conclusively in a succession of productions at Covent Garden, this one recorded not actually 'live' but immediately after stage performances. Sir Colin Davis, the leading Berlioz conductor of the day, fired his forces to give the kind of reading that could only have emerged from experience of the work in the opera house. He is fully aware of the epic quality of the story and no one else has quite so successfully conveyed the score's dramatic stature, its nobility and its tragic consequences. There are many splendid performances on this set, but in the end it is the sense of a team effort, of a cast, chorus and orchestra utterly devoted to the task in hand that is so boldly declared. The recording matches the quality of the music-making.

Leonard Bernstein
American 1918-1990

Bernstein. ORCHESTRAL WORKS. **New York Philharmonic Orchestra/ Leonard Bernstein.** CBS Maestro CD44773. Items marked [a] from 72405 (5/66), [b] Philips SBBL652 (2/62).
Candide—Overture[a]. West Side Story—Symphonic dances[b]. On the Town—Three dance episodes[a]. On the Waterfront—Symphonic suite[b].

55' ADD 2/91   ♩P

Broadway and Hollywood form a backcloth to all the music on this disc. A maniacally driven Overture to Bernstein's third Broadway musical, *Candide*, sets the style from the outset with the conductor intent on squeezing every last ounce from both his music and players. The orchestra can sound hard-pressed at times and details get smudged, especially so in the cavernous acoustic, but the dazzling zest of this approach is totally winning and, when the music does relax into more tender moments, the pathos is overwhelming. In the Symphonic dances from *West Side Story*, few orchestras could better the NYPO's intuitive feel for the dance rhythms and cross accents, the rampaging Latin percussion barrage, the screaming trumpet writing, or the theatre-pit instrumental balance. The Three Dance Episodes from Bernstein's first musical, *On the Town*, are more overtly eclectic, with hints of Gershwin alongside allusions to Stravinsky, whilst the magnificent score for the film, *On the Waterfront*, finds Bernstein inventively complementing the highlights and deep shadows of Elia Kazan's visual style, and the savagery of the plot. As his own best interpreter, Bernstein goes straight for the key features of all these scores and inspires his orchestra to produce its best.

Bernstein. Songfest[a]. Chichester Psalms[b]. [a]**Clamma Dale** (sop); [a]**Rosalind Elias,** [a]**Nancy Williams** (mezs); [a]**Neil Rosenshein** (ten); [a]**John Reardon** (bar); [a]**Donald Gramm** (bass); [b]soloist from the **Vienna Boys' Choir;** [b]**Vienna Jeunesse Choir;** [a]**National Symphony Orchestra of Washington,** [b]**Israel Philharmonic Orchestra/Leonard Bernstein.** DG 415 965-2GH. Texts and, where appropriate, translations included. Item marked [a] from 2531 044 (11/78), [b] 2709 077 (9/78) which was recorded at a performance in the Philharmonie, Berlin during August 1977.

62' ADD 5/86

"I, too, am America", is the message of Leonard Bernstein's orchestral song-cycle *Songfest*. The subject of the work is the American artist's emotional, spiritual and intellectual response to life in an essentially Puritan society, and, more specifically, to the eclecticism of American society and its many problems of social integration (blacks, women, homosexuals and expatriates). As expected from a composer/conductor equally at home on Broadway or in Vienna's Musikverein, the styles range widely. The scoring is colourful, occasionally pungent, always tuneful. Bernstein's soloists are well chosen and sing with feeling. This vivid live recording of the *Chichester Psalms offers* the full orchestral version and the performers all give their utmost.

Bernstein. SONGS AND DUETS. **Judy Kaye** (sop); **William Sharp** (bar); [a]**Sara Sant'Ambrogio** (vc); **Michael Barrett, Steven Blier** (pfs). Koch International Classics 37000-2. Texts included.
Arias and Barcarolles. ON THE TOWN—Some other time; Lonely town; Carried away; I can cook. WONDERFUL TOWN—A little bit in love. PETER PAN—Dream with me[a]. Songfest—Storyette, H.M.; To what you said[a].

59' DDD 6/90

One of Bernstein's last compositions was the song-cycle *Arias and Barcarolles*, a work that gets its title from a remark made by President Eisenhower after hearing the composer play Mozart and Gershwin at the White House in 1960. "You know, I liked that last piece—it's got a *theme*. I like music with a theme, not all them arias and barcarolles." Well, Bernstein may have enjoyed a reputation as a conductor quite at home amongst the 'arias and barcarolles' of the repertoire, but as a composer his language would have surely spoken directly to Eisenhower. Tunes were his meat and drink, and he certainly knew how to write them. *Arias and Barcarolles* is about irony, capturing head-on clashes of emotion experienced in childhood, growing-up and everyday life. Bernstein draws on his own experiences—Jewish weddings, boyhood, bringing up children and so on. The two soloists interweave with different levels of consciousness and different outlooks. Initially difficult to grasp, these little vignettes, skilfully developed and harnessing the quintessential Bernstein, repay acquaintance. The remainder of the disc speaks directly to the heart and senses; here are a stream of Bernstein's most delicious melodies performed with style, wit and a great deal of elegance. This is the part of the record that speaks directly to the senses. Judy Kaye and William Sharp are nicely matched, and the piano duo team supply ideal accompaniments. It is no wonder that this enchanting record has garnered so many plaudits.

Bernstein. WEST SIDE STORY. **Dame Kiri Te Kanawa** (sop) Maria (Nina Bernstein); **José Carreras** (ten) Tony (Alexander Bernstein); **Tatiana Troyanos** (mez) Anita; **Kurt Ollmann** (bar) Riff; composite chorus and orchestra from 'on and off' Broadway/**Leonard Bernstein** with **Marilyn Horne** (mez). DG 415 253-2GH2. Including "On the Waterfront"—Israel Philharmonic Orchestra/Bernstein. From 2532 051 (7/82) and recorded live in May 1981. Notes and text included.

A complete recording of a full-blooded musical with five leading operatic stars? Here's 'crossover' with a vengeance! Before this recording Bernstein had not conducted the original full-length score. To have his presence at the sessions was clearly an enormous benefit—not only in his authoritative conducting but in his influence over the starry cast, all of whom respond with zest to his direction. The recording quality is dry and immediate, to enhance the dramatic impact of the score, but there is plenty of bloom on the voices. The suite from Bernstein's music for the 1954 film *On the Waterfront* is terse and powerful and provides an appropriate make-weight.

Bernstein. CANDIDE. **Jerry Hadley** (ten) Candide; **June Anderson** (sop) Cunegonde; **Adolph Green** (ten) Dr Pangloss, Martin; **Christa Ludwig** (mez) Old lady; **Nicolai Gedda** (ten) Governor, Vanderdendur, Ragotski; **Della Jones** (mez) Paquette; **Kurt Ollmann** (bar) Maximilian, Captain, Jesuit father; **Neil Jenkins** (ten) Merchant, Inquisitor, Prince Charles Edward; **Richard Suart** (bass) Junkman, Inquisitor, King Hermann Augustus; **John Treleaven** (ten) Alchemist, Inquisitor, Sultan Achmet, Crook; **Lindsay Benson** (bar) Doctor, Inquisitor, King Stanislaus; **Clive Bayley** (bar) Bear-Keeper, Inquisitor, Tsar Ivan; **London Symphony Chorus and Orchestra/Leonard Bernstein.** DG 429 734-2GH2. Notes and text included.

And it came to pass that Leonard Bernstein's prodigal son finally found immortality. *Candide*'s chequered history, its many trials and tribulations, can almost rival that of its hapless hero. But here it is—all of it, at last—musical comedy, grand opera, operetta, satire, melodrama, all rolled into one. We can thank John Mauceri for much of the restoration work: his 1988 Scottish Opera production was the spur for this long-awaited recording and prompted exhaustive reappraisal. Numbers like "We Are Women", "Martin's Laughing Song" and "Nothing More Than This" have rarely been heard, if at all. The last mentioned, Candide's 'aria of disillusionment', is one of the enduring glories of the score, reinstated where Bernstein always wanted it (but where no producer would have it), near the very end of the show. Bernstein called it his "Puccini aria", and that it is—bitter-sweet, long-breathed, supported, enriched and ennobled by its inspiring string counterpoint. And this is but one of many forgotten gems.

Who but a Bernstein could have seen Voltaire's irreverent satire in terms of central-European operetta traditions? The horrors of the Spanish Inquisition ("Oh what a day for an auto-da-fe!") turned Gilbert and Sullivanesque romp laced with cheap flamenco; Cunegonde's hypocrisy brilliantly encapsulated in the mad mocking coloratura of "Glitter and Be Gay" (Gounod was never this much fun); everywhere whiffs of Lehár and Johann Strauss waltzes, Offenbach galops; and of course Bernstein's own sweeter than sweet lyricism—ultimately the heart of the matter in such numbers as "It Must Be So", "The Ballad of Eldorado" (Bernstein's favourite), the aforementioned "Nothing More Than This" and the great choral finale "Make Our Garden Grow". Of course, the style of the show lends itself to the kind of high-level 'operatic' casting that was to prove something of a problem in the composer's own *West Side Story* recording. No such

Leonard Bernstein [photo: DG/Bayat]

embarrassment here. Indeed, it was an inspiration on someone's part (probably Bernstein's) to persuade the great and versatile Christa Ludwig (so "Easily Assimilated") and Nicolai Gedda (in his sixties and still hurling out the top Bs) to fill the principal character roles. To say they do so ripely is to do them scant justice. Bernstein's old sparring partner Adolph Green braves the tongue-twisting and many-hatted Dr Pangloss with his own highly individual form of *sprechstimme*, Jerry Hadley sings the title role most beautifully, *con amore*, and June Anderson has all the notes, and more, for the faithless, air-headed Cunegonde. It is just a pity that someone didn't tell her that discretion is the better part of comedy. "Glitter and Be Gay" is much funnier for being played straighter, odd as it may sound. Otherwise, the supporting roles are all well taken and the LSO Chorus have a field-day in each of their collective guises.

Having waited so long to commit every last note (or thereabouts) of his cherished score to disc, there are moments here where Bernstein seems almost reluctant to move on. His tempos are measured, to say the least, the score fleshier now in every respect: even that raciest of Overtures has now acquired a more deliberate gait, a more opulent tone. But Bernstein would be Bernstein, and there are moments where one is more than grateful for his indulgence: the grandiose chorales, the panoramic orchestrascapes (sumptuously recorded), and of course, that thrilling finale—the best of all possible Bernstein anthems at the slowest of all possible speeds—and why not (prepare to hold your breath at the choral *a capella*). It's true, perhaps, that somewhere in the midst of this glossy package there is a more modest show trying to get out, but let's not look gift horses in the mouth.

Franz Adolf Berwald
Swedish 1796-1868

***Berwald.* SYMPHONIES. Gothenburg Symphony Orchestra/Neeme Järvi.** DG 415 502-2GH2.
No. 1 in G minor, "Sérieuse"; No. 2 in D major, "Capricieuse"; No. 3 in C major, "Singulière"; No. 4 in E flat major.

② 1h 51' DDD 12/85 ❓

Franz Berwald is certainly not an everyday name, but his almost total exclusion from concert programmes is inexcusable. The opening of the *Sinfonie singulière* is simple in technique but provides a rich germ for development. The *Sinfonie capricieuse* has momentary whiffs of Mendelssohn but as with all of Berwald's music parallels are not made easily. The smiling world of the last symphony, the E flat, finds Berwald in light-hearted mood proffering a particularly charming and classical *Scherzo*. Paired on the second disc with the earlier *Sinfonie sérieuse* the darker hues of that work seem to glow more impressively. Järvi's advocacy of these works is totally committed and the Gothenburg Symphony Orchestra play splendidly with some fine wind articulation. The recording is well-detailed and crisp.

Heinrich Biber

Biber. Mensa sonora. Sonata violino solo representativa in A major[a]. **Cologne Musica Antiqua/Reinhard Goebel** ([a]vn). Archiv Produktion 423 701-2AH.

62' DDD 11/89

Biber was one of the greatest German composers of his generation, furthermore enjoying a reputation as a virtuoso violinist of the first rank. This invigorating and stylish disc embraces both aspects of Biber's talent. *Mensa sonora* is a six-part anthology of music which occupies territory belonging to the chamber sonata and the suite. This is delightful music, strongly dance-orientated and with a marked feeling for gesture. These qualities, and others too, are affectingly realized by Reinhard Goebel and his impeccably drilled ensemble in such a way that a listener might be excused for leaving the comfort of an armchair and taking to the floor. By way of an entr'acte between the first three and the last three parts of the anthology, Goebel gives a virtuoso performance of Biber's *Sonata violino solo representativa* in which a nightingale, cuckoo, cockerel, frog, and other creatures make themselves heard; a cat wreaks havoc with them but is in turn sent packing by a musketeer. Many tricks of the violinist's trade are on display and Goebel revels in them all. A splendid achievement by all concerned.

Biber. Mystery Sonatas. **John Holloway** (vn); **Davitt Moroney** (org/hpd); **Tragicomedia** (Stephen Stubbs, lte/chitarrone; Erin Headley, va da gamba/lirone; Andrew Lawrence-King, hp/regal). Virgin Classics Veritas VCD7 90838-2.

② 2h 11' DDD 5/91

Biber was among the most talented musicians of the late seventeenth century. He was a renowned violinist and his compositions, above all for the violin, are technically advanced and strikingly individual. The 15 *Mystery Sonatas* with their additional *Passacaglia* for unaccompanied violin were written in about 1678 and dedicated to Biber's employer, the Archbishop of Salzburg. Each Sonata is inspired by a section of the Rosary devotion of the Catholic Church which offered a system of meditation on 15 Mysteries from the lives of Jesus and His mother. The music is not, strictly speaking, programmatic though often vividly illustrative of events which took place in the life of Christ. All but two of the 16 pieces require *scordatura* or retuning of the violin strings; in this way Biber not only facilitated some of the fingerings but also achieved sounds otherwise unavailable to him. The Sonatas are disposed into three groups of five: Joyful, Sorrowful and Glorious Mysteries whose contrasting states are affectingly evoked in music ranging from a spirit reflecting South German baroque exuberance to one of profound contemplation. John Holloway plays with imaginative sensibility and he is supported by a first-rate continuo group whose instruments include baroque lute, chitarrone, viola da gamba, a 15-string lirone, double harp and regal.

Harrison Birtwistle

Birtwistle. Carmen Arcadiae Mechanicae Perpetuum (1978). Silbury Air (1977). Secret Theatre (1984). **London Sinfonietta/Elgar Howarth.** Etcetera KTC1052.

58' DDD 4/88

Birtwistle is only 'difficult' if you are convinced in advance that he is going to be, or if you have read somewhere about the obscure numerical techniques that he uses to help him compose. Forget them: they're his concern, not the listener's; you don't get to understand Bach by reading textbooks on counterpoint. Jump straight in, with ears and mind open, and the sheer exhilaration of his music, its alluringly strange patterns and textures, its suggestions of mysterious ritual, above all the unmistakable sense of a composer in total control of a rich and resourceful language, will soon draw you in. The fact that it cannot be wholly comprehended at a single hearing is no drawback, but a positive bonus: this is music that changes each time you hear it, as a landscape changes when you explore different paths through it. The performances throughout are vividly virtuosic and the recording has tremendous impact.

Birtwistle. Endless Parade[a].
Blake Watkins. Trumpet Concerto.
Maxwell Davies. Trumpet Concerto. **Håkan Hardenberger** (tpt); [a]**Paul Patrick** (vib); **BBC Philharmonic Orchestra/Elgar Howarth.** Philips 432 075-2PH.

79' DDD 6/91

This is very much Håkan Hardenberger's record. The balance places him firmly in front of the orchestra, and his style of playing—bright in tone, often with a strong vibrato—underlines his dominance. Fortunately he has the technical skill and expressive flexibility to stand up to the spotlight, and the result (which also owes much to the unobtrusive excellence of Elgar Howarth and the BBC Philharmonic) is imposing and enthralling. You are left in no doubt that contemporary trumpet writing has much more to offer than varieties of fanfare at one extreme and sentimental brass-band melody at the other. Sir Peter Maxwell Davies and Michael Blake Watkins each in their very different ways devise large-scale symphonic structures in order to give the soloist the widest perspectives within which to place his often dazzlingly florid thematic lines. The trumpet virtuoso today needs to be able to shape and project phrases which might tax a flautist or a clarinettist, and Hardenberger does so with staggering consistency. Sir Harrison Birtwistle's *Endless Parade* is perhaps the most exhilarating of all, less lyric in style than the two concertos but supremely assured as drama, now abrasively comic, now sinisterly serious. It crowns a disc that would be memorable without it.

Birtwistle. PUNCH AND JUDY. **Stephen Roberts** (bar) Punch; **Jan DeGaetani** (mez) Judy, Fortune-teller; **Phyllis Bryn-Julson** (sop) Pretty Polly, Witch; **Philip Langridge** (ten) Lawyer; **David Wilson-Johnson** (bar) Choregos, Jack Ketch; **John Tomlinson** (bass) Doctor; **London Sinfonietta/David Atherton.** Etcetera KTC2014. Notes and text included. From Decca Headline HEAD24/5 (9/80).

② 1h 43' ADD 12/89

In *Punch and Judy* Sir Harrison Birtwistle and his inspired librettist Stephen Pruslin succeeded in giving characters normally presented as simple caricatures an almost mythic power and substance. As opera *Punch and Judy* may owe more to such Stravinskian fables as *Renard* than to the great lyric tragedies of the Monteverdi/Wagner tradition, yet even in *Punch and Judy* the music is most memorable in moments of reflection—sinister, poignant, or both. Though different performers have presented the work brilliantly in the theatre since this recording was made, it is hard to imagine a more effective account of the opera on disc. The singers are expert and well contrasted, with none of the ranting and approximation that this kind of expressionistic vocal writing often elicits. Moreover, the London Sinfonietta are at their most responsive, as well they might be given the outstandingly musical direction of David Atherton, who conducted the opera's première at Aldeburgh in 1968. The analogue recording may sound a trifle shallow by the latest standards, but it leaves you in no doubt as to the brilliance and resourcefulness of Birtwistle's vocal and instrumental design.

Georges Bizet

French 1838-1875

Bizet. Symphony in C major[a]. L'Arlésienne—Suite No. 1[b]; Suite No. 2 (arr. Guiraud)[b]. [a]**French Radio National Symphony Orchestra, [b]Royal Philharmonic Orchestra/Sir Thomas Beecham.** EMI CDC7 47794-2. Item marked [a] from ASD388 (4/61), [b] ASD252 (2/59).

65' ADD 11/87

Bizet's only symphony was written within the space of a month just after his seventeenth birthday. It is an easy piece to listen to, fairly light-weight and with a hint of the mature composer-to-be in a long and beautiful oboe solo. But it has many conventional, immature features too, and needs special advocacy in performance. Beecham had a genius for making second-rate works seem masterpieces and his recording has tremendous flair, imagination and affection. From the incidental music for *L'Arlésienne* Bizet salvaged four pieces and re-orchestrated them for full orchestra in the form of what we know now as Suite No. 1. After his death Bizet's friend Ernest Guiraud re-scored four more numbers to make up Suite No. 2. The music has a marvellous sense of colour and atmosphere and Bizet's inspired invention reaches great heights of expression. It is difficult to imagine a more inspired, more sympathetic and beautifully played performance, for Beecham makes the music live and breathe in a way that is head and shoulders above any other conductor. The recordings were made in 1959 and 1956 respectively but both sound rich and clear.

Bizet. L'Arlésienne—Suites Nos. 1 and 2. Carmen—Suites Nos. 1 and 2. **Montreal Symphony Orchestra/Charles Dutoit.** Decca 417 839-2DH.

73' DDD 6/88

These four suites draw on Bizet's incidental music to Daudet's play and his most celebrated opera, and in performance they need qualities of subtlety and delicacy as well as an earthy vitality, which they receive here in full measure. The playing of the Montreal Symphony Orchestra under Charles Dutoit is consistently satisfying and there are some impressive contributions from the solo flautists. The recording is vivid and rich yet natural-sounding; only in a few places might one feel that big tuttis with percussion are too resonant. At 73 minutes this CD is generous in quantity as well as quality, and is distinctly impressive as music, performance and sheer sound.

Bizet. Jeux d'enfants.
Ravel. Ma mère l'oye—ballet.
Saint-Saëns. Le carnaval des animaux[a]. [a]**Julian Jacobson, [a]Nigel Hutchinson** (pfs); members of **London Symphony Orchestra/Barry Wordsworth.** Pickwick IMP Classics PCD932.

63' DDD 4/90

These three works make a very attractive programme and as a mid-price issue this CD is desirable indeed. No attempt is made to sensationalize the *Carnival of the Animals*, which is played with just ten instrumentalists as the composer intended, but there is plenty of wit and brilliance from the pianists Julian Jacobson and Nigel Hutchinson, not only in their charmingly droll own number (No. 11) which relegates them firmly to the animal kingdom but also in the work as a whole. The violinists' donkeys (No. 8) are no less amusing, and the cello 'swan' in No. 13 is serenely touching, but all the players are good and the finale is rightly uproarious. Barry Wordsworth's sense of style in this French repertory is no less evident in the Bizet *Children's Games* and Ravel's *Mother Goose*, which in the latter case is the entire score of the ballet and not just the more familiar suite taken from it. We may single out such pleasures as the gently stated and lovingly shaped "Berceuse" and "Petit mari, petite femme" in the Bizet, but all is charmingly done and then in the Ravel we are transported at once into a child's fairyland of infinite delicacy, wit and tenderness which is crowned unforgettably by the inspired final number, *The Fairy Garden*. A special word of praise to the LSO's oboists, so important in Ravel's score. EMI's Studio No. 1 in Abbey Road provides a beautifully atmospheric recording, close but not glaring.

Bizet. CARMEN. **Julia Migenes** (mez) Carmen; **Plácido Domingo** (ten) Don José; **Faith Esham** (sop) Micaëla; **Ruggero Raimondi** (bass) Escamillo; **Lilian Watson** (sop) Frasquita; **Susan Daniel** (mez) Mercédès; **Jean-Philippe Lafont** (bar) Dancairo; **Gérard Garino** (ten) Remendado; **François Le Roux** (bar) Moralès; **John Paul Bogart** (bass) Zuniga; **French Radio Chorus; French Radio Children's Chorus; French National Orchestra/ Lorin Maazel.** Erato 2292-45207-2. Notes, text and translation included. From NUM75113 (3/84).

③ 2h 31' DDD 9/85

Bizet. CARMEN. **Victoria de los Angeles** (sop) Carmen; **Nicolai Gedda** (ten) Don José; **Janine Micheau** (sop) Micaëla; **Ernest Blanc** (bar) Escamillo; **Denise Monteil** (sop) Frasquita; **Marcelle Croisier, Monique Linval** (sops) Mercédès; **Jean-Christophe Benoit** (bar) Dancairo; **Michel Hamel** (ten) Remendado; **Bernard Plantey** (bar) Moralès; **Xavier Depraz** (bass) Zuniga; **Les Petits Chanteurs de Versailles; French National Radio Chorus and Orchestra/Sir Thomas Beecham.** EMI CDS7 49240-2. Notes, text and translation included. From ASD331/3 (5/60).

③ 2h 41' ADD 6/88

With some justification, *Carmen* is reckoned to be the world's most popular opera. Its score is irresistible, its dramatic realism riveting, its sense of *milieu* unerring, though it has to be remembered that the work was not an immediate triumph. Too many recordings have blown up the work to proportions beyond its author's intentions but here Maazel adopts a brisk, light-weight approach that seems to come close to what Bizet wanted. Similarly Julia Migenes approaches the title part in an immediate, vivid way, exuding the gipsy's allure in a performance that suggests Carmen's fierce temper and smouldering eroticism, and she develops the character intelligently into the fatalistic person of the card scene and finale. Her singing isn't conventionally smooth but it is compelling from start to finish. Plácido Domingo has made the part of Don José very much his own, and here he sings with unstinting involvement and a good deal of finesse. Ruggero Raimondi is a macho Toreador though Faith Esham is a somewhat pallid Micaëla.

While the Maazel set remains a strong recommendation, Beecham's 32-year-old reading remains supreme in many respects. It has a peculiar individuality and style all its own and a degree of elegance in the conducting that seems a lost quality today. Beecham's feeling for the wit and charm of Bizet's miraculous score doesn't preclude his understanding of the tragic passion of the last two acts. If De Los Angeles is not quite as immediately alluring or earthy as Migenes, she manages to capture almost every facet of the complex and difficult role. Gedda turned in one of his most persuasive and musical performances as José, one full of good singing wanting only Domingo's dark, doomed intensity. Blanc is an idiomatic, powerful Escamillo, Micheau a stylish if somewhat dry-toned Micaëla. The supporting cast, chorus and orchestra are all authentically French. The recording is a bit restricted in range by modern standards, but has a perfect balance between voice and orchestra.

Bizet. LES PECHEURS DE PERLES. **Barbara Hendricks** (sop) Leila; **John Aler** (ten) Nadir; **Gino Quilico** (bar) Zurga; **Jean-Philippe Courtis** (bass) Nourabad; **Chorus and Orchestra of the Capitole, Toulouse / Michel Plasson.** EMI CDS7 49837-2. Notes, text and translation included.

② 12h 7' DDD 1/90

Let a tenor and a baritone signify that they are willing to oblige with a duet, and the cry will go up for *The Pearl Fishers*. It's highly unlikely that many of the company present will know what the duet is about—it recalls the past,

Barbara Hendricks   *[photo: EMI/Isserman]*

proclaims eternal friendship and nearly ends up in a quarrel—but the melody and the sound of two fine voices blending in its harmonies will be quite sufficient. In fact there is much more to the opera than the duet, or even than the three or four solos which are sometimes sung in isolation; and this recording goes further than previous versions in giving a complete account of a score remarkable for its unity as well as for the attractiveness of individual numbers. It is a lyrical opera, and the voices need to be young and graceful. Barbara Hendricks and John Aler certainly fulfil those requirements, she with a light, silvery timbre, he with a high tenor admirably suited to the tessitura of his solos. The third main character, the baritone whose role is central to the drama, assumes his rightful place here: Gino Quilico brings genuine distinction to the part, and his aria in Act 3 is one of the highlights. Though Plasson's direction at first is rather square, the performance grows in responsiveness act by act. It is a pity that the accompanying notes are not stronger in textual detail, for the full score given here stimulates interest in its history. One of the changes made in the original score of 1863 concerns the celebrated duet itself, the first version of which is given in an appendix. It ends in a style that one would swear owed much to the 'friendship' duet in Verdi's *Don Carlos*—except that Bizet came first.

Michael Blake Watkins   *Refer to Index*   British 1948

Arthur Bliss

Bliss. Piano Concerto, Op. 58[a]. March, Op. 99, "Homage to a Great Man". [a]**Philip Fowke** (pf); **Royal Liverpool Philharmonic Orchestra/David Atherton.** Unicorn-Kanchana Souvenir UKCD2029. From DKP9006 (9/81).

44' DDD 8/90

Bliss's Piano Concerto, written for the New York World Fair in 1939, is a deliberate essay in the grand manner, full of big, rhetorical gestures and opulent Rachmaninovian melodies. This performance does it full justice in a recording that has transferred well from LP, though some may find the sound rather unreverberant in places. Bliss was half-American and the music seems to reflect also the exuberance of the United States. It is romantic music in the best sense, not only in its richness of orchestration and the Lisztian virtuosity of the solo part, commandingly played by Philip Fowke—listen to the double octaves at the start—but in the sheer beauty of the meditative quieter passages, as when flute and oboe accompany the soloist's musings in the recapitulation section of the first movement. The *March of Homage* is a reminder of how splendidly Bliss fulfilled the role of Master of the Queen's Music. The homage is to Churchill and the work was broadcast just before the great man's funeral in 1965. In a short time, it goes to the heart of the matter. David Atherton and the RLPO are completely at home in these two fine works.

Bliss. Checkmate—suite.
Lambert. Horoscope—suite.
Walton. Façade—Suites Nos. 1 and 2. **English Northern Philharmonia/ David Lloyd-Jones.** Hyperion CDA66436.

74' DDD 3/91

A programme devoted to British ballet music may raise eyebrows—is there any? Yes, not least because ballet played an important part in the London theatre in the first half of this century: Beecham and Boult conducted in London for Diaghilev's *Ballets Russes*, while Lambert was for many years the Musical Director of the Vic-Wells Ballet, one of several fine native companies. Not surprisingly, the three works represented here all owe something to the example of Stravinsky, not least in their rhythmic verve and colourful instrumentation, but each has individuality too and it is good to have the fine ballet scores by Bliss and Lambert, for these composers are too neglected. Of course, Walton's splendidly witty *Façade* was not written as a ballet, but it works admirably as such. It was Lambert who conducted the première in 1931 of Frederick Ashton's stage version; and seven years later, with the same choreographer, came that of his own *Horoscope*, a love story in which the female lead was created by Margot Fonteyn. This is music that bubbles over with vivacity, good tunes and in places (such as the finale) real romantic warmth. Bliss's *Checkmate* was inspired by the game of chess and turns the stage into a chessboard (thus anticipating Tim Rice's musical), but here, too, one of the characters represents Love and the music, though forceful, also has a romantic element. All three of these scores are played with real flair by a conductor and orchestra that have specialized in British music, and the recording has clarity and atmosphere. The booklet essay by Christopher Palmer is both informative and stylish.

Ernest Bloch   *Refer to Index*

John Blow

British bapt. 1649-1708

Blow. VENUS AND ADONIS. **Nancy Argenta** (sop) Cupid; **Lynne Dawson** (sop) Venus; **Stephen Varcoe** (bar) Adonis; **Emily Van Evera** (sop) Shepherdess; **John Mark Ainsley, Charles Daniel** (tens), **Gordon Jones** (bass) Shepherds; **Rogers Covey-Crump** (ten) Huntsman; **Chorus; London Baroque/Charles Medlam.** Harmonia Mundi HMC90 1276. Notes and text included.

50' DDD 9/88

This is seventeenth-century court entertainment with nothing lacking in its charm and elegance. We know that Blow's mini opera was first performed in Oxford in 1681, with Moll Davies, the mistress of Charles II in the role of Venus. Her nine-year-old daughter, Lady Mary Tudor, must have been a particularly gifted child to have been able to sing and act the part of Cupid, and we can well imagine the delight of the court at such scenes as the spelling lesson with the infant Cupids. As for us, we can enjoy the accomplished performance of an expert cast, with the sprightliness of Nancy Argenta as Cupid matched only by the gently dramatic flexibility of Lynne Dawson and Stephen Varcoe in the title roles. Even the members of the chorus and those with lesser parts have all been hand-picked, and London Baroque are in their element. Yet nothing is exaggerated or overdone. What is outstanding in this performance is the fact that although we have sound alone, it is so cleverly recorded that we have the delightful illusion that the opera is actually taking place before our very eyes.

Luigi Boccherini

Italian 1743-1805

Boccherini. Symphonies—D minor, Op. 12 No. 4, G506, "La casa del Diavolo"; A major, Op. 12 No. 6, G508; A major, Op. 21 No. 6, G498. **London Festival Orchestra/Ross Pople.** Hyperion CDA66236.

54' DDD 9/87

Boccherini may not have been the most purposeful of composers of his time, but he was certainly one of the most endearing. Not for him the sturdy, strongly argued symphonic structures of a Haydn, in which each note has its place and its meaning, but rather pieces, coloured by the relaxed and sunny south, that indulge in graceful lines and tellingly manipulated detail. Boccherini loved playing with textures and producing sounds that are pleasurable in themselves; he also liked experimenting with musical forms, and one of the three symphonies here has as its finale just a slow introduction followed by a replay of part of the first movement. The symphony here from Op. 21 is a slight piece, with playful themes in its first movement, a refined little *Andantino* to follow and a cheerful minuet. The other two are on a larger scale, with quite expansive opening movements and in one case a wistful minor-key *Larghetto*, the other a charming minor-key gavotte, to follow. The D minor symphony ends with a reworking of the movement we know as the "Dance of the Furies" from Gluck's *Orphée*. The spirit of the music is happily captured in these performances even though modern instruments are used. The articulation is delightfully clear, light and rhythmic, and the tempos are lively; clearly Ross Pople has a sympathetic feeling for Boccherini.

Boccherini. CELLO CONCERTOS. **David Geringas** (vc); **Orchestra da Camera di Padova e del Veneto/Bruno Giuranna.** Claves CD50-8814/16. No. 1 in E flat major, G474; No. 2 in A major, G475; No. 3 in D major, G476; No. 4 in C major, G477; No. 5 in D major, G478; No. 6 in D major, G479; No. 7 in G major, G480; No. 8 in C major, G481; No. 9 in B flat major; No. 10 in D major, G483; No. 11 in G major, G573; No. 12 in E flat major.

③ 3h 24' DDD 7/89

"Boccherini: 12 Concerti per il Violoncello" proclaims the cover, a little ambitiously, perhaps—for Boccherini probably didn't compose that many. David Geringas has had to exercise a little ingenuity to reach this figure (two of the concertos are almost certainly spurious), but it was probably worth the effort, and the set is a thoroughly enjoyable one in its undemanding way. His intonation is virtually perfect, even high up on the A string, his passage-work is clean, his rhythms are crisp, and he produces (not using a period instrument) a light but pleasingly resonant tone. Listen in particular to the slow movements (such as those of G477 or G483) for eloquence and neatly timed detail. Geringas provides his own cadenzas, including one that quotes Mozart. A very pleasing release. The recording quality and balance are exemplary.

Boccherini. Guitar Quintets—No. 3 in B flat, G447; No. 9 in C major, G453, "La ritirata di Madrid". **Pepe Romero** (gtr); **Academy of St Martin in the Fields Chamber Ensemble** (Iona Brown, Malcolm Latchem, vns; Stephen Shingles, va; Denis Vigay, vc). Philips Musica da Camera 426 092-2PC. From 9500 789 (10/81).

51' ADD 6/90

Boccherini was asked by his friend and patron, the Marquis of Benavente, for some chamber music in which he, a guitarist of now-unknown ability—as was Boccherini, might take part. He responded by adapting a number of his existing works (mostly piano quintets) as guitar quintets, of which eight are known; in his catalogue of Boccherini's works Gérard assigns the numbers G445-53 to these works, but G452 represents four 'lost' quintets—which explains why one of eight is labelled No. 9. The Quintet G447 is based on the Piano Quintet, Op. 57/2, but G453 is of mixed parentage: the first three movements are derived from the Piano Quintet, Op. 56/3, but the fourth is adapted from a String Quintet (Op. 30/6), *La musica notturna delle strade di Madrid*. In this last, a military parade (in the form of a theme and 12 variations) approaches, passes and disappears into the distance via dynamic 'hairpins'. The original forms of these works, long on charm, grace and refined craftsmanship, are now rarely heard, but their survival as guitar quintets is fully justified in superb (and superbly recorded) performances such as those in this recording.

Alexander Borodin

Russian 1833-1887

Borodin. Symphony No. 2 in B minor. In the Steppes of Central Asia. Prince Igor—Overture; March; Dance of the Polovtsian Maidens; Polovtsian Dances. **John Alldis Choir; National Philharmonic Orchestra/Louis Tjeknavorian.** RCA Victor Silver Seal VD60535. From RL25098 (8/77).

64' ADD 8/77

A nicely turned, sumptuously recorded concert comprising Borodin's most
popular symphony in harness with the familiar orchestral items from his only

opera, *Prince Igor*. Tjeknavorian revels in the Symphony's frequent dramatic
outburst and opulent tunes (sampling the first movement should convince
anyone), while the hand-picked National Philharmonic—well known for their
virtuoso performances of classic film scores under this disc's producer, Charles
Gerhardt—is enthusiastically assisted by the John Alldis Choir in the March and
Dances from *Prince Igor*. Add a warmly played account of the appealing *In the
Steppes of Central Asia* and you have a most attractive selection, expertly
transferred from fine-sounding tapes. One hopes that it will soon be joined by
the remaining two symphonies in Tjeknavorian's Borodin cycle.

Borodin. String Quartets—No. 1 in A major; No. 2 in D major. **Borodin
Quartet** (Mikhail Kopelman, Andrei Abramenkov, vns; Dmitri Shebalin, va;
Valentin Berlinsky, vc). EMI CDC7 47795-2. From EMI Melodiya ASD4100 (3/
82).

66' DDD 5/88

These quartets are delightful music, and they are played here by the aptly-named
Borodin Quartet with a conviction and authority that in no way inhibits panache,
spontaneity and sheer charm. Doubtless the most popular music of Borodin and
the other members of the Russian 'Five' will always be their colourful orchestral
and stage music, but no CD collector should ignore these chamber works. Their
style derives from a mid-nineteenth-century Russian tradition of spending happy
hours in music-making at home and also from the refreshing musical springs of
folk-song. This performance offers not only first-rate playing from artists who
'have the music in their blood' but also a warm and convincing recorded sound.

Borodin. String Quartet No. 2 in D major[a].
Shostakovich. String Quartet No. 8 in C minor, Op. 110[a].
Tchaikovsky. String Quartet No. 1 in D major, Op.11[b]. [a]**Borodin Quartet**
(Rostislav Dubinsky, Jaroslav Alexandrov, vns; Dmitri Shebalin, va; Valentin
Berlinsky, vc); [b]**Gabrieli Quartet** (Kenneth Sillito, Brendan O'Reilly, vns; Ian
Jewel, va; Keith Harvey, vc). Decca 425 541-2DM. Items marked [a] from
SXL6036 (2/63), [b] SDD524/5 (10/77).

76' ADD 5/90

The programme adopted here deserves wide emulation: take the contents of a
highly reissue-worthy LP and hunt for something appropriate to supplement it.
The Borodin Quartet's affection for the composer after whom they named
themselves was evidently still warmly fresh when this performance was recorded.

The Borodin String Quartet [photo: Virgin Classics/Wood

The quiet charm of the piece (it was
fondly dedicated to Borodin's wife)
comes over beautifully. They are
Shostakovich specialists, too, and their
account of his most famous quartet is
one of the noblest and most vehement
it has ever received: superbly virtuoso
and hair-raisingly expressive. But
what should preface these two
performances? An English quartet in
Tchaikovsky might not seem the
obvious choice, but it works very
well, with the Gabrieli showing a fine
responsiveness to the work's singing
qualities and its refined colour, even

in passages which can seem as though Tchaikovsky would just as soon have been writing for string orchestra. They (recorded in 1976) receive a rather closer recorded sound than the Borodin (whose performances date from 1962) but all three still sound very well.

Borodin. PRINCE IGOR. **Boris Martinovich** (bar) Igor; **Nicolai Ghiuselev** (bass) Galitsky; **Nicolai Ghiaurov** (bass) Konchak; **Kaludi Kaludov** (ten) Vladimir; **Angel Petkov** (ten) Eroshka; **Stoil Georgiev** (bass) Skula; **Mincho Popov** (ten) Ovlur; **Stefka Evstatiev** (sop) Yaroslavna; **Alexandrina Milcheva** (contr) Konchakovna; **Elena Stoyanova** (sop) Nurse, Polovtsian Girl; **Sofia National Opera Chorus; Sofia Festival Orchestra/Emil Tchakarov.** Sony Classical CD44878. Notes, text and translation included.

③ 3h 30' DDD 6/90

Borodin's principal occupation as Professor of Chemistry often left him with little time to devote to composition, with the result that many of his compositions would often take years to complete. *Prince Igor* was no exception; even after 18 years of work it remained unfinished at his death in 1887, and it was finally completed by Rimsky-Korsakov and Glazunov. Borodin's main problem with *Prince Igor* was the daunting task of turning what was principally an undramatic subject into a convincing stage work. In many ways he never really succeeded in this and the end result comes over more as a series of epic scenes rather than a musical drama. Despite this, however, one is nevertheless left with an impression of a rounded whole, and it contains some of Borodin's most poignant and moving music, rich in oriental imagery and full of vitality. Tchakarov conducts a performance that is both vigorous and refined, and there are some excellent performances from the principal singers too—Boris Martinovich makes a particularly strong Igor and Nicolai Ghiuselev and Nicolai Ghiaurov in the roles of Prince Galitsky and the Polovtsian Khan Konchak deserve special mention also. This Sony issue is a particularly welcome addition to the catalogue as it represents the only *complete* version of the opera on disc.

Pierre Boulez

French 1925-

Boulez. Pli selon pli. **Phyllis Bryn-Julson** (sop); **BBC Symphony Orchestra/Pierre Boulez.** Erato 2292-45376-2. From NUM75050 (5/83).

68' DDD 3/89

Pli selon pli (1957-62) is one of the great pillars of post-war musical modernism. If that proclamation merely makes it sound forbidding, then it could scarcely be less appropriate. 'Pillar' it may be, but as exciting in its moment-to-moment shifts of colour and contour, and as compelling in its command of large-scale dramatic design as anything composed since the great years of Schoenberg and Stravinsky. Easy, no: enthralling and rewarding—yes. This is no grand, single-minded work in the great Germanic symphonic tradition, but a sequence of distinct yet balanced responses to aspects of the great symbolist poet Mallarmé. In this his second recording of the piece Boulez is prepared to let the music expand and resonate, the two large orchestral tapestries enclosing three "Improvisations", smaller-scale vocal movements in which the authority and expressiveness of Phyllis Bryn-Julson is heard to great advantage. The sound is brilliantly wide-ranging and well-balanced, and while the contrast between delicacy and almost delirious density embodied in *Pli selon pli* does take some getting used to, to miss it is to miss one of modern music's most original masterworks.

Boulez. Rituel (1974-75). Messagesquisse (1976). Notations 1-4 (1978). **Orchestre de Paris/Daniel Barenboim.** Erato 2292-45493-2.

41' DDD 10/90

Obviously enough, this disc wins no prizes for length. It is nevertheless important in several significant respects. Only rarely do we have the chance to hear Boulez's music, not only under a conductor other than the composer, but a conductor whose whole artistic background is so different to Boulez's own. Barenboim clearly has his own point of view, and the technical skill to realize it convincingly with a first-class French orchestra. Boulez himself now tends to underline the public ceremonial of *Rituel* (a tribute to the Italian composer and conductor Bruno Maderna), whereas Barenboim, restraining the cumulative clangour of the music's dialogues between the implacable reiterations of gongs and tamtams and the seven other instrumental groups, preserves more of the intimacy of personal regret and loss. *Rituel* is unusual for Boulez in the clear-cut logic of its gradually evolving form, and Barenboim does well to convey that logic without making the whole design seem too predictable for its own good. He is equally attentive to the need to balance striking details with a feeling for overall shape in the shorter but no less personal structures of *Notations* and *Messagesquisse*. The recording is outstanding in its spaciousness and tonal range.

William Boyce

British 1711-1779

Boyce. SYMPHONIES. **The English Concert/Trevor Pinnock** (hpd). Archiv Produktion 419 631-2AH.
No. 1 in B flat major; No. 2 in A major; No. 3 in C major; No. 4 in F major; No. 5 in D major; No. 6 in F major; No. 7 in B flat major; No. 8 in D minor.

60' DDD 9/87

Boyce's *Eight Symphonys* (to follow his own spelling) were written over a period of some 20 years, as overtures for court odes and theatre pieces; later he collected them for publication and use as concert music. They are typically English, in a variety of ways: their tunefulness, their eccentricities of melody and rhythm, their refusal to obey any of the rules about style. And if you think, on hearing the trumpets and drums of No. 5, that Boyce is giving way to Handel's influence (it's very like the *Fireworks Music*), pause a moment: this piece dates from 1739, ten years earlier than the Handel work. The freshness and the vivacity of Boyce's invention are beautifully caught in these performances by Trevor Pinnock and The English Concert, with their sure feeling for tempo, their sprightly dance rhythms, and indeed their understanding of the gentle vein of melancholy.

Boyce. Solomon—a serenata. **Bronwen Mills** (sop) She; **Howard Crook** (ten) He; **The Parley of Instruments/Roy Goodman.** Hyperion CDA66378. Text included.

76' DDD 11/90

Boyce's *Solomon* is not a biblical oratorio, like Handel's, but an extremely secular serenata based on *The Song of Solomon*—in short, a celebration of nature and of

Roy Goodman   *[photo: Hyperion/Schillinger*

erotic love. It has just two 'characters', He and She, and most of their music is amorous—all of it gracefully written, some of it unsophisticatedly jolly, some markedly sensual. The most famous number is "Softly arise, O southern breeze!", for tenor with an eloquent bassoon obbligato and throbbing strings. For the most part the listener will be reminded of Handel's *Acis and Galatea*, with its typically pastoral features such as nature imitations (there are trilling birds and Purcellian frosty shivers); no one could fail to be charmed by this appealing, very English work. The singers here, Bronwen Mills and Howard Crook, are both of them good stylists, not perhaps as naturally sensuous in tone or phrasing as they might be but natural and fluent and showing an instinctive feeling for the shape of Boyce's lines, and they give due weight to the words. Roy Goodman conducts expertly with a period-instrument band, and the result is a gently beguiling performance.

Johannes Brahms

German 1833-1897

Brahms. Piano Concerto No. 1 in D minor, Op. 15ᵃ. Intermezzosᵇ—E flat major, Op. 117 No. 1; C major, Op. 119 No. 3. **Sir Clifford Curzon** (pf); ᵃ**London Symphony Orchestra/George Szell.** Decca 417 641-2DH. Item marked ᵃ from SXL6023 (12/62), ᵇ SXL6041 (5/63).

57' ADD 10/87

This is a classic recording of the concerto, one which teamed a supremely civilized pianist with a conductor renowned for ruling with a rod of iron when directing his own orchestra, the Cleveland. In London, the results were quite magical; Szell's approach, while never less than totally authoritative has a warmth and smile to it that was often lacking in the States. Curzon is, quite simply, peerless. With a work like the Brahms First Piano Concerto a total rapport between piano and orchestra is vital simply because there are passages when the soloist must accompany the orchestra quite as much as vice versa. The two solo works are carried off with a beautiful sense of poetry and poise and all in all this is a magnificent achievement, well worth having.

Brahms. Piano Concertosᵃ—Nos. 1 and 2. Fantasias, Op. 116ᵇ. **Emil Gilels** (pf); ᵃ**Berlin Philharmonic Orchestra/Eugen Jochum.** DG 419 158-2GH2. Items marked ᵃ from 2707 064 (12/72), ᵇ2530 655 (7/76).

② 2h 6' ADD 9/86   Ⓑ

Emil Gilels was an ideal Brahms interpreter and his account of the two concertos with Eugen Jochum, another great Brahmsian, is one of the inspired classics of the gramophone. The youthful, leonine First Concerto and the expansive, lyrical Second were both played for the first time by Brahms himself, and it would be difficult to imagine any performances coming closer to the spirit of his music than these. They should not be missed and their value is further enhanced by the addition of the autumnal Fantasias, Op. 116. The recording, too, is natural and has plenty of concert hall ambience and an ideal balance between soloist and orchestra. This set cannot be too strongly recommended.

Brahms. Violin Concerto in D major, Op. 77. **Itzhak Perlman** (vn); **Chicago Symphony Orchestra/Carlo Maria Giulini.** EMI CDC7 47166-2. From ASD3385 (11/77).

♪ 43' ADD 1/87 Ⓑ

Brahms. Violin Concerto in D major, Op. 77. **David Oistrakh** (vn); **French Radio National Orchestra/Otto Klemperer.** EMI Studio CDM7 69034-2. From Columbia SAX2411 (11/61).

♪ 41' ADD 12/89 Ⓑ

Brahms. Violin Concerto in D major, Op. 77.
Mendelssohn. Violin Concerto in E minor, Op. 64. **Xue-Wei** (vn); **London Philharmonic Orchestra/Ivor Bolton.** ASV CDDCA748.

♪ 67' DDD 4/91 Ⓑ

Giulini conducts the opening of this work in a strong and serious fashion, and at a moderate tempo. The unhurried pace indeed seems dangerously slow for the soloist, but then Perlman enters the scene and all is found to be well. His magisterial playing, ardent, powerful, and with magnificent breadth of phrase and tone makes for a very satisfying first movement. The *Adagio* has a good solo oboe from Ray Still; here Perlman's playing is reflective at first and then it becomes more overtly passionate as the movement develops. The last movement's 'gipsy' rondo finale makes an effective contrast, with plenty of sharp attack and rhythmic bite. The late 1970s recording is of good tonal quality and well balanced.

When the earlier EMI recording was made, it was not possible to bring Oistrakh and Klemperer together in London, so the veteran conductor travelled to Paris, and to an unfamiliar orchestra. We are told that the sessions were not without incident and provided a headache or two for the producer Walter Legge. But there is no hint of this in one of the finest versions of the concerto ever recorded for conductor and soloist seem in perfect artistic accord. Oistrakh's account of the first movement is richly communicative and deeply affecting, and in the slow movement his glorious tone quality and eloquent, soaring lyricism suit the music perfectly. The finale is executed in a strong, ruggedly good-humoured fashion and throughout the work the excellent French orchestra play with magnificent strength and commitment under Klemperer's magisterial direction. The recording is attractively spacious and has plenty of tonal lustre.

Congratulations to ASV for finding a much more appropriate coupling for the Mendelssohn than the amiable but decidedly second-rate Bruch G minor Concerto. But the outstanding advantage of this recording is the quality and exceptional freshness of Xue-Wei's playing. His Mendelssohn is that rare kind of performance that makes one hear a very familiar work as though for the first time, and there's a similar sense of discovery in the Brahms. There may be a few rough edges here and there—and the way he pushes forward in the great *Andante* melody of the Mendelssohn might not be to everyone's taste—but in both works what Xue-Wei turns out has the immediacy, urgency and sweep of a live performance. This is very much a young man's performance, and like a lot of young players Xue-Wei can be expansive, but he never loses his feel for the long phrase, and the central climax in the first movement of the Brahms is pulse-quickening stuff. Recommended to enthusiasts and jaded palates alike.

Brahms. Double Concerto in A minor, Op. 102[a]. Piano Quartet No. 3 in C minor, Op. 60[b]. **Isaac Stern** (vn); [b]**Jaime Laredo** (va); **Yo-Yo Ma** (vc); [b]**Emmanuel Ax** (pf); [a]**Chicago Symphony Orchestra/Claudio Abbado.** CBS Masterworks CD42387.

68' DDD 6/88

The grave, declamatory utterances at the beginning of the Double Concerto tell us much about the nature of what will follow. They can also reveal a great deal about the two soloists who enter in turn with solo cadenzas separated by thematic orchestral material. Perhaps surprisingly it is the much younger man,

Yo-Yo Ma, who brings out most strongly the noble gravity of the composer's inspiration, while the relative veteran Isaac Stern is more melodious and spontaneous-sounding. The music's steady but unhurried paragraphs are very well handled by Claudio Abbado and the excellent Chicago Symphony Orchestra is responsive and pretty faithfully balanced with the soloists. This is a performance to satisfy rather than to thrill, perhaps, but satisfy it does. The recording is rich and rather reverberant, notably in orchestral tuttis. The powerful C minor Piano Quartet is also well played and provides a substantial partner to the concerto. Apparently

Claudio Abbado   *[photo: DG/Bayat]*

Brahms once said that it had the mood of a man thinking of suicide, but one hastens to say that it is nothing like as gloomy as that would suggest.

Brahms. Serenades—No. 1 in D major, Op. 11[a]; No. 2 in A major, Op. 16[b]. **London Symphony Orchestra/István Kertész.** Decca Weekend 421 628-2DC. Item marked [a] from SXL6340 (5/68), [b] SXL6368 (2/69).

76' ADD   £

Brahms. Serenades—No. 1 in D major, Op. 11; No. 2 in A major, Op. 16. **Vienna Symphony Orchestra/Gary Bertini.** Orfeo C008101A.

76' ADD 6/90

Brahms's two serenades were his first published works for orchestra alone. He composed his First Serenade as a nonet for flute, two clarinets, horn, bassoon and strings but later rescored it for larger forces as well as expanding it structurally. It has many features which look forward to his mature symphonic works but at the same time it has a lightness of touch reminiscent of the classical serenades of Mozart and Haydn. The Second Serenade uses a much smaller orchestra than the First, and texturally it differs in not using violins at all. The atmosphere is serene, bucolic even, and one is constantly reminded of folk-dances. Kertész's 1967 readings of these two delightful works have long been celebrated. On CD they sound remarkably fresh, and it says much for Decca's engineering that even unremastered they rival some more modern digital recordings in sound-quality. At budget price they are definite bargains.

The main impression one has from the Orfeo performances is of mellow warmth, a cosy German humour and a feeling for the dance, for Gary Bertini takes a pleasantly flexible view of the music and the Vienna Symphony Orchestra follow him well with some particularly attractive woodwind playing. It is good to have both these longish works together on a single disc. The recording is pleasingly rich, though with a touch of edge to the woodwind in the treble register.

Brahms. Hungarian Dances Nos. 1-21—orchestrations. **Vienna Philharmonic Orchestra/Claudio Abbado.** DG 410 615-2GH. From 2560 100 (3/83).
Brahms: Nos. 1, 3 and 10. *Hallén:* No. 2. *Juon:* No. 4. *Schmeling:* Nos. 5 and 6. *Gál:* Nos. 7, 8 and 9. *Parlow:* Nos. 11-16. *Dvořák:* Nos. 17-21.

| 48' DDD 9/84 | Ⓑ |

To play the 21 *Hungarian Dances* through at one sitting is not recommended: far better for the CD user to choose a group of four or five and then just sit back and enjoy some charming and vivacious music, full of good tunes. High spirits predominate in the first set; in the second set there is more a mixture of liveliness and minor key 'gipsy' melancholy, though the introspection never becomes more than skin-deep. Abbado persuades the VPO to play with much brilliance and an engaging rhythmic lift and lightness of touch. These are highly enjoyable performances and the sound-quality emphasizes the nature of the playing, clear and brilliant, if a little lacking in warmth.

Brahms. Symphony No. 1 in C minor, Op. 68. **London Philharmonic Orchestra/Klaus Tennstedt.** EMI Eminence CD-EMX2160. From EL270019-1 (6/84).

| 48' DDD 11/84 |

Brahms. Symphony No. 1 in C minor, Op. 68. Tragic Overture, Op. 81. Academic Festival Overture, Op. 80. **London Philharmonic Orchestra/ Eugen Jochum.** EMI Laser CDZ7 62604-2. From SLS5093 (10/77).

| 69' ADD 12/89 | £ Ⓑ |

Tennstedt's is a sturdy, measured account of the symphony, though by no means lacking in drama or expressive conviction. He keeps the music continually on the move and his shapely phrasing and sensitive rubato prevent it from sounding four-square. Brahms's orchestration can sound stodgy and bottom-heavy, but Tennstedt makes sure that each detail emerges clearly while keeping a close watch on internal balance. Some fine playing from the London Philharmonic Orchestra adds to the attractiveness of this disc: the strings respond enthusiastically to Brahms's sweeping melodic lines, and the woodwind are especially eloquent in the *Adagio*. Balance, presence and dynamic range are well judged and although the treble has a slightly grainy quality, the overall sound-quality is pleasing.

Jochum's 1976 recordings still retain all of their character in digital transfer. He draws from the LPO the depth and richness of timbre that Brahms needs without allowing the sound to lose its solidity and transparency, and this is conveyed with an agreeable spaciousness and warmth. Jochum's is not the most immediately arresting reading of the First Symphony in the catalogue: he eschews overpowering drama at the opening and refrains from driving the music relentlessly on; nor does he linger over the great theme of the final movement. His view is exceptionally long term and, like the finest claret, this is a reading primed for a greatness that will develop with age and further acquaintance. By contrast, the *Academic Festival* Overture is treated to all the zest it deserves, with Jochum retaining a sense of proportion in its most boisterous passages, and the

Tragic Overture proves the ideal foil to the finale of the First Symphony, which precedes it. Altogether a disc well worth exploring.

Brahms. Symphony No. 2 in D major, Op. 73.
Schubert. Symphony No. 8 in B minor, D759, "Unfinished". **Philharmonia Orchestra/Herbert von Karajan.** EMI Studio CDM7 69227-2. From SXLP30513 (5/81).

64' ADD 4/88

Brahms. Symphony No. 2 in D major, Op. 73. Tragic Overture, Op. 81.
Chicago Symphony Orchestra/Sir Georg Solti. Decca 414 487-2DH. From SXL6925 (9/79).

59' ADD 8/85

After the seriousness of the First Symphony, Brahms was able to relax in the Second and, whilst still maintaining close control of the thematic unity of the work, could allow the most genial, open-air aspects of his style full vent. The glorious opening horn calls of the first movement and the bucolic woodwind ensemble of the third attest to this feeling and although the moving slow movement sets a more serious note, the finale finds Brahms at his most rumbustious.

Karajan was in high spirits for this 1955 performance, revelling in the zest of the Philharmonia. The coupled performance of Schubert's No. 8 echoes the warmth of tone this orchestra summons for the Brahms, and Karajan astutely balances the romantic tunefulness of this work with its underlying vein of melancholy. This early example of stereo recording beautifully illustrates just how well skill and imagination can overcome limited technical resources. It is a delight to hear such clear, straightforward presentation of orchestral sound.

Solti's Brahms is tough, purposeful and uncompromising and the basic pulse of each movement is quickly established and single-mindedly maintained throughout. This does not mean, however, that Solti is ungenerous or unyielding—there is plenty of warmth and intensity in the *Adagio* of the symphony, and the solo playing is often very beautiful—but overall one senses that he is perhaps more concerned to acknowledge Brahms's debt to Beethoven than to Schubert or Schumann. This impression is strongest in the outer movements, which in this performance are unusually urgent and exhilarating. The recording is clear and immediate, though never too close for comfortable listening.

Brahms. Symphony No. 3 in F major, Op. 90. Tragic Overture, Op. 81. Schicksalslied, Op. 54[a]. [a]**Ernst-Senff Choir; Berlin Philharmonic Orchestra/Claudio Abbado.** DG 429 765-2GH.

68' DDD 1/91

Brahms. Symphony No. 3 in F major, Op. 90[a]. Variations on a Theme by Haydn, "St Antoni"[b]. **Columbia Symphony Orchestra/Bruno Walter.** CBS Masterworks CD42531. From CD42022 (9/86). Item marked [a] from M3P 39631 (7/85), [b] Philips SABL185 (2/61).

52' ADD 9/86

The DG disc is gloriously programmed for straight-through listening. Abbado gets off to a cracking start with an urgently impassioned *Tragic Overture* in which the credentials of the Berlin Philharmonic to make a richly idiomatic, Brahmsian sound—already well accepted—are substantially reaffirmed. A wide-eyed, breathtaking account of the *Schicksalslied* ("Song of Destiny") follows to provide sound contrast before the wonders of the Third Symphony are freshly explored.

This is a reading of the Symphony to be savoured; it is underpinned throughout by a rhythmic vitality which binds the four movements together with a forward thrust, making the end inevitable right from the opening bars. Even in the moments of repose and, especially, the warmly-felt *Andante*, Abbado never lets the music forget its ultimate goal. Despite this, there are many moments of wonderful solo and orchestral playing along the way in which there is time to delight, and Abbado seems to bring out that affable, Bohemian-woods, Dvořák-like element in Brahms's music to a peculiar degree in this performance. The Symphony is recorded with a particular richness and some may find the heady waltz of the third movement done too lushly, emphasized by Abbado's lingering tempo. Nevertheless, this is splendid stuff, and not to be missed.

The engineers have done a grand job in revitalizing Walter's 1960 recordings, but even they cannot totally disguise moments of overloading and touches of thin stridency. Forget the sound, then, and listen to the performances and it soon becomes apparent why this disc can still be recommended. Bruno Walter, just a couple of years before his death, still exuded more energy and vitality than many a conductor many years his junior, and he had all that wealth of experience behind him. The Brahms symphonies were old friends and the warmth of that relationship effuses from every note of this performance. There are only a couple of performances that really seem to get to grips with the Third Symphony's meaning and this is one of them. There is control here, yet above all the orchestra sounds as though it has been allowed its head—it can rely on Walter to shape the larger paragraphs but, given a luscious melody or fruity harmonies, it need not fear restraint. The *Variations* are kept more under rein, yet even here the result is still remarkably vital. This disc is a testament to a great conductor.

Brahms. Symphony No. 4 in E minor, Op. 98. **Vienna Philharmonic Orchestra/Carlos Kleiber.** DG 400 037-2GH. From 2532 003 (4/81).

| 39' DDD 9/85 | Ⓑ |

Brahms. Symphony No. 4 in E minor, Op. 98[a].
Liszt. Les préludes, S97[b]. **Philharmonia Orchestra/Herbert von Karajan.** EMI Studio CDM7 69228-2. Item marked [a] from SXLP30505 (5/81), [b] SXLP30450 (2/81).

| 56' ADD 4/88 | Ⓑ |

Kleiber's reading of Brahms's Fourth Symphony is highly individual and thought-provoking but those listeners who know Kleiber from his thrilling recordings of Beethoven's Fifth and Seventh Symphonies and are expecting similarly uncompromising, high-tension performances with enormous muscular energy are in for a surprise! His reading certainly has plenty of muscle, but he shows considerable patience and generosity in his handling of Brahms's long, constantly developing melodic lines. Sound is generally good, though the bass may need assistance on some equipment.

Karajan's is also a fine performance. Tempos are by and large fairly measured and the phrasing has a good deal of breadth, so that one is made very aware of the work's structure and its cumulative development towards the climax of the finale. But although the outline of the performance is objective and unhurried there is, too, a marked sense of momentum and line, with detail not at all neglected. The Philharmonia play with much personality and spirit, and the woodwind section is a particular joy to hear; the sound is so clear, spacious and beautifully warm that nobody would guess that it dates from May 1955, when EMI had only just started to record in stereo. *Les préludes* was recorded in 1958 and has excellent sound too. Karajan's conducting banishes any sense of vulgarity from the work and he gives the score a certain nobility and strength not often found in other performances.

Brahms. String Sextets—No. 1 in B flat major, Op. 18; No. 2 in G major, Op. 36. **Raphael Ensemble** (James Clarke, Elizabeth Wexler, vns; Sally Beamish, Roger Tapping, vas; Andrea Hess, Rhydian Shaxson, vcs). Hyperion CDA66276.

74' DDD 1/89

Completed after the First Piano Concerto, but still comparatively early works, the Sextets are typified by lush textures, ardent emotion, and wonderfully memorable melodic lines. The first is the warmer, more heart-on-the-sleeve piece, balancing with complete naturalness a splendidly lyrical first movement, an urgent, dark set of intricate variations, a lively rustic dance of a *Scherzo*, and a placidly flowing finale. The Second Sextet inhabits at first a more mysterious world of half-shadows, occasionally rent by glorious moments of sunlight. The finale, however, casts off doubt and ends with affirmation. Both works are very susceptible to differing modes of interpretation, and the Raphael Ensemble has established very distinctive views of each, allowing the richness of the texture its head without obscuring the lines, and selecting characteristically distinct tone qualities to typify the two works. The recording is clear and analytic without robbing the sound of its warmth and depth. Altogether an impressive recording début for this ensemble.

Brahms. Clarinet Quintet in B minor, Op. 115[a].
Mozart. Clarinet Quintet in A major, K581[b]. **Gervase de Peyer** (cl); Members of the **Melos Ensemble** (Emanuel Hurwitz, Ivor McMahon, vns; Cecil Aronowitz, va; Terence Weill, vc). EMI CDM7 63116-2. Item marked [a] from ASD620 (3/65), [b] ASD605 (9/64).

65' ADD 11/89   £ 9p

There can be few who hear the opening to Brahms's Clarinet Quintet who fail to succumb to the main subject's tender and haunting melancholy—surely one of Brahms's most poignant utterances and certainly one guaranteed to send tingles down the spine. Gervase de Peyer's warm, full-bodied tone and liquid playing is a delight to the ear, and the autumnal beauty of the work is captured particularly well in this affectionate and thoughtful performance. Unlike the Mozart Quintet, which treats the clarinet very much as a concertante instrument, Brahms integrates the clarinet into the overall texture, skilfully blending and juxtaposing the characteristic timbre with that of the strings into an homogeneous whole, a quality that comes over exceptionally well in this performance. The Mozart

Quintet makes an ideal contrast to the autumnal glow of the Brahms, and receives an equally fine and engaging performance, if perhaps lacking just that extra bit of magic that makes the Brahms so irresistible. The Melos Ensemble convey the work's geniality and freshness from beginning to end, and the slow movement is imbued with great serenity and beauty. The 1964 recordings have retained a remarkable freshness, and are both naturally balanced and beautifully clear. At mid-price this reissue should not be missed.

Brahms. Piano Quintet in F minor, Op. 34. **Maurizio Pollini** (pf); **Quartetto Italiano** (Paolo Borciani, Elisa Pegreffi, vns; Dino Asciolla, va; Franco Rossi, vc). DG 419 673-2GH. From 2531 197 (9/80).

| 43' AAD 6/87 |

Brahms. Piano Quintet in F minor, Op. 34. **André Previn** (pf); **Musikverein Quartet** (Rainer Küchl, Eckhard Seifert, vns; Peter Götzel, va; Franz Bartolomey, vc). Philips 412 608-2PH. From 412 608-1PH (11/85).

| 41' DDD 1/86 |

Brahms. Piano Quintet in F minor, Op. 34.
Schumann. Piano Quintet in E flat major, Op. 44. **Jenö Jandó** (pf); **Kodály Quartet** (Attila Falvay, Tamás Szabo, vns; Gábor Fias, va; János Devich, vc). Naxos 8 550406.

| 67' DDD 2/91 £ |

This work was originally composed as a string quintet with two cellos. Brahms's influential friend Joseph Joachim then subjected the composition to a good deal of criticism, and Brahms took this to heart so much that he converted the quintet into a sonata for two pianos. As this version also was not well received Brahms turned to another friend, Clara Schumann, and as a result of her advice the work emerged in a third form, for piano quintet. This powerfully argued work gives little indication of its varied origins. The long first movement has a particularly strong yet highly romantic vein of expression, and in their performance Pollini and his colleagues bring out particularly well its stormy, dramatic nature. In the slow movement the performers bring a certain restless, questing quality to Brahms's rich lyricism and the *Scherzo*, perhaps the most inventive movement, is quickly and urgently expressed. The rondo-finale is a very substantial movement in its own right and is given its full weight by the five excellent players. The recording is clear and very immediate.

Previn's high regard for the work is evident in the cogency and eloquence of his playing, and he listens and responds well to the Musikverein Quartet, who match his vision with playing of high concentration. Here is chamber music-making of very satisfying quality. Happily the sound and recorded balance is excellent.

Maybe the Hungarian players on the Naxos disc don't have the refinement of the finest ensembles, and in the second main theme in the first movement of the Schumann the cellist sounds an honest player rather than a Rostropovich, but the feeling is right. The Brahms Quintet, which is the later and bigger work, is also most enjoyable, with the right blend of passion and mystery, and although we may look for a more Schubertian warmth in the slow movement, generally the feeling is right and perhaps only purists will regret that unlike some other ensembles the Hungarians omit the exposition repeat in the first movement, for even so it is still the longest at over 11 minutes although their tempo in no way drags and indeed has the right urgency. The recording is not quite as good as the playing, being a little plummy and reverberant, but it is perfectly serviceable and at this bargain price no collector wanting this coupling need hesitate.

Brahms. Piano Quartets—No. 1 in G minor, Op. 25; No. 2 in A major, Op. 26; No. 3 in C minor, Op. 60. **Isaac Stern** (vn); **Jaime Laredo** (va); **Yo-Yo Ma** (vc); **Emanuel Ax** (pf). Sony Classical CD45846.

| (2) 2h 8' DDD 3/91 |

These three piano quartets belong to the middle of Brahms's life. They have all the power and lyricism that we associate with his music, as well as the fine craftsmanship that he acquired when young and, with the high standards he set himself, demonstrated in every work thereafter. The mood of the music is again Brahmsian in that alongside a wealth of melodic and harmonic invention there are some shadows: all we know of Brahms's life suggests that he was never a happy man. But if this is reflected in the music, and especially the C minor Quartet, we can recognize the strength of intellect and will that keeps all in proportion so that there is no overt soul-bearing. These quartets are big pieces which often employ a grand manner, though less so in No. 2 than the others. For this reason, the present performances with their exuberant sweep are particularly telling, and although no detail is missed the players offer an overall strength. Top soloists in their own right, they combine their individual gifts with the ability to play as a well integrated team. The recording is close but not overwhelmingly so. Only the booklet, with notes in four languages, mars at least some copies of this issue, for it has some blank pages and details of the movements are missing, as are parts of the English and Italian notes.

Brahms. String Quartets—C minor, Op. 51 No. 1; A minor, Op. 51 No. 2. **Takács Quartet** (Gábor Takács-Nagy, Károly Schranz, vns; Gábor Ormai, va; András Fejer, vc). Decca 425 526-2DH.

66' DDD 9/90

Brahms. String Quartets—A minor, Op. 51 No. 2; B flat major, Op. 67. **Orlando Quartet** (John Harding, Heinz Oberdorfer, vns; Ferdinand Erblich, va; Stefan Metz, vc). Ottavo OTRC68819.

75' DDD 6/90

Few composers have ever been more self-critical than Brahms. He is said to have suppressed some 20 string quartets before writing one he deemed worthy of publication, and by then he was 40 years old. The C minor work was quickly followed by a second in A minor in the same year of 1873, and just two years later he produced his third and last in the major key of B flat. As yet, Hungary's Takács Quartet has only recorded the first two. But on the strength of such vivid playing and vibrant reproduction, few collectors are likely to be content until given the third. Though these four artists have now been together long enough to play as one, they are in fact still young enough to bring up every phrase with the immediacy of a new discovery. The two powerfully challenging flanking movements of the C minor work are sustained with splendid strength and drive. Yet how sensitively and subtly they convey the vulnerable heart concealed behind the classical façade in the second subject of the opening *Allegro*, for instance, and again, of course, in the work's two gentler central movements. They at once enter the more lyrical world of the first two movements of the A minor work, with its reminders of the motto themes adopted by both the composer himself and his great friend, the half-Hungarian violinist, Joachim. And how they relish the zest of the Hungarian-spiced finale.

The Orlando Quartet perform the last two quartets with affecting empathy for the music's beauty and radiance, its dramatic power and tender delicacy. These are warm, generous performances which clearly look forward to the autumnal shadows that were later to cross Brahms's music. The out-of-doors vigour of the first movement of Op. 67 may seem tamed because of this but, in the long term, this unusual interpretation makes a convincing case for itself by subduing the contrast between the movements and consequently making the whole work more coherent. In Op. 51 No. 2, one is immediately struck by how well the Orlando's rather slowish speed for the opening *Allegro non troppo* works, providing time for its intricacies to register and its heart-on-the-sleeve emotions to establish themselves. The characterful acoustic of Old-Catholic Church in Delft allows the music to breathe and the work's romantic centre to expand. Altogether, then, the Ottavo disc also substantially pushes forward the cause of these often misunderstood masterworks.

Brahms. PIANO TRIOS. **Beaux Arts Trio** (Isidore Cohen, vn; Bernard Greenhouse, vc; Menahem Pressler, pf). Philips 416 838-2PH2.
No. 1 in B major, Op. 8; No. 2 in C major, Op. 87; No. 3 in C minor, Op. 101; A major, Op. posth. (attrib. Brahms).

② 1h 59' DDD 1/88

The great bonus of this particular recording is the inclusion of the A major posthumous work, discovered among a batch of manuscripts in Bonn at the beginning of this century, and now authenticated as Brahms's own work. The joy of the Beaux Arts performances of all the works is their obvious sense of delight in just that relaxed, intimate sort of music-making which takes time and space enough to sing through the broad river-flow of both opening movements, and to get dug into the contrasting developmental material with great gusto. Their C major Trio shows them getting down to business: they give a real sense of clambering, of the traversal of time in their ebullient working-through of rhythm and key. There are times when they can sound over-busy; but the Trio offer here the affectionate, fallible, but ever-generous powers of communication, recorded in a warm, close acoustic.

Brahms. Piano Trio No. 1 in B major, Op. 8.
Ives. Piano Trio. **Fontenay Trio** (Michael Mücke, vn; Niklas Schmidt, vc; Wolf Harden, pf). Teldec 2292-44924-2.

57' DDD 4/90

This is certainly a very curious coupling, but anybody who is interested in both works need not hesitate, for performances are first-rate. Ives's Piano Trio was written in 1904-05 and revised in 1911. If what we hear is the final 1911 version without any later changes then the work is remarkably forward-looking

Charles Ives   [photo: Koch International/Tyler

for its day. The first *moderato* movement has some intriguing patterns and sonorities and is followed by "TSIAK" (This Scherzo Is A Joke). Then comes a more substantial finale, where Ives's writing becomes more expressive, almost romantic. The Fontenay Trio play the work with obvious dedication, great understanding and high expertise. Their account of the Brahms Trio is also very distinguished. This was the composer's first published chamber work, but revised in his late years. The Fontenays play the first movement with a good deal of strength, but in a generous-spirited fashion, with considerable flexibility of phrase. Their account of the Scherzo has great conviction and they maintain tension and pulse throughout the Adagio. They round off the work with a majestically delivered finale. This outstanding disc is superbly recorded.

Brahms. Piano Trio No. 2 in C major, Op. 87.
Dvořák. Piano Trio No. 1 in B flat major, B51. **Fontenay Trio** (Michael Mücke, vn; Niklas Schmidt, vc; Wolf Harden, pf). Teldec 2292-44177-2

64' DDD 2/90

These two works were written within a few years of each other. In 1875, when Dvořák wrote his Piano Trio No. 1 (he revised it a little later), he was still an emerging talent. Brahms, the older composer by eight years, was very much an established figure when he completed his Second Piano Trio in 1882. The Dvořák work still has a spirit of youthfulness, which is reflected faithfully in the Fontenay Trio's spontaneous-seeming, beautifully poised and generously phrased performance. There is an unhurried, affectionate quality in their playing which is highly attractive and they seem to be enjoying the recording process greatly. In the mature, masterful Brahms work the Fontenay's playing has similar virtues. They project the music with great understanding and a superb sense of style. The tonal quality of the two string players is warm and sonorous and all three artists are technically immaculate. Teldec have crowned this disc with an excellent recording which clearly has taken place in an appropriately small chamber, but one which possesses plenty of resonance.

Brahms. Horn Trio in E flat major, Op. 40[a].
Franck. Violin Sonata in A major. **Itzhak Perlman** (vn); [a]**Barry Tuckwell** (hn); **Vladimir Ashkenazy** (pf). Decca 414 128-2DH. From SXL6408 (5/69).

> 56' AAD 4/85

Anyone who thinks of chamber music as predominantly an intellectual medium should easily be persuaded otherwise by these two mellow works of the late nineteenth century. Brahms is the more classically shaped of the two, while the third movement of the Franck Sonata is a "recitative-fantasia" whose quiet eloquence seems more than a little to foreshadow Debussy. Here, as in the strictly canonic theme of the finale, Franck shows us that even baroque techniques can be turned with no apparent effort to romantic ends. In the Brahms Horn Trio, Perlman and Ashkenazy are joined by another virtuoso in the person of Barry Tuckwell; but it is not their dazzling technical command that we notice so much as their musicianly subtlety. In the rich textures of this work we are reminded of the composer's inspiration by the beauty of the Black Forest and also of his grief at the recent loss of his beloved mother. The combination of these three instruments is rare to say the least, but the engineer has balanced them satisfactorily.

Brahms. Clarinet Sonatas, Op. 120—No. 1 in F minor; No. 2 in E flat major.
Weber. Grand duo concertant, J204. **Paul Meyer** (cl); **François-René Duchable** (pf). Erato 2292-45480-2.

> 66' DDD 9/90

It was the clarinettist Richard Mühlfeld who inspired Brahms to write his clarinet music, a Quintet with strings and these two sonatas, and as in the similar case of Anton Stadler and Mozart, it happened towards the end of his life. Again like Mozart, Brahms displays the richly lyrical aspect of the instrument as well as its force, agility and big compass ranging from tenor to high soprano. Perhaps the generally mellow nature of the writing owes something also to the composer's recognition that he was in the autumn of his life. Paul Meyer and François-René Duchable treat these sonatas lovingly and unhurriedly, and in the first movement of the E flat major they give us all the warmth implied by the composer's marking *amabile*. Although it is the second sonata, this work is played first; but in any case both were written in the same year and the rather more urgent and passionate F minor Sonata follows on naturally. Even here, the two artists take a broad and graceful view of the music, and its essential seriousness and occasional melancholy come across, not least in the eloquent sad tread of the slow movement. Weber's *Grand duo concertant* is quite different, being a melodious and vivacious piece with a strong element of wit and even the theatre about it, and there is a pleasing Gallic panache and elegance to this performance as well as dexterity and fine ensemble. The recording is admirably clear as well as being

faithful to both instruments.

Brahms. Cello Sonatas—No. 1 in E minor, Op. 38; No. 2 in F major, Op. 99. **Steven Isserlis** (vc); **Peter Evans** (pf). Hyperion CDA66159. From A66159 (10/85).

> 50' DDD 4/86

Brahms worked on his Cello Sonata No. 1 over a period of three years, from 1862 to 1865. Originally the work included an *Adagio*, but this was destroyed by the composer before publication, and as a result we have a three-movement sonata consisting of a somewhat dark-hued, questing *Allegro non troppo*, a central *Allegretto quasi menuetto*, which has a slight eighteenth-century pastiche flavour, and a bold, tautly argued *Allegro* finale. The F major Sonata of 1886 is a bigger work in every way. It was one of three chamber works written during a summer stay in Switzerland, and the glorious scenery stimulated Brahms to compose in a warm, open-hearted fashion. Steven Isserlis plays throughout both works with an impressive tone-quality and an immaculate technique. Though his sympathy for the music is everywhere evident, he does lack the last ounce of interpretative insight. But with fine playing from the pianist Peter Evans, and a very good, natural sounding recording, this is a disc which will give much pleasure.

Brahms. Violin Sonatas—No. 1 in G major, Op. 78; No. 2 in A major, Op. 100; No. 3 in D minor, Op. 108. **Josef Suk** (vn); **Julius Katchen** (pf). Decca Ovation 421 092-2DM. From SXL6321 (1/68).

> 68' ADD 5/88   £

Brahms was 45 when he began to work on the first of these Sonatas and he completed the final one some ten years later. These products of his mature genius are certainly the greatest works written in this form since Beethoven's. Though they are lovingly crafted and have a predominant air of lyricism, there is great variety of melody and of mood. The invention always sounds spontaneously conceived and they fit the CD format like a kid glove. Suk's control over nuance is magical whilst Katchen has a complete understanding of the style. In every way these are performances that truly deserve to be labelled as classics and the naturally vivid recorded sound brings them to life with magnificent immediacy.

Brahms. Piano Sonata No. 3 in F sharp minor, Op. 5. **Zoltán Kocsis** (pf). Hungaroton HCD12601.

> 40 DDD 1/85

Brahms composed his three piano sonatas early in life, completing the Third during his important friendship with Robert Schumann. It is a work of colossal scale and dimension, possessing a grandeur that seems to cry out for comparison with Beethoven's last compositions. The listener's attention is seized right at the outset by the massive opening theme that sweeps through the movement and there follows a meditative Andante, a gypsy-like Scherzo and an almost funereal Intermezzo. The final movement brings this huge structure to a resounding close. Zoltán Kocsis brings youthful ardour to this vivid work, relishing its moments of rapt intensity as well as its torrential verve. The recording is full and rich.

Brahms. Four Ballades, Op. 10.
Weber. Piano Sonata No. 2 in A flat major, J199. **Alfred Brendel** (pf). Philips 426 439-2PH.

> 53' DDD 6/91

It is hard to imagine piano music by German romantic composers more different than these works by Weber and Brahms, the former being full of fluent expressiveness and the latter of introspection. Part of the reason is that Weber was one of the earliest romantics and Brahms a late one, and their dates do not even overlap; but besides this, in character they were unalike, Weber being a brilliant, nervous man of the theatre and Brahms a shy, dour Northerner. Setting aside the chronological order that he follows in his valuable booklet essay, Alfred Brendel plays the Brahms *Ballades* first, and does so with force and momentum, not least in No. 1 with its evocation of the grim Scottish ballad about a patricide that is quoted in the score. Considering that the composer was only 21 when he wrote these pieces, they are surprisingly sombre, and although No. 3 is a kind of scherzo (which Schumann called demonic) all are in a minor key. This music is hardly easy listening, but the authority of the playing is compelling. The Weber "Grand Sonata" in A flat major is a four-movement work, lasting over half an hour, which was once better known than it is now: the elegant writing sometimes reminds us of his *Invitation to the Dance*, and we can also see why Liszt and Chopin admired him and learned from him. Though the music is discursive, as Liszt and Chopin are not, it is in excellent hands here and Brendel holds things together in a way that would elude lesser artists. There are awkwardnesses and naïveties here, but the work is still one of great interest and the playing most persuasive. Fine, faithful piano sound.

Brahms. Two Rhapsodies, Op. 79—B minor; G minor. 16 Waltzes, Op. 39. Six Piano Pieces, Op. 118. **Stephen Kovacevich** (pf). Philips 420 750-2PH. From 6514 229 (4/83).

53' DDD 4/88

The Op. 79 Rhapsodies have been described as the "most temperamental" of all Brahms's later keyboard works. It would certainly be hard to imagine more vehement performances than those given by Kovacevich, thanks to his robust tone, trenchant attack and urgent tempos—perhaps even a shade too fast for the *Molto passionato, ma non troppo allegro* of the second. But the pleading second subject of No. 1 in B minor brings all the requisite lyrical contrast. The Waltzes, too, have their tenderer moments of *Ländler*-like sentiment and charm. However, they emerge faster and more excitable than usual, as if Kovacevich were trying to remind us of Brahms's old love of Hungary no less than his new love of Vienna. "It is wonderful how he combines passion and tenderness in the smallest of spaces" was Clara Schumann's comment on the miniatures and the phrase fits Kovacevich's warmly responsive account of the Op. 118 set just as well. The piano is faithfully and fearlessly reproduced in what sounds like a ripely reverberant venue.

Brahms. Variations and Fugue on a Theme by Handel, Op. 24.
Reger. Variations and Fugue on a Theme by Telemann, Op. 134. **Jorge Bolet** (pf). Decca Ovation 417 791-2DM. From SXL6969 (11/81).

59' ADD 2/90   £ ⁹ₚ

Brahms. Variations and Fugue on a Theme by Handel, Op. 24. Four Ballades, Op. 10. Variations on a Theme by Schumann, Op. 9. **Jorge Federico Osorio** (pf). ASV CDDCA616.

68' DDD 11/88

The Decca issue is one of Bolet's finest studio recordings. Although his playing was very much founded on the great virtuoso tradition there is never a sense of mere virtuosity for its own sake, though his technical command and imposing virtuosity (as these recordings bear witness) are never in doubt. The Brahms *Variations and Fugue on a Theme by Handel* is one of the great masterpieces of variation form and has always maintained a high place in the piano repertoire.

Jorge Bolet *[photo: Decca/Easten*

The theme (taken from Handel's three "Lessons for Harpsichord") is simplicity itself, though around the simplicity Brahms weaves an imaginative profusion of ideas. His love of Bach can be detected in the highly contrapuntal textures and which find their ultimate *coup de grâce* in the enormously effective concluding fugue. Reger's magnificent set of variations date from 1914 and was his last major work for the solo piano. It shares with the Brahms a remarkable mastery of counterpoint, and its Herculean technical demands place it out of bounds to all but the most accomplished of pianists. Under Bolet's hands all musical and technical difficulties are quashed, and both here and in the Brahms his clarity of texture and balance of parts is most impressive. The recording is vivid and naturally balanced.

Jorge Federico Osorio is a Mexican-born pianist whose teachers included Wilhelm Kempff, and he brings to this music a real feel for its style as well as fine technical resource; tempos are well judged and textures no less so, and altogether the playing is most compelling. The recording of the piano is unusually good even by today's high standards, with a resonant bass and a spacious acoustic, and it encompasses Brahms's biggest climaxes remarkably well, with the vigorous Third Ballade being specially striking here. This piano music is not the easiest to play and interpret, but this CD brings us fine performances from an artist who fully understands the music, and the playing of the *Schumann Variations* should help to re-establish this rather neglected work in the piano repertory.

Brahms. PIANO WORKS. **Julius Katchen** (pf). Decca 430 053-2DM6. Variations on a Theme by Paganini, Op. 35. Variations and Fugue on a Theme by Handel, Op. 24 (both from SXL6218, 4/66). Four Ballades, Op. 10 (SXL6160, 5/56). Variations on a Theme by Schumann, Op. 9. Variations on an Original Theme, Op. 21 No. 1. Variations on a Hungarian Song, Op. 21 No. 2 (all from SXL6219, 3/66). Waltzes, Op. 39. Two Rhapsodies, Op. 79 (both from SXL6160, 5/65). Piano Sonatas—No. 1 in C major, Op. 1; No. 2 in F sharp minor, Op. 2 (both from SXL6129, 12/64); No. 3 in F minor, Op. 5. Scherzo in E flat minor (both from SXL6228, 6/66). Piano Pieces—Op. 76. Fantasias, Op. 116 (both from SXL6118, 9/64); Op. 118; Op. 119. Three Intermezzos, Op. 117 (all from SXL6105, 5/64). Hungarian Dances (with Jean-Pierre Marty, pf. SXL6217, 12/65).

⑥ 6h 28' ADD 2/91

The American pianist Julius Katchen, who died in 1969 at the age of 42, was a virtuoso much in demand for his performance of such works as the Rachmaninov Second Concerto, but he was also a philosophy graduate who brought intellectual force and subtlety to his playing. Brahms was a special favourite of his, and these performances recorded in the 1960s have real distinction, for he is at home in all the areas of the composer's world, ranging from the youthful ardour of the sonatas and *Paganini* Variations to the autumnal musings of the later pieces such as the intermezzos and fantasias, which are shorter but say much in little and sometimes show a wistful sunset glow. The immensely difficult *Paganini* Variations, based on a theme used by several other composers, show the leonine side both of Brahms and the pianist: this is an outstandingly athletic performance, powerful and yet sometimes more delicate too, and if there's a touch of hardness to the piano tone, that is not out of place. The *Handel* Variations are more varied in mood and texture and link up more with the world of the Two Rhapsodies in which storm and lyricism are finely balanced here, while the humour, tenderness, twilight mystery and sadness of the late pieces are perfectly realized, as are the lilt of the Waltzes and the gipsy bravura of the Hungarian Dances, in 11 of which Katchen plays as a duettist with Jean-Pierre Marty.

Brahms. PIANO WORKS. **Radu Lupu.** Decca 417 599-2DH. Items marked [a] from SXL6504 (5/71), [b] SXL6831 (11/78).
Rhapsodies, Op. 79—No. 1 in B minor[a]; No. 2 in G minor[b]. Three Intermezzos, Op. 117[a]. Six Piano Pieces, Op. 118[b]. Four Piano Pieces, Op. 119[b].

71' ADD 8/87 **B**

Brahms. PIANO WORKS. **François-René Duchable.** Erato 2292-45477-2.
Theme and Variations in D minor. Three Intermezzos, Op. 117. Two Rhapsodies, Op. 79. Variations on a Theme by Paganini, Op. 35.

63' DDD 3/91 **B**

Brahms's late piano music inhabits a very special world, equally appealing to the sentimental as to the intellectually inclined listener. A poignant sense of resignation, of autumnal wistfulness, is allied to consummate mystery of compositional technique, and these elements are mutually transformed, producing an effect impossible to capture in words. Radu Lupu's playing captures it, though. Listen to the quiet rapture as he sleepwalks into the last section of Op. 117 No. 3 or the revelation in Op. 118 No. 2 that the inversion of the theme is even more beautiful than its original statement. One senses a complete identity with the composer's thoughts, and it is to be doubted whether any finer recording of these works has ever been made.

Nevertheless, François-René Duchable is an extremely gifted pianist who has the technique to do justice to Brahms's dauntingly challenging *Paganini* Variations and does so to notable effect in his 1989 recording made in a well chosen Swiss location. Technique here means more than the necessary dexterity, of course, and he also gives us poise and poetry. This is aristocratic playing of a work which has the average concert pianist struggling to achieve accuracy at an acceptable pace (wise amateurs do not even attempt it) and it gives much pleasure, not least because Duchable also keeps the momentum going from one variation to the next and so avoids the sectional effect that we hear from some other artists in this music, even good ones. The other pieces are finely done, too. The Op. 117 Intermezzos have a quiet persuasiveness, and the two passionate Rhapsodies are exciting in keyboard terms yet always lyrical as well. We also have a rarity in the D minor Theme and Variations which is a transcription of a famous slow movement in the String Sextet, Op. 18. The recording is a good one, and the trace of hardness in the piano's treble register that one notices in the *Paganini* Variations is not out of place.

Brahms. CHORAL WORKS. [a]**Jard van Nes** (mez); **San Francisco Symphony Chorus and Orchestra/Herbert Blomstedt.** Decca 430 281-2DH. Texts and translations included.
Gesang der Parzen, Op. 89. Nänie, Op. 82. Schicksalslied, Op. 54. Begräbnisgesang, Op. 13. Alto Rhapsody, Op. 53[a].

63' DDD 8/90

Brahms is such a familiar figure that it is salutary to be reminded that one area of his work, choral music, remains mostly unknown to collectors save for the

Herbert Blomstedt   *[photo: Decca/Stoddard*

German Requiem and *Alto Rhapsody*. This is a pity, for this composer who was also a distinguished choral conductor drew some of his finest inspiration from this medium. This issue includes the *Rhapsody*, warmly and movingly sung by Jard van Nes, but its importance lies in the fact that it also does much to give us a better knowledge of other big pieces too. Don't be put off by the sombre subject matter—including *Begräbnisgesang*, "A Song of the Fates" (a tremendous piece), another work about fate itself and not one but two funeral hymns!—but listen instead to thrilling choral singing and orchestral playing under the direction of a conductor who believes passionately in the music. "Plenty of strength, light and drama" is what *Gramophone*'s critic found in this programme when it first came out, and to that I would add that the San Francisco Symphony Chorus sing the German texts with complete conviction. If this music makes us regret that Brahms wrote no opera, we may at least feel that here is something not far short of it even though it was not intended for the stage; to see what I mean, listen only to the *Schicksallied* which is the first work performed. A good recording complements the quality of performance, though ideally the choral textures could be clearer.

Brahms. MOTETS. **Trinity College Choir, Cambridge/Richard Marlow.** Conifer CDCF178. Texts and translations included.
Op. 29—Es ist das Heil uns kommen her; Schaffe in mir, Gott. Psalm 13, Op. 27 (with Richard Pearce, org). Op. 110—Ich aber bin elend; Ach, arme Welt, du trügest mich; Wenn wir in höchsten Nöten sein. Ave Maria, Op. 12 (Pearce). Op. 109—Unsere Väter; Wenn ein starker Gewappneter; Wo ist ein so herrlich Volk. Geistliches Lied, Op. 30 (James Morgan, org). Op. 37—O bone Jesu; Adoramus te Christe; Regina coeli, Op. 74—Warum ist das licht gegeben dem Mühseligen?; O Heiland, reiss die Himmel auf.

· 65' DDD 2/90

The Choir of Trinity College, Cambridge have the remarkable gift of making music heavily overladen with contrapuntal wizardry sound, not only inevitable, but extraordinarily lovely. This recording of the complete set of Brahms's motets may be recommended unreservedly. The singing is of a high quality and the acoustic of the chapel serve to enhance both the clarity and the blend. The motets range from a fairly straightforward chorale style of writing to some very substantial double-choir composition. A few pieces are written for female voices only—not for nothing was Brahms conductor of the Hamburg Frauenchor and thus well-acquainted with that medium—the performance of these pieces by the high voices of the Trinity Choir is a model of lightness, lucidity and skill. The ingenious *Regina coeli* comes across with something of the sprightliness of an Elizabethan ballet (albeit with alleluias instead of Fa-la-

la-ing!). This is a disc calculated to delight both the Brahms specialist and all music lovers.

Brahms. LIEDER. **Thomas Allen** (bar); **Geoffrey Parsons** (pf). Virgin Classics VC7 91130-2. Texts and translations included.
Wir wandelten, Op. 96 No. 2. Der Gang zum Liebchen, Op. 48 No. 1. Komm bald, Op. 97 No. 5. Salamander, Op. 107 No. 2. Nachtigall, Op. 97 No. 1. Serenade, Op. 70 No. 3. Geheimnis, Op. 71 No. 3. Von waldbekränzter Höhe, Op. 57 No. 1. Dein blaues Auge hält so still, Op. 59 No. 8. Wie bist du, meine Königin, Op. 32 No. 9. Meine Liebe ist grün, Op. 63 No. 5. Die Kränze, Op. 46 No. 1. Sah dem edlen Bildnis, Op. 46 No. 2. An die Nachtigall, Op. 46 No. 4. Die Schale der Vergessenheit, Op. 46 No. 3. In Waldeseinsamkeit, Op. 85 No. 6. Wiegenlied, Op. 49 No. 4. Sonntag, Op. 47 No. 3. O wüsst ich doch den Weg zurück, Op. 63 No. 8. Minnelied, Op. 71 No. 5. Feldeinsamkeit, Op. 86 No. 2. Ständchen, Op. 106 No. 1. Von ewiger Liebe, Op. 43 No. 1. Die Mainacht, Op. 43 No. 2. Botschaft, Op. 47 No. 1.

62' DDD 9/90

Brahms's songs are, on the whole, intimate, one-to-one statements. They rarely approach the nature of public announcements and thus only occasionally explore extreme loudness: they are ideally suited to home listening. The darkening timbre of Thomas Allen's voice makes it increasingly suited to Brahms, and his characteristic, though far from common, qualities of heroic breath control and vital, lissom phrasing compound his affinity with this music. The songs make best use of the distinctive parts of his range and this, wedded to Allen's innate musicianship, sets a solid foundation for an engrossing recital. Geoffrey Parsons picks up these features and mirrors them in the searching piano parts, bringing light and shade, clarity and mist to support the voice. The recital as a whole is well thought out: the songs have clear, unifying links in terms of mood and gesture, but there is enough variety here to retain interest throughout. A pleasantly close recording of the voice emphasizes subtleties of tonal shading, and the more subdued setting of the piano allows it to make its effect without overpowering the singer. A disc to delight both novice and seasoned listener alike, then.

Brahms. LIEDER. **Olaf Bär** (bar); **Geoffrey Parsons** (pf). EMI CDC7 49723-2. Texts and translations included.
Sechs Gesänge, Op. 3. Lieder und Gesänge, Op. 32. Liedern und Gesängen von Georg Friedrich Daumer, Op. 57—Von waldbekränzter Hohe; Wenn du nur zuweilen lächelst; Ach, wende diesen Blick; In meiner Nächte Sehnen; Strahlt zuweilen auch ein mildes Licht; Die Schnur, die Perl an Perle; Unbewegte laue Luft. Vier Lieder, Op. 96. Lieder, Op. 59—Regenlied; Nachklang.

66' DDD 5/88

Brahms, who suffered much in the cause of love and never had a completely satisfactory relationship with a woman, was a master at expressing the pain of unrequited or rejected love, nowhere more so than in No. 6 of Op. 32, "Du sprichs dass ist mich täuschte", an outright masterpiece. Bär, one of the most perceptive of current-day Lieder interpreters, sings it with direct feeling. That is a hallmark of this whole cheerfully-prepared recital, a consistency of approach, based on the even projection of tone and sensitive enunciation of words. Time and again, Bär phrases with just the right response to words and music. He is admirably supported by his regular partner, Geoffrey Parsons, who

seconds the baritone with playing that at once underpins the singer and offers its own insights into Brahms, such as the wonderful way the composer intertwines voice and piano, yet keeps them independent. The recording has a natural presence to it.

Brahms. LIEDER. **Anne Sofie von Otter** (mez); **Bengt Forsberg** (pf). DG 429 727-2GH. Texts and translations included.
Zigeunerlieder, Op. 103—No. 1-7 and 11. Dort in den Weiden, Op. 97 No. 4. Vergebliches Ständchen, Op. 84 No. 4. Die Mainacht, Op. 43 No. 2. Ach, wende diesen Blick, Op. 57 No. 4. O kühler Wald, Op. 72 No. 3. Von ewiger Liebe, Op. 43 No. 1. Junge Lieder I, Op. 63 No. 5. Wie rafft' ich mich auf in der Nacht, Op. 32 No. 1. Unbewegte laue Luft, Op. 57 No. 8. Heimweh II, Op. 63 No. 8. Mädchenlied, Op. 107 No. 5. Ständchen, Op. 106 No. 1. Sonntag, Op. 47 No. 3. Wiegenlied, Op. 49 No. 4. Zwei Gesänge, Op. 91 (with Nils-Erik Sparf, va).

`61' DDD 4/91`

Many of the lieder here are but meagrely represented in current catalogues, so that this recital is all the more welcome, particularly in view of the perceptive musicality of both singer and pianist. They show a fine free (but unanimous!) flexibility in the *Zigeunerlieder*, with a dashing "Brauner Bursche" and "Röslein dreie" and a passionate "Rote Abendwolken"; but there is also lightness, happy in "Wisst ihr, wann mein Kindchen", troubled in "Lieber Gott, du weisst"; and Otter's coolly tender tone in "Kommt dir manchmal in den Sinn" touches the heart. Also deeply moving are the profound yearning and the loving but anxious lullaby in the two songs with viola obbligato (most sensitively played). Elsewhere, connoisseurs of vocal technique will admire Otter's command of colour and legato line in the gravity of *O kühler Wald*, the stillness of *Die Mainacht* and the intensity of *Von ewiger Liebe*, and her lovely *mezza voce* in the *Wiegenlied* and the partly repressed fervour of *Unbewegte laue Luft*; but to any listener her remarkable control, her responsiveness to words and, not least, the sheer beauty of her voice make this a most rewarding disc, aided as she is by Forsberg's characterful playing.

Brahms. Ein deutsches Requiem, Op. 45. **Elisabeth Schwarzkopf** (sop); **Dietrich Fischer-Dieskau** (bar); **Philharmonia Chorus and Orchestra/ Otto Klemperer.** EMI CDC7 47238-2. Notes, text and translation included. From Columbia SAX2430/31 (2/62).

`69' ADD 6/87`

Brahms. Ein deutsches Requiem, Op. 45. **Charlotte Margiono** (sop); **Rodney Gilfry** (bar); **Monteverdi Choir; Orchestre Révolutionnaire et Romantique/John Eliot Gardiner.** Philips 432 140-2PH. Text and translation included.

`66' DDD 4/91`

Brahms's *German Requiem*, a work of great concentration and spiritual intensity, is, rather surprisingly, the creation of a man barely 30 years old. He turned for his text not to the liturgical Mass but to the German translations of the Old Testament. It is decidedly *not* a Requiem of 'fire and brimstone' overshadowed by the Day of Wrath; instead it is a work for those who mourn, those who remain in sorrow ("As one whom his mother comforteth, so I will comfort you", sings the soprano in a soaring hymn of grief-assuaging beauty). The texture is sinuous and Brahms employs the orchestra with great delicacy as well as enormous muscular energy. Klemperer's reading of this mighty work has long been famous: rugged, at times surprisingly fleet and with a juggernaut power. The superb Philharmonia are joined by their excellent Chorus and two magnificent soloists—Elisabeth Schwarzkopf offering comfort in an endless stream of pure tone and Fischer-Dieskau, still unequalled, singing with total absorption. A great performance beautifully enhanced on CD.

The pungency of a small chorus and the incisive edge provided by the orchestra of period instruments, the Orchestre Révolutionnaire et Romantique, makes for a fresh reappraisal of a work that can all too often sound turgid and dull. Gardiner has written of the work's radiance, optimism and full-bloodedness and he instils these characteristics into his performance. The reduced forces employed mean that great subtlety can be drawn out of the score—words are meticulously cared for, dynamic nuances observed and, above all, strong and secure attack ensure a genuine intensity of expression. The soloists are good too, with the young American baritone Rodney Gilfry quite outstanding, offering firm, warm and beautifully rounded tone throughout. Charlotte Margiono, set a little far back in the aural perspective, is a sweet and suitably conciliatory soprano soloist. For anyone who has in the past found Brahms's *Ein deutsches Requiem* difficult to come to terms with then this pioneering period instrument set is probably the one to win the most converts.

Frank Bridge
British 1879-1941

Bridge. Suite for strings.
Butterworth. A Shropshire Lad. Two English Idylls. The Banks of Green Willow.
Parry. Lady Radnor's Suite. **English String Orchestra / William Boughton.** Nimbus NI5068.

> 61' DDD 10/88

No one who loves British music of the romantic period will need much introduction to the three pieces by George Butterworth that begin this programme. His poignant orchestral rhapsody *A Shropshire Lad* somehow seems to presage his death at the age of 31 in the trenches of World War I (it has been called "his own requiem") and took its inspiration from A.E. Housman's poetry, itself laden with half-suppressed longings and a passionate identification with doomed youth; and though the *Two English Idylls* and *The Banks of Green Willow* (with a folk melody introduced by the clarinet) are brighter, these too have a certain sadness along with pastoral charm. Sir Hubert Parry was another Britisher whose music reveals a sensitive heart, though he hid it under a country-squire exterior, and his *Lady Radnor's Suite* was composed in 1894 for an aristocratic friend who heard it first at her castle near Salisbury; its six movements form a sequence of neo-classical dances ending with a somewhat Irish-sounding *Gigue*. Frank Bridge was admired by his pupil, Britten, as England's foremost composer, and his Suite for strings of 1910 shows his mastery of string writing and textures. William Boughton and the English String Orchestra are persuasive advocates of this music and the recording is pleasantly resonant.

Bridge. Piano Quintet in D minor.
Elgar. Piano Quintet in A minor, Op. 84. **Coull Quartet** (Roger Coull, Philip Gallaway, vns; David Curtis, va; John Todd, vc); **Allan Schiller** (pf). ASV CDDCA678.

> 70' DDD 1/90

These two endearingly evocative works are clearly linked by their characteristic tendency to refer to something unnamed outside of themselves. This was typical of Bridge's style at the time (the Quintet was composed in 1905, revised in

1912) but for Elgar in 1919 it represented a culmination of the inner doubts and public sorrows that virtually ended his compositional career. Much of Bridge's finest music is to be found in his chamber works and, besides an enormous inventiveness, he always displays in them a keen sense of just proportion. In revising the Piano Quintet, he took the opportunity to integrate the Scherzo into the slow movement, producing a more balanced structure, and resolving many of the inadequacies inherent in the work in its earlier guise. The performers here bring out that elegant shape most skilfully without undermining the passing delights to be savoured along the way. Elgar's Quintet is, for the most part, treated to a lighter touch than usual, emotional intensity being focused towards the central slow movement, and Allan Schiller's less dominating contribution allows the engineers to attain a subtle balance of strings and piano often missing in other recordings. Such an apt coupling is worth trying.

Bridge. PIANO WORKS, Volume 1. **Peter Jacobs.** Continuum CCD1016. Arabesque. Capriccios—No. 1; No. 2. A Dedication. A Fairy Tale Suite. Gargoyle. Hidden Fires. In Autumn. Three Miniature Pastorals—Set 1; Set 2. A Sea Idyll. Three Improvisations for the Left Hand. Winter Pastoral.

73' DDD 9/90

Peter Jacobs here plays piano pieces composed by Bridge between 1905 and 1928. They will be unfamiliar to most listeners and are well worth exploration. It is not too much to say that they represent an English-music equivalent of Fauré with something of the spirit of Brahms's late pieces too. This is especially true of Bridge's pre-1914 works, where the clarity of the harmony avoids any over-lush treatment of such titles as *Sea Idyll*. The charm of the *Fairy Tale Suite* and of the *Miniature Pastorals*, both dating from 1917, belong to the world of Ravel's *Ma mère l'oye*. But the second set of *Pastorals*, composed in 1921, reflects the devastating effect the First World War had on Bridge. Delightful though they still are, these pieces have lost their innocence and are the work of a disillusioned man. During the 1920s, Bridge's harmonic style grew more radical and moved nearer to atonality, as can be heard in *A Dedication* and *In Autumn*. Jacobs's performances reflect not only his command of the technique required for this music but his total belief in its quality. He has done Bridge a service and the recording engineers have backed him to the hilt.

Benjamin Britten

British 1913-1976

Britten. Piano Concerto, Op. 13[a]. Violin Concerto, Op. 15[b]. [b]**Mark Lubotsky** (vn); [a]**Sviatoslav Richter** (pf); **English Chamber Orchestra/ Benjamin Britten.** Decca London 417 308-2LM. From SXL6512 (8/71).

67' ADD 10/89

Just after Britten's performances were released on LP in 1971, the composer admitted with some pride that Sviatoslav Richter had learned his Piano Concerto "entirely off his own bat", and had revealed a Russianness that was in the score. Britten was attracted to Shostakovich during the late 1930s, when it was written, and the bravado, brittleness and flashy virtuosity of the writing, in the march-like finale most of all, at first caused many people (including Lennox Berkeley, to whom it is dedicated) to be wary of it, even to think it somehow outside the composer's style. Now we know his music better, it is easier to accept, particularly in this sparkling yet sensitive performance. The Violin Concerto dates from the following year, 1939, when Britten was in Canada, and it too has its self-conscious virtuosity, but it is its rich nostalgic lyricism which strikes to the heart and the quiet elegiac ending is unforgettable. Compared to Richter in the other work, Mark Lubotsky is not always the master of its hair-raising difficulties, notably in the scherzo, which has passages of double artificial harmonics that even Heifetz wanted simplified before he would play it (Britten refused), but this is still a lovely account. Fine recording, made in The Maltings at Snape.

Britten. Cello Symphony, Op. 68[a]. Sinfonia da Requiem, Op. 20[b]. Cantata misericordium, Op. 69[c]. [a]**Mstislav Rostropovich** (vc); [c]**Sir Peter Pears** (ten); [c]**Dietrich Fischer-Dieskau** (bar); [c]**London Symphony Chorus and Orchestra**, [a]**English Chamber Orchestra**, [b]**New Philharmonia Orchestra/Benjamin Britten**. Decca London 425 100-2LM. Text and translation included. Item marked [a] from SXL6138 (12/64), [bc] SXL6175 (9/65).

75' ADD 9/89

This mid-price disc offers two of Britten's finest works, the *Cello Symphony* and the *Sinfonia da Requiem*. The latter was written in 1940 and is one of the composer's most powerful orchestral works, harnessing opposing forces in a frighteningly intense way. From the opening drumbeat the *Sinfonia* employs sonata form in a dramatically powerful way, though the tone is never fierce or savage; it has an implacable tread and momentum. The central movement, "Dies irae", however, has a real sense of fury, satirical in its biting comment—the flutter-tongued wind writing rattling its defiance. The closing "Requiem aeternam" is a movement of restrained beauty. On this recording from 1964 the New Philharmonia play superbly. The Cello Symphony, written in 1963 as part of a series for the great Russian cellist Mstislav Rostropovich, was the first major sonata-form work written since the *Sinfonia*. The idea of a struggle between soloist and orchestra, implicit in the traditional concerto, has no part here; it

is a conversation between the two. Rostropovich plays with a depth of feeling that has never quite been equalled in other recordings and the playing of the ECO has great bite. The recording too is extraordinarily fine for its years. The *Cantata misericordium*, one of Britten's lesser known works, was written in 1962 as a commission from the Red Cross. It takes the story of the Good Samaritan and is scored for tenor and baritone soloists, chorus, string quartet and orchestra. It is a universal plea for charity and here receives a powerful reading. This is a must for any collection of Britten's music.

Britten. The Young Person's Guide to the Orchestra, Op. 34.
GLORIANA—Courtly dances.
Prokofiev. Peter and the Wolf, Op. 67[a]. **Royal Philharmonic Orchestra/
André Previn** ([a]narr). Telarc CD80126. Text included where appropriate.

55' DDD 5/87   **B**

Britten. The Young Person's Guide to the Orchestra, Op. 34[a]. Simple
Symphony, Op. 4[b]. Variations on a Theme of Frank Bridge, Op. 10[c]. [a]**London
Symphony Orchestra;** [bc]**English Chamber Orchestra/Benjamin Britten.**
Decca 417 509-2DH. Item marked [a] from SXL6110 (9/64), [b] SXL6405 (6/69),
[c] SXL6316 (11/67).

61' ADD 1/87   P **B**

Britten. The Young Person's Guide to the Orchestra, Op. 34. Symphony for
cello and orchestra, Op. 68[a]. PETER GRIMES—Four Sea Interludes, Op. 33a.
Pärt. Cantus in memory of Benjamin Britten. [a]**Truis Mørk** (vc); **Bergen
Philharmonic Orchestra/Neeme Järvi.** BIS CD420.

75' DDD 6/89   **B**

In *Peter and the Wolf* André Previn is an ideal guide to the components of the
orchestra, for his relaxed, friendly delivery creates just the right atmosphere,
while through the magic of tape editing he also contrives to conduct a neatly
characterized performance, vividly recorded. Britten's *Young Person's Guide to the
Orchestra,* adapted from a theme by Purcell, came about through a film which
would demonstrate to children the instruments of the orchestra. This brilliantly
inventive work is excellently played by the RPO though Previn's direction is a
shade reserved. The attractive Courtly dances from Britten's opera *Gloriana*
complete an attractive disc.

Britten's performance of his *Young Person's Guide* wisely omits the now rather
dated text. He adopts quick tempos that must be demanding even for the LSO
players, along with more spacious ones for the more introspective sections. This
is beautiful playing, with all kinds of memorable touches. Britten's own
childhood music is also here, in the shape of the delightfully fresh *Simple
Symphony*. This fine CD then ends with more variations, the young composer's
tribute to his teacher Frank Bridge. It is marvellous music, of astonishing wit and
often intensely serious too, and the composer's own performance with the ECO
is uniquely authoritative.

The BIS issue is a well-planned disc and it was a particularly good idea to
include Pärt's *Cantus*, scored for strings and a bell which tolls throughout the
work to most hypnotic effect. Järvi's interpretation of Britten's Cello Symphony
is more lyrical and relaxed than most, with a nostalgic touch that softens the
edges of the score. But he still imparts the necessary vigour, irony and starkness
to this enigmatic composition. The solo part is magnificently played by Truis
Mørk, whose expressive phrasing is matched by the virtuosic brilliance of his
playing. The Bergen Philharmonic gives an admirable account of the orchestral
score and is also fully conversant with the *Peter Grimes* Interludes and the *Young
Person's Guide*. The recording is clear and well-balanced, allowing the music to
create its own atmosphere.

Britten. Canadian Carnival, Op. 19. Violin Concerto, Op. 15[a].
Britten/Berkeley. Mont Juic, Op. 12. [a]**Lorraine McAslan** (vn); **English
Chamber Orchestra/Steuart Bedford.** Collins Classics 1123-2.

58' DDD 12/90   S

However, Lorraine McAslan's playing and interpretation of the Violin Concerto
must take its place among the classic Britten performances. In intensity and

insight it is ahead of any of its rivals, and outstrips them all by reason of the superbly clear and balanced recording and of the marvellous performance of the orchestral score. Soloist and conductor are in no doubt that this is a big work and they stress the tragedy implicit in it (it reflects Britten's emotions about the Spanish Civil War). McAslan's playing of the formidably difficult *scherzo* is a *tour de force* and she brings a vibrant passion to the concluding *Passacaglia*. A deeply moving performance by one of Britain's outstanding young violinists. This enterprising disc also includes two rarer Britten works, one of them only half by him. This is *Mont Juic*, a suite of Catalan dances, composed jointly with Lennox Berkeley (the last two movements are Britten's) and a witty, colourful, tuneful pieces that deserves to be better known. *Canadian Carnival* was composed in 1940, makes delightful use of the folk-song *Alouette* and is much indebted to Copland. Not major Britten, but refreshingly unusual.

Britten. The Prince of the Pagodas, Op. 57. **London Sinfonietta/Oliver Knussen.** Virgin Classics VCD7 91103-2.

② 1h 59' DDD 7/90

It is not surprising that this two-disc set won the 1990 *Gramophone* award in the Engineering category, for it is technically superlative (recorded in St Augustine's Church, Kilburn). But its primary importance is that Oliver Knussen has recorded the complete score of Britten's only ballet, restoring 20 minutes of music that had not previously been heard. Britten's 1957 recording for Decca had over 40 cuts, including four entire dances. It is extraordinary that the inclusion of this extra music should drastically alter the perspective of the whole work, but it does—it seems a better piece altogether, its debt to Tchaikovsky, Prokofiev and Stravinsky less obvious. Much connected with the production of the ballet at Covent Garden turned sour for Britten and this may have been reflected in his conducting of the recording. Knussen's interpretation is far more loving and effective and the playing of the London Sinfonietta is outstanding for individual virtuosity and for the richness and sparkle of the ensemble. This is that rare commodity, a disc that sheds entirely new light on a composition, and it should be in the collection of everyone who values Britten's—and British—music.

Britten. String Quartet No. 3, Op. 94.
Tippett. String Quartet No. 4 (1978). **Lindsay Quartet** (Peter Cropper, Ronald Birks, vns; Robin Ireland, va; Bernard Gregor-Smith, vc). ASV CDDCA608.

53' DDD 5/88

Neither Britten nor Tippett had written a string quartet for over 30 years when they returned to the medium in the 1970s. Both composed a masterpiece. In Britten's case there was the poignancy of its being the last major work he completed, yet there is no sign of declining powers in a work that pays homage to Shostakovich as well as to the special qualities of the Amadeus Quartet for whom it was written. The Lindsay Quartet's interpretation is very different; it is emotionally more intense and one can rarely be unaware of the shadow over the score, with its thematic references to Britten's last opera, *Death in Venice*. The last movement, a Passacaglia from which all passion has been drained to leave a serene air of resignation, is played very slowly. Tippett's Fourth Quartet has a lyrical and impassioned slow movement at its core and the predominant impression is one of energy and vigour. The music has such abundance that it seems to be bursting the confines of the medium and it is no surprise to learn that Tippett authorized an arrangement for string orchestra, not that the Lindsays sound at all strained by this vibrant score. The playing is masterful and the recording is admirably clear.

Britten. PIANO WORKS. **Stephen Hough,** [a]**Ronan O'Hora** (pfs). Virgin Classics VC7 91203-2.
Holiday Diary, Op. 5. Three Character Pieces (1930). Night Piece (1963). Sonatina romantica (1940)—Moderato; Nocturne. 12 Variations on a Theme (1931). Five Waltzes (1923-5 and 1969). Two Lullabies (1936)[a]. Mazurka elegiaca Op. 23 No. 2[a]. Introduction and Rondo alla burlesca, Op. 23 No. 1[a].

    80' DDD 8/91

Though a fine pianist, Britten wrote surprisingly little for his own instrument, admitting in later life that he found it unsatisfying. Thus even with the inclusion of boyhood pieces unpublished in his lifetime there is not enough solo piano music to fill a single disc, and Stephen Hough is joined by Ronan O'Hora for three two-piano works. The biggest item here is the one that comes first, the *Holiday Diary* of 1934, four pieces of which Britten wrote to a friend a decade later, "I have an awfully soft spot for them still—they just recreate that unpleasant young thing BB in 1934—but who enjoyed being BB all the same!!" They have schoolboyish titles like "Early morning bathe" and "Funfair", and show an attractive youthful energy, but the final piece called "Night" is unusual in being slow and mysterious instead of a conventional brilliant finale. Stephen Hough has a coolly sharp way with this music, which is perhaps right for the buttoned-up young Britten that was revealed in the collection of his letters and diaries published last year. Not all the music here is distinguished, but it is well written; it is enlightening, too, to hear the influence of the composer's teacher, Ireland, in the *Three Character Pieces* and of Hindemith in the athletic *12 Variations*. Hough's playing has exemplary clarity and poise throughout, and the *Night Piece* of 1963 is beautifully atmospheric, while the two-piano music is also well delivered by thoughtful artists working well together. A clear and faithful recording complements this valuable issue.

Britten. Spring Symphony, Op. 44[a]. Cantata Academica, Op. 62[b]. Hymn to St Cecilia[c]. [ab]**Jennifer Vyvyan** (sop); [a]**Norma Procter,** [b]**Helen Watts** (contrs); [ab]**Sir Peter Pears** (ten); [b]**Owen Brannigan** (bass); [a]**Emanuel School Boys' Choir;** [a]**Chorus and Orchestra of the Royal Opera House, Covent Garden;** [bc]**London Symphony Chorus;** [b]**London Symphony Orchestra/** [a]**Benjamin Britten,** [bc]**George Malcolm.** Decca London 425 153-2LM. Texts and translation included. Item marked [a] from SXL2264 (5/61), [b] and [c] L'Oiseau-Lyre SOL60037 (10/61).

    74' ADD 1/90

Britten's famous recording of the *Spring Symphony* has acquired a brightness on CD that has the effect of lightening his entire palette by a perceptible degree or two. It is a jubilantly bright piece, of course, and the enthusiasm of the performance is so great that many listeners will not object. There is now a slight acidity to the choral sound which could be a drawback for some listeners but, since this is the only recording of the symphony currently available, most people will be happy to live with it. The *Cantata Academica* suffers less from this flaw and Britten's reading relishes its lightly-worn learned humour so much (and the fact that the solos were so obviously written as wittily affectionate portraits of the singers who were to record them) that it is part of the essential Britten discography. The *Hymn to St Cecilia* is also nicely done.

Britten. Les illuminations, Op. 18[a]. Simple Symphony, Op. 4. Phaedra, Op. 93[a]. [a]**Christiane Eda-Pierre** (sop); **Jean-Walter Audoli Instrumental Ensemble/Jean-Walter Audoli.** Arion ARN68035.

56' DDD 6/89

It is good to have, at last, a recording of Britten's *Les illuminations* that is sung by a French singer and played by a French orchestra under a conductor from the same country. She and her colleagues bring a clean refinement to this score, and although other performances may have more excitement and sensuous charm this is one to appreciate for its sharp intelligence and Gallic clarity of judgement. Having written that Christiane Eda-Pierre is French-speaking, one must at once add that her English in *Phaedra* is also very good. Oddly enough, Britten here set a text which was originally in French (the translation is by the American poet Robert Lowell), and his music powerfully conveys the classical intensity of Racine's play on the subject of the Greek queen who falls into a forbidden love for her stepson Hippolythus and takes poison to escape a guilt that has become intolerable. Though called a cantata, *Phaedra* is really a miniature opera for a single singer (it was written for Dame Janet Baker) and it contains some of Britten's most effective writing for the female voice. The *Simple Symphony* which separates these two vocal works is altogether different, being based on music dating from the composer's happy childhood and having a fresh and often touching quality. The recording is as crisp as the performances.

Britten. Serenade for tenor, horn and strings, Op. 31[a]. Les illuminations, Op. 18[b]. Nocturne, Op. 60[c]. [abc]**Sir Peter Pears** (ten); [c]**Alexander Murray** (fl); [c]**Roger Lord** (cor a); [c]**Gervase de Peyer** (cl); [c]**William Waterhouse** (bn); [ac]**Barry Tuckwell** (hn); [c]**Dennis Blyth** (timp); [c]**Osian Ellis** (hp); [ac]strings of the **London Symphony Orchestra,** [b]**English Chamber Orchestra/**[abc]**Benjamin Britten.** Decca 417 153-2DH. Texts included. Item marked [a] from SXL6110 (9/64), [b] SXL6316 (11/67), [c] SXL2189 (5/60).

73' ADD 8/86

No instrument was more important to Britten than the human voice and, inspired by the musicianship and superb vocal craftsmanship of his closest friend, he produced an unbroken stream of vocal works of a quality akin to those of Purcell. Three of his most haunting vocal pieces are featured on this wonderful CD. The performances date from between 1959 and 1966 with Pears in penetratingly musical form, even if the voice itself was by now a little thin and occasionally unsteady. The ECO and LSO are superb in every way and of course Britten was his own ideal interpreter. The recordings are vintage Decca, i.e. excellent.

Britten. CHORAL WORKS. **London Sinfonietta** [a]**Voices and** [b]**Chorus/ Terry Edwards.** Virgin Classics VC7 90728-2. Texts included.
A Boy was Born, Op. 3 (with St Paul's Cathedral Boys' Voices)[b]. Hymn to St Cecilia (1942)[a]. A.M.D.G. (1939)[b]. A Shepherd's Carol (1944)[b].

64' DDD 10/88

Since Britten's death, a number of his works have been released from his archive which he had either suppressed or forgotten in his lifetime. All these 'discoveries' have been pure gain, but some more than others. Among the major 'lost' compositions is A.M.D.G. (*Ad maiorem Dei gloriam*), seven settings of poems by Gerard Manley Hopkins. They are difficult but very rewarding; "God's Grandeur" is an exciting song, making virtuoso demands on the choir, and in "O Deus, ego amo te", the religio-erotic fervour is striking. *A Boy was Born*, written when Britten was 19, is in some ways the most advanced choral work in his whole output. The deservedly popular and well-loved Auden setting, *Hymn to St Cecilia*, is here performed by five solo voices, a procedure which had Britten's approval and is surprisingly effective, especially in this superb performance. Recording quality is alpha-plus.

Britten. SACRED CHORAL MUSIC. [a]**Sioned Williams** (hp); **Westminster Cathedral Choir/David Hill** with [b]**James O'Donnell** (org). Hyperion CDA66220. From A66220 (12/86). Texts included.
A Ceremony of Carols, Op. 28[a]. Missa brevis, Op. 63[b]. A Hymn to the Virgin (1934). A Hymn of St Columba (1962)[b]. Jubilate Deo in E flat major (1961)[b]. Deus in adjutorum meum (1945).

49' DDD 2/88

A Ceremony of Carols was Britten's first work for boys' voices but already shows his natural feeling for texture and rhythm. It sets nine medieval and sixteenth-century poems between the "Hodie" of the plainsong Vespers. The sole accompanying instrument is a harp, but given the right acoustic, sensitive attention to the words and fine rhythmic control the piece has a remarkable richness and depth. The Westminster Cathedral Choir perform this work beautifully; diction is immaculate and the acoustic halo surrounding the voices gives a festive glow to the performance. A fascinating *Jubilate* and *A Hymn to the Virgin*, whilst lacking the invention

David Hill   *[photo: Hyperion*

and subtlety of *A Ceremony*, intrigue with some particularly felicitous use of harmony and rhythm. *Deus in adjutorum meum* employs the choir without accompaniment and has an initial purity that gradually builds up in texture as the psalm (No. 70) gathers momentum. The *Missa brevis* was written for this very choir and George Malcolm's nurturing of a tonal brightness in the choir allowed Britten to use the voices in a more flexibile and instrumental manner than usual. The effect is glorious. St Columba founded the monastery on the Scottish island of Iona and Britten's hymn sets his simple and forthright prayer with deceptive simplicity and directness. The choir sing this music beautifully and the recording is first rate.

Britten. Saint Nicolas, Op. 42[a]. Rejoice in the Lamb, Op. 30[b]. [a]**David Hemmings,** [b]**Michael Hartnett** (trebs); [b]**Jonathan Steele** (alto); [a]**Sir Peter Pears,** [b]**Philip Todd** (tens); [b]**Donald Francke** (bass); [a]**Girls' Choir of Sir John Leman School, Beccles;** [a]**Boys' Choir of Ipswich School Preparatory Department;** [b]**Purcell Singers;** [a]**Aldeburgh Festival Choir and Orchestra/Benjamin Britten** with [a]**Ralph Downes,** [b]**George Malcolm** (orgs). Decca London mono 425 714-2LM. Texts included. Item marked [a] from LXT5060 (7/55), [b] LXT5416 (5/58).

64' ADD 9/90

This disc is a further example of Decca's wisdom in transferring to CD its historic collection of Britten/Pears performances of the former's music; and, incidentally, it shows how extremely good the recordings were in the first place. The performance of the cantata *Rejoice in the Lamb*, composed just after Britten returned to England from America during the war, was made in 1958 and remains unsurpassed. The mood of the work's touching setting of Christopher Smart's innocent but soul-searching poem is perfectly caught by the performers, who include George Malcolm as the organist. Britten's writing for the organ here is full of invention, whether he is illustrating Smart's cat Jeoffry "wreathing his body seven times round with elegant quickness" or the "great personal valour" of the mouse who defies Jeoffry. The Purcell Singers, impeccable in clarity of diction, and the soloists, are first-rate. *Saint Nicolas* was recorded even earlier, in Aldeburgh Church in 1955. The treble soloist is David Hemmings who had created Miles in *The Turn of the Screw* the previous year, and Pears sings the role he had created at the first Aldeburgh Festival in 1948. This disc is indispensable for the quality of the performance and as documentary evidence of the standard of the festival in its early years.

Britten. War Requiem, Op. 66. **Galina Vishnevskaya** (sop); **Sir Peter Pears** (ten); **Dietrich Fischer-Dieskau** (bar); **Simon Preston** (org); **Bach Choir**; **Highgate School Choir**; **London Symphony Chorus**; **Melos Ensemble**; **London Symphony Orchestra/Benjamin Britten.** Decca 414 383-2DH2. Texts and translations included. From SET252/3 (5/63).

② 81' ADD 4/85

Britten's *War Requiem* is the composer's most public statement of his pacifism. The work is cast in six movements and calls for massive forces: full chorus, soprano soloist and full orchestra evoke mourning, supplication and guilty apprehension; boys' voices with chamber organ, the passive calm of a liturgy which points beyond death; tenor and baritone soloists with chamber orchestra, the passionate outcry of the doomed victims of war. The 1963 recording manages to reflect these distinctions very well indeed. The soloists for whom the work was written convey superbly the harrowing impact of the Wilfred Owen poems and under the composer's direction the performance has an unsurpassed authority. Compact Disc conveys the contrasts between the many long passages of quiet music and the awe-inspiring climaxes extremely well, of course, and the only pity is the rather high level of hiss on the original tapes. Otherwise, every aspect of the recording is quite beyond reproach.

Britten. CURLEW RIVER. **Sir Peter Pears** (ten) Madwoman; **John Shirley-Quirk** (bar) Ferryman; **Harold Blackburn** (bass) Abbot; **Bryan Drake** (bar) Traveller; **Bruce Webb** (treb) Voice of the Spirit; **English Opera Group/Benjamin Britten** and **Viola Tunnard.** Decca London 421 858-2LM. Text included. From Decca SET301 (1/66).

69' ADD 9/89

This "parable for church performance" is the first of three such works that Britten wrote in the 1960s, not long after the *War Requiem*, and it too breathes a strongly religious spirit while being far removed from conventional church music. Set in the fenland of East Anglia as a medieval Christian mystery play, it tells the story of a madwoman who, seeking the young son stolen from her, comes to, and finally crosses, the Curlew River, only to meet with the spirit of the dead boy who gives her his blessing. The story derives from a classical *Noh* play that the composer had seen in Tokyo a few years before, and following the Japanese tradition he used an all-male cast, a bold step that proved successful since he had an exceptional artist to play the Madwoman in the shape of Peter Pears. Sir Peter brings great dignity and depth to this role, one of his favourites among the many by Britten that he created, and the other principals are fine too, notably John Shirley-Quirk as the Ferryman and Bruce Webb as the Boy, both also from the original cast. The seven instrumentalists who participate are first rate, and under the composer's direction this is a moving experience and a recording of historic importance, made most atmospherically in Orford Church in Suffolk, where the work had its first performance.

Britten. THE RAPE OF LUCRETIA[a]. Phaedra, Op. 93[b]. [a]**Sir Peter Pears** (ten) Male Chorus; [a]**Heather Harper** (sop) Female Chorus; [ab]**Dame Janet Baker** (mez) Lucretia; [a]**John Shirley-Quirk** (bar) Collatinus; [a]**Benjamin Luxon** (bar) Tarquinius; [a]**Bryan Drake** (bar) Junius; [a]**Elizabeth Bainbridge** (mez) Bianca; [a]**Jenny Hill** (sop) Lucia; **English Chamber Orchestra/** [a]**Benjamin Britten,** [b]**Steuart Bedford.** Decca London 425 666-2LH2. Notes and texts included. Item marked [a] from SET492/3 (6/71), [b] SXL6847 (7/77).

② 2h 4' ADD 5/90

Other transfers in this series represent a celebration of the art of Peter Pears as well as that of Benjamin Britten, but this set brings Janet Baker into the limelight. She takes the title roles in two works that, though divided by nearly 30 years, are still closely linked. Dame Janet gives of her best in strongly drawn, sympathetic portrayals of the two classical 'heroines', Phaedra and Lucretia, but, despite this, neither lady becomes particularly endearing and Britten describes their fates with an underlying coolness that countermands the immediate brilliance of the sounds he creates. Nevertheless, there is so much in both works that is typical of Britten's genius that, coupled together, they form a very significant facet of his work. *The Rape of Lucretia* was Britten's first chamber opera. *Phaedra*, based on Racine's *Phèdre*, was one of the composer's final works and capped his long-time empathy with French culture. Both receive performances that do them full justice, though the recording of the latter could be a shade more lucid for its date. Steuart Bedford's conducting matches that of Britten in the earlier recording remarkably well and the whole now presents a particularly attractive package.

Britten. A MIDSUMMER NIGHT'S DREAM. **Alfred Deller** (alto) Oberon; **Elizabeth Harwood** (sop) Tytania; **Sir Peter Pears** (ten) Lysander; **Thomas Hemsley** (bar) Demetrius; **Josephine Veasey** (mez) Hermia; **Heather Harper** (sop) Helena; **Stephen Terry** (spkr) Puck; **John Shirley-Quirk** (bar) Theseus; **Helen Watts** (contr) Hippolyta; **Owen Brannigan** (bass) Bottom; **Norman Lumsden** (bass) Quince; **Kenneth Macdonald** (ten) Flute; **David Kelly** (bass) Snug; **Robert Tear** (ten) Snout; **Keith Raggett** (ten) Starveling; **Richard Dakin** (treb) Cobweb; **John Prior** (treb) Peaseblossom; **Ian Wodehouse** (treb) Mustardseed; **Gordon Clark** (treb) Moth; **Choirs of Downside and Emanuel Schools; London Symphony Orchestra/ Benjamin Britten.** Decca London 425 663-2LH2. Notes and text included. From SET338/40 (5/67).

② 2h 24' ADD 5/90

From the first groanings of the Athenian wood, marvellously conjured by glissando strings, through to Puck's final adieu to the audience, Britten's adaptation of *A Midsummer Night's Dream* is a cascade of insight and invention, married to a clear and memorable tunefulness. Although this 1966 performance in many ways represents a definitive account of the opera, the work allows for a wide variety of interpretation. The role of Oberon, for example, is here filled with an other-worldly detachment by Alfred Deller, yet the fairy king's threatening and ambiguous sexuality has been strongly drawn by others in the opera house. A recording of the strength of this present issue does tend to inhibit the introduction on disc of other, equally viable, alternative views. Nevertheless, the transfer to CD of this performance was imperative and although the original vinyl set was splendidly vital, the recording now shines even brighter and the performance is still more lovable. There's not a weak link to be found, and the final ensemble, "Now until the break of day", retains the same power to move with its breathtaking beauty as it had a quarter of a century ago when it was first recorded.

Britten. PAUL BUNYAN. **Pop Wagner** (bar) Narrator; **James Lawless** (spkr) Paul Bunyan; **Dan Dressen** (ten) Johnny Inkslinger; **Elisabeth Comeaux Nelson** (sop) Tiny; **Clifton Ware** (ten) Slim; **Vern Sutton** (ten), **Merle Fristad** (bass) Two Bad Cooks; **James Bohn** (bar) Hel Helson; **Phil Jorgenson, Tim Dahl, Thomas Shaffer, Lawrence Weller** (tens/bars) Four Swedes; **James McKeel** (bar) John Shears; **James Westbrock** (ten) Western Union Boy; **Maria Jette** (sop) Fido; **Sue Herber** (mez) Moppet; **Janis Hardy** (mez) Poppet; **Plymouth Music Series Chorus and Orchestra/Philip Brunelle.** Virgin Classics VC7 90710-2. Notes and text included.

② 1h 53' DDD 8/88 ❓

Paul Bunyan was Britten's first opera and the libretto, characteristically witty, allusive and coruscating in its dexterity, is by W.H. Auden. By an extraordinary feat of creative imagination, these two exiled young Englishmen wrote an opera that is idiomatically American. Britten's score is a dazzling achievement, with songs in the form of blues, parodies of spirituals and Cole Porter, and remarkable anticipations of his own later works. Paul Bunyan is a mythical American folk-hero, never seen on-stage and whose part is spoken. The principal singing roles are those of his assistant Johnny Inkslinger, his Swedish foreman Hel Helson, a "man of brawn but no brains", his daughter Tiny, and a collection of cooks, farmers, cats and dogs. The work was none too favourably reviewed by the Americans in 1941 and Britten was only persuaded to look at it again in 1974 as a therapeutic exercise after his serious heart operation. This is its first recording and it is an unqualified success. It is not a work that requires star voices; teamwork and a generally good standard are the chief requirements and these are forthcoming. Each individual performance is neatly characterized and there is just enough homespun quality to remind us of the work's origins. Diction is exemplary and the American accents are genuine. Philip Brunelle conducts with real affection and understanding and the booklet is a superb piece of documentation. It is difficult to imagine a better performance.

Britten. ALBERT HERRING. **Sir Peter Pears** (ten) Albert Herring; **Sylvia Fisher** (sop) Lady Billows; **Johanna Peters** (contr) Florence Pike; **April Cantelo** (sop) Miss Wordsworth; **John Noble** (bar) Mr George; **Edgar Evans** (ten) Mr Upfold; **Owen Brannigan** (bass) Mr Budd; **Joseph Ward** (ten) Sid; **Catherine Wilson** (mez) Nancy; **Sheila Rex** (mez) Mrs Herring; **Sheila Amit** (sop) Emmie; **Anne Pashley** (sop) Cis; **Stephen Terry** (treb) Harry; **English Chamber Orchestra/Benjamin Britten.** Decca London 421 849-2LH2. Notes and text included. From SET274/6 (10/64).

2h 18' ② ADD 6/89 🎵P

Britten's chamber-opera has found a renewed place in the public's affection since Sir Peter Hall's celebrated production at Glyndebourne in 1985. The audience was once again charmed by the freshness and joyfulness of this delightful piece, an English ensemble work if ever there was one. Based on a Maupassant short story *Le rosier de Madame Husson*, Eric Crozier's libretto transports the story from France to Britten's native East Anglia. It tells of a market town's hunt for a May Queen to be crowned at the annual May Festival. None of the female candidates pass muster, leaving the honour to a boy, Albert Herring. This hand-picked cast, directed with evident affection and incomparable skill by the composer, could hardly be bettered. Peter Pears makes a perfect Albert, hesitant, callow but ultimately dignified; Sylvia Fisher is a domineering Lady Billows; April Cantelo twitters engagingly as Miss Wordworth; Owen Brannigan is splendid as the local policeman, Superintendent Budd. Indeed there isn't a weak link. The English Chamber Orchestra play superbly and the recording sounds quite superb for its years. All in all, this is a classic performance of an enchanting piece.

Britten. THE TURN OF THE SCREW. **Sir Peter Pears** (ten) Prologue, Quint; **Joan Cross** (sop) Mrs Grose; **Arda Mandikian** (sop) Miss Jessel; **Jennifer Vyvyan** (sop) Governess; **David Hemmings** (treb) Miles; **Olive Dyer** (sop) Flora; **English Opera Group Orchestra/Benjamin Britten.** Decca London mono 425 672-2LH2. Notes and text included. From LXT5038/9 (8/55).

② 1h 45' ADD 5/90

Sir Colin Davis's magnificent Philips recording of *The Turn of the Screw* has yet to be transferred to CD, but Britten's own 1954 version, made with the original cast not long after the work's first performance, wants for virtually nothing—even the mono sound has a vigour and clarity that many a modern stereo recording would do well to match. Part of the lasting success of this recording is a result of Britten's use of a chamber ensemble to provide the orchestral background to the singers—this could be captured with much greater space and accuracy than would have been possible at that time with a full orchestra, and provided the opportunity to push farther the expressive potential

of the chamber opera genre. Britten paces the work's chilling, insidious tale of good and evil so that it compounds, variation by variation, towards the tragic triumph of its conclusion. The key roles of Quint and the Governess, which subtly explore so many ramifications of male/female relationships, are definitively portrayed by Peter Pears and Jennifer Vyvyan, and the rest of the cast emulate the same high standard of musical distinction allied to sensitive characterization. This is, then, much more than an issue of only documentary interest.

Britten. DEATH IN VENICE. **Sir Peter Pears** (ten) Gustav von Aschenbach; **John Shirley-Quirk** (bar) Traveller, Elderly Fop, Old Gondolier, Hotel Manager, Hotel Barber, Leader of the Players, Voice of Dionysus; **James Bowman** (alto) Voice of Apollo; **Kenneth Bowen** (ten) Hotel Porter; **Peter Leeming** (bass) Travel Clerk; **Iris Saunders** (sop) Strawberry-seller; **English Opera Group Chorus; English Chamber Orchestra/Steuart Bedford.** Decca London 425 669-2LH2. Notes and text included. From SET581-3 (11/74).

② 2h 25' ADD 5/90

A special place is reserved for *Death in Venice* in the affections of most Britten aficionados, for not only is it one of his finest works but it also contains strong autobiographical associations. With his heart condition worsening as he composed, Britten feared that he might not live to complete the opera. Those troubles, coupled with his doubts about the value of what he had achieved in his life and career, found intense resonances in the plot and words of Myfanwy Piper's libretto. To us lesser mortals, his doubts might seem incomprehensible, yet they served to deepen and enrich the many layers of meaning that the music of *Death in Venice* encompasses. Recorded in The Maltings at Snape in 1974, this performance, so imaginatively and accurately directed by Steuart Bedford, brings the listener quickly to the work's chief themes. Pears's dominating presence as Aschenbach inevitably helps this process, yet much of the praise may go to the recording, which gives the singers an immediacy that, though rare in the opera house, is ideal for home listening. With magnificent support from the rest of the cast and the ECO, Pears, more than ever, seems Britten's alter ego here and the whole production a direct projection of the composer's mind.

Britten. PETER GRIMES. **Sir Peter Pears** (ten) Peter Grimes; **Claire Watson** (sop) Ellen Orford; **James Pease** (bass) Captain Balstrode; **David Kelly** (bass) Hobson; **Owen Brannigan** (bass) Swallow; **Lauris Elms** (mez) Mrs Sedley; **Jean Watson** (contr) Auntie; **Marion Studholme** (sop) First Niece; **Iris Kells** (sop) Second Niece; **Raymond Nilsson** (ten) Bob Boles; **John Lanigan** (ten) Rector; **Sir Geraint Evans** (bar) Ned Keene; **Chorus and Orchestra of the Royal Opera House, Covent Garden/Benjamin Britten**. Decca 414 577-2DH3. Notes and text included. From SXL2150/52 (10/59).

③ 2h 22' ADD 4/86 Ⓑ

This is the definitive recording which, in 1958, introduced the opera to many listeners and one which has never been superseded in its refinement or insight. Britten's conducting, lithe, lucid and as inexorable as "the tide that waits for no man", reveals his work as the complex, ambiguous drama that it is. Sir Peter Pears, in the title-role which was written for him, brings unsurpassed detail of nuance to Grimes's words while never losing sight of the essential plainness of the man's speech. The rest of the cast form a vivid portrait gallery. The recording is as live and clear as if it had been made yesterday and takes the listener right on to the stage. The bustle of activity and sound effects realize nicely Britten's own masterly painting of dramatic foreground and background.

Leo Brouwer   *Refer to Index*   *Cuban 1939-*

Max Bruch   *German 1838-1920*

Bruch. Violin Concerto No. 1 in G minor, Op. 26. Scottish Fantasy, Op. 46. **Cho-Liang Lin** (vn); **Chicago Symphony Orchestra/Leonard Slatkin.** CBS Masterworks CD42315. From IM42315 (3/87).

53' DDD 7/87 Ⓠℙ Ⓑ

Bruch. Violin Concerto No. 1 in G minor, Op. 26.
Mendelssohn. Violin Concerto in E minor, Op. 64. **Scottish Chamber Orchestra/Jaime Laredo** (vn). Pickwick IMP Red Label PCD829.

53' DDD 1/87 £ Ⓑ

Bruch. Violin Concerto No. 1 in G minor, Op. 26.
Dvořák. Violin Concerto in A minor, Op. 53. **Tasmin Little** (vn); **Royal Liverpool Philharmonic Orchestra/Vernon Handley.** Classics for Pleasure CD-CFP4566.

60' DDD 7/90 £ Ⓑ

When the CBS disc first appeared in 1987 Edward Greenfield was moved to write in *Gramophone*: "this is one of the most radiantly beautiful violin records I have heard for a long time". This seems to say it all. Cho-Liang Lin's playing is of the highest order here, with technically flawless performances of both works performed with such consummate ease that it leaves one with a sense of amazement. His handling of the first main subject in the Concerto's first movement has passion and intensity without resorting to sentimentality or over-indulgence, and a real feeling of excitement and momentum is generated as it leads to a truly magical account of the *Adagio*, where Lin's silky smooth tone is heard to its full advantage in the beautifully rapt and sustained melodic line. Bravura excitement returns in the finale which couples nobility and strength with warmth and tenderness. The *Scottish* Fantasy makes a welcome alternative to the normal Mendelssohn Concerto coupling. This is a less known and rarely recorded work, but is no less attractive or rewarding, especially in so persuasive and brilliant a performance as this. Leonard Slatkin and the Chicago Symphony Orchestra provide excellent and sympathetic support throughout. The recording is well balanced.

For anyone seeking the inevitable coupling, the Pickwick issue offers the best available version at any price. Laredo and the Scottish Chamber Orchestra obviously enjoy a close rapport, and the orchestral playing is marvellously alive and responsive, even when Laredo's attention must have been fully engaged by the solo part. His playing is technically immaculate and his tone is pure and sweet. In the Bruch concerto he plays with great sensitivity and sympathy and without any spurious seeking after effect: the *Adagio*, for instance, is projected with a quiet, reflective dignity and the finale has an abundance of natural, joyful energy. The Mendelssohn concerto is most poetically brought off, too, with the most natural, easy phrasing in the first movement, a beautifully shaped, most affecting slow movement, and a finale which has the most delicious, zestful spontaneity. It sounds very much as if Laredo and his orchestra thoroughly enjoyed making these recordings. The recording quality is attractively warm and clear.

The CFP disc is a most welcome issue and a fine bargain. In fact, Dvořák's Concerto is not as well known as it should be. As a boy, the composer played the violin for dancing in his native village, and thus he understood the instrument well, but after he composed this work in 1879 he became discouraged when his chosen soloist Joseph Joachim demanded revisions, and although Joachim then played it through for him, he himself was now dissatisfied with the work and made further changes before its première by another violinist in 1883. Today it is hard to see what was wrong, especially when the music is played here by a very gifted young soloist in a sympathetic partnership with an attentive conductor and the Royal Liverpool Philharmonic Orchestra in fine form. Tasmin Little's tone is rich and clear, and she shapes all this music with ardour, while the splendidly Bohemian-style finale really dances. The better known First Concerto of Bruch (another work on which the composer sought Joachim's advice) has a connection with Liverpool, for in 1881 the composer became the conductor of the city's Philharmonic Society and he directed a performance of it there in the following year. This music is also given with sweetness and considerable strength, and the recording made in the Liverpool Philharmonic Hall has good body and a natural balance.

Bruch. Kol Nidrei, Op. 47.
Lalo. Cello Concerto in D minor.
Saint-Saëns. Cello Concerto No. 1 in A minor, Op. 33. **Matt Haimovitz** (vc); **Chicago Symphony Orchestra/James Levine.** DG 427 323-2GH.
59' DDD 6/89

Although not himself Jewish, Bruch's inspiration for *Kol Nidrei* was the Jewish prayer for the eve of Yom Kippur and the Hebrew melodies associated with it. The result is eloquent indeed, with the solo cellist acting as a kind of cantor whose music seems to speak for a whole race. Lalo's Concerto is also music that has its share of rhetoric, though much of it is in a brilliant style suited to the concerto form. Saint-Saëns offers something different again, with three linked sections of considerable charm and ingenuity. The young cellist, Matt Haimovitz, displays a remarkable talent and an excellent recording complements the fine playing of both soloist and orchestra in all three works.

Anton Bruckner *Austrian 1824-1896*

Bruckner. SYMPHONIES. **Berlin Philharmonic Orchestra/Herbert von Karajan.** DG Karajan Symphony Edition 429 648-2GSE9.
No. 1 in C minor (Linz version)[b]; No. 2 in C minor (ed. Nowak[b]. Both 2740 264, 6/82); No. 3 in D minor (1889 version, ed. Nowak[b]. 2532 007, 7/81); No. 4 in E flat major, "Romantic"[a] (2530 674, 10/76); No. 5 in B flat major[a] (2702 101, 10/78); No. 6 in A major[a] (2531 295, 11/80); No. 7 in E major[a] (2707 102, 4/78); No. 8 in C minor (ed. Haas[a]. 2707 085, 5/76); No. 9 in D minor[a] (2530 828, 6/77).

| ⑨ 8h 40' | [a]ADD | [b]DDD | 3/91 |

It is often said that the essence of good Bruckner conducting is a firm grasp of structure. In fact that's only a half-truth. Of course one must understand how Bruckner's massive statements and counterstatements are fused together, but a performance that was nothing but architecture would be a pretty depressing experience. Karajan's understanding of the slow but powerful currents that flow beneath the surfaces of symphonies like the Fifth or Nos. 7-9 has never been bettered, but at the same time he shows how much more there is to be reckoned with: strong emotions, a deep poetic sensitivity (a Bruckner symphony can evoke landscapes as vividly as Mahler or Vaughan Williams) and a gift for singing melody that at times rivals even Schubert. It hardly needs saying that there's no such thing as a perfect record cycle, and this collection of the numbered Bruckner symphonies (unfortunately Karajan never recorded "No. 0") has its weaknesses. The early First and Second Symphonies can be a little heavy-footed and, as with so many Bruckner sets, there's a suspicion that more time might have been spent getting to know the fine but elusive Sixth—and there's an irritating throw-back to the days of corrupt Bruckner editions in the first big crescendo of the Fourth Symphony (high swooping violins—nasty!)—but none of these performances is without its major insights, and in the best of them—particularly Nos. 3, 5, 7, 8 and 9—those who haven't stopped their ears to Karajan will find that whatever else he may have been, there was a side to him that could only be described as 'visionary'. As for the recordings: climaxes can sound a touch overblown in some of the earlier symphonies, but on the whole the image is well-focused and atmospheric. A valuable set, and a landmark in the history of Bruckner recording.

Bruckner. Symphony No. 0 in D minor, "Die Nullte" (rev. 1869). Overture in G minor. **Berlin Radio Symphony Orchestra/Riccardo Chailly.** Decca 421 593-2DH.

| 58' | DDD | 1/90 |

It should be remembered that Bruckner wrote all his symphonies (including this one) after he was 40, indeed the bulk of *Die Nullte* that we encounter here was written after his official No. 1, and can be regarded as the progenitor of much that was to come in Bruckner's symphonic output: many of the motives can be found in later symphonies, the obvious example being the opening ostinato which later provided the underlay to the opening of the Third Symphony. Chailly's

thoroughly convincing performance takes a fairly spacious view of the work, with much emphasis on nobility, poise and dynamic shaping. And if at times he comes dangerously close to sentimentality in the Andante, in the end it is his feeling of serenity and warmth that win us over. This is superbly contrasted with the exuberance and urgency that he conveys in the dance-like Scherzo. At times the strings have a tendency to sound a little thin in the trio section, but this is more than compensated for in the lyrical and graceful playing of the Berlin RSO. The Overture in G minor, dating from 1862, makes a welcome filler and receives a similarly warm and persuasive performance. The recording is warm and well balanced.

Bruckner. Symphonies—No. 1 in C minor (1866 version)[a]; No. 5 in B flat major (orig. version)[b]. **Berlin Philharmonic Orchestra/Herbert von Karajan.** DG 415 985-2GH2. Item marked [a] from 2740 264 (6/82), [b] 2702 101 (10/78).

② 2h 12' DDD/ADD 6/87

Bruckner. Symphony No. 1 in C minor (1891 version). **Berlin Radio Symphony Orchestra/Riccardo Chailly.** Decca 421 091-2DH.

54' DDD 8/88

The First Symphony is a fully mature example of Bruckner's symphonic style. The very start, with its sturdy onward treading March, broken into by a chirpy little theme, was a startling innovation and the work contains other now familiar Brucknerian trademarks. Karajan projects it in a vital, ebullient fashion with a fine control of the music's ebb and flow. By the time Bruckner completed the Fifth Symphony, his style had become more complex and he allowed his ideas to develop at considerable length. This monumental work is handled superbly by Karajan. He has an unerring grasp of the work's structure, so that it seems to flow naturally and inevitably from beginning to end. The BPO's playing is superlative, and the 1977 analogue recording is rather better than that of the First Symphony.

Although Bruckner tinkered with the score of his Fifth Symphony, it was not until 1891 that he produced a full revision. Despite leaving the overall structure of the work virtually untouched, his rethinking of the details went so far as almost to produce a new work, certainly one more akin to his last two symphonies than his earlier ones. Whereas the earlier score has a freshness and simplicity that the latter lacks, the latter has a maturity of expression and technical assurance that the previous version fails to attain. Both are most worthy of a place on the CD shelves.

Chailly produces an uncompromising reading of this later version. He emphasizes those features that distinguish it from the original and chooses his speeds carefully to match the weight of the orchestration and the intensity of the expression. With a full-blooded, wide-ranging recording he can afford to pull out the orchestral stops and to highlight the dynamic contrasts, knowing that the inner details will remain audible in the thickest textures and solidity of timbre will not be sacrificed in the thinnest. This is certainly the most approachable of Bruckner symphonies for the uninitiated, particularly in this performance.

Bruckner. Symphony No. 3 in D minor. **Berlin Philharmonic Orchestra/ Herbert von Karajan.** DG 413 362-2GH. From 2532 007 (7/81).

54' DDD 8/84

Bruckner's Third Symphony exists in three versions and Karajan opts for the final, 1889 version; not that there is anything 'late' about his reading. He conducts long stretches of the score with unusual clarity and intensity and the whole performance is very dramatic but radiant, too, in the lyrical interludes. It is also surprisingly earthy and countrified in the several peasantish dance subjects which Bruckner winningly introduces. Some minor imprecisions in ensemble occur, the more or less inevitable by-products of what were probably long and very live takes. That is unavoidable though the recording itself is superb. On LP it was a great threat to domestic harmony; on CD it is even more so.

Bruckner. Symphony No. 4 in E flat major, "Romantic" (1888). **Philharmonia Orchestra/Otto Klemperer.** EMI Studio CDM7 69127-2. From Columbia SAX2569 (5/65).

61' ADD 12/88

Bruckner. Symphony No. 4 in E flat major, "Romantic" (1874, rev. Nowak). **Staatskapelle Dresden/Herbert Blomstedt.** Denon C37-7126.

67' DDD 2/85

Bruckner. Symphony No. 4 in E flat major, "Romantic" (1880, ed. Nowak). **Berlin Philharmonic Orchestra/Eugen Jochum.** DG Privilege 427 200-2GR. From SLPM139134/5 (5/67).

64' ADD 9/89

Bruckner's Fourth is the most immediately approachable of his symphonies and with its lovely horn solo has surely one of the most evocative openings of any symphony, whilst the 'Hunting' *Scherzo* uses the full horn section with rhythmical exuberance to equal atmospheric effect. The listener is ever conscious of the structural power of the piece, like a great building, with four impressive rooms, each leading to the other in perfect architectural balance.

Of all conductors Klemperer most conveys this feeling of structure; its power is undeniable and he is supported by magnificent Philharmonia playing. The 1965 recording is given added brilliance in the digital remastering, but its weight and amplitude remain. Blomstedt has the advantage of first-class modern digital recording, and the playing and body of tone made by his Dresden orchestra are gloriously rich. He too shows a fine sense of the work's architecture, and his reading has a special combination of intensity and poetic feeling—his slow movement is particularly eloquent. This is a mellower view and the rich ambience of the recording suits it well.

For many the inspirational qualities of Jochum's reading are most satisfying of all. He is one

of the few conductors to make real sense of Bruckner's block-like formal structures and his long-term harmonic movements; yet he also finds time to bring out the composer's humanity and tenderness. His control of the music's flow seems uncannily inevitable. Tempos tend to be on the slow side, but Jochum is so persuasive that one feels the rightness of his pacing and in his control of the work's great climaxes he is never hectoring: there is a nobility of conception here that is very moving. The sound is noticeably analogue in origin but still has a fine dynamic and frequency spread which enhances rather than detracts from this outstanding performance.

Bruckner. Symphony No. 5 in B flat major. Te Deum[a]. [a]**Karita Mattila** (sop); [a]**Susanne Mentzer** (mez); [a]**Vinson Cole** (ten); [a]**Robert Holl** (bass); [a]**Bavarian Radio Chorus; Vienna Philharmonic Orchestra/Bernard Haitink.** Philips 422 342-2PH2. Text and translation included.

② 1h 40' DDD 11/89

Completed in 1876 and slightly modified a couple of years later, Bruckner's Fifth was not then performed in its original version until 1935. Its subsequent dissemination has done much to help our understanding of the composer's work for, being more orchestrally spartan and emotionally self-contained, it is fairly atypical of his canon of symphonies. Haitink's 1972 recording with the Concertgebouw remained for many years the yardstick by which other performances of the work could be judged, but this new version for CD looks like acceding to that role. Using the VPO here, Haitink returns the work to its roots, drawing upon the native feel that these players have for the Austrian dance rhythms that Bruckner exploits so effectively in the Scherzo's third movement. He gives the players their collective head in the slower moments of the work, broadening the tempo to allow them to enrich expression and tonal weight. The recording also allows for this, and the result is as passionate and idiomatic as could be wished for. The coupled *Te Deum* is a glorious realization of what Bruckner considered "the pride of my life", filling to the limit the awesome Viennese acoustic.

Bruckner (ed. Haas). Symphony No. 6 in A major. **New Philharmonia Orchestra/Otto Klemperer.** EMI Studio CDM7 63351-2. From Columbia SAX2582 (9/65).

55' ADD 3/90

No Brucknerian will want to be without Klemperer's legendary performance, indeed it has long been regarded as perhaps the finest recorded interpretation of this symphony. Part of Klemperer's success lies in his unerring ability to project the symphony's architectural and organic content through Bruckner's ever changing terrain. His vigorous and resolute approach is apparent from the outset, where the opening ostinato string figure, crisp and rhythmically assured, tell us that this is no routine performance. His handling of Bruckner's frequent *fortissimo* 'blaze ups' is always dramatic, exhilarating and sonorous, whilst never destroying the beautifully clear and lucid textures he achieves throughout the symphony. The adagio is one of Bruckner's most sublime creations. Klemperer's choice of tempo may seem fast here, but is entirely justified by the resulting sense of momentum and forward drive: and you will be hard pressed to find a better rendering of the tender and expansive second theme as it burgeons out of the sombre introduction. The Scherzo, with its incessant bass and cello ostinato tread is given a subtle and evocative reading, building the tension superbly before resolving into the haunting and mysterious trio section with its Tristanesque horn calls. The recording, made in the Kingsway Hall in 1964, is excellent.

Bruckner. Symphony No. 7. **Staatskapelle Dresden / Herbert Blomstedt.** Denon C37-7286.

> 68' DDD 8/86 **B**

Bruckner's gloriously long-breathed Seventh Symphony is, of all his works, the one most indebted to the music of Wagner. Although the Third was dedicated to this composer, it is the Seventh which is closer in spirit and tonal colour to that of Wagner. Herbert Blomstedt's performance of this great work is glorious—well judged, beautifully played and with just the right blend of eloquence and tension. The recording is excellent.

Bruckner. Symphony No. 8 in C minor. **Vienna Philharmonic Orchestra / Herbert von Karajan.** DG 427 611-2GH2.

> ② 83' DDD 10/89 **B**

As if by some strange act of providence, great conductors have often been remembered by the immediate posthumous release of some fine and representative recording. With Karajan it is the Eighth Symphony of Bruckner, perhaps the symphony he loved and revered above all others. It is the sense of the music being in the hearts and minds and collective unconscious of Karajan and every one of the 100 and more players of the Vienna Philharmonic that gives this performances its particular charisma and appeal. It is a wonderful reading, every bit as authoritative as its many predecessors and every bit as well played but somehow more profound, more humane, more lovable if that is a permissible attribute of an interpretation of this Everest among symphonies. The end of the work, always astonishing and uplifting, is especially fine here and very moving. Fortunately, it has been recorded with plenty of weight and space and warmth and clarity, with the additional benefit of the added vibrancy of the Viennese playing. The sessions were obviously sufficiently happy for there to shine through moments of spontaneous power and eloquence that were commonplace in the concert hall in Karajan's later years, but which recordings can't always be relied upon to catch.

Bruckner. Symphony No. 9 in D minor. **Columbia Symphony Orchestra / Bruno Walter.** CBS Maestro CD44825. From Philips SABL179 (6/61).

> 59' ADD 6/90 £ **P**

Bruckner. Symphony No. 9. **Berlin Philharmonic Orchestra / Herbert von Karajan.** DG 419 083-2GH. From 2530 828 (6/77).

> 62' ADD 9/86 **P** **B**

Walter's is a classic recording, almost the Alpha and Omega of Bruckner Ninth performance, refurbished in mellow digital garb. He takes an expansive, almost relaxed view of the work and coaxes from the Columbia Symphony Orchestra a performance of eloquent power. Although there is some lack of refinement over details, the broad sweeps are taken to their expressive extremes with the orchestra balanced to produce an enormous, full-bodied sound at *fortissimo*. In the first movement, the weavings of the second subject are made particularly telling by this large-scale approach, and it pays off magnificently in the closing slow movement, where all the tensions created in the first movement and Scherzo are gloriously resolved. The towering textures and affirmative repetitions have a spacious grandeur that few other conductors even approach. Bruckner intended a finale to follow but Walter reads the work as though he hadn't, perhaps establishing the Brucknerites's preference for seeing the third movement as the apotheosis of the composer's life work. Many fine versions of this work, in more up-to-date sound, are now available on CD, yet any devotee of Bruckner's Ninth could not feel complete without this one.

Nevertheless, no conductor has understood this astonishing score, intellectually and intuitively, more completely than Karajan. His performance has, from first note to last, a blazing eloquence and a depth of commitment you will encounter nowhere else. The Berlin playing is equal to the occasion. The recording, exceptionally vivid, was sometimes difficult to tame on LP, but the CD version gives unalloyed pleasure.

Bruckner. CHORAL WORKS. **Corydon Singers; English Chamber Orchestra Wind Ensemble/Matthew Best.** Hyperion CDA66177. Texts and translations included. From A66177 (2/86).
Mass No. 2 in E minor. Libera me in F minor (Colin Sheen, Roger Brenner, Philip Brown, tbns). Aequali for three trombones, Nos. 1 and 2 (Sheen, Brenner, Brown).

53' DDD 9/86

Bruckner's E minor Mass, unlike its two companions in D minor and F minor, employs a wind band as its instrumental base. This rich accompaniment creates a powerful foundation to the spaciously conceived vocal parts whilst the clarity of the writing gives the work a grandeur and feeling of architectural stability more often encountered in mightier works. This fine recording uses the ample acoustics of St Alban, Holborn in London to telling effect. The performances are extremely good, matched by a recording of a kind at which Hyperion excel.

Bruckner. SACRED CHORAL WORKS. **Bavarian Radio [a]Chorus and [b]Symphony Orchestra; [c]Chorus of the Deutsche Oper, Berlin; [c]Berlin Philharmonic Orchestra/Eugen Jochum.** DG 423 127-2GX4. Texts and translations included.
Masses[ab]—No. 1 in D minor (with Edith Mathis, sop; Marga Schiml, contr; Wieslaw Ochman, ten; Karl Ridderbusch, bass; Elmar Schloter, org. From 2720 054, 3/73); No. 2 in E minor (2720 054, 3/73); No. 3 in F minor (Maria Stader, sop; Claudia Hellmann, contr; Ernst Haefliger, ten; Kim Borg, bass; Anton Nowakowski, org. SLPM138829, 3/63). Te Deum[c] (Stader; Sieglinde Wagner, contr; Haefliger; Peter Lagger, bass; Wolfgang Meyer, org. SLPM139117/18, 5/66). Psalm 150[c] (Stader. SLPM139399, 5/69).
Motets[a]—Virga Jesse; Ave Maria; Locus iste; Tota pulchra es (Richard Holm, ten; Nowakowski); Ecce sacerdos magnus (Ludwig Laberer, Josef Hahn, Alfons Hartenstein, tbns; Hedwig Bilgram, org. All from SLPM139135, 5/67); Os justi; Christus factus est; Vexilla regis (SLPM139138, 5/69); Affrentur regi (Laberer, Hahn, Hartenstein); Pange lingua (both from 2720 054).

④ 3h 47' ADD 9/88

Bruckner's first notable composition was a Requiem in D minor and is important because it contains fingerprints of Bruckner's symphonic style, as does the Mass No. 3 in F minor. But undoubtedly the *Te Deum* is Bruckner's greatest choral work, a mighty affirmation of faith in C major but with interludes of tenderness and warmth in which a solo violin is used expressively. The performances on this disc are a notable tribute to the art of the conductor Eugen Jochum and were made between 1963 and 1972. They have been transferred to CD with total success and the singing of the respective choirs is thrilling. Maria Stader and Kim Borg are the best of the soloists in the F minor Mass, with Stader also outstanding in the *Te Deum*. The discs are invaluable, too, for containing 10 short motets, most of which will be unfamiliar to many listeners. The seraphic *Ave Maria* and a particularly touching *Pange lingua* are typical of the quality of music and performance enshrined here.

Ferruccio Busoni
Italian-German 1866-1924

Busoni. Piano Concerto, Op. 39. **Volker Banfield** (pf); **Bavarian Radio Chorus; Bavarian Radio Symphony Orchestra/Lutz Herbig.** CPO CPO999 017-2.

| 73' AAD 7/89 | |

Busoni. Piano Concerto, Op. 39. **Garrick Ohlsson** (pf); Men's voices of the **Cleveland Orchestra Chorus; Cleveland Symphony Orchestra/ Christoph von Dohnányi.** Telarc CD80207.

| 72' DDD 4/90 | |

Busoni. Piano Concerto, Op. 39. **Peter Donohoe** (pf); men's voices of the **BBC Singers; BBC Symphony Orchestra/Mark Elder.** EMI CDC7 49996-2. Recorded at a performance in the Royal Albert Hall, London on August 5th, 1988.

| 74' DDD 1/91 | |

Busoni's must be the longest piano concerto every written. Because of its length and its unusual proportions it can easily seem sprawling. Busoni gave a clue to avoiding this impression by describing the concerto in architectural terms: the central movement as a huge nave or dome, buttressed by the introduction and finale, with the scherzos envisaged as 'scenes from life', played out in the open air between the three great buildings. It is in the characterization of the music that Herbig is most successful. He is especially good at projecting Busoni's individual orchestral sound (helped by a very natural recording) and it is by this means that he makes the choral finale seem both necessary and culminatory. The sound here is quite magical. Herbig must surely have read the stage directions for the play from which Busoni drew his text; they describe Aladdin's magic cavern, with jewelled fruit growing on metal trees, and it is the rocks themselves that sing the concerto's concluding mystical hymn. The scale of Busoni's playing matches the grandeur of the work's conception, and if a few of the quieter moments lack a touch of delicacy or fantasy this is amply outweighed by his fire and virtuosity elsewhere.

Garrick Ohlsson won the Busoni Competition in Italy as long ago as 1966 and obviously believes passionately in the work. He brings to it great virtuosity and intellectual strength, while Christoph von Dohnányi and the Cleveland Orchestra (and Men's Chorus in the finale) give him excellent support. Doubts may remain as to whether this enormous structure with its mystical final message ("Lift your hearts...Feel Allah near", sings the chorus) holds up against the charge of windiness, but it is done here with such commitment and panache that even the doubters must surely salute the demonstration of a kind of genius. Ohlsson uses a Bösendorfer piano that produces just the right kind of big, craggy tone as well as being capable of delicacy when needed. The recording is outstanding, and index marks are usefully provided in the long *Pezzo serioso* which is the third movement.

However, the sense of adventure and discovery inherent in this work is nowhere better realized than in the mould-breaking 1988 Proms reading from Donohoe and Elder. Their devotion to the work is evident in every bar, and the concentration that they apply to it does not waver from start to finish: the enrapt attention of the audience bears eloquent testament to this. The price you pay for this degree of integrity, typical of live performance, is relatively slight—balance is not always ideal, especially with the mens' voices in the final movement, and the orchestral sound has a certain fullness that a studio would probably have mitigated. But be warned: this is not a performance to be sampled—it works wonderfully as a whole and once begun it seems impossible not to see it through to the end.

Busoni. THE MAJOR PIANO WORKS. **Geoffrey Douglas Madge.** Philips 420 740-2PH6. Booklet included. Recorded at performances at the Royal Conservatorium, The Hague, Holland during 1986.
24 Preludi, Op. 37. Zwei Tänzstücke, Op. 30a. Ballettszene No. 4, Walzer und Galopp, Op. 33a. Racconti fantastici, Op. 12. Variationen und Fuge in freier Form über Fr. Chopins c-moll Präludium, Op. 22. Macchiette Medioevali, Op. 33. Stücke, Op. 33b. Elegien. Suite Campestre, Op. 18. Zehn Variationen über ein Präludium von Chopin Op. 22 (second version). Fantasia contrappuntistica (first version). Choral Vorspiel über ein Bachsches Fragment. Nuit de Noël. Indianisches Tagebuch. Fantasia nach Johann Sebastian Bach. Sonatina No. 1. Sonatina No. 2. Sonatina No. 3 ad usum infantis. Sonatina No. 4 in diem nativitatis Christi MCMXVII. Sonatina No. 5 brevis "in signo Joannis Sebastiani Magni". Sonatina No. 6 super Carmen. Drei Albumblätter. Notturni, Prologo. Perpetuum mobile. An die Jugend. Sieben kurze Stücke zur Pflege des polyphonen Spiels. Prélude et Etude en Arpèges. Toccata: Preludio, Fantasia, Ciaccona.

⑥ 6h 25' DDD 4/88

Cautious newcomers to Busoni's music may find a six-and-a-half-hour bumper bundle of it rather off-putting. But you do get a clearer idea of what sort of composer Busoni was from this great bran-tub than from concentrating exclusively on the masterpieces. Busoni's self-imposed task was one of musical unification. His gifts as a formidably equipped virtuoso, together with his roots in late Romanticism, gave him a strong commitment to the traditions of Liszt, Brahms and Schumann (we can hear the latter two in the astonishingly ambitious and precocious Preludes, written in his mid-teens; Liszt is clearly audible in the Ballet Scene, Op. 33a). Busoni's head and much of his heart, however, were devoted to Bach, while his ears were keenly open to what was going on around him. He became convinced that an inclusive language, rooted in Bach but welcoming all that was innovatory in his successors, was the firmest foundation on which to build paths to the future. His attempts to find his own path are chronicled in this absorbing collection. Alongside the masterpieces (the two great *Fantasias*, the *Toccata* and the *Sieben kurze Stücke*), there are many pages of audacious mastery in the Sonatinas and the *Elegien* and many of unashamed barnstorming pianism. Geoffrey Douglas Madge explores Busoni's musical autobiography and testament with huge enjoyment and technical assurance and with a truly Busonian sense of adventure. An exciting achievement, with the bold architecture of the music paralleled by a richly sonorous recording.

Busoni. Fantasia contrappuntistica (1910)[a]. Fantasia nach J. S. Bach (1909)[a]. Toccata[b]. **John Ogdon** (pf). Continuum CCD1006. Items marked [a] from Altarus AIR-2-9074 (10/88), [b] new to UK.

60' AAD 7/89

Busoni's *Fantasia contrappuntistica* is of legendary difficulty, density and length and pianists seem very reluctant to learn it. Ogdon plays it with consummate virtuosity, clarity and sustained concentration, and alongside the technical assurance there is a firm intellectual grasp of Busoni's prodigious structure and a lofty eloquence in expressing his faith. It is a formidable feat of musicianship as well as pianism. The two other pieces are more personal; many may find them even more moving. The *Fantasia nach J.S. Bach* is freer in structure than the *Fantasia contrappuntistica* and with its dedication to his father's memory it is as though Busoni has chosen particularly beloved and appropriate pages for his tribute, adding his own meditations on them. The very late *Toccata* is a resurgence of the Faustian vein that runs throughout Busoni's work, but now dark and pessimistic. The three works add up to a sort of triple self-portrait and Ogdon characterizes them finely. Busoni's piano-writing demands a huge range of sonority as well as endurance and sheer dexterity; in these performances (and this superb recording) Busoni's piano is rendered full-size.

Busoni. DOKTOR FAUST. **Dietrich Fischer-Dieskau** (bar) Doktor Faust; **William Cochran** (ten) Mephistopheles; **Anton de Ridder** (ten) Duke of Parma; **Hildegard Hillebrecht** (sop) Duchess of Parma; **Karl Christian Kohn** (bass) Wagner, Master of Ceremonies; **Franz Grundheber** (bar) Soldier, Natural Philosopher; **Manfred Schmidt** (ten) Lieutenant; **Marius Rintzler** (bass) Jurist; **Hans Sotin** (bass) Theologian; **Bavarian Radio Chorus and Symphony Orchestra/Ferdinand Leitner.** DG 20th Century Classics 427 413-2GC3. Notes, text and translation included. From 139291/3 (9/70).

⏱ ③ 2h 36' ADD 8/89

Doktor Faust has never become a popular repertory piece. Its musical subtleties, they say, are too learned for general consumption—yet those subtleties are dressed in the most alluring, indeed magical sonorities. Busoni rather too readily assumes, they say, that listeners will be as soaked in the various versions of the Faust legend as he was. He omits huge chunks of it (there is no Gretchen, for example) so that he can concentrate on the tragico-heroic essentials—but his

Dietrich Fischer-Dieskau   [photo: EMI]

Faust is a grander and more humane creation as a consequence. On disc especially, where its dark sayings can be mulled over at leisure, it sounds more and more like a *necessary* opera: an idealistic model of what the form is capable of, a meditation on themes, both musical and philosophical, that have never been more relevant than they are now. This excellently remastered recording is 20 years old, and the work was extensively cut to get it on to three LPs (ironically enough its playing time is now just marginally too long for two CDs). It is a superb performance, though, dominated by Fischer-Dieskau's grandly eloquent assumption of the title-role. Cochran is frighteningly intense in the impossibly high tenor role of Mephistopheles, and all the secondary characters are cast strongly, with the exception of Hillebrecht's worn and rather squally Duchess. Firm direction from Leitner, very accomplished choral singing, and a fine sense of real stage space surrounding the action.

George Butterworth   *Refer to Index*   British 1885-1916

Dietrich Buxtehude

Buxtehude. ORGAN WORKS. **Ton Koopman.** Novalis 150 048-2. Played on the Arp-Schnitger organ of St Ludgeri's, Norden.
Prelude and Ciacona in C major, BuxWV137. Eine feste Burg ist unser Gott, BuxWV184. Passacaglia in D minor, BuxWV161. Nun komm, der Heiden Heiland, BuxWV211. In dulci jubilo, BuxWV197. Fuga in C major, BuxWV174. Puer natus in Bethlehem, BuxWV217. Prelude in D major, BuxWV139. Nun lob, mein Seel, den Herren, BuxWV212. Prelude in G minor, BuxWV163. Wie schön leuchtet der Moregenstern, BuxWV223. Prelude in G minor, BuxWV149.

57' DDD 6/90

A most welcome by-product of the 'CD revolution' has been the generous exposure given to those composers whose music, if not their names, has been familiar only to those with specialized interest. For readers of potted histories of music Buxtehude will be known primarily as the man whose organ playing was considered sufficiently impressive for the young J.S. Bach to walk 400 miles to hear. But as for his music, even organists are largely unaware of the vast amount he wrote for that instrument. Yet there are those who would claim that, had it not been for the towering genius of Bach, Buxtehude would today be considered as one of the 'great' composers of the baroque age. Those of an inquisitive disposition who would like a representative cross-section of Buxtehude's organ music on a single disc will find this one ideal. From the big, flamboyant, virtuoso works (such as the Prelude in G minor) to the delightful miniatures which had a particularly strong influence on the young Bach (including a frivolous Gigue Fugue) here is Buxtehude on top form. Ton Koopman gives them all sturdy, no-nonsense performances on a full-blooded, earthy instrument dating from Buxtehude's time, and the recording has great presence.

William Byrd

Byrd. MASSES AND MOTETS. **The Tallis Scholars/Peter Phillips.** Gimell CDGIM345. From BYRD345 (5/84).
Mass for five voices. Mass for four voices. Mass for three voices. Motet—Ave verum corpus a 4.

67' DDD 3/86

Byrd was a fervently committed Roman Catholic and he helped enormously to enrich the music of the English Church. His Mass settings were made for the many recusant Catholic worshippers who held services in private. They were published between 1593 and 1595 and are creations of great feeling. The contrapuntal writing has a much closer texture and fibre than the Masses of Palestrina and there is an austerity and rigour that is allowed to blossom and expand with the text. The beautifully restrained and mellow recording, made in Merton College Chapel, Oxford, fully captures the measure of the music and restores the awe and mystery of music that familiarity has sometimes dimmed.

The Tallis Scholars [photo: Barda

John Cage

American 1912-

Cage. Sonatas and Interludes for prepared piano. **Gérard Frémy** (prepared pf).
Etcetera KTC2001. From ETC2001 (12/83).

70' DDD 9/88

John Cage made two major discoveries when he invented the 'prepared piano' in
1946. The first was that to insert nuts, bolts, rubber wedges and bits of plastic
between the strings of a piano does not make it sound hideously nasty but, if
done with care and precision, turns it into an orchestra of delicately chiming,
bright, fragile and gamelan-like sounds. The second discovery was that this 'new'
instrument had to be treated with great subtlety. The result is the most
mysteriously lucid score he has ever written, a sequence of quiet rituals and
arabesque gestures, of silences in which hazes of resonance die away. Transparent
textures and low dynamic levels predominate, but the work is by no means
incidentless. There is a fairly clear progress from the briefer, quieter, more
hesitant earlier Sonatas to the bigger and more dramatic gestures of Sonatas 9 to
12. To hear the Sonatas and Interludes complete and in sequence, at least once
in a while, is a wonderfully ear-cleansing experience, a demonstration of how
potent, beautiful and startlingly fresh the simplest of musical events can be. The
discovery led Cage into an entranced contemplation of the sounds around us that
we cannot accept as 'music', and these pieces raise questions about how we
listen and how we hear that will not go away. Frémy's absorbed and absorbing
performance has the composer's approval and the transparent clarity of the
recording is ideal.

Thomas Campion

British 1567-1620

Campion. AYRES. **Drew Minter** (alto); **Paul O'Dette** (lute). Harmonia
Mundi HMU90 7023. Texts included.
Beauty, since you so much desire. Love me or not. Your faire lookes. Never
love unlesse you can. O never to be moved. The sypres curten of the night is
spread. Awake thou spring of speaking grace. Come you pretty false-ey'd
wanton. So tyr'd are all my thoughts. Fire, fire. Pin'd I am and like to dye.
Author of light. See where she flies. Faire if you expect admiring. Shall I come
sweet love to thee? It fell on a sommers daie. Kinde are her answers. Beauty is
but a painted hell. Sweet exclude me not. Are you what your faire lookes
expresse? I care not for these ladies. Never weather-beaten saile.

58' DDD 6/91

Thomas Campion wrote even more lute songs than John Dowland, though it
must be said that, unlike Dowland, he composed nothing else. His songs are
marked by a careful marriage of music with speech-rhythms but they are less
demonstrative than those of Dowland, whose penchant for dramatic harmonic
underlining he did not share. They are nevertheless very rewarding, beautiful in
their individual way, and often catchy; another respect in which Campion
differed from Dowland (and others) was that he wrote both the music and the
lyrics. This recording contains a selection from Campion's published books of
1601, 1613 and 1617, and their texts range from the devout (*Never weather-beaten
saile; Author of light*) to the bawdy—but subtle enough to give Mary Whitehouse
no offence (*Beauty, since you so much desire; It fell on a sommers daie*), with an
extensive middle ground of songs concerning the pleasure and pains of love.
Drew Minter's vocal quality is excellent and Paul O'Dette's lute accompaniments are exemplary; if Campion could do as well single-handed, he was

indeed talented. Full texts are given (also in French and German) in the booklet, together with concisely informative annotation by Robert Spencer.

André Campra *French 1660-1744*

Campra. Messe de Requiem. **Elisabeth Baudry, Monique Zanetti** (sops); **Josep Benet** (alto); **John Elwes** (ten); **Stephen Varcoe** (bar); **La Chapelle Royale Chorus and Orchestra/Philippe Herreweghe.** Harmonia Mundi HMC90 1251.

43' DDD 9/87

Two outstandingly beautiful *Messes des Morts* were composed in France during the late baroque period. The earlier was by Jean Gilles, the later by André Campra. Both were Provençal composers and both were connected at least by the fact that Campra directed a performance of the other's Mass at Gilles's funeral in 1705. As well as being a gifted composer of sacred music—he succeeded Delalande as composer to the Chapelle Royale— Campra was a successful and innovative theatre composer. This is reflected in his ability to handle the components of an elaborate sacred work such as this Requiem Mass in a colourful and dramatic manner. But it is the quiet intensity and profoundly contemplative character of the Requiem which more deeply affect our senses. Listeners, too, may be struck by the music's individuality which almost, perhaps, forges a link with Fauré's *Requiem* some two hundred years later. Philippe Herreweghe is attentive to points of style and has assembled a strong cast of singers among whom John Elwes and Stephen Varcoe are outstanding. The voices of La Chapelle Royale are clear in texture and pleasantly blended and the Orchestra, too, makes an effective contribution. The work is well recorded and, by-and-large, eloquently performed.

Campra. TANCREDE. **François Le Roux** (bar) Tancred; **Daphné Evangelatos** (contr) Clorinda; **Catherine Dubosc** (sop) Herminie; **Pierre-Yves Le Maigat** (bass-bar) Argant; **Gregory Reinhart** (bass) Ismenor; **Colette Alliot-Lugaz** (sop) Peace, Female Warrior, Dryad; **Dominique Visse** (alto) Wood-nymph; **Alison Wells** (sop) Shepherdess; **Andrew Murgatroyd** (ten) Warrior, Magician; **Christopher Royall** (alto), **Jeremy White** (bass) Magicians; **The Sixteen; Grande Ecurie et la Chambre du Roy/Jean-Claude Malgoire.** Erato Musifrance 2292-45001-2. Notes, text and translation included. Recorded at a performance in the Théâtre de l'Archevêche, Aix-en-Provence in July 1986.

② 2h 2' DDD 6/90

André Campra carried on the Lullian tradition of *tragédies en musique* but made his own distinctive contribution to the development of dramatic forms with *opéra-ballet*. *Tancrède*, however, is a *tragédie* and proved to be one of Campra's most successful serious operas. It was first performed in 1702 and held the stage at frequent intervals until 1764. The story is loosely based on the legend of Tancred and Clorinda in Tasso's epic poem *Gerusalemme Liberata*. In its overture, prologue and five acts and its generous assortment of instrumental movements, *Tancrède* follows the pattern set by Lully. The present recording, made from a production of the work which took place during the 1986 Aix-en-Provence Festival does not include all of Campra's music but is trimmed to a two-hour entertainment. The performance is enjoyable notwithstanding a few disappointments both in the singing and playing. Catherine Dubosc, François Le Roux and Gregory Reinhart are the most impressive of the principal soloists but some of the minor roles are well sung, too. Jean-Claude Malgoire's direction is more sharply focused than in some other of his recordings and the project as a whole gives a fair account of an appealing work. Full texts are included in French, English and German.

Joseph Canteloube

French 1879-1957

Canteloube. CHANTS D'AUVERGNE, Volume 2. Triptyque. **Frederica von Stade** (mez); **Royal Philharmonic Orchestra/Antonio de Almeida.** Sony Classical CD37837. Texts and translations included. From IM37837 (7/86).
Là-haut, sur le rocher. Jou l'pount d'o Mirabel. Hé beyla-z-y-dau fé. Lou boussou. Pastourelle. Malurous qu'o uno fenno. Obal, din lo coumbèlo. La pastrouletta è lou chibaliè. Quand z'eyro petitoune. Pastouro sé tu m'aymo. Pastorale. La pastoura al camps. Lou diziou bé.

• 61' DDD 10/86 Ⓑ

The intriguing combination of innocence and sophistication, a favourite feature in several of the arts, is alluringly exemplified in Canteloube's now famous settings of folk-songs from his native corner of France—lusciously ornate, beautifully and ingeniously scored free arrangements of basically simple material. Von Stade's purity of tone is ideally suited to this: she tells the little tales (mostly of shepherdesses) with an engaging directness, entering with spirit into the gaiety of the song about feeding the donkey or the rollicking irony of "Unhappy he who has a wife", and providing some characterization for the mixed pathos and humour of the dialogue between Jeanneton and the hunchback. Canteloube's remarkable invention gives the RPO a real outing, providing elaborate washes of sound in the *Pastorale* (which is cognate with the celebrated *Baïlèro*) and dizzy chromaticisms in "At the Mirabel bridge". For sheer sensuous beauty, however, the prize should surely go to *Là-haut, sur le rocher* (the only one here in French: the rest are in the original *langue d'oc*). Canteloube also made various other collections of Auvergnat songs, besides composing symphonic works and two operas—none of which we ever hear. But von Stade does include here, besides 16 of the *Chants d'Auvergne*, his remarkable *Triptyque*, composed a decade earlier, ecstatic rhapsodies on pantheistic poems by Roger Frène (who ought to have been credited): the rapturous romanticism of these, sung with passion by von Stade, whets an appetite to know more of Canteloube's music.

Elliott Carter

American 1908-

Carter. Piano Concerto (1964-5)[a]. Variations for Orchestra (1954-5). [a]**Ursula Oppens** (pf); **Cincinnati Symphony Orchestra/Michael Gielen.** New World NW347-2. Recorded at performances in the Music Hall, Cincinnati, Ohio in October 1984 and October 1985.

• 45' DDD/ADD 4/87

Live recordings of complex contemporary works are a risky enterprise and there are certainly a few rough and ready aspects to be heard in these performances. But they are trivial in the extreme beside the excitement and commitment of artists who have read beyond the notes into the spirit of this tough but exhilarating music. Carter is so important because, while a radical in the sense of moving well beyond transitional ideas of melody and harmony, he uses his new techniques to achieve an amazing directness of expression. The Variations and the

Piano Concerto complement each other very well. In the Variations, echoes of the past can still be heard, and the moods are playful and aspiring, predominantly optimistic. The Concerto is darker, with elements of the tragic represented by the tension between the soloist and the orchestral mass. The result is far from negative, even so, since the soloist's material has all the delicacy and flamboyance of Carter at his most imaginative. This music is the perfect antidote to an overdose of Philip Glass or John Adams, and the recordings, despite the occasional contributions from the audience, are perfectly adequate.

Carter. MISCELLANEOUS WORKS. [a]**Phyllis Bryn-Julson** (sop); [b]**Heinz Holliger** (ob); [c]**Sophie Cherrier** (fl); [c]**André Trouttet** (cl); [d]**Ensemble Intercontemporain/Pierre Boulez.** Erato 2292-45364-2. Text included. Oboe Concerto[bd]. Esprit rude/esprit doux[c]. Penthode[d]. A Mirror on which to Dwell[ad].

> 63' DDD 2/90

Elliott Carter has had a gratifyingly productive old age. Only one of the works on this disc, *A Mirror on which to Dwell*, was composed before 1980, and we can now appreciate how its beautifully refined sonorities and needle-sharp balancing of formal coherence against shapely text-setting marked the start of a new phase

to which all the other works included belong. The brief flute/clarinet duet, *Esprit rude/esprit doux*, was a sixtieth-birthday gift for Boulez in 1985, and *Penthode* was completed that same year for Boulez's Ensemble Intercontemporain. The title refers to the four groups of five instruments which this rich and fascinating score explores with all Carter's characteristic subtlety of differentiation and interaction. As for the Oboe Concerto, the contrast of melody-spinning soloist and context-setting ensemble inspires Carter to an even more spontaneous outpouring of intricate yet always characterful polyphony. The performance

Pierre Boulez   *[photo: Erato/Sarrat]*

by Heinz Holliger is quite simply definitive, and the other works are also very well done in an excellently clear and well-balanced recording.

Carter. STRING QUARTETS. **Arditti Quartet** (Irvine Arditti, David Alberman, vns; Levine Andrade, va; Rohan de Saram, vc). Etcetera KTC1065/6. *KTC1065:* String Quartets—No. 1; No. 4. *KTC1066:* String Quartets—No. 2; No. 3. Elegy.

> ② 59' 45' DDD 5/89   Ⓠ[P]

The Arditti Quartet can play the most complex modern music with confidence as well as accuracy. Their performances radiate enjoyment and enthusiasm, not just a dour determination to convey what is on the printed page with maximum precision. Carter's four quartets span 35 years (1951-86) and, with the early *Elegy* of 1943, chart with exemplary clarity his spiritual and stylistic odyssey. Starting with a shapely neo-classicism quite close to that of Copland, he moved around 1950 into a world nearer that of early twentieth-century Viennese expressionism, whilst retaining an expansive form and rhythmic buoyancy which is characteristically American. In the Third Quartet you sense a kind of crisis within this expressionism, overwhelming in its unsparing vehemence and stretching the medium to breaking point. In his later works the crisis recedes and the Fourth Quartet finds room for lighter moods and calmer considerations. The Second Quartet is perhaps the jewel of the collection, but all four quartets in this finely-recorded set, performed as they are with such authority and commitment, repay repeated as well as concentrated listening.

John Casken
British 1949-

Casken. GOLEM. **Adrian Clarke** (bar) Maharal; **John Hall** (bass-bar) Golem; **Patricia Rozario** (sop) Miriam; **Christopher Robson** (alto) Ometh; **Paul Wilson** (ten) Stoikus; **Richard Morris** (bar) Jadek; **Paul Harrhy** (ten) Stump; **Mary Thomas** (sop) Gerty; **Music Projects London/Richard Bernas.** Virgin Classics VCD7 91204-2. Notes, text and translation included.

② 99' ADD 8/91

It is fitting that *Golem* should have won for its composer the first Britten Award for composition in 1990—not because John Casken's music sounds remotely like Britten's, but because the spirit of his opera does have things in common with the humanly focused rituals of Britten's own Parables for church performance. The story of *Golem* specifically shuns a Christian context, and although it deals with some of the same issues as, for example, the parable of the prodigal son, it has a tragic outcome: no happy ending here. Even so, the need for human beings to achieve a positive balance between thought and feeling is as important in *Golem* as it is in *Curlew River*. Maharal, the embodiment of human authority, creates a Golem—a man from clay—to serve him and society. But he fails to anticipate or control the consequences of his action, and in the end is driven to destroy his wayward but willing creation. As with all such symbolic tales', the dangers of falling into alienatingly schematic formulae are considerable. But Casken is remarkably successful in ensuring that, through his music, the story has a convincing social context and a strong basis in human feeling. If you are so inclined, you can approach the music by way of its associations with more familiar idioms: here with Birtwistle, there with Maxwell Davies, sometimes with Ligeti, Lutoslawski or Berio. But it soon becomes clear that Casken has evolved a distinctively personal 'brew' from the rich mix of mainly expressionist source-materials that underpin his style, and the result is a first opera—performed and recorded with admirable conviction—that is also a major achievement.

Herbert Chappell   *Refer to Index*
British 1934-

Gustave Charpentier
French 1860-1956

G. Charpentier. LOUISE. **Ileana Cotrubas** (sop) Louise; **Plácido Domingo** (ten) Julien; **Gabriel Bacquier** (bar) Father; **Jane Berbié** (sop) Mother; **Michel Sénéchal** (ten) Noctambulist, King of the Fools; **Lyliane Guitton** (mez) Irma; **Ambrosian Opera Chorus; New Philharmonia Orchestra/Georges Prêtre.** Sony Classical CD46429. Text and translation included. From CBS 79302 (10/76).
③ 2h 52' ADD 6/91

The generation gap, headstrong youth and 'free love', the pillars of the plot of *Louise*, could suggest a subject of contemporary relevance; but the scene here is

Paris in 1900, where a naïve little seamstress (a lot more realistic than Mimì) becomes besotted with a handsome but feckless young poet (a great deal less sentimental than Rodolfo) with whom she goes to live, despite her parents' opposition. Her mother, worn out by poverty, treats her sternly, but her hard-working, respectable father has so deep an affection for her that, when she decides to remain with her lover although her father is ill, his final outburst against Parisian loose morals is all the more bitter. His is the most fully drawn character in this unromanticized story of ordinary working-class people (curiously, only the authentic street-vendors' cries seem contrived), and Bacquier is an almost ideal interpreter of it, capturing every nuance of the tormented father's emotions: Berbié brings distinction to her much smaller role as the mother. Cotrubas is extremely appealing, both in her tonal purity (in a technically very exacting part) and her sensitivity to words, and vividly depicts Louise's innocent charm. Julien is an entirely two-dimensional figure, but that really does not excuse his role being sung most of the time at an ardent, open-throated *forte* (thrilling as the sound is that Domingo produces). He creates several problems of balance for which the producer must shoulder some of the blame, as he should also for some ill-judged perspectives and some slips in the French. There is a vast array of small parts, on the whole very ably taken by members of the 1976 Ambrosian Opera Chorus (several of whom have since become well known in their own right), and Prêtre conducts sympathetically.

Marc-Antoine Charpentier
French c.1645-50 d.1704

Charpentier. CANTICUM AD BEATAM VIRGINEM MARIA. **Le Concert des Nations/Jordi Savall.** Auvidis Astrée E8713. Texts and translations included.
Canticum in honorem Beatae Virginis Mariae inter homines et angelos, H400. Prélude a 3, H509. Pour la conception de la Vierge, H313. Nativité de la Vierge, H309. Prélude pour Salve regina a 3, H23a. Salve regina a 3, H23. Pour la fête de l'Epiphanie, H395. Prélude pour le Magnificat a 4, H533. Magnificat a 4, H80. Stabat mater pour des religieuses, H15. Litanies de la vierge, H83.

75' DDD 2/90

The music on this disc is a skilful compilation of disparate pieces by Charpentier all connected with Marian devotion. The two most extended works are the *Canticum in honorem Beatae Virginis Mariae* and the *Litanies de la Vierge*; the first is intimate yet ardent in expression and takes the form of a dialogue between man and angels. Charpentier was a master of small-scale dramatic forms such as these and Jordi Savall brings passion and a lively sense of theatre to this one. The *Litanies* are more contemplative, sometimes profoundly so, but they are not without a quiet radiance and Savall convincingly explores their expressive vocabulary. Hardly less appealing is the beautiful *Stabat mater pour des religieuses*, written for soprano soloist with unison soprano chorus. Charpentier may well have composed it for the nuns of the convent of Port Royal, though Savall in fact uses male voices for the refrains retaining the soprano for the serene and ethereal solos. The remaining pieces are more modestly conceived but extremely effective in this thoughtfully constructed context. Savall creates a marvellous sense of occasion, bringing the music to life with Mediterranean verve. Lively continuo realizations, in which a theorbo plays a prominent part, are a constant delight as indeed is so much else in this captivating performance. Small vocal and instrumental insecurities matter little when interpretative skill is on such a level as this. The booklet is well documented with full texts in several languages. Faithful and vibrant recorded sound set the seal on a distinguished project.

Charpentier. SACRED CHORAL WORKS. [a]**Greta de Reyghere,** [b]**Isabelle Poulenard,** [b]**Jill Feldman** (sops); [c]**Ludwig van Gijsegem** (ten); [d]**Capella Ricercar/Jerome Léjeune** with [e]**Bernard Foccroulle,** [f]**Benoit Mernier** (orgs). Ricercar RIC052034.

Magnificat pour le Port Royal, H81[abde]. Messe pour le Port Royal, H5[abcde]. O clementissime Domine Jesu, H256[abe]. Dixit Dominus pour le Port Royal[abdf]. Laudate Dominum pour le Port Royal, H227[abdf]. Stabat mater pour les religieuses, H15[bdf]. **Raison:** Pièces d'orgue[d].

67' DDD 1/89

There are several distinctive features about the music (composed for the nuns of Port Royal) included on this delightful disc, the most striking of them being that the vocal writing is, of course, for female voices only. That may seem a confining discipline but is anything but that in the hands of a composer as resourceful as Charpentier. What is lacking in complexity and textural richness is more than compensated for by subtle inflexion, warm fervour and a radiance of sound. This is especially so in the *Magnificat*, a ravishingly beautiful setting for three voices. Here the solo sections are interspersed with a vocal ensemble refrain whose affecting suspensions haunt the memory. The most elaborate work is the *Messe pour le Port Royal* where the voices are deployed in a masterly fashion, ringing the changes between varying ensembles and vocal dispositions. Short organ solos which would have played a part in the 'Mass' were not included in Charpentier's original score since they would have probably been improvised. Sensibly, organ music by his contemporary, André Raison has been inserted at the appropriate places and very fine it sounds, too.

Charpentier. LE MALADE IMAGINAIRE. **Isabelle Poulenard, Jill Feldman** (sops); **Guillemette Laurens** (mez); **Gilles Ragon** (ten); **Michel Verschaeve, Bernard Deletré, Jean-Louis Bindi, Jean-Paul Fouchécourt** (basses); **Les Musiciens du Louvre/Marc Minkowski.** Erato MusiFrance 2292-45002-2. Notes, text and translation included.

73' DDD 6/90

Comédie-ballet was a dramatic form developed by Molière in which music played both an integral and incidental part. Lully was his earliest collaborator but, following a quarrel Molière turned to Charpentier to provide music. *Le malade imaginaire*, first performed in 1673, was the playwright's last *comédie-ballet* and the one to which Charpentier made his most substantial contribution. Here it is the medical profession which comes under Molière's merciless scrutiny with an hypochondriac, his deceitful wife and doctors who know everything about disease except the cure of it. This recording omits the spoken dialogue but includes almost all of Charpentier's music; and delightful it is, too, in its engaging variety of airs and dances. The orchestra is colourful, consisting of flutes, recorders, oboes and strings together with some surprising sounds in the third of three *intermèdes* which follow the prologue. Here, besides castanets, drums and tambourines, Charpentier calls for apothecary's mortars, once cast in a bell foundry and for this recording lent by a Paris antiquarian: such is the lure of authenticity these days! Marc Minkowski, Les Musiciens du Louvre and a strong ensemble of solo voices combine to give a refreshingly unbuttoned performance of the music, little of which has previously been available to record collectors. The recording is excellent and comes with full texts in French, English and German.

Charpentier. ACTEON. **Dominique Visse** (alto) Actéon; **Agnès Mellon** (sop) Diane; **Guillemette Laurens** (mez) Junon; **Jill Feldman** (sop) Arthébuze; **Françoise Paut** (sop) Hyale; **Les Arts Florissants Vocal and Instrumental Ensemble/William Christie.** Harmonia Mundi Musique d'abord HMA190 1095. From HM1095 (5/83).

47' AAD

Poor old Actaeon; if you recall, he was discovered hiding in the bushes while the goddess Diana and her followers were bathing. Without being given a chance to explain himself properly Diana turns him into a stag, whereupon he is torn to pieces by his own hounds. That is the version of the legend followed in Charpentier's opera. The score contains many ingredients of Lullian *tragédie-lyrique*, with a profusion of fine choruses and dances. William Christie and Les Arts Florissants bring stylistic unity, lively temperament and a sharp awareness of rhythmic and harmonic nuances to this music. The soloists make distinctive and accomplished contributions and the whole opera is performed with a fervour and intensity which emphasizes the poignant plot. No French text or translation are included in the CD booklet, but a useful synopsis takes their place. The recording is excellent.

Charpentier. MEDEE. **Jill Feldman** (sop) Médée; **Gilles Ragon** (ten) Jason; **Agnès Mellon** (sop) Creuse; **Jacques Bona** (bass) Créon; **Sophie Boulin** (sop) Nérine; **Philippe Contor** (bass) Oronte; **Les Arts Florissants Chorus and Orchestra/William Christie.** Harmonia Mundi HMC90 1139/41. Notes, text and translation included. From HM1139/41 (11/84).

③ 3h 2' AAD 3/85

Médée is Charpentier's dramatic masterpiece in the conventional French baroque form of a prologue and five acts and was first performed in 1693. Thomas Corneille based his libretto on the story of the sorceress Medea as told by Euripides and the opera begins after the arrival of Jason and Medea at Corinth in the "Argo"; thus the adventure of the Golden Fleece has already taken place.

Charpentier's music is well able to rise to the occasion and does so with chilling effect in the memorable witchcraft scenes of Act 3. Jill Feldman's Medea contains many layers of expressive subtlety and her command of French declamation is impressive. Agnès Mellon is affecting as the innocent and sincere Creuse and Gilles Ragon an articulate and suitably complacent Jason. The chorus and orchestra of Les Arts Florissants have their rough patches but William Christie directs a thrilling performance of a work representing one of the finest achievements of French baroque musical drama. The recording was

William Christie   *[photo: Harmonia Mundi*

made in a lively and sympathetic acoustic but you will need a magnifying glass to read the libretto.

Ernest Chausson

French 1855-1899

Chausson. Concerto in D major for piano, violin and string quartet, Op. 21[a]. String Quartet in C minor, Op. 35. **Jean-Philippe Collard** (pf); [a]**Augustin Dumay** (vn); [a]**Muir Quartet** (Lucy Stoltzman, Bayla Keyes, vns; Steven Ansell, va; Michael Reynolds, vc). EMI CDC7 47548-2. From EL270381-1 (3/87).

66' DDD 10/87

Though the instruments required for Chausson's Concerto would imply a sextet, Chausson's insistence on the term 'concerto' points to a different relationship between the instruments contrasting the two solo players with the string quartet. Whatever its formal design, the work is brimful with rich, passionate melody and the scoring is luminous, with the solo piano and violin spinning ever longer tendrils of light and colour around the fibrous texture of the quartet. Jean-Philippe Collard tackles the difficult piano part with aplomb and plays with his usual poetry and feeling for line. The Muir Quartet assume centre stage in Chausson's unfinished String Quartet, a lovely work which through its three movements gives a more rigorous and crafted feeling. The recording perhaps gives the sense of the players huddled in the midst of a large stage, but the focus is good and the piano tone in the Concerto rich and full.

Fryderyk Chopin

Polish 1810-1849

Chopin. Piano Concertos—No. 1 in E minor, Op. 11; No. 2 in F minor, Op. 21. **Murray Perahia** (pf); **Israel Philharmonic Orchestra/Zubin Mehta.** Sony Classical CD44922. Recorded at performances in the Mann Auditorium, Tel Aviv in 1989.

76' DDD 6/90

Warm applause from the audience is not the only pointer to the fact that these are live concert recordings. The playing itself is full of that "inspirational heat-of-the-moment" long known to mean more to Murray Perahia than mere streamlined studio correctness. The miracle is the way his urgency of feeling finds an outlet in playing of such super-sensitive finesse. Nearly always he favours slightly faster tempo than many of his rivals on disc, giving the first movements of both works a strong sense of direction in response to their *risoluto* markings. Mehta and the Israel Philharmonic might even be thought over-resolute, at the cost of a measure of the music's aristocratic elegance. But tonal balance is good, and progressively in each work a close-tuned partnership is achieved. Both rapt slow movements are sung with an exquisite tonal purity as well as embellished with magical delicacy. Their contrasting middle sections nevertheless bring eruptions of burning intensity. The dance-inspired finales have a scintillating lightness and charm recalling Perahia, the fingertip magician, in Mendelssohn. Even if not in the five-star class, the recorded sound is the equal of anything to be heard in rival CD versions of these two endearing reminders of the young Chopin's last year in Warsaw before leaving his homeland for ever.

Chopin. Piano Concerto No. 2 in F minor, Op. 21[a].
Tchaikovsky. Piano Concerto No. 1 in B flat minor, Op. 23[b]. **Vladimir Ashkenazy** (pf); **London Symphony Orchestra/**[a]**David Zinman,** [b]**Lorin Maazel.** Decca Ovation 417 750-2DM. Item marked [a] from SXL6174 (9/65), [b] SXL6058 (6/63).

66' ADD 1/89

This coupling serves as a highly impressive showcase for Ashkenazy's talents. He was around 30 when the recordings were made and every bar reveals a maturity and relaxed mastery that many artists only achieve much later in their careers. Around 45 years separate the composition of the concertos and one is very aware in listening to them of the transition from an essentially classical form into something symphonic in scope. In the Chopin the moments of reverie are carefully divided from the heroic passages and Ashkenazy finds exactly the right concentrated mood for each. In the Tchaikovsky he avoids making the piece appear as an unequal contest between soloist and orchestra and opts for a lucid and unhurried way with the music. There is plenty of spontaneity and virtuosity in the reading as well. As in the Chopin, he regulates his piano tone with wonderful ease, so as to lend each episode its distinct character. The quality of the recorded sound really is exemplary for the date and the conductors are in complete sympathy with the aspirations of the pianist.

Chopin. PIANO WORKS. Volume 8. **Vladimir Ashkenazy** (pf). Decca 410 122-2DH. From 410 122-1DH (3/84).
Mazurkas, Op. 30—No. 1 in C minor; No. 2 in B minor; No. 3 in D flat major; No. 4 in C sharp minor. Op. 33—No. 1 in G sharp minor; No. 2 in D major; No. 3 in C major; No. 4 in B minor. *Nocturnes,* Op. 32—No. 1 in B major; No. 2 in A flat major; C minor, Op. posth. Impromptu in A flat major, Op. 29. Largo in E flat major, Op. posth. Scherzo in B flat minor, Op. 31. Waltz in F major, Op. 34 No. 3. Variation No. 6 in E major, "Hexameron".

52' DDD 7/84

Though Ashkenazy's decision to offer a mix of genres on a disc instead of a chronological sequence may be questioned, the result is probably more satisfactory for listening, since one has here a real recital of varied music. It ranges from the extrovert brilliance of the B flat minor Scherzo and the F major *Grande valse brillante*, Op. 34 No. 3, through the elegantly wistful 'salon' mood of the A flat major Nocturne and the surprisingly varied and dramatic Mazurkas, to mere chips from the composer's workbench like the *Largo* in E flat major and the C minor Nocturne which were both unpublished until 1938. Ashkenazy's affinity with Chopin in all his moods is the justification for such a complete survey as this and only very occasionally might one feel a need for even more mystery and spontaneity. As for the sound-quality, it is bright but very faithful and never approaches harshness even in the most powerful passages. This is a noble recording.

Chopin. PIANO WORKS. **Peter Katin** (pf). Olympia OCD254.
Nocturnes—E minor, Op. 72 No. 1; C sharp minor, Op. posth. Op. 9—No. 1
in B flat minor; No. 2 in E flat major; No. 3 in B major. Op. 15—No. 1 in F
major; No. 2 in F sharp major; No. 3 in G minor. Op. 27—No. 1 in C sharp
minor; No. 2 in D flat major. Op. 32—No. 1 in B major; No. 2 in A flat
major; C minor. Op. 37—No. 1 in G minor; No. 2 in G major. Op.
48—No. 1 in C minor; No. 2 in F sharp minor. Op. 55—No. 1 in F minor;
No. 2 in E flat major. Op. 62—No. 1 in B major; No. 2 in E major.
Impromptus—No. 1 in A flat major, Op. 29; No. 2 in F sharp major, Op. 35;
No. 3 in G flat major, Op. 51. Fantaisie-impromptu in C sharp minor, Op. 66.

② 2h 20' DDD 12/89 £

Here at medium price are 140 minutes of great piano music finely played. Katin
is a quietly persuasive artist rather than a virtuoso and he brings an entirely
appropriate sense of intimacy to this Chopin recital of nocturnes and
impromptus. The approach is chronological and complete, so that in the
nocturnes the E minor and the *Lento con gran espressione* in C sharp minor come
first, although they were published posthumously, and we also hear the rarely
played C minor (without opus number) which only came to light in 1937, a
century after its composition. Rubato is used freely but tastefully and melodies
really sing, so that a good balance is achieved between emotional richness and
the fastidiousness that was also part of Chopin's musical nature. The impromptus
are well done too, with the famous *Fantaisie-impromptu* played according to a
manuscript source and so with rather fewer ornaments than usual. The recording
was made in an Oslo church with a fine acoustic and an instrument that the
pianist finds "exceptionally sympathetic", as the booklet tells us and his own
programme notes are almost as poetic as the music itself, as when he writes of
the E flat major Nocturne, Op. 55/2, that "a coda of sheer magic seems to
descend from a height and passes into infinity"—which is not purple prose but a
statement demonstrably true of the music and the performance.

Chopin. PIANO WORKS. **Martha Argerich.** DG Galleria 415 836-2GGA.
24 Preludes, Op. 28. Preludes—C sharp minor, Op. 45; A flat major, Op.
posth. (all from 2530 721, 2/78). Barcarolle in F sharp major, Op. 60
(SLPM138672, 1/68). Polonaise in A flat major, Op. 53 (SLPM139317, 5/68).
Scherzo in B flat minor, Op. 31 (2530 530, 6/75).

62' ADD 4/88 P Ⓑ

Professor Zurawlew, the founder of the Chopin Competition in Warsaw was
once asked which one of the prizewinners he would pick as having been his
favourite. Looking back over the period 1927-75, the answer came back
immediately: "Martha Argerich". This CD could explain why. There are very few
recordings of the 24 Preludes that have such a perfect combination of
temperamental virtuosity and compelling artistic insight. Argerich has the
technical equipment to do whatever she wishes with the music. Whether it is in
the haunting, dark melancholy of No. 2 in A minor or the lightning turmoil of
No. 16 in B flat minor, she is profoundly impressive. It is these sharp changes of
mood that make the performance scintillatingly unpredictable. In the *Barcarolle*
there is no relaxed base on which the melodies of the right hand are
constructed, as is conventional, but more the piece emerges as a stormy odyssey
through life, with moments of visionary awareness. Argerich, it must be said, is
on firmer ground in the *Polonaise*, where her power and technical security reign
triumphant. The CD ends with a rippling and yet slightly aggressive reading of
the second Scherzo. This is very much the playing of a pianist who lives in the
'fast lane' of life. The sound quality is a bit reverberant, an effect heightened by
the fact that Argerich has a tendency to over-pedal.

***Chopin*. PIANO WORKS. Daniel Barenboim** (pf). EMI Eminence CD-EMX2117. From ASD2963 (5/74).
Fantaisie in F minor, Op. 49. Berceuse in D flat major, Op. 57. Barcarolle in F sharp major, Op. 60. Polonaise-fantaisie, Op. 61. Souvenir de Paganini. Variations brillantes, Op. 12.

53' ADD 11/89

We usually associate Barenboim with the classical repertory, and perhaps Beethoven in particular, but this Chopin disc reminds us that he has a fine insight into this composer too. He avoids choosing from Chopin's several sets of pieces (preludes, nocturnes, studies and so on) and instead offers works that, for one reason or another, stand on their own. The *Fantaisie* is a work of surging emotion that in places suggests a patriotic march, and the *Berceuse* that follows provides a total contrast with its rocking lullaby mood. The *Barcarolle* takes us to a different world again, that of Venice and a wonderful kind of gondola song presented in rich piano textures and sumptuous harmonies. As for the *Polonaise-fantaisie*, it is a strangely beautiful piece—Chopin himself had trouble on deciding what to call it—that reveals itself almost hesitantly and goes on through a kaleidoscope of moods to a brilliant and triumphant coda. Brilliance is the key note of the last two pieces, the first being based on a famous tune used by Paganini for one of his violin pieces called *The Carnival of Venice*—or more popularly, "O mamma mia"! Most stylish playing throughout this recital and excellent piano sound that doesn't show its age from EMI's Abbey Road studio.

***Chopin*. PIANO WORKS. Krystian Zimerman.** (pf). DG 423 090-2GH.
Ballades—No. 1 in G minor, Op. 23; No. 2 in F major, Op. 38; No. 3 in A flat major, Op. 47; No. 4 in F minor, Op. 52. Barcarolle in F sharp major, Op. 60. Fantasie in F minor, Op. 49.

60' DDD 10/88 ⓑ

Chopin's choice of the previously unused literary title of "ballade" for the four great works with which this recital begins suggests that they may well have been inspired by tales of his country's past. Certainly Krystian Zimerman, a Pole himself, unfolds all four with a rare appreciation of their freely self-evolving narrative style, almost as if he were composing the music himself while going along. His timing here and there might be thought a little self-indulgent in its lingerings but he never rushes his fences. The overall impression left by his playing is one of uncommon expansiveness, upheld by a splendidly full, warm, rich recording. Despite his very slow tempo in the F minor Fantasie he still manages to suggest that patriotic fires were very much aflame in the composer at the time. The *Barcarolle* is as seductively sensuous as it is passionate.

***Chopin*. Etudes, Opp. 10 and 25. Maurizio Pollini** (pf). DG 413 794-2GH. From 2530 291 (11/72).

56' ADD 5/85

The 24 *Etudes* of Chopin's Opp. 10 and 25, although dating from his twenties, remain among the most perfect specimens of the genre ever known, with all technical challenges—and they are formidable—dissolved into the purest poetry. With his own transcendental technique (and there are few living pianists who can rival it) Pollini makes you unaware that problems even exist—as for instance in Op. 10 No. 10 in A flat, where the listener is swept along in an effortless stream of melody. The first and last of the same set in C major and C minor have an imperious strength and drive, likewise the last three impassioned outpourings of Op. 25. Lifelong dislike of a heart worn on the sleeve makes him less than intimately confiding in more personal contexts such as No. 3 in E and

No. 6 in E flat minor from Op. 10, or the nostalgic middle section of No. 5 in E minor and the searing No. 7 in C sharp minor from Op. 25. Like the playing, so the recording itself could profitably be a little warmer from time to time, but it is a princely disc all the same, which all keyboard *aficionados* will covet.

Chopin. Piano Sonatas—No. 2 in B flat minor, Op. 35; No. 3 in B minor, Op. 58. **Maurizio Pollini** (pf). DG 415 346-2GH.

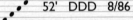

52' DDD 8/86

Maurizio Pollini   *[photo: DG/Umboh*

These two magnificent romantic sonatas are Chopin's longest works for solo piano. The passion of the B flat minor Sonata is evident throughout, as is its compression (despite the overall length)—for example, the urgent first subject of its first movement is omitted in the recapitulation. As for its mysterious finale, once likened to "a pursuit in utter darkness", it puzzled Chopin's contemporaries but now seems totally right. The B minor Sonata is more glowing and spacious, with a wonderful *Largo* third movement, but its finale is even more exhilarating than that of the B flat minor, and on a bigger scale. Pollini plays this music with overwhelming power and depth of feeling; the expressive intensity is rightly often disturbing. Magisterial technique is evident throughout and the recording is sharp-edged but thrilling.

Clemens non Papa
Franco/Flemish c.1510-c.1556

Clemens Non Papa. SACRED CHORAL WORKS. **The Tallis Scholars/ Peter Phillips.** Gimell CDGIM013.
Missa Pastores quidnam vidistis. Motets—Pastores quidnam vidistis; Tribulationes civitatum; Pater peccavi; Ego flos campi.

54' DDD 12/87

This recording is a feast for the ear. Thanks to the Tallis Scholars a great and prolific sixteenth-century Flemish master has been rescued from almost total oblivion. Peter Phillips once pinpointed two major requirements for the performance of polyphonic music, namely, tuning and sonority. From that standpoint one can, indeed, just lean back and enjoy every moment of this recording, because it fulfils amply both requirements. I was particularly impressed by the perfection of its implementation in the long extended eight-part motet *Pater, peccavi*, which describes the confession to his father of the Prodigal Son on his return to the family home. The eight voices are so well controlled and in such perfect accord that they generate an atmosphere of total serenity and confidence consistent with the theme of the text. Similar qualities are displayed in the Scholars' performance of the parody Mass *Pastores quidnam vidistis* and of its parent motet. The crafting of the performance is matched only by the carefully-wrought structuring of the music itself. In the Mass, the tuning and the rich sonority are bound together by a series of strong, interweaving arching phrases and by a slowly descending scale passing from voice to voice towards the end of certain movements.

Louis-Nicolas Clérambault *French 1676-1749*

Clérambault. DRAMATIC CANTATAS[a]—Orphée; Zéphire et Flore; Léandre et Héro. Sonata, "La Magnifique". [a]**Julianne Baird** (sop); **Music's Re-creation.** Meridian CDE84182. Texts and translations included.

65' DDD 1/91

The *cantate française* was vigorously cultivated in France during the first three decades of the eighteenth century. A master, indeed *the* master of the form was Louis-Nicolas Clérambault. Like his contemporary Couperin, he was skilful in blending features of the Italian style with those of his native France. Clérambault published five books of chamber cantatas between 1710 and 1726 as well as composing some half dozen others. Julianne Baird and Music's Re-creation have chosen a captivating programme which includes Clérambault's masterpiece, *Orphée*. Baird's declamation is stylish, her diction clear and her intonation dependable. She breathes life into each of the cantatas and, notwithstanding a somewhat harsh violin tone, is sympathetically accompanied by the instruments. This is a disc which explores an important and engaging area of French baroque musical life. The performances have strengths and weaknesses but it is the former which prevail, and the music emerges with bright colours and graceful gestures. Additionally, the programme includes Clérambault's attractive but seldom-performed trio sonata *La Magnifique*. Recorded sound is effective.

Eric Coates *British 1886-1957*

Coates. ORCHESTRAL WORKS. [a]**Royal Liverpool Philharmonic Orchestra/Sir Charles Groves**; [b]**London Symphony Orchestra/Sir Charles Mackerras**; [c]**City of Birmingham Symphony Orchestra/ Reginald Kilbey.** Classics for Pleasure CFPD4456. From CFPD414456-3 (11/86).
Saxo-Rhapsody. Wood Nymphs. Music Everywhere (Rediffusion March). From Meadow to Mayfair. The Dam Busters—march ([a]all from Columbia TWO226, 12/68); London. Cinderella—phantasy. London Again ([a]TWO321, 12/70). The Merrymakers—miniature overture. Summer Days—At the dance. By the Sleepy Lagoon. The Three Men—Man from the sea. The Three Bears—phantasy ([b]CFP40279, 3/78). Calling all Workers—march. The Three Elizabeths ([c]TWO361, 12/71).

② 2h 9' ADD £

Eric Coates reached a vast public through the use of his music as signature tunes for radio programmes such as "In Town Tonight" ("Knightsbridge" from the *London Suite*), "Music While You Work" (*Calling all Workers*) and "Desert Island Discs" (*By the Sleepy Lagoon*). The cinema furthered the cause with the huge success of *The Dam Busters* march. There is much more to his music, though, than mere hit themes. Suites such as *London, London Again, From Meadow to Mayfair* and *The Three Elizabeths* offer a wealth of delights and are all the better for the juxtaposition of their contrasted movements. The two tone-poems for children, *Cinderella* and *The Three Bears* are splendidly apt pieces of programme music—simple to follow, ever charming, never trite. The miniature overture *The*

Merrymakers and the elegant waltz "At the dance" (from the suite *Summer Days* are other superb pieces of light music, whilst the *Saxo-Rhapsody* shows Coates in somewhat more serious mood. Throughout there is a rich vein of melody, and an elegance and grace of orchestration that makes this music to listen to over and over again with ever increasing admiration. The three conductors and orchestras featured adopt a no-nonsense approach that modestly suggests that his music should not be lingered over, never taken too seriously. Considering that the Mackerras items were first issued in 1956 (the rest being from 1968-71), the sound is of astonishingly good and remarkably uniform quality. This is a veritable feast of delightful music and, at its low price, a remarkable bargain.

Aaron Copland

American 1900-1990

Copland. ORCHESTRAL WORKS. [a]**Raymond Mase** (tpt); [a]**Stephen Taylor** (cor ang); **Orpheus Chamber Orchestra.** DG 427 335-2GH.
Appalachian Spring—suite. Quiet city[a]. Short Symphony (No. 2). Three Latin-American Sketches.

61' DDD 8/89

This disc will be of value to devotees of and newcomers to Copland's music alike. For the devotee, interest will be aroused not only by the *Three Latin-American Sketches*, but also by the inclusion of the 1958 version of the *Appalachian Spring* suite which uses the chamber orchestra scoring of the original ballet in place of the more frequently heard version for full orchestra. The lighter scoring gives the music a greater degree of luminosity and transparency, and also serves to highlight the crispness and buoyancy of Copland's rhythmic invention, especially when the performance is as fine as it is here; string textures are beautifully clear, and there are some wonderful solo performances from the woodwind players. The *Short* Symphony, with its obvious influences of Stravinsky (*cf.* Symphony in Three Movements) and Jazz is given a very rhythmically alert and vital performance, with much attention paid to subtle dynamic shading. Special mention must also be made to the solo playing of Raymond Mase and Stephen Taylor in *Quiet city* whose first-class performances create a very evocative and elegiac soundscape. With the *Three Latin-American Sketches* we return once more to the rhythmic drive that so often pervades Copland's music. The second and third dances were written in 1959; the first was added in 1971, presumably to give a more formal balance to the set, resulting in a fast-slow-fast sequence. The recorded sound is of the highest quality.

Copland. ORCHESTRAL WORKS. **St Paul Chamber Orchestra/Hugh Wolff.** Teldec 2292-46314-2.
Appalachian Spring (orig. version). Music for the Theatre. Quiet City. Three Latin American Sketches.

76' DDD 7/91

Much of what is best about Copland's vernacular music is encapsulated on this well-filled disc. Invigorating rhythms (derived from jazz, Latin-American dance, or American folk-music) and soulful musings, scored with painstaking delicacy, sit happily side-by-side in these works. *Music for the Theatre* is the earliest piece, premièred by Koussevitzky and the Boston Symphony Orchestra in 1925; its toe-tapping jauntiness reflects Copland's delight in jazz at that time, and his sidelong glances at Stravinsky and Satie. *Quiet City*, of 1940, with its effective coupling of trumpet and cor anglais, provides a reposeful heart to the programme, reflected in the simply beautiful "Paisaje mexicana", the second of the *Latin American*

Sketches, finished in 1971. The original, chamber version of *Appalachian Spring* (1944) completes the disc with more dance rhythms, made all the more immediate by the use of smaller forces. The performances tie the works together through a keen sense of idiom: rhythmic lift and vitality drive the faster movements and the more meditative are either allowed to be peacefully simple or enriched by a finely poised degree of pathos that never cloys. A recording that manages to combine brightness with intimate warmth is a special bonus.

Copland. Symphony No. 3ᵃ. Quiet Cityᵇ. ᵇ**Philip Smith** (tpt); ᵇ**Thomas Stacy** (cor ang); **New York Philharmonic Orchestra/Leonard Bernstein.** DG 419 170-2GH. Item marked ᵃ recorded at a performance in the Avery Fisher Hall, New York during December 1985.

54' DDD 11/86

Copland intended this symphony as a 'grand gesture' and there is no doubt at any point in Bernstein's performance that a big statement is being made. There is passionate earnestness in the opening movement and tremendous impact to the brass and drums at the beginning of the scherzo, the central mood of the *andantino* is one of vibrant intensity, while the finale is a public address of great splendour. It is undoubtedly the 'positive' aspects of the work that have made its reputation and they could hardly be more eloquently stated: the dance-like rhythms are crisp and springy, the *Fanfare for the common man* is magnificently sonorous and the noble conclusion of the work is vastly impressive. *Quiet City* is given a no less deeply felt reading. The symphony's live recording obviously took place before an uncommonly healthy audience: not a cough is to be heard and the sound has plenty of power and edge but not quite enough richness to the bass; high strings sometimes take on a dazzling glare. The much more reticently scored *Quiet City*, made in the studio, has no such problems.

Copland. Billy the Kid—ballet. Rodeo—ballet. **St Louis Symphony Orchestra/Leonard Slatkin.** EMI CDC7 47382-2. From EL270398-1 (7/86).

56' DDD 11/87 **(B)**

Between 1938 and 1944 Copland wrote the three ballet scores which somehow managed to epitomize the American character in music: *Billy the Kid, Rodeo* and *Appalachian Spring*. Here we have the complete scores of the two 'Westerns', which are usually given in somewhat abridged form. *Billy* is built around a collection of cowboy ballads and is the more obviously symphonic, whilst *Rodeo* is closer to a dance suite. Slatkin and the St Louis Symphony Orchestra give spirited performances of these works, refined as well as brilliant and the recording, transferred at a rather lower level than usual, is very well defined and atmospheric, conveying both the broad horizons of the prairie and the violent exchanges to marvellous effect.

Copland. THE TENDER LAND. **Elisabeth Comeaux** (sop) Laurie; **Janis Hardy** (mez) Ma Moss; **Maria Jette** (sop) Beth; **LeRoy Lehr** (bass) Grandpa Moss; **Dan Dressen** (ten) Martin; **James Bohn** (bar) Top; **Vern Sutton** (ten) Mr Splinters; **Agnes Smuda** (sop) Mrs Splinters; **Merle Fristad** (bass) Mr Jenks; **Sue Herber** (mez) Mrs Jenks; **Chorus and Orchestra of The Plymouth Music Series, Minnesota/Philip Brunelle.** Virgin Classics VCD7 91113-2. Notes and text included.

② 1h 47' DDD 8/90

Aaron Copland was a father figure of American music, and Leonard Bernstein expressed a lifelong admiration when he called him "the best we have". Yet though a generation separates them, *The Tender Land* had its première in 1954 just three years before *West Side Story*. Both opened in New York, but while Bernstein's piece is set there and portrays a violent urban America, Copland's belongs to the wide Midwest and the quiet of a farming home. It was written for young singers and has a wonderful freshness, a clean 'plainness' which Copland compared to that of his ballet *Appalachian Spring*. The story tells how the young girl Laurie Moss falls in love with Martin, a travelling harvester who visits her mother's farm, and after being left by him still decides to leave home and make her own way in the world. It has been criticized as undramatic, and its partly spoken dialogue and small cast have also gone against it—Copland later wryly called opera "la forme fatale" and never wrote another—but whatever its viability on stage, on record it provides a satisfying experience and this Minnesota performance has just the right flavour, offering simplicity and sensitivity without affectation. The conductor is himself a Midwesterner who writes that his young cast "have their roots in this particular soil" which is the heartland of America. The recording is every bit as fresh as the music.

Arcangelo Corelli

Italian 1653-1713

Corelli. 12 Concerti grossi, Op. 6. **The English Concert/Trevor Pinnock.** Archiv Produktion 423 626-2AH2.
No. 1 in D major; No. 2 in F major; No. 3 in C minor; No. 4 in D major; No. 5 in B flat major; No. 6 in F major; No. 7 in D major; No. 8 in G minor; No. 9 in F major; No. 10 in C major; No. 11 in B flat major; No. 12 in F major.

② 2h 10' DDD 1/89

In his working life of about 40 years Corelli must have produced a great deal of orchestral music, yet the 12 *Concerti grossi*, Op. 6 form the bulk of what is known to have survived. Their original forms are mostly lost but we know that those in which in which they were published in Amsterdam by Estienne Roger had been carefully polished and revised by the composer—and that they were assembled from movements that had been written at various times. The first eight are in *da chiesa* form, the last four in *da camera* form—without and with named dance movements respectively, and the number of their movements varies from four to seven. Each features the interplay of a group of soloists, the *concertino* (two violins and a cello) and the orchestra, the *ripieno*, the size of which Corelli stated to be flexible. These are masterpieces of their genre, one that was later developed by, notably, Bach and Handel, and they are rich in variety. The scores leaves scope for embellishment, not least in cadential and lining passages, and the players of The English Concert take full advantage of them. Regarding the overall performances, suffice it to say that this recording won a *Gramophone* Award in 1990.

William Cornysh

British d.1523

Cornysh. CHORAL WORKS. **The Tallis Scholars/Peter Phillips.** Gimell CDGIM014. Texts and translations included.
Salve regina. Ave Maria, mater Dei. Gaude virgo mater Christi. Magnificat. Ah, Robin. Adieu, adieu, my heartes lust. Adieu courage. Woefully arrayed. Stabat mater.

65' DDD 4/89

William Cornysh, the leading English composer of his generation, was creative, original to a degree of waywardness, sometimes tender, often ecstatic and he served both Henry VII and Henry VIII, holding the post of Master of the Children of the Chapel Royal. The highly skilled trebles he trained to tackle his own most exacting music are replaced, here, by two of the Scholars' most agile, boyish sopranos. The musical pyrotechnics they throw off with such apparent ease give one a good idea of what so delighted the ears of sixteenth-century audiences. The varied programme includes the magnificent *Salve regina*, which unfolds in never-ending volutes of melody, whilst the *Stabat mater*, depicting the sufferings of Mary, reveals Cornysh at his most powerfully imaginative. The relish with which The Scholars understand Cornysh's music makes this a disc of quite exceptional beauty.

François Couperin

French 1668-1733

F. Couperin. Pièces de clavecin—onzième ordre; treizième ordre. **Huguette Dreyfus** (hpd). Denon C37-7070.

 44' DDD

This is a selection of attractive and inventive pieces from this important French composer's Eleventh and Thirteenth Order (or collection) of harpsichord music. The recital is most convincingly played, though the rubato that perhaps regrettably now seems an accepted feature of performances of music of the period will not be to all tastes and the registration and dynamic level of the instrument could be more colourfully varied. The recording is clear and faithful.

F. Couperin. HARPSICHORD WORKS. **Kenneth Gilbert.** Harmonia Mundi Musique d'abord HMA190 351/60 (two triple- and two double-disc sets). *HMA 190 351/3*—Premier livre de clavecin: Ordres—1 (from RCA LSB4067, 9/72); 2 (LSB4077, 2/73); 3 and 4 (LSB4087, 5/73); 5 (LSB4098, 8/73). *HMA190 354/6*—Deuxième livre de clavecin: Ordres—6 and 7 (RCA LHL1 5048, 1/75); 8. L'art de toucher le clavecin (LHL1 5049, 1/75). Ordres—9 and 10 (LHL1 5050, 2/75); 11 and 12 (LHL1 5051, 2/75). *HMA190 357/ 8*—Troisième livre de clavecin: Ordres—13 (new to UK); 14 to 19 (all from RCA SER5720/23, 4/75). *HMA190 359/60*—Quatrième livre de clavecin: Ordres—20 to 27 (LHL4 5096, 12/75).

 ④x4 2h 32' 3h 11' 2h 30' 2h 32' ADD 10/89

Couperin's solo harpsichord music, collected in four volumes and published between 1713 and 1730, represents one of the highest peaks of baroque keyboard repertory. Its elusive and, indeed allusive style, however, frequently

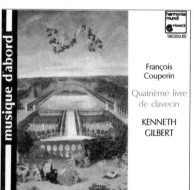

François Couperin

Quatrième livre de clavecin

KENNETH GILBERT

gets the better of would-be performers and it is doubtless partly for this reason that only five complete versions of this music have been issued commercially. Kenneth Gilbert has long been acknowledged a master of French baroque interpretation and his performance of Couperin's 27 *Ordres*—the word implies something between a suite and an anthology—though now 20 years old, has not been surpassed. Indeed, it is no mean tribute to his informed approach that these interpretations strike today's audiences as being as stylish as when they were first issued in 1971. Gilbert scrupulously adheres to aspects of performance by which the composer himself set such store. Couperin was precise about ornamentation and related matters and Gilbert is meticulous in his observance of them. Unequal rhythms are applied discerningly but with a natural ease that variously brings out the nobility, the grandeur, and the tenderness of the music. There is, in short, a wonderful variety of affects to be found in these pieces and Gilbert seldom if ever disappoints us in his feeling for them. From among the most infinite delights to be found in this impressive and satisfying project we may, perhaps, mention the *Ordres* Nos. 6, 7, 8 and 26 in their entirety, and the exquisitely shaped seventh prelude from *L'art de toucher le clavecin* are outstanding examples of Gilbert's artistry. Small technical deficiencies in the remastering appear almost negligible in the face of so much that is rewarding. These are performances to treasure for a lifetime.

F. Couperin. HARPSICHORD WORKS. **Skip Sempé.** Deutsche Harmonia Mundi RD77219.
L'art de toucher le clavecin: Préludes—C major; D minor; G minor; B flat major; F minor; A major. *Premier livre:* Troisième ordre—Allemande La ténébreuse; Courantes I and II; Sarabande La lugubre; L'espagnolète; Chaconne La favorite. Cinquième ordre—Sarabande La dangereuse; Les ordes. *Dieuxième livre:* Sixième ordre—Les baricades mistérieuses. Huitième ordre— La Raphaéle; Allemande L'Ausoniène; Courantes I and II. Sarabande L'unique; Gavotte; Rondeau; Gigue; Passacaille. *Troisième livre:* Quinzième ordre—Le dodo ou L'amour au berçeau. *Quatrième livre:* Vingt-troisième ordre—L'arlequine. Vingtquatrième ordre—Les vieux seigneurs.

72' DDD 1/91

Couperin's subtly expressive harpsichord music is amongst the most elusive in the French baroque repertory to the performer. The American, Skip Sempé, has an intuitive understanding of it and conveys to the listener the grandeur, the wit and metaphor variously present in Couperin's dances and delicately coloured character pieces. Sempé's programme is thoughtfully chosen both for its capacity to show off the composer's considerable if restrained emotional range, and in its inclusion of pieces which have helped to bring his music to a wide audience. So we find the enigmatically titled rondeau *Les baricades mistérieuses*, an enchanting pastoral "Rondeau in B flat" which Bach could not resist including in the *Music Book* for his wife Anna Magdalena, the great B minor *Passacaille* and *L'arlequine*, evoking the spirit of Commedia dell'Arte together with pieces which may be less familiar but no less rewarding on acquaintance. This is a delightful programme and an ideal introduction to Couperin's music for anyone not yet familiar with a veritable poet of the harpsichord. Sympathetically recorded and imaginatively presented.

F. Couperin. Trois leçons de ténèbres. Motet—Victoria! Christo resurgenti. Magnificat. **Mieke van der Sluis** (sop); **Guillemette Laurens** (mez); **Pascal Monteilhet** (lute); **Marianne Muller** (va da gamba); **Laurence Boulay** (hpd, org). Erato MusiFrance 2292-45012-2. Texts and translations included.

61' DDD 8/90

Couperin's three *Leçons de ténèbres*, dating from the second decade of the eighteenth century, are masterly examples of a peculiarly French sacred musical idiom. Sung during Holy Week, their texts are drawn from the *Lamentations of Jeremiah* interspersed with ornamental, melismatic phrases inspired by ritualistic Hebrew letters. The subtle blend of Italian monody with French court air, which characterizes Couperin's *Leçons* and those of his predecessor Charpentier, seems to have made appeal both at court and wider afield. Mieke van der Sluis and

Guillemette Laurens are experienced singers with alluring voices, a fluent grasp of style and acute sensibilities. Each is allotted one of the two *Leçons* for single voice while in the third, for two voices, they blend together in a well balanced radiance of sound. The remaining pieces, a *Magnificat* and a very beautiful Easter Motet are both two-voice settings which come across with warmth and conviction. These singers convey with subtlety music which ranges in temperament from exuberant Italianate polyphony to noble, contemplative utterances such as the setting of the words "quoniam viderunt ignominiam eius" in the second *Leçon*. The vocalists are supported throughout by a stylish, unobtrusive continuo team which includes the director of the performances, Laurence Boulay.

Claude Debussy   *French 1862-1918*

Debussy. ORCHESTRAL WORKS. **French Radio National Orchestra/ Jean Martinon.** EMI Studio CDM7 69589-2. From SLS893 (2/75).
Children's Corner—suite (orch. Caplet). Petite Suite (orch. Büsser). Danse sacrée et danse profane (with Marie-Claire Jamet, hp). La boîte à joujoux (orch. Caplet).

73' ADD 10/89

When on form, as here, Jean Martinon and the French Radio National Orchestra could always give persuasive accounts of Debussy, and this programme taken from their complete set of his orchestral music brings, for the most part, smaller and less familiar works. Three of them are transcriptions, but both André Caplet and Henri Büsser had an acute understanding of Debussy's instrumental world, so that this orchestral version of the *Petite Suite* arguably has even more charm than the original one for piano duet. *Children's Corner* is a hard nut for the most skilful transcriber to crack (the first piece here is even supposed to evoke piano exercises!) but Caplet makes a good job of the suite as a whole and there are many imaginative touches, with the double-bass sounding more elephantine than any pianist can in No 2, "Jimbo's Lullaby", and the oboe nicely suggesting the pipe played by "The little shepherd". There is an odd change of tempo at 1'20" in "The snow is dancing", however, which suggests an editor's hand. The two strangely archaic *Danses* for harp and strings are finely shaped. But the real rarity here is *La boîte à joujoux*, a children's puppet ballet which the composer only partially orchestrated and was not staged until after his death. Altogether this is Debussy playing of wit and tenderness, not to be missed by anyone who loves his music. The recordings, made in 1973 in the Salle Wagram, Paris, are fresh and colourful.

Debussy. ORCHESTRAL WORKS. **French Radio National Orchestra/ Jean Martinon.** EMI Studio CDM7 69668-2. From SLS893 (2/75).
Fantaisie for piano and orchestra (Aldo Ciccolini, pf). La plus que lente (orch. cpsr). Première rapsodie for clarinet and orchestra (Guy Dangain, cl). Rapsodie (orch. Roger-Ducasse. Jean-Marie Londeix, sax). Khamma (orch. Koechlin. Fabienne Boury, pf). Danse (orch. Ravel).

75' ADD 10/89

This fourth volume of Debussy's complete orchestral works—interpreting the terms liberally to include other men's orchestrations of compositions he left in piano versions—confirms Martinon's standing as a Debussian of notable insight: perhaps the most revealing item here is his remarkably flexible and sensitive *La plus que lente*, which the composer scored, oddly enough, with a prominent part

for the cimbalom. Of the three larger *concertante* works (his only other, the
dances for harp and orchestra, is on a previously issued disc) the best,
intrinsically, is the clarinet *Rapsodie*, written as a Conservatoire test-piece and full
of delicate sensuousness, but with a Puckish final section. The three-movement
Fantaisie with piano (which isn't allowed out on its own very much) was an early
work that Debussy withdrew as uncharacteristic (moments before d'Indy was to
conduct it, thus earning his permanent hostility), but its meditative Lento has an
attractive languor: the saxophone *Rapsodie*, commissioned (but never received) by
the lady president of the Boston Orchestral Club, found Debussy experimenting
with an exotic idiom in his attempt to suit the instrument. But exoticism
rampant is the characteristic of the Egyptian ballet *Khamma* (in which the heroine
dances herself to death before the sun god Amon-Ra in her plea to avert the
destruction of her town): the composer himself did not think much of it, but
many now feel it has been under-valued, and parts of it are very lovely. The
playing of orchestra and soloists is first-class throughout the disc, which never
suggests that its contents were recorded in 1973/74.

Debussy. Images. Prélude à l'après-midi d'un faune. **London Symphony
Orchestra/André Previn.** EMI CDC7 47001-2. From ASD3804 (12/79).

48' ADD 2/84

Debussy's *Images* are among the supreme masterpieces of musical impressionism,
translating the subtle colourings of his piano music into equally delicate
orchestral terms. The second *Image*, "Ibéria", is both the longest and most
colourful of the three, relying as it does on the sharp rhythms of Spanish folk-
music. It is often performed on its own, but stands out all the more effectively
here, thanks both to Previn's crisp control of rhythm and colour, and to being
placed in context with the other two works, both also with nationalistic
overtones but more elusive, less extrovert. "Gigues", using the Northumbrian
folk-tune, the *Keel Row*, for all its jolly rhythms, conveys melancholy, while
"Rondes de printemps", using French folk-tunes, evokes in the subtlest terms the
festivities of May Day. These performances stand out not only for their sharp
focus but for the actual sound; the three-dimensional realism and sense of
presence, coupled with outstandingly fine balance, have never been altogether
surpassed.

Debussy. La mer[a]. L'après midi d'un faune[a].
Ravel. Daphnis et Chloé—Suite No. 2[a]. Boléro[b]. **Berlin Philharmonic
Orchestra/Herbert von Karajan.** DG Galleria 427 250-2GGA. Items marked
[a] from SLPM138 923 (3/65), [b] SLPM139 010 (11/66).

64' ADD 7/89

Debussy. La mer. Prélude à l'après-midi d'un faune. Jeux—poème dansé.
London Philharmonic Orchestra/Serge Baudo. EMI Eminence CD-
EMX9502. From EMX2090 (8/86).

52' DDD 10/87

Debussy. ORCHESTRAL WORKS. **Montreal Symphony Orchestra/
Charles Dutoit.** Decca 430 240-2DH.
La mer. Jeux. Le martyre de Saint Sébastien. Prélude à l'après-midi d'un faune.

75' DDD 2/91

The DG disc preserves one of Karajan's finest recordings showing his deep
affinity with French music and displaying a delicacy and feeling for colour that he
is too often denied by his detractors. The *Daphnis* suite is magnificently
conducted and played. The merest whisper of sound is lovingly tended and the

climax of the great evocation of dawn is perfectly placed. The *Prélude* is a gorgeous interpretation, you can almost feel the warmth of the afternoon sun playing on the faun, and Karlheinz Zöller's flute playing is ravishing. *La mer* receives quite a powerful reading, muscular and flexible with Karajan riding the storm masterfully. The *Boléro* shows a great orchestra and conductor in perfect harmony and has remained one of Karajan's party-pieces. The sound is very fine and the performances countless times superior to Karajan's digital re-recordings. A must for admirers of French music and Karajan alike.

However, three of Debussy's most popular and most beautifully coloured works gathered on a single bargain-price disc is hard to resist, especially when Serge Baudo draws some quite exquisite playing from the LPO who have rarely sounded better. *L'après-midi d'un faune*, in particular, has a languour and mediterranean warmth that wonderfully evokes the lines of Mallarmé's poem. This is a spectacularly recorded collection that shows that good things need not cost the most!

The undeservedly unfamiliar *Le martyre de Saint Sébastien* is undoubtedly the most compelling reason for acquiring the Decca disc. *Le martyre* is music of disturbing allure, a powerful mix of mystical and sensual rapture, dark undercurrents and strange pastoralism. The sheer sorcery of Debussy's orchestration is relished to the full by Dutoit and his players. Dutoit's *Jeux* is less successful than some in its capacity to suggest the *risqué* amorous side-play of the young man and two girls, as is the Decca sound, with its relatively distant woodwind balance in delineating the essential interplay of timbres. Dutoit's *La mer*, though, has immense drive and vitality. The listener is swept forward on a tide of bracing rhythms and cross currents. Others have found more atmosphere and enchantment in this score, but few such propulsive energy. The articulation and thrust of the lower strings at the start of the last movement has to be heard to be believed.

Debussy. Nocturnes[a]. Jeux—poème dansé. [a]**Collegium Musicum Amstelodamense; Concertgebouw Orchestra, Amsterdam/Bernard Haitink.** Philips 400 023-2PH. From 9500 674 (11/80).

> 43' ADD 6/83

In all three movements of the *Nocturnes* Haitink succeeds in projecting their colourful atmosphere to masterly effect. Again, in *Jeux* he captures its sense of mystery and the playing of the Concertgebouw Orchestra is incomparable. This release won a *Gramophone* Award, both for the realism and naturalness of the recording and the artistry of the performance. It is one of those issues that sets a standard by which subsequent versions will be judged.

Debussy (orch. Ravel). Danse. Sarabande.
Milhaud. La création du monde.
Prokofiev. Symphony No. 1 in D major, Op. 25, "Classical". Sinfonietta in A major, Op. 48. **Lausanne Chamber Orchestra/Albert Zedda.** Virgin Classics VC7 91098-2.

> 63' DDD 5/90

Prokofiev's *Classical* Symphony and *Sinfonietta* make ideal couplings. Their light, translucent textures and scoring, and immediately memorable tunes also make them an ideal introduction for those approaching Prokofiev's music for the first time. The *Classical* Symphony began life as an exercise in translating the formal proportions and elegance of Haydn's music into a twentieth-century style, whilst at the same time retaining an originality and spontaneity. Prokofiev said of its title: "I called it the 'Classical' symphony for the fun of it, to 'teese the geese', and in the secret hope that I would prove to be right if the symphony really did turn out to be a piece of classical music". Well, as it turned out, that's exactly what did happen, and it has been charming audiences ever since. The *Sinfonietta* predates the symphony by seven years (though it is heard on this disc in its revised version of 20 years later) but it shares the same 'classical' approach and effervescent high spirits of the symphony. Milhaud's jazz-inspired score, *La création du monde*, evolved from a collaboration with the writer Blaise Cendrars, and was given its première by the Ballet Suédois in 1923; its steamy, sultry music illustrates the creation of the world as depicted by African folklore. Ravel's two orchestrations of Debussy's piano pieces, *Sarabande* and *Danse* round off this attractive disc nicely. The Lausanne Chamber Orchestra directed by Alberto Zedda play with charm, character and warmth in performances that are amongst the finest available. The warm, slightly resonant recording is exceptionally fine.

Debussy. CHAMBER WORKS. [cd]**Roger Bourdin** (fl); [a]**Arthur Grumiaux** (vn); [d]**Colette Lequien** (va); [b]**Maurice Gendron** (vc); [d]**Annie Challan** (hp); [a]**István Hajdu,** [b]**Jean Françaix** (pfs). Philips Musica da Camera 422 839-2PC. From SAL3644 (4/68).
Violin Sonata[a]. Cello Sonata[b]. Syrinx[c]. Sonata for Flute, Viola and Harp[d].

45' ADD 1/89

Debussy. CHAMBER WORKS. **Nash Ensemble** ([e]Delphine Seyrig, narr; [bce]Philippa Davies, [e]Lenore Smith, fls; [a]Marcia Crayford, vn; [b]Roger Chase, va; [d]Christopher van Kampen, vc; [be]Marisa Robles, [e]Bryn Lewis, hps; Ian Brown, [ad]pf/[e]cel)/[e]**Lionel Friend.** Virgin Classics VC7 91148-2. Text and translation included.
Violin Sonata[a]. Sonata for flute, viola and harp[b]. Syrinx[c]. Cello Sonata[d]. Chansons de Bilitis (1901)[e].

68' DDD 4/91

The mystique that surrounds Debussy's late sonatas (six were intended but only three were completed before death intervened) sometimes inhibits performers from taking the music at its face value. These are direct, clean-boned compositions that benefit immeasurably from the sort of straightforward treatment they receive here from Philips. The Cello Sonata was written first, in 1915, and was followed later that year by the Sonata for Flute, Viola and Harp.

The Nash Ensemble   *[photo: Virgin Classics]*

The Violin Sonata was added, after a creative hiatus, in 1917 and, to some extent, it looks back to the clarity and single-mindedness that Debussy's earlier music exhibited. The flute solo, *Syrinx*, is an interloper, written in 1913 to illustrate Gabriel Mourey's *Psyche*. The playing in all these works is a delight, never forced nor understated, but finding an easy balance of form and expression. The recording tidily defines the placing of the instruments across the soundstage whilst allowing just enough blending to provide a real sense of ensemble. If you've had trouble coming to terms with these works before, this disc should set you on the right path.

On the Virgin disc the sonatas receive sensitive and perceptive performances, but that of the one for flute, viola and harp (with each instrument retaining its individuality) is particularly compelling: truly affecting are the raptures of the Nash team's reading and the unaffected simplicity, "smiling through its tears", of its second movement. The 1914 war had spurred Debussy into labelling himself, proudly, as "musicien français", and the quasi-archaic, bare texture of the Cello Sonata was a symptom of his wish to evoke the glories of the golden age of French classicism. Christopher van Kampen proves himself an eloquent interpreter of it, and Marcia Crayford catches something of the elusive, intangible quality of the Violin Sonata, though the placing of both artists (particularly the latter) in a rather hollow-sounding recording venue creates some problems of balance with their excellent pianist Ian Brown. There is a subtle, graceful sensuousness in Philippa Davies's performance. Also inspired by ancient Greece were the *Chansons de Bilitis* (written two years after Debussy's three songs of the same title), which consist of musical topping-and-tailing of a number of erotic poems, originally to accompany a performance of nude *tableaux vivants*: the music was later re-worked into the *Epigraphes antiques*. The quietly expressive reader here is the distinguished actress Delphine Seyrig, who died in October 1990: this recording is something in the nature of an *In memoriam*.

Debussy. String Quartet in G minor, Op. 10.
Ravel. String Quartet in F major. **Quartetto Italiano** (Paolo Borciani, Elisa Pegreffi, vns; Piero Farulli, va; Franco Rossi, vc). Philips Silver Line 420 894-2PSL. From SAL3643 (5/68).

57' ADD 10/88 Ⓑ

Coupling the Debussy and Ravel string quartets has become something of a cliché in the record industry, but these two masterpieces do make a very satisfying pair in which similarities and differences complement each other to advantage. Both composers were around 30 when they wrote them and the medium seems to have drawn from them something unusually personal and expressive which is especially intense in the slow movements, although there is ample colour and vitality in the scherzos and the brilliant finales. These performances by the Italian Quartet were hailed as superlative when they first appeared and although there have been others of comparable quality since then, this is still one of the finest of chamber music records and especially desirable at medium price. The CD transfer is excellent and catches all the nuances of the playing.

Debussy. Violin Sonata in G minor[a]. Sonata for flute, viola and harp[b].
Franck. Violin Sonata in A major[a].
Ravel. Introduction and Allegro[b]. [a]**Kyung Wha Chung** (vn); [b]**Osian Ellis** (hp); [a]**Radu Lupu** (pf); [b]**Melos Ensemble.** Decca 421 154-2DM. Items marked [a] from SXL6944 (9/80), [b] SOL60048 (9/62).

67' ADD 1/90 £ Ⓠ Ⓟ

This must be one of the best CD bargains around, with three masterpieces from the French tradition in excellent performances that have won the status of recording classics. Kyung Wha Chung and Radu Lupu are a fine duo who capture and convey the delicacy and poetry of the Franck Sonata as well as its rapturous grandeur, and never can the strict canonic treatment of the great tune in the finale have sounded more spontaneous and joyful. They are no less successful in the different world of the elusive Sonata which was Debussy's last work, with its smiles through tears and, in the finale, its echoes of a Neapolitan tarantella. The 1977 recording is beautifully balanced, with a natural sound given to both the violin and piano. The Melos Ensemble recorded the Ravel *Introduction and Allegro* 15 years before, but here too the recording is a fine one for which no allowances have to be made even by ears accustomed to good digital sound; as for the work itself, this has an ethereal beauty that is nothing short of magical and Osian Ellis and his colleagues give it the most skilful and loving performance. To talk about this disc as one for every collection savours of cliché, but anyone who does not have it may safely be urged to make its acquisition.

Debussy. Sonata for cello and piano (1915)[a].
Schubert. Sonata in A minor, D821, "Arpeggione"[b].
Schumann. Fünf Stücke im Volkston, Op. 102[a]. **Mstislav Rostropovich** (vc); **Benjamin Britten** (pf). Decca 417 833-2DH. Items marked [a] from SXL6426 (10/70), [b] SXL2298 (1/62).

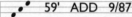

59' ADD 9/87

Mstislav Rostropovich   *[photo: Sarrat*

Benjamin Britten was also supremely gifted as conductor and pianist and on this disc we hear him interpreting the music of others. The Schubert Sonata is an engaging work, whilst the five Schumann pieces have a rustic simplicity and strength which these performers turn entirely to Schumann's advantage. Debussy's Sonata is a more intense, temperamental work and its main subtleties reveal themselves only after many hearings. Britten and Rostropovich bring to all these works a depth of understanding which it would be hard to imagine bettered. Certainly a collector's item, this CD ought to be part of every chamber music collection. The analogue recordings have transferred extremely well.

Debussy. MUSIC FOR TWO PIANOS. **Stephen Coombs, Christopher Scott.** Hyperion CDA66468.
En blanc et noir. Prélude à l'après-midi d'un faune. Lindaraja. Trois nocturnes (trans. Ravel). Danse sacrée et danse profane.

59' DDD 1/90

The number of works written for two pianos is small, perhaps because not many concert venues past or present possess two good, well-matched instruments, and masterpieces written for this combination of instruments is still smaller. But Debussy's suite *En blanc et noir* is certainly among them. Written in 1915 during the First World War, it is one of his last works and its second movement evokes the grimness of a battle scene and is dedicated to the memory of a young friend recently killed in action. The other two movements sparkle with mysterious life, their mood elusive but compelling. Stephen Coombs and Christopher Scott are young artists who joined forces as duo pianists in 1985, and on the evidence of this playing they are extremely skilful and sensitive. This is a lovely performance, alert to every nuance of Debussy's thought. The other works are no less well done, and although with the exception of the brief Spanish-style *Lindaraja* they are all transcriptions rather than pieces originally written for two pianos, the playing is so good that we are able to forget the lack of an orchestra and enjoy them in this format. The recorded sound is admirable and atmospheric, and the Monet picture of water-lilies on the booklet cover beautiful and

appropriate.

Debussy. PIANO WORKS. **Zoltán Kocsis.** Philips 412 118-2PH.
Suite bergamasque (1905). Images oubliées (1894). Pour le piano (1901).
Estampes (1903).

> 55' DDD 4/85   P

Debussy. PIANO WORKS. **Zoltán Kocsis.** Philips 422 404-2PH.
Images, Books 1 and 2. D'un cahier d'esquisses. L'isle joyeuse. Deux arabesques.
Hommage à Haydn. Rêverie. Page d'album. Berceuse héroïque.

> 62' DDD 2/90   Ⓑ

Three decades ago you could have counted on the fingers of one hand the
performers who really had the measure of Debussy's piano style. Today there are
many, but even so the Hungarian pianist Zoltán Kocsis stands out as especially
idiomatic. On the first disc here, he plays four earlyish sets of pieces of which all
but the *Suite bergamasque* are in the composer's favourite triptych form that he
also used in *La mer*. The most 'classical' of them are the oddly titled *Pour le
piano*, in which the Prelude echoes Bach's keyboard writing, and the *Suite
bergamasque* with its eighteenth-century dances, but even in the latter work we
find the composer's popular "Claire de lune" memorably impressionistic in its
evocation of moonlight. In the *Estampes*, the last pieces played, he displayed a
still more fully developed impressionism in musical pictures of the Far East,
Moorish Spain and lastly a mysteriously rainswept urban garden. The rarity here
is the *Images oubliées*, pieces dating from 1894 that Debussy left unpublished,
doubtless because he reworked material from them in the *Estampes* and very
obviously in the Sarabande of *Pour le piano*, but they are fine in their own right
and here we can compare the different treatments of the similar ideas. Zoltán
Kocsis brings refinement and brilliance to all this music and the piano sound is
exceptionally rich and faithful.

The second Debussy recital by the same artist can be welcomed as a revealing
portrait of the composer, its items discerningly offsetting the familiar with the
less-known. It also brings playing not only of exceptional finesse, but at times of
exceptional brilliance and fire. The main work is of course *Images*, its two sets
completed in 1905 and 1907 respectively, by which time the composer was
already master of that impressionistic style of keyboard writing so different from
anything known before. For superfine sensitivity to details of textural shading
Kocsis is at his most spellbinding in the first two numbers of the second set,
"Cloches à travers les feuilles" and "Et la lune descend sur le temple qui fût". He
is equally successful in reminding us of Debussy's wish to "forget that the piano
has hammers" in the atmospheric washes of sound that he conjures (through his
pedalling no less than his fingers) in *D'un cahier d'esquisses*. The sharp, clear
daylight world of *L'isle joyeuse* reveals a Kocsis exulting in his own virtuosity and
strength as he also does in the last piece of each set of *Images*, and even in the
second of the two familiar, early *Arabesques*, neither of them mere vapid drawing-
room charmers here. The recording is first rate. Both discs are highly
recommendable.

Debussy. Etudes, Books 1 and 2; **Mitsuko Uchida** (pf). Philips 422 412-
2PH.

> 47' DDD 7/90   S

Near the beginning of his career, Debussy's *Prélude à l'après-midi d'un faune*
(1894) opened the door (so it is often said) for modern music. His late works,
including three chamber sonatas and the set of twelve piano studies (1915),
opened another door, through which perhaps only he could have stepped. But his
death from cancer in 1918 at the age of 56 put paid to that prospect. The
harmonic language and continuity of the *Studies* is elusive even by Debussy's

standards, and it takes an artist of rare gifts to play them 'from within', at the same time as negotiating their finger-knotting intricacies. Mitsuko Uchida is such an artist. On first hearing perhaps rather hyperactive, her playing wins you over by its bravura and sheer relish, eventually disarming criticism altogether. This is not just the finest-ever recorded version of the *Studies*; it is also one of the finest examples of recorded piano playing in modern times, matched by sound quality of outstanding clarity and ambient warmth.

Debussy. Préludes—Books 1[a] and 2[b]. **Walter Gieseking** (pf). EMI Références mono CDH7 61004-2. Item marked [a] from Columbia 33CX1098 (1/54), [b] 33CX1304 (11/55).

· 70' AAD 4/88 £

The Debussy *Préludes* have the rare distinction of appealing equally to the amateur and to the most sophisticated professional. And pianistic difficulty apart, their immediate charm as impressionistic evocations is as strong as the lasting fascination of their constructional intricacies. As repertoire pieces the technically more straightforward pieces demand considerable imaginative resources and tonal refinement, and Walter Gieseking was the epitome of this kind of artistry. His recordings of the *Préludes* have rightly remained touchstones for impressionist pianism. The subtlety of Gieseking's soft playing, his hyper-sensitive pedalling, his ability to separate textural strands and yet achieve an overall blended effect, are unsurpassed. Since the piano on these mid-1950s recordings is ideally regulated, since the recording quality is wholly acceptable and since both books of *Préludes* are accommodated on a single mid-price CD, it goes without saying that this is an exceptionally desirable issue.

Debussy. MELODIES. **Anne-Marie Rodde** (sop); **Noël Lee** (pf). Etcetera KTC1048. Texts and translations included.
Jane. Caprice. Rondeau. Aimons-nous et dormons. La fille aux cheveux de lin. Calmes dans le demi-jour. Sept poèmes de Banville. Proses lyriques. Trois Poèmes de Stéphane Mallarmé.

· 53' DDD 4/88

Very few CDs so far have been devoted to Debussy's songs, but in any case this one is exceptional in that it includes six that he composed before the age of 20 and seven to poems by Thédore de Banville, of which this is the first recording. The sweetness and freshness of Anne-Marie Rodde's voice, her purity of intonation, her security in the high register, and not least her understanding of style and the exemplary clarity of her enunciation make her a near-ideal interpreter of this repertoire, and she is sympathetically and ably partnered by Noël Lee. In a few places the piano is on the loud side, but otherwise the recording is excellent.

Debussy. La damoiselle élue[a]. Prélude à l'après-midi d'un faune. Images (1905-12)—No. 2, Ibéria. [a]**Maria Ewing** (sop) Damoiselle; [a]**Brigitte Balleys** (contr) Narrator; **London Symphony** [a]**Chorus and Orchestra/Claudio Abbado.** DG 423 103-2GH. Text and translation included.

· 49' DDD 3/88

La damoiselle élue is scored for soprano, women's chorus and orchestra and sets verses from Dante Gabriel Rossetti's *The Blessed Damozel*. It is cast into four short movements and owes a clear debt to Wagner's *Parsifal*. The *Prélude à l'après-midi d'un faune* was Debussy's first real masterpiece and this evocation of Mallarmé's

poem introduced a whole palette of new, supremely beautiful sounds, combining them into a musical structure both concise and subtly complex. Once heard it can never be forgotten. "Ibéria" is the central component of the orchestral set of *Images* and its three movements employ the rhythms and harmonies of Spanish music to conjure up a perfect picture of the Spanish/Mediterranean climate in its various moods. A fine Debussyan, Abbado penetrates to the heart of all these works and is given fine orchestral support throughout. Maria Ewing is an impressive Damoiselle and the women of the LSO chorus are in excellent voice. The recording is most successful, with good atmosphere and clarity.

Michel Delalande
French 1657-1726

Delalande. Te Deum. Super flumina. Confitebor tibi, Domine. **Véronique Gens, Sandrine Piau, Arlette Steyer** (sops); **Jean-Paul Fouchécourt, François Piolino** (tens); **Jérôme Corréas** (bass); **Les Arts Florissants/ William Christie.** Harmonia Mundi HMC90 1351. Texts and translations included.

64' DDD 7/91

Delalande was the greatest court musician of his generation and a gifted composer of 'grands motets', some 64 of which survive. William Christie has chosen three of them for this recording and in varying ways they illustrate Delalande's considerable strengths when working in this medium. The 'grand motet' was an elaborately constructed piece with solos, ensembles and choruses all supported with a variety of instrumental combinations. These performances are full of affecting gestures, and telling insights to the music and it is all stylishly interpreted though some listeners might take issue over details. Christie's shaping of phrases is eloquent and his articulation crisp though the latter is not always helpfully served by a recording which tends to diffuse the larger sound of singers and instruments rather than focus it. There are some notable solo contributions, outstanding among which is that of the soprano, Sandrine Piau; she is well-matched by another soprano, Véronique Gens though the *haute-contre* or high tenor, Jean-Paul Fouchécourt sounds a little strained in his uppermost notes. A rewarding disc in spite of a few rough edges in both singing and playing.

Leo Delibes
French 1836-1891

Delibes. Sylvia—ballet suite[a]. Coppélia—ballet suite[b].
Gounod. FAUST—ballet music[a]. [a]**Budapest Philharmonic Orchestra/ János Sándor;** [b]**Berlin Radio Symphony Orchestra/Heinz Fricke.** LaserLight 15 616. Item marked [b] from 10 073 (12/86).

57' DDD 5/90 £

There are some most attractive bargains to be found on various inexpensive CD labels, and this LaserLight collection provides an excellent example. It combines familiar suites from Delibes's two most popular ballet scores with the ballet music that Gounod composed for the Walpurgis Night scene of his opera *Faust*. The music is throughout supremely tuneful, always elegant, and mixing the grace and charm of, say, Delibes's ravishing waltzes with the liveliness of the Csárdás from *Coppélia* and some of the rousing *Faust* items. Whether it be Heinz Fricke and the Berlin Radio Symphony Orchestra in *Coppélia* or János Sándor and the Budapest Philharmonic in *Sylvia* or *Faust*, the interpretations are all finely judged, bringing out all that is natural in the music, without succumbing to the temptation to add extra, artificial excitement. The orchestral playing also is of a higher order of refinement. The recordings are all digital originals and are of splendid clarity, dynamic range and naturalness.

Delibes. Sylvia—ballet[a].
Massenet. LE CID—ballet music[b]. [a]**New Philharmonia Orchestra,** [b]**National Philharmonic Orchestra/Richard Bonynge.** Decca Ovation 425 475-2DM2. Item marked [a] from SXL6635/6 (6/74), [b] SXL6812 (11/76).

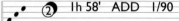
② 1h 58' ADD 1/90

If the scenario and Merante's choreography for *Sylvia* are somewhat lacking in inspiration, the same could hardly be said of Delibes's music for the ballet. "What charm, what elegance, what a wealth of melody, rhythm and harmony", Tchaikovsky was to write after hearing the score for the first time. With this work Delibes made a substantial advance in the lasting quality of ballet music,

Richard Bonynge   *[photo: Decca/Chlala]*

one that was then to be taken even further in the great masterworks of the genre by Tchaikovsky. First produced in Paris in 1876, *Sylvia* marked a new political age, the brilliance of the Second Empire which spawned *Coppélia* having recently collapsed to be replaced by a new republic. The exuberance of the earlier ballet, though still present in abundance, is now balanced by a unifying emotional undercurrent that suggests a more realistic awareness of the cost of joy. The ballet from Massenet's opera, *Le Cid* (1885), bristles with those well-known tunes that are so often difficult to put a name to. If anything, the National Philharmonic are a touch more technically adroit here than are the New Philharmonia in the Delibes, where Richard Bonynge's hard-driven approach occasionally leaves the orchestra little space for subtlety in the quieter corners of the work. Nevertheless, both performances are first rate and excellent value.

Delibes. Coppélia—ballet. **National Philharmonic Orchestra/Richard Bonynge.** Decca 414 502-2DH2.

② 92' DDD 12/86

Where other conductors may approach ballet recordings with the stage movements in mind, Bonynge sees them very much as an aural experience in their own right. He is ever ready to push the score along and provide all the excitement he can engender. For the armchair listener who may find some of the linking passages a shade tedious this may be just what is required. It may be that such numbers as the celebrated mazurka are approached a shade too aggressively and that the frequent recourse to *fortissimo* climaxes can become a shade wearying and obscure the native charm of a score such as this. On the other hand, orchestral effects such as those in the music of the automata come across with extra vividness, and set numbers such as the Act 2 "Boléro" and the "Valse des heures" achieve a quite thrilling effect. There is beautiful orchestral playing and the digital sound helps a great deal to create an overall effect of undemanding and rewarding listening.

Delibes. LAKME. **Dame Joan Sutherland** (sop) Lakmé; **Alain Vanzo** (ten) Gérald; **Gabriel Bacquier** (bar) Nilakantha; **Jane Berbié** (sop) Mallika; **Claud Calès** (bar) Frederick; **Gwenyth Annear** (sop) Ellen; **Josephte Clément** (sop) Rose; **Monica Sinclair** (contr) Miss Benson; **Emile Belcourt** (ten) Hadji; **Monte-Carlo Opera Chorus; Monte-Carlo National Opera Orchestra/Richard Bonynge.** Decca Grand Opera 425 485-2DM2. Synopsis, text and translation included. From SET387/9 (5/69).

> ② 2h 18' ADD 12/89

Like Pinkerton in *Madama Butterfly* (but not a cad like him), the British officer Gérald has succumbed to the exotic charm of the East: in particular, though engaged to a high-born English girl, he has become infatuated with the Brahmin priestess Lakmé, who returns his love, despite the fact that her father is bitterly hostile to the British and is plotting against them. A tragic outcome (with the help of a poisonous plant) is predictable: you might call this a Plain Tale from the Raj. This recording of Delibes's opera, though over 20 years old, still sounds fresh and clean. In Alain Vanzo it has a near-ideal lyric tenor hero; Gabriel Bacquier is suitably dark-hued as Lakmé's vengeful father; and in the title-role Joan Sutherland produces strikingly beautiful tone and seemingly effortless precision in florid passages (as in that famous showpiece the "Bell song"). Her words, however, are difficult to make out, owing to her weak consonants—a rare failing of hers, but one which her admirers have learnt to tolerate. In all other respects this is a very recommendable issue (especially at medium price).

Frederick Delius
British 1862-1934

Delius. Violin Concerto (1916). Suite (1888). Légende (1895). **Ralph Holmes** (vn); **Royal Philharmonic Orchestra/Vernon Handley.** Unicorn-Kanchana DKPCD9040. From DKP9040 (7/85).

> 53' DDD 9/85

Two pleasing early works and a mature masterpiece make up an enterprising disc. The Suite is full of easy-going charm and the influence of Grieg is very much evident. This is the work's first recording. The *Légende* has also only been known in recent years, through Delius's own violin and piano reduction, since the original orchestral parts were lost. Fortunately the original manuscript survives and new parts have been copied. The late Ralph Holmes had a delightfully fresh and affectionate approach to both works, and the RPO and Handley lend him ideal support. In the complex and melodically inspired Violin Concerto Holmes gives an ardent, lyrical account of the solo part and Handley conducts with great sensitivity. A high quality recording well captures Delius's magical sound-world.

Delius. Florida—suite. North Country Sketches. **Ulster Orchestra/Vernon Handley.** Chandos CHAN8413. From ABRD1150 (7/86).

> 67' DDD 12/86

Florida was Delius's first purely orchestral work and though a frankly derivative score, with scarcely a hint of the mature composer to be, it is skilful and attractive, with plenty of good tunes, including the well-known "La calinda". In a beautifully refined and detailed recording Handley unfolds the music easily and naturally, so that its natural warmth and charm speak to us very directly. The four *North Country Sketches*, by contrast, show the mature Delius at his very finest. Recalling youthful emotions inspired by the Yorkshire countryside, it is a work of extraordinary power and imagination. Handley is acutely sensitive to the score's numerous fine details and he understands the ebb and flow of the musical argument to perfection. He is particularly successful in achieving a good balance of textures during the climaxes and he is aided both by the refined playing of the Ulster Orchestra and the outstanding quality of recording.

Delius. Florida—suite. Paris: The Song of a Great City. Brigg Fair: An English Rhapsody. **Bournemouth Symphony Orchestra/Richard Hickox.** EMI CDC7 49932-2.

76' DDD 5/91

This disc will be of immense value to Delians as it contains the only modern recording available (at the time of writing) of *Paris*. Both in the enormous orchestral forces employed and in the techniques for using them Delius does not disguise his debt to Richard Strauss, and he conjures an expansive nocturnal portrait of the city as evocative and colourful as is Vaughan Williams's of London in his Second Symphony of over a decade later. As in the earlier *Florida* Suite and the later masterpiece *Brigg Fair*, the Bournemouth Orchestra play gloriously. In opulence of tone, so important for these works, they yield nothing to more prestigious rivals, and Hickox shows himself a born Delian. One of Beecham's most memorable achievements in *Brigg Fair* was the cultivation of a gorgeous heat haze of string tone, something Hickox seems to have successfully inherited. His tempos are slower than Beecham's but his concentration and control of the long paragraphs sustain interest. A very desirable issue, whose attraction is enhanced by glowing, suitably distanced three dimensional sound.

Delius. ORCHESTRAL WORKS. **Hallé Orchestra/Vernon Handley.** Classics for Pleasure CD-CFP 4568.
Brigg Fair—An English Rhapsody. In a Summer Garden. Eventyr. A Song of Summer.

56' DDD 8/90

Beecham laid a heavy interpretative hand on the scores of Delius, and the composer's approval of the results suggests that such adjustments of orchestral balance are essential to an idiomatic reading of this canon of works. Vernon Handley has latterly adopted Beecham's mantle in this respect, and has taken advantage of modern recording developments to lay down quite a number of the composer's chief works. His readings exalt both the hedonistic delight in life that much of Delius's music displays and intimations of the spiritual dimension that derive from the composer's pantheistic view of the world. This present disc represents remarkable value for money, combining as it does well-known works with some that few would claim to be on intimate terms with, all in a bargain package. The Hallé drive home all the points Handley wishes to make with an intuitive feel for the style and potential of the music. The recording has the fullness and clarity that is so typical of the venue, Manchester's Free Trade Hall, qualities that are normally so difficult to capture on tape. Clean CD transfers of 1981 originals make the disc doubly commendable.

Beecham Conducts Delius. THE COMPLETE STEREO RECORDINGS.
Royal Philharmonic Orchestra/Sir Thomas Beecham. EMI CDS7
47509–8. Items marked [a] from ASD357 (8/60), [b] ASD329 (9/60), [c] ASD518
(4/63), [d] SXLP30440 (10/80).
Over the Hills and Far Away (ed. Beecham)[b]. Sleigh Ride[a]. Irmelin—Prelude[c].
Dance Rhapsody No. 2[b]. Summer Evening (ed. and arr. Beecham)[c]. Brigg Fair:
An English Rhapsody[a]. On hearing the first Cuckoo in Spring[a]. Summer Night on
the River[a]. A Song before Sunrise[a]. Marche Caprice[a]. Florida Suite (ed. and arr.
Beecham)[b]. Songs of Sunset (with Maureen Forrester, contr; John Cameron, bar;
Beecham Choral Society)[d]. Fennimore and Gerda—Intermezzo (ed. and arr.
Beecham)[a].

| ② 2h 27' ADD 6/87 | Ⓑ |

The names of Frederick Delius and Sir Thomas Beecham are inseparable. In the
early days of Beecham's career it was Delius who convinced him that his role in
life was not as pianist or composer, but as a conductor. Beecham was to more
than repay his debt to the composer, for not only did he become Delius's
uniquely understanding advocate, but helped to establish him as a major
twentieth-century composer. The present set bears eloquent testimony in
offering all the orchestral music (plus the *Songs of Sunset*) which Beecham
recorded in stereo. Beecham's affinity with Delius was both instinctive and
inspirational—the composer seldom made practical suggestions to him, yet
expressed total satisfaction with the conductor's magical phrasing and natural
pacing. Beecham was also a master of balance and this is perhaps a major reason
why these early stereo recordings produce such beautiful textures of sound.
Because Delius was a skilful miniaturist the shorter pieces are completely
enchanting, from the veiled strings and luminous woodwind which draw a
delicate watercolour of the *First cuckoo in Spring*, to the sultry, even sentient,
atmosphere of *Summer Night on the River*, glowing like an impressionistic painting,
while the *Sleigh Ride* has a twinkling piquancy. But it is Delius's masterpiece,
Brigg Fair, that one remembers most of all. Here the Delian rapture is
wonderfully evoked at the opening with the plaintive oboe's pastoral piping
answered by the softly pliant flute. Throughout the orchestral playing is quite
marvellous and at the centre, the long-breathed string melody, finally echoed by
the horn, has an unforgettable lazy somnambulance redolent of an idyllic English
summer afternoon. The *Florida Suite* was written on an American orange
plantation and it introduces one of the composer's most famous dance tunes, *La
calinda*. Deliciously orchestrated, its mood changes from delicacy to robust high
spirits, with the piece ending with a languorous horn solo. This collection
presents us with a special kind of musical ecstasy, essentially innocent and
wonderfully refined, which no one has since matched.

Delius. THE FENBY LEGACY. **Royal Philharmonic Orchestra/Eric
Fenby.** Unicorn-Kanchana DKPCD9008/09. Texts included where appropriate.
From DKP9008/09 (10/81).
Songs of Farewell (with Ambrosian Singers). Idyll (Felicity Lott, sop; Thomas
Allen, bar). Fantastic Dance. A Song of Summer. Cynara (Allen). Irmelin
Prelude. A Late Lark (Anthony Rolfe Johnson, ten). La calinda (arr. Fenby).
Caprice and Elegy (Julian Lloyd Webber, vc). Two Aquarelles (arr. Fenby).
FENNIMORE AND GERDA—Intermezzo (new to UK).

| ② 1h 45' DDD 12/87 |

It was Fenby's visit to the home of Delius in rural France that re-established the
stricken composer's link with the outside world. Fenby became Delius's
amanuensis and the tangible results of his French visit are offered here on a pair
of CDs which make a perfect supplement to Beecham's EMI set. The *Irmelin*

Prelude is the most famous but the most important are the more ambitious and equally evocative *Song of Summer*, and the *Songs of Farewell* set to words from his favourite American poet, Walt Whitman. The characteristically opaque choral textures tend to obscure the words at times, but this is of relatively small importance for Delius was mainly concerned with the sounds and colours of intertwining his ambitious chorus and equally large orchestra. The *Idyll* is an ardent love duet and its erotic element is in no doubt. The other orchestral pieces are characteristically appealing Delian miniatures, played with passionately romantic feeling and a real sense of ecstasy by the RPO; while in the choral music Fenby achieves the richest colours and wonderfully hushed *pianissimos*.

Delius. ORCHESTRAL SONGS. [a]**Felicity Lott** (sop); [b]**Sarah Walker** (mez); [c]**Anthony Rolfe Johnson** (ten); [d]**Ambrosian Singers; Royal Philharmonic Orchestra/Eric Fenby.** Unicorn-Kanchana DKPCD9029. Notes and texts included. From DKP9029 (12/84).
The song of the high hills (1911)[d]. Twilight fancies (1889)[b]. Wine roses (1897)[b]. The bird's story (1889)[a]. Let springtime come (1897)[a]. Il pleure dans mon coeur (1859)[c]. Le ciel est, par dessus le toit (1895)[a]. La lune blanche (1910)[c]. To daffodils (1915)[b]. I-Brasil (1913)[c].

· · 56' DDD 3/85

The song of the high hills is one of Delius's most original masterpieces. Scored for a large orchestra and chorus it evokes with extraordinary power and beauty the grandeur and the spirit of nature. Eight of the nine songs with orchestra were scored by the composer himself, and *To daffodils* was orchestrated by Eric Fenby. They all reflect in one manner or another Delius's favourite theme of the transience of love. The soloists are admirable, but Sarah Walker's three contributions are particularly perceptive. Fenby and the RPO accompany with total understanding and the recording is superlative.

Delius. A VILLAGE ROMEO AND JULIET. **Arthur Davies** (ten) Sali; **Helen Field** (sop) Vreli; **Thomas Hampson** (bass) The Dark Fiddler; **Barry Mora** (bar) Manz; **Stafford Dean** (bass) Marti; **Samuel Linay** (treb) Sali as a child; **Pamela Mildenhall** (sop) Vreli as a child; **Arnold Schönberg Choir; Austrian Radio Symphony Orchestra/Sir Charles Mackerras.** Argo 430 275-2ZH2. Notes and text included.

· · (2) 111' DDD 12/90   ⑨ P

This was one of the recordings with which the Argo label was re-launched and very distinguished it proved to be. *A Village Romeo and Juliet* is the Delius opera that has held the stage while his others have appeared from time to time as

curiosities. The reasons are twofold: it is dramatically the strongest and musically the most inspired. There have been two previous complete recordings (one conducted by Beecham), but this is incomparably the best, not least because the recording quality itself is so high. It was made in Vienna, with an Austrian orchestra and choir; the latter's English is impeccable. It would be insular to regard this work as English music, for it belongs to the 1900 ambience of Strauss and Mahler and that no doubt is why this cosmopolitan performance is so idiomatic. Sir Charles Mackerras conducts the opera with total authority and understanding. He demonstrates that to inspire orchestral playing as subtle and sensuous as this was not Beecham's Delian prerogative only. As the two young lovers who choose death rather than this world's worldliness, Helen Field and Arthur Davies are ideally cast, the soprano in particular giving a lustrous and moving performance. As The Dark Fiddler, the enigmatic figure whose claim to a disputed strip of land is the lynchpin of the plot, the American baritone Thomas Hampson is first-rate. The final scene of the opera, with the lovers' duet and the distant voices of "the travellers passing by", is magical as music, performance and recording.

Franco Donatoni
Italian 1927-

Donatoni. Tema[a]. Cadeau[a].
Ligeti. Six Etudes, Book 1[b]. Trio for violin, horn and piano[c]. [bc]**Pierre-Laurent Aimard** (pf); [c]**Maryvonne Le Dizès-Richard** (vn); [c]**Jacques Deleplancque** (hn); [a]**Ensemble Intercontemporain/Pierre Boulez.** Erato 2292-45366-2.

68' DDD 4/90

It's quite rare for a disc of recent music to present that often intimidating phenomenon in as appealing a manner as this one. Both composers are in their sixties, and Ligeti, the best-known of the two, is represented by two of his better later scores. The Horn Trio is perfectly conceived for this strange, Brahms-inspired combination, and Ligeti makes no technical or expressive compromises. This is music of diverse and at times dark emotions, its contrasts threatening to burst the bounds of its well-defined structures. The *Etudes* also marry technical sophistication with emotional depth, especially the staggering No. 6, "Autumn in Warsaw". Donatoni's music has been relatively rarely heard in recent years, but the two works from the 1980s recorded here reveal an infectious vitality and confidence, an infallible ear for novel sonority married to a trenchant command of well-balanced forms and an abundance of well-shaped, often witty ideas. Both pieces were written for the Ensemble Intercontemporain, and they reward the composer with highly expert performances—not that the Ligeti pieces lack this expertise either. The recording as such is very fine, even if the problems of balance created by the Horn Trio have necessitated a less natural sound than is evident elsewhere on the disc.

Gaetano Donizetti
Italian 1797-1848

Donizetti. DON PASQUALE. **Sesto Bruscantini** (bar) Don Pasquale; **Mirella Freni** (sop) Norina; **Leo Nucci** (bar) Dr Malatesta; **Gösta Winbergh** (ten) Ernesto; **Guido Fabbris** (ten) Notary; **Ambrosian Opera Chorus; Philharmonia Orchestra/Riccardo Muti.** EMI CDS7 47068-2. Notes, text and translation included. From SLS143436 (4/84).

② 2h 3' DDD 8/88

In this delightful opera Donizetti's inspiration is unfaltering, and he manages to combine sentiment and comedy in equal proportions. The somewhat hard-hearted treatment of old Pasquale's weakness for the lovely Norina, and the ruse she and Malatesta play on him are eventually dissolved in the triumph of love over cynicism. Riccardo Muti is a stickler for fidelity to the score, playing it complete and insisting on his cast singing the written notes and nothing else. Donizetti blossoms under such loving treatment. It is a reading, brisk and unvarnished, that demands one's attention throughout, and the playing of the Philharmonia is splendidly vital. As Pasquale, Bruscantini sings with the benefit of long experience in defining line and words. Leo Nucci sings a smiling, resourceful Malatesta, at once Pasquale's friend and the author of the trick played on him. Gösta Winbergh is an accurate and fluent Ernesto, and Mirella Freni, the Norina, delivers her difficult aria with all her old sense of flirtatious fun: but when the joke has gone too far, she finds just the plaintive tone to express Norina's doubts and regret.

Donizetti. LA FILLE DU REGIMENT. **Dame Joan Sutherland** (sop) Marie; **Luciano Pavarotti** (ten) Tonio; **Spiro Malas** (bass) Sulpice; **Monica Sinclair** (contr) Marquise of Berkenfield; **Jules Bruyère** (bass) Hortensius; **Eric Garrett** (bar) Corporal; **Edith Coates** (contr) Duchess of Crakentorp; **Alan Jones** (ten) Peasant; **Chorus and Orchestra of the Royal Opera House, Covent Garden/Richard Bonynge.** Decca 414 520-2DH2. Notes, text and translation included. From SET373/4 (11/68).

② 1h 47' ADD 11/86

This is one of those obliging operas which allow you to forget just how many tuneful and charming melodies they contain, thus affording the delight of surprised recognition. On record the good humour comes through without too much underlining, and the *bravura* singing (dazzling flights of scales, staccatos, trills and high notes) puts a brilliant shine on the whole entertainment. Pavarotti has a full share in this: his solo "Ah, mes amis" is one of the most celebrated tenor recordings ever made. As so often with Sutherland one misses a firm singing-line in the simpler melodies, and there is also the depressing pronunciation, where 'fait' sounds like 'feu' and 'coquette' sounds like 'coquutte'. Still, there is much to be marvelled at, much to enjoy; a performance and an opera not to be missed.

Donizetti. L'ELISIR D'AMORE. **Katia Ricciarelli** (sop) Adina; **José Carreras** (ten) Nemorino; **Domenico Trimarchi** (bar) Dulcamara; **Leo Nucci** (bar) Belcore; **Susanna Rigacci** (sop) Giannetta; **Turin Radio Symphony Chorus and Orchestra/Claudio Scimone.** Philips 412 714-2PH2. Notes, text and translation included. From 412 714-1PH2 (2/86).

② 2h 7' DDD 6/86

The plot of *L'elisir d'amore* is a variant of the much used theme of the fake love potion. Here the potion is pedalled in a Basque village by the charlatan Doctor Dulcamara and purchased by the shy young Nemorino to help him win the love of the village girl Adina. Donizetti composed the score at high speed, and his burst of creative activity resulted in a piece of tremendous fluency and immensely fertile melodic invention. With his tender, smooth vocal production, Carreras is ideal for the part of Nemorino, culminating in a beautiful performance of the aria "Una furtiva lagrima" at the point where he finds he has truly won Adina's affection. As Adina, Katia Ricciarelli produces an equally affecting, properly Italianate performance. Indeed the genuinely Italianate style is an aspect of the performance as a whole, and an important one in such a charmingly intimate piece as this. As Sergeant Belcore, Nemorino's rival for Adina's affections, Leo Nucci offers a performance full of verve and fun, and Domenico Trimarchi is a splendidly swaggering Doctor Dulcamara. Claudio Scimone paces the work excellently, displaying a light, buoyant touch and chorus and orchestra are splendidly full-blooded. The recorded sound is natural and open, and each act is commendably contained on a single disc of generous running time. Anyone who does not know this opera should remedy the omission forthwith. Anyone who does should need no further urging.

Donizetti. LUCIA DI LAMMERMOOR. **Dame Joan Sutherland** (sop) Lucia; **Luciano Pavarotti** (ten) Edgardo; **Sherrill Milnes** (bar) Enrico; **Nicolai Ghiaurov** (bass) Raimondo; **Huguette Tourangeau** (mez) Alisa; **Ryland Davies** (ten) Arturo; **Pier Francesco Poli** (ten) Normanno; **Royal Opera House Chorus and Orchestra, Covent Garden/Richard Bonynge.** Decca 410 193-2DH3. Notes, text and translation included. From SET528/30 (5/72).

③ 2h 20' ADD 11/85

Donizetti. LUCIA DI LAMMERMOOR. **Maria Callas** (sop) Lucia; **Giuseppe di Stefano** (ten) Edgardo; **Tito Gobbi** (bar) Enrico; **Raffaele Arié** (bass) Raimondo; **Anna Maria Canali** (mez) Alisa; **Valiano Natali** (ten) Arturo; **Gino Sarri** (ten) Normanno; **Maggio Musicale Fiorentino Chorus and Orchestra/Tullio Serafin.** EMI mono CMS7 69980-2. Notes, text and translation included. From Columbia 33CX1131/2 (3/54).

② 1h 51' ADD 10/89   £

Donizetti. LUCIA DI LAMMERMOOR. **Maria Callas** (sop) Lucia; **Giuseppe di Stefano** (ten) Edgardo; **Rolando Panerai** (bar) Enrico; **Nicola Zaccaria** (bass) Raimondo; **Luisa Villa** (mez) Alisa; **Giuseppe Zampieri** (ten) Arturo; **Mario Carlin** (ten) Normanno; **Chorus of La Scala, Milan; Berlin RIAS Symphony Orchestra/Herbert von Karajan.** EMI mono CMS7 63631-2. Recorded at a performance in the Berlin State Opera on September 29th, 1955.

② 1h 59' ADD 2/91

Donizetti's rousing *Lucia di Lammermoor* is the greatest of his serious operas, a jewel of Italian *bel canto* writing and one of the great survivors of all changes of operatic fashion. Most notably it has the celebrated mad scene with which Sutherland made her name in 1959. Here she is at her most ravishing, with her firm, limpid soprano performing vocal acrobatics that surely cannot fail to thrill, encompassing notes that defy belief. She is supported by a remarkably fine team of singers, including one of the great tenors of our age at a relatively early stage in his career. Decca have provided a suitably clear recording to enhance the general effect, and use a music text that is absolutely complete yet not a moment too long.

Serafin was the conductor who had played such a crucial part in establishing Callas's full potential, Despite the ups-and-downs of their relationship, di Stefano was 'her' tenor, and with Gobbi she made several of the most dramatic of all duets on records. In this opera she had some of the greatest triumphs of her career, and in doing so restored to favour a whole school of opera that had come to be regarded as passé. This was 1953, and her voice had passages of rare beauty as we hear in the Love Duet, "Verranno a te", and "Soffriva nel pianto" in

Dame Joan Sutherland   *[photo: Decca/Steiner*

Act 2. The solos in Act 1 and the famous Mad Scene have that dramatic vividness and depth of feeling which at the time came as such a revelation. And, as always with Callas, any phrase of recitative is liable to go to the heart with an intensity no less penetrating than that of the great arias.

The 1955 Berlin Festival recording provides a genuine extension of the Callas Lucia known to listeners through the above studio performances. The Fountain scene is still subtler in its shadings, the verse in "Verranno a te" still more affecting in its simplicity. The Mad scene has more space and the contrasts of tone have richer dramatic effect. Di Stefano, too, sings like one inspired, and Karajan conducts with real love for the music. The recorded sound is vivid and faithful apart from an occasional distortion of upper notes. Though the applause is restricted, one knows that the spirit of deep enjoyment is abroad in the house and that when people refer to this as a "legendary performance" there is, for once, no need to reach for the salt-cellar.

John Dowland

British c.1563-1626

Dowland. Lachrimae, or Seaven Teares. **Dowland Consort/Jakob Lindberg** (lte). BIS CD315. From LP315 (10/86).

66' 12/86

John Dowland was described by a contemporary as "a cheerful person" but the darker side of his nature is evident in many of his works. In *Lachrimae, or Seaven Teares* he constructed seven marvellous pavans based on its opening motif and set for five viols and lute. They are followed by 14 other compositions, some of which bear dance titles whilst others are dedicated to particular persons. The melancholy consequences of technical inadequacy often suffered by viol consorts are entirely absent here and the problem of balancing the lute is solved to perfection in this marvellous recording. If Renaissance music were to be represented by only one disc it should perhaps be this one.

Dowland. SONGS. **Nigel Rogers** (ten); **Paul O'Dette** (lte). Virgin Classics Veritas VC7 90726-2. Texts included.
The First Booke of Songes—Come away, come sweet love; Come heauy sleepe; Wilt thou unkind thus reaue me of my hart:; If my complaints could passions moue; My thoughts are wingd with hopes; Awake sweet loue thou art returnd. The Second Booke of Songs—Sorow sorow stay, lend true repentant teares; Fine knacks for ladies; Flow my teares; Shall I sue, shall I seeke for grace?; I saw my Lady weepe. The Third and Last Booke of Songs—When Phoebus first did Daphne loue; Say loue if euer thou didst finde; Fie on this faining, is loue without desire; Weepe you no more, sad fountaines. A Pilgrimes Solace— Loue those beames that breede; Sweete stay a while, why will you: To aske for all thy loue; Were euery thought an eye; Shall I striue with wordes to moue.

61' DDD 11/88

The contents of Dowland's three *Bookes of Songes* and *A Pilgrimes Solace*, some 85 items, form the heart of the English lute-song repertoire, unexcelled expressions of the full gamut of human emotions—that of carnal desire is clothed in discreetly poetic terms. Nigel Rogers and Paul O'Dette cover the emotional range in their cross-section of all four sources. The lute accompaniments are not mere backcloths but integral parts of the musical texture; Dowland doubtless performed the songs single-handed, as do some of today's artists, but when singer and lutenist are not the same person each can concentrate on his/ her own (often difficult) role, and when the partnership is felicitous—as is the present one—the songs emerge in all their expressive glory. Rogers imparts the proper ethos to every song and his pure-velvet voice is faithfully matched at every step by O'Dette's accompaniment. He liberally ornaments the lines and, though some may disagree with the practice, as each stanza is set to exactly the same music, it lends variety. The recording is crystal-clear—so much so that the printed texts provided in the inlay booklet might be regarded as a luxury.

Dowland. The Second Booke of Songs (1600). **Emma Kirkby** (sop); **John York Skinner** (alto); **Martyn Hill** (ten); **David Thomas** (bass); **Consort of Musicke/Anthony Rooley** (lte). L'Oiseau-Lyre 425 889-2OH. Texts included. From DSLO528/9 (9/77).

> 70' ADD 8/91

This recording originally appeared in 1977 as part of Florilegium's complete Dowland cycle and, such projects seeming a little less likely to get off the ground nowadays, it's good to see it being re-released on CD. The Second Booke of Songs dates from 1600 and contains two of Dowland's most famous compositions *Flow my teares* and *I saw my lady weepe*, though here these are presented unusually (and not entirely convincingly) as vocal duets. In fact there is a surprisingly wide variety of vocal and instrumental combinations throughout the disc, from consort song to four-part vocal to the more familiar sound of solo voice and lute, all of which were suggested as performance possibilities by Dowland himself. It is partly as a result of this that the recording retains its freshness in spite of its age, but it would be wrong to ignore the contribution made by the intelligent and sensitive singing of Emma Kirkby and Martyn Hill, both of whom sound completely in their element.

David Del Tredici
American 1937-

Del Tredici. Steps[a] (1990). Haddock's Eyes[b] (1985). [b]**David Tel Tredici** (pf); [b]**Susan Naruki** (sop); [b]**Claire Bloom** (narr); [a]**New York Philharmonic Orchestra;** [b]**New York Philharmonic Ensemble/Zubin Mehta.** New World NW80390-2.

> 54' DDD

The (extraordinary) music of David Del Tredici has had relatively little exposure on disc so far, which is rather surprising given the approachability and melodiousness of its style. Del Tredici first came to public attention in 1976 when Solti conducted the first performance of *Final Alice*—a large and colourful monodrama scored for amplified soprano and orchestra. The subject matter of *Final Alice*—Lewis Carroll's *Alice in Wonderland*—has become an almost singular preoccupation with Del Tredici since 1968 and has formed the inspiration to nearly all of his compositions since. *Steps* for orchestra is an exception, though even here something of the surreal, dream-like quality of the *Alice* stories permeates this fascinating and richly imaginative score. *Steps* is cast in one movement, divided into four interconnected sections: "Giant Steps", "The Two-Step", "Giant Giant Steps" and "Stepping Down" and has been described by Del Tredici as "a monster—violent, powerful, inexorable ... my most dissonant tonal piece". Mehta and the New York Philharmonic give a stunningly virtuosic performance of this 'jabberwocky' of a piece and make a strong case for Del Tredici as one of America's most imaginative living composers. *Haddock's Eyes*, if the title hasn't already given it away, is one of

Del Tredici's many 'Alice'-inspired works, and is a wonderfully affectionate setting of the "White Knight's Song" from *Through the Looking-Glass* scored for soprano, narrator and chamber ensemble. Susan Naruki's performance is a real *tour-de-force* as she spills out Carroll's words and Del Tredici's music in an ever and ever increasing hysterical frenzy. A marvellous introduction to the music of this fascinating American composer.

Maurice Duruflé

French 1902-1986

Duruflé. ORGAN WORKS. **John Scott.** Hyperion CDA66368. Played on the organ of St Paul's Cathedral, London.
Prélude sur l'introit de l'Epiphanie. Prélude et fugue sur le nom d'Alain, Op. 7. Suite, Op. 5. Scherzo, Op. 2. Prélude, adagio et choral varié sur le "Veni creator spiritus", Op. 4 (with the men's voices of St Paul's Cathedral Choir). Fugue sur le carillon des heures de la Cathédrale de Soissons, Op. 12.

· 70' DDD 1/91

The *Requiem* is Duruflé's best-known work. But as an organist it was only natural that the bulk of his music was written for that instrument. While six pieces which comfortably fit on to a single CD may not seem much to show for a lifetime's devotion to the organ, such a meagre output is entirely the result of extreme fastidiousness: Duruflé was almost obsessively self-critical revising his compositions many times over before releasing them for publication. The result is music in which no note is superfluous and where emotional intensity has unusually direct impact. Many characteristics of the *Requiem* will be instantly picked up here by the discerning listener, not least the copious use of plainsong. A singularly beautiful addition to this recording is the use of men's voices to chant verses of *Veni creator spiritus*. But while Duruflé's deeply-felt, sometimes pained expression permeates most of this music, there are flashes of gaiety: in a simply delicious *Siciliano* (from the Suite) and in the bubbly *Scherzo*. John Scott's performances are truly exceptional. Technically he is impressive and he readily bares his sensitive musical soul to release the full beauty of these pieces. Hyperion have made a wonderful job in recording at St Paul's, achieving an ideal blend between clarity and atmosphere. The echo at this venue can have, and does here, a stunning effect: just savour that glorious aftertaste which seems to linger into eternity each time Scott's hands leave the keys.

Duruflé. Requiem[a]. Four Motets. [a]**Ann Murray** (mez); [a]**Thomas Allen** (bar); **Corydon Singers;** [a]**English Chamber Orchestra/Matthew Best** with [a]**Thomas Trotter** (org). Hyperion CDA66191. Texts and translations included. From A66191 (5/86).

· 51' DDD 4/87

The Requiem is adapted from a suite of organ pieces Duruflé based on plainsong from the Mass for the Dead. Although it expresses the same tranquility and optimism as the Fauré Requiem, Duruflé's language is firmly based in the twentieth century. The Requiem exists in three versions: one uses a full orchestra; another has just cello and organ accompaniment, while the "middle version" of 1961, used here, employs a small orchestra. The performance is admirable in its quiet expressiveness, and Matthew Best conducts with skill and sensitivity. The *Quatre Motets* inhabit a similar world to that of the Requiem and are also based on Gregorian chant. The recording is not ideally clear, but is

more than adequate.

Henri Dutilleux

French 1916-

Dutilleux. Violin Concerto, "L'arbre des songes"[a].
Maxwell Davies. Violin Concerto[b]. **Isaac Stern** (vn); [a]**French National Orchestra/Lorin Maazel;** [b]**Royal Philharmonic Orchestra/André Previn.** CBS Masterworks CD42449.

56' DDD 2/88

This is a unique coupling in many respects, not least among them the fact that both concertos were written for this soloist. The Dutilleux Concerto, unlike the traditional bravura vehicle, is more integrated, more inward looking with the slower passages radiating a distinctive haunting beauty. The Maxwell Davies work also offers comparatively few opportunities for display, although its technical demands are virtuosic indeed, and includes numerous allusions to the dances of the Scottish highlands. Stern gives confident and involving performances of both works, projecting a wide range of colour and conveying an understanding of and confidence in their musical values. The recordings are good.

André Previn   *[photo: Maede*

Antonin Dvořák

Czechoslovakian 1841-1904

Dvořák. Cello Concerto in B minor, B191.
Tchaikovsky. Variations on a Rococo theme, Op. 33. **Mstislav Rostropovich** (vc); **Berlin Philharmonic Orchestra/Herbert von Karajan.** DG 413 819-2GH. From SLPM139044 (10/69).

60' ADD 3/85

Dvořák's Cello Concerto dominates the repertoire and above all it needs a larger-than-life soloist and a balancing orchestral partnership. As an interpreter of the work Rostropovich reigns supreme and he has recorded it six times. Undoubtedly the collaboration with Karajan was the most fruitful, with these two great artists striking sparks off one another, resulting in Rostropovich's tendency to romantic indulgence seeming natural and inspirationally spontaneous against the sweep of the background canvas supplied by the Berlin Philharmonic players. It is an admirable performance, helped by a superb, naturally balanced recording. What better coupling than Tchaikovsky's elegant and tuneful *Rococo* Variations, a work displaying the composer's affinity with his beloved Mozart—there never seems to be a note too many. Again, Rostropovich and Karajan are in their element, with the Berlin orchestra providing many inimitable touches, and the result is sheer delight.

Dvořák. Violin Concerto in A minor, B108. Romance in F minor, B39.
Kyung Wha Chung (vn); **Philadelphia Orchestra/Riccardo Muti.** EMI
CDC7 49858-2.

	47' DDD 11/89

Dvořák. Violin Concerto in A minor, B108[a].
Sibelius. Violin Concerto in D minor, Op. 47[b]. **Salvatore Accardo** (vn);
[a]**Concertgebouw Orchestra, Amsterdam,** [b]**London Symphony
Orchestra/Sir Colin Davis.** Philips Silver Line 420 895-2PSL. Item marked [a]
from 9500 406 (2/81), [b] 9500 675 (10/80).

	68' ADD 10/88	£

Considering the popularity of his Cello Concerto, Dvořák's concerto for violin
has never quite caught on with the general public. But a top class performance
can convince us that the neglect is unfair. Kyung Wha Chung plays the concerto
with the right blend of simplicity and brilliance, Slavonic warmth and folk-like
quality, and the Philadelphia Orchestra under Riccardo Muti give her the right
kind of support, unobtrusive enough to make us forget that the orchestral
writing is not Dvořák at his most instrumentally imaginative, yet positive enough
to provide more than just a discreet background. Ultimately, we probably enjoy
the concerto most for its Bohemian lilt, a quality we feel in the violin's very first
entry and that is present again in ample measure in the rondo finale—a
movement of unfailingly dancing rhythm and considerable charm that here
receives a sparkling performance. The delicately scored Romance in F minor that
completes the programme is a slightly earlier work than the Violin Concerto
and, it has been said, suggests a leisurely walk through the Bohemian countryside
with someone who knows it well. The recorded sound is well defined and
faithful, capturing Chung's fine tonal palette.

Accardo and Sir Colin Davis also give a refined presentation of the work
and the purity of the soloist's tone and intonation is a joy in itself. In addition
to the Dvořák, we are offered the Sibelius—all at mid-price, too! Again
Accardo is masterly: there is no attempt to play to the gallery, and in
the slow movement he achieves the repose and nobility this music calls for but
rarely attains. The finale has splendid zest and yet there is an aristocratic feel to
the whole which is just what this work needs. Other virtuosi may have more
'glitz', but Accardo is more natural and unforced, his virtuosity is effortless
and the musical rewards rich. First-class orchestral playing and excellent
recorded sound.

Dvořák. Piano Concerto in G minor, B63[a].
Schumann. Introduction and Allegro appassionato, Op. 92. **András Schiff**
(pf); **Vienna Philharmonic Orchestra/Christoph von Dohnányi.** Decca
417 802-2DH. Item marked [a] recorded at a performance in the Musikverein,
Vienna during November 1986.

	53' DDD 1/89

It seems extraordinary that the Piano Concerto is not all that well known. For a
long time it was thought unpianistic, but András Schiff gives a fresh and agile
account of what is a delightful score. He is very well partnered by von Dohnányi
and the Vienna Philharmonic Orchestra, and the playing is singularly sure for a
live performance. The music is unmistakably Dvořák's, though in this relatively
early work we do not find the consistently Bohemian flavour that is actually
stronger in his later music. Schumann wrote his *Introduction* while under the
literary influence of Byron's dramatic poem *Manfred* with its tormented hero.
Here is another relatively neglected piece, but it has considerable atmosphere
and is once again persuasively performed. Clear yet spacious recording in both

works.

Dvořák. ORCHESTRAL WORKS. **Ulster Orchestra/Vernon Handley.** Chandos CHAN8453.

In nature's realm, B168. Carnival, B169. Othello, B174. Scherzo capriccioso, B131.

53' DDD 7/86

This disc not only gives the catalogue a fine recording of four of Dvořák's most charming orchestral works but it allows us to hear the three overtures as the composer originally intended them—one after the other. Dvořák became interested in the idea of a three-movement symphonic work on the theme of

nature, life and love in 1892 shortly before leaving for the United States. Heard as a trilogy these three works have great impact; their rapt involvement and unforced lyricism carrying all the hallmarks of the composer. The programme closes with an earlier work, the ever popular *Scherzo capriccioso*, which amid the energy and colour introduces a glorious waltz theme. Vernon Handley has already shown what an accomplished Dvořákian he is and together with the Ulster Orchestra here makes a winning partnership.

Vernon Handley   *[photo: Van Walsum*

Dvořák. Serenades—E major, B52; D minor, B77. **Academy of St Martin in the Fields/Sir Neville Marriner.** Philips 400 020-2PH. From 6514 145 (5/82).

51' DDD 4/83

These two serenades are works full of melody and good humour, bubbling over with tuneful zest, but always inventive and skilfully scored. The gracefully elegant E major Serenade here receives a wonderfully cultivated reading which never overlooks the subtleties of the part-writing. The D minor is a slightly grittier piece and also benefits from Marriner's attentive guidance. Tempos are finely judged and well related throughout and the fast sections have a lovely zip and panache. The recording is excellent too, the strings having just the right bloom without sacrificing the music's essential intimacy.

Dvořák. Slavonic Dances, Opp. 46 and 72. **Rheinland-Pfalz State Philharmonic Orchestra/Leif Segerstam.** BIS CD425.

78' DDD 7/89

There is immense character and vitality in these 16 pieces, originally written as piano duets and only later orchestrated with great success. As a boy, Dvořák had played the fiddle for village dancing and here as a mature artist he drew on his experience. The German orchestra play this music as to the manner born, with great panache and warmth, under their chief conductor Leif Segerstam. Although the Dances are played in the published order, he interestingly suggests another possible programming in which "the 16 dances relate according to key and tempo to form four miniature symphonies". But whichever way one plays these pieces, they bubble over with melody, rhythmic verve and sheer delight. The recording misses no detail and the dynamic range is a full *pianissimo* to *fortissimo*. Collectors will note the exceptionally generous length of 78 minutes.

Dvořák. SYMPHONIES AND ORCHESTRAL WORKS. [a]**Berlin Philharmonic Orchestra,** [b]**Bavarian Radio Symphony Orchestra/Rafael Kubelik.** DG 423 120-2GX6.

Symphonies[a]—No. 1 in C minor, B9, "The Bells of Zlonice"; No. 2 in B flat major, B12; No. 3 in E flat major, B34; No. 4 in D minor, B41; No. 5 in F major, B54; No. 6 in D major, B112 (all from 2720 066, 10/73); No. 7 in D minor, B141 (2530 127, 10/71); No. 8 in G major, B163 (139 181, 3/67); No. 9 in E minor, B178, "From the New World" (2720 066, 10/73). Scherzo capriccioso, B131[b] (2530 466, 11/75). Carnival Overture, B169[b] (2530 785, 2/78). The wood dove, B198[b] (2530 713, 11/76).

⑥ 7h 5' ADD 10/88 £

Here is a way for the collector who already knows Dvořák's Nos. 7-9 to come to grips with the other symphonies at not too great an expense. Kubelik's performances of the three familiar works have earned the highest praise for their combination of drama and freshness. He is equally impressive in No. 6, a splendid and characteristic work which deserves to rank alongside the last three, and often in the earlier symphonies he manages to disguise some of the immaturity of the writing, bringing out the dance derivations vivaciously, while slow movements gain from the consistently fine playing of the Berlin Philharmonic Orchestra. The shorter works make enjoyable bonuses and the remastered recording sounds fresh and transparent, yet has a warm ambience too. This is excellent value.

Dvořák. Symphony No. 5 in F major, B54. Othello, B174. Scherzo capriccioso, B131. **Oslo Philharmonic Orchestra/Mariss Jansons.** EMI CDC7 49995-2.

64' DDD 7/90 **B**

Of all the romantic composers, it is probably Dvořák who best evokes a sunlit, unspoiled and relatively untroubled picture of nineteenth-century country life. Light and warmth radiate from his Fifth Symphony, composed in just six weeks of the year 1875 when he was in his early thirties. It has been called his "Pastoral Symphony", and it is easy to see why, especially in a performance as fresh and sunny as this one. Mariss Jansons brings out all the expressiveness and heart of the music without exaggerating the good spirits and playful humour that are so characteristic of the composer, and one would single out for praise the fine wind playing of the Oslo Philharmonic Orchestra (and not least its golden-toned horns) were it not for the fact that the strings are no less satisfying. The lyrical *Andante con moto* brings out the fine interplay of the instrumental writing, the bouncy *Scherzo* is uninhibited without going over the top and the exciting finale has plenty of momentum. The other two pieces are also nicely done, the *Scherzo capriccioso* having both lilt and vigour and the rarely played *Othello* Overture (a late work) being a suitably dramatic response to Shakespeare's tragedy. The recording is warm and clear.

Dvořák. Symphony No. 6 in D major, B112.
Janáček. Taras Bulba. **Cleveland Orchestra/Christoph von Dohnányi.** Decca 430 204-2DH.

66' DDD 7/91

Dohnányi here turns to a radiant work that until now has been relatively neglected on CD. With its obvious echoes of Brahms's Second Symphony this is a work which, for all its pastoral overtones, gains from refined playing, and quite apart from the imaculate ensemble, the Cleveland violins play ethereally, as in the melody at the start of the slow movement. Dohnányi does not miss the earthy qualities of the writing either, and the impact of the performance is greatly enhanced by the fullness and weight of the recording. This is altogether a superb account of No. 6. There is also the bonus of Dohnányi's unexpected makeweight, *Taras Bulba*. The account here is very Viennese in style and warmly expressive against its opulent background. However, if Janáček is your first priority, then Mackerras's version, coupled with the *Sinfonietta* (reviewed elsewhere in this *Guide*) is the obvious choice, for he characterfully persuades his truly Viennese musicians to sound more like Czechs, playing brilliantly with a sharp attack very apt for the composer's music. But those who want a radiant account of the Dvořák will find comparable joy in the characterful Janáček rhapsody.

Dvořák. Symphonies—No. 7 in D minor, B141[a]; No. 8 in G major, B163[b]. **Royal Concertgebouw Orchestra, Amsterdam/Sir Colin Davis.** Philips Silver Line 420 890-2PSL. Item marked [a] from 9500 132 (2/77), [b] 9500 317 (10/79).

| 74' ADD 1/89 | £ |

Dvořák's Seventh and Eighth Symphonies represent the peak of his symphonic creativity. The Seventh Symphony has a wider range of mood than the Eighth with its potently atmospheric opening and eloquent and life-enhancing finale. The Eighth also has its moments of strong drama but the overall mood is one of extrovert geniality. Sir Colin Davis has the full measure of both works, he finds exhilaration and vitality alongside a spontaneous lyricism. Whether in the eloquently played slow movements or the contrasted scherzos, his pacing is perfectly judged and in both finales there is flair and excitement. Not surprisingly the Royal Concertgebouw Orchestra is wonderfully responsive to his freshness of approach, and these two highly satisfying performances are superbly played. The digital remastering has been very beneficial: the orchestra is naturally balanced with detail clear within an attractively warm ambience. Offered at mid-price this reissue is an undoubted bargain.

Dvořák. Symphony No. 9 in E minor, B178, "From the New World"[a]. American Suite[b]. [a]**Vienna Philharmonic Orchestra/Kirill Kondrashin;** [b]**Royal Philharmonic Orchestra/Antál Dorati.** Decca 430 715-2DM. From [a]SXDL7510 (7/80), [b]410 735-2DH2 (3/85).

| 63' DDD 8/91 | |

Dvořák. Symphony No. 9 in E minor, B178, "From the New World". **Cleveland Orchestra/Christoph von Dohnányi.** Decca 414 421-2DH. From 414 421-1DH (11/86).

| 41' DDD 1/87 | Ⓑ |

Dvořák. Symphony No. 9 in E minor, B178, "From the New World"[a]. Carnival Overture, B169[b]. Scherzo capriccioso, B131[c]. **London Symphony Orchestra/István Kertész.** Decca Ovation 417 724-2DM. Item marked [a] from SXL6291 (11/67), [b] SXL6253 (11/66), [c] SXL6044 (7/63).

| 65' ADD 12/87 | Ⓑ |

Dvořák. Symphony No. 9 in E minor, B178, "From the New World"[a]; Symphonic Variations, B70[b]. **London Philharmonic Orchestra/Zdenek Macal.** Classics for Pleasure CD-CFP9006. Item marked [a] from CFP40382 (11/82), [b] CFP40345 (1/81).

| 66' DDD 9/87 | £ |

Kondrashin's *New World* caused something of a sensation when originally transferred to CD. Here was a supreme example of the clear advantages of the

Christoph von Dohnányi [photo: Decca/Sayer]

new medium over the old and the metaphor of a veil being drawn back between listener and performers could almost be extended to a curtain: the impact and definition of the sound is quite remarkable.

However, Decca are never a company to rest on their laurels and in 1986 Christoph von Dohnányi provided an equally attractive and even more direct and spectacularly recorded version of the Ninth. The performance is in some respects less dramatic than Kondrashin's and has the disadvantage of omitting the first movement exposition repeat. But the easy lyricism of the music-making, combined with a natural vitality, brings not only great warmth in the playing but a strong affinity with the Czech idiom.

To bring yet further competition Decca have also reissued Kertész's famous LSO version from the late 1960s, a wonderfully fresh account, notable for its sense of flow and ideal choice of tempos, and the hushed intensity of the slow movement. Coupled with sparkling performances of the *Carnaval Overture* and *Scherzo capriccioso* this makes a formidable bargain at mid-price.

At not far short of 70 minutes and with a bargain price, the Macal issue might be worth considering even if the performances were of only satisfying quality. As it is, they are thrilling. The LPO play with enormous vivacity and authenticity for their Czech conductor and the sheer earthy strength and pastoral freshness of the music comes over without any lapse into crudity. The *Symphonic Variations* is a rather earlier work and is distinctly ungainly, but is here treated with ingenuity and invention as well as some humour.

Dvořák. String Sextet in A major, B80[a].
Martinů. Serenade No. 2. String Sextet (1932)[a]. **Academy of St Martin in the Fields Chamber Ensemble** (Kenneth Sillito, Malcolm Latchem, vns; Robert Smissen, [a]Stephen Tees, vas; [a]Stephen Orton, [a]Roger Smith, vcs). Chandos CHAN8771.
50' DDD 5/90

There is little which links the music of Dvořák and Martinů except a common Czech background, but the ASMF Chamber Ensemble respond well to both composers' styles and the result is a highly enjoyable, well-contrasted programme. Martinů's smart metropolitan 1930s style is encapsulated in the brief, but rather trifling *Serenade*. The Sextet is a longer and a more substantial work, still written in a busy, neo-classical style and effective in its way. These two works inspire an alert, spick-and-span response in the ASMF players. Their style in the warmly romantic Dvořák work is appropriate, too. In the first movement their tempo variations are quite marked, and the playing is highly expressive. The second movement *Dumka* has effectively strong accents and is followed by a fast, exhilarating third movement *Furiant*. The finale comprises a set of variations, each episode of which is vividly characterized in this performance. The recording was made in a church, but fortunately the acoustic is generous without having unwanted resonances and the balance is good.

Dvořák. Piano Quartets—No. 1 in D major, B53; No. 2 in E flat major, B162. **Domus** (Krysia Osostowicz, vn; Timothy Boulton, va; Richard Lester, vc; Susan Tomes, pf). Hyperion CDA66287.

70' DDD 3/89

Apart from the so-called *American* Quartet Dvořák's chamber music is too seldom heard. The two piano quartets are delightful works and like so much of his music seem to inhabit a world of apparently limitless melodic invention. The three movements manage to combine a sophistication of form with a folk-song-like simplicity. However, the piano's role is much more inventive in the E flat major Quartet and meets the string players as an equal partner rather than being seen merely as a subservient accompanist. Texture is uppermost in this latter work and Dvořák brings off some delicious instrumental coups.

Domus is an uncommonly fine piano quartet and they bring to this music a freshness and unanimity of approach that is hugely rewarding. The recorded sound, too, is very fine.

Dvořák. String Quartet No. 12 in F major, B179, "American". Cypresses, B152—Nos. 1, 2, 5, 9 and 11.
Kodály. String Quartet No. 2, Op. 10. **Hagen Quartet** (Lukas Hagen, Annette Bik, vns; Veronika Hagen, va; Clemens Hagen, vc). DG 419 601-2GH.

61' DDD 5/87

Surely no work in the string quartet repertoire expresses so much contentment and joy as Dvořák's *American* Quartet. The very youthful Hagen Quartet penetrate the work's style, with its dance-like rhythms and open-hearted, folky melodies, very successfully and they produce an attractively full-bodied tone-quality. With Kodály's brief Quartet No. 2 we enter a very different world. As in Dvořák's quartet there is a folk-music influence, but here it is the music of Kodály's native Hungary, which by its very nature is more introspective. The Hagen Quartet again capture the work's nationalistic flavour very adroitly. Dvořák's youthful *Cypresses* were originally voice and piano settings of poems which reflected the composer's love for a singer and are played with an affecting simplicity and warmth. The recording is a little too cavernous, but not so much as to spoil the enjoyment afforded by this excellent disc.

Dvořák. String Quartet No. 12 in F major, B179, "American"[a].
Schubert. String Quartet No. 14 in D minor, D810, "Death and the Maiden"[b].
Borodin. String Quartet No. 2 in D major—Notturno[a]. **Quartetto Italiano** (Paolo Borciani, Elisa Pegreffi, vns; Piero Farulli, va; Franco Rossi, vc). Philips Silver Line 420 876-2PSL. Items marked [a] from SAL3618 (8/67), [b] SAL3708 (5/69).

75' ADD 3/89   £ Ⓑ

This is a cherishable coupling of two of the finest quartets in the repertoire. The Quartetto Italiano bring to the Schubert, with its drama and passion so close to the surface, great panache and involvement. The singing theme of the second movement receives a grave intensity that is all too elusive. Similarly Dvořák's *American* Quartet is given exactly the right quality of nostalgia and ease that the work requires. The charming finale, one of Dvořák's most enchanting movements, is given a real folk-like sense of fun. As a bonus the Quartet play the celebrated *Notturno* slow movement from Borodin's Second Quartet; charming though it is it really deserves to be heard in context. The 1960s recordings sound well.

***Dvořák*. RUSALKA. Gabriela Beňačková-Cápová** (sop) Rusalka; **Wieslaw Ochman** (ten) Prince; **Richard Novák** (bass) Watergnome; **Věra Soukupová** (contr) Witch; **Drahomíra Drobková** (mez) Foreign Princess; **Jana Jonášová, Daniela Sounová-Brouková** (sops), **Anna Barová** (contr) Woodsprites; **Jindřich Jindrák** (bar) Gamekeeper; **Jiřina Marková** (sop) Turnspit; **René Tuček** (bar) Hunter; **Prague Philharmonic Chorus; Czech Philharmonic Orchestra/Václav Neumann.** Supraphon 11 03641-2. Notes, text and translation included.

③ 156' DDD 7/86

Dvořák's opera contains some of his most enchanting and haunting music. It tells the tragic story of the water nymph Rusalka who falls in love with a mortal prince. Gabriela Beňačková-Cápová's Rusalka is glorious, the voice full, lithe and with a beautiful soaring legato. She sings the famous Moon song quite magically. Richard Novák is a gruff though benign Watergnome, Wieslaw Ochman an ardent prince and Věra Soukupová a splendidly ominous witch. Václav Neumann directs the Czech Philharmonic with a command of the idiom that is totally engaging. The recording is very fine and the dynamic range quite extraordinarily vivid.

Edward Elgar

British 1857-1934

***Elgar*. Cello Concerto in E minor, Op. 85[a]. Sea Pictures, Op. 37[b].**
[a]**Jacqueline du Pré** (vc); [b]**Dame Janet Baker** (mez); **London Symphony Orchestra/Sir John Barbirolli.** EMI CDC7 47329-2. From ASD655 (12/65).

70' ADD 5/86

***Elgar*. Cello Concerto in E minor, Op. 85.**
***Bloch*. Schelomo. Steven Isserlis** (vc); **London Symphony Orchestra/ Richard Hickox.** Virgin Classics VC7 90735-2.

51' DDD 7/89

This is a classic recording, offering two performances by soloists at the turning point of their careers. Jacqueline du Pré's performance of the Elgar Concerto is extraordinarily complete: the cello sings, cries almost, with burning force in its upper registers; *pianissimos* barely whisper; pizzicatos ring with muted passion; those moments of palpitating *spiccato* bowing convey more than is almost imaginable. The LSO perform as if inspired; hardly surprising given Barbirolli's magical accompaniment. Dame Janet Baker's *Sea Pictures* are no less masterly. The young voice is glorious rich but agile, her diction superb whilst some of the exquisite floated high notes simply defy description. The 1965 sound is quite spectacular its very immediacy and vividness grab one at the outset and don't let go.

Nevertheless, the Virgin issue presents a brave, imaginative, highly-individual account of the Elgar Concerto—as personal in its perception of the piece as the classic Du Pré/Barbirolli recording. With Isserlis, the emotional tug is considerably less overt, the emphasis more on shadow and subtext than open heartache. Yet the inner-light is no less intense, the phrasing no less rhapsodic in manner than Du Pré. In short, understated but certainly not under-characterized. Hickox and the LSO prove model collaborators, and thanks also to an impeccably balanced recording, the give and take between soloist and orchestra in one of Elgar's most perfectly crafted scores, is seamless. Turning to the unique coupling, it almost goes without saying that the LSO bring all their well-oiled filmic skills to bear on Bloch's soulful King Solomon portrait, trumpets and

horns positively outreaching themselves in the outrageous biblical climaxes.
Isserlis does not stint himself, either, pouring forth his darkest and most
impassioned colours, and the big Watford Town Hall acoustic opens out
splendidly to accommodate it all.

Elgar. Violin Concerto in B minor, Op. 61. **Nigel Kennedy** (vn); **London
Philharmonic Orchestra/Vernon Handley.** EMI CD-EMX2058. From
EMX412058-1 (12/84).

| 54' DDD 12/85 | Ⓑ |

Even after the success of his First Symphony, Elgar's self-doubt persisted and
caused his creative instincts to look inward. He could identify with his own
instrument, the violin, as his own lonely voice pitted against an orchestra which
might represent the forces of the outside world. Usually a concerto consisted of
a big first movement, then a lyrical slow movement and a lighter finale: Elgar's
finale, which balanced the first movement in weight, was unique, and at first the
50-minute-long work daunted all but the bravest soloists. Nigel Kennedy's
technique is such that the work's formidable difficulties hold no terrors for him;
his playing is first and foremost immaculate in its execution, complemented by
Handley's sensitive accompaniment. But it is more than that. He has a pure
silvery tone-quality which is a joy to hear; his response to Elgar's vision is
unfailingly sympathetic and understanding, and his projection of it is fresh and
stimulating. The natural concert hall sound is excellent in quality, with important
orchestral detail always registering clearly.

Elgar. Variations on an original theme, "Enigma", Op. 36[a].
Falstaff—Symphonic Study, Op. 68[b]. [a]**Philharmonia Orchestra;** [b]**Hallé
Orchestra/Sir John Barbirolli.** EMI Studio CDM7 69185-2. Item marked [a]
from ASD548 (11/63), [b] ASD610-11 (12/64).

| 65' ADD 11/88 | Ⓑ |

This coupling restores to the catalogue at a very reasonable price two key Elgar
recordings of works which Sir John Barbirolli made very much his own.
Barbirolli brought a flair and ripeness of feeling to the *Enigma* with which Elgar
himself would surely have identified. Everything about his performance seems
exactly right. The very opening theme is phrased with an appealing combination
of warmth and subtlety, and variation after variation has a special kind of
individuality, whilst for the finale Barbirolli draws all the threads together most
satisfyingly. *Falstaff* is a continuous, closely integrated structure and again
Barbirolli's response to the music's scenic characterization is magical while he
controls the overall piece, with its many changes of mood, with a naturally
understanding flair. The original recordings perhaps sounded more sumptuous
but on CD there is more refined detail and greater range and impact to the
sound.

Elgar. The Wand of Youth—Suites Nos. 1 and 2, Opp. 1*a* and 1*b*. Nursery
Suite (1931). **Ulster Orchestra/Bryden Thomson.** Chandos CHAN8318.
From ABRD1079 (8/83).

| 63' DDD 10/84 |

Elgar's orchestral music shows an astonishingly wide range of sensibility. The
patriotic writing has all the pageantry and rumbustious vigour of an era, before
the First World War, when Great Britain believed in itself and seemed to know
just where it was heading. The Symphonies, which are on the grandest scale,
with flowing and surging melodic lines, distil much of this confidence, yet there

Bryden Thomson [photo: Chandos/Curzon]

are already fleeting suspicions and doubts, while the Cello Concerto, the composer's *fin de siècle* masterpiece, confirms the disillusion of an age in its valedictory heart-aching intensity. Elgar's music for children remains very special, and in its innocence of atmosphere stands apart from the rest of his output. The two *Wand of Youth* Suites evoke a dream world untainted by adult unreasonableness. Vignettes like the gentle "Serenade", the delicious "Sun dance" with its dainty chattering flutes, and the fragile charm of the delicate "Fairy pipers" are utterly delightful. Orchestral textures are exquisitely radiant while the robust numbers bring elements of direct contrast, as in "Fairies and Giants" or "Wild bears", which have the bright primary colours of toy trains and nursery boisterousness. The origins of this music date from Elgar's own childhood, even though the *Nursery Suite* is quite a late work, and has the haunting nostalgia of the output from the final decade of his life. The wistful charm of "The Serious Doll" and "The Sad Doll" is unforgettable, and the approaching and departing "Wagon" shows a wonderfully sure touch in handling the orchestra. Bryden Thomson has the full measure of the disarming simplicity of Elgar's writing, and the Ulster Orchestra play this music with great affection and finesse. The warm Ulster acoustic is matched by vivid stereo projection and this fairly early digital recording has stood the test of time.

Elgar. Symphony No. 1, Op. 55. **Royal Philharmonic Orchestra/André Previn.** Philips 416 612-2PH. From 416 612-1PH (6/86).

52' DDD 7/86

Elgar. Symphony No. 1 in A flat major, Op. 55. In the South, Op. 50 ("Alassio"). **London Philharmonic Orchestra/Leonard Slatkin.** RCA Victor Red Seal RD60380.

74' DDD 6/91

At the age of 50, after the success of the *Enigma* Variations and three great oratorios, Elgar created the melody which would become the opening motto theme of his First Symphony. This was a turning point in his career, and nearly all his remaining major works were orchestral. Previn's finely shaped and alert exposition of the motto theme material sets the scene for a reading which throughout glows with something of the unique warmth and vitality Elgar achieved in his own 1930 recording, though Previn's tempos are a little slower and his phrasing is a little more relaxed. The scherzo is, however, brimful of nervous energy, the *Adagio* is shaped lovingly yet with dignified restraint and the outer movements have plenty of impetus. If the sound lacks the last ounce of warmth it is nevertheless full-bodied and clear.

Leonard Slatkin is a conductor whose passion for British music has become something of a crusade, and a listener hearing him in Elgar's First Symphony without knowing the artists could well think that this was a performance under a conductor such as Sir Adrian Boult, long steeped in a tradition which was part of his national heritage. But good music knows no bounds (after all, you don't have to be Austrian to play Mozart!) and Slatkin's understanding of this composer is abundantly clear throughout. In all this, of course, he has the splendid co-operation of the London Philharmonic Orchestra, who have the skill also to manage his rapid tempo for the *Allegro molto* second movement—a pace that is not far, in fact, from the composer's own. There is no trace of sentimentality or dated quality in the treatment of the mighty first movement, either, for here is real grandeur and not just grandiose utterance while the noble sadness of the coda has especial beauty. The other movements are hardly less fine, for the richly textured *Adagio* is most eloquently done and the finale is thrilling. The overture *In the South* which begins the disc is brilliantly vivid, dramatic as well as conveying the Mediterranean sunlight and warmth which the composer experienced on the Italian Riviera. Elgar's massive though subtle scoring can present problems to engineers; here they are magnificently solved and the sound is rich yet detailed with excellent bass.

Elgar. Symphony No. 2 in E flat major, Op. 63. **London Philharmonic Orchestra/Vernon Handley.** Classics for Pleasure CD-CFP4544. From CFP40350 (7/81).

54' ADD 10/88 £ Ⓑ

For those brought up on a diet of Boult's Elgar, this reading of the Second Symphony should not seem particularly alien. Although Handley does not push the climaxes quite as far as Boult or savour the moments of grief with the same personal sense of loss, his view is essentially from the same vantage point; and if his interpretation is a touch more restrained then that is no bad thing in music that is so embroidered around with fleeting, though distracting, wonders. Handley is very much an Elgarian for the present day, interpreting afresh this passionate music in the light of what we now know of its composer. The LPO are his ideal companions in this, for the work is an old friend for them and they show themselves fully imbued with its idiom and sensitive to its slightest nuance. A rich recording, with an extended dynamic range, an astutely-judged balance, and just the right degree of resonance, complements the dedicated playing and puts the finishing touch to a genuinely bargain issue.

Elgar. MUSIC FOR STRINGS. ªJosé-Luis Garcia, ªMary Eade (vns); ªQuentin Ballardie (va); ªOlga Hegedus (vc); English Chamber Orchestra/Sir Yehudi Menuhin. Arabesque Z6563. From ABQ6563 (1/87). Introduction and Allegroª. Chanson de nuit (arr. Fraser). Chanson de matin (arr. Fraser). Three Characteristic Pieces—No. 1, Mazurka. Serenade for strings in E minor. Salut d'amour (arr. Fraser). Elegy.

45' DDD 6/87

Elgar's pieces for string orchestra contain some of his greatest music and certainly the *Introduction and Allegro, Serenade* and *Elegy* included in this delightful programme embody quintessential Elgar. Sir Yehudi Menuhin's readings dig deep into the hearts of these works, drawing out the nostalgia and inner tragedy that underpins even some of the most seemingly high-spirited of Elgar's music. The lighter pieces allow relief from the intensity of the major works, thus making that intensity all the more effective. The English Chamber Orchestra is more than capable of providing first-rate soloists from its own ranks, and the quartet extracted for the *Introduction and Allegro* is suitably virtuosic. Both performers and engineers have produced an ideal integration of this solo group with the main string body, and the generally effervescent sound suits the celebratory nature of the piece. There are a number of other collections of such music available on CD, but this issue should certainly not go unsampled.

Elgar. String Quartet in E minor, Op. 83.
Walton. String Quartet in A minor. **Gabrieli Quartet** (Kenneth Sillito, Brendan O'Reilly, vns; Ian Jewel, va; Keith Harvey, vc). Chandos CHAN8474. From ABRD1185 (1/87).

> 56' DDD 10/87

This nicely recorded disc couples two fine English string quartets in highly accomplished performances by the Gabrieli Quartet. They are both imaginatively conceived works, powerfully projected. The Elgar Quartet is his only surviving quartet and the Gabrieli give a strong, sinuous reading revealing its toughness and range as well as its obvious beauties. Walton's String Quartet also has a similar vitality and exciting, rhythmic fervour that the composer's later reworking for string orchestra tends to dilute. The recording is faithful and exceptionally clean.

Elgar. VIOLIN WORKS. **Nigel Kennedy** (vn); **Peter Pettinger** (pf). Chandos CHAN8380. From ABRD1099 (7/84).
Violin Sonata in E minor, Op. 82. Six Very Easy Melodious Exercises in the First Position, Op. 22. Salut d'amour, Op. 12 (with Steven Isserlis, vc). Mot d'amour, Op. 13. In the South—Canto popolare (In Moonlight). Sospiri, Op. 70. Chanson de nuit, Op. 15 No. 1. Chanson de matin, Op.15 No. 2.

> 55' DDD 8/85

As a violinist himself, Elgar wrote idiomatically for the instrument, and this music shows the expressive variety that he achieved. The Sonata in E minor was his last work for the instrument and is the centrepiece of the recital. It is the only big work here, a dramatic utterance that the artists play with power and poetry. If the Sonata is a key work to the understanding of this composer, so too in its own way is the lilting piece called *Salut d'amour*, which is among his most popular. The *Chanson de nuit* and *Chanson de matin* are charming miniatures while the *Six Very Easy Melodious Exercises in the First Position* (written for his niece) are tiny pieces which can surely not have received a more elegant performance. A good digital recording catches Kennedy's fine tone and complements an attractive issue.

Elgar. CHORAL MUSIC. **Bristol Cathedral Choir/Malcolm Archer** ([a]org), with **Anthony Pinel** (org). Meridian CDE84168.
The Apostles, Op. 49—The Spirit of the Lord. Ave verum corpus, Op. 2 No. 1. Drakes Broughton (Hymn Tune). Give unto the Lord, Op. 74. God be merciful unto us (Psalm 67). Great is the Lord, Op. 67 (with Stephen Foulkes, bar; Bristol Cathedral Special Choir). Imperial March, Op. 32 (trans. Martin)[a]. Te Deum and Benedictus, Op. 34.

> 60' DDD 10/89

When we think of Elgar's choral music we quite rightly remember the great oratorios—*Gerontius, The Apostles, The Kingdom*. The Bristol Cathedral Choir and their former Director of Music, Malcolm Archer, have looked to smaller-scale pieces to fill this delightful CD. Unlike so many English composers Elgar was not brought up in the Anglican church with its strong musical tradition: not for him countless settings of the *Magnificat* and *Nunc Dimittis* or innumerable organ voluntaries. Indeed he wrote only one specifically liturgical piece, the beautifully simple setting of *Ave verum corpus*, and the *Imperial March*, which Archer plays here with such gusto, is a transcription of a fine orchestral piece in the *Pomp and Circumstance* tradition. Other music on this disc includes a pleasant hymn-tune, a run-of-the-mill psalm-chant and items written for major festival occasions, such as *Te Deum and Benedictus* in F and the thrilling choral showpiece *Great is the Lord*. These 'festival' pieces were intended to have orchestral accompaniments, but Anthony Pinel's always imaginative and skilful organ playing is a most satisfactory alternative. The choir have been well trained for these recordings and produce some stirring and inately sensitive performances in the pleasantly warm acoustic of Bristol Cathedral.

Elgar. The Kingdom, Op. 51ᵃ. ORCHESTRAL TRANSCRIPTIONS. ᵃ**Yvonne Kenny** (sop); ᵃ**Alfreda Hodgson** (contr); ᵃ**Christopher Gillett** (ten); ᵃ**Benjamin Luxon** (bar); ᵃ**London Philharmonic Choir; London Philharmonic Orchestra/Leonard Slatkin.** RCA Victor Red Seal RD87862. Notes and text included.
Bach (trans. Elgar): Fantasia and Fugue in C minor, BWV537. *Handel* (trans. Elgar): Overture in D minor.

② 1h 56' DDD 3/89

Elgar intended *The Kingdom* to be the second of three oratorios recounting the events which led to the founding of the Christian church. Poor box-office returns from the first performances of *The Apostles* and of *The Kingdom* discouraged him from completing the project. What a shame! Hearing such a powerful performance as this, one is left in no doubt that *The Kingdom* ranks among the finest of all oratorios. Leonard Slatkin measures his performance with a breadth and expansiveness which suits such momentous subject matter. He isn't afraid of slow tempos and it pays off handsomely; the climaxes, when they come, have real impact and the essentially reflective character of the music is all the more convincing. The orchestra and choir respond to his deeply-felt approach with fervour and the recording, made in EMI's Abbey Road studio, is outstanding. The two orchestral transcriptions of Bach and Handel provide slightly disappointing fillers; not because the performances are anything less than first-rate, but simply because these are little more than Elgar fiddling around in a way which today smacks of dubious taste.

Elgar. The Dream of Gerontius, Op. 38ᵃ. The Music Makers, Op. 69ᵇ. ᵇ**Dame Janet Baker** (mez); ᵃ**Helen Watts** (contr); ᵃ**Nicolai Gedda** (ten); ᵃ**Robert Lloyd** (bass); ᵃ**John Alldis Choir;** ᵃᵇ**London Philharmonic Choir,** ᵃ**New Philharmonia Orchestra;** ᵇ**London Philharmonic Orchestra/Sir Adrian Boult.** EMI CDS7 47208-8. Notes and texts included. Items marked ᵃ from SLS987 (5/76), ᵇ ASD2311 (5/67).

② 2h 16' ADD 1/87   Ⓑ

Elgar. The Dream of Gerontius, Op. 38ᵃ. Sea Pictures, Op. 37ᵇ. **Dame Janet Baker** (mez); ᵃ**Richard Lewis** (ten); ᵃ**Kim Borg** (bass); ᵃ**Hallé Choir;** ᵃ**Sheffield Philharmonic Chorus;** ᵃ**Ambrosian Singers;** ᵇ**London Symphony Orchestra,** ᵃ**Hallé Orchestra/Sir John Barbirolli.** EMI Studio CMS7 63185-2. Texts included. Item marked ᵃ from ASD648/9 (10/65), ᵇ ASD655 (12/65).

② 2h 2' ADD 12/89   £ Ⓑ

Elgar's best-known oratorio is the nearest he ever came to writing an opera. The story of the anguished Gerontius in his death throes and his momentary vision of Heaven was set by Elgar in the most graphic terms, and the principals are like characters in music-drama. Throughout most of its history Sir Adrian Boult was a renowned interpreter of the work, but it was only late in his life that he came to record it. The results were both worth waiting for and rewarding in their own right, capturing its intensity of emotion while never allowing the structure to weaken through too much affection. Nicolai Gedda may not be the ideal interpreter of the title-role, but Boult persuaded him to catch something of its fervour. Helen Watts's Angel was in the best tradition of singing that sympathetic part—warm but firm—whilst Robert Lloyd is heard to strong effect in both bass roles. The London Philharmonic Choir and the New Philharmonia sing and play to the top of their collective best. The spacious recording is a fine match for the calibre of the reading.

Barbirolli's *Gerontius* is not quite so pristine, with more noticeable tape hiss and a few glitches. Although the playing from the Hallé lacks a degree of technical refinement, Barbirolli's direction proved inspirational and the orchestra's legendary depth of string tone carries all before it. Richard Lewis, the stalwart of so many concert performances, was not in best voice for this recording, suffering from a cold, but Dame Janet and Kim Borg are more than equal to their roles, and the composite chorus is remarkably convincing in its urgency and commitment. Whilst this is not the version of *Gerontius* that you might turn to for technical perfection (though you'd be hard put to it to find fault with Janet Baker's performance here), it is an affectionate reading from Barbirolli, and one that proves profoundly satisfying. The transcendentally radiant account of *Sea Pictures* is still holding up unbelievably well after a quarter of a century and makes a valuable coupling.

George Enescu   Romanian 1881-1955

Enescu. OEDIPE. **José van Dam** (bass-bar) Oedipus; **Barbara Hendricks** (sop) Antigone; **Brigitte Fassbaender** (mez) Jocasta; **Marjana Lipovšek** (contr) The Sphinx; **Gabriel Bacquier** (bar) Tiresias; **Nicolai Gedda** (ten) Shepherd; **Jean-Philippe Courtis** (bass) Watchman; **Cornelius Hauptmann** (bass) High Priest; **Gino Quilico** (bar) Theseus; **John Aler** (ten) Laius; **Marcel Vanaud** (bar) Creon; **Laurence Albert** (bass) Phorbas; **Jocelyne Taillon** (mez) Merope; **Les Petits Chanteurs de Monaco; Orféon Donostiarra; Monte-Carlo Philharmonic Orchestra/Lawrence Foster.**
EMI CDS7 54011. Notes, text and translation included.

② 2h 37' DDD 11/90

It is a sad commentary on the musical world's perception that except in Enescu's native Romania this remarkable opera—not merely his masterpiece (over which he pondered for more than 15 years) but a work of international stature—should have received little more than a handful of performances since it was first heard 55 years ago. Those who know Enescu only from his popular early *Romanian Rhapsodies* will here find a composer of infinitely greater stature, employing a highly individual and eclectic style that includes exotic folk elements, strong influences from his teacher Fauré, and an ultra-sophisticated harmonic idiom, subtle instrumentation and ecstatic quality akin to the music of his near-contemporary Szymanowski. The opera's plot covers the entire Greek legend, from the initial warning to Laius through the events of *Oedipus rex* to *Oedipus in Colonna*; and one of the problems of mounting the work has been that the principal personage is on the stage virtually throughout except in the prologue. In this title-role José van Dam, always an artist of the first rank, presents one of his most memorable performances, encompassing the wide range of moods (and equally varied vocal techniques) with consummate mastery. But the casting throughout—individual mention would be invidious—is superb, stars being engaged even for minor roles; and Lawrence Foster, who has consistently championed Enescu's music, draws impressive playing from the Monte Carlo orchestra, capturing the score's delicacy as well as its violence, and ensuring that its complex texture remains clear.

Manuel de Falla   *Spanish 1876-1946*

Falla. El sombrero de tres picos[a]. El amor brujo[b]. [a]**Colette Boky** (sop); [b]**Huguette Tourangeau** (mez); **Montreal Symphony Orchestra/Charles Dutoit.** Decca 410 008-2DH. From SXDL7560 (7/83).

62' DDD 8/83   **Ⓑ**

Here is a partnership of charismatic music-making and engineering of great flair in a superb recording acoustic, elements which combine to produce one of Decca's most famous CDs. With the sound so wonderfully atmospheric and vivid and with seductive orchestral playing, Dutoit shows his natural feeling for Spanish Flamenco rhythms. Both scores have been recorded very successfully before, but never with more magnetism. Whether in the delicious lilt of "Pantomime" or the spectacular opening of *El sombrero de tres picos* ("The three-cornered hat"), with its voluble timpani "Olés!" and castanets, this is music-making of the most compulsive kind, projected with great realism.

Falla. El amor brujo—ballet (orig. version)[a]. El corregidor y la molinera[b]. [b]**Jill Gomez** (sop); [a]**Claire Powell** (mez); **Aquarius/Nicholas Cleobury.** Virgin Classics VC7 90790-2. Texts and translations included.

75' DDD 1/90

In choosing to record here the original, chamber-orchestra version of *El amor brujo*, Nicholas Cleobury in no way tries to compete on equal terms with the many brilliant, full-orchestral realizations of the later ballet and suite available on disc. He makes his effect through the new dramatic light that this more complete version throws on the work and the increased feeling of space that is given to the orchestral textures. *El corregidor y la molinera* is also given in its earliest mime-play version for chamber orchestra: it was later reworked as the ballet, *El sombrero de tres picos* ("The Three Cornered Hat"). Here the later version has additions that one would not wish to be without, but this embryonic form is pleasing enough in its own right and gives great insights into de Falla's working methods. This CD, then, is something of a coup, made all the more desirable by the excellent quality of the performances from Claire Powell and Jill Gomez—both colourful and intense in their respective roles—and Aquarius, who bring a triumph of subtlety to the reduced orchestral parts. The recording retains their vivacity without becoming too intimate.

Falla. EL RETABLO DE MAESE PEDRO[a]. **Matthew Best** (bass) Don Quijote; **Adrian Thompson** (ten) Maese Pedro; **Samuel Linay** (treb) El Trujamán; **Maggie Cole** (hpd).
Milhaud. LES MALHEURS D'ORPHEE[b]. **Malcolm Walker** (bar) Orphée; **Anna Steiger** (sop) Eurydice; **Paul Harrhy** (ten) Maréchal, Le sanglier; **Patrick Donnelly** (bass) Le charron; **Matthew Best** (bass) Le vannier, L'ours; **Gaynor Morgan** (sop) Le renard, La soeur Jumelle; **Patricia Bardon** (sop) Le loup, La soeur Ainée; **Susan Bickley** (mez) Le soeur Cadette.
Stravinsky. RENARD[c]. **Hugh Hetherington, Paul Harrhy** (tens); **Patrick Donnelly, Nicolas Cavallier** (basses); **Christopher Bradley** (cimbalom); [abc]**Matrix Ensemble/Robert Ziegler.** ASV CDDCA758. Texts and translations included.

77' DDD 7/91

Three complete operas on one disc lasting 77 minutes must be good value, and especially so when they are important works from the first quarter of this century. One thing they have in common is that all were commissioned by the

American-born Princess de Polignac, a patroness of music who exercised considerable flair in her choice of gifted artists in a Paris that was then full of them. The performances here by Robert Ziegler and his Matrix Ensemble are full of flair and his chosen singers for the three works (who include the convincingly Spanish boy treble Samuel Linay as El Trujamán in the Falla) sound at home in Spanish, French and Russian in turn. As presented here, Falla's puppet-opera is full of Iberian colour and verve, and although Milhaud's piece on the Orpheus legend is not so striking or dramatic it still has beauty and is elegantly and expressively sung and played. But the best music is still to come in Stravinsky's magnificently earthy and vivid 'barnyard fable' *Renard*, not a long work but a dazzling one, where this performance of great panache simply bursts out of one's loudspeakers to transport us instantly to a farmyard of old Russia. There's excellent cimbalom playing here from Christopher Bradley. The libretto of all three works is usefully provided in the booklet, together with an English translation. The recording is first class, being both immediate and atmospheric.

Gabriel Fauré

French 1845-1924

Fauré. ORCHESTRAL WORKS. [a]**Lorraine Hunt** (sop); [b]**Jules Eskin** (vc); [c]**Tanglewood Festival Chorus; Boston Symphony Orchestra/Seiji Ozawa.** DG 423 089-2GH. Text and translation included where appropriate. Pelléas et Mélisande (with Chanson de Mélisande—orch. Koechlin)[a]. Après un rêve (arr. Dubenskij)[b]. Pavane[c]. Elégie[b]. Dolly (orch. Rabaud).

> 56' DDD 1/88

Fauré's music for Maeterlinck's play *Pelléas et Mélisande* was commissioned by Mrs Patrick Campbell and to the usual four movement suite Ozawa has added the "Chanson de Mélisande", superbly sung here by Lorraine Hunt. Ozawa conducts a sensitive, sympathetic account of the score, and Jules Eskin plays beautifully in both the arrangement of the early song *Après un rêve* and the *Elégie*, which survived from an abandoned cello sonata. The grave *Pavane* is performed here in the choral version of 1901. *Dolly* began life as a piano duet, but was later orchestrated by the composer and conductor Henri Rabaud. Ozawa gives a pleasing account of this delightful score and the recording is excellent.

Fauré. Piano Quartets—No. 1 in C minor, Op. 15; No. 2 in G minor, Op. 45. **Domus** (Krysia Osostowicz, vn; Robin Ireland, va; Timothy Hugh, vc; Susan Tomes, pf). Hyperion CDA66166. From A66166 (10/86).

> 62' DDD 10/86

Fauré. Piano Quartet No. 1 in C minor, Op. 15[a]. Piano Trio in D minor, Op. 120. **Beaux Arts Trio** (Isidore Cohen, vn; Peter Wiley, vc; Menahem Pressler, pf); [a]**Kim Kashkashian** (va). Philips 422 350-2PH.

> 53' DDD 6/90

The First Piano Quartet reveals Fauré's debt to an earlier generation of composers, particularly Mendelssohn. Yet already it has the refined sensuality, the elegance and the craftsmanship which were always to be hallmarks of his style and it is a thoroughly assured, highly enjoyable work which could come from no other composer's pen. The Second Quartet is a more complex, darker work, but much less ready to yield its secrets. The comparatively agitated, quicksilver scherzo impresses at once, however, and repeated hearings of the

complete work reveal it to possess considerable poetry and stature. Just occasionally one could wish that the members of Domus had a slightly more aristocratic, commanding approach to these scores, but overall the achievement is highly impressive, for their playing is both idiomatic and technically impeccable. The recording has an appropriately intimate feel to it and is faithful and well-balanced.

The Beaux Arts Trio are one of the most celebrated of ensembles and together with the violist Kim Kashkashian

The Beaux Arts Trio   [photo: Philips/Steiner]

they bring the right balance of passion and poise to the C minor Quartet's first movement, one that in lesser hands can seem discursive. The wry, prickly humour of the deft scherzo and the profound yet reticent romantic feeling of the *Adagio* are fully realized here too, as is the mysterious agitation of the finale. The D minor Piano Trio dates from 1923, over 40 years after the Piano Quartet and only a year before the composer's death, and is no less moving for being sometimes elliptical and questioning in utterance; this touching yet enigmatic music, though Gallic in feeling, is unlike any other French music of its time, though we may see expressive parallels to it in aspects of the novel sequence *A la recherche du temps perdu* which Marcel Proust was bringing to completion at this time. The recording made in the Snape Maltings is on the close side but broadly satisfying, although the piano sound in the Trio is a little compressed.

Fauré. Violin Sonatas—No. 1 in A major, Op. 13[a]; No. 2 in E minor, Op. 108[a].
Franck. Violin Sonata in A major[b]. **Arthur Grumiaux** (vn); [a]**Paul Crossley,** [b]**György Sebok** (pfs). Philips Musica da Camera 426 384-2PC. Items marked [a] from 9500 534 (7/79), [b] 9500 568 (10/80).

73' ADD 7/90

Fauré was only 31, and on the crest of his first great love affair, when writing his radiantly lyrical A major Violin Sonata. But curiously he allowed four decades to elapse before following it up with the E minor Sonata, by which time deafness, no less than the dark background of war, had drawn him into a more recondite world of his own. As portraits of the composer in youth and full artistic maturity the two works make an ideal coupling. But here, as a bonus, we are also given César Franck's one and only Violin Sonata, written at 64, bringing the playing time to the very generous total of almost an hour-and-a-quarter. It would be hard to find any two artists closer to Fauré's own heart than the intimately attuned Grumiaux and Crossley. Their original LP was immediately hailed as the best available way back in 1979. And despite fine newcomers in recent years (not forgetting Krysia Osostowicz and Susan Tomes) this mellow CD transfer still triumphs over all the catalogue's rivals. An unerring sense of style goes hand in hand with very beautiful, finely nuanced tone and an immediacy of expression suggesting joyous new discovery. Even if Sebok's piano emerges a little more plummy than Crossley's, the Franck Sonata, too, appeals through its warmth of heart.

Fauré. PIANO WORKS. **Pascal Rogé**. Decca 425 606-2DH.
Impromptus—No. 2 in F minor, Op. 31; No. 3 in A flat major, Op. 34.
Nocturnes—No. 1 in E flat minor, Op. 33 No. 1; No. 2 in B major, Op. 33
No. 2; No. 3 in A flat major, Op. 33 No. 3; No. 4 in E flat major, Op. 36;
No. 5 in B flat major, Op. 37. Trois Romances sans paroles, Op. 17.
Barcarolles—No. 1 in A minor, Op. 26; No. 2 in G major, Op. 41; No. 4 in A
flat major, Op. 44. Valse-caprice No. 1 in A major, Op. 30.

> 72' DDD 5/90

Fauré. PIANO WORKS. **Kathryn Stott** (pf). Conifer CDCF138. From
CFC138 (8/86).
Impromptus—No. 1 in E flat major; No. 2 in F minor; No. 3 in A flat major.
Nocturnes—No. 1 in E flat minor; No. 4 in E flat major; No. 6 in D flat
major. Barcarolles—No. 1 in A minor; No. 4 in A flat major; No. 5 in F sharp
minor; No. 6 in E flat major. Three songs without words.

> 63' DDD 6/87

Fauré's piano music spans a period of all but 40 years: but these discs illustrate
only its early manifestations. He was still finding his feet, at first much under the
influence of Schumann, Chopin and Saint-Saëns (as can be heard in the first
Valse-caprice), but later of Liszt, who befriended him and whose example is
observable in the powerful climaxes of the second *Barcarolle*. An excellent pianist
himself, in these early works he delighted in diverse and inventive experiments
in texture and in harmonic subtleties, which Pascal Rogé handles with
understanding and charm. Particularly notable are the purity of his rapid runs
and decorative passagework, his sensitive dynamic nuances and the clarity of his
part-playing. Overall, his interpretations, less extrovert than those of some of his
rivals, are characterized by a refinement that is eminently apt to this fastidious
composer. In one or two places the resonant acoustic slightly clouds detail, but
for the most part the recorded quality is pleasurably warm.

Kathryn Stott, too, shows much sympathy for Fauré's style. Her use of rubato
is natural and expressive, and she responds to the gently changing emotional
content of the music with considerable sensitivity. Her playing is most enjoyable
and the piano tone is very lifelike.

Fauré. La bonne chanson, Op. 61[a]. Piano Trio in D minor, Op. 120[b]. [a]**Sarah
Walker** (mez); [a]**Nash Ensemble**; [b]**Marcia Crayford** (vn); [b]**Christopher
van Kampen** (vc); [b]**Ian Brown** (pf). CRD CRD3389. Text and translation
included. From CRD1089 (4/81).

> 44' ADD 5/90

In *La bonne chanson*, generally considered the finest of Fauré's song-cycles, he
perfectly matched the ecstatic moods of Verlaine's love-poems to the young girl
who was to become his wife; but though the sentiments expressed are those of a
man and the songs were first performed by a baritone, they are more usually
sung by a female voice. Sarah Walker, with her warm, voluptuous tone, poetic
sensibility, shaping of phrases and, not least, excellent French, makes an
admirable interpreter of their passionate lyricism. Fauré's own arrangement of
the original piano accompaniment for string quintet and piano is played with
tonal finesse by the Nash Ensemble. The final song, "L'hiver a cessé", refers to
the music of the previous eight, summing up the atmosphere of radiant devotion
that pervades the cycle. The Piano Trio, composed 30 years later when Fauré
was 77, was his penultimate work and represents him at his most direct and
compact: the artists here are responsive to its subtle harmonic thinking and judge
its expressive weight to a nicety, preserving the grace of this essentially elegant,
if elusive, work.

Fauré. Requiem, Op. 48 (original 1894 version)[a].
Fauré/Messager. Messe des Pêcheurs de Villerville[b]. [a]**Agnès Mellon** (sop);
[a]**Peter Kooy** (bar); [b]**Jean-Philippe Audoli** (vn); [a]**Leo van Doeselaar** (org);
**Petits Chanteurs de Saint-Louis; Paris Chapelle Royale Chorus;
Musique Oblique Ensemble/Philippe Herreweghe.** Harmonia Mundi
HMC90 1292. Texts included.

56' DDD 4/89

Fauré's original conception of his Requiem was as a chamber work, but when
the work was published it was scored for full orchestra. There is no evidence
that Fauré did any more than acquiesce in preparing this 'concert-hall version' of
his score. Even accepting that an amplification of the instrumentation is needed
when the work is played in large halls, a rediscovery of the score as it existed
before publication has long seemed desirable. New and convincing sources have
now been discovered by the Fauré authority Jean-Michel Nectoux:·a complete
set of orchestral parts, apparently prepared for Fauré's use, some of them in his
own hand and all corrected by him. The resulting score is as near to authentic
Fauré as we shall get and this first recording of Nectoux's edition is ideal. It uses
boys' voices in the upper parts (as did Fauré himself) and a convincingly boy-like
soprano in the "Pie Jesu". The orchestra is of ideal size and is beautifully
balanced in a sympathetic acoustic. As a charming bonus we have another act of
Fauréan 'restoration', the original version of what later became the *Messe basse*,
with its pretty accompaniment for string quintet, wind trio and harmonium and
its two long-suppressed extra movements by Messager. An enchanting record as
well as an important document.

Gerald Finzi

British 1901-1956

Finzi. Cello Concerto, Op. 40.
Leighton. Veris gratia—suite, Op. 9[a]. **Rafael Wallfisch** (vc); [a]**George
Caird** (ob); **Royal Liverpool Philharmonic Orchestra/Vernon Handley.**
Chandos CHAN8471.

66' DDD 10/86

Finzi wrote his Cello Concerto for the Cheltenham Festival of 1955. At this time
he had suffered from leukaemia for four years and he knew that he had not long
to live. This knowledge served only to enhance his deep-seated awareness of and
preoccupation with questions concerning life's transience, and the result is a
work which is large in scale and reflects dark, troubled emotions. Raphael
Wallfisch gives a moving and eloquent account of the solo part: he plays with a
rich quality of tone, and Vernon Handley provides a sympathetic accompaniment.
Kenneth Leighton was still a student when Finzi took an interest in his work.
Finzi was conductor of the Newbury String Players, and for this group Leighton
wrote his suite *Veris gratia*, a melodious, lyrical work in four movements,
inspired by Helen Waddell's translation of *Medieval Latin Lyrics*. The performance
is all that could be desired, and is set in a high quality recording.

Finzi. ORCHESTRAL WORKS. [a]**Alan Hacker** (cl); **English String
Orchestra/William Boughton.** Nimbus NI5101.
Love's Labour's Lost—Suite, Op. 28. Clarinet Concerto in C minor, Op. 31[a].
Prelude in F minor, Op. 25. Romance in E flat major, Op. 11.

65' DDD 12/88

There are several other Finzi issues available which include the Clarinet
Concerto. Alan Hacker, however, encompasses all his colleagues' virtues,

providing special insights and revelling in the brilliant writing. He also adds something extra—an almost mystical realization of the music's poetic vision which is deeply moving. This is in spite of the fact that the string-playing sometimes lacks polish and precision. Finzi wrote incidental music for a BBC production of *Love's Labour's Lost* and expanded it for a later open-air production. It is tuneful, graceful music, but one cannot feel that the stage was Finzi's world. The disc is completed by two interesting early pieces for strings, the *Prelude* and *Romance*, both wholly characteristic of the composer and very well played.

Finzi. The Fall of the Leaf, Op. 20. New Year Music nocturne for orchestra, Op. 7.
Moeran. Sinfonietta. Serenade in G major. **Northern Sinfonia / Richard Hickox.** EMI CDC7 49912-2.

— 62' DDD 2/90

All Saints' Church, Quayside, in Newcastle upon Tyne imparts a lively resonance to these brilliantly lit performances from the Northern Sinfonia, lending ripeness and space to the already glowing colours of such quintessentially British works. Moeran's *Serenade* and *Sinfonietta*, which frame the two shorter pieces by Finzi,

Richard Hickox   [photo: EMI / MacDomnic]

are late works of direct and appealing expression. The *Serenade* is suite-like, with four dance movements plus a Prologue and Epilogue, and is brightly scored for small orchestra. The *Sinfonietta* has only three movements, though the second is a theme with six variations, and the whole is suffused with images of Radnorshire's moorland. Its darker moments tie it more closely in mood with Finzi's *The Fall of the Leaf*, a work left only partly scored at the composer's death. Howard Ferguson has made a marvellous job of completing the piece and we can but be glad that such a gloriously poignant example of Finzi's art is now available. His *Nocturne*, without being as effusively emotional, also makes a lasting impression in these strong, dedicated readings from Richard Hickox. The straightforward approach does not preclude poetry and it is difficult to think of these works receiving more sympathetic performances.

Finzi. Dies Natalis, Op. 8[a]. Farewell to Arms, Op. 9[a]. Clarinet Concerto in C minor, Op. 31[b]. [a]**Martyn Hill** (ten); [b]**Michael Collins** (cl); **City of London Sinfonia / Richard Hickox.** Virgin Classics VC7 90718-2. Texts included.

— 61' DDD 8/88

This enterprising disc contains what can probably be regarded as Finzi's two best-known works, *Dies Natalis* and the Clarinet Concerto, and a rarity, the *Farewell to Arms*. *Dies Natalis* is a masterpiece of sustained rapture, the perfect metamorphosis into music of the metaphysical poet Traherne's Blake-like vision of the innocence and wonder with which we come into the world. Words and music belong together and the unending melody never loses its power to entrance the sympathetic listener. Martyn Hill sings beautifully and Richard Hickox's conducting ensures a memorable interpretation. The Clarinet Concerto with its elegiac slow movement inhabits a similar world. But Finzi is capable of more than pastoral reverie, as the restless first movement and the delightfully relaxed and witty *rondo-finale* demonstrate. Michael Collins is an agile, poetic and virtuosic soloist, his mellow and pleasing tone faithfully captured by the recording.

Gioseffo-Hectore Fiocco
Belgian-Italian 1703-1741

G-H. Fiocco. Pièces de clavecin, Op. 1. **Ton Koopman** (hpd). Auvidis Astrée E7731.

② 86' AAD 3/90

The Belgian-born Gioseffo-Hectore Fiocco was, in spite of his name, at least as francophile as italophile, at least to judge by these two harpsichord suites (published *c.*1730). The suites contain mixtures of French and italianate movements, as well as a few in the more *galant* style of *les goûts réünis*. Couperin's influence is evident in such external details as the titles, ornamentation—although a good proportion of that is the stylish invention of Ton Koopman—and the exquisite melancholy; but Fiocco also mastered the forms, textures and harmonic progressions epitomized by Couperin's music. And while Fiocco never surpassed the sublimity of his model, he did compose powerful and often sombre music worthy of wider circulation. Each suite is a microcosm of contemporary forms. The G major encompasses many contrasts of mood and style (*L'italiene*—surely a parody of Handel—is followed by the Couperinesque *La Françoise*). For all the French movements, Fiocco's first suite ends with a four-movement Italian sonata, in which Vivaldi might have taken pride. The D minor suite is less structured: there are dance movements graced with interesting technical challenges (especially in the Ramellian *Sauterelles*), three *rondeaux* and a lively, stylistically integrated finale (*La Frinqante*). Throughout, Koopman plays masterfully, interestingly and with unimpeachable taste. He has written the extremely informative booklet, revealing much about both the music and his approach to playing. The variety and aptness of his own ornamentation in both French and italianate movements can serve as a valuable guide: this is the crux of his performance which brings the music to life.

Cesar Franck
Belgian/French 1822-1890

Franck. Symphony in D minor[a]. Symphonic Variations, Op. 46[b]. [b]**Alexis Weissenberg** (pf); [a]**Orchestre de Paris**, [b]**Berlin Philharmonic Orchestra/Herbert von Karajan.** EMI Studio CDM7 69008-2. Item marked [a] from ASD2552 (9/70), [b] ASD2872 (5/73).

58' ADD 9/87 Ⓑ

Franck was 65 when he composed his Symphony. It is a powerfully written three-movement work strongly conceived in bold orchestral colours and containing one of those melodies that linger in the memory for days. Karajan's performance makes much of its strong Germanic characteristics; he perfectly understands its architecture and conceives the work on a grand scale. The playing of the Paris Orchestra is very fine indeed, combining the strength of vision of the conductor with a uniquely Gallic quality only a French orchestra possesses. The *Symphonic Variations* was composed some three years after the Symphony and shows a wittier side to the composer. Alexis Weissenberg makes a strong case for the work and is partnered sympathetically by Karajan. The recordings are good and the two different venues match well on the disc.

Franck. ORGAN WORKS. **Jean Guillou.** Dorian DOR90135. Played on the organ of St Eustache, Paris.
Cantabile in B major. Chorales—No. 1 in E major; No. 2 in B minor; No. 3 in A minor. Fantaisie in A major. Fantaisie in C major. Final in B flat major. Grande Pièce Symphonique. Pastorale in E major. Pièce Héroïque in B minor. Prélude, Fugue et Variation. Prière in C sharp minor.

② 2h 27' 6/90

Franck. ORGAN WORKS. **Michael Murray.** Telarc CD80234. Played on the Cavaillé-Coll organ of Saint Sernin Basilica, Toulouse.
Fantaisie in A major. Cantabile in B major. Pièce Héroïque in B minor. Fantaisie in C major. Grande Pièce Symphonique. Prélude, Fugue et variation. Pastorale. Prière in C sharp minor. Final in B flat major. Chorales—No. 1 in E major; No. 2 in B minor; No. 3 in A minor.

② 2h 29' DDD 7/90

Although Franck wrote a great many small pieces for organ it was with these 12 (the 'masterworks' as the Telarc disc styles them) that he established an organ music tradition which French composers to this day have followed. Jean Guillou is certainly in that tradition. He is a virtuoso organist and gifted improviser (as was Franck) and his own organ music is in the large, colourful, symphonic mould effectively created by Franck. As part of that living tradition Guillou obviously doesn't feel constrained by what Franck actually wrote down. He modifies the original almost to the point of eccentricity: much of what you hear here bears little relation to the published text. But if you are willing to listen with an open mind and don't believe that what the composer wrote has to be considered sacrosanct you will be rewarded with some breathtaking virtuosity and a spectacular recorded sound.

Michael Murray, on the other hand, is entirely respectful of tradition. There is about his performances something akin to reverence. He is completely faithful to the finest detail of the score, and the authenticity of these performances is underlined by being recorded on an instrument contemporaneous (just) with Franck and still in virtually unaltered shape; this was the kind of organ sound that inspired Franck to write these pieces. Authentic and respectful as they are, Murray's performances are beautifully played. Like most American organists he seems to have a natural gift for direct communication; a gift wholeheartedly supported by Telarc's exceptionally fine recording.

Franck. Les Béatitudes. **Diana Montague, Ingeborg Danz** (mezzos); **Cornelia Kallisch** (contr); **Keith Lewis, Scot Weir** (tens); **Gilles Cachemaille** (bar); **John Cheek, Juan Vasle, Reinhard Hagen** (basses); **Stuttgart Gächinger Kantorei and Radio Symphony Orchestra/ Helmuth Rilling.** Hänssler 98 964. Text and translation included.

② 2h 11' DDD 7/91

Without going as far as some of Franck's disciples—d'Indy, for example, called *Les Béatitudes* "the greatest work for a long time in the development of the art"—

Franck F

it has to be conceded that sections of the work, such as parts four and five, contain music of great beauty, and that the rich texture and extremely effective orchestration in all of it are impressive. It was intended not as a narrative oratorio in the Handel-Haydn-Mendelssohn tradition but as a series of contemplative devotional studies; and stylistically it shows both an affinity to the Liszt-Wagner school and an anticipation of the Impressionists. The predominantly slow tempos of the Prologue and eight Beatitudes, unenterprising rhythmic invention and the structural uniformity of the sections (each consisting of high-toned but pedestrian moralistic verse followed by the Biblical quotation) flaw the impact of the oratorio as an entity; but this is a case of the parts being greater than the whole. Helmuth Rilling (if over-inclined to exaggerate ritardandos) here delivers a very fine performance, certainly superior to the two current previous recordings, with an excellent chorus and orchestra and some first-rate soloists: radiant singing from Diana Montague and incisively menacing tone from John Cheek as the voice of Satan. Good presentation material and good recording.

Domenico Gallo   *Refer to Index*   *Italian, born c.1730*

George Gershwin   *American 1898-1937*

Gershwin. ORCHESTRAL WORKS. [a]**Earl Wild** (pf); **Boston Pops Orchestra/Arthur Fiedler.** RCA Papillon GD86519. Item marked [a] from VICS1308 (7/73), [b] new to UK, [c] SB6580 (9/64).
Rhapsody in Blue[a]. Piano Concerto in F major[b]. An American in Paris[c]. Variations on "I got rhythm"[b].

70' ADD 11/87   £

Arthur Fiedler   *[photo:BMG Classics*

The ideal pianist for Gershwin is one who combines the instinctive feel for Broadway musical rhythm with the control, dexterity and power of the classical virtuoso, and Earl Wild is pretty close to that ideal. The other vital ingredient is an orchestra and conductor with a similar blend of skills, and here the Boston Pops with Arthur Fiedler fits the bill as closely as any. This is one of the few symphony-orchestra versions of the *Rhapsody in Blue* which does not make one yearn for the leaner, punchier textures of the original jazz-band orchestration; and what a relief to hear the Concerto and *An American in Paris* avoiding both the constraint and the self-conscious freedom to which most classics-only orchestras are prone. The inclusion of the immensely resourceful *Variations on "I got rhythm"* gives the disc a further edge over its competitors. Recording quality is clean-cut and free from trickery, although in its somewhat constricted perspective it just falls short of the highest standards.

***Gershwin Gold*. Royal Philharmonic Orchestra/Andrew Litton** ([a]pf).
RPO CDRPO8008.
Rhapsody in Blue (orig. version). George Gershwin Song-book (arr. solo
pf)—Swanee[a]; Nobody but you[a]; Do it again[a]; Clap yo hand[a]. Who cares? (orch.
by Hershy Kay from the George Gershwin Song-book)—Strike up the band;
Sweet and low down; Somebody loves me; Bidin' my time; 'S wonderful/That
certain feeling; Do do do/Lady be good; The man I love; I'll build a stairway to
paradise; Embraceable you; Fascinatin' rhythm; Who cares?; My one and only;
Liza; I got rhythm.

60' DDD 9/87

***Simon Rattle—The Jazz Album*. London Sinfonietta/Simon Rattle.**
EMI CDC7 47991-2.
Milhaud: La création du monde (with John Harle, sax). **Gershwin:** Rhapsody
in Blue (orig. version. Peter Donohoe, pf). **Creamer and Layton:** After
you've gone (Jeremy Taylor, ten). **Kahn, Erdman, Meyers and Schoebel:**
Nobody's sweetheart. **Stravinsky:** Ebony Concerto (Michael Collins, cl).
Harris and Young: Sweet Sue (Harvey and the Wallbangers). **Bernard and
Black:** Dardanella. **Donaldson and Kahn:** Makin' whoopee! (Harvey and the
Wallbangers). **Donaldson and Whiting:** My blue Heaven (Harvey and the
Wallbangers). **McPhail and Michels:** San. **Bernstein:** Prelude, Fugue and
Riffs (Collins; Donohoe).

74' DD 12/87

Both of these discs contain highly cherishable accounts of Gershwin's *Rhapsody in
Blue* in the original jazz-band version. The young American pianist and conductor
Andrew Litton proves himself to be an uncommonly fine Gershwin
pianist—loose-limbed, rhythmically flexible and possessing just that right degree
of *laissez faire*. The RPO respond to his intuitive approach with idiomatic playing
and ideal abandon. Peter Donohoe, too, gives a fine performance, more closely
controlled than Litton's with some acute rhythmic pointing and a 'bite' that
proves irresistible. *Rhapsody* apart the discs couldn't differ more. Rattle offers a
gloriously languid performance of Milhaud's sultry *Création du monde*, crisp
readings of Stravinsky's *Ebony Concerto* and Bernstein's *Prelude, Fugue and Riffs* and
a number of orchestrations made for the Paul Whiteman Band including a
delicious account of *Makin' whoopee!*. The London Sinfonietta play the music with
total command. Litton's coupling, a splendid Hershy Kay medley based on
Gershwin songs entitled *Who Cares?* is equally enticing. Both discs are winners.

***Gershwin*. Rhapsody in Blue[a]. An American in Paris. Piano Concerto in F
major[a]. London Symphony Orchestra/André Previn** ([a]pf). EMI CDC7
47161-2. From ASD2754 (11/71).

64' ADD 9/86   Ⓑ

***Gershwin*. An American in Paris[a]. Rhapsody in Blue[b]. [a]Columbia Symphony
Orchestra; [b]New York Philharmonic Orchestra/Leonard Bernstein**
(pf[a]). CBS Maestro CD42611. From Philips SABL160 (10/60).

35' ADD 11/90

Few CDs remastered from analogue LPs show an improvement in sound-quality
so striking as Previn's Gershwin triptych. The digital remastering has
transformed the effect of the music-making, giving both the *Rhapsody* and *An
American in Paris* a vibrant, vivid clarity, without serious loss of body, and in the
Concerto the strings sound particularly fresh, creating the most attractively warm
timbre in the lyrical theme of the first movement. There are many felicities in
these performances and *An American in Paris* is infectiously volatile, with a strong

rhythmic inflection for the great blues tune when it enters on the trumpet. In the *Rhapsody* there is much chimerical detail from Previn and the lack of inflation is very telling. One is glad to see the Concerto is at last establishing itself in the concert hall for it is full of memorable tunes. Previn's version is highly distinguished, with the lyricism of the slow movement evocatively caught and the brilliant finale a *tour de force*.

Bernstein conducted and played the music of Gershwin with the same naturalness as he brought to his own music. Here, *An American in Paris* swings by with an instinctive sense of its origins in popular and film music; no stilted rhythms or four-squareness delay the work's progress, and where ripe schmaltz is wanted, ripe schmaltz is what we get, devoid of all embarrassment. *Rhapsody in Blue* is playful and teasing, constantly daring us to try to categorize its style, and then confounding our conclusions. Although the solo passages from individual players are beautifully taken, both orchestras pull together magnificently to capture the authentic flavour of Gershwin's idiom, and Bernstein pushes them to transcend the printed score. His own playing in the *Rhapsody* is tantalizingly unpredictable. The recording is clear and bright, perhaps a touch hard-edged, and a little of the richness of the original LP issue might have been preferred by some, especially as the editing is now made more obvious, but the sound suits the works. The only major criticism would be of the stingy overall timing of the disc—but with these performances quality compensates.

Gershwin (arr. Wild). PIANO TRANSCRIPTIONS. **Earl Wild.** Chesky CD32.
Fantasy on "Porgy and Bess". Improvisation in the form of a Theme and Three Variations on "Someone to watch over me". Seven Virtuoso Etudes: I got rhythm; Lady be good; Liza; Embraceable you; Somebody loves me; Fascinatin' rhythm; The man I love.

59' DDD 10/90

This disc is one of those remarkable contemporary documents of great pianism, to be treasured and brought out for comparison whenever the virtuosos of earlier ages are cited. Earl Wild not only matches many of the giants in technical dexterity and musical insight, but also mirrors the ability of a number to produce enthralling glosses on the music of others in the form of almost ridiculously taxing transcriptions. Here, Gershwin is the subject of Wild's wonderful flights of fancy, a particularly appropriate choice as Gershwin himself produced transcriptions of a number of his own songs, obviously considering them ideal vehicles for jazz-type transformation. Wild magically combines a modern improvisational technique with a Lisztian attention to form, development and unity, producing works that repay repeated listening. The *Porgy and Bess* Fantasy achieves what the best of Liszt's works in the genre do—it conveys the flavour of the opera to those who do not know it, prompting them to hear the original, and gives added insight into the music for those who are already familiar with it. The solid-toned Baldwin piano, captured with effective truthfulness by the recording, is the ideal instrument for such inspirational performances.

Kiri Sings Gershwin. Dame Kiri Te Kanawa (sop); **New Princess Theater Orchestra/John McGlinn.** EMI CDC7 47454-2.
Including—Somebody loves me, Love walked in, Summertime, The man I love, Things are looking up.

> 46' DDD 10/87

Gershwin. OVERTURES. **New Princess Theater Orchestra/John McGlinn.** EMI CDC7 47977-2.
A Damsel in Distress—suite. Stiff upper lip. Girl Crazy. Of Thee I Sing (all orch. Robert Russell Bennett). Tip-toes (orch. John Ansell, Gershwin and Larry Moore). Oh, Kay! (orch. Hilding Anderson). Primrose.

> 42' DDD 12/87

These two recordings featuring the New Princess Theater Orchestra were made possible by the discovery of a cache of scores, with original orchestrations, in the Warner Brothers warehouse in New Jersey. "Kiri Sings Gershwin" is a remarkably successful disc finding Te Kanawa on sparkling form. The up-tempo presentation may take a little getting used to (*Love is here to stay* is really rather swift) but the record has a wonderful verve that is quite intoxicating. The overtures disc is brim full with good tunes, beautifully orchestrated. For bite and sheer rhythmic exuberance these performances take a lot of beating. John McGlinn, who has done much of the musical detective work on the orchestrations, directs wholly idiomatically. The recordings are a little fierce in the 'pop' style, with a slightly tiring edge lent to this already quite fizzy music. But these are treasurable mementoes of the 1920s and 1930s.

Gershwin. GIRL CRAZY. Cast includes **Lorna Luft, David Carroll, Judy Blazer, Frank Gorshin, David Garrison, Vicki Lewis, chorus and orchestra/John Mauceri.** Elektra Nonesuch 7559-79250-2. Notes and text included.

> 73' DDD 2/91

Girl Crazy is certainly one of the most hit-filled shows the Gershwins ever penned as the rousing Overture alone, with its references to "But not for me", "I got rhythm", "Bidin' my time" and "Embraceable you", immediately and irresistibly confirms. But these are not the only knockout numbers that pepper this terrific score; "Could you use me?", "Sam and Delilah" and "Treat me rough" are equally deserving of the term 'showstopper'. The show's basic setting, a Dude Ranch (where eastern playboys spent their vacation pretending to be western cowboys), may be uniquely American (which could explain why the show did not cross the Atlantic) but any unfamiliarity the overseas listener may have with the plot's finer points will in no way mar enjoyment of this completely captivating recording. One of the chief pleasures to be had from the current crop of Broadway reconstructions is the opportunity of hearing the songs with their original orchestrations, and Robert Russell Bennett's here are no exception. John Mauceri and his hand-picked orchestra respond with infectious gusto to every nuance of Bennett's delightful arrangements and throughout the score they successfully evoke the jazzy atmosphere of 1930s Broadway. Each of the soloists and chorus, too, are all just right, bringing off their respective numbers with tremendous verve and a real feel for the idiom. Packaged with an incredibly lavish and informative booklet (96 pages in all) this issue is an absolute treasure.

Gershwin. PORGY AND BESS. **Willard White** (bass) Porgy; **Cynthia Haymon** (sop) Bess; **Harolyn Blackwell** (sop) Clara; **Cynthia Clarey** (sop) Serena; **Damon Evans** (bar) Sportin' Life; **Marietta Simpson** (mez) Maria; **Gregg Baker** (bar) Crown; **Glyndebourne Chorus; London Philharmonic Orchestra/Simon Rattle**. EMI CDS7 49568-2. Notes and text included.

③ 3h 9' DDD 6/89

Gershwin. PORGY AND BESS—excerpts. **Leontyne Price, Barbara Webb, Berniece Hall, Maeretha Stewart** (sops); **Miriam Burton** (mez); **John W. Bubbles, Robert Henson** (tens); **William Warfield, McHenry Boatwright, Alonzo Jones** (bars); **RCA Victor Chorus and Orchestra/ Skitch Henderson**. RCA Victor Gold Seal GD85234. From SB6554 (1/64). Act 1—Introduction; Summertime; A woman is a sometime thing; Gone, gone, gone. Act 2—I got plenty o' nuttin; Bless you is my woman now; It ain't necessarily so; What you want wid Bess? I loves you Porgy. Act 3—There's a boat dat's leavin'; Oh Bess; Oh Lawd, I'm on my way.

48' ADD 4/89

The company, orchestra and conductor from the outstanding 1986 Glyndebourne production recreate once more a very real sense of Gershwin's 'Catfish Row' community on EMI's complete recording. Such is the atmosphere and theatricality of this recording, we might easily be back on the Glyndebourne stage; you can positively smell the drama in the key scenes. From the very first bar it's clear just how instinctively attuned Simon Rattle and this orchestra are to every aspect of a multi-faceted score. The cast, too, are so *right*, so much a part of their roles, and so well integrated into the whole, that one almost takes the excellence of their contributions for granted. Here is one beautiful voice after another, beginning in style with Harolyn Blackwell's radiant "Summertime", which at Rattle's gorgeously lazy tempo, is just about as beguiling as one could wish. Willard White conveys both the simple honesty and inner-strength of Porgy without milking the sentiment and Haymon's passionately sung Bess will go wherever a little flattery and encouragement take her. As Sportin' Life, Damon Evans not only relishes the burlesque elements of the role but he really *sings* what's written a lot more than is customary. But the entire cast deliver throughout with all the unstinting fervour of a Sunday revivalist meeting. Sample for yourself the final moments of the piece—"Oh Lawd, I'm on my way"—if that doesn't stir you, nothing will.

The RCA issue is unashamedly a vehicle for the glorious voice of Leontyne Price, a notable Bess in her early career. Her voice was at its peak of form and beauty in 1963 when this disc was made and the richness and pliancy across the

entire register is quite breathtaking. William Warfield's Porgy is almost overshadowed by such luxuriance of tone but it is good to have on record what was a celebrated portrayal. Another splendid assumption is John W. Bubbles's Sportin' Life, a wonderfully rounded characterization. The orchestral support is lively and theatrical and for anyone hesitant about investing in Rattle's fine complete recording of the opera, this highlights disc has a lot to offer.

Willard White   *[photo: Gramophone*

Carlo Gesualdo

Italian c.1561-1613

Gesualdo. MADRIGALS. **Les Arts Florissants** [a]**Vocal and** [b]**Instrumental Ensembles/William Christie.** Harmonia Mundi HMC90 1268. Texts and translations included.
Madrigals[a]—Ahi, disperata vita. Sospirava il mio cor. O malnati messaggi. Non t'amo, o voce ingrata. Luci serene e chiare. Sparge la morte al mio Signor nel viso. Arde il mio cor. Occhi del mio cor vita. Mercè grido piangendo. Asciugate i begli ochi. Se la mia morte brami. Io parto. Ardita Zanzaretta. Ardo per te, mio bene. *Instrumental items*[b]—Canzon francese. Io tacerò. Corrente, amanti.

55' DDD 10/88

The music and life of Gesualdo, Prince of Venosa, have become inextricably linked for their controversy and pungency. There is a strange allure to the music of this man who murdered his wife because of her adultery; it drags the vocal art to extremes just as he pushed his own life to the very brink of acceptability. William Christie has gathered together a selection of Gesualdo's five-voice madrigals which ideally trace the composer's development in the realms of expression and distorted beauty. Les Arts Florissants are ever alive to the strangeness of this remarkable music and never smooth out the textures and harmonic excrescences. The clashes of tonalities, used to powerful expressive effect, are relished and the acoustic adds immensely to the fine portrayal of colour and nuance. Christie, somewhat controversially, adds some instrumental parts to the madrigals, historically defensible but stylistically questionable. That said, this is a remarkable and highly enjoyable introduction to one of the great experimenters of Western Music.

Orlando Gibbons

British 1583-1625

Gibbons. CHURCH MUSIC. **King's College Choir, Cambridge/Philip Ledger** with **John Butt** (org) and [a]**London Early Music Group.** ASV Gaudeamus CDGAU123. FROM DCA514 (6/82).
Canticles—Magnificat and Nunc dimittis, "Short Service"; Magnificat and Nunc dimittis, "Second Service". *Full Anthems*—Almighty and Everlasting God; Lift up your heads; Hosanna to the Son of David. *Verse Anthems*[a]—This is the record of John; See, see, the Word is incarnate; O Thou, the central orb. *The Hymnes and Songs of the Church*—Now shall the praises of the Lord be sung; O Lord of Hosts; A song of joy unto the Lord we sing; Come, kiss me with those lips of thine. *Organ works*—Voluntary; Fantasia for double organ; Fantasia.

53' DDD 4/86

Gibbons had close links with King's College, Cambridge, where he himself was a chorister. Little wonder, then, that the choir today frequently performs the music of one of its most illustrious musical sons! This programme is fully representative of Gibbons's output, with the two Services, several hymns, three organ pieces and examples of both his full and his verse anthems. Of these last, *This is the record of John* is particularly delectable. Michael Chance sings the alto solo with remarkable control, to the gentle accompaniment of the five viols, and in alternation with the full choir. His wonderful vocal quality 'makes' this record, but the solo trebles are notable for their poise, professionalism and first-class diction. The three organ pieces, elegantly played by John Butt, arc of special interest, because of the place they hold in the development of keyboard music. Gibbons, himself renowned for his playing, was once described by the French Ambassador as 'the best finger of that age'.

Umberto Giordano
Italian 1867-1948

Giordano. ANDREA CHENIER. **Luciano Pavarotti** (ten) Andrea Chenier; **Leo Nucci** (bar) Gerard; **Montserrat Caballé** (sop) Maddalena; **Kathleen Kuhlmann** (mez) Bersi; **Astrid Varnay** (sop) Countess di Coigny; **Christa Ludwig** (mez) Madelon; **Tom Krause** (bar) Roucher; **Hugues Cuénod** (ten) Fleville; **Neil Howlett** (bar) Fouquier-Tinville, Major-domo; **Giorgio Tadeo** (bass) Mathieu; **Piero De Palma** (ten) Incredible; **Florindo Andreolli** (ten) Abate; **Giuseppe Morresi** (bass) Schmidt; **Ralph Hamer** (bass) Dumas; **Welsh National Opera Chorus; National Philharmonic Orchestra/ Riccardo Chailly.** Decca 410 117-2DH2. Notes, text and translation included. From 411 117-1DH3 (11/84).

② 1h 47' DDD 2/85

Andrea Chenier, set at the start of the French Revolution, is a potent blend of the social and the emotional. The three main characters, the aristocratic Maddalena, the idealistic poet Chenier and the fiercely republican Gerard, are caught up in a triangle that pits love against conscience, independence against society. The opera has many well-known set numbers high on any list of favourites must be Chenier's so-called *Improviso* in Act 1 where he bursts out in a spontaneous poem on the power of love, or Maddalena's glorious and moving "La mamma morta" in the Third Act where she describes how her mother gave up her life to save her. Giordano had a real theatrical flair for the 'big moment' and he paces the work masterfully. The tunes seem to flow endlessly from his pen and the characters have real flesh and blood. The cast is strong, with Caballé and Pavarotti making a powerful central pair. Riccardo Chailly conducts the excellent National Philharmonic with flair and feeling and the whole opera is beautifully recorded.

Philip Glass
American 1937-

Glass. Music in 12 Parts. **Philip Glass Ensemble/Philip Glass.** Virgin Venture CDVEBX32.

③ 3h 27' DDD 6/90

There are many who consider *Music in 12 Parts* to be one of Glass's finest works. On one level its mesmeric coruscations of sound are a kind of musical equivalent to a sensory deprivation tank (and that's not meant as an insult); on another, more serious level, it's a vast lexicon of minimalist techniques that offer the listener a fascinating insight into Glass's intellectual and aesthetic ideas. His travels in North Africa and India, and in particular his studies with Ravi Shankar's drummer Allah Rakha had a profound effect on his musical creativity, and resulted in the now familiar fingerprints of Glass's style. *Music in 12 Parts* is epic in its proportions—on CD it lasts nearly three hours, with each part roughly 20 minutes in duration (though individual parts can last considerably longer in concert performances), and its demands on the performers (keyboards, flutes, saxophones and a vocalizing soprano) are virtuosic in the extreme. The best way to experience it is in its entirety, though Glass allows (and encourages) the listener to make all manner of re-

Philip Glass

orderings and manipulations of its 12 movements. Brilliantly performed and recorded.

Alexander Glazunov

Glazunov. Violin Concerto[a].
Prokofiev. Violin Concerto No. 2[b].
Sibelius. Violin Concerto[c]. **Jascha Heifetz** (vn); [a]**RCA Victor Symphony Orchestra/Walter Hendl;** [b]**Boston Symphony Orchestra/Charles Münch;** [c]**Chicago Symphony Orchestra/Walter Hendl.** RCA Red Seal RD87019. Items marked [a] and [b] from GL89833 (9/86), [c] GL89832 (9/86).

69' ADD 10/86

Here are three great concertos on one CD, all of them classics of the gramophone which have never been equalled, let alone surpassed. Heifetz made the première recording of all three concertos in the 1930s and his interpretations have particular authority. The recordings here were all issued in the early 1960s and in their digital refurbishment sound remarkably good. Heifetz's golden tone shines more brightly than ever and his technical virtuosity and profound musicianship remain dazzling. The performances can only be described as stunning and they remain an indispensable part of any collection.

Glazunov. SYMPHONIES. **USSR Ministry of Culture State Symphony Orchestra/Gennadi Rozhdestvensky.** Olympia OCD100/1.
OCD100—No. 1 in E major, Op. 5, "Slavyanskaya"; No. 7 in F major, Op. 77, "Pastoral'naya". *OCD101*—No. 4 in E flat major, Op. 48; No. 5 in B flat major, Op. 55.

② **70' 70' ADD 8/86** ❓

It is always easy to underestimate the Glazunov symphonies. There is no doubt that this set of performances from Rozhdestvensky and the splendid orchestra, give them a 'new look'. There is a sophistication in the playing to match the elegance of Glazunov's often highly engaging wind scoring—especially in the scherzos, always Glazunov's best movements—but there is a commitment and vitality too, which makes all the music spring readily to life. In Rozhdestvensky's hands the fine *Adagio* of No. 1 sounds remarkably mature while the *Andante* movements of Nos. 5 and 7 are romantically expansive in a very appealing way. The Fourth Symphony is a highly inventive piece throughout and held together by a moto theme; and the better-known Fifth does not disappoint when the presentation is so persuasive. On both discs the recording is brightly lit without being too brittle, and has plenty of fullness too. For anyone looking for new nineteenth-century symphonies to explore, this would be a good place to start.

Christoph Gluck

Gluck. LE CINESI. **Kaaren Erickson** (sop) Sivene; **Alexandrina Milcheva** (contr) Lisinga; **Marga Schiml** (contr) Tangia; **Thomas Moser** (ten) Silango; **Munich Radio Orchestra/Lamberto Gardelli.** Orfeo C178891A. Notes, text and translation included.

66' DDD 1/90

Gluck's version of Metastasio's *Le cinesi* ("The Chinese ladies") was composed for the Habsburg Empress, Maria Theresa, in 1754. Within the space of a single act, the text and music of the opera-serenade brightly illuminates the relationships between the three women and the man in a series of contrasting vignettes. Using a single, exotic set, the characters devise an afternoon's entertainment; trying first a brilliantly contrived scene from a hypothetical heroic opera, then a pastorale and finally a comedy (in which the romantic undercurrents between the man and two of the women are explored), they resolve instead to dance. The Munich Radio Orchestra under Lamberto Gardelli deliver a thoroughly modern performance (replete with 'resonant' harpsichord). Of the soloists, Alexandrina Milcheva as Lisinga and Thomas Moser as Silango in particular give polished performances. Having been roused from a 200-year sleep, Gluck's jewel-like *Cinesi* seems set to attract a wide spectrum of amateur and professional performances.

Gluck. IPHIGENIE EN AULIDE. **Lynne Dawson** (sop) Iphigénie; **José van Dam** (bass) Agamemnon; **Anne Sofie von Otter** (mez) Clytemnestre; **John Aler** (ten) Achille; **Bernard Deletré** (bass) Patrocle; **Gilles Cachemaille** (bass) Calchas; **René Schirrer** (bass) Arcas; **Guillemette Laurens** (mez) Diane; **Ann Monoyios** (sop) First Greek woman, Slave; **Isabelle Eschenbrenner** (sop) Second Greek woman; **Monteverdi Choir; Lyon Opéra Orchestra/John Eliot Gardiner.** Erato 2292-45003-2. Notes, text and translation included.

② 2h 12' DDD 6/90

Gluck's first reform opera for Paris has tended to be overshadowed by his other *Iphigénie*, the *Tauride* one. But it does contain some superb things, of which perhaps the finest are the great monologues for Agamemnon. On this recording, José van Dam starts a little coolly; but this only adds force to his big moment at the end of the second act where he tussles with himself over the sacrifice of his daughter and—contemplating her death and the screams of the vengeful Eumenides—decides to flout the gods and face the consequences. To this he rises in noble fashion, fully conveying the agonies Agamemnon suffers. The cast in general is strong. Lynne Dawson brings depth of expressive feeling to all she does and her Iphigénie, marked by a slightly grainy sound and much intensity, is very moving. John Aler's Achille too is very fine, touching off the lover and the hero with equal success, singing both with ardour and vitality. There is great force too in the singing of Anne Sofie von Otter as Clytemnestre, especially in her outburst "Ma fille!" as she imagines her daughter on the sacrificial altar. John Eliot Gardiner's Monteverdi Choir sing with polish, perhaps seeming a little genteel for a crowd of angry Greek soldiers baying for Iphigénie's blood. But Gardiner gives a duly urgent account of the score, pressing it forward eagerly and keeping the tension at a high level even in the dance music. A period-instrument orchestra might have added a certain edge and vitality but this performance wants nothing in authority or drama and can be securely recommended.

Gluck. IPHIGENIE EN TAURIDE. **Diana Montague** (mez) Iphigénie; **John Aler** (ten) Pylade; **Thomas Allen** (bar) Oreste; **Nancy Argenta** (sop); **Sophie Boulton** (mez) First and Second Priestesses; **Colette Alliot-Lugaz** (sop) Diana; **René Massis** (bass-bar) Thoas; **Monteverdi Choir; Lyon Opera Orchestra/John Eliot Gardiner.** Philips 416 148-2PH2. Notes, text and translation included.

② 2h 3' DDD 6/86

Many Gluckists reckon *Iphigénie en Tauride* to be the finest of his operas; and although the claims of *Orfeo* are also very strong the breadth and grandeur of this score, the vigour of its declamatory writing, the intensity with which the situations of Iphigénie and Oreste are depicted and the ultimate integration of music and drama produce a uniquely powerful musical realization of classical tragedy. John Eliot Gardiner's sense of dramatic concentration and his intellectual control make him an ideal interpreter; the impassioned accompanied recitatives and the taut, suggestive accompaniments to the arias are particularly impressive, and the dance music is gracefully done. It might, however, have been better if a period orchestra had been used; this one, though efficient and responsive, cannot quite articulate the music as Gluck intended and tends to be string-heavy in the modern manner. Vocally, the set is distinguished above all by Diana Montague's Iphigénie, sung with due nobility and a finely true, clean middle register, and Thomas Allen's noble and passionate Oreste; John Aler's Pylade is warm and flexible and René Massis provides a suitably barbaric Thoas. In all a noble account, the best available on disc, of a remarkable opera.

Gluck. ORFEO ED EURIDICE. ORPHEE ET EURYDICE—ballet music. **Jochen Kowalski** (alto) Orfeo; **Dagmar Schellenberger-Ernst** (sop) Euridice; **Christian Fliegner** (treb) Amor; **Berlin Radio Chorus; Carl Philipp Emanuel Bach Chamber Orchestra/Hartmut Haenchen.** Capriccio 60 008-2. Notes, text and translation included. Orphée et Eurydice—Air de furies; Ballet des ombres heureuses; Air vif; Menuet; Chaconne.

② 1h 54' DDD 1/90

Not very long ago, the standard view of Gluck's *Orfeo ed Euridice* was that a compromise text, between the Italian original of 1762 and the French revised version of 1774, was desirable, allowing performers and listeners to have the best of both worlds. But nowadays people are beginning to realize that Gluck may have known what he was doing when he wrote these two versions, and that each has its own integrity. And certainly the more focused and more concentrated of the two is the Vienna original, in Italian. But following this means foregoing two of the most admired and striking numbers, the "Dance of the Furies" and the flute solo "Dance of the Blessed Spirits". On this recording of the Italian version these two dances, and three others, are sensibly included as an appendix. The rich, flexible alto of Jochen Kowalski as Orfeo is very impressive; he is impassioned in the series of ariosos and recitatives that form the central part of Act 1 and his smooth and even, refined tone compels admiration. Haenchen draws very capable singing from the Berlin Radio Chorus. This version is a modern one, when period instruments might have been more appropriate, but Kowalski's very beautiful singing will be the deciding factor for many listeners.

Charles François Gounod
French 1818-1893

Gounod. Symphony No. 1 in D major. Petite symphonie. **Bizet** (ed. Hogwood). L'Arlésienne—excerpts. **Saint Paul Chamber Orchestra/Christopher Hogwood.** Decca 430 231-2DH. L'Arlésienne—Prélude; Minuetto; Entr'acte; Mélodrame; Pastorale; Carillon.

67' DDD 7/91

This is a disc to delight, from a pair of French composers who are well matched, for Gounod taught Bizet and spoke tearfully at his funeral. It also reminds us of Gounod's skill outside the opera house, although there is nothing especially French about this symphony that he seems to have written almost as a tribute to Mendelssohn, whom he came to know personally and admired as a musician. In other words, this is the more classical kind of nineteenth-century music and its

origin in the romantic era is only revealed in its unashamed charm and elegance—the only way here, perhaps, in which Gounod shows his Gallic nationality. Christopher Hogwood and his expert players of the Saint Paul Chamber Orchestra are perfectly at ease in this work and the performance of the *Petite symphonie* for nine wind instruments is no less stylish. In Bizet's incidental music for Daudet's play *L'Arlésienne*, Hogwood's touch is no less sure. He has gone back to the original theatre scoring rather than playing the better-known orchestral suites that were made later, which means an odd instrumental combination including seven violins but only one viola, a saxophone and a piano, plus the restoration of some

Christopher Hogwood [*photo: Decca*]

original keys. The recording is spacious and detailed, and one only wishes that Decca had provided separate tracks for the six Bizet pieces.

Gounod. FAUST—ballet music.
Offenbach (arr. Rosenthal). Gaîté parisienne—ballet. **Montreal Symphony Orchestra/Charles Dutoit.** Decca 411 708-2DH. From 411 708-1DH (3/84).

— 59' DDD 7/84

The very title of Offenbach's *Gaîté parisienne* tells us that this is unashamedly music to delight. However, it is not the composer's own but rather one given to a collection of his music arranged by Ravel's pupil Manuel Rosenthal for Léonide Massine and his Ballets Russes de Monte Carlo in 1938. The ballet is set in a Parisian night club and includes many attractive dance pieces as well as the celebrated Can-can from *Orpheus in the Underworld* and the Barcarolle from *The Tales of Hoffman*. We may forget all about Marlowe's play when we come to the *Faust* ballet, for originally Gounod's opera had no such thing as this elaborate danced section in which the *femmes fatales* of history paraded before Faust. But it seems that the Paris Opéra insisted on it. The music is in different style from Offenbach but still lilting and highly attractive. Dutoit and his excellent Montreal orchestra are admirable in this music, and if there's a trace of brashness in the noisier sections of the Offenbach that is justified by the nature of the music itself.

Gounod. FAUST. **Plácido Domingo** (ten) Faust; **Mirella Freni** (sop) Marguérite; **Nicolai Ghiaurov** (bass) Méphistophélès; **Thomas Allen** (bar) Valentin; **Michèle Command** (sop) Siébel; **Jocelyne Taillon** (mez) Marthe; **Marc Vento** (bar) Wagner; **Paris Opéra Chorus and Orchestra/Georges Prêtre.** EMI CDS7 47493-8. Notes, text and translation included. From SLS5170 (9/79).

— ③ 3h 10' ADD 4/87

For a full century after its première, Gounod's *Faust* was the most popular opera in the international repertoire. Georges Prêtre draws from his Paris orchestra and chorus, and his international cast, a sense of line which creates a truly Gallic lyricism which British performances too often find hard to achieve. Even the minor parts have an authority and authenticity all their own. Nicolai Ghiaurov's Méphistophélès provides rich body-colour for the cast's palette: his *diablerie* is both chill and sensual, and he has a fine line in black comedy where it is needed. This is, however, very much Domingo's *Faust*, and he brings to the role the appropriate tenderness but also torment and remorse in a performance of potently sustained intensity. But it is also Mirella Freni's opera: hers is a Marguérite of both innocence and spirit, with nerves and senses fully engaged in a claustrophobic *angoisse*.

Percy Grainger

American/Australian 1882-1961

Grainger. ORCHESTRAL WORKS. **Philip Martin** (pf); [a]**Moray Welsh** (vc); **Bournemouth Sinfonietta/Kenneth Montgomery.** Chandos CHAN8377. From RCA RL25198 (5/79).
Youthful Suite—Rustic dance; Eastern intermezzo. Blithe Bells (free ramble on a theme by Bach, "Sheep may safely graze"). Spoon River. My Robin is to the Greenwood Gone. Green Bushes. Country Gardens (orch. Schmid). Mock Morris. Youthful Rapture[a]. Shepherd's Hey. Walking Tune. Molly on the shore. Handel in the Strand (orch. Wood).

55' ADD 8/85

None of the 13 items on this disc is longer than nine minutes, and they are carefully planned to make an attractive sequence for continuous listening. The two items from the *Youthful Suite* were composed when Grainger was but 17 years old and are quite advanced harmonically for 1898-9. *Blithe Bells* is a somewhat florid arrangement of Bach's "Sheep may safely graze", and then we have *Spoon River*, an arrangement of an old American fiddle tune. *My Robin is to the Greenwood Gone, Green Bushes* and the famous *Country Gardens* are all based on English folk-tunes, but the cheerful *Mock Morris* is an original pastiche. *Handel in the Strand* is a set of variations on Handel's *Harmonious Blacksmith* whilst the charming *Walking Tune* for wind quintet came to Grainger's mind when on a walking tour. There's no doubt that Kenneth Montgomery has a strong sympathy for Grainger's music, and he directs lively performances. The recording acoustic is a little reverberant but the sound quality is otherwise good.

Grainger. ORCHESTRAL WORKS. **Melbourne Symphony Orchestra/ Geoffrey Simon.** Koch International Classics 37003-2.
The Warriors. Hill-Song No. 1. Irish Tune from County Derry, BFMS20. Hill-Song No. 2. Danish Folk-Music Suite. **Traditional Chinese** (harmonized Yasser, arr. Grainger, orch. Sculthorpe): Beautiful fresh flower.

67' DDD 11/90 ❓

It was Sir Thomas Beecham who first suggested to Percy Grainger the idea of writing a ballet, and though in the event a commission was not forthcoming Grainger went ahead with the work that was to become without doubt one of his largest and most extravagant works—The Warriors. Although it has only a relatively short duration—18 minutes—its demands in every other aspect are gargantuan; in addition to an already large orchestra he calls for six horns, three pianos, a large-tuned percussion section (including wooden and steel marimbas and tubular bells), an off-stage brass section and—if necessary—three conductors! (though in this recording Geoffrey Simon takes on the task single handed), with the musical material deriving from no less than 15 themes and motifs. Grainger described the piece as "an orgy of war-like dances, processions and merry-making broken, or accompanied by amorous interludes"—a sort of "warriors of the world unite". It was described by Delius (the work's dedicatee) as "by far Grainger's greatest thing" and indeed it seems to encapsulate and condense the very essence of Grainger's wild and free-roaming spirit.

The two *Hill-Songs* were a response to "the soul-shaking hillscapes" of West Argyllshire after a three-day hike in the Scottish Highlands. Like many of Grainger's compositions they exist in various scorings from the two-piano and solo piano arrangements to the chamber orchestra version of 1923 heard in this recording. Their organic, unbroken flow of melodic ideas and rhythmically complex writing create a bracing, evocative impression of the spirit of the Highlands. The remaining works on the disc consist of the attractive *Danish Folk-Music Suite*, notable for the two haunting ballads "The Power of Love" and "The Nightingale and the Two Sisters" and three short folk-song arrangements from China, Denmark and Ireland. Geoffrey Simon and the Melbourne Symphony Orchestra positively revel in this music, and the excellent recording is clear and spacious. An essential disc for those with an adventurous spirit.

Grainger. SYMPHONIC BAND MUSIC. **Michigan State University Symphonic Band/Keith Brion,** [a]**Kenneth G. Bloomquist.** Delos DE3101. *Grainger:* Molly on the Shore, BFMS23. Country Gardens (1953). The Immovable Do (1939). Colonial Song, S1. In a Nutshell— No. 4, Gum-suckers' March (1942)[a]. Ye Banks and Braes o' Bonnie Doon, BFMS32. Children's March, "Over the Hills and Far Away", RMTB4. Country Gardens (arr. Sousa)[a]. *Fauré* (arr. Grainger): Tuscan serenade, Op. 3 No. 2. *Franck* (arr. Grainger): Chorale. *Bach* (arr. Grainger): March in D. O Mensch, bewein' dein' Sünde gross, BWV622.

57' DDD 4/91

Percy Grainger is one of those composers who refuse to fall into any of the categories which critics use to place creative artists so as to fit them into their view of musical history. Being Australian must have helped to make him different, and although much of his musical formation was European—he studied piano with Busoni and became a friend of Grieg and Delius—he was also inspired at the Paris Exhibition of 1900 by an Indonesian *gamelan* orchestra and an Egyptian wind ensemble. His experience of wind bands was later also much enlarged by his service from 1917-19 in the US Army Band, in which he played the oboe or soprano saxophone. It seems right, therefore, that it is an American band that plays the dozen pieces on this CD, which includes such popular numbers as *Country Gardens,* in a Grainger treatment that must bring a smile of pleasure to the face of all but the most gloomy listener, with Sousa's bouncy arrangement of the same music coming later in the programme for good measure. Some of these pieces are derived from British folk music, but by no means all as the list above shows, and in fact the *Gum-suckers' March* was inspired by his home state of Victoria, Australia. This is delightful and inventive music by a real original, and the playing of the Michigan State University Symphonic Band under two good conductors does it justice, as does the clean, if sometimes slightly tubby, recording. The booklet note by the Grainger specialist Dana Perna steers us skilfully through some unfamiliar music.

Grainger. PIANO WORKS, Volume 1. **Martin Jones.** Nimbus NI5220. Andante con moto. Bridal Lullaby. Children's March. Colonial Song. English Waltz. Handel in the Strand. Harvest Hymn. In a Nutshell—suite. In Dahomey. Mock Morris. Peace. Sailor's Song. Saxon Twi-play. The Immovable Do. To a Nordic Princess. Walking Tune.

72' DDD 4/90 ❓

This is the best of Percy Grainger, and it would be hard to imagine it better played. Most of these pieces are better-known in Grainger's lavish and colourful orchestrations, but they seem to have more pith and urgency to them in their piano versions, even where those were not the originals. The luscious *To a Nordic Princess* has more energy to it in this form, and the slow movement of *In a Nutshell*, far from the lyrical interlude that it can sound in orchestrated form, emerges as a very direct and almost shockingly poignant self-image of Grainger. Even the popular trifles, *Handel in the Strand* and *Mock Morris*, take on added zest at the crisp and airy tempos that Martin Jones chooses; even more importantly the haunting lyricism of *The Immovable Do* and the deep nostalgia of *Colonial Song* are liberated by restoration to Grainger's own instrument. They need something like Grainger's own flamboyantly virtuoso pianism, of course, and one of the reasons that they are far more familiar in their orchestral guise is that they make hair-raising demands of the pianist. Jones is fully equal to them; indeed, he goes well beyond meeting those demands and sounds as though he is positively enjoying himself. A hugely enjoyable collection; the rather disembodied recording is a quirk rather than a real drawback.

Enrique Granados

Spanish 1867-1916

Granados. Danzas españolas, Op. 37. **Alicia de Larrocha** (pf). Decca 414 557-2DH. From SXL6980 (3/82).

♪ 56' ADD 10/85

Not long before he drowned, in 1916, when his ship was sunk by a German submarine, Granados had felt that his compositional career was being opened up by the deep vein of genuine Spanish feeling that he was increasingly able to tap in his music. His piano suite, *Goyescas*, and the opera based on it were, perhaps,

Alicia de Larrocha   *[photo: Decca/Steiner]*

the most convincing and individual expression of that sentiment, but the numerous shorter pieces for piano that he produced, some of which were collected together in the sets of *Danzas españolas*, also showed real sparks of that same nationalism, even though they were still clearly rooted in the common European harmonic and melodic language of the later romantic period. These sparks need to be emphasized in performance by an artist who has an intuitive feel for them, and there is none better suited than Alicia de Larrocha, who has both the technical control and emotional insight to make the most of this music. Her playing, even at moments of highest constraint, has an undercurrent of powerful forces striving to be released; when the constraint is lifted, the effect is tumultuous. Thankfully, the recording can cope. The result is an almost definitive issue of this intriguing collection.

Granados. Goyescas—suite for piano. **Alicia de Larrocha** (pf). Decca 411 958-2DH. From SXL6785 (12/77).

♪ 57' ADD 3/89

The Granados *Goyescas* are profoundly Spanish in feeling, but the folk influence is more of court music than of the flamenco or *cante hondo* styles which reflect gipsy and Moorish influence. This set of seven pieces was given its first performance by the composer in 1911, and his own exceptional ability as a pianist is evident in its consistently elaborate textures. That performance took place in Barcelona, and as Granados's compatriot and a native of that very city Alicia de Larrocha fully understands this music in its richly varied moods; a fact which tells in interpretations that have a compelling conviction and drive. Thus, she can dance enchantingly in such a piece as "El Fandango de candil", while in the celebrated "Maiden and the nightingale", No. 4 of the set, we listen to a wonderful outpouring of Mediterranean emotion, all the more moving for its avoidance of excessive rubato and over-pedalling. A splendid disc of one of the twentieth century's piano masterpieces, which was atmospherically recorded in the former Decca studios in West Hampstead in 1976 and has transferred well to CD.

Edvard Grieg

Norwegian 1843-1907

Grieg. Piano Concerto in A minor, Op. 16.
Schumann. Piano Concerto in A minor, Op. 54. **Stephen Kovacevich** (pf); **BBC Symphony Orchestra / Sir Colin Davis.** Philips 412 923-2PH. From 6500 166 (3/72).

61' ADD 10/86

Grieg. Piano Concerto in A minor, Op. 16[a].
Tchaikovsky. Piano Concerto No. 1 in B flat minor, Op. 23[b]. [a]**Sir Clifford Curzon** (pf); **London Symphony Orchestra / Øivin Fjeldstad;** [b]**Vienna Philharmonic Orchestra / Sir Georg Solti.** Decca Weekend 417 676-2DC. Item marked [a] from LW5350 (7/59), [b] SXL2114 (6/59).

64' AAD 1/89

Grieg. Piano Concerto in A minor, Op. 16.
Schumann. Piano Concerto in A minor, Op. 54. **Murray Perahia** (pf); **Bavarian Radio Symphony Orchestra / Sir Colin Davis.** CBS Masterworks CD44899. Recorded at performances in the Philharmonie Gasteig, Munich during 1987 and 1988.

60' DDD 5/89

Grieg. Piano Concerto in A minor, Op. 16.
Schumann. Piano Concerto in A minor, Op. 54. **Pascal Devoyon** (pf); **London Philharmonic Orchestra / Jerzy Maksymiuk.** Classics for Pleasure CD-CFP4574.

63' DDD 2/91

Since the advent of the LP the Grieg and Schumann concertos have been ideally paired and the performances on the Philips disc have set the standard by which all other versions are judged. The scale of both is perfectly managed. The Grieg, with its natural charm and freshness, has power too (witness the superb first movement cadenza), but poetry dominates and climaxes must never seem hectoring, as both these artists fully understand. The romanticism of the Schumann Concerto is particularly elusive on record, with its contrasting masculine and feminine elements difficult to set in ideal balance. But here there is no sense of any problem, so naturally does the music flow, the changing moods being seen within the overall perspective. There is refinement and strength, the virtuosity sparkles, the expressive elements are perfectly integrated with the need for bravura. This CD remastering of a very well balanced and felicitous recording gives both performances a new lease of life.

Sir Clifford Curzon shows excellent rapport with both orchestras and conductors and strikes right to the heart of both pieces, bringing a freshness to

Sir Georg Solti   *[photo: Decca/Purdom*

these well-used classics that prompts the listener to experience anew delights that might otherwise have passed unnoticed. Ageing though these recordings might now be, they are still finely detailed in their CD garb, and although the Grieg has the greater warmth and weight, neither is lacking in these qualities. At the price, then—irresistible.

The performances on the CBS disc are amongst the finest. Perahia's innate sense of musicality and poetry bring out the nostalgic lyricism of these works extremely well, though he is equally well at home with the more bravura passages (as for instance in the cadenza of the Grieg). Sir Colin Davis and the Bavarian RSO provide excellent support and the recordings, which were taken from public concerts in Munich (the sound is as clean as any studio recording), are warm and well balanced.

Quality performances, fine recording and a bargain price also earns the CfP disc a strong recommendation. In fact, it's worth saying that although the piano soloist is less spotlit than usual, the balance is very natural and one misses no detail of Pascal Devoyon's playing. He is also attentive to detail in just the right way: every musical point is there, and yet he doesn't call our attention to it so that it sounds mannered. The London Philharmonic Orchestra under Jerzy Maksymiuk are entirely sympathetic partners, too: listen to their dialogue with the pianist in the central Intermezzo movement of the Schumann to see how well the gentle exchange of musical ideas is managed. Although some collectors may despair of hearing a performance of the Grieg Concerto with the spontaneity and freshness it deserves, this new CD has a good chance of convincing them that its essential innocence is still there to be revealed by the best artists. The lovely slow movement is magical, but so is much else, not least the wonderful F major section in the finale beginning with an exquisite flute solo that takes us straight to a Norwegian fjord at sunrise. Indeed, these performances are equal to the classic account by Stephen Kovacevich reviewed above.

Grieg. Norwegian Dances, Op. 35. Lyric Suite, Op. 54. Symphonic Dances, Op. 64. **Gothenburg Symphony Orchestra/Neeme Järvi.** DG 419 431-2GH.

68' DDD 1/87

Grieg's music has that rare quality of eternal youth: however often one hears it, its complexion retains its bloom, the smile its radiance and the youthful sparkle remains undimmed. Though he is essentially a miniaturist, who absorbed the speech rhythms and inflections of Norwegian folk melody into his bloodstream, Grieg's world is well defined. Both the *Norwegian Dances* and the *Symphonic Dances* were originally piano duets, which Grieg subsequently scored: Järvi conducts both with enthusiasm and sensitivity. In the *Lyric Suite* he restores "Klokkeklang" (Bell-ringing), which Grieg omitted from the final score: it is remarkably atmospheric and evocative, and serves to show how forward-looking Grieg became in his late years. The recording is exceptionally fine and of wide dynamic range; the sound is very natural and the perspective true to life.

Grieg. Peer Gynt—incidental music[a]. Sigurd Jorsalfar—incidental music, Op. 22[b]. [a]**Barbara Bonney** (sop); [a]**Marianne Eklöf** (mez); [b]**Kjell Magnus Sandve** (ten); [a]**Urban Malmberg**, [a]**Carl Gustaf Holmgren** (bars); **Gösta Ohlin's Vocal Ensemble; Pro Musica Chamber Choir; Gothenburg Symphony Orchestra/Neeme Järvi.** DG 423 079-2GH2. Texts and translations included.

(2) 2h 4' DDD 2/88 · B

Grieg. Peer Gynt—incidental music[a]. Symphonic Dance, Op. 64 No. 2[b]. Concert Overture, Op. 11, "In Autumn"[c]. **Ilse Hollweg** (sop); **Beecham Choral Society; Royal Philharmonic Orchestra/Sir Thomas Beecham.** EMI Studio CDM7 69039-2. Item marked [a] from ASD258 (1/59); [b] ASD518 (4/63); [c] SXLP30530 (2/82).

58' ADD 1/89 · B

Grieg's incidental music was an important integral part of Ibsen's *Peer Gynt*. From this score Grieg later extracted the two familiar suites but DG's issue represents the first ever complete recording of Grieg's original work. Even the music which accompanies dialogue is included, with actors speaking Ibsen's lines, and the effect enhances the music's expressive power. Texts and translations are provided, so that it is easy to put the music in its dramatic context. Room is also found for another example of Grieg's incidental music, this time for Bjørnstjerne Bjørnson's play *Sigurd Jorsalfar*. Usually we hear just the concert suite of three movements, but again Järvi has recorded for the first time the complete eight-movement original score with chorus and tenor soloist. Here is an enterprising and stimulating issue which both instructs and gives much pleasure. The recording quality is good.

Sir Thomas Beecham's recording of ten of the numbers from *Peer Gynt* goes back to 1957 but still sounds well and is most stylishly played. He includes the best known ("Anitra's Dance" is a delicate gem here) plus "Solveig's Song" and "Solveig's Cradle Song". Beecham uses the soprano Ilse Hollweg to advantage, her voice suggesting the innocence of the virtuous and faithful peasant heroine. There's also an effective use of the choral voices which are almost inevitably omitted in ordinary performances of the two well-known orchestral suites: the male chorus of trolls in the "Hall of the Mountain King" are thrilling, and the women in the "Arabian Dance" have charm. The other two pieces are worth having also; *Symphonic Dance* is a later, freshly pastoral work, while the overture *In Autumn* is an orchestral second version of an early piece for piano duet.

Grieg. LYRIC PIECES—excerpts. **Emil Gilels** (pf). DG 419 749-2GH. From 2530 476 (3/75).
Arietta, Op. 12 No. 1. Berceuse, Op. 38 No. 1. Butterfly, Op. 43 No. 1. Solitary Traveller, Op. 43 No. 2. Album-leaf, Op. 47 No. 2. Melody, Op. 47 No. 3. Norwegian Dance, "Halling", Op. 47 No. 4. Nocturne, Op. 54 No. 4. Scherzo, Op. 54 No. 5. Homesickness, Op. 57 No. 6. Brooklet, Op. 62 No. 4. Homeward, Op. 62 No. 6. In ballad vein, Op. 65 No. 5. Grandmother's minuet, Op. 68 No. 2. At your feet, Op. 68 No. 3. Cradlesong, Op. 68 No. 5. Once upon a time, Op. 71 No. 1. Puck, Op. 71 No. 3. Gone, Op. 71 No. 6. Remembrances, Op. 71 No. 7.

56' ADD 10/87

This record is something of a gramophone classic. The great Russian pianist Emil Gilels, an artist of staggering technical accomplishment and intellectual power, here turns his attention to Grieg's charming miniatures. He brings the same insight and concentration to these apparent trifles as he did to towering masterpieces of the classic repertoire. The programme proceeds chronologically and one can appreciate the gradual but marked development in Grieg's harmonic and expressive language—from the folk-song inspired early works to the more progressive and adventurous later ones. Gilels's fingerwork is exquisite and the sense of total involvement with the music almost religious in feeling. This is a wonderful recording: pianistic perfection.

Grieg. LYRIC PIECES, Volume 1. **Peter Katin** (pf). Unicorn-Kanchana Souvenir UKCD2033.
Book 1, Op. 12; Book 2, Op. 38; Book 3, Op. 43; Book 4, Op. 47.
63' DDD 9/90

Between 1867 and 1901, Grieg published ten sets of short piano pieces called *Lyric Pieces*, using an adjective which implies something expressive, songlike and on a small scale. Only one of the 29 here lasts more than four minutes and the shortest lasts just 40 seconds, yet they are not mere chips from the composer's work-bench but instead beautifully crafted miniatures in the tradition of Schumann's *Scenes from Childhood*. Although in the past pianists often played them in public, today we hardly ever hear them in the concert hall where, as Peter Katin points out in his booklet note, we usually get "far weightier fare". In fact a recorded performance is all the more welcome in that some of their intimacy is lost in an auditorium and Grieg certainly intended them to be heard in domestic surroundings. Some are 'easy' in the sense that the notes are not hard to play even for learners, but even so we gain immensely from the shaping of tone and rhythm that a fine artist can bring, especially when he so clearly loves the music. It is worth adding that there is plenty of variety here: thus Book 1 ends with a vigorous *National Song* that is very unlike the gentle little *Arietta* with which it begins. There are so many delights that it's hard to list special ones, but we would not go wrong if we lighted on the freshly charming *Butterfly, Little Bird* and *To the Spring* in Book 3, which remind us that Nature was often Grieg's inspiration. Pleasantly clean sound, with a touch of hardness in bigger passages.

Ivor Gurney

British 1890-1937

Gurney. The Western Playland[b]. Ludlow and Teme[a].
Vaughan Williams. On Wenlock Edge[a]. [a]**Adrian Thompson** (ten); [b]**Stephen Varcoe** (bar); **Delmé Quartet** (Galina Solodchin, John Trusler, vns; John Underwood, va; Jonathan Williams, vc); **Iain Burnside** (pf). Hyperion CDA66385. Texts included.
69' DDD 9/90

A.E. Housman's set of 63 poems *A Shropshire Lad*, published in 1896, inspired many English composers at the turn of the century. There was something in the deeply-felt but restrained emotions of Housman that seemed to catch the prevailing mood in England at the time. Best-known of all these settings must be Vaughan Williams's cycle of six, *On Wenlock Edge*. Among the most beautiful of these is the magical "Bredon Hill" with its evocative bell-like chords from the piano and the gentle swaying of the string quartet. Iain Burnside and the Delmé Quartet produce some wonderfully rich and colourful sounds to accompany Adrian Thomson who sings the whole cycle with suitably youthful fervour. Much less well known, but most unjustifiably so, are the two settings by Ivor Gurney, one of the finest yet most underrated of British song composers this century. Using the same economic instrumentation as Vaughan Williams and with equally marvellous effect, these two song-cycles possess a wealth of wonderful music. Even more than Vaughan Williams, Gurney seems to have penetrated the very heart of Housman's words, and text and music coalesce completely. Here is English song-writing at its absolute zenith. Stephen Varcoe's beautifully sensitive account of *The Western Playland* really should be in the collection of anyone who appreciate fine singing and sublime music.

Reynaldo Hahn

Venezuelan-French 1875-1947

Hahn. Premières Valses. Le rossignol éperdu—excerpts. **Catherine Joly** (pf). Accord 20054-2.

67' DDD 5/90

The very epitome of the suave, exquisite frequenter of fashionable Paris salons, Reynaldo Hahn has until recently been little recognized as a composer except for one or two songs. Moreover, the charming *Ciboulette* (the most successful of his many stage works) and the fact that he enjoyed a reputation as a Mozart conductor and that for the last two years of his life he was music director of the Paris Opéra, prove that he was no mere dilettante. The chain of ten *Premières Valses*, it is true, reflects the atmosphere of the salons, but their wide diversity of moods and their informed passing salutations to Chopin and Schubert betoken a cultivated and inventive mind. More serious are the 25 pieces selected from the later, little-known *Le rossignol éperdu*, which are travel vignettes of a literary provenance (a pity that the introductory quotations are not given here), a kind of musical diary mostly pervaded by a dark nostalgia: in this, as elsewhere in Hahn, melody is paramount. Catherine Joly plays everything here with the utmost subtlety of dynamics, rhythm and coloration. This disc opens up a new storehouse of miniatures—only three last as long as three minutes—which will be appreciated by the discriminating.

Hahn. CIBOULETTE. **Mady Mesplé** (sop) Ciboulette; **José van Dam** (bass-bar) Duparquet; **Nicolai Gedda** (ten) Antonin; **Colette Alliot-Lugaz** (sop) Zénobie, La Comtesse de Castiglione; **François Le Roux** (bar) Roger; **Monique Pouradier-Duteil** (sop) Françoise; **Jean-Christophe Benoit** (bar) Le Père Grenu, Le Marquis; **Claude Vierne** (mez) Madame Grenu, La Baronne; **Marcel Quillévéré** (ten) Auguste, Victor, Tranchu, Butler; **Jacques Loreau** (ten) Landlord, Grissart, Mayor; **Carole Bajac** (sop) Young girl, Madame de Presles; **Jean Laforge Choral Ensemble; Monte-Carlo Philharmonic Orchestra/Cyril Diederich.** EMI CDS7 49873-2. Notes, text and translation included. From EMI Pathé Marconi 2C 167 73105/06 (7/83).

② 1h 55' DDD 1/90

Hahn's *Ciboulette* harks back wistfully to the Paris of 1867. There are charming set numbers, such as Ciboulette's entrance song, the duet "Comme frère et soeur" and a big waltz number in Act 3, but what is so striking about the score is the declamatory nature of so much of the writing and the chamber textures of the scoring. The prelude to Act 2 is an especially beautiful piece of descriptive writing. The recording is cast from strength. Mady Mesplé caresses the vocal line tenderly and charmingly, her Act 2 song "Moi j' m'en fous" being an especial delight. No less admirable are José van Dam as Duparquet, manager of Les Halles, and Nicolai Gedda as the aristocratic Antonin, who manages to fall asleep in a cabbage truck and ends up fulfilling a fortune-teller's prophesy by marrying the market girl, Ciboulette. Colette Alliot-Lugaz and Jean-Christophe Benoit head a strong supporting team and Cyril Diederich conducts with an obvious feel for the tenderness of Hahn's score. EMI's clear, spacious digital recording helps to make this a set of rare delight.

George Frederic Handel

Handel. ORGAN CONCERTOS. **Simon Preston** (org); **The English Concert/Trevor Pinnock.** Archiv Produktion 413 465-2AH2. From 413 465-1AH2 (10/84).
Op. 4—No. 1 in G minor; No. 2 in B flat major; No. 3 in G minor; No. 4 in F major; No. 5 in F major; No. 6 in B flat major; No. 14 in A major.

Handel's highly acclaimed skill as a virtuoso organist was a significant factor in attracting audiences. His organ concertos are rich in catchy tunes, with some of the long *Allegros* sailing along with unstoppable momentum. But there are great treasures in the slow movements too—the *Andante* from No. 4 in F is full of colour and the solo part performs wonders of invention over a simple foundation of chords. The other F major Concerto, No. 5, short and charming, is an adaptation of a recorder sonata. Number 6 in B flat was originally intended for the harp, and that is how it is given here, played enchantingly by Ursula Holliger. There is a confident unity between Trevor Pinnock's English Concert, playing authentic instruments, and the soloist. Between them they convey a spirit of intimate music-making which makes ideal home listening. The recording is excellent.

Handel. Concerti grossi, Op. 3. **The English Concert/Trevor Pinnock** (hpd). Archiv Produktion 413 727-2AH.

The abundant variety of these concertos is in the number and character of their movements, and in the ways in which a comparatively limited palette of instrumental colour is exploited. Collectively they show Handel's enthusiasm for the Italian style and his ability to write the good tunes it required. The recorded performances capture the youthful freshness of Handel's imagination, enhanced by graceful embellishments by the soloists where appropriate. The sound, too, is appropriate, coming from 'period' instruments Handel would recognize, recorded with great clarity and with good balance—the continuo harpsichord is comfortably audible and, played by Pinnock himself, always worth hearing.

Handel. Concerti grossi, Op. 6 Nos. 1-4. **The English Concert/Trevor Pinnock.** Archiv Produktion 410 897-2AH. From 2742 002 (11/82).
No. 1 in G major; No. 2 in F major; No. 3 in E minor; No. 4 in A minor.

Handel. Concerti grossi, Op. 6 Nos. 5-8. **The English Concert/Trevor Pinnock.** Archiv Produktion 410 898-2AH. From 2742 002 (11/82).
No. 5 in D major; No. 6 in G minor; No. 7 in B flat major; No. 8 in C minor.

Handel. Concerti grossi, Op. 6 Nos. 9-12. **The English Concert/Trevor Pinnock.** Archiv Produktion 410 899-2AH. From 2742 002 (11/82).
No. 9 in F major; No. 10 in D minor; No. 11 in A major; No. 12 in B minor.

Handel. Concerti grossi, Op. 6 Nos. 1-12. **Guildhall String Ensemble.**
RCA Victor Red Seal RD87895/RD87907/RD87921.

RD87895—No. 1 in G major; No. 2 in F major; No. 3 in E minor; No. 4 in A minor. *RD87907*—No. 5 in D major; No. 6 in G minor; No. 7 in B flat major; No. 8 in C minor. *RD87921*—No. 9 in F major; No. 10 in D minor; No. 11 in A major; No. 12 in B minor.

③ 44' 60' 56' DDD 2/90 Ⓑ

Handel's 12 *Concerti grossi* have from four to six movements and are mostly in *da chiesa* form, i.e. without dance movements. They were written within one month in the autumn of 1739 (an average of two movements per day!) and when a great composer is thus carried on the tide of urgent inspiration it usually shows, as it does here in the flow of felicitous invention and memorable tune-smithing. The range of musical idioms used throughout is impressive and to them all Handel imparts his own indelible and unmistakable stamp. Trevor Pinnock's account contains much that is satisfying: polished ensemble, effectively judged tempos, a natural feeling for phrase, and a buoyancy of spirit which serves Handel's own robust musical language very well. Crisp attack, a judicious application of appoggiaturas and tasteful embellishment further enhance these lively performances. Pinnock varies the continuo colour by using organ and harpsichord and also includes Handel's autograph (though not printed) oboe parts for Concertos Nos. 1, 2, 5 and 6; where they occur a bassoon is sensibly added to fulfil the customary three-part wind texture of the period. Recorded sound is clear and captures something of the warm sonorities of the instruments.

The ideal way to hear this music is on period instruments, but if this is not to your taste you may with a clear conscience choose to have them on modern ones—providing they are as well used as they are by the Guildhall String Ensemble. This music was written to be enjoyed and that is how it is treated, stylishly and with a fresh enthusiasm that produces some brisk tempos, in this well balanced and clean-sounding recording. As the discs are separately available you can test the water with a cautious toe, but having done so you are likely to opt for total immersion.

Handel. Water Music. **Simon Standage, Elizabeth Wilcock** (vns); **The English Concert/Trevor Pinnock** (hpd). Archiv Produktion 410 525-2AH. From 410 525-1AH (1/84).

54' DDD 2/84 Ⓑ 🖉

Handel. Water Music. **Consort of London/Robert Haydon Clark.** Collins Classics 10152.

63' DDD Ⓑ

The *Water Music* was written for a river journey made by King George I and his retinue in 1717 and falls into three groups of suites in different keys (F, D and G major). Some of the tunes such as the Alla hornpipe are now familiar to many people who may not even know where they come from, or who wrote them. The English Concert play the music with a mixture of gaiety, verve and regal pomp, using period instruments and performing practices that enable us to hear it as closely as possible to the way it would have been heard in 1717.

Handel had earlier written a Concerto in F, which he revised and transposed to form the first two movements of the final ('trumpet') Suite (in D major) of the *Water Music*. In the Collins recording these two movements are added, in their original forms, at the end of the Suite in F—which makes a pleasant bonus, even if the King did not hear them thus. The Consort of London uses modern instruments, so that the music sounds at concert pitch ('authentic' performances emerge about half a tone lower) and they do so with the utmost intelligence—notably in the transparent sound of the strings—and alertness to good style. The pristine quality of the recorded sound helps to make this another very attractive way of hearing this much-loved music.

Handel. Music for the Royal Fireworks. Concerti a due cori—No. 2 in F major; No. 3 in F major. **The English Concert/Trevor Pinnock.** Archiv Produktion 415 129-2AH.

	54' DDD 8/85	♩ s Ⓑ

The *Concerti a due cori* (concertos for two choirs of instruments) are in fact written for a string band and two wind bands, each consisting (in the two concertos above) of oboes, horns and bassoon. The famous *Fireworks* music was written to enliven a firework display in Green Park and although King George III wanted as many warlike instruments as possible, Handel preferred to add a sizeable string band. The quality and balance of the sound are radically affected by the instruments used—period or modern. The English Concert use the former with a skill that makes this a very pleasant experience. You can enjoy this magnificent music with superb sound from the CD.

Handel. KEYBOARD SUITES. **Scott Ross** (hpd). Erato 2292-45452-2. Suites de pièces pour le clavecin (1720)—A major; F major; D minor; E minor; E major; F sharp major; G minor; F minor.

	② 1h 52' DDD 2/90	

Handel published these eight Suites in London together with a foreword, explaining that, as many copies of them were in circulation, he was doing so in order to set the record straight. The format of the baroque suite had by then become that of the sequence—allemande, courante, sarabande, gigue, usually preceded by a prelude and often with other, lighter dances separating the last two of the sequence, but Handel perceived no duty to conform to it. The F major Suite follows the standard pattern but has a fugue instead of a prelude, the A major Suite deviates in having no sarabande; five others admix dances with 'abstract' movements (including three fugues, two sets of variations and a passacaglia), whilst the F major Suite is a 'dance-less' *sonata da chiesa*. The music, displaying elements of French, Italian and German styles, reflects Handel's own cosmopolitan nature and tastes. To show an empathy with these diverse facets of Handel's world a performer needs a firm grasp of stylistic matters such as the rhythmic freedoms of rubato and *inégalités*, and the introduction of embellishments of various kinds; the late Scott Ross, beautifully recorded in charge of a reproduction of a French instrument of 1733, had all these attributes in abundance.

Handel. ITALIAN CANTATAS. **Emma Kirkby** (sop); **Michel Piguet** (ob, rec); **Rachel Beckett** (rec); **Charles Medlam** (va da gamba); **Jane Coe** (vc cont); **Academy of Ancient Music/Christopher Hogwood** (hpd). L'Oiseau-Lyre Florilegium 414 473-2OH. Texts and translations included. Tu fedel? tu costante?; Mi palpita il cor; Alpestre monte; Tra le fiamme.

	55' DDD 3/86	

Three of the cantatas in this issue belong to Handel's Italian period whilst the fourth, *Mi palpita il cor*—in its version for soprano, oboe and continuo—probably dates from his first years in England. There is a wealth of fine music to be found in this comparatively neglected area of Handel's output and the composer seldom if ever disappoints us in the subtlety with which he captures a mood or colours an image. The partnership of Emma Kirkby with solo instrumentalists and members of the Academy of Ancient Music is a rewarding one. Her singing is light in texture, fluent and effective in phrasing, and is ideally equipped to bring out the many nuances both of text and music. All concerned contribute towards lively performances under the stylistically informed direction of Christopher Hogwood.

Handel. L'Allegro, il Penseroso ed il Moderato. **Patrizia Kwella, Marie McLaughlin, Jennifer Smith** (sops); **Michael Ginn** (treb); **Maldwyn Davies, Martyn Hill** (tens); **Stephen Varcoe** (bar); **Monteverdi Choir; English Baroque Soloists/John Eliot Gardiner.** Erato 2292 45377-2. Notes, text and translation included. From STU71325 (11/80).

② Ih 55' DDD 7/85

Handel was the leading opera composer of the age, but when his fortunes in this sphere began to decline he started to develop other dramatic forms, notably those of the English ode and oratorio. Early in 1740 he turned to two great

poems of Milton's youth and composed a masterpiece. This was the ode *L'Allegro, il Penseroso ed il Moderato*. Charles Jennens, the librettist, skilfully adjusts and alternates Milton's poems with their strongly contrasting humours to suit the best interests of the music. John Eliot Gardiner has recorded the work

The Monteverdi Choir and English Baroque Soloists   [*photo: DG/Masotti*

almost complete with a small orchestra of period instruments and a first-rate cast of soloists. Patrizia Kwella and Maldwyn Davies are memorable in the beguiling duet, "As steals the morn", one of many arias which reveal Handel's acute sensibility to the natural landscape. The Monteverdi Choir is characteristically well-disciplined in Handel's varied and evocative choruses savouring the colourful images of the poems and responding effectively to Gardiner's stylish direction. The recorded sound is clear and resonant and full texts are provided in English, French and German.

Handel. Aci, Galatea e Polifemo[a]. Recorder Sonatas[b]—F major, HWV369; C major, HWV365; G major (trans. F major), HWV358. **Emma Kirkby** (sop) Aci; **Carolyn Watkinson** (contr) Galatea; **David Thomas** (bass) Polifemo; [b]**Michel Piquet** (rec); [b]**John Toll** (hpd); **London Baroque/Charles Medlam** ([b]vc). Harmonia Mundi HMC90 1253/4. Notes, text and translation included. Item marked [a] new to UK, [b] from HMC1190/91 (9/86).

② Ih 46' DDD 11/87

Handel's English pastoral *Acis and Galatea* has always been one of his most popular works, but not many of its admirers are aware that he had written a completely different treatment of the same story ten years earlier (when he was 23) for a ducal wedding in Naples. In this version modern ears need to adjust to Acis (a young shepherd lad) being represented by a soprano (originally a castrato), while the nymph Galatea is a contralto. The work is full of invention and instrumental colour, and there are several memorably beautiful items in the score, such as the opening duet (with the lovers' voices intertwining), and above all Acis's dying farewell after the jealous giant Polyphemus has crushed him under a huge rock. To suggest the giant's vast size Handel employed a prodigious vocal range of two-and-a-half octaves, which has proved the chief obstacle to performances of the work, here receiving a very enjoyable first recording. All three singers are excellent and so is the technical quality.

Handel. Acis and Galatea. **Norma Burrowes** (sop) Galatea; **Anthony Rolfe Johnson** (ten) Acis; **Martyn Hill** (ten) Damon; **Willard White** (bass) Polyphemus; **Paul Elliot** (ten); **English Baroque Soloists/John Eliot Gardiner.** Archiv Produktion 423 406-2AH2. Notes, text and translation included. From 2708 038 (9/78).

② 95' ADD 8/88

John Eliot Gardiner made this recording of Handel's masque during the late 1970s when the revival of period instruments was still in a comparatively early stage. Listeners may detect weaknesses both in intonation and in ensemble from time to time but, nevertheless, Gardiner's performance is lively and stylistically assured. He paces the work dramatically revealing nuances both in the text and in the music. The solo team is a strong one and there are especially fine contributions from Norma Burrowes and Anthony Rolfe Johnson. This is an enjoyable performance of an enchanting work.

Handel. Alceste[a]. Comus[b]. [a]**Emma Kirkby**, [a]**Judith Nelson**, [b]**Patrizia Kwella**, [a]**Christina Pound** (sops); [ab]**Margaret Cable**, [a]**Catherine Denley** (mezs); [a]**Paul Elliott**, [a]**Rogers Covey-Crump** (tens); [ab]**David Thomas**, [a]**Christopher Keyte** (basses); **Academy of Ancient Music/ Christopher Hogwood.** L'Oiseau-Lyre Florilegium 421 479-2OH. Texts included. Item marked [a] from DSLO581 (12/80), [b] DSLO598 (8/82).

74' ADD 3/89

The *Alceste* music was written towards the end of Handel's life as masque-like interludes for a production of Tobias Smollett's play. They were never used in that form and were later employed by the composer for *The Choice of Hercules*. The musical numbers Handel created would seem to have provided a kind of musical commentary on the text of the play itself. It consists primarily of arias and choruses with occasional orchestral interludes. One of the highlights is definitely the lovely setting of "Gentle Morpheus, son of night", exquisitely sung here by Emma Kirkby. Paul Elliott, too, sings with great style. The bonus item, *Comus*, consists of three songs linked by choral refrains. They are beautifully done with the AAM playing with great style throughout, and the recordings are finely managed.

Handel. Alexander's Feast[a]. Concerto Grosso in C major, HWV318. [a]**Donna Brown** (sop); [a]**Carolyn Watkinson** (contr); [a]**Ashley Stafford** (alto); [a]**Nigel Robson** (ten); [a]**Stephen Varcoe** (bar); [a]**Monteverdi Choir, English Baroque Soloists/John Eliot Gardiner.** Philips 422 055-2PH2. Text included. Recorded at a performance during the 1987 Göttingen Handel Festival, Germany.

② 98' DDD 11/88

Alexander's Feast was the first work Handel had set by a major English poet (Dryden) and it was also the first time he allotted the principal male part to a tenor instead of the castrato heroes of his Italian operas. These two factors, combined with much fine music, scored with great brilliance and imagination, ensured the immediate success of *Alexander's Feast*. It is strange that nowadays it is seldom performed so this recording would have been very welcome even had it not been so full of vitality and so stylishly performed (though perhaps with more sophisticated detail than the eighteenth century would have managed). The Monteverdi Choir and the soloists are all Gardiner regulars, though the pure-voiced Canadian soprano Donna Brown is a fairly recent (and welcome) acquisition; and the English Baroque Soloists have ample opportunities to shine—especially the violins, although the natural horns' lusty entry in the bucolic "Bacchus, ever fair and young" is exhilarating.

Handel. Athalia. **Dame Joan Sutherland** (sop) Athalia; **Emma Kirkby** (sop) Josabeth; **Aled Jones** (treb) Joas; **James Bowman** (alto) Joad; **Anthony Rolfe Johnson** (ten) Mathan; **David Thomas** (bass-bar) Abner; **New College Choir, Oxford; Academy of Ancient Music/Christopher Hogwood.** L'Oiseau-Lyre 417 126-2OH2. Notes and text included. From 417 126-1OH2 (11/86).

② 2h 2' DDD 2/87

Although *Athalia* was a huge success when first performed and has long been recognized as a masterly work, not only is this its first complete recording, but barely a note of it has previously appeared in the catalogues, apart from a couple of excerpts in transcriptions. With lip service constantly paid to Handel, this has been a startling neglect; but fortunately the conspiracy of silence has now been broken with a performance that does justice to this remarkable piece. Handel's treatment of form is exceptionally flexible, his characterization is vivid, and his musical invention is at its most exuberant: the opening Sinfonia (alertly played under Hogwood) immediately whets the appetite. Emma Kirkby delights by the freshness and limpidity of her tone and by the absolute precision and charm of her trills and ornamentation whilst James Bowman sings accurately but is unimaginative in his treatment of words. In the title-role Joan Sutherland makes the most of the apostate queen's vengeful outbursts, and her enunciation is much clearer than usual. There are splendid florid solos for David Thomas and Anthony Rolfe Johnson, and Aled Jones as the boy king sings his one aria with beautifully controlled tone and impeccable intonation. The chorus sings enthusiastically and makes a shattering entry in the brilliant opening of Act 2—which is certainly the number to sample for anyone wishing to know what this fine work is like.

Handel (reconstr. Dixon). Carmelite Vespers (1707). [a]**Taverner Choir; Taverner Players/Andrew Parrott.** EMI Reflexe CDS7 49749-2. Texts and translations included.
Dixit Dominus (with Jill Feldman, Emily Van Evera, sops; Margaret Cable, contr; Joseph Cornwell, ten; David Thomas, bass)[a]. Laudate pueri Dominum (Emma Kirkby, sop)[a]. Te decus virgineum (Mary Nichols, contr.). Nisi Dominus (Cable; Cornwell; Thomas)[a]. Haec est regina virginum (Kirkby). Saeviat tellus (Feldman). Salve regina (Van Evera). Plainchant for the Second Vespers of the Feast of Our Lady of Mount Carmel.

② 2h 1' DDD 6/89

You will not find this work listed in any catalogue of Handel's music, though the *Dixit Dominus, Laudate pueri* and *Nisi Dominus* are fairly well known. But in Rome in 1707 Handel was commissioned by Cardinal Colonna to provide music for the festival of Our Lady of Mount Carmel, the patroness of the Carmelite order: we know that the music was on a lavish scale, but no details have been preserved of exactly what was performed (or even whether all of it was exclusively by Handel). Graham Dixon has constructed a hypothetical version of the service, making use of Handel compositions of the time (especially those which should have had no other reason for their existence) as well as appropriate plainsong. The Taverner Choir is tonally assured and intelligent in its use of words; the Taverner Players are lively and efficient, and the experienced soloists are mostly in very good form—though it is curious to find a female alto (unknown in Roman churches) in so meticulously scholarly a reconstruction. Andrew Parrott secures stylish and buoyant performances but adopts rather brisk tempos.

However, the overall atmosphere is very convincing, and this collection brings out some splendid music. Particularly attractive is an unfamiliar *Haec est regina*, sung with delightful freshness by Emma Kirkby; and plainchant enthusiasts will appreciate the smoothly fluent singing of *Laudate Jerusalem* and *Ave maris stella*.

Handel. ITALIAN DUETS. **Gillian Fisher** (sop); **James Bowman** (alto); **The King's Consort/Robert King.** Hyperion CDA66440. Texts and translations included.
A miravi io son intento. Conservate, raddoppiate. Fronda leggiera e mobile. Langue, geme e sospira. Nò, di voi non vuo fidarmi. Se tu non lasci amore. Sono liete, fortunate. Tanti strali al sen. Troppo crudo.

64' DDD 4/91

Handel's duets were written for high-class domestic music-making during his Italian years and his brief period in Hanover; then he composed some additional ones in London in the 1740s. Mostly they consist of two or three movements in a free contrapuntal style, the voices imitating one another, then turning each other's ideas in a new direction, then the two coming together to round off the section. Some are cheerful and spirited (it was from one of his duets, not on the present disc, that Handel developed the choruses "For unto us" and "All we like sheep" in *Messiah*); others are highly chromatic and expressive, for example, the beautiful, heartfelt first movement of *Langue, geme e sospira* and that of *Se tu non lasci amore*, with its languishing moans and sighs—most, of course, are about the pleasurable pains of unrequited love. The two soloists here, both experienced Handelians, know just how to make the most of this music, letting their voices intertwine, dawdling faintly on the dissonances, shaping the runs purposefully, using the words to good effect; the accompaniments are tastefully done, with lute and organ relieving the predominant harpsichord. Altogether a happy disc.

Handel. Chandos Anthems, Volume 4—The Lord is my light, HWV255; Let God arise, HWV256. **Lynne Dawson** (sop); **Ian Partridge** (ten); **The Sixteen Chorus and Orchestra/Harry Christophers.** Chandos Chaconne CHAN0509. Texts included.

49' DDD 7/90

The Chandos Anthems, which Handel composed during his residence at Canons, Edgware, Middlesex, in the years around 1720, have not had a complete recording before. The Sixteen have now completed their set of these appealing pieces, church music on a modest scale composed for the Duke of Chandos's private worship. Essentially intimate in style, they nevertheless have a touch of

the ceremonial about them, echoing Purcell and the English tradition but at the same time reinterpret that tradition in a broad, urbane manner, attuned to the worldliness of the Anglican establishment of the time. Probably they were intended for performance by a very small group, but Harry Christopher's ensemble is well scaled to the music and his chorus sing for the most part with spirit, especially in the quicker music. Ian Partridge sings with his usual impeccable taste and judgement in the tenor solo music; the other soloist here is the soprano Lynne Dawson, whose glowing tone and diamantine passage-work are one of the chief delights of this pleasing disc.

Handel. ARIAS FOR MONTAGNANA. **David Thomas** (bass); **Philharmonia Baroque Orchestra/Nicholas McGegan.** Harmonia Mundi HMU90 7016. Texts and translations included.
Acis and Galatea—Avampo ... Ferito son d'Amore. Athalia—Ah, canst thou but prove me! Deborah—Barak, my son ... Awake the ardour; They ardours warm ... Swift inundation; Tears, such as tender fathers shed. Esther—I'll hear no more ... Pluck root and branch; Turn not, O Queen; How art thou fall'n. Ezio—Perchè tanto tormento? ... Se un bell'ardire; Folle è colui ... Nasce al bosco; Che indegno! ... Già risonar. Orlando—Mira, prendi l'essempio! ... Lascia Amor; Impari ognun da Orlando ... O voi, del mio poter ... Sorge infausta una procella. Sosarme—Addio, principe scrupoloso ... Fra l'ombre e gli orrori; Quanto più Melo ... Sento il core; Tanto s'eseguirà ... Tiene Giove. Tolomeo, re di egitto—Piangi pur.

● 68' DDD 8/90

Antonio Montagnana was a Venetian who sang bass parts in London in Handel's time: which means that his voice and his capacities gave shape to many of the bass parts Handel composed— it being the custom, in those times, for a composer to write the music to the singer's specific abilities. And Handel's music tells us that Montagnana was a singer quite out of the ordinary, as remarkable, in fact, as his impersonator here, the English bass David Thomas. Some of the arias are big, blustery pieces, suitable for unscrupulous villains or sturdy military men, but others show Montagnana (and Thomas) as what came to be called a *basso cantante* (listen to the eloquent one from *Tolomeo*), and there are sheer virtuoso pieces too (conspicuously those from *Sosarme*). Some of them range from what is practically a tenor compass right down to *basso profondo* regions. Thomas is an astonishing singer, agile to a degree, able to encompass all that Montagnana did and indeed to add apt ornamentation at times; the articulation is precise and energetic, the tone true and even across two-and-a-half octaves, and always there is a touch of wit and spirit behind the singing. Nicholas McGegan's band provides sharp, slightly choppy support.

Handel. Messiah. **Arleen Auger** (sop); **Anne Sofie von Otter** (mez); **Michael Chance** (alto); **Howard Crook** (ten); **John Tomlinson** (bass); **The English Concert Choir; The English Concert/Trevor Pinnock.** Archiv Produktion 423 630-2AH2. Text included.

● ② 2h 30' DDD 11/88

Handel (arr. Mozart/Sargent). Messiah. **Elsie Morison** (sop); **Marjorie Thomas** (contr); **Richard Lewis** (ten); **James Milligan** (bass); **Huddersfield Choral Society; Royal Liverpool Philharmonic Orchestra/Sir Malcolm Sargent.** Classics for Pleasure CD-CFPD4718. From Columbia SAX2308/10 (12/59).

● ② 2h 24' ADD 5/91

Handel first performed his oratorio *Messiah* in 1742 and subsequently made several revisions. Trevor Pinnock more or less follows the pattern of Handel's later performances of the work thus including the music composed in 1745 and 1750; but the combination of solo voices chosen by Pinnock does not precisely correspond with that used by Handel on any known occasion and The English Concert Choir, furthermore, consists of male and female voices whereas Handel envisaged an all male chorus of boys and men. This is a stylish and affectionate performance with a first-rate team of soloists, lively choral singing and fine instrumental playing both obbligato and in ensemble. Pinnock has almost unfailingly sound judgement where Handel's tempos are concerned and he directs the work from the harpsichord with fervour and authority. Few listeners will be disappointed by the uniformly high standard of solo singing and Anne Sofie von Otter and Michael Chance give especially winning performances of their solos. Full texts are included in an informative booklet and the recorded sound is clear and resonant.

For many years Sir Malcolm Sargent's *Messiah* with the Royal Choral Society was a much loved annual event which attracted a capacity audience in the Royal Albert Hall. There was nothing ossified about this tradition of performing Handel's masterpiece on the largest scale, for Sargent's reading never lost its freshness, and he had good reasons for his stylistic approach. The present recording uses a chorus of 100, which is completely contrary to the propaganda of the authenticists, who cite the smallness of the choir at Handel's own early performances. But Sargent suggests that "Handel was renowned for his big effects, for wanting twice as many voices in the chorus as usual", and goes on to describe large-scale performances of *Messiah*, with nearly 300 choristers and a huge orchestra, occurring within 25 years of Handel's death. He also tells us that under his baton "the orchestra play the original Handel string, trumpet and drum parts, plus orchestrations which I have arranged, unhesitatingly adopting any good ideas from earlier, experienced editors". In matters of scoring he is a law unto himself, using clarinets among the woodwind and commenting that "their tone colour blends well, and although it is true that they are an anachronism, I must point out that conductors who object to them are themselves an anachronism! They should not be there at all. The conductor as such was not known in Handel's day. Direction was done from the keyboard." Sargent's view of the work is unashamedly spacious and grand. His tempos are slower than we expect today, and the reason the work fits comfortably on a pair of CDs is because he also observes traditional cuts (although his annual London performance with the Royal Choral Society was always complete). Sargent has splendid soloists for his recording, and they respond to his histrionic approach without losing purity of line. The famous numbers, "O thou that tellest", "He was despised" (Marjorie Thomas singing movingly), Elsie Morison's freshly radiant "I know that my Redeemer liveth" and the dramatic male solos, "The trumpet shall sound" and "Why do the nations so furiously rage together", all emerge with great spontaneity. The majestic choruses are equally impressive, especially "Hallelujah" (which is worth standing up for) and the grandiloquent concluding "Worthy is the Lamb" and "Amen". There is vitality here beside authority and breadth, and it is refreshing to hear this famous interpretation, recorded in 1959, emerging as such a vivid listening experience, for the transfer to CD has worked miracles with the original sound. The choral focus is immeasurably improved, and the soloists are clearly and naturally projected, yet flattered by the warm ambience.

Handel. Israel in Egypt. **Nancy Argenta, Emily Van Evera** (sops); **Timothy Wilson** (alto); **Anthony Rolfe Johnson** (ten); **David Thomas, Jeremy White** (basses); **Taverner Choir and Players/Andrew Parrott.** EMI CDS7 54018-2. Text included.

② 2h 15' DDD 2/91

If anyone needs to assure themselves as to whether the English choral tradition is alive and well, they need only buy this CD. *Israel in Egypt*, of all Handel's works, is the choral one *par excellence*—so much so, in fact, that it was something of a failure in Handel's own time because solo singing was much preferred to choral by the audiences. Andrew Parrott gives a complete performance of the work, in its original form: that is to say, prefaced by the noble funeral anthem for Queen Caroline, as adapted by Handel to serve as a song of mourning by the captive Israelites. This first part is predominantly slow, grave music, powerfully elegiac; the Taverner Choir show themselves, in what is testing music to sing, firm and clean of line, well focused and strongly sustained. The chorus have their chances to be more energetic in the second part, with the famous and vivid Plague choruses—in which the orchestra too play their part in the pictorial effects, with the fiddles illustrating in turn frogs, flies and hailstones. And last, in the third part, there is a generous supply of the stirring C major music in which Handel has the Israelites give their thanks to God, in some degree symbolizing the English giving thanks for the Hanoverian monarchy and the Protestant succession. Be that as it may, the effect is splendid. The solo work is first-rate, too, with Nancy Argenta radiant in Miriam's music in the final scene and distinguished contributions too from David Thomas and Anthony Rolfe Johnson.

Handel. Saul. **Lynne Dawson, Donna Brown** (sops); **Derek Lee Ragin** (alto); **John Mark Ainsley, Neil Mackie, Philip Salmon, Philip Slane** (tens); **Alastair Miles, Richard Savage** (basses); **Monteverdi Choir; English Baroque Soloists/John Eliot Gardiner.** Philips 426 265-2PH3. Recorded at performances in the Stadthalle, Göttingen, Germany, in June 1989.

③ 2h 39' DDD 8/91

Saul is considered by many to be one of the most arresting music dramas in the English language, even though it is officially classed as an oratorio. In it Handel explores in some psychological depth the motivations of his characters, most notably that of the eponymous anti-hero, whose tantrums caused by envy and his searching for supernatural intervention are all vividly delineated; so is the friendship of David and Jonathan and the different characters of Saul's daughters, Merab and Michal. In yet another compelling performance of Handel under his baton, John Eliot Gardiner—in this live recording made at the Göttingen Handel Festival—fulfils every aspect of this varied and adventurous score, eliciting execution of refined and biting calibre from his choir and orchestra. The young British bass Alastair Miles captures Saul in all his moods. John Mark Ainsley and Derek Lee Ragin are both affecting as Jonathan and David; so are Lynne Dawson and Donna Brown as Michal and Merab. There are a few cuts, but they aren't grievous enough to prevent a firm recommendation.

Handel. Susanna. **Lorraine Hunt, Jill Feldman** (sops); **Drew Minter** (alto); **Jeffrey Thomas** (ten); **William Parker** (bar); **David Thomas** (bass); **Chamber Chorus of the University of California, Berkeley; Philharmonia Baroque Orchestra/Nicholas McGegan.** Harmonia Mundi HMC90 7030/2. Notes and text included.

③ 2h 58' DDD 10/90

Susanna is one of the least often heard of Handel's oratorios. A tale, from the *Apocrypha*, of the betrayal of a beautiful and virtuous woman, in her husband's absence, by two lascivious elders when she rejects their importunities, it gives Handel opportunities for a wide range of music—there are amorous pieces for Susanna and her husband, idyllic rural ones when she is in the garden with her maid, sharply drawn pictures of the elders (one an insinuating tenor, the other a more menacing bass), and several powerful expressions of devoutness, rectitude and faith. It has been called "an opera of village life", and it does contain touches of character and comedy; but in this very fine performance one is never in doubt that it is much more than that, a deeply serious work, whose climaxes come in noble, solemn music such as Susanna's "Bending to the throne of glory" (a B minor aria with rich, five-part strings, grave yet glowing) and the chorus at the end, when she is found to be faultless, in praise of divine justice. Lorraine Hunt sings Susanna's music here with considerable power and focus of tone, rising to the great moments, and also charming and graceful in the lesser ones such as the bathing aria in Part 2. As her husband, the gentle counter-tenor Drew Minter is sensitive and controlled, while the elders are graphically drawn by Jeffrey Thomas and David Thomas. The choral singing by this Californian group, under English direction, is clear and firm in line, direct in rhythm, and Nicholas McGegan's handling of the Baroque orchestra is live and assured, with the tempos and the sense of the music always surely judged.

Handel. FLAVIO. **Jeffrey Gall** (alto) Flavio; **Derek Lee Ragin** (alto) Guido; **Lena Lootens** (sop) Emilia; **Bernarda Fink** (contr) Teodata; **Christina Högman** (sop) Vitige; **Gianpaolo Fagotto** (ten) Ugone; **Ulrich Messthaler** (bass) Lotario; **Ensemble 415/René Jacobs.** Harmonia Mundi HMC90 1312/3. Notes, text and translation included.

② 2h 36' DDD 7/90

Flavio is one of the most delectable of Handel's operas. Although it comes from his 'heroic' period, it is not at all in the heroic mould but rather an ironic tragedy with a good many comic elements. Does that sound confusing?—well, so it is, for you never know quite where you are when King Flavio of Lombardy starts falling in love with the wrong woman, for although this starts as an amusing idle fancy it develops into something near-tragic, since he imperils everyone else's happiness, ultimately causing the death of one counsellor and the dishonour of another. The delicately drawn amorous feeling is like nothing else in Handel, and in its subtle growth towards real passion and grief is handled with consummate skill. The opera, in short, is full of fine and exceptionally varied music, and it is enhanced here by a performance under René Jacobs that, although it takes a number of modest liberties, catches the moods of the music surely and attractively, with shapely, alert and refined playing from the admirable Ensemble 415. And the cast is strong. The central roles, composed for two of Handel's greatest singers, Cuzzoni and Senesino, are done by Lena Lootens, a delightfully natural and expressive soprano with a firm, clear technique, and the counter-tenor Derek Lee Ragin, who dispatches his brilliant music with aplomb and excels in the final aria, a superb minor-key expression of passion. The singers also include Bernarda Fink as the lightly amorous Teodata and Christina Högman, both fiery and subtle in the music for her lover, and the capable Jeffrey Gall as the wayward monarch. Altogether a highly enjoyable set, not flawless but certainly among the best ever Handel opera recordings.

Handel. HERCULES. **Jennifer Smith** (sop) Iole; **Sarah Walker** (mez) Dejanira; **Catherine Denley** (mez) Lichas; **Anthony Rolfe Johnson** (ten) Hyllus; **John Tomlinson** (bass) Hercules; **Peter Savidge** (bar) Priest of Jupiter; **Monteverdi Choir; English Baroque Soloists/John Eliot Gardiner.** Archiv Produktion 423 137-2AH3. Notes and text included. From 2742 004 (6/83).

③ 2h 33' DDD 1/88

Handel's *Hercules* is neither opera nor sacred oratorio though it contains elements of both. The story of Dejanira's jealousy of her husband Hercules and of his agonizing death on wearing a poisoned robe which she sends him is brought to life by Handel with typically vivid characterization and in an altogether masterly fashion. Dejanira is sung by Sarah Walker with intensity of feeling, and a fine sense of theatre; Handel capturing the various shades of her character with deep psychological insight and consummate musical genius. Most of the other characters, though skilfully drawn, do not develop to a comparable extent.

Jennifer Smith makes an effectively youthful and fresh-sounding princess Iole, and

John Tomlinson a resonant and authoritative Hercules. The chorus reflects the varied emotions emerging as a result of the action and respond to Handel's requirements in a lively, articulate fashion. Orchestral playing on period instruments is comparably alert with clean ensemble and several fine obbligato contributions. Clear, resonant recorded sound and exemplary presentation with full text.

Handel. ORLANDO. **James Bowman** (alto) Orlando; **Arleen Auger** (sop) Angelica; **Catherine Robbin** (mez) Medoro; **Emma Kirkby** (sop) Dorinda; **David Thomas** (bass) Zoroastro; **Academy of Ancient Music/Christopher Hogwood.** L'Oiseau-Lyre 430 845-2OH3. Notes, text and translation included.

③ 2h 38' DDD 8/91

Handel's operas represent the greatest expanse of underexplored musical territory ever to have been written by a major composer. For cherishers of verismo the formalism of Handel's theatrical world no doubt presents a problem or two, but for listeners willing to accept the (not so very restricting) conventions within which the composer worked there are wonderful discoveries to be made. *Orlando* is as good a place as any to start looking. Its pastoral tale of

unrequited love and resultant madness is retold by Handel with customary sympathy and psychological insight; and, needless to say, he provides some ravishing music along the way. Christopher Hogwood is not, perhaps, a born opera conductor, but he has assembled a fine cast for this recording, which benefits, too, from being based on a touring production. Thus, though one might feel that there is a slight lack of dramatic weight and pacing in this performance, such faults are redeemed by the polished and confident contributions of its five experienced baroque singers. James Bowman is intelligent and passionate in the title-role, Arleen Auger frequently thrilling as the object of his hopeless love, and the remaining parts are all perfectly suited to the particular strengths of their interpreters. Definitely a Handel recording worth having.

Arleen Auger   [photo: Hyperion/Barda]

Handel. SOLOMON. **Carolyn Watkinson** (mez) Solomon; **Nancy Argenta** (sop) Solomon's Queen; **Barbara Hendricks** (sop) Queen of Sheba; **Joan Rodgers** (sop) First Harlot; **Della Jones** (mez) Second Harlot; **Anthony Rolfe Johnson** (ten) Zadok; **Stephen Varcoe** (bass) A Levite; **Monteverdi Choir; English Baroque Soloists/John Eliot Gardiner.** Philips 412 612-2PH2. Notes, text and translation included.

③ 2h 16' DDD 12/85   ◖p ◖s Ⓑ

This oratorio is a somewhat static affair but one filled with the most serene and affecting music. The three acts set forth three aspects of Solomon's majesty. The first deals with his piety and marital bliss, the second with his wisdom in his famous judgement as to which of two harlots is the mother of a child, the third to the visit of the Queen of Sheba. Handel set the scene in a wonderful contrast of pomp and ceremony with the pastoral, his choruses always apt to the mood to be depicted. The scene between the two harlots is brilliantly characterized, the airs for the other principals in Handel's most felicitous vein, while the Sinfonia depicting the Queen of Sheba's entrance is justly famous. The Monteverdi Choir sing with mellifluous tone and precise articulation and the authentic instruments of the English Baroque Soloists play for John Eliot Gardiner with style and virtuosity. The soloists are well chosen with special praise for Nancy Argenta as Solomon's Queen. The recording does full justice to every aspect of the colourful score and it would be hard to imagine a performance that was a better advocate for Handel's cause.

Howard Hanson *Refer to Index* *American 1896-1981*

Roy Harris *American 1898-1979*

Harris. Symphony No. 3 (1939).
Schuman. Symphony No. 3 (1941). **New York Philharmonic Orchestra/ Leonard Bernstein.** DG 419 780-2GH. Recorded at a performance in the Avery Fisher Hall, New York in December 1985.

51' DDD 11/87

If you already know music by Gershwin and Copland and wish to explore the work of other American composers then these two symphonies provide the ideal opportunity. Harris's short Third Symphony of 1939 is in one continuous movement, which however falls into five sections—Tragic, Lyric, Pastoral, Fugue-Dramatic and Dramatic-Tragic. The style is austere without being in the least forbidding; the musical arguments are terse but easy to follow, the orchestral sound solid but not opaque. When first performed the symphony was an instant critical and popular success, as was Schuman's Third Symphony when premièred two years later. Harris's influence on his slightly younger colleague is apparent, but Schuman has a rather more brilliant orchestral style and the mood of the work, cast in two movements, each of which has two connected sections, is a little more outgoing. The New York Philharmonic has this kind of music in its bones, and it gives superlative performances under its former chief conductor, whose sympathy and insight into the music of his older contemporaries has always been notable. The recordings are superlative.

Jonathan Harvey *Refer to Index* *British 1939*

Joseph Haydn *Austrian 1732-1809*

Michael Haydn *Austrian 1737-1806*

Haydn. Horn Concerto No. 1 in D major. Symphony No. 31 in D major, "Hornsignal".
M. Haydn. Horn Concerto in D major. **Anthony Halstead** (natural hn); **Hanover Band/Roy Goodman.** Nimbus NI5190.

61' DDD 11/89

This disc is something of an eulogy to the natural, valveless horn of the

eighteenth century. Here it is played with panache by Anthony Halstead whose firm control of a notoriously difficult instrument together with accomplished musicianship ensures performances of assurance and finesse. The two Horn Concertos by the brothers Haydn come over well though they are not, perhaps, especially memorable pieces. Virtuoso horn playing is required and Halstead provides it with brilliant passagework, clearly articulated phrases and a characterful sound. The remaining work on the disc is Haydn's well-known Symphony No. 31, *Hornsignal*; here, the composer requires not one but four horn players who collectively make an imposing phalanx. Haydn's appealing sense of humour caters for various varieties of horn signal loudly barked out or beguilingly *piano* as the case may be. In the lyrical Adagio there is a prominent role allotted the solo violin, whilst in the finale, a set of variations, Haydn gives further solos to cello, flute, horns, violin and violone. The contributions are a little variable here but nevertheless spontaneous and affectionate playing such as this should win friends. Effective recorded sound.

Haydn. Trumpet Concerto in E flat major, HobVIIe/1[a]. Cello Concerto in D major, HobVIIb/2[b]. Violin Concerto in C major, HobVII/1[c]. [c]**Cho-Liang Lin** (vn); [b]**Yo-Yo Ma** (vc); [a]**Wynton Marsalis** (tpt); [a]**National Philharmonic Orchestra/Raymond Leppard;** [b]**English Chamber Orchestra/José Luis Garcia;** [c]**Minnesota Orchestra/Sir Neville Marriner.** CBS Masterworks CD39310. From IM39310 (1/85).

· 59' DDD 1/86 Ⓑ

This compilation of three Haydn concertos has a different soloist and orchestra for each. The young American trumpeter Wynton Marsalis has all the fluency one could wish for and an instrument allowing a full three octaves (E flat—E flat) to be displayed in his own cadenza to the first movement. Although this is an efficient performance, it in no way approaches the class of the next one. The cellist Yo-Yo Ma is very different as a performer: though equally a master of his instrument, and indeed a virtuoso who seems incapable of producing an ugly sound or playing out of tune, one feels a deep emotional involvement in all he does. Also, the recording in this D major Cello Concerto is unusually faithful in blending the cello well into the ensemble without ever covering it. Ma is supported by the excellent English Chamber Orchestra and the qualities of integration and ensemble under their leader's direction are all that one could wish for. In the C major Violin Concerto the skilful Cho-Liang Lin has the benefit of a most sympathetic conductor in Sir Neville Marriner, but he cannot match Ma's subtlety and commitment.

Haydn. Violin Concertos—C major, HobVIIa/1; G major, Hob VIIa/4. Concerto for violin, keyboard and strings in F major, HobXVIII/6[a]. [a]**Justin Oprean** (pf); **European Community Chamber Orchestra/Adelina Oprean** (vn). Hyperion Helios CDH88037.

· 61' DDD 1/90 £

Apart from his Trumpet Concerto, we don't usually associate Haydn with concerto form, but he did write a number of concertos, and not surprisingly they prove to be well worth getting to know. The three of them here are all from around his thirtieth year, and although by his standards they are a little old-fashioned and owe something to Italian models they are delightful music, tuneful and life-affirming. They are also very well written for the violin, and for the keyboard too (originally it was the organ, but here a piano is convincingly used) in the case of the Double Concerto in F major that begins the programme. The violinist Adelina Oprean has a sweet tone but plenty of attack too, and in terms of style her playing seems unfailingly right; the same may be said of her direction of this fine orchestra of strings and harpsichord and also of the cadenzas

273

she supplies to all three works. The recording of this attractive disc was made in a North London church and it sounds very lifelike, with just a natural degree of ambience. At medium price this CD is excellent value.

Haydn. SYMPHONIES. **Philharmonia Hungarica/Antál Dorati.** Decca 430 100-2DM32. Also available as eight four-disc sets.
425 900-2DM4 (270 minutes)—Nos. 1-16. *425 905-2DM4* (274 minutes)—Nos. 17-33. *425 910-2DM4* (283 minutes)—Nos. 34-47. *425 915-2DM4* (273 minutes)—Nos. 48-59. *425 920-2DM4* (251 minutes)—Nos. 60-71. *425 925-2DM4* (269 minutes)—Nos. 72-83. *425 930-2DM4* (286 minutes)—Nos. 84-95. *425 935-2DM4* (286 minutes)—Nos. 96-104. Symphony "A" in B flat major. Symphony "B" in B flat major. Sinfonia concertante in B flat major.

③② 36h 31' ADD 6/91 £ 9 p

Though there are now two period-instrument Haydn cycles underway (from Goodman on Hyperion and Hogwood on L'Oiseau-Lyre), this pioneering modern-instrument cycle recorded by Antál Dorati and his band of Hungarian exiles between 1969 and 1973 is going to be a hard act to follow. When first issued on LP Dorati's performances won almost universal praise for their style and verve, their eager and imaginative engagement with the music's astonishing, protean inventiveness. And in their very overdue CD incarnation, in eight sets of four discs each, they still have little to fear from most of the competition. Remarkably, in such an extended project, there is hardly a whiff of routine: time and again the orchestra seems to play out of its skin for Dorati, the strings sweet-toned and luminous, the wind deft and resourceful, savouring to the full the wit and whimsy of Hadyn's writing. And though one might have reservations about this or that symphony, Dorati's actual interpretations are often exemplary, combining rhythmic resilience and a splendid overall sweep with an unusual care for detail.

Aficionados of period performances may feel that the strings, especially in the earlier symphonies, are too numerous and too liberal with vibrato. But the buoyancy of Dorati's rhythms and the crispness of the strings' articulation constantly preclude any suggestion of undue opulence. Most of the early symphonies (in which Dorati uses a discreetly balanced harpsichord continuo) are captivatingly done: *Allegros* dance and leap and slow movements are shaped with finesse and affection. Listen, for instance, to the beautiful neo-baroque D minor *Andante* in No. 4, or the grave *siciliano* in No. 12, a particularly appealing, warm-textured work. And in the second box, containing Nos. 17-33, Dorati brings a characteristic breadth and intensity of line to the opening *Adagios* of No. 21 (a notably mature and eloquent movement, this) and No. 22, the so-called *Philosopher*. The famous *Hornsignal*, No. 31, is also irresistibly done, with rollicking, ripe-toned horns; and practically the only disappointment in the first two boxes is the *Lamentatione*, No. 26, where both the tragic first movement and the quizzical final minuet are too smooth and sluggish.

A number of the minuets in the middle-period symphonies (those written between the late 1760s and the early 1780s) are also distinctly leisurely, lacking Dorati's usual rhythmic spring—cases in point are those in Nos. 43, 52 and 49 (the last funereally slow). And one or two of the passionate minor-keyed symphonies, especially Nos. 39 and 52, are, like No. 26, wanting in fire and dramatic thrust. But in many of these works of Haydn's first full maturity (several still virtually unknown) Dorati gives penetrating, shrewdly judged performances. Highlights among the rarer symphonies include No. 41, with its pealing trumpets and high horns (stunningly played), the expansive No. 42, done with real breadth and grandeur, and the subtle, lyrical No. 64, whose sublime *Largo* is sustained at the slowest possible tempo. In one or two works (notably the large-scale D major, No. 61, and the so-called *Laudon*, No. 69), Dorati

Antál Dorati   [photo: Decca]

might seem too frothy and frolicsome. And just occasionally (as in the outrageous six-movement *Il Distratto*, No. 60) he can underplay the earthy, rumbustious side of Haydn's complex musical personality.

Two of the most desirable boxes of all are those containing Symphonies Nos. 72-83 and 84-95—though some collectors may find it inconvenient that both the "Paris" and the "London" sets are split between boxes. Most of the pre-Paris symphonies are still underrated: but works like Nos. 76, 77 and 81 reveal a new, almost Mozartian suavity of manner and a sophistication of thematic development influenced by the Op. 33 String Quartets, while the two minor-keyed symphonies, Nos. 78 and 80, have notably powerful, concentrated first movements. If Dorati is a shade too comfortable in No. 80 he is superb elsewhere on these discs. Though the competition from rival performances now begins to hot up, he can more than hold his own in the "Paris" set: listen to the mingled grace and strength he brings to Nos. 85 and 87, with their clear, gleaming textures, or his dramatic urgency in the first movement of the misleadingly named *La Poule*, No. 83.

As for the "London" Symphonies, Dorati's readings are as detailed and attentive as any on the market, though at times he can underestimate the music's boldness, grandeur and dangerous wit. This is partly a question of tempos (some distinctly on the slow side) and accent, but also of the variable prominence accorded the brass and timpani—in several works, notably Nos. 94, 96 and, most seriously, the flamboyant, aggressive Nos. 97 and 100, these instruments are too recessed to make their full dramatic effect. Elsewhere, though, the balance is more satisfying: and in symphonies like Nos. 93, 103 and 104 Dorati combines power, incisiveness and symphonic breadth with an unusual sensitivity to the lyrical poignancy which underlies much of Haydn's later music.

The recordings, outstanding in their day, still sound pretty impressive, with a fine spaciousness and bloom, even if the violins can acquire a touch of glare above the stave. All in all, a magnificent, life-enhancing series that has contributed vastly to our deeper understanding of Haydn's genius over the last two decades. Whatever integral cycles may appear in the future, Dorati's will stand as one of the gramophone's grandest achievements.

Haydn. Symphonies—No. 6 in D major, "Le matin"; No. 7 in C major, "Le midi"; No. 8 in G major, "Le soir". **The English Concert/Trevor Pinnock** (hpd). Archiv Produktion 423 098-2AH.

65'   DDD   1/88

These symphonies represent the times of day; *Le matin* portrays the sunrise, and there is a storm in *Le soir*, but otherwise there is not a lot that could be called programmatic. But Haydn did take the opportunity to give his new colleagues in the princely band something interesting to do, for there are numerous solos here, not only for the wind instruments but for the section leaders—listen especially to the *Adagio* of No. 6, with solo violin and prominent flutes and cello, a delectable piece of writing. Inventively, the music is uneven; the concerto-like style was not wholly harmonious with Haydn's symphonic thinking. But there is plenty of spirited and cheerful music here, and that is well caught in these vivacious performances by Trevor Pinnock and his band, with their brisk tempos and light textures; the playing is duly agile, and the period instruments give a bright edge to the sound.

Haydn. SYMPHONIES. **Academy of Ancient Music/Christopher Hogwood.** L'Oiseau-Lyre 430 082-2OH3.
No. 21 in A major; No. 22 in E flat major, "The Philosopher"; No. 23 in G major; No. 24 in D major; No. 28 in A major; No. 29 in E major; No. 30 in C major, "Alleluja"; No. 31 in D major, "Hornsignal"; No. 34 in D minor.
③ 3h 10' DDD 12/90

As 'the father of the symphony', Haydn had over 100 children! So a complete recorded cycle is a major undertaking for any company, and the one launched with the present issue uses authentic instruments and a slightly lower pitch than modern 'concert' ones. Details of these instruments are listed in the four-language booklet, which has 70 pages including an explanation of the grouping of these works into 15 volumes—the present one, oddly enough, being No. 4 and covering the years 1764-65. The Academy of Ancient Music is usually a small orchestral body, supporting the contention expressed by Joseph Webster that Haydn's orchestra at this time was of about 13 to 16 players and that there was no keyboard continuo. In other words, there is no harpsichord to fill out textures, but although some listeners may miss it initially the playing soon convinces. The music itself cannot be summarized briefly, but as usual with Haydn, even these relatively unfamiliar pieces are inventive and often beautiful. The playing has zest, but however brisk the tempo chosen for quick movements they never degenerate into mere bustle, although other performers may take a less tense view than Christopher Hogwood. There are real discoveries to be made here, beginning with the nervous, dramatic finale to Symphony No. 21, and they also include minuets such as the enigmatic ones to Nos. 28 and 29. Similarly, slow movements have dignity, grace and often a quiet humour too, while phrasing is intelligent and affectionate and textures well balanced. Indeed, Hogwood's wind and string players alike are precise and stylish. Repeats are faithfully observed. Finally, the recording is clear and atmospheric.

Haydn. Symphonies—No. 26 in D minor, "Lamentatione"; No. 52 in C minor; No. 53 in D major, "L'Impériale". **La Petite Bande/Sigiswald Kuijken.** Virgin Classics Veritas VC7 90743-2.
62' DDD 3/89

This period instrument coupling contains some sprightly and imaginative playing. Symphony No. 26, is sub-titled *Lamentatione* and the nickname alludes to Haydn's use of Gregorian chant in the first two movements. The C minor Symphony No. 52 is a dramatic work, vividly capturing a mood of restless, brooding expectancy. Symphony No. 53, *L'Impériale*, has a glorious confidence and authority to it; the title, scholars suppose, refers to the Empress Maria Theresa. It has an air of sophistication and nobility worthy of Austria's great ruler and receives a vivid and accomplished recording. The sound throughout is warm and ingratiating.

Haydn. SYMPHONIES. **The English Concert/Trevor Pinnock.** Archiv
Produktion 429 756-2AH.
No. 42 in D major; No. 44 in E minor, "Trauer"; No. 46 in B major.

| 63' DDD 9/90 |

These are inspiriting performances of three of Haydn's greatest symphonies from
the so-called "Sturm und Drang" years of the early 1770s. Storm and stress is
most evident in the *Trauer* ("Mourning"), whose outer movements push the
contemporary musical language to new limits of violent intensity; the nickname,
incidentally, derives from the sublime *Adagio*, which Haydn is said to have
wanted played at his funeral. Symphony No. 46 is probably the only eighteenth-
century symphony in the key of B major. And with the outlandish tonality go
extremes of expression: the first movement is astonishingly tense and dark-hued
for a work of this period in the major key, while the finale is Haydn at his most
bizarrely humorous. The other work on the disc, No. 42, is a real rarity, and
may well come as a revelation to many. Both the first and second movements
have an expansiveness and a harmonic breadth new in Haydn's symphonic music;
and the finale is a delightful early example of the racy, popular style which
colours so many of his later symphonies. Using an orchestra of around 20
players, as Haydn himself would have done, Pinnock gives vital, characterful
readings, with a blend of sophistication and earthiness ideally suited to the
composer. The string playing is supple and sweet-toned—no wire-wool
associations here—and the expertly played oboes and horns cut through
pungently in the tuttis. Outer movements are boldly projected, their often
exceptional rhythmic and harmonic tension powerfully controlled. All three slow
movements are done with finesse and a beautiful sense of line (none of the
exaggerated 'squeezed' phrasing favoured in some authentic performances),
though the *Adagio* of No. 44 has a slightly too easy, *grazioso* feel. More
controversial are the minuets, taken very smartly indeed, with a loss of dignity
and grandeur in Nos. 42 and 46. But these truthfully recorded performances can
be recommended to anyone who is not ideologically opposed to period
instruments.

Haydn. Symphony No. 44 in E minor, "Trauer".
Mozart. Symphony No. 40 in G minor, K550. **St John's Smith Square
Orchestra/John Lubbock.** Pickwick IMP Red Label PCD820.

| 55' DDD 8/86 | £

Here is a performance of Mozart's No. 40 that looks deeper than the often overstated surface qualities of charm and grace, resulting in a darker and more
sinister account of this highly original work. The elusive opening is skilfully
handled, creating a fine air of expectancy. The orchestra's phrasing is always
intelligent and well articulated, and in the *Andante* they capture the restlessness
of spirit and subtle hesitations. Beautiful phrasing also pervades the *Minuet*, which
acts like an impatient upbeat to the finale, emphasized by its vague and abrupt
ending. The despairing and impassioned finale has energy and vigour as the
dramatic tension builds towards the harmonically daring development section,
notable in this performance for some excellent horn playing. Haydn's *Trauer*
Symphony receives a fine performance too, if perhaps lacking a little of the
sustained vigour and tension found in the Mozart. It is one of Haydn's finest
"Sturm und Drang" symphonies, and the first movement is noted for its dramatic
strength and dynamic contrast. The *Adagio* is beautifully played in this tender and
serene performance; this movement was reputed to be a particular favourite of
Haydn's, and he requested it to be played at his funeral (hence the nickname
Trauer). The finale regains the energy and vigour found in the Mozart, and the
clarity of the recording highlights the contrapuntal texture very well indeed.
Rewarding performances at a bargain price.

Haydn. Symphony No. 49, "La passione".
Schubert. Symphony No. 5 in B flat major, D485. **St John's Smith Square Orchestra/John Lubbock.** Pickwick IMP Classics PCD819.

| 53' DDD 1/86 | £ |

Although this reading of Schubert's charming Fifth Symphony will certainly pass muster, with straightforward playing that emphasizes the more naîve aspects of the piece, the gold on this disc is to be found in the coupled performance of Haydn's darkly urgent *La passione* Symphony. Completed in 1768, during Haydn's "Sturm und Drang" period, this work begins with a brooding *Adagio* and is followed by a vigorous, intense *Allegro di molto*. A dour *Menuetto*, with a brighter, oboe and horn dominated Trio for contrast, intervenes before the dramatic, rather brief closing *Presto*, that strangely adumbrates Mendelssohn in places. The total effect is marvellously disturbing, especially so in this involved, purposeful reading from Lubbock and the Smith Square Orchestra. They clearly have the measure of this piece and communicate its burning originality with force. Especially impressive is the way that the spirit of romanticism flourishes here without the just proportion of classicism being split asunder. The enclosed ambience of the recording intensifies the introversion of this Symphony, reflecting the isolation that Haydn welcomed at his employer's palace at Esterhaza, where he composed the work.

Haydn. Symphonies—No. 78 in C minor; No. 102 in B flat major. **Orpheus Chamber Orchestra.** DG 429 218-2GH.

| 46' DDD 5/90 | ♩P |

The Orpheus Chamber Orchestra play without a conductor, but their account of these two Haydn symphonies is splendidly precise. The key of C minor was unusual enough when No. 78 was composed in 1782 and Haydn's invention still makes the work a disturbing one, particularly when the first movement and the finale are taken at this spanking pace, surely faster than it would have been in Haydn's time but brought off well here. The quality that comes across strongly here is one of urgent energy, and even in the Adagio the articulation and dynamics keep one from cosily relaxing; but there is nothing wrong with that if the results stand on their own merits as here. We find a vivid energy also in Symphony No. 102, but although the orchestra recognize the brighter mood, sometimes one looks for more playfulness and 'smiling' quality to provide expressive contrast. Nevertheless the playing is highly skilful and though this is not a long CD, collectors wishing to investigate the relatively unfamiliar Symphony No. 78 or an alternative view of No. 102 will be rewarded, not least by the pleasing recorded quality.

Haydn. Symphonies—No. 82 in C major, "L'ours"; No. 83 in G minor, "La poule". **Concertgebouw Orchestra, Amsterdam/Sir Colin Davis.** Philips 420 688-2PH.

| 52' DDD 2/88 | ♩P   ♩S |

Haydn. Symphonies—No. 82 in C major, "L'ours"; No. 83 in G minor, "La poule"; No. 84 in E flat major. **Orchestra of the Age of Enlightenment/ Sigiswald Kuijken.** Virgin Classics Veritas VC7 90793-2.

| 78' DDD 2/90 | ✑ |

Haydn's development as a symphonic composer was given a boost in the early 1780s by a commission from the Paris "Concert de la Loge Olympique". That society's orchestra was a much larger one than Haydn had written for hitherto and he was inspired to produce some of his finest works in this form, larger in scale, more complex in structure and with a wider range of expression. This is at once shown in the arresting first movement of Symphony No. 82, *The Bear*, which has something of a military character. A spacious, flowing *Allegretto* and a stately Minuet are followed by a finale which has a first subject akin to a bear dance, over a bagpipe-like drone—hence the symphony's nickname. A certain feeling of agitation pervades the minor-key first movement of Symphony No. 83, *The Hen*, whose cackling subsidiary theme gives the work its somewhat misleading nickname. A slow *Andante* then provides a sense of calm after a storm, and the Minuet and trio shows the resurgence of Haydn's good-natured optimism, with the finale positively bubbling over with high spirits. Sir Colin Davis and the Concertgebouw Orchestra unerringly go to the heart of Haydn's endearing musical personality, and the wit, the charm and the zest of each score is wonderfully realized. The recording quality is superlative.

There are a lot of happy details and interesting revelations in Kuijken's recording of three of the *Paris* symphonies on period instruments. Although the recording is decidedly on the resonant side, the symphonies come up sounding pleasantly fresh with these spruce rhythms and lively tempos and a balance that lets the woodwind detail come sharply through. Kuijken tends to use fast tempos for the minuets, which is in line with current early music orthodoxy, but he might have done well to reflect on the significance of the *allegretto* markings in those of Nos. 83 and 84, which imply something a little more measured than this. Number 84, a symphony we do not often hear, fares particularly well here, with a fine rhythm to the opening movement and an alert and pointed finale.

Haydn. Symphonies—No. 85 in B flat major, "La reine"; No. 86 in D major; No. 87 in A major. **Orchestra of the Age of Enlightenment/Sigiswald Kuijken.** Virgin Classics Veritas VC7 90844-2.

79' DDD 5/90

The mention of period instruments can make people fear (with occasional good reason) that they will hear playing less notable for persuasiveness than for bluntness and sometimes roughness of interpretation and execution. If so, this recording should open minds, for the playing is clean yet fully stylish and expressive and there is no question of accepting dull string tone or poor woodwind intonation in the name of the god Authenticity. The period flavour is there all right (listen for example to the clean sound of the oboe and bassoon in Symphony No. 85, and the crisp strings and overall texture) but it convinces. So do the tempos, phrasing, dynamics and articulation, the latter being sharper than with most modern orchestras and making the latter sound heavy by comparison. To this fine playing under young the Belgian conductor you might add that these three symphonies are masterpieces of Haydn's wonderful Indian summer of his sixties, that the 1989 recording in EMI's Abbey Road Studios is atmospheric in the right degree, and that a total length of nearly 80 minutes results in a most attractive CD. The booklet gives useful details of the instruments played in each work, mostly eighteenth-century originals in the case of the strings with modern replicas for wind and nineteenth-century timpani in Symphony No. 86.

Haydn. Symphonies—No. 90 in C major; No. 93 in D major. **Orchestra of the Eighteenth Century/Frans Brüggen.** Philips 422 022-2PH. Recorded at performances in The Netherlands during 1987.

51' DDD 5/88

These performances are of a calibre which deserve to be noticed. Amongst the many delights of this recording are the mellow sound and warm textures of the wind instruments and the generally high level of technical expertise with which they are played. Haydn's wind writing is usually interesting, sometimes witty and, especially in the case of the horns, often extremely difficult to play. These fine players surmount most of the difficulties with an admirable degree of self-assurance and Brüggen's direction is always lively. Lovers of Haydn's music should find much that is rewarding in this issue.

Haydn. LONDON SYMPHONIES. **Austro-Hungarian Haydn Orchestra/ Adám Fischer.** Nimbus NI5200/4.
No. 93 in D major; No. 94 in G major, "Surprise"; No. 95 in C minor; No. 96 in D major, "Miracle"; No. 97 in C major; No. 98 in B flat major; No. 99 in E flat major; No. 100 in G major, "Military"; No. 101 in D major, "Clock"; No. 102 in B flat major; No. 103 in E flat major, "Drumroll"; No. 104 in D major, "London".

⑤ 5h 16' DDD 12/89   Ⓑ

Together these symphonies form a grand apotheosis to Haydn's symphonic output, into which he poured everything he had learned in his 50 years of creativity. Haydn's aim was always to please both the ordinary music lover and the expert, and nowhere is this more evident than in these wonderful symphonies. These are elegant and stylish performances, with generally unhurried tempos which allow the music's natural wit and elegance to surface without duress. The weighty Adagio introductions are given plenty of poise and stature without resorting to pomposity or overstatement, while the following Allegros have the perfect blend of exuberance and finesse. The dance rhythms of the Menuets are on the whole finely pointed and there is much buoyancy and spiritedness in these movements. The famous "Clock Menuet" from No. 101 is delivered with a delicious sense of tongue-in-cheek seriousness, and the Menuet from the *Surprise* is delightfully swaggish. The playing throughout this set is very fine indeed, Fischer obtains some beautifully turned phrasing from his players, and the wind section deserve special mention for their pure intonation and sweetness of tone. The overall impression of these performances is one of *joie de vivre*. The finely balanced recordings are slightly reverberant, though never to the point of obscuring detail or articulation, with a warm and atmospheric acoustic. This set provides an excellent bargain for anyone who prefers the consistency of one conductor's approach, and who would rather not shop around for individual performances with the inevitability of duplications.

Haydn. Symphonies—No. 92 in G major, "Oxford"; No. 104 in D major, "London". **English Sinfonia/Sir Charles Groves.** Pickwick IMP Classics PCD916.

  55' DDD 6/89

Haydn. Symphonies—No. 91 in E flat major; No. 92 in G major, "Oxford". **Concertgebouw Orchestra, Amsterdam/Sir Colin Davis.** Philips 410 390-2PH. From 410 390-1PH (3/84).

  51' DDD 4/85   ⁹ₚ ⁹ₛ

Haydn. Symphonies—No. 102 in B flat major; No. 104 in D major, "London". **English Chamber Orchestra/Jeffrey Tate.** EMI CDC7 47462-2. From EL270451-1 (3/87).

  57' DDD 5/87

In 1790, with the death of Prince Nicholas Esterházy, Haydn found himself free to travel and compose for whom he chose. He was quickly signed up by Johann Peter Salomon, who brought him to London in 1791 and 1794 for two highly successful seasons. During his stay, Haydn composed the twelve symphonies, known collectively as the *London* symphonies (though only the last, No. 104,

Sir Charles Groves [photo: Vandyck]

bears the name of the capital), specifically for his English audiences. During the first visit, Haydn accepted an honorary doctorate from Oxford and, not having time to compose a work specially for the occasion, performed Symphony No. 92. The work has since borne the name of the University city, in honour of the event. Both the works on this disc have, in common with the other *London* symphonies, a directness and depth of meaning that show Haydn at the very peak of his compositional powers. Typically, though, they require a lightness of touch in performance to allow the essential elegance of their idiom to make full impact. Sir Charles Groves gets the balance of intensity and shapeliness just right, and the relaxed, ideally distanced recording is the perfect complement.

Symphony No. 91 only seems less exalted by comparison with such heights, for it too shows not only the finest degree of craftsmanship of which Haydn was capable but also those hints of other-worldliness that underpin much of his greatest and most mature compositions. Sir Colin Davis and the Concertgebouw play with honesty and simple, unpretentious musicianship; an approach that makes these performances very successful. Although much work must have gone into creating such artless simplicity, it seems as though the music plays itself and the listener has a direct line with the composer's ideas. The timeless *Adagio* of the Oxford provides a fine example and Davis produces pure emotions that are very moving. With first-rate, natural sound these recordings demand a place in any collection.

Tate's *London* Symphonies have all the attributes found in his readings of Nos. 100 and 103: relaxed tempos, freshness of approach and a buoyancy that keeps the music flowing and animated. Perhaps at times there is a touch more weight in these performances, but that is as it should be, as these Symphonies are inclined towards ebulliency and grandeur—qualities that are superbly brought out in Symphony No. 104. The *Adagio* of No. 102 has suavity and elegance, and the following *Menuetto*'s dance rhythms are strongly projected, demonstrating Tate's ability to adapt to Haydn's sharply contrasting moods. Once again the recorded sound is warm and finely balanced, with perhaps a shade more bite and brilliance to the upper strings.

Haydn. Symphonies—No. 93 in D major; No. 94 in G major, "Surprise"; No. 96 in D major, "The Miracle". **Concertgebouw Orchestra, Amsterdam/Sir Colin Davis.** Philips 412 871-2PH. From 6725 010 (6/82).

68' DDD 1/86

The ever popular *Surprise* Symphony needs no introduction, but it should be pointed out that the *Miracle* and No. 93 are in no way inferior, either in melodic inspiration or compositional ingenuity. These performances are some of the finest to appear in recent years. Above all, Sir Colin Davis shows a strong feeling for the ebullient humour that lies at the heart of this music: slow movements are highly expressive without ever becoming sentensious, and the *allegros* do indeed "dance and leap" (Haydn's own description) with elegant quickness. The playing of the Concertgebouw Orchestra is lively, quick-witted and deliciously refined, and the recordings are attentive, well balanced and warmly atmospheric.

Haydn. Symphonies—No. 100 in G major, "Military"; No. 104 in D major, "London". **Concertgebouw Orchestra, Amsterdam/Sir Colin Davis.** Philips 411 449-2PH. From 9500 510 (3/79).

> 54' ADD 10/84

The *Military* proved to be one of Haydn's most popular symphonies when it was first performed in 1794, creating such a frenzy in the audience that the Symphony had to be repeated many times during Haydn's stay in London. Its fascination with the public was mainly due to Haydn's inclusion in the second and fourth movements of the then fashionable Turkish instruments: cymbals, triangle, and bass-drum, which gave the work a rather military character. This is another marvellous Haydn disc from Sir Colin Davis and the Concertgebouw Orchestra. The interpretations are splendidly idiomatic, and the playing of the Concertgebouw is a continual delight. The overall impression is of brightness, wit and untramelled energy and though the original recording is pre-digital, the range and clarity of the sound are as fine as in any contemporary issue.

Haydn. String Quartets—C major, Op. 20 No. 2; B flat major, Op. 50 No. 1; D minor, Op. 76 No. 2, "Fifths". **Lindsay Quartet** (Peter Cropper, Ronald Birks, vns; Robin Ireland, va; Bernard Gregor-Smith, vc). ASV CDDCA622. Recorded at a performance in the Wigmore Hall, London during the "Genius of Haydn" Festival in September 1987.

> 63' DDD 9/88

The second of the *Sun* Quartets (Op. 20) has a gently paced but rich first movement, a dramatic *Capriccio* that gives way to a lyrical *arioso*, flowing into a far from formal Minuet and Trio, and a fugal finale which develops in whispers until vigorous homophony finally prevails. Haydn dedicated his Op. 50 set (the *Prussian* Quartets) to King Friedrich Wilhelm, an amateur cellist, and they are marked by the thematic economy typified in the first movement of No. 1. The finale is another sonata-form movement, likewise sparing with its material, en route to which is a delightful theme, three variations and coda (*Adagio non lento*), and a robust Minuet with a tip-toeing Trio. Count Joseph Erdödy was the dedicatee of the Quartets Op. 76 (1797) and are abundantly nicknamed. The whole work is a torrent of invention, Haydn at his most compelling. These recordings were made live in the Wigmore Hall, a virtual guarantee of a sympathetic acoustic: the presence of an audience can be hazardous, but here it served only to stimulate the Lindsay Quartet to performances so riveting that there isn't so much as a sniffle to be heard—only the richly earned applause at the end of each work.

Haydn. String Quartets, Op. 54—No. 1 in G major; No. 2 in C major; No. 3 in E major. **Lindsay Quartet** (Peter Cropper, Robin Ireland, vns; Ronald Birks, va; Bernard Gregor-Smith, vc). ASV CDDCA582.

> 66' DDD 8/87

All three quartets are in the usual four-movement form but with many surprises: in No. 1, the false recapitulation in the first movement, the dark modulations in the following sonata-form *Allegretto* and the Hungarian-gipsy flavour (anticipated in the Minuet) and mischievousness of the final Rondo. Number 2 has a rhapsodic fiddler in its second movement, a nostalgic Minuet with an extraordinarily anguished Trio, and an *Adagio* finale in which a *Presto* section turns out to be no more than an episode. A notable feature of No. 3 is its tenary-form *Largo cantabile*, the centre of which is more like a mini-concerto for the first violin; 'Scotch snaps' pervade the Minuet, and pedal points the finale. The performances (and the recording) are superb, marked by unanimity, fine tone, suppleness of phrasing, and acute dynamic shaping; in the second movement of No. 1 there are hushed passages whose homogeneity and quality of sound is quite remarkable. Even more remarkable would be the Haydn lover who found this recording resistible.

Haydn. String Quartets—D major, Op. 64 No. 5, "Lark"; C major, Op. 54 No. 2. **Gabrieli Quartet** (Kenneth Sillito, Brendan O'Reilly, vns; Ian Jewel, va; Keith Harvey, vc). Chandos CHAN8531.

39' DDD 11/87

These are fabulous works, supremely inventive and remarkably innovative, with movements very much integrated into a symphonic-type structure. Few who hear the magical opening of Op. 64 No. 5 can fail to respond to Haydn's arrestingly simple opening. Few, too, could remain unmoved by the depth of emotion conveyed in Haydn's slow movements, by his impassioned melodic lines and astonishing harmonic daring. These are unquestionable masterpieces and are as central to the quartet repertoire as are the greatest essays in the medium from Mozart or Beethoven. The Gabrieli Quartet play very beautifully, demonstrating a deep understanding of both the moment and the movement.

Haydn. String Quartets—E flat major, Op. 71 No. 3; C major, Op. 74 No. 1. **Salomon Quartet** (Simon Standage, Micaela Comberti, vns; Trevor Jones, va; Jennifer Ward Clarke, vc). Hyperion CDA66098. From A66098 (3/84).

59' AAD 12/87

The two Quartets heard here are particularly fine examples of Haydn's late period. Written especially for performance in the concert hall, as opposed to the drawing room, they are much more 'public' in stance than his earlier quartets, with a deliberately more sonorous, almost orchestral, approach which is better tailored to a larger acoustic. They are more public too in having, all of them except one, a symphonic-like opening flourish. The emotional focal point of both is the second, slow movement and it is here that Haydn produces some of his most daring harmonic innovations, his most forward-looking effects in instrumentation. The aptly-named Salomon Quartet specialize in the performance of music from the eighteenth century and they play on instruments of the period. Balancing its more serious vein, Haydn's music is elsewhere full of wit and spirit and the Salomons are very responsive to every turn he takes, revelling in his constant inventiveness. Highly recommended.

Haydn. Apponyi String Quartets—F major, Op. 74 No. 2; G minor, Op. 74 No. 3, "The Rider". **Salomon Quartet** (Simon Standage, Micaela Comberti, vns; Trevor Jones, va; Jennifer Ward Clarke, vc). Hyperion CDA66124. From A66124 (9/84).

53' DDD 3/87

The period instruments of the Salomon Quartet give a deliciously clean-edged feel to these Quartets. With minimal use of vibrato they bring an extraordinary intensity to the concentrated writing of the two slow movements. The sheer rightness of the rhythms give these performances a solid foundation best felt in the unwavering pulse of the minuets' reprise after the trios. The finale of the G minor Quartet, the movement which gives it its nickname *The Rider*, has tremendous sparkle and wit, greatly enhanced by the silvery tone of the top strings and the very immediate feel of bow on gut in the bouncing accompaniment. The recording is all you could wish for: clean, focused but nicely spacious. A delightful disc.

Haydn. String Quartets, Op. 76—No. 4 in B flat major; No. 5 in D major; No. 6 in E flat major. **Takács Quartet** (Gábor Takács-Nagy, Károly Schranz, vns; Gábor Omai, va; András Fejér, vc). Decca 425 467-2DH.

68' DDD 1/90

In these three quartets from a set of six published in 1797, one can only be delighted by the sheer invention that Haydn showed in his sixties. This youthful Hungarian ensemble bring to this music a freshness that does not inhibit them from the necessary underlining of this or that point. The *Sunrise* Quartet is invigorating in the first movement and lyrically broad in the Adagio, and the

syncopated minuet and lilting finale are no less delightful. The D major Quartet starts with an Allegretto suggesting a set of variations but then moves into a section in new keys before ending with a brisk coda. The slow movement's *cantabile e mesto* marking is fully realized, as is the major-minor contrast of the minuet and the playful Presto finale, which begins with an unmistakable joke of six bars that sound more like the end of a movement. The third of these quartets begins with variations that culminate in a fugato; the slow movement (called a fantasia) is another original, and this is followed by a

The Takács Quartet   [*photo: Decca*]

witty scherzo and a finale in which scale fragments participate in a game of dizzy contrapuntal complexity. The recording, made in a London church, is immediate yet atmospheric, although with a touch of glare that tone controls will tame.

Haydn. String Quartets—G major, Op. 77 No. 1; F major, Op. 77 No. 2; D minor, Op. 103 (unfinished). **Mosaïques Quartet** (Erich Höbarth, Andrea Bischof, vns; Anita Mitterer, va; Christophe Coin, vc). Auvidis Astrée E8799.

62' DDD 2/90

Anyone who thinks that period-instrument performance means austerity and coolness should listen to this disc. Here is a group of youngish French players, using instruments of the kind Haydn would have heard, played (as far as we can know) in a style he would have been familiar with: the result is a disc full of expressive warmth and vigour. The opening of Op. 77 No. 1 is done duly gracefully, but with a sturdy underlying rhythm and the Scherzo is as crisp and alive as one could ask for. Then the first movement of the F major work is very beautifully done, with many sensitive details; and the lovely second movement is happily leisurely, so that the players have ample room for manoeuvre and the leader makes much of his opportunities for delicate playing in the filigree-like high music. The players show a real grasp of the structure and they know when to illuminate the key moments, with a touch of extra deliberation or a little additional weight of tone. These performances, clearly recorded, are competitive ones not merely within the protected world of 'early music' but in the bigger, 'real' world too!

Haydn. PIANO SONATAS. **Emanuel Ax** (pf). CBS Masterworks CD44918. *Sonatas:* C minor, HobXVI/20; F major, HobXVI/23; C major, HobXVI/48; C major, HobXVI/50.

⏺ **64' DDD 12/89**

Here is another powerful antidote to the notion of Haydn as a kind of clever comedian—and it seems the point still has to be made. Emanuel Ax avoids romantic overstatement throughout these performances; the interpretation sounds as if it's felt from within the notes, rather than applied to them. Ax can bring out the high seriousness of the great C minor Sonata's first movement without trying to 'Beethovenize' the drama, while in Sonata No. 60 he can pass from childlike humour in the opening theme to taut symphonic argument without a trace of incongruity. Most impressive of all though is his feeling for dramatic shape: the slow first movement of Sonata No. 58 grows steadily to a powerful final climax—as, with very different effect, does the C minor's opening *Moderato*: there's something truly tragic about the final resolution. The slight distant reverberation is a little disconcerting at first—as though Ax were playing to a large deserted auditorium—but it's soon accepted.

Haydn. PIANO WORKS. **Alfred Brendel** (pf). Philips 416 643-2PH4. Booklet included.
Sonatas—C minor, HobXVI/20; E flat major, HobXVI/49 (both from 9500 774, 8/81); E minor, HobXVI/34; B minor, HobXVI/32; D major, Hob XVI/42 (412 228-1PH, 8/85); C major, HobXVI/48; D major, HobXVI/51; C major, Hob XVI/50 (6514 317, 11/83); E flat major, HobXVI/52; G major, HobXVI/40; D major, HobXVI/37 (416 365-1PH, 12/86). Fantasia in C major, HobXVI/4. Adagio in F major, HobXVI/9 (412 228-1PH, 8/85). Andante with variations in F minor, Hob XVI/6 (416 365-1PH, 12/86).

⏺ ④ **52' 55' 37' 61' ADD/DDD 3/87**

The Sonatas collected in this set are some magnificent creations wonderfully well played by Alfred Brendel. Within the order and scale of these works Haydn explores a rich diversity of musical languages, a wit and broadness of expression that quickly repays attentive listening. It is the capriciousness as much as the poetry that Brendel so perfectly attends to; his playing, ever alive to the vitality and subtleties, makes these discs such a delight. The sophistication innate in the simple dance rhythms, the rusticity that emerges, but above all, the sheer *joie de vivre* are gladly embraced. Brendel shows in this music what makes a merely technically accomplished player a truly great one—his continual illumination of the musical ideas through intense study pays huge dividends. The recording quality varies enormously between the various works and though the close acoustic on some of the later discs could be faulted for allowing one to hear too much of the keyboard action, it certainly brings one into vivid contact with the music.

Haydn. Mass in D minor, "Nelson"[a]. Te Deum in C major, HobXXIIIc/2.
[a]**Felicity Lott** (sop); [a]**Carolyn Watkinson** (contr); [a]**Maldwyn Davies** (ten); [a]**David Wilson-Johnson** (bar); **The English Concert and Choir/Trevor Pinnock.** Archiv Produktion 423 097-2AH. Texts and translations included.

⏺ **50' ADD 2/88**

The British Admiral had ousted the Napoleonic fleet at the Battle of the Nile just as Haydn was in the middle of writing his *Nelson* Mass. Although the news could not have reached him until after its completion, Haydn's awareness of the international situation was expressed in the work's subtitle, "Missa in Augustiis", or "Mass in times of fear". With its rattle of timpani, its pungent trumpet calls, and its highly-strung harmonic structure, there is no work of Haydn's which cries out so loudly for recording on period instruments; and it is the distinctive sonority and charged tempos of this performance which sets it apart from its competitors. The dry, hard timpani and long trumpets bite into the dissonance of the opening *Kyrie*, and the near vibrato-less string playing is mordant and urgent. The fast-slow-fast triptych of the *Gloria* is set out in nervously contrasted speeds, and the *Credo* bounces with affirmation. Just as the choral singing is meticulously balanced with instrumental inflection, so the soloists have been chosen to highlight the colours in Pinnock's palette. This is an unusually exciting recording.

Haydn. Die Jahreszeiten. **Gundula Janowitz** (sop); **Werner Hollweg** (ten); **Walter Berry** (bass); **Chorus of the Deutsche Oper, Berlin; Berlin Philharmonic Orchestra/Herbert von Karajan.** EMI CMS7 69224-2. Text and translation included. From SLS969 (9/73).

● ② 2h 33' ADD 7/88 £

Haydn's oratorio *The Seasons* is a work full of charm and rustic good humour. Karajan has always been a stylish Haydn conductor, not surprisingly opting for a rather heavier approach than some of his colleagues, but never failing to find the ideal pace and tempo. His feeling for atmosphere finds outlet in his masterly portrayal of the freezing of winter and the spring's warming and melting—the Berlin strings are superb. The chorus brings real colour and rustic abandon to their contributions and throw themselves into the feast-tide celebrations with great verve. The soloists are well chosen. Gundula Janowitz makes a radiant Hanna, blending a simple, untrammelled beauty of expression in her recitatives with a mellower, warmer tone for her arias. Walter Berry is a robust Simon and Werner Hollweg brings a fine artistry to bear on the rich melodies given to Lukas—his *mezza voce* singing is a real delight. The balance between soloists, chorus and orchestra is nicely handled. At mid price this is a most recommendable version of a work brimful of bucolic charm and high spirits.

Haydn. Die Schöpfung. **Edita Gruberová** (sop); **Josef Protschka** (ten); **Robert Holl** (bass); **Arnold Schönberg Choir; Vienna Symphony Orchestra/Nikolaus Harnoncourt.** Teldec 2292-42682-2. Notes, text and translation included. Recorded at performances in the Konzerthaus, Vienna on April 10th and 11th, 1986.

● ② 1h 55' DDD 4/87 Ⓑ

Haydn. Die Schöpfung (sung in English). **Emma Kirkby** (sop); **Anthony Rolfe Johnson** (ten); **Michael George** (bass); **Choir of New College, Oxford; Academy of Ancient Music Chorus and Orchestra/ Christopher Hogwood.** L'Oiseau-Lyre 430 397-2OH2. Text included.

● ② 99' DDD 3/91

It was a glimpse of the heavens through the telescope of his astronomer friend, William Herschel, which gave Haydn the final excited impetus to compose his great oratorio, *The Creation*. Any performance which fails to recreate a comparable sense of awe is wasting its time. Harnoncourt here awakes just that sense of delight and wonder in both his performers and his listeners. The soloists are well-picked: neither too operatic nor too ethereal for their purpose. Robert Holl's Raphael is at once man and god, awesome and authoritative; Josef

Protschka a Uriel tremulous with joy; and Edita Gruberová both radiant and heroic as Gabriel and Eve.

The claims to historical authenticity made on behalf of Hogwood's performance of Haydn's oratorio, *The Creation,* are diffuse and overstated, but that need not worry the listener overmuch, for what counts is the performance itself. It is the second to have been recorded using period instruments but the first to use Peter Brown's new performing edition based on appropriate sources. The Academy of Ancient Music fields an orchestra, here expanded to 115 players together with the Choir of New College, Oxford and a strong solo vocal group. The results are mostly satisfying and the performance greatly enhanced by a sympathetic recorded balance which captures the distinctive character of period instruments. When Haydn published the first edition, it included both German and English texts and it would seem probable that he intended one or other to be sung according to the nationality of the audience. This version is sung in English, a feature that many listeners will find illuminating. All-in-all this is an enterprising project which has largely succeeded in achieving its aim as outlined by the Director of the performance, Christopher Hogwood "to recapture in sound, scale and text the performances conducted by the composer". The booklet contains full texts in four languages and an informative essay.

Haydn. Stabat mater. **Patricia Rozario** (sop); **Catherine Robbin** (mez); **Anthony Rolfe Johnson** (ten); **Cornelius Hauptmann** (bass); **The English Concert and Choir/Trevor Pinnock.** Archiv Produktion 429 733-2AH.

> 69'　DDD　9/90

Haydn's deeply expressive *Stabat mater* for soloists, choir and orchestra is all too seldom performed. Composed in 1767 it hints strongly at the *Sturm und Drang* idiom that was to characterize Haydn's music over the next few years. Boldly contrasting juxtapositions, vivid dynamic shading, chromaticism, syncopation and gently sighing gestures all contribute towards an expressive intensity which affectingly complements the celebrated Latin poem. Trevor Pinnock has assembled a fine quartet of soloists whose voices, singly and in varying ensembles are sympathetically partnered by warm-sounding and stylish playing by The English Concert. The choir of The English Concert is effective, too, with well-balanced ensemble and textural clarity. One of the most alluring numbers of the work is the quartet and chorus, "Virgo virginium praeclara" in which all the various components of Haydn's forces join in a fervent, sorrowful prayer of sustained beauty. The recording is ideally resonant yet capturing many details of colour and nuance present in the character of period instruments. The booklet includes the full text of the poem in three languages.

Hans Werner Henze

German 1926-

Henze. SYMPHONIES. ªBerlin Philharmonic Orchestra; ᵇLondon Symphony Orchestra/Hans Werner Henze. DG 20th Century Classics 429 854-2GC2. Items marked ª from SLPM139203/4 (1/67), ᵇ 2530 261 (11/72). No. 1 (1947, rev. 1963)ª; No. 2 (1949)ª; No. 3 (1949-50)ª; No. 4 (1955)ª; No. 5 (1962)ª; No. 6 (1969)ᵇ.

> ② 2h 30'　ADD　12/90

Hans Werner Henze is one of the few remaining composers to continue the German symphonic tradition, which make these authoritative recordings all the more invaluable and welcome. Henze was only 21 when he produced his First

Hans Werner Henze   *[photo: DG/Auerbach*

Symphony, and though it clearly owes much to Bartók, Stravinsky and Hindemith it is nevertheless a remarkable work for a composer so young. The Second Symphony, completed only two years after the First, is a dark and sombre work, and orchestrated in a style closer to Berg and Schoenberg than any later composer. It is here, also, that his preoccupation with the theatre begins to emerge, until in the Third, Fourth and Fifth Symphonies it becomes integrally part of the structure. The Third dates from the period when he was artistic director of the Wiesbaden Ballet, and its three movements: "Invocation of Apollo", "Dithyramb" and "Conjuring Dance" clearly evoke the spirit of the dance, within the formal structure of its symphonic argument. The Fourth and Fifth Symphonies quote heavily from his operas *König Hirsch* and *Elegy for Young Lovers*, and also begin to reflect his move from Germany to Italy, which brought about a greater feeling of 'arioso' lyricism and poetry to his style. The most radical is the Sixth, which dates from 1969 whilst Henze was living in Cuba, and we find him confronting and re-examining not only his own personal past (and political affiliations), but also the 'bourgeois' new music of the time. A valuable set that repays more and more with repeat hearings.

Victor Herbert

American/Irish 1859-1924

Herbert. Cello Concertos—No. 1 in D major, Op. 8; No. 2 in E minor, Op. 30. Five Pieces for cello and strings (trans. Dennison). **Lynn Harrell** (vc); **Academy of St Martin in the Fields/Sir Neville Marriner.** Decca 417 672-2DH.
Cello Pieces—Yesterthoughts; Pensée amoureuse; Punchinello; Ghazel; The Mountain Brook.

    67'   DDD 10/88

Victor Herbert is best known nowadays as the composer of romantic American operettas. However, in his early days he was a cello virtuoso and composed many works for the instrument. The second of his two cello concertos is a powerful piece that is said to have influenced Dvořák to compose his own concerto for the instrument. The First Concerto remained in manuscript until recently and now provides a most rewarding surprise, since it offers the same characteristics of romantic warmth and subtle interplay of soloist and orchestra with even more melodic appeal. The second movement, with a sprightly scherzo section framed by an affecting andante, and ending with the soloist at the very top of the 'cello register, is a real winner. Lynn Harrell brings to the works not only virtuoso technique but an emotional intensity and variety of tone missing in previous recordings of the Second Concerto, and both accompaniment and recording are first class. The inclusion of transcriptions of five of Herbert's short pieces adds up to a very well-filled and immensely rewarding collection.

Hildegard of Bingen

German 1098-1179

Hildegard of Bingen. Sequences and Hymns. **Gothic Voices/ Christopher Page** with **Doreen Muskett** (symphony); **Robert White** (reed drones). Hyperion CDA66039. Texts and translation included. From A66039 (7/82).
Columba aspexit. Ave, generosa. O ignis spiritus. O Jerusalem. O Euchari. O viridissima virga. O presul vere civitatis. O Ecclesia.

44' DDD 7/85

Before 1981 Abbess Hildegard of Bingen was little more than a shadowy name in a brief paragraph in the music history text-books. Christopher Page and Gothic Voices have changed all that, revealing her to the world as one of the "greatest creative personalities of the Middle Ages". Hildegard once described herself as a "feather on the breath of God", writing and composing under divine impulsion. Now, with the arrival of this remarkable recording, a selection of her hymns and sequences has had new life breathed into it by these refreshingly unsophisticated performances. The music is all single line monody, freely composed in a modal idiom that owes much to the sort of music Hildegard was singing every day in choir. But these pieces are infused with a lyricism, sometimes even an ecstasy, that are entirely her own, and which seem to have a particular appeal to modern ears. This CD is an outright winner that merits a place in every collection.

Paul Hindemith

German 1895-1963

Hindemith. Horn Concerto (1950)[a].
R. Strauss. Horn Concertos[b]—No. 1 in E flat major, Op. 11; No. 2 in E flat major. **Dennis Brain** (hn); **Philharmonia Orchestra/**[a]**Paul Hindemith,** [b]**Wolfgang Sawallisch.** EMI CDC7 47834-2 . Item marked [a] from HLS7001 (3/72), [b] Columbia mono 33CX1491 (11/57).

49' ADD 10/87

The First Horn Concerto, written at the age of 18, turned out to be Richard Strauss's first really successful composition, already typical in many respects of the mature composer to be. The Second Concerto dates from 1942 and looks back to his early years. The later concerto shows an obviously much more experienced hand at work: the scoring is more resourceful and adventurous, the structure of the work more sophisticated. Hindemith wrote his only horn concerto in 1949 for Dennis Brain, whose score he later inscribed with the words "To the unsurpassed original performer of this piece from a grateful composer". The work is quite short and unusual in construction, with two very brief quicker movements succeeded by a longer slow movement in the form of a palindrome. After Strauss's warm romanticism Hindemith's work seems a little severe at first, but it has its own very distinct character and wit. It would be difficult to imagine more accomplished, more confident and exuberant performances than these by Dennis Brain. The Hindemith was recorded in stereo, and is in good sound: the Strauss concertos were recorded in mono only, and the orchestral sound was never good for its date. This transfer has even less body than the original LP, but fortunately Brain's unique and instantly recognizable tone quality comes through unscathed.

Hindemith. Mathis der Maler—symphony. Trauermusik[a]. Symphonic Metamorphosis on Themes of Carl Maria von Weber. [a]**Geraldine Walther** (va); **San Francisco Symphony Orchestra/Herbert Blomstedt.** Decca 421 523-2DH.

· 55' DDD 10/88

Hindemith. Mathis der Maler—symphony. Symphonic Metamorphosis on Themes of Carl Maria von Weber. Konzertmusik for strings and brass, Op. 50. **Israel Philharmonic Orchestra/Leonard Bernstein.** DG 429 404-2GH. Recorded at performances in the Frederic R. Mann Auditorium, Tel Aviv in April 1989.

· 67' DDD 5/91

Hindemith. Symphonic Metamorphosis on Themes of Carl Maria von Weber. **Reger.** Variations and Fugue on a Theme of Mozart, Op. 132. **Bavarian Radio Symphony Orchestra/Sir Colin Davis.** Philips 422 347-2PH.

· 55' DDD 9/90

The charge sometimes levelled against Hindemith of being dry and cerebral utterly collapses in the face of Blomstedt's disc. Masterly craftsmanship and virtuosity there is in plenty; but the powerful emotions of *Mathis der Maler* and the festive high spirits of the *Symphonic Metamorphosis* could not be denied except by those who wilfully close their ears. Each of the three movements of the *Mathis* symphony is based on a panel of Grünewald's great Isenheim altar. The eventual glorious illumination of "The angels" folk-tune, the poignant slow movement and the blazing triumphant Allelujas after the desperate struggle with the demons in the finale have a searing intensity in this performance, which also presents Hindemith's elaborate web of counterpoints with the utmost lucidity. For brilliant and joyously ebullient orchestral writing few works can match that based on Weber's piano duets and his *Turandot* overture: here the San Francisco woodwind and brass have a field day. In addition, this warmly recommended disc contains a heartfelt performance of the touching elegy on the death of King George V which Hindemith wrote overnight in 1936.

One can't help feeling that, had it been available, Tony Palmer would have used Bernstein's account of the *Mathis der Maler* Symphony for his South Bank Show film on Hindemith's masterpiece. Arguably the Israel woodwinds are not as spirited as Decca's version and the heart is too readily on the sleeve for the sad, withdrawn second movement, but the impact of St Anthony's torments in the finale is thrillingly graphic with Bernstein literally hurling the music's imagery at us. Here the winds of Hell blow at nothing less than hurricane force. The *Konzertmusik* and *Symphonic Metamorphosis* were both written for American orchestras, but although Bernstein was not on home ground for this recording, it's hard to imagine a more exuberant swing and swagger in the big band echoes of both works. The DG engineering is appropriately dry and clear, the balance, perhaps, co-ordinated as much from the mixing desk as the conductor, but there's no denying that the impact of the recording with the conductor's exhalations, exhortations and reinforced podium much in evidence is as physical as that of the performances. One of Bernstein's last recordings, this one unmistakably live, and a disc to treasure.

Debussy once dismissed variation technique as "an easy way of making a lot out of a little". It is certainly astonishing what Reger manages to make out of Mozart's little theme (one of those tunes you know, even if you didn't know that you knew it) and the long journey to the inevitable king-sized fugue is full

of late romantic nostalgia, fantasy and an enlivening lightness of touch. If, to quote Wilfred Mellers, Reger's "chromatic elaboration did not follow Tristan into a transfigured night", his writing for strings is surely as sensuous as in Schoenberg's early masterpiece. The flavour of Davis's performance of Hindemith's *Symphonic Metamorphosis* is more Anglo-Bavarian than American but, as in the Reger, the playing is superb and the sound very natural.

Hindemith. When Lilacs Last in the Door-yard Bloom'd (Requiem for those we love). **Jan DeGaetani** (mez); **William Stone** (bar); **Atlanta Symphony Chorus and Orchestra/Robert Shaw.** Telarc CD80132. Text included.

· 62' DDD 7/87

Taking as his text Walt Whitman's poem, a work laden with imagery and layers of association, written to mourn the death of President Lincoln, Hindemith adds further layers of meaning to this already intense poem. He was commissioned to compose the work by Robert Shaw for his New York-based Collegiate Chorale so it is appropriate and gratifying to be recommending a recording made some 40 years later by that same Robert Shaw. Hindemith's setting of the poem perfectly moulds itself to Whitman's somewhat sectionalized approach and the virtuosity involved is balanced, if not outweighed, by the sheer power and beauty of the music. Like the lilacs of Whitman's poem the music has a pungency that lingers long after the piece has ended. Shaw's grasp of the subtleties and powerful imagery of the text is total and his experience of the work pays enormous dividends in this moving performance. William Stone is a very sympathetic and sweet-toned baritone matched by Jan DeGaetani's pure mezzo. Shaw's choral and orchestral forces point up every subtlety and the recording is first rate.

Gustav Holst

British 1874-1934

Holst. The Planets, H125. Women's voices of the **Montreal Symphony Chorus; Montreal Symphony Orchestra/Charles Dutoit.** Decca 417 553-2DH.

· 53' DDD 4/87   Ⓑ

Holst. The Planets, H125[a]. The Perfect Fool, H150—ballet music[b]. Egdon Heath, H127[b]. [a]Women's voices of the **London Philharmonic Choir; London Philharmonic Orchestra/**[a]**Sir Georg Solti,** [b]**Sir Adrian Boult.** Decca London 425 152-2LM. Item marked [a] from SET628 (3/79), [b] SXL6006 (9/62).

· 74' ADD 12/89   £ Ⓑ

Holst's brilliantly coloured orchestral suite, *The Planets*, is undoubtedly his most famous work and its success is surely deserved. The musical characterization is as striking as its originality of conception: the association of "Saturn" with old age, for instance, is as unexpected as it is perceptive. Bax introduced Holst to astrology and while he wrote the music he became fascinated with horoscopes, so it is the astrological associations that are paramount, although the linking of "Mars" (with its enormously powerful 5/4 rhythms) and war also reflects the time of composition. Throughout, the work's invention is as memorable as its vivid orchestration is full of infinite detail. No recording can reveal it all but this one comes the closest to doing so. Dutoit's individual performance is in a long line of outstanding recordings.

The second Decca issue brings together three excellent Holst performances on one mid-price CD, with a total playing time of nearly 74 minutes to boot: superb value for money if ever there was. The sleeve-note to the *Planets* informs us that Solti listened to Holst's own recording of 1926 before recording this disc. Those who are familiar with Holst's account will notice that although the timings of some movements differ, Solti has remained faithful to Holst's view that rhythmic incisiveness and clarity of detail are of the utmost importance in this work. Holst said that "Mars, the Bringer of War" should sound "unpleasant and terrifying", and it is those qualities that are brought out in Solti's relentless and icy account. The rhythmic vitality of his performance is heard to great effect in "Jupiter", with the big tune in the middle (later to be set as a hymn to the words "I vow to thee my country") sounding beautifully poised and heartfelt. Timings are at their most divergent in "Saturn, the Bringer of Old Age", where Solti adds nearly three minutes to Holst's reading, but the effectiveness of Solti's chosen tempo is undeniable. The two Boult recordings make a generous fill-up. His *Egdon Heath* is wonderfully atmospheric and the exuberance and colour of *The Perfect Fool* is vividly captured. The digital transfer is very fine indeed, with no loss of warmth or presence.

Holst. CHORAL MUSIC. **Holst Singers and [a]Orchestra/Hilary Davan Wetton.** Hyperion CDA66329. Texts included.
Two psalms, H117[a]. Six choruses, H186[a]. The evening watch, H159. Seven Partsongs, H162[a]. Nunc dimittis, H127.

.• 65' DDD 1/90

It is incomprehensible that so much of Holst's wonderful music for chorus should still remain comparatively unknown to the general listening public. Hyperion must be particularly commended on the care and attention that have obviously been devoted to the fine recording and production here. Hilary Davan Wetton took on the mantle of Director of Music at St Paul's Girls' School in Hammersmith, the position held by Holst himself from 1905 until his death in 1934, and the spirit of the venue seems to suffuse both the performances and the recording. Featuring a chorus and orchestra dedicated to Holst's music, these readings capture exactly the sonorities that the composer implies in his scores and the spiritual world that the works inhabit. It is perhaps invidious to single out from a programme of such consistent quality a couple of items of particular merit, but the two short unaccompanied pieces for eight-part choir, *The evening watch* and the appropriately concluding *Nunc dimittis* are both outstanding and worthy of special attention.

Arthur Honegger
French/Swiss 1892-1955

Honegger. ORCHESTRAL WORKS. **Bavarian Radio Symphony Orchestra/Charles Dutoit.** Erato 2292 45242-2. From NUM75254 (4/86). Symphony No. 1. Pastorale d'été. Three symphonic movements—Pacific 231; Rugby; No. 3.

.• 55' DDD 12/86 ❓

Honegger's First Symphony is a highly impressive work, concisely and effectively constructed in what might be generally described as a neo-classical style; and the scoring is attractive and skilful. His evocation of dawn on a summer's day in *Pastorale d'été*, scored for small orchestra with exquisite, quiet beauty, is surely a miniature masterpiece, and both *Pacific 231* (1924) and *Rugby* (1928) are brilliantly contrived essays in imaginative scoring and the use of cross-rhythms. Honegger was distressed by a critical notion that he was trying to imitate the sound of a steam locomotive and specific moves in a game of rugby: he insisted that the two scores conveyed only a general impression of a train journey and the atmosphere of Colombes stadium. So offended was he that he called the third companion piece merely *Mouvement symphonique No. 3*, but it is a little less effective than its two bedfellows. These vigorous performances are excellent.

Honegger. Symphonies—No. 2 for strings and trumpet; No. 3, "Liturgique". **Berlin Philharmonic Orchestra / Herbert von Karajan.** DG 20th Century Classics 423 242-2GC. From 2530 068 (7/73).

59' ADD 6/88

Honegger. Symphonies—No. 2 for strings and trumpet; No. 4, "Deliciae basiliensis". **Bavarian Radio Symphony Orchestra / Charles Dutoit.** Erato 2292-45247-2.

54' DDD

The classic DG recording is unlikely to be surpassed. The Second Symphony is a powerfully atmospheric piece written during the grim years of the German occupation. It is a searching, thoughtful piece, appropriately dark in colouring which eventually breaks into the light with its chorale melody played on the trumpet. The *Liturgique* is a powerhouse of energy and its slow movement is among Honegger's most glorious inspirations. The playing of the Berlin Philharmonic is sumptuous in tone, vibrant with energy and encompasses an enormously wide range of dynamics and colour. One can only marvel at the quality of sound they achieve in both the beautiful slow movements and their virtuosity in the finale of No. 3. Astonishing performances and an indispensable disc for all lovers of modern music.

Charles Dutoit   [photo: Decca / Gamble]

The Fourth Symphony of 1946, sub-titled "Deliciae Basiliensis", reflects Honegger's friendship with Paul Sacher, conductor of the Basle Chamber Orchestra, and the pleasure he drew from the town of Basle and the surrounding countryside. And so the work has a tranquil, contented atmosphere. Dutoit clearly has a particular sympathy for this music and he directs thoroughly committed and well-conceived performances.

Honegger. Jeanne d'Arc au bûcher. **Françoise Pollet, Michèle Command** (sops); **Nathalie Stutzman** (contr); **John Aler** (ten); **Marthe Keller, Georges Wilson, Pierre-Marie Escourrou, Paola Lenzi** (narrs); **Chorus and Children's Voices of French Radio; French National Orchestra / Seiji Ozawa.** DG 429 412-2GH. Text and translations included. Recorded at a performance in the Basilique Saint-Denis, Paris, in June 1989.

69' DDD 4/91

Honegger described *Joan of Arc at the stake* as a "dramatic oratorio", but it is a work almost impossible to categorize, the two chief characters—Joan and Brother Dominc—being speaking parts, but with a chorus (now commenting on, now involved in, the action), a children's chorus, and a curiously constituted orchestra including saxophones instead of horns, two pianos and, most notably, an ondes martenot which, with its banshee shriek, bloodcurdlingly reinforces the climax as Joan breaks her earthly chains. The action is partly realistic, partly symbolic, unfolding in quasi-cinematic flashbacks. The musical techniques and styles employed by Honegger are extraordinarily varied, with humming and shouting besides singing, and with elements of polyphony, folk-song, baroque dances and jazz rhythms; yet all is fused together in a remarkable way to produce a work of gripping power and, in the final scenes, almost intolerable emotional intensity: the beatific *envoi* "Greater love hath no man ..." is a passage that catches the throat and haunts the mind for long afterwards. Ozawa fully captured the work's dramatic forces in this public performance, which has been skilfully served by the recording engineers; Marthe Keller vividly portrays Joan's bewilderment, fervour and agony, John Aler makes a swaggering Procus, and Françoise Pollet is radiant-voiced as the Virgin. Even more than *Le roi David*, this is Honegger's masterpiece.

Honegger. Le roi David[a]. Mouvement symphonique No. 3. La tempête—Prélude. [a]**Christiane Eda-Pierre** (sop); [a]**Martha Senn** (contr); [a]**Tibère Raffalli** (ten); [a]**Daniel Mesgiuch** (narr); [a]**Annie Gaillard** (rec); [a]**Kühn Children's Chorus; [a]Prague Philharmonic Chorus; Czech Philharmonic Orchestra/Serge Baudo.** Supraphon CO-1412/13. Text and translation included.

② 83' DDD 6/88

Honegger was thought of early in this century as a modernist as influential as Stravinsky and Bartók, but then fell into a certain neglect. However, today he is rightly seen as an important figure although with no special school or followers. *Le roi David* (1921) is a symphonic psalm in three parts that tells of the shepherd boy David who slays Goliath and becomes ruler of Israel. This music is brimful of invention, colour (sometimes oriental) and passion, and the French conductor Serge Baudo has a crisp, dramatically alert narrator in Daniel Mesgiuch as well as a heroic David in the tenor Tibère Raffalli and a fine Witch of Endor in Martha Senn. The chorus and orchestra seem completely at home with the idiom, so that such big set pieces as the "Dance before the Ark" that ends Part 2 are overwhelmingly exciting. The recording is clear yet atmospheric and encompasses the enormous climaxes. Unlike its predecessors, Honegger's Symphonic Movement No. 3 has no title, though at least one critic thought it portrayed a ski jumper! It is a lively piece, and the Prelude to Shakespeare's *Tempest* again shows the composer's skill in handling powerful ideas orchestrally. These other pieces are worth having and they help to fill the two CDs, but one may regret that at 68 minutes or so, *Le roi David* was not more economically accommodated on just one.

Herbert Howells
British 1892-1983

Howells. Requiem (1936)[a]. Take him, earth, for cherishing (1963). *Vaughan Williams.* Mass in G minor (1922)[b]. Te Deum in G major (1928)[c]. [a]**Mary Seers** (sop); [ab]**Michael Chance** (alto); [ab]**Philip Salmon** (ten); [ab]**Jonathan Best** (bass); **Corydon Singers/Matthew Best** with [c]**Thomas Trotter** (org). Hyperion CDA66076. Texts included. From A66076 (8/83).

60' AAD 10/87

Vaughan Williams's unaccompanied Mass in G minor manages to combine the common manner of Elizabethan liturgical music with those elements of his own folk-music heritage that make his music so distinctive, and in so doing arrives at something quite individual and new. The work falls into five movements and its mood is one of heartfelt, if restrained, rejoicing. Herbert Howells wrote his unaccompanied Requiem in 1936, a year after the death of his only son. The work was not released in his lifetime but was reconstructed and published in 1980 from his manuscripts. It is a most hauntingly beautiful work of an obviously intensely personal nature. *Take him, earth, for cherishing* was composed to commemorate the assassination of President John F. Kennedy. The text is an English translation by Helen Waddell of Prudentius's fourth-century poem, *Hymnus circa Exsequias Defuncti*. Again it demonstrates the great strength of Howells's choral writing, with a clear outline and aptly affecting yet unimposing harmonic twists. The Corydon Singers give marvellous performances of these works and the sound is very fine indeed. An hour of the finest English choral music and not to be missed.

Howells. SACRED CHORAL AND ORGAN WORKS. [a]**Christopher Dearnley** (org); **St Paul's Cathedral Choir, London/John Scott.** Hyperion CDA66260. Texts included.
Collegium regale—canticles. Six Pieces for organ—No. 3, Master Tallis's Testament[a]. Like as the hart. Behold, O God our defender. Psalm-Preludes, Set 2—No. 1, De profundis[a]. Take him, earth, for cherishing. St Paul's—canticles.

62' DDD 9/88

This admirable disc is a fine tribute to the memory of Herbert Howells. The choir has used with enormous skill everything St Paul's Cathedral has to offer in the way of acoustical potential: space, resonance—even its echo—a lively response to timbre and volume; all of it justly timed and finally captured in a superb recording. The canticles for Morning Prayer (*Te Deum and Jubilate*) and those for Evensong (*Magnificat* and *Nunc Dimittis*) provide a framework for the organ pieces and the motets, all of them enhanced and enriched by the variety of sonorities obtainable as much from the building itself as from the music. Together, these works epitomize the life and death of this most English of English composers. The choice and planning of the programme is particularly skilful: each piece seems to lead to the next with total inevitability. Behind that lies a measure of expertise and professionalism one rarely encounters; but it passes almost unnoticed simply because the ear is totally satisfied and charmed.

Johann Hummel
Austrian 1778-1837

Hummel. Piano Concertos—A minor, Op. 85; B minor, Op. 89. **Stephen Hough** (pf); **English Chamber Orchestra/Bryden Thomson.** Chandos CHAN8507.

66' DDD 4/87

This is a staggering disc of Hummel's piano concertos played by Stephen Hough. The most obvious comparison is with the piano concertos of Chopin, but whereas those works rely on the grace and panache of the piano line to redeem an often lacklustre orchestral role, the Hummel works have finely conceived orchestral writing and certainly no shortage of original ideas. The piano part is formidable, combining virtuosity of a very high order indeed with a vigour and athleticism that does much to redress Hummel's somewhat tarnished reputation. The A minor is probably the better known of the two works here, with a thrilling rondo finale, but the B minor is no less inventive with some breathtaking writing in the piano's upper registers. This record makes strong demands to be heard: inventive and exciting music, a masterly contribution from

Stephen Hough, fine orchestral support from the ever sympathetic ECO under Bryden Thomson and, last but not least, a magnificent Chandos recording.

Hummel. Piano Quintet in E flat major, Op. 87.
Schubert. Quintet in A major, D667, "Trout". **Schubert Ensemble of London** (Jacqueline Shave, vn; Roger Tapping, va; Jane Salmon, vc; Peter Buckoke, db; William Howard, pf). Hyperion Helios CDH88010.

··• 61' DDD 6/90

Both works here offer turn-of-the-century Viennese warmth and geniality in full measure, the centuries in question being of course the eighteenth and nineteenth, and Schubert being a native of Vienna while Hummel made his home there. They are also classical in structure, and the Hummel Quintet especially so, which is not surprising since he was a pupil of Mozart and Haydn and a musical conservative compared to Beethoven, with whom he formed a lasting relationship that nevertheless had its ups and downs. The scoring of his Quintet is unusual, with the four strings featuring a double bass instead of being the usual two violins, viola and cello, and evidently this work was known to Schubert when he composed his *Trout* Quintet for the same combination, although it also reflected the instruments played by the music-loving friends in a provincial town for whom it was written. It is this work, with its famous variation-form fourth movement on the theme of the song *Die Forelle*, which begins the programme, and the playing by the Schubert Ensemble of London is vivid yet affectionate, with a recording quality that is on the full side as regards piano tone but still pleasantly natural. They are no less agreeable stylistically in the Hummel, which is more theatrical in its gestures but makes no pretence of offering romantic self-expression or real profundity, and if the first movement seems on the fast side and a touch breathless, they could argue that its marking *Allegro e risoluto assai* justifies this.

Englebert Humperdinck

German 1854-1921

Humperdinck. HANSEL UND GRETEL. **Anne Sofie von Otter** (mez) Hansel; **Barbara Bonney** (sop) Gretel; **Hanna Schwarz** (mez) Mother; **Andreas Schmidt** (bar) Father; **Barbara Hendricks** (sop) Sandman; **Eva Lind** (sop) Dew Fairy; **Marjana Lipovšek** (contr) Witch; **Tölz Boys' Choir; Bavarian Radio Symphony Orchestra/Jeffrey Tate.** EMI CDS7 54022-2. Notes, text and translation included.

··• ② 1h 43' DDD 11/90   9 P

Humperdinck's delightful and ever popular fairy-tale opera is presented here in an appealing, well paced and unsentimental performance, and though Tate brings out the Wagnerian influence of the work (Humperdinck was greatly admired by Wagner and was musical assistant in preparation for the first performance of *Parsifal*) it is never made to sound heavyweight or protracted. Indeed, Tate's tempos are generally faster than normal and these give the opera a persuasive sense of flow and direction. Though carefully avoiding over-sentimentality (especially in the "Evening Hymn" and "Dream Pantomime") Tate nevertheless brings a natural warmth and charm to the work both in his beautifully crafted phrasing and his subtle and sympathetic approach to the opera. The soloists are particularly well chosen. Anne Sofie von Otter and Barbara Bonney are especially fine in their fresh and youthful portrayal of the young children and Marjana Lipovšek's superb performance as the Witch (avoiding the often melodramatic and histrionic characterization found in other recordings) deserves special mention. The beautiful warm and spacious recording is exceptionally clear and is ideally balanced in terms of voices and orchestra. Destined to become a classic.

Vincent d'Indy *French 1851-1931*

d'Indy. Symphonie sur un chant montagnard français (Symphonie cévenole)[a].
Martinů. Rhapsody-Concerto for viola and orchestra[b]. [a]**Michel Block** (pf);
[b]**Rivka Golani** (va); **Berne Symphony Orchestra/Peter Maag.** Conifer
CDCF146. From CFC146 (6/87).

48' DDD 10/88

Two works of special interest and very different character. Vincent d'Indy's
Symphony on a French Mountaineer's Song is no more a symphony than the
Martinů is a concerto, and it is not quite a concertante work either, for it
eschews virtuosity. Yet it is a strong piece with genuine melodic appeal and
nobility of feeling, which deserves a stronger place in the repertory. Michel
Block makes out a strong case for it and the orchestral playing is thoroughly
committed. Martinů's music is enjoying greater exposure in his centenary year;
his is a strongly individual voice whose powerful symphonies are at long last
coming into their own. The *Rhapsody-Concerto* for viola and orchestra comes
from 1952 and is one of the finest works of his last years. It is a two-movement
work, not quite a viola concerto though there are elements of dialogue and
display, but it is primarily gentle and reflective, particularly in these artists'
hands. There is nothing spectacular or high-powered about these performances
under Peter Maag: it is playing of the old school that allows the music to speak
for itself.

Charles Ives *American 1874-1954*

Ives. A Symphony: New England Holidays[b]. The Unanswered Question (orig.
and rev. versions)[a]. Central Park in the Dark. [a]**Adolph Herseth** (tpt);
Chicago Symphony [b]**Chorus and Orchestra/Michael Tilson Thomas.**
CBS Masterworks CD42381.

63' DDD 10/88

The essential Charles Ives is here and Tilson Thomas proves a most engrossing
guide. *Holidays* is a kind of American *Four Seasons*—one tone-poem per National
holiday; each a wonderfully resourceful canvas from the ultimate 'American'
composer. There can be no mistaking Tilson Thomas's profound affection for
these scores: not least the simple home-spun honesty of the quieter reflective

paragraphs—sepia memories of times
past. The nostalgic winterscape of
"Washington's Birthday" is most
beautifully realized. So too are the
opening pages of "Decoration Day",
as the townsfolk of Danbury,
Connecticut, gather for their annual
procession to the Civil War
veterans' graves. As for those rowdy
Ivesian collages, the cacophonous
mêlées of "Washington's Birthday"
and, more notoriously, "The Fourth
of July", Tilson Thomas and his CBS
engineers have worked wonders with
their keen ears and some ingenious
sleight of hand at the mixing
console. You'll catch more of the

Michael Tilson Thomas *[photo:CBS*

'tunes' than you might have thought possible: internal clarity is most impressive, the tonal depth of the recording likewise. So don't be surprised that the Jew's harp more than holds its own during the demented "barn dance" sequence of "Washington's Birthday"! No less impressive is the conductor's concentrated way with the two remaining pieces—classics of their kind.

Ives. Symphonies—Nos. 1 and 4 (including original hymn settings). **Chicago Symphony Orchestra/Michael Tilson Thomas.** Sony Classical CD44939. 77' DDD 2/91

It could be worth asking a musical friend to listen to the start of Ives's First Symphony here and (presuming he doesn't already know the work) then to identify the composer. It seems almost impossible that anyone would get the answer right, for this tuneful, vigorous music hardly suggests the wild-eyed 'ornery crittur' and iconoclast represented to many listeners by much of Ives's later music; Dvořák, Mahler and Nielsen all flash through the mind, which is significant because all three drew their deepest inspiration from folk music, as did Ives himself. The explanation is that this is an early work written in 1898 as an exercise for music graduation at Yale; but make no mistake, it shows that this composer in his twenties knew a good deal about symphonic writing and (as the slow second movement, complete with Dvořákian cor anglais, demonstrates) about writing melodies as well. The Fourth Symphony with all its wild and wilful complexities is another matter, for the good tunes (which are sometimes those of hymns and Gospel songs) are interwoven with astonishing boldness into a score of daunting individuality and complexity. This disc also includes some of these hymn tunes in their original form with voices, one however, *Beulah Land*, being an organ solo played on a modern instrument that sounds splendidly authentic. The conductor Michael Tilson Thomas has a proven affinity with Ives's music, and these authoritative performances have a touching strength, while the recording too does justice to some of the most challenging music ever to come out of America.

Ives. Symphony No. 4 (1910-16). **John Alldis Choir; London Philharmonic Orchestra/José Serebrier.** Chandos CHAN8397. From ABRD 1118 (9/85). 33' ADD 1/86

There are wonderful accounts of the problems, both logistical and musical, involved in mounting a performance of Ives's Symphony No. 4, but the CD buyer has the opportunity with this remarkable performance to ignore all those and concentrate on what the music is about. The sound that results from that hard and dedicated work by so many people is not particularly alien or difficult to understand, however multi-layered or devious it may become. The warm, open expression of the third-movement Fugue, for example, so redolent of Mahler and early Copland, only holds terrors for those too close to it. The complexities of the final movement, not quite made fully lucid in this fine recording, do need some working at by the listener, but the rewards are great: Ives said of it that it was "an apotheosis of the preceding content, in terms that have something to do with the reality of existence and its religious experience". He wrote the Symphony between 1910 and 1916, though it was not performed in its entirety until 1965, and it marked an artistic high-point in his career, containing in its mere 33 minutes much that was best and most revolutionary about his music. This pioneering disc is a must for any collection.

Ives. ORCHESTRAL WORKS. **New York Philharmonic Orchestra/ Leonard Bernstein.** DG 429 220-2GH. Recorded at performances in Avery Fisher Hall, New York during 1987 and 1988.
Symphony No. 2. The Gong on the Hook and Ladder. Tone Roads—No. 1. A set of 3 Short Pieces—Largo cantabile, Hymn. Hallowe'en. Central Park in the Dark. The Unanswered Question.

68' DDD 8/90

Although Bernstein thought of Ives as a primitive composer, these recordings reveal that he had an undeniably deep affinity for, and understanding of, Ives's music. The Second Symphony (written in 1902 and first performed in 1951) is a gloriously beautiful work, still strongly rooted in the nineteenth century yet showing those clear signs of Ives's individual voice that are largely missing from the charming but lightweight First Symphony. Bernstein brings out all its richness and warmth without wallowing in its romantic elements, and he handles with utter conviction the multi-textures and the allusions to popular tunes and snatches from Bach, Brahms and Dvořák, to name but a few. The standard of playing he exacts from the NYPO, both here and in the disc's series of technically demanding shorter pieces, is remarkably high with the depth of string tone at a premium—and the engineers retain this to a degree unusual in a live recording. Altogether an essential disc for any collection.

Ives. Piano Sonata No. 2, "Concord, Mass., 1840-60".
M. Wright. Piano Sonata (1982). **Marc-André Hamelin** (pf). New World NW378-2.

58' DDD 9/89

From time to time composers dream of a totally free music, transcending traditional modes of thought, floating on waves of pure untrammelled inspiration. Charles Ives, who seems to have anticipated most European developments by decades, made the dream a remarkable reality. Based on a trial-and-error approach to harmony, notated largely without bar-lines and structured only by the dictates of Ives's inner vision, the *Concord* Sonata attempts to convey the essence of writers associated with the town of Concord, Massachusetts. The music covers a colossal range of mood, from the intrepid philosophical journeys of "Emerson", to the kaleidoscopic variety of "Hawthorne", the homeliness of "the Alcotts" and finally the inner expanses of "Thoreau". Comparison with Beethoven's *Hammerklavier* may seem imprudent, but there is no clearer precedent in the piano repertoire for such a combination of visionary and technical demands. Marc-André Hamelin, a 27-year-old Canadian, is one of the chosen few who can measure up to both aspects and Maurice Wright's Sonata is a by no means negligible fill-up. Both works are excellently recorded. A disc mainly for the adventurous, but the potential rewards of this particular adventure are immense.

Leos Janáček
Czech 1854-1928

Janáček. ORCHESTRAL WORKS[a].
Smetana. THE BARTERED BRIDE—Overture[b].
Weinberger. SCHWANDA THE BAGPIPER—Polka and Fugue[c]. **Pro Arte Orchestra/Sir Charles Mackerras.** EMI Phoenixa CDM7 63779-2. Items marked [a] from Pye Golden Guinea GSGC14004 (5/64), [b] CSEM75007 (12/59), [c] CEM36014 (4/59).

Janáček: Sinfonietta. THE MAKROPOLOUS CASE— Prelude. KATA KABANOVA—Prelude. FROM THE HOUSE OF THE DEAD—Prelude. Jealousy.

61' ADD 1/91 £ 9p

It is astonishing to think that a generation ago Janáček was still a little known composer and that now a recorded programme of Czech music can devote most of its space to him and use Smetana's *Bartered Bride* Overture as a fill-up! But his music merits it, and the very first notes blared out by the brass in his *Sinfonietta* remind us of the strength and originality of this unique musical personality, a man born in 1854, just 13 years after Dvořák, whose music nevertheless seems very much of the twentieth century. This is a performance of the *Sinfonietta* which is unequivocally "red in tooth and claw", as someone wrote when it first came out—and it sounds truthfully coarse-grained, rich and powerful in a way that simply defies us to believe that the recording in Walthamstow Town Hall was made in 1959. A cooler appraisal, if such a thing is desirable with this music and playing, of course reminds us that there is some inevitable tape hiss, but it never distracts. In the four operatic preludes (i.e. overtures) the sheer physical and emotional heat of the playing is quite extraordinary. Indeed, this is music of utterly abundant life-affirmation played with 110 per cent commitment by an excellent orchestra under the young Charles Mackerras. The two fillers date from the same 1959 sessions in London and are no less alive.

Janáček. Sinfonietta. Taras Bulba—rhapsody for orchestra. **Vienna Philharmonic Orchestra/Sir Charles Mackerras.** Decca 410 138-2DH. From SXDL7519 (7/81).

48' DDD 11/83

This has long been a favourite coupling and in these thoroughly idiomatic performances the effect is spectacular. Of course these are far more than just orchestral showpieces. Both works were fired by patriotic fervour—*Taras Bulba* by Czechoslovakia's struggle towards independence, the *Sinfonietta* by the city of Brno, the composer's adopted home town. Both works display a deep-seated passion for the basic elements of music and yield unprecedented levels of excitement. To get the most out of *Taras Bulba* you really need all its gory programmatic details (of battles, betrayal, torture and murder) to hand. The *Sinfonietta* needs no such props; its impact is as irresistible and physically direct as a massive adrenalin injection. If the listener is to revel in this music a corresponding sense of abandon in the playing is even more important than precision. The Vienna Philharmonic supplies a good measure of both and Sir Charles Mackerras's commitment and understanding are second to none, while the high-level recording captures every detail in vivid close-up.

Janáček. The diary of one who disappeared[a]. String Quartet No. 1, "Kreutzer Sonata"[b]. [a]**Clara Wirz** (mez); [a]**Peter Keller** (ten); [a]**Lucerne Singers/Mario Venzago** (pf); [b]**Doležal Quartet** (Bohuslav Matousek, Josef Kekula, vns; Karel Doležal, va; Vladimir Leixner, vc). Accord 22031-2.

57' AAD 4/90

Both of these works reflect Janáček's innocently ecstatic love for a woman very much younger than himself, but both are also multi-layered. In the quartet the ostensible subject is Tolstoy's novella about a guilty and ultimately fatal love affair, but Janáček also described the piece as a protest against the subjection of women. The *Diary* is fascinatingly ambiguous, too: the poems on which it is based were published as the work of an unlettered peasant, all that he had left behind after abandoning home, family and friends to follow an alluring gipsy girl.

There have been suggestions that the supposed authorship of the poems was a hoax, but their very mysterious anonymity makes it possible to hear the cycle both as a gripping drama and as a dream-like metaphor.

That dual quality is finely conveyed in this performance of the *Diary* by a combination of directness (the dusky-voiced and intimately insinuating Clara Wirz is the gipsy Zefka to the life; the 'wordless song' at the centre of the cycle—the original poem consisted of nothing more than three suggestive asterisks—is vividly climactic) and mysterious poetry: the off-stage women's chorus both magical and real. Peter Keller has a light but ardent voice, well-suited to conveying the young man's wonder at what is happening to him and his diction is praiseworthily clear (a pity that only French translations of the Czech texts are provided). The quartet, alas, though performed with impetuous urgency and passion, receives a dry, harsh and nasal recording. But this account of the *Diary* will be a recurring pleasure.

Janáček. JENUFA. **Elisabeth Söderström** (sop) Jenůfa; **Wieslaw Ochman** (ten) Laca; **Eva Randová** (mez) Kostelnička; **Petr Dvorský** (ten) Steva; **Lucia Popp** (sop) Karolka; **Marie Mrazová** (contr) Stařenka; **Václav Zitek** (bar) Stárek; **Dalibor Jedlička** (bass) Rychtar; **Ivana Mixová** (mez) Rychtarka; **Vera Soukopová** (mez) Pastuchyňa, Tetka; **Jindra Pokorná** (mez) Barena; **Jana Janasová** (sop) Jano; **Vienna State Opera Chorus; Vienna Philharmonic Orchestra/Sir Charles Mackerras.** Decca 414 483-2DH2. From D276D3 (9/83).

② 2h 10' DDD 12/85

Janáček's first operatic masterpiece is a towering work which blends searing intensity with heart-stopping lyricism. It tells of Jenůfa and her appalling treatment as she is caught between the man she loves and one who eventually comes to love her. But dominating the story is the Kostelnička, a figure of huge strength, pride and inner resource who rules Jenůfa's life and ultimately kills Jenůfa's baby. Eva Randová's characterization of the role of the Kostelnička is frightening in its intensity but also has a very human core. The two men are well cast and act as fine foils to Elisabeth Söderström's deeply impressive Jenůfa. The Vienna Philharmonic play beautifully and Mackerras directs magnificently. The recording is all one could wish for and the booklet is a mine of informed scholarship.

Janáček. THE CUNNING LITTLE VIXEN. The Cunning Little Vixen—orchestral suite (arr. V. Talich)[a]. **Lucia Popp** (sop) Vixen, Young vixen; **Dalibor Jedlička** (bass) Forester; **Eva Randová** (mez) Fox; **Eva Zikmundová** (mez) Forester's wife, Owl; **Vladimir Krejčik** (ten) Schoolmaster, Gnat; **Richard Novák** (ten) Priest, Badger **Václav Zítek** (bar) Harašta; **Beno Blachut** (ten) Pásek; **Ivana Mixová** (mez) Pásek's wife, Woodpecker, Hen; **Libuše Marová** (contr) Dog; **Gertrude Jahn** (mez) Cock, Jay; **Eva Hríbiková** (sop) Frantik; **Zuzana Hudecová** (sop) Pepik; **Peter Saray** (treb) Frog, Grasshopper; **Miriam Ondrášková** (sop) Cricket; **Vienna State Opera Chorus; Bratislava Children's Choir; Vienna Philharmonic Orchestra/Sir Charles Mackerras.** Decca 417 129-2DH2. Notes, text and translation included. From D257D2 (5/82). Item marked [a] new to UK.

② 1h 49' DDD 11/86

Janáček used the most unlikely material for his operas. For *The Cunning Little Vixen* his source was a newspaper series of drawings, with accompanying text, about the adventures of a vixen cub and her escape from the gamekeeper who

Lucia Popp [photo: EMI]

raised her. The music is a fascinating blend of vocal and orchestral sound—at times ludicrously romantic, at others raw and violent. Sir Charles Mackerras's Czech training has given him a rare insight into Janáček's music and he presents a version faithful to the composer's individual requirements. In the title-role, Lucia Popp gives full weight to the text while displaying all the richness and beauty of her voice. There is a well-chosen supporting cast of largely Czech singers, with the Vienna Philharmonic to add the ultimate touch of orchestral refinement. Decca's sound is of demonstration quality, bringing out all the violent detail of Janáček's exciting vocal and orchestral effects.

Janáček. OSUD (sung in English). **Helen Field** (sop) Mila Valková; **Philip Langridge** (ten) Zivný; **Kathryn Harries** (sop) Mila's Mother; **Peter Bronder** (ten) A poet, A student, Hrazda; **Stuart Kale** (ten) Dr Suda; **Welsh National Opera Chorus and Orchestra/Sir Charles Mackerras.** EMI CDC7 49993-2. English text included.

79' DDD 9/90

The story of *Osud* ("Fate") concerns a tragic relationship between a composer (Zivný) and a girl (Míla) whose mother throws both herself and her daughter to their deaths; the composer has produced an unfinished opera about his life with the girl, and as he finished explaining it to a group of his students he too is felled by a blow of fate. Composed in 1904-6, immediately after *Jenufa, Osud* had to wait more than 50 years for its first production; and it was not until 1984 and David Pountney's staging for English National Opera that opera-goers in Britain realized they had been missing one of Janáček's most inspired works. Philip Langridge played Zivný in that production, and his singing here shows complete identification with and mastery of the role. Indeed, given the cast involved, under the guidance of the master-Janáčekian Sir Charles Mackerras, it should not be surprising that the whole performance radiates conviction and a sense of theatre. EMI's recording quality is superb and there are authoritative notes and a full libretto. Anyone who is allergic to opera in English should perhaps think carefully before buying; otherwise this can be confidently recommended, especially to anyone who thinks there is no such thing as a neglected masterpiece.

Scott Joplin

American 1868-1917

Joplin. PIANO WORKS. **Dick Hyman** (pf). RCA Victor Gold Seal GD87993.
Maple Leaf Rag. Original Rags. Swipesy. Peacherine Rag. The Easy Winners. Sunflower Slow Drag. The Entertainer. Elite Syncopations. The Strenuous Life. A Breeze from Alabama. Palm Leaf Rag. Something Doing. Weeping Willow. The Chrysanthemum. The Cascades. The Sycamore.

58' ADD 10/89

The Rag is a simple dance form characterized by the device of syncopation, whereby a strong accent is displaced from its expected place on the first beat of the bar to a subsidiary beat. The effect of this is to give a lift or 'swing' to the rhythm. Traditional Negro folk and popular music provided the basis for this form, which in itself was one of the bases for the development of jazz. Scott Joplin was the most skilled composer of rags, and he wrote over 50 pieces between 1899 and 1904. In 1973 the film, *The Sting*, used Joplin's rag *The Entertainer*, and this was a strong element in a revival of his music. Dick Hyman recorded all of Joplin's rags in 1975, and this disc gives us a selection of 16 items. He manages to invest each piece with its own distinct character, and his buoyant, witty playing in a clear but slightly shallow recording is very attractive.

Josquin Desprez
French .c1440-1521

Josquin Desprez. SACRED CHORAL WORKS. **Hilliard Ensemble/Paul Hillier.** EMI CDC7 49960-2. Texts and translations included.
Missa Hercules dux Ferrariae. Pater noster/Ave Maria. Miserere mei Deus. Tu solus qui facis mirabilia. **Gombert:** Lugebat David Absalon.

68' DDD 5/90

Few groups have made as consistent a contribution to early polyphony on disc as the Hilliard Ensemble under its director, Paul Hillier. Some listeners, already familiar with other versions of the *Miserere* may feel this one to be on the slow side but, on the other hand both here and in the Mass *Hercules dux Ferrariae*, a fine product of the composer's mature period, the Hilliard Ensemble penetrates beyond the surface to reach the heart of the music. And in so doing the singers uncover many precious details and savour many nuances in Josquin's score. With great justification, perhaps, listeners might take issue with the Ensemble in its somewhat cool performance of the impassioned *Lugebat David Absalon*, probably by Nicolas Gombert (*c.*1500-*c.*1556); but few if any will be other than thrilled by its reading of Josquin's four-part motet *Tu solus qui facis mirabilia*. Thoughtful and thought-provoking performances, sympathetically recorded and accompanied by full texts and translations.

Josquin Desprez. Missa L'homme armé super voces musicales. Missa L'homme armé sexti toni.
Anonymous. L'homme armé. **The Tallis Scholars/Peter Phillips.** Gimell CDGIM019. Text and translation included.

74' DDD 7/89

Towards the end of the Middle Ages it became customary to use popular secular melodies instead of the usual plainchant themes as the basis for composing polyphonic Masses. One such was the fifteenth-century melody *L'homme armé* ("Beware of the armed man"), a melody that may have originated as a crusader song. These settings would provide endless opportunities for a composer to demonstrate his contrapuntal skills. In the first of Josquin's two settings, *Super voces musicales*, he uses the tune over and over again, beginning each time on successive ascending degrees of the six-note scale Ut-Re-Mi-Fa-Sol-La, so that it rises higher and higher as the Mass progresses. Sometimes the melody appears back to front from half way through the piece on to the end. In the *Sexti toni* Mass the tune is transposed so that F rather than G is the final note. The listener's enjoyment is in no way lessened by all this contrapuntal ingenuity. The music flows along with unsurpassed ease and beauty, displaying that unique quality of seeming inevitability which characterizes all great music. It is well matched by the expertise and enthusiasm of The Tallis Scholars and their first-class recording engineers.

Josquin Desprez. Missa Pange lingua. Missa La sol fa re mi. **The Tallis Scholars/Peter Phillips.** Gimell CDGIM009.

62' DDD 3/87

Throughout his long life Josquin Desprez was held in enormous esteem by his contemporaries and of his 18 surviving Masses the two gathered on this disc

Peter Phillips   *[photo: Gimell*

come from different periods in his life. The *Missa La sol fa re mi* dates from 1502 and, as its name implies, is based on the notes A,G,F,D,E. From this motif the Mass emerges, a technical feat at which Josquin excelled (and of a kind which he often seemed to set himself as a challenge). The repetition of this theme is carried out with such sophistication that one is hardly aware of its recurrence so many times. The *Missa Pange lingua* is a much later work based on the plainchant written for the feast of Corpus Christi. It has a freedom of invention and harmonic richness that, at times, seem to take us far away from the restraints of a theme-based composition. The eight singers of The Tallis Scholars (who, incidentally, use female voices for the soprano line) make a beautiful sound: rich, integrated but always willing to bring out the melodic subtleties presented to them in this most glorious of renaissance music. The recording matches the excellence of the performance.

Giya Kancheli

Georgian 1935-

Kancheli. Symphonies—No. 3 (1973)[a]; No. 6 (1980)[b]. [a]**Gamlet Gonashvili** (ten); [b]**Archil Kharadze**, [b]**Giya Chaduneli** (vas); **Georgia State Symphony Orchestra/Dzansug Kakhidze.** Olympia Explorer OCD401.

60' ADD 9/90

Kancheli. Symphonies—No. 4, "In Commemoration of Michaelangelo" (1975); No. 5 (1976). **Georgia State Symphony Orchestra/Dzansug Kakhidze.** Olympia OCD403.

51' ADD 4/91

Giya Kancheli is the author of seven symphonies and widely respected amongst Soviet musicians. His homeland is an entirely different entity from Russia, and in its climate, food and customs it is a far cry from most westerners' views of the Soviet Union. Bordering on the Black Sea, Turkey and Armenia, it is a land of starkly contrasted mountains and valleys, which seem to find a parallel in the inner landscape of Kancheli's music.

All four symphonies on these discs are single-movement works of around 25 minutes' duration and all commute between poles of profound meditation and violent pulsating energy. In the Fourth and Fifth Symphonies the quiet music is in part a matter of explicitly childlike episodes—music-box-type ideas, or delicate, tuneful fragments of tune on a harpsichord— so that the juxtaposition with blocks of full orchestral sound (sometimes recalling Stravinsky's Russian ballets) registers as a violation of innocence. So, in common with many of his Soviet contemporaries, most famously Schnittke, Kancheli operates with extreme stylistic oppositions. But his musical personality is far more austere and more focused than Schnittke's, and the overall effect of his music is closer to the ritualistic world of the Estonian Arvo Pärt. Each of the symphonies is riveting on first hearing and each grows more and more impressive on repeated listening. Indeed, a claim could be entered for Kancheli as one of the four finest living symphonists (say, with Tippett, Simpson and Sallinen).

Dzansug Kakhidze has been a friend and colleague of Kancheli since their student days in the mid-1950s. He draws performances of spellbinding intensity from his excellent Georgian orchestra, and the recordings are vivid and immediate, just as the music demands. For the record it has to be noted that the Third Symphony comes out a whole tone sharp, courtesy of less than state-of-the-art Georgian technology; but the character of the music remains 99% intact. One would hesitate to recommend one disc over the other, except to say that the Fourth Symphony is marginally less memorable than the others.

Jerome Kern
American 1885-1945

Kern. SHOW BOAT. Cast includes **Teresa Stratas, Frederica von Stade, Jerry Hadley, Bruce Hubbard, Karla Burns; Ambrosian Chorus; London Sinfonietta/John McGlinn.** EMI CDRIVER1. Notes and text included.

③ 3h 42' DDD 11/88

This three-CD *Show Boat* is a remarkable, inspired achievement that is far from being an example of a musical swamped by the misguided use of operatic voices. *Show Boat* was composed on a large scale for singers of accomplishments far above those we often hear in the theatre today, and here it is given its due.

John McGlinn [photo: EMI/Steiner]

"Make believe", "Ol' man river", "Can't help lovin' dat man", "Why do I love you?" and "You are love" have been sung by countless singers over the years, but in beauty and style the performances here can surely never have been rivalled. The love duets between Frederica von Stade and Jerry Hadley are stunningly beautiful and Bruce Hubbard's firm, honeyed baritone has absolutely nothing to fear from comparisons with Paul Robeson. Teresa Stratas's "Can't help lovin' dat man" is quite ravishing.

But the success of this set is due above all to the enthusiasm and dedication of its conductor, John McGlinn. His avowed aim has been to include all the music Kern wrote for the piece over the years for various stage and film productions. Much of this appears in a lengthy and fascinating appendix; but the main text itself includes not only full-length versions of numbers traditionally much shortened but other magnificent items dropped during try-outs and only rediscovered in a Warner Brothers warehouse in 1982. Not least he has restored the original orchestrations of Robert Russell Bennett. The London Sinfonietta clearly revels in them, not least the jazz-flavoured elements of the final Act. The Ambrosian Chorus, too, has a field day in the rousing choral numbers. Bright, spacious recorded sound helps to make this a quite magnificent, quite irresistibly enjoyable achievement.

Aram Khachaturian *Russian 1903-1978*

Khachaturian. Violin Concerto in D minor (1940).
Tchaikovsky (orch. Glazunov). Méditation, Op. 42 No. 1. **Itzhak Perlman** (vn); **Israel Philharmonic Orchestra/Zubin Mehta.** EMI CDC7 47087-2. From EL270108-1 (3/85).

46' DDD 7/85

The twentieth century has had its share of great violin concertos. Khachaturian's is not quite that, in the sense that it never attempts the heights and depths we find in his Soviet colleagues Prokofiev and Shostakovich; but it is a work of considerable charm, beautifully written. Shostakovich once pointed out that a "national and folk idiom" was evident in everything his friend wrote, and Khachaturian's Armenian origin is agreeably evident in the melodic and harmonic contours of the lilting second theme in the first movement and the *Andante sostenuto* that follows. It goes without saying that Itzhak Perlman plays this work with total technical command and persuasive feeling, and the result is most enjoyable even if one feels in some places, such as the first movement's long cadenza, that musical inspiration is being spread rather thin. The finale, however, is predictably exciting. The Tchaikovsky *Méditation* coupling is well worth having, both for its intrinsic quality and also because it was originally planned as the slow movement of his own Violin Concerto. Good accompaniment from Mehta and the Israel Philharmonic Orchestra and a bright recording.

Khachaturian. Gayaneh—Sabre dance; Dance of the Rose Maidens; Dance of the Kurds; Lezghinka.
Offenbach/Rosenthal. Gaîté Parisienne—ballet. **Boston Pops Orchestra/Arthur Fiedler.** RCA Victrola VD87734. From SF5036 (9/59).

46' ADD 9/89 £

The Boston Pops are at their best here, in the sort of music they do so well. The four numbers from Khachaturian's *Gayaneh* might have benefited from the inclusion of the Lullaby but, as they stand, they form an effective short suite, played with fire and precision. The ballet, *Gaîté Parisienne*, is a compilation of items by Offenbach, taken from a richly varied array of sources from *The Tales of Hoffman* and *Orpheus in the Underworld*, through to *Le voyage dans la lune* and *Tromb al Cazar* (all, sadly, left undocumented in the minimal insert notes to this issue). Manuel Rosenthal's gloriously over-the-top orchestrations gave the choreographer, Massine, some initial misgivings but, on the recommendation of Stravinsky, he went ahead and created the ballet that was first produced by the Ballet Russe de Monte Carlo in 1938. Percussion and brass are very much in evidence in the score and Fiedler emphasizes their role in this almost manically high-spirited reading. The extreme brightness of the recording, that verges on edginess at times, compounds the effect. The inevitable hiss from the analogue originals is not too intrusive and the whole production is carried along by the sheer vitality and rhythmic drive of the performance.

Khachaturian. Spartacus—ballet. Gayaneh—ballet. **London Symphony Orchestra / Aram Khachaturian.** EMI Eminence CD-EMX2119. From ASD3347 (5/77).
Spartacus—Variation of Aegina; Adagio of Spartacus and Phrygia; Entrance of Harmodius and Adagio of Aegina and Harmodius; Dance of the Gaditanae—The Rebels' Approach. *Gayaneh*—Lezghinka; Lullaby; Storm; Sabre Dance; Mountaineers; Invention.

55'   ADD   3/89

Apart from the Violin Concerto *Gayaneh* is Khachaturian's finest score, and *Spartacus*, though more uneven and prone to vulgarity, also has some exuberantly inspired individual numbers. The most famous is the expansively passionate "Adagio of Spartacus and Phrygia", made famous by the BBC TV series, "The Onedin Line". Whoever it was that made the choice of this sweeping string tune to accompany a sailing ship against a spectacular oceanic panorama, helped to ensure that Khachaturian's theme (which has nothing to do with the sea) became a top classical 'pop'. *Gayaneh* does not offer a romantic melody on this scale, but it has a rather lovely "Lullaby" and a number of folk-styled dance movements bubbling over with incandescent slavonic energy; the "Sabre Dance" almost bursts at the seams with explosive vitality. The composer's exhilarating 1977 performances have all the energy and ardour one expects from the Russian temperament, and the LSO respond with enthusiasm, the composer making sure that good ensemble go hand-in-hand with fervour. The originally spectacularly reverberant recording has been somewhat clarified for CD, but the digital remastering retains all the vividness; its impact and colour are undeniable.

Zoltán Kodály   *Refer to Index*   *Hungarian 1882-1967*

Fritz Kreisler   *Refer to Index*   *Austrian 1875-1962*

Franz Krommer   *Bohemian 1759-1831*

Krommer. Double Clarinet Concertos[ab]—E flat major, Op. 35; E flat major, Op. 91.
Rossini. Variations in C major for clarinet and chamber orchestra[a].
Introduction, Theme and Variations in B flat major for clarinet and orchestra[a].
[a]**Sabine Meyer,** [b]**Wolfgang Meyer** (cls); **Württemberg Symphony Orchestra / Jörg Faerber.** EMI CDC7 49397-2.

62'   DDD   7/89

The sleeve note claims that Krommer is more than "a prolific producer of pleasant, undemanding music"; but if only on the evidence of these concertos, it seems a good description of the composer of so many charming, refreshing pieces. Krommer is a minor composer in the best sense, and his concertos are good examples of his natural inventiveness and fluent craftsmanship when faced with a particular challenge. Not surprisingly, he has much recourse here to passages with the two instruments in thirds or sixths, and on witty or tender imitation. The invention is lively, the harmony simple and effective, the orchestration clear, expert and graceful. The siblings Meyer understand this music very well, and produce playing that is fresh and nimble, beautifully unanimous yet contrasted. One cannot imagine it being better done. Wolfgang Meyer fires off the pyrotechnics of Rossini's C major Variations coruscatingly, leaving sister Sabine to deal with the rather more extended and ambitious *Introduction, Theme and Variations*. There seems little to separate the two players in skill and virtuosity. Both performances are great fun. The recording is bright and warm.

Edouard Lalo

Lalo. Symphonie espagnole, Op. 21. Violin Concerto in F major, Op. 20. **Augustin Dumay** (vn); **Toulouse Capitole Orchestra/Michel Plasson.** EMI CDC7 49833-2.

 59' DDD 2/90

Even if Dumay had not made something special here of Lalo's gorgeously exotic *Symphonie espagnole*, this disc would be worth having for his absorbed, penetrating account of the fascinating Violin Concerto of 1874. He is particularly effective in the graceful *Andantino* of this latter work, gently shaping its well-turned phrases and capturing the poise of each held note as though a ballet dancer on points. The purposeful finale is brought off with vigour and virtuosic dash, counterbalancing the more pedestrian opening *Allegro*. The popular *Symphonie* is imbued with all the élan and charm suggested by its whistleable tunes and crisp orchestration. Like the Concerto, this work was written for Sarasate but, in honour of that great virtuoso, it is completely suffused with a Spanish warmth and, most noticeably, the rhythm of the habanera. The Toulouse Capitole Orchestra seem to need little encouragement from Michel Plasson to bring this rhythm to life and to use it as a unifying theme throughout the work. The recording venue, the Halle-aux-Grains in Toulouse, provides resonant support to the sound, especially effective, for example, in the pizzicatos of the *Scherzando* second movement, but the engineers have still kept the textures clean and the whole is genially listenable.

Constant Lambert *Refer to Index*

Orlando Lassus

Lassus. CHANSONS, MOTETS, MADRIGALS AND LIEDER. **King's Singers.** (Jeremy Jackman, Alastair Hume, altos; Robert Chilcott, ten; Anthony Holt, Simon Carrington, bars; Colin Mason, bass). EMI CDC7 49158-2. Texts and translations included.
Chansons—Bon jour et puis quelles nouvelles?; Bon jour mon coeur; Dessus le marché d'Arras; Il esteoit une religieuse; Au feu venez-moy; Paisible domaine; O vin en vigne; Vignon vignon vignette; La nuict froide et sombre; Quand mon mary vient; Toutes les nuitz. *Motets*—Musica Dei donum optimi; Omnia tempus habent. *Madrigals*—Matona mia cara; Come la notte ogni fiamella; Chi chilichi?; Cantai hor piango; Ardo si ma non t'amo. *Lieder*—Hört zu ein news Gedicht; Ein guten Raht wil geben ich; Im Mayen hört man die Hanen krayen.

 51' ADD 11/88

If the King's Singers had existed in the time of Lassus, he might have composed these pieces especially for them: the fun, humour, piquancy, nonsense patter, boisterous good cheer, but also the gentle irony, amorous lyricism, meditative musing and occasional moralizing are all right up their street. Indeed, composer and interpreters could hardly have been better matched. *Bon jour mon coeur* is a delight with its freshness and the beauty of its rhythmic declamation, *Quand mon mary* is enjoyable for the excitement of its breathless knock-about peasant humour and for its rich Germanic extravagance and so is *Hört zu ein news Gedicht*, the "new song composed concerning noses short or long", where Cyrane would have discovered an unbeatable rival! The King's Singers are in top form and in *Chi chilichi?* their humorous interpretation adds enormously to the fun. Full texts and excellent translations are a bonus.

Lassus. SACRED CHORAL WORKS. **The Tallis Scholars/Peter Phillips.** Gimell CDGIM018. Texts and translations included.
Missa Osculetur me. Motets—Osculetur me; Hodie completi sunt; Timor et tremor; Alma Redemptoris mater a 8; Salve regina mater a 8; Ave regina caelorum Il a 6; Regina coeli a 7.

| • • • | 49' DDD 7/89 | 𝄞ₛ ✍ |

The Tallis Scholars have produced another winner with this recording, performing a fairly recently discovered and relatively unknown masterpiece: the mellifluous *Missa Osculetur me*, built on the composer's own motet of the same title. The Mass, with its two alternating and interlocking choirs and its two solo quartets, presents a fascinating study in the use of vocal textures. Indeed, this is equally true of the motets, variously scored for six, seven and eight voices. The Pentecost motet *Hodie completi sunt*, sung by men's voices, is particularly effective. It bursts into its final "alleluias" after a sustained crescendo of tremendous power. The weirdly chromatic *Timor et tremor* presents a rich, full sound, lightened when the sopranos indulge in lively syncopation towards the end. Such variety is exploited to the full by the Scholars: the listener can hear each strand of the web, and enjoy not only the final blend but also the sheer quality of each and every voice.

Ludwig Lebrun *Refer to Index*   German 1752-1790

Jean-Marie Leclair   *French 1697-1764*

Leclair. FLUTE SONATAS. **Barthold Kuijken** (fl); **Wieland Kuijken** (va da gamba); **Robert Kohnen** (hpd). Accent ACC58435/6D. From ACC8435/6 (7/85).
ACC58435D—Op. 1: No. 2 in C major. Op. 2: No. 1 in E minor; No. 3 in C major; No. 5 in G major. *ACC58436D*—Op. 1: No. 6 in E minor. Op. 2: No. 8 in D minor; No. 11 in B minor. Op. 9: No. 2 in E minor; No. 7 in G major.

| • • • | ② 50' 59' DDD 2/86 | ✍ |

Leclair's Flute Sonatas are technically among the most advanced of their period; only Bach's make comparable demands on the soloist. The music is subtle and much of its charm lies in the successful assimilation and juxtaposition of French and Italian styles. In Leclair's hands the "reunion of tastes" is considerably and brilliantly advanced. Fast movements are outwardly clad in Italian dress, yet French dance measures sometimes lie concealed within. Slow movements are usually of a more overtly French character brought out in ornamentation, gesture and the rhythmic inflexions of courtly dances such as the menuet and gavotte. Kuijken gives fluent and stylistically assured performances, chasing the elusive qualities of the music with unhurried grace and a warm rounded tone. His is a baroque flute and on occasion he is inclined to be smothered by an over-assertive continuo team; but Kuijken's feeling for gesture, his informed use of unequal rhythms and his quietly passionate affair with this great flute literature assures performances that are enduringly satisfying.

Leclair. SCYLLA ET GLAUCUS. **Donna Brown** (sop) Scylla; **Howard Crook** (ten) Glaucus; **Rachel Yakar** (sop) Circé; **Catherine Dubosc** (sop) Dorine, Sicilian girl; **Françoise Golfier** (sop) Cupid; **Agnès Mellon** (sop) Venus; **René Schirrer** (bar) Licas; **Elisabeth Vidal** (sop) Temire; **André Murgatroyd** (ten) Propetide I; **Nicolas Robertson** (ten) Propetide II; **Philip Salmon** (ten) Shepherd; **Elizabeth Priday** (sop) Shepherdess; **Richard Stuart** (bar) Sylvan; **Francis Dudziak** (bar) Hecate, Sylvan; **Monteverdi Choir; English Baroque Soloists/John Eliot Gardiner.** Erato 2292-45277-2. Notes, text and translation included.

③ 2h 50' DDD 4/88

Leclair was foremost an instrumental composer and *Scylla et Glaucus* was his sole contribution to the French operatic stage. There are three principal characters in the drama and they have been strongly cast in Donna Brown (a warmly appealing Scylla), Howard Crook (effortlessly negotiating the highest reaches of his tessitura) and in Rachel Yakar (as Circé). Circé is Leclair's most colourful role and the potency of her magic is vividly captured in the music of Act 4. The Monteverdi Choir and English Baroque Soloists under the informed and lively direction of John Eliot Gardiner set the seal on a splendid achievement. The recorded sound is clear and a full libretto is legibly presented in the accompanying booklet.

Franz Lehár
Austrian/Hungarian 1870-1948

Lehár. DIE LUSTIGE WITWE. **Josef Knapp** (bar) Baron Mirko Zeta; **Hanny Steffek** (sop) Valencienne; **Eberhard Waechter** (bar) Graf Danilo Danilowitsch; **Elisabeth Schwarzkopf** (sop) Hanna Glawari; **Nicolai Gedda**(ten) Camille Rosillon; **Kurt Equiluz** (ten) Vicomte Cascada; **Hans Strohbauer** (ten) Raoul de St Brioche; **Franz Böheim** (buffo) Njegus; **Philharmonia Chorus and Orchestra/Lovro von Matačić.** EMI CDS7 47178-8. Notes, text and translation included. From Columbia SAN101/2 (5/63).

② 80' AAD 4/86 Ⓑ

Lehár. DIE LUSTIGE WITWE. **Benno Kusche** (bar) Baron Mirko Zeta; **Helen Donath** (sop) Valencienne; **Hermann Prey** (bar) Graf Danilo Danilowitsch; **Edda Moser** (sop) Hanna Glawari; **Siegfried Jerusalem** (ten) Camille Rosillon; **Norbert Orth** (ten) Vicomte Cascada; **Friedrich Lenz** (ten) Raoul de St Brioche; **Horst Sachtleben** (spkr) Njegus; **Bavarian Radio Chorus; Munich Radio Orchestra/Heinz Wallberg.** EMI Studio CMS7 69940-2. From HMV SLS5202 (10/80).

② 82' ADD 7/89 £ Ⓑ

The Merry Widow contains some marvellous melodies and although versions have come and gone none have ever managed to oust the classic 1962 recording with Elisabeth Schwarzkopf. She is a merry widow without equal, conveying with her rich and alluring voice the ebullience and glamour of the character as in no other recording. EMI's preference for a baritone (rather than tenor) Danilo in successive recordings has not always been successful, but here Eberhard Waechter encompasses the role without difficulty and gives a rousing portrayal of the playboy embassy *attaché*. As the second couple, Nicolai Gedda is in typically radiant voice, whilst Hanny Steffek makes a charming and vibrant Valencienne. Josef Knapp is a spirited ambassador.

If von Matačić's tempos are at times a little on the fast side, this is fully justified by the extra excitement achieved. At the same time there are moments of tenderness, as in the beautifully paced "Vilja" song, which comes off to perfection with

Nicolai Gedda   [photo: EMI

Schwarzkopf's beautifully held final note. The contribution of the "Königliche-Pontevedrinische Hof-Tamburrizzakapelle" to provide authentic Balkan atmosphere at Hanna's party is just one of the delightful touches of Walter Legge's production that go to make this a very special recording. The pity is that the score is given less than absolutely complete and that the CD changeover comes in the middle of Act 2. However, the artistry and sheer enjoyment of the recording are unmatched. It is one of those occasions when everything seems to come off perfectly.

Wallberg's version of *The Merry Widow* has come as close as any to ousting the earlier EMI recording from favour and it should certainly be considered by anyone wanting a CD of Lehár's masterpiece. If Edda Moser does not have the allure of Schwarzkopf, she is anything but dull and always sings intelligently and enjoyably, Prey sings commandingly and with an evident taste for the girls of Maxim's. There is particular appeal, though, from the supporting roles, with Siegfried Jerusalem and Helen Donath singing beautifully as the second couple. Moreover, they are allocated their full quota of numbers, with the delightful "Zauber der Häuslichkeit" duet (omitted from the earlier recording) showing Donath in especially captivating form. Benno Kusche, too, is his usual, splendidly fruity-voiced self as the ambassador. If Wallberg never quite generates the excitement that Matačić does, he is none the less an admirable conductor who always allows the score to speak for itself. Besides the inclusion of the additional number already mentioned, this set has three other advantages over its rival; firstly, the disc change is sensibly placed between Acts 1 and 2; secondly, the analogue sound has been digitally remastered to produce a clearer, more spacious result and finally, there is a price advantage. Provided that one does not mind the lack of a libretto, this set has undoubted attractions.

Kenneth Leighton   *Refer to Index*   *British 1929-1989*

Ruggero Leoncavallo

Italian 1857-1919

Leoncavallo. PAGLIACCI[a]. **Joan Carlyle** (sop) Nedda; **Carlo Bergonzi** (ten) Canio; **Giuseppe Taddei** (bar) Tonio; **Ugo Benelli** (ten) Beppe; **Rolando Panerai** (bar) Silvio.
Mascagni. CAVALLERIA RUSTICANA[a]. **Fiorenza Cossotto** (mez) Santuzza; **Adriane Martino** (mez) Lola; **Carlo Bergonzi** (ten) Turiddu; **Giangiacomo Guelfi** (bar) Alfio; **Maria Gracia Allegri** (contr) Lucia; **Chorus and Orchestra of La Scala, Milan/Herbert von Karajan.**
Opera Intermezzos. Berlin Philharmonic Orchestra/Herbert von Karajan. DG 419 257-2GH3. Notes, texts and translations included. Items marked [a] from SLPM139205/07 (10/66), [b] SLPM139031 (6/69).
Verdi: La traviata—Prelude, Act 3. **Puccini:** Manon Lescaut—Intermezzo. Suor Angelica—Intermezzo. **Schmidt:** Notre Dame—Intermezzo. **Massenet:** Thaïs—Meditátion (with Michel Schwalbé, vn). **Giordano:** Fedora—Intermezzo. **Cilea:** Adriana Lecouvreur—Intermezzo. **Wolf-Ferrari:** I gioiello della Madonna—Intermezzo. **Mascagni:** L'amico Fritz—Intermezzo.

③ 3h 18' ADD 10/87 Ⓑ

Cav and *Pag* as they are usually known have been bedfellows for many years. Lasting for about 75 minutes each, they have some similarities. Both works concern the passions, jealousies and hatred of two tightly-knit communities—the inhabitants of a Sicilian town and the players in a travelling troupe of actors. *Cavalleria rusticana* ("Rustic chivalry") concerns the triangular relationship of mother, son and his rejected lover. Played against a rich musical tapestry, sumptuously orchestrated, the action is played out during the course of an Easter day. Bergonzi is a stylish, ardent Turiddu whose virile charms glitter in his every phrase and Fiorenza Cossotto makes a thrilling Santuzza motivated and driven by a palpable conviction; her contribution to the well-known Easter hymn scene is gripping. But the real hero of the opera is Karajan, whose direction of this powerful work is magnificent. Conviction and insight also instil *Pagliacci* with excitement and real drama. A troupe of actors arrive to give a performance of a *commedia dell'arte* play. The illustration of real love, life and hatred is portrayed in the interplay of Tonio, Silvio, Nedda and her husband Canio. As the two rivals, Bergonzi and Taddei are superb. Taddei's sinister, hunchbacked clown, gently forcing the play-within-the-play closer to reality until it finally bursts out violently is a masterly assumption, and Karajan controls the slow build-up of tension with a grasp that few conductors could hope to equal. The Scala forces respond wholeheartedly and the 1965 recording sounds well. The third disc is filled by a selection of very rich, very soft-centred opera intermezzos.

Anatoli Liadov

Russian 1855-1914

Liadov. ORCHESTRAL WORKS. **Slovak Philharmonic Orchestra/ Stephen Gunzenhauser.** Marco Polo 8220348.
Baba-Yaga, Op. 56. Intermezzo in B flat major, Op. 8 No. 1. Pro starinu—Ballade in D major, Op. 21b. The enchanted lake, Op. 62. Village scene by the inn—Mazurka, Op. 19. Nénie, Op. 67. Polonaise, Op. 49. Polonaise in D major, Op. 55. Kikimora, Op. 63. From the Apocalypse, Op. 66.

58' DDD 10/86

Liadov was a superb miniaturist and as a professor of composition at the St Petersburg Conservatory he had an interestingly potent influence on the music of
his younger contemporaries. His finest works are jewel-like in the depth and

luminosity of colour they embody and the finesse with which they are worked. His short tone-poem, *The enchanted lake*, immediately establishes in a few delicate strokes the dank mystery of his subject; *Baba-Yaga* conjures up in only three minutes the menace of the mythical witch in flight; *Kikimora*, so well admired by Stravinsky, summons from out of hushed menace the demon wife of the house spirit, Domovoi. Listening to Liadov's works in succession highlights his problem with more protracted formal structures, but a programme such as this one is worth dipping into for the choice morsel or two. Each of these performances drives straight to the heart of the mood Liadov has in mind and the recording more than adequately captures the sparkle and solidity of the orchestral sound. For anyone interested in Liadov or the flowering of late-romanticism in music, this disc is well worth sampling.

Gyorgy Ligeti   *Refer to Index*   *Hungarian 1923-*

Franz Liszt   *Hungarian 1811-1886*

Liszt. Piano Concertos—No. 1 in E flat major, S124; No. 2 in A major, S125. **Sviatoslav Richter** (pf); **London Symphony Orchestra/Kyrill Kondrashin.** Philips 412 006-2PH. From SABL207 (5/62).

> 39' ADD 12/84   Ⓑ

Liszt. Piano Concertos—No. 1 in E flat major, S124; No. 2 in A major, S125. Totentanz, S525. **Alfred Brendel** (pf); **London Philharmonic Orchestra/ Bernard Haitink.** Philips Silver Line 426 637-2PSL. From 6500 374 (10/73).

> 56' ADD 11/90   £ ⁹ₚ Ⓑ

If the first disc is short in playing time it is long in artistry. Two great performances recorded in 1961 are preserved here in very good sound, especially in regard to the piano tone. Concerto No. 1 is the shorter and more immediately attractive of the two, its quieter passages containing music of delicate poetry and nobility that contrasts effectively with the 'heroic' virtuoso sections. The Second Concerto is a more inward work and is a less ostensibly virtuoso piece. Richter has a breathtaking technique, but it is more the aristocratic manner of his playing, and the eloquence and concentration of his phrasing which command admiration. The LSO seem inspired by the soloist, and they provide playing of high quality for Kondrashin.

Alfred Brendel's name has long been associated with Liszt's music, and in his recording of the two concertos and the wonderfully macabre *Totentanz* he is in superlative form, even judged by his own high standards. So are the London Philharmonic Orchestra and Bernard Haitink, and the sheer electricity, charm and scary *diablerie* of this brilliantly pianistic music is realized here to the full. The programme begins with the Second Concerto, which opens quietly, and though it has its full share of fireworks thereafter it is also a work of considerable lyricism and quiet eloquence. The First Concerto is still more of a bravura piece, but here too there are moments of great delicacy to which the artists do equal justice. The *Totentanz* was inspired by Orcagna's frescoes of the *Last Judgement at Pisa*, which Liszt saw in 1838 while on a visit to Italy with his mistress the Countess d'Agoult, and is a work of uncanny power and Mephistophelian glitter, cast in the form of variations of the *Dies irae* theme, which in an inspired performance such as this may be guaranteed soon to have any sympathetic listener on the edge of his or her seat if not actually falling off it. The recording goes back 20 years to 1972 but remains astonishingly vivid, not least in the all-important piano sound, and at medium price this is a disc that offers quite exceptional value.

Liszt. ORCHESTRAL WORKS. [a]**Shura Cherkassky** (pf); **Berlin Philharmonic Orchestra/Herbert von Karajan.** DG 415 967-2GH2. Fantasia on Hungarian Folk-themes, S123[a]. Mazeppa, S100 (both from 138 692, 9/61). Les préludes, S97 (139 037, 6/69). Mephisto Waltz No. 2, S111 (2530 244, 10/72). Hungarian Rhapsodies: No. 2 (2530 698, 8/76), No. 4, S359 (135 031, 4/68); No. 5 (2530 698, 8/76). Tasso, lamento e trionfo, S96 (2530 698, 8/76).

② 2h 1' ADD 9/86 Ⓑ

It was Liszt who first used the term "symphonic tone-poem" to describe the orchestral pieces he composed depicting stories and events. This set is a compilation of Liszt recordings made by Karajan over a period of some 15 years, and it is apparent that here is a composer who constantly stimulates the BPO's conductor to his freshest and most imaginative performances. There is a remarkable consistency of style in the playing, which is everywhere fresh, alert and has an abundance of energy and spirit, and the orchestra respond to their director with virtuoso playing of a high order. The *Fantasia* is an ideal vehicle for Cherkassky's brilliant, improvisatory style and although this particular recording was made a quarter of a century ago the piano tone and indeed the orchestral sound are very good. In fact the recordings all sound excellent, despite the difference in their dates of origin.

Liszt. A Faust Symphony, S108. **Alexander Young** (ten); **Beecham Choral Society; Royal Philharmonic Orchestra/Sir Thomas Beecham.** EMI CDM7 63371-2. From ASD317/18 (4/60).

70' ADD 2/88 £

Liszt's *Faust Symphony* is not in any way a conventional symphony, for it has three movements, in which the basic material is a series of short themes which are subjected to various techniques of alteration and transformation. Each movement portrays a character from Goethe's *Faust* but no attempt is made to follow the story. Beecham's 1958 recording has never been surpassed. The way he draws out the contrasts and characterizes each episode is masterly, and yet he maintains a strong sense of line throughout the long and complicated structure. To the "Gretchen" movement he brings a miraculous delicacy and grace, while the finale has extraordinary energy for a conductor in his eightieth year. The RPO's playing is inspired, and all the singing is good. In the new transfer there is a slight edge to the sound, but the basic quality is good.

Liszt. HUNGARIAN RHAPSODIES, S244—Nos. 1-19. **Roberto Szidon** (pf). DG Galleria 423 925-2GGA2. From 2720 072 (10/73). No. 1 in C sharp minor; No. 2 in C sharp minor; No. 3 in B flat major; No. 4 in E flat major; No. 5 in E minor, "Héroïde-Elégiaque"; No. 6 in D flat major; No. 7 in D minor; No. 8 in F sharp minor, "Capriccio"; No. 9 in E flat major, "Carnival in Pest"; No. 10 in E major; No. 11 in A minor; No. 12 in C sharp minor; No. 13 in A minor; No. 14 in F minor; No. 15 in A minor, "Rákóczy"; No. 16 in A minor, "For the Munkascy festivities in Budapest"; No. 17 in D minor; No. 18 in F sharp minor, "On the occasion of the Hungarian Exposition in Budapest"; No. 19 in D minor.

② 2h 23' ADD 3/89 £

Liszt's 19 Hungarian Rhapsodies contain some formidably difficult music of tremendous flavour and colour. Liszt first encountered gipsy music when he returned to Hungary in 1840 and he was quite entranced with the abandon and ecstasy it seemed capable of inspiring. Although the rhapsodies are perfectly able to stand on their own they can also be seen as an entity, a work with disparate but linked elements. The first 15 pieces (the last four date from the 1880s) therefore form a unified creation. The clash of tempo, tonality and rhythm has a strong place in Liszt's rhapsodies and the colours and timbres of the gipsy band are beautifully captured by this wizard of the keyboard with almost diabolic accuracy. The last four rhapsodies, in common with his other works from late in his career, have a haunted, introspective quality that makes them sound more abstract than their earlier counterparts. This recording has always been highly regarded and hearing it again on CD it is easy to understand why. There is a panache and verve that is so vital for the inner life of this music.

Liszt. PIANO WORKS. **Alfred Brendel** (pf). Philips 410 040-2PH. From 6514 147 (11/82).

Piano Sonata in B minor, S178. Légendes, S175—St François d'Assise: la prédication aux oiseaux; St François de Paule marchant sur les flots. La lugubre gondola Nos. 1 and 2, S200/1-2.

62' DDD 10/83 ⓑ

Liszt. PIANO WORKS. **Maurizio Pollini.** DG 427 322-2GH. Items marked [a] recorded at a performance in the Grosser Saal, Musikverein, Vienna on May 30th, 1988.

Piano Sonata in B minor, S178. Nuages gris, S199[a]. Unstern: sinistre, disastro, S208. La lugubre gondola I, S200[a]. R. W.—Venezia, S201[a].

46' DDD 7/90 ⓑ

Alfred Brendel   [photo: Philips

Liszt's Piano Sonata is one of the monuments of the romantic period and is the only sonata which the greatest pianist of musical history wrote for his instrument. It is in one long movement that has its component parts contained within a mighty sonata structure. Unfortunately it is also a work that has often been misunderstood and when treated chiefly as a virtuoso warhorse and vehicle for self-display the Sonata loses its dignity and poise. Alfred Brendel has lived with this music for decades, and his love and understanding of it are evident. Technically it is not flawless, but the blend of the various qualities needed—power, dignity, dexterity, sheer excitement, charm and above all structural cohesion is admirable. The two *St Francis* Legends and the funereal *Gondola* pieces are more than a fill-up and enhance this fine disc, revealing as they do other aspects of the composer.

Pollini is also one of the select few pianists who can keep all the Sonata's diverse elements in balance, so that his reading has a sense of wholeness rarely encountered in this work, even though others may have been even more illuminating in one or other aspect. Deutsche Grammophon's recording is of the highest quality. It would be unwise to expect too much of the late pieces, however. These are widely held to be prophetic of early twentieth-century modernism, but Pollini's way with them is rather detached (though pianistically judged to perfection) and the recording mixes live and studio performances to disconcerting effect.

***Liszt*.** PIANO WORKS. **Stephen Hough.** Virgin Classics VC7 90700-2.
Mephisto Waltz No. 1, S514. Venezia e Napoli, S162—Tarantella. Rhapsodie
espagnole, S254. Harmonies poétiques et religieuses, S173—Bénédiction de Dieu
dans la solitude; Pensée des morts. Légendes, S175—St François d'Assise: la
prédication aux oiseaux.

75' DDD 6/88

***Liszt*.** PIANO WORKS. **Jorge Bolet.** Decca 411 803-2DH.
Venezia e Napoli, S162. Années de pèlerinage. Troisième année, S163—No. 4,
Les jeux d'eaux à la Villa d'Este. Harmonies poétiques et religieuses,
S173—Bénédiction de Dieu dans la solitude. Ballade No. 2 in B minor, S171.

58' DDD 12/85

The most popular of the virtuoso pieces on the Hough disc is of course the first
Mephisto Waltz, played here with pronounced contrasts of dazzling diablerie and
seductive lyricism. The Italy-inspired *Tarantella* confirms Hough's technical
brilliance in breathtakingly fast repetition of single notes, while throughout the
dance he preserves an exceptional textural clarity. Characterization in the
Rhapsodie espagnole's variations is enhanced by a wide range of tone colour,
though just once or twice his scintillating prestidigitation militates against
breadth. But there is certainly no lack of that quality in *Pensée des morts*, the
fourth and most introspectively searching of the *Harmonies poétiques et religieuses*,
whose broodings are sustained with quite exceptional intensity as well as
expanding into a magnificently sonorous climax. The simple holiness of *St
François d'Assise: la prédication aux oiseaux* is conveyed with pellucid delicacy.
Finally comes the deeply consolatory *Bénédiction de Dieu dans la solitude*, where
Hough is even able to convince us that its "heavenly lengths" (17' 45") are not a
moment too long. The excellent recording artfully contrasts the crispness of the
three virtuoso pieces with Hough's more sustained sonority in religious
reflection.

The Decca recital also gives an unusually well-rounded picture of Liszt's piano
writing, what with the flurries of *Les jeux d'eaux à la Villa d'Este* (the most
important single precursor of French pianistic impressionism), the devotional
inwardness of *Bénédiction de Dieu dans la solitude* and the easy flowing grace of
"Gondoliera" and "Canzona" from *Venezia e Napoli*. Jorge Bolet's spacious
approach allows the ear to savour every detail, never at the expense of musical
flow and only at some small cost to physical exhilaration in the display pieces.
The impression of warm, consoling lyricism is enhanced by the faithfulness of an
exceptionally fine recording.

***Liszt*.** 12 Transcendental Studies, S139. **Claudio Arrau** (pf). Philips 416 458-
2PH. From 6747 412 (2/78).

67' ADD 6/86

Liszt published the *Douze Etudes en Douze Exercices* in 1826, when he was 15. He
later expanded all but one to form the basis of his horrendously difficult *Grandes
etudes* of 1838 (24 were intended but only 12 completed). Sensitivity to the
technical limitations of other virtuosos eventually overcame him, and in 1852 he
published a revised, 'easy' version, entitled the *Douze Etudes d'Exécution
Transcendante*, which he dedicated to his teacher, Carl Czerny. It is in this
(merely fiendishly difficult) form, with its fanciful titles for ten of the pieces,
that the work is usually performed today. Only a very few pianists of each
generation can begin to make music of these works in the way Liszt expected.
The technique required goes well beyond simple virtuosity and all too often
performances sink in a tumultuous sea of the scales and arpeggios that Liszt
intended should only provide a background tint. Maintaining speed is the other
major problem, for the great melodies must flow and sing as though the myriad

of other notes that interpose are hardly there. Arrau has for many years been one of the select band capable of this work and in this stable, well-defined recording from the mid 1970s he produces the account against which most others are measured.

Liszt. ORGAN WORKS. **Gunther Kaunzinger.** Novalis 150 069-2. Recorded on the organ of the Stiftsbasilika, Waldsassen, Germany. Prelude and Fugue on the name B-A-C-H, S260. Evocation à la Chapelle Sixtine, S658. Variations on "Weinen, Klagen, Sorgen, Zagen", S673. Fantasia and Fugue on "Ad nos, ad salutarem undam", S259.

72' DDD 2/91

Liszt's prodigious skill at the piano was legendary. But he was also a most capable organist and in the later years of his life he turned more and more to the organ, making transcriptions and reworkings for it of his own and other composers' music. As for original organ compositions he wrote a mere handful. The *Fantasia and Fugue* on the chorale *Ad nos, ad salutarem undam* (from Meyerbeer's opera *La Prophète*) is a work of considerable stature and virtuosity almost unparalleled in the organ's repertory. Although barely a third the length of the *Fantasia and Fugue*, the *Prelude and Fugue on B-A-C-H* is also a virtuoso showpiece paying homage to the composer who Liszt regarded as a supreme master. Homage is also paid to Bach in the Variations on *Weinen, Klagen, Sorgen, Zagen*, a theme Liszt took from Bach's Cantata No. 21. The *Evocation* of the Sistine Chapel combines Allegri's *Miserere* and Mozart's *Ave verum* in a deeply religious work which was, for Liszt, a profound statement of faith. Gunther Kaunzinger gives an outstanding performance of the *Fantasia and Fugue*, and in the other pieces his playing has great authority. He is served by a fine, if rather thick-sounding instrument, and a clean, full-blooded recording.

Liszt. ORGAN WORKS. **Reubke.** Sonata on the 94th Psalm. **Thomas Trotter** (org). Argo 430 244-2ZH. Played on the organ of the Münster zur Schönen Unsrer Lieben Frau, Ingolstadt, Germany. *Liszt:* Prelude and Fugue on the name B-A-C-H, S260. Gebet, S265 (arr. Gottschalg). Orpheus S98 (arr. Schaab). Prometheus, S99 (trans. Guillou).

73' DDD 2/91

This is a spectacular organ record, made on a big modern instrument in the very resonant acoustic of the Church of Our Lady, at Ingolstadt in Germany, which Thomas Trotter plays with great flair. The music is no less spectacular, belonging as it does to the nineteenth century and a full-blooded romantic tradition. The longest piece is the Reubke Sonata, music by a composer who died at 24 and is virtually unknown except to organists, and even to them by just this one work. It is a mighty one-movement sonata which reflects the influence of his teacher Liszt, to whom he went in 1856 shortly after the older man completed his great Piano Sonata, and was inspired by the powerful text of *Psalm* No. 94, which calls for God's judgement upon the wicked. Liszt himself is represented here by another work of surging strength, the *Prelude and Fugue* on the letters of the name Bach (the notes B flat, A, C, B natural), which make for a tightly chromatic motif yielding great harmonic and contrapuntal possibilities, not least in the fugue. This work begins the recital, and is followed by the same composer's serene tone poem in praise of music which he called *Orpheus*. Then comes the Reubke, and the other Liszt items follow it and thus make a sort of triptych with the longest work (the Sonata) as the centrepiece. Though two of the Liszt pieces are transcriptions rather than original organ works, they are effective in this form.

Henry Litolff   *Refer to Index*   *French 1818-1891*

Albert Lortzing   *German 1801-1851*

Lortzing. UNDINE. **Monika Krause** (sop) Undine; **Josef Protschka** (ten) Hugo; **Christiane Hampe** (sop) Bertalda; **John Janssen** (bar) Kühleborn; **Klaus Häger** (bass) Tobias; **Ingeborg Most** (contr) Marthe; **Heinz Kruse** (ten) Veit; **Andreas Schmidt** (bass) Hans; **Günter Wewel** (bass) Heilmann; **Dirk Schortemeier** (spkr) Messenger; **Cologne Radio Chorus and Orchestra/Kurt Eichhorn.** Capriccio 60 017-2. Text and translation included.

② 2h 37' DDD 3/91

A pity, in a way, that this couldn't have been a video recording, for *Undine*, a curious mixture of the fantastic and the prosaically bourgeois, has one of the most spectacular (though enormously difficult to stage) endings in all opera: the knight Hugo's castle is (in full view) inundated, and he and his living water-nymph Undine (who has been put on earth to find out whether humans, who have souls, are superior to nature-spirits, who have none) are united in a crystal palace at the bottom of the sea. A lot more than he deserved, for having fallen in love with this pretty and ingenuous creature and married her, he had been faithless; but Lortzing allowed himself to be persuaded to give the work a happy ending. His setting of this fable is undemandingly melodious, frequently folk-like, and extremely skilfully scored; and the veteran Kurt Eichhorn secures first-class orchestral playing and choral singing. The sopranos—Undine and the haughty princess who is discovered to be low-born—are less impressive than the men, who are extremely well cast. Protschka as the fickle knight excels in his big 'nightmare' aria in Act 4, Janssen makes a menacing Prince of the Waters, and Kruse is efficient, if sounding over-classy for a mere squire with a weakness for the bottle. Gaps left between the ends of musical numbers and the ensuing dialogues (which are well produced) rather weaken the dramatic flow; but all in all this first complete recording for 25 years of this romantic opera is greatly to be welcomed.

Jean-Baptiste Lully   *Italian-French 1632-1687*

Lully. ATYS. *Prologue*—**Bernard Deletré** (bass) Le Temps; **Monique Zanetti** (sop) Flore; **Jean-Paul Fouchécourt** (bass), **Gilles Ragon** (ten) Zephirs; **Arlette Steyer** (sop) Melpomene; **Agnès Mellon** (sop) Iris. *Tragédie-lyrique*—**Guy de Mey** (ten) Atys; **Agnès Mellon** (sop) Sangaride; **Guillemette Laurens** (mez) Cybèle; **Françoise Semellaz** (sop) Doris; **Jacques Bona** (bass) Idas; **Noémi Rime** (sop) Mélisse; **Jean-François Gardeil** (bass) Célénus; **Gilles Ragon** (ten) Le sommeil; **Jean-Paul Fouchécourt** (ten) Morphée, Trio; **Bernard Deletré** (bass) Phobétor, Sangar; **Michel Laplénie** (ten) Phantase; **Stephan Maciejewski** (bass) Un songe funeste; **Isabelle Desrochers** (sop) Trio; **Véronique Gens** (sop) Trio; **Les Arts Florissants Chorus and Orchestra/William Christie.** Harmonia Mundi HMC90 1257/9. Notes, text and translation included.

③ 2h 50' DDD 7/87

Once upon a time Lully's melodies were the property of the common people. Not so today when, apart from occasional revivals and broadcasts, his operas are largely forgotten. *Atys* is reputed to have been Louis XIV's favourite opera and here William Christie and a fine line-up of soloists bring the work to life in a most compelling way. There are some beautiful choruses and ensembles throughout the opera which should make wide and immediate appeal; but it is in the Third Act where Lully treats his audience to a *sommeil* or sleep scene that much of the most arresting and original music is contained. Recorded sound is effective and the booklet contains the full libretto.

Witold Lutoslawski

Polish 1913-

Lutoslawski. ORCHESTRAL WORKS. [a]**Louis Devos** (ten); [b]**Roman Jablónski** (vc); [b]**Katowice Radio Symphony Orchestra;** [ad]**Warsaw National Philharmonic Orchestra;** [cd]**Jan Krenz;** [ab]**Witold Lutoslawski.** Polskie Nagrania Muza PNCD042.
Paroles tissées[a]. Cello Concerto[b] (both from EMI 1C 165 03231/6, 7/79).
Postlude I[bc]. Livre pour orchestre[d].

64' ADD 9/90

This volume featuring CD transfers of ageing recordings stands up to today's competition better than most. Although they date from between 1964 and 1976, the recordings still retain much of the clarity and detail of these first-rate performances. Jan Krenz makes a fine job of the intricate textures of that concentrated masterpiece, *Livre pour orchestre* and the somewhat similarly structured Cello Concerto, dedicated to Rostropovich, finds here a committed advocate in Roman Jablónski. These two works date from 1968 and 1970 respectively. *Paroles tissées* predates the first of these by three years and, superficially, seems very different in style with open textures and chamber-music balances. If the tenor here, Louis Devos, lacks the poetry of Sir Peter Pears, for whom the work was written, he nevertheless does the work justice and points its many delights. The first of the three Postludes (1958-63), which opens the disc, shows Lutoslawski's musical antecedents much more clearly than the other works, but it is still a remarkable piece for a composer who, only a few years before, had been producing music that only too well complied with the requirements of a Poland still in the cultural grip of Stalinist dictates.

Lutoslawski. Partita for violin, orchestra and obbligato solo piano (1985)[a].
Chain 2 for violin and orchestra (1984)[b].
Stravinsky. Violin Concerto in D[c]. **Anne-Sophie Mutter** (vn); [a]**Phillip Moll** (pf); [ab]**BBC Symphony Orchestra/Witold Lutoslawski;** [c]**Philharmonia Orchestra/Paul Sacher.** DG 423 696-2GH.

56' DDD 2/89

This disc contains some spell-binding violin playing in a splendidly lifelike recording, and it's a bonus that the music, while unquestionably 'modern', needs no special pleading: its appeal is instantaneous and long-lasting. Anne-Sophie Mutter demonstrates that she can equal the best in a modern classic—the Stravinsky Concerto—and also act as an ideal, committed advocate for newer works not previously recorded. The Stravinsky is one of his liveliest neo-classical pieces, though to employ that label is, as usual, to underline its rough-and-ready relevance to a style that uses Bach as a springboard for an entirely individual and unambiguously modern idiom. Nor is it all 'sewing-machine' rhythms and pungently orchestrated dissonances. There is lyricism, charm, and above all humour: and no change of mood is too fleeting to escape the razor-sharp responses of this soloist and her alert accompanists, authoritatively guided by the veteran Paul Sacher. Lutoslawski's music has strongly individual qualities that have made him perhaps the most approachable of all contemporary composers. This enthralling collaboration between senior composer and youthful virtuoso is not to be missed.

Guillaume de Machaut

French c.1300-1377

Machaut. Messe de Nostre Dame.
Anonymous. Plainsong Prayers for the Feast of the Nativity of Our Lady.
Taverner Consort and Choir/Andrew Parrott. EMI Reflexe CDC7 47949-2. Notes, texts and translations included. From ASD143576-1 (3/84).

51' DDD 8/88

Machaut. Messe de Nostre Dame. Je ne cesse de prier (lai "de la fonteinne"). Ma fin est mon commencement. **Hilliard Ensemble/Paul Hillier.** Hyperion CDA66358. Texts and translations included.

54' DDD 3/90

Machaut's *Messe de Nostre Dame* is the earliest known setting of the Ordinary Mass by a single composer though we cannot be certain either that Machaut wrote it at one time or even that he initially intended to bring its six movements together. The music is splendid but though each of these performances seeks 'authenticity' the chosen path towards it is markedly different. Paul Hillier is the

Andrew Parrott [photo: EMI]

more modest of the two directors in the extent to which he 'reconstructs', and he employs two voices only to a part. Andrew Parrott, on the other hand, places the Mass in a liturgical context with Propers, bells and celebrants; furthermore, he transposes the music down a fourth employing only tenors and basses as soloists. Each performance has its own strengths and weaknesses and one might almost say that neither on its own offers the listener a wholly satisfying account of Machaut's music. Listeners will probably find that the textures achieved by the Hilliard Ensemble are lighter and more expressive than those of the other, transposed down a fourth. But the notion of presenting the music in the context of a Mass, thereby allowing for important contrasts between chant and polyphony is effective, and Parrott's reconstruction contains an engaging and proper sense of occasion. Both versions include texts and translations and both should be heard.

Roman Maciejewski

Polish 1910-

Maciejewski. Missa pro defunctis. **Zdzislawa Donat** (sop); **Jadwiga Rappé** (contr); **Jerzy Knetig** (ten); **Janusz Niziolek** (bass); **Warsaw Philharmonic Choir and Orchestra/Tadeusz Strugala.** Polskie Nagrania Muza PNCD039.

② 2h 11' DDD 9/90

This Requiem was Roman Maciejewski's attempt to come to terms with the catastrophic events of the Second World War and also with his disillusionment with the pre-war avant-garde. It took him until 1959 to finish it, and it had to wait another 16 years for its first performance in Los Angeles—apparently a very emotional event. One of the most extraordinary things about the Requiem though is the way that it anticipates recent developments in music, particularly the rejection of difficult atonalism in favour of sensuous modal harmonies and hypnotic repetitions. Occasionally one may be reminded of the Holst of *Neptune* or the *Rig Veda* hymns—and that's a significant comparison, because whatever else he is, Maciejewski is not a minimalist. In the most beautiful movements— the "Graduale", "Tractus" or "Recordare" for instance—the patterns provide the background to some finely expressive vocal and instrumental writing. It is in these meditative movements rather than in the big apocalyptic numbers that Maciejewski really shows his strength, but he manages to keep the listener hooked right to the end. Performances and recording may lack the final layer of polish, but intense feelings are communicated. A real discovery.

Elizabeth Maconchy *British 1907-1990*

Maconchy. String Quartets, Nos. 5-8. **Bingham Quartet** (Stephen Bingham, Mark Messenger, vns; Brenda Stewart, va; Miriam Lowbury, vc). Unicorn-Kanchana DKPCD9081.

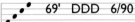 69' DDD 6/90

Elizabeth Maconchy was a pupil, and later a lifelong friend, of Vaughan Williams. But her music owes little to the British nationalist tradition inspired by folk-song; rather, she has always shown a natural inclination towards what she calls the "difficult and challenging medium" and "impassioned debate" of the string quartet, with its form and interplay between four balanced voices. This second disc in Unicorn-Kanchana's enterprising series of these works brings us music written between 1948 and 1967, played with intelligence and commitment by a young British ensemble. The fact that Quartets Nos. 5-8 all fit on to a single CD itself tells us something about their terse, pithy nature; Bartók is the most obvious model (and sometimes too obvious for comfort, as in the finale of No. 5 and the form of No. 7), but we also often find, in the slow movements particularly, a quiet, edgy lyricism that is very much an aspect of the composer's own voice and an attractive one. The recording has warm yet detailed sound. In the accompanying booklet, the composer is usefully informative and her daughter's biographical note is also valuable, though making rather extravagant claims.

Albéric Magnard *French 1865-1914*

Magnard. Symphony No. 2 in E major, Op. 6. Hymne à la justice, Op. 14. Ouverture, Op. 10. **Toulouse Capitole Orchestra/Michel Plasson.** EMI CDC7 49080-2.

67' DDD 1/89

Magnard's music has been somewhat eclipsed by that of Debussy. Nevertheless his own personality is evident from the very first bars of his Second Symphony, which manage to sound unexpected yet convincing, and the freshness of what Magnard had to say is a feature throughout the whole of this big work, with its grandly constructed first movement, dance-like second, songful third (again with a striking opening and perhaps the most memorable in its rich lyricism) and vivacious finale. Michel Plasson and his Toulouse Capitole Orchestra are notably good in this kind of repertory, and they are richly if not always quite clearly recorded. This is not yet one of the great orchestras, but theirs is a strong and understanding presentation of unfamiliar music that deserves to be better known. Like the symphony, the *Hymn to Justice* and *Overture* belong to the period 1892-1902 and remind us what fine music was then coming out of France.

Gustav Mahler

Austrian 1860-1911

Mahler. SYMPHONIES. **Bavarian Radio Symphony Orchestra/Rafael Kubelík.** DG 429 042-2GX10.
Symphonies—No. 1 (from SLPM139331, 5/68); No. 2, "Resurrection" (Edith Mathis, sop; Norma Procter, contr; Bavarian Radio Chorus 139332/3, 4/70); No. 3 (Marjorie Thomas, contr; Tölz Boys' Choir; Bavarian Rad. Chor. SLPM139337/8, 9/68); No. 4 (Elsie Morison, sop. SLPM139339, 12/68); No. 5 (2720 033, 10/71); No. 6 (139341/2, 11/69); No. 7 (2720 033); No. 8 (Martina Arroyo, Erna Spoorenberg, Mathis, sops; Júlia Hamari, Procter, contrs; Donald Grobe, ten; Dietrich Fischer-Dieskau, bar; Franz Crass, bass; Regensburg Cathedral Boys' Choir; Munich Motet Choir; Bavarian Rad. Chor; North German Radio Chorus; West German Radio Chorus, 2720 033); No. 9 (SLPM139 345/6, 12/67); No. 10—Adagio (139341/2).

⑩⑩ 10h 51' ADD 5/90 £ 9ᵖ

There are well over 150 recordings of Mahler's symphonies listed in *The Classical Catalogue*, so anyone approaching them for the first time is faced with the daunting problem of which versions he should invest in. This reissue may well be something of a solution. For here we have a distinguished and highly commendable cycle of the symphonies at bargain price that provides an excellent opportunity for the newcomer to explore the symphonies at a relatively low cost. Kubelík's cycle is still one of the most completely satisfying on disc. There is a breadth and consistency of vision in these interpretations, that comes only from a conductor who has a deep understanding and a long association with this music. The most successful

performances are perhaps Symphonies Nos. 1, 4, 5, 7 and 9. The First, notable for its fresh, youthful account and clearly defined textures, is still one of the finest versions available. The Fourth is equally as impressive, with lively tempos and excellent orchestral playing. There is a strong sense of direction and structural unity in this performance and Elsie Morison's warm and poetic performance in the finale is a real delight. Kubelík's reading of Symphonies Nos. 5 and 7 have not always met with the credit that they deserve. The Fifth is a very individual performance, though certainly not lacking in

Rafael Kubelík [photo: DG]

intensity or power. Kubelík avoids dwelling too much on the tragic elements in the first movement of the Seventh and instead tries to build out of the devastation of the Sixth Symphony's finale. The Ninth is a very strong performance indeed, with great clarity of detail and a strong sense of architecture.

It would of course be foolish to suggest that Kubelík's cycle is without flaws—the Second Symphony, although not without intensity, lacks perhaps the drama and spirituality of, say, Klemperer or Rattle and the same could be said of the Third. The Eighth is a fine performance superbly recorded and with some excellent singing from the soloists, but is ultimately outclassed by the superb recordings of Solti and Tennstedt. The recordings are all clear, spacious and naturally balanced and were recorded in the warm and resonant acoustic of the Munich Herkulessaal between 1967 and 1971. A considerable bargain.

Mahler. Symphony No. 1. **Royal Concertgebouw Orchestra, Amsterdam/Leonard Bernstein.** DG 431 036-2GBE. Recorded at performances in the Concertgebuw, Amsterdam in October 1987.

56' DDD 3/89

A great performance from a great Mahlerian impressively caught 'in the act' at Amsterdam's Concertgebouw hall. Bernstein's view of the piece has changed comparatively little over the years and fundamentals such as tempos remain more or less consistent. And yet the whole experience sounds newer, fresher; certain phrases have filled out, the expression is appreciably freer and easier now. How acutely Bernstein still *hears* Mahler's early-morning 'silence' at the outset: the dewy haze of string harmonics, the richly harmonized horns, their dreamy reveries broken only by sudden *fortissimo* pizzicatos (like startled animals) in the violins. All this is most beautifully and subtly chronicled by the Royal Concertgebouw players. In the bucolic inner movements, Bernstein characteristically relishes the coarse-cut sonorities. Accenting is trenchant and weighty in the lumbering scherzo, and the corny gipsy-cum-café music of the third movement is ideally tawdry. Furthermore, Bernstein's inspired account of the finale is a performance like no other—in atmosphere, in galvanic energy, in repose or in triumph. The recording, like the performance, is vivid and immediate. A very hard act to follow.

Mahler. Symphony No. 2, "Resurrection". **Arleen Auger** (sop); **Dame Janet Baker** (mez); **City of Birmingham Symphony Chorus and Orchestra/ Simon Rattle.** EMI CDS7 47962-8. Text and translation included. From EX270598-3 (10/87).

② 86' DDD 12/87

The folk-poems from *Des knaben Wunderhorn*, with their complex mixture of moods and strong ironic edge, formed the basis of Mahler's inspiration for the Second Symphony. It is a work of huge scope, emotionally as well as physically taxing, and here it receives a performance that remarkably rekindles the feeling of a live performance with a quite breathtaking immediacy. The CBSO play magnificently and Rattle's attention to the letter of the score never hinders his overall vision of this masterpiece. The recording is superb.

Mahler. Symphony No. 3. **Norma Procter** (contr); **Wandsworth School Boys' Choir; Ambrosian Singers; London Symphony Orchestra/Jascha Horenstein.** Unicorn-Kanchana Souvenir UKCD2006/07. Text and translation included. From RHS302/03 (12/70).

② 97' ADD 11/88

Every now and again, along comes a Mahler *performance* that no serious collector can afford to be without. Horenstein's interpretation of the Third Symphony is an outstanding example and its reissue on CD at mid-price is a major addition to the Mahler discography. No other conductor has surpassed Horenstein in his total grasp of every facet of the enormous score. Even though the LSO strings of the day were not as powerful as they later became, they play with suppleness and a really tense sound, especially appropriate in the kaleidoscopic first movement, where changes of tempo and mood reflect the ever-changing face of nature. Horenstein gives the posthorn solo to a flügelhorn, a successful experiment. His light touch in the middle movements is admirable, and Norma Procter is a steady soloist in "O Mensch! Gib acht!", with the Wandsworth School Boys' Choir bimm-bamming as if they were all Austrian-born! Then comes the *Adagio* finale, its intensity and ecstasy sustained by Horenstein without dragging the tempo. The recording is not as full and rich in dynamic range as some made recently, but it is still a classic.

Mahler. Symphony No. 4 in G major. **Kathleen Battle** (sop); **Vienna Philharmonic Orchestra/Lorin Maazel.** CBS Masterworks CD39072. From IM39072 (3/85).

61' DDD 1/86

Mahler. Symphony No. 4 in G major. **Felicity Lott** (sop); **London Philharmonic Orchestra/Franz Welser-Möst.** EMI Eminence CD-EMX2139. Text and translation included.

63' DDD 12/88

"With sincere and serene expression" says Mahler's footnote in the finale—"absolutely without parody!" And that is exactly how Lorin Maazel, Kathleen Battle and the Vienna Philharmonic Orchestra respond to this music: the grotesqueries of the scherzo are nicely underplayed; the darker outbursts of the slow movement are not overloaded with *Angst*; and there is nothing wry or sentimentally nostalgic about "Die himmlischen Freuden". Instead, there is warmth, tenderness and, especially in the closing movement, a kind of heart-easing simplicity, enhanced by the purity and uncloying sweetness of Kathleen Battle's singing. The recording is warm-toned and beautifully balanced and the dynamic range is impressive, though never unrealistic.

Franz Welser-Möst, however, sheds new light on this Symphony with a reading that is the most expansive on disc so far. This has the effect of placing the work more in the context of Mahler's symphonic line. 'Expansive' is very much the word, the slow movement being the most controversial in this respect. Welser-Möst takes a leisurely 25 minutes here (most performances average 19 or 20 minutes) but the effect is quite magical and convincing, with never a hint of sluggishness, and the final climax and closing pages of this movement are truly revelatory and uplifting. The phantasmagoria of the first movement is well captured too, from the optimistic opening to the fairy-tale horror of the development's climax, where the trumpet's fanfare looks both back to the Second and Third Symphonies and forward to the opening of the Fifth. The LPO's performance is top rate, with some ravishing and full-bodied string playing, and Welser-Möst's meticulous attention to detail is highlighted by a spacious and well-defined recording.

Mahler. Symphony No. 5. **Vienna Philharmonic Orchestra/Leonard Bernstein.** DG 423 608-2GH. Recorded at a performance in the Alte Oper, Frankfurt during September 1987.

75' DDD 8/88

Mahler. Symphony No. 5. **New Philharmonia Orchestra/Sir John Barbirolli.** EMI Studio CDM7 69186-2. From ASD2518 (12/69).

74' ADD 11/88

Mahler's Fifth begins with a funeral march, in which the military bugle-calls he heard as a boy sound through the textures, leading to a central *scherzo* full of nostalgia for Alpine lakes and pastures, a soulful *Adagietto* for strings which we now know was a love-letter to his future wife and ends with a triumphant, joyous *rondo-finale*. It has been called Mahler's *Eroica* and that is not a far-fetched description. In recent years Bernstein tended to go 'over the top' in Mahler, but here he is at his exciting best and the Vienna Philharmonic responds to him as only it can to a conductor with whom it has a special relationship. The recording is exceptionally clear and well-balanced, so that many subtleties of detail in the scoring emerge but are not over highlighted. The symphony again sounds the daringly orchestrated piece that bewildered its first audiences, only now we realize the genius of it all. Structure, sound and emotion are held in ideal equilibrium by Bernstein in this enthralling performance.

Sir John's Mahler No. 5 has a special place in everyone's affections: a performance so big in spirit and warm of heart as to silence any rational discussion of its shortcomings. Despite some controversially measured tempos and ensemble in the vehement second movement that is not all it should be, this reading has a unity and strength of purpose and an entirely idiomatic response to Mahlerian colour and cast. But most important of all, it has that very special Barbirolli radiance, humanity—call it what you will—the celebrated *Adagietto* is, needless to say, in very caring hands indeed. Something of a classic, then (and EMI have made a wonderful job of the digital remastering), though one to regard as a supplement to the stunning Bernstein account.

Mahler. Symphony No. 6 in A minor[a]. Five Rückert Lieder[b]. [b]**Christa Ludwig** (mez); **Berlin Philharmonic Orchestra/Herbert von Karajan.** DG 415 099-2GH2. Notes, texts and translations included. Item marked [a] from 2707 106 (7/78), [b] 2707 082 (12/75).

② 102' ADD 4/85

Mahler. Symphony No. 6. **City of Birmingham Symphony Orchestra/ Simon Rattle.** EMI CDS7 54047-2.

② 86' DDD 11/90

Mahler. Symphony No. 6. Kindertotenlieder[a]. [a]**Thomas Hampson** (bar); **Vienna Philharmonic Orchestra/Leonard Bernstein.** DG 427 697-2GH2. Recorded at a performance in the Grosser Saal, Musikverein, Vienna in September and October 1988

② 115' DDD 1/90

Mahler's tragic Sixth Symphony digs more profoundly into the nature of man and Fate than any of his earlier works. It also celebrates his attachment to his wife and Muse Alma. The symphony, however, closes in desolation, a beat on the bass drum, a coffin lid closing. Karajan's reading of this great work is superb, profoundly observed and imaginatively coloured. The *Rückert Lieder*, which complete the set, show how Mahler's song writing changed as he moved away from the folk-song world of *Des Knaben Wunderhorn* to the sparer, emotionally tauter and spiritually more concentrated poetic world of Friedrich Rückert. Christa Ludwig brings her rich, burnished tones to these glorious songs and is sensitively accompanied by Karajan, whose handling of the important wind lines is masterly. It restores one's taste for life after the bleakness of the symphony's close.

Nevertheless, Rattle is a natural Mahlerian and his emotional and intellectual grasp of the first movement of the Sixth is outstanding. Tempos are perfectly judged and there's a tremendous feeling of architectural unity here. The beautiful *Alma* theme is played with a great deal of elation and affection, with inner parts superbly detailed (the descanting horns sound wonderful) and upper strings are perfectly phrased and radiant. Rattle has strong feelings about the ordering of the central movements, belonging to the school of thought that Mahler originally intended the *Andante* to precede the *Scherzo* (most conductors perform them as published—*Scherzo* first, *Andante* second) so it comes as no surprise to find the more controversial order in Rattle's recording (it's only fair to mention that EMI have split these movements between the two discs, thus ruling out any ideas listeners may have in craftily altering the sequence). Rattle's account of the *Andante* is extraordinarily beautiful—magical in the extreme, with some particularly intense and lovely solos from the players of the CBSO, and in the finale Rattle calculatingly builds the intensity and anguish to an almost unbearable degree when we reach the third and final hammer blow (which Rattle reinstates in this performance) after which all is darkness until the spine-chilling final chord in A minor. The recording is well balanced and superbly engineered.

Bernstein's reading was a live recording at a concert, with all the electricity of such an occasion, and the Vienna Philharmonic Orchestra respond to the conductor's dark vision of Mahler's score with tremendous bravura. Fortunately, the achingly tender slow movement brings some relief, but with the enormous finale lasting over 30 minutes we must witness a resumption of a battle to the death and the final outcome. The coupling is a logical one, for the *Kindertotenlieder* takes up the theme of death yet again. But it is in a totally different, quieter way: these beautiful songs express a parent's grief over the loss of a child, and although some prefer a woman's voice here the sensitive Thomas Hampson makes a good case for a male singer. The recording of both works is so good that one would not know it was made 'live', particularly as the applause is omitted.

Mahler. Symphony No. 7. **Chicago Symphony Orchestra/Claudio Abbado.** DG 413 773-2GH2. From 413 773-1GH2 (3/85).

② 79' DDD 4/85

Mahler provided no programme for this Symphony but it can be logically viewed as a progression through various shades of darkness until a finale is reached, providing light and hope. Abbado's performance has a clear-sighted lucidity which serves this work well. The first movement has a fine coherence, and a forward-moving thrust; the distinctive separate characters of the inner movements are sharply drawn, and throughout the symphony Abbado draws playing of brilliance and refinement from the Chicago orchestra. The recording has an ideal clarity too, and a presence which boldly illuminates Mahler's fantastic scoring.

Mahler. Symphony No. 8. **Elizabeth Connell, Edith Wiens, Felicity Lott** (sops); **Trudeliese Schmidt, Nadine Denize** (contrs); **Richard Versalle** (ten); **Jorma Hynninen** (bar); **Hans Sotin** (bass); **Tiffin Boys' School Choir; London Philharmonic Choir and Orchestra/Klaus Tennstedt.** EMI CDS7 47625-8. Notes, text and translation included. From EX270474-3 (3/87).

② 82' DDD 5/87

Mahler's extravagantly monumental Eighth Symphony, often known as the *Symphony of a Thousand*, is the Mahler symphony that raises doubts in even his most devoted of admirers. Its epic dimensions, staggering vision and sheer

profligacy of forces required make it a 'difficult work'. Given a great live performance it will sway even the hardest of hearts; given a performance like Tennstedt's, reproduced with all the advantages of CD, home-listeners, too, can be mightily impressed (and so, given the forces involved, will most of the neighbourhood!)—the sheer volume of sound at the climax is quite overwhelming. The work seeks to parallel the Christian's faith in the power of the Holy Spirit with the redeeming power of love for mankind and Tennstedt's performance leaves no doubt that he believes totally in Mahler's creation. It has a rapt, almost intimate, quality that makes this reading all the more moving. The soloists are excellent and the choruses sing with great conviction.

Mahler. Symphony No. 9 in D major. **Berlin Philharmonic Orchestra/ Herbert von Karajan.** DG 410 726-2GH2. Recorded at performances in September 1982 at the Berlin Festival.

② 85' DDD 8/84   P Ⓑ

Mahler. Symphony No. 9 in D major. **Berlin Philharmonic Orchestra/Sir John Barbirolli.** EMI Studio CDM7 63115-2. From ASD596/7 (9/64).

78' ADD 11/89   £ P Ⓑ

Mahler's Ninth is a death-haunted work, but is filled, as Bruno Walter remarked, "with a sanctified feeling of departure". Rarely has this Symphony been shaped with such understanding and played with such selfless virtuosity as it was by Karajan and the Berlin Philharmonic in a legendary series of concerts in 1982. The performance is electric and intense, yet Karajan—ever the enigmatic blend of fire and ice—has the measure of the symphony's spiritual coolness. Karajan had previously made a fine studio recording of the Ninth but this later concert performance is purer, deeper, and even more dauntingly intense. The digital recording has great clarity and a thrilling sense of actuality; no symphony in the repertoire benefits more than this one from the absolute quietness that CD allows. When the history of twentieth-century music-making comes to be written this performance will be seen as one of its proudest landmarks.

Barbirolli's famous recording of Mahler's Ninth Symphony has also long been considered as one of the finest accounts on disc. It is reputed that Barbirolli spent over 50 hours rehearsing this Symphony when he first conducted it with the Hallé Orchestra in 1954. This recording made ten years later with the Berlin Philharmonic certainly contains all the hallmarks of a conductor who possesses a deep understanding of and affection for the work. The result is very special indeed. Barbirolli took great pains over this recording, even to the point of rearranging the recording schedules so that the last movement *Adagio* was recorded in one of the evening sessions, giving the players a chance to "get in the right mood" as he put it. The first movement is primed with intensity and emotion, and Mahler's vast arch-like structure is never allowed to flag or falter for a moment. Contrapuntally this movement is the most complex that Mahler ever wrote, and Barbirolli's handling of these textures is imbued with a clarity and sense of purpose seldom found. The sarcasm and irony of the central movements are superbly drawn, and the *Rondo Burleske* has a savage ferocity of demonic proportions. The stoical *Adagio*-finale is given a reading of transcendental beauty, intensity and passion. The recording, like the playing, is warm, sumptuous and atmospheric and apart from some faint tape hiss, shows little sign of ageing. Highly recommended.

Mahler. (Cooke perf. ver.). Symphony No. 10.
Schoenberg. Verklärte Nacht, Op. 4. **Berlin Radio Symphony Orchestra/Riccardo Chailly.** Decca 421 182-2DH2.

② 1h 50' 3/88

There is no doubt that Chailly is convinced of Deryck Cooke's performing version of the Tenth Symphony. He conducts with the authority that comes from a total understanding of the score. His tempos are generally slower than in previous recordings and the emotional temperature is somewhat lower, but Chailly highlights the thematic connections between movements and his interpretation of the problematical second *scherzo* is the finest on disc. Where Chailly differs from other conductors is in muffling the drum strokes at the start of the finale—not as terrifying a sound as the startling thwacks in other recordings, but perhaps realistically nearer to the sound that so moved Mahler as a New York fireman's cortège passed below his hotel window. The solo flautist and trumpeter are magnificent in this finale, as are the violins in their last statement of the movement's sublime climactic melody. Just how good the orchestra's string section is as a whole may be heard in its lyrical performance of Schoenberg's *Verklärte Nacht*, which makes a well-chosen adjunct to the symphony. Both works are exceptionally well recorded in the satisfying acoustic of the Jesus-Christus Kirche, Berlin.

Mahler. LIEDER.
Wolf. LIEDER. **Anne Sofie von Otter** (mez); **Ralf Gothóni** (pf). DG 423 666-2GH. Texts and translations included.
Mahler: Des Knaben Wunderhorn—No. 2, Verlorne Müh; No. 7, Rheinlegendchen; No. 9, Wo die schönen Trompeten blasen; No. 10, Lob des hohen Verstands. Lieder und Gesang—No. 1, Frühlingsmorgen. No. 2, Erinnerung. No. 4, Serenade aus Don Juan. No. 5, Phantasie aus Don Juan No. 7, Ich ging mit Lust durch einen grünen Wald. No. 8, Aus! Aus!. **Wolf:** Heiss mich nicht reden (Mignon I). Nur wer die Sehnsucht (Mignon II). So lasst mich scheinen (Mignon III). Kennst du das Land (Mignon). Frühling übers Jahr. Frage nicht. Die Spröde. Der Schäfer. Gesang Weylas.

· 59'   DDD   6/89

Anne Sofie von Otter's first record of Lieder has proved an outright winner. She obviously owes something of a debt to Christa Ludwig and Brigitte Fassbaender, but she nonetheless establishes a personality and style of her own. Technically she is virtually faultless, and she brings to her performance a nice combination of interpretative insight and emotional involvement. These assets are at once

evident in the four settings by Hugo Wolf of Mignon's enigmatic utterances from *Wilhelm Meister*. Each is perceptively characterized by von Otter and her admirable partner Ralf Gothóni, bringing before our eyes the suppressed grief and longing of the sad waif so unerringly portrayed by Wolf. They then find, by contrast, a pleasing simplicity for the next three songs before returning to a more intense manner for the marvellous *Gesang Weylas*.

For the Mahler the pair adopt another style and just the right one. Humour and lightness, where relevant, rightly dominate their accounts of the pieces from *Des Knaben Wunderhorn*. Von Otter's singing is playful without ever becoming coy or mannered. In the more serious "Ich ging mit Lust" the singer's melding of line and tone is near-ideal. "Wo die schönen Trompeten blasen" may be taken at a dangerously slow tempo, but this in a way enhances the mesmeric mood of the song. The seldom-heard settings from Molina's *Don Juan*, especially the alluring "Serenade", are precisely tuned to the music in hand. Altogether this is a delightful and more-than-promising début.

Anne Sofie von Otter   [photo: DG/Somoroff]

Mahler. Das Lied von der Erde. **Christa Ludwig** (mez); **Fritz Wunderlich** (ten); **Philharmonia Orchestra, New Philharmonia Orchestra/Otto Klemperer.** EMI CDC7 47231-2. From SAN179 (1/67).

> 64' ADD 12/85

Mahler. Das Lied von der Erde. **Brigitte Fassbaender** (mez); **Thomas Moser** (ten); **Cyprien Katsaris** (pf). Teldec 2292-46276-2. Text and translation included.

> 61' DDD 6/90 ❓

One of the great orchestral song cycles grew, like the Ninth Symphony, out of Mahler's sense of the imminence of his own death. The text is based on poems from the Chinese T'ang dynasty and their delicate sense of the transience of things chimed perfectly with Mahler's mood. His music is luminously beautiful but shot through with a recurring sense of irony, anguish and imminent loss. Of the recordings on CD Otto Klemperer's 1966 version remains the best sung, best played, and most characterfully and illuminatingly conducted of all. Walter Legge's recording is admirably balanced, allowing us to hear every word and nuance of Wunderlich's incomparable singing. Christa Ludwig also benefits from the unvarnished clarity of the recording; like Wunderlich, she gives a performance which for beauty of tone and truth of inflection remains unsurpassed in living memory. Klemperer's reading is cast in the stoic vein and is uniquely chilly in the haunting second movement. But for all its grimness and gauntness and sharply etched detailing, Klemperer's is also a reading of great compassion. Above all, it is that rare thing: a performance in which the work seems to be being discovered anew in every bar.

The première recording of the composer's own piano version of *Das Lied von der Erde* provides us with a valuable insight into Mahler's creative processes. As Stephen E. Hefling's informative booklet-notes point out this is not just a piano transcription of the orchestral score, but a valid performing version in its own right; an observation reinforced not only by Mahler's own remark that "*what* one writes has always seemed to me more important than what it is scored *for*" but also by the fact that he worked on both the piano and orchestral versions almost simultaneously. The orchestral version of *Das Lied von der Erde* (a symphony in all but name) represents a perfect synthesis of the two genres that occupied his entire creative career—the symphony and the song, which make it all the more fitting to have the opportunity to hear the more intimate keyboard setting presented here. Any lingering doubts one may still have about the validity or necessity for such a recording are soon dispelled by the commitment and persuasiveness of the performances. Thomas Moser and Brigitte Fassbaender give intense and moving performances throughout (Fassbaender's "Der Abschied" is particularly impressive) and both respond well to the more subtle approach required for this more intimate, almost Lieder-like version. Cyprien Katsaris deserves much praise too for his sympathetic and virtuoso performance of the piano part. An essential purchase for any serious Mahlerian.

Mahler. Des Knaben Wunderhorn. **Elisabeth Schwarzkopf** (sop); **Dietrich Fischer-Dieskau** (bar); **London Symphony Orchestra/George Szell.** EMI CDC7 47277-2. From SAN218 (1/69).

> 48' ADD 11/88

Mahler's reputation rests primarily on his ten symphonies, but running alongside these magnificent works are his great song cycles. The poems of *Des Knaben Wunderhorn* ("The youth's magic horn") are drawn from a collection written in a deliberately 'folk' style. They are often humorous, ironic (as in the military settings), surreal or eerily strange. Mahler's use of the orchestra is delicate and sensitive; he rarely employs its full might but conjures from it a wide variety of colours and sounds. Schwarzkopf and Fischer-Dieskau sing the songs magnificently, drawing from the texts every verbal nuance and subtle shading and Szell's accompaniments are outstanding.

Mahler. Lieder eines fahrenden Gesellen[a]. Kindertotenlieder[b]. Rückert Lieder[c]. **Dietrich Fischer-Dieskau** (bar); [a]**Philharmonia Orchestra/Wilhelm Furtwängler;** [b]**Berlin Philharmonic Orchestra/Rudolf Kempe;** [c]**Daniel Barenboim** (pf). EMI CDC7 47657-2. Texts and translations included. Item marked [a] from mono ALP1270 (10/55), [b] mono BLP1081 (5/56), [c] SLS5173 (6/80).

> 62' ADD 6/87

Mahler. Kindertotenlieder[a]. Rückert Lieder[b]. Lieder eines fahrenden Gesellen[a]. **Dame Janet Baker** (mez); [a]**Hallé Orchestra;** [b]**New Philharmonia Orchestra/Sir John Barbirolli.** EMI CDC7 47793-2. Texts and translations included. Items marked [a] from ASD2338 (2/68), [b] ASD2518/19 (12/69).

> 65' ADD 12/87

The songs of the *Lieder eines fahrenden Gesellen* ("Songs of a Wayfarer") are directly quoted from Mahler's First Symphony and the same fresh, springtime atmosphere is shared by both works. The orchestration has great textural clarity and lightness of touch. The *Kindertotenlieder*, more chromatically expressive than the earlier work, tap into a darker, more psychologically complex vein in Mahler's spiritual and emotional make-up. The *Rückert Lieder* are not a song cycle as such but gather in their romantic awareness and response to the beauties of the poetry a unity and shape that acts to bind them. Heard in their piano version they sound more advanced harmonically than when performed with an orchestra. Though recorded some 25 years apart Fischer-Dieskau's intensity of approach remains consistent throughout and, given such great musicians as accompanists, scales rare heights of emotional projection. The 1950s recordings sound remarkably fine in this remastering.

Together, Baker and Barbirolli reach a transcendental awareness of Mahler's inner musings. Barbirolli draws from the Hallé playing of great delicacy and precision. These readings give nothing to Dietrich Fischer-Dieskau's magnificent performances and establish a clear case for having both versions in your collection.

Marin Marais
French 1656-1728

Marais. PIECES DE VIOLE DU CINQUIEME LIVRE. **Wieland Kuijken, Kaori Uemura** (vas da gamba); **Robert Kohnen** (hpd). Accent ACC78744D. Suites—G minor; A minor. Chaconne in G major. Dialogue. Le jeu du volant. Le tableau de l'opération de la taille. La poitevine. Le tombeau pour Marais le Cadet.

> 65' DDD 2/88

Marais. PIECES DE VIOLE DU CINQUIEME LIVRE. **Jordi Savall** (bass viol); **Hopkinson Smith** (theorbo); **Ton Koopman** (hpd) with **Jean-Michael Damian** (spkr). Auvidis Astrée E7708. Suites—G minor; E minor/major. Le tableau de l'opération de la taille. Le tombeau pour Marais le Cadet.

> 52' DDD 2/88

Wieland Kuijken and Jordi Savall are two of the finest modern-day players, and each in his way an exponent of the French tradition. It is nevertheless fascinating to compare the differences in their interpretation of these exquisite and highly idiomatic pieces from Marais's final miscellany which—but for the startling (and ultimately quite amusing) *Bladder Stone Operation*—have until now been rarely performed. Kuijken's playing is always serious and often profound; it is beautifully controlled and deeply eloquent. Savall betrays his Spanish blood by playing expansively and with panache; there is more variety in his sound, more delicacy and jauntiness. Though it is a matter of taste which recording one might choose on artistic grounds, the recording quality of Savall's performance is in fact superior.

Frank Martin
Swiss 1890-1974

Martin. Concerto for seven wind instruments, timpani, percussion and string orchestra (1949)[a]. Etudes for string orchestra (1955-6)[a]. Petite symphonie concertante (1945)[b]. **Suisse Romande Orchestra/Ernest Ansermet.** Decca Enterprise [a]stereo/[b]mono 430 003-2DM. Items marked [a] from SXL2311 (6/62), [b]LXT2631 (12/51).

58' ADD 12/90

Frank Martin's music surely lays to rest Harry Lime's celebrated remark (through the lips of Orson Welles in *The Third Man*) that Switzerland's major achievements are the cuckoo clock and milk chocolate! Martin only came to prominence in this country after the Second World War through performances of his *Petite symphonie concertante* for harp, harpsichord, piano and double string orchestra and *Le vin herbé*, his oratorio based on the Tristan theme. His centenary celebrations were distinctly muted by 1991 Mozart standards but Decca has at least reissued on this CD the very first recording of the *Petite symphonie concertante*, arguably his masterpiece, and here given a performance of great concentration, authority and atmosphere. The recording made in 1951 sounded pretty state-of-the-art at the time but now calls for tolerance but no such allowances need be made for the sound in the Concerto for seven wind instruments and the *Etudes* for string orchestra, recorded in the 1960s which are exceptionally fresh and vivid. The middle movement of the Concerto is one of his most haunting creations. It sounds eminently characterful and idiomatic, as do the Suisse Romande strings in the ingenious *Etudes*. This is a good place to start your exploration of this underrated and rewarding master.

Martin. Mass for double chorus.
Poulenc. Mass in G major. Quatre petites prières de Saint François d'Assise. Salve regina. **Christ Church Cathedral Choir, Oxford/Stephen Darlington.** Nimbus NI5197. Texts included.

59' DDD 12/89

This recording of the Poulenc Mass stands up well against its competitors, with a sense of artistic finish, absolute security in the singing and an attractive forwardness and freshness of sound: specially notable is the beautifully tranquil *Benedictus*. The smaller Poulenc pieces are also expressively performed; but the chief attraction of the disc is the little-known Mass by Frank Martin, which he wrote in the 1920s while still completing his lengthy studies. It is a deeply impressive work, its eight-part *a cappella* texture richly contrapuntal, with strong overtones of plainchant in the *Kyrie* though elsewhere highly original (for example, in the impressionistic bell-sounds of the *Sanctus*): not until later did Martin adopt his individual brand of dodecaphony. The Christ Church Cathedral Choir (whose trebles are very likeable) sing splendidly—flexible and well moulded in their phrasing, stirring in their capture of the feelings of utter joy in *Et resurrexit*. The recording gives just the right amount of reverberation. A notable addition to the recorded repertoire.

Martin. Requiem. **Elisabeth Speiser** (sop); **Ria Bollen** (contr); **Eric Tappy** (ten); **Peter Lagger** (bass); **Lausanne Women's Chorus; Union Chorale; Ars Laeta Vocal Ensemble; Suisse Romande Orchestra/Frank Martin.** Jecklin Disco JD631-2. Text and translation included. Recorded at a performance in Lausanne Cathedral on May 4th, 1973. From Jecklin 190 (12/85).

47' ADD 1/90

If Frank Martin were to be represented by one work, it should be this rather than the celebrated *Petite Symphonie concertante* for harp, harpsichord, piano and strings. The Requiem is a remarkable and beautiful score. It comes from Martin's last years, and was written after a Mediterranean cruise he made in 1971 and inspired by three cathedrals, St Mark's in Venice, the Montreale in Palermo and the Greek temples of Paestum near Naples. It is a work of vision and elevation of spirit and casts a strong spell. There is a dramatic power and a serenity that are quite new. The short *In Paradisum* is inspired and has a luminous quality and a radiance that is quite otherworldly. The 83-year-old composer conducts a completely dedicated and authoritative performance: it might well be improved upon at one or two places in terms of ensemble or security, but the spirit is there. The Swiss Radio recording is eminently truthful and well-balanced and offers a natural enough acoustic, the audience reasonably unobtrusive. It is a sorry comment on our times that music of this calibre has so far enjoyed so little exposure: it deserves to be heard every bit as often as the Fauré Requiem.

Bohuslav Martinů

Czech 1890-1959

Martinů. SYMPHONIES. **Bamberg Symphony Orchestra/Neeme Järvi.** BIS CD362/3, CD402.
CD362—No. 1 (1942); No. 2 (1943). *CD363*—No. 3 (1944); No. 4 (1945). *CD402*—No. 5 (1946); No. 6 (1953).

③ 61' 63' 59' DDD 9/87 12/88

Martinů began composing at the age of ten and later studied and lived in Paris, America and Switzerland. Despite his travels he remained a quintessentially Czech composer and his music is imbued with the melodic shapes and rhythms

of the folk-music of his native homeland. The six symphonies were written during Martinů's years in America and in all of them he uses a large orchestra with distinctive groupings of instruments which give them a very personal and unmistakable timbre. The rhythmic verve of his highly syncopated fast movements is very infectious, indeed unforgettable, and his slow movements are often deeply expressive, most potently, perhaps, in that of the Third Symphony which is imbued with the tragedy of war. The Bamberg

[photo: Chandos

orchestra play marvellously and with great verve for Järvi, whose excellently judged tempos help propel the music forward most effectively. His understanding of the basic thrust of Martinů's structures is very impressive and he projects the music with great clarity. The BIS recordings are beautifully clear, with plenty of ambience surrounding the orchestra, a fine sense of scale and effortless handling of the wide dynamic range Martinů calls for. Enthusiastically recommended.

Martinů. Nonet (1959). Trio in F major (1944). La Rêvue de Cuisine. **The Dartington Ensemble** (William Bennett, fl; Robin Canter, ob; David Campbell, cl; Graham Sheen, bn; Richard Watkins, hn; Barry Collarbone, tpt; Oliver Butterworth, vn; Patrick Ireland, va; Michael Evans, vc; Nigel Amherst, db; John Bryden, pf. Hyperion CDA66084.

50' DDD

The last few years or so have seen a steadily increasing interest in the music of Martinů. This beautifully balanced programme of chamber music may not be wholly representative of his style, but it's certainly an enjoyable and entertaining disc, and is as good a starting place as any for those approaching his music for the first time. His style has often been described as eclectic; his early works reveal the influence of Debussy and impressionism, and later, in the 1920 and 1930s, jazz and neo-classicism play an increasingly important role in his work. However, Martinů was no dilettante; for all his borrowings and years of exile from his homeland he remained essentially a Czech composer with a strong and original voice. The concert suite from the ballet *La Rêvue de Cuisine* ("The Kitchen Review") dates from 1930 whilst he was resident in Paris. There are plenty of high jinks and comedy in this agreeable and unpretentious work and the sound and influence of the Paris jazz bands are clearly discernible in the dance-inspired movements. The outer movements of the Trio in F major inhabit a similarly bright and cheerful world, and these are contrasted well with the lyrical beauty of the central *Adagio*. The *Nonet*, completed shortly before his death in 1959, is a serene and sunny work, neo-classical in design with its Haydnesque themes and its clarity of texture with a deep nostalgia for his Czech homeland from which he had been separated for so many years. The Dartington Ensemble give fine, committed performances and the recording has warmth and perspective. An essential disc for enthusiasts and toe-dippers alike.

Martinů. The epic of Gilgamesh. **Eva Depoltová** (sop); **Stefan Margita** (ten); **Ivan Kusnjer** (bar); **Ludek Vele** (bass); **Milan Karpíšek** (spkr); **Slovak Philharmonic Choir; Slovak Philharmonic Orchestra/Zdeněk Košler.** Marco Polo 8 223316. Translation included.

56' DDD 4/91

Gilgamesh is a long Assyrian-Babylonian poem recorded on cuneiform tablets in or before the seventh century BC which predates Homer by at least 1,500 years. Martinů was fascinated not only by the poem, the oldest literature known to mankind, but its universality—"the emotions and issues which move people have not changed ... they are embodied just as much in the oldest literature known to us as in the literature of our own time ... issues of friendship, love and death. It is dramatic; it pursues me in my dreams", he wrote. It certainly inspired in him music of extraordinary vision and intensity as well as enormous atmosphere. The *Epic* tells how Gilgamesh, King of Uruk, hears about the warrior Enkidu, a primitive at home among the works of nature with only animals as friends. He sends him a courtesan to whom he loses his innocence; the King then befriends him but they quarrel and fight before their friendship is really cemented. The second and third parts of the oratorio centre on the themes of death and immortality; the second tells of Enkidu's death and Gilgamesh's grief, his plea to the gods to restore Enkidu and his search for immortality, and the third records his failure to learn its secrets. *Gilgamesh* deals with universal themes and is Martinů at his most profound and inspired. There are no weaknesses in the cast (and the Gilgamesh of Ivan Kusnjer is very impressive indeed), and the chorus and orchestra respond very well to Zdeněk Košler's direction. The recording maintains a generally natural balance between the soloists, narrator, chorus and orchestra, and the somewhat resonant acoustic is used to good advantage. Those who do not know this extraordinary work of Martinů's last years should investigate it without delay.

Jules Massenet *French 1842-1912*

Massenet. MANON[a]. **Victoria de los Angeles** (sop) Manon; **Henri Legay** (ten) Des Grieux; **Michel Dens** (bar) Lescaut; **Jean Borthayre** (bass) Comte des Grieux; **Jean Vieuille** (bar) De Brétigny; **René Hérent** (ten) Guillot; **Liliane Berton** (sop) Poussette; **Raymonde Notti** (sop) Javotte; **Marthe Serres** (sop) Rosette; **Chorus and Orchestra of the Paris Opéra-Comique/Pierre Monteux.**
Chausson. Poème de l'amour et de la mer[b]. **Victoria de los Angeles** (sop); **Lamoureux Orchestra/Jean-Pierre Jacquillat.** EMI [a]mono/[b]stereo CMS7 63549. Notes and text included. Item marked [a] from HMV ALP1394/7 (11/56), [b] ASD2826 (3/73).

③ 3h 9' ADD 8/90

This has always been the classic version of Massenet's most popular opera. Pierre Monteux was one of the most eminent interpreters of French music in the gramophone's history, and he here draws authentically idiomatic playing from the Opéra-Comique Orchestra of 35 years ago. The tradition they between them

embody has been more-or-less lost in the interim which makes the reappearance of this set that much more welcome and important. And who could resist de los Angeles in the title role? She embodies to perfection, as she did on stage, Manon's endearing, sensual and flirtatious characteristics, and manages to convert them into a reading that is true to all Massenet's copious demands on his singers. Add to that the sheer beauty of the soprano's voice at the time and you have a good enough reason for acquiring these discs. Henri Legay's Des Grieux is hardly less affecting. He is the amorous, highly charged and obsessed lover to the life and

Victoria de los Angeles [photo: EMI/Steiner]

matches his Manon in obedience to Massenet's requirements. As the smaller parts are cast with other French singers familiar with Massenet's idiom every need is fulfilled. The recording sounds very reasonable for its day. Chausson's *Poème* makes an apt filler if by the early seventies the tonal bloom on de los Angeles's voice was much less in evidence.

Massenet. WERTHER. **Alfredo Kraus** (ten) Werther; **Tatiana Troyanos** (mez) Charlotte; **Matteo Manuguerra** (bar) Albert; **Christine Barbaux** (sop) Sophie; **Jules Bastin** (bass) Bailiff; **Philip Langridge** (ten) Schmidt; **Jean-Philippe Lafont** (bar) Johann; **London Philharmonic Orchestra/ Michel Plasson.** EMI CMS7 69573-2. Notes and text included. From SLS5183 (2/80).

② 2h 17' ADD 4/89 £

Massenet. WERTHER. **José Carreras** (ten) Werther; **Frederica von Stade** (mez) Charlotte; **Thomas Allen** (bar) Albert; **Isobel Buchanan** (sop) Sophie; **Robert Lloyd** (bass) Bailiff; **Paul Crook** (ten), **Malcolm King** (bass) Bailiff's friends; **Linda Humphries** (sop) Katchen; **Donaldson Ball** (bar) Bruhlmann; **Children's Choir; Royal Opera House Orchestra, Covent Garden/Sir Colin Davis.** Philips 416 654-2PH2. Notes, text and translation included. From 6769 051 (10/81).

② 2h 11' ADD 2/87

Werther is considered by many as Massenet's outright masterpiece. Here he reaches his zenith in the supple combination of a lyrical and a parlando style. Based faithfully on Goethe's novel, the work exposes movingly the feelings of the lovelorn poet Werther and those of his beloved Charlotte. The EMI recording benefits from Michel Plasson's instinctive feeling for the very individual shape of a Massenet phrase and for impassioned identification with the work's direct emotions. He

José Carreras [photo: Philips]

draws sensuous and eloquent playing from the LPO. Alfredo Kraus has been for many years a leading interpreter of the title role, which he understands to the full. He is to the life the self-pitying, tortured poet, obsessed by his love for the unattainable Charlotte and delivers Werther's many solos with an innate feeling for the poet's predicament. His Charlotte is the equally admirable Tatiana Troyanos, who perfectly catches the undercurrent of emotional conflict in Charlotte's being. Hers is a big-hearted, committed interpretation, but one that doesn't want for subtlety or interpretation. The two principals are well supported by the singers of the secondary roles, especially Christine Barbaux's properly eager and girlish Sophie. The recording is full and natural.

In Sir Colin Davis's recording the changing seasons, which form a backdrop to Werther's own manic swings between dream and reality, joy and despair, are recreated in exuberant and vibrant detail. The Royal Opera Orchestra play their very best: the solo detail, in every sentient response to Massenet's flickering orchestral palette, operates as if with feverishly heightened awareness. Carreras sees the force of the will to self-destruction in the character as dominating even the passages of brooding lyricism. Charlotte, struggling between the responsibilities of her bourgeois home life and the emotional turmoil in which she sees much of herself reflected in Werther, is sung by Frederica von Stade with winning simplicity and idiomatic French style. Young Sophie, whom Massenet made more important than Goethe did, becomes a true *oiseau d'aurore* in the voice of Isobel Buchanan, while Thomas Allen, characteristically, finds unusual breadth in the role of poor, spurned Albert.

Peter Maxwell Davies

British 1934-

Maxwell Davies. Symphony No. 4[a]. Trumpet Concerto[b]. [b]**John Wallace** (tpt); [a]**Scottish Chamber Orchestra/Sir Peter Maxwell Davies.** Collins Classics 1181-2.

73' DDD 6/91

Sir Peter Maxwell Davies has survived the transition from *enfant terrible* to *éminence grise* with equanimity—perhaps because he was always less 'terrible' than he seemed, and is still far from seriously 'grise'. From his earliest works to his most recent—the Trumpet Concerto and Fourth Symphony date from the late 1980s—he has used his delight in system-building to generate ambitious and complex structures that vibrate with no less complex but utterly uninhibited emotions. The Concerto is the immediately accessible of the two: the nature of the solo instrument, and Maxwell Davies's willingness not to jettison all the conventions of the concerto genre see to that. The work was written for John Wallace, and while it would be wrong to say that he makes light of its difficulties—at times you could swear that only a flautist could get round such florid writing—he succeeds brilliantly in demonstrating that the difficulties serve musical ends. The Symphony has less immediately arresting ideas, but when the music is savoured, returned to, and allowed time to weave its spells, its rewards become progressively more apparent. These recordings capture the composer's own highly-charged readings with commendable fidelity.

Maxwell Davies. Miss Donnithorne's Maggot[a]. Eight Songs for a Mad King[b]. [a]**Mary Thomas** (sop); [b]**Julius Eastman** (bar); **The Fires of London/Sir Peter Maxwell Davies.** Unicorn-Kanchana DKPCD9052. Texts included. Item marked [a] new to UK, [b] from RHS308 (12/71).

67' ADD/DDD 3/88

King George III in his madness sang the music of his beloved Handel; he also used a miniature mechanical organ in attempts to teach caged birds to sing for him. Eliza Donnithorne, on the other hand, was jilted at the church door and reacted by making the rest of her life an endless wedding-morning. She did not sing, so far as we know, but her crazed monologues are as haunted, in Maxwell Davies's phantasmagoria, by memories of martial music and by overtones of all those Italian opera heroines who went 'mad in white satin' as the King's are by distorted Handel, by folk-songs and the twittering of birds and by grotesque foxtrots. The range of vocal effects required of the two soloists is punishing: howls and screeches and extremes of pitch for the vocalist in *Eight Songs*, burlesque coloratura warblings and swoopings for the soprano in *Miss Donnithorne*. The hysterical intensity of the music is pretty taxing for the listener, too, but he is rewarded in *Eight Songs* by a breathtaking kaleidoscope of vivid allusion, invention and parody, and in *Miss Donnithorne* by a harsh poignancy as well. Both pieces are vehicles for virtuoso performance, from the instrumentalists as well as the singers, and one can scarcely imagine either being done better than it is here. The very immediate recording adds substantially to their uncomfortable impact.

Billy Mayerl
British 1902-1959

Mayerl. PIANO WORKS. **Eric Parkin.** Chandos CHAN8848.
Four Aces Suite (1933)—No. 1, Ace of Clubs; No. 4, Ace of Spades. Mistletoe
(1935). Autumn crocus (1932). Hollyhock (1927). White heather (1932). Three
Dances in Syncopation, Op. 73. Sweet William (1938). Parade of the Sandwich-
Board Men (1938). Hop-O'-My-Thumb (1934). Jill all alone (1955). Aquarium
Suite (1937). **Mayerl/Croom-Johnson:** Bats in the Belfry (1935). Green
tulips (1935).

 50' DDD 11/90

Billy Mayerl was a Londoner of partly German parentage who became a brilliant
pianist and a composer whose piano pieces, immensely popular between the
wars, successfully bridge the gap between ragtime and, let's say, Frank Bridge
and John Ireland in their lighter piano moods. In this way, he was a middle-of-
the-road figure like Eric Coates, and for that reason he later came to be
neglected by jazz aficionados and classical buffs alike as representing no pure
'tradition'. Today, it's a delight to return to tuneful music which has such
originality, wit, and sparkle as well as being superbly written for the piano.
Listen to the very first number (the *Ace of Clubs*), and you at once hear the
charm and sharp sophistication of Mayerl's style, which is worthy of his
contemporaries Noël Coward and Cole Porter, to say nothing of Gershwin.
Though it's a pity we don't have all the 'Aces' of this four-part suite here, that's
because Eric Parkin recorded the other two on an earlier CD devoted to this
composer on which we also find the famous piece *Marigold*. Parkin is right inside
this music and his playing is stylistically spot on in its tonal warmth, crisp
articulation and rhythmic zest. This is a delightful disc. Quite a few classical
music lovers, if given a one-way ticket to a desert island and a medium-size
suitcase, would gladly sacrifice some Schoenberg for modern music as attractive
and well played as this.

Felix Mendelssohn
German 1809-1847

Mendelssohn. Violin Concertos—E minor, Op. 64; D minor. **Viktoria
Mullova** (vn); **Academy of St Martin in the Fields/Sir Neville
Marriner.** Philips 432 077-2PH.

 50' DDD 5/91

Since the competition is strong to say the least, new accounts of 'the'
Mendelssohn Violin Concerto have to be rather special to make their way in the
catalogue, but that of Viktoria Mullova and the ASMF under Sir Neville Marriner
falls into the category of distinguished additions. The deliberate mention of the
orchestra and conductor here is because this work is emphatically not a
showpiece for a soloist in the way that Paganini's or Wieniawski's violin
concertos are. Instead it offers a real dialogue with orchestra although there are
plenty of opportunities for violin virtuosity as well. Mullova's sweet and
somehow youthful tone is beautifully matched here by Marriner and his
orchestra, which in turn does not sound so big as to overwhelm the often
intimate character of the music. The recording helps, too, with its natural
balance between the soloist and the orchestral body. The reference above to this
E minor work as 'the' Mendelssohn Violin Concerto is because after his death it
was found that as a boy of 13 he also composed the one in D minor which here
makes a useful coupling. Of course it shows the influence of classical models,
including Mozart, but the slow movement has an attractive warmth and the

finale a zest and drive that owes something to gipsy music. Maybe in less than expert hands it could sound ordinary, but not when it is done as stylishly as here.

Mendelssohn. A Midsummer Night's Dream—Overture; Scherzo; Nocturne; Wedding March.
Schubert. Rosamunde—Overture; Ballet music in G minor; Entracte in B flat major; Entracte in B minor. **Concertgebouw Orchestra, Amsterdam/ George Szell.** Philips Concert Classics 426 071-2PCC. From mono ABL3238 (3/59).

> 59' ADD 4/90   £ (B)

The magic of Mendelssohn and the big-heartedness of Schubert are the perfect complement in these affecting readings from Szell and the Concertgebouw. The brief selection of items from the incidental music to *A Midsummer Night's Dream* is played with a lightness of touch and an uncluttered attitude towards the fairy elements of the music's programmatic background. The effect is only limited by moments of less than exact ensemble. *Rosamunde* suffers no such qualification. Here the work's pathos is touchingly underlined in playing of restrained refinement, and the contrasting sections of joy are captured with full tone and rhythmic bite. Rarely has the balance of these elements in *Rosamunde* been so astutely maintained. In the most tender passages, the woodwind of the Concertgebouw suggest a touching frailty that belies the confident assertions of the bolder sections and hints at the strongly personal statement that this music encompasses. The richness of the Schubert is well sustained by the engineers and if the Mendelssohn is a touch less vivid, this is no serious demerit in such a bargain issue.

Mendelssohn. OVERTURES. **Bamberg Symphony Orchestra/Claus Peter Flor.** RCA Victor Red Seal RD87905.
Die Hochzeit des Camacho, Op. 10. A Midsummer Night's Dream, Op. 21 (from RD87764, 10/88). Meeresstille und glückliche Fahrt, Op. 27. Ruy Blas, Op. 95. Athalie, Op. 74. The Hebrides, Op. 26, "Fingal's Cave".

> 59' DDD 1/89

Claus Peter Flor   [photo: BMG]

The Marriage of Camacho Overture was written in 1825, two years before the masterly evocation of *A Midsummer Night's Dream*, with its gossamer fairies, robust mortals and pervading romanticism, and already demonstrates the teenager composer's enormous musical facility and organizational skills, together with the high quality of his invention. *Calm sea and prosperous voyage* (1828) anticipates *The Hebrides* of a year later, and celebrates an ocean voyage on a sailing ship. *Ruy Blas* is a jolly, slightly melodramatic, but agreeably tuneful piece and *Athalie* is also attractive in its melodic ideas. *Fingal's Cave* with its beauty and dramatic portrayal of Scottish seascapes matches the Shakespearian overture in its melodic inspiration (the opening phrase is hauntingly unforgettable) and shows comparable skill in its vivid orchestration. Flor directs wonderfully sympathetic and spontaneous performances, with the Bamberg Symphony Orchestra playing gloriously. There is abundant energy and radiant lyrical beauty in the playing and each piece is unerringly paced and shaped. The glowing recording gives a wonderful bloom to the orchestral textures without preventing a realistic definition. There has never been a collection of Mendelssohn's overtures to match this and it will give enormous pleasure in every respect.

Mendelssohn. SYMPHONIES AND OVERTURES. **London Symphony Orchestra/Claudio Abbado.** DG 415 353-2GH4.
Symphonies—No. 1 in C minor, Op. 11; No. 2 in B flat major, Op. 52, "Lobgesang" (with Elizabeth Connell, Karita Mattila, sops; Hans-Peter Blochwitz, ten); No. 3 in A minor, Op. 56, "Scottish"; No. 4 in A major, Op. 90, "Italian"; No. 5 in D major, Op. 107, "Reformation". Overtures—The Hebrides, Op. 26, "Fingal's Cave"; A Midsummer Night's Dream, Op. 21. The Fair Melusina, Op. 32. Octet in E flat major, Op. 20—Scherzo.

④ 4h 5' DDD 1/86

This is a msot valuable collection and Abbado impresses at once in the First Symphony by his serious yet lively account of the score: his approach to the *Lobgesang* is warm and joyful and though he cannot quite rid the work of its Victorian flavour, his performance is fresh and restores the music's charm and innocence. He has a good chorus at his disposal and three dedicated, skilful soloists. In the more familiar *Scottish* Symphony Abbado again invests the work with warmth and stature, never rushing or driving too hard: the familiar *Italian* Symphony, too, gains from his affectionate, respectful yet sparkling approach. Even the *Reformation* Symphony, which can seem even more coloured by Victorian religious sentiment than the *Hymn of Praise*, emerges as a vigorous, uplifting work, with the hymn tunes played in cheerful, direct fashion. Only in the three overtures, where Abbado's tempos and phrasing are strangely idiosyncratic (though never less than interesting), do the performances depart from a very high standard indeed. Throughout the set the LSO respond to Abbado with lean, virile playing. The recordings have a pleasing, natural sound, with a particularly good balance in the choral item.

Mendelssohn. Symphony No. 2 in B flat major, Op. 52, "Lobgesang".
Elizabeth Connell, Karita Mattila (sops); **Hans-Peter Blochwitz** (ten); **London Symphony Orchestra/Claudio Abbado.** DG 423 143-2GH. From 415 353-1GH4 (1/86).

74' DDD

Long a favourite of British choral societies this work has many well-known passages and will probably chime a chord of recognition with most people. There is some striking music in it—the tenor's celebrated questioning, "Watchmen, will the night soon pass?" is but one—here beautifully sung by Hans-Peter Blochwitz. The soprano's *Andante* "Ich harrete des Herrn" shows Mendelssohn's gift for melodic shaping at its most inspired. The LSO and chorus perform this work with obvious devotion and Abbado once more shows his mettle as a first-rate Mendelssohnian.

Mendelssohn. Symphonies—No. 3 in A minor, Op. 56, "Scottish"; No. 4 in A major, Op. 90, "Italian". **London Symphony Orchestra/Claudio Abbado.** DG 3D-Classics 427 810-2GDC. From 415 353-2GH4 (1/86).

71' DDD 2/90 £ Ⓑ

Mendelssohn. Symphonies—No. 3 in A minor, Op. 56, "Scottish"; No. 4 in A major, Op. 90, "Italian". **London Classical Players/Roger Norrington.** EMI Reflexe CDC7 54000-2.

65' DDD 11/90 Ⓑ ✒

There have already been individual discs extracted from Abbado's well-thought of set of Mendelssohn's orchestral music, but this most recent well-filled issue is probably the most generally appealing, coupling two of the best loved works in two of the most astute performances of the set—and all at bargain price. Although there are many more challenging readings of these two symphonies elsewhere on CD, Abbado's is a soundly middle-of-the-road view, drawing refined, understated playing from the LSO that is especially effective, for example, in the more brooding moments of the first movement of the *Scottish*. Abbado captures keenly here the ambience of the ruined chapel of Holyrood House in Edinburgh, so imbued with the tragedy of Mary, Queen of Scots, that first inspired Mendelssohn in this work. The restrained recording suits this symphony better than it does the brilliant lights of the *Italian*, though even there the understated playing makes its own, peculiarly poignant effect. At the price, then, this is certainly an issue to consider.

In any performance of the *Scottish* Symphony on period instruments there are bound to be losses: the modern symphony orchestra is wonderfully capable of realizing the brooding mists and powerful outbursts of the first movement in a way that lighter-toned instruments cannot hope to emulate. But turn to the *Scherzo* and the validity of using authentic instruments becomes immediately apparent. Here, the wind timbres are so intriguing in themselves, the woodwinds so individual, the horns so ruggedly outdoor, that another level of meaning within this music is revealed to us. The *Adagio* now becomes much more classical, shorn of its late-romantic angst, rendering the intimations of full-blooded romanticism to become all the more telling. The opening of the *Italian* is predictably vivacious, with soft-timbred flutes blending with the strings rather than trying to compete, and when they come to the fore again in the *Saltarello*, playing a breathy duet, the effect is magical. Lively speeds adopted by Norrington in both works may seem hurried on first hearing, but their rightness for the forces used and the acoustic of the venue establishes itself with repeated listening. A well-balanced, not too brightly lit recording serves both symphonies well.

Mendelssohn. Symphony No. 5 in D major, Op. 107, "Reformation"[a]. **Schumann.** Symphony No. 3 in E flat major, Op. 97, "Rhenish"[b]. **Berlin Philharmonic Orchestra/Herbert von Karajan.** DG Galleria 419 870-2GGA. Item marked [a] from 2720 068 (12/73), [b] 2720 046 (9/72).

69' ADD 4/88 £

This is just the sort of repertoire at which Karajan excels; his Schumann is strongly characterized, firmly driven and beautifully shaped and his Mendelssohn often achieves a delicacy of touch that belies the size of orchestra employed. Karajan's set of the Schumann symphonies made in 1971 was a notable success and the *Rhenish* speaks for them all. Here the powerful thrust of the work is gorgeously conveyed by the Berlin strings and the spontancity of the music-making is striking. The Mendelssohn makes an ideal companion, since in scale the *Reformation* embraces wide vistas and far horizons. Laden with references to Protestant worship, Mendelssohn paints a picture of security and solidity achieved over many years and much struggle. Karajan maybe overemphasizes the epic qualities of the work but the playing of the orchestra is superb. The recordings have 'dried-out' a little in the transfer, but still sound well.

Mendelssohn. Symphonies for string orchestra—No. 9 in C minor; No. 10 in B minor; No. 12 in G minor. **London Festival Orchestra/Ross Pople.** Hyperion CDA66196. From A66196 (7/86).

```
54'  DDD  6/87
```

Mendelssohn's 12 *String Symphonies* are an endless source of delight. They were written between the ages of 12 and 14, and came to light in an East Berlin library only as recently as 1950, dispelling the myth that the famous Octet of 1825 was an isolated masterpiece of his early development. The string writing is polished and mature, and they reveal a grasp of form and melodic invention that is quite remarkable. Much of the spirit and vitality of these works look forward to the later symphonies, and also serves to demonstrate the unique path that Mendelssohn choose to follow; a path that was neither classical nor fully romantic, instead lying somewhere between the two. To comment on each work individually would be unnecessary, save to say that they are all immediately appealing and engaging, and that their youthful high spirits and warmth shine through from beginning to end, especially when the performances are as fine as they are here. Ross Pople's immaculate attention to detail and balance, coupled with his obvious conviction and enthusiasm add all the more to the enjoyment of these delightful and rewarding works. Well worth exploring.

Mendelssohn. PIANO WORKS. **Murray Perahia; [a]Academy of St Martin in the Fields/Sir Neville Marriner.** CBS Masterworks CD42401. Items marked [a] from IM76376 (7/75), [b]IM37838 (5/85). Piano Concertos[a]—No. 1 in G minor, Op. 25; No. 2 in D minor, Op. 40. Prelude and Fugue in E major/minor, Op. 35 No. 1[b]. Variations sérieuses in D minor, Op. 54[b]. Andante and Rondo capriccioso, Op. 14[b].

```
70'  ADD/DDD  11/87
```

Though conflict and suffering, the experiences on which Beethovenian music is supposed to feed, were foreign to Mendelssohn's nature, ardour, inspiration, soulfulness and fiery energy he had in abundance. So although both these concertos, products of the composer's twenties, are in minor keys, they have little of the pathos or drama that that might lead one to expect. It is for their consummate ease and naturalness, their ability to make the listener feel as though he is soaring, that they are valued. Not too many pianists are suited by temperament, or indeed equipped by technique, for such music. Murray Perahia undoubtedly is. His dazzling fingerwork and his sensitivity to the direction of harmony are delightful, and he knows just how to step aside to let the more relaxed slow movements make their point. Slight fizziness on the string sound and a less than ideally regulated piano detract but little from one's enjoyment; and CBS have made partial amends by adding 26 minutes from a solo Mendelssohn recital which shows Perahia on top form.

Mendelssohn. Octet in E flat major, Op. 20. String Quintet No. 2 in B flat major, Op. 87. **Academy of St Martin in the Fields Chamber Ensemble.** Philips 420 400-2PH. From 9500 616 (3/80).

```
63'  ADD  11/87                                    (B)
```

Mendelssohn was as remarkable a prodigy as Mozart and one can only speculate with sadness what marvels he might have left us had he lived longer. Had death

claimed him at 20 we would still have this glorious Octet, a work of unforced
lyricism and a seemingly endless stream of melody. The Academy Chamber
Ensemble, all fine soloists in their own right, admirably illustrate the benefits of
working regularly as an ensemble for they play with uncommon sympathy. The
string quintet is a work of greater fervour and passion than the Octet but it is
characterized by the same melodiousness and unfettered lyricism with plenty of
opportunities for virtuoso playing, which are well taken. The recordings, made
in 1978, give a pleasant and warm sheen to the string colour of the ensemble.

Mendelssohn. String Quintet No. 1 in A major, Op. 18[a]. Octet in E flat
major, Op. 20. **Hausmusik** ([a]Monica Huggett, [a]Pavlo Beznosiuk, Paull
Boucher, Jolianne von Einem, vns; [a]Roger Chase, [a]Simon Whistler, vas;
[a]Anthony Pleeth, Sebastian Comberti, vcs). EMI CDC7 49958-2.

63' DDD 9/90

Hausmusik is an impressive chamber group, led by Monica Huggett, with
Anthony Pleeth the principal cellist. They use original instruments, and create
fresh, transparent textures, yet there is no lack of warmth and those horrid
bulges on phrases which disfigure some early music performances are mercifully
absent. Mendelssohn's miraculous Octet was written in 1825 when the composer
was 16 and the almost equally engaging Quintet, with its gently nostalgic
Intermezzo dates from a year later. The performances here fizz with vitality in
outer movements where pacing is brisk and sparkling, yet never sounds rushed.
The famous *Scherzo* in the Octet is wonderfully fleet, and articulated with a
disarming, feather-light precision, and the *Presto* finale has real exhilaration. Yet
the expressive music sings with unforced charm. Excellent, realistic recording,
with enough resonance for bloom without clouding. If you are only familiar with
the Octet the Quintet could prove a real bonus.

Mendelssohn. STRING QUARTETS. **Melos Quartet** (Wilhelm Melcher,
Gerhard Voss, vns; Hermann Voss, va; Peter Buck, vc). DG 415 883-2GCM3.
From 2740 267 (11/82).
E flat major (1823); No. 1 in E flat major, Op. 12; No. 2 in A minor, Op. 13;
No. 3 in D major, Op. 44 No. 1; No. 4 in E minor, Op. 44 No. 2; No. 5 in E
flat major, Op. 44 No. 3; No. 6 in F minor, Op. 80. Andante, Scherzo,
Capriccio and Fugue, Op. 81 Nos. 1-4.

③ 3h 19' ADD 12/87

Mendelssohn's chamber music is relatively unknown except for the delightful
Octet, so this wonderfully played and totally captivating set provides an ideal
opportunity for acquainting oneself with these shamefully underrated quartets.
The early quartets are fresh and brightly lit and are obvious forerunners of the
more mature pieces that were to follow. The recordings are a little fierce so you
have to find a comfortable volume at which to play them but these are really
rewarding works and at mid price well worth trying. The Melos Quartet clearly
believe in every note they play. The set contains a quite outstanding booklet.

Mendelssohn. Piano Trios—No. 1 in D minor, Op. 49; No. 2 in C minor,
Op. 66. **Guarneri Trio** (Mark Lubotsky, vn; Jean Decroos, vc; Daniele
Dechenne, pf). Globe GLO5007.

57' DDD 9/89

The First Piano Trio is a beautifully crafted work, richly melodious yet not
without moments of tension and drama. His only other trio, in C minor, was
composed six years later, and this too is an impressive piece, which uses a

solemn chorale theme known to Bach (*Vor deinem Thron tret' ich*) to express his longing for a better world. But although the finale of the D minor is rather serious, neither of these works is at all tragic despite their minor keys, and neither has a really slow movement, while the two scherzos dance along in the composer's best fairy-playful manner, that of the Second Trio taken here at a pace which must tax even these skilful players. The Guarneri Trio play this music with wit and expressive force, keeping the right balance between romantic feeling and classical poise. The recording is a model of clarity, with well-judged slight reverberation.

Mendelssohn. Violin Sonatas—F minor, Op. 4; F major (1838). **Shlomo Mintz** (vn); **Paul Ostrovsky** (pf). DG 419 244-2GH.
· 51' DDD 8/87

The surprise here is the early F minor Violin Sonata, which is a work of strong character and an amazing achievement for a boy of 14. It is true that the sonata bears the influence of Beethoven and Mozart, but these influences are somehow assimilated and translated in a way that results in the work having its own very distinct personality. Obviously Mintz and Ostrovsky believe strongly in the work, and rightly do not play it down as a piece of juvenilia. Their response to the slow central movement is equally sensitive and beautifully phrased, and the last movement *Allegro agitato* is taut and well-argued. The F major Sonata shows all the elements of Mendelssohn's mature style, and is an altogether more urbane work than its predecessor. Again the soloists deserve high praise for their sympathetic response to the score. The excellent recording does full justice to Mintz's beautiful violin tone.

Mendelssohn. SONGS WITHOUT WORDS. **Lívia Rév** (pf). Hyperion CDA66221/2.
Books—No. 1, Op. 19; No. 2, Op. 30; No. 3, Op. 38; No. 4, Op. 53; No. 5, Op. 62; No. 7, Op. 85; No. 8, Op. 102. G minor, Op. posth.
② 2h 6' DDD 12/87

Perhaps more than any other piano pieces from the early nineteenth century, Mendelssohn's *Songs without words* seem to sum up a comfortable bourgeois aesthetic cultivated by a newly established middle class in Western Europe. Today fashion dictates that we should look slightly askance at this music and consider it merely bland and anodyne, lacking the passion and depth of some

greater masters. But the fact that Mendelssohn's art is polite and refined does not mean it is characterless and superficial, and these pieces offer much beauty and variety. Lívia Rév plays with dexterity and panache in the brisker pieces and sensitivity in all, and we can admire without reservation her deft yet refined handling of the rapid No. 5 in F sharp minor, and the similarly marked Nos. 10 and 21, to say nothing of No. 34, "The Bee's Wedding". In slower pieces, one may feel that she is a little too lingering but at least this doubtless makes us take the

Lívia Rév [*photo: Hyperion*]

music's expressive content more seriously than we might otherwise do. On the other hand, the famous "Duetto" (No. 18) is refreshingly unsentimental. The piano sound is convincing and attractive; the accompanying booklet unusually informative.

Mendelssohn. PIANO WORKS. **Murray Perahia** (pf). CBS Masterworks CD37838. From IM37838 (5/85).
Piano Sonata in E major, Op. 6. Prelude and Fugue in E minor/major, Op. 35 No. 1. Variations sérieuses in D minor, Op. 54. Andante and Rondo capriccioso in E minor, Op. 14.

50' DDD

This is a beautifully controlled and very welcome glimpse of a side of Mendelssohn rarely encountered in the concert-hall. Perahia's exquisitely fleet fingerwork and finely controlled pianism matches the weight of the music ideally. The four pieces represented here are not of equal stature but there are certainly some fine things. The *Variations sérieuses* is Mendelssohn's best-known work for the piano—as the title might imply there is a darker, maybe even melancholy flavour to the theme and the subsequent variations have real substance. Here and in the other works, particularly the delightful *Rondo capriccioso*, Perahia's performance overlooks nothing in mood or atmosphere.

Mendelssohn. Elijah. **Elly Ameling** (sop); **Annelies Burmeister** (contr); **Peter Schreier** (ten); **Theo Adam** (bass); **Leipzig Radio Chorus; Leipzig Gewandhaus Orchestra/Wolfgang Sawallisch.** Philips 420 106-2PH2. Text and translation included. From SAL3730/32 (9/69).

② 2h 11' ADD 2/88

Mendelssohn's *Elijah* received its first performance (in its English version) in Birmingham in 1846; thanks to the vigour and excitement of the writing the occasion was a resounding success, requiring of its performers encore after encore. This 1968 recording made with the Leipzig Gewandhaus Orchestra (which Mendelssohn himself conducted) uses the German version and the performance is quite simply superb. Sawallisch clearly believes in every note of this score and his team of soloists, with Theo Adam outstanding in the title-role, is very fine, as are the chorus. The recording wears its years lightly. This is one of the great choral records of recent decades.

Olivier Messiaen
French 1908-

Messiaen. Quatuor pour la fin du temps. **Tashi** (Richard Stoltzman, cl; Ida Kavafian, vn; Fred Sherry, vc; Peter Serkin, pf). RCA Victor Gold Seal GD87835. From RL11567 (7/77).

47' ADD 4/89

Written in a prisoner-of-war camp in German-occupied Poland, the *Quatuor pour le fin du temps* ("Quartet for the End of Time") is a key work in Messiaen's output, an apocalyptic vision of remarkably precise vividness. The location of the camp (it was far enough north for a brilliant display of the Aurora borealis), its harsh privations (malnutrition caused Messiaen to dream in colour), even the lack of musical resources—all these seem to have contributed to the work's graphic urgency. Precision and vividness are required of any performance of it, and these players provide both in abundance. A difficult combination of vision and virtuosity is achieved here, backed by a scrupulously balanced recording.

Messiaen. Visions de l'Amen. **Alexandre Rabinovitch, Martha Argerich** (pfs). EMI CDC7 54050-2.

48' DDD 12/90

The *Visions de l'Amen* were composed in Paris in 1943, shortly after Messiaen's return from a German prison camp where he had written the more famous *Quatuor pour la fin du temps*. These two works share similar apocalyptic concerns, a similar time-scale, and a similar vacillation between religious agony and ecstasy. The two-piano medium, with the addition of a stereophonic dimension to sounds usually fixed in space, is well suited to such evocations; on the other hand it only takes a momentary poor synchronization or the slightest discrepancy of tuning between the instruments to destroy the atmosphere. With Argerich and Rabinovitch (a Russian who has lived in France since 1974) the atmosphere is electric throughout and the visionary aspect of the music is fully realized. They achieve near-perfect synchronization, not by caution and compromise, but by allowing the musical initiative to pass from one player to the other—a much more exciting and musically rewarding strategy. EMI's recording is slightly too distant to allow for a full measure of clamorous cataclysm; otherwise it does full justice to the playing.

Messiaen. Catalogue d'oiseaux (1956-8)—Books 1-3. **Peter Hill** (pf). Unicorn-Kanchana DKPCD9062.
Book 1—Le Chocard des Alpes; Le Loriot; Le Merle bleu. Book 2—Le Traquet Stapazin. Book 3—Le Chouette Hulotte; L'Alouette Lulu.

59' DDD 5/88

Messiaen describes himself as 'ornithologist-musician', but he is a landscape-painter of genius as well. Though each piece in his catalogue bears the name of a single bird, each is really an evocation of a particular place (very often at a particular season and time of day), and most of the pieces contain the carefully transcribed and meticulously labelled songs of many birds. His imagery is naïve but the catalogue's huge range of sonority and gesture, its eloquently visionary intensity and its descriptive power make it one of the peaks of twentieth-century piano literature. It is so long (the complete catalogue plays for about two-and-three-quarters hours) and so difficult that the peak is seldom scaled. The work is fortunate to have found such an interpreter as Peter Hill. He is a complete master of its rhythmic complexity and its finger-breaking defiance of the pianistically possible, but he never loses sight of the fact that the cycle's main objective is to evoke a sense of place, of light and temperature even, and thereby to awake awe in the listener at the majesty and sublimity of creation.

Messiaen. La nativité du Seigneur[a]. Le banquet céleste[b]. **Jennifer Bate** (org). Unicorn-Kanchana DKPCD9005. Played on the organ of Beauvais Cathedral. Item marked [a] from DKP9005 (6/82), [b] DKP9018 (2/83).

62' DDD 2/88

La nativité du Seigneur comprises nine meditations on themes associated with the birth of the Lord. Messiaen's unique use of registration gives these pieces an extraordinarily wide range of colour and emotional potency and in Jennifer Bate's hands (and feet) it finds one of its most persuasive and capable advocates. Bate is much admired by the composer and is so far the only organist to have recorded his complete works for the instrument. *Le banquet céleste* was Messiaen's first published work for the organ and is a magical, very slow-moving meditation on a verse from St John's Gospel (VI, 56). The very faithful recording captures both the organ and the large acoustic of Beauvais Cathedral to marvellous effect.

Messiaen. Livre du Saint Sacrement. **Jennifer Bate** (org). Unicorn-Kanchana DKPCD9067/8. Recorded on the organ of L'Eglise de la Sainte-Trinité, Paris.

② 2h 9' DDD 10/87   9ₚ

The crowning achievement of Messiaen's unique cycle of music for the organ, the *Livre du Saint Sacrement* is also his largest work for the instrument. It is an intensely personal score based on the cornerstone of Messiaen's Catholic faith, the Blessed Sacrament, and spans a wide range of emotions from hushed, private communion to the truly apocalyptic. Jennifer Bate gave the British première of the work in 1986, following which Messiaen invited her to record it using his own organ at the Trinity Church in Paris. He was on hand throughout the sessions so in every sense this performance carries the stamp of authority. The recording is a model of clarity and it is hard to imagine the complex and often very subtle textures of this music being better conveyed. This is a magnificent achievement and should be heard by all who profess an interest in the music of our time.

Messiaen. ORGAN WORKS, Volume 1. **Hans-Ola Ericsson.** BIS CD409. Played on the organ of Lulea Cathedral, Sweden.
L'Ascension. Le banquet céleste. Apparition de l'église éternelle. Diptyque.

64' DDD

This disc contains Messiaen's first organ works written between 1928 and 1934, and they are among his most expressive and attractive pieces. The titles bear testament to his profound Christian faith and his visionary approach to music. His earliest composition, *Le banquet céleste* represents the Holy Communion with long drawn-out manual chords supporting a pedal line which represents the drops of Christ's blood. *Diptyque* is subtitled "essay on earthly life and eternal happiness" and after a bustling, rather sour opening the transformation to the celestial peace is quite unnerving. Most visionary of all, the *Apparition de l'eglise éternelle* portrays the coming into view among swirling clouds of the eternal church and then its subsequent fading away. Incessant hammer blows can be heard from the organ pedals. *L'Ascension* was the first of Messiaen's large-scale cycles for the instrument, and was itself a transcription of an orchestral work. Hans-Ola Ericsson has a richly romantic vein in his soul which he willingly bares here. He produces some lovely playing, especially in the slower pieces, and is supported by a mellow organ tone which is well captured in this fine recording.

Messiaen. Des canyons aux étoiles (1974)[a]. Oiseaux exotiques (1956). Couleurs de la cité céleste (1963). **Paul Crossley** (pf); [a]**Michael Thompson** (hn); [a]**James Holland** (xylorimba); [a]**David Johnson** (glockenspiel); **London Sinfonietta/Esa-Pekka Salonen.** CBS Masterworks CD44762.

② 2h 2' DDD 2/89

Anyone who has ever responded to Messiaen's *Turangalîla* Symphony should certainly experience its counterpart. *Des canyons aux étoiles* is an awed contemplation of the marvels of the earth and the immensity of space, both seen as metaphors and manifestations of divinity. And yet of the two works it is *Des canyons* that most startlingly conjures up visual, physical images in sound.

It is often ravishing music but also often hard-edged and dazzlingly bright. The two shorter works in the collection make interesting points of reference. In *Oiseaux exotiques* Messiaen delights in intensifying birdsong by transposing it to quite un-bird-like instruments: brass, percussion and the piano. And if you imagine that an exclusively religious meditation like *Couleurs de la cité céleste* will be hushed, prayerful and mysterious, watch out. It speaks of rainbows and of trumpets, abysses and measureless spaces, blinding light and jewel-like colour, and the work is scored accordingly for strident clarinets, xylophones, brass and metal percussion: it is one of the loudest scores he has ever written. Both these sound-tributaries flow into *Des canyons aux étoiles*, one of this century's masterpieces of instrumental writing, and it is good to have such a virtuoso performance of it. Paul Crossley produces prodigies of brilliant dexterity throughout all three works and he is worthily backed by Salonen and the Sinfonietta players. The recording is as clear as can be, but not without atmosphere.

Messiaen. La nativité du Seigneur[a]. La Transfiguration de Notre Seigneur Jésus-Christ[b]. **[b]Michael Sylvester** (ten); **Paul Aquino** (bar); **[b]Westminster Symphonic Choir; [b]Wallace Mann** (fl); **[b]Loren Kitt** (cl); **[b]János Starker** (vc); **[b]Frank Ames** (marimba); **[b]Ronald Barnett** (vibraphone); **[b]John Kane** (xylorimba); **[b]Yvonne Loriod** (pf); **[a]Simon Preston** (org); **[b]Washington National Symphony Orchestra/Antál Dorati.** Decca Enterprise 425 616-2DM2. Notes, text and translation included. Item marked [a] played on the organ of Westminister Abbey and from Argo ZRG5447 (3/66), [b] HEAD1-2 (5/74).

② 2h 30' ADD 9/90

Considering that *La Transfiguration de Notre Seigneur Jésus-Christ* represents one of the most important landmarks in Messiaen's output, it is somewhat surprising that this pioneering account from the 1970s remains the only recording of this work—and even this remained out of circulation for some time. Happily it has been reissued, and at medium price too. Its neglect undoubtedly has something to do with the work's monumental proportions and equally monumental forces required for performance (it requires an orchestra of over 100 players, a choir of 100 voices as well as a group of seven instrumental soloists). The texts centre around the Gospel narrative of the Transfiguration, interspersed with meditative movements drawn from various biblical and theological texts. Messiaen's fondness for formal symmetry dictates the structure; the work is divided into two groups of seven pieces, which in turn contain internal symmetries and reflections within each part. Stylistically it contains all the ingredients that we have come to associate with Messiaen's music—plainsong, Indian and Greek rhythms and birdsong, in this case a staggering 80 different species. At the time of its composition it represented the summation of Messiaen's art and achievement. Dorati's structural control over this immense work is little short of miraculous, and there are some deeply committed performances from the instrumental soloists too; particularly notable are Yvonne Loriod and János Starker. Not content with giving us just one bargain, Decca have also included as an added bonus Simon Preston's marvellous 1965 recording of *La nativité du Seigneur*. Both works are exceptionally well recorded.

Luis de Milán
Spanish c.1500-c.1561

Milán. Libro de musica de vihuela de mano, "El maestro"—excerpts. **Hopkinson Smith** (vihuela). Auvidis Astrée E7748. Texts and translations included.

51' DDD 5/91

Luis Milán's anthology of vihuela music, *El maestro* was printed in 1535 or 1536 and was the first of its kind for the instrument. It contains villancios and romances, sets of diferencias, dances, transcriptions of sacred and secular polyphony, fantasias and tientos. Some of the pieces can easily be sung as well as played and in such cases in the manuscript the melody appears in red figures to

assist the singer. This disc, however, contains only pieces for solo vihuela
including four of Milán's six beautiful pavanas, nine fantasias and three tientos.
Hopkinson Smith is a skilled and sympathetic player who has given careful
thought to his programme, laying it out in four groups corresponding to the
modes carefully documented in Milán's imaginative anthology. All in all it makes
for fascinating listening, and the disc is very well recorded allowing us to
appreciate the subtleties of the gut-string sound of the instrument.

Darius Milhaud *French 1892-1974*

Milhaud. La création du monde—ballet, Op. 81. Le boeuf sur le toit—ballet,
Op. 58. Saudades do Brasil, Op. 67 (orch. composer). **Orchestre National de
France/Leonard Bernstein.** EMI CDC7 47845-2. From ASD3444 (2/78).
Saudades do Brasil—No. 7, Corcovado; No. 8, Tijuca; No. 9, Sumare; No. 11,
Larenjeiras.

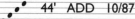 44' ADD 10/87

Leonard Bernstein [photo: DG/Bayat]

Milhaud spent a year in Brazil and
quickly fell in love with its colours, its
rhythms and its carnival freedom. Back
in Paris, these sounds had a profound
effect on his music. *Le boeuf sur le toit*,
set in a bar in prohibition America,
has a fantastic scenario with a score to
match—vivid, vital, lithe and jazzy.
The ballet, *La création du monde*,
illustrates the creation of the world as
depicted in African folklore. The 17-
piece orchestra portrays the primeval
awakening and the gradual emergence
of human life from a formless mass.
The music is alternately vigorously
jazz-inspired and tenderly restrained,
the saxophone giving the textures a lovely veiled quality. The dances from 12
Saudades do Brasil are portraits of Rio de Janeiro in its various states revealing
enormous sympathy and affection and are quite beautifully played. This is one of
the finest things Bernstein has done and the orchestra respond to his loose-
limbed and intensely rhythmic direction superbly.

Ernest Moeran *British 1894-1950* *Refer to Index*

Claudio Monteverdi *Italian 1567-1643*

Monteverdi (ed Parrott/Keyte). Vespro della Beata Vergine. **Taverner
Consort; Taverner Choir; Taverner Players/Andrew Parrott.** EMI CDS7
47078-8. From EX270129-3 (5/85).

② 1h 52' DDD 10/85

For a generation, performances have revelled in the colossal aspect of this work:
huge choirs, generously-sized orchestras of modern instruments and lavish
interpretations, all of which go hand in hand with a such a view of the music.

Without question, splendour was part of Monteverdi's conception, but it was the splendour of ritual that he had in mind. It is this ritualistic aspect that Andrew Parrott restores in this special recording. Plainchant and instrumental sonatas mix authentically with Monteverdi's music; changes are made to the printed order of items to conform to the requirements of the *Vespers* service; several movements are transposed downwards to make them easier on the voice. If the result undermines the conventional view of the *Vespers* as an unbroken chain of glorious concert pieces, culminating in the huge, high-pitched Magnificat, then it does so to the advantage of Monteverdi's original intentions. Parrott brings together the cream of today's early-music specialists and both the playing (entirely on period instruments) and the singing are of the highest order. Few liturgical reconstructions on record have worked so well as this one does. It is a noble and moving experience.

Monteverdi. SACRED VOCAL MUSIC. [a]**Emma Kirkby** (sop); [b]**Ian Partridge** (ten); [c]**David Thomas** (bass); **The Parley of Instruments/Ray Goodman** (vn) with **Peter Holman** (chbr org). Hyperion CDA66021. From A66021 (10/81).
La Maddalena—Prologue: Su le penne de'venti[c]. Confitebor tibi, Domine[abc]. Iste confessor Domini sacratus[b]. Laudate Dominum, Omnes gentes[c]. Confitebor tibi, Domine[ab]. Confitebor tibi, Domine[a]. Ab aeterno ordinata sum[c]. Nisi Dominus aedificaverit domum[abc]. Deus tuorum militum sors et corona[abc].

43' DDD 7/85

This is a delightful selection of lesser-known shorter sacred pieces. There are five psalm settings, each one perfectly distinct from the others; a setting of a passage from *Proverbs* depicting a fantastic vision of creation, two hymn settings and finally, the Prologue to a liturgical drama, *La Maddalena*. The writing has much in common with the madrigalian style: in the first place, it is episodic; it also vividly dramatizes the sense of the words and demands a sensitive response on the part of the singers. For example, the phrase "sanctum et terribile nomen eius" is highlighted by a dignified, slow-moving theme at "sanctum" followed by speedy vocal jittering on "terribile"! The singers have countless opportunities to display both their mastery of vocal techniques and their sensitivity to the text. In general they show restraint and avoid overdoing the pyrotechnics: the music never seems to deviate from its sacred purpose; it always retains a sense of decorum.

Wolfgang Amadeus Mozart
Austrian 1756-1791

Mozart. Sinfonia concertante in E flat major, K364/K320d[a]. Concertone in C major for two violins, oboe, cello and orchestra, K190/K186e[b]. **Itzhak Perlman** (vn); **Pinchas Zukerman** ([a]va, vn); [b]**Chaim Jouval** (ob); [b]**Marcel Bergman** (vc); **Israel Philharmonic Orchestra/Zubin Mehta.** DG 415 486-2GH. Item marked [a] from 2741 026 (11/83), [b] new to UK.

60' DDD 12/85

The first of these works was recorded in 1982 at a concert in Tel Aviv, and represents live music making at its best. Itzhak Perlman's friend Pinchas Zukerman is, like him, a violinist of international reputation, but in the last decade or so he has also played the viola, and since they have a similar approach to the *Sinfonia concertante,* they make for possibly the most desirable pair of soloists that one could hope to bring together for a performance of this melodious work. All is of the finest quality, but the exquisite slow movement stands out memorably even so, "with the silvery image of the violin set against the richer viola tone" as it has been said. Zubin Mehta accompanies sensitively too, with an Israel Philharmonic seemingly inspired by the occasion, and this Mozart playing is exceptional even by today's high standards. The recording is excellent although the soloists sound closer than they would in the concert hall, and audience noise is minimal with no applause. Recorded in the studio, the *Concertone* is another unusually named work, written when Mozart was 18, and has two solo violins plus roles for oboe and cello; this too is most enjoyable and the oboist Chaim Jouval plays with firm yet sweet tone.

Mozart. Sinfonias concertante—E flat major, K364/320*d*[a]; E flat major, KAnh9/C14·01/297*b*[b]. [b]**Stephen Taylor** (ob); [b]**David Singer** (cl); [b]**Steven Dibner** (bn); [b]**William Purvis** (hn); [a]**Todd Phillips** (vn); [a]**Maureen Gallagher** (va); **Orpheus Chamber Orchestra.** DG 429 784-2GH.

63' DDD 4/91   Ⓑ

The Orpheus Chamber Orchestra are a conductorless ensemble of some 25 players, formed in 1972, who have made several successful Mozart records; and here is another. The soloists in the *Sinfonia concertante* for violin and viola are well blended with the orchestral body yet are distinguishable from it and from each other, while the playing in the *Allegro maestoso* first movement is energetic yet not over-emphasized or forced along and the cadenza here is finely shaped. The beautiful central slow movement is warm yet gentle, with a quiet unflagging

strength underlying the sensitivity of the soloists in their thoughtful dialogue, and the finale is vivid without breathlessness. The other work with four wind soloists is also very pleasing, with no weaker member in the solo quartet; here is a good tonal, rhythmic and interpretative blend. If in comparison with some other performances it may seem a trifle understated in places, that is no serious fault in music such as this, which speaks pretty eloquently for itself, and the players miss none of the wit of the cheery variation-form finale. The recording accorded to both these sinfonias concertantes, which was made at the State University of New York, is both natural and pleasing.

Wolfgang Amadeus Mozart

Mozart. Sinfonia concertante in E flat major, K296*b*[a]. Horn Quintet in E flat major, K407/386*c*[c]. Quintet in E flat major for piano and wind, K452[c]. [ac]**Derek Wickens** (ob); [ac]**Robert Hill** (cl); [ac]**Martin Gatt** (bn); [b]members of the **Gabrieli Quartet** (Kenneth Sillito, vn; Kenneth Essex, va; Kenneth Harvey vc); [c]**John Ogdon** (pf); [a]**English Chamber Orchestra/Barry Tuckwell** ([bc]hn). Decca 421 393-2DH. From 410 283-1DH3 (8/84).

73' DDD 9/88

This is a happily chosen compilation of three lesser-known Mozart works, offering a handy way of adding them to a collection without duplication. The *Sinfonia concertante* is not the one featuring violin and viola as soloists, but a delectable lightweight work with wind instruments to the fore. Playing here is smiling and stylish, the lovely slow movement has the lightest touch and is elegantly gracious. The Horn Quintet with its spirited finale, will appeal to anyone who enjoys the concertos while the Piano and Wind Quintet is one of Mozart's masterpieces. Mozart had a very special way with blending woodwind (and horn) and here with the piano as a dominating catalyst he gives us a three movement piece which is infectiously inventive from the first bar to the last. Barry Tuckwell is the personality common to all three performances, and it is he who dominates the Horn Quintet; elsewhere he takes his place with his colleagues, but also directs the *Sinfonia concertante*. The digital recording is very realistic, the players might well be sitting at the end of your listening room.

Mozart. Violin Concertos—No. 3 in G major, K216; No. 4 in D major, K218; No. 5 in A major, K219. **Christian Altenburger** (vn); **German Bach Soloists/Helmut Winscherman.** LaserLight 15 525.

75' DDD 5/90

The violin concertos remind us that, apart from being one of the leading pianists of his day, Mozart was also a more-than-capable violinist. Whilst working with the court orchestra of the Prince-Archbishop of Salzburg, he completed, in 1775, five prime examples of the genre; these were intended as entertainment music for the court, and were to feature himself as soloist. The concertos have much in common with Mozart's cassations, divertimentos and serenades, which also highlight the solo violin and have other concerto-like elements in them. But their lightweight means of expression in no way diminishes their long-term appeal, for Mozart could not but fill them to the brim with wonderful ideas. High spirits are much in evidence in Christian Altenburger's performance of the last three of these concertos, and the restrained size of the accompanying ensemble, along with its crisp, unfussy playing, makes for a relaxed, celebratory atmosphere. The engineers have kept the performers in agreeable balance, placing the soloist far enough forward for his sound to retain its immediacy and vivacity, yet still keeping the German Bach Soloists in sharp focus. Stripped of the usual romantic overkill that they receive from most of the big-name soloists, these concertos now emerge as surprisingly refreshing, youthful works of great charm.

Mozart. Clarinet Concerto in A major, K622[a]. Clarinet Quintet in A major, K581[b]. **Thea King** (basset cl); [b]**Gabrieli String Quartet** (Kenneth Sillito, Brendan O'Reilly, vns; Ian Jewel, va; Keith Harvey, vc); [a]**English Chamber Orchestra/Jeffrey Tate.** Hyperion CDA66199. From A66199 (3/86).

64 DDD 9/86

Mozart. Clarinet Concerto in A major, K622[a]. Flute and Harp Concerto in C major, K299/297c[b]. [a]**Emma Johnson** (cl); [b]**William Bennett** (fl); [b]**Osian Ellis** (hp); **English Chamber Orchestra/Raymond Leppard.** ASV CDDCA532. From DCA532 (6/85).

54' DDD

The two works on the Hyperion disc are representative of Mozart's clarinet writing at its most inspired; however, the instrument for which they were written differed in several respects from the modern clarinet, the most important being its extended bass range. Modern editions of both the Concerto and the Quintet have adjusted the solo part to suit today's clarinets, but on this recording Thea King reverts as far as possible to the original texts, and her playing is both sensitive and intelligent. Jeffrey Tate and the ECO accompany with subtlety and discretion in the Concerto, and the Gabrielli Quartet achieve a fine sense of rapport with King in the Quintet. Both recordings are clear and naturally balanced, with just enough distance between soloist and listener.

The ASV recording followed swiftly on the success of Emma Johnson as the BBC's 1984 "Young Musician of the Year", and it certainly bears out her success. This is tasteful and fluent playing: rather less a performance memorable for special beauty and subtlety of tone and delivery or the revelatory quality which is impossible to define but easily recognized when present—though the *Adagio* has a simple eloquence. However, it is still admirably sure and direct. The Concerto for Flute and Harp brings together two instruments of exquisite beauty. Not surprisingly, the music is delightful, with the two soloists pouring forth golden melody and rippling arpeggios. William Bennett and Osian Ellis are among today's finest players, too, and the recording is very natural, although one might have liked a little more brightness to their sound and could feel that the well-modulated orchestral playing under Raymond Leppard could have more sheer sparkle. Only your preference in respect of coupling can determine the choice between these two recordings

Mozart. HORN CONCERTOS. **Dennis Brain** (hn); **Philharmonia Orchestra/Herbert von Karajan.** EMI Références mono CDH7 61013-2. From Columbia 33CX1140 (10/54).
No. 1 in D major, K412; No. 2 in E flat major, K417; No. 3 in E flat major, K447; No. 4 in E flat major K495.

55' ADD 2/88 £ ⓅⒷ

Mozart. HORN CONCERTOS. **English Chamber Orchestra/Barry Tuckwell** (hn). Decca 410 284-2DH. From 410 284-1DH3 (8/84).
No. 1 in D major, K412; No. 2 in E flat major, K417; No. 3 in E flat major, K447; No. 4 in E flat major K495.

52' DDD 11/84 Ⓑ

Dennis Brain set the yardstick by which all subsequent performances of these concertos would be measured. The security of his technique, the smooth, easy tone and subtle, almost understated expression were all exceptional for the early 1950s, and only the leading horn players of subsequent generations have been able to approach his degree of finesse. Karajan was the ideal accompanist and together they produced performances of great humanity. Although the mono sound is now somewhat lacking in string warmth, it is clean and detailed enough to allow the years to fall away, and for Brain to speak directly to us.

Barry Tuckwell proves that he is one of only a meagre handful of players who can equal Brain's artistry in these works. For some, Brain's view, always urbane and intuitively Mozartian, will remain a first choice, whilst others will prefer the more up-to-date sound of the later recording—despite the comparative thickness of the horn timbre engendered by close miking—and Tuckwell's more overtly virtuosic approach and broader tone quality. The ECO, always the most sensitive of accompanists, are on fine form, their effectiveness limited only by an acoustic that traps lower middle-register detail. With excellent insert notes from Lionel Salter, and Barry Tuckwell himself, this is an issue that may be safely recommended to all wanting a first, second, or subsequent version of these works for their collection.

Mozart. Flute Concerto No. 1 in G major, K313/285c. Andante in C major, K315/285e. Flute and Harp Concerto in C major, K299/297cᵃ. **Susan Palma** (fl); ᵃ**Nancy Allen** (hp); **Orpheus Chamber Orchestra.** DG 427 677-2GH.

58' DDD 3/90 Ⓟ

Mozart described the flute as "an instrument I cannot bear" in 1778 before composing his G major Flute Concerto for the Dutch amateur Ferdinand DeJean

The Orpheus Chamber Orchestra   *[photo: DG/Steiner]*

However, he was incapable of writing poor music and this is a work of much charm and some depth that comes up with admirable freshness in this performance by Susan Palma. She is a remarkably gifted player and a member of the no less skilled Orpheus Chamber Orchestra, a conductor-less ensemble of 24 players who shape the music with unfailing skill and unanimity so that everything is alert, lithe and yet sensitive. Palma's tone is liquid and bright, and she offers fine tonal nuances too, while her cadenzas are no less well imagined. The Concerto for Flute and Harp, written for another amateur player (the Count de Guines) to play with his harpist daughter, combines these two beautiful instruments to celestial effect; again the soloists are highly skilled and beyond that, they are perfectly matched. Palma is as delightful as in the other work and the spacious *Andante* in C major that separates the two concertos, while Nancy Allen makes an exquisite sound and also articulates more clearly than many other harpists in this work. The balance between the soloists and the orchestra is natural and the recording from New York's State University has a very pleasing sound.

Mozart. Oboe Concerto in C major, K314/285.
R. Strauss. Oboe Concerto in D major. **Douglas Boyd** (ob); **Chamber Orchestra of Europe/Paavo Berglund.** ASV CDCOE808. From COE808 (7/87).

> 44' DDD 11/87

This coupling links two of the most delightful oboe concertos ever written. Mozart's sprightly and buoyant work invests the instrument with a chirpy, bird-like fleetness encouraging the interplay of lively rhythm and elegant poise. Boyd's reading of this evergreen work captures its freshness and spontaneity beautifully. If the Mozart portrays the sprightly side of the instrument's make-up the Strauss illustrates its languorous ease and tonal voluptuousness. Again Boyd allows himself the freedom and breadth he needs for his glowing interpretation; he handles the arching melodies of the opening movement and the witty staccato of the last with equal skill. Nicely recorded.

Mozart. Serenade in B flat major for 13 wind instruments, K361. **Academy of St Martin in the Fields Wind Ensemble/Sir Neville Marriner.** Philips 412 726-2PH.

> 49' DDD 5/87

Here is the finest of Mozart's open-air works for wind ensemble. Although the title of "Gran Partita" on the original manuscript may not be Mozart's own the serenade's length of almost 50 minutes fully justifies such a title. Mozart himself described the work, rather more aptly, as "a great wind piece of a very special kind". Sir Neville Marriner is at his very best in repertoire such as this, and he has at his disposal some of Britain's finest wind players. Together they create a performance which reflects Mozart's inspiration to ideal effect. Tempos are all beautifully judged to give the music a good forward momentum and coherence while providing ample room for the most elegant phrasing, and the score's variations in mood are skilfully drawn out. The recording is warm and falls naturally and pleasantly on the ear.

Mozart. Serenade in D major, K250/248*b*, "Haffner". **Josef Suk** (vn); **Prague Chamber Orchestra/Libor Hlaváček.** Supraphon Gems 2SUP0006.

54' AAD 12/87 £

Mozart. Serenade in D major, K250/248*b*, "Haffner"[a]. March in D major, K249, "Haffner". [a]**Iona Brown** (vn); **Academy of St Martin in the Fields/ Sir Neville Marriner.** Philips 416 154-2PH. From 416 154-1PH (3/86).

58' DDD 9/86

The Serenade in D, subtitled after its dedicatee Elizabeth Haffner, is one of Mozart's most joyful and festive works. Its eight movements encompass a wide range of emotions and the essentially dance-based structure is enriched, as is often found in Mozart's serenades, by the interpolation of what amounts to a miniature violin concerto at its heart. Josef Suk has a very positive approach to his solo role, his tone being firm, his decorative trills very clear-cut. His manner is reflected by the playing of the Prague Chamber Orchestra as a whole—Hlaváček drawing from them correspondingly precise and robust playing, suitably festive, pointing up the celebratory purpose for which the work was conceived. Some may prefer a lighter musical approach with perhaps more variety in the phrasing but this is a very acceptable version and a good introduction to one of the composer's most utterly charming works.

Marriner's is a desirable disc even if you already possess the *Haffner* Serenade, for playing such as this brings out the genial warmth of Mozart's inspiration to the full. The little March that precedes the main work seems to wear a smile for all its rhythmical neatness and precision, and that too is surely as it should be. Recorded in London in 1984, the Academy of St Martin in the Fields is in top form and Iona Brown is an immaculate violinist in the solo role which surfaces in what is in effect a kind of violin concerto that Mozart incorporated into the eight movements that make up the larger whole of the Serenade. It has a particularly lovely *Andante*, which is the Serenade's second movement, and a bustling and brilliant rondo-finale. The sound is full yet detailed, with natural reverberation.

Mozart. Divertimentos—B flat major, K287/271*h*; D major, K205/167*a*. **Salzburg Mozarteum Camerata Academica/Sándor Végh.** Capriccio 10 271.

59' DDD 11/89

Mozart's Divertimento, K287 is a six-movement work cast on quite a large scale, and is scored for two violins, viola, two horns and bass, a combination which presents some difficulties of balance. One solution is to use a full orchestral string section, as did Toscanini and Karajan in their recordings, but this can bring its own problems, for Mozart demands playing of virtuoso standard in this score, and anything less than this is ruthlessly exposed. Sandor Végh's smallish string band is of high quality, and has a pleasantly rounded tone quality. The engineers have managed to contrive a satisfactory balance which sounds not at all unnatural, and the sound quality itself is very good. Végh directs an attractive, neatly-pointed performance of the work, one which steers a middle course between objective classicism and expressive warmth. The

Divertimento, K205, has five movements, but none lasts longer than five minutes, and the work is much shorter and more modest than K287. Scoring in this case is for violin, viola, two horns, bassoon and bass, to provide another difficult but well resolved problem for the engineers. Végh directs another characterful, delightful performance, to round off a very desirable disc.

Mozart. Divertimentos—D major, K251; B flat major, K270. Serenade in D major, "Serenata notturna". **Orpheus Chamber Orchestra.** DG 415 669-2GH.

• 49' DDD 4/86

The Orpheus Chamber Orchestra has made some remarkably fine recordings. This was among the first of them, but it offers absolutely assured Mozart playing, both in terms of ensemble skills and sheer stylistic flair. The music is well chosen, and as delightful as we may expect from Mozart in divertimento and serenade mood, and as played here, the dances really do dance and the marches march, while the more lyrical slower movements sing as gracefully as anyone could wish. The *Serenata notturna* is a work of especial charm, and the performance here has the right blend of quiet pomp and elegance, with fine violin solos in the Minuet and playful finale. Although the photo of the orchestra in the booklet shows 25 players including flutes and a dozen strings, it also says that there are 26 in the orchestra (16 string and 10 wind). But elsewhere the players listed and named amount to only ten, and what we have here are chamber-music performances of the three works with just one instrument to a part; however, the timpanist who plays in the Serenade is not listed, or for that matter illustrated. The recording is clear if with a tolerable touch of edginess to the violin tone.

Mozart. Divertimentos—D major, K205/167a[a]; D major, K334/320b[b]. March in D major, K290/167ab[a]. **Franz Liszt Chamber Orchestra/[a]János Rolla, [b]Frigyes Sándor.** Hungaroton White Label HRC080.

• 67' ADD 5/90   £

The Franz Liszt Chamber Orchestra of Budapest is a fine ensemble, and here they play two of Mozart's divertimentos with a crisp, lithe style and pleasant and well varied tone. The bigger work here is the first, K334, which has a Theme (in D minor) and Variations as its second movement and a well known Minuet as its third. The earlier Divertimento, also in D major, is preceded by the little March, K290, which was also evidently played at its first performance at a garden party in 1773. Neither work is deep music, as the title tells us, but each entertains delightfully and the minuets, of which there are four in all, dance with both gravity and grace. Excellent recording in a resonant acoustic that does not obscure detail and of course the super-bargain price is another attraction, while there is an informative booklet note provided too.

Mozart. PIANO CONCERTOS. **English Chamber Orchestra/Daniel Barenboim** (pf). EMI CZS7 62825-2.
No. 1 in F major, K37; No. 2 in B flat major, K39; No. 3 in D major, K40; No. 4 in G major, K41 (all from SLS5031, 1/76); No. 5 in D major, K175 (ASD2484, 11/69); No. 6 in B flat major, K238 (ASD3032, 11/74); No. 8 in C major, K246 (ASD3033, 1/75); No. 9 in E flat major, K271 (ASD2484); No. 11 in F major, K413/387a (ASD2999, 9/74); No. 12 in A major, K414/385p (ASD2956, 2/74); No. 13 in C major, K415/387b (ASD2357, 4/68);

No. 14 in E flat major, K449; No. 15 in B flat major, K450 (both ASD2434, 11/68); No. 16 in D major, K451 (ASD2999); No. 17 in G major, K453 (ASD2357); No. 18 in B flat major, K456 (ASD2887, 7/73); No. 19 in F major, K459 (ASD2956); No. 20 in D minor, K466 (ASD2318, 7/67); No. 21 in C major, K467 (ASD2465, 2/69); No. 22 in E flat major, K482 (ASD2838, 11/72); No. 23 in A major, K488 (ASD2318); No. 24 in C minor, K491 (ASD2887); No. 25 in C major, K503 (ASD3033); No. 26 in D major, K537, "Coronation" (ASD3032); No. 27 in B flat major, K595 (ASD2465). Rondo in D major, K382 (ASD2838).

⟨1⟩⟨10⟩ 11h 1' ADD 6/90   £

Here are all 27 of Mozart's piano concertos plus the D major Rondo, K382, on ten medium-priced discs giving a total of eleven hours listening. The skills of Daniel Barenboim and the English Chamber Orchestra in this repertory are well proven, and his account of these concertos, directed from the keyboard, is spacious and satisfying. This artist has always been a master of clean exposition

and structure, and from the early Concertos to the late masterpieces such as Nos. 21, 24 and 27 he is a sure guide with a full awareness of Mozart's inventive and expressive range. Sometimes one may feel that he allows a rather romantic self-indulgence to creep in, and in the more dramatic music (e.g. in the D minor and C minor concertos) he may be thought too powerfully Beethovenian— incidentally, he uses a Beethoven cadenza, as arranged by Edwin Fischer, in the first movement of the first of these. Ideally, too, we might prefer a smaller body of strings than was used in these performances from the late 1960s and early 1970s.

Daniel Barenboim   [*photo: Teldec/Martin*]

But these are only small reservations, given the high overall standard, and certainly this is a major achievement. The recordings sound well, with mellow piano tone and good balance.

84

Mozart. Piano Concertos—No. 15 in B flat, K450; No. 16 in D major, K451. **English Chamber Orchestra/Murray Perahia** (pf). CBS Masterworks CD37824.

50' DDD

It is difficult to do justice to interpretations of this calibre in a short review. Perahia's delicious shaping of even the most elaborate phrases and his delicacy and refinement of tone impress throughout these performances. The two works are admirably contrasted: K450 is on the whole light and high-spirited, while the first movement of K451 is almost Beethovenian in its grandeur and purposefulness, and both concertos have typically beautiful slow movements. Recordings are superb: an overly attentive microphone could have done irreparable damage to Perahia's legato, but here the distance is finely judged and

the soloist/orchestra balance is exemplary.

Mozart. Piano Concertos—No. 19 in F major, K459; No. 27 in B flat major, K595. **András Schiff** (pf); **Salzburg Mozarteum Camerata Academica/ Sándor Végh.** Decca 421 259-2DH.

59' DDD 3/89

Listening to this disc one is immediately struck by a quality rarely encountered in so much music-making today. It is civilized, urbane, 'old fashioned' even, but always alive to the inner vitality of the music. It is also pleasant to encounter music-making where both soloist and conductor evidently enjoy playing together and achieve an almost chamber-music intimacy. Sándor Végh conducts with sympathy, panache and an evident love of the music. His hand-picked orchestra are quite outstanding with some remarkable wind playing. András Schiff responds with equal amounts of sympathy, giving razor-sharp articulation to the music. It is subtle pianism, performed with taste. The recording is generous, initially slightly disconcerting (reverberance somewhat diminishing the piano's impact) but one soon adjusts, aided by perceptive musicianship at its very best.

Mozart. PIANO CONCERTOS. **English Chamber Orchestra/Murray Perahia** (pf). CBS Masterworks CD42241 and CD42243. Items marked [a] from 76651 (4/78), [b] 76731 (5/80), [c] 76481 (5/76).
CD42241—No. 20 in D minor, K466[a]; No. 27 in B flat major, K595[b].
CD42243—No. 11 in E major, K413[a]; No. 12 in A major, K414[b]; No. 14 in E flat major, K449[c].

② 62' 70' ADD/DDD 9/87

These discs happily epitomise some of the best qualities of the complete Perahia/ ECO set. Always intelligent, always sensitive to both the overt and less obvious nuances of this music, Perahia is firstly a true pianist, never forcing the instrument beyond its limits in order to express the ideas, always maintaining a well-projected singing touch. The superb ECO reflect his integrity and empathy without having to follow slavishly every detail of his articulation or phrasing. K414 and K413 are charming and typically novel for their time, but do not break new ground in quite the way that K449 does. Here, Mozart's success in the theatre may have suggested a more dramatic presentation and working of ideas for this instrumental genre. K595 is a work pervaded by a serenity of acceptance that underlies its wistfulness. Mozart had less than a year to live, and the mounting depression of his life had already worn him down, yet there is still a sort of quiet joy in this music. The vast range of styles, emotions, and forms that these few works encompass are evocatively celebrated in these performances, and admirably captured in civilized recordings.

Mozart. Piano Concertos—No. 20 in D minor, K466; No. 21 in C major, K467. **Mitsuko Uchida** (pf); **English Chamber Orchestra/Jeffrey Tate.** Philips 416 381-2PH.

62' DDD 7/86 **Ⓑ**

Mozart. Piano Concertos—No. 20 in D minor, K466; No. 27 in B flat major, K595. **Sir Clifford Curzon** (pf); **English Chamber Orchestra/Benjamin Britten.** Decca 417 288-2DH. From SXL7007 (2/83).

65' ADD 10/86 **Ⓑ**

Mitsuko Uchida's Mozart is quite without parallel. Her manner is strong and intense but free from any kind of romantic excess. For her every note matters, even when the piano writing is largely decorative, and yet her playing never sounds sententious. In the shaping of the tiniest phrase, or in the pacing of the longest movement, she shows the same remarkable insight and sensitivity. As a result, her performances are elegant as well as moving. She is fortunate in having Jeffrey Tate, another perceptive and deeply serious Mozartian, as a musical partner. Their obvious rapport adds considerably to the impact of the D minor Concerto and to the more intimate charm of the C major. Fine recordings, with soloist and orchestra convincingly balanced.

Sir Clifford Curzon's playing is also extraordinarily alert and concentrated: shaping and shading of even the minutest details is superbly subtle, while each movement as a whole has a sense of grand inevitability. This ability to focus intently upon foreground detail without losing the sense of the overall shape is one of the hallmarks of Curzon's genius, and one could be thankful that he was able to find such an understanding and sympathetic accompanist as Benjamin Britten. Their partnership in this music radiates a sense of shared joy in music-making. There is a quick fade-in at the start of K595, slightly blunting the effect of the opening tutti, but otherwise the transfers are excellent.

Mozart. Piano Concertos—No. 21 in C major, K467; No. 24 in C minor, K491. **Robert Casadesus** (pf); **Cleveland Orchestra/George Szell.** CBS Maestro CD42594. From SBRG72234 (7/65).

57' ADD 2/90 Ⓑ

Mozart. Piano Concertos—No. 21 in C major, K467; No. 25 in C major, K503. **Stephen Kovacevich** (pf); **London Symphony Orchestra/Sir Colin Davis.** Philips Concert Classics 426 077-2PC. From 6500 431 (4/74).

59' ADD 2/90 £ Ⓟ Ⓑ

Mozart. Piano Concerto No. 21 in C major, K467[a].
Schumann. Piano Concerto in A minor, Op. 54[b]. **Dinu Lipatti** (pf);
[a]**Lucerne Festival Orchestra;** [b]**Philharmonia Orchestra/ Herbert von Karajan.** EMI Références mono CDH7 69792-2. Item marked [a] recorded at a performance in the Kunsthaus, Lucerne on August 23rd, 1950 and from Columbia 33C1064 (1/61), [b] LX1110/3 (11/48).

58' ADD 7/89 Ⓟ Ⓑ

Although the sound can at times be, by turns, a touch astringent and woolly in the now ageing CBS recordings, there is no disguising the infectious enthusiasm of Casadesus's playing, nor the sympathetic support given him by the Cleveland Orchestra under Szell. The dreamy *Andante* of K467, the piano musing over a pacing accompaniment, is taken with unhindered flow, articulation and dynamics creating the effect rather than fluctuations in speed. The shifts in pace of the following *Allegro vivace assai* are all the more surprising and effective then. The drama of K491 is darkly portrayed, both soloist and conductor fully taking on board the significance Mozart attached to the work's key. In the final movement they imbue the theme with the utmost simplicity, rendering the subsequent variations all the more sinister, even those of the brightest, unshadowed expression. The end is, therefore, doubly tragic. If, despite all their attractions, you are still not drawn to these performances, then at least the amazing cadenzas, unmistakably by Saint-Saëns, should be heard.

The Philips disc may contain fairly standard readings but Stephen Kovacevich makes the concertos sparkle with crystalline tone, perfectly even, though shapely passagework, and a total dedication to conveying the music's directness of expression. In the *Andante*s, his absorption with the sheer perfection of the sound ideally transmits the inner light of the work, and in the faster movements he delights in their fluidity and rhythmic vitality. Sir Colin Davis seems well in tune with the soloist's intentions but, though the LSO generally provides a pleasingly coherent accompaniment, the whole is let down on occasions by obtrusive width of vibrato and moments of sour chording from the woodwind. That aside, there is little here that is other than delightful. The recording sets the soloist fairly far

George Szell

forward and provides plenty of orchestral detail, so any anomalies are particularly obvious: Kovacevich's playing blooms under these conditions, his avoidance of overstatement made all the more pertinent.

Lipatti recorded the Schumann Concerto in 1948 and the sound is more true to life, and better balanced, than anything heard in Mozart's K467 taken from a concert performance two years later. But it's the playing that counts. There was only one Lipatti, as a younger generation of CD collectors can now, happily, discover for themselves. He is known to have expressed doubts about his readiness to record the Schumann and after its emergence, he wondered if his playing might have been a little too "confined". Such fears were groundless. The reading combines spontaneous youthful freshness and élan with absolute truthfulness to the letter of the score. The music's poetry is conveyed without self-conscious 'interpretation' and its sentiment never degenerates into sentimentality. When undertaking the Mozart in Lucerne in 1950, the miraculous reprieve wrought by cortisone was ending. But nearly 40 years on, the vitality and commitment of the performance make it impossible to believe that leukaemia was to claim his life in less than four months. It's a collector's piece, despite less than ideal reproduction, all the more so for allowing us to hear Lipatti's own cadenzas in the first movement and the last.

Mozart. Piano Concertos—No. 22 in E flat major, K482[a]; No. 23 in A major, K488[b]. **Daniel Barenboim** (pf); **English Chamber Orchestra/Daniel Barenboim.** EMI CDM7 69122-2. Item marked [a] from ASD2838 (11/72), [b] ASD2318 (7/67).

62' ADD 6/88

These two concertos make a good coupling, especially in these affecting, elegant readings from Barenboim and the ECO. What Barenboim may have lacked in authenticity of instruments or style when recording these concertos about 20 years ago, he more than made up for in authenticity of spirit and musicianship. Both the slow movements of these works are especially fine, poised, shapely, and heartfelt: Barenboim employs both great subtlety and great simplicity, keeping the listener on the edge of his seat waiting for even the slightest of gestures that can open the way to new meanings. The faster, outer movements are ideally paced and although dexterity obviously plays a part in their successful realization, it never intrudes. We have here two performances of the highest calibre from a soloist and orchestra of the front rank. They will bear much repetition, and the close yet well-spaced recordings lend an easy, genial feel to the proceedings.

Mozart. Cassations—G major, K63; B flat major, K99/63*a*. Adagio and Fugue in C minor, K546. **Salzburg Camerata/Sándor Végh.** Capriccio 10 192.

51' DDD 3/88

Mozart's cassations, a term usually applied to music that was intended for performance in public, often outdoors, are works of great charm and vitality. How lovely it must have been to catch this graceful, elegant music floating out into the night air. The solemn *Adagio and Fugue*, K546, written originally around a two-piano composition and later arranged for strings, shows Mozart looking back to the baroque era, and the great form of that age, the fugue. It has a solemnity and gravity beautifully captured by this fine band of musicians. Sándor Végh, one of the most celebrated chamber-musicians of our age, brings a wealth of musical understanding to these rarely heard works imbuing them with an old-world humanity.

Mozart. ORCHESTRAL WORKS. **Orpheus Chamber Orchestra.** DG 429 783-2GH.

Ein musikalischer Spass, K522. Contredanses—C major, K587, "Der Sieg vom Helden Koburg"; D major, K534, "Das Donnerwetter"; C major, K535, "La Bataille"; G major, K610, "Les filles malicieuses"; E flat major, K607/605a, "Il trionfo delle donne". Gallimathias musicum, K32. German Dances—K567; K605; C major, K611, "Die Leyerer". March in D major, K335 No. 1.

69' DDD 4/91

After all the Mozart with which we have been bombarded during his bicentenary year, it is a mark of his greatness that an issue such as this comes up with an incomparably engaging freshness. The celebrated *Musikalischer Spass* ("Musical Joke") which begins the disc is never so crudely funny that it wears thin, but make no mistake, the jokes are there in just about every passage, whether they are parodying third-rate music or wobbly playing, and oddly enough sound still more amusing when the performance is as stylishly flexible as this one by the conductorless Orpheus Chamber Orchestra. One of the tunes here (that of the finale on track four) is that of the BBC's *Horse of the Year* programme—and what a good tune it is, even at the umpteenth repetition as the hapless composer finds himself unable to stop. The rest of this programme is no less delightful and includes miniature pieces supposedly describing a thunderstorm, a battle, a hurdy-gurdy man and a sleigh-ride (with piccolo and sleigh-bells). There is also a *Gallimathias musicum*, a ballet suite of dainty little dances averaging less than a minute in length, which Mozart is supposed to have written at the age of ten. Whatever the case this CD, subtitled "A Little Light Music", provides proof of his genius, though differently from his acknowledged masterpieces. The recording is as refined as anyone could wish yet has plenty of impact.

Mozart. 17 Church Sonatas. **Ian Watson** (org); **Classical Orchestra of the King's Consort/Robert King** (org). Hyperion CDA66377.

60' DDD 11/90

At the age of 16 Mozart was appointed Konzertmeister to the Prince-Archbishop of Salzburg. Opportunities for composing large-scale church music in this post were rather restricted since the Archbishop had ruled that music for the Mass had to be kept to an absolute minimum: the whole service could not exceed 45 minutes. One area where a brief musical interlude was required was between the readings of the Epistle and Gospel. Normally for this Mozart would improvise on the organ, but on special occasions he made use of an instrumental ensemble. These 17 Epistle Sonatas were the result. Most composers would have found little scope in such short pieces (none lasts much more than four minutes). Mozart, the supreme genius, came up with 17 tiny yet perfectly-proportioned gems, full of interest, originality and charm. The later sonatas use the organ in something approaching a solo role; indeed the last one, K336, is like a self-contained concerto movement complete with cadenza. In this recording Ian Watson is a most agile and stylish soloist. As ever Robert King and the King's Consort show total involvement in the music and play with refreshing enthusiasm.

Mozart. SYMPHONIES. **The English Concert/Trevor Pinnock** (hpd).
Archiv Produktion 431 679-2AH.
No. 25 in G minor, K183/173*db*; No. 26 in E flat major, K184/161*a*; No. 29
in A major, K201/186*a*.

53' DDD 7/91

The bicentenary year brought so many Mozart issues (and reissues) that there is a
danger that with its passing some of them may quickly be forgotten. However,
this one has enough personality to keep its place in the catalogue, and that
quality comes across instantly at the start of Symphony No. 26, which is played
first. Admittedly the marking is *molto presto*, but even so the listener may be
startled by the brisk pace and the near-aggressive vigour of this sound. This is a
performance with period instruments (note the veiled string tone in quiet
passages), yet there is also something modern about the spotless efficiency of it
all and one wonders whether Mozart heard or intended performances like this
and if Trevor Pinnock's penchant for pace and sheer energy is sometimes
excessive. Set aside that doubt, however, and one must admire the polish and
ensemble of this playing, and make no mistake, there is sensitivity too, as the
Andante shows. This miniature symphony lasts less than nine minutes and its
three movements are played without a break. Predictably, Pinnock brings out all
the "storm and stress" drama of the G minor Symphony, but there is mystery
too in the strangely gliding slow movement and the quiet start of the finale. The
elegantly genial A major is nicely shaped, too, and only in the finale might one
wish for more space for the music to sound. A vivid and well balanced recording
complements this expert playing.

Mozart. SYMPHONIES. **Capella Istropolitana/Barry Wordsworth.**
Naxos 8 550113, 8 550119, 8 550164, 8 550186, 8 550264 and 8 550299.
8 550113 (65 minutes): No. 25 in G minor, K183/173*dB*; No. 32 in G major,
K318; No. 41 in C major, K551, "Jupiter". *8 550119* (69 minutes): No. 29 in A
major, K201/186*a*; No. 30 in D major, K202/186*b*; No. 38 in D major, K504,
"Prague". *8 550164* (61 minutes): No. 28 in C major, K200/189*k*; No. 31 in D
major, K297/300*a*, "Paris"; No. 40 in G minor, K550. *8 550186* (62 minutes):
No. 34 in C major, K338; No. 35 in D major, K385, "Haffner"; No. 39 in E
flat major, K543. *8 550264* (65 minutes): No. 27 in G minor, K199/161*b*; No.
33 in B flat major, K319; No. 36 in C major, K425, "Linz". *8 550299* (62
minutes): No. 40 in G minor, K550; No. 41 in C major, K551, "Jupiter".

⑥ 6h 24' DDD 4/91 £ Ⓑ

Collectors who complain about the price of CDs will find their prayers answered
in this marvellous Naxos set of the 15 greatest symphonies of Mozart, digitally
recorded, yet offered at super-bargain price. Moreover, for those who do not
need them all, Naxos have combined the two greatest, No. 40 in G minor and
the *Jupiter* on a single disc, which at its modest price should surely find a place
in every collection, for it is exceptionally satisfying in every respect. The Capella
Istropolitana was founded in 1983, drawing for its players on members of the
Slovak Philharmonic Orchestra. The orchestra has already recorded a wide range
of baroque music for Naxos and through these discs is gaining a reputation for
freshness of musical presentation and polish of ensemble that recalls the early
days of the Academy of St Martin in the Fields. Like the first series of Argo
ASMF recordings, the impression is that the players really care about the music;
there is not a whiff of routine about the music-making. And, as observed in the
original *Gramophone* review, "there is an inescapable feeling of fine players
enjoying themselves". They are fortunate to have a musical director as sensitive
in matters of style and phrasing as Barry Wordsworth, a British conductor, who
began his conducting career with the Royal Ballet. His star is ascending very
quickly into the firmament, and these discs represent his finest achievement so

far. His gift of spontaneity in the recording studio is of course helped by the natural response of his orchestra, which is surely exactly the right size for Mozart. One of his greatest gifts is his sense of pacing, which seems unerring. One has only to turn to the two most famous works (Nos. 40 and 41) to find that tempos are perfectly interrelated. Yet one can go back to the delightful early G minor Symphony (No. 25) and find the *Allegro con brio*, exactly that, and the following *Andante* bringing balm to the senses, with a warmly relaxed *espressivo*. Yet there is never a feeling that the momentum is flagging, for a gently sustained tension beneath the surface of the music keeps it flowing onwards. This is even more striking in the poignant elegy of the *Andante* of No. 29, with its exquisitely gentle cantilena in the violins, while the gracious melodies of the *Andantes* of the *Haffner* (No. 35) and the *Prague* (No. 38) are shaped with disarming beauty. The Introduction of the first movement of the *Prague* is particularly imposing (clearly Mozart wanted to make a strong impression at its first performance): then follows a bright, alert *Allegro*, here full of the spirited momentum one also finds in the finale of No. 29 and the brightly, vivacious outer movements of No. 28. This is an early masterpiece that has only recently been receiving its full due from the general public. Symphony No. 39, a great favourite of many, has another portentous introduction, made the more impressive here by the hard-sticks used on the timpani. Its merry finale (comparable with the genial *Allegro molto* of No. 34) almost anticipates Mendelssohn in its sparkle, and the bright colours from the woodwind. The key of A major means that in the *Allegros* of No. 29 the horns are pitched high, and how wonderfully they shine out over the strings in the finale. Indeed, another aspect of these discs is their excellent balance, with the orchestra believably set out in front of the listener in a natural concert hall acoustic that is warm, yet not too resonant for clarity. Barry Wordsworth is wholly sensible in the matter of repeats, observing them in the expositions of first movements (where they are needed so that the main themes register firmly with the listener, before the argument of their development begins), and in the finales only where they are necessary to establish the appropriate character of the work. As in the *Jupiter*, where the repeat emphasizes the power and breadth of the closing movement, with its great culminating fugal denouement. In all this is a superb set, among the very finest new offerings made during the Mozart bicentennial. To quote further from the original *Gramophone* review, "In every way these are worthy rivals to the best full-price versions". Unless you insist on original instruments they will give very great satisfaction. There are adequate notes (only the disc with Nos. 28, 31 and 40 is deficient in this respect) and they currently cost around £22 for the six discs, which provide around five-and-a-half hours of the greatest music ever written.

Mozart. Symphonies—No. 25 in G minor, K183/173*dB*; No. 28 in C major, K200/189*k*; No. 29 in A major, K201/186*a*. **Prague Chamber Orchestra/ Sir Charles Mackerras.** Telarc CD80165.

78' DDD 9/88

Here are three symphonies from Mozart's late teens, written in his native Salzburg, in crisply articulated performances. The first of them is a "Sturm und Drang" piece in a key that the composer reserved for moods of agitation. Mackerras takes the orchestra through the big opening *Allegro con brio* of No. 25 with drive and passion, although it is unlikely that Mozart would have expected a Salzburg orchestra in the 1770s to play as fast as this skilful body of Czech players. The gentle *Andante* comes therefore as a relief, though here too Mackerras keeps a firm rhythmic grasp on the music, and indeed a taut metrical aspect is a feature of all three symphonies as played here, so that minuets dance briskly and purposefully and finales bustle. However, the sunlit warmth of the beautiful A major Symphony, No. 29, comes through and the bracing view of the other two symphonies is a legitimate one, though giving little or nothing in the direction of expressive lingering, much less towards sentimental indulgence. The Prague Chamber Orchestra is an expert ensemble, not over-large for this style of music and the recording is admirably clear although a little reverberant. A well-filled disc.

Mozart. Symphonies—No. 27 in G major, K199/161*b*; No. 28 in C major, K200/189*k*; No. 34 in C major, K338. **English Sinfonia/Sir Charles Groves.** Pickwick IMP Classics PCD933.

63' DDD 3/90

Most music lovers are familiar with half a dozen or so of the Mozart symphonies, but there are others worth exploring too, and this account of three of them is most agreeably done. In the quicker movements, Sir Charles Groves and the English Sinfonia are deft yet alert, but they also respond to nuance, while in the slow movements the playing is quietly expressive. There is an unforced quality about the interpretation overall that is attractive, though some listeners might feel that individual works need fuller characterization. Nevertheless, the playing is always stylish and faithful, and No. 34 is well projected in its sturdy utterance. One curious fault, at least on the copy reviewed here, is that the track for the bustling finale of this latter symphony (Track 10) begins too early and takes in the last phrase of the *Andante di molto*; however, this will not be noticed if the two are played consecutively, as that phrase, ending with a perfect cadence in F major, is followed by an appropriate small pause. The recording has a natural balance and reverberation.

Mozart. Symphonies—No. 29 in A major, K201/186*a*; No. 32 in G major, K318; No. 33 in B flat major, K319. **English Sinfonia/Sir Charles Groves.** Pickwick IMP Classics PCD922.

61' DDD 11/89 **Ⓑ**

Mozart. Symphonies—No. 29 in A major, K201/186*a*; No. 33 in B flat major, K319. **English Baroque Soloists/John Eliot Gardiner.** Philips 412 736-2PH. From 412 736-1PH (4/86).

44' DDD 8/86 **Ⓑ**

The bright and attractive performances of Sir Charles Groves are crisply articulated and yet with the right degree of lyricism, even in quick movements. The quality of playing that comes across above all is élan, but this 'dash' is never allowed to drive the music forward so that we overlook delights on the way, and overall one feels that Sir Charles gets the balance right between 'just playing the notes' and allowing them to sound mannered. The slow movements remind us of the excellence of the wind players in the English Sinfonia, and the strings sing most fetchingly. Tempos are well judged too, and how good it is to hear the *Allegro moderato* first movement of Symphony No. 29 (which some conductors bustle through) presented with poise, delicacy and even tenderness—and yet also with the necessary feeling of energy. The recording is clear yet with enough atmosphere to suggest an expert band in rococo surroundings. The medium price is another attraction.

The Philips performances on period instruments sound entirely idiomatic and John Eliot Gardiner has taken pains to avoid anything anachronistic. But perhaps the most striking effect of playing this music on 'authentic' instruments is the gain in textural clarity and the improved orchestral balance: the woodwind stand out distinctly without microphonic assistance and it is no longer necessary to subdue the horns. Performances are marvellously fresh and vital, and the attentive and sympathetic recordings ensure that nothing is lost. Both works are highly inventive and rich in melodic interest, although it is the earlier symphony, No. 29, which impresses most—an astonishing achievement for an 18 year old!

Mozart. Symphonies—No. 31 in D major, K297, "Paris" (first version); No. 34 in C major, K338. **English Baroque Soloists/John Eliot Gardiner.** Philips 420 937-2PH.

48' DDD 7/88

Mozart. Symphonies—No. 31 in D major, K297/K300a, "Paris"; No. 33 in B flat major, K319; No. 34 in C major, K338. **Prague Chamber Orchestra/Sir Charles Mackerras.** Telarc CD80190.

65' DDD 3/90

The three-movement *Paris* Symphony was written during Mozart's visit to the capital in 1778. A request for a slow movement that was less complex than the first he produced spurred him to compose one of his finest works in the genre, showing a new structural tension, with all superfluous material, however fine, pared away. On both of these recordings, we have the chance directly to compare the old and new slow movements, as they are played consecutively. The less blatant Symphony No. 34 is performed on the Philips disc with the addition of the Minuet K409, which may have been intended for the work's Viennese revival two years after the Symphony's composition. Both of Gardiner's versions of the symphonies are performed on period instruments, with a keen sense of their significance but without any undue aggrandizement. There is a natural ease and flow in his readings that allows the listener simply to sit back and enjoy the music's glorious charm and shapeliness. The recording provides fine scope for the subtleties of the playing, especially in the more exposed sections for woodwinds, to be fully appreciated.

Although Sir Charles Mackerras does not choose to use period instruments, he is a most dedicated Mozartian, going to a variety of original manuscripts and orchestral parts in order to provide what he considers to be the composer's final thoughts on each of the works coupled here. He also uses a reduced-scale orchestra and harpsichord continuo to help recreate these masterworks. The performances themselves need no further validation, though, for Mackerras infuses all with a vitality and style that easily keeps his audience on the edge of their seat, eager to miss no inspired detail or well-turned phrase. The Prague Chamber Orchestra rise to the challenge he sets them with fleet dexterity in the faster movements and poised, heartfelt expression in the *Andantes*, all produced against a backcloth of adroit textural balance. The open, large-scale acoustic tends to upset these best endeavours in the loudest passages, but elsewhere the sound is first-class, with a fine feeling of space in Prague's characterful Castle of Dobris.

Mozart. Symphonies—No. 31 in D major, K297/300a, "Paris"; No. 38 in D major, K504, "Prague". **English Sinfonia/Sir Charles Groves.** Pickwick IMP Classics PCD892.

55' DDD 9/88

Groves's no-nonsense approach to music of the classical era pays dividends with these two masterworks. He loves this music but, rather than harbouring too precious an infatuation, he greets it with the warm embrace of long acquaintance, letting his natural sense of style control any romantic excess that might otherwise ensue. He brings to these performances the poise of a great performer, unhurried even in the fastest sections, palpably delighting in the fact that repeats provide the opportunity to hear more of this wonderful music. The three movements of both these symphonies require careful balancing if they are not to seem too lightweight and too close to the operatic-overture beginnings of the genre. Sir Charles achieves this by bringing out the warmth of the slow movements, with their elegant phrasing, and avoiding an overdriven and frenetic feel to the finales, by the use of well-judged tempos. The recording, agreeable in most respects, lacks impact in the loudest sections but the overall result is still a happy example of music-making at its best.

Mozart. Symphonies—No. 35 in D major, K385, "Haffner"[a]; No. 36 in C major, K425, "Linz"[a]. Rondo for violin and orchestra in B flat major, K269[b]. [a]**Bavarian Radio Symphony Orchestra/Rafael Kubelík;** [b]**Saint Paul Chamber Orchestra/Pinchas Zukerman** (vn). CBS Masterworks CD44647.

57' DDD 9/89 Ⓑ

These are very satisfying accounts of the *Linz* and *Haffner* Symphonies. Kubelík's ability to project a strong sense of architecture and formal balance is remarkable, and this is reflected on the small scale too, with melodic phrases beautifully shaped and refined. The outer movements of both works are consistently well paced with plenty of rhythmic drive, vitality and drama, with Kubelík never allowing his grip on the symphonic argument to falter or slacken. His unfussy approach in the *Andante* of the *Haffner* allows the pastoral freshness of this movement to surface with ease, and in the *Menuetto* much is made of the contrast between loud and soft, emphasizing the Haydnesque qualities of this movement. The Bavarian orchestra respond well to Kubelík's approach with playing that is warm, full-toned and very assured. The disc also contains an extra bonus in the shape of the *Rondo* in B flat, originally written as an alternative finale to the Violin Concerto No. 1, K207, and is played here in a very attractive performance. The recorded sound has warmth and presence.

Mozart. Symphonies—No. 36 in C major, K425, "Linz"; No. 38 in D major, K504, "Prague". **English Chamber Orchestra/Jeffrey Tate.** EMI CDC7 47442-2. From EL270306-1 (1/86).

67' DDD 11/86

Mozart. Symphonies—No. 36 in C major, K425, "Linz"; No. 38 in D major, K504, "Prague". **Prague Chamber Orchestra/Sir Charles Mackerras.** Telarc CD80148.

66' DDD 10/87

Mozart. Symphonies—No. 38 in D major, K504, "Prague"; No. 39 in E flat major, K543. **Bavarian Radio Symphony Orchestra/Rafael Kubelík.** CBS CD44648.

56' DDD 2/90 P

Mozart wrote his *Linz* Symphony in great haste (five days to be precise), but needless to say there is little evidence of haste in the music itself, except perhaps that the first movement has all the exuberance of a composer writing on the wing of inspiration. The slow movement with its siciliano rhythm certainly has no lack of serenity, although it has drama too. The *Prague* Symphony was written only three years later, yet Mozart's symphonic style had matured and the work is altogether more ambitious and substantial. It has a superbly expansive *Andante*, most imaginatively orchestrated, which Tate makes the very most of by observing the repeat. There is no minuet and the *Presto* finale provides a sparkling release of tension. For those who enjoy Mozart on a sensible scale, yet using modern instruments, Tate's performances will surely seem near ideal, for they match finesse and warmth of phrasing with vitality and a fine sense of overall structure. The digital recording is forward and clear, yet has plenty of body.

A glorious spaciousness surrounds Sir Charles's performances. The recording venue is reverberant, yet there is no loss of detail, and the fullness of the sound helps to add weight to climaxes without going beyond the bounds of volume that Mozart might have expected. Sir Charles captures the joy and high spirits that these symphonies embody without in any way undermining their greatness. This vivacity is emphasized by the east-European sound of the Prague Chamber Orchestra, with the out-of-doors timbre of its winds which provides a pleasing contrast both with those of the standard British and Germanic orchestras and specialist, authentic ensembles. Mackerras does, however, adopt some aspects of the modern approach to Mozart performance: he includes harpsichord continuo,

Jeffrey Tate   [photo: Decca

his minuets are taken trippingly, one-to-a-bar, and he prefers bowing that is crisper, more detached, and pointed. Phrasing and articulation are taken with a natural grace and without overemphasis, dynamics being graded to provide drama at the right moments. The very rightness of the result is recommendation enough.

Symphony No. 39 has a more expansive, four-movement structure than No. 38 that draws attention to its great stature. Mozart substituted two clarinets for the more usual oboes in this work and his use of them gives the Symphony a distinctive colouring that frequently shapes the nature of the melodic lines and harmonic balance. In the relaxed, clean CBS recordings, Kubelík shows himself alive to the subtleties of emphasis that give these two works their individual personalities, and the Bavarian Radio orchestra displays both the technique and empathy required to give them weighty meaning without the intrusion of heavy articulation. Both first movements find a fine sense of direction and the finales fairly dance along.

Mozart. Symphonies—No. 39 in E flat major, K543[a]; No 41 in C major, K551, "Jupiter"[b]. **Staatskapelle Dresden/Sir Colin Davis.** Philips 410 046-2PH. Item marked [a] from 6514 205 (7/83), [b] 6514 206 (9/83).

> 66' DDD 6/84

Mozart. Symphonies—No. 39 in E flat major, K543; No. 41 in C major, K551, "Jupiter". **London Classical Players/Roger Norrington.** EMI Reflexe CDC7 54090-2.

> 66' DDD 6/91

Disc buyers who like their Mozart free from romantic exaggeration and other dubious traditional accretions but who don't warm to the experiments of the period instruments school need look no further than the Sir Colin Davis recording. These are direct, no-nonsense performances, steering a confident middle path between overly personal interpretation on the one hand and clinical intellectualism on the other. Each instrumental line is elegantly shaped and the orchestra respond warmly to Davis's stylish direction. Recordings are clear and well balanced, with the weight and distance of the horns, trumpets and timpani (always a problem in conventional instrument performances) judged to a nicety.

Roger Norrington's performances of the classical repertory usually carry a few surprises. This CD starts off with one: the slow introduction to the E flat Symphony is no broad, dignified prelude but an impassioned, almost hectic piece of rhetoric, shot through with the fierce thwacks of the period timpani; and when the main *Allegro* comes its tuttis, full of sharp accents, are restless and brilliant in effect. There is an alert, quickish account of the *Andante*, a powerfully propelled minuet and a finale which forswears the usual wit in favour of sturdiness and seriousness. It's a new view of the work, not particularly a period-instrument one, nor a specially sympathetic one, but it is certainly riveting and brings out unfamiliar aspects of the music. The *Jupiter* is again rather hard driven in the outer movements, and not readily responsive to mood, and there are one or two seeming lapses of taste; but although the *Andante* is none too *cantabile*, and decidedly on the quick side, the tone of unease, almost of menace, behind it is telling. These are not, then, conventional performances, nor beguiling ones, but a tough and original view of the music, often very dramatic, and always invigorating. If you like your Mozart docile and soothing, don't try it.

Mozart. Symphonies—No. 40 in G minor, K550; No. 41 in C major, K551, "Jupiter". **English Chamber Orchestra/Jeffrey Tate.** EMI CDC7 47147-2. From EL270154-1 (2/85).

| 64' DDD 7/85 | Ⓑ |

Mozart. Symphonies—No. 40 in G minor, K550; No. 41 in C major, K551, "Jupiter". **Bavarian Radio Symphony Orchestra/Rafael Kubelík.** CBS Masterworks CD44649.

| 58' DDD 9/89 | Ⓑ |

Mozart. Symphonies—No. 40 in G minor, K550; No. 41 in C major, K551, "Jupiter". **Prague Chamber Orchestra/Sir Charles Mackerras.** Telarc CD80139.

| 71' DDD 5/87 | Ⓑ |

Mozart. Symphonies—No. 40 in G minor, K550; No. 41 in C major, K551, "Jupiter". **Cleveland Orchestra/George Szell.** CBS Maestro CD42538.

| 53' ADD 5/90 | Ⓑ |

Jeffrey Tate's approach to both these works is fresh and vigorous and, while he has obviously laboured long and hard over these scores, there isn't the faintest suggestion of contrivance or self-conscious novelty-seeking. His lucid articulation and attention to detail give the music a distinctive textural clarity. There is a monumental quality about these interpretations but this by no means precludes expressive intimacy, for human interest is there too. The playing of the English Chamber Orchestra is a constant delight, and the recording is admirably clear and realistically balanced.

Kubelík's account of Mozart's Symphony No. 40 is noble and poised; cool, and yet not without feeling or emotion. Some may wince at the way he teases out phrase lengths (purists beware!) especially the drooping semitone string figures in the exposition, but others will find them beautifully turned and elegant. He brings an aloofness to this work that is not entirely out of place; the intense and melancholic *Andante* has a veiled, far-off quality, as if suspended between two worlds. The Menuetto is given an unusually slow and deliberate tempo (no brusqueness or ebullience here) which has an unsettling and disquieting effect that seems totally apt before it launches into the troubled spirit of the finale; here Kubelík is suitably restless and impetuous, as the Symphony speeds headlong towards its destiny—the *Jupiter*.

This receives a strong, if perhaps less individual performance, and like his recordings of the *Haffner* and *Linz* Symphonies there is a fine sense of architectural balance; the outer movements are brisk and alert in tempo, with the contrapuntal textures in the finale superbly controlled. The recording is very fine.

Sir Charles Mackerras observes all repeats in these works but adopts lively tempos, establishing the balanced weighting of sections as Mozart wanted without allowing the whole to become over-ponderous. His method is not, however, to dash headlong at the various movements, but to allow space and light into the textures and to retain an underlying feeling of repose in the most urgent sections. Even the fastest movements, then, are not rushed and the intensity of expression never becomes overdone. The results are sometimes startling, but Mackerras and the Prague Chamber Orchestra have the innate musicianship to bring off these innovations with an unerring sense of style. The easy flow and delight of these pieces are reminiscent of Sir Thomas Beecham's approach to music-making, even though the interpretations are far removed from his world. Just listening to this sportive, yet exultant performance of the finale of the *Jupiter*, with its dazzling contrapuntal devices, the listener is prompted to recall that Mozart's greatness lay so much in his ability to rise above the misery of his situation to create music that, whilst profoundly meaningful, could still retain a strong element of childlike playfulness.

It may seem strange to go back to 1956 for a cheaper recommendation of this coupling, yet it is a feature of all art that there is no aesthetic progress, only change and variety. How Szell and the Cleveland saw these towering masterpieces over 35 years ago remains just as valid now as then. These orchestral players were as technically equipped to play these works as the best of modern performers and the precision of their ensemble and the richness of the body of tone they produced could outdo that of many an orchestra of today. Just listen to the timbral variety and warmth of expression in either of these slow movements to realize the validity of this. Although the concept of authenticity in performance was not fully under way at that time, Szell was able to rely on his innate musicality and sense of style to direct performances that are, nonetheless, true to Mozart. Musicality knows no progress, either. Technology, by contrast, can progress and it's a happy irony that developments in the sound processing field have enabled these performances to speak to us with nearly as much impact as in the best of modern productions.

Mozart. Oboe Quartet in F major, K370. Adagio in C major for cor anglais, two violins and cello, K580b[a]. Divertimento in D major, K251[bcd]. **Heinz Holliger** (ob, [a]cor ang); [b]**Hermann Baumann**, [c]**Michel Gasciarrino** (hns); [d]**Henk Guldemond** (db); **Orlando Quartet** (István Párkányi, Heinz Oberdorfer, vns; Ferdinand Erblich, va; Stefan Metz, vc). Philips 412 618-2PH.

51' DDD 11/85

The Oboe Quartet is a work that has received little critical attention. When compared to the Clarinet Quintet it is not of especial character, save perhaps in its attractive final *Rondo* with its dancing main theme and florid oboe passages. The *Adagio* in C major was left incomplete, including directions for instrumentation. It is a serious piece in the composer's poignantly chromatic later manner: one phrase anticipates the opening of the motet *Ave verum corpus* of two years later, but this may be coincidence. The recordings are clear and firm, and the playing has similar qualities. Mozart's Divertimento in D major, K251, written for his sister's 25th birthday, is quite long with its six movements, and buoyant in mood as befits the occasion.

Mozart. Divertimento in E flat major for string trio, K563ª. Six Preludes and Fugues (after Bach), K404dᵇ—No. 1 in D minor; No. 2 in G minor; No. 3 in F major. **Grumiaux Trio** (Arthur Grumiaux, vn; Georges Janzer, va; Eva Czako, vc). Philips 416 485-2PH. Item marked ª from SAL3664 (8/68), ᵇ 6500 605 (5/75).

> 62' ADD 11/87

Mozart. Divertimento in E flat major for string trio, K563. Duos for violin and viola—G major, K423; B flat major, K424. **Dénes Kovács** (vn); **Géza Németh** (va); **Ede Banda** (vc). Hungaroton White Label HRC072.

> 73' ADD 5/90 £

There cannot be many major works by great composers that are undoubted masterpieces and yet remain still relatively little known, but Mozart's Divertimento for string trio is certainly one of them. The late Arthur Grumiaux leads his Trio here in a very skilful and sensitive performance, and they bring out the tragic power of the *Andante* in a way that cannot fail to impress and move a sympathetic listener. This is a work that all who love Mozart should know, and this performance is persuasive and very well recorded, so that one would not guess that the date of the sessions was 1967. The three Preludes followed by Fugues in three contrapuntal parts were recorded in 1973 and while not personal in the obvious sense they have a special interest of their own for students of this composer.

Though the Hungaroton performance of the Divertimento is less subtle than that of the Grumiaux Trio, it is fresh and clean and at a super-bargain price and a length of over 70 minutes this CD is most recommendable, particularly as the recording is well balanced and has a natural sound. With his sweet, clear tone, the violinist Dénes Kovács also leads positively in the two duos with viola, which are too attractive and substantial to be thought of as miniatures or curiosities—those wishing to sample may try the slow movement of either work. Incidentally, the Duo, K424, is in B flat major, not B major as the booklet states: Mozart never used the latter as a main key for a work, though Haydn did.

Mozart. String Quartets—D major, K575; F major, K590. **Salomon Quartet** (Simon Standage, Micaela Comberti, vns; Trevor Jones, va; Jennifer Ward Clarke, vc). Hyperion CDA66355.

> 61' DDD 4/91

It is not always that the sound of a string quartet is as easy on the ear as here, and although the recording has fine clarity and bloom it really seems as if this is thanks to the unusually sensitive playing of the four artists using modern replicas of fine period instruments. The result sounds authentic, in the best sense of that much-misused word, and an attractive warmth is imparted to the music. Along with that the members of the Salomon Quartet phrase thoughtfully and affectionately, articulate springily and exercise good judgement in their choice of tempos, not least that of the opening *Allegretto* of the D major Quartet, an unusual pace for a Mozart first movement. Just here and there one might wish for the greater humour, vigour and momentum that other ensembles find, say in the finale of the same work, but the playing is still highly enjoyable and it is a further plus that repeats are faithfully observed. The quartets themselves are the first and third of his three *Prussian* quartets written in 1789-90 for the cello-playing King Friedrich Wilhelm of Prussia—hence their sometimes prominent cello writing and also, probably, the not excessive technical demands placed upon the players. The recording has already been praised and it remains only to add that although it is a little close, lacking really soft dynamics, the intimacy of the playing style still pleases and the instruments are well balanced.

Mozart. "HAYDN" STRING QUARTETS. **Chilingirian Quartet** (Levon Chilingirian, Mark Butler, vns; Nicholas Logie, va; Philip de Groote, vc). CRD CRD3362/4. From CRD1062/4 (12/80).

CRD3362—G major, K387; D minor, K421/*417b. CRD3363*—E flat major, K428/*421b*; B flat major, K458, "Hunt". *CRD3364*—A major, K464; C major, K465, "Dissonance".

③ 59' 56' 68' ADD 9/90

The Chilingirian Quartet — [photo: Chandos/Chlala]

Though the Chilingirian may yield to quartets like the Melos and the Alban Berg in sheer virtuosity, their performances of these six inexhaustible works represent some of the most thoughtful, naturally expressive Mozart playing in the catalogue. Unlike some of their more high-powered rivals their manner is essentially private, devoid of both surface gloss and self-conscious point-making. Tempos tend to be rather slower than average, especially in the outer movements of the *Hunt* and the *Dissonance* and in some of the minuets. But any lack of bite and *brio* is more than offset by the Chilingirian's breadth of phrase and unusual care for inner detail. The A major, Beethoven's favourite among Mozart's quartets, is especially successful, done with a gentle, luminous intensity, the minuet spare and absorbed, the variations shaped with a real sense of cumulative growth. If the 6/8 *Andantes* of K421 and K428 are a touch too deliberate (the latter hardly *con moto* as Mozart asks), the Chilingirian's profound reflective tenderness, here and in the other slow movements, brings its own rewards. The quality of the interpretations is matched by that of the recordings, which is intimate, truthful and rounded, with the four instruments nicely separated.

Mozart. String Quartets—G major, K387; D minor, K421. **Bartók Quartet** (Peter Komlos, Sandor Devich, vns; Géza Németh, va; Károly Botvay, vc). Hungaroton White Label HRC129.

59' ADD 10/89 £

Mozart. String Quartets—D minor K421; C major, K465, "Dissonance". **Salomon Quartet** (Simon Standage, Micaela Comberti, vns; Trevor Jones, va; Jennifer Ward-Clarke, vc). Hyperion CDA66170. From A66170 (12/85).

63' DAD 4/87

Although the string quintet is usually cited as the chamber-music medium into which Mozart poured his most profound thoughts, his canon of some 23 string quartets contains so much that is typical of his genius that to write those works off as being of lesser interest would be to mistake their importance and stature. Quartets Nos. 14-19, effusively dedicated to Haydn, are rightfully the most famous, for in these works Mozart was successfully able to combine, as never before, elements of both the string quartet's entertaining, public face and its more intimate aura of friends relaxing in genial music-making. The Bartók Quartet innately emphasizes this last element, for each of the players produces a distinctively different timbre and adopts an intriguingly individual approach to the technical posers set by the composer. As a whole, their view of the music, though not without its moments of surprising interpretation, always maintains a restrained awareness of its idiomatic bounds and the recording similarly conveys immediacy without over-inflation.

The thoughtful, warm yet often incisive playing (the violin tone altogether lacks gloss) on the Hyperion recording, with period instruments, leads to performances that are finely shaped and beautifully clear in detail. The minuets tend to be quickish by modern standards, which is in line with the latest thinking about how they were done in Haydn and Mozart's time, and makes good musical sense. These performances may not represent the ultimate word on the music but they have real integrity and are very satisfying.

Mozart. String Quintets—complete. **Grumiaux Trio** (Arthur Grumiaux, vn; Georges Janzer, va; Eva Czako, vc); **Arpad Gerecz** (vn); **Max Lesueur** (va). Philips 416 486-2PH3. From 6747 107 (1/76).

③ 2h 49' ADD 7/86

Mozart's early string quintets are well-made and enjoyable works but not a great deal more than that. His latter compositions in the genre are, however, an entirely different matter. They are extraordinary works and the addition of the second viola seems to have encouraged him to still greater heights. Although recorded in 1973 this survey has been well transferred and the quality is warm and expansive. The performances have something of a southern warmth too, with Grumiaux's tone in particular a delight to the ear. He and his colleagues have found a good rapport: tempos are well-chosen, and all the playing is alert and stylish.

Mozart. Piano Quartets—G minor, K478; E flat major, K493. **Mozartean Players** (Stanley Ritchie, vn; David Miller, va; Myron Lutzke, vc; Steven Lubin, fp). Harmonia Mundi HMU90 7018.

64' DDD 3/91

Mozart's piano quartets, composed about the time of *Figaro* and the great piano concertos, lend themselves particularly well to performance on period instruments. The balance between strings and piano, and the way the piano can come through the string sound, is quite different on modern ones from what Mozart had in his mind when he set these works down, and it is refreshing to hear the kind of sound he envisaged. And particularly in performances as affectionate as these. Stanley Ritchie's smooth and graceful playing of the violin part is an especial delight, most of all in the long and shapely lines of the outer movements of the E flat work; Steven Lubin at the fortepiano is relaxed, too, and almost too responsive at times, letting the rhythms soften to make a point even if occasionally at the expense of the general momentum. And it would be better if he did not so often spread chords to make an expressive effect. But in the G minor work there is much happy illumination of detail. Those who prefer performances of a rather relaxed kind, in preference to tauter, more purposeful ones, will find much to enjoy here.

Mozart. Wind Serenades—E flat major, K375; C minor, K388/384a. Wind soloists of the **Chamber Orchestra of Europe/Alexander Schneider.** ASV CDCOE802. From COE802 (6/85).

47' DDD 5/88

Although a collection of wind serenades may possibly be too much of a good thing, the alertness of the playing here prevents any musical or tonal monotony. The C minor Wind Serenade that is played first is surprisingly passionate, whereas the E flat major is simpler expressively. Each work is for an octet consisting of two oboes, clarinets, bassoons and horns, and the players here have an excellent tonal blend and interpretative unanimity. Their musical style too is good, being vital yet flexible.

Mozart. Sonatas for piano and violin—E flat major, K481; A major, K526; F major, K547. **Szymon Goldberg** (vn); **Radu Lupu** (pf). Decca 425 420-2DM. From 13BB 207/12 (11/75).

⠶ 62' ADD 10/89

Mozart designated his violin sonatas as "for keyboard and violin", in that order but they match the two different instruments so that the matter of 'just temperament' which differentiates them and sometimes vexes musicologists is made unimportant. Here, indeed, is a wonderfully civilized interchange of ideas, and with playing of this quality coming at medium price this CD represents an attractive proposition. Delicacy is often the order of the day; yet there are passages of considerable strength too and no one will accuse these artists of lacking dash where it is called for in the quicker movements, while the eloquence of slow ones (for example, that of the E flat major Sonata) draws real passion from them. Well judged tempos are another plus, and the rhythmically complex first movement of the A major Sonata has a delightful spring to it. The oddly shaped F major Sonata, with a central *Allegro* flanked by *Andantes*, is charming too. The analogue recording from the mid-seventies has a good dynamic range and the Kingsway Hall location has atmosphere yet clear detail, with Goldberg and Lupu nicely balanced.

Mozart. FLUTE QUARTETS. **William Bennett** (fl); **Grumiaux Trio** (Arthur Grumiaux, vn; Georges Janzer, va; Eva Czako, vc). Philips Musica da Camera 422 835-2PC. From 6500 034 (6/71).
D major, K285; G major, K285a; C major, KAnh171/285b; A major, K298.

⠶ 49' ADD 10/89

Mozart. FLUTE QUARTETS. [a]**János Szebenyi** (fl); [b]**Béla Kovács** (cl); [a]**András Kiss** (vn); [a]**László Bársony,** [b]**Géza Németh** (vas); [a]**Károly Botvay** (vc); [b]**Ferenc Rados** (pf). Hungaroton White Label HRC128.
D major, K285; G major, K285a; C major, KAnh171/285b; A major, K298. Clarinet trio in E flat major, "Kegelstatt", K498[b].

⠶ 70' ADD 10/89   £

Mozart. FLUTE QUARTETS. **Jean-Pierre Rampal** (fl); **Isaac Stern** (vn); **Salvatore Accardo** (va); **Mstislav Rostropovich** (vc). CBS Masterworks CD42320.
D major, K285; G major, K285a; C major, KAnh171/285b; A major, K298.

⠶ 52' DDD 9/87

Though he confessed that he did not much like the flute, Mozart was incapable of writing dull or poorly constructed music, and as it happens we know that he gave especial attention to the D major Flute Quartet, rewriting part of its finale, while its *Adagio* with its pizzicato accompaniment has a liquid beauty that utterly suits the instrument. This is all attractive music, and the four pieces played on the Philips disc include two charming sets of variations. The playing is of a high order, for William Bennett is an agile and sensitive flautist with a sure sense of the Mozart style, while the Grumiaux Trio, always reliable in this composer, blend beautifully with him tonally. Tempos are well judged also, always a good test of the understanding of the music. The recording dates from 1969, but

nothing in the sound suggests this save perhaps a lack of real *pianissimo*, while the instruments are nicely balanced by the Philips engineers in a slightly (but not excessively) reverberant acoustic.

Hungaroton's generously filled disc gives us the Clarinet Trio as well as the four flute quartets. The Clarinet Trio acquired its nickname (meaning 'skittle alley') because Mozart is supposed to have conceived it while bowling. The performances of the flute quartets are less consciously refined than those of William Bennett and the Grumiaux Trio but sound delightfully spontaneous—though that word is not intended to suggest any lack of precision, and indeed the ensemble is excellent, for example in the difficult pizzicato accompaniment in the *Adagio* of the D major Quartet. János Szebenyi has a fine tone, rich yet delicate, and that of the clarinettist Béla Kovács in the Trio is pleasing too. With good playing and a natural recorded balance, this is an attractive bargain.

The glitterati assembled for the CBS performances make no attempt at authenticity of timbre or style, yet the simple directness of their approach, married with sublime musicianship, has an authenticity all of its own.

Mozart. PIANO WORKS. **András Schiff.** Decca 421 369-2DH. Variations on "Ah, vous dirai-je, maman", K265/300*e*. Andante in F major, K616. Rondo in A minor, K511. Adagio in C major, K356/617*a*. Minuet in D major, K355/576*b*. Gigue in G major, K574. Adagio in B minor, K540. Variations on "Unser dummer Pöbel meint", K455.

72' DDD 10/88

This young Hungarian can boast fingers second to none when dazzling prestidigitation is the order of the day. Here, however, we meet him not as a virtuoso but as a musician. Nothing in the recital makes heavy technical demands, but since everything dates from Mozart's last decade, each note in a sense is laden. And Schiff brings this home with a rare understanding of the eloquence of simplicity. The Variations themselves testify to Mozart's ever-burgeoning ingenuity of invention as time ran on—and out. In the field of the so-called miniature, surely no composer has ever written anything more profound than the A minor *Rondo* and B minor *Adagio*, both beautifully timed and shaded here. The harmonically audacious *Minuet* in D and the teasing G major *Gigue* in their turn bring just the right contrast from the *Andante* in F for Mechanical Organ and the *Adagio* in C for Glass Harmonica, which in their Elysian purity touch the heart just that much more for having both grown from Mozart's very last spring. In sum, a disc to be treasured.

Mozart. SONATAS FOR PIANO AND VIOLIN. **Oscar Shumsky** (vn); **Artur Balsam** (pf). ASV CDDCS404. Sonatas—C major, K296; G major, K301/293*a*; E flat major, K302/293*b*; C major, K303/293*c* (all from ALH930, 9/83); E minor, K304/300*c* (ALH944, 2/84); A major, K305/293*d* (ALH930); D major, K306/300*l* (ALH944); F major, K376/374*d* (ALH950, 9/84); F major, K377/374*e* (ALH954, 2/85); B flat major, K378/317*d* (ALH944); G major, K379/373*a* (ALH950); E flat major, K380/387*f* (ALH954); B flat major, K454; E flat major, K481 (both ALH964, 5/86); A major, K526; F major, K547 (ALH967, 10/86). Variations—G major, K359/374*a*, "La bergère Célimene"; G minor, K360/374*b*, "Hélas! j'ai perdu mon amant" (ALH950).

④ 4h 48' ADD 3/90

The potential endurance test of listening to 16 violin sonatas and two sets of variations becomes an exquisite feast when the music is by Mozart and the performers are Balsam and Shumsky. These four discs cover less than half of Mozart's total output in the genre but include what may be considered the

Oscar Shumsky [photo: ASV]

mature part of that canon. The first sonata here dates from 1778 and the last from 1788, yet the development that Mozart had wrought in the form in those brief ten years is astounding. The last sonata, K547, is something of a trifle but the three that precede it, K454, K481 and K526, are all major works of substantial proportions, works that have moved far from the idea of the form that Mozart inherited—a piano sonata with violin accompaniment. Both performers on these discs are seasoned chamber music players and this shows time and again in the amount of give and take that shapes these readings. Balsam's fluent finesse, that is especially effective in the running piano passagework of the faster movements, is nicely balanced by Shumsky's pungent tone and precise, well-considered articulation. The compiled recordings do not always sit easily beside each other but generally sustain a high level of involvement and integrity. The whole represents a major recording achievement.

Mozart. SONATAS FOR PIANO AND VIOLIN. **Frank Peter Zimmermann** (vn); **Alexander Lonquich** (pf). EMI CDC7 49712-2.
C major, K296; E flat major, K302/293*b*; D major, K306/300*l*; F major, K377/374*e*.

• 71' DDD 9/89

These are crisp and enjoyable performances given by gifted young German artists. Once or twice one might query the tempo chosen for a movement—for example the *Andantino cantabile* of K306 may be a trace leisurely—and the booklet wrongly gives the key of the C major Sonata, K296, as G major; but this is clean and stylish playing from a duo with excellent unanimity of approach, although just occasionally one might wish for a more openly expressive treatment of this or that phrase, for example when the piano introduces the gently undulating theme of the *Andante sostenuto* in K296. The recording is beautifully clear, though a little lacking in atmosphere, and the balance between the instruments could not be bettered.

Mozart. Piano Sonata in D major, K448.
Schubert. Fantasia in F minor, D940. **Murray Perahia, Radu Lupu** (pfs). CBS Masterworks CD39511. From IM39511 (3/86).

• 42' 10/86

One of the highlights of concert-going at Snape in the 1980s was to hear Lupu and Perahia, two of the greatest pianists of our era, performing together as one, and yet retaining their own, very individual identities. This disc is a happy reminder of that experience; it was recorded live at The Maltings and it captures exactly that peculiarly characterful, wayward acoustic that has been the bane of so many recording engineers. Having an audience present makes the job infinitely simpler, yet the task is still not an easy one. The performances that are so admirably conveyed here are not of the conventional block-buster type. Neither of these pianists has made tickets to their recitals as difficult to grasp as the Grail by producing virtuosic histrionics. Perfect tone control, total dedication to the inner life of the music, satisfying originality of vision, and a beguiling spontaneity have made their solo performances special; together they show themselves to be selfless chamber musicians of the highest order, capable of lifting already great music to a higher plain. Despite the warm tone of the instruments and ambience, their Mozart is totally classical in ethos, their Schubert divinely other-worldly. One of the desert island's life-sustaining Eight.

Mozart. MASONIC MUSIC. [a]**Werner Krenn** (ten); [b]**Tom Krause** (bar); [c]**Edinburgh Festival Chorus; György Fischer** ([d]org/[e]pf); [f]**London Symphony Orchestra/István Kertész.** Decca Serenata 425 722-2DM. Texts and translations included. From SXL6409 (10/69).
Lobegesang auf die feierliche Johannisloge, K148[ae]. Dir, Seele des Weltalls, K429/K468[a][acf]. Lied zur Gesellenreise, K468[ae]. Die Maurerfreude, K471[acf]. Maurerische Trauermusik, K477[f]. Zerfliesset heut', geliebte Brüder, K483[acd]. Ihr unsre neuen Leiter, K484[acd]. Die ihr des unermesslichen Weltalls, K619[ae]. Laut verkünde unsre Freude, K623[abcf]. Lasst uns mit geschlungnen Händen, K623[a][cd].

> 53' ADD 11/90

In the late eighteenth century, the Freemasons' belief in a human brotherhood and mutual responsibility that was independent of birth or wealth was a force for social change which proved so strong and influential that Masonry was banned in Austria not long after Mozart's death. Since he, Haydn and Beethoven were all Masons, it is clear that this secretive society meant much to several major artists, and in Mozart's case this is reflected in the many Masonic works he composed, of which the opera *Die Zauberflöte* is the most celebrated. This disc offers a number of other Masonic pieces, mostly little known, some of which were actually used in Viennese Lodges. They begin with a simple tenor hymn in praise of brotherhood, and include several other vocal pieces, some honouring God the 'Great Architect'; there is also the powerful *Masonic Funeral Music* of 1785, written for an unusual orchestral body (including a double-bassoon) just 11 months after the composer was admitted to the Viennese Lodge 'Beneficence', with its name implying the doing of good works. These performances sound dedicated as well as being skilful, with the tenor soloist Werner Krenn sounding particularly suited to the music with its touch of solemn earnestness. The recording does not show its age of over 20 years and balances the various vocal and instrumental forces well.

Mozart. (ed. Schmitt/Gardiner). Mass in C minor, K427/417a. **Sylvia McNair** (sop); **Diana Montague** (mez); **Anthony Rolfe Johnson** (ten); **Cornelius Hauptmann** (bass); **Monteverdi Choir; English Baroque Soloists/John Eliot Gardiner.** Philips 420 210-2PH. Text and translation included.

> 54' DDD 5/88

Mozart (ed. Maunder). Mass in C minor, K427/417a. **Arleen Auger, Lynne Dawson** (sops); **John Mark Ainsley** (ten); **David Thomas** (bass); **Winchester Cathedral Choir; Winchester College Quiristers; Academy of Ancient Music/Christopher Hogwood.** L'Oiseau-Lyre Florilegium 425 528-2OH. Text and translation included.

> 51' DDD 7/90

Mozart left unfinished the work that ought to have been the choral masterpiece of his early Viennese years but there is enough of it to make up nearly an hour's music—music that is sometimes sombre, sometimes florid, sometimes jubilant. This recording, using a period-instrument orchestra (though a mixed rather than an all-male choir), offers a strongly characterized account of the music. The solo singing is distinguished, too—Diana Montague brings her usual clarity of line to the music for the second soprano, while Sylvia McNair is breathtaking in her purity of tone and line: first at her initial entry in the "Christe", later in the "Et incarnatus", beautifully refined in detail, passionately devout in feeling and expressive of wonderment at the mysteries of which she sings.

Christopher Hogwood avoids any charge of emotional detachment in his steady and powerful opening *Kyrie*, monumental in feeling, dark in tone; and he brings ample energy to the big, bustling choruses of the *Gloria*—and its long closing fugue is finely sustained. The clarity and ring of the boys' voices serve him well in these numbers. There is a strong solo team, headed by Arleen Auger in radiant, glowing voice and, as usual, singing with refined taste; Lynne Dawson joins her in the duets, John Mark Ainsley too in the trio. But this is essentially a "soprano mass"—Mozart wrote it, after all, with the voice of his new wife (and perhaps thoughts of the much superior one of her sister Aloysia) in his mind—and Auger, her voice happily stealing in for the first time in the lovely "Christe", excels in the florid and expressive music of the "Et incarnatus" (where Richard Maudner has supplied fuller string parts than usual, perhaps fuller than Mozart would have done had he finished the work). Hogwood directs with his usual spirit and clarity.

Mozart. Requiem, K626 (completed by Süssmayr and others). **Margaret Price** (sop); **Trudeliese Schmidt** (mez); **Francisco Araiza** (ten); **Theo Adam** (bass); **Leipzig Radio Chorus; Staatskapelle Dresden/Peter Schreier.** Philips 411 420-2PH. From 6514 320 (3/84).

· · 51' DDD 6/84   **B**

Mozart's last unfinished work is presented as a strong unity, sure of itself and of its interpretative standpoint. Drama is generated not through superimposed expressive emphases, but by the hard working of its orchestral and choral part-writing. This earthy robustness is counterbalanced by a sensitivity to phrasing and timbre which acknowledges the other-worldly too. The sopranos of the Leipzig Radio Chorus contribute a most finely sustained *Lacrimosa*, and the soprano of Margaret Price rises out of the opening "Requiem" and the last invocation of eternal light with a unique and luminous poise. She is part of a firmly balanced team of soloists, all of whom bring the liveliness of individual character to their parts without ever threatening the equilibrium of their closely integrated writing. The recording, full-bodied and never over-flattering, matches Schreier's reading in its concentration of focus, and does full justice to the colour and clarity of the playing.

Mozart. CONCERT ARIAS. [a]**Lena Lootens** (sop); [b]**Christoph Prégardien** (ten); **La Petite Bande/Sigiswald Kuijken.** Virgin Classics Veritas VC7 90753-2. Texts and translations included.
Misero! o sogno ... Aura che intorni spiri, K431/425b[b]. A questo seno deh vieni ... Or che il cielo, K374[a]. Si mostra la sorte, K209[b]. Voi avete un cor fedele, K217[a]. Clarice cara, K256[b]. Va, dal furor portata, K21/19c[b]. Ah, lo previdi! ... Ah, t'invola agl'occhi miei ... Deh, non varcar, K272[a]. Se al labbro mio non credi, K295[b]. Bella mia fiamma ... Resta, oh, cara, K528[a].

· · 74' DDD 8/89

While much has been written and said about authentic instruments over these last few years, the subject of 'authentic voices' is altogether more elusive—for
obvious reasons, the most obvious one being that none survive from the

eighteenth century. The two young artists represented on this appealing disc would sound a good deal more like the singers for whom Mozart composed than do most of the singers who fill, and whose voices fill, our large opera houses. Lena Lootens, a sweet and unspoilt soprano, shows graceful phrasing and clean, light coloratura in the early aria *Voi avete un cor fedele*; but in one for the distraught Andromeda, *Ah, lo previdi!*, she produces ample histrionic power, and she also distinguishes herself in the demanding *Bella mia fiamma*, an aria written, it seems, to test the powers of an old friend of Mozart's with its chromaticisms and its high-lying music. Christoph Prégardien, a tenor with a real gift for shapely phrasing, shows a command of Mozartian line in the elegant cantilena of *Misero! o sogno* and again in the sympathetically written *Se al labbro mio non credi*. With the alert, rhythmic accompaniments provided by Sigiswald Kuijken and his Petite Bande, this is altogether an appealing disc.

Mozart. LIEDER. **Barbara Hendricks** (sop); [a]**Goran Söllscher** (gtr); [b]**Maria João Pires** (pf); [c]**Lausanne Chamber Orchestra/Mika Eichenholz.** EMI CDC7 54007-2. Texts included.
Abendempfindung, K523[b]. Als Luise die Briefe, K520[b]. An Chloe, K524[b]. Ch'io mi scordi di te … Non temer, amato bene, K505[bc]. Dans un bois solitaire, K308/295b[b]. Ich würd, auf meinem Pfad, K390/340c[b]. Die ihr des unermesslichen Weltalls, K619[b]. Die kleine Spinnerin, K531[b]. Komm, liebe Zither, komm, K351/367b[a]. Das Lied der Trennung, K519[b]. Un moto di gioia, K579[b]. Oiseaux, si tous les ans, K307/284d[b]. Ridente la calma, K152/210a[b]. Sehnsucht nach dem Frühling, K596[b]. Sei du mein Trost, K391/340b[b]. Das Veilchen, K476[b]. Die Verschweigung, K518[b]. Der Zauberer, K472[b]. Die Zufriedenheit, K473[b].

🎵 63' DDD 7/91

Few would claim that Mozart was one of the great composers of Lieder; it fell to Schubert, Schumann and Brahms to perfect this particular genre. Mozart himself never really seemed entirely happy with the form and in all he wrote only 33 individual songs. Perhaps this is a little surprising since in his operas Mozart showed himself to be a supreme composer for the human voice. Indeed this CD ends with a delightful performance of the concert aria *Ch'io mi scordi di te* in which both the singer and pianist are projected as soloists above the orchestra in an enchanting re-working of material from *Idomeneo*. But while his solo songs certainly don't contain his best music, his wonderful gifts of lyrical expression shine through: provided, of course, they are given sensitive and intelligent performances. They most certainly are here. Barbara Hendricks sings with poise and elegance and is beautifully supported by Maria João Pires. They never try to overstate their case by underlining too heavily the touches of genius in Mozart's subtle word-painting at the expense of the fundamentally simple and open character of the songs. All in all a captivating disc, although it is something of a disappointment that EMI have chosen not to include translations of the Italian, French and German texts.

Mozart. ARIAS. **Elisabeth Schwarzkopf** (sop); [a]**London Symphony Orchestra/George Szell;** [bcd]**Philharmonia Orchestra/**[bc]**Carlo Maria Giulini,** [d]**Sir John Pritchard.** EMI CDC7 47950-2. Texts and translations included. Items marked [a] from ASD2493 (3/70), [b] Columbia SAX2381/4 (6/61), [c] SAX2369/72 (2/61), [d] Columbia mono 33CX1069 (12/53).
Concert arias[a]—Ch'io mi scordi di te, K505 (with Alfred Brendel, pf); Vado ma dove?, K583; Alma grande e nobil core, K578; Nehmt meinem Dank, K383. LE NOZZE DI FIGARO—Porgi amor[b]; E Susanna non vien! … Dove sono[b]; Non so più[d]; Voi che sapete[d]; Giunse alfin il momento … Deh vieni, non tradar[d]. DON GIOVANNI—Ah, fuggi il traditor[c]; In qual eccessi … Mi tradi quell'alma

ingrata[c]; Batti, batti, o bel Masetto[d]; Vedrai, carino[d]; Crudele? ... Non mi dir[d].
IDOMENEO—Zeffiretti lusinghieri[d].

72' ADD 11/87

This superb collection gathers together some of the finest Mozart singing heard
in the last four decades. The shading and shaping Schwarzkopf brings to this
glorious music everywhere displays a style and panache only achieved by study
aided by insight. Take for example her majestic but human Countess and her
sympathetic Donna Elvira. Both are unmannered and have a depth of personality
so often missing in today's interpreters. Given the luxury of so fine a pianist as
Alfred Brendel in the celebrated *Ch'io mi scordi di te*, this is five-star Mozart
interpretation indeed.

Mozart. OPERA AND CONCERT ARIAS. **Olaf Bär** (bar); **Ute Selbig**
(sop)[a]; **Falke Thummler, Holger Merkel, Martin Kolditz** (trebs)[a];
Staatskapelle Dresden/Hans Vonk. EMI CDC7 49565-2. Texts and
translations included.
Mentre ti lascio, o figlia, K513. Un bacio di mano, K541. LA FINTA
GIARDINIERA—Der verliebte Italiener. LE NOZZE DI FIGARO—Bravo,
signor padrone! ... Se vuol ballare; Non più andrai; Tutto é disposto ... Aprite
un po' quegli occhi; Hai già vinta la causa! ... Vedrò, mentr'io sospiro. DON
GIOVANNI—Deh vieni alla finestra; Finch' han dal vino. COSI FAN
TUTTE—Donne mie, la fate a tanti. ZAIDA—Nur mutig, mein Herze. DIE
ZAUBERFLOTE—Der Vogelfänger bin ich ja; Ein Mädchen oder Weibchen;
Papagena! Papagena! Papagena![a].

54' DDD 9/89

Olaf Bär   [photo: EMI/Platt]

Olaf Bär is very much the
baritone of the moment, but as
yet his representation in the
operatic catalogues remains
slight. So until we've the
opportunity to hear him in a
complete role this nicely wide
ranging recital will suit the bill.
Bär sings the standard Mozartian
baritone roles with great aplomb
and a nicely differentiated style
for each. His Papageno, a role
he'd surely excel in on stage is a
real, rounded character and his
Don Giovanni, perhaps softer
grained than is usual, is a noble
figure. Bär sings the insertion
aria *Mentre ti lascio, o figlia*, a
father's sad leave-taking from his daughter written for use in an opera by
Paisiello, with a wonderful sense of line and genuine dramatic involvement. The
Staatskapelle Dresden and Hans Vonk accompany well, and the recording is
good.

Mozart. LE NOZZE DI FIGARO. **Claudio Desderi** (bar) Figaro; **Gianna
Rolandi** (sop) Susanna; **Richard Stilwell** (bar) Count Almaviva; **Felicity Lott**
(sop) Countess Almaviva; **Faith Esham** (mez) Cherubino; **Anne Mason** (sop)
Marcellina; **Artur Korn** (bass) Bartolo; **Ugo Benelli** (ten) Don Basilio;
Alexander Oliver (ten) Don Curzio; **Federico Davià** (bass) Antonio; **Anne
Dawson** (sop) Barbarina; **Glyndebourne Chorus; London Philharmonic**

Orchestra/Bernard Haitink with **Martin Isepp** (hpd). EMI CDS7 49753-2. Notes, text and translation included.

> ③ 2h 58' DDD 7/88 Ⓑ

Mozart. LE NOZZE DI FIGARO. **Giuseppe Taddei** (bar) Figaro; **Anna Moffo** (sop) Susanna; **Eberhard Waechter** (bar) Count Almaviva; **Elisabeth Schwarzkopf** (sop) Countess Almaviva; **Fiorenza Cossotto** (mez) Cherubino; **Dora Gatta** (sop) Marcellina; **Ivo Vinco** (bass) Bartolo; **Renato Ercolani** (ten) Don Basilio, Don Curzio; **Piero Cappuccilli** (bass) Antonio; **Elisabetta Fusco** (sop) Barbarina; **Philharmonia Chorus and Orchestra/Carlo Maria Giulini.** EMI CMS7 63266-2. Notes, text and translation included. From Columbia SAX2381/4 (6/61).

> ② 2h 33' ADD 1/90 £ 9ₚ Ⓑ

Le nozze di Figaro ("The marriage of Figaro") is comically inventive (though subtly spiked with irony), musically fleet and theatrically well-nigh perfect. The plot revolves around the domestic arrangements of the Count and Countess and their servants Figaro and Susanna, and more specifically around the male/female struggle in the household. Plots involving disguise and much hiding lead effortlessly through this most enchanting of operas to a rousing chorus when, in true Mozartian style, the world is restored to rights and everyone is just that bit chastened and a little wiser. With a cast of very accomplished singers Haitink re-creates a real sense of ensemble and shared music-making. The LPO play delightfully and Martin Isepp's witty continuo playing is a joy. A lovely set.

Giulini stresses the opera's Italian virtues of line and ebullience of spirit, and with a largely Italian (or Italian-descended) cast Da Ponte's words are given due attention. At the centre is Schwarzkopf's Countess, done with exceptional grace and pathos, and matched in weight by Waechter's imposing, irascible Count. There is a strong, darkish Figaro from Taddei, a vivacious Susanna from Moffo and from Cossotto a Cherubino of unusual fullness. But it is Giulini who is the real star here, in his immaculate pacing of the score, his constant concern, above all, with a shapely, beautiful and carefully timed musical line as well as luminous orchestral textures, nowhere sacrificing the music to the senses as more modern performances are often inclined to do. The virtues may be old-fashioned ones, but the musical experience is of a high order.

Mozart. COSI FAN TUTTE. **Elisabeth Schwarzkopf** (sop) Fiordiligi; **Christa Ludwig** (mez) Dorabella; **Hanny Steffek** (sop) Despina; **Alfredo Kraus** (ten) Ferrando; **Giuseppe Taddei** (bar) Guglielmo; **Walter Berry** (bass) Don Alfonso; **Philharmonia Chorus and Orchestra/Karl Böhm.** EMI CMS7 69330-2. Notes, text and translation included. From SAN103/6 (5/63).

> ③ 2h 45' ADD 11/88 £ 9ₚ Ⓑ

Mozart. COSI FAN TUTTE. **Karita Mattila** (sop) Fiordiligi; **Anne Sofie von Otter** (mez) Dorabella; **Elzbieta Szmytka** (sop) Despina; **Francisco Araiza** (ten) Ferrando; **Thomas Allen** (bar) Guglielmo; **José van Dam** (bass-bar) Don Alfonso; **Ambrosian Opera Chorus; Academy of St Martin in the Fields/Sir Neville Marriner.** Philips 422 381-2PH3. Notes, text and translation included.

> ③ 3h 11' DDD 11/90 9ₚ Ⓑ

Così fan tutte has been very lucky on disc, and besides the delightful EMI set there have been several other memorable recordings. However, Böhm's cast could hardly be bettered, even in one's dreams. The two sisters are gloriously sung—Schwarzkopf and Ludwig bring their immeasurable talents as Lieder singers to this sparkling score and overlay them with a rare comic touch. Add to that the stylish singing of Alfredo Kraus and Giuseppe Taddei and the central quartet is unimpeachable. Walter Berry's Don Alfonso is characterful and Hanny Steffek is quite superb as Despina. The pacing of this endlessly intriguing work is immaculate. The emotional control of the characterization is masterly and Böhm's totally idiomatic response to the music is without peer. It is as close as you could wish to get to ideal Mozart, and its mid price only serves to makes this a truly desirable issue.

Nevertheless, Marriner's set ranks as a very strong alternative. His pacing is throughout naturally and firmly paced, and he manages more successfully than other recent conductors to create a sense of the opera house in the studio. With his own smallish band in alert and responsive form and the instruments well balanced with the singers, one can sit back and enjoy some finely articulated and lively singing of six well-integrated voices. There is no weakness in the cast, but the Ferrando of Araiza (technically secure in his three, difficult arias) and the Guglielmo of Thomas Allen are particularly successful as regards Mozartian style and refined, seductive tone. Their voices blend well as do those of Mattila and von Otter as the girls. If one has a passing doubt about Mattila's sense of pitch, she consoles us with her warm, even tone. Von Otter bubbles with fun and her tone is fresh and firm. Van Dam is a keen-voiced and wily Alfonso, Szmytka a vivid Despina. All enter willingly into the high spirits and the sentiments of Mozart's flawless, ever-fascinating opera, and together make up a splendid ensemble.

Mozart. DON GIOVANNI. **Thomas Allen** (bar) Don Giovanni; **Carol Vaness** (sop) Donna Anna; **Keith Lewis** (ten) Don Ottavio; **Maria Ewing** (mez) Donna Elvira; **Elizabeth Gale** (sop) Zerlina; **Richard Van Allan** (bass) Leporello; **John Rawnsley** (bar) Masetto; **Dimitri Kavrakos** (bass) Commendatore; **Glyndebourne Festival Chorus; London Philharmonic Orchestra/Bernard Haitink.** EMI CDS7 47037-8. Notes, text and translation included. From SLS143665-3 (7/84).

③ 2h 52' DDD 12/84 Ⓑ

Mozart. DON GIOVANNI. **Eberhard Waechter** (bar) Don Giovanni; **Dame Joan Sutherland** (sop) Donna Anna; **Elisabeth Schwarzkopf** (sop) Donna Elvira; **Graziella Sciutti** (sop) Zerlina; **Luigi Alva** (ten) Don Ottavio; **Giuseppe Taddei** (bar) Leporello; **Piero Cappuccilli** (bar) Masetto; **Gottlob Frick** (bass) Commendatore; **Philharmonia Chorus and Orchestra/Carlo Maria Giulini.** EMI CDS7 47260-8. Notes, texts and translation included. From Columbia SAX2369/72 (2/61).

③ 2h 42' ADD 12/87 Ⓑ

Mozart. DON GIOVANNI. **Håkan Hagegård** (bar) Don Giovanni; **Arleen Auger** (sop) Donna Anna; **Della Jones** (mez) Donna Elvira; **Barbara Bonney** (sop) Zerlina; **Nico van der Meel** (ten) Don Ottavio; **Gilles Cachemaille** (bar) Leporello; **Bryn Terfel** (bass-bar) Masetto; **Kristinn Sigmundsson** (bass) Commendatore; **Drottningholm Theatre Chorus and Orchestra/Arnold Ostman.** L'Oiseau-Lyre 425 943-2OH3. Text and translation included.

③ 2h 51' DDD 12/90 Ⓟ Ⓑ ✒

Haitink's is a performance of assured musical pacing which, with a vividly matched team of soloists, is refined in a sturdily well-balanced recording. Those familiar with the production will recognize at once its chillingly saturnine Don Giovanni as portrayed by Thomas Allen who conveys a sensuousness which knows no true tenderness. His women are unusually strongly characterized. Donna Anna and Donna Elvira face each other as fearfully contrasted victims of both Giovanni and themselves. Richard Van Allan's chiaroscuro of wit, audacity and sulking petulance, of foreground servility and background resentment, make this one of the most entertaining and thought-provoking Leporellos on disc. And the same imaginative response to every nuance of Mozart's musical subtext runs like an electric current through this performance's recitatives. With Martin Isepp's tingling harpsichord continuo acting as invisible director and stage manager, it is here that the musical and dramatic heart of the work really beats; and for private listening on this count alone the performance can hardly be bettered.

Nevertheless, Giulini's 30-year-old version has always been most recommendable and here he captures all the work's most dramatic characteristics, faithfully supported by the superb Philharmonia forces of that time. Then he had one of the most apt casts ever assembled for the piece. Waechter's Giovanni combines the demonic with the seductive in just the right proportions, Taddei is a high-profile Leporello, who relishes the text and sings with lots of 'face'. Elvira was always one of Schwarzkopf's most successful roles: here she delivers the role with tremendous intensity. Sutherland's Anna isn't quite so full of character but it is magnificently sung. Alva is a graceful Ottavio. Sciutti's charming Zerlina, Cappuccilli's strong and Italianate Masetto and Frick's granite Commendatore are all very much in the picture. The recording still sounds well.

The L'Oiseau-Lyre issue is Mozart opera with a difference—and for once the difference is not a gimmick but the feeling that we really are closer to the original. Ostman's Don Giovanni is a young man and the other characters are no less human beings living at a dangerous pace, so that there is urgency as well as realism in his treatment of the score. The effect is as powerful as if one had cleaned away accretions of dust from a picture, and makes one feel that Ostman has removed inappropriate later traditions from this summit of music drama. Håkan Hagegård and Gilles Cachemaille, although both baritones, are fully contrasted as the Don and his servant-confidant Leporello, though indeed Ostman thinks of them as in a sense brothers belonging to different classes. Also fine are the ladies who in their different ways react to Giovanni's charm and self-will: listen, for example to "La ci darem la mano" (CD1, track 15), to hear outstanding singing and characterization. In fact these singer-actors are real to a degree that we sometimes despair of finding in more conventional accounts of this opera, and it seems no surprise when we learn that the 'real' Giovanni and Zerlina (Barbara Bonney) were married shortly after the recording. The orchestra, playing period instruments, are no less fine. The third CD includes the alternative or additional material that Mozart wrote for the Viennese production following the Prague première. This is a *Don Giovanni* to delight, and it has been beautifully recorded.

Mozart. IDOMENEO. **Anthony Rolfe Johnson** (ten) Idomeneo; **Anne Sofie von Otter** (mez) Idamante; **Sylvia McNair** (sop) Ilia; **Hillevi Martinpelto** (sop) Elettra; **Nigel Robson** (ten) Arbace; **Glenn Winslade** (ten) High Priest; **Cornelius Hauptmann** (bass) Oracle; **Monteverdi Choir; English Baroque Soloists/John Eliot Gardiner.** Archiv Produktion 431 674-2AH3. Notes, text and translation included. Recorded at performances in the Queen Elizabeth Hall, London on June 8th, 11th and 19th, 1990.

③ 3h 31' DDD 6/91

This is unquestionably the most vital and authentic account of the opera to date on disc. We have here what was given at the work's first performance in Munich plus, in appendices, what Mozart wanted, or was forced, to cut before that première and the alternative versions of certain passages, so that various combinations of the piece can be programmed by the listener. Gardiner's direct, dramatic conducting catches ideally the agony of Idomeneo's terrible predicament—forced to sacrifice his son because of an unwise row. This torment of the soul is also entirely conveyed by Anthony Rolfe Johnson in the title role to which Anne Sofie von Otter's moving Idamante is an apt foil. Sylvia McNair is a diaphanous, pure-voiced Ilia, Hillevi Martinpelto a properly fiery, sharp-edged Elettra. With dedicated support from his own choir and orchestra, who have obviously benefited from a long period of preparation, Gardiner matches the stature of this noble *opera seria*. The recording catches the excitement which all who heard the live performances will recall.

Mozart. DIE ENTFÜHRUNG AUS DEM SERAIL. Welch ängstliches Beben, K389 (completed and orch. E. Smith). **Christiane Eda-Pierre** (sop) Konstanze (Renate Pichler); **Norma Burrowes** (sop) Blondchen (Pia Werfel); **Stuart Burrows** (ten) Belmonte (Friedhelm Ptok); **Robert Tear** (ten) Pedrillo (Franz Rudnick); **Robert Lloyd** (bass) Osmin (Herbert Weicker); **Curd Jürgens** (spkr) Pasha Selim; **John Alldis Choir; Academy of St Martin in the Fields/Sir Colin Davis.** Philips 416 479-2PH2. Notes, text and translation included. From 6769 026 (9/80).

② 2h 14' ADD 5/88

It is the sense of immediacy about this set that has always made it the most attractive of the *Entführung* recordings. Some interpreters may go for greater breadth, others for sharper colouring; but Sir Colin Davis gets it right in his lively reading, modest and even quite intimate in scale—the Academy of St Martin in the Fields plays with the fineness of a chamber group for him—but also immensely spirited. In spite of the fact that a different cast is used for the spoken dialogue and no-one took the trouble to ensure that the voices matched properly, there is a real sense of theatre about this recording; as the Overture ends you feel a sense of expectancy as if the curtain is about to rise and a distinct whiff of greasepaint comes through the speakers.

It is a strong cast but without any specially remarkable individual performances. Christiane Eda-Pierre seems a little cautious at first as Konstanze but rises to a commanding "Martern aller Arten", firm, clear and accurate. Belmonte's graceful expressions of ardour are in Stuart Burrows's capable hands: a poised performance that pays due attention to Belmonte's dignity and good breeding. There is a splendidly alive and intelligent Pedrillo from Robert Tear and a Blondchen of considerable charm from Norma Burrowes; while Robert Lloyd, as Osmin, somehow manages to produce a fat man's voice—he copes well with the bottom notes, too, and shows plenty of verbal athleticism. Not, then, a spectacular cast, but one that impresses for its liveliness and its spirited interaction and which with Davis's pointed and alert direction ensures a persuasive reading of this vernal masterpiece.

Mozart. DIE ZAUBERFLOTE. **Margaret Price** (sop) Pamina; **Peter Schreier** (ten) Tamino; **Luciana Serra** (sop) Queen of Night; **Kurt Moll** (bass) Sarastro; **Mikael Melbye** (bass-bar) Papageno; **Maria Venuti** (sop) Papagena; **Robert Tear** (ten) Monostatos; **Theo Adam** (bass-bar) Speaker; **Marie McLaughlin** (sop), **Ann Murray, Hanna Schwarz** (mezs) First, Second and Third Ladies; Members of the **Dresden Kreuzchor; Leipzig Radio Chorus; Staatskapelle Dresden/Sir Colin Davis.** Philips 411 459-2PH3. Notes, text and translation included. From 411 459-1PH3 (9/84).

③ 2h 40' DDD 1/85

This opera, of all Mozart's, is the one potentially to offer the richest rewards for armchair listening, and Sir Colin Davis's Dresden performance uniquely combines a lively sense of theatre with a finely-imagined, chamber-musical reading of the score. Sarastro is, in Kurt Moll's rolling bass, the very epitome of age-old wisdom, whilst Luciana Serra's Queen of Night shoots out all the spangles, but also finds a wan, unearthly sadness in her *Mutterherz*, making her first, slow aria one of the high points of this recording. Peter Schreier's princely Tamino contains a steely heroism within a silver tenor, his phrasing and verbal pointing sharpened by many of the *apercus* of a Lieder singer. This Pamina, Margaret Price, is a magic flute in her own right; and the wind soloists of the Staatskapelle, Dresden are always aware of their special vocation, too: their introduction to the opera's finale is a distillation of the fine balance of timbre and tempo throughout this performance.

John Mundy   *Refer to Index*   *British c. 1555-1630*

Modest Mussorgsky   *Russian 1839-1881*

Mussorgsky. Pictures at an Exhibition (orch. Ravel). A night on the bare mountain (arr. Rimsky-Korsakov). **Cleveland Orchestra/Lorin Maazel.** Telarc CD80042. From 10042 (3/80).

Mussorgsky. Pictures at an Exhibition (orch. Ravel). A night on the Bare Mountain (orch. Rimsky-Korsakov).
Ravel. Valses nobles et sentimentales. **New York Philharmonic Orchestra/Giuseppe Sinopoli.** DG 429 785-2GH.

Giuseppe Sinopoli   *[photo: DG/Barda]*

It would be unthinkable for any collection of outstanding CDs to omit the Telarc disc, one of the first and still one of the most spectacular demonstrations of how first-rate recording can enhance the realism of a big nineteenth-century orchestra. The closing climax of "The Great Gate of Kiev", at the end of Mussorgsky's *Pictures*, has an amplitude and impact of the kind to send a tingle of excitement to the nape of the listener's neck: the splendidly sonorous Cleveland brass produce an effect that is quite riveting. This is not to minimize the contribution of the orchestra itself, which play superbly throughout, for Maazel's reading is strongly characterized, from the chattering children in "Tuileries" to the sinister "Catacombs" sequence, with the trombones again featured arrestingly. The acoustic is admirably suited to this music, allowing the *fortissimos* to expand gloriously and providing a glowing warmth to the gentler moments. Just one grumble: as this was an early CD the separate 'pictures' are not cued.

Sinopoli's recording of *Pictures at an Exhibition* has great panache and is full of subtle detail and sharply characterized performances. Of course none of this would be possible without the marvellous virtuosity of the New York Philharmonic, whose brass section play with a wonderful larger-than-life sonority (just what's needed in this colourful extravaganza) and whose woodwind section produce playing of considerable delicacy and finesse, as for example in "Tuileries" and the "Ballet of the Unhatched Chicks". Sinopoli clearly revels in the drama of this work and this is nowhere more noticeable than in his sinister readings of "Catacombs" and "Baba-Yaga". *A night on the Bare Mountain* is no less impressive, where again the flair and dazzling virtuosity of the NYPO have an almost overwhelming impact. Less successful are Ravel's *Valses nobles et sentimentales* which are perhaps a little too idiosyncratic for an individual recommendation despite some superb performances and moments of great beauty. The sound is beautifully balanced and engineered.

Mussorgsky. Pictures at an Exhibition—original piano version[a].
Mussorgsky (orch. Ashkenazy). Pictures at an Exhibition[b]. [b]**Philharmonia Orchestra/Vladimir Ashkenazy** ([a]pf). Decca 414 386-2DH. Item marked [a] from SXDL7624 (4/83), [b] 410 121-1DH (11/83).

🎵 67' DDD 5/86	Ⓑ

Mussorgsky. Pictures at an Exhibition.
Tchaikovsky (arr. Pletnev). The Sleeping Beauty, Op. 66—excerpts. **Mikhail Pletnev** (pf). Virgin Classics VC7 91169-2.
The Sleeping Beauty—Introduction; Danse des pages; Vision d'Aurore; Andante; La feéargent; Le chat botté et la chatte blanche; Gavotte; Le canari qui chante; Chaperon rouge et la loup; Adagio; Finale.

🎵 64' DDD 4/91	Ⓑ

Decca's highly imaginative coupling arises out of Vladimir Ashkenazy's dual career as a pianist and conductor. In fact he appears here in yet another role, that of transcriber for orchestra; for as he tells us revealingly in his informative notes, he always thinks in orchestral colours when he plays the piano, and now his imagination has allowed him to realize those colours in orchestral terms as well, and with success, drawing sharper lines than Ravel in his famous transcription. It is worth saying too that he has been able to correct "a number of textual errors" in Ravel's score that occurred because they were in the only piano copy available to the French composer. There's tremendous personality in Ashkenazy's piano playing, although some listeners may find the almost metallic intensity of his sound as here recorded a bit overwhelming at times, in the opening of the *Pictures*, the heavy ox-wagon tread of "Bydlo, "The Market at Limoges" and "Baba Yaga". A tiny point which should make musicologists think is that tempos are mostly slower in the orchestral version although the same artist is in charge—entirely convincingly, but one wonders why. Certainly this is great Russian music performed by a great Russian artist, and the recordings which were both made in London's Kingsway Hall in 1982 are fine.

Mikhail Pletnev brings a strong personality to whatever he does, and his *Pictures* are no exception, with subtlety and intensity in such quieter pieces as "The Old Castle" and a tremendous urgency and sense of space in the really big numbers like "Baba-Yaga" and of course the monumental final "Great Gate of Kiev". In both these latter pieces, and most obviously the "Gate", the pianist adds some notes of his own which sound musically convincing; although purists with an eye on Mussorgsky's score will shake their heads and say that he has gone over the top, others will forgive him for being, as it seems, simply carried away by the sheer dynamic sweep of performance. Pletnev's mastery of atmosphere is also well illustrated by the conversation of the two Jews Goldenberg and Schmuyle and his evocation of the black "Catacombs". All this is enhanced by a wonderfully vivid recording. The Tchaikovsky ballet transcriptions made by Pletnev himself are much more than a fill-up. They are splendidly conceived in piano terms and his playing here is so stylish as to be in a class quite of its own.

Mussorgsky. SONGS. **Boris Christoff** (bass); [a]**Alexandre Labinsky,** [b]**Gerald Moore** (pfs); **French Radio National Orchestra**/[a]**Georges Tzipine.** EMI Références mono CHS7 63025-2. [a] from ALP1652/5 (1/59), [b] DB21383 (2/52). Notes, texts and translations included.

③ 3h 11' ADD 8/89 £ P

This set is undoubtedly one of the all-time glories. Unavailable on LP for many years, its welcome reappearance on CD should make it a 'must' for any worthwhile collection on account of both its content and execution. Listening through the set without interruption gives one a wonderful idea of the range and variety of Mussorgsky's writing and leaves one amazed at the virtuosity of Christoff's singing. This is unquestionably the famous bass's most importance legacy to music simply because one cannot imagine another singer attempting so many of these songs so successfully. The composer's range of characterization is veritably Dostoyevskian. Even on the first disc, in the earlier and slightly less remarkable songs, he offers a range of personalities and emotions until then unexplored in Russian song. In their interpretation, Christoff brings before us a whole cast of characters portrayed with an amazing palette of sound-colours, everything from the utterly ferocious to the gentlest whisper. The second disc brings many of the better-known songs, all arrestingly interpreted, and the *Nursery* cycle, in which Christoff manages to adapt his dark tone miraculously to a convincing impersonation of a small boy. On the final disc, we hear predictably penetrating performances of the other two cycles. Christoff catches the bleak gloom of *Sunless* and the histrionic force of *Songs and Dances of Death* (though unfortunately a corrupt orchestration is used), some lesser songs and finally a rollicking *Song of the Flea*. Labinsky is a vivid, imaginative pianist. All in all, a set to treasure.

Mussorgsky. BORIS GODUNOV. **Alexander Vedernikov** (bass) Boris Godunov; **Vladislav Piavko** (ten) False Dmitri; **Irina Arkhipova** (mez) Marina; **Vladimir Matorin** (bass) Pimen; **Artur Eizen** (bass) Varlaam; **Andrei Sokolov** (ten) Prince Shuisky; **Anatoli Mishutin** (ten) Missail; **Yuri Mazurok** (bar) Rangoni; **Glafira Koroleva** (mez) Feodor; **Elena Shkolnikova** (sop) Xenia; **Nina Grigorieva** (mez) Nurse; **Ludmila Simonova** (mez) Hostess; **Janis Sporgis** (ten) Simpleton; **Alexander Voroshilo** (bar) Shchelkalov; **Yuri Elnikov** (ten) Lavitsky, Khrushchov, Boyar; **Vladimir Silaev** (bar) Chernikovsky; **Spring Studio Children's Chorus; USSR TV and Radio Large Chorus and Symphony Orchestra**/**Vladimir Fedoseyev.** Philips 412 281-2PH3. Notes, text and translation included. From 412 281-1PH4 (12/84).

③ 3h 18' ADD 3/85

Boris is often regarded as the quintessential Russian opera as it embodies in a highly-charged dramatic scheme the best of Russian folk idioms and word setting. After the composer's death, Rimsky-Korsakov extensively reworked the opera and it is in various versions of his revised score that the work is best known today. But although he did a great service in keeping the opera in the repertoire, many would regard Mussorgsky's original version to be superior. To have an all-Russian production for this opera has not always been of such benefit as one might expect, with the delight in watery vocal tone and wide vibrato sometimes obscuring the music's direction, but on this recording the overall dedication and empathy of the performers produces a vital and soul-searching interpretation that easily compensates for lack of the stage's visual drama. Much of the opera's success lies with the strength of the title-role and here Alexander Vedernikov scores with a psychologically penetrating account of the great Tsar's mental, spiritual, and physical decline. Fedoseyev conducts with complete understanding of the essence of each scene, and draws excellent singing and playing from the chorus and orchestra. Though the wide-spread recording sessions have not been fully integrated, the overall effect is appropriate to the sequence of events and in no way distracts from this moving production.

Conlon Nancarrow

Mexican 1912-

Nancarrow. Studies for Player Piano, Volumes 3 and 4. **Nancarrow**. Wergo WER60166/7-50.
Studies—Nos. 1, 2*a*, 2*b*, 7, 8, 9, 10, 11, 12, 13, 15, 16, 17, 18, 19, 21, 23, 24, 25, 27, 28, 29, 33, 34, 36, 43, 46, 47 and 50.

② 1h 55' DDD 7/91

It is self-evident that towards the ending of our century we are enabled via recordings to hear a wealth of music that could not come the way of even the most travelled concert-goer, and one could hardly pick on a better example than this music written by a now octogenarian composer probably over 40 years ago, although we cannot be sure since his reply to scholars interested in dates has been "it's nobody's business"! We do at least know that he started composing for player piano (or if you prefer, pianola) not long after World War II. The reason was that his music was too complex for human performers, and electronic means were not yet available; and he worked with two 'custom-altered' instruments, punching their paper rolls directly so as to create elaborate rhythms and textures. The result as heard here is extraordinary, sometimes sounding jazzy (as in track 2 on disc 1), reminding us that Nancarrow was a jazz trumpeter, and at others maniacally but agreeably 'way out', as when showers of notes assault the listener at ultra-fast tempos. On disc 1, try Studies Nos. 15 and 21 for this, on disc 2 No. 17; No. 21 has a treble line starting at an amazing 37 notes to the second but then getting steadily slower while a slower bass line gets steadily faster to an unbelievable 111 notes a second! Yet basically the music is tonal and often fairly tuneful, with a good range of ideas (some Bachian) and there is more dynamic variety than the idea of mechanical reproduction suggests. The booklet note by James Tenney is most informative but demands mathematical intellect from the reader. In sum, this is an astonishing issue for the adventurous, recorded in 1988 on the 1927 Ampico reproducing piano in the composer's studio in Mexico City.

Carl Nielsen

Danish 1865-1931

Nielsen. Violin Concerto, Op. 33[a].
Sibelius. Violin Concerto in D minor, Op. 47[b]. **Cho-Liang Lin** (vn); [a]**Swedish Radio Symphony Orchestra**, [b]**Philharmonia Orchestra/Esa-Pekka Salonen.** CBS Masterworks CD44548.

69' DDD 1/89

Oddly enough no one has previously recorded the two greatest Nordic violin concertos on one disc and the result is a triumphant success. This is the best recording of the Sibelius Concerto to have appeared for more than a decade and probably the best ever of the Nielsen. Cho-Liang Lin brings an apparently effortless virtuosity to both concertos. He produces a wonderfully clean and silvery sonority and there is no lack of aristocratic finesse. Only half-a-dozen years separate the two concertos, yet they breathe a totally different air. Lin's perfect intonation and tonal purity excite admiration and throughout them both there is a strong sense of line from beginning to end. Esa-Pekka Salonen gets excellent playing from the Philharmonia Orchestra in the Sibelius and almost equally good results from the Swedish Radio Symphony Orchestra. This should take its place among the classic concerto records of the century.

Nielsen. Violin Concerto, FS61[a]. Flute Concerto, FS119[b]. Clarinet Concerto, FS129[c]. [d]**Toke Lund Christiansen** (fl); **Niels Thomsen** (cl); [a]**Kim Sjøgren** (vn); **Danish National Radio Symphony Orchestra/Michael Schønwandt.** Chandos CHAN8894.

80' DDD 4/91

Nielsen's six symphonies range over the best part of his creative life and have inevitably overshadowed his other work. This well-filled CD brings all three concertos together: the Violin Concerto comes from the period of the Third Symphony and the two wind concertos were written after the Sixth during the last years of his life. Nielsen planned to write five concertos, one for each member of the Copenhagen Wind Quintet. Kim Sjøgren may not command the purity of tone of Cho-Liang Lin but he has the inestimable advantage of totally idiomatic orchestral support: Michael Schønwandt has an instinctive feeling for this music—and this shows throughout the whole disc. The perspective between soloist and orchestra is well-judged (Sjøgren is never larger than life) and so is the internal balance. In the Flute Concerto, which veers from Gallic wit to moments of great poetic feeling, Toke Lund Christiansen is an excellent soloist. He has no want of brilliance or authority and his performance also has plenty of character. Niels Thomsen's account of the Clarinet Concerto is one of the very finest now before the public. If there is any music from another planet, this is it! There is no attempt to beautify the score nor to overstate it: every dynamic nuance and expressive marking is observed by both the soloist and conductor. Thomsen plays as if his very being is at stake and Michael Schønwandt secures playing of great imaginative intensity from the Danish Radio Orchestra.

Nielsen. Symphonies—No. 1 in G minor, FS16; No. 6, "Sinfonia semplice", FS116. **San Francisco Symphony Orchestra/Herbert Blomstedt.** Decca 425 607-2DH.

67' DDD 2/90

Nielsen. Symphony No. 1 in G minor, FS16. Flute Concerto, FS119[a]. An imaginary trip to the Faroe Islands—rhapsody overture, FS123. [a]**Patrick Gallois** (fl); **Gothenburg Symphony Orchestra/Myung-Whun Chung.** BIS CD454.

63' DDD 8/90

Nielsen always nurtured a special affection for his First Symphony—and rightly so, for its language is natural and unaffected. It has great spontaneity of feeling and a Dvořákian warmth and freshness. Blomstedt's recording is one of the best to have appeared for some years. It is vital, beautifully shaped and generally faithful to both the spirit and the letter of the score. The recording, too, is very fine: the sound has plenty of room to expand, there is a very good relationship between the various sections of the orchestra and a realistic perspective. Blomstedt gives a powerful account of the Sixth, too, with plenty of intensity and an appreciation of its extraordinary vision. It is by far the most challenging of the cycle and inhabits a very different world from early Nielsen. The intervening years had seen the cataclysmic events of the First World War and Nielsen himself was suffering increasingly from ill health. Blomstedt and the fine San Fransisco orchestra convey the powerful nervous tension of the first

Carl Nielsen   [*photo: Royal Danish Embassy*

movement and the depth of the third, the *Proposta seria*. He is splendidly served by Decca's recording team.

Nielsen's symphonies cover the same period as those of Sibelius though the two composers developed very differently. The First Symphony (1892) bears the imprint of Brahms, Dvořák and Svendsen but Nielsen never disowned it—and rightly so. A young man's work written while he was still a member of the Royal Danish Orchestra, it remains wonderfully fresh and full of ardour. Myung-Whun Chung conducts as if he were born and bred in Denmark. There is a splendid sense of line, and he is always attentive to phrasing but never fussy or narcissistic. Throughout the piece he knows how to build up to a climax and keep detail in the right perspective. As always the Gothenburg Orchestra play with enthusiasm and spirit, and though they must have lived with this music all their lives, they play with the enthusiasm of first discovery. The rhapsody overture is not one of Nielsen's best works but the Flute Concerto most emphatically is. This performance is most strongly characterized by Patrick Gallois who plays with effortless virtuosity and an expressive eloquence that is never over or understated. His purity of line is quite striking, his dynamic range wide, the tone free from excessive vibrato and his approach fresh. Nielsen himself spoke of the conflict between the Arcadian solo instrument which "prefers pastoral atmospheres; the composer is therefore obliged to submit to its sweetness—if he does not wish to be branded as a barbarian", and Gallois splendidly conveys this spirit. The wonderful acoustic of the Gothenburg Hall is vividly captured and the engineering is first class.

Nielsen. Symphonies—No. 2, FS29, "The Four Temperaments"; No. 3, FS60, "Sinfonia espansiva"[a]. [a]**Nancy Wait Fromm** (sop); [a]**Kevin McMillan** (bar); **San Francisco Symphony Orchestra/Herbert Blomstedt.** Decca 430 280-2DH.

67'   DDD   8/90

This record couples two of Nielsen's most genial symphonies, both of which come from the earliest part of the century, in performances of the very first order. The Second (1902), inspired by the portrayal of *The Four Temperaments* (Choleric, Phlegmatic, Melancholic, Sanguine) that he had seen in a country inn, has splendid concentration and fire and, as always, from the right pace stems the right character. Moreover the orchestra sounds as if it is fired at having encountered this music, for there is a genuine excitement about their playing. Indeed Blomstedt's accounts are by far the most satisfying to have appeared for some time. The Third *Espansiva*, is even more personal in utterance than *The Four Temperaments*, for during the intervening years Nielsen had come much further along the road of self-discovery. His melodic lines are bolder, the musical paragraphs longer and his handling of form more assured. It is a glorious and richly inventive score whose pastoral slow movement includes a part for two wordless voices. Blomstedt gives us an affirmative, powerful reading and in the slow movement, the soprano produces the required ethereal effect. The Decca sound is very detailed and full-bodied, and in the best traditions of the company. Blomstedt's *Espansiva* has greater depth than most rival accounts; the actual sound has that glowing radiance that characterizes Nielsen, and the tempo, the underlying current on which this music is borne, is expertly judged—and nowhere better than in the finale. Blomstedt is an experienced guide in this repertoire and this shows, while his orchestra play with refreshing enthusiasm.

Nielsen. Symphony No. 3, Op. 27, "Sinfonia espansiva"[a]. Clarinet Concerto, Op. 57[b]. MASKARADE—Overture. [a]**Pia Raanoja** (sop); [a]**Knut Skram** (bar); [b]**Olle Schill** (cl); **Gothenburg Symphony Orchestra/Myung-Whun Chung.** BIS CD321.

68' DDD 8/86

This is vivid and idiosyncratic music. Here at times is not so much a sublimation of human thought and feeling as a deliberate voicing and portrayal of personal whims and traits, warts and all—as in the Clarinet Concerto. It will startle anyone hoping for an elegant flow of liquid melody but there is some fun and much skill on display. The *Maskarade* Overture is easier stuff: it belongs to a comic opera and sets the scene well enough, but is so brief at under five minutes that it sounds rather abrupt on its own. As for the Third Symphony it has much of the vigour and purpose that the title suggests. These performances are vivid and the recording is good.

Nielsen. Symphonies—No. 4, FS76, "Inextinguishable"; No. 5, FS97. **San Francisco Symphony Orchestra/Herbert Blomstedt.** Decca 421 524-2DH.

72' DDD 10/88   **B**

This Decca recording presents two of Nielsen's most popular and deeply characteristic symphonies on one CD. Both are good performances that can hold their own with any in the present catalogue, and as recordings they are better. The Fourth Symphony occupied Nielsen between 1914 and early 1916 and reveals a level of violence new to his art. The landscape is harsher; the melodic lines soar in a more anguished and intense fashion (in the case of the remarkable slow movement, "like the eagle riding on the wind", to use the composer's own graphic simile). The title *Inextinguishable* tries to express in a single word what only the music alone has the power to fully express: "the element will to life". Blomstedt's opening has splendid fire: this must sound as if galaxies are forming; he is not frightened of letting things rip. The finale with its exhilarating dialogue between the two tympanists comes off splendidly. The Fifth Symphony of 1922 is impressive, too: it starts perfectly and has just the right glacial atmosphere. The climax and the desolate clarinet peroration into which it disolves are well handled. The recording balance could not be improved upon: the woodwind are decently recessed (though clarinet keys are audible at times), there is an almost ideal relationship between the various orchestra sections and a thoroughly realistic overall perspective. Blomstedt has a good rapport with his players who sound in excellent shape and respond to these scores to the manner born.

Nielsen. SAUL AND DAVID. **Aage Haugland** (bass) Saul; **Peter Lindroos** (ten) David; **Tina Kiberg** (sop) Mikal; **Kurt Westi** (ten) Jonathan; **Anne Gjevang** (contr) Witch of Endor; **Christian Christiansen** (bass) Samuel; **Jørgen Klint** (bass) Abner; **Danish National Radio Choir and Symphony Orchestra/Neeme Järvi.** Chandos CHAN8911/12. Notes, text and translation included.

② 2h 4' DDD 3/91

Although Scandinavia has produced a number of great dramatists and an abundance of world-famous singers, scarcely a handful of operas have reached the international repertoire. *Saul and David* is one of them. It comes from the period immediately preceding the Second Symphony and inhabits much the same world. Nielsen served in the Orchestra of the Royal Theatre for many years and became its conductor when Svendsen retired, and so knew the operatic repertoire from the inside. Before he began work on Saul he wrote, "The plot must be the 'pole' that goes through a dramatic work; the plot is the trunk; words and sentences are fruits and leaves, but if the trunk is not strong and healthy, it is no use that the fruits look beautiful". His librettist, Einar Christiansen certainly provided a strong 'pole', and in this splendid Chandos version sung in the original Danish we are at last able to hear it as both author and composer intended. However intelligent and sensitive a translation may be, something valuable is lost when the original language is abandoned (as it is when Mussorgsky, Janáček or Debussy are sung in translation). It is on Saul that the opera really focuses: his is the classic tragedy of the downfall of a great man through some flaw of character and it is for him that Nielsen (and the splendid Aage Haugland) mobilizes our sympathy. Haugland's portrayal is thoroughly full-blooded and three-dimensional, and he builds up the character with impressive conviction. The remainder of the cast is also good and the Danish Radio Choir does justice to the powerful choral writing, some of it strongly polyphonic, which distinguishes the score. The action is borne along effortlessly on the essentially symphonic current of Nielsen's musical thought. What is, of course, so striking about this piece is the sheer quality and freshness of its invention, its unfailing sense of line and purpose! No attempt is made at stage production but thanks to the committed performers under Neeme Järvi, the music fully carries the drama on its flow. The conductor paces the work to admirable effect and the Chandos recording made in collaboration with the Danish Radio is well-balanced and vivid.

Michael Nyman

British 1944-

Nyman. String Quartets—No. 1 (1985); No. 2 (1988); No. 3 (1990).
Balanescu Quartet (Alexander Balanescu, Jonathan Carney, vns; Kate Musker, va; Anthony Hinnigan, vc). Argo 433 093-2ZH.

63' DDD 8/91 ❓

The liveliness of Michael Nyman's musical imagination here combines with the Balanescu Quartet's sparkling performance style to create one of the most enticing recitals of new chamber music released in recent years. Those who associate Nyman with pastiche, parody and wit will feel particularly at home with the First Quartet, which takes as its starting point a piece by the Elizabethan virginalist John Bull. A loose variation form binds together various acts of dismemberment and reassembly, some of them reverent, others emphatically not so. The Second Quartet, designed for dance and loosely inspired by Indian models of cyclic rhythm, is gritty where its predecessor is cheeky. In complete contrast, the Third Quartet models itself on Nyman's soundtrack for a BBC documentary on the 1988 Armenian earthquake; a solemn nobility here replaces the vivacity of the two partner pieces. Those who view Nyman as a lightweight or a mere joker need look no further than this piece to have their views put into disarray.

Johannes Ockeghem

Franco/Flemish c.1410-1497

Ockeghem. SACRED CHORAL WORKS. **Hilliard Ensemble/Paul Hillier.**
EMI Reflexe CDC7 49798-2. Texts and translations included.
Missa prolationum. Motets—Alma redemptoris mater; Salve regina I; Salve
regina II; Intemerata dei mater; Ave Maria.

68' DDD 9/89 ?

The Hilliard Ensemble   *[photo: EMI/Carnegie*

Johannes Ockeghem, one of the greatest fifteenth-century composers, served at the court of Charles I, Duke of Bourbon and later at the French court, under Charles VII of France and his successor Louis XI. Ockeghem's *Missa prolationum* is a masterpiece of musical ingenuity, yet it comes across in this magnificent recording with apparent inevitability, a work of high lyricism and a far cry from some dry technical exercise. The group of five Marian motets opens with the light and joyful *Alma redemptoris mater*, the chant melody transposed up a fifth and paraphrased here in the top part. Of the two settings of the *Salve regina* the first is probably not by Ockeghem himself but by one of his contemporaries, Philippe Basiron. Scored for four voices, it is quietly contemplative. The third motet, *Intemerata dei mater* explores with gravity and a remarkable vocal blend the darker sonorities of the lower voices. The gem of the collection must surely be the little *Ave Maria*, though I think the second *Salve regina*—which is certainly by Ockeghem—is possibly more representative of the composer's wide-ranging genius. This is a gorgeous recording, greatly to be recommended to anyone who is building up a collection of early music.

Jacques Offenbach

German/French 1819-1880

Offenbach. ORPHEE AUX ENFERS. **Michel Sénéchal** (ten) Orpheus;
Mady Mesplé (sop) Eurydice; **Charles Burles** (ten) Aristeus-Pluto; **Michel
Trempont** (bar) Jupiter; **Danièle Castaing** (sop) Juno; **Jane Rhodes** (mez)
Public Opinion; **Bruce Brewer** (ten) John Styx; **Michèle Command** (sop)
Venus; **Jane Berbiè** (mez) Cupid; **Michèle Pena** (sop) Diana; **Jean-Philippe
Lafont** (bar) Mars; **André Mallabrera** (ten) Mercury; **Les Petits Chanteurs
à la Croix Potencée; Toulouse Capitole Chorus and Orchestra/Michel
Plasson.** EMI CDS7 49647-2. Notes, text and translation included. From
SLS5175 (3/80).

② 140' ADD 1/89

For most people *Orpheus in the Underworld*, with its mythological satire and its celebrated 'can-can', epitomizes Offenbach's French musical world. In effect Offenbach composed the work twice, since he later expanded the original two-act version by adding ballet sequences and several extra songs. It is this full four-act version that we have here on two very well-filled discs. Mady Mesplé, the Eurydice, is a highly assured performer and Michel Sénéchal, the Orpheus, sings with splendid lightness and flair. There are equally effective contributions from other principal singers and there are cameo performances, too, all displaying a fine understanding of the true Offenbach style. Michel Plasson handles Offenbach's music with rare insight. He captures the tenderness of such moments as Eurydice's "Invocation to death" as readily as the high spirits and ebullience of so much else, showing the ability to vary tempo that is such an important element of Offenbach's writing. With a recording that offers a good balance of sound and a good sense of perspective, this is as good a representation of what Offenbach was all about as one is likely to find.

Offenbach. LA BELLE HELENE. **Jessye Norman** (sop) Hélène; **John Aler** (ten) Paris; **Charles Burles** (ten) Menelaus; **Gabriel Bacquier** (bar) Agamemnon; **Jean-Philippe Lafont** (bar) Calchas; **Colette Alliott-Lugaz** (mez) Orestes; **Jacques Loreau** (bar) Achilles; **Roger Trentin** (ten) Ajax I; **Gérard Desroches** (ten) Ajax II; **Nicole Carreras** (sop) Bacchis; **Adam Levallier** (spkr) Slave; **Toulouse Capitol Chorus and Orchestra/Michel Plasson.** EMI CDS7 47157-8. Notes, text and translation included. From EX270171-3 (12/85).

② 1h 46' DDD 9/86

La Belle Hélène is Offenbach's satirical treatment of the story of Helen of Troy. Though others of his operettas may show individual aspects of his genius to greater effect, there is perhaps none that combines so well the charm, the sparkle, the melodic verve and the musical humour that are his musical trademarks. Despite having American singers in the two leading roles, this is nonetheless a very French version, and there is excellent support from a team of seasoned French performers. Plasson has learned how to keep an Offenbach score tripping along, and such rousing ensemble numbers as the "March of the Kings" and the Act 2 finale help to make this a joyful and exciting experience.

Offenbach. LES BRIGANDS. **Tibère Raffalli** (ten) Falsacappa; **Ghislaine Raphanel** (sop) Fiorella; **Colette Alliot-Lugaz** (sop) Fragoletto; **Michel Trempont** (bar) Pietro; **Christian Jean** (ten) Carmagnola; **Francis Dudziak** (ten) Domino; **Pierre-Yves le Maigat** (bass-ten) Barbavano; **Valérie Millot** (sop) Princess of Granada; **Michel Fockenoy** (ten) Adolphe de Valladolid, A page; **Jean-Luc Viala** (ten) Comte de Gloria-Cassis; **Thierry Dran** (ten) Duke of Mantua; **François le Roux** (bar) Baron de Campotasso; **Bernard Pisani** (ten) Antonio; **René Schirrer** (bar) Captain of the Carabinieri; **Jacques Loreau** (bar) Pipo; **Chorus and Orchestra of the Lyon Opéra/John Eliot Gardiner.** EMI CDS7 49830-2. Notes, text and translation included.

② 1h 45' DDD 2/90

If *Les Brigands* does not count amongst the best-known of Offenbach's works, it has a consistently attractive score and some outstanding individual numbers. It also has one of the wittiest of the libretti supplied by the masters Meilhac and Halévy. The comment that "one should steal according to the position that one occupies in society" is as valid a comment on corruption today as it was in the final throes of Second Empire Paris. As for anyone interested in influences on Gilbert and Sullivan (specifically *The Pirates of Penzance*), they might note not only the comic carabinieri who always arrive too late to capture their prey but also the beautiful double chorus in Act Three. W.S. Gilbert in fact wrote an English version of the work, which was staged to considerable effect in London a few years back. The piece has generally remained much better known on the continent, though, and this recording is based upon a production at Lyon in 1988. It fully shows the benefits of stage preparation, with John Eliot Gardiner directing with an attractive lightness of touch, allowing Offenbach's scoring and tempo markings to whip up the excitement as required. Of the singers, the light tenor Tibère Raffalli leads the way admirably as the brigand chief, whilst Ghislaine Raphanel is no less attractively sweet-voiced as his daughter Fiorella. Bernard Pisani pulls off the treasurer's hilarious song with splendid aplomb, and there is also the usual fine bunch of supporting characters. The recording is clear and natural, with some excellent action effects to complete a splendid representation of a typical Offenbach *tour de force*.

Offenbach. LES CONTES D'HOFFMANN. **Plácido Domingo** (ten) Hoffmann; **Dame Joan Sutherland** (sop) Olympia, Giulietta, Antonia, Stella; **Gabriel Bacquier** (bar) Lindorf, Coppélius, Dapertutto, Dr Miracle; **Huguette Tourangeau** (mez) La Muse, Nicklausse; **Jacques Charon** (ten) Spalanzani; **Hugues Cuénod** (ten) Andres, Cochenille, Pitichinaccio, Frantz; **André Neury** (bar) Schlemil; **Paul Plishka** (bass) Crespel; **Margarita Lilowa** (mez) Voice of Antonia's Mother; **Roland Jacques** (bar) Luther; **Lausanne Pro Arte Chorus; Du Brassus Chorus; Suisse Romande Chorus and Orchestra/Richard Bonynge.** Decca 417 363-2DH2. Notes, text and translation included. From SET545/7 (11/72).

② 2h 23' ADD 11/86

Offenbach died after finishing the piano score of *The Tales of Hoffmann* plus the orchestration of the First Act and a summary of the scoring of the rest, which was then completed by Ernest Guiraud. The work became an instant popular success, but not exactly as the composer conceived it. Bonynge's recording returns to Offenbach's original conception as far as seems practicable, but includes certain desirable extra numbers such as the inserted arias for Dapertutto and Coppélius—both of which would be sorely missed—and restores a fine missing quartet to climax the Epilogue. It is essential that the four main soprano roles are taken by one singer, here Dame Joan Sutherland in superb form, and the four faces of villainy (Lindorf, Coppélius, Dapertutto and Dr Miracle) must also be given to a single artist, here the magnificent Gabriel Bacquier. Plácido Domingo is outstanding as Hoffmann (and it is not easy to be convincing in a role that demands ingenuous amorous liaisons with first a clockwork doll, then a courtesan and finally an opera star, determined to sing herself to death). He sings with optimistic fervour throughout all his disappointments, while Huguette Tourangeau is most appealing as his companion and confidante, Nicklausse. Bonynge directs with splendid vitality and romantic feeling and finds the right lightness of touch for the doll scene. The whole performance goes with a swing and Decca's recording, vividly atmospheric, is fully worthy of it.

Carl Orff
German 1895-1982

Orff. Carmina burana. **Sheila Armstrong** (sop); **Gerald English** (ten); **Thomas Allen** (bar); **St Clement Danes Grammar School Boys' Choir; London Symphony Chorus and Orchestra/André Previn.** EMI CDC7 47411-2. Text and translation included. From ASD3117 (10/75).

63' DDD 12/86

There are at least 15 digital recordings of Orff's flamboyant and inspired cantata, using Latin texts taken from a thirteenth-century manuscript, and it is a work that particularly benefits from the range and clarity of digital techniques. Nevertheless, Previn's 1975 version sweeps the board. Not only has the performance a unique bite and exuberance, plus at times an infectious joy, but the three soloists are outstanding and the recording has been most effectively remastered to seem fresher than ever. For once all three soloists are splendid. If Thomas Allen especially catches the attention, the tenor, Gerald English, is excellent too and the soprano, Sheila Armstrong, is suitably ravishing in her love songs, with words explicitly conveying that they are about physical love-making. The boys, too, obviously relish the meaning of the lyrics, which they put over with much gusto. Indeed, this pantheistic celebration of life's earthy pleasures could hardly be more vividly projected: the recording is a triumph.

Niccolo Paganini
Italian 1782-1840

Paganini. Violin Concertos—No. 1 in D major, Op. 5; No. 2 in B minor, Op. 7, "La campanella". **Salvatore Accardo** (vn); **London Philharmonic Orchestra/Charles Dutoit.** DG 415 378-2GH. From 2740 121 (11/75).

69' ADD 2/87   (B)

Paganini's violin music was at one time thought quite inaccessible to lesser mortals among the violin-playing fraternity, but as standards of technique have improved master technicians are now able to do justice to such works as these concertos. Salvatore Accardo is certainly among them, and we can judge his skill as early as the opening violin solo of the First Concerto. This is typical of the style, with its authoritative and rhetorical gestures and use of the whole instrumental compass, but so is the second theme which in its refinement and songlike nature demands (and here receives) another kind of virtuosity expressed through a command of tone, texture and articulation. Dutoit and the London Philharmonic Orchestra have a mainly subordinate role, certainly when the soloist is playing, but they fulfil it well and follow Accardo through the kind of rhythmic flexibilities which are accepted performing style in this music and which for all we know were used by the virtuoso performer-composer himself. The 1975 recording is faithful and does justice to the all-important soloist.

Paganini. 24 Caprices, Op. 1. **Itzhak Perlman** (vn). EMI CDC7 47171-2. From SLS832 (6/72).

72' ADD 7/88

This electrifying music with its dare-devil virtuosity has long remained the pinnacle of violin technique, and they encapsulate the essence of the composer's style. For a long time it was considered virtually unthinkable that a violinist should be able to play the complete set; even in recent years only a handful have produced truly successful results. Itzhak Perlman has one strength in this music that is all-important, other than a sovereign technique—he is incapable of playing

with an ugly tone. He has such variety in his bowing that the timbre of the instrument is never monotonous. The notes of the music are despatched with a forthright confidence and fearless abandon that are ideal. The frequent double-stopping passages hold no fear for him. Listen to the fire of No. 5 in A minor and the way in which Perlman copes with the extremely difficult turns in No. 14 in E flat; this is a master at work. The set rounds off with the famous A minor Caprice, which inspired Liszt, Brahms and Rachmaninov, amongst others, to adapt it in various guises for the piano.

| *Itzhak Perlman*   [*photo: EMI/Hunstein*]

Giovanni Palestrina

Palestrina. SACRED CHORAL WORKS. **Christ Church Cathedral Choir, Oxford/Stephen Darlington.** Nimbus NI5100. Texts and translations included.
Missa Dum complerentur. *Motets*—Super flumina Babylonis; Exsultate Deo; Sicut cervus; O bone Jesu, exaudi me a 8; Dum complerentur a 6.

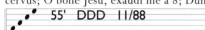 55' DDD 11/88

The full potential of this choir gradually unfolds as they sing through the movements of Palestrina's parody mass *Dum complerentur dies pentecostes*—one of the 22 masses the composer based on one of his own earlier motets. The choir's approach to the Pentecost mass is generally restrained and they find greater scope in the five motets, ending with a brilliant performance of *Dum complerentur* upon which the Mass is built. They clearly revel in its cascading descending phrases in all six voices, which they pour forth jubilantly. Darker, more sombre colours are displayed in *Super flumina Babylonis*, whilst rejoicing and exuberance characterize *Exsultate Deo*, with its crisp treble lead. Anyone coming fresh to this type of music will benefit by following the excellent notes.

Palestrina. SACRED CHORAL WORKS. **Westminster Cathedral Choir/ James O'Donnell.** Hyperion CDA66316. Texts and translations included.
Masses—Viri Galilaei; O Rex gloriae. *Motets*—Viri Galilaei; O Rex gloriae.

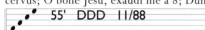 68' DDD 1/90

This is music in which Westminster Cathedral Choir excel: their response to the richly reverberant acoustic is warm and generous; they perform with the ease and freedom of kinship—a far cry from the studied perfection of many other choirs. Each motet is heard before its reworking as a Mass. The six-part scoring of *Viri Galilaei* (two trebles, alto, two tenors and bass) invites a variety of combinations and textures, culminating in the joyful cascading Alleluias at the end of Part I and the jubilant ascending series in Part II. In the Mass the mood changes from triumph to quiet pleading—a change partly due to revised scoring: the two alto parts beneath the single treble produce a more subdued sound. The Choir clearly relishes this exploration of the deeper sonorities: in the *Creed* one entire section is entrusted to the four lowest voices. The four-part motet *O Rex gloriae* is lithe and fast-moving. The corresponding Mass, largely syllabic in style, gives the Choir the chance to demonstrate their superb command of phrasing and accentuation: the Latin comes over with intelligibility and subtlety. Listen, also, to the wonderful solo boys' trio in the "Crucifixus", and for the carefully crafted canons in the *Benedictus* and the *Agnus Dei*.

Hubert Parry

Parry. Symphonies—No. 3 in C major, "English"; No. 4 in E minor. **London Philharmonic Orchestra/Matthias Bamert.** Chandos CHAN8896.

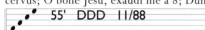 76' DDD 1/91

It is encouraging to find a Swiss conductor, Matthias Bamert, championing Parry's music in the Chandos cycle of the symphonies and some choral works of which this was the first issue. He is clearly a convinced enthusiast and brings to the music a probing passion that eluded Boult in his last years when he recorded some Parry with the same orchestra. The discovery here is the Fourth Symphony, first performed (conducted by Hans Richter) in 1889, revised in

1910, performed twice in its new version and then forgotten for nearly 80 years. It is a deeply personal work, almost confessional in its repressed passion. The first movement (16 minutes) is on an immense scale, covering an emotional range comparable with Elgar's Second (which it preceded). The Third Symphony is more conventional, an English equivalent of Schumann's *Rhenish*. Its sunny exuberance and the lightness of the scoring make it highly attractive. Performance and recording are both admirable. Highly recommended.

Parry (ed J. Dibble). Nonet in B flat major[a].
Stanford. Serenade (Nonet) in F major, Op. 95[b]. **Capricorn** ([b]Elizabeth Layton, [b]Iain King, vns; [b]Paul Silverthorne, va; [b]Timothy Mason, vc; [b]Judith Evans, db; [ab]Helen Keen, fl; [a]Christopher O'Neal, [a]Katie Clemmow, obs; [ab]Anthony Lamb, [a]Julian Farrell, cls; [ab]Gareth Newman, [a]Jean Owen, bns; [ab]Michael Baines, [a]Stephen Bell, hns). Hyperion CDA66291.

53' DDD 9/89

Those who are fond of the nonets by Spohr and Rheinberger might well like to try Stanford's Serenade, Op. 95, scored for an almost similar line-up of winds and strings. Like those two greater works, it inhabits a world of grace and melodic charm, only occasionally essaying more turbulent emotions. Written in 1905, the work was immediately admired both for its spontaneity and clean structural lines. Parry's Nonet for winds, composed in 1877, was more of a student work and owes allegiances to Brahms's Op. 16 Serenade, which Parry had studied in fine detail. Whilst it lacks the glorious tunefulness of Dvořák's D minor Serenade, completed in the following year, it is by no means without interest and has many moments of well-judged scoring, harmonic surprise, and melodic shapeliness. Capricorn give both Nonets the solidity of a dedicated performance, allowing the richness of resonance that comes from expert chording, and the subtlety of understated, yet well-turned phrasing, to draw the listener's attention towards the best qualities of the works. All is revealed in a typically first-class recording from Hyperion, that does not shout its quality but gets on with its job unobtrusively.

Arvo Pärt

Pärt. Passio Domini nostri Jesu Christi secundum Johannem (1982). **Michael George** (bass) Jesus; **John Potter** (ten) Pilate; **Hilliard Ensemble** (Lynne Dawson, sop; David James, alto; Rogers Covey-Crump, ten; Gordon Jones, bass—Evangelist quartet; Elizabeth Layton, vn; Melinda Maxwell, ob; Elisabeth Wilson, vc; Catherine Duckett, bn; Christopher Bowers-Broadbent, org); **Western Wind Chamber Choir/Paul Hillier.** ECM New Series 837 109-2. Text and translation included.

71' DDD 2/89

It's a mark of the extent to which Arvo Pärt identifies with the distant musical past that in setting the words of the St John Passion he should look not to J.S. Bach for his model, but rather to the ritualistic severity of plainchant and polyphony of the pre-Baroque era. The *Passion* is, indeed, an austere work even by Pärt's own standards. Without question it is the sheer restraint of the music, combined with the tension that gradually accumulates over a vast span of time that lends the work its special nobility and pathos. Pärt relies on simple but potent recitation formulae, which he entrusts to small consorts of voices variously accompanied by a tiny (but tellingly handled) instrumental ensemble. So underplayed is most of the narration that the tiniest emphasis, piquancy of

harmony or addition of colour makes its presence felt, often to exquisite and moving effect. Add to this a committed performance by a superb team, an evocatively resonant church acoustic and a quite unexpected bonus—the sound of the wind haunting the building—and the net effect is one of the most powerful twentieth-century musical responses to a Christian theme currently available.

Krzysztof Penderecki   *Refer to Index*   *Polish 1933-*

Giovanni Pergolesi   *Italian 1710-1736*

Pergolesi. Stabat mater[ab]. Salve regina in A minor[a]. In coelestibus regnis[b]. [a]**Gillian Fisher** (sop); [b]**Michael Chance** (alto); **King's Consort / Robert King.** Hyperion CDA66294.

| ♪ 54' DDD 11/88 | |

Pergolesi. Stabat mater[a]. Salve regina in C minor. **Emma Kirkby** (sop); [a]**James Bowman** (alto); **Academy of Ancient Music / Christopher Hogwood.** L'Oiseau-Lyre Florilegium 425 692-2OH. Texts and translations included.

| ♪ 52' DDD 2/90 | |

Pergolesi's *Stabat mater*, written in the last few months of his brief life, enjoyed a huge popularity throughout the eighteenth century. But modern performances often misrepresent its nature, either through over-romanticizing it or by transforming it into a choral work. Of the various versions available, the Hyperion performance is one of the most successful and the most rewarding. The two soloists are excellent, Gillian Fisher combining tonal purity and finesse of phrasing, and Michael Chance showing himself an alto of outstanding accomplishment and artistry; and the ensemble of solo strings with archlute and

organ (Robert King himself) is exemplary. Pergolesi's emotional effects, such as his piled-up suspensions or broken rhythms, have an intensity that is admirably caught—but never exaggerated—in this stylish and tasteful performance. The disc also includes some sweet legato singing in the *Salve regina* in A minor, and a very brief cheerful motet about the blissful abode of the saints. First-class recording too.

None of the *Stabat mater*'s qualities is overlooked in Hogwood's affecting performance, for Emma Kirkby and James Bowman are well-versed in the stylistic conventions of baroque and early classical music—and their voices afford a pleasing partnership. Both revel in Pergolesi's sensuous vocal writing, phrasing the music effectively and executing the ornaments with an easy grace. Singers and instrumentalists alike attach importance to sonority, discovering a wealth of beguiling effects in Pergolesi's part writing. In the *Salve regina* in C minor, the better known of two settings by Pergolesi, Emma Kirkby gives a compelling performance, pure in tone, expressive and poignant, and she is sympathetically supported by the string ensemble. The recording is pleasantly resonant and does justice to Pergolesi's translucent textures. Full texts are included.

Pérotin

French c.1160-c.1225

Pérotin. SACRED CHORAL WORKS. **Hilliard Ensemble** (David James, alto; John Potter, Rogers Covey-Crump, Mark Padmore, Charles Daniels, tens; Gordon Jones, bar)/**Paul Hillier** (bar). ECM New Series 837 751-2. Texts included.
Pérotin: Viderunt omnes. Alleluia, Posui adiutorium. Dum sigillum summi Patris. Alleluia, Nativitas. Beata viscera. Sederunt principes. *Anonymous Twelfth Century:* Veni creator spiritus. O Maria virginei. Isias cecinit.

68' DDD 2/90

Today the music of a great choirmaster of Notre Dame in Paris is accessible to all of us thanks to the dedication, stylistic flair and remarkable skill of the seven male singers who make up the Hilliard Ensemble. There are nine pieces here, of which three are anonymous. Five of them are in *conductus* style, with one rhythm even if there is more than one vocal part, and the others in *organum* with more independent writing—an example of *conductus* is *Beata viscera*, a flowing meditation on the Virgin birth for solo countertenor above a quiet drone bass, while the opening *Viderunt omnes* in four parts is in *organum,* as is the rhythmically remarkable *Allelulia, Posui Adiutorium*. Such music as this evokes the great gothic cathedrals of France such as Notre Dame and Chartres, buildings of the same period, and its intense luminous quality has something of the power of their architecture, carving and stained glass, giving a great craftsmanship and a sense of lofty grandeur that is allied to simplicity of faith. There's an excellent booklet note by Paul Hillier. The recording was made in Boxgrove Priory and, rightly, it has plenty of reverberation.

Walter Piston

USA 1894-1976

Piston. Symphony No. 2 (1943)[a].
Ruggles. Sun-treader (1926-31)[b].
Schuman. Violin Concerto (1959)[c]. [c]**Paul Zukofsky** (vn); **Boston Symphony Orchestra/Michael Tilson Thomas.** DG 20th Century Classics 429 860-2GC. Items marked [a] and [c] from 2530 103 (7/71), [b] 2530 048 (4/71).

75' ADD 1/91

Though British collectors know their Gershwin, Copland, Bernstein, and maybe some Ives, Carter, Glass or Adams, there are still unfamiliar areas of American music and the composers here are major figures. The most radical is Ruggles, whose music is as uncompromising as Ives's though without that composer's folksy quality; not surprisingly, he was long neglected and *Sun-treader* waited 35 years for its American première at the time of his ninetieth birthday. This tough, big-scale piece is played first, and with considerable expressive force, under Michael Tilson Thomas, who was in his twenties when these recordings were made but had already made a name as a conductor willing to explore unfamiliar repertory, and the sound needs no apology for its age, being detailed and satisfying. Schuman and Piston are later figures than Ruggles, and both were distinguished teachers though in no way academic in their composing styles. The Schuman Concerto has violin writing that is lively as well as sometimes calmly lyrical (although the orchestration tends to be heavy), and Paul Zukofsky is a strong soloist. But Piston's Second Symphony, though a shorter work, has more to offer with its melodic sweep and well varied textures (the *Adagio* second movement has climaxes worthy of Shostakovich) and an element of lightness and even tunefulness that the Schuman lacks, while the structure convinces, too, as being well thought out. An important and well filled issue, and one that is especially desirable at medium price.

Amilcare Ponchielli *Italian 1834-1886*

Ponchielli. LA GIOCONDA. **Maria Callas** (sop) La Gioconda; **Fiorenza Cossotto** (mez) Laure Adorno; **Pier Miranda Ferraro** (ten) Enzo Grimaldo; **Piero Cappuccilli** (bar) Barnaba; **Ivo Vinco** (bass) Alvise Badoero; **Irene Companeez** (contr) La Cieca; **Leonardo Monreale** (bass) Zuane; **Carlo Forte** (bass) A Singer, Pilot; **Renato Ercolani** (ten) Isepo, First Distant Voice; **Aldo Biffi** (bass) Second Distant Voice; **Bonaldo Giaiotti** (bass) Barnabotto; **Chorus and Orchestra of La Scala, Milan/Antonio Votto.** EMI mono CDS7 49518-2. Notes, text and translation included. From Columbia SAX2359/61 (11/60).

③ 2h 47' DDD 2/88

Ponchielli's old warhorse has had a bad press in recent times, which seems strange in view of its melodic profusion, Ponchielli's unerring adumbration of Gioconda's unhappy predicament and of the sensual relationship between Enzo and Laura. But it does need large-scale and involved singing—just what it receives here on this 32-year-old set. Nobody could fail to be caught up in its conviction. Callas was in good and fearless voice when this set was made, with the role's emotions perhaps enhanced by the traumas of her own life at the time. Here her strengths in declaiming recitative, her moulding of line, her response to the text are all at their most arresting. Indeed she turns what can be a maudlin act into true tragedy. Ferraro's stentorian ebullience is most welcome. Cossotto is a vital, seductive Laura. Cappuccilli gives the odious spy and lecher Barnaba a threatening, sinister profile, whilst Vinco is a suitably implacable Alvise. Votto did nothing better than this set, bringing out the subtlety of the Verdi-inspired scoring and the charm of the "Dance of the Hours" ballet. The recording still sounds excellent.

Francis Poulenc *French 1899-1963*

Poulenc. Concerto in D minor for two pianos and orchestra[a]. Piano Concerto. Aubade. **François-René Duchable,** [a]**Jean-Philippe Collard** (pfs); **Rotterdam Philharmonic Orchestra/James Conlon.** Erato 2292-45232-2. From NUM75023 (2/86).

59' DDD 8/88

The *Aubade* is a most delicious ballet score, with clear-cut rhythms, aggressive Stravinskian harmonic clashes, and an abundance of good melodies, some jolly, some sentimental. Duchable and Conlon give a good account of the score, though they are sometimes a little too straight-faced. The Concerto for two pianos is another brilliant *divertissement*. The first movement has a superficially neo-classical style, but pert little tunes crop up to dispel any temporary seriousness. There follows a *Larghetto* which possesses genuine elegance and melodic beauty, and then there is a final energetic romp. The shortish Piano Concerto is another *jeu d'esprit* in three movements, but the style is noticeably that of the later Poulenc. Though the recording tends to favour the soloists it is otherwise very satisfactory.

Poulenc. Organ Concerto[a].
Saint-Saëns. Symphony No. 3 in C minor, Op. 78, "Organ"[b]. **George Malcolm, [b]Anita Priest** (orgs); [a]**Academy of St Martin in the Fields/ Iona Brown; [b]Los Angeles Philharmonic Orchestra/Zubin Mehta.**
Decca Ovation 417 725-2DM. Item marked [a] from SXL6482 (1/71), [b] Argo ZRG878 (7/79).

56' ADD 12/87

The performance of Saint-Saëns's Symphony is full of vitality, with the orchestral exuberance in the first movement not detracting from the crispness of ensemble; the slow movement begins gravely but then the climax sings out passionately on the violins, with the bright sound adding to the projection. The scherzo has splendid bite and the crisp detail of the recording brings out, with attractive delicacy, the filigree ornamentation of the great organ theme of the finale—the organ itself massive enough for anyone. The orchestral focus is not absolutely sharp at the culmination but the sound is still pretty impressive. After a suitable pause, George Malcolm then begins the Poulenc Concerto and its genial mood—the *allegro* of the first movement has irrepressible rhythmic flair—is very much in harmony with the Saint-Saëns idiom. The work is in seven distinct sections, each linked, but each an individual vignette, to offer a series of strong contrasts. The fourth and fifth sections, *Tempo allegro molto agitato*, and *Très calme: Lent* place melodrama and serenity in immediate proximity and remind one of music to accompany a silent movie. The Concerto is immensely diverting and the overall effect is very stylish indeed.

Poulenc. CHAMBER MUSIC. [a]**Paris Wind Quintet** (Jacques Castagner, fl; Robert Casier, ob; André Boutard, cl; Gérard Faisandier, bn; Michel Bergès, hn) and various artists. EMI CZS7 62736-2. Items marked [b] from EMSP553 (3/76), [c] EMI Pathé Marconi 2C 165 12519-22 (2/81).
Violin Sonata[b] (Sir Yehudi Menuhin, vn; Jacques Février, pf). Cello Sonata[b] (Pierre Fournier, vc; Février). Trio for oboe, bassoon and piano[c] (Février; Robert Casier, ob; Gérard Faisandier, bn). Sextet for piano and wind quintet[ac] (Février). Flute Sonata[b] (Michel Debost, fl; Février). Oboe Sonata[b] (Maurice Bourgue, ob; Février). Clarinet Sonata[b] (Michel Portal, cl; Février). Elégie for horn and piano[b] (Alan Civil, hn; Février). Sonata for two clarinets[b] (Portal, Maurice Gabai, cl). Sonata for clarinet and bassoon[b] (Portal, Amaury Wallez, bn). Sonata for horn, trumpet and trombone[b] (Civil; John Wilbraham, tpt; John Iveson, trbn).

② 2h 25' ADD 12/89 £

Except for his works with voice, this collection contains the whole of Poulenc's chamber music, from the 1918 Sonata for two clarinets to the 1962 oboe and clarinet Sonatas; and though there is plenty of evidence of his frivolous side (as in the early Sonata for three brass instruments and the scherzo of the Cello Sonata), the conspectus also reveals the melancholy which underlay several of his best works. Three were specifically elegiac—the Oboe Sonata in memory of his friend Prokofiev, that for clarinet for Honegger, and the horn *Elégie* for Dennis Brain; but it is worth noting that the first movement of the Flute Sonata is also marked *Allegro malinconico*. The standard of performance throughout this set, by a number of distinguished French and British artists, is of the highest: while Poulenc was happiest with wind instruments, Menuhin and Fournier are both most persuasive even against the composer's exuberant piano parts. His piano writing is such that not even so understanding a player as Février can help dominating too much in the Sextet (a diffuse work); but apart from this, and a decidedly too close positioning of the two wind instruments in the Trio for oboe, bassoon and piano, the recording quality of the set is very acceptable. At medium price this valuably comprehensive survey is a bargain.

Poulenc. PIANO WORKS. **Pascal Rogé.** Decca 417 438-2DH.
Les soirées de Nazelles (1930-36). Deux novelettes—No. 1 in C major (1927); No. 2 in B flat minor (1928). Novelette "sur un thème de M de Falla" (1959). Pastourelle (arr. pf). Trois mouvements perpétuels (1918). Valse (1919). 15 Improvisations (1932-59)—No. 1 in B minor; No. 2 in A flat major; No. 3 in B minor; No. 6 in B flat major; No. 7 in C major; No. 8 in A minor; No. 12 in E flat major, "Hommage à Schubert"; No. 13 in A minor; No. 15 in C minor, "Hommage à Edith Piaf". Trois Pièces (1928).

67' DDD 7/87

Poulenc. PIANO WORKS. **Pascal Rogé.** Decca 425 862-2DH.
Humoresque (1934). Nocturnes (1929-38). Suite in C (1920). Thème varié (1951). Improvisations—No. 4 in A flat major (1932); No. 5 in A minor (1932); No. 9 in D major (1934); No. 10 in F major, "Eloge des gammes" (1934); No. 11 in G minor (1941); No. 14 in D flat major (1958). Two Intermezzos (1934). Intermezzo in A flat major (1943). Villageoises (1933). Presto in B flat major (1934).

63' DDD 4/91

These beautifully recorded and generously filled discs offer a rich diversity of Poulenc's output. On the first disc, the masterly *Soirées de Nazelles* were improvised during the early 1930s at a country house in Nazelles as a memento of convivial evenings spent together with friends. It paints a series of charming portraits—elegant, witty and refined. The *Trois mouvements perpétuels* are, like so many of the works represented here, light-hearted and brief, improvisatory in flavour and executed with a rippling vitality. The *Improvisations* constantly offer up echoes of the piano concertos with their infectious rhythmic drive—the

Pascal Rogé   [photo: Decca

"Hommage à Schubert" is a tartly classical miniature in three-time played with just the right amount of nonchalant ease by Pascal Rogé. The "Hommage à Edith Piaf" is a lyrical and touching tribute—obviously deeply felt.

The *Humoresque* which opens the second recital is open-air and open-hearted in style, yet songlike too in its melodic richness. The simplicity of this music is deceptive, as is that of the warmly caressing C major Nocturne that follows, for both pieces need subtle phrasing, rubato and the kind of textures only obtainable through the most refined use of the sustaining pedal. Rogé has these skills, and he is also fortunate in having an excellent piano at his disposal as well as a location (the Salle Wagram in Paris) that gives the sound the right amount of reverberation. There are many delights in this music and the way it is played here: to mention just one, listen to the masterly way that the composer and pianist together gradually bring around the flowing freshness of the C major Nocturne towards the deeply poignant feeling of the close. Both discs hold the listener's attention effortlessly from one piece to the next, and though suitable for any time of day they make perfect late-night listening. They should especially delight, and to some extent reassure, anyone who deplores the absence of charm and sheer romantic feeling in much of our century's music.

Poulenc. CHORAL WORKS. **The Sixteen/Harry Christophers.** Virgin Classics VC7 91075-2. Texts and translations included.
Figure humaine. Quatre motets pour un temps de pénitence. Laudes de Saint Antoine de Padoue. Quatre motets pour le temps de Noël. Quatre petites prières de Saint François d'Assise.

62' DDD 3/90

Poulenc. CHORAL WORKS. [a]**Donna Carter** (sop); [b]**Christopher Cock** (ten); **Robert Shaw Festival Singers/Robert Shaw.** Telarc CD80236. Texts and translations included.
Mass in G major[a]. Quatre motets pour le temps de Noël. Quatre motets pour un temps de pénitence. Quatre petites prières de Saint François d'Assise[b].

52' DDD 10/90

Poulenc made a particularly substantial contribution to the body of twentieth-century French works for *a capella* chorus, and one of his finest works for the medium receives a splendid performance on this disc. *Figure humaine*, described as a Cantata, a setting of eight poems by Paul Eluard, was written during the Second World War as an expression of the urgent, libertarian feeling of a nation suffering under an oppressive yoke. Poulenc stretches the technical resources of the double mixed chorus to its maximum in order to convey the profundity of the emotions rawly displayed in the verse, and it is the triumph of this performance that The Sixteen not only cope with these difficulties with seeming ease but allow the music to soar, a symbol of the transcendence of the human spirit in the face of adversity. The coupled motets, littered with remarkable, jewel-like delights of affecting harmonic shifts, contrasts of chordal placings, and melodic twists, receive a similarly thoughtful and technically expert treatment from this front-ranking chorus. The recording is well balanced, with the basses allowed to make a solid, full effect that is to some tastes, but may be a little overdone for other listeners. None of the present CD competition can offer such a blending of fine qualities.

Virgin's fine account of Poulenc's sacred music was recorded in the church of St Pierre de Gramat, near Rocamadour in the south of France. It was there that Poulenc, following the death of a friend, rediscovered his Catholic faith. The Robert Shaw Festival Singers comprise a homogeneous-sounding, highly professional group. The soloists Donna Carter and Christopher Cock are effective, too. But perhaps what makes this disc special, apart from its touching association with the composer, himself, is the skilful way in which Robert Shaw places his forces at the service of the church's ample resonance. In this way his singers are able to bring a subtle range of emotions to the music, delicately coloured and almost infinitely varied. Not that everything here fares equally well in such a spacious acoustic, but it would be hard to imagine more affecting performances than these under similar circumstances.

Poulenc. Gloria[a]. Piano Concerto[b]. Les biches—ballet suite[c]. [a]**Norma Burrowes** (sop); [b]**Cristina Ortiz** (pf); **City of Birmingham Symphony Orchestra and** [a]**Chorus/Louis Frémaux.** EMI CDM7 69644-2. Items marked [ab] from SQ ASD3299 (12/76), [c]ASD2989 (5/74).

62' ADD 1/89

Poulenc is a difficult figure to classify, and the frivolities and Gallic charm of his music go hand in hand with a deep if unorthodox religious feeling and an occasional sadness. His admiration for light music and for classical figures as different as Schubert and middle-period Stravinsky are reflected in the melodic richness and rhythmic bounce of his music, so that a movement such as the "Laudamus te" of his *Gloria* sounds at first as if Stravinsky's *Symphony of Psalms* had been rewritten by a twentieth-century Offenbach, while the soprano solo "Dominus Deus" that follows has a Franckian fervour. But like Stravinsky, Poulenc made everything he borrowed delightfully his own. The Piano Concerto and the ballet suite *Les biches* are no less delightful and touching. This is music to give pleasure, not to be intellectualized or analysed. Good performances and satisfying digital transfer from 1970s originals.

Michael Praetorius
German 1571-1621

Praetorius. Terpsichore—excerpts. **New London Consort/Philip Pickett.** L'Oiseau-Lyre Florilegium 414 633-2OH.

51' DDD 11/86

For the full range of late Renaissance instruments, impressively played and brimming over with good humour, this is unquestionably the finest disc in the catalogue. Schryari, racketts, crumhorns, sorduns, theorboes, archlutes, viols, regal: all these and lots more, played by some of Britain's finest exponents and recorded with dazzling clarity. Moreover, should you be at all unsure about the difference between the sound of a shawm and a rauschpfeife, for example, you will find all the instruments used carefully itemized for each of the 31 different dances presented here. And the insert reproduces the pictures of these instruments that Praetorius himself published in his massive *Syntagma musicum*. The dances themselves are chosen from over 300 that Praetorius published in his *Terpsichore* of 1612. They are the perfect vehicle for this array of machinery. Pickett and his musicians go to work on them with considerable verve and the result fairly fizzles.

Sergey Prokofiev
Russian 1891-1953

Prokofiev. Violin Concertos—No. 1 in D major, Op. 19; No. 2 in G minor, Op. 63. **Dmitry Sitkovetsky** (vn); **London Symphony Orchestra/Sir Colin Davis.** Virgin Classics VC7 90734-2.

49' DDD 12/88

Sitkovetsky rediscovers page after page of these concertos and the First is little short of revelatory. Rarely can the tenuous balance between the lyrical and the diabolical have proved so unsettling. From the 'once upon a time' opening, with its beautiful spun-silk melody, to the disruptive, increasingly agitated development which ensues, Sitkovetsky never once sacrifices accuracy for drama or vice versa. His technical prowess throughout is extraordinary.
At the other end of the expressive spectrum, the long *Romeo and Juliet*-like cantabile of the Second Concerto's *Andante* is gloriously true and free—almost as if the line were being created in the playing of it. Sir Colin Davis proves the ideal collaborator, his firm rhythmic arm much in evidence. If the recording is somewhat close and overbearing, with soloist and orchestra thrown into sharp foreground relief, in the light of such marvellous music-making, there is no need to quibble.

Prokofiev. PIANO CONCERTOS. **Vladimir Ashkenazy** (pf); **London Symphony Orchestra/André Previn.** Decca 425 570-2DM2. From 15BB 218 (10/75).
No. 1 in D flat major, Op. 10. No. 2 in G minor, Op. 16. No. 3 in C major, Op. 26. No. 4 in B flat major, Op. 53, "for the left hand". No. 5 in G major, Op. 55.

② 2h 6' ADD 3/90

While it's true that the Prokofiev piano concertos are an uneven body of work, there's enough imaginative fire and pianistic brilliance to hold the attention even in the weakest of them, while the best by common consent Nos. 1, 3 and 4 have stood the test of time very well. As indeed have these recordings the set first appeared in 1975, but the sound is fresher than many contemporary digital issues, and Ashkenazy has rarely played better. Other pianists have matched his brilliance and energy in, say, the Third Concerto, but few very few have kept up such a sure balance of fire and poetry. The astonishingly inflated bravura of the Second Concerto's opening movement is kept shapely and purposeful even the out-of-tune piano doesn't spoil the effect too much. And the youthful First has the insouciance and zest its 22-year-old composer plainly intended. Newcomers to the concertos should start with No. 3: so many facets of Prokofiev's genius (including that wonderfully piquant lyricism) are here, and Ashkenazy shows how they all take their place as part of a kind of fantastic story. But there are rewards everywhere, and the effort involved in finding them is small. Why hesitate?

Prokofiev. Piano Concerto No. 3 in C major, Op. 26[a].
Tchaikovsky. Piano Concerto No. 1 in B flat major, Op. 23[b]. **Martha Argerich** (pf); [a]**Berlin Philharmonic Orchestra/Claudio Abbado;** [b]**Royal Philharmonic Orchestra/Charles Dutoit.** DG 415 062-2GH. Item marked [a] from 138349 (2/68), [b] 2530 112 (10/71).

63' ADD 5/85

By general consensus Martha Argerich's 1971 recording of Tchaikovsky's B flat minor Piano Concerto is still among the best of the currently available recordings. The opening of the first movement sets the mood of spaciousness and weight, with the lovely secondary material bringing poetic contrast. The *Andantino* has an appealing delicacy, with the centrepiece dazzling in its light-fingered virtuosity to match the exhilaration of the last movement. The admirably balanced recording has plenty of spectacle, the strings are full and firm and the piano image is strikingly real and tangible. The unexpected but inspirational coupling was one of Argerich's début recordings, and for those less familiar with Tchaikovsky's twentieth-century compatriot, the music itself will come as a refreshing surprise. The apparent initial spikiness soon dissolves with familiarity and Prokofiev's concerto reveals itself as very much in the romantic tradition. Its harmonies are more pungent than those of Tchaikovsky, but the melodic appeal is striking and the

| *Martha Argerich*   [*photo: DG/Steiner*]

sheer vitality of the outer movements is irresistible as projected by Martha Argerich's nimble fingers.

Prokofiev. Piano Concerto No. 5 in G major, Op. 55[a].
Rachmaninov. Piano Concerto No. 2 in C minor, Op. 18[b]. **Sviatoslav Richter** (pf); **Warsaw Philharmonic Orchestra/[a]Witold Rowicki, [b]Stanislaw Wislocki.** DG 415 119-2GH. Item marked [a] from 138075 (3/60), [b] 138076 (1/60).

58' ADD 6/85

Prokofiev was to find no more dedicated an advocate for his keyboard works than Richter. So how good that this artist's now legendary account of the Fifth Piano Concerto has been granted a new lease of life on CD. Although it has never enjoyed the popularity of Prokofiev's Nos. 1 and 3, here, however, attention is riveted from first note to last. Richter delights in the music's rhythmic vitality and bite, its melodic and harmonic unpredictability. Both piano and orchestra are so clearly and vividly reproduced that it is difficult to believe the original recording dates back to 1959. Though betraying its age (1960) slightly more, notably in the sound of the keyboard itself, Rachmaninov's No. 2 is no less gripping. Not all of Richter's tempos conform to the score's suggested metronome markings, but his intensity is rivalled only by his breathtaking virtuosity. Never could the work's opening theme sound more laden, more deeply and darkly Russian.

Prokofiev. ORCHESTRAL WORKS. [a]**Sting** (narr); [b]**Stefan Vladar** (pf); **Chamber Orchestra of Europe/Claudio Abbado.** DG 429 396-2GH. Peter and the wolf, Op. 67[a]. Symphony No. 1 in D, Op. 25, "Classical". March in B flat minor, Op. 99. Overture on Hebrew Themes, Op. 34*bis*[b].

50' DDD 4/91

Abbado and the multi-talented Sting offer a lively and beautifully crafted account of Prokofiev's ever popular *Peter and the wolf*. The choice of Sting as narrator is clearly aimed at a younger audience who would otherwise never give this delightful work a second glance. Any fears that the original freshness of Prokofiev's creation may be lost in favour of a less formal approach are soon dispelled—Sting is an effective and intelligent story-teller capable of capturing the imagination of adults and children alike, and there is never a feeling of contrivance or mere gimmickry. The orchestral playing is a real delight too; sharply characterized and performed with great affection. The *Overture on Hebrew Themes* is more commonly heard in its drier, more acerbic version for clarinet, piano and string quartet, but makes a welcome and refreshing appearance on this disc in Prokofiev's own arrangement for small orchestra. Abbado's elegant and graceful reading of the *Classical* Symphony is one of the finest in the catalogue, and is particularly notable for its beautifully shaped phrasing, clarity of inner detail and crisp articulation.

Prokofiev. Romeo and Juliet—ballet, Op. 64: excerpts. **Berlin Philharmonic Orchestra/Esa-Pekka Salonen.** CBS Masterworks CD42662. Act 1—No. 7, The Prince gives his orders; No. 8, Interlude; No. 9, Preparing for the Ball; No. 10, Juliet as a young girl; No. 11, Arrival of the guests; No. 12, Masques; No. 13, Dance of the Knights; No. 19, Balcony scene; No. 20, Romeo's Variation; No. 21, Love Dance. Act 2—No. 22, Folk Dance; No. 25, Dance with the mandolins; No. 33, Tybalt and Mercutio fight; No. 35, Romeo decides to avenge Mercutio's death; No. 36, Finale. Act 3—No. 39, The last farewell; No. 48, Morning Serenade. Epilogue—No. 51, Juliet's Funeral; No. 52, Death of Juliet.

56' DDD 8/88

Prokofiev. Romeo and Juliet—ballet, Op. 64. **Cleveland Orchestra/Lorin Maazel.** Decca 417 510-2DH2. From SXL6620/22 (9/73).

② 2h 21' ADD 2/87

Prokofiev. Romeo and Juliet—excerpts from Suites Nos. 1 and 2, Op. 64*b*/*c*. **Cleveland Orchestra/Yoel Levi.** Telarc CD80089.

50' DDD 2/87

Lorin Maazel   [photo: Sony Classical]

Prokofiev's *Romeo and Juliet* is one of the greatest of all Russian ballets and a masterly successor to Tchaikovsky's works. The melodic invention, always consistently inspired, the harmonic flavour, often pungent, and the individual and brilliantly colourful orchestration bring the ear constant diversity and stimulation. The CBS collection of excerpts offers 19 items from more than 50 and they have been admirably selected to follow the musical characterization and narrative line of the story. The marvellous playing of the Berlin Philharmonic captures the passion of the star-crossed lovers with moving expressive feeling, yet the lighter dances are presented with finesse and grace. "Juliet as a young girl" is a delightful portrait, and "Tybalt and Mercutio fight" could hardly be more gripping, while the "Dance with the mandolins" is deliciously played. The final tragedy of the "Death of Juliet" is most powerfully projected in a recording which has spaciousness and clarity, depth and atmosphere.

Lorin Maazel also conducts a magnificent performance of the score, and draws playing of great virtuosity, tonal weight and exactness of ensemble from the Cleveland Orchestra. The strings have a remarkable depth of tone, though they play with great delicacy when needed, while the piquant woodwind blend suits the music exactly. The recording was first issued in 1973 and was of demonstration quality then; it has been exceedingly well transferred to CD and still sounds first rate.

Yoel Levi's rapport with the Cleveland Orchestra is remarkable, too, and the music has marvellous eloquence, particularly in the big *pas de deux* of Romeo and Juliet. There is much delicacy of feeling and the shorter characteristic dances have the most engaging colour, while the "Death of Tybalt" generates power and bite. But it is the fervour of the lovers, so indelibly caught in Prokofiev's music, which has put this ballet alongside the great classical ballets in public favour, and the music's lyrical yearning passion is made highly involving by the committed Cleveland players. The recording is very much in the demonstration class, with a spectacularly wide dynamic range and radiant string timbres

Prokofiev. Symphonies—No. 1 in D major, Op. 25, "Classical"; No. 4 in C major, Op. 112 (rev. 1947 version). **Scottish National Orchestra/Neeme Järvi.** Chandos CHAN8400. From ABRD1137 (11/85).

52' DDD 3/86 **Ⓑ**

Prokofiev. Symphonies—No. 3 in C minor, Op. 44; No. 4 in C major, Op. 47 (original 1930 version). **Scottish National Orchestra/Neeme Järvi.** Chandos CHAN8401. From ABRD1138 (11/85).

59' DDD 5/86 **Ⓑ**

Prokofiev. Symphonies—No. 1 in D major, Op. 25, "Classical"; No. 5 in B flat major, Op. 100. **Los Angeles Philharmonic Orchestra/André Previn.** Philips 420 172-2PH.

58' DDD 11/87 **Ⓑ**

Few twentieth-century symphonies have quite the immediate melodic appeal of Prokofiev's *Classical* Symphony. It is so familiar that its perfect proportions, its effervescent high spirits and its striking originality tend to be taken for granted. Järvi gives an altogether exhilarating account of it. The slow movement has real tenderness and the finale is wonderfully high spirited. It is coupled with a rarity, the Fourth Symphony which draws on material from his ballet, *The prodigal son*. The balletic origins of the symphony are obvious, both in terms of its melodic substance and organization. Prokofiev drastically revised the score in 1947 and the extent of this overhaul will be evident from the fact that the 1930 version takes 23 minutes and the revision 37. The first two movements are much expanded, the orchestration is richer and among other things a piano is added. Järvi's totally committed accounts of both versions are recorded with remarkable fidelity and presence. Järvi is also entirely at home with the Third Symphony (a reworking of ideas from the opera *The fiery angel*) and is particularly successful in conveying the sense of magic and mystery in the *Andante*. The opening idea is austere but lyrical, and the music to which it gives rise is extraordinarily rich in fantasy and clothed in an orchestral texture of great refinement and delicacy. With its whirlwind of activity, the scherzo evokes the strange, supernatural and 'possessed' atmosphere of the opera.

Prokofiev is a composer with whom Previn has a strong natural affinity and his recording is an almost unqualified success. Once an artist has found the speed which ideally suits his view of a work, details of phrasing, articulation and colour fall naturally into place. Thus the first movement of the Fifth Symphony seems to be exactly right, everything flowing naturally and speaking effectively, sweeping up to an exhilarating and high-spirited scherzo. In the slow movement Previn gets playing of genuine eloquence from the Los Angeles orchestra. He also gives an excellent account of the *Classical* Symphony, this perennially fresh score sounding beautifully natural with impressive detail, range and body. This is a splendid issue and must rank among the finest versions now available; highly recommended.

Prokofiev. Symphony No. 6 in E flat minor, Op. 111. Waltz Suite, Op. 110—Nos. 1, 5 and 6. **Scottish National Orchestra/Neeme Järvi.** Chandos CHAN8359. From ABRD1122 (5/85).

57' DDD 7/85

Although it appeared after the end of the war, the Sixth Symphony reflects much of the anguish and pain of those years, and it certainly strikes a deeper vein of feeling than any of its companions. It begins in a way that leaves no doubt that it is made of sterner stuff, the brass and lower strings spitting out a few notes that are so striking and bitter that the relatively gentle main theme comes as a surprise. Järvi has an intuitive understanding of this symphony, and indeed the whole Prokofiev idiom, and he shapes the details as skilfully as he does its architecture. The various climaxes are expertly built and the whole structure is held together in a masterly fashion. As a make-weight there are three movements from the *Waltz Suite*, in which Prokofiev draws from the ballet, *Cinderella*, and the opera, *War and Peace*. The recording is remarkably vivid and well detailed with a particularly rich bass.

Prokofiev. Symphony No. 7 in C sharp minor, Op. 131. Sinfonietta in A major, Op. 48. **Scottish National Orchestra/Neeme Järvi.** Chandos CHAN8442. From ABRD1154 (4/86).

. . ● 51' DDD 7/86

The two pieces on this disc come from the opposite extremes of Prokofiev's career, the *Sinfonietta* from the beginning and the Symphony from the end. Both have that blend of wit and fantasy that Prokofiev made so his own. The Seventh Symphony is a relaxed and genial composition, some of whose ideas recall the fairy-tale atmosphere of *Cinderella*. The *Sinfonietta* is a tuneful, delightful piece that ought to be as popular as the *Classical* Symphony or *Peter and the Wolf*. Järvi is totally inside this music and the Scottish National Orchestra play splendidly for him. The recording has great range and depth, effectively conveying the impression of a concert hall experience.

Prokofiev. Violin Sonatas—No. 1 in F minor, Op. 80; No. 2 in D major, Op. 94*a*. **Shlomo Mintz** (vn); **Yefim Bronfman** (pf). DG 423 575-2GH.

. . ● 56' DDD 2/89	9 P

Prokofiev. Violin Sonata No. 2 in D major, Op. 94*bis*.
Ravel. Violin Sonata (1927).
Stravinsky. Divertimento. **Viktoria Mullova** (vn); **Bruno Canino** (pf). Philips 426 254-2PH.

. . ● 61' DDD 8/90

Both Prokofiev sonatas are wartime pieces; both follow the classical four-movement plan and both must be numbered among Prokofiev's very finest achievements. There the similarities end, for the First is declamatory, agonized and predominantly introspective, whereas the Second, originally for flute and piano, is untroubled, intimate and consoling. This essential difference in character presents a challenge which not all duos have risen to. Mintz and Bronfman have got right to the heart of the matter, however, and if their First Sonata is still marginally the finer that is only because it is on a truly rare level of insight. Both players deploy a wide range of colour and accent, s uperbly captured in a bright but not over-reverberant acoustic, and they are united in their nuanced response to Prokofiev's lyricism and motoric drive. In the extraordinary first movement coda of the First Sonata, they create an atmosphere of almost hypnotic numbness, and it is a pity that one terrible edit breaks the spell here (the violin tone changes abruptly in mid-bar). But that is the only serious defect in what is a truly outstanding recital.

Prokofiev's Second Sonata needs a performance that is fully committed to its violin garb. It receives that in force on the Philips disc, Mullova relishing its challenge. Stravinsky's Divertimento is a 1933 transcription of music from his enchanting ballet, *Le baiser de la fée*, which is in turn founded on the music of Tchaikovsky. Mullova and Canino take it 'as found' rather than being beholden to its origins, allowing the work's own logic to sustain emotional impact. The superb security of their playing, coupled with an acute sense of the work's direction, makes a strong case for it being included in every violinist's recital repertoire. The Ravel Sonata, finished in 1927, is characterized by a strident 'Blues' second movement, followed by a *Perpetuum mobile* finale which serve, on reflection, to set the more conventional opening movement in stark relief. Some may find this reading a touch too solid to reflect the impressionism of Ravel's idiom, but its purposefulness cannot be doubted. In all three works, Canino is an ideally sensitive, but far from passive, accompanist and together these superb musicians create an engrossing recital that is well worth investigating.

Prokofiev. Piano Sonata No. 6 in A major, Op. 82.
Ravel. Gaspard de la nuit. **Ivo Pogorelich** (pf). DG 413 363-2GH. From 2532 093 (6/83).

52' DDD 11/84

Although Prokofiev's Sixth Sonata is less well known than its successors, it is every bit as brilliant and if anything more inventive. Ivo Pogorelich has remarkable technical address, as is evident from these performances, and he plays with a mixture of abandon and discipline that is enormously exhilarating. Ravel's evocations of Aloysius Bertrand's prose poems in *Gaspard de la nuit* is a *tour de force*, one of the most totally pianistic works in the whole keyboard repertoire.

Ivo Pogorelich   *[photo: DG/Bayat]*

Pogorelich produces a remarkable range of keyboard colour and the recording does justice to his dynamic range. His account of "Le gibet" is particularly imaginative and chilling.

Prokofiev. Visions fugitives, Op. 22.
Scriabin. PIANO WORKS. **Nikolai Demidenko** (pf). Conifer CDCF204.
Scriabin: Piano Sonatas—No. 2 in G sharp minor, Op. 19, "Sonata-fantasy"; No. 9 in F major, Op. 68, "Messe noire". Etudes—F sharp minor, Op. 8 No. 2; B major, Op. 8 No. 4; E major, Op. 8 No. 5; F sharp major, Op. 42 No. 3; F sharp major, Op. 42 No. 4; F minor, Op. 42 No. 7. Four Pieces, Op. 51. Vers la flamme, Op. 72.

73' DDD 8/91

The remarkable talent of Nikolai Demidenko is heard here to its full advantage. The Scriabin items not only display the breadth of Demidenko's expressive powers, but also serve to illustrate Scriabin's astonishing transition from post-romantic to the visionary modernist. The early *Sonata-fantasy* of 1892-7 (surely one of his most beautiful and sensuous pieces) is played here with much poetry and affection, and the final movement (an exhilarating *Presto* in 3/4 time) is a fine example of Demidenko's precision, clarity and immaculate pedal control. With the six etudes and the *Four Pieces*, Op. 51 that follow the listener is taken on a fascinating journey that culminates in the volatile sound-worlds of the Ninth Sonata and *Vers la flamme*. These nebulous, shadowy works are delivered with an extraordinary degree of intensity and perception. His account of Prokofiev's *Visions fugitive* is in a class of its own. Each tiny miniature is jewelled to perfection, and his acute sense of colour and tonal variation make this one of the finest performances on disc. A remarkable début recording in every respect.

Prokofiev. Alexander Nevsky, Op. 78[a].
Rachmaninov. The Bells, Op. 35[b]. [b]**Sheila Armstrong** (sop); [a]**Anna Reynolds** (mez); [b]**Robert Tear** (ten); [b]**John Shirley-Quirk** (bar); **London Symphony Chorus and Orchestra/André Previn.** EMI Studio CDM7 63114-2. Item marked [a] from ASD2800 (7/72), [b] ASD3284 (12/76). Texts and translations included.

78' ADD 10/89 £

One of the remarkable musical partnerships of the seventies was that of André Previn and the London Symphony Orchestra, for their special blend of communication and enthusiasm produced electrifying results. Some of their finest recordings were made for EMI, two of which have been combined on this CD reissue. Previn's account of Prokofiev's *Alexander Nevsky* has tremendous energy and power, which is aided and abetted by the dramatic and colourful singing of the LSO chorus. Anna Reynolds's solo in the "Fields of Death" is very fine too, where her rich, velvety tone and plangent reading create a moving contrast to the excitement of "The Battle on the Ice" movement. Rachmaninov's choral symphony *The Bells* was recorded four years later, but is no less impressive or compelling. This is certainly one of the most satisfying performances on disc, with splendid performances from orchestra, chorus and soloists. The wonderfully crisp and detailed orchestral playing is noticeable from the very beginning and the first appearance of the chorus is guaranteed to send tingles down any listener's spine. Both performances on this disc are served with outstandingly good recorded sound and at 78 minutes this mid-price CD offers exceptional value for money.

Prokofiev. THE LOVE FOR THREE ORANGES (sung in French). **Gabriel Bacquier** (bar) King of Clubs; **Jean-Luc Viala** (ten) Prince; **Hélène Perraguin** (mez) Princess Clarissa; **Vincent Le Texier** (bass-bar) Leandro; **Georges Gautier** (ten) Truffaldino; **Didier Henry** (bar) Pantaloon, Farfarello, Master of Ceremonies; **Gregory Reinhart** (bass) Tchelio; **Michèle Lagrange** (sop) Fata Morgana; **Consuelo Caroli** (mez) Linetta; **Brigitte Fournier** (sop) Nicoletta; **Catherine Dubosc** (sop) Ninetta; **Jules Bastin** (bass) Cook; **Béatrice Uria Monzon** (mez) Smeraldina; **Chorus and Orchestra of Lyon Opéra/Kent Nagano.** Virgin Classics VCD7 91084-2. Notes, text and translation included.

② 1h 42' DDD 12/89

A wonderfully zany story about a prince whose hypochondriac melancholy is lifted only at the sight of a malevolent witch tumbling over, in revenge for which she casts on him a love-spell for three oranges: in the ensuing complications he encounters an ogre's gigantic cook who goes all gooey at the sight of a pretty ribbon, princesses inside two of the oranges die of oppressive desert heat, and the third is saved only by the intervention of various groups of 'spectators' who argue with each other on the stage. The music's brittle vivacity matches that of the plot, and though there are no set-pieces for the singers and there is practically no thematic development—the famous orchestral March and Scherzo are the only passages that reappear—the effervescent score is most engaging. The performance, conducted by the new musical director of the Lyon Opéra, is full of zest, with lively orchestral playing and a cast that contains several outstanding members and not a single weak one; and the recording is extremely good. Those desirous of so doing can delve into the work's symbolism and identify the objects of its satire—principally Stanislavsky's naturalistic Moscow Arts Theatre: others can simply accept this as a thoroughly enjoyable romp.

Giacomo Puccini

Puccini. OPERA ARIAS. **Leontyne Price** (sop); **New Philharmonia Orchestra/Edward Downes.** RCA RD85999. Texts and translations included. Items marked [a] from SER5674 (12/73), [b] ARL1 0840 (4/76), [c] SER5589 (1/71), [d] new to UK.
LA BOHEME[a]—Sì, mi chiamano Mimì; Donde lieta uscì; Quando me'n vo'soletta. EDGAR[a]—Addio, mio dolce amor. LA RONDINE[a]—Ore dolce e divine. TOSCA[a]—Vissi d'arte. MANON LESCAUT[a]—In quelle trine morbide; Sola, perduta, abbandonata. LE VILLI[a]—Se come voi. MADAMA BUTTERFLY—Bimba, bimba, non piangere (with Elizabeth Bainbridge, mez; Plácido Domingo, ten; New Philh/Nello Santi)[b]; Un bel dì, vedremo[a]. LA FANCIULLA DEL WEST[a]—Laggiù nel Soledad. GIANNI SCHICCHI[c]—O mio babbino caro (London Symphony Orchestra/Downes). TURANDOT[d]—In questa reggia (Daniele Barioni, ten; Ambrosian Opera Chorus; New Philh/Santi).

 71' ADD 2/88

Puccini. OPERA ARIAS. **Montserrat Caballé** (sop); **London Symphony Orchestra/Sir Charles Mackerras.** EMI CDC7 47841-2. Texts and translation included. From ASD2632 (2/71).
TURANDOT—Signore, ascolta; Tu che di gel sie cinta. MADAMA BUTTERFLY—Un bel dì vedremo; Tu, tu, piccolo iddio. MANON LESCAUT—In quelle trine morbide; Sola, perduta, abbandonata. GIANNI SCHICCHI—O mio babbino caro. TOSCA—Vissi d'arte. LA BOHEME—Sì, mi chiamano Mimì; Donde lieta uscì. LE VILLI—Se come voi. LA RONDINE—Chi il bel sogno di Doretta.

 44' ADD 10/87

These two immensely cherishable discs show off a couple of the most beautiful voices of recent decades. Leontyne Price's smokey soprano is gloriously displayed and even in roles one would not expect of her, such as Turandot, her artistry and feeling for line reaps rich rewards. Montserrat Caballé's lighter voice is also used to ravishing effect in a similarly wide-ranging programme. She focuses primarily on Puccini's 'little women', singing the role of Liù rather than Turandot, capturing her vulnerability as well as her resolve. Her phrasing is quite superb and always used to illuminate the characterization. Mackerras, sensitively aided by the London Symphony Orchestra, accompanies with feeling.

Puccini. LA BOHEME. **Jussi Björling** (ten) Rodolfo; **Victoria de los Angeles** (sop) Mimì; **Robert Merrill** (bar) Marcello; **Lucine Amara** (sop) Musetta; **John Reardon** (bar) Schaunard; **Giorgio Tozzi** (bass) Colline; **Fernando Corena** (bass) Benoit, Alcindoro; **William Nahr** (ten) Parpignol; **Thomas Powell** (bar) Customs Official; **George de Monte** (bar) Sergeant; **Columbus Boychoir; RCA Victor Chorus and Orchestra/Sir Thomas Beecham.** EMI mono CDS7 47235-8. Notes, text and translation included. From ALP1409/10 (1/57).

 ② 1h 48' ADD 6/87   P B

To recommend a 30-year-old mono recording of *La bohème* over all the more glamorously star-studded and sumptuously recorded versions that have appeared since may seem perverse, but the Beecham version is a true classic which has never been surpassed. This intimate opera is not about two super-stars showing off how loudly they can sing their top Cs, but about a poverty-stricken poet's love for a mortally-ill seamstress. De los Angeles's infinitely-touching Mimì and Björling's poetic, ardent Rodolfo are backed by consistently fine and characterful ensemble work making this the most realistic version ever recorded. The recording of course shows its age, but this is scarcely noticeable as page after page of the score come freshly alive again: not a *tour-de-force* of vocalism, not a sequence of famous arias with bits of dialogue between but a lyric tragedy of wrenching pathos and truth.

Puccini. MADAMA BUTTERFLY. **Renata Scotto** (sop) Madama Butterfly; **Carlo Bergonzi** (ten) Pinkerton; **Rolando Panerai** (bar) Sharpless; **Anna di Stasio** (mez) Suzuki; **Piero De Palma** (ten) Goro; **Giuseppe Morresi** (ten) Prince Yamadori; **Silvana Padoan** (mez) Kate Pinkerton; **Paolo Montarsolo** (bass) The Bonze; **Mario Rinaudo** (bass) Commissioner; **Rome Opera House Chorus and Orchestra/Sir John Barbirolli.** EMI CMS7 69654-2. Notes, text and translation included. From SAN184/6 (9/67).

② 2h 22' ADD 5/89 · ⓑ

This is not quite the best sung *Butterfly* available but Barbirolli ensures that it is the most richly and enjoyably Italianate. Italian opera was in his blood and as a cellist at Covent Garden, playing under Puccini's direction, and as a conductor whose formative years were spent in the theatre (his Covent Garden début was in this very opera), Barbirolli's pleasure in returning to the world of opera is audible throughout this recording. The rapport between him and the Italian orchestra is close and affectionate; it is a heart-warming performance, subtle and supple in the pacing of the love duet, urgently passionate in the great outbursts. Scotto is a touching Butterfly, with all the tiny and crucial details of characterization delicately moulded. There have been more dashing Pinkertons than Bergonzi, but not many who have so effectively combined suavity of sound with neatness of phrasing and good taste. Panerai is a first-class Sharpless and di Stasio a sympathetic Suzuki; there are no weak links elsewhere, and the recording is decent enough for its date, if a bit narrow in perspective and with the singers rather forwardly placed. Barbirolli's *Butterfly* has several distinguished rivals on CD, but for a performance that will remind you of the first time you fell in love with this opera it has permanent value and great eloquence.

Puccini. LA FANCIULLA DEL WEST. **Carol Neblett** (sop) Minnie; **Plácido Domingo** (ten) Dick Johnson; **Sherrill Milnes** (bar) Jack Rance; **Francis Egerton** (ten) Nick; **Robert Lloyd** (bass) Ashby; **Gwynne Howell** (bass) Jake Wallace; **Paul Hudson** (bass) Billy Jackrabbit; **Anne Wilkens** (sop) Wowkle; **Chorus and Orchestra of the Royal Opera House, Covent Garden/Zubin Mehta.** DG 419 640-2GH2. Notes, text and translation included. From 2709 078 (9/78).

② 2h 10' ADD 11/87

Puccini. LA FANCIULLA DEL WEST. **Renata Tebaldi** (sop) Minnie; **Mario del Monaco** (ten) Dick Johnson; **Cornell Macneil** (bar) Jack Rance; **Piero de Palma** (ten) Nick; **Silvio Maionica** (bass) Ashby; **Giorgio Tozzi** (bass) Jake Wallace; **Dario Caselli** (bass) Billy Jackrabbit; **Biancamaria Casoni** (mez) Wowkle; **Santa Cecilia Academy Chorus and Orchestra, Rome/ Franco Capuana.** Decca Grand Opera 421 595-2DM2. Text and translation included. From SXL2039/41 (12/58).

② 2h 13' ADD 1/89 · £

This opera depicts the triangular relationship between Minnie, the saloon owner and 'mother' to the entire town of gold miners, Jack Rance, the sheriff and Dick Johnson (alias Ramerrez), a bandit leader. The music is highly developed in Puccini's seamless lyrical style, the arias for the main characters emerge from the texture and return to it effortlessly. The vocal colours are strongly polarized with the cast being all male except for one travesti role and Minnie herself. The

Plácido Domingo *[photo: DG*

score bristles with robust melody as well as delicate scoring, betraying a masterly hand at work. On the DG recording Carol Neblett is a strong Minnie, vocally distinctive and well characterized, whilst Plácido Domingo and Sherrill Milnes make a good pair of suitors for the spunky little lady. Zubin Mehta conducts with real sympathy for the idiom and the orchestra respond well.

Franco Capuana conducts a performance that never forces the pace or overplays a climax, and as a company production it is an admirable piece of work. Of the three principals, Tebaldi as 'the girl' might be expected to constitute the main

attraction, del Monaco as the hero the main liability, with Macneil as nasty Jack Rance something in between. In the event, the men do very well indeed, for both are well-suited and del Monaco is both thrilling and surprisingly tender. Tebaldi, by contrast, is a mixed blessing. Cackling at the miners' confusion about the Old Testament and still more at the idea of any man wanting water with his whisky, she establishes the tough side of Minnie's character, but does not make it immediately clear why everyone is so fond of her. She gives a good standard performance, but her best singing comes near the end of the opera in Minnie's touching appeal to the miners before riding off into the sunset.

Puccini. MANON LESCAUT. **Maria Callas** (sop) Manon Lescaut; **Giuseppe di Stefano** (ten) Des Grieux; **Giulio Fioravanti** (bar) Lescaut; **Franco Calabrese** (bass) Geronte; **Dino Formichini** (ten) Edmondo; **Fiorenza Cossotto** (mez) Singer; **Carlo Forti** (bass) Innkeeper; **Vito Tatone** (ten) Dancing-master; **Giuseppe Maresi** (bass) Sergeant; **Franco Ricciardi** (ten) Lamplighter; **Franco Ventrigilia** (bass) Captain; **Chorus and Orchestra of La Scala, Milan/Tullio Serafin.** EMI CDS7 47393-8. Notes, text and translation included. From EX290041 (3/86).

② 2h ADD 9/86

Manon Lescaut is not by any means the most lucidly constructed of Puccini's works, but the youthful ardour of it all combined with his already evident skill as an orchestrator make it an attractive work to encounter both in the theatre and on disc. Manon herself needs a touch of the capriciousness of a spoilt child in her portrayal and only Maria Callas has really encompassed all its needs; she is the character to the life, her verbal pointing subtle as always. As Des Grieux, Giuseppe di Stefano is her ardent partner, and their duets are as impassioned and desperate as they should be. Serafin's conducting is attuned to the needs of Puccini's score. His pacing is exemplary, serving the cause of the work's overall shape and the intricate detail of the scoring, drawing authentic sounds from the forces of La Scala. The sound may leave something to be desired but that hardly seems important bearing in mind the arresting nature of the performance.

Puccini. TOSCA. **Maria Callas** (sop) Tosca; **Giuseppe di Stefano** (ten) Cavaradossi; **Tito Gobbi** (bar) Scarpia; **Franco Calabrese** (bass) Angelotti; **Angelo Mercuriali** (ten) Spoletta; **Melchiorre Luise** (bass) Sacristan; **Dario Caselli** (bass) Sciarrone, Gaoler; **Alvaro Cordova** (treb) Shepherd Boy; **Chorus and Orchestra of La Scala, Milan/Victor de Sabata.** EMI mono CDS7 47175-8. Notes, text and translation included. From Columbia 33CX1094/5 (12/53).

⸿ ② Ih 48' ADD 9/85 ♀ P Ⓑ

Puccini. TOSCA. **Leontyne Price** (sop) Tosca; **Giuseppe di Stefano** (ten) Cavaradossi; **Giuseppe Taddei** (bar) Scarpia; **Carlo Cava** (bass) Angelotti; **Piero De Palma** (ten) Spoletta; **Fernando Corena** (bass) Sacristan; **Leonardo Monreale** (bass) Sciarrone; **Alfredo Mariotti** (bass) Gaoler; **Herbert Weiss** (treb) Shepherd Boy; **Vienna State Opera Chorus; Vienna Philharmonic Orchestra/Herbert von Karajan.** Decca Grand Opera 421 670-2DM2. Text and translation included. From RCA SER5507/08 (11/63).

⸿ ② Ih 54' ADD I/89 £ Ⓑ

In the course of *Tosca*'s history there have been many notable interpreters, but few have been able to encompass so unerringly the love, jealousy and eventual courage of Tosca as well as Maria Callas. Her resinous, sensuous tone, her wonderful diction, and her inborn passion filled every phrase of the score with special and individual meaning. In 1953 she was in her early prime, the tone seldom prey to those uneasy moments on high that marred her later recordings, and with the vital, vivid conducting of Victor de Sabata, her performance has rightly attained classic status. Giuseppe di Stefano is the ardent Cavaradossi, his tone forward and vibrant in that way peculiar to Italians. Tito Gobbi's cynical, snarling Scarpia, aristocratic in manner, vicious in meaning, remains unique in that part on record. The mono recording stands up well to the test of time.

Karajan's 30-year-old set also sounds just as well recorded as many modern versions, well balanced and full of atmosphere. It remains one of his most enjoyable incursions into the Puccini repertory. His mastery of line and pacing, even when that is sometimes unduly slow, give his reading immense dramatic power in which he is splendidly supported by his Vienna forces. Leontyne Price's supple and gorgeous voice encompasses most of the demands of the title role, intense in expression and at the peak of her vocal powers. Di Stefano may have been a shade past his peak but colours his voice so subtly and sings with such passion that passing vocal inadequacies are forgiven. Taddei's Scarpia is a highly detailed, suavely sung reading that stands up well to the test of time. Not as taut on the whole as the De Sabata performance, this has a breadth and power that equals it.

Puccini. TURANDOT. **Dame Joan Sutherland** (sop) Princess Turandot; **Luciano Pavarotti** (ten) Calaf; **Montserrat Caballé** (sop) Liù; **Tom Krause** (bar) Ping; **Pier Francesco Poli** (ten) Pang, Prince of Persia; **Piero De Palma** (ten) Pong; **Sir Peter Pears** (ten) Emperor Altoum; **Nicolai Ghiaurov** (bass) Timur; **Sabin Markov** (bar) Mandarin; **Wandsworth School Boys' Choir; John Alldis Choir; London Philharmonic Orchestra/Zubin Mehta.** Decca 414 275-2DH2. From SET561 (9/73).

⸿ ② Ih 57' ADD 5/85

Turandot is a psychologically complex work fusing appalling sadism with self-sacrificing devotion. The icy Princess of China has agreed to marry any man of royal blood who can solve three riddles she has posed. If he fails his head will roll. Calaf, the son of the exiled Tartar king Timur, answers all the questions easily and when Turandot hesitates to accept him, magnanimously offers her a riddle in return—"What is his name?". Liù, Calaf's faithful slave-girl, is tortured but rather than reveal his identity kills herself. Turandot finally capitulates announcing that his name is Love. Dame Joan Sutherland's assumption of the title role is statuesque, combining regal poise with a more human warmth, whilst Montserrat Caballé is a touchingly sympathetic Liù, skilfully steering the character away from any hint of the mawkish. Pavarotti's Calaf is a heroic figure in splendid voice and the chorus is handled with great power baying for blood at one minute, enraptured with Liù's nobility at the next. Mehta conducts with great passion and a natural feel for Puccini's wonderfully tempestuous drama. Well recorded.

Puccini. SUOR ANGELICA. **Ilona Tokody** (sop) Suor Angelica; **Eszter Póka** (mez) Princess; **Zsuzsa Barlay** (mez) Mother Superior, Lay Sister II; **Maria Teresa Uribe** (mez) Sister Superior; **Tamara Takács** (mez) Mistress of the Novices, Sister of the Infirmary; **Katalin Pitti** (sop) Suor Genovieffa; **Magda Pulveri** (sop) Suor Osmina; **Zsuzsa Misura** (sop) Suor Dolcina, Lay Sister I; **Janka Békás** (sop) First Nursing Sister; **Margit Keszthelyi** (sop) Second Nursing Sister; **Ildikó Szönyi** (sop) Novice; **Hungarian State Opera Chorus and Orchestra/Lamberto Gardelli.** Hungaroton HCD12490-2.

> 52' DDD

Suor Angelica risks sentimentality telling of a young nun confined to a convent to atone for the scandal of having given birth to a child out of wedlock. She is visited by her aunt, the frosty Princess, who tells Angelica of the death of her son. Angelica resolves on suicide and as her life ebbs away sees a vision of the Holy Virgin. The orchestration is lush and the texture can become monotonous with its preponderance of female voices. The lament "Senza mamma" is the opera's 'hit', and when sung in so winning a way as here by Ilona Tokody, achieves a moving sense of the young girl's spiritual innocence and nobility of purpose. The other parts are sung competently and the choral passages are nicely balanced. Gardelli directs a highly sympathetic performance, never overlooking the score's felicitous detail. The recording is clear if a little generous of acoustic.

Henry Purcell

British 1659-1695

Purcell. SONATAS, Volume 3. **Purcell Quartet** ([a]Catherine Mackintosh, Elizabeth Wallfisch, vns; Richard Boothby, va da gamba; [b]Robert Woolley, org). Chandos CHAN8763.
Ten Sonatas in Four Parts, Z802-11—No. 3 in A minor; No. 4 in D minor; No. 5 in G minor; No. 6 in G minor; No. 7 in G major; No. 8 in G minor (with two variant movements); No. 9 in F major; No. 10 in D major. Organ Voluntaries, Z717-20[b]—No. 2 in D minor; No. 4 in G major. Prelude for Solo Violin in G minor, ZN773[a].

> 63' DDD 12/89

For lovers of Purcell this recording promises an hour of sheer delight. The performers play upon instruments of choice, one violin (Jan Bouwmeester, 1669) being contemporary with the composer, the other a fine-toned eighteenth-century Italian instrument. Both gamba and chamber organ are modern reconstructions based on seventeenth-century English models. The acoustics of Orford Church ensure warmth and clarity and even give you the extraordinary feeling that the players are actually present in your sitting-room, with the strings close beside you and the organ only a step away. Many listeners will be familiar with Purcell's *Sonatas in Four Parts*: generations of young fiddlers have been brought up on pieces like the *Golden* Sonata (No. 9) or the famous Chaconne

(No. 6). This performance, with its sensitivity, ease and wit should therefore arouse happy memories. It all seems so simple, yet what perfection of detail!—small points, such as the choice of the order in which the sonatas are played, ensuring smooth transitions and apt contrasts; the adoption of appropriately graded tempos; the delicacy, grace and elegance of the music, but also the mysteriously expressive chromaticism and certain moments of unexpected exploratory harmony.

Purcell. AYRES FOR THE THEATRE. **The Parley of Instruments/Peter Holman.** Hyperion CDA66212.
Abdelazer, Z570—suite. Timon of Athens, Z632—No. 1, Overture; No. 20, Curtain tune. The Gordion Knot Unty'd, Z597—suite. Bonduca, Z574—suite. The Virtuous Wife, Z611—suite. Chacony in G minor, Z730.

57' DDD 9/87

This well recorded disc gathers some of Purcell's most delightful incidental music for the many theatrical productions his music graced. Listeners familiar with Britten's *The Young Person's Guide to the Orchestra* will recognize the theme plucked from *Abdelazer* and here given a very sprightly gait. There is some outstanding instrumental playing—with some virtuoso natural trumpet playing from Crispian Steele-Perkins—and tempos are consistently crisper and more alert than normal. The collection also includes Purcell's well-known *Chacony* in a brisk performance—it may have originated in the theatre anyway and so makes a logical addition. This delightful disc is far more generously cued than the sleeve would have one believe, and makes for pleasing listening in an intimate recording acoustic.

Purcell. CHORAL WORKS. **Taverner Choir; Taverner Players/Andrew Parrott.** EMI Reflexe CDC7 49635-2. Texts included.
Ode for St Cecilia's Day, 1683—Welcome to all the pleasures, Z339 (with John Mark Ainsley, Charles Daniels, tens). Funeral Sentences—Man that is born of a woman, Z27; In the midst of life, Z17a; Thou know'st, Lord, Z58b. Ode for Queen Mary's Birthday, 1694—Come ye sons of art, away, Z323 (Emily Van Evera, sop; Timothy Wilson, alto; Ainsley, Daniels; David Thomas, bass). Funeral Music for Queen Mary—March and Canzona, Z860. Thou know'st, Lord, Z58c.

55' DDD 2/90

This is a satisfying anthology of vocal music by Purcell which includes the masterly and memorable *Come ye sons of art, away*. Andrew Parrott, as so often, has some surprises in store for the unsuspecting listener; here he performs the famous duet "Sound the trumpet" not with two counter-tenors but with two voices of contrasting timbres and registers: a countertenor and a tenor, albeit a high one. This has been achieved by a choice of low pitch for the entire work and the results are convincing. Likewise, the air "Sound the viol", traditionally counter-tenor's property, has been allotted

to a high tenor. Parrott brings this beautiful work to life with insight, affection and rigorous attention to all aspects of style. Much else on the disc is comparably successful and, if the music does not always maintain the dizzy heights of *Come ye sons of art* it is never far below. Outstanding from a musical and interpretative standpoint are the profoundly affecting *Funeral Sentences* and *Funeral Music for Queen Mary* both of which are notably well served by EMI in its sympathetic recording.

Purcell. THEATRE MUSIC. **Joy Roberts, Judith Nelson, Emma Kirkby, Elizabeth Lane, Prudence Lloyd** (sops); **James Bowman** (alto); **Martyn Hill, Paul Elliott, Alan Byers, Peter Bamber, Rogers Covey-Crump, Julian Pike** (tens); **David Thomas, Christopher Keyte, Geoffrey Shaw, Michael George** (basses); **Taverner Choir; Academy of Ancient Music/ Christopher Hogwood** (hpd). L'Oiseau-Lyre 425 893-2OM6. Texts included. Abdelazar, Z570. Distressed Innocence, Z577. The Married Beau, Z603. The Gordian Knot Unty'd, Z597 (all from DSLO504, 6/76). Sir Anthony Love, Z588. Bonduca, Z574. Circe, Z575 (DSLO527, 2/78). The Virtuous Wife, Z611. The Old Bachelor, Z607. Overture in G minor, Z770. Amphitryon, Z572 (DSLO55Q, 12/79). The Comical History of Don Quixote, Z578 (DSLO534, 11/78). The Double Dealer, Z592. The Richmond Heiress, Z608. The Rival Sisters, Z609. Henry the Second, King of England Z580. Tyrannic Love, Z613 (DSLO561, 4/81). Overture in G minor, Z772. Theodosius, Z606. The Libertine, Z600. The Massacre of Paris, Z604. Oedipus, Z583 (DSLO590, 3/ 82). Overture in D minor, Z771. The History of King Richard II, Z581. Sir Barnaby Whigg, Z589. Sophonisba, Z590. The English Lawyer, Z594. A Fool's Preferement, Z571. The Indian Emperor, Z598. The Knight of Malta, Z599. Why, my Daphne, why complaining?, Z525. The Wifes' Excuse, Z612. Cleomenes, Z576. Regulus, Z586. The Marriage-hater Match'd, Z602 (414 173-1OH, 7/85). Love Triumphant, Z582. Rule a Wife and have a Wife, Z587. The Female Virtuosos, Z596. Epsom Wells, Z579. The Maid's Last Prayer, Z601. Aureng-Zebe, Z573. The Canterbury Guests, Z591. The Fatal Marriage, Z595. The Spanish Friar, Z610. Pausanias, Z585. The Mock Marriage, Z605. Oroonoko, Z584 (414 174-1OH, 9/85). Pavans—A major, Z748; A minor, Z749; B flat major, BWV750; G minor, BWV751; G minor, Z752. Trio Sonata for violin, bass viol and organ, Z780. Chaconne, Z730 (DSLO514, 10/77).

(6) 6h 54' ADD/DDD 4/91

A six-CD anthology of vocal and instrumental music by Purcell is as rich and rewarding in its variety as it is indispensable to our picture of this English genius. Although Restoration England continued to take an interest in theatre music from abroad towards the end of the seventeenth century she began to develop staged musical entertainments along hybrid lines of her own. Most of the music contained here dates from the last six years of Purcell's life when plays, from Shakespeare to Shadwell were seldom staged without songs, instrumental interludes and dances. Purcell's legacy to the Restoration stage contains jewels of almost priceless worth and these are lovingly burnished by Christopher Hogwood, the Academy of Ancient Music and an excellent group of vocalists; choruses are imaginatively sung by the Taverner Choir under Andrew Parrott's direction. It would be difficult to isolate any particular songs and dances from such a vast treasure-trove but few may be able to resist Emma Kirkby's saucy "Lads and Lasses, blithe and gay" (*Don Quixote*), Martyn Hill's "Thus to a ripe, consenting maid" (*The Old Bachelor*), the ravishing trio "With this sacred charming wand" (*Don Quixote*) or the "Scotch tune" from *Amphitryon*. Performances are lively and stylish if not always polished but that, one suspects, is as authentic a touch as anything else here. The booklet contains texts of all the songs and the discs are pleasantly recorded.

Purcell. Hail, bright Cecilia. **Emma Kirkby** (sop); **Michael Chance, Kevin Smith** (altos); **Rogers Covey-Crump, Charles Daniels, Paul Elliott, Neil Jenkins, Andrew King** (tens); **Michael George, Simon Grant, David Thomas, Richard Wistreich** (basses); **Robert Woolley** (org); **Taverner Choir and Players/Andrew Parrott.** EMI Reflexe CDC7 47490-2. Text included.

57' DDD 1/87

Purcell's Ode in praise of the patroness of music is but one of a whole series of such works written by various composers between 1683 and 1703 for festivities held at the Stationer's Hall in London. Purcell had written the first ode for these gatherings and was later asked to make a setting of words by the Royal Chaplain Nicholas Brady. Throughout its 13 sections poet and composer hymn the praises of the various instruments of music. Purcell's limpid music beautifully and tastefully adorns this most gracious of poetry and vividly observes both its vigour and sublimity. The Taverner Consort, Choir and Players comprise some of the finest musicians in the early-music field and with such fresh and versatile voices as Emma Kirkby's, Rogers Covey-Crump's and Michael Chance's, to single out but three, singing the praises of music, who could complain? The recording is clear, spacious and natural-sounding.

Purcell. DIDO AND AENEAS. **Dame Janet Baker** (sop) Dido; **Patricia Clark** (sop) Belinda; **Eileen Poulter** (sop) Second Woman; **Raimund Herincx** (bass) Aeneas; **Monica Sinclair** (contr) Sorceress; **Rhianon James** (mez) First Witch; **Catherine Wilson** (mez) Second Witch; **John Mitchinson** (ten) Sailor; **Dorothy Dorow** (sop) Spirit; **St Anthony Singers; English Chamber Orchestra/Anthony Lewis.** Decca Serenata 425 720-2DM. From L'Oiseau-Lyre 1961 SOL60047 (3/62).

53' ADD 12/90

Dame Janet Baker   [*photo: Hyperion*]

This 30-year-old recording, now happily available on CD, has never really been surpassed in excellence. It is arguably the best performance of Purcell's tightly-constructed opera—better even than Flagstad's and Schwarzkopf's rendering back in the fifties and certainly equal to more recent recordings. It is a collector's item, with Janet Baker, in the role of Dido, rising to the height of her vocal powers. Her first aria, "Ah! Belinda I am prest", is full of tender foreboding and her final lament powerfully grief-stricken. She is well supported by Patricia Clark, Dido's light-hearted confidante. Monica Sinclair reveals herself as a truly sinister, though somewhat unevenly-voiced Sorceress. The hero's role in the opera is minimal, but Raimund Herincx matches up well to the heroine in their famous final duet. The St Anthony Singers give ample proof of their versatility producing, as required by the score, cackling witches, boozy sailors and rabble or merely a crowd of gently gossiping English courtiers running for shelters from the elements. The strings of the English Chamber Orchestra are supported by Thurston Dart on the harpsichord continuo—a definite plus, this, and a reminder of the tragically early death of a brilliant performer who combines, here as always, both discretion and inspired imagination.

Purcell. THE FAIRY QUEEN. **Nancy Argenta, Lynne Dawson, Isabelle Desrochers, Willemijn van Gent, Veronique Gens, Sandrine Piau, Noéme Rime** (sops); **Charles Daniels, Jean-Paul Fouchécourt, Mark le Brocq, Christophe le Paludier** (altos); **Bernard Loonen, Françoise Piolino, Thomas Randle** (tens); **François Bazola** (bar); **Jérôme Corréas, George Banks-Martin, Bernard Deletré, Thomas Lander, Richard Taylor** (basses); **Les Arts Florissants/William Christie.** Harmonia Mundi HMC90 1308/9. Notes and text included.

② 2h 8' DDD 1/90

Purcell's *The Fairy Queen*, loosely based by an anonymous seventeenth-century literary hack on Shakespeare's *A Midsummer Night's Dream*, was one of the composer's last works. Like all his other works for the London public theatres, *The Fairy Queen* is not so much an opera in the accepted sense, but more a sequence of masque-like interludes together with dances and instrumental music designed to punctuate the play. William Christie's exciting account of this magical score grew directly from a staging of the piece at the 1989 Aix-en-Provence Festival, and it retains all the immediacy and conviction of an interpretation born of genuine theatrical experience. The orchestra is large for the period, but it allows Christie to exploit all the nuances of Purcell's writing, from the wit of the Scene of the Drunken Poet to the delicate sadness of the Act Five Plaint,

The Fairy Queen [photo: Harmonia Mundi/Ely

wistfully delivered by Lynne Dawson. The high point is the deliciously comic exchange between Bernard Deletré and Jean-Paul Fouchécourt in the dialogue between Corydon and Mopsa, sharply characterized and given an added humorous edge by the remaining traces of Gallic pronunciation. This is a sheer delight to listen to, and a must for anyone keen to hear some of the finest English music of the seventeenth century.

Sergey Rachmaninov

Russian/American 1873-1943

Rachmaninov. Piano Concerto No. 1 in F sharp minor, Op. 1[a]. Rhapsody on a Theme of Paganini, Op. 34[b]. **Vladimir Ashkenazy** (pf); [a]**Concertgebouw Orchestra, Amsterdam,** [b]**Philharmonia Orchestra/Bernard Haitink.** Decca 417 613-2DH.

52' DDD 12/87

Showpiece that it is, with its lush romantic harmonies and contrasting vigorous panache, the First Concerto has much to commend it in purely musical terms and although its debts are clear enough (most notably perhaps to Rimsky-Korsakov), it stands on its own two feet as far as invention, overall design and musical construction are concerned. The *Paganini* Rhapsody is one of the composer's finest works and arguably the most purely inventive set of variations to be based on Paganini's catchy tune ever written. The wealth of musical invention it suggested to Rachmaninov is truly bewildering and his control over what can in lesser hands become a rather laboured formal scheme is masterly indeed. Ashkenazy gives superb performances of both works and the Concertgebouw and the Philharmonia are in every way the perfect foils under Bernard Haitink's sympathetic direction. There is weight, delicacy, colour, energy and repose in equal measure here and it is all conveyed by a full-bodied and detailed recording.

Rachmaninov. Piano Concerto No. 2 in C minor, Op. 18. Rhapsody on a Theme of Paganini, Op. 34. **Vladimir Ashkenazy** (pf); **London Symphony Orchestra/André Previn.** Decca Ovation 417 702-2DH. From SXLF6565/7 (9/72).

> 58' ADD 7/87   £ Ⓑ

Works for Piano and Orchestra. **Cristina Ortiz** (pf); **Royal Philharmonic Orchestra/Moshe Atzmon.** Decca 414 348-2DH. From 414 348-1DH (5/86).
Addinsell: Warsaw Concerto. *Litolff:* Concerto symphonique No. 4 in D minor, Op. 102—Scherzo. *Gottschalk* (orch. Hazell): Grande fantaisie triomphale sur l'hymne national brésilien, RO108. *Rachmaninov:* Piano Concerto No. 2 in C minor, Op. 18.

> 58' DDD 9/86   Ⓑ

Rachmaninov. Piano Concertos—No. 2 in C minor, Op. 18[a]; No. 3 in D minor, Op. 30[b]. **Sergei Rachmaninov** (pf); **Philadelphia Orchestra/ [a]Leopold Stokowski; [b]Eugene Ormandy.** RCA Red Seal mono RD85997. Item marked [a] from HMV DB1333/7 (11/29), [b] DB5709/13 (12/40).

> 66' ADD 10/88   ꝗP Ⓑ

Rachmaninov. Piano Concerto No. 3 in D minor, Op. 30[a]. PRELUDES[b]. **Vladimir Ashkenazy** (pf); **[a]London Symphony Orchestra/André Previn.** Decca Ovation 417 764-2DM. Item marked [a] from SXLF6565/7 (9/72), [b] 5BB 221/2 (2/76).
Preludes—C sharp minor, Op. 3 No. 2; B flat major, Op. 23 No. 2; G minor, Op. 23 No. 5; B minor, Op. 32 No. 10; D flat major, Op. 32 No. 13.

> 70' ADD 10/88   Ⓑ

Rachmaninov. Piano Concertos—No. 2 in C minor, Op 18; No. 3 in D minor, Op. 30. **Earl Wild** (pf); **Royal Philharmonic Orchestra/Jascha Horenstein.** Chandos Collect CHAN6507. First released on Reader's Digest in 1966.

> 66' ADD 2/91   ꝗP Ⓑ

Rachmaninov. Piano Concerto No. 2 in C minor, Op. 18. Rhapsody on a Theme of Paganini, Op. 34. **Jenö Jandó** (pf); **Budapest Symphony Orchestra/György Lehel.** Naxos 8 550117.

> 58' DDD 10/90   £ Ⓑ

The C minor Concerto of Rachmaninov symbolizes romanticism at its ripest. Its combination of poetry and sensuous warmth with languorously memorable melodic lines balanced by exhilarating pianistic brilliance happily avoids any suggestion of sentimentality. The simple chordal introduction from the soloist ushers in one of the composer's most luscious tunes, yet the slow movement develops even greater ardour in its melodic contour, and the composer holds back a further haunting expressive idea to bring lyrical contrast to the scintillating finale.

Ashkenazy's 1972 performance with Previn has now been reissued as a superb mid-price bargain, coupled with an exhilarating performance of the *Rhapsody on a theme of Paganini*, where the famous 18th Variation blossoms with passionate fervour. The Concerto is no less involving, the first movement building to an engulfing climax, the *Adagio* radiantly beautiful, perhaps the finest on disc. The recording represents Decca vintage analogue sound at its best and the remastering is extremely successful, rich, well balanced and vivid.

However, Decca have since produced a highly-recommendable digital alternative from Ortiz and the RPO. The couplings are apt. The genuinely inspired pastiche *Warsaw Concerto* by Richard Addinsell has a principal theme worthy to stand alongside those of Rachmaninov and its layout shows satisfying craftsmanship. Ortiz plays this main theme with great affection and she is equally beguiling in the delicious Litolff *Scherzo*. The effect here is of elegance rather than extrovert brilliance: this is reserved for the Gottschalk *Grande fantaisie triomphale*, which is played with a splendid panache that almost covers its inherent vulgarity and certainly emphasizes its ingenuous charm. Throughout the recording balance is realistic and the reverberation adds the most attractive bloom.

The RCA recordings sound every bit as old as they are, ill-defined in the bass and decidedly short on tonal allure from either piano or orchestra. So it takes a rather special kind of performance to earn this CD a place in the *Guide*. To have the composer's own view of two such familiar works is valuable enough in itself and to many listeners brought up on more modern styles of playing Rachmaninov's interpretations will seem startlingly different. Not that they are freer or more romantic; rather the reverse—tempos are generally faster, expressive lingerings generally avoided. The end result is to reveal more clearly the architecture of the music and its dynamic force rather than its communication of feeling.

Ashkenazy's recording of the Third Concerto complements the composer's own. It is more conspicuously expressive, more heroic and more yielding by turns, it is uncut, it includes the more massive of the first movement cadenzas, and it enjoys a full-blooded modern recording. There is a tendency to bang away when the chords are coming thick and fast and to overdo expressive lingerings; also, Previn's accompaniment is fine but not outstandingly idiomatic. But these points do not outweigh the advantages of what, especially at mid-price, is currently the top recommendation for this concerto on CD. A selection of five of Rachmaninov's most popular Preludes enhances the attractions of the disc.

Wild's 1965 recording with Horenstein comes into the connoisseur category. All the urgent bravura is here, and the heart-on-the-sleeve emotions, but a strong discipline controls the overall framework. Excessive fluctuations in speed and mawkish poring over details are carefully avoided to produce an almost classical structural poise. The Third Concerto, with its sometimes overplayed degree of introspection, particularly benefits from this approach and together these readings illustrate the best qualities of Rachmaninov's work in this genre.

The highly recommendable Naxos coupling of these two favourite Rachmaninov works for piano and orchestra did much to establish the reputation of its Hungarian soloist, Jenö Jandó as an artist of distinction, and at the same time shows that a super bargain label could offer a quality of music-making and digital recording to compare with the finest issues at premium price. The Concerto opens simply, and unfolds with languorous warmth; the performance has character from the very opening bars. Jandó shows a natural feeling for the ebb and flow of the Rachmaninovian phrase, and having started at a relatively measured pace, the first movement expands excitingly at its bold climax. The *Adagio* is beautifully played by soloist and orchestra alike and the finale brings exhilarating zest and a ripe romantic blossoming for its famous lyrical melody. The *Rhapsody on a Theme of Paganini* is even finer: it has all the necessary flamboyance and bravura, yet there is no sense of virtuosity just for its own sake, and the work's detail and variety of mood are revealed in the most spontaneous way, not least the plangent arrival of the *Dies irae*. The romantic expansiveness at Variation No. 18 is followed by a postlude of gentle nostalgia from the soloist; then he sets off again in sparkling fashion and there is plenty of excitement in the closing Variations. György Lehel's accompaniments are splendidly supportive in both works, and the balance between the piano and orchestra, very good in the concerto, seems ideally judged in the *Rhapsody*, while the recorded sound is first rate in every way. The individual Variations are not cued, but this remains an astonishing bargain.

Rachmaninov. ORCHESTRAL WORKS. **London Symphony Orchestra/ André Previn.** EMI Studio CDM7 69025-2. Items marked ᵃ from ASD3259 (9/76), ᵇ ASD3284 (12/76), ᶜ ASD3369 (8/77).
Symphonic Dances, Op. 45ᵃ. The isle of the dead, Op. 29ᵃ. Vocalise, Op. 34 No. 14ᵇ (arr. composer). ALEKOᶜ—Intermezzo; Women's Dance.

> • 71' ADD 9/87

André Previn's affinity with the music of Rachmaninov is evident and few people give the symphonic works the same weight of authority or attention to detail. This issue gathers some of his finest performances. The *Symphonic Dances* have a rhythmic crispness that Previn willingly softens where the string writing gains in texture and fullness. The elegant waltz theme is laid over the sprightly accompaniment with just the right nonchalance. *The isle of the dead* receives an appropriately mysterious interpretation and the *Vocalise* is prepared for even the most addicted sweet-tooth. The programme closes with the two extracts from *Aleko*—nicely shaded and beautifully shaped. The LSO play superbly and the recording has been finely remastered.

Rachmaninov. SYMPHONIES. **Concertgebouw Orchestra, Amsterdam/ Vladimir Ashkenazy.** Decca 421 065-2DM3. Item marked ᵃ from SXDL7603 (11/83), ᵇ SXDL7563 (7/82), ᶜ SXDL7531 (6/83).
Symphonies—No. 1 in D minor, Op. 13ᵃ; No. 2 in E minor, Op. 27ᵇ; No. 3 in A minor, Op. 44ᶜ; Youth Symphonyᶜ.

> • ③ 2h 30' DDD 12/87

Rachmaninov's symphonies possess a melodic memorability and lyrical ardour to match the piano concertos. The Second in E minor was the first to gain general recognition, with its sweeping string melodies and gloriously expansive slow movement; No. 3, written some 20 years after the Second Symphony, has hardly

less melodic appeal, and is notable for a hauntingly nostalgic *molto cantabile* melody which acts as secondary theme in the first movement. His First was a failure at its première and Rachmaninov abandoned it in despair; it languished unplayed for two decades but has now gained universal acceptance for its emotional power and the rugged strength of the finale. Ashkenazy is particularly successful in bringing this fine work vibrantly to life. Here, as in the other symphonies, his volatile tempos and passionately spontaneous control of rubato within the spacious romantic paragraphs create the most involving ebb and flow of tension, with the lyrical melodies always blossoming readily. Throughout all three symphonies the expressive urgency of the playing of the Concertgebouw, with moments of serenity and glowing expansiveness to balance the ardour, give the utmost satisfaction to the listener. Each work moves forward with striking spontaneity and the splendid digital recording is vividly detailed and gloriously full in its textures; the slight edge of the strings in the Second Symphony adds bite to the performance, rather than detracting from the interpretation. As a bonus Ashkenazy offers the early *Youth* Symphony composed when Rachmaninov was 18, immature in its Tchaikovskian influences, but pleasingly fresh in invention.

Rachmaninov. Symphony No. 3 in A minor, Op. 44[a].
Shostakovich. Symphony No. 6 in B minor, Op. 54[b]. **London Symphony Orchestra/André Previn.** EMI Studio CDM7 69564-2. Item marked [a] from ASD3369 (8/77), [b] ASD3029 (12/74).

75' ADD 12/88 £

Previn's highly praised recording of Rachmaninov's Third Symphony came at the peak of a very successful period in the EMI studios, the Shostakovich, hardly less fine, was done three years earlier. They make a splendid and distinguished mid-price coupling showing the symbiosis Previn had with the LSO at that time. The string section play Rachmaninov's lyrical themes with a rapturous romantic sweep and the nervous intensity of the reading is immensely gripping. The first movement of the Shostakovich Sixth is an expansive *Largo*, longer than the other two movements put together, especially when Previn's treatment is so eloquently spacious; the scherzo which follows is full of wit, and the ebullient finale seems optimistic, but maybe things are not what they seem. Previn is clearly deeply involved in this powerful score and so are his players and the remastered recording is full and clear without too much loss of ambience in the clarification process.

Rachmaninov. WORKS FOR TWO PIANOS AND PIANO FOUR AND SIX HANDS. **Brigitte Engerer, Oleg Maisenberg.** Harmonia Mundi HMC90 1301/02.
Russian Rhapsody in E minor. Suites—No. 1, Op. 5, "Fantaisie-tableaux"; No. 2, Op. 17. Polka italienne (1906). Romance in G major (1893). Six Duets, Op. 11. Two pieces for six hands (with Elena Bachkirova). Symphonic Dances, Op. 45*a*.

② 2h 11' DDD 3/90

Rachmaninov's four- and six-hand piano music covers his whole composing career, from the *Russian Rhapsody* of 1891 to the *Symphonic Dances* of nearly 50 years later (the latter being better known in Rachmaninov's orchestral version). It is a rewarding repertoire, even if it is only with the *Symphonic Dances* that it is appropriate to speak of a masterpiece. One reason why these works get so much less exposure than the solo piano music is the inherent problem of the two-piano or duet medium—the need to synchronize the instantaneous attacks of two pianists can easily stifle their expressive freedom (and to leave attacks unsynchronized can sound terribly amateurish). Engerer and Maisenberg have a shared understanding of the idiom which helps them around this problem, and their performances are fluent, warmly expressive and cleanly recorded. Recording quality gourmets should note that not all the pieces were recorded on the same occasion or with the same set-up of instruments—in the second movement of the First Suite the two pianos even appear to swap channels. It should also be said that the Second Suite, a favourite with students and adventurous amateurs, is a little less exciting as a performance than the rest of the programme. Apart from those things, this is an exceptionally fine issue.

Rachmaninov. Piano Sonatas—No. 1 in D minor, Op. 28; No. 2 in B flat minor, Op. 36 (original version). **Gordon Fergus-Thompson** (pf). Kingdom KCLCD2007.

73' DDD 6/89

Familiar though Rachmaninov is as a composer of piano concertos, his two Piano Sonatas have not as yet attained anything like the same level of popularity. But here is a recording that couples them together in performances that are both persuasive and masterly. Gordon Fergus-Thompson has the technique and the temperament to do full justice to this music. In his later life, Rachmaninov made considerable cuts in his Second Sonata, but today the tendency is to return to his original, which is what Fergus-Thompson does here to good advantage. In this form the Sonata lasts some 28 minutes, but it does not outstay its welcome; and as a matter of fact the First Sonata is longer at nearly three-quarters of an hour. Both sonatas contain thrilling and highly personal music, and they have been well recorded.

Rachmaninov. 24 Préludes[a]. Piano Sonata No. 2 in B flat minor, Op. 36[b.] **Vladimir Ashkenazy** (pf). Decca 414 417-2DH2. Item marked [a] from 5BB 221/2 (2/76), [b] SXL6996 (9/82).

② 1h 46' ADD 11/85

These recordings were outstanding on LP and they sound even better in CD format. Ashkenazy gets as close as possible to making the C sharp minor *Prelude* sound fresh, and one might also note the becalmed melancholy of Op. 23 No. 1, the exquisite management of the different threads in the texture of Op. 23 No. 4, the supple flow of Op. 23 No. 6. Superficially the two sets of *Preludes* are similar, yet in reality they are a lot different. Closely linked to the quality of Ashkenazy's interpretations is the fact that he brings to this music a technique perfectly adapted to Rachmaninov's way of writing for the piano in these works, a good illustration being Op. 23 No. 9, which is an *étude* rather than a prelude. The Sonata also receives a magnificent performance, though one whose recorded sound is less sumptuous than that of the *Preludes*. These two CDs of Ashkenazy's are unlikely to be surpassed in terms of sheer mastery of this composer's music.

Rachmaninov. The bells, Op. 35[a]. Vocalise, Op. 34 No. 14[b]. *Tchaikovsky.* Romeo and Juliet (orch. Taneyev)—duet[ac]. Festival Coronation March in D major. [abc]**Suzanne Murphy** (sop); [ab]**Keith Lewis** (ten); [a]**David Wilson-Johnson** (bar); **Scottish National** [a]**Chorus and Orchestra/Neeme Järvi.** Chandos CHAN8476. Notes and English texts included.

63' DDD 2/87

Rachmaninov had grown up in a land where different kinds of church bells were often heard, and their sound evoked in him vivid childhood memories. Edgar Allan Poe's evocation of four human states and their bell connotations seemed to Rachmaninov an ideal basis for a four-part choral symphony. This is well realized byJärvi, though perhaps the urgency of the "Loud Alarum Bells" could be expressed more vehemently. The soloists are not ideal, but a rich, atmospheric recording provides a suitable vehicle for some lusty though well-disciplined choral singing. *Vocalise* is reasonably well sung, as is the Tchaikovsky

Romeo and Juliet duet. After Tchaikovsky's death Taneyev discovered and then put together sketches for the operatic duet recorded here: no doubt he was aided by the fact that the duet re-uses material from the Fantasy overture. *The Festival Coronation March* was written to celebrate the 1883 crowning of Tsar Alexander III.

Rachmaninov. Vespers, Op. 37. **Corydon Singers/Matthew Best.** Hyperion CDA66460. Text and translation included.

66' DDD 7/91

Rachmaninov's piano concertos and solo pieces are among the most popular of classical works, but he covered a wider range than this and his setting of the Vespers (or to use his own title, *All-night vigil*) has long been admired by the few outside Russia who knew it. It uses a liturgical text of the Russian Church for the services of Vespers (starting at sunset), Matins and The First Hour (Prime), and is deeply religious in feeling, for although the composer did not always adhere to the faith of his childhood he was married in church and thought much about the beliefs of his forefathers. After he wrote this work in a mere two weeks of 1915, one of his friends said that basses who could sing a low C, to say nothing of the B flat at the end of the fifth section, "were as rare as asparagus at Christmas" and that was in Russia, famous for its low basses! Nevertheless, Matthew Best and his Corydon Singers rise (or rather fall) splendidly to this occasion, and overall their style, tonal quality and pronunciation are alike convincingly authentic, with fine alto and tenor soloists; indeed, hearing John Bowen in the *Nyne Otpushchaeshi* ("Nunc dimittis") one could imagine oneself at a real Orthodox service, especially as the recording was made in a church. There's an excellent booklet note and the text is given in a transliteration from the original Cyrillic script into our own Roman alphabet, with an English translation. This is music of spiritual beauty that fully embodies the Russian Orthodox saying that "the mind should enter the heart".

Jean-Philippe Rameau
French (1683-1764)

Rameau. HARPSICHORD WORKS. **Trevor Pinnock.** CRD3310, CRD3320 and CRD3330. Items marked [a] from CRD1010 (2/75), [b] CRD1020 (6/76), [c] CRD1030 (5/77).
CRD3310[a]—Nouvelles suites de pièces de clavecin—A minor. Pièces de clavecin—Suite in E minor. *CRD3320*[b]—Premier livre de pièces de clavecin—Suite in A minor. La Dauphine. Cinq pièces pour clavecin seul (Pièces de clavecin en concerts). La pantomime. *CRD3330*[c]—Pièces de clavecin—Suite in D minor/major. Nouvelles suites de pièces de clavecin—G major/minor.

③ 52' 43' 52' ADD 8/88

Most of the pieces from Rameau's first book of solo harpsichord music bear standard dance titles, but this practice became increasingly rare in the later, more mature books. His fantasy is instead exercised in character pieces with strange titles, the significance of some of which is clear, e.g. *Les trois mains* (which sounds as though the player has three hands) and *Le rappel des oiseaux* (you can hear the bird-calls), though others remain unexplained. Rameau admired his predecessors, Couperin and D'Anglebert, but his music is more sinewy, clear and less heavily ornamented than theirs. By all accounts Rameau was a severely serious man, as many of these pieces confirm, but Pinnock's wonderfully fluent and flexible performances help to reveal the many other human faces of his music, including the humorous one of *La poule* (the hen) and *La boiteuse* (the limping one), and of course the extrovertly virtuosic one. The quality of the recording is no less stunning than that of the playing—on replicas of three different period instruments.

Rameau. PLATEE. **Gilles Ragon** (ten) Platée; **Jennifer Smith** (sop) La Folie, Thalie; **Guy de Mey** (ten) Thespis, Mercure; **Vincent le Texier** (bass-bar) Jupiter, A satyr; **Guillemette Laurens** (mez) Junon; **Bernard Deletré** (bass) Cithéron, Momus; **Véronique Gens** (sop) L'Amour, Clarine; **Michel Verschaeve** (bass) Momus; **Françoise Herr Vocal Ensemble; Musiciens du Louvre/Marc Minkowski.** Erato MusiFrance 2292-45028-2. Notes, text and translation included.

② 2h 15' DDD 9/90

The *comédie-lyrique, Platée* is one of Rameau's masterpieces. It dates from 1745 when it was performed at Versailles as part of the celebrations for the Dauphin's marriage to the Infanta Maria-Theresa of Spain. The story concerns Platée, a nymph of unprepossessing appearance who is the butt of a cruel joke which leads her to believe that she will be the bride of Jupiter, no less. The theme may appear heartless but the music most certainly is not, and the charades, disguises and comic figures, evoking Carnival spirit, providing Rameau with almost unparalleled opportunities to display his unique genius as an orchestrator. There is hardly a weak moment in the score and anyone hitherto intimidated by this giant of the French baroque will find in *Platée* an enchanting introduction to Rameau's music. The performance under Marc Minkowski's direction is full of life and mischievous little insights. The solo cast is strong with Gilles Ragon in the high tenor travesti role of Platée and Jennifer Smith dazzlingly virtuosic and high-spirited as La Folie. This is, in short, a robust and well-paced account of a captivating work. The score is presented without cuts and with only a very few repeats omitted. The recorded sound is bright and effective and the accompanying booklet contains full texts in French, English and German.

Rameau. ZOROASTRE. **John Elwes** (ten) Zoroastre; **Greta de Reyghere** (sop) Amélite; **Mieke van der Sluis** (sop) Erinice; **Agnès Mellon** (sop) Céphie; **Gregory Reinhart** (bass) Abramane; **Jacques Bona** (bar) Oramasés, Voice from the Underworld; **Michel Verschaeve** (bass) Zopire; **François Fauché** (bass) Narbanor; **Philippe Cantor** (ten) God of Revenge; **Ghent Collegium Vocale; La Petite Bande/Sigiswald Kuijken.** Deutsche Harmonia Mundi Editio Classica GD77144. Notes, text and translation included. From HM1999813 (5/84).

③ 3h 4' ADD 7/90

Zoroastre was first performed in Paris in 1749 and was Rameau's penultimate serious opera or *tragédie en musique*. It was fairly well received but not without criticism concerning, above all, the librettist, Cahusac's text. When the work was revived in 1756 shifts of emphasis were made within the plot and it is this later version which is performed here. The story deals with the conflict between Light (Good) and Darkness (Evil) central to Zoroastrianism. Rameau brings to life the chief protagonists Zoroastre and Abramane with consummate skill and his characteristic feeling for colour is seldom absent from the many fine choruses, airs and instrumental dances. John Elwes (tenor) sings the title role with a firm grasp of the French baroque idiom, while Gregory Reinhart (bass) makes a formidable opponent in the person of Abramane with clear diction and a commanding vocal presence. The three principal female roles are sung with equal assurance though their voices are perhaps insufficiently distinctive from one another to make the strong contrasts implicit in their characters. Agnès Mellon as the innocent Céphie is, nonetheless, a particularly happy piece of casting. Sigiswald Kuijken directs the performance with insight into and affection for Rameau's subtle art and the recording comes with an informative booklet in French, English and German.

Maurice Ravel

French 1875-1937

Ravel. PIANO WORKS. **Jean-Philippe Collard** (pf); **French National Orchestra/Lorin Maazel.** EMI CDC7 47386-2.
Piano Concerto in G major. Piano Concerto in D major for the left hand (from ASD3845, 6/80). Pavane pour une infante défunte. Jeux d'eau. La valse (with Michel Béroff, pf. From EMI Pathé Marconi 2C 167 73025/7, 5/81).

65' ADD 10/86

Charm and sheer *joie de vivre* are the characteristic features of the G major Concerto. Two vigorous outer movements flank a poised *Adagio* whose beautiful melody was in part inspired by a similar flowing theme in Mozart's Clarinet Quintet. The Left-hand Concerto, in one movement, was written at the same time but is darker and more turbulent, though no less convincing and beautiful. Both works incorporate jazz elements, bright in the G major work and more sinister in the other. Jean-Philippe Collard is vivid always, with excellent rhythmic verve yet missing no felicitous detail, and the more tender passages are unfailingly affectionate. Lorin Maazel is a fine Ravel interpreter as well as a sympathetic, alert accompanist and the French National Orchestra is in top form. The two solo piano pieces and the marvellous but disturbing *La valse* are a welcome bonus to this delightful disc. The 1979 recording is excellent.

Ravel. Piano Concerto in G major.
Rachmaninov. Piano Concerto No. 4 in G minor, Op. 40. **Arturo Benedetti Michelangeli** (pf); **Philharmonia Orchestra/Ettore Gracis.** EMI CDC7 49326-2. From ASD255 (10/58).

47' ADD 9/88

Arturo Benedetti Michelangeli   [photo: DG/Reichardt]

Temperamentally it might seem that neither piece on this disc is ideally suited to the aloof, magisterial image that Michelangeli cultivates. The Ravel is a witty, jazzy-influenced score; the Rachmaninov is full of big-hearted nostalgia and heroic virtuosity. Michelangeli's achievement is to let those elements speak for themselves, and, by his refinement and awareness of long lines of musical thought, to bring out a sense of wholeness which is absent from the vast majority of other interpretations—apart from which the sheer virtuosity is breathtaking. Two passages stand out as examples of indisputably great music-making—the climax of Rachmaninov's first movement, prepared with gripping dramatic intensity and unleashed with astonishing force, and the exquisitely refined unfolding of the solo opening to Ravel's sublime slow movement. The Philharmonia, obviously sensing a special presence at the keyboard, play out of their skins; EMI have lavished all the care on the digital remastering that the performance deserve.

Ravel. Daphnis et Chloé—ballet[a]. Rapsodie espagnole[b]. Pavane pour une infante défunte[b]. [a]**Chorus of the Royal Opera House, Covent Garden; London Symphony Orchestra/Pierre Monteux.** Decca Historic 425 956-2DM. Item marked [a] from SXL2164 (12/59), [b] SXL2312 (7/62).

74' ADD 5/90   **Ⓑ**

Ravel. Daphnis et Chloé—ballet. **Montreal Symphony Chorus and Orchestra/Charles Dutoit.** Decca 400 055-2DH. From SXDL7526 (6/81).

56' DDD 3/83   **Ⓑ**

Diaghilev's ballet *Daphnis et Chloé*, based on a pastoral romance by the ancient Greek poet Longus, was first produced in June 1912, with Nijinsky and Karsavina in the title roles and choreography by Mikhail Fokine. Pierre Monteux conducted the first performance, and 47 years later he recorded his peerless interpretation for Decca. Though the Second Suite from the ballet is familiar to concert-goers and makes an effective piece in its own right, the full score, with wordless chorus, conveys still greater atmosphere and magic. No work of more sheer sensual beauty exists in the entire orchestral repertoire, and Monteux was its perfect interpreter. He conducts with a wonderful sense of clarity and balance: every important detail tells, and there is refinement of expression, yet inner strength too. The LSO play with superlative poetry and skill, and the chorus is magnificent in its tonal blend and colour. The *Rapsodie espagnole* and *Pavane* are also given ideal performances, and the recordings show off Decca's exceedingly high standards during the late 1950s and early 1960s.

On the second Decca disc the ballet is given not only a gloriously rich and understanding performance but a sumptuous recording to match. This swiftly became the CD medium's most cherished demonstration recording and indeed the sound is not only refined in its texturing of detail, but is beautifully balanced and warmly co-ordinated. Dutoit's reading is both brilliant and ardently committed, with the celebrated crescendo of "Daybreak" sounding radiant.

Ravel. Ma mère l'oye—ballet.
Saint-Saëns. Carnival of the Animals[a]. [a]**Joseph Villa; [a]Patricia Prattis Jennings** (pfs); **Pittsburgh Symphony Orchestra/André Previn.** Philips 400 016-2PH. From 9500 973 (2/82).

49' DDD 4/83

The sheer beauty of sound and the delicacy of the textures to be found in Ravel's exquisitely written ballet score must surely soften the hardest heart. Previn's performance is very tender, warm and affectionate, and very enjoyable. Saint-Saëns's "Zoological Fantasy" of 1886 inhabits a very different world, though like Ravel's score it was also written for children. But this time the idea is to divert and amuse through a series of 14 short, brilliantly orchestrated studies which portray animals such as the elephant, hens and cocks and also more strange beasts such as pianists and fossils. All the Pittsburgh orchestral soloists enter with relish into the jokes—there are quotations from other composers' works—and the two pianists have just the right tongue-in-cheek, busy manner.

Ravel. ORCHESTRAL WORKS. **Montreal Symphony Orchestra/Charles Dutoit.** Decca 410 254-2DH. From 410 254-1DH (8/84).
Ma mère l'oye—ballet. Pavane pour une infante défunte. Le tombeau de Couperin. Valses nobles et sentimentales (1911).

67' DDD 11/84

There is no more magical score than Ravel's *Ma mère l'oye* ("Mother Goose"). It has the elegance and perfection of Mozart, yet the translucence of the scoring is a Ravelian hallmark. *Le tombeau de Couperin* also shows the composer at his most elegant. This neo-classical evocation again demonstrates an affinity with a different age from Ravel's own, yet the delicious orchestral colour essentially belongs to the twentieth century. The *Valses nobles et sentimentales*, more melodically diffuse, have comparable subtlety. This is a very different work from *La valse* and much more characteristic of the essence of the composer. The Montreal orchestra show a natural rapport with these scores and their playing is warmly sympathetic yet not indulgent, so that the delicacy of texture is never over-laden. It is difficult to think of many other discs where everything comes together so perfectly to serve the composer's inspiration.

Ravel. ORCHESTRAL WORKS. **Montreal Symphony Orchestra/Charles Dutoit.** Decca 410 010-2DH. From SXDL7559 (9/82).
Boléro. Alborada del gracioso. Rapsodie espagnole. La valse.

51' DDD 8/83

Ravel. Alborada del gracioso. Rapsodie espagnole. Le tombeau de Couperin. La valse. **Orchestre de Paris/Herbert von Karajan.** EMI Studio CDM7 63526-2. From ASD2766 (3/72).

57' ADD 11/90

Ravel's *Boléro* is now so popular and universally familiar that it is easy to forget its originality. Dutoit plays it magnetically as a steady, remorseless crescendo and its power and marvellous command of orchestral colour are freshly revealed. The glittering *Alborada del gracioso* and the sensuous and exciting *Rapsodie espagnole* readily demonstrate the special feeling French composers had for the Spanish idiom, with diaphanous textures to capture the sultry quality of the Mediterranean evening and offset the sparkle of the Flamenco dance rhythms. *La valse* begins in the mists and expands to a breathtaking climax with a vision of countless dancing couples whirling round in an intoxicating infinity of space; then cruelly and abruptly the imagery disintegrates into silence. This CD is a model of its kind while the music-making combines a feeling for spectacle with the utmost refinement of detail.

Purists might argue that Karajan's Ravel was impressionistic on the surface and Romantic at its core, with no room for the symbolist currents that so distinguish the composer's style. Yet it is still so alluringly attractive to listen to that we would be foolish to ignore it for those reasons. His collection of popular works illustrates exactly Karajan's ability to combine his fascination with sonic beauty and his keen sense of structure: details are important here, but only to give substance to the long-term meaning of the music. The Orchestre de Paris play magnificently. Their intonation is not always as positive as that of some other major orchestras, but the spirit of the music is unerringly captured and the French tones are distinctively presented, even in those works that evoke Spain and Vienna. The woodwind playing in *Le tombeau de Couperin* is wistfully redolent of an earlier age and its pastoral context, and in *La valse* the impressionistic mists that Karajan summons are entirely appropriate, even cited by the composer in his commentary on the work. A spacious, warm recording is the cherry on the top of this delicious gateaux.

Ravel. ORCHESTRAL WORKS. **Orchestre de Paris / Jean Martinon.** EMI Studio CDM7 69565/6-2. From SLS5016 (10/75).
CDM7 69565-2—Boléro. Shéhérazade (1899)—Ouverture de féerie. Rapsodie espagnole. Menuet antique. La valse. *CDM7 69566-2*—Daphnis et Chloé—ballet (with Paris Opéra Chorus). Valses nobles et sentimentales.

> ♪♪ ② 64' 73' ADD 12/88 £

Appropriately enough, the best performance and recording here are of the finest work, the complete *Daphnis et Chloé* ballet. Martinon was a conductor of impeccable taste who fully understood this music and who here shapes the glorious score with great delicacy, seductiveness and tingling energy: it is a reading to rank among the most recommendable now available. The *Rapsodie espagnole* is perhaps less atmospheric, but clean-cut and lucid. The obstinately popular *Boléro* often proves difficult for conductors to find its right pace, but Martinon manages it admirably, on the way extracting some wry humour in its cumulative repetitions. The two Viennese-inspired works here come off less well because of their recorded quality, *Valses nobles et sentimentales* shrill in its *fortissimos*, *La valse* too harsh. A rarely-heard curiosity in this collection is the early *Shéhérazade* overture.

Ravel. WORKS FOR PIANO DUET. **Louis Lortie, Hélène Mercier** (pfs). Chandos CHAN8905.
Boléro. Introduction and Allegro. La valse. Ma mère l'oye. Rapsodie espagnole.

> ♪♪ 65' DDD 3/91

Ravel. MUSIC FOR TWO PIANOS. **Stephen Coombs, Christopher Scott** (pfs). Gamut Classics GAMCD517.
Frontispice. Introduction and Allegro. La valse. Rapsodie espagnole. Sites auriculaires—Entre cloches. Shéhérazade—Ouverture de féerie.

> ♪♪ 56' DDD 2/91

Louis Lortie is an excellent Ravel pianist and he and his fellow-Canadian Hélène Mercier have played as a duo since their student days in Montreal. Their performance of *Ma mère l'oye* is as delicate and tender as befits a piece written for children, but it also has the passion which is also part of a child's world, not least in the deep sense of joyful wonder of the final movement called "The Fairy Garden", which opens up to our inner vision the kind of childhood paradise that for all but the rarest mortals is forever lost, like innocence, as we reach adulthood. The *Rapsodie espagnole* is also done with great refinement, and although some collectors might like it more overtly sensual this is a performance to place beside the more familiar orchestral version of the same music. So is the *Boléro* in Ravel's own two-piano transcription, for although the piece might seem to depend wholly on orchestral colour it comes off well when played as excitingly as this at a fairly taut tempo. Again, the *Introduction and Allegro* may seem to depend on the sound of a chamber ensemble including harp, but this keyboard transcription made by the composer is beautiful. The programme ends with an account of *La valse* which offers playing that can only be described in superlatives or in terms of Dionysiac frenzy; this is a glowing, sumptuous dream-turning-to-nightmare that should not be missed by anyone who cares about Ravel's music and yet again reveals what an extraordinarily unsettling masterpiece this is. The recording made in the Snape Maltings is outstanding, detailed yet atmospheric.

Coombs and Scott formed a duo in 1985 and their outstanding début recording of Debussy will be found elsewhere in the *Guide*. Now they have turned their attention to Ravel, and the result is also very satisfying. They play with such style and sensitivity that the works in the composer's own piano transcriptions have more than documentary interest, while *Entre cloches* and

Frontispice are original works for two pianos. We may note, however, that *Ma mère l'oye* is not here, and nor is *Boléro*; the latter work was recorded and edited, but finally the artists and producer decided that it did not succeed in keyboard form, which one may regret since other duos, like Lortie and Mercier, have recorded it successfully. The richly atmospheric yet delicate recording is another plus for this attractive disc.

Ravel. PIANO WORKS, Volume 1. **Vlado Perlemuter.** Nimbus NIM5005. Items marked [a] from 2102 (7/79), [b] 2101 (7/79). Miroirs[a]. Jeux d'eau[b]. Pavane pour une infante défunte[b]. Gaspard de la nuit[b].

59' AAD 1/84 ♩ P

It would be foolish to deny that technical wizardry is essential to the performance of Ravel's piano music, so much of which was intended to stretch the limits of virtuosity, but depth of imagination and poetry are, if anything, even more important to its successful recreation. It is with this latter quality that Vlado Perlemuter scores so heavily. In his performances you can lose yourself, absorbed totally by the worlds he summons. His technical mastery lies less with fleet fingers than with supple pedalling and the enormous range of tone colours that he employs, with *pianissimo* chords that are distant soundings, and semiquaver passagework that ripples and scintillates. As one who studied with Ravel, Perlemuter has much to say about these works that is of archival as well as artistic value, but in, say, "Oiseaux tristes" from *Miroirs*, how Ravel might have wanted the work played on one or two occasions in the past is not as important as the depth of natural insight that this pianist brings to the score. Nimbus's preferred resonant acoustic suits both this music and Perlemuter's style of playing well, supporting the textures warmly without limiting clarity where it is required. The recording contributes substantially to the success of this altogether unique project.

Ravel. VOCAL AND ORCHESTRAL WORKS. [a]**Maria Ewing** (mez); **City of Birmingham Symphony Orchestra/Simon Rattle.** EMI CDC7 54204-2. Text and translation included. Fanfare pour "L'éventail de Jeanne". Shéhérazade[a]. Alborada del gracioso. Miroirs—La vallée des cloches (arr. Grainger). Ma mère l'oye. La valse.

75' DDD 8/91 ♩ P Ⓑ

A paean of British critical praise greets almost every new issue from this team with monotonous regularity, so it is gratifying, in this instance, to note *Diapason*'s (the French contemporary to *Gramophone*) reviewer finding Rattle's *Ma mère l'oye* of a "striking delicacy" and "releasing an indescribable emotion" (apologies to Rémy Louis for a wholly inadequate translation). In the past there have been instances of Rattle's intensive preparation for setting down a much loved masterpiece precluding spontaneity in the end result. Not here. Along with the customary refinement and revelation of texture, there is a sense of Rattle gauging the very individual

Simon Rattle   [photo: EMI/Macdomnic]

fantasy worlds of this varied programme with uncanny precision: an aptly child-like wonder for *Ma mère l'oye*'s fairy tale illustrations; the decadence and decay that drive *La valse* to its inevitable doom; and the sensual allure of the Orient in *Shéhérazade* providing a vibrant backdrop for soprano Maria Ewing's intimate confessions. Space does not permit enthusing about the three shorter items that make up this indispensable (and generously filled) disc, recorded with stunning realism. Try it for yourself and marvel at the astonishing range of Ravel's imagination.

Ravel. L'HEURE ESPAGNOLE. **Jane Berbié** (sop) Concepción; **Jean Giraudeau** (ten) Torquemada; **Gabriel Bacquier** (bar) Ramiro; **José van Dam** (bass-bar) Don Inigo Gomez; **Michel Sénéchal** (ten) Gonzalve; **French Radio National Orchestra/Lorin Maazel**. DG 423 719-2GH. Notes, text and translation included. From SLPM138 970 (10/65).

46' ADD 3/89

For genuinely witty operas *L'heure espagnole* is in a class of its own; and to do it justice it needs a conductor with an alert ear for all Ravel's minutely judged and ingeniously scored jests (the automata in the shop, the story of the toreador's watch, the jangling of the pendulum as the grandfather clock is hoisted on to the muleteer's brawny shoulder) and no conductor is more mentally alert than Maazel. It also requires a cast all of whom relish the verbal nuances and adopt the *quasi-parlando* style that the composer asked for; and these desiderata are met in this classic, and unequalled, 1965 performance. All the singers give excellent characterizations—Berbié as the frustrated and exasperated young wife, Bacquier as the simple, somewhat bemused muleteer who is happy to oblige, Sénéchal as the poet whose head is too far in the clouds to attend to practicalities, van Dam as the fatuous portly banker, and Giraudeau as the doddery old watchmaker who at the end shows an unexpectedly astute business sense. A delicious work, in a performance to savour.

Ravel. L'ENFANT ET LES SORTILEGES. **Françoise Ogéas** (sop) Child; **Jeanine Collard** (contr) Mother, Chinese cup, Dragonfly; **Jane Berbié** (sop) Sofa, She Cat, Squirrel, Shepherd; **Sylvaine Gilma** (sop) Fire, Princess, Nightingale; **Colette Herzog** (sop) Bat, Little Owl, Shepherdess; **Heinz Rehfuss** (bar) Armchair, Tree; **Camille Maurane** (bar) Grandfather Clock, Tom Cat; **Michel Sénéchal** (ten) Teapot, Little Old Man (Mr Arithmetic), Frog; **Chorus and Children's Voices of French Radio; French Radio National Orchestra/Lorin Maazel**. DG 423 718-2GH. Notes, text and translation included. From SLPM138675 (6/61).

43' ADD 3/89

This is a Desert Island Disc if ever there was one. Every musical and verbal point in Ravel's brilliantly ingenious, deliciously witty and entirely enchanting score is brought out by a well-nigh perfect cast, backed by orchestral playing of the first class; and the recording is as vivid as anyone could wish. The story is that of a petulant brat who breaks the china, pulls the cat's tail, pricks the pet squirrel with a pen-nib, puts the fire out by upsetting the kettle on it, tears the wallpaper and his books and snaps off the pendulum of the grandfather clock—only to find that all these come to life and turn on him. Their anger is appeased only when he tends the squirrel's paw; and finally the naughty child, having seen the error of his ways, falls tearfully into his mother's arms. Everyone will have their own favourite passages but the last pages of the opera, in particular, are hauntingly beautiful. An absolute gem of a disc.

Thomas Ravenscroft

British c.1590-c.1633

Ravenscroft. THERE WERE THREE RAVENS. **Consort of Musicke/ Anthony Rooley.** Virgin Classics Veritas VC7 91217-2. Texts included.
A Round of three Country dances in one. A wooing Song of a Yeoman of Kents
Sonne. Browning Madame. The crowning of Belphebe. The Cryers Song of
Cheape-Side. Laboravi in gemitu meo. The Marriage of the Frogge and the
Mouse. Martin said to his man. Musing mine owne selfe all alone. Ne laeteris
inimica mea. Of all the birds that ever I see. There were three ravens. Three
blinde Mice. To morrow the Fox will come to towne. Wee be Souldiers three.
The wooing of Hodge and Malkyn. Yonder comes a courteous knight.
Instrumental works—Fancy No. 1. Fantasia No. 4. Viol Fancy a 5.

61' DDD 8/91

Thomas Ravenscroft was a learned musician (even a pedant in some respects)
who is perhaps best known for his 1621 collection of psalms; and to illustrate
that side of him this disc contains two deeply expressive Latin motets and some
attractive and skilfully written fantasias for viols. However, as a likeable and
lively-minded person, he also delighted in writing music for entertainment,
"mirth and jocund melody", and in 1609 printed the first known collection in
England of catches and rounds, under the title *Pammelia*. From this and two
similar subsequent volumes the Consort of Musicke have made a selection which
they themselves obviously thoroughly enjoyed performing and whose enjoyment
is infectious. (The assumption of a variety of accents, from Cockney for a
Cheapside crier's song to a Somerset-dialect wooing dialogue for once does not
seem an irritating gimmick.) Anthony Rooley has skilfully arranged the
programme to present a diversity of types, pace and scoring; but among the
highlights here are the melancholy *Musing mine owne selfe all alone* and *There were
three ravens* and the merry *The Marriage of the Frogge and the Mouse* and the saucy
Yonder comes a courteous knight.

Max Reger

Refer to Index   *German 1873-1916*

Steve Reich

American 1936-

Reich. Different Trains (1988)[a]. Electric Counterpoint (1987)[b]. [a]**Kronos
Quartet** (David Harrington, John Sherba, vns; Hank Dutt, va; Joan Jeanrenaud,
vc); [b]**Pat Metheny** (gtr). Elektra-Nonesuch 7559-79176-2.

42' DDD 6/89

The name 'minimalist' clings to Steve Reich, but in fact there's little that can be
called minimal in works of the richness and comparative complexity of *Octet* or
The Desert Music, where all that's left of his earlier style is a taste for pulsating
rhythms, short-term circular repetitions and a sonorous harmoniousness. *Different
Trains* also combines strong ideas with superb craftsmanship, and it is carried
out with total confidence. The programme is autobiographical: Reich evokes
his long childhood train journeys across America in the aftermath of the
Second World War, and ponders on the parallel but enforced train journeys
undertaken by Jewish refugees in Europe. A tinge of melancholy darkens the
otherwise excited mood of music, which draws most of its imagery from the
driving motor-rhythms of steam trains, constantly punctuated by the evocative
sound of whistles, and scraps of recorded interviews. *Different Trains* is given an
exemplary reading by the Kronos Quartet, and it is nicely complemented by

Pat Metheny's performance of the short *Electric Counterpoint* for live and multi-tracked acoustic guitars.

Ottorino Respighi

Respighi. Symphonic Poems—Pines of Rome; Fountains of Rome; Roman Festivals. **Montreal Symphony Orchestra/Charles Dutoit.** Decca 410 145-2DH. From SXDL7591 (9/83).

60' DDD 11/83		Ⓑ

Respighi. Symphonic Poems—Pines of Rome; Fountains of Rome. The birds—suite[a]. [a]**William Bennett** (fl); **London Symphony Orchestra/István Kertesz.** Decca Weekend 425 507-2DC. From SXL6401 (7/69).

56' ADD 4/90	£ ⁹ᵖ	Ⓑ

Respighi's three orchestral showpieces inspired by Rome have often been dismissed as merely musical picture-postcards, but in ripely committed performances like this, stunningly recorded, there are few works to match them in showing off the glories of a modern orchestra in full cry. Dutoit's performance is as brilliant as any, but it also finds a vein of warm expressiveness in the writing as well as rhythmic point, so adding to the vividness of atmosphere. This is a work which benefits more than most from CD, when quite apart from the quality of recording over the widest range of dynamics and frequency, the perils of LP end-of-side distortion are eliminated, and separate bands allow you to pick out individual movements in each work, even though the music is continuous.

The musicality and keen attention to detail of Kertesz's performances stand out against some of the more superficially glossy and brilliant versions on disc. The joy and exuberance of children playing is marvellously evoked in the 'Petrushka'-like opening movement of *Pines*, and in the sensuous and lovely "Pines of the Janiculum" Kertész creates a magical nocturnal atmosphere in which there are some seductively expressive solos from the clarinet, violin and cello. "Pines on the Appian Way" lacks perhaps the sheer excitement of Dutoit's recording, but nevertheless succeeds in its objective of sending tingles up and down ones spine. *Fountains* is equally as impressive; the serenity of the gently flowing "Fountains of the Valle Guilia at dawn" is gorgeously captured, and the full virtuosity of the LSO can be heard in the stormier waters of "The Fountain of Trevi at Mid-day". The ever popular suite *The birds* provides an excellent contrast to the richly scored symphonic poems. These delightful and charming arrangements of compositions by seventeenth and eighteenth century composers (Rameau, Pasquini, etc.) receive superb performances, with some exceptionally fine playing from the wind section. The recording is vividly realistic with a very wide dynamic range. A classic recording.

Respighi. The birds. Ancient airs and dances for lute. **Australian Chamber Orchestra/Christopher Lyndon Gee.** Omega OCD191007.

73' DDD 8/89	

Respighi's skill as a transcriber of other men's music sometimes makes us forget his own real creative gifts as exemplified in his evocative *Pines of Rome* and other orchestral works. *The birds* is a suite consisting of something between transcriptions of older music and original pieces, rather as happens in Stravinsky's *Pulcinella*, and the result is delightful. Thus, "The Dove", a seventeenth-century lute piece by Jacques Gallot, is transformed into an expressive oboe solo (beautifully played here) with a delicate, twittering accompaniment, while "The Hen" comes from a keyboard piece by Rameau and "The Nightingale" is an atmospheric nocturnal arrangement of an old English folk-tune. The scoring is charmingly imaginative and a wide variety of instruments are heard, including brass, harp and metallophones. The *Ancient airs and dances* are rather more straightforward as transcriptions, but even here there is charming invention. The Australian Chamber Orchestra under the stylish direction of Christopher Lyndon Gee proves to be an expert, refined body of players and the recording, made in Sydney, is successfully balanced with good texture and dynamic range.

Respighi. Violin Sonata in B minor.
R. Strauss. Violin Sonata in E flat major, Op. 18. **Kyung-Wha Chung** (vn); **Krystian Zimerman** (pf). DG 427 617-2GH.

> 52' 2/90 ♩P ♩S

This is wonderful violin playing, as richly romantic as both works often demand, but with a wide range of colour to underline the subtleties and the varying tones of voice that both employ. To add to the coupling's appeal, Kyung-Wha Chung's pianist is a musician of exceptional subtlety who is clearly as intent as she is to demonstrate that both sonatas deserve a position much closer to the centre of the repertory than they have so far been given. In the Strauss in particular they succeed eloquently. It is often described as the last work of his apprentice years, but in this performance the mature Strauss steps out from the shadow of Brahms so often and so proudly that its stature as his 'real' Op. 1 seems confirmed. The Respighi is a lesser piece, no doubt, but its melodies and its rhapsodic manner are attractive, and Chung's warm response to Respighi's idiomatic way with the instrument (he was a violinist himself) is infectious. Good and natural-sounding balance between violin and piano is not easy to achieve, but the recording here, significantly helped by Zimerman's combination of poetry and alert responsiveness, is outstandingly successful.

Julius Reubke *Refer to Index* *German 1834-1858*

Nicolay Rimsky-Korsakov *Russian 1844-1908*

Rimsky-Korsakov. Scheherazade, Op. 35. Capriccio espagnol, Op. 34. **London Symphony Orchestra/Sir Charles Mackerras.** Telarc CD80208.

> 60' DDD 10/90 ♩P ♩S Ⓑ

Rimsky-Korsakov. Scheherazade, Op. 35[b]. [a]**Beecham Choral Society; Royal Philharmonic Orchestra/Sir Thomas Beecham.**
Borodin. PRINCE IGOR—Polovtsian Dances[a]. EMI CDC7 47717-2.
Item marked [a] from SXLP30171 (10/74), [b] ASD251 (10/58).

> 58' ADD 9/87 Ⓑ

Sir Charles Mackerras throws himself into this music with expressive abandon, but allies it to control so that every effect is realized and the London Symphony Orchestra play this familiar music as if they were discovering it afresh. Together they produce performances that are both vivid and thoughtful, while the solo violin in *Scheherazade*, who represents the young queen whose storytelling skills prolong and finally save her life in the court of the cruel Sultan Shahriar (portrayed by powerful brass), is seductively and elegantly played by Kees

Sir Thomas Beecham   *[photo: EMI*

Hulsmann, not least at the wonderfully peaceful end to the whole work. The finale featuring a storm and shipwreck is superbly done, the wind and brass bringing one to the edge of one's seat and reminding us that Rimsky-Korsakov served in the Russian Navy and well knew the beauty and danger of the sea. This sensuous and thrilling work needs spectacular yet detailed sound, and that is what it gets here, the 1990 recording in Walthamstow Town Hall being highly successful and giving us a CD that many collectors will choose to use as a demonstration disc to impress their friends. The performance and recording of the *Capriccio espagnol* is no less of a success, and this issue is worth every penny of its full price.

Beecham's classic version of *Scheherazade* deserves a special place in every discerning CD collection. Over 30 years have elapsed since this recording, but the passage of time has had no detrimental effect, and it is still capable of holding its own against even the most recent of digital rivals. This is a spell-binding performance of considerable depth and power, made even greater by a recording that has warmth, clarity and wide dynamic range. The wonderfully exotic atmosphere is captured exceedingly well, helped by some marvellous orchestral playing: the solo bassoon's characterful portrait of the Prince in the opening of the second section; the beautiful arabesque woodwind passages, and not least the beguiling performance of the solo violin (played here by Steven Staryk) representing Scheherazade's voice as it leads us through this colourful landscape. Beecham's performance of Borodin's "Polovtsian Dances" have great energy and vitality, but the recorded sound is less flattering here with an element of coarseness and a noticeable amount of tape hiss.

Joaquin Rodrigo

Spanish 1901-

Rodrigo. Concierto de Aranjuez (1939). Fantasía para un gentilhombre (1955). **John Williams** (gtr); **Philharmonia Orchestra/Louis Frémaux.** CBS Masterworks CD37848. From IM37848 (7/84).

53'   DDD   7/85

Rodrigo. Concierto de Aranjuez. Fantasía para un gentilhombre. **Villa-Lobos.** Guitar Concerto. **Göran Söllscher** (gtr); **Orpheus Chamber Orchestra.** DG 429 232-2GH.

65'   DDD   6/90

The *Concierto de Aranjuez* is a romantic work whose success remains unparalleled. Rodrigo's recipe for both works on this recording is to express his reverence for past traditions in terms of his own, neo-classical musical language—lush tunes and harmonies, some courtly formality and a soupçon of mischievous spikiness. The *Fantasía* (the *Gentilhombre* is Segovia) pays its respects also to a great guitarist of the seventeenth century, Gaspar Sanz, some of whose themes are winsomely reworked by Rodrigo. Both works call for a high degree of virtuosity but difficulties present no problem to Williams, who brings to both pieces the proper blend of expressiveness and poise. To describe a recording as 'vivid' has become a cliché but in this case it is inevitable.

All three works on the DG issue contain elements of Latin fire and temperament, fully exploited by many other soloists, but Söllscher, a Swede of aristocratic musicality, also shows the other side of their coin in his sensitive, thoughtful and immaculately played performances. The Orpheus Chamber Orchestra manage wonderfully well without a conductor (so too did their eponym!), following Söllscher with the attentiveness of members of a string quartet, and the recording engineers are equally alert to everyone else concerned. These are 'the thinking man's' versions of these three works.

Sigmund Romberg   *Hungarian/American 1887-1951*

THE STUDENT PRINCE (Romberg/Donelly). Cast includes **Marilyn Hill Smith, Rosemary Ashe, Diana Montague, David Rendall, Bonaventura Bottone, Neil Jenkins, Jason Howard, Norman Bailey, Donald Maxwell; Ambrosian Chorus; Philharmonia Orchestra/John Owen Edwards.** TER Classics CDTER2 1172.

② 1h 40' DDD 3/91

Although we think of the 1920s as a period of great success for the musical comedies of the Gershwins and Rodgers and Hart it was, too, a glorious decade for Sigmund Romberg, who scored three personal triumphs with his operettas *The Student Prince*, *The Desert Song* and *New Moon*. Each of these scores exudes an air of confidence both in the sweep of their melodic lines, and the vigorous choral writing that has stood the test of time rather better than the flimsy story lines that support them. In order to include as much of Romberg's score as feasible, it has been necessary to include some rather embarrassing cues that certainly defeats one of the more senior members of the cast, which in the main is the same team that was assembled by TER for their outstanding recording of *Kismet*, with John Owen Edwards once again drawing assured playing from the Philharmonia. In addition to David Rendall sporting boyish good humour in the title role, there are distinctive contributions from Bonaventura Bottone leading the Drinking song, Norman Bailey in "Golden days" and a lovely version of the Lehár-like duet, "Just we two" from Diana Montague and Steven Page. The one slight disappointment in this line-up is Marilyn Hill Smith who on this occasion can't escape a charge of blandness, and a touch of shrillness on the high Cs of "Come boys, let's be gay boys". That apart, there is no hesitation in extending a warm welcome to this much-needed new recording which surprises more than once by the charm of its lesser known numbers: the Act 2 gavotte, for instance, and the sophistication of Romberg's handling of the score's big duet, "Deep in my heart" and the humorous chorus, "Student life".

Moritz Rosenthal   *Refer to Index*   *Polish 1862-1946*

Gioachino Rossini

Rossini. BALLET MUSIC. **Monte Carlo National Opera Orchestra/ Antonio de Almeida.** Philips 422 843-2PBA. From 6780 027 (12/76).
Le Siège de Corinthe. Moïse et Pharaon. Guillaume Tell. Otello.

> 73' ADD 12/76

Being an Italian composer, Rossini devoted most of his career to writing operas (and enjoying good food and wine) and since he worked latterly in Paris he also composed dances to satisfy the demand of the Parisian public for a balletic element even in serious pieces of music theatre such as his (and Verdi's) *Otello*.

Gioachino Rossini

The *Siege of Corinth* was the thirty-sixth of his 39 operas and includes his first French 'ballet', consisting of just two dances. The story of the great Hebrew prophet Moses in his next opera is epic, but that did not stop him from providing lilting dance music here too, borrowed from two much earlier operas hopefully unknown to his French audience. *William Tell*, his last opera, tells of the heroic Swiss patriot, and here too the dance element is prominent, with the well known *Pas de six* especially attractive and a 'Tyrolean choir' singing in the next number, while the *Otello* music was again raided from early operas for a Paris production in 1844. For a sheer feeling of *joie de vivre* Rossini is a composer hard to beat and this is a delightful collection, played with great style and nicely recorded.

Rossini. OVERTURES. **Orpheus Chamber Orchestra.** DG 415 363-2GH.
Tancredi. L'Italiana in Algeri. L'inganno felice. La scala di seta. Il barbiere di Siviglia. Il Signor Bruschino. La cambiale di matrimonio. Il turco in Italia.

> 52' DDD 10/85

Rossini. OVERTURES. **Philharmonia Orchestra/Herbert von Karajan.**
EMI CDM7 63113-2. Items marked [a] from Columbia SAX2378 (3/61), [b] SAX2274 (9/59).
Overtures—L'Italiana in Algeri[a]; Semiramide[a]; Il barbiere di Siviglia[a]; Guillaume Tell[a]; La scala di seta[a]; La gazza ladra[a]. GUILLAUME TELL—Overture; Pas de trois et choeur tyrolien[b].

> 64' ADD 11/89

There are numerous collections of Rossini overtures in the catalogue, but this DG one is special: not only is the recording first-rate, presenting the orchestra with a splendidly tangible sense of presence, but the performances exude life and delight in the music. The Orpheus CO plays without conductor, yet the ensemble is exact, expression and tempo fluctuations are beautifully fluid, and balance is just right for these very theatrical works. Rossini would rarely have had a large orchestra available to him in the Italian theatre pit of his time, and

the wind-dominated texture that is heard from this chamber ensemble is probably closer to his expectations than the string-heavy balance of most symphony orchestras. The woodwind playing here is warm and full of individuality, and each work is driven by a lively sense of rhythm that only flags on the odd few occasions. What is perhaps most refreshing about this issue is the way the inherent humour of the music is allowed to raise an ongoing chuckle, rather than being forced to a belly laugh.

Background hiss is one of the few indicators of the age of Karajan's otherwise vivacious and full-bodied recordings. This is vintage Karajan, at ease with the orchestra and the music, prepared to rest on his heels and let the natural good humour of the music make its own effect. He takes the traditional, concert view of these overtures, treating them as mini tone-poems. The performances are none the worse for that, and they provide ideal home listening, with lashings of dynamic contrast and well-paced crescendos, full-toned woodwind solos and weighty string playing. The "Pas de trois et choeur tyrolien" from *Guillaume Tell*, added to make up time on this CD, make an effective intermezzo for the programme and provide the listener who only knows the Overture with an intriguing taste of the opera's other delights. The Philharmonia plays all with practised ease, obviously pleased to find their conductor in such an affable mood.

Rossini. Stabat mater. **Helen Field** (sop); **Della Jones** (mez); **Arthur Davies** (ten); **Roderick Earle** (bass); **London Symphony Chorus; City of London Sinfonia/Richard Hickox.** Chandos CHAN8780. Text and translation included.

> 59' DDD 3/90

This used to be a ripe nineteenth-century favourite, and many a proudly bound vocal score at present languishing in a pile of second-hand music would testify to a time when its owner felt enabled, with its help, to combine the pleasure of church-going with the duty of attendance at the opera. The words are those of Jacopone da Todi's sacred poem, but Rossini's music is dramatic, exciting and sometimes almost indecently tuneful. Certainly the soloists have to be recruited from the opera company; the soprano who launches out into the "Inflammatus" must be generously supplied with high Cs as well as the power to shoot them over the heads of full choir and orchestra, while the tenor at one alarming moment is asked for a top D flat and has to ring out the melody of his "Cujus animam" with tone to match the trumpets which introduce it. In all four soloists, grace and technical accomplishment are as important as range and power; they must also have the taste and discipline to work harmoniously as a quartet. In this recording they certainly do that, and neither are they lacking in range or technique; if there is a limitation it is rather in richness of tone and in the heroic quality which the solos mentioned above ideally need. Even so, individually and collectively, they compare well with most of their competitors on record, and the choral and orchestral work under Hickox is outstanding.

Rossini. Petite messe solennelle. **Helen Field** (sop); **Anne-Marie Owens** (mez); **Edmund Barham** (ten); **John Tomlinson** (bass); **David Nettle, Richard Markham** (pfs); **Peter King** (harmonium); **City of Birmingham Symphony Orchestra Chorus/Simon Halsey.** Conifer CDCF184. Text and translation included.

> 78' DDD 10/90

Of Rossini's later works, none has won such affection from the general listening public as the *Petite messe solennelle*. He called it "the final sin of my old age" and, as with the other of his *pêches de vieillesse*, he declined to have it published. Editions issued in 1869, the year after his death, failed to retain his original scoring and contained numerous inaccuracies, yet these have been the basis of most subsequent recordings of the work. This disc presents the mass in a revelatory new Oxford University Press edition by Nancy Fleming, using two pianos in addition to a fine, French harmonium. That alone would mark it out for prime consideration, even if the reading were only passable, but here we have the bonus of dedicated, heartfelt performances from all involved. Above all, the scale of the work is finely captured—it was intended for chamber performance and both writing and scoring reflect the intimacy of Rossini's ideas. Much praise must go to Simon Halsey for so clearly establishing the parameters for this performance, and to the recording engineers for making it all seem so convincing. The whole issue establishes a new benchmark for assessing recordings of this work.

Rossini. OPERA ARIAS. **Della Jones** (mez); [a]**Richard Hickox Singers; City of London Sinfonia/Richard Hickox.** Chandos CHAN8865. Texts and translations included.
L'ITALIANA IN ALGERI—Quanta roba! ... Cruda sorte! Amor tiranno![a]. LA DONNA DEL LAGO—Mura felici ... O quante lacrime finor versai. IL SIGNOR BRUSCHINO—Ah, voi condur volete ... Ah, donate i caro sposo. ADELAIDE DI BORGOGNA—Soffri la tua sventura; Salve, Italia, un dì regnante[a]. OTELLO—Assisa apiè d'un salice (with Carol Smith, sop). IL BARBIERE DI SIVIGLIA—Una voce poco fà. BIANCA E FALLIERO—Tu non sai qual colpo atroce. LA CENERENTOLA—Nacqui all'affanno ... Non più mesta[a] (Smith; Katherine Steffan, mez; Harry Nicholl, Gerard Finley, tens; Simon Birchall, bass).

· ·: 68' DDD 2/91

In the court of the mezzo-soprano, Rossini would be composer-laureate. He wrote for the mezzo voice most extensively and excitingly, providing opportunities for comedy and pathos, for a pure, even melodic line and for brilliant displays of virtuosity. He exploited the whole vocal range, two octaves or more, yet was considerate in keeping the 'lie' or *tessitura* of the notes within the comfortable middle of the voice, avoiding strain at either extreme. Above all, he put the mezzo-soprano into the centre of the stage: for once, she, and not the full, high soprano, would be the star. Over the last 30 or 40 years many famous singers have been associated with these roles. Marilyn Horne and Teresa Berganza perhaps come to mind first, while most recently added to the line has been Cecilia Bartolli. None has coped more ably with the technical demands than Della Jones. She is fluent and precise, and exercises an easy mastery over the most difficult passage-work. She can express tenderness and concern (as in *La cenerentola*), but most of all these are *spirited* performances, some of them, too, in little-known music such as the arias from *Adelaide di Borgogna* and *Bianca e Falliero*. The acoustic may be a trifle too reverberant, but both the singing and the playing are so well defined that any loss of clarity is minimal.

Rossini. LE COMTE ORY. **John Aler** (ten) Le Comte Ory; **Sumi Jo** (sop) Comtesse Adèle; **Diana Montague** (mez) Isolier; **Gino Quilico** (bar) Raimbaud; **Gille Cachemaille** (bar) La Gouverneur; **Maryse Castets** (sop) Alice; **Raquel Pierotti** (mez) Ragonde; **Francis Dudziac** (ten) First Chevalier; **Nicholas Rivenq** (bar) Second Chevalier; **Chorus and Orchestra of Lyon Opera/John Eliot Gardiner.** Philips 422 406-2PH2. Notes, text and translation included.

· ·: ② 132' DDD 10/89

Rossini's last comedy had its première in 1828 and for English audiences it came delightfully to new life at Glyndebourne in 1955. The recording made under Vittorio Gui with the Glyndebourne cast deservedly keeps its place in the affections of many listeners, but this recent version has great merit of its own, including some excellent singing, a fuller text and clearer, more spacious, recorded sound. More than most, it is an opera that needs to be seen, especially the part where Ory and his men disguised as nuns are solicitously cared for by the ladies whom they hope to vanquish in the few hours remaining before their husbands return from the Crusades. Still, all is played vividly, and the ear catches the infection of laughter much as sight does in the theatre. Gardiner's direction has pace and point, and his young-sounding cast have a natural grace and lightness of touch. Outstanding among them is the Korean-born soprano Sumi Jo, charming in tone and style, highly accomplished in the rapid scale-work and high coloratura abounding in her part. Her duet with Ory in Act 2 is one of the high-spots; one among many, it has to be added, for all of the principal singers add something distinctive and delightful when their turn comes. Best of all perhaps is the concerted work of the whole company in the finale of Act 1: the very essence of Rossinian comedy is here, and one can hardly imagine a performance more happily combining refinement and exhilaration.

Rossini. LA GAZZA LADRA. **Katia Ricciarelli** (sop) Ninetta; **William Matteuzzi** (ten) Giannetto; **Samuel Ramey** (bass) Gottardo; **Bernadette Manca di Nissa** (contr) Pippo; **Luciana d'Intinto** (mez) Lucia; **Ferruccio Furlanetto** (bar) Fernando Villabella; **Roberto Coviello** (bass) Fabrizio Vingradito; **Oslavio di Credico** (ten) Isacco; **Pierre Lefebre** (ten) Antonio; **Francesco Musinu** (bass) Giorgio; **Marcello Lippi** (bass) Ernesto; **Prague Philharmonic Choir; Turin Radio Symphony Orchestra/Gianluigi Gelmetti.** Sony Classical CD45850. Notes, text and translation included. Recorded at performances in the Teatro Rossini, Pesaro in August 1989.

③ 3h 14' DDD 10/90

Recorded live during the 1989 Rossini Opera Festival in Pesaro, and suffused with the atmosphere of the venue, this performance sports a first-class line-up of soloists, a strong chorus and an enthusiastic orchestra. Ricciarelli, though perhaps a little rich-toned for the role of a country girl, stylishly ornaments her part and brings great authority and conviction to the role. Similarly, Samuel Ramey, as the Mayor, is particularly telling; but even the smallest parts are effectively done. The score employed here is unusually close to that used when this "Melodrama in due atti" first saw the light of day at La Scala in 1817, and as such gives us a good idea of Rossini's intentions for the work, unencumbered by the 'improvements' of later hands; the sentiments of the original play by d'Aubigny and Caigniez, that so moved Parisian audiences of 1815 and 1816, are once again made vital and relevant. Most importantly, the conductor, Gianluigi Gelmetti, must be commended for pacing the opera so astutely: Act 1 seems relatively low-key at first hearing, but emotion steadily builds in the long Act 2 to culminate in a stunning finale.

Rossini. GUILLAUME TELL. **Gabriel Bacquier** (bar) Guillaume Tell; **Montserrat Caballé** (sop) Mathilde; **Nicolai Gedda** (ten) Arnold; **Kolos Kovacs** (bass) Walter Furst; **Gwynne Howell** (bass) Melcthal; **Mady Mesplé** (sop) Jemmy; **Jocelyne Taillon** (mez) Hedwige; **Louis Hendrikx** (bass) Gessler; **Charles Burles** (ten) Fisherman; **Ricardo Cassinelli** (ten) Rudolph; **Nicholas Christou** (bar) Leuthold; **Ambrosian Opera Chorus; Royal Philharmonic Orchestra/Lamberto Gardelli.** EMI CMS7 69951-2. Notes and text included. From SLS970 (11/73).

④ 3h 58' ADD 3/89

Rossini's last opera was not only his grandest but also the very epitome of operatic grandeur. In length alone it involves a formidable commitment, but more fundamental are the span of the scenes, the amplitude of the forces employed and the range of mood and feeling from simple rustic happiness to a passionate affirmation of liberty hard-won in the face of cruelty and personal loss. Near the end of the whole epic work, as the sky clears, literally and figuratively, there comes a passage of inspired sublimity, with an effect worthy of *Fidelio*; it also is built with Rossini's favourite device of the crescendo, but having its excitement now transfigured and ennobled, so that even if Rossini had composed more operas one feels he could hardly have gone beyond this. Though frequently given in Italian, it was written to a French text and the language gives a strong initial advantage to this recording over its notable rivals. Among the principals Bacquier is a dignified, elderly-sounding Tell, Caballé a tender yet patrician Mathilde, Gedda a lyrical Arnold who fortifies his voice manfully for the heroic passages. Gardelli conducts with control and flexibility; the orchestral playing and chorus work are alike admirable, as are the clarity and sense of presence in the recorded sound.

Rossini. SEMIRAMIDE. **Dame Joan Sutherland** (sop) Semiramide; **Marilyn Horne** (mez) Arsace; **Joseph Rouleau** (bass) Assur; **John Serge** (ten) Idreno; **Patricia Clark** (sop) Azema; **Spiro Malas** (bass) Oroe; **Michael Langdon** (bass) Ghost of Nino; **Leslie Fryson** (ten) Mitrane; **Ambrosian Opera Chorus; London Symphony Orchestra/Richard Bonynge.** Decca 425 481-2DM3. Notes, text and translation included. From SET317/19 (10/66).

③ 2h 48' ADD 2/90 £ ⑨ P

Wagner thought it represented all that was bad about Italian opera and Kobbe's *Complete Opera Book* proclaimed that it had had its day—but then added what looked like second thoughts, saying that "were a soprano and contralto to appear in conjunction in the firmament the opera might be successfully revived". That was exactly what happened in the 1960s, when both Sutherland and Horne were in superlative voice and, with Richard Bonynge, were taking a prominent part in the reintroduction of so many nineteenth-century operas which the world thought it had outgrown. This recording brought a good deal of enlightenment in its time. For one thing, here was vocal music of such 'impossible' difficulty being sung with brilliance by the two principal women and with considerable skill by the men, less well-known as they were. Then it brought to many listeners the discovery that, so far from being a mere show-piece, the opera contained ensembles that possessed quite compelling dramatic intensity. People who had heard of the duet "Giorno d'orroré" (invariably encored in Victorian times) were surprised to find it remarkably unshowy and even expressive of the ambiguous feelings of mother and son in their extraordinary predicament. It will probably be a long time before this recording is superceded, admirably vivid as it is in sound, finely conducted and magnificently sung.

Rossini. IL SIGNOR BRUSCHINO. **Bruno Praticò** (bar) Gaudenzio; **Natale di Carolis** (bass-bar) Bruschino padre; **Patrizia Orciani** (sop) Sofia; **Luca Canonici** (ten) Florville; **Pietro Spangnoli** (bar) Filiberto; **Katia Lytting** (mez) Marianna; **Fulvio Massa** (ten) Bruschino figlio, Commissario; **Turin Philharmonic Orchestra/Marcello Viotti.** Claves CD50-8904/5. Text included.

② 84' DDD 10/89

It may take a wise father to know his own son, but even a fool can recognize a complete impostor: that, roughly, is the upshot of this little comedy in which the young Rossini tried out several ideas that were going to come in handy later on, and which is still revived from time to time to act as a pleasant part of a double-bill or a curtain-raiser. It is a pity that this recording could not have run in harness, for 84 minutes on two discs hardly constitutes good value these days. Still, the performance is likeable and at present has no competitor on CD. The singers are young and fresh-voiced; they miss a few tricks which their elders might have brought to the catch-phrases and the supposedly unexpected turn of events, but we are spared the conventional buffo clowning, with its exaggerated diction and falsetto squeaks. The best feature is the playing of the accomplished Turin orchestra under Marcello Viotti. The score is delightfully melodious and inventive, and the delicacy of orchestral texture as well as the spring of its rhythms can be well appreciated here, starting, of course, with the Overture and its famous raps of the second violins' bows on their music-stands which brought the musicians out on strike at the première in 1813.

Rossini. IL TURCO IN ITALIA. **Maria Callas** (sop) Fiorilla; **Nicolai Gedda** (ten) Narciso; **Nicola Rossi-Lemeni** (bass) Selim; **Mariano Stabile** (bar) Poet; **Franco Calabrese** (bass) Geronio; **Jolanda Gardino** (mez) Zaida; **Piero De Palma** (ten) Albazar; **Chorus and Orchestra of La Scala, Milan/ Gianandrea Gavazzeni.** EMI mono CDS7 49344-8. Notes, text and translation included. From Columbia 33CXS1289, 33CX1290/91 (10/55).

② 1h 53' ADD 12/87 £ ⁹ₚ

The triumph of *L'Italiana in Algeri* in 1813 prompted Rossini to write a successor the following year. The ideas are similar, the basic propositions being that foreigners are funny (especially if from the Middle East or the wrong side of the Mediterranean) and that old gentlemen must look out for trouble if they associate with young ladies who are both pretty and witty. The orchestral score sparkles and charms, the principal roles demand plenty of personality as well as vocal accomplishment, and the ensembles gather momentum with the madcap exhilaration of a fairground roundabout. It may seem strange to come upon Maria Callas in the midst of all this, for comedy may not appear to be an element in which she would thrive. But in fact she succeeds brilliantly, not only in her solos and in the deft inflections of recitative but also in ensemble-work as a member of the company, playing her part in happy collaboration with the others. These include the veteran Mariano Stabile and the young Nicolai Gedda, neither of whom has as much to do as one would wish; Rossi-Lemeni as the Turk and Franco Calabrese as the old husband sing with zest, and all take heart from the practised skill of Gavazzeni at the helm. The old recording comes up like new, and though some cuts have been made in the score they hardly detract from the enjoyment of so polished an entertainment.

Rossini. IL BARBIERE DI SIVIGLIA. **Thomas Allen** (bar) Figaro; **Agnes Baltsa** (mez) Rosina; **Domenico Trimarchi** (bar) Dr Bartolo; **Robert Lloyd** (bass) Don Basilio; **Francisco Araiza** (ten) Count Almaviva; **Matthew Best** (bass) Fiorello; **Sally Burgess** (mez) Berta; **John Noble** (bar) Official; **Ambrosian Opera Chorus; Academy of St Martin in the Fields/Sir Neville Marriner** with **Nicholas Kraemer** (fp). Philips 411 058-2PH3. Notes, text and translation included. From 6769 100 (6/83).

③ 2h 27' DDD 4/84 Ⓑ

The Overture gives the clue: this is to be a real *Barbiere* on the boards. Incisive, sprung rhythms, cheeky, rather than seductive, woodwind and a sense of fun as much as of intrigue characterize this performance from start to finish. It has a lot to do with Marriner's phrasing and rollicking sense of Rossinian style, to which the orchestra of the Academy respond so readily. But the barometer of this performance is its recitatives, and with Nicholas Kraemer's astute playing of a sweet-toned fortepiano in place of a spidery harpsichord, the voltage of the Rosina/Figaro encounters and the comic timing of Bartolo and Basilio is excitingly high. It keeps the soloists on their toes, too; and they are a strong team. The outstanding recommendation of this *Barbiere,* though, is its Rosina. From the first bars of "Una voce poco fa", Agnes Baltsa shows that this "dolce amorosa" can turn to the sting of a viper, too: the dark recesses of her chest voice and the brilliance of her high register flash in turn to follow every volatile mood of the role in a searching performance of superb dramatic timing.

Rossini. IL VIAGGIO A REIMS. **Cecilia Gasdia** (sop) Corinna; **Katia Ricciarelli** (sop) Madama Cortese; **Lella Cuberli** (sop) Contessa di Folleville; **Lucia Valentini Terrani** (mez) Marchesa Melibea; **Edoardo Gimenez** (ten) Cavalier Belfiore; **Francisco Araiza** (ten) Conte di Libenskof; **Samuel Ramey** (bass) Lord Sidney; **Ruggero Raimondi** (bass) Don Profondo; **Enzo Dara** (bar) Barone di Trombonok; **Leo Nucci** (bar) Don Alvaro; **Prague Philharmonic Chorus; Chamber Orchestra of Europe/Claudio Abbado.** DG 415 498-2GH3. Notes, text and translation included. Recorded at performances at the 1984 Rossini Opera Festival, Pesaro, Italy.

③ 2h 16' DDD 1/86

Il Viaggio à Reims   [*photo: Capellini-Venezia*]

Composed as an elaborate and sophisticated entertainment for the coronation of Charles X, *Il viaggio a Reims* marked Rossini's début in Paris as the international superstar which his dazzling and innovative Italian career had justly made him. Musically it is bewitching: an intoxicant that gives sustained sensuous pleasure quite independent of the libretto. The rediscovery and assembly of the complete score, which Rossini partially dismantled and expertly reallocated to *Le Comte Ory,* is the brilliant scholarly achievement of Janet Johnson and Philip Gosset. The set is also a triumph for Claudio Abbado, the finest Rossini conductor of our day, and for DG whose munificence helped make possible the assembly of that dazzling array of vocal talent which the piece needs. The recording is a miracle of clarity and brilliance, with the kind of electricity in the atmosphere which is virtually impossible to reproduce in studio conditions.

Albert Roussel

French 1869-1937

Roussel. Symphonies—No. 1 in D minor, Op. 7, "Le poème de la forêt"; No. 3 in G minor, Op. 42. **French National Orchestra/Charles Dutoit.** Erato 2292-45254-2. From NUM75283 (2/87).

59' DDD 6/87

Roussel's First Symphony is not a symphony in the usual sense at all, but more a cycle of four tone-poems. When the first of these, "Soir d'été", was performed Roussel did not envisage any further seasonal depictions of nature, but after "Renouveau" was written it was quickly followed by "Forêt d'hiver" and "Faunes et Dryades"—this last piece having autumnal connotations to complete Roussel's own 'Four Seasons'. The completed Symphony was Roussel's first major orchestral work, and although it is more romantic than his later works it already has characteristic fingerprints in his use of the orchestra. The Third Symphony is a very outgoing work in conventional four movement form, with characteristic 'motor' rhythms, and breezy, rather terse melodies—except in the *Scherzo*, which almost has the air of a jaunty popular song. Dutoit's performances are quite admirable in their clarity and understanding of Roussel's contrasted styles. The orchestra have just the right timbre and the recording is superb.

Roussel. Symphonies—No. 2 in B flat major, Op. 23; No. 4 in A major, Op. 53. **French National Orchestra/Charles Dutoit.** Erato 2292-45253-2.

60' DDD 6/87

This disc couples one of Roussel's most often-played symphonies with one of his least. The Fourth Symphony is a late work written only a few years before his death, and is a delightful score, the product of a richly-stocked imagination. It has a dark and powerful slow movement, a most infectiously engaging scherzo and a captivating finale. The Second Symphony is a rarity. It is abundantly resourceful and full of colour, and the scoring is refined and opulent. Dutoit gets playing of great vitality from this great French orchestra, dynamic markings are scrupulously observed but it is not just the letter but the spirit of the score that is well served. The Erato engineers do full justice to the dark and richly-detailed orchestral textures and the sound is particularly imposing in the definition of the bottom end of the register. Not to be missed.

Edmund Rubbra
British 1901-1986

Rubbra. ORCHESTRAL WORKS. **Philharmonia Orchestra/Norman Del Mar.** Lyrita SRCD202.
Symphonies—No. 3, Op. 49; No. 4, Op. 53. A Tribute, Op. 56. Resurgam—overture, Op. 149.

73' DDD 11/90

This is a first recording of either symphony after half-a-century of indifference and neglect! Yet the opening of the Fourth Symphony is one of the most beautiful things not just in Rubbra but in all present-day English music. It is often said that Rubbra's music is "not of our time but could not have been written at any other", to which one might add that it could not have been composed anywhere other than England. It is predominantly pastoral in feeling but there is little sense of what Constant Lambert called the 'cow-pat' school (though as the seventieth-birthday tribute included on this disc shows, Rubbra certainly revered Vaughan Williams). It is obvious from the first bars of each work that this music possesses eloquence and nobility and clearly tells of deep and serious things. The opening pages of the Fourth Symphony are free from any kind of artifice and their serenity and quietude resonate long in the memory. The overture, *Resurgam*, is a late work, also of great beauty, written in response to a commission from the Plymouth Orchestra, and another first recording. It commemorates the rebuilding of the Church of St Andrew, destroyed by Nazi bombers in 1941. Only its tower remained intact on whose north door of its tower stood one word, *Resurgam* ("I will rise again"). The performances by the Philharmonia Orchestra under Norman Del Mar are dedicated and the recorded sound offers superb clarity and presence with transparent well-defined textures. An important and rewarding issue.

Carl Ruggles   *Refer to Index*   *American 1876-1971*

Camillc Saint-Saëns   *French 1835-1921*

Saint-Saëns. PIANO CONCERTOS. **Pascal Rogé** (pf); [a]**Philharmonia Orchestra,** [b]**Royal Philharmonic Orchestra,** [c]**London Philharmonic Orchestra/Charles Dutoit.** Decca 417 351-2DH2. From D244D3 (10/81). No. 1 in D major, Op. 17[a]; No. 2 in G minor, Op. 22[b]; No. 3 in E flat major, Op. 29[c]; No. 4 in C minor, Op. 44[a]; No. 5 in F major, Op. 103, "Egyptian"[b].

(2) 2h 21' ADD 12/86

Saint-Saëns's First Concerto was written when the composer was 23 years old, and it is a sunny, youthful, happy work conventionally cast in the traditional three-movement form. A decade later he wrote the Second Concerto in a period of only three weeks. This concerto begins in a mood of high seriousness rather in the style of a Bach organ prelude; then this stern mood gives way to a jolly fleet-footed scherzo and a *presto* finale: it is an uneven work, though the most popular of the five concertos. The Third Concerto is perhaps the least interesting work, whilst the Fourth is the best of the five. It is in effect a one-movement work cast in three ingeniously crafted sections. Saint-Saëns wrote his last, the *Egyptian*, in 1896 to celebrate his 50 years as a concert artist. Mirroring the sights and sounds of a country he loved, this is another brilliant work. Pascal Rogé has a very secure, exuberant sense of rhythm, which is vital in these works, as is his immaculate, pearly technique. Dutoit is a particularly sensitive accompanist and persuades all three orchestras to play with that lean brilliance which the concertos demand. The recordings are true and well-balanced.

Saint-Saëns. SYMPHONIES. [a]**Bernard Gavoty** (org); **Orchestre National de l'ORTF/Jean Martinon.** EMI CZS7 62643-2.
A major; F major, "Urbs Roma"; No. 1 in E flat major, Op. 2; No. 2 in A minor, Op. 55; No. 3 in C minor, Op. 78, "Organ"[a].

(2) 2h 36' ADD 5/91   (B)

Saint-Saëns's four early symphonies have rather tended to be eclipsed by the popularity of his much later *Organ* Symphony. It's easy to see why the latter, with its rich invention, its colour and its immediate melodic appeal has managed to cast an enduring spell over its audiences, but there is much to be enjoyed in the earlier symphonies too. The A major dates from 1850 when Saint-Saëns was just 15 years old and is a particularly attractive and charming work despite its debt to Mendelssohn and Mozart. The Symphony in F major of 1856 was the winning entry in a competition organized by the Societé Sainte-Cécile of Bordeaux but was immediately suppressed by the composer after its second performance. The pressures of writing for a competition no doubt contribute to its more mannered style but it nevertheless contains some impressive moments, not least the enjoyable set of variations that form the final movement. The Symphony No. 1 proper was in fact written three years before the *Urbs Roma* and shares the same youthful freshness of the A major, only here the influences are closer to Schumann and Berlioz. The Second Symphony reveals the fully mature voice of Saint-Saëns and in recent years has achieved a certain amount of popularity which is almost certainly due in part to this particularly fine recording. Inevitably we arrive at the *Organ* Symphony, and if you don't already have a recording then you could do a lot worse than this marvellously colourful and flamboyant performance. Indeed, the performances throughout this generous set are persuasive and exemplary. A real bargain and well worth investigating.

Saint-Saëns. Symphony No. 3 in C minor, Op. 78, "Organ". **Peter Hurford** (org); **Montreal Symphony Orchestra/Charles Dutoit.** Decca 410 201-2DH. From SXDL7590 (3/83).

> 34' DDD 3/84   ♀ S Ⓑ

Saint-Saëns. Symphony No. 3 in C minor, Op. 78, "Organ". **Daniel Chorzempa** (org); **Berne Symphony Orchestra/Peter Maag.** Pickwick IMP Red Label PCD847.

> 37' DDD 4/87   £ Ⓑ

Saint-Saëns completed his Third Symphony at the peak of his career, in 1886, the same year in which he composed the *Carnaval of the Animals* (although this latter work was not given public performance until after his death). He was a renowned virtuoso pianist, had been described by Liszt as the world's greatest organist, and was recognized abroad, and especially in England, as France's leading composer; it was for a Philharmonic Society's commission that he produced this Symphony. It is packed with splendour. Its huge orchestra, including triple woodwind and a generous brass section, is joined by piano duet and greatly enriched by the majestic organ part. It is the presiding presence of the organ which quickens the listener's heart-beat and which inevitably makes this the *Organ* Symphony. The magnificent finale is all highly artificial and theatrical, but wholly absorbing every time. It is a perfect demonstration piece. Dutoit spaces his dynamic effects for maximum clarity, so that nothing is ever missed. Compact Disc opens up the score amazingly: it is impossible to resist turning towards the timpani and the triangle.

Pickwick's issue presents a performance of great charm and vigour in a work that can easily become over-heavy or too studied. The use of the organ has given rise to many problems in recording the work, especially ones of balance and tuning. Here the producer, Tony Faulkner, has overcome these difficulties with alacrity and the Berne orchestra are given the freedom to produce both powerful blocks of sound and delicately controlled textures. The much under-recorded veteran Swiss conductor, Peter Maag, controls all with an innate understanding of the work's overall structure. Dutoit's version may have more sumptuous or arresting sound, but this must be a first choice at its price.

Saint-Saëns. SAMSON ET DALILA. **Jon Vickers** (ten) Samson; **Rita Gorr** (mez) Dalila; **Ernest Blanc** (bar) High Priest of Dagon; **Anton Diakov** (bass) Abimélech, Old Hebrew Man; **Rémy Corazza** (ten) A Philistine Messenger; **Jacques Potier** (ten) First Philistine; **Jean-Pierre Hurteau** (bass) Second Philistine; **René Duclos Choir; Paris Opéra Orchestra/Georges Prêtre.** EMI CDS7 47895-8. Notes, text and translation included. From SAN117/9 (12/63).

> ② 2h 1' ADD 7/88

Religious earnestness and pagan revelry form an uneasy partnership, and *Samson et Dalila* can seem a tawdry entertainment, despite the melodic inventiveness and the skilful musical workmanship. Yet given a good performance, as is heard in this recording, it retains extraordinary vitality, charm and strength. Jon Vickers has a Herculean voice, with reserves of power and massive conviction of purpose that make him the very man to dislodge the pillars of the temple. Rita Gorr was one of the most powerful singers of her time, and her Dalila has all the requisite strength and firmness. Chorus and orchestra do well, and Prêtre earns gratitude for avoiding pretentiousness and exaggeration.

Antonio Salieri *Italian 1750-1825*

Salieri. AXUR, RE D'ORMUS. **Andrea Martin** (bar) Axur; **Curtis Rayam** (ten) Atar; **Eva Mei** (sop) Aspasia; **Ettore Nova** (bass) Biscroma, Brighella; **Ambra Vespasiani** (mez) Fiammetta, Smeraldina; **Massimo Valentini** (bass) Arteneo; **Michele Porcelli** (bar) Altamor; **Mario Cecchetti** (ten) Urson; **Sonia Turchetta** (contr) Elamir; **Giovanni Battista Palmieri** (ten) Arlecchino; **Guido d'Arezzo Choir; Russian Philharmonic Orchestra/ René Clemencic.** Nuova Era 6852/4. Notes, text and translation included. Recorded at performances in the Teatro di Rinnovati, Sienna between August 19th-23rd, 1989.

 ③ 2h 44' DDD 12/90 ❓

This work, which has good claims to be reckoned Salieri's masterpiece, was composed in 1787, the time of *Don Giovanni*, with which it shares a librettist, Da Ponte. Unlike Mozart's work, *Axur* is a serious opera, and indeed it had originally been a *tragédie lyrique*, written for Paris; this Italian reworking, for Vienna, retains much of the nobility of manner and exalted style associated with the French form, especially in the music for the central characters. Listen for example to the big two-part aria in the second act for the hero, Atar, or the thrilling scene for him in Act 3—a link, this, between the operas of Salieri's mentor Glück and the serious operas of Rossini. Do not look here for the human quality, the wit, the warmth, of a Mozart; Salieri was a different kind of composer, and his music is lofty and solemn, also occasionally stilted, pretentious and dry. But it is skilful music, bold in harmony and inventive in orchestration and is well worth trying. The plot is rather a silly one, not much helped by its passages of comic relief. But the singing here serves it well. Curtis Rayam is outstanding as Atar, with his smooth, graceful and expressive tenor; Eva Mei gives pleasure too in the *prima donna* role of Aspasia, with an attractive glow to her voice and no shortage of passion. René Clemencic's direction, if not ideally stylish or disciplined, nevertheless gives a very fair i dea of an opera that truly merits an occasional revival. The live recording evokes, sometimes almost too vividly, the atmosphere of an Italian opera house.

Aulis Sallinen *Finnish 1935-*

Sallinen. Symphony No. 5, Op. 57, "Washington Mosaics"[a]. Chamber Music III, Op. 58, "The Nocturnal Dances of Don Juanquixote"[b]. Solo Cello Sonata, Op. 26[c]. [bc]**Arvo Noras** (vc); [b]**Finlandia Sinfonietta**, [a]**Helsinki Philharmonic Orchestra/Okko Kamu.** Finlandia FACD370.

71' DDD 10/89 ❓

Sallinen's operas have proved enormously successful and his symphonies have struck a highly responsive chord among the wider musical public. Their success prompted Rostropovich to commission the present Symphony, which he conducted for the first time in 1985. Its overall form is symmetrical: the outer

movements (*Washington Mosaics* I and II) are the most substantial and frame three shorter middle movements, all called intermezzi. All three are strong in atmosphere and the orchestral sonorities are unfailingly resourceful and imaginative. The first movement has some Stravinskian overtones and there is a good sense of movement, and elsewhere in the Symphony there are passing affinities with Britten and Shostakovich. There is a strong feeling for nature, and the work casts a strong spell. It is marvellously played by the Helsinki orchestra under Okko Kamu: the recording is open with plenty of air around the sound and no want of detail, and the many colours of the Symphony are vividly brought to life. Neither of the other pieces is anywhere near as strong but the disc is well worth having just for the Symphony.

Erik Satie
French 1866-1925

Satie. PIANO WORKS. **Anne Queffélec.** Virgin Classics VC7 90754-2. Six Gnossiennes. Véritables préludes flasques. Vieux séquins et vieilles cuirasses. Chapitres tournés en tous sens. Three Gymnopédies. Embryons desséchés. Je te veux valse. Sonatine bureaucratique. Heures séculaires et instantanées. Le Picadilly. Avant-dernières pensées. Sports et divertissements.

76' DDD 5/89 Ⓑ

Satie. PIANO WORKS. **Pascal Rogé** (pf). Decca 410 220-2DH. From 410 220-1DH (6/84). Three Gymnopédies. Je te veux—valse. Quatre préludes flasques. Prélude en tapisserie. Nocturne No. 4. Vieux séquins et vieilles cuirasses. Embryons desséchés. Six Gnossiennes. Sonatine bureaucratique. Le Picadilly.

61' DDD 10/84 Ⓑ

Satie. PIANO WORKS. **Peter Dickinson.** Conifer CDCF183. Chapitres tournés en tous sens. Croquis et agaceries d'un gros bonhomme en bois. Je te veux. Le Piccadilly. Pièces froides. Le piège de Méduse. Poudre d'or. Préludes du fils des étoiles. Prélude en tapisserie. Sonatine bureaucratique. Sports et divertissements. Three gymnopédies. Trois véritables préludes flasques (pour un chien). Vexations.

77' DDD 12/90 Ⓑ

Satie is a composer who defies description. His piano music has the same quirky originality as his life and his love of flying in the face of convention are

crystallized in these fascinating miniatures. Anne Queffélec has made an excellent selection of Satie piano music starting with the famous and well-loved *Gnossiennes* and also including the *Gymnopédies*, works of a chaste almost ritualistic stillness. Also included are the wicked *Véritables préludes flasques (pour un chien)* containing his celebrated parody of Chopin's funeral march, credited typically à la Satie as a quotation "from the famous mazurka by Schubert". The programme ends with the

Anne Queffélec   *[photo: Virgin Classics*

whimsical and charming *Sports et divertissements* played with just the right air of mock seriousness. The recorded quality is good. It is a hard-hearted and humourless listener who cannot respond to the often childlike charm and evident warm and guileless heart of this very individual composer. Pascal Rogé plays these short pieces with the right kind of childlike gravity and sensuousness and the Decca recording is excellent.

In the booklet, we are told that Dickinson has sought to present "the essential Erik Satie", and he has succeeded admirably in his selection; the gravity and/or humour of these pieces is perfectly caught and conveyed, and as regards the latter quality the slightly understated playing in, say, *Le piège de Méduse* is right for this enigmatic composer. The three *Gymnopédies* provide a good test of Satie performance as well as being his most popular work, and Peter Dickinson is dead on target in his blend of gravity, sadness and tenderness—one almost writes "suppressed tenderness", given that their rarely understood titles evokes ceremonial dances of ancient Sparta performed by naked boys. There's also charm in plenty in the *café-concert* waltzes called *Poudre d'or* and *Je te veux*, and though not distinguished as music they have a fetching Gallic variety of schmaltz, while the Rosicrucian music of *Le fils des étoiles* is impressively serious. Maybe there are some damp squibs among the fireworks that Satie tossed casually at the listener, but with playing of this commitment there are no *longueurs* or bosh shots. The recording, made by Bob Auger in the Snape Maltings, has piano sound that is immediate yet well textured.

Alessandro Scarlatti

Italian 1660-1725

A. Scarlatti. Variations on "La folia"[a]. Cantatas[b]—Correa nel seno amato; Già lusingato appieno. [b]**Lynne Dawson** (sop); **Purcell Quartet** (Catherine Mackintosh, Elizabeth Wallfisch, vns; Richard Boothby, va da gamba; [a]Robert Woolley, hpd). Hyperion CDA66254. Texts and translations included.

52' DDD 3/90

To their series devoted to *La folia* variations, the Purcell Quartet have added this CD of music by Alessandro Scarlatti, who set the familiar tune in startlingly original harpsichord couplets. Robert Woolley plays 30 of them—many with striking touches of chromaticism—in glorious fashion; it is hard to imagine a performance that could match his wonderfully disciplined yet witty virtuoso one, which culminates in arpeggiated harp effects. Most of this disc, however, is devoted to two 'unfoliated' cantatas in which the Purcell Quartet is joined by the bewitching voice of Lynne Dawson. *Correa nel seno amato* is a pastoral cantata, the natural imagery of the text beautifully reflected in the music. The opening sinfonia and lyrical opening recitative are characterful and sensitively paced. Both singer and quartet capitalize on the chromatic inflexions and echoes in "Idolo amato". "Già lusingato appieno" is unusual for its textual references to an 'English hero'—possibly James II—bidding farewell to his family as he goes into exile. Among the highlights are the movements of collaboration between voice and strings, as in "Cara sposa" with its concertante violins, and "Sento l'aura", in which slow trills and echoes are made to sound like "whispering breezes". Just as in "Correa nel seno amato", Dawson commands the listener's attention from the very first notes of recitative with her beautifully weighted projection of the text. Both cantatas end with magical epilogues cast in recitative.

Domenico Scarlatti *Italian 1685-1757*

D. Scarlatti. KEYBOARD SONATAS. **Virginia Black** (hpd). CRD CRD3442.
A major, Kk113; E major, Kk380; E major, Kk381; D minor, Kk213; D major, Kk119; D minor, Kk120; C major, Kk501; C major, Kk502; F minor, Kk466; G major, Kk146; F sharp major, Kk318; F sharp major, Kk319; A major, Kk24.

60' DDD 6/87

D. Scarlatti. KEYBOARD SONATAS. **Trevor Pinnock** (hpd). CRD CRD3368. From CRD1068 (5/81).
G major, Kk124; C minor, Kk99; G major, Kk201; B minor, Kk87; E major, Kk46; C major, Kk95; F minor/major, Kk204*a*; D major, Kk490; D major, Kk491; D major, Kk492; G major, Kk520; G major, Kk521; C major, Kk513.

61' ADD 12/86

D. Scarlatti. KEYBOARD SONATAS, Volume 25. **Gilbert Rowland** (hpd). Keyboard KGR1025CD.
D minor, Kk9; E major, Kk46; E minor, Kk98; C minor, Kk129; A major, Kk208; A major, Kk209; B flat major, Kk360; B flat major, Kk361; G major, Kk454; G major, Kk455; C major, Kk514; C major, Kk515.

51' DAD 10/89

D. Scarlatti. KEYBOARD SONATAS. **Vladimir Horowitz** (pf). CBS Masterworks CD42410. Items marked [c] recorded at a concert in Carnegie Hall, New York in 1968. Items marked [a] from SBRG72117 (7/63), [b] SBRG72274 (8/65), [c] 72720 (1/69).
D major, Kk33[b]; A major, Kk39[b]; A minor, Kk54[b]; G major, Kk55[c]; D major, Kk96[b]; G major, Kk146[b]; E major, Kk162[b]; E minor, Kk198[b]; A major, Kk322[a]; E major, kk380[c]; G major, Kk455[a]; F minor, Kk466[b]; E flat major, Kk474[b]; F minor, Kk481[b]; D major, Kk491[b]; F major, Kk525[b]; E major, Kk531[a].

61' AAD 5/89

D. Scarlatti. KEYBOARD SONATAS. **Valda Aveling** (hpd). Classics for Pleasure CD-CFP4538. From HMV HQS1365 (2/77).
Sonatas—E major, Kk28; D minor, Kk52; C major, Kk132; C major, Kk133; n A major, Kk208; A major, Kk209; D major, Kk490; D major, Kk491; D major, Kk492; B flat major, Kk544; B flat major, Kk545.

52' ADD 1/91   ♩P ♩S **Ⓑ**

A highly accomplished harpsichordist, Domenico Scarlatti's influence on keyboard composition was enormous giving the short sonatas a freedom of form, range of expression and technical complexity quite unlike anything previously written for the medium. His sonatas call for extremes of virtuosity and a quick-silver technique. Virginia Black proves herself a worthy exponent and offers in her well-balanced recital three pairs of sonatas as well as five separate sonatas. Though much of the music demands a powerful sense of momentum and furious brilliance from the player, Black shows how expressive much of the music can be if treated with sensitivity, gently introducing a little rubato and allowing the music to breathe more freely. The harpsichord is beautifully recorded and altogether this programme offers a vivid and most enjoyable introduction to the art of Scarlatti.

Pinnock presents 13 of these very varied pieces with all the vivacity and panache his admirers have learned to expect. One advantage of this particular compilation is that it avoids some very well-known sonatas to introduce others of equal character and invention. Though the recording is close and on the harsh side it should not deter anyone from an interesting and useful issue in which the last sonata of all, Kk513, is especially charming and evocative with its lilting siciliana rhythm and musette effects.

Volume 25 of Gilbert Rowland's complete Scarlatti sonata series contains eight Kirkpatrick-paired sonatas and four singletons, offering an enjoyable cross section of Scarlatti's output in this genre—as astonishing in its stylistic variety as in its quantity. If you are a keyboard player you will recognize the ways Scarlatti tested his pupils' technique; whether you are or not, you can thoroughly enjoy his musical creativity—and share Gilbert Rowland's love for it.

Horowitz's chosen 17 at once prove the point made in the booklet that this composer's music is not just "mostly fast, light and requiring only articulation and dexterity". He finds room for more than a few that are "poetic, nostalgic and even dreamy, very much in the bel canto style". Whatever the tempo or mood, his playing is as memorable for its pin-point precision and textural clarity as it is for its potency of characterization. All in all it would be difficult to imagine these works played with a keener reconciliation of the demands of period style and the resources of the modern piano, with its richer range of colour. The CD transfer is excellent.

Valda Aveling's love-affair with Scarlatti has been a long one. She revels in the abundant opportunities he provides for nimble and garrulous fingerwork, she relishes the frequent flashes of wit that probably made Maria Barbara smile—and wince when the joke was at the expense of her fingers, and she holds her head high in the stately procession of Kk490. Best of all, she makes one aware that there was a genuine human being at Scarlatti's keyboard, and is at her own, never more than in the sadly beautiful Kk208; once, after playing this in a recital, she turned to the audience and said "Isn't that *gorgeous*—isn't it a lovely tune!"—and of course it *is*. The scholarship is always there but it is never dry; it has been absorbed into Aveling's bloodstream. The harpsichord itself has mod cons that Scarlatti never had at his disposal but they are put to the service of the music, never used merely to tickle the ear. If Scarlatti is listening from some unseen vantage point, these sentient performances (and the superb recording of them) could well be putting an approving smile on *his* face too.

Giacinto Scelsi
Italian 1905-1988

Scelsi. CHAMBER WORKS. [a]**Michiko Hirayama** (sop); [a]**Frank Lloyd** (hn); [a]**Maurizio Ben Omar** (perc); **Arditti Quartet** (Irvine Arditti, David Alberman, vns; Levine Andrade, va; Rohan de Saram, vc)/[a]**Aldo Brizzi.** Salabert Actuels SCD8904/05.
String Quartets Nos. 1-5. String Trio (1958). Khoom[a] (1962).

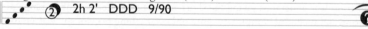

② 2h 2' DDD 9/90

Even in the twentieth century, an age of rampant musical individualism, Giacinto Scelsi stands out as an independent spirit. One authority claims convincingly that he was neither "a sublime visionary" nor "a bungling amateur" so much as "an inspired naïf", similar in some ways to Charles Ives except that there is nothing Ivesian about the pared-down luminosity of Scelsi's later works. The five String Quartets chart a remarkable journey from the relatively traditional expansiveness and assured technique of No. 1 (1944) to the later styles which, in a nutshell, seek (with even greater assurance) as many subtle—often microtonal—inflexions of as few notes as possible. As a result there's an intensity to which so-called minimalism rarely aspires and what might seem impersonal experiments with pure sound take on compelling shapes and forms. Apart from the Quartets this admirable set contains the seminal String Trio of 1958 and a striking vocal work from the early 1960s. Authoritatively performed, effectively recorded, well annotated, the set provides an ideal introduction to an authentically modern and still too little known composer, who has many of the attributes of genius.

Alfred Schnittke

Russian 1934-

Schnittke. Concerto Grosso No. 1[a]. Quasi una sonata[b]. Moz-Art à la Haydn[c]. [ac]**Tatiana Grindenko** (vn); **Yuri Smirnov** ([a]hpd/[a]prep pf/[b]pf); **Chamber Orchestra of Europe**/[a]**Heinrich Schiff,** [bc]**Gidon Kremer** ([a]vn). DG 429 413-2GH. Recorded at a performance in the Kammermusiksaal, Berlin in September 1988.

62'   DDD   9/90

For a single representative of Alfred Schnittke's work you could choose nothing better than the first *Concerto Grosso* of 1977. Here are the psychedelic mélanges of baroque and modern, the drastic juxtapositions of pseudo-Vivaldi with pseudo-Berg, producing an effect at once aurally exciting and spiritually disturbing. The

piece has been recorded several times over, but never with the panache of Gidon Kremer and friends and never with the vivid immediacy of this live DG recording (in fact the solo violins are rather too closely miked for comfort, but that's only a tiny drawback). *Quasi una sonata* was originally composed in 1968 for violin and piano and it was something of a breakthrough piece for Schnittke as he emerged from what he called "the puberty rites of serialism", letting his imagination run riot for the first time. No-one could call it a disciplined piece, but if

Gidon Kremer   *[photo: DG/Bayat]*

that worries you, you should leave Schnittke alone anyway. The transcription for solo violin and string orchestra is an ingenious one and Kremer again supplies all the requisite agonized intensity. *Moz-Art à la Haydn* is a very slight piece of work, and it really depends on visual theatricality to make its effect. Still, it complements the other two pieces well enough, and the disc as a whole makes an excellent introduction to a composer currently enjoying an enormous vogue.

Schnittke. Concerto Grosso No. 4/Symphony No. 5. Pianissimo. **Gothenburg Symphony Orchestra/Neeme Järvi.** BIS CD427.

49'   DDD   8/90

Since the mid-1960s Alfred Schnittke has formulated a manner of composition in which different styles are juxtaposed in the same piece. He calls the procedure 'polystylism', and the effect is often arrestingly dramatic, a reincarnation in modern (or rather, post-modern) terms of the stylistic collisions in Ives, Mahler, Stravinsky and Shostakovich (to name Schnittke's most influential forebears). The idea behind the main piece on this disc is a gradual transition from a *Concerto Grosso*, with solo parts for violin, oboe and harpsichord, to a full-blown tragic Symphony. The in-between stage is a movement paraphrasing the incomplete slow movement of Mahler's early Piano Quartet. As so often with Schnittke there is a strong element of Hammer Horrors melodrama in the writing; but there is also a concentration and a rhythmic drive which make the overall experience an overwhelming one (contrasted with the fill-up, which is a crudely schematic piece of work). The Royal Concertgebouw Orchestra premièred the *Concerto Grosso/Symphony* in 1988 and a recording from them is expected in due course; but that will have to be something special if it is to rival the full-blooded playing of the Gothenburg Symphony Orchestra, recorded in their own hall with its famously sympathetic acoustic.

Schnittke. String Quartets—No. 1 (1966); No. 2 (1980); No. 3 (1983). **Tale Quartet** (Tale Olsson, Patrik Swedrup, vns; Ingegerd Kierkegaard, va; Helena Nilsson, vc). BIS CD467.

62' DDD 7/90

Schnittke's achievement—and you can hear him acquiring increasing mastery of it through these three quartets, covering a 17-year period—is to stay on the right side of the fine line that separates expressionistic modernism from self-indulgent musical chaos. The First Quartet risks the most in its eagerness to equal if not to outdo the most extravagant devices that the *avant-garde* style (in 1966) had to offer. By 1980 Schnittke was sadder, wiser and much more responsive to the long shadow of history. In the Third Quartet, in particular, that responsiveness initially involves a riveting dialogue between Schnittke himself and the disparate but formidable trio of Lassus, Beethoven and Shostakovich, and gradually develops into a compelling meditation on the associations and incompatibilities of past and present. Nobody in their right minds would want to hear all three quartets at a sitting. Schnittke's music needs the contrast of something more classically restrained and consolatory in character—the quartets of Haydn or Mozart, perhaps. Yet even if Schnittke's Quartets are too immediate, too unmediated to demand instant elevation to the category of 'Master-work', they are memorable in a manner that, unlike much modern music, puts no barriers between composer and listener, and they are brilliantly performed and recorded here.

Arnold Schoenberg
Austrian/Hungarian 1874-1951

Schoenberg. Verklärte Nacht, Op. 4. Variations for Orchestra, Op. 31. **Berlin Philharmonic Orchestra/Herbert von Karajan.** DG 415 326-2GH. From 2711 014 (3/75).

52' ADD 3/86 Ⓑ

The decadence of German culture in the 1920s and 1930s is already very apparent in the saturated romanticism of *Verklärte Nacht* (1899), the most lusciously sentient work ever conceived for a string group. By comparison the *Variations for Orchestra* comes at the peak of the composer's atonal period and is perhaps the most impressive and imaginative demonstration of the possibilities of this compositional method. Thus the two works on this CD are pivotal in Schoenberg's career and Karajan and the Berlin Philharmonic make the very best case for both works. It is impossible not to respond to the sensuality of *Verklärte Nacht* in their hands, while the challenging *Variations* also make a profound impression. The recording matches the intensity of the playing brilliantly.

Schoenberg. Chamber Symphonies—No. 1, Op. 9; No. 2, Op. 38. Verklärte Nacht, Op. 4 (arr. string orch). **Orpheus Chamber Orchestra.** DG 429 233-2GH.

69' DDD 7/90 ♩P ♩S Ⓑ

In the late twentieth century there's increasing evidence that the early twentieth century's most radical music is becoming so easy to perform that it may at last be losing its terrors for listeners as well as players. This can only be welcomed, provided that performances do not become bland and mechanical, and the unconducted Orpheus Chamber Orchestra triumphantly demonstrate how to combine fluency with intensity. If you like your Schoenberg effortful—to feel that the players are conquering almost insuperable odds—these recordings may not be for you. But if you like spontaneity of expression that is never an end in itself, and communicates Schoenberg's powerfully coherent forms and textures as well as his abundant emotionalism, you should not hesitate. This CD is the first to place Schoenberg's two Chamber Symphonies alongside *Verklärte Nacht*, whose original version for string quartet was the prime mover of so many later developments, in Schoenberg and others. Here, in *Verklärte Nacht*, is Schoenberg the late-romantic tone poet, the equal of Richard Strauss: the First Chamber Symphony shows Schoenberg transforming himself from late-romantic into expressionist, while in the Second the recent American immigrant, in the 1930s, looks back to his romantic roots and forges a new, almost classical style. With superb sound, this is a landmark in recordings of twentieth-century music.

Schoenberg. PIANO MUSIC. **Maurizio Pollini.** DG 20th Century Classics 423 249-2GC. From 2530 531 (5/75).
Three Piano Pieces, Op. 11. Six Little Piano Pieces, Op. 19. Five Piano Pieces, Op. 23. Piano Suite, Op. 25. Piano Pieces, Opp. 33*a* and 33*b*.

50' ADD 6/88 £

When Pollini claims these as probably the most important piano pieces of the twentieth century he does so with good reason. For example, the Op. 11 pieces are generally reckoned the first wholly atonal work and the Prelude of Op. 25 was Schoenberg's first 12-note piece. Not surprisingly they are tough going for the uninitiated. Schoenberg expects the listener to come all the way to meet him, however uninviting the journey may appear; and getting to the sense behind the notes has defeated plenty of would-be exponents, for it tolerates no weakness of technical or musical equipment. Fortunately, Pollini is just about the ideal guide across Schoenberg's bleak ridges and past his sudden avalanches, and for combined intellectual and pianistic mastery he stands unchallenged. DG's recording is clear and lifelike and at mid-price this CD is superb value.

Franz Schubert

Austrian 1797-1828

Schubert. SYMPHONIES. **Chamber Orchestra of Europe/Claudio Abbado.** DG 423 651-2GH5.
Symphonies—No. 1 in D major, D82; No. 2 in B flat major, D125; No. 3 in D major, D200; No. 4 in C minor, D417, "Tragic"; No. 5 in B flat major, D485; No. 6 in C major, D589; No. 8 in B minor, D759, "Unfinished"; No. 9 in C major, D944, "Great". Grand Duo in C major, D812 (orch. J. Joachim). Rosamunde, D644—Overture, "Die Zauberharfe".

⑤ 5h 20' DDD 2/89

For this covetable box-set Abbado has had original sources researched in order to restore bars and details that have been missed out by later editors and to expurgate those added by some, Brahms included, who felt Schubert's originals did not quite balance! For those who know these Symphonies in the later, corrupted versions, these performances can be startling at times, and real eye-openers. The balance of the first movement of the Fourth Symphony, for example, where eight bars added by Brahms to the exposition have been cut, is so radically altered that the effect persists throughout the work, and changes its meaning. Such dedication to Schubert's intentions must be applauded, and the more so because Abbado also draws from his small orchestra of brilliant young performers playing of the utmost sympathy and commitment. The whole set sounds like a labour of love. It has the occasional weaker point but, as a whole, it sustains a remarkably high standard, and the admirably-detailed recordings permit an unstrained appreciation of the finer qualities of the playing.

Schubert. Symphonies—No. 3 in D major, D200; No. 4 in C minor, D417, "Tragic". Overture in D major, D590, "In the Italian style". **Stockholm Sinfonietta/Neeme Järvi.** BIS CD453.

62' DDD 4/90

Schubert's orchestral style is well realized in this Stockholm recording of three of his early works. The "Italian style" of the Overture was undoubtedly gleaned from Rossini, whose music reached and conquered Vienna at around the time of Schubert's twentieth birthday; but the Mediterranean lightness and wit are all the more interesting for being lit with a melodic and harmonic warmth that is Schubert's own. Let us admit that the Stockholm Sinfonietta are not an absolutely first class band by the present high international standards, as the woodwind playing around the 6'20" mark here reminds us, but under Neeme Järvi they give this music a very fetching youthful vivacity and freshness. The Third Symphony does not sound like the work of an 18-year-old composer, and though here too we are aware of influences, Mozart's above all, the scoring and the dramatic use of thematic material look forward to later Schubert and the chirpy *Allegretto* and tarantella-like finale (another Italian influence) are delightful. Schubert himself used the subtitle *Tragic* for the Fourth Symphony, and perhaps we find such a mood only in the first movement, but there are some clouds elsewhere too and the 'minuet' has an odd quirkiness. A mellow sound, a bit thick and bassy in places but agreeable.

Schubert. Symphonies—No. 3 in D major, D200; No. 5 in B flat major, D485; No. 6 in C major, D589. **Royal Philharmonic Orchestra/Thomas Beecham.** EMI Studio CDM7 69750-2.

78' ADD 8/90

Beecham was well into his seventies when he made these recordings with the Royal Philharmonic, the orchestra he had founded in 1946. His lightness of touch, his delight in the beauty of the sound he was summoning, the directness of his approach to melody, and his general high spirits will all dominate our memory of these performances. But listening again, we may be reminded that Beecham could equally well dig deep into the darker moments of these works. Schubert's elation was rarely untroubled and the joy is often compounded by its contrast with pathos—Beecham had that balance off to a tee. It should be noted that Beecham does not take all the marked repeats and he doctored some passages he considered over-repetitive. However, these recordings may also serve as a reminder of the wonderful heights of musicianship that his players achieved, as in the Trio of the Third Symphony's *Minuet*, where a simple waltz-like duet between oboe and bassoon attains greatness by the shapeliness, ease and poignancy of its execution. Despite some signs of age, these recordings still preserve the brilliance of their readings and the tonal quality of this orchestra. Altogether, a disc to lift the heaviest of spirits.

Schubert. Symphonies—No. 5 in B flat major, D485; No. 8 in B minor, D759, "Unfinished". **Vienna Philharmonic Orchestra/Sir Georg Solti.** Decca 414 371-2DH.

58' DDD 9/85

Schubert's lyrical, early romantic style is unmistakable and if the Fifth Symphony still uses eighteenth-century style it has a nineteenth-century warmth of expression. In its more complex use of form, its use of a bigger orchestra and in its greater expressive power Schubert's Eighth Symphony looks forward, even to Brahms and Bruckner. It scarcely matters that Schubert left the work unfinished, for as its vast popularity proves, the symphony in its surviving two-movement form makes a satisfying whole. In the Fifth symphony the most difficult hurdle for a conductor is the *Andante*, which in unskilled hands can seem a long movement indeed. Solti avoids monotony with great skill, keeping the music alive with tiny and entirely appropriate expressive inflections. Elsewhere his lightness of touch and phrase and his airy rhythms produce a very pleasing performance. He brings more serious intent to the *Unfinished* Symphony, with strong, purposeful conducting at slowish tempos; yet the firm outlines are often softened by warm and affectionate phrasing. The VPO are persuaded to play at their very best and the recording is clear and immediate.

Schubert. Symphony No. 8 in B minor, D759, "Unfinished"[a].
Schumann. Symphony No. 3 in E flat major, Op. 97, "Rhenish".
[a]**Philharmonia Orchestra/Giuseppe Sinopoli;** [b]**Los Angeles Philharmonic Orchestra/Carlo Maria Giulini.** DG 3D-Classics 427 818-2GDC. Item marked [a] from 410 862-2GH (4/84), [b] 2532 040 (6/82).

63' DDD 4/90

This is not the most immediately obvious of couplings, especially as it features two different orchestras with two different conductors, but the result is surprisingly effective. It shows that the works share a certain companionship of feeling, made particularly obvious by these two readings of them. Sinopoli's view

Carlo Maria Giulini [photo: DG/Wolf]

of the *Unfinished* will be, for most listeners, a love or hate issue. The work's most operatic moments are keenly emphasized, with the pace habitually adjusted to draw out the last ounce of drama from the music. Some will find this revelatory and intensely emotional; others will be too aware of the manipulation that is being perpetrated. Giulini is much more direct for the Schumann. Never an easy symphony to pace or balance, the *Rhenish* can often be made to work movement by movement, whilst the whole fails to make overall sense. Giulini does not fall into that trap, and if other conductors have drawn more juice from the individual movements, few have matched Giulini's onward momentum throughout the work. The sound, that copes so well with the bloom of Schubert's orchestration, is not so kind to Schumann's fuller textures, recorded a couple of years earlier, and there are moments when the listener might wish for extra light to shine on the inner parts. Nevertheless, this inspired coupling should provide plenty of food for thought.

Schubert. Symphony No. 9 in C major, D944, "Great". **Vienna Philharmonic Orchestra/Sir Georg Solti.** Decca 400 082-2DH. From SXDL7557 (10/82).

55' DDD 3/83

Schubert. Symphony No. 9 in C major, D944, "Great". **London Philharmonic Orchestra/Sir Adrian Boult.** EMI Studio CDM7 69199-2. From ASD2856 (11/72).

54' ADD 4/88

Schubert's *Great* C major Symphony, so called as to differentiate it from his earlier symphony in the same key, is one of the greatest of all classical symphonies and an indispensable part of any collection. Long thought to be from the last year of his life, it is now placed in 1825-26 and so has an earlier number (849) in the Deutsch catalogue. Its glories are too familiar to need further enumeration and since the advent of the Compact Disc more than 30 new versions have appeared. Sir Georg Solti's account with the Vienna Philharmonic was one of the first and remains one of the best. For sheer all-round excellence of performance and recording it would be hard to beat. Solti's reading is concentrated yet spacious, leisurely but never wanting in impulse, measured in its responses and never overdriven. It can confidently be recommended even to those who are not always in sympathy with this conductor. The Decca recording has all the clarity, detail and tonal finesse one expects from this source.

Sir Adrian Boult was 83 when his version was recorded but he very clearly retained all his powers of shaping this big work as a whole. At the same time, details of phrasing, articulation and textures are given a measured loving care that never degenerates into mannerism. That this symphony is a mighty work is evident throughout, and its qualities of energy and dignity are also kept in a good balance. Perhaps by modern standards we may judge the sound to be rather bassy and reverberant, but it still allows detail to emerge in a natural way.

Schubert. String Quintet in C major, D956. **Cleveland Quartet** (Donald Weilerstein, Peter Salaff, vns; Atar Arad, va; Paul Katz, vc) with **Yo-Yo Ma** (vc). CBS Masterworks CD39134. From IM39134 (4/85).

54' DDD 8/86

The String Quintet is extraordinarily fertile in melodic invention and Schubert frames it in a rich harmonic language alive to the many rhythmic subtleties. The Cleveland Quartet and Ma capture the urgency and ardour of the long first movement but also take the beautiful second subject at the requested *pp*—a rare but welcome observation. The intense second movement with its pizzicato bass line is well done too and greatly helped by the recording, which is attentive without being too close (there's no excessive breathing): the five players are well spread across the stereo image. The closing *Allegretto*, the shortest movement, is nicely sprung, giving it a slightly folk-like gait. A fine disc in an already well-represented catalogue.

Schubert. Piano Quintet in A major, D667, "Trout"[a]. String Trios[b]—B flat major, D471; B flat major, D581. **Grumiaux Trio** (Artur Grumiaux, vn; Georges Janzer, va; Eva Czako, vc); [a]**Jacques Cazauran** (db); [a]**Ingrid Haebler** (pf). Philips Musica da Camera 422 838-2PC. Item marked [a] from SAL3621 (10/67), [b] SAL3782 (6/70).

63' ADD 10/89

Schubert. Piano Quintet in A major, D667, "Trout"[a]. String Quartet in D minor, D810, "Death and the Maiden"[b]. [a]**Sir Clifford Curzon** (pf); [a]members of the **Vienna Octet** (Willi Boskovsky, vn; Gunther Breitenbach, va; Nikolaus Hübner, vc; Johann Krump, db); [b]**Vienna Philharmonic Quartet** (Boskovsky, Otto Strasser, vns; Rudolf Streng, va; Robert Scheiwein, vc). Decca 417 459-2DM. Item marked [a] from SXL2110 (6/59), [b] SXL6092 (5/64).

71' ADD 6/88 £

Schubert. Piano Quintet in A major, D667, "Trout". **Clemens Hagen** (vn); **Veronika Hagen** (va); **Lukas Hagen** (vc); **Alois Posch** (db); **András Schiff** (pf). Decca 411 975-2DH. From 411 975-1DH (2/85).

44' DDD 4/85

Schubert composed the *Trout* Quintet in his early twenties for a group of amateur musicians in the town of Steyr in Upper Austria, which lies upon the River Enns and was then reputed for its fine fishing and keen fishermen. The Quintet was certainly tailored for special circumstances, but like all great occasional music it stands as strongly as ever today, with its freshly bubbling invention and sunny melodiousness. Arthur Grumiaux is always a stylish violinist, but his natural refinement never inhibits the natural high spirits of the music, while Ingrid Haebler is no less stylish. The single movement for string trio that is D471 was written even earlier in the composer's short life, in 1816, while the four-movement Trio in the same key followed it a year later; these too are played deftly yet with the right kind of simplicity. The recordings are satisfactory but have a little residual tape hiss; in the trios it may be useful to make some treble reduction, since the sound here is brighter.

Willi Boskovsky's gentle and cultured mind is very much responsible for the success of these performances of Schubert's two best-known chamber works. In the delectable *Trout* Quintet there is real unanimity of vision between the players, as well as an immaculate attention to the details of the scoring. Clifford Curzon's part in the performance is memorable especially for his quiet playing—the atmosphere is magical in such moments. Everywhere there is a great awareness of the delicacy and refinement of Schubert's inventiveness. The *Death and the Maiden* Quartet is no less successful. Schubert's strikingly powerful harmonies, together with a sustained feeling of intensity, all go to heighten the urgency of the first movement. Despite this, string textures are generally kept light and feathery. In the *Andante* all is subtly understated and although a mood of tragedy is always lurking in the background, never is it thrown at the listener. Boskovsky's understanding of the music is very acute and the performance cannot fail to satisfy even the most demanding. These are two vintage recordings and in the quartet the quality of sound is quite remarkable.

Schubert's *Trout* Quintet is played on the later Decca recording by a professional Viennese family group, joined by the naturally musical András Schiff, and the result combines freshness with concentration to hold the listener in rapt attention from the first note to the last. To emphasize that this is a team project, the Decca engineers have perceptively balanced the piano within the string group, and that adds to the feeling of spontaneous musical integration. The recorded sound is eminently vivid and realistic.

Schubert. Octet in F major, D803. **Academy of St Martin in the Fields Chamber Ensemble** (Kenneth Sillito, Malcolm Latchem, vns; Stephen Shingles, va; Denis Vigay, vc; Raymund Koster, chbr bass; Andrew Marriner, cl; Timothy Brown, hn; Graham Sheen, bn). Chandos CHAN8585.

60' DDD 8/88   **B**

Schubert used material from previous years in composing this work which ostensibly has a serenade-like character, but shows a great depth of feeling, almost pathos at times. Schubert was already afflicted with the illness which was to dog the rest of his short life, and in the six-movement Octet he looked back nostalgically to happier days. It is one of his great masterpieces. The ASMF Chamber Ensemble have recorded the Octet on two occasions, but this Chandos version is considerably the better of the two. The engineers have succeeded in resolving problems of balance posed by the unequal power of solo strings and wind with great skill, and the sound itself is superlatively fine. The players respond eagerly to the Octet's song-like spontaneity, and they manage to capture its relaxed, Viennese flavour in a very authentic style, but they also understand and express with rare eloquence the work's underlying profundity of expression.

Schubert. String Quartets—D minor, D810, "Death and the Maiden"; C minor, D703, "Quartettsatz". **Lindsay Quartet** (Peter Cropper, Ronald Birks, vns; Robin Ireland, va; Bernard Gregor-Smith, vc). ASV CDDCA560. From DCA560 (7/86).

52' DDD 3/87

Der Tod und das Mädchen ("Death and the Maiden") Quartet is a work composed entirely in the minor key and draws its title from the song based on the poem by Matthias Claudius which Schubert had set in 1817. Not unlike the famous song *Erlkönig, Der Tod und das Mädchen* takes the form of a dialogue between life and death, here the maiden and the scythe-bearing figure of death. Schubert uses this song as the basis for the second movement's set of variations. How much he intended the mood of the poem to permeate the entire quartet is impossible to tell; suffice it to say that performing tradition has tended to emphasize the dark, death-centred character of the piece. The Lindsay Quartet bring their usual intense and febrile approach to what is appropriately Schubert's most intense chamber work. If at times the expression threatens to become orchestral in scope it never obscures the composer's vision. The recording allows plenty of air around the players without diminishing their powers of attack.

Schubert. Impromptus—D899; D935. **Murray Perahia** (pf). CBS Masterworks CD37291. From 37291 (1/84).

63' 4/85   **q P**

Schubert. Impromptus—D899; D935. **Krystian Zimerman** (pf). DG 423 612-2GH.

65' DDD 5/91

Though an able pianist, Schubert was not a concert-giving virtuoso out to conquer an international public with large-scale bravura works. The music-making he most enjoyed was at informal parties (they came to be known as Schubertiads) in the homes of music-loving friends, hence the very large number of miniatures—with the *Impromptus* among them—that flowed unceasingly from his pen. Whereas so much of what he wrote was never published in his lifetime, he had the satisfaction of seeing all eight *Impromptus* in print the year before he died. And their popularity has never waned, as the quickest glance at any catalogue at once makes clear. Inevitably Murray Perahia has strong rivals all equally deserving of a place in *The Good CD Guide*. His own version nevertheless constantly enchants with its pellucid tone and spontaneous spring-like freshness. Note the rippling lightness of the triplets in No. 2 in E flat and the pinpoint clarity of his semiquaver articulation in No. 4 in A flat in the first set, likewise the dancing lilt he brings to the variations of No. 3 in B flat and his respect for the *scherzando* expressively qualifying the *allegro* in No. 4 in F minor in the second set. None are 'over-loaded'. The recording is no less pleasing.

Zimerman's searching and very personally committed account of these eight pieces comes as a keen reminder that they are as representative of the composer in full maturity as any of the later piano sonatas. With his wide tonal range and bold response to climaxes, he sometimes even brings to mind how this music might have sounded had Schubert chosen to score it for an orchestra of that day. The recording itself very faithfully reproduces the mellow warmth of his own sound-world. Zimerman's desire to shed new light on the familiar has sometimes in recent years made us too aware of an interpreter at work. That danger is not wholly averted in his elasticity of pulse in the emotionally ambivalent D899 No. 1 in C minor/major, and equally his coquetry in some of the variations of D935 No. 3 in B flat. But for the most part it is a joy to hear these pieces at once so intensely experienced and lyrically sung. Though the earlier version from Perahia will always keep its place on library shelves, this new issue can now join it.

Schubert. PIANO WORKS. **András Schiff.** Decca 425 638-2DH. Allegretto in C minor, D915. Drei Klavierstücke, D946. 12 Ländler, D790. Vier Impromptus, D935.

74' DDD 7/90

Throughout his life Schubert was as irresistibly drawn to the keyboard miniature as he was to the realm of song. On this disc András Schiff assembles a choice assortment of these shorter pieces, playing them with the youthful freshness and charm with which Schubert himself must so often have delighted his friends at those convivial evenings of domestic music-making that came to be known as Schubertiads. Most familiar, of course, are the last four *Impromptus*, dating from the year before he died but inexplicably left unpublished for the next 12 years. For these Schiff favours fleeter tempos than we often hear (notably for the Second in A flat), giving each piece an effortless lyrical flow. The three *Klavierstücke* of his last year, with their strong internal contrasts, are richly characterized, yet again Schiff resists all temptation to over-interpret or emotionally inflate. The minor/major bittersweetness of the C minor *Allegretto*, written for Schubert's "dear friend", Ferdinand Walcher, on his departure from Vienna in April 1827, is brought home with the same disarming simplicity. Lighter relief comes in the 12 *Ländler* of 1823 (always so dear to Brahms, who owned the manuscript and eventually arranged for their publication), where Schiff prefers imaginative vitality to *schmalz*. The recording (made in Vienna's Konzerthaus) respects his light-fingered textural clarity.

Schubert. Fantasy in C major, D760, "Wanderer".
Schumann. Fantasia in C major, Op. 17. **Murray Perahia** (pf). CBS Masterworks CD42124.

52' DDD 12/86

The *Wanderer* Fantasy is a work in four linked movements using a motto theme that is variously transformed as the work proceeds, a technique that we find later in such works as Liszt's Piano Concertos and Franck's Symphony. It is a vigorous piece and in some ways somewhat classical and symphonic in utterance, strong in rhetoric as well as poetry. On the other hand, Schumann's *Fantasia*, written some 16 years later around 1837, is more obviously pianistic (of the two composers it was he who was the better pianist) and inspired more clearly by the romantic spirit that had already developed in music during Schubert's lifetime. Both works are major landmarks of the piano repertory, and Murray Perahia plays them with an unerring sense of their different styles as well as impeccable technical command. He is unfailingly exciting and uplifting in the quicker music, but it is probably in the slower and more expressive sections that his nobly personal eloquence is most strikingly revealed. Two different American locations were used for these performances, but the second of them (for the Schumann) allows a richer and more atmospheric piano sound.

Schubert. Piano Sonata in A minor, D845. Drei Klavierstücke, D946. **Alfred Brendel** (pf). Philips 422 075-2PH.

| 61' DDD 10/89 |

Schubert. Piano Sonatas—A minor, D845[a]; G major, D894[b]. **Radu Lupu** (pf). Decca 417 640-2DH. Item marked [a] from SXL6931 (12/79), [b] SXL6741 (5/76).

| 74' ADD 6/87 |

The coupling of Brendel and Schubert inspires confidence. Though love of the music alone, as pianists know, is not enough to master these pieces, it is essential, and in this big A minor Sonata (a key that was somehow especially important to Schubert) Brendel presents us with a drama that is no less tense for being predominantly expressed in terms of shapely melody. There is a flexibility in this playing that reminds us of the pianist's own comment that in such music "we feel not masters but victims of the situation": he allows us plenty of time to savour detail without ever losing sight of the overall shape of the music, and the long first movement and finale carry us compellingly forwards, as does the scherzo with its urgent energy, while the *Andante* second movement, too, has the right kind of spaciousness. In the *Three Piano Pieces* which date from the composer's last months, Brendel is no less responsive and imaginative. Richly sonorous digital recording in a German location complements the distinction of the playing on this fine Schubert disc.

Radu Lupu also understands Schubert's style as do few others and the way in which he is able to project this essentially private world is extraordinary. His tone is unfailingly clear, and this adds substantially to the lucidity of the readings. The simplicity of the opening themes of the A minor Sonata is a marvel of eloquence and when it is reset in the development section of the first movement one is amazed to hear Lupu transforming it into something far more urgent and full of pathos. The G major Sonata again fires Lupu's imagination and in the Minuet third movement he uses a considerable amount of rubato for the dance; its solid rhythmic pulse is an ideal foil to offset the extraordinary transitions of the finale that follows. The recorded sound does full justice to the colour of the pianist's tone.

Schubert. Piano Sonatas—D major, D850; A minor, D784. **Alfred Brendel** (pf). Philips 422 063-2PH.

| 63' DDD 11/88 |

There is an extraordinary amount of highly experimental writing in Schubert's piano sonatas. The essence of their structure is the contrasting of big heroic ideas with tender and inner thoughts; the first impresses the listener, the second woos him. The two works on this CD are in some ways of a varying scale. The D major lasts for 40 minutes, the A minor for around 23. However, it is the latter that contains the most symphonically inspired writing—it sounds as if it could easily be transposed for orchestra. Alfred Brendel presents the composer not so much as the master of lieder-writing, but more as a man thinking in large forms. Although there are wonderful quiet moments when intimate asides are conveyed with an imaginative sensitivity one remembers more the urgency and the power behind the notes. The A minor, with its frequently recurring themes, is almost obsessive in character whilst the big D major Sonata is rather lighter in mood, especially in the outer movements. The recorded sound is very faithful to the pianist's tone, whilst generally avoiding that insistent quality that can mar his loudest playing.

Schubert. Piano Sonatas—A major, D959; B flat major, D960. **Melvyn Tan** (fp). EMI Reflexe CDC7 49631-2.

> 67' DDD 9/89

Schubert. Piano Sonata in B flat major, D960. **Stephen Kovacevich** (pf). Hyperion CDA66004. From A66004 (2/83).

> 42' DDD 4/87

Schubert. Piano Sonata in B flat major, D960. Fantasia in C major, D760, "Wanderer". **Alfred Brendel** (pf). Philips 422 062-2PH.

> 58' DDD 1/90

Readers should perhaps be reminded that Melvyn Tan is only in his thirties. In years to come he will probably play the last two and greatest of Schubert's keyboard sonatas with a deeper poise. But for the moment we can be grateful for his refreshing reminder that when writing them, Schubert (albeit with only another two months to live) was not an elderly philosopher but like Tan himself,

Melvyn Tan   [photo: EMI/Garnham]

a highly impressionable young man. To meet the composer still more closely on his own ground he uses a reproduction by Derek Adlam of an 1814 Nannette Streicher fortepiano, which comes over with vibrant warmth in a recording made in the Long Gallery of Doddington Hall, Lincoln. The most controversial feature of the disc is the unusually brisk tempo he adopts for both slow movements, as if trying to lighten their sorrow. In other contexts, such as the second subject of the A major Sonata's first movement, there are occasional rhythmic idiosyncrasies which might, after repeated hearings, begin to sound a little mannered. Yet the spontaneity of his youthful response to passing marvels remains irresistible, likewise his virility in both Scherzos and his strong sense of direction in the B flat major Sonata's finale.

Stephen Kovacevich offers a deeply felt and comprehensive experience of Schubert's last Piano Sonata seemingly acknowledging all shades of meaning, yet retaining a marvellous sense of wholeness (and a marvellous pianistic poise as well). In this context his heart-stopping withdrawals of tone (especially in the first two movements) are profoundly moving. At full price, without coupling, and with slightly veiled sound-quality, this may seem like an extravagant purchase—but musical riches of this kind are impossible to put a price on.

Brendel meets Schubert on his own ground, exulting in the *con fuoco* panache of the earlier work, and just as keenly revealing the 'other-worldliness' of Schubert's farewell. For immediacy of response, it would be hard to name any player more aware of Schubert's own impressionability—the impressionability of a composer who died young enough to have known only "the poignancy and rapture of first sensations". Some might feel that Brendel's reaction to the mood of the moment at times results in over-elasticity of pulse, as in his drastic slowings-down for the lyrical second subject in the *Wanderer*'s first movement. But never mind. Whatever he does is done with enough conviction to make you feel, at the moment of listening, that there could be no other way. The recording is both rich and clear.

Schubert. LIEDER. **Felicity Lott** (sop); **Graham Johnson** (pf). Pickwick IMP Classics PCD898.
Die Forelle, D550. An Sylvia, D891. Heidenröslein, D257. Du bist die Ruh, D776. Der Musensohn, D764. An die Musik, D547. Auf dem Wasser zu singen, D774. Sei mir gegrüsst, D741. Litanei, D343. Die junge Nonne, D828. Ave Maria, D839. Im Frühling, D882. Gretchen am Spinnrade, D118. Nacht und Traüme, D827. Ganymed, D544. Mignon und der Harfner, D877. Seligkeit, D433.

65' DDD 10/88 £

This mid-price disc of Schubert Lieder presents many of his best-loved songs in attractive, fresh performances. Felicity Lott shows her complete command of the genre. Secure tone, confident phrasing, exemplary control of breathing, combined with an understanding of the idiom are evident throughout. They help to make songs such as *Du bist die Ruh, Nacht und Träume* and *Ganymed* a pleasure from start to finish. Throughout she cleverly varies her tone and style: for instance, light for *Ganymed*, smiling for *Seligkeit*, sombre for *Litanei*. The more dramatic songs are dealt with strongly and in *Die junge Nonne*, she creates the right sense of unease conquered by serenity. In everything she is superbly supported by Graham Johnson's pertinent and perceptive playing, which recalls that of his mentor Gerald Moore in its softness of touch and clarity of detail.

Schubert. LIEDER, Volume 1. **Dame Janet Baker** (mez); **Graham Johnson** (pf). Hyperion CDJ33001. Texts and translations included.
Der Jüngling am Bache, D30. Thekla, D73. Schäfers Klagelied, D121 (first version). Nähe des Geliebten, D162 (second version). Meerestille, D216. Amalia, D195. Die Erwartung, D159 (second version). Wandrers Nachtlied, D224. Der Fischer, D225 (second version). Erster Verlust, D226. Wonne der Wehmut, D260. An den Mond, D296. Das Geheimnis, D250. Lied, D284. Der Flüchtling, D402. An den Frühling, D587 (second version). Der Alpenjäger, D588 (second version). Der Pilgrim, D794. Sehnsucht, D636 (second version).

70' DDD 10/88

Schubert. LIEDER, Volume 6. **Anthony Rolfe Johnson** (ten); **Graham Johnson** (pf). Hyperion CDJ33006. Texts and translations included.
Die Nacht, D534 (completed by Anton Diabelli). Jagdlied, D521 (with chorus). Abendstern, D806. Abends unter der Linde, D235. Abends unter der Linde, D237. Der Knabe in der Wiege, D579. Abendlied für die Entfernte, D856. Willkommen und Abschied, D767. Vor meiner Wiege, D927. Der Vater mit dem Kind, D906. Des Fischers Liebesglück, D933. Die Sterne, D939. Alinde, D904. An die Laute, D905. Zur guten Nacht, D903 (chorus).

♪ **73' DDD 6/90**

Schubert. LIEDER, Volume 7. **Elly Ameling** (sop); **Graham Johnson** (pf).
Hyperion CDJ33007. Texts and translations included.
Minona, D152. Der Jüngling am Bache, D192. Stimme der Liebe, D187.
Naturgenuss, D188. Des Mädchens Klage, D191. Die Sterbende, D186. An den
Mond, D193. An die Nachtigall, D196. Die Liebe (Klärchens Lied), D210.
Meeresstille, D215a. Idens Nachtgesang, D227. Von Ida, D228. Das Sehnen,
D231. Die Spinnerin, D247. Wer kauft Liebesgötter?, D261. An den Frühling,
D283. Das Rosenband, D280. Liane, D298. Idens Schwanenlied, D317. Luisens
Antwort, D319. Mein Gruss an den Mai, D305. Mignon, D321. Sehnsucht,
D310 (two versions).

♪ **71' DDD 8/90**

Schubert. LIEDER, Volume 8. **Sarah Walker** (mez); **Graham Johnson**
(pf). Hyperion CDJ33008. Texts and translations included.
An den Mond, D259. Romanze, D114. Stimme der Liebe, D418. Die
Sommernacht, D289. Die frühen Gräber, D290. Die Mondnacht, D238. An den
Mond in einer Herbstnacht, D614. Die Nonne, D208. An Chloen, D462.
Hochzeit-Lied, D463. In der Mitternacht, D464. Trauer der Liebe, D465. Die
Perle, D466. Abendlied der Fürstin, D495. Wiegenlied, D498. Ständchen, D920
(with chorus). Bertas Lied in der Nacht, D653. Der Erlkönig, D328.

♪ **72' DDD 10/90** ♩ P Ⓑ

Schubert. LIEDER, Volume 10. **Martyn Hill** (ten); **Graham Johnson** (pf).
Hyperion CDJ33010. Texts and translations included.
Der Sänger, D149. Auf einen Kirchhof, D151. Am Flusse, D160. An Mignon,
D161. Vergebliche Liebe, D177. An die Apfelbäume, wo ich Julien erblickte,
D197. Seufzer, D198. Auf den Tod einer Nachtigall, D201. Der Liebende,
D207. Adelwold und Emma, D211. Der Traum, D213. Die Laube, D214. Der
Weiberfreund, D271. Labetrank der Liebe, D302. An die Geliebte, D303.
Harfenspieler I, D325.

♪ **74' DDD 5/91** ♩ P Ⓑ

Schubert. LIEDER, Volume 11. **Brigitte Fassbaender** (mez); **Graham
Johnson** (pf). Hyperion CDJ33011. Texts and translations included.
An den Tod, D518. Auf dem Wasser zu singen, D774. Auflösung, D807. Aus
Heliopolis I, D753. Aus Heliopolis II, D754. Dithyrambe, D801. Elysium,
D584. Der Geistertanz, D116. Der König in Thule, D367. Lied des Orpheus,
D474. Nachtstück, D672. Schwanengesang, D744. Seligkeit, D433. So lasst mich
scheinen, D727. Thekla, D595. Der Tod und das Mädchen, D531. Verklärung,
D59. Vollendung, D989. Das Zügenglöcklein, D871.

♪ **65' DDD 8/91**

The Hyperion Schubert Edition goes from strength to strength and all three discs
here are outstanding. Dame Janet Baker has always espoused the cause of rare
Schubert since the early days of her career and here she seems rejuvenated and
inspired by Johnson to recapture all her old sense of questing as she tackles
many songs that must be new to her. The selection is made entirely from
settings of Goethe and Schiller, and Baker responds strongly to some often quite
taxing songs. Right through she demonstrates again her unerring ability to seize
the mood and character of a song and project it with imaginative bravura. In
each case she makes you listen to the familiar as much as the unfamiliar with an
enthusiasm that matches her own adventurous approach. In support Graham
Johnson illustrates Schubert's mastery of the piano.

The Rolfe Johnson volume is devoted to nocturnal matters and it finds the
mellifluous tenor in his most inspired form. The soft grain of his tone and his
perceptive phrasing are to the fore throughout his long recital. The variety in the

Brigitte Fassbaender   *[photo: Hyperion / Crowthers]*

readings match the variety in the music and very few points go unremarked: intensity and sensitivity here go hand in hand.

So do they on the equally recommendable disc that features Ameling and Johnson. Once again the pianist and the originator of the series picks songs that are suited to the singer in the limelight. Ameling has made many very special Schubert recitals on disc over the years but here she seems inspired in the many rare and marvellous songs chosen for her to surpass even her own achievements. She sheds the years in producing performances that are of particular beauty and eloquence, not to forget her total command of technique and phrasing. Again there is a judicious mixture of the familiar and the unfamiliar, with the latter eliciting several forgotten masterpieces.

On Volume 8, with the theme of "Schubert and the Nocturne", are many marvels, not least a wondrous setting of *An den Mond in einer Herbstnacht* where Schubert minutely reflects the detail of a lovely poem about the moon being, as Johnson comments in his interesting notes, "all-seeing and all-encompassing". The Klopstock setting, *Die Sommernacht*, is another moon-saturated piece, where recitative and melody ideally match the cut of the poem. In more extrovert vein there is the gothic horror of Goethe's *Die Nonne* and the dreadful story of Rosalie von Montavert's interment in *Romanze*. To match these eerie ballads are Schubert's first settings of Goethe's beautiful *An den Mond* and the magically lilting *Ständchen* (Grillparzer) for mezzo and men's chorus. Yet another vein is struck in the still, timeless *Die Mondnacht* (Kosegarten). To crown the achievement comes a hair-raising version of *Der Erlkönig*. All these varying moods and types of setting are unerringly voiced by Sarah Walker (at home in the dramatic as she is in the lyrical or pensive) and played by Johnson, superb in *Erlkönig*. Both excel themselves. The recording is well balanced.

Johnson's choice of songs on Volume 10 are all well suited to Hill's plaintive tenor and slightly reticent manner. And what songs they are! It remains a mystery why so many outright masterpieces should have been neglected for so long, most notably perhaps the settings of the poet Ludwig Hölty, in all of which Hill's subtle word-painting and Johnson's finely shaped playing are unassumingly right. Many might have been written for this partnership to interpret. The two Goethe settings are on a similar level of inspiration. Then there is the first recording ever of the 27-minute narrative, *Adelwold und Emma*, a cornucopia of Schubertian invention, here fully realized. With a generous timing of 74 minutes this is a recital that will afford long-lasting and deep pleasure.

In Volume 11 of the series, we are given highly individual performances typical of Fassbaender in their intensity of manner. Graham Johnson has devised for her a programme with an emphasis on Death, with a capital 'D'. The songs range in breadth and colour from the eloquent swansong, *Nachtstück*, through the black humour of *Geistertanz*, the mystery of *Mignon (So lasst mich scheinen),* the impassioned exaltation of *Aus Heliopolis I*, to the majestic power of *Auflösung*. This series of thoughts about eternity and the Promised Land reaches its zenith in the quirky but magnificent Schiller view of heaven in *Elysium*, a cantata influenced by Beethoven. Fassbaender also throws new light on two songs usually associated with lighter voices—*Auf dem Wasser zu singen* and *Seligkeit*. As in other discs in this series, Johnson contributes well-varied playing and authoritative notes.

Schubert. LIEDER. **Nancy Argenta** (sop); **Melvyn Tan** (fp). EMI Reflexe
CDC7 54175-2. Texts and translations included.
Gott im Frühlinge, D448. Nachtviolen, D752. Der Wanderer an den Mond,
D870. Der Musensohn, D764. An die Nachtigall, D497. Der Schmetterling,
D633. Abendstern, D806. Schwestergruss, D762. Der Wachtelschlag, D742.
Nacht und Träume, D827. Liebhaber in alien Gestalten, D558. Auf dem Wasser
zu singen, D774. Die Forelle, D550. Kennst du das Land, D321. Heiss mich
nicht reden, D877 No. 2. So lasst mich scheinen, D877 No. 3. Nur wer die
Sehnsucht kennt, D877 No. 4. Heimliches Lieben, D922. An die Entfernte,
D765. Seligkeit, D433. Erster Verlust, D226. Rastlose Liebe, D138. Der Hirt
auf dem Felsen, D965 (with Erich Hoeprich, cl).

74' DDD 7/91

Here is a collection of Schubert Lieder performed by two highly respected
musicians who have a remarkably close musical partnership. What makes this CD
unusual is that Nancy Argenta is rarely heard in music of this period. The use,
not of a modern piano, but of a fortepiano (the kind of instrument more familiar
to Schubert) is also of particular interest here. It is an utter delight to hear
Argenta's interpretations of such familiar repertoire. It's almost as if she is
discovering it for the first time and her enthusiasm and enjoyment of each new
song is most infectious. The fortepiano has a nimble, sprightly quality which
gives an extra dimension of buoyancy in *Der Wanderer an den Mond* and *Der
Musensohn*. There is a danger that it can become a little too twangy to our
twentieth century ears, but we must not forget that Melvyn Tan is one of the
foremost exponents of the fortepiano and knows exactly how to measure his
accompaniments so that we quickly forget that this is not the instrument we hear
almost every day of our lives.

Schubert. LIEDER[a].
Schumann. LIEDER[b]. **Elly Ameling** (sop); **Jörg Demus** (pf). Deutsche
Harmonia Mundi Editio Classica GD77085. Texts and translations included.
Items marked [a] from BASF BAC3088 (2/75), [b] Deutsche Harmonia Mundi 1C
065 99631 (11/78).
Schubert: Der Hirt auf dem Felsen, D965 (with Hans Deinzer, cl). Seligkeit,
D433. Gretchen am Spinnrad, D118. Du liebst mich nicht, D756. Heimliches
Lieben, D922. Im Frühling, D882. Die Vögel, D691. Der Jüngling an der
Quelle, D300. Der Musensohn, D764. **Schumann:** Myrthen, Op. 25
Widmung; Der Nussbaum. Aufträge, Op. 77 No. 5. Sehnsucht, Op. 51 No. 1.
Frage, Op. 35 No. 9. Mein schöner Stern, Op. 101 No. 4. Lieder Album für
die Jugend, Op. 79—Schmetterling; Käuzlein; Der Sandmann; Marienwürmchen;
Er ists's; Schneeglöckchen. Erstes Grün, Op. 35 No. 4. Die Sennin, Op. 90
No. 4. Sehnsucht nach der Waldgegend, Op. 35 No. 5. Jasminenstrauch, Op. 27
No. 4. Liederkreis, Op. 39—Waldesgespräch. Loreley, Op. 53 No. 2. Die
Meerfee, Op. 125 No.]1.

69' ADD 5/90

This recital has been compiled from two LPs dating from the mid 1960s when
the soprano, Elly Ameling was at the height of her career. The older and
perhaps more beautiful of the two is the Schubert recital in which Elly Ameling
is accompanied on a fortepiano by Jörg Demus. It was an early gesture towards
'authenticity' and this is reflected both in the choice of piano and in the early
clarinet played by Hans Deinzer in the most celebrated of the songs *Der Hirt auf
dem Felsen*. But whatever the merits of the approach, and they are in this instance
considerable, it is the superlative singing of Elly Ameling that sets the seal of
distinction on this beautiful recital. *Gretchen am Spinnrad* is exquisitely felt, *Im
Frühling* fervent, wistful and perhaps unrivalled in its freshness of tone and

warmth of sentiment. This is a performance to treasure for a lifetime, leaving an indelible mark upon the sensibilities. There is not one disappointment here and the atmosphere one imagines to have suffused a Schubertiade is at times almost unbearably strong. The Schumann songs are no less well sung but, with a more up-to-date sounding piano the atmosphere is somewhat less heady. But these are affecting performances and no-one with a love of the repertory could fail to be enchanted by them. Full texts are provided in German and English and the sound, capturing much that was most attractive in recording techniques of the period, is appealing. An outstanding achievement.

Schubert. LIEDER. **Peter Schreier** (ten); **András Schiff** (pf). Decca 425 612-2DH. Texts and translations included.
Schwanengesang, D957. Herbst, D945. Der Wanderer an den Mond, D870. Am Fenster, D878. Bei dir allein, D866 No. 2.

> 63' DDD 6/90

Though *Schwanengesang* is not a song-cycle but a collection of Schubert's last (or 'swan') songs by their first publisher, it is generally felt to form a satisfying sequence, with a unity of style if not of theme or mood. This is certainly not weakened by the addition here of the four last songs which were originally omitted, all of them settings of poems by Johann Seidl. Seidl is one of the three poets whose work Schubert used in these frequently sombre songs and it is strange to think that all concerned in their creation were young men, none of the poets being older than Schubert. The listener can scarcely be unaware of a shadow or sometimes an almost unearthly radiance over even the happiest (such as "Die Taubenpost", the last of all) and that is particularly true when the performers themselves have such sensitive awareness as here. Peter Schreier is responsive to every shade of meaning in music and text; graceful and charming in "Das Fischermädchen", flawlessly lyrical in "Am Meer", he will sometimes risk an almost frightening raw-boned cry as in the anguish of "Der Atlas" and "Der Doppelgänger". András Schiff's playing is a miracle of combined strength and delicacy, specific insight and general rightness. One of the great Lieder recordings, and not merely of recent years.

Schubert. LIEDER. **Elisabeth Speiser** (sop); **John Buttrick** (pf). Jecklin Disco JD630-2. Texts and translations included.
Abendbilder, D650. Abschied, D475. Am Grabe Anselmos, D504. An mein Herz, D860. Beim Winde, D669. Frühlingsglaube, D686. Ganymed, D544. Strophe aus Die Götter Griechenlands, D677. Gretchen am Spinnrade, D118. Heimliches Lieben, D922. Im Abendrot, D799. Der Knabe, D692. Lachen und Weinen, D777. Lied der Anne Lyle, D830. Nachtstück, D672. Die Rose, D745. Schlaflied, D527. Sehnsucht, D879. Der Wanderer an den Mond, D870. Wanderers Nachtlied, D224. Der Winterabend, D938.

> 75' ADD 2/91 Ⓑ

Sometimes it is an unfashionable artist who yields more gratifying insights into a composer's music than a more familiar one. That is the case here where Elisabeth Speiser, a soprano who has been unassumingly on the scene for some time now, calls on her experience to look into the heart of a group of Schubert songs, familiar and unfamiliar, on a very well-filled CD. Time and again she goes to the heart of the matter through the thoughtfulness of her phrasing and the acuity of her verbal emphases. That would be of little avail if it were not for the sheer beauty of Speiser's singing. Though she recalls at times Irmgard Seefried and Margaret Price, she has a plaintive quality in her tone very much her own. All this makes her ideally fitted to the programme she has chosen, which has the sub-title "Schöne Welt, wo bist du ...?" ("Beautiful world, where are you ...?"). She and her admirable pianist John Buttrick have chosen well from Schubert's many songs dealing with the search for a peace and happiness mostly just beyond reach. For instance, the grief of *Am Grabe Anselmos*, the longing of *Der Wanderer an den Mond*, the unease amidst happy surroundings of *Frühlingsglaube* are moods all caught and held, with speeds ideal, line clear and accents precisely placed. These are typical of the whole.

Schubert. Die schöne Müllerin, D795. **Olaf Bär** (bar); **Geoffrey Parsons** (pf). EMI CDC7 47947-2. Text and translation included.

65' DDD 8/87

Schubert. Die schöne Müllerin, D795. **Dietrich Fischer-Dieskau** (bar); **Gerald Moore** (pf). DG 415 186-2GH (9/85).

62' ADD 9/85

Schubert. Die schöne Müllerin, D795. **Siegfried Lorenz** (bar); **Norman Shetler** (pf). Capriccio 10 220. Texts included.

68' DDD 5/90

Schubert. Die schöne Mullerin, D795. **Peter Schreier** (ten); **András Schiff** (pf). Decca 430 414-2DH. Texts and translations included.

63' DDD 5/91

The 20 songs of *Die schöne Müllerin* portray a Wordsworthian world of heightened emotion in the pantheistic riverside setting of the miller. The poet, Wilhelm Müller, tells of solitary longings, jealousies, fears and hopes as the river rushes by, driving the mill-wheel and refreshing the natural world. Olaf Bär has a most beautiful voice: warm and flexible and, more importantly, possessing the interpretative means of expressing the poetry. Fischer-Dieskau brings experience and intelligence to the inner life of both poetry and music. His flexible but distinctive tone-quality is fined down for the reflective songs and swelled to stentorian directness for the more resonant ones. On both recordings the accompanists bring insight and flair; sound quality is clean and natural.

Siegfried Lorenz and his dynamic accompanist, Norman Shetler, steals a march on much of the rest of the field by presenting the work with such unadorned freshness, captured in a recording of ideally distanced intimacy. Lorenz has a youthful vocal quality that accords beautifully with the sentiment of the verse, yet his maturity allows him to bring out the universal resonances that underpin the cycle, without having to resort to overemphasis. Norman Shetler is hardly an accompanist, for he ensures that the important piano part equals that of the vocalist, without in any way unduly dominating it: the result is an ideal musical partnership of give and take. Both performers have a lively sense of rhythm and a long-sighted view of pacing and balance within the cycle, so the prospects look good for this version to hold up well under the onslaught of repeated listening. Try before you buy, but if this is not possible you will not be disappointed with this recommendation.

However, Schreier's partnership with a notable Schubert pianist, András Schiff, surpasses all its predecessors and should be part of any worthwhile collection of Lieder. With his plangent tone, now more disciplined than ever, allied to his poignant and finely accented treatment of the text, Schreier gives moving expression to the youth's love and loss, nowhere more so than in his colloquy with the stream, "Der Müller und der Bach". Everything in his reading has been carefully thought through yet the result sounds wholly spontaneous and natural. To his role Schiff brings an inquiring mind, deft and pliant fingers and an innate feeling for Schubertian phraseology. He probes as deep into the music's meaning, perhaps deeper than any before him yet without giving the accompaniment undue prominence or calling attention unduly to the piano. More than anything, it is as a unified concept that this reading achieves its greatness. It is recorded with an ideal balance between voice and piano, in a sympathetic acoustic.

Schubert. Winterreise, D911[a]. Piano Sonata in C major, D840, "Reliquie"[b]. **Peter Schreier** (ten); **Sviatoslav Richter** (pf). Philips 416 289-2PH2. Text and translation included. Item marked [a] from 416 194-1PH2 (2/86)—recorded at a performance in the Semperoper, Dresden on February 17th, 1985; [b] 416 292-1PH (2/86)—recorded at a performance in Leverkusen, West Germany on December 12th, 1979.

② 2h 3' ADD/DDD 3/86 Ⓑ

Schubert. Winterreise, D911. **Olaf Bär** (bar); **Geoffrey Parsons** (pf). EMI CDC7 49334-2. Text and translation included.

75' DDD 11/89 Ⓑ

Schubert. Winterreise, D911. **Brigitte Fassbaender** (mez); **Aribert Reimann** (pf). EMI CDC7 49846-2. Text and translation included.

70' DDD 7/90 Ⓑ

Winterreise can lay claim to be the greatest song cycle ever written. It chronicles the sad, numbing journey of a forsaken lover, recalling past happiness, anguishing over his present plight, commenting on how the snow-clad scenery reflects or enhances his mood. Although the songs were written for a tenor, very often in recent years they have been sung by lower voices, which made the appearance of Peter Schreier's recording all the more welcome, particularly as he was partnered by Sviatoslav Richter. Schreier's plangent tenor and finely moulded phrasing are supported by almost limitless breath control. Richter's playing is communicative in a refined and subtly modulated way. The live recording has the attendant drawback of coughs at the most untoward moments, but the feeling of being present at a real occasion overrides it. Richter offers Schubert's *Reliquie* Sonata as a substantial filler in a mesmeric performance.

Bär's account is more resigned in its utterance but just as moving, yet he still seems able to encompass the best of the other school, evincing quite as much anguish and bitterness as Schreier. Throughout Bär's treatment of the text, pointed but unexaggerated, is masterly and with as clean a line as anyone when legato is called for. He also manages an extraordinary range of colour and accent in his reading, matching the immediacy in his projection of the broken man's feelings. In all this he is admirably and faithfully supported by Geoffrey Parsons. The recording is worthy of such a notable interpretation.

Although we normally hear a man sing this cycle, there is a precedent for a female interpreter in the past (Elena Gerhardt) and it has been followed by at least three mezzos today. Undoubtedly the most compelling among them is Brigitte Fassbaender whose reading is full of the agony of the soul portrayed by Schubert. However idiosyncratic she may be, Fassbaender's subtleties of phrase and verbal nuance always arise from the inner meaning of the poems and their settings. Her bold and arresting performance makes the listener hear the most searing of all cycles anew, and she is supported in her highly individual reading by the searching and frequently revelatory playing of Aribert Reiman. This isn't an easy or comforting interpretation, but it is one that consistently reaches the heart of the matter.

Schubert. Masses—G major, D167[a]; E flat major, D950[b]. [a]**Dawn Upshaw,** [b]**Benita Valente** (sops); [b]**Marietta Simpson** (mez); [a]**David Gordon,** [b]**Jon Humphrey,** [b]**Glenn Siebert** (tens); [a]**William Stone** [b]**Myron Myers** (bars); **Atlanta Symphony Chamber Chorus; Atlanta Symphony Chorus and Orchestra/Robert Shaw.** Telarc CD80212. Text and translation included.

· · 78' DDD 9/90

Schubert. Mass in E flat major, D950[a]. Tantum Ergo, D962[b]. Offertorium, D963[c]. [a]**Helen Donath,** [b]**Lucia Popp** (sops); [ab]**Brigitte Fassbaender** (mez); [a]**Francisco Araiza,** [bc]**Peter Schreier** (tens); [ab]**Dietrich Fischer-Dieskau** (bar); **Bavarian Radio Chorus and Symphony Orchestra/Wolfgang Sawallisch.** EMI Studio CDM7 69223-2. Items marked [a] from SLS5278 (5/83), [bc] SLS5254 (2/83).

· · 71' DDD 9/90

Schubert's second Mass, D167, was written in six days during 1815, his eighteenth year. This small-scale, tuneful work, given only a light accompaniment of strings and organ, conformed closely with what was expected of Schubert by his teacher, Salieri, and has many moments of simple charm, expressive of a simple faith. The Mass in E flat was completed, along with *Tantum Ergo* and the *Offertorium*, in the autumn of 1828, the year of Schubert's death, and is clearly the work of a composer at the height of his powers, intent on extending the boundaries of expression whilst still having to retain some of the conventions of formal liturgical structure. The accompaniment here is for the full orchestra of the time, minus flutes, and the dramatic impact of these resources is exploited to the full. Yet more than this, it is the revolutionary harmonic ideas that single this Mass out for special note, orchestral colours emphasizing the drastic shifts and subtle slides. The composer's faith had, by this time, become more individual, less conformist, and there are hints in this work of that reassessment. Robert Shaw and his Atlanta forces set the two works in stark contrast, underlining the individual qualities of each. The choral singing is of a high order and there is an underlying detachment in their approach that fits well with the intended use of this music; operatic emotion would hardly have been in keeping. Sawallisch, with the benefit of cleaner sound, can get away with more forceful, enriched expression and his is, perhaps, the preferable reading of D950. The coupled *Tantum Ergo* and *Offertorium* have splendid soloists who capture the Austrian flavour of these works well, showing them to be typical of that line of liturgical music that ran from Mozart to Bruckner. Both discs would grace the CD player and are sufficiently dissimilar to merit equal attention.

Schubert. FIERRABRAS. **Josef Protschka** (ten) Fierrabras; **Karita Mattila** (sop) Emma; **Robert Holl** (bass) Charlemagne; **Thomas Hampson** (bar) Roland; **Robert Gambill** (ten) Eginhard; **László Polgár** (bass) Boland; **Cheryl Studer** (sop) Florinda; **Brigitte Balleys** (contr) Maragond; **Hartmut Welker** (bar) Brutamonte; **Arnold Schönberg Choir; Chamber Orchestra of Europe/Claudio Abbado.** DG 427 341-2GH2. Notes, text and translation included. Recorded at performances in the Theater an der Wien, Vienna in May 1988.

· · ② 2h 24' DDD 10/90

The pathetic comment that Schubert "wrote more beautiful music than the world has time to know" is gradually being corrected as more of his almost completely neglected works are being brought to light. This opera was commissioned in 1823 in Vienna but, because of the Rossini craze, the departure of several German singers and a consequent managerial upheaval, not produced, and Schubert received no payment for it, either: it remained in limbo until it was published almost 60 years after his death. The 1988 performances in Vienna,

Claudio Abbado   *[photo: DG/Schirmer]*

from which this recording was taken, revealed the riches of his score, which—especially in Act 2, contains an astonishing sequence from a lovely duet for two girls and a forceful quintet to an unaccompanied chorus and a moving recognition scene—are overwhelming. The plot, a complicated web of medieval chivalry, love, honour and war at the courts of Charlemagne and a defeated but vengeful Moorish prince (whose daughter is secretly in love with the Frankish knight Roland, and his son Fierrabras with Charlemagne's daughter, who however has been dallying with the knight Eginhard), would have been enough to defeat an experienced operatic composer; and Schubert, without a hand to guide him, allowed his matchless lyrical invention to swamp dramatic pace, though there *is* drama too, in the rescue by the Moorish princess of Roland and his fellow ambassadors for peace from the prison in which they have basely been thrown. The orchestral writing is splendid and very characteristic, and Abbado misses no opportunity to underline its strength—perhaps a trifle at the expense of the voices, who are not always ideally balanced in ensembles: the choruses are brilliantly handled. The well-integrated cast is very satisfactory: chief honours go to Karita Mattila as Charlemagne's daughter, to Josef Protschka as the noble Moorish prince ready to sacrifice himself to shield her, and to Robert Gambill as the guilt-ridden Eginhard. The spoken dialogue is omitted but printed in full in the admirably produced booklet.

William Schuman   *Refer to Index*   *American 1910-*

Robert Schumann   *German 1810-1856*

Schumann. Violin Concerto in D minor. Fantasie in C major, Op. 131.
Thomas Zehetmair (vn); **Philharmonia Orchestra/Christoph Eschenbach.** Teldec 2292-44190-2.

♪ 45' DDD 4/90

Schumann had barely six months of normal working life left to him when writing his only two works for violin and orchestra in the autumn of 1853. Both were inspired by the 22-year-old Joachim, who though immediately taking the *Fantasie* into his repertory, subsequently decreed that the Concerto was unworthy of its composer and should be suppressed. But thanks to his great-niece, Jelly d'Aranyi who, guided by 'supernatural messages', secured its publication and performance in 1938, we now all know that any shortcomings in the somewhat episodic finale are more than redeemed by the quality of the first two movements, particularly the nostalgically beautiful *Langsam*. For Thomas Zehetmair's rapt playing of that movement alone, the disc would be invaluable. Though questionably deliberate in tempo in the finale, the performance as a whole emerges as a labour of love from soloist, orchestra and conductor alike, very sumptuously recorded. All musicians will be grateful for the Concerto's coupling with the *Fantasie*, a work hitherto unobtainable on CD. Here the disposition of the solo part and its interplay with the orchestra suggest that Joachim himself may have proffered a few helpful performing suggestions. Though not wholly seamless, the sonata-form argument is memorable for its recall of the inspired introductory theme in both the development section and coda. With their close attunement and fine balance, the warmly lyrical Zehetmair and Eschenbach certainly explain Joachim's own enthusiasm for this now unjustly neglected work.

Schumann. SYMPHONIES. **Staatskapelle Dresden/Wolfgang Sawallisch.** EMI Studio CDM7 69471-2, 69472-2. From SLS867 (2/74).
CDM7 69471-2—No. 1 in B flat major, Op. 38, "Spring"; No. 4 in D minor, Op. 120. Overture, Scherzo and Finale, Op. 52. *CDM7 69472-2*—No. 2 in C major, Op. 61; No. 3 in E flat major, Op. 97, "Rhenish".

② 77' 71' ADD 11/88 5/89 Ⓑ

Schumann's symphonies come in for a lot of criticism because of his supposed cloudy textures and unsubtle scoring, but in the hands of a conductor who is both skilful and sympathetic they are most engaging works. These two mid-price CDs, brightly transferred, return to circulation the contents of a much admired set. Sawallisch's conducting is sensible, alert and very pleasing and he achieves great lightness in the First and Fourth Symphonies. The Second and Third Symphonies, larger and more far-reaching in their scope, again benefit from Sawallisch's approach. The Dresden orchestra play superbly, with a lovely veiled string sound and a real sense of ensemble. These are real bargains and with the *Overture, Scherzo and Finale* thrown in for good measure, definitely not to be missed.

Schumann. Symphonies—No. 1 in B flat major, Op. 38, "Spring"; No. 4 in D minor, Op. 120. **Royal Concertgebouw Orchestra/Riccardo Chailly.** Decca 425 608-2DH.

63' DDD 12/90 Ⓢ Ⓑ

Recent recordings of Schumann Symphonies have sought to bring new insights often at the expense of beauty of tone, or the composer's perceived romanticism. Here is one which triumphantly proves that Schumann, played on modern instruments without radical interpretative standpoints, need not be a stale or bloated experience. Listening to this disc, one wonders why critics used to constantly berate poor Schumann for his inept orchestration. The lean, but wonderfully expressive, Concertgebouw strings are equal partners with the fresh and characterful woodwind (rarely, if ever, has this balance been so well managed); Chailly's direction is warm, precise, both taut and yielding in all the right places. Sawallisch's indispensable set of the seventies on EMI offers playing of more energy and determination in the Fourth, but the recording lacks the detail and transparent textures of this newcomer. Indeed the pristine clarity and three dimensional depth of Decca's sound is one of this disc's principal joys.

Schumann. Symphonies—No. 3 in E flat major, Op. 97, "Rhenish"; No. 4 in D minor, Op. 120. **London Classical Players/Roger Norrington.** EMI CDC7 54025-2.

57' DDD 3/91

Spearheading the authentic brigade's excursion into romantic repertoire, it's surprising how euphonious Roger Norrington's ensemble sounds here. Gone is the braying brass obscuring fragile strings that is often a feature of period performance. As in his recent Schubert discs, Norrington controls his forces with an acute ear and intelligence for what is germane to the music, and the brass only 'open up' where structure demands it, or where the overall balance would be unaffected. The strength of purpose, separated violin desks and close balance are often reminiscent of the best of Klemperer's work for EMI in the sixties. There is too a similar lack of concern for mere beauty of sound. Textural revelations aside (they are too numerous to mention), the most striking feature of these accounts is their strict adherence to Schumann's explicit indications of tempo: the middle movements of both symphonies are much faster than usual. Some collectors may initially feel short changed on graceful singing lines and variety of moods but compensation lies in the revitalization of the music's rhythms, and its sense of direction. The Fourth Symphony, in particular, is experienced in one single sweep. It's a pity, here, in music that should be continuous, that the CD contains breaks between the first three movements.

Schumann. WORKS FOR CELLO. **Yo-Yo Ma** (vc); [b]**Emanuel Ax** (pf); [a]**Bavarian Radio Symphony Orchestra/Sir Colin Davis.** CBS Masterworks CD42663.
Cello Concerto in A minor, Op. 129[a]. Fantasiestücke, Op. 73[b]. Adagio and Allegro in A flat major, Op. 70[b]. Funf Stücke im Volkston, Op. 102[b].

61' DDD 10/88

While others couple Schumann's endearing Concerto with other concertos, Yo-Yo Ma adopts the most logical course and gives us the rest of Schumann's music for cello and piano. His account of the Concerto is keenly affectionate and Sir Colin Davis gives him the most sympathetic support. Both soloist and conductor are in harmony and thoroughly attuned to the sensibility of this music. The Concerto comes from 1850, the same period as the *Rhenish* Symphony, and so is a relatively late work. Schumann called it a "Concert piece for cello with orchestral accompaniment", and is particularly successful in balancing the roles of both. The CBS recording is particularly successful with nicely rounded and mellow tone: the balance between soloist and orchestra is just about right and the various elements in the orchestral picture blend admirably. The sound suits Schumann's well-upholstered scoring. The three pieces that complete this disc are well projected and full of feeling with sensitive and well-characterized playing from Emanuel Ax. This belongs in any self-respecting Schumann collection and even though Ma exaggerates his *pianissimo* tone once or twice, his is playing of great refinement which serves this lovely music well.

Schumann. Violin Sonatas—No. 1 in A minor, Op. 105; No. 2 in D minor, Op. 121. **Gidon Kremer** (vn); **Martha Argerich** (pf). DG 419 235-2GH.

49' DDD 1/87

The rapidity of composition of the two violin sonatas (four and six days respectively) is nowhere evident except perhaps in the vigour and enthusiasm of the music. Argerich and Kremer, both mercurial and emotionally charged performers, subtly balance the ardent Florestan and dreamily melancholic Eusebius elements of Schumann's creativity. This is even more striking in the Second Sonata, a greater work than its twin, thematically vigorous with a richness and scope that make it at once a striking as well as ideally structured work. Kremer and Argerich have established a close and exciting duo partnership and this fine recording shows what like minds can achieve in music so profoundly expressive as this.

Schumann. Piano Sonata No. 1 in F sharp minor, Op. 11. Fantasia in C major, Op. 17. **Maurizio Pollini** (pf). DG 423 134-2GH. From 2530 379 (5/74).

> 63' ADD 5/88

These works grew from Schumann's love and longing for his future wife Clara. Both performances are superb, not least because they are so truthful to the letter of the score. By eschewing all unspecified rubato in the *Fantasia*, Pollini reminds us that the young Schumann never wrote a more finely proportioned large-scale work; this feeling for structure, coupled with exceptional emotional intensity, confirms it as one of the greatest love-poems ever written for the piano. His richly characterized account of the Sonata is refreshingly unmannered. Certainly the familiar charges of protracted patterning in the faster flanking movements are at once dispelled by his rhythmic *élan*, his crystalline texture and his ear for colour. The sound re-emerges with all its original clarity on CD.

Schumann. Kreisleriana, Op. 16. Etudes symphoniques, Op. 13. **Dmitri Alexeev.** EMI CDC7 49845-2.

> 72' DDD 11/89

Schumann. Kinderszenen, Op. 15. Kreisleriana, Op. 16. **Martha Argerich** (pf). DG 410 653-2GH. From 410 653-1GH (3/84).

> 52' DDD 5/84

Although Alexeev's *Kreisleriana* is a worthy contender in a hotly contested area of the market, it is for his *Etudes symphoniques* that this disc merits such a strong recommendation. In live performance, Maurizio Pollini on DG is hard to better in this latter work, but his own CD does not fully reflect the deep involvement

Robert Schumann

he has with this music. Alexeev here matches Pollini's propulsion through the devious ramifications of the noble theme, equalling his clarity of line and textural balance whilst embracing a more passionate realization of the music's bravura. His virtuosity is always put at the service of the music and his pacing of the disparate sections is so well thought through that he seizes the attention from the opening chord to the final lifting of the pedal. In this performance, Alexeev integrates the work's five supplementary variations into the general flow, between *Etudes* 7 and 8. As it is, Alexeev, recorded with spacious clarity and veracious dynamic and tonal range, emerges as a prime choice in this masterwork.

An effective performance of Schumann's 13 little pieces must be spontaneous and fresh-sounding yet sensitive to every detail. Martha Argerich fulfils these requirements for the most part, although some may find her treatment of certain of the *Kinderszenen* a little brisk. The *Kreisleriana,* however, is especially suited to her natural impetuosity; its sections are capricious and tenderly song-like by turns. Both works are marvellous examples of piano romanticism and the recording is delightfully natural.

Schumann. Dichterliebe, Op. 48. Liederkreis, Op. 39. **Olaf Bär** (bar); **Geoffrey Parsons** (pf). EMI CDC7 47397-2. From EL270364-1 (6/86).

54' DDD 9/86

The 16 songs of *Dichterliebe* ("A poet's love") form not so much a cycle as a sequence of *tableaux* charting the many emotions of the lover, from the wonder at the beauties of nature to the stoic resignation at love's fickleness. This is young man's music—ardent, vigorous and heartfelt. From Olaf Bär we have a young man's response—virile, firm of tone and warmly beautiful, never hectoring or over-insistent. This is mature singing of surpassing elegance. In the softer, dusky contours of the *Liederkreis* Bär demonstrates his fine legato and again impresses with his varied expressive range, capturing both the sense of mystery and the bitter-sweet quality of such songs as "Zwielicht" or "Wehmut". Geoffrey Parsons offers sensitive accompaniments and the recording assists Bär's immaculate diction, though never at the piano's expense.

Schumann. Szenen aus Goethes Faust. **Elizabeth Harwood, Jenny Hill, Jennifer Vyvyan, Felicity Palmer** (sops); **Meriel Dickinson, Margaret Cable, Pauline Stevens** (mezs); **Alfreda Hodgson** (contr); **Sir Peter Pears, John Elwes, Neil Jenkins** (tens); **John Noble, Dietrich Fischer-Dieskau, John Shirley-Quirk** (bars); **Robert Lloyd** (bass); **Wandsworth School Choir; Aldeburgh Festival Singers; English Chamber Orchestra/ Benjamin Britten.** Decca 425 705-2DM2. Notes, text and translation included. From SET567/8 (12/73).

1h 58' ADD 7/90

It was with Goethe's mystical closing scene, never approached by any composer before, that Schumann began his *Scenes from Faust* in 1844, when around the age of 34. The impending Goethe centenary celebrations sufficiently rekindled his life-long enthusiasm for the subject for three Gretchen-inspired scenes to follow in the summer of 1849, and three more Faust-inspired scenes the next year. But it was not until 1853 that he finally added the overture, and the work was never performed in its entirety until six years after his death. Even today it remains enough of a rarity for Benjamin Britten's revelatory revival in June 1972, to stand out as one of the most memorable of all his Aldeburgh Festival's many glories. So hats off to Decca for this CD reissue of the LP recording made at The Maltings in Snape shortly afterwards, with some, if not all, of the festival cast—incidentally a recording happily timed for first release on Britten's sixtieth birthday in November 1973.

Whereas in Goethe's closing scene (Part 3) we are reminded of the lyrical Schumann, the great surprise of the work is the drama of the subsequently composed Parts 1 and 2. Not for nothing had Schumann by this time moved from a Mendelssohn-dominated Leipzig to a Wagner-stirred Dresden. The late and still sorely lamented Elizabeth Harwood is a touchingly vulnerable, pure toned Gretchen, while Fischer-Dieskau responds with quite exceptional immediacy and intensity to Faust's blinding, visionary dreams and moment of death. As Mephistopheles and Ariel, John Shirley-Quirk and Sir Peter Pears are equally outstanding for their sensitive tonal shading and shapely line. Under Britten's inspired direction all soloists are splendidly upheld by the ECO, and last but not least, by the Aldeburgh Festival Singers and Wandsworth School Choir who sing with as much flexibility and character in their various guises as anyone on the platform. The CD reproduction is excellent.

Schumann. LIEDER. **Peter Schreier** (ten); **Christoph Eschenbach** (pf).
Teldec 2292-46154-2. Texts and translations included.
Liederkreis, Op. 24. Liederkreis, Op. 39. Dichterliebe, Op. 48. Myrthen,
Op. 25—No. 1, Widmung; No. 2, Freisinn; No. 3, Der Nussbaum; No. 7,
Die Lotosblume; No. 15, Aus den hebräischen Gesängen; No. 21, Was
will die einsame Träne?; No. 24, Du bist wie eine Blume; No. 25, Aus den
östlichen Rosen; No. 26, Zum Schluss, Lieder-Album für die Jugend, Op.
79—No. 4, Frühlingsgruss; No. 7, Zigeunerliedchen; No. 13, Marienwürmchen;
No. 26, Schneeglöckchen. Zwölf Gedichte, Op. 35—No. 3, Wanderlied; No. 4,
Erstes Grün; No. 8, Stille Liebe; No. 11, Wer machte dich so krank?; No. 12,
Alte Laute. Liebesfrühling, Op. 37—No. 1, Der Himmel hat eine Träne
geweint; No. 5, Ich hab in mich gesogen; No. 9, Rose, Meer und Sonne. Fünf
Lieder, Op. 40. Mein schöner Stern!, Op. 101 No. 4. Nur ein lächelnder Blick,
Op. 27 No. 5. Geständnis, Op. 74 No. 7. Aufträge, Op. 77 No. 5. Meine
Rose, Op. 90 No. 2. Kommen und Schneiden, Op. 90 No. 3. Lieder und
Gesange, Op. 51—No. 1, Sehnsucht; No. 3, Ich wandre nicht. An den Mond,
Op. 95 No. 2. Dein Angesicht, Op. 127 No. 2. Lehn deine Wang, Op. 142
No. 2. Der arme Peter, Op. 53 No. 3.

③ 2h 45' DDD 6/91

This is a very fair conspectus of Schumann's genius as a Lieder composer and all
the offerings are authoritatively performed. They include recommendable
accounts of the three cycles apt for a male singer to tackle. Schreier with
Eschenbach, who has made a special study of the composer, make the most of
Dichterliebe and the two *Liederkreise*, identifying themselves with the various
moods and characters depicted within. Schreier's idiomatic and pointed
diction and accents allied to Eschenbach's exploratory and imaginative way with
Schumann's highly individual writing for piano would be hard to better. The
remainder of these three well-filled CDs is given over to single songs and to
discerning choices from groups other than the cycles. Here are the most telling
pieces from *Myrthen* and from the 12 Kerner settings, Op. 35. Late
Schumann is acknowledged to be a more doubtful quantity, but he could still
write great songs such as the poignant *Meine Rose* and the lovely Heine setting,
Dein Angesicht. To these, as to the delightful *Zigeunerliedchen*, and much else, this
pair of superb performers bring their unfailing artistry, always seeking and
finding the heart of the matter. The well-balanced recording is an unobtrusive
support.

Schumann. LIEDER. **Eberhard Waechter** (bar); **Alfred Brendel** (pf).
Decca 425 949-2DM. Texts and translations included. From SXL2310 (6/62).
Dichterliebe, Op. 48. Liederkreis, Op. 24—Schöne Wiege meiner Leiden; Mit
Myrten und Rosen. Lehn deine Wang an meine Wang, Op. 142 No. 2. Mein
Wagen rollet langsam, Op. 142 No. 4.

41' ADD 6/91

This recording of *Dichterliebe*, 30 years old and somewhat overlooked when
first issued, is one of the most satisfying ever made of the cycle by virtue of
Waechter's total identification with the jilted man's sorrow expressed in
warm, vibrant, wholehearted, never self-conscious singing. Here the romantic
thoughts, melancholy, anger, torment, resignation, so memorably achieved in
Schumann's setting of Heine, receives an answering identification on
Waechter's part. Nowhere else in Schumann's output are the voice and piano
so closely entwined as if in a single outpouring of inspiration. Here that
achievement is fully realized through Brendel's discerning, probing execution.
Always achieving rapport with his partner, Brendel is here caught before he
became the famous pianist he is today. Anybody listening to his marvellously

perceptive accounts of Schumann's ingenious postludes would hear what a masterly pianist he already was. The extra songs are given with just as much illumination on both sides.

Heinrich Schütz

Schütz. SACRED CHORAL WORKS. **Monteverdi Choir; English Baroque Soloists; His Majesties Sagbutts and Cornetts/John Eliot Gardiner.** Archiv Produktion 423 405-2AH. Texts and translations included. Freue dich des Weibes deiner Jugend, SWV453 (with Frieder Lang, ten). Ist nicht Ephraim mein teuer Sohn, SWV40. Saul, Saul, was verfolgst du mich, SWV415. Auf dem Gebirge, SWV396 (Ashley Stafford, Michael Chance, altos). Musicalische Exequien, SWV279-81 (Lang).

· 51' DDD 11/88

Unlike so much of Schütz's huge output, made up largely of short motet-like settings, the *Musicalische Exequien* is a work of ample proportions; the opening "concerto in the form of a burial Mass" alone runs to more than 20 minutes of music. But it is not mere size that makes this work so striking. It is also a work of impressive solemnity. For all the exuberance trained into him through early contact with Venice in the age of the Gabrielis, in his mature works Schütz's distinguishing quality is his sobriety and austere nobility. Without question the climax of the *Musicalische Exequien* comes in the concluding "Nunc dimittis", an extraordinary setting in which a semi-chorus, half-heard from the dark recesses of the church, punctuates the main text with its own exquisite words, "Blessed are the dead which die in the Lord". Both here and in the selection of four short motets, the Monteverdi Choir sing with authority and great beauty, revealing in the process the true colours of music which in the wrong hands all too often is made to seem grey.

Schütz. St Matthew Passion, SWV479. **Paul Elliott** (ten) Evangelist; **Hilliard Ensemble/Paul Hillier** (Christus). EMI Reflexe CDC7 49200-2. Text and translation included. From EL270018-1 (4/85).

· 55' DDD 2/89

If Bach's two passions are masterpieces of reflection, encouraging the listener to ponder the meanings and mysteries that lie behind the Crucifixion story, then the passions of Heinrich Schütz are models instead of dramatic story-telling. Whereas Bach's libretti draw freely on contemporary poetry, Schütz's settings adhere closely to the Biblical narratives. In the *St Matthew Passion*, Schütz's principal medium is a unique form of monody, part plainchant, part recitative, which is delivered by solo voices without any accompaniment whatsoever. Severe as this speech-song may appear initially, in fact it allows for an extraordinary range of nuance, and in the hands of such sensitive performers as the Hilliard Ensemble, Schütz's monodies come alive in a powerfully communicative way. Without question this is not a disc that one would choose to play as background music, nor can it be listened to in snatches. It demands the closest attention, and reveals its secrets only when heard through from start to finish. In this impressive performance, finely paced and delivered in excellent German, the Hilliard Ensemble show it to be a work of exquisite pathos and power.

Alexander Scriabin

Russian 1872-1915

Scriabin. Piano Concerto in F sharp minor, Op. 20[a]. Prometheus, Op. 60[b]. Le poème de l'extase, Op. 54[c]. [ab]**Vladimir Ashkenazy** (pf); [b]**Ambrosian Singers;** [ab]**London Philharmonic Orchestra,** [c]**Cleveland Orchestra/ Lorin Maazel.** Decca 417 252-2DH. Items marked [a] and [b] from SXL6527 (1/72), [c] SXL6905 (9/79).

66' ADD 4/89

This CD gives us the essential Scriabin. The Piano Concerto has great pianistic refinement and melodic grace as well as a restraint not encountered in his later music. With *Le poème de l'extase* and *Prometheus* we are in the world of *art nouveau* and Scriabin in the grip of the mysticism (and megalomania) that consumed his later years. They are both single-movement symphonies for a huge orchestra: *Prometheus* ("The Poem of Fire") calls for quadruple wind, eight horns, five trumpets, strings, organ and chorus as well as an important part for solo piano in which Ashkenazy shines. The sensuous, luminous textures are beautifully conveyed in these performances by the LPO and the Decca engineers produce a most natural perspective and transparency of detail, as well as an appropriately overheated sound in the orgasmic world of *Le poème de l'extase*.

Scriabin. ORCHESTRAL WORKS. **Philadelphia Orchestra/Riccardo Muti.** EMI CDS7 54251-2. Text and translation included.
Symphonies—No. 1 in E major, Op. 26 (with Stefania Toczyska, mez; Michael Myers, ten; Westminster Choir. From EL270270-1, 3/86); No. 2 in C minor, Op. 29 (CDC7 49859-2, 11/90); No. 3 in C minor, Op. 43, "Le divin poème" (CDC7 49115-2, 4/89). Le poème de l'extase, Op. 54 (Frank Kaderabek, tpt. CDC7 54061-2). Prometheus, Op. 60, "Le poème du feu" (Dmitri Alexeev, pf; Philadelphia Choral Arts Society, CDC7 54112-2).

③ 3h 8' DDD 7/91

Harken all hedonists! Herein are contained all Scriabin's symphonies—the *Poem of Ecstasy* and *Prometheus* couldn't possibly be referred to by anything as mundane as mere symphonic numbers—at last in performances that mingle dramatic fervour with an ability to float all those gorgeous *cantabiles*; and achieve climaxes that radiate enlightenment and, yea, cause the very earth to move. The first two Symphonies find the budding luminary still bound by the fetters of tradition (such stars in the firmament as Liszt, Tchaikovsky and Wagner exerting a strong

gravitational pull). *The Divine Poem* (No. 3) shows Scriabin's universe magnificently broadening, using an enormous orchestra (to match the expanded mission), whilst the single movement *Poem of Ecstasy* and *Prometheus* represent the full flowering of his genius, and manage some startling musical innovations in the process. High Priest Riccardo Muti has at his command an orchestra whose opulent tones are here at their legendary best and a group of technical acolytes who see to it that the mystical waves of sound are aptly tidal.

Riccardo Muti *[photo: Philips/Steiner*

Scriabin. Symphony No. 1, Op. 26. **Stefania Toczyska** (mez); **Michael Myers** (ten); **Westminster Choir; Philadelphia Orchestra/Riccardo Muti.** EMI CDC7 47349-2. From EL270270-1 (3/86).

51' DDD 7/86

Cast in six movements this First Symphony evolves in a way that is often genuinely grand rather than merely grandiose, and the composer is more prodigal of invention than in some more characteristic later music where minimal thematic material is exposed to protracted and all too often febrile treatment. If in doubt as to whether you will like it, try the playful and delicately scored scherzo fourth movement. The finale, starting with a rhythmically very square exchange between the two soloists, is to a text by the composer himself. A committed performance such as this one from Muti and his Philadelphia players and singers does much for the work, and the recording is good.

Scriabin. Symphony No. 2 in C minor, Op. 29.
Tchaikovsky. Hamlet—fantasy overture, Op. 67. **Philadelphia Orchestra/ Riccardo Muti.** EMI CDC7 49859-2.

67' DDD 11/90

The trouble with 'bad' recordings of Scriabin's Second Symphony is that they make you feel that the composer was trying too hard to give his symphony formal unity by using the opening theme as the basis for most of the succeeding ones. Another trouble is that lack of faith in the score has often led conductors to tart it up with extra percussion—in their defence they might protest that Scriabin was a Russian, and that the Russians loved their cymbals. It occurs to this writer that Scriabin's intention to relate his expressive ideas symphonically was paralleled by a concern to orchestrate them with a nod to some of his more fastidious European forebears. A recipe for tedium? In Muti's hands, not for a second. With the Philadelphia Orchestra at their expressive and cultured best, full and glowing EMI sound, Muti provides triumphant vindication of Scriabin's values. Tchaikovsky's *Hamlet* is often unfavourably compared with his *Romeo and Juliet*. (Balakirev once wickedly observed that the love scene was the moment where Hamlet hands Ophelia an ice cream.) An entertaining but irrelevant remark. From the *Manfred*-like opening, the music takes its dark, oppressive and explosive course with unerring dramatic thrust and continuity. In a performance such as Muti's, it stands proudly alongside *Romeo and Juliet*, not in its shadow.

Scriabin. Symphony No. 3 in C minor, Op. 43, "Le Divin poème". Le poème de l'extase, Op. 54. **New York Philharmonic Orchestra/ Giuseppe Sinopoli.** DG 427 324-2GH.

70' DDD 6/89

Scriabin's "Divine Poem" is a gorgeous tapestry of shot colours and sinuous arabesques, portraying languorous and ecstatic emotions, visionary states and scarcely communicable ecstasies, but it is also a piece of music with a beginning, a middle and an end. What makes Sinopoli's account so special is his refined care for balance, both of texture and of tempo, and his choice of the "Poem of Ecstasy" as the obvious coupling. There is a fine sense, in both works, that you really are hearing every note that Scriabin wrote, and that foreground and background are both audible but never confused with each other. The secret seems to be a very precise control of the subtle slackenings and hastenings of tempo that are essential to Scriabin's idiom, and after one has relished all the impossible richnesses of this music it is an absorbing experience to go back for a repeat hearing to work out how Sinopoli does it. He couldn't have done it, of course, without orchestral playing of great subtlety and responsiveness and a recording that combines richness with exceptional clarity. Here he has both, and the result is both sumptuous and vital.

Scriabin. PIANO SONATAS. **Håkon Austbø.** Simax PSC1055.
No. 1 in F minor, Op. 6; No. 4 in F sharp, Op. 30; No. 5, Op. 53; No. 7, Op. 64, "White Mass"; No. 9, Op. 68, "Black Mass".
· 63' DDD 5/90

In the early years of this century the future of the great musical forms was much debated, and Scriabin was among those whose solutions fuelled the debate. He it was who, following Liszt, transmuted the symphony into the "poem"; and again building on Liszt's example he settled on a single-movement format for his last six piano sonatas (Nos. 6 to 10). This format was to be the container for mystical soul-states running the gamut from almost total inertia to delirious ecstasy. The pianist who wishes to do justice to such music has to have an uncommon gift for empathy—faultless elucidation of the score will get him nowhere near the heart of the matter. The Norwegian-born Håkan Austbø, now resident in Holland, captures precisely the multi-faceted fanaticism of Scriabin's imaginative world, and he even manages to suggest that the First Sonata is a worthy member of the canon rather than an early dry run. There have been other larger-than-life interpreters (Sofronitsky, Horowitz and Richter among them) whose recordings anyone seriously interested in this repertoire must seek out. But in his less demonstrative way Austbø says just as much about the essence of Scriabin, and his sensitivity to atmosphere even manages to turn a marginally over-reverberant acoustic to his advantage.

Dmitry Shostakovich
Russian 1906-1975

Shostakovich. Concerto in C minor for piano, trumpet and strings, Op. 35[a]. Piano Concerto No. 2 in F major, Op. 102. The Unforgettable Year 1919, Op. 89—The assault on beautiful Gorky. **Dmitri Alexeev** (pf); [a]**Philip Jones** (tpt); **English Chamber Orchestra/Jerzy Maksymiuk.** Classics for Pleasure CD-CFP4547. From CFP414416-1 (11/83).
· 48' DDD 1/89 £

Shostakovich's Piano Concertos were written under very different circumstances, yet together they contain some of the composer's most cheerful and enlivening music. The First, with its wealth of perky, memorable tunes, has the addition of a brilliantly-conceived solo trumpet part (delightfully done here by Philip Jones) that also contributes to the work's characteristic stamp. The Second Concerto was written not long after Shostakovich had released a number of the intense works he had concealed during the depths of the Stalin era. It came as a sharp contrast, reflecting as it did the optimism and sense of freedom that followed the death of the Russian dictator. The beauty of the slow movement is ideally balanced by the vigour of the first, and the madcap high spirits of the last. The poignant movement for piano and orchestra from the Suite from the 1951 film *The Unforgettable Year 1919*, "The assault on beautiful Gorky", provides an excellent addition to this disc of perceptive and zestful performances by Alexeev. He is most capably supported by the ECO under Maksymiuk, and the engineers have done them proud with a recording of great clarity and finesse. A joyous issue.

Shostakovich. Violin Concertos—No. 1 in A minor, Op. 99; No. 2 in C sharp minor, Op. 129. **Lydia Mordkovitch (vn); Scottish National Orchestra/Neeme Järvi.** Chandos CHAN8820.

69' DDD 4/90

These two heartfelt violin concertos are fine examples of Shostakovich's genius. It is the First, composed in 1948 for David Oistrakh, that is the better known and some people think it the finer work; but the Second was written for the same violinist two decades later and Lydia Mordkovitch, who studied with him in Moscow, reveals its sparer lines no less successfully than the big romantic gestures of No. 1. Her tone has a dark warmth that suits the soliloquizing lyrical music of these pieces admirably, but she is also not afraid to be uncompromisingly rough and tough (more so than Oistrakh himself) in the delivery of the scherzo and finale of the First Concerto as well as its great cadenza. Neeme Järvi is himself a committed performer of the Shostakovich symphonies who well understands the composer's style, and the Scottish National Orchestra sounds as Russian as anyone could wish, even to the tone of its brass section, which has the fine principal horn that both concertos require. The recording of the solo violin is closer than one would hear in the concert hall—Glasgow's City Hall in this case—and at times (for example, the cadenza of the First Concerto) positively tactile and percussive in effect, but with playing such as this few will complain. The orchestral sound is rich in the Chandos tradition and if it occasionally almost overwhelms the ear that is maybe what the composer intended. An exciting disc.

Shostakovich. Cello Concertos—No. 1 in E flat major, Op. 107; No. 2, Op. 126. **Heinrich Schiff (vc); Bavarian Radio Symphony Orchestra/Maxim Shostakovich.** Philips 412 526-2PH. From 412 526-1PH (8/85).

61' DDD 10/85

These two concertos make an obvious and useful 'coupling' for they are both vintage Shostakovich. Indeed, the First occupies a commanding position in the post-war repertory and is probably the most often-heard modern cello concerto. If the Second Concerto has not established itself in the repertory to anywhere near the same extent, the reason may be that it offers fewer overt opportunities for display. It is a work of grave beauty, inward in feeling and spare in its textures. It is pensive, intimate and withdrawn and on first encounter its ideas seem fugitive and shadowy, though the sonorities have a characteristic asperity. The recording's balance is generally excellent: very natural yet very clear, and there is quite outstanding definition and realism.

Shostakovich. Symphony No. 4 in C minor, Op. 43. **Scottish National Orchestra/Neeme Järvi.** Chandos CHAN8640.

61' DDD 12/89

Shostakovich withdrew the Fourth Symphony before its first performance and one can readily see why: Stalin would have loathed it. It is a work of extraordinary bitterness and anger, curdled with dissonance, raucous derision and eerie unease, the very model of what a Soviet symphony should not be, but at the same time the teeming cauldron from which much of the troubling ambiguity of Shostakovich's later style was cast. It needs a performance that takes risks, not least of setting the listener's teeth on edge and of terrifying him out of his wits. Järvi is prepared to allow his orchestra to yell at times to allow the occasional ugly, poisoned sound in a work that boils with discontent but also with sheer unreleased creative energy. No one who admires the Fifth Symphony should be without a recording of the Fourth that presents its towering frustration and disquiet at full strength. Järvi does so more successfully than any other conductor. Both his orchestra and the recording engineers hang on like grim death. The effect can only be described as magnificently appalling.

Shostakovich. Symphony No. 5 in D minor, Op. 47. Ballet Suite No. 5, Op. 27*a*. **Scottish National Orchestra/Neeme Järvi.** Chandos CHAN8650.

76' DDD 4/90 Ⓑ

Shostakovich. Symphony No. 5 in D minor, Op. 47[a]. Cello Concerto No. 1 in E flat major, Op. 107[b]. [a]**New York Philharmonic Orchestra/Leonard Bernstein;** [b]**Yo-Yo Ma** (vc); [b]**Philadelphia Orchestra/Eugene Ormandy.** CBS Maestro CD44903. Item marked [a] from 35854 (12/80), [b] 37840 (3/84).

77' DDD 4/90 £ Ⓑ

Shostakovich. Symphony No. 5 in D minor, Op. 47. Five Fragments, Op. 42. **Royal Philharmonic Orchestra/Vladimir Ashkenazy.** Decca 421 120-2DH.

56' DDD 6/88 Ⓑ

Shostakovich. Symphonies—No. 5 in D minor, Op. 47; No. 9 in E flat major, Op. 70. **Atlanta Symphony Orchestra/Yoel Levi.** Telarc CD80215.

78' DDD 6/90 P Ⓑ

There are more Shostakovich Fifths than you can shake a stick at in the CD catalogue at present, and several of them are very good. Järvi's makes perhaps the safest recommendation of them all: it has a generous coupling (which cannot be said of many of its rivals), it has no drawbacks (save, for some tastes, a slight touch of heart-on-sleeve in the slow movement) and a number of distinct advantages. A profound seriousness, for one thing, and an absolute sureness about the nature of the finale, which many conductors feel the need to exaggerate, either as brassy optimism or as bitter irony. Järvi takes it perfectly straight, denying neither option, and the progression from slow movement (the overtness of its emotion finely justified) to finale seems more natural, less of a jolt than usual. The SNO cannot rival the sheer massiveness of sound of some of the continental orchestras who have recorded this work, but while listening one hardly notices the lack, so urgent and polished is their playing. A very natural and wide-ranging recording, too, and the lengthy Suite (eight movements from Shostakovich's early ballet *The Bolt*, forming an exuberantly entertaining essay on the various modes that his sense of humour could take) makes much more than a mere fill-up.

Bernstein's overall approach to the Fifth is unashamedly warm and romantic, and is certainly one of the most weighty and impressive performances in the catalogue. Drama and tension are superbly sustained throughout the first movement, and it comes as no surprise to find the Mahlerian qualities of the work strongly projected both here and in the following *Allegretto*. The hushed and expressive playing from the NYPO strings at the beginning of the *Largo* is quite extraordinary, and Bernstein conveys the tragic intensity and introspective mood of this movement with consummate skill. The finale, avoiding any trace of irony or sarcasm, brings the Symphony to a triumphant and optimistic conclusion. The recording conveys all the electricity and presence of a live performance, while also having the clarity and precision one normally only finds in a studio recording.

Yo-Yo Ma's intense, compelling account of the First Cello Concerto is perhaps second only to Rostropovich's world première recording. Technically Ma is without flaw in this work. The outer movements are full of fire and rhythmic vitality, and in the slow movement and following cadenza he plays with great lyrical beauty and intensity. The recording is warm and well balanced. A remarkable bargain.

The collaboration of a Russian-born conductor and a Western orchestra works splendidly on the Decca issue. There have been more spectacular orchestral displays and more spectacular recording qualities, but rarely a more convincing alliance of idiomatic detail and structural insight. If one movement has to be singled out let it be the *largo*, often regarded as the emotional core of the work and interpreted here with intense inwardness and no trace of artificiality. Best results will be obtained at a slightly higher volume setting than usual, and even then glamorous orchestral sounds should not be expected—they're not what this music is about. The *Five Fragments* contain some of Shostakovich's quirkiest invention and are a rare and welcome bonus to a fine disc.

The Atlanta Symphony Orchestra's performances are among the best Shostakovich symphony recordings in recent years. One of the great lessons to be learned from them is that if you take careful note of Shostakovich's markings and then meticulously consider what he meant by them you will find that a good many of the music's interpretative problems are already solved. Which sounds easy, but when the poignant *Largo* of the Ninth Symphony sounds so achingly sad, but without a trace of applied histrionics to point the emotion, or when in the corresponding movement of the Fifth you are aware of a breathlessly hushed suspense without the slightest suspicion that this is the engineers' doing, you realize just how much Levi's painstaking study has achieved. He could not have achieved so much, of course, without superbly responsive orchestral playing and an unobtrusively lucid recording. The result is that we seem closer to Shostakovich himself than in many readings and better able to respond to the works as symphonies.

Shostakovich. Symphonies—No. 6 in B minor, Op. 54; No. 11 in G minor, Op. 103, "The year 1905"[a]. Overture on Russian and Kirghiz Folk Themes, Op. 115[b]. **Concertgebouw Orchestra, Amsterdam/Bernard Haitink.** Decca 411 939-2DH2. Item marked [a] from 411 939-1DH2 (6/85), [b] SXDL7577 (6/83).

② 1h 45' DDD 8/85

Shostakovich's Sixth and Eleventh Symphonies are both real challenges to the interpreter. The Sixth consists of a sombrely noble but deeply uneasy slow movement enigmatically followed by two scherzos but no apparent finale. The

Eleventh, a sequence of bold, poster-like images of the abortive 1905 uprising in Russia, makes extensive use of a number of tunes that are not Shostakovich's own (revolutionary songs of the period, mostly) and are not wholly suited to a symphonic structure on such a scale. The orchestral playing throughout both works is of the utmost splendour: the darkly glittering sonorities of the Sixth Symphony finely judged, the exhausting demands of its two fast movements heroically met; the sheer power and attack of the Eleventh, of the strings especially, rendered with precision as well as weight. The recording is very clean, natural and spacious.

Shostakovich (arr. Atovm'yan). The gadfly—suite, Op. 97*a*. **USSR Cinema Symphony Orchestra/Emin Khachaturian.** Classics for Pleasure CD-CFP4463. From EMI ASD3309 (2/77).

42' ADD 4/89 £

This film score belongs to the 1950s, a period when the composer produced some of his finest and most characteristic work, and if this is hardly profound or very personal Shostakovich it is still often striking, usually charming and unmistakably his. In a way the bargain price goes with the music: this is emphatically not top-drawer Shostakovich but it is worth having and the 1962 Melodiya recording has come up well in the present digital remastering. Sample No. 6 in the Suite, the entertaining "Galop", to see how the composer could be absolutely simple yet effective; sample the following "Introduction into the Dance" to hear how he could turn conventional phrases into something genuinely touching. The Suite shows how much music from the film was worth preserving and it has been well arranged by Lev Atovm'yan from the original score. The USSR Cinema Symphony Orchestra plays it as to the manner born.

Shostakovich Two Pieces for String Quartet (1931)[a]. Seven Romances on Poems of Alexander Blok, Op. 127[b]. Piano Quintet in G minor, Op. 57[c]. [b]**Elisabeth Söderström** (sop); [c]**Vladimir Ashkenazy** (pf); **Fitzwilliam Quartet** (Christopher Rowland, [ac]Jonathan Sparey, vns; [ac]Alan George, va; Ioan Davies, vc). Decca 411 940-2DH.

64' DDD 2/87

This is powerful music and very well performed, but not comfortable listening. The piano writing in the Quintet could hardly be further from the older Russian tradition of Rachmaninov in its sparse texture, although there is a fortitude and perhaps even nobility in the Quintet as a whole. In the much later *Seven Romances on Poems of Alexander Blok* the accompanying piano trio is used mostly in different combinations of instruments and only complete in the final song: the poems are full of sombre introspective images (for example, "a black dream oppresses my heart" in No. 6) that are all too faithfully reflected in the music. But the intensity of the performances here commands admiration. Elisabeth Söderström's Russian seems wholly idiomatic, and in the Quintet the Fitzwilliam Quartet are by no means upstaged by Ashkenazy's icy power.

Shostakovich. String Quartets—No. 1 in C major, Op. 49; No. 3 in F major, Op. 73; No. 4 in D major, Op. 83. **Brodsky Quartet** (Michael Thomas, Ian Belton, vns; Paul Cassidy, va; Jacqueline Thomas, vc). Teldec 2292-46009-2.

72' DDD 6/90

The young Brodsky Quartet are in the course of issuing a complete cycle of Shostakovich's string quartets and on this evidence it should be well worth collecting. The First, Third and Fourth Quartets make a particularly absorbing coupling, with hinted depths and plans for further exploration clearly audible beneath the acknowledgements to quartet tradition in the First (which also has a touch of very likeable open-eyed naivety to it), an enormous step forward to the grandeur of the Third's impassioned slow movement and a path forward firmly indicated by the troubled ambiguities and poignancies of the Fourth. The Brodsky will have the range for the complete cycle, there seems no doubt of that; already there is a fine balance between bigness of gesture and an expressive but strong lyricism. They are especially good at pacing and concentration over a long span, too, and they leap the technical hurdles with ease. A very clean and direct but rather close recording, but the sense of being amidst such responsive players, almost watching their intentness, has its own rewards.

Shostakovich. String Quartet No. 8, Op. 110.
Tippett. String Quartet No. 3. **Duke Quartet** (Louise Fuller, Martin Smith, vns; John Metcalfe, va; Ivan McCready, vc). Factory Classical FACD246.

51' DDD 1/90

Shostakovich's Eighth is his most 'public' quartet, a sustained and bitter outcry at oppression and inhumanity. Its official dedication is "in memory of the victims of fascism and war"; but its copious self-quotations and its incessant use of the composer's musical monogram DSCH (D, E flat, C, B in German notation) makes it clear that the work is 'about' far more than the aftermath of the Second World War. Tippett's Third, by contrast, is in a sense his most private quartet, a prolonged and at times visionary wrestling with the shade of Beethoven, containing audacious formal experiments. By choosing for their recording début two of the most technically and expressively demanding works in the repertory, the young Duke Quartet certainly nailed their colours to the mast. They are powerfully communicative players, with what seems like a burning desire to convey the protesting grief of the Shostakovich and the sometimes inward, sometimes ecstatic musings of the Tippett. They have the virtuoso technique and the ample tone to achieve this. No less important, they have a very firm sense of the music's impulse; whether the movement is fast or slow, there is a strong feeling of forward impetus and clearly perceived destination. The recording, appropriately enough, brings these passionately urgent readings very close to the listener.

Shostakovich. Piano Quintet in G minor, Op. 57ª. String Quartets—No. 7 in F sharp minor, Op. 108; No. 8 in C minor, Op. 110. ªSviatoslav **Richter** (pf); **Borodin Quartet** (Mikhail Kopelman, Andrei Abramenkov, vns; Dmitri Shebalin, va; Valentin Berlinsky, vc). EMI CDC7 47507-2. From EL270338-1 (11/85).

70' ADD 10/87

The Seventh and Eighth Quartets are separated by only one opus number and both works inhabit a dark and sombre sound world. The Seventh is dedicated to the memory of his first wife, Nina, who died in 1954 and is one of his shortest and most concentrated quartets. The Eighth Quartet provides a perfect introduction to Shostakovich's music. It is very much an autobiographical work. The Piano Quintet is almost symphonic in its proportions, lasting some 35 minutes and has been popular with audiences ever since its first performance in 1940. Much of its popularity stems from Shostakovich's highly memorable material, particularly in the boisterous and genial Scherzo and finale movements. The Borodin Quartet play with great authority and conviction and in the Seventh Quartet there is a fine sense of poetry and intimacy. Richter's performance of the Piano Quintet matches the grandeur of the work, with playing that has tremendous power and strength. The recording, taken from a live performance, is rather dry with a slightly hard piano sound, but this does little to distract from so commanding a performance as this. The earlier studio recordings of the string quartets are well recorded. An excellent introduction to the chamber music of Shostakovich.

Shostakovich. 24 Preludes and Fugues, Op. 87. **Tatyana Nikolaieva** (pf). Hyperion CDA66441/3.

③ 2h 46' DDD 3/91

Even if you didn't know that Shostakovich had written his 24 Preludes and Fugues specially for Tatyana Nikolaieva it would be difficult not to sense the unique authority. The playing isn't without the odd small blemish here and there (memory lapses?) and the reverberant acoustic adds a sustaining pedal effect of its own in one or two places, but for playing of such strength, character and insight one would willingly put up with far worse. Inevitably particular pieces linger in the memory—the impassioned F sharp minor Fugue, the dancing A major Prelude or the haunted stillness of the B flat minor Fugue—but the most impressive aspect of Nikolaieva's interpretation is the way she communicates her belief that these 24 small pieces add up to a complete musical experience—after this it's very difficult to disagree: the monumental D minor Fugue really does feel like the final stage in a long and fascinatingly varied process. If you still think that Shostakovich's contribution to piano literature is relatively insignificant, try this.

Jean Sibelius
Finnish 1865-1957

Sibelius. Violin Concerto in D major, Op. 47 (original 1903-04 version and final 1905 version). **Leonidas Kavakos** (vn); **Lahti Symphony Orchestra/ Osmo Vänskä.** BIS CD500.

75' DDD 4/91

In the 1950s the BBC Third Programme regularly broadcast a series called "Birth of an opera" which traced the evolution of an operatic masterpiece from gestation to first performance. This disc could almost be called "Birth of a Concerto", for it offers Sibelius's first thoughts alongside the final version of the Violin Concerto. After its unsuccessful first performance in Helsinki in 1904, the composer decided to overhaul it and putting the two versions alongside each other is an absorbing experience. One is first brought up with a start by an incisive figure just over a minute into the proceedings after which the orchestra does all sorts of 'unexpected' things! In the unaccompanied cadenza 21 bars later (2'11") there is some rhythmic support while to the next idea on cellos and bassoon (fig. 2), the soloist contributes decoration. And then at seven bars before fig. 3 (3'41") a delightful new idea appears which almost looks forward to the light colourings of the later *Humoresques*. Although it is a great pity that it had to go, there is no doubt that the structural coherence of the movement gains by its loss both here and on its reappearance. It is the ability to sacrifice good ideas in the interest of structural coherence that is the hallmark of a good composer. The fewest changes are in the slow movement which remains at the same length. As in the case of the Fifth Symphony where the revision is far more extensive than it is here the finished work tells us a great deal about the quality of Sibelius's artistic judgment, and that, of course, is what makes him such a great composer. This disc offers an invaluable insight into the workings of his mind, and even in its own right, the 1904 version has many incidental beauties to delight us. Leonidas Kavakos and the Lahti Orchestra play splendidly throughout and the familiar concerto which was struggling to get out of the 1903-04 version emerges equally safely in their hands.

Sibelius. SYMPHONIES. **Philharmonia Orchestra/Vladimir Ashkenazy.** Decca 421 069-2DM4.
Symphonies—No. 1 in E minor (from 414 534-1DH, 5/86); No. 2 in D major (SXDL7513, 11/80); No. 3 in C major (414 267-1DH, 8/85); No. 4 in A minor (SXDL7517, 5/81); No. 5 in E flat major (SXDL7541, 1/82); No. 6 in D minor (414 267-1DH, 2/85); No. 7 in C major (SXDL7580, 8/83).

④ 3h 52' ADD/DDD 12/87

Of all the cycles of Sibelius's symphonies recorded during recent years this is one of the most consistently successful. Ashkenazy so well understands the thought processes that lie behind Sibelius's symphonic composition just as he is aware, and makes us aware, of the development between the Second and Third Symphonies. His attention to tempo is particularly acute and invariably he strikes just the right balance between romantic languor and urgency. The Philharmonia play for all they are worth and possess a fine body of sound. The recordings are remarkably consistent in quality and well complement the composer's original sound-world.

Sibelius. Symphony No. 1 in E minor, Op. 39. Karelia—suite, Op. 11. **Philharmonia Orchestra/Vladimir Ashkenazy.** Decca 414 534-2DH.

57' DDD 5/86   **B**

The First Symphony has strong Tchaikovskian echoes, even though the colouring and personality of Sibelius are still greatly in evidence. Ashkenazy and the Philharmonia Orchestra give a strongly projected account of the score: the first movement has real grip and this performance conveys a powerful sense of its architecture. But throughout the work Ashkenazy evokes the Sibelian landscape with instinctive sympathy and the sheer physical excitement this score engenders is tempered by admirable control. The recording has superb detail and clarity of texture, and there is all the presence and body one could ask for. The playing of the Philharmonia Orchestra is of the very first order. The popular *Karelia* Suite makes an admirable make-weight and is beautifully played and recorded.

Sibelius. Symphony No. 2 in D major, Op. 43. Romance in C major, Op. 42. **Gothenburg Symphony Orchestra/Neeme Järvi.** BIS CD252.

48' DDD 10/84   **B**

The Second Symphony possesses a combination of Italianate warmth and Nordic intensity that has ensured its wide popular appeal. None of his other symphonies has enjoyed such immediate and enduring success. If it inhabits much the same world as the First, it views it through more subtle and refined lenses. As in the First Symphony, it is the opening movement that makes the most profound impression. Its very air of relaxation and effortlessness serves to mask the inner strength it has. Järvi's version has sinew and fire and the Gothenburg orchestra are splendidly responsive and well disciplined. There is an unerring sense of purpose and direction: the momentum never slackens and yet nothing seems over-driven. The performance is concentrated in feeling and has freshness and honesty. The short but charming *Romance* in C for strings, written at about the same time, is an excellent make-weight.

Sibelius. Symphonies—No. 3 in C major, Op. 52; No. 7 in C major, Op. 105. **City of Birmingham Symphony Orchestra/Simon Rattle.** EMI CDC7 47450-2. From EL270496-1 (4/87).

51' DDD 8/87

Sibelius's Third Symphony is a striking advance on his first two; whilst they speak the same language as the music of Tchaikovsky and Grieg, the Third strikes us because of its spareness of texture and concentration of ideas. The weight of string tone associated with Sibelius is here apparent and carries tremendous expressive power. The finale, in particular, is a remarkable movement possessing a power and inevitability that evolve from the Symphony's unusual structure. Sibelius's last symphony, also in C major, shows how far his gift for concentration had taken him. It is his shortest symphony; a single 23-minute movement originally entitled *Fantasia Sinfonica*. Its brevity by no means impedes its scale and scope and in it Sibelius weaves together a series of motivic ideas that fuse and gain in strength as the work unfurls. Both performance and recording are very fine.

Sibelius. Symphonies—No. 4 in A minor, Op. 63[a]; No. 6 in D minor, Op. 104[b]. **Berlin Philharmonic Orchestra / Herbert von Karajan.** DG 415 107-2GH. Item marked [a] from SLPM138974 (6/66), [b] SLPM139032 (10/68).

> 63'   ADD   6/85

Sibelius. Symphonies—No. 4 in A minor, Op. 63; No. 5 in E flat major, Op. 82. **San Francisco Symphony Orchestra / Herbert Blomstedt.** Decca 425 858-2DH.

> 68'   DDD   7/91

Both of the symphonies on the DG disc are dark almost sombre pieces, lacking the harmonic colouring and textural richness of many of the other compositions from this period. The Fourth is cast in greys and silvers rarely employing the orchestral resources at their most opulent, preferring instead a sparer, more restrained weave. Sibelius employs a motto theme which, like so many works that seem to lie under a shadow cast by Fate, adds to its powerful sense of internal unity. The Sixth Symphony too is a work of restraint and sombre colour. Again the composer eschews vibrant surface life to dig deep in the soul and the music receives a strong sense of unity through the use of motifs but here they have a rich modal flavour that place the work apart as a product of the carefree 1920s. Karajan has long been a champion of Sibelius's music and the icy depths of the Berlin strings, their peerless winds and dark, baying brass add a powerful sense of inevitability to these two scores. The early 1960s recording are very good.

  Herbert Blomstedt's performances are very impressive indeed. First, he gets exactly the right kind of sound from the San Francisco orchestra: the strings are cultured without being too sumptuous, the wind and brass are beautifully blended and the overall sound is lean and refined. Secondly, the music unfolds so naturally and logically, and in a totally unforced way. This is impressive in both symphonies, and so is the feeling for texture Blomstedt shows. In both the first and the slow movement of the Fourth Symphony there is an impressive sense of communion with nature. It is never possible to say that one record is the 'best', particularly when there are so many fine versions of both symphonies in circulation, but there is no doubt that this is one of the best records of both symphonies to have appeared for a very long time, and the recording is altogether state-of-the-art.

Sibelius. Symphonies—No. 5 in E flat major, Op. 82[a]; No. 7 in C major, Op. 105[b]. **Berlin Philharmonic Orchestra / Herbert von Karajan.** DG 415 108-2GH. Item marked [a] from SLPM138973 (9/65), [b] SLPM139032 (10/68).

> 55'   ADD   6/85

The Fifth Symphony, like No. 7, is epic and heroic in character, and the finale has a tremendous feeling of momentum as well as an awe-inspiring sense of the majesty of nature. The one-movement Seventh is the most extraordinary of his symphonies and the most sophisticated in its approach to form. Karajan has recorded the Fifth no fewer than four times and the best is undoubtedly this DG version made in 1965. It has grandeur and nobility and, it goes without saying, superlative orchestral playing. The transfer to CD is so successful that it would be difficult to guess its age. This is a classic account of the Fifth.

Sibelius. ORCHESTRAL WORKS. **Berlin Philharmonic Orchestra/ Herbert von Karajan.** DG 413 755-2GH. From 413 755-1GH (10/84). Finlandia, Op. 26. Legends, Op. 22—No. 2, The swan of Tuonela. Kuolema, Op. 44—Valse triste. Tapiola, Op. 112.

| 44' DDD 1/85 | ♩ P |

Karajan was a lifelong Sibelian and this CD brings what is arguably his greatest account of *Tapiola*, that extraordinary vision of the primaeval Northern forests—though to be frank you can't go far wrong with any of his performances of it! But never has it sounded more mysterious or its dreams more savage; never have the wood-sprites "weaving their magic secrets" come more vividly to life and never has the build-up to the storm ever struck a more chilling note of terror. Once in his later years Sibelius spoke of Karajan having a very special feeling for his music and listening to his account of The swan you can see why! He captures its powerful, brooding atmosphere to perfection and the remaining two pieces, *Valse triste* and *Finlandia* are hardly less impressive. At 44 minutes playing-time this may seem short measure, but if it is short on quantity, it is long on quality and that applies to the recording too.

Sibelius. ORCHESTRAL WORKS. [a]**Royal Philharmonic Orchestra;** [b]**BBC Symphony Orchestra;** [c]**London Philharmonic Orchestra/Sir Thomas Beecham.** EMI Beecham Edition mono CDM7 63397-2.
The Tempest—incidental music, Op. 109 (from Philips ABR4045, 12/55)[a]. Scènes historiques: Op. 25—No. 3, Festivo; Op. 66 (both from Columbia 33C1018, 11/53)[a]. Karelia Suite, Op. 11—No. 1, Intermezzo; No. 3, Alla marcia (HMV DB6248. Recorded 1945)[b]. Finlandia, Op. 26 (Columbia LX704, 4/38)[c].

| 73' ADD 7/90 | £ ♩ P |

In 1925 Sibelius was commissioned to write incidental music for a lavish production of Shakespeare's The Tempest at the Royal Theatre, Copenhagen. As this theatre also houses the Royal Danish Opera, he had a large orchestra at his disposal. After its successful production the following year he arranged two suites from the music, publishing the Prelude separately. Beecham's 1955 recording of the two suites has long enjoyed legendary status—and has never really been equalled, let alone surpassed. (Beecham omits the Prelude here, perhaps because it appears in truncated form at the end of the Second Suite.) The "Oak Tree" is haunting and the "Chorus of the Winds" is pure magic in his hands: it is a joy to hear the rapt *ppp* string tone he secured and in the Intermezzo that follows. The 1952 performances of four of the *Scènes historiques* have a similar ring of authenticity that transcend sonic limitations—which, incidentally, are few. The *Karelia* Intermezzo recorded in 1945 is curiously cavalier but the "Alla marcia" finds him back on form. The *Finlandia* is rather drily recorded but grippingly played. But it is *The Tempest* music that makes this CD a must.

Sibelius. ORCHESTRAL WORKS. **Royal Philharmonic Orchestra/Sir Thomas Beecham.** EMI Beecham Edition CDM7 63400-2.
Pelléas et Mélisande—incidental music, Op. 46. The Oceanides, Op. 73. Symphony No. 7 in C major, Op. 105 (all from HMV ASD468, 7/62). Tapiola, Op. 112 (ASD518, 4/63).

| 76' ADD 7/90 | £ ♩ P |

Beecham's championship of Sibelius began in earnest in the 1930s when he made a number of pioneering records of his music including the Violin Concerto with Heifetz. One of the special things about Beecham's Sibelius was its sheer

sonority: there was a fresh, vernal sheen on the strings quite different from the opulence of Koussevitzky or Karajan but with all their flexibility and plasticity of phrasing, and a magic that is easier to discern than define. Moreover his feeling for atmosphere in Sibelius was always matched by a strong grip on the architecture. This CD collects some of his greatest performances from the early days of stereo—*Pelléas, Tapiola* and *The oceanides*. His *Pelléas* is glorious and remains unsurpassed in atmosphere and poetic feeling, though Karajan some three decades later runs it pretty close. But Beecham conveys that pale wintry light in the "Pastorale", when the strings enter (track 5, 00'50" onwards) as does no other conductor. When he visited Sibelius in 1955 shortly before his ninetieth birthday, the composer asked him to record *The Oceanides*, and his performance remains altogether special in its handling of light and colour, as well as the control of climax. Beecham recorded *Tapiola* twice, once immediately after the war and then again in 1955, and though he did not actually pass the present recording for publication it is still pretty superb. He makes the magic of the forest depths very telling and though his account of the Seventh Symphony does not quite match it, this CD still remains an indispensable part of a Sibelius collection. Amazing sound for its period.

Sibelius. Piano Quintet in G minor (1890)[a]. String Quartet in D minor, Op. 56, "Voces intimae". **Gabrieli Quartet** (John Georgiadis, Brendan O'Kelly, vns; Ian Jewel, va; Keith Harvey, vc) with [a]**Anthony Goldstone** (pf). Chandos CHAN8742.

74' DDD 2/90

Only a few months after its composition in 1890, Sibelius dismissed his Piano Quintet as "absolute rubbish". It is far from that, though Busoni's description of it as "wunderschön" is rather overdoing things. The first movement is probably the finest though the *Andante,* too, has a lot of good music in it, if let down by a rather lame, march-like second theme. The scherzo is attractive and very neatly played. To maximize contrast, these artists reverse the order of the scherzo and the *Andante* so that the two slow movements are separated. Although the finale is less satisfactory in terms of structure, it has a good deal of spirit and some memorable ideas. Anthony Goldstone is consistently imaginative and intelligent throughout and the Gabrielis play with conviction. The *Voces intimae* Quartet comes from Sibelius's maturity—between the Third and Fourth symphonies. It is a masterly score and is selflessly played. The fourth movement certainly needs more bite and forward movement; yet the scherzo could not be done with greater delicacy and finesse—and no one comes closer than they to the spirit of this music in the closing bars of the slow movement or the celebrated bars that Sibelius marked "voces intimae".

Sibelius. SONGS. **Anne Sofie von Otter** (mez); **Bengt Forsberg** (pf). BIS CD457. Texts and translations included.
Arioso, Op. 3. Seven Songs, Op. 17. Row, row duck (1899). Six Songs, Op. 36. Five Songs, Op. 37. Pelleas and Melisande, Op. 46—The three blind sisters. Six Songs, Op. 88. Narcissus (1918).

57' DDD 6/90	?

In all, Sibelius composed about 100 songs, mostly to Swedish texts but his achievement in this field has, naturally enough, been overshadowed by the symphonies. Most music-lovers know only a handful like "Black roses", Op. 36 No. 1, and "The Tryst" and the most popular are not always the best. Sibelius's output for the voice has much greater range, diversity and depth than many people suppose. For collectors used to hearing them sung by a baritone, the idea of a soprano will seem strange but many of them were written for the soprano Ida Ekman. Anne Sofie von Otter not only makes a beautiful sound and has a feeling for line, but also brings many interpretative insights to this repertoire. The very first song from the Op. 17 set is a marvellous Runeberg setting, "Since then I have questioned no further" and it was this that Ida Ekman sang for Brahms! Von Otter captures its mood perfectly and has the measure of its companions too. Her account of "Black roses" is particularly thrilling and she is very persuasive in the weaker Op. 88 set. She sings throughout with great feeling for character and her account of "Astray", Op. 17 No. 6, has great lightness of touch and charm. The Opp. 36 and 37 sets are among the finest lyrical collections in the whole of Sibelius's song output, and they completely engage this artist's sensibilties. These are performances of elegance and finesse; Bengt Forsberg proves an expert and stylish partner and both artists are well recorded.

Robert Simpson
British 1921-

Simpson. Symphony No. 3[a]. Clarinet Quintet[b]. [b]**Bernard Walton** (cl); [b]**Aeolian Quartet** (Sydney Humphreys, Raymond Keenlyside, vns; Margaret Major, va; Derek Simpson, vc); [a]**London Symphony Orchestra/Jascha Horenstein.** Unicorn-Kanchana Souvenir UKCD2028. Item marked [a] from UNS225 (9/70), [b] UNS234 (8/71).

66' ADD 6/90

The British have been accused of chauvinism, but by no way of thinking can this be said to apply to British opinion of native composers, which has often been disparaging, as both Elgar and Britten found to their cost until the pendulum swung the other way, and it is disgraceful that Robert Simpson has only recently been recognized as the major figure that he is although he has been a symphonist for 40 years and not long ago wrote his Tenth Symphony. This is not the place to apportion blame, but rather to say that many of us are doing some belated

catching up with this composer who proves that one doesn't have to be a serialist or minimalist to write music that is personal and worth hearing. His Third Symphony (1962) is not easy listening, though, for it offers an uncompromising argument forcefully scored, but it also reveals real purpose and repays the close acquaintance that a recording allows. The sound here is from 1970 and has a rather cramped acoustic quality, but it is still acceptable and the performance by the LSO under Horenstein, an early Simpson champion, brings out the strength of the writing, not least in the big second movement (there are only two)

Robert Simpson   *[photo: Hyperion/Dijkema]*

which the composer calls "Nature music, in a sense" and which, after a hushed start on violins, steadily grows in pace and excitement though ending quietly. The Clarinet Quintet (1968) is in five connected sections, and though it has some dourness it is finely written and well played here, so that careful listening brings rewards. Both works were recorded under the composer's supervision.

Simpson. Symphony No. 9 (1987). **Bournemouth Symphony Orchestra/ Vernon Handley.** Hyperion CDA66299. Also includes an illustrated talk on the work by the composer.

68' DDD 12/88

Simpson's Ninth Symphony made a tremendous impact on its appearance in 1987 and this CD is excellent in every way. As in the Sixth and Seventh Symphonies, Simpson's mastery of musical motion takes the breath away. The sense of power and energy in reserve is almost tangible at the very outset and once hooked the attention is held through a patiently unfolded 'chorale prelude', a battering scherzo, a disembodied slow movement and an awe-inspiring finale. A superb modern symphony, an excellent performance, self-effacing sound-quality, informative sleeve-notes, a fascinating illustrated talk by the composer—what more could you want?

Simpson. String Quartets—No. 3 (1954)[a]; No. 6 (1975)[a]. String Trio (Prelude, Adagio and Fugue). **Delmé Quartet** (Galina Solodchin, [a]John Trusler, vns; John Underwood, va; Jonathan Williams, vc). Hyperion CDA66376.

72' DDD 7/90

Simpson has said that if he were restricted to writing only one kind of music it would have to be string quartets, and his cycle of 14 such works to date is gradually becoming recognized as a major contribution to the genre. It is something of a shock to hear the familiar bounding momentum and knotty, argumentative tone of the recent Simpson so fully formed no less than 37 years ago in the Third Quartet; the shock consists partly of amazement that the quality of this music took so long to dawn on so many critics. Twenty years later the Sixth Quartet is the last of a trilogy closely modelled on Beethoven's three *Razumovsky* Quartets—a curious exercise, but one which produces fascinating results, especially in the haunting slow movement. Another jump, this time of 12 years, takes us to the String Trio of 1987. This resourceful work is cast in an apparently baroque mould of Prelude, Adagio and Fugue, but in fact sounds wholly modern in its combative energy. Clean, well-balanced playing from the Delmé Quartet, backed up by the same virtues in Hyperion's engineering.

Simpson. STRING QUARTETS. **Delmé Quartet** (Galina Solodchin, Jeremy Williams, vns; John Underwood, va; Stephen Orton, vc). Hyperion CDA66117, CDA66127. Items marked [a] from A66117 (9/84), [b] A66127 (11/84). CDA66117—No. 7 (1977)[a]; No. 8 (1979)[a]. CDA66127—No. 9 (1982)[b].

② 51' 58' ADD 2/90

Robert Simpson's main musical preoccupation has been with the restoration of a sense of forward motion—one of the principal achievements of the great Viennese classics. And it is natural that this preoccupation should have been worked out in those classical genres *par excellence*, the symphony and string quartet. The Seventh and Eighth Quartets reflect the astronomical and entomological interests of their respective dedicatees, whilst the Ninth is a piece of unashamed creative virtuosity—32 variations and a fugue on the minuet from Haydn's Symphony No. 47, and all of them, like the original theme, palindromic (that is, they go backwards from the halfway point—the challenge being to make the music sound as good both ways). The Delmé Quartet's dedicated performance reveal all three works as major contributions to the quartet literature. The recordings, though less than ideal in 'bloom', are adequate.

Edith Sitwell   *Refer to Index*   *British 1887-1964*

Bedrich Smetana   *Bohemian 1824-1884*

Smetana. Má vlast. THE BARTERED BRIDE—Overture; Polonaise; Furiant; Skočná. **Vienna Philharmonic Orchestra/James Levine.** DG 419 768-2GH2.

② 96' DDD 10/87

Smetana. Má vlast. **Suisse Romande Orchestra/Wolfgang Sawallisch.** RCA Red Seal RD83242.

74' ADD 11/86

Smetana. Má vlast. **Royal Liverpool Philharmonic Orchestra/Libor Pešek.** Virgin Classics VC7 91100-2.

76' DDD 7/90

Smetana's great cycle of six tone-poems, *Má vlast*, celebrating the countryside and legendary heroes and heroines of Bohemia, in Levine's recording receives the performance it has been waiting for since the long deleted version by Karel Ančerl. This is a work of immense national significance encapsulating many of the ideals and hopes of that country. The Overture and dances from Smetana's *The bartered bride* make a vivid and popular coupling. The VPO play this music for all it is worth and the recording is clear and open. As a single-disc alternative to Levine's DG version, Wolfgang Sawallisch directs an imaginative and vigorous account of this lovely score. The Swiss orchestra may lack the bloom and finesse of their Viennese colleagues but they have been well served by the engineers, and rarely disappoint.

Libor Pešek is himself a native of Prague and brings great affection and strength to this music, and the Royal Liverpool Philharmonic Orchestra of, which he is Music Director, play as if to the manner born, while the recording, made in Liverpool's Philharmonic Hall, is vivid but very natural. Though the second piece, *Vltava,* is the best known of this great cycle, to appreciate it fully one should really hear it right through for its nobly cumulative effect, as this 76-minute CD allows, and when one does so Smetana's use of the powerful Hussite hymn melody "You who are God's warriors" in the last two pieces is all the more moving, not least at this time of great changes and major challenges in Czechoslovakia.

Smetana. String Quartets—No. 1 in E minor, "From my life" (1876); No. 2 in D minor (1882-83). **Smetana Quartet.** Supraphon C37S-7338. From 411 2130 (3/80).

46' ADD 1/86

Although we think of Smetana as first and foremost an operatic composer, his two string quartets are also important. The First is frankly programmatic and autobiographical: the call of destiny in the first movement; the lilting second reminiscing on his carefree youth and the last, the recognition of "national awareness in art" and the first warning of impending deafness. The work is almost as central to the chamber-music repertoire as Dvořák's *American* Quartet or Borodin's Second—and every bit as tuneful. The Second comes from 1882-8 when deafness had overtaken him and is, as Smetana himself put it, "the presentation of the whirl of music in a man who has lost the power of hearing".

The eponymous Smetana Quartet have long championed both works and this recording remains the classic version of these pieces.

Ethel Smyth

British 1858-1944

Smyth. Mass in D major[a]. THE BOATSWAIN'S MATE—Suppose you mean to do a given thing. March of the Women[b]. **Eiddwen Harrhy** (sop); [a]**Janis Hardy** (contr); [a]**Dan Dressen** (ten); [a]**James Bohn** (bass); **Plymouth Festival** [ab]**Chorus and Orchestra/Philip Brunelle.** Virgin Classics VC7 91188. Texts and translation included.

75' DDD 8/91

Dame Ethel Smyth's Mass was performed by the Royal Choral Society under Sir Joseph Barnby in 1893, when *Musical Opinion* found in it "many pages of supreme beauty, for which parallels must be sought in the masterpieces of the great choral writers". *The Musical Times* detected royal patronage, which "explained all, prevented the action of the committee from being assailed, and revealed Miss Smyth in the character of a very fortunate person". Whatever the cause, her good fortune then deserted her, for the Mass was not heard again till 1924, when *The Musical Times* decided after all that "its genuine character and its vehemence make it intrinsically worth hearing". Now in 1991 it gains its first recording, not from London or Birmingham (where the second performance took place) but Minnesota. Time, certainly, has done nothing to weaken its effects. "Parallels … in the masterpieces of the great choral writers" do indeed come to mind, most notably the Beethoven of the *Missa solemnis*, but what impresses now is the individuality and scale of the achievement. The *Kyrie*, for instance, may start like a text-book fugue with echoes of Bach's B minor Mass, but it soon develops along its own lines, and the declamatory use of the choir, the quickening pace, growing intensity and unforeseen turns of form and style are expressions of an almost fiercely independent spirit at work. Each movement has its special strength, and the *Gloria*, transposed from its normal place in the Mass, provides a joyfully rumbustious finale. The attractive solo from *The Boatswain's Mate* makes one wish to hear the rest of the opera (and the other five), while the *March of the Women* or *Suffragettes' Battle Hymn* recalls another part of that contentious and vigorous life. The performances carry conviction; recorded sound is adequate except that, as usual, one would like the choir to be more forward.

Fernando Sor

Spanish 1778-1839

Sor. GUITAR WORKS. **Lex Eisenhardt.** Etcetera KTC1025. From ETC1025 (11/85).
Variations on the Scottish Air, "Ye banks and braes", Op. 40. Six Airs from Mozart's "Die Zauberflöte", Op. 19. Le calme—caprice, Op. 50. Sonata No. 2 in C minor, Op. 25.

49' DDD 1/89

In May 1819 *Die Zauberflöte* was performed in London and it may have been there that Sor heard it—and was stimulated to write his famous Variations (Op. 9) on *Das klinget so herrlich*, published in 1821; two years later, when he was living in Russia, he made simple, charming settings of six more airs from the opera which he sent to his publisher in Paris. Variations were in the salon-musical air that Sor regularly breathed and those on *Ye banks and braes* may have resulted from his hearing the tune in London, or perhaps, reflected the contemporary continental taste for Scottish melodies, shared by Beethoven, Haydn and (in London) J.C. Bach. By 1832 Sor had returned to Paris, where he dedicated the elegant little Caprice *Le calme* to one of his lady students. Of the few guitar composers of the time who ventured to write full-scale sonatas, Sor was the most lyrical, adventurous in departing from the guitar's most grateful keys, and fastidious in his craftsmanship; the Sonata Op. 25 is the finest of his works in this genre. Lex Eisenhardt plays all this music most persuasively and is clearly recorded in a generous acoustic.

Charles Villiers Stanford   *Irish/British 1852-1924*

Stanford. Symphony No. 3 in F minor, Op. 28, "Irish". Irish Rhapsody No. 5 in G minor, Op. 147. **Ulster Orchestra/Vernon Handley.** Chandos CHAN8545.

56' DDD 1/88

The Third Symphony is marvellously well written and incorporates traditional Irish folk melodies in a rich palette of ideas, presenting these ingredients in a Brahmsian orchestral environment which nevertheless retains a perfectly individual voice. Few can resist the deft jig-scherzo of its second movement or can remain unmoved by the beautiful slow movement. The coupling is the *Irish Rhapsody* No. 5. Written some 30 years after the symphony it again draws heavily on Irish tunes and inflexions, with vigorous outer sections and a seamlessly beautiful, nostalgic central episode. The Ulster Orchestra play magnificently, giving a performance that would be hard to match let alone surpass, and the recording is a truly magnificent example of the art.

Stanford. Symphony No. 4 in F major, Op. 31. Irish Rhapsody No. 6, Op. 191[a]. Oedipus tyrannus, Op. 29— Prelude. [a]**Lydia Mordkovitch** (vn); **Ulster Orchestra/Vernon Handley.** Chandos CHAN8884.

65' DDD 3/91

Chandos's exploration of the wilder—or, at any rate, unfamiliar—shores of British music has led them to record all the Stanford symphonies in excellent sound. The Fourth Symphony was commissioned by Berlin, where it was first performed in 1889. Its first audience would no doubt have recognized the twin

influences of Brahms and Dvořák, but if they had any sense would have put them to the back of their minds as they enjoyed the light and luminous orchestration. Although the finale is the weakest moment, it is melodically enchanting. The Sixth *Irish Rhapsody* is a rarity, dating from 1922, two years before the composer's death when he was out of fashion and knew it. Perhaps this accounts for the sense of isolation in this haunting piece for violin and orchestra, played most eloquently by Lydia Mordkovitch and conducted with rare understanding by Vernon Handley. The Ulster Orchestra's playing of all the music on the disc is admirable.

| *Lydia Mordkovitch*   *[photo: Chandos/Curzon*

Wilhelm Stenhammar *Swedish 1871-1927*

Stenhammar. Serenade, Op. 31 (with the "Reverenza" movement).
Gothenburg Symphony Orchestra/Neeme Järvi. BIS CD310.

● 44' DDD 2/87

The Serenade for Orchestra is without doubt Stenhammar's masterpiece, an imaginative and magical work, full of memorable ideas and delicate orchestral colours. But it was not an immediate success and after the appearance of his Second Symphony, Stenhammar returned to the Serenade removing one of the movements and revising the outer ones. The jettisoned *Reverenza* survives in the Swedish Royal Academy Archives and Järvi has chosen to restore the movement to its original place. The *Reverenza* has some of the melancholy charm of Elgar and its refined texture enriches this wholly enchanting piece. The performance here is eloquent and committed. Glorious music, sensitively played and finely recorded, this must be recommended with all possible.

Stenhammar. SONGS. [a]**Anne Sofie von Otter** (mez); [b]**Håkan Hagegård** (bar); [a]**Bengt Forsberg**, [b]**Thomas Schuback** (pfs). Musica Sveciae MSCD623. Texts included.
In the forest[a]. Ingalill[b]. Fylgia[a]. My ancestor had a great goblet[b]. I was dear to you[b]. The girl came from meeting her lover[a]. The girl tying on Midsummer's Eve[a]. A fir tree stand alone[a]. The ballad of Emperor Charles[b]. Leaning against the fence[a]. The girl to her aged mother[a]. To a rose[a]. Under the maple tree at dusk[b]. Were I a small child[b]. A barrel-organ ballad[b]. Melody[a]. Star eye[a]. At the window[a]. Old dutchman[b]. Moonlight[a]. Adagio[a]. The Wanderer[b]. The Star[b]. Mistress Blond and Mistress Brunett[b]. A ship is sailing[b]. When through the room[b]. Why so swift to retire?[b]. Voyage to the happy country[b]. Prince Aladdin of the lamp[b]. Love song[b].

● 74' DDD 7/90   ❓

Alongside his many accomplishments as composer and conductor Stenhammar was a pianist of some renown. He played with most of the major conductors of his day including Hans Richter and Richard Strauss, and was a noted interpreter of the Brahms concertos as well as his own. His late Beethoven was also much admired, as was his chamber music playing. What is less well-known is that he was much in demand as an accompanist, and toured extensively in that capacity. At home in his childhood, the family could muster a vocal quartet, for which he composed a number of small pieces though most of his youthful output was for solo voice, for which he wrote throughout his life. This CD brings no fewer than 30 songs into the catalogue and is the most comprehensive survey yet to appear. They cover his whole career from *In the forest*, written when he was only 16, through to his very last work, a love song from 1924. The bulk come from the 1890s and 1900s including *The girl came from meeting her lover* (or "The Tryst") made famous by Sibelius's slightly later setting. (In this instance Stenhammar's is the more subtle setting.) Some of the earlier songs are a bit conventional but they never fall below a certain level of distinction, and some are captivating. They can be original and forward-looking as in *Prince Aladdin of the lamp*, or have an unaffected naturalness and charm as in *A barrel-organ ballad*, both of which are good tracks to sample. But they are all beautifully fashioned with not a note out of place and the product of a man of fastidious taste and poetic feeling. The majority are allotted to Håkan Hagegård and Thomas Schuback, who accompanies superbly. Anne Sofie von Otter is a joy throughout. The original texts are all given with detailed summaries in English, and there is an authoritative and scholarly essay, which is a model of its kind.

Karlheinz Stockhausen

German 1928-

Stockhausen. Stimmung. **Singcircle/Gregory Rose.** Hyperion CDA66115.
Text and translation included. From A66115 (10/84).

70' DDD 2/87

Stimmung relies totally on vocal harmonics formed from six notes centred
around various words. The six voices work closely together following a leading
singer into sympathetic treatments of tempo, rhythm and dynamic. When
the voices have achieved an 'identity' another singer leads into the next section.
Of the 51 sections of the work (all individually cued on this CD) 29 employ
a 'magic name' drawn from a diversity of cultures, others employ erotic
poetry written by the composer himself. The variety of timbres created by
the quite extraordinarily virtuosic group Singcircle is astonishing—the
mesmerizing web of sounds at times seems to reject any association with the
human voice. This is a very acquired taste but really does deserve to be
heard. Fascinating!

Johann Strauss I

Austrian 1804-1849

J. Strauss I. Radetzky March.
J. Strauss II. WALTZES AND POLKAS. **Vienna Philharmonic
Orchestra/Willi Boskovsky** (vn). Decca Ovation 417 747-2DM. From Decca
recordings made between 1958-74.
J. Strauss II: DIE FLEDERMAUS—Overture. Perpetuum mobile.
Accelerationen—Waltz. Unter Donner und Blitz—Polka. Morgenblätter—Waltz.
Persischer Marsch. Explosionen—Polka. Wiener Blut—Waltz. Pizzicato Polka.
Egyptischer Marsch. Künstlerleben—Waltz. Tritsch-Tratsch—Polka.

65' ADD

There have been no finer recordings of Johann Strauss than those by Boskovsky
and the Vienna Philharmonic. The velvety sheen and elegance of the orchestra's
sound, combined with the unique lilt that comes so naturally to Viennese
players, produced magical results. For this compilation Decca have sensibly
mixed seven of the most famous waltzes and polkas from those sessions with
other popular Strauss compositions in various rhythms, from the celebrated *Die
Fledermaus* Overture, through popular polkas and novelty pieces (for *Perpetuum
mobile* Boskovsky himself can be heard explaining that it has no ending) to the
ever-popular *Radetzky March*. The recorded sound is not up to the most modern
digital standards, but re-processing has produced a remarkably homogeneous
sound for recordings originating over a 15-year period.

Johann Strauss II

Austrian 1825-1899

J. Strauss II. WALTZES. **Hallé Orchestra/Bryden Thomson.** Classics for
Pleasure CD-CFP9015.
An der schönen, blauen Donau. Künstlerleben. Wein, Weib und Gesang.
Accelerationen. Wiener Blut. Frühlingstimmen. G'schichten aus dem
Wienerwald. Kaiser-Walzer.

72' DDD 12/87

British orchestras rarely acquit themselves in Strauss waltzes as well as the Hallé
do here. The music is allowed to speak for itself and flows elegantly on its way.

All the key orchestral effects that mean so much to the pieces are here, including the zither in *Tales from the Vienna Woods*. Even more noteworthy is the fact that *Wine, Woman and Song* includes the rarely heard, lengthy introduction that Strauss provided for its first performance as a piece for male chorus. Indeed, these are all very complete versions, including repeats that are frequently omitted. There is thus all the more opportunity to revel in these glorious melodies of this highly satisfying bargain collection.

J. Strauss II. DIE FLEDERMAUS. **Elisabeth Schwarzkopf** (sop) Rosalinde; **Nicolai Gedda** (ten) Eisenstein; **Rita Streich** (sop) Adele; **Erich Kunz** (bar) Falke; **Karl Dönch** (bar) Frank; **Helmut Krebs** (ten) Alfred; **Rudolf Christ** (ten) Orlofsky; **Erich Majkut** (ten) Blind; **Franz Böheim** (bar) Frosch; **Luise Martini** (sop) Ida; **Philharmonia Orchestra and Chorus/ Herbert von Karajan.** EMI CHS7 69531-2. From Columbia 33CX1309-10 (11/55).

② 1h 50' ADD 11/88 ⑨ P Ⓑ

J. Strauss II. DIE FLEDERMAUS (with Gala Sequence). **Hilde Gueden** (sop) Rosalinde; **Waldemar Kmentt** (ten) Eisenstein; **Erika Köth** (sop) Adele; **Walter Berry** (bass) Falke; **Eberhard Waechter** (bar) Frank; **Giuseppe Zampieri** (ten) Alfred; **Regina Resnik** (mez) Orlofsky; **Peter Klein** (ten) Blind; **Erich Kunz** (bar) Frosch; **Hedwig Schubert** (sop) Ida; **Vienna State Opera Chorus; Vienna Philharmonic Orchestra/Herbert von Karajan.** Decca 421 046-2DH2. Notes, text and translation included. From SET201/03 (11/60).

② 2h 23' ADD 12/87 Ⓑ

Anyone less concerned with modernity of sound than with enjoying a well-proven, classic interpretation of Strauss's operetta masterpiece can readily be recommended to EMI's 1955 recording. Herbert von Karajan, whose preference for slow tempos and beauty of sound above all else was then still in the future, here directs with affection and *élan*. Amongst the principals Elisabeth

Elisabeth Schwarzkopf   *[photo: EMI/Wilson*

Schwarzkopf leads the cast majestically and ravishingly. Notably in the *csárdás*, her firm lower notes swell gloriously into a marvellously rich and individual register. As her maid, Adele, Rita Streich is an agile-voiced, utterly charming foil, launching her "Laughing Song" with deliciously credible indignation. Nicolai Gedda also enters into the fun with supreme effect. Throughout he sings with youthful ardour and freshness, but he also has a high old time impersonating the stammering Dr Blind in the Act 3 trio.

Erich Kunz's rich, characterful baritone is also heard here to good effect as Dr Falke, the character who arranges the 'bat's revenge' which forms the story of *Die Fledermaus*. Unconventionally, the young Prince is played by a tenor rather than the mezzo-soprano for whom the role was written. Purists may object, but the result is dramatically convincing, and musically could hardly be bettered when the singer is the sweet-toned Rudolf Christ. Altogether this set can still rival any later one in theatrical effectiveness and EMI have done a good job in refurbishing it, with the disc-break sensibly placed between Acts 1 and 2.

Die Fledermaus has always been a speciality in Vienna so any performance that has the Vienna Philharmonic Orchestra 'in the pit' starts with an immediate advantage. That explains the additional choice of Karajan's 1960 recording which includes the ballet and also has the famous and now historic 'gala' in the party scene where we can hear Tebaldi singing the Viljalied from *The Merry Widow*, Nilsson singing "I could have danced all night", Björling "Dein ist mein ganzes Herz", and Simionato and Bastianini "Anything you can do, I can do better". The casting leaves little to be desired and Karajan presides with a deft hand. The 30-year-old recording is in no way put in the shade by more recent efforts.

Richard Strauss

German 1864-1949

R. Strauss. Horn Concertos[a]—No. 1 in E flat major, Op. 11; No. 2 in E flat major. Oboe Concerto in D major[b]. Duett-Concertino[c]. [a]**Peter Damm** (hn); [b]**Manfred Clement** (ob); [c]**Manfred Weise** (cl); [c]**Wolfgang Liebscher** (bn); **Staatskapelle Dresden/Rudolf Kempe.** EMI Studio CDM7 69661-2. FROM SLS5067 (10/76).

* 79' ADD 6/89 £ 9 P

This is a skilful compilation, bringing together Strauss's finest solo concertos. The First Horn Concerto has great panache, not surprising for a 19-year-old whose father was principal horn in the Munich Court Orchestra. It is a graceful piece and one which nevertheless has considerable humour. The other works on the disc date from Strauss's maturity and they all share his exquisitely vocal style of composition: fluid, subtle and unrestrainedly melodious. The Oboe Concerto is particularly fine and could quite easily be seen as an instrumental equivalent of the delicious *Four Last Songs*. The soloists, all drawn from the ranks of the Staatskapelle Dresden, play with consummate skill and a real feel for Strauss's idiom. Kempe conducts superbly.

R. Strauss. Don Juan, Op. 20[a]. Tod und Verklärung, Op. 24[b]. Also sprach Zarathustra, Op. 30[c]. **Vienna Philharmonic Orchestra/Herbert von Karajan.** Decca Ovation 417 720-2DM. Item marked [a] from SXL2269 (5/61), [b] SXL2261 (4/61), [c] SXL2154 (8/59).

* 75' ADD 12/87 9 P (B)

The orchestral playing here is magnificent—the sheer ecstatic fervour of the violins brings out all the sexuality of the glorious *Don Juan* love-music, while at the end the feeling of the desolate ebbing away of all feeling is marvellously conveyed. *Also sprach Zarathustra* is full of subtle detail, and the CD background quiet brings the most potent atmospheric feeling, as is immediately instanced by the hushed string entry of "The dwellers in the world beyond". The punch of the brass and again the soaring violins in "Of joys and passions" compensates for any lack of amplitude while the "Dance Song" has a special rhythmic lilt from an orchestra famous for their feeling for the dance idiom. The transfiguration theme of *Tod und Verklärung* is another instance where the leonine timbre of the VPO brings a new dimension. All in all, this is a splendid triptych, confirming Karajan as a great and indeed uniquely perceptive Straussian.

R. Strauss. Don Quixote, Op. 35[a]. Le bourgeois gentilhomme—suite, Op. 60[b]. [a]**Leonard Rubens** (va); [a]**Paul Tortelier** (vc); **Royal Philharmonic Orchestra/Sir Thomas Beecham.** EMI Great Recordings of the Century mono CDH7 63106-2. Item marked [a] from HMV DB6796/800 (4/49), [b] DB6643, DB6646/8 (11/49).

66' ADD 9/89   **q** P

Although *Don Quixote* has been well served on record, this recording must be chosen for its special qualities of insight. It combines the youthful freshness of the young soloist at the beginning of his career, who only a few years earlier had played the work under Strauss himself, with the wisdom and maturity of a lifelong advocate of the composer. Moreover, the composer was present not only during the recording of *Don Quixote* but also during some of the movements from *Le bourgeois gentilhomme*, which are given with such sparkle here. Beecham was one of the few conductors to bring a rare kind of delicacy and lightness to Strauss's scores, nowhere more so than in *Le bourgeois gentilhomme*. Tortelier brings to *Don Quixote* nobility and great poetic insight and no reader of whatever generation is likely to be disappointed by the quality of the orchestral playing. Indeed it is pretty electrifying, with the newly-formed RPO on their best form.

R. Strauss. Aus Italien, Op. 16. Don Juan, Op. 20. **Berlin Philharmonic Orchestra/Riccardo Muti.** Philips 422 399-2PH.

61' DDD 9/90

Muti's interpretation of *Aus Italien*, Strauss's early 'symphonic fantasy', composed after a holiday in Italy, glows and glistens with Southern warmth and colour. The Berlin Philharmonic revels in the masterly scoring and its rich sound is fully captured by the Philips recording. Muti achieves a splendid balance and one can almost feel the heat of the sun as the young Strauss glories in his first experience of the land that has inspired so many composers. The performance of *Don Juan* is also extremely good, but Muti's interpretation favours excessively slow tempos in the romantic episodes.

R. Strauss. Eine Alpensinfonie, Op. 64. **Concertgebouw Orchestra, Amsterdam/Bernard Haitink.** Philips 416 156-2PH. From 416 156-1PH (4/86).

50' DDD 7/86   **q** S

R. Strauss. Eine Alpensinfonie, Op. 64. Don Juan, Op. 20. **San Francisco Symphony Orchestra/Herbert Blomstedt.** Decca 421 815-2DH.

70' DDD 6/90   **(B)**

The *Alpine* Symphony is the last of Richard Strauss's great tone-poems and is in many ways the most spectacular. The score is an evocation of the changing moods of an alpine landscape and the huge orchestral apparatus of over 150 players encompasses quadruple wind, 20 horns, organ, wind machine, cowbells, thunder machine, two harps and enhanced string forces. Its pictorialism may be all too graphic but what virtuosity and inspiration Strauss commands. Haitink gives a magisterial account of this long underrated score and the playing of the Concertgebouw Orchestra is of the highest order of virtuosity. The recording reproduces every strand in the complex texture with clarity and does full justice to its wide dynamic range.

   Herbert Blomstedt's *Eine Alpensinfonie* also penetrates beyond the pictorialism into the work's deeper elements. It emerges as a gigantic hymn to nature on a Mahlerian scale. Tempos are slower, but these are justified by the noble expansiveness of the final pages, towards which the whole performance moves with impressive inevitability. The San Francisco Symphony's playing is magnificent, with subtle use of vibrato by the strings and superb performances, individual and corporate, by the wind sections. The recording is on a spacious scale to match the performance, the big climaxes really thrilling and the whole well balanced. The *Don Juan* performance is fine too.

R. Strauss. Symphonia domestica, Op. 53. **Berlin Philharmonic Orchestra/Herbert von Karajan.** EMI Studio CDM7 69571-2. From ASD2955 (4/74).

44' ADD 1/89

What this disc lacks in total playing time, it more than makes up for by the quality and dedication of the performance. This is a classic reading of Op. 53 from Karajan and the Berlin Philharmonic, embodying their special affinity for Strauss's music. The work lays powerful traps for the unwary conductor—the domestic delights can, all too easily, acquire the amateur triviality of the home movie but Karajan allows the sentiments to ring true by letting them speak for themselves. The domestic incidents are vividly portrayed but not parodied, the more romantic sections are allowed their head, but not overdriven. Karajan also has a clear idea of the music's direction, and passing details are not permitted to hinder his path or obscure his view. With refined playing typical of the Berlin Philharmonic's standard and a wide-ranging, subtle recording, this issue does not put a foot wrong.

R. Strauss. Metamorphosen for 23 solo strings. Tod und Verklärung, Op. 24. Drei Hymnen, Op. 71[a]. [a]**Felicity Lott** (sop); **Scottish National Orchestra/ Neeme Järvi.** Chandos CHAN8734. Texts and translations included.

72' DDD 3/90

R. Strauss. Metamorphosen for 23 solo strings. Tod und Verklärung, Op. 24. **Berlin Philharmonic Orchestra/Herbert von Karajan.** DG 410 892-2GH. From 2532 074 (5/83).

52' DDD 2/84

There is plenty of competition among recordings of *Metamorphosen* and *Tod und Verklärung*, but what makes this Chandos disc so attractive is that it contains the first CD recording of the *Drei Hymnen*, Op. 71, settings of poems by Hölderlin about aspects of love, not erotic love so much as love of nature and one's country. They were composed in 1921 for the Wagnerian soprano Barbara Kemp and require a very large orchestra. In their outpouring of soprano ecstasy, they anticipate the *Four Last Songs* and would be as well known were they not so difficult to perform. Felicity Lott is no Wagnerian, but she has the Straussian qualities of silvery tone and expressive radiance. Although she is occasionally tested by the sustained intensity of these songs, she sings them rapturously while Järvi and the Scottish orchestra give her fine support. Järvi's interpretation of *Metamorphosen* is urgent and compelling and the performance of *Tod und Verklärung* likewise. The recording is up to Chandos's high standard for its Järvi Strauss cycle, although the resonance of the hall used for the recordings may not be to every collector's liking.

In Karajan's handling of *Metamorphosen* power is held in reserve, until the climactic C major eruption just before the coda, with thrilling effect—everything, one feels, has been in some way a preparation for this moment, and the final turn to the minor acquires greater poignancy and dramatic force as a result. The playing of the Berlin Philharmonic strings is magnificent, and the recording manages to be both spacious and intimate. After this, the prospect of another long stretch of C minor may seem a little daunting, but *Tod und Verklärung* provides a strong contrast to the much later *Metamorphosen*, and once again Karajan's superbly controlled and intense reading ensures a gripping musical experience.

R. Strauss. Ein Heldenleben, Op. 40. **Staatskapelle Dresden / Herbert Blomstedt.** Denon C37-7561.
46' DDD 12/85

R. Strauss. Ein Heldenleben, Op. 40. Till Eulenspiegels lustige Streiche, Op. 28. **London Symphony Orchestra / Michael Tilson Thomas.** Sony Classical CD44817.
63' DDD 5/89

R. Strauss. Ein Heldenleben, Op. 40. Don Juan, Op. 20. **Royal Liverpool Philharmonic Orchestra / Libor Pešek.** Virgin Classics VC7 91171-2.
64' DDD 5/91

The hero of *Ein Heldenleben* ("A Hero's Life") is Strauss himself and the heroine, his wife, the legendary Pauline. Written when he was in his mid thirties it is the most exuberant and confident of the great symphonic poems. Herbert Blomstedt shapes this performance with both authority and poetry. The musical argument is finely judged and beautifully paced: one can tell from the start that we are in for a thoroughly idiomatic performance, for Blomstedt sounds a genuinely heroic note and generates keen dramatic excitement. The characterization of the critics, of Pauline (there is superb violin playing from the leader, Peter Mirring, in this episode) and the battle come off with great vividness. The orchestral playing is glorious throughout and the recording is refreshingly natural.

Strauss burst on the musical world as a young man with an almost insolent mastery of form, instrumentation and tone painting plus an ebullient personality. Though not one to wallow in self-pity, he resembled other romantics in sometimes using music to portray himself, as in his *Symphonia domestica* and the opera *Intermezzo*. In *Ein Heldenleben*, he went still further by displaying himself as a *Held* or hero. But he was too intelligent and had too much sense of humour to regard himself as a Nietzschean superman and this 'hero's life' is that of a composer whose enemies include a pack of carping critics—portrayed in the second section of the work as acidly grumbling wind instruments whose music is marked 'very sharp and pointed'! But our hero is encouraged and consoled by his wife, represented by a solo violin, and there are also sections evoking his valiant battles and his works of peace. For all its egoism, this is opulent music and captivatingly extroverted. Michael Tilson Thomas gives a wonderfully positive account of this music, and though he does not pull out all the stops too soon, there is thrilling bravura to spare in the battle scene in *Heldenleben*, while the orchestral strings sound sumptuous and the love music with the solo violin is deeply tender. The picaresque adventures of that lovable rascal *Till Eulenspiegels* are no less attractive,

Libor Pešek   *[photo: Virgin Classics*

sparkling with life and wit, too. The recording is rich yet detailed, with the vast orchestra held in fine perspective.

Virgin Classics has also given us one of the best of several outstanding recordings of *Ein Heldenleben* in the current catalogue and has the additional virtue of demonstrating what a fine orchestra Libor Pešek has in Liverpool. His is a recording of startling clarity; the battle scene is a notable example of this quality, for all its sound and fury. The thrusting tempo of the introductory section follows Strauss's own example, and if the love scene is rather more indulgent, it never cloys or sags. The disc is enhanced by an outstanding performance of *Don Juan*, its opening rocket-like in its youthful ardour. On this showing, in this music, the RLPO need fear comparison with none.

R. Strauss. Schlagobers, Op. 70. **Tokyo Metropolitan Symphony Orchestra/Hiroshi Wakasugi.** Denon CO-73414.

75' DDD 1/90

Strauss's second large-scale ballet score, *Schlagobers* ("Whipped Cream"), was written for Vienna, where it was first performed in 1924. It was not a success, partly because it did not suit the national mood at a time of food shortages and hyper-inflation! Composed as a frothy piece, designed wholly for pleasure, it also was unfavourably compared with the Strauss of *Elektra* and *Heldenleben*. How good it is, therefore, to have this complete recording so that we may savour the work on its own terms, as a soufflé, full of inimitable wit and parody, deliciously orchestrated. This is the Strauss of *Le bourgeois gentilhomme*, the invention not perhaps as effortlessly sustained but very enjoyable just the same. Wakasugi and the Tokyo Metropolitan Symphony Orchestra, who have already recorded the earlier *Josephslegende* ballet, perform this very different music with much skill and charm. The recording is outstandingly fine and the presentation of the disc notes and indexing is exceptional.

R. Strauss. Four Last Songs (1948)[a]. ORCHESTRAL SONGS. **Elisabeth Schwarzkopf** (sop); [a]**Berlin Radio Symphony Orchestra;** [b]**London Symphony Orchestra/George Szell.** EMI CDC7 47276-2. Notes, texts and translations included. Items marked [a] from ASD2888 (7/66), [b] ASD2493 (3/70). *Orchestral songs*—Muttertändelei, Op. 43 No. 2[a]; Waldseligkeit, Op. 49 No. 1[a]; Zueignung, Op. 10 No. 1[a]; Freundliche Vision, Op. 48 No. 1[a]; Die heiligen drei Könige, Op. 56 No. 6[b]; Ruhe, meine Seele, Op. 27 No. 1[b]; Meinem Kinde, Op. 37 No. 3[b]; Wiegenlied, Op. 41 No. 1[b]; Morgen, Op. 27 No. 4 (with Edith Peinemann, vn)[b]; Das Bächlein, Op. 88 No. 1[b]; Das Rosenband, Op. 36 No. 1[b]; Winterweihe, Op. 48 No. 4.

54' ADD 12/85

Richard Strauss's *Four Last Songs*, besides being one of the greatest song cycles ever written for the female voice, are a perfect summation not only of a career which had spanned more than six decades but also of the romantic era itself. Modern recordings of these twilight songs appear at intervals but none can surpass this legendary 1966 account by Elisabeth Schwarzkopf most beautifully accompanied by George Szell. Tonal beauty, a penetrating intelligence and an unequalled attention to the subtleties of the words make this the version to have. The voice arches gloriously in one long parabola to the close. Szell's conducting is perfect: attentive, long-breathed and ever poetic—the Berlin RSO quite the equal of their celebrated neighbours. The remainder of the disc is devoted to a generous selection of orchestral songs and here too there are countless felicities. The recording is warm, well balanced and natural, with the voice in a realistic relationship to the orchestra.

R. *Strauss*. LIEDER[a]. Metamorphosen for 23 solo strings. [a]**Gundula Janowitz** (sop); **Academy of London/Richard Stamp.** Virgin Classics VC7 90794-2. Texts and translations included.
Lieder—Ruhe, meine Seele, Op. 27 No. 1; Waldseligkeit, Op. 49 No. 1; Freundliche Vision, Op. 48 No. 1; Morgen!, Op. 27 No. 4; Befreit, Op. 39 No. 4; Meinem Kinde, Op. 37 No. 3; Winterweihe, Op. 48 No. 4; Wiegenlied, Op. 41 No. 1; Die heiligen drei Könige aus Morgenland, Op. 56 No. 6.

60' DDD 2/91

Gundula Janowitz has given some of the most beautiful performances of the music of Richard Strauss in the last three decades. Why no one asked her to record more songs during her heyday is a great mystery, but here is a quite lovely collection that shows her musicality and fine feeling for the Strauss idiom at its best. Obviously, given the passing of the years, she is happiest in the gentler, more legato numbers where her quite exquisite breath control and beauty of tone reap rich rewards—the floated line in *Wiegenlied* is absolutely ravishing and her feeling for words has, if anything, deepened over the years. She instils appropriate drama into the ecstatic *Die heiligen drei Könige aus Morgenland*, a lovely song. Throughout the disc the Academy of London play with great feeling and a good regard for the sound-world that Richard Strauss's music demands. As a very substantial make-weight, Richard Stamp and his orchestra offer a sensitive reading of Strauss's heart-rending *Metamorphosen*, that threnody for the great opera-houses of Germany destroyed by Allied bombing during the Second World War. The complex lines are interwoven with care and sensitivity, and the work's true character emerges powerfully in this passionate performance. The recording is rich and clear. A delightful disc.

R. *Strauss*. LIEDER.
Wolf. LIEDER. **Barbara Bonney** (sop); **Geoffrey Parsons** (pf). DG 429 406-2GH. Texts and translations included.
R. *Strauss*: Du meines Herzens Krönelein, Op. 21 No. 2; Meinem Kinde, Op. 37 No. 3; Ich schwebe wie auf Engelsschwingen, Op. 48 No. 2; Die Nacht, Op. 10 No. 3; Morgen, Op. 27 No. 4; Allerseelen, Op. 10 No. 8; Mein Auge, Op. 37 No. 4; Schön sind, doch kalt die Himmelssterne, Op. 19 No. 3; Ich wollt' ein Sträusslein binden, Op. 68 No. 2; Ständchen, Op. 17 No. 2. **Wolf:** Mörike Lieder—Der Knabe und das Immlein; Er ist's; Das verlassene Mägdlein; Begegnung; Nimmersatte Liebe; Verborgenheit. Eichendorff Lieder—Verschwiegene Liebe. Italienisches Liederbuch—Auch kleine Dinge. Spanisches Liederbuch—In dem Schatten meiner Locken. Bescheidene Liebe.

55' DDD 8/90

Bonney's clear, bell-like tone and faultless technique are heard at their most appealing here. Adding to her purely vocal accomplishments is the imagination behind the singing. Cannily choosing some of Wolf's most approachable songs, she proceeds to interpret them with unaffected, stylish singing. She finds truth in simplicity, avoiding the need for any over-detailed word painting; at the same time she unerringly finds the right mood and timbre for each piece. *Das verlassene Mägdlein* is properly empty and weary, *Begegnung* smiling and playful, *Nimmersatte Liebe* sensuous, *Verschwiegene Liebe* easily playful. Her Strauss might sometimes benefit from more flowing tempos, but the phrasing is as inevitable and natural as it is in the Wolf. Most attractive here is the conjuring up of unnamed threats in *Die Nacht* and the proper rapture in *Ständchen*. Parsons is at his most free-ranging and keen. Both artists are well supported by an open, forward recording. Anyone wanting a representative choice of these composers' songs need look no further.

R. Strauss. SALOME. **Birgit Nilsson** (sop) Salome; **Gerhard Stolze** (ten) Herod; **Grace Hoffman** (mez) Herodias; **Eberhard Waechter** (bar) Jokanaan; **Waldemar Kmentt** (ten) Narraboth; **Josephine Veasey** (mez) Page; **Tom Krause** (bar) First Nazarene; **Nigel Douglas** (ten) Second Nazarene; **Zenon Koznowski** (bass) First Soldier; **Heinz Holecek** (bass) Second Soldier; **Theodore Kirschbichler** (bass) A Cappadocian; **Liselotte Maikl** (sop) A Slave; **Vienna Philharmonic Orchestra/Sir Georg Solti.** Decca 414 414-2DH2. Notes, text and translation included. From SET228 (3/62).

② 99' ADD 7/85

With the Vienna Philharmonic in full cry and the Decca engineers capturing the violently erotic splendour of the sound, this set, like the opera, caused something of a stir when it first appeared and one can hear why even more vividly on CD. Nilsson marvellously captures Salome's decadent sensuality and produces a softer grain to her voice than some at the time thought her capable of, while the well-known solidity of her singing was unimpaired. Gerhard Stolze makes a suitably fevered, unhinged sound as the near-crazed Herod, Eberhard Waechter is a forceful, visionary-sounding John the Baptist, Waldemar Kmentt a properly ardent Narraboth (the soldier so infatuated with Salome's charms that he commits suicide when she shows no interest in him). The supporting cast, recruited from the Vienna State Opera and Covent Garden, is strong.

R. Strauss. ARIADNE AUF NAXOS. **Jessye Norman** (sop) Ariadne; **Juia Varady** (sop) Composer; **Edita Gruberová** (sop) Zerbinetta; **Paul Frey** (ten) Bacchus; **Dietrich Fischer-Dieskau** (bar) Music Master; **Olaf Bär** (bar) Harlequin; **Gerd Wolf** (bass) Truffaldino; **Martin Finke** (ten) Scaramuchio, Dancing Master; **Eva Lind** (sop) Naïad; **Marianne Rørholm** (contr) Dryad; **Julie Kaufmann** (sop) Echo; **Rudolf Asmus** (spr) Major-domo; members of the **Leipzig Gewandhaus Orchestra/Kurt Masur.** Philips 422 084-2PH2. Notes, text and translation included.

② 1h 58' DDD 11/88

Not everybody finds Jessye Norman a truly Straussian soprano, but the sheer opulence of her singing, its dignity and poise, are to be cherished. Julia Varady's Composer is full of fire and, where required, tenderness and although she is perhaps not quite at her best here, it is still a formidable performance, bright, incisive and crystalline in the trills in the big aria. Outstanding among the men are Olaf Bär as Harlequin—the best on disc—and Fischer-Dieskau as a gruff Music Master. Many *Ariadne* performances have foundered on the singing of Bacchus, but Paul Frey recalls the achievements of Helge Roswaenge in the role and makes the final duet the climactic experience that Strauss intended. Exquisite playing by the instrumentalists from the Leipzig Gewandhaus Orchestra and inspired conducting by Kurt Masur make this a highly successful issue.

R. Strauss. ELEKTRA. **Birgit Nilsson** (sop) Elektra; **Regina Resnik** (mez) Clytemnestra; **Marie Collier** (sop) Chrysothemis; **Tom Krause** (bar) Orestes; **Gerhard Stolze** (ten) Aegistheus; **Vienna Philharmonic Orchestra/Sir Georg Solti.** Decca 417 345-2DH2. Notes, text and translation included. From SET354/5 (11/67).

② 1h 48' 12/86

Elektra is the most consistently inspired of all Strauss's operas and derives from Greek mythology, with the ghost of Agamamenon, so unerringly delineated in

the opening bars, hovering over the whole work. The invention and the intensity of mood are sustained throughout the opera's one-act length, and the characterization is both subtle and pointed. It is a work peculiarly well-suited to Solti's gifts and he has done nothing better in his long career in the studios. He successfully maintains the nervous tension throughout the unbroken drama and conveys all the power and tension in Strauss's enormously complex score which is, for once, given complete. The recording captures the excellent singers and the Vienna Philharmonic in a warm, spacious acoustic marred only by some questionable electronic effects.

R. Strauss. DIE FRAU OHNE SCHATTEN. **Cheryl Studer** (sop) Empress; **René Kollo** (ten) Emperor; **Ute Vinzing** (sop) Dyer's Wife; **Alfred Muff** (bass-bar) Barak the Dyer; **Hanna Schwarz** (mez) Nurse; **Andreas Schmidt** (bar) Spirit Messenger; **Julie Kaufmann** (sop) Voice of the Falcon; **Cyndia Sieden** (sop) Guardian of the threshold of the Temple; **Paul Frey** (ten) Voice of a young man; **Marjana Lipovšek** (sop) Voice from above; **Jan-Hendrick Rootering** (bass) One-eyed Brother; **Kurt Rydl** (bass) One-armed Brother; **Kenneth Garrison** (ten) Hunchback Brother; **Tölz Boys' Choir; Bavarian Radio Chorus and Symphony Orchestra/Wolfgang Sawallisch.** EMI CDS7 49074-2. Notes, text and translation included.

③ 3h 11' DDD 9/88

This was the most ambitious operatic project on which Strauss and his librettist Hugo von Hofmannsthal collaborated. It is both fairy-tale and allegory, with clear references to Mozart's *Die Zauberflöte*. The music, on the other hand, is Wagnerian in its scale and breadth. This Sawallisch recording presents the score uncut, something that has rarely happened in the theatre and not hitherto on discs. Chief beneficiary is the role of the Nurse and Hanna Schwarz's glorious performance emphasizes the insensitive folly of reducing the contribution of one of Strauss's most important female creations. Barak's wife was based on Strauss's wife Pauline and is musically a forerunner of Christine (Pauline again) in *Intermezzo*. If Ute Vinzing is one of the disappointments of the set, her voice often unsteady and lacking the necessary variety of tone-colour, Alfred Muff, on the other hand, is a splendid Barak, gruff, tender, and compassionate according to need. The Empress is marvellously sung by Cheryl Studer and there is magnificent playing by the Bavarian Radio Symphony Orchestra under Sawallisch's inspired and wholly sympathetic direction.

R. Strauss. CAPRICCIO. **Elisabeth Schwarzkopf** (sop) The Countess; **Eberhard Waechter** (bar) The Count; **Nicolai Gedda** (ten) Flamand; **Dietrich Fischer-Dieskau** (bar) Olivier; **Hans Hotter** (bass-bar) La Roche; **Christa Ludwig** (mez) Clairon; **Rudolf Christ** (ten) Monsieur Taupe; **Anna Moffo** (sop) Italian Soprano; **Dermot Troy** (ten) Italian Tenor; **Karl Schmitt-Walter** (bar) Major-domo; **Philharmonia Orchestra/Wolfgang Sawallisch.** EMI mono CDS7 49014-8. Notes, text and translation included. From Columbia 33CX1600/02 (3/59).

② 2h 15' ADD 9/87

The plot of *Capriccio* centres on the Countess and her two suitors, a poet and a composer. The opera moves as surefootedly as one would expect of this master, to its closing scene, one of Strauss's most magical, in which the Countess speculates on her predicament. Right from the opening notes of this classic performance, where the string sextet evokes the mood so delicately, one can sense that this is a recording that will never be equalled. There is not a weak link in the chain and the cast couldn't be more perfectly matched. Though the recording is in mono it sounds quite magnificent.

R. Strauss. DER ROSENKAVALIER. **Elisabeth Schwarzkopf** (sop) Die Feldmarschallin, First Orphan; **Otto Edelmann** (bass) Baron Ochs; **Christa Ludwig** (mez) Octavian, Second Orphan; **Eberhard Waechter** (bar) Faninal; **Teresa Stich-Randall** (sop) Sophie; **Ljuba Welitsch** (sop) Marianne; **Paul Kuen** (ten) Valzacchi; **Kerstin Meyer** (contr) Annina, Third Orphan; **Nicolai Gedda** (ten) Italian Tenor; **Franz Bierbach** (bass) Police Commissioner; **Erich Majkut** (ten) Marschallin's Major-domo; **Gerhard Unger** (ten) Faninal's Major-domo, Animal Seller; **Harald Pröghlöf** (bar) Notary; **Karl Friedrich** (ten) Landlord; **Anny Felbermayer** (sop) Milliner; **Loughton High School for Girls and Bancroft's School Choirs; Philharmonia Chorus and Orchestra/Herbert von Karajan.** EMI CDS7 49354-2. Notes, text and translation included. From Columbia SAX2269/72 (11/59).

③ 3h 11' ADD 1/88   Ⓑ

Der Rosenkavalier concerns the transferring of love of the young headstrong aristocrat Octavian from the older Marschallin (with whom he is having a affair) to the young Sophie, a girl of *nouveau riche* origins who is of the same

generation. The portrayal of the different levels of passion is masterly and the Marschallin's resigned surrender of her ardent young lover gives opera one of its most cherishable scenes. The comic side of the plot concerns the vulgar machinations of the rustic Baron Ochs and his attempts to seduce the disguised Octavian (girl playing boy playing girl!). The musical richness of the score is almost indescribable with stream after stream of endless melody, and the final trio which brings the three soprano roles together is the crowning glory of a masterpiece of our century. This magnificent 1957 recording, conducted with genius by Karajan and with a cast such as dreams are made of, has a status unparalleled and is unlikely to be challenged for many a year. The

Herbert von Karajan   *[photo: EMI*

Philharmonia play like angels and Elisabeth Schwarzkopf as the Marschallin gives one of her greatest performances. The recording, lovingly remastered, is outstanding.

Igor Stravinsky

Russian/French/American 1882-1971

Stravinsky. ORCHESTRAL WORKS. a**Columbia Symphony Orchestra;** b**CBC Symphony Orchestra/Igor Stravinsky.** CBS Masterworks CD42432/3.
CD42432—The Firebirda (from SBRG72046, 9/62). Scherzo à la russea. Scherzo fantastique, Op. 3b. Fireworks, Op. 4a (all from GM31, 2/82).
CD42433—Petrushkaa (Philips SABL175, 4/61). The Rite of Springa (SABL174, 4/61).

② 63' 65' ADD 9/88   ♩ P Ⓑ

It's not just authentic folk-songs, such as the one which dominates the solemn yet joyous finale, which give *Firebird* its national identity, but a host of colouristic and harmonic touches as well. Stravinsky's recordings of his own works have a quality it is tempting to call 'definitive'. Others have been more highly inflected in one way or another, but almost always at some cost to the overall excitement and long-term durability of the interpretation. Listen to the hush which comes over the opening of the final tableau—nothing but the finest control of long-term pacing could make that passage feel so right. The Columbia Symphony Orchestra was actually a pick-up band assembled by CBS for recording only; but it numbered many of the finest players in America and its performances on this CD are world-class. Digital remastering reveals the panache and precision more clearly than ever before and fortunately there is less trickery with the microphones than CBS sometimes indulged in. The same goes for the three scherzos. Perhaps the juvenile *Scherzo fantastique* is over-extended, and *Fireworks*, the piece which alerted Diaghilev to Stravinsky's talent and prompted the *Firebird* commission, fails to live up to the promise of its opening (as well as cribbing shamelessly from Dukas's *Sorcerer's apprentice*). But the *Scherzo à la russe* is a masterpiece in miniature.

Stravinsky. Concerto in E flat major, "Dumbarton Oaks". Pulcinella[a]—ballet (with original inspirations). [a]**Bernadette Manca di Nissa** (mez); [a]**David Gordon** (ten); [a]**John Ostendorf** (bass); **St Paul Chamber Orchestra/Christopher Hogwood.** Decca 425 614-2DH.
*Inspirations—**Gallo***: Trio Sonatas—No. 1 in G major: Moderato; No. 2 in B flat major: Presto, Presto; No. 7 in G minor: Allegro (Romuald Tecco, Thomas Kornacker, vns; Peter Howard, vc; Hogwood, hpd). ***Pergolesi***: Cello sinfonia (Howard, Joshua Koestenbaum, vcs; Hogwood).

66' DDD 6/90

Both *Dumbarton Oaks* and *Pulcinella* are deeply involved with the eighteenth century and the benefit of involving an eighteenth-century specialist in performing them is, firstly, that he will adopt a scholarly attitude to both pieces (Hogwood has sorted out one or two textual problems in *Dumbarton Oaks* by going back to the sources, just as if Stravinsky were an obscure composer of concerti grossi) and secondly that he will be likely to try out some of what he knows of period performing practice on these products of Stravinsky's kleptomaniac (his own word) forays into the eighteenth century.

So, we have on the whole non-legato, eighteenth-century style bowing among the strings (expressive slurs and slides only where Stravinsky asks for them), an implicit assumption that if a note appears in the score it is intended to be heard and a feeling, in both works, of an inherently vocal, Italianate grace to the sustained lines. Together with clean, crisp rhythms (this music dances more often than it pounds) and a deft pointing of accents it makes for great freshness and zest and a clear demonstration of Stravinsky's deep love for and understanding of the past and of the wholly twentieth-century creative response it awoke in him. The fragments of eighteenth-century music that Stravinsky used as a basis for *Pulcinella* make an entertaining supplement, but how one misses his inspired 'distortions' while listening to them. Admirable playing throughout, acceptable soloists and a first-class recording.

Stravinsky. WORKS FOR VIOLIN AND PIANO AND SOLO VIOLIN. **Isabelle van Keulen** (vn); [a]**Olli Mustonen** (pf). Philips 420 953-2PH2. Suite italienne (1932)[a]. Ballad (1947)[a]. Petrushka—Danse russe[a]. Chanson russe (1937)[a]. Pastorale (1933)[a]. Divertimento (1932)[a]. Duo concertante (1931-2)[a]. Tango (arr. Mustonen)[a]. Elegie (1944—arr. vn solo). Prelude et ronde des princesses (1929)[a]. The Firebird[a]—Berceuse (1929); Scherzo (1933). La Marseillaise (1919—arr. vn solo). Chants du rossignol et Marche chinoise (1932)[a].

② 96' DDD 8/89

Stravinsky once scribbled down a chord and asked violinist Samuel Dushkin if it was playable—"Of course not" was the reply. But when Dushkin tried it out it proved not only playable but unusually striking in its effect. Stravinsky proceeded to build his Violin Concerto of 1931 around this discovery. That same year the two musicians decided to form a concert duo and Stravinsky rapidly produced new works and transcriptions for them to take on tour. Again and again Stravinsky's ability to re-imagine his music in a new medium is astonishing—nowhere more so than in the essentially pianistic (so one might have thought) "Danse russe" from *Petrushka*. And with the restrained seriousness of the *Duo concertante* the complete programme adds up to far more than a succession of circus tricks. The two young musicians on this recording match Stravinsky's relish down to the tiniest detail and when more serious matters are broached their intelligence is as conspicuous as their virtuosity. The piano is admittedly a fraction too far forward, but not so as to detract in any significant way from the verve and flair of the playing.

Stravinsky. Symphony of Psalms[a]. Symphony in Three Movements[b]. Symphony in C major[c]. [a]**Toronto Festival Singers;** [ab]**CBC Symphony Orchestra,** [c]**Columbia Symphony Orchestra/Igor Stravinsky.** CBS Masterworks CD42434. Text and translation included. Items marked [a] and [c] from SBRG72181 (8/64), [b] SBRG72038 (9/62).

70' ADD 12/88

The chance of adding Stravinsky conducting his own music to your CD collection is hardly one to be missed. Time and again he stresses the rhythmic drama of his music and seeks out the bold contrasts of timbre in his orchestration. The purity of ideas in the Symphony in C and the warlike, motoristic pacing of the *Symphony in Three Movements* stand in stark relief with each other, despite their similarities of scoring and method. He seems to be at pains to let the music generate its own expression rather than impose grand gestures upon it, and revels in the rather bland, uniform sound of the Toronto Festival Singers in the *Symphony of Psalms*. The recordings of the two instrumental symphonies are well matched, with much of the inner complexity laid bare, though they both suffer from an aura of artificiality. The *Symphony of Psalms* still has thickened, mid-range textures but, like the other two works, has greatly benefited from this remixing for CD transfer.

Stravinsky. Les noces[a]. Mass[b]. [a]**Anny Mory** (sop); [a]**Patricia Parker** (mez); [a]**John Mitchinson** (ten); [a]**Paul Hudson** (bass); **English Bach Festival Chorus;** [b]**Trinity Boys' Choir;** [a]**Martha Argerich,** [a]**Krystian Zimerman,** [a]**Cyprien Katsaris,** [a]**Homero Francesch** (pfs); [a]**English Bach Festival Percussion Ensemble;** [b]members of the **English Bach Festival Orchestra/ Leonard Bernstein.** DG 20th Century Classics 423 251-2GC. Texts and translations included. From 2530 880 (2/78).

44' ADD 6/88   £

Like *Les noces*, the *Mass* presents a fundamental ritual experience, here the sacrament of worship rather than marriage. It does so in a similar depersonalized way but with the emphasis on stillness and awe rather than driving rhythmic energy. In its austerity the *Mass* is the gateway to the later serial Stravinsky of the 1950s and 1960s. The English Bach Festival Chorus, joined by the Trinity Boys' Choir in the *Mass*, carry the burden of the all-important choral parts, and do so triumphantly. The glamorous line-up of the pianists (Argerich, Zimerman, Katsaris, Francesch) supplies the expected panache in *Les noces* and the vocal soloists are first-rate. Bernstein co-ordinates the ensemble superbly and ensures that the sense of wonder underlying both works is fully conveyed. In DG's digital remastering the original analogue recording sounds in mint condition.

Franz von Suppé

Austrian 1819-1895

Suppé. OVERTURES. **Academy of St Martin in the Fields / Sir Neville Marriner.** EMI CDC7 54056-2.

Leichte Kavallerie. Tantalusqualen. Die Irrfahrt um's Glück. Die Frau Meisterin. Ein Morgen, ein Mittag, ein Abend in Wien. Pique-Dame. Wiener Jubel. Dichter und Bauer.

61' DDD 10/90

Suppé. OVERTURES. **Hungarian State Opera Orchestra / János Sándor.** LaserLight 15 611.

Overtures—Leichte Kavallerie; Fatinitza; Pique Dame; Dichter und Bauer; Banditenstreiche; Die schöne Galathéee; Flotte Bursche; Ein Morgen, ein Mittag, ein Abend in Wien. O du mein Osterreich—march.

63' DDD 11/90

Suppé's overtures are delightful creations brimming with melodic invention, and Marriner brings out all their warmth and infectious vitality in his highly successful interpretations. The orchestra respond to their conductor's obvious enthusiasm for this music with great aplomb, their expressive playing breathing new life into the more familiar items, like *Leichte Kavallerie* ("Light Cavalry") and *Dichter und Bauer* ("Poet and Peasant"). But what makes this winning collection so valuable is the inclusion of four Suppé rarities, *Tantalusqualen*, *Die Irrfahrt um's Glück*, *Wiener Jubel* (which contains one of those seductively big tunes that will haunt you for days) and *Die Frau Meisterin*, all of which are constructed with great skill and deserve to be more widely known. Sparkling, crisp recorded sound provides the final icing on the cake.

Although János Sándor does not quite capture the excitement of Marriner's performances, his collection is nonetheless extremely enjoyable and should not be overlooked. Some robust, committed playing from the Hungarian orchestra and a pleasingly clean digital recording make this a particularly attractive bargain price issue.

Arthur Sullivan

British 1842-1900

Sullivan. THE GONDOLIERS. **John Reed** (bar) The Duke of Plaza-Toro; **Jeffrey Skitch** (bar) Luiz; **Kenneth Sandford** (bass) Don Alhambra de Bolero; **Thomas Round** (ten) Marco Palmieri; **Alan Styler** (bar) Giuseppe Palmieri; **Michael Wakeham** (bar) Antonio, Annibale; **Joseph Riordan** (ten) Francesco; **George Cook** (bass) Giorgio; **Gillian Knight** (mez) The Duchess of Plaza-Toro; **Jennifer Toye** (sop) Casilda; **Mary Sansom** (sop) Gianetta; **Joyce Wright** (mez) Tessa; **Dawn Bradshaw** (sop) Fiametta; **Ceinwen Jones** (mez) Vittoria; **Dorothy Gill** (contr) Giulia; **Jeanette Roach** (contr) Inez; **D'Oyly Carte Opera Chorus; New Symphony Orchestra / Isidore Godfrey.** Decca 425 177-2LM2. From SKL4138-40 (11/61).

② 1h 59' ADD 1/90

Although *The Gondoliers* is one of the longer Gilbert and Sullivan works, Decca unusually recorded it with dialogue not once but twice. This is the older of the two versions, but decidedly the better. It offers an admirable sample of the D'Oyly Carte Opera Company around 1960, when it had some of the strongest performers of the post-War years. The performers' enjoyment of their roles readily comes through, and their lightness of delivery is totally appropriate for this, the sunniest of Sullivan's scores. Thomas Round and Alan Styler make most characterful gondoliers, the former being especially effective in "Take a pair of sparkling eyes". Mary Sansom and Joyce Wright are no less charming *contadine*, John Reed a suitably dry Duke, Gillian Knight a somewhat youngish-sounding Duchess and Kenneth Sandford a lightish-voiced but humorous Don Alhambra. There is good chorus work too, but perhaps the most important factor in the all-round strength of performance such as this is the conducting of Isidore Godfrey. He managed to make the music sparkle night after night in the theatre and does so here. The *cachucha* is quite captivatingly done. Despite its age, the spacious recorded sound comes up well.

Sullivan. THE MIKADO. **John Ayldon** (bass) Mikado; **Colin Wright** (ten) Nanki-Poo; **John Reed** (bar) Ko-Ko; **Kenneth Sandford** (bass) Pooh-Bah; **Michael Rayner** (bar) Pish-Tush; **John Broad** (bass) Go-To; **Valerie Masterson** (sop) Yum-Yum; **Peggy Ann Jones** (mez) Pitti-Sing; **Pauline Wales** (sop) Peep-Bo; **Lyndsie Holland** (contr) Katisha; **D'Oyly Carte Chorus; Royal Philharmonic Orchestra/Royston Nash.** Decca 417 296-2DY2. From SKL5158/9 (1/74).

② 90' ADD

Considering that it is the most popular of the Savoy Operas, *The Mikado* has been less well represented on disc than others of the series. Moreover, despite the popularity of some of Gilbert's spoken lines, it is one of the works that has never been recorded with dialogue. Of the recordings currently available on CD, this 1973 D'Oyly Carte Opera Company version is the one to have. The outstanding vocal performance comes from Valerie Masterson, a former member of the stage company, who is utterly delectable in "The sun whose rays". In John Reed and Kenneth Sandford there are seasoned performers of the male comic parts, and their important comic numbers ("I've got a little list" and "To sit in solemn silence") go well. If other singers are technically less good, they nevertheless contribute to a lively overall performance that is, indeed, much more than the sum of its parts. This is due particularly to the excellent choral and orchestral contributions, with Royston Nash keeping the score moving imposingly along. The spacious recorded sound also plays its part in the recording's success, by enabling the listener to appreciate Sullivan's orchestral skill and his ability to give point to the lyrics with appealing instrumental touches.

Sullivan. TRIAL BY JURY[a]. **Ann Hood** (sop) Plaintiff; **Thomas Round** (ten) Defendant; **Kenneth Sandford** (bar) Counsel; **John Reed** (bar) Judge; **Donald Adams** (bass-bar) Usher; **Anthony Raffell** (bass-bar) Foreman of the Jury; **D'Oyly Carte Opera Chorus; Orchestra of the Royal Opera House, Covent Garden/Isidore Godfrey.** From SKL4579 (4/64).
Sullivan. THE YEOMEN OF THE GUARD. **Anthony Raffell** (bass-bar) Sir Richard Cholmondeley; **Philip Potter** (ten) Col Fairfax; **Donald Adams** (bass-bar) Sergeant Meryll; **David Palmer** (ten) Leonard Meryll, First Yeoman; **John Reed** (bar) Jack Point; **Kenneth Sandford** (bar) Wilfred Shadbolt; **Thomas Lawlor** (bass) Second Yeoman; **Elizabeth Harwood** (sop) Elsie Maynard; **Ann Hood** (sop) Phoebe Meryll; **Gillian Knight** (mez) Dame Carruthers; **Margaret Eales** (sop) Kate; **D'Oyly Carte Opera Chorus, Royal Philharmonic Orchestra/Sir Malcolm Sargent.** From SKL4624-5 (11/64). Decca 417 358-2LM2.

② 2h 5' ADD 1/90   £ 9p

The D'Oyly Carte Opera Company's 1964 recording of *Yeomen of the Guard* was

one of the finest of all their recordings and certainly the most desirable CD version. For it Decca imported Sir Malcolm Sargent, who directs an interpretation of Sullivan's most imposing comic opera score that is at once spacious and commanding but at the same time breathes far more life than his earlier version for EMI. Decca also brought in the much lamented Elizabeth Harwood to display the beauties of the soprano writing that Sullivan provided for the role of Elsie Maynard. In support, the traditional D'Oyly Carte musical theatre style of performance is preserved through the contribution of various leading members of the permanent company of the time, including Ann Hood, Kenneth Sandford, Donald Adams and Gillian Knight, and John Reed as Jack Point. As if this fine performance could not stand up on its own, Decca have generously coupled a *Trial by Jury* recording of similar vintage, conducted in sparkling fashion by Isidore Godfrey and featuring Thomas Round as a suitably caddish defendant. The recorded sound in both cases remains remarkably good, making an altogether irresistible coupling of two of Sullivan's finest stage scores.

Karol Szymanowski
Polish 1882-1937

Szymanowski. String Quartets[a]—No. 1 in C major, Op. 37; No. 2, Op. 56. **Lutoslawski.** String Quartet[b]. **Penderecki.** String Quartet No. 2[b]. **Varsovia Quartet** (Boguslaw Bruczkowski, Krzysztof Bruczkowski, vns; Artur Paciorkiewicz, va; Wojciech Walasek, vc). Olympia OCD328. Items marked [a] from Pavane ADW7118 (10/85), [b]new to UK.

> **68' AAD 6/89**

Szymanowski's sound world is totally distinctive: there is an exotic luxuriance, a sense of ecstasy and longing, a heightened awareness of colour and glowing, almost luminous textures. The two quartets are separated by a decade: the First, whose sense of ecstasy and longing permeates its opening, is a subtle and deeply-felt performance and much the same must be said of the Varsovia account of No. 2. Again heady perfumes and exotic landscapes are in evidence, though with his increasing interest in folk-music, the finale has slight overtones of Bartók. There are magical things in both works and the Varsovia play marvellously throughout. Lutoslawski's Quartet has a highly developed and refined feeling for sonority and balance, and generally speaking succeeds in holding the listener, whereas the Penderecki is perhaps less substantial and for much of its time the sound world seems to aspire to the condition of electronic music. The Varsovia Quartet play excellently and are recorded in a warm and fresh acoustic. A most rewarding issue.

Szymanowski. PIANO WORKS. **Dennis Lee.** Hyperion CDA66409. Four Studies, Op. 4. Metopes, Op. 29. Fantasy, Op. 14. Masques, Op. 34.

> **64' DDD 7/91**

Szymanowski is to Polish music what Bartók was to Hungarian, in that he revived his country's musical creativity and enriched its repertory in the early part of this century. Like Bartók, too, he was attracted to Richard Strauss's harmonic and instrumental opulence, and sometimes drew upon his native folk music and allowed it to influence his works. But here the resemblance ends, for this Pole was a hothouse romantic more akin to Scriabin, and his piano music resembles his in being characteristically luxuriant and decadent in a *fin de siècle* way. Like Scriabin's, his earlier pieces owe much to Chopin, as we hear at once in the Four Etudes. Dennis Lee plays them persuasively, and these studies (of which the melodiously poignant third was a favourite of Paderewski) have charm as well as brilliance. But already in No. 4 we find the more chromatic style to which Szymanowski's music was soon to adhere and into which we are immediately plunged in "Isle of the Sirens", the first of the *Metopes* of 1915: their title suggests scenes depicted in antique Greek friezes. Here are what someone has called "swarms of notes", and this lushness is characteristic of the other works too, but though the constant runs and trills and the shifting harmony may cloy some palates, in certain moods this music can carry one away into a world of mystery, especially when it is played with this quiet authority. A valuable Szymanowski anthology, with piano sound that is pleasing though not in the demonstration class.

Toru Takemitsu

Takemitsu. PIANO WORKS. **Roger Woodward** (pf). Etcetera KTC1103.
Items marked [a] recorded at a performance in the Art Gallery of New South Wales, Sydney on September 16th, 1990.
Corona[a]. The Crossing[a]. Far Away. Les yeux clos. Litany. Pause uninterrupted. Piano Distance. Rain Tree Sketch.

· · • 78' DDD 6/91   ❓

The piano works on this disc illustrate particularly well the three stages in Takemitsu's development as a composer. The early pieces such as *Pause uninterrupted* of 1952-9 and *Piano Distance* (1969) reveal the influences of Scriabin, Debussy and Messiaen together with more modernist hints of composers such as Boulez and Stockhausen, whilst *Corona, The Crossing* and *Far Away* reveal his interest in the experimental music of composers such as John Cage. The remaining works, *Rain Tree Sketch, Litany* and *Les yeux clos* date from 1980-90 and represent his return to a more traditional, less radical style of composition. Despite his varied approach to writing Takemitsu has always maintained a distinct personal voice, and his unique, skilful blend of eastern aesthetics with western contemporary trends has earned him a prominent position in the world of contemporary music. His music is always highly coloured, sensuous and even when he is at his most extreme, as in *Corona* or *Far Away*, there is always a great sense of beauty and poetry. Roger Woodward has had a long association with Takemitsu and his music plays with authority and affection.

Thomas Tallis

Tallis. SACRED CHORAL WORKS. **The Hilliard Ensemble/Paul Hillier.**
ECM New Series 833 308-2. From 833 308-1 (4/88).
Lamentations of Jeremiah the Prophet a 5. Salvator mundi II a 5. O sacrum convivium a 5. Mass a 4. Absterge Domini a 5.

· · • 54' DDD   ✒

The Hilliard Ensemble appear here in sombre mood. They sing with restraint and gravity a programme of quite uncommon beauty, in the main austere and penitential. Apart from the Mass for Four Voices, most of these pieces would have been written during the reign of Elizabeth I, when Latin had ceased, in England, to be the official language of liturgy. *Salvator Mundi* and *O sacrum convivium* are short five-part antiphons from the feasts of the Exaltation of the Cross and Corpus Christi respectively. The singers respond to both with perfect objectivity, appearing to have greater affinity with the final piece, *Absterge Domine,* which is forward-looking in its delicate sensitivity to the words. The whole performance is distinguished by the careful shaping of every musical phrase and the impressive vocal quality—a glorious richness devoid of any vibrato.

Tallis. SACRED CHORAL WORKS. [a]**Taverner Consort;** [b]**Taverner Choir/Andrew Parrott.** EMI Reflexe CDC7 49555-2, CDC7 49563-2. Texts and translations included.
CDC7 49555-2—Videte miraculum[b]. Homo quidam[b]. Audivi vocem[a]. Candidi facti sunt Nazarei[b]. Dum transisset Sabbatum[b]. Honor, virtus et potestas[b]. Hodie nobis[a]. Loquebantur variis linguis[b]. In pace, in idipsum[a]. Spem in alium (with Wim Becu, bass sackbut; Paul Nicholson, Alan Wilson, orgs)[ab]. *CDC7 49563-2*—Gaude gloriosa Dei mater[ab]. Te lucis ante terminum … Procul recedant somnia I[a]. Miserere nostri[a]. Salvator mundi I[a]. Salvator mundi[b]. Lamentations of Jeremiah[a]. O sacrum convivium[b]. Suscipe, quaeso Domine[b]. O nata lux[b]. In jejunio et fletu[a].

② 62' 68' DDD 5/89

Tallis, one of the greatest composers of sacred music, has been sympathetically and generously acknowledged by Andrew Parrott and the Taverner Choir with two separately available discs of Latin church music. They include 12 pieces from the Cantiones Sacrae of 1575, the two *Lamentations of Jeremiah*, and the masterly 40-part responsary *Spem in alium* written, it would seem, in reply to a similarly ambitious one by Tallis's Italian contemporary, Alessandro Striggio. The performances are characterized by translucent textures, a wonderful feeling for structure and a fluent understanding of the composer's contrapuntal ingenuity. Certainly there are occasional hints of vocal strain in the uppermost reaches of the part writing but they do little to spoil an affectionate, technically assured account of thrilling music. Among many impressive features to be found in these discs is the performance of the *Gaude gloriosa Dei mater,* spacious in dimension, rich in counterpoint and concluding with an extended "Amen". Parrott illuminates the music with his own deep understanding of it, but above all with the skilful deployment of vocal talent that he has at his command.

Tallis. MOTETS. **The Tallis Scholars/Peter Phillips.** Gimell CDGIM006. Spem in alium. Salvator mundi (I, II). Sancte Deus, sancte fortis. Gaude gloriosa Dei mater. Miserere nostri. Loquebantur variis linguis.

43' DDD 3/86 Ⓑ

In Thomas Tallis's celebrated *Spem in alium* the Roman Catholic composer pleads to his queen for tolerance of his faith in the language he knows best, the tongues of collected voices. The result is humbling, overwhelming and quite lovely. The Tallis Scholars directed by Peter Phillips offer this monumental work in their glorious Tallis programme. The blend of voices, capped by a penetrating soprano line, makes a versatile and tremendously powerful instrument. *Gaude gloriosa* deploys the choir with a richness of texture and gradual accumulation of voices that are used to hymn Queen Mary for being "the means of salvation", the restorer of the faith. The recording, made in Merton College Chapel, Oxford, is beautifully handled. The space and shape of the building virtually appear before one's ears and eyes as the music unfolds.

Tallis. Missa Salve intemerata virgo.
Taverner. Mass a 4, "Western Wynde". Song, "Western Wynde". **St John's College Choir, Cambridge/George Guest.** EMI Eminence CD-EMX2155.

58' DDD 2/90

The St John's College Choir, Cambridge under its recently-retired Director, George Guest gives fervent and firmly structured performances of Masses by two great masters of English sixteenth-century sacred vocal music. Taverner, the earlier composer of the two was innovative in his use of a secular cantus firmus, the tune of *Western Wynde* throughout the Mass. In the present performance, a solo tenor introduces the listener to this famous and beautiful sixteenth century song which in the Mass is treated to 36 variations. Tallis's five-part Mass *Salve intemerata virgo* is based on his own motet of that name. Its masterly counterpoint is lucidly sustained and is balanced in such a way as to highlight details in vocal character and texture. Nowhere, perhaps, is this more movingly demonstrated than in the second *Agnus Dei* where the four lower voices pursue a course of vocalization on the syllable 'O' of "nobis". This and the re-entry of the trebles for the final invocation is affectingly realized by Guest and his accomplished choir. The recording is sympathetic but the booklet omits the Latin texts.

Giuseppe Tartini   *Refer to Index*   *Italian 1692-1770*

John Tavener   *British 1944-*

Tavener. Ikon of Light (1984)[a]. Funeral Ikos[b]. Carol—The Lamb[c]. [a]Members of the **Chilingirian Quartet** (Mark Butler, vn; Csaba Erdelyi, va; Philip de Groote, vc); **Tallis Scholars/[ab]Peter Phillips,** [c]**John Tavener.** Gimell CDGIM005. Texts and translations included. From 1585-05 (12/84).

55' DDD 6/91

John Tavener first met with critical acclaim in 1968 with his dramatic cantata on biblical (and not so biblical) texts—*The Whale*. There followed a series of works (*Ultimos Ritos, Celtic Requiem* and the opera *Therese* to name but three) in which Tavener seemed to be re-examining and questioning the very nature of his faith and his relationship with his creator, and this culminated in his being received, in 1977, into the Russian Orthodox Church. Since then many of his works have been inspired by Russian Orthodox texts and the quietly omnipotent image of the ikon. One such work, and arguably an important turning point in his approach to composition, is the *Ikon of Light*. This penetrating and visionary work is a setting of the "Mystic Prayer to the Holy Spirit" by mystical poet St Simeon, the New Theologian. To describe the opening as luminous would be an understatement. Five repetitions of the word *Phos* ("Light"), each proportionally longer than the previous, are interspersed by the sound of a distant string trio (representing the Soul's yearning for God) before dissolving into the radiantly polyphonic music of the second movement "Dhoxa" ("Glory"). As an expression of faith in contemporary art it is without doubt one of the most important works of the last 20 years, and deserves to win many friends and renewed recognition for this often undervalued and extraordinarily gifted composer. The austere and simple, yet equally moving *Funeral Ikos*—a setting of the Greek funeral sentences for the burial of priests—and the gentle stillness of the now popular carol *The Lamb* complete this richly rewarding disc. Beautifully performed and vividly recorded.

John Taverner

British c.1490-1545

Taverner. Missa Gloria Tibi Trinitas. Kyrie a 4, "Leroy". Dum transisset Sabbatum. **The Tallis Scholars/Peter Phillips.** Gimell CDGIM004. From 1585-04 (12/84).

47' DDD 7/86

Taverner's Mass *Gloria Tibi Trinitas* is a gloriously rich work showing a strong awareness of continental styles that was a hallmark of the cultural life encouraged by Henry VIII until he broke with Rome. Taverner was appointed the first choirmaster of Cardinal College, Oxford (now Christ Church) and it seems almost certain that the Mass was composed for that choir. Musicians today accept the work's superiority and though there are several excellent recordings currently in the catalogue, Peter Phillips's recording with The Tallis Scholars is perhaps the most exciting, splendidly recorded in the chapel of Merton College, Oxford.

Pyotr Ill'yich Tchaikovsky

Russian 1840-1893

Tchaikovsky. Piano Concerto No. 1 in B flat minor, Op. 23[a]. Violin Concerto in D major, Op. 35[b]. [a]**Emil Gilels** (pf); [a]**New York Philharmonic Orchestra/Zubin Mehta;** [b]**Pinchas Zukerman** (vn); [b]**Israel Philharmonic Orchestra/Zubin Mehta.** CBS Masterworks CD44643. Item marked [a] from 36660 (5/81), [b] IM39563 (10/85).

69' DDD 9/89

Tchaikovsky. Piano Concerto No. 1 in B flat minor.
Dohnányi. Variations on a Nursery Song. **András Schiff** (pf); **Chicago Symphony Orchestra/Sir Georg Solti.** Decca 417 294-2DH. From 417 294-1DH (10/86).

59' DDD 12/86

Pyotr Ill'yich Tchaikovsky

The factor of cost which sometimes worries people buying CDs is put into perspective here, with a mid-price disc lasting nearly 70 minutes and containing Tchaikovsky's two most popular concertos, works which we would in the past normally have bought on separate LPs, and played by top-class artists who for all their virtuosity put expression first and foremost and bring considerable charm to the music. The Piano Concerto No. 1 is a 1979 live performance from New York, and has all the excitement which that implies, a kind of urgency that keeps you at the edge of your seat. Emil Gilels is in his best form, which is saying something, and the New York Philharmonic under Zubin Mehta are caught up in this fine music-making. The recording does not bring the piano as close as we are accustomed to, perhaps, but that is no bad thing, and though there are some noticeable audience noises, few people will consider this too high a price to pay for being present, as it were, on a memorable occasion. In the Violin Concerto, Pinchas Zukerman joins the same conductor in Tel Aviv in 1984. This time the orchestra is the Israel Philharmonic, and here too we have a thrilling live performance of one of the great violin concertos by a soloist and conductor entirely in sympathy with the music. Applause follows both performances, but sensibly it is faded fairly quickly.

Schiff's reading of the Tchaikovsky war-horse is very competitive, with the piano finely integrated with the orchestra in the tuttis and picking a telling line above the texture in the quieter moments. His reading is not as aggressive as some, and this provides a useful alternative view of the work. But if that is not enough to tempt you, the coupling of Dohnányi's *Variations on a Nursery Song* makes this issue even more attractive. From its portentous opening, through its bathetically simple theme, to the joyous delights of the finale, this is a work that, for all its humour, is not to be underestimated. Schiff and Solti certainly could not be accused of that, for they give it their all, treating each idea with utter conviction. Schiff's immaculate fingerwork is particularly effective in the filigree passagework and Solti's firm hand on the tiller ensures that the whole functions as a rounded and balanced structure. The clean recording allows all performers to take the dynamic range to its limits, allowing even the snowflake delicacy of Variation No. 5 to be deliciously sustained, whilst the opening of Variation No. 11 has all the power and impact you could hope for.

Tchaikovsky. 1812—Overture, Op. 49. Capriccio italien, Op. 45. MAZEPPA—Cossack Dance. **Cincinnati Symphony Orchestra/Erich Kunzel.** Telarc CD80041. From DG10041 (4/80).

35' DDD 12/83

Kunzel's recording of the *1812* is an unashamed hi-fi spectacular, so much so that purchasers are warned that the cannon at the end can damage loudspeakers with their extreme volume. At the time of the recording it is claimed that windows nearby were shattered. In the *Capriccio italien* too, another colourful popular favourite, this version uses the full range of high-fidelity digital sound with the bass drum very prominent and astonishingly vivid in its exploitation of the lowest register. The forwardness of such effects may detract from the purely musical qualities of the performances, which are strong and energetic without being so perceptive or so exciting as some, though very well played. Particularly enjoyable is the third item, the vigorous and colourful "Cossack Dance".

Tchaikovsky. Swan Lake, Op. 20. **Royal Opera House Orchestra, Covent Garden/Mark Ermler.** Royal Opera House Records ROH301/03.

③ 2h 33' DDD 12/89

Tchaikovsky. Swan Lake, Op. 20. **Philharmonia Orchestra/John Lanchbery.** EMI CDS7 49171-2. From SLS5271 (11/82).

② 2h 34' DDD 9/89

It is a measure of its greatness that *Swan Lake* has survived the many trials and tribulations of its chequered history. Its first performance met with only moderate success in 1877; critics found its form and orchestration original, but generally considered it unsuitable for dance. It remained in the repertoire, however, until 1883, during which time it had undergone gross distortions at the hands of various choreographers, even to the point of having nearly a third of Tchaikovsky's music replaced by music from other composers's ballets. It was not until two years after Tchaikovsky's death that a truly successful production was mounted and today *Swan Lake* is rightfully recognized as a masterpiece, greatly loved by dancers and audiences alike.

The Orchestra of the Royal Opera House, Covent Garden, must have performed this music more times than they care to remember. However, this is no routine performance; in fact, the result is very special indeed. Their playing glows with a freshness of an orchestra performing the music for the first time and you would be hard put to find a recording where the strings play so beguilingly or with such romantic fervour as they do here, with every phrase beautifully crafted and elegant. The brass sound splendid too, playing with great panache and sonority. All this is helped by the marvellously sumptuous recording, set in a warmly resonant acoustic. Ermler's tempos are generally more expansive than his rivals, adding about ten minutes to the overall duration, although Conifer's decision to spread the ballet over three discs seems rather curious, as it could easily have been fitted on to two well filled CDs. That aside, this is still the first choice and is a recording that the orchestra can be very proud of.

Lanchbery's near-complete recording (two numbers from Act 2 had to be omitted for space reasons) proves that the usually recorded highlights are only special delights from a score that is brimful of them and has no weak moments. It is played here with immense affection and rhythmic gusto by the Philharmonia Orchestra under a conductor who has over 30 years of experience directing ballet in the theatre and knows just how to pace a scene for maximum effect. The accompanying booklet gives a full synopsis of the action and lists the various numbers which each occupy a separate track.

Tchaikovsky. The Sleeping Beauty, Op. 66. **Philharmonia Orchestra/John Lanchbery.** EMI CDS7 49216-2. From HMV SLS5272 (11/82).

② 2h 39' DDD 3/89

The Sleeping Beauty is the most intractable of the three great Tchaikovsky ballets; it is very long and the story line is slender and produces very little action. It does, however, have wonderful things: the "Panorama" of Act 2 is one of the composer's finest melodic ideas, while the "Pas de six" of Act 1 and the contrasted Fairy dances of Act 3 bring the same almost Mozartian grace (combined with Tchaikovsky's own very special feeling for orchestral colour) that he displays in the *Nutcracker* characteristic dances, which turn simple ballet vignettes into great art. This 1982 recording from Lanchbery and the Philharmonia on top form enjoys a good modern recording and sounds splendid. There is zest and a fine sense of drama without any loss of classical grace, and there is a great feeling of vitality. This set is sure to provide a great deal of listening pleasure.

Tchaikovsky. The Nutcracker—Ballet[a]. QUEEN OF SPADES—Duet of Daphnis and Chloë[b]. [b]**Cathryn Pope** (sop); [b]**Sarah Walker** (mez); [a]**Tiffin Boys' School Choir; London Symphony Orchestra/Sir Charles Mackerras.** Telarc CD80137.

② 88' DDD 5/87   ⁹ₛ Ⓑ

Tchaikovsky. The Nutcracker—Ballet[a].
Rossini/Respighi. La boutique fantasque[b]. [a]**Suisse Romande Orchestra/ Ernest Ansermet;** [b]**Israel Philharmonic Orchestra/Sir Georg Solti.** Decca Weekend 425 509-2DC2. Item marked [a] from SXL2092/3 (4/59), [b] SXL2007 (10/58).

② 2h 4' AAD 12/9   £ Ⓑ

The *Nutcracker* ballet shows Tchaikovsky's inspiration at its most memorable and the orchestration creates a unique symbiosis with the music. The ballet is based on a grotesque tale by E.T.A. Hoffmann, but in the ballet it becomes more of a fairy story, with only the eccentric Drosselmeyer who provides the heroine, Clara, with the Nutcracker at a Christmas party, reflecting anything of the mood of the original narrative. Tchaikovsky's music, a stream of wonderful tunes, radiantly, piquantly or glitteringly scored, as the character of each demands, contains much that enchants the listener which is not included in the famous Suite, notably the "Waltz of the Snowflakes" (with its wordless chorus) and the glorious climbing melody that accompanies the journey through the pine forest to the Magic Castle. Under Mackerras the music glows with colour and has superb vitality; the stunningly rich Telarc recording helps too. This is a wonderful entertainment from the first bar to the last and the documentation is admirable. As a bonus we are offered a charming duet from the *Queen of Spades*.

Whilst the *Nutcracker* from the Suisse Romande and Ansermet may not feature dazzling technical display from the orchestra or the rich sonic kaleidoscope of the Telarc production, its interpretative qualities still keep it a firm favourite. Ansermet's knack of fixing on just the right tempo for each of the multifarious sections helps not just every individual section make sense, but it also shapes the overall form so that the complete ballet acquires a satisfying structure. Outside the theatre, *The Nutcracker* can seem to be just a motley collection of unrelated numbers, but not in this performance. Less than 30 years separated the first production of *Nutcracker* (1892) and Respighi's arrangement of pieces by Rossini for his one act ballet, *La boutique fantasque* (1919). Yet, even though the original music used for the latter is firmly of the nineteenth century and Respighi makes obvious allusion to later romantic ballet idioms, there is still a world of difference between the two. This contrast is strongly drawn by Solti's dynamic reading of the Respighi, its primary-colour brilliance forcing the Israel Philharmonic to pull out all the stops. The close recording is the ideal complement.

Tchaikovsky. Romeo and Juliet—Fantasy Overture. The Nutcracker—Suite, Op. 71a. **Berlin Philharmonic Orchestra/Herbert von Karajan.** DG 410 873-2GH. From 410 873-1GH (2/84).

· ·ᐟ **44' DDD 4/84**

It might be argued that *Romeo and Juliet* is the most successful symphonic poem in the repertoire, economically structured, wonderfully inspired in its melodies and with the narrative and final tragedy depicted with imaginative vividness. Karajan brings out all the intensity of the composer's inspiration and the playing of the Berlin Philharmonic creates much excitement. *The Nutcracker* shows the other side of the composer's personality—for he could relax to write the most wonderfully crafted light music—and the suite is utter perfection. Each of the *danses caractéristiques* is a miracle of melody and orchestration and their charm never cloys, especially when they are played so winningly and with such polish. The recording is admirably clear and well balanced and though a little more warmth would have made the upper strings sweeter in the ballet music, this remains a very recommendable disc.

Tchaikovsky. Piano Concerto No. 2 in G major, Op. 44 (orig. version). **Peter Donohoe** (pf); **Bournemouth Symphony Orchestra/Rudolf Barshai** with **Nigel Kennedy** (vn); **Steven Isserlis** (vc). EMI CDC7 49124-2. From EL270603-1 (8/87).

· ·ᐟ **47' DDD 11/87**

This piano concerto has always lived in the shadow of its famous predecessor. The Concerto was first performed by Tchaikovsky's pupil Sergei Taneyev, who

Nigel Kennedy [photo: EMI/Jebb]

then suggested that the long first and second movements be cut. Tchaikovsky made three small cuts himself, but the score was not published until after his death, in a version which had still more drastic cuts made by another pupil, Alexander Siloti. It is through this version that the world has judged the Concerto to be an inferior piece. When, as in this recording, the original score is played, with the important solo violin and cello parts in the slow movement restored, a work of much greater stature is revealed. Peter Donohoe plays the work with enormous dash and conviction. Barshai and the Bournemouth orchestra give him magnificent support, and the slow movement is adorned by the most beautiful playing from Kennedy and Isserlis. The high artistic qualities of this performance are well-complemented by a bold, wide-ranging recording.

Tchaikovsky. Violin Concerto in D major, Op. 35[a].
WORKS FOR VIOLIN AND PIANO[b]. Itzhak Perlman (vn); [b]**Janet Goodman Guggenheim** (pf); [a]**Israel Philharmonic Orchestra/Zubin Mehta.** EMI CDC7 54108-2. Recorded at performances in [a]Philharmonic Hall, Leningrad on May 2nd, 1990 and [b]Tchaikovsky Hall, Moscow on April 30th, 1990.
Bazzini: La ronde des lutins, Op. 25. *Bloch:* Baal shem—Nigun. *Kreisler:* Liebeslied. *Prokofiev* (arr. Heifetz): The Love for Three Oranges—March. *Tartini:* Violin Sonata in G minor, "The devil's trill". *Tchaikovsky* (arr. Kreisler): String Quartet No. 1 in D major, Op. 11—Andante. *Wieniawski* (arr. Kreisler): Caprice in A minor.

72' DDD 2/91

Itzhak Perlman is one of the great violinists of our time, and this recording has a special interest in that it provides a memento of his first visit to the Soviet Union in the spring of 1990, which happens also to have been the first visit of the Israel Philharmonic Orchestra and the conductor Zubin Mehta. Among the pluses here is a sense of immediacy that belong to live performance before an audience, and for this most collectors will accept the debit side, which frankly includes a fair amount of audience noise including applause not only at the end of pieces—note that in Russia, the slow handclap is a mark of special enthusiasm!—but, for example, when the violinist announces some of the pieces he played at his Moscow concert with piano (this occupies the seven tracks after the three that are taken up with the Tchaikovsky Concerto, played in Leningrad). Judging by the odd murmurs, rustles and bumps on this disc, Soviet concert audiences who are obviously enjoying themselves are none too silent either while the music is actually happening, and if you think this could matter a lot to you, listen to the slow movement of the Concerto before purchasing this CD. Otherwise, there's little to fear and much to delight, for the violin playing is masterly in its vibrant eloquence and bravura, and Mehta and the orchestra accompany most attentively in the Concerto although the recording (excellent of Perlman) could ideally have captured more detail of their contribution. The wonders of violin virtuosity in the final piece with piano by Bazzini draw gasps of delighted amazement from the Moscow audience, as well they might!

Tchaikovsky. SYMPHONIES. **Berlin Philharmonic Orchestra/Herbert von Karajan.** DG 429 675-2GSE4.
No. 1 in G minor, Op. 13, "Winter daydreams"; No. 2 in C minor, Op. 17, "Little Russian"; No. 3 in D major, Op. 29, "Polish" (all from 2740 219, 11/79); No. 4 in F minor, Op. 36 (2530 883, 6/78); No. 5 in E minor, Op. 64 (2530 699, 8/76); No. 6 in B minor, Op. 74, "Pathétique" (2530 774, 6/77).

⊙ ④ 4h 24' ADD 1/89 £ 9ₚ

If the trouble and expense of selecting and buying the Tchaikovsky symphonies individually for your collection does not appeal, you could do far worse than go for this bargain set of the six numbered ones shoe-horned into four CDs. Splitting Symphonies Nos. 2 and 5 across two discs is an inconvenience, but the performances more than compensate. Karajan recorded Symphonies Nos. 4, 5 and 6 numerous times but DG have selected the best of the bunch for this set. He treats these works as true symphonies, extensions of the classical genre, rather than the multi-movement tone-poems that they so often become under other batons. He maintains subtle structural shaping at all times: the *Pathétique* is not allowed to brood too soon and this makes the final bars all the more effective; No. 5 is given its head to blaze away at the climax points, yet balance is never lost. Karajan's readings of the three earlier symphonies are also outstanding, easily keeping pace with the competition. Symphony No. 2, for example, is given a particularly effective lift by the selection of buoyant tempos in the faster movements; the ballet elements of No. 3 are keenly brought out and this adds poignancy to the juxtaposition of dance and symphonic form typical of Tchaikovsky's musical character. An added bonus to this set is the consistency of approach that derives from having the same orchestra for all works. That special quality of sound, that marked the Berlin Philharmonic as one of the world's greatest orchestras, lends a depth and unity to recordings made throughout the latter half of the 1970s. If they do not always have the clarity and detail of a fully up-to-date production, they still serve the performances well and generally retain a rich body of orchestral sound without restricting appreciation of the finer points.

Tchaikovsky. SYMPHONIES. [abc]**Philharmonia Orchestra,** [d]**New Philharmonia Orchestra/Vladimir Ashkenazy.** Decca 425 586-2DM3.
No. 4 in F minor, Op. 36[a] (from SXL6919, 12/79); No. 5 in E minor, Op. 64[b] (SXL6884, 5/78); No. 6 in B minor, Op. 74, "Pathétique"[c] (SXL6941, 8/81). Manfred Symphony, Op. 58[d] (SXL6853, 9/78).

⊙ ③ 3h 12' ADD 3/90 £ Ⓑ

There are many fine recordings of Tchaikovsky's last three symphonies in the catalogue to choose from, but there is something particularly special about Ashkenazy's marvellous readings. These were among the recordings that confirmed Ashkenazy's status as a conductor of considerable powers. Repackaged as they are here on three mid-price CDs they represent exceptional value for money. Despite having been recorded over a period of three years, there is a remarkable consistency in style, quality and approach. Particularly striking is the way in which he underplays the obvious emotional qualities of these works by avoiding any over sentimentality or self indulgence. Instead we are given strong, dramatic and purposeful readings that are unafraid to probe beneath the surface of these most intimate utterances. The Philharmonia's string playing has a wonderful pureness of tone and there is some delicious wind playing too, particularly in the scherzos, where lightness, accuracy and crisp articulation are required. The Fourth Symphony has plenty of vigour and dramatic weight, but there is subtlety too, especially in his close attention to dynamic shading. The transition from *Scherzo* to finale is splendid and the finale itself is a real *tour de force*. A remarkably warm and lyrical reading of the Fifth Symphony follows and in the *Pathétique* it is once again his freshness and spontaneity, together with a strong sense of forward momentum and purpose, that makes this so compelling a performance. And for desert—simply one of the finest readings of the *Manfred* Symphony on disc. The vivid analogue recordings (some of Decca's very best) have lost none of their lustre or clarity in their transfer to CD. Strongly recommended.

Tchaikovsky. Symphonies—No. 1 in G minor, Op. 13, "Winter daydreams"[a]; No. 2 in C minor, Op. 17, "Little Russian"[b]; No. 3 in D major, Op. 29, "Polish"[c]. **Concertgebouw Orchestra/Bernard Haitink.** Philips 420 751-2PM2. Item marked [a] from 9500 777 (4/81), [b] 9500 444 (6/79), [c] 9500 776 (8/81).

② 2h 4' ADD 6/90

All too often conductors approach these early symphonies with the hindsight of the later, more passionate symphonies in mind, often resulting in an over-indulgence that seems inappropriate in these earlier, more optimistic symphonies. Haitink however, responds in a much more sympathetic and direct manner, with clean-limbed performances that have poise, nobility and great charm, coupled with a freshness of approach that allows the music to speak for itself. Symphony No. 1, *Winter daydreams*, is given a marvellously atmospheric reading, especially in the sub-titled first and second movements —"Reveries of a Winter Journey" and "Land of Desolation, Land of Mists" and his choice of tempos throughout are perfectly judged. The Second Symphony, *Little Russian*, is amongst the finest in the catalogue at any price. Here Haitink responds in a most persuasive way to Tchaikovsky's symphonic structure and draws from the Concertgebouw performances of remarkable clarity and detail. The Third is also very fine and again it is his direct and fresh approach that is most convincing though perhaps it lacks the passion found in some performances, it is more than compensated for in the charm and eloquence of the playing. For the collector who already possesses the more popular symphonies Nos. 4, 5 and 6, this set provides the perfect opportunity to complete the cycle with performances of the highest quality at an unbeatable price. The recordings are exceptionally fine and have lost none of their warmth in this transfer to CD. Strongly recommended.

Tchaikovsky. Symphony No. 3, Op. 29, "Polish". **Oslo Philharmonic Orchestra/Mariss Jansons.** Chandos CHAN8463.

45' DDD 7/86

Unusually, this symphony has five movements: the first is the longest, and consists of a subdued introduction followed by a bracing, very positive *Allegro brillante*. A graceful, waltz-like intermezzo follows and then there is the slow movement proper, marked *Andante elegiaco*. The *Scherzo* is a bouncing, whirling affair, with delicate, wispy figurations. A final quicker movement with a rousing climax brings the symphony to a confident conclusion. This is not an easy work to bring off effectively in performance, for the material is not always so immediately memorable as in other Tchaikovsky symphonies, and it is sometimes awkwardly constructed. Mariss Jansons comes through the test with flying colours. He secures playing of high virtuosity from the Oslo orchestra, and the recording has splendid clarity and presence.

Tchaikovsky. Symphony No. 4 in F minor, Op. 36. **Oslo Philharmonic Orchestra/Mariss Jansons.** Chandos CHAN8361. From ABRD1124 (7/85).

42' DDD 9/85		**B**

Tchaikovsky. Symphonies—No. 4 in F minor, Op. 36[a]; No. 5 in E minor, Op. 64[b]; No. 6 in B minor, Op. 74, "Pathétique[c]. **Leningrad Philharmonic Orchestra/Evgeny Mravinsky.** DG 419 745-2GH2. Items marked [a] from SLPM138657 (6/61), [b] SLPM138658 (10/61), [c] SLPM138659 (11/61).

② 2h 9' ADD 8/87		P	**B**

A high emotional charge runs through Jansons's performance of the Fourth, yet this rarely seems to be an end in itself. There is always a balancing concern for the superb craftsmanship of Tchaikovsky's writing: the shapeliness of the phrasing; the superb orchestration, scintillating and subtle by turns; and most of all Tchaikovsky's marvellous sense of dramatic pace. Rarely has the first movement possessed such a strong sense of tragic inevitability, or the return of the 'fate' theme in the finale sounded so logical, so necessary. The playing of the Oslo Philharmonic Orchestra is first rate: there are some gorgeous woodwind solos and the brass manage to achieve a truly Tchaikovskian intensity. Recordings are excellent: at once spacious and clearly focused, with a wide though by no means implausible dynamic range.

Mariss Jansons [photo: EMI/Huf]

Mravinsky's classic 1960s recordings make a fine, and reasonably priced, alternative to Jansons's superb Chandos issues. Mravinsky's control of his orchestra is total, and the sheer energy he can unleash at climaxes is breathtaking. His rhythmic control is remarkable and is used at all times to follow the letter of the score. The sincerity and spirit of the music-making is without question. The recordings have an immediacy and depth that has greatly benefited from the remastering.

Tchaikovsky. Symphony No. 5 in E minor, Op. 64. **Oslo Philharmonic Orchestra/Mariss Jansons.** Chandos CHAN8351.

43' DDD 3/85		P **B**

Many of the remarks made about Mariss Janson's performance of the Fourth Symphony also apply here, though it should be stressed that there isn't the vaguest hint of sameness about his interpretations. One's impressions in the Fifth are very different: one remembers the rich dark tones of the clarinets in the first movement's introduction, the beautiful tone and elegant phrasing of the horn in the *Andante cantabile*, the ardent, sweeping intensity of the strings at climaxes and, above all, Jansons's extraordinarily coherent vision of the Symphony as a complete utterance. It doesn't matter whether you're hearing the Symphony for the first time or the 1,000-and-first; Jansons is the version to have.

Tchaikovsky. Symphony No. 6 in B minor, Op. 74, "Pathétique". **Oslo Philharmonic Orchestra/Mariss Jansons.** Chandos CHAN8446. From ABRD1158 (1/87).

44' DDD 5/87

Tchaikovsky's autobiographical *Pathétique* Symphony carries an extraordinary musical intensity, the whole drenched in an emotional despair that drains away almost to a state of total inertness in the closing stages. It is a work that, when given a powerful reading in concert, closes in silence leaving the audience drained and unbearably moved. Jansons brings to his reading of this great work an acuteness and detail that never imbalance the wider shape of the Symphony, but which none the less illuminate its many subtleties. The Oslo orchestra play superbly and possess the same compelling weight of tone that so distinguishes their other recordings in this much-praised series. The recording is very fine indeed.

Tchaikovsky. Manfred Symphony, Op. 58. **Oslo Philharmonic Orchestra/ Mariss Jansons.** Chandos CHAN8535.

53' DDD 5/88

This Symphony "in Four Scenes" was inspired by a reading of Byron's dramatic poem. Tchaikovsky seems to have felt great affection for the work but was unsure of its structural validity. It has proved difficult to bring off successfully in performance, despite the straightforward appeal of much of its melodic invention. In this performance, Jansons selects rather fast tempos for the most part and manages to bring out the warmth of the melodic writing whilst holding the whole work together most convincingly. The Oslo Philharmonic responds with adroit vivacity. Spectacularly open sound complements all the best qualities of this performance, securing here what is likely to be a prime recommendation for quite some time to come.

Tchaikovsky. String Quartets—No. 1 in D major, Op. 11; No. 2 in F major, Op. 22; No. 3 in E flat minor, Op. 30. Souvenir de Florence, Op. 70[a]. **Borodin Quartet** (Mikhail Kopelman, Andrei Abramenkov, vns; Dmitri Shebalin, va; Valentin Berlinsky, vc) with [a]**Yuri Bashmet** (va); [a]**Natalia Gutman** (vc). EMI CDS7 49775-2.

(2) 2h 20' ADD 8/88

Tchaikovsky's writing for string quartet shows considerable mastery, and all three works have an open-hearted fluency and a high quality of invention. There are no hints of constraint, and it seems that Tchaikovsky enjoyed the task of writing for a gentler medium. The Third Quartet has an elegiac quality throughout, with a particularly deeply-felt slow movement. The First Quartet, with the famous *Andante cantabile* slow movement, has a delightfully spring-like, outgoing lyrical character, and is the most popular of the three: the Second Quartet has a slightly greater range of expression, and the movements are more contrasted in mood. The Borodin Quartet play these works with a fine sense of style, and their readings are totally free of mannerisms and interpretative quirks. They are particularly impressive in the way that they float the long melodies in Tchaikovsky's slow movements, though they can play with plenty of brilliance when required. In *Souvenir de Florence* the two extra players combine happily with the Quartet. The recordings have plenty of presence and warmth.

Tchaikovsky. Piano Trio in A minor, Op. 50. **Vladimir Ashkenazy** (pf); **Itzhak Perlman** (vn); **Lynn Harrell** (vc). EMI CDC7 47988-2. From ASD4036 (7/81).

49' DDD 12/87

The very popularity of Tchaikovsky's orchestral music has overshadowed his much smaller output of chamber and instrumental music. The Piano Trio was composed to honour the memory of Nicholas Rubinstein, whose personal kindness Tchaikovsky never forgot (in spite of their temporary rift over the First Piano Concerto). The Trio was originally performed on the first anniversary of Rubinstein's death and despite its length, it enjoys something approaching popularity these days, thanks to the quality of its thematic invention and its obvious depth of feeling. This version is absolutely complete, and with the unforced yet deeply expressive playing that the performers bring to the music, it is also strongly recommendable.

Tchaikovsky. EUGENE ONEGIN. **Bernd Weikl** (bar) Onegin; **Teresa Kubiak** (sop) Tatyana; **Stuart Burrows** (ten) Lensky; **Júlia Hamari** (mez) Olga; **Nicolai Ghiaurov** (bass) Gremin; **Anna Reynolds** (mez) Larina; **Enid Hartle** (mez) Filippyevna; **Michel Sénéchal** (ten) Triquet; **Richard Van Allan** (bass) Zaretsky; **William Mason** (bass) Captain; **John Alldis Choir; Orchestra of the Royal Opera House, Covent Garden/Sir Georg Solti.** Decca 417 413-2DH2. Notes, text and translation included. From SET596/8 (6/75).

② 2h 23' ADD 8/87

In *Eugene Onegin* the young, sensitive Tatyana falls in love with the blasé dandy Onegin only to be bluntly rejected. Onegin's emotional insensitivity leads to the death of his friend Lensky in a duel, but he realizes his mistake and confronts his true feelings for Tatyana. The seven scenes of *Onegin* do not follow the usual narrative progression of a Mozart or Verdi opera, but rather present a series of situations like cartoon pictures, concentrated and emotionally precise. Tchaikovsky's intense sympathy with Tatyana's unrequited love is evident and in the famous Letter scene he gives her some of his most exquisite music, highlighting every emotional twist and turn she encounters. This recording is well conceived and sounds very good in this transfer.

Tchaikovsky. THE QUEEN OF SPADES. **Wieslaw Ochman** (ten) Hermann; **Stefka Evstatieva** (sop) Lisa; **Penka Dilova** (mez) Countess; **Ivan Konsulov** (bar) Count Tomsky; **Yuri Mazurok** (bar) Prince Yeletsky; **Stefania Toczyska** (mez) Paulina; **Angel Petkov** (ten) Chekalinsky; **Peter Petrov** (bass) Surin; **Mincho Popov** (ten) Chaplitsky, Major-domo; **Stoil Georgiev** (bass) Narumov; **Wesselina Katsarova** (mez) Governess; **Rumyana Bareva** (sop) Masha; **Elena Stoyanova** (sop) Prilepa; **Gouslarche Boys' Choir; Svetoslav Obretenov National Chorus; Sofia Festival Orchestra/Emil Tchakarov.** Sony Classical CD45720. Notes, text and translation included.

③ 2h 39' DDD 12/90

Recordings of what many consider to be Tchaikovsky's greatest opera have been few and far between, and none too satisfactory so that this new and excellent performance is a most welcome addition to the catalogue. It is one of a series of Russian operas issued by Sony and conducted by Tchakarov, who rises magnificently to the challenge of this work's astonishing originality of concept and structure. He is splendidly supported by his Bulgarian forces, his

Bulgarian chorus and orchestra singing and playing with vigour tempered by sensitivity. The set has been carefully cast. Ochman's anguished, intensely subjective, slightly crazed Hermann could hardly be bettered in either interpretation or singing. Evstatieva makes a vibrant, highly strung Lisa, just right. Mazurok's authoritative Yeletsky and Konsulov's properly gruff Tomsky are other assets. Dilova's old Countess may not be as characterful as some but the part is well sung, as are the smaller roles, including Toczyska's Paulina. The recording is full of the right, haunted atmosphere in the private scenes, big scale in the public ones.

Georg Philipp Telemann   *German 1681-1767*

Telemann. ORCHESTRAL WORKS. **Stephen Preston** (fl); **John Turner** (rec); **Clare Shanks** (ob d'amore); **Friedmann Immer, Michael Laird, Iain Wilson** (tpts); **Monica Huggett** (va d'amore); **Academy of Ancient Music/Christopher Hogwood** (hpd). L'Oiseau-Lyre Florilegium 411 949-2OH. From DSDL701 (1/83).
Concerto in D major for three trumpets, strings and continuo. Quadro in B flat major. Concerto in E minor for recorder and flute. Concerto polonois. Concerto in E major for flute, oboe d'amore, viola d'amore, strings and continuo.

   54' DDD 8/84

Telemann's distinctive eclecticism, uniting Italian energy and brilliance with French delicacy of expression, is often irresistibly appealing. Sometimes, too, his music is seasoned with Polish folk rhythms, melodies which had always fascinated the composer. Telemann claimed to have found difficulty in writing concertos but he nevertheless composed well over a hundred of them. This modest selection contains two of his finest works in the form, the Concertos in E major and E minor. The delicately blended textures of the first provide a wonderful example of Telemann's instrumental writing in which the solo parts are clearly outlined in registers that emphasize their individual character. In the second, the partnership of flute and recorder creates an engagingly subtle tonal palette, especially in the slow movements while the finale is a swirling dance in Telemann's best Polish manner. The performances capture the spirit of the music delightfully with Christopher Hogwood providing stylish direction.

Telemann. ORCHESTRAL WORKS. **Cologne Musica Antiqua/Reinhard Goebel.** Archiv Produktion 413 788-2AH.
Suite in C major. Concertos—B flat major; F major; A minor.

   49' DDD 3/85

Telemann's love for the French overture suite is in little doubt, if only because he wrote so many of them. A notably fine example of his skill in this medium exists in the Suite in C major. The programmatic element is a strong one and most of its movements have titles relating to figures from classical myth. Reinhard Goebel and Cologne Musica Antiqua vividly evoke the aquatic fun and games of Aeolus, Thetis, Neptune, Zephyr, Tritons, Naiads and the like in a varied sequence of French dance movements. These are prefaced by a splendid Overture in the French manner. The remainder of the disc is given over to three of Telemann's concertos for pairs of treble recorder and oboes, with bassoon and strings. They are attractive pieces, two of them having not been previously recorded and the crisp woodwind playing makes the most of this graceful, unassuming repertoire. Clear recorded sound and informative presentation.

Telemann. 12 Fantaisies for transverse flute. **Barthold Kuijken** (transverse fl). Accent ACC57803D.

48' DDD 9/85

Telemann's music reached full maturity during the 1730s and in the flute *Fantaisies* we find pieces of sustained concentration, varied invention and easy grace. As so often with this composer the idiom is frequently forward-looking, hinting not only at the incipient 'galant' style but also at the acutely sensitive style (*emfindsamer Stil*) later developed above all in the keyboard music of Telemann's godson and successor at Hamburg, C.P.E. Bach. Barthold Kuijken plays a baroque flute which is strikingly different in sound from a present day instrument. His technique is secure, his articulation clear and communicative, and his phrasing pleasingly shaped. He is able to feel beyond what is written on the printed page and this pays off handsomely in movements such as the *Largo* of the B minor *Fantaisie*. Set in contrast with 'affective' pieces such as these are captivating little dances like the pastoral finale of the *Fantaisie* No. 5. Recorded sound is first-rate.

Telemann. Musique de table—Productions I-III. **Vienna Concentus Musicus/Nikolaus Harnoncourt.** Teldec Das Alte Werk 2292-44688-2.

④ 4h 21' DDD 10/89

Telemann. Musique de table—Productions I-III. **Cologne Musica Antiqua/ Reinhard Goebel.** Archiv Produktion 427 619-2AH4.

④ 4h 14' DDD 10/89

By some curious quirk of fate Archiv Produktion and Teldec have managed not once but twice simultaneously to issue complete recordings of Telemann's three-part orchestral and instrumental anthology *Musique de table*. Notwithstanding what must have seemed commercially bad timing we should be grateful to both companies for instigating performances which, though uneven in places are by and large outstandingly successful. Both Nikolaus Harnoncourt and Reinhard Goebel direct ensembles of period instruments but what each does with them is in striking contrast with the other. In matters of instrumental finesse Goebel's Musica Antiqua Cologne has the edge on the Vienna Concentus Musicus and listeners will hardly fail to recognize disciplined and lively playing of an high order throughout this set. Nevertheless rigorous precision of this kind is sometimes at the cost of spontaneity and lyricism and it is in these respects that Harnoncourt's performances may well strike a more sympathetic chord in the listener.

Nowhere are the two approaches more divergent, perhaps, than in the beautiful G major Quartet of the First Production of the *Musique de table*. There Harnoncourt captures the gently sighing, *galant* gestures of the opening movement with sympathy and insight while Goebel is rhythmically stiff, and self-consciously mannered. But the positions are frequently reversed especially at such times when Harnoncourt's group sounds comparatively rough in ensemble or when occasionally it makes heavy weather over rhythmic patterns. To conclude on a positive note, neither version of Telemann's *magnum opus* is likely to cause disappointment. Ultimately it must be a question of taste and temperament. It may well be some while before such performances as these are equalled let alone bettered. Fine recorded sound and helpful documentation are features of both issues.

Telemann. Ino[a]. Overture-Suite in D major. [a]**Barbara Schlick** (sop); **Cologne Musica Antiqua/Reinhard Goebel.** Archiv Produktion 429 772-2AH. Text and translation included.

54' DDD 4/91

Telemann's dramatic cantata *Ino* (1765) is the product of an Indian summer which the composer enjoyed during the decade 1755-1765. He was, in fact, 84 when he composed *Ino* but we could easily be forgiven for believing it to be the work of a composer half his age. The Enlightenment poet Ramler's text is based on one of Ovid's *Metamorphoses* and concerns Ino, daughter of Cadmus and Hermione. She married Athamos who went mad, murdered one of their sons and attempted murder on the other. Ino, with husband in hot pursuit hurls herself into the sea clutching her child. Neptune comes to her aid, transforms her into the goddess Leukothea and her son into the god Palaemon. Telemann, with music often strikingly up-to-date and wonderfully fresh in spirit brings the tale to life in a manner hardly equalled and never surpassed by any of his earlier dramatic works. Barbara Schlick sounds cool in the face of such adversity as Ovid and Ramler place in her path, but there is an underlying passion in her interpretation and the result is musically satisfying. That is also true of Cologne Musica Antiqua under the informed and enthusiastic direction of Reinhard Goebel. This stylish ensemble comes into its own in a performance of another product of Telemann's Indian summer, the Overture-Suite in D major (1765). A feast for lovers of this composer's music and one which offers delights that no baroque music enthusiast should overlook. Outstanding.

Telemann. Der Tag des Gerichts[a]. Pimpinone oder Die Ungleiche Heyrath[b]. Paris Quartets Nos. 1 and 6[c]. [a]**Gertraud Landwehr-Herrmann** (sop); [a]**Cora Canne-Meijer** (contr); [a]**Kurt Equiluz** (ten); [a]**Max van Egmond** (bass); [a]**Vienna Boys' Choir**, [a]**Hamburg Monteverdi Choir**, [a]**Vienna Concentus Musicus/Nikolaus Harnoncourt**; [b]**Ute Spreckelsen** (sop) Vespetta; [b]**Siegmund Nimsgern** (bass) Pimpinone; [b]**Ensemble Florilegium Musicum/Hans Ludwig Hirsch** with [b]**Herbert Tadiezi** (hpd). [c]**Quadro Amsterdam** (Frans Brüggen, fte; Jaap Schröder, vn; Anner Bylsma, vc; Gustav Leonhardt, hpd). Teldec 2292-42722-2. Text and translations included. From Telefunken Das Alte Werk SAWT9484-5 (3/67).

③ 3h 7' ADD

It says much for Harnoncourt's performing style that this recording of Telemann's last oratorio comes across as freshly and stylishly today as it did on its first appearance in the 1960s. The soloists include Kurt Equiluz and Max van Egmond, and van Egmond's declamation of Devotions aria, "Da kreuzen

Nikolaus Harnoncourt   *[photo: Teldec*

verzebrende Blitze" ("consuming lightnings cross each other") is just one among many thrilling details in this vivid realization of Telemann's music. The remainder of the cast is impressive, too, with outstanding contributions from two soloists of the Vienna Boys' Choir. This is Harnoncourt at his best. Telemann's comic intermezzo, *Pimpinone* was probably first performed between the acts of Handel's *Tamerlano* in Hamburg in 1725. Pimpinone, an elderly bachelor, is looking for a maid. He engages Vespetta who persuades him to marry her, only to play fast and loose with his affections and his cash. This is a stylish performance under the direction of Hans Ludwig Hirsch, with especially fine singing from Nimsgern. Two of Telemann's *Paris* Quartets make a delightful filler.

Michael Tippett

British 1905-

Tippett. ORCHESTRAL WORKS. ^c**Heather Harper** (sop); ^{abc}**London Symphony Orchestra/Sir Colin Davis;** ^d**Chicago Symphony Orchestra/ Sir Georg Solti.** Decca London 425 646-2LM3.
Symphonies—No. 1[a] (from Philips 9500 107, 10/76); No. 2[b] (Argo ZRG535, 1/68); No. 3[c] (Philips 6500 662, 1/75); No. 4[d], Suite in D for the Birthday of Prince Charles[d] (both from Decca SXDL7546, 8/81).

③ 2h 51' ADD/DDD 7/90

These four symphonies comprise one of the most considerable contributions to the genre by a British composer this century. Numbers 1 and 2 are examples of Tippett's earlier, still relatively traditional language, while Nos. 3 and 4 are more radical. Bounding energy is the predominant quality of Nos. 1 and 2, an energy whose individual attributes are by no means diminished by associations with Stravinsky. But Tippett's more personal, magical lyricism is also prominent, especially in the marvellous slow movement of No. 2, and this lyricism forms a clear link to the more reflective passages of No. 3. This glorious, 55-minute work evolves from purely instrumental arguments about active and reflective states of mind into a series of songs (for soprano) that confront some of the most urgent social issues of our time. Though arguing the need to counter violence and repression with tolerance and love, the music offers its own irreconcilable confrontation between allusions to Beethoven's Ninth and Bessie Smith-style blues, swept up into a stark coda as uncompromising in its modernism as anything in Tippett's output. After this the Symphony No. 4 is less hectic, though no less diverse in its materials, a half-hour single movement of dazzling colours and vivid emotions. Although the performances occasionally remind us of the difficulties Tippett presents to his interpreters, and the recordings are not, on the whole, of the latest digital vintage, this is—thanks mainly to the commitment and persuasiveness of Sir Colin Davis—a set of considerable distinction.

Tippett. Concerto for double string orchestra. Fantasia concertante on a Theme of Corelli[a]. Songs for Dov[b]. ^b**Nigel Robson** (ten); ^a**John Tunnell,** ^a**Rosemary Ellison** (vns); ^a**Kevin McCrae** (vc); **Scottish Chamber Orchestra/Sir Michael Tippett.** Virgin Classics VC7 90701-2. Texts included.

71' DDD 6/88

A recording by the composer is always an event and this enterprising disc finds Sir Michael at the helm of a very responsive and finely-recorded Scottish Chamber Orchestra. The Concerto receives a very broad reading, one sensitive to the complexity of texture and dynamic, drawing it very much away from the tradition of the English string serenade. The *Corelli* Fantasia too has a breadth and textural concern. The soloists are good and because of the small forces involved it has a crispness it so importantly needs. The highlight on the disc is undoubtedly the strange but haunting *Songs for Dov* in a quite outstanding interpretation by Nigel Robson who has obviously worked long and hard on them. He integrates the barking and howling into the vocal line so well and really captures the spirit of these songs (do persevere with them, they are difficult at first!). The recording is very good.

Tippett. String Quartets—No. 1 in A major; No. 2 in F major; No. 3. **Lindsay Quartet** (Peter Cropper, Ronald Birks, vns; Roger Bigley, va; Bernard Gregor-Smith, vc). Decca London 425 645-2LM. From L'Oiseau-Lyre DSLO10 (12/75).

71' ADD 2/90

Sir Michael Tippett's first three String Quartets, all relatively early pieces, are a fascinating alembic from which, we can now see, much of his later music was distilled. In particular they are a record of his enormously fruitful and self-questioning dialogue with Beethoven. Many of Tippett's closest musical affinities are with traditions remote from Beethoven (folk-song, the English madrigalists, Tudor church music, blues and spirituals) and in these Quartets we hear him forging a language to which Beethoven and Byrd and Bessie Smith have all contributed. To hear all three in sequence is absorbing, and casts revealing light on the uses to which he subsequently put that language. That Tippett eventually did write a Fourth Quartet (and that a Fifth is promised shortly) we owe to the artists who made this cleanly well-focused recording. Long experience of playing these works has given them the assurance to make light of their formidable technical difficulties, but has not robbed them of their delight in the sheer exuberance of invention they contain. It is infectious: no wonder their playing prompted the composer to take up the medium again.

Tippett. CHORAL WORKS. **Christ Church Cathedral Choir/Stephen Darlington.** Nimbus NI5266. Texts included.
Dance, Clarion Air. The Weeping Babe. Plebs angelica. Bonny at Morn (with Michael Copley, Maurice Hodges, Evelyn Nallen, recs). Crown of the Year (Medici Quartet—Paul Robertson, David Matthews, vns; Ivo-Jan van der Werff, va; Anthony Lewis, vc; Copley, Hodges, Nallen; John Anderson, ob; Colin Lawson, cl; Graham Ashton, tpt; Peter Hamburger, Martin Westlake, Jeremy Cornes, perc; Martin Jones, pf). Music (Jones, pf). A Child of our Time—Five Negro Spirituals.

51' DDD 1/91

Here is choral singing of the very highest order sumptuously recorded in the mellow surrounds of the Abbey at Dorchester-on-Thames. Under Stephen Darlington the men and boys of Christ Church Cathedral Choir sing with precision, immaculate control and great sensitivity. They achieve an almost perfect blend: no voice stands out in isolation, there are no rough edges and the whole effect is of a single, immensely versatile musical instrument. Of course there is a price to be paid: any individuality or character in the voices has had to be subjugated. So it's probably something of a mistake to project singers from the choir as soloists in the four Spirituals from *A Child of our Time*. There are no reservations about anything else on this lovely disc. The principal work, *Crown of the Year*, was written in 1958 for a children's choir supported by very economical instrumental resources, Surprisingly this hasn't been recorded before; yet as this performance demonstrates most vividly, it is a colourful and vibrant work full of joy and vigour and incorporating such familiar tunes as "For he's a jolly good fellow". With the exception of the captivating *Bonny at Morn*, which uses a trio of fluttering recorders as a descant to a beautifully sung unison line, the other pieces on this CD are unaccompanied. The music is Tippett in his most simple and magical vein. Performed and recorded with such excellence the whole thing is a delight to the ear.

Tippett. A Child of Our Time (1939-41). **Jessye Norman** (sop); **Dame Janet Baker** (mez); **Richard Cassilly** (ten); **John Shirley-Quirk** (bar); **BBC Singers; BBC Choral Society; BBC Symphony Orchestra/Sir Colin Davis.** Philips 420 075-2PH. Text included. From 6500 985 (11/75).

64' ADD 11/87 **B**

A Child of Our Time takes as its narrative kernel the shooting in 1938 of a minor German diplomat by a 17-year-old Jew, Herschel Grynspan, and so causing one of the most savage anti-Jewish pogroms seen in Nazi Germany. But the universality of the dilemma of an individual caught up in something he cannot control gives it a much broader relevance. Just as Bach used the Lutheran hymns for the chorale sections within his Passions, so Tippett uses the negro spiritual to tap a similarly universal vein. The soloists provide the narrative thread against the more reflective role of the chorus but they come together forcefully in the spirituals. Sir Colin Davis directs a powerful and atmospheric performance and his soloists are very fine. The 1975 recording sounds well in this remastering.

Tippett. The Mask of Time. **Faye Robinson** (sop); **Sarah Walker** (mez); **Robert Tear** (ten); **John Cheek** (bass); **BBC Singers; BBC Symphony Chorus and Orchestra/Andrew Davis.** EMI CDS7 47705-8. From EX270567-3 (5/87). Recorded at a performance in the Royal Festival Hall, London, in March 1986.

② 92' DDD 10/87

A huge work in two parts, each lasting some 45 minutes, *The Mask of Time* comprises ten 'scenes', the five in Part One more obviously mythological in character and moving from the 'creation' of the cosmos to the emergence of civilization and an earthly paradise, and those in Part Two more to do with the individual in history. The work calls for four soloists, chorus and large symphony orchestra and presents all manner of difficulties in performance and recording with its contrasting of full-blown episodes (with typically thrilling brass and percussion writing) and intimate chamber-like ensembles. There are many unforgettable moments in this deeply felt and thought-provoking score, and none more moving than Tippett's post-Hiroshima threnody for "those who have never had a life". This performance is superb, Andrew Davis demonstrating a fine grasp of the overall structure as well as the fine detail of this complex work. The live recording, too, is first-rate. This is by no means an easy work to assimilate, but those prepared to give it open-minded consideration will find themselves richly rewarded.

Tippett. KING PRIAM. **Norman Bailey** (bar) Priam; **Heather Harper** (sop) Hecuba; **Thomas Allen** (bar) Hector; **Felicity Palmer** (sop) Andromache; **Philip Langridge** (ten) Paris; **Yvonne Minton** (mez) Helen; **Robert Tear** (ten) Achilles; **Stephen Roberts** (bar) Patroclus; **Ann Murray** (mez) Nurse; **David Wilson-Johnson** (bar) Old man; **Peter Hall** (ten) Young guard; **Kenneth Bowen** (ten) Hermes; **Julian Saipe** (treb) Paris, as a boy; **Linda Hirst** (sop) Serving woman; **London Sinfonietta Chorus; London Sinfonietta/David Atherton.** Decca London 414 241-2LH2. Notes and text included. From D246D3 (11/81).

② 2h 8' DDD 1/90

King Priam is the exception among Tippett's five operas in taking its plot from
existing literature. But the text itself is Tippett's own, and the dramatic

Sir Michael Tippett   *[photo: Nimbus/Shenai*

themes—the horrors of war, the torments of families whose destinies and choices create only tragedy—reverberate in various ways in many of his other works, though never again with the stark immediacy and sense of despair embodied here. It is astonishing how so uncompromising an opera can leave the listener more exhilarated than depressed: it must be something to do with witnessing human creativity asserting its power so convincingly. And Tippett's power here extends well beyond the blood and gore of the Trojan War. Even more moving and compelling is the mutual compassion of those who share bereavement, and the tortured hope of the one character (Achilles) who imagines what life might be like "after the war"—though he too will die in battle. No praise can be too high for this performance, in which a fine cast and the matchless London Sinfonietta are galvanized by David Atherton into an account which achieves maximum expressive fidelity while also affirming the opera's great structural strength. The recording does not seek to reproduce a theatrical ambience, but it is totally convincing in its own terms.

Michael Torke

American 1961-

Torke. CHAMBER AND ORCHESTRAL WORKS. **Michael Torke** (pf); [a]**Edmund Niemann, Nurit Tilles** (pf, four hands); [b]**James Pugliese** (xylophone); [c]**Gary Schall** (marimba); **London Sinfonietta**/[d]**Kent Nagano,** [e]**David Miller.** Argo 430 209-2ZH.
The Yellow Pages[e]. Slate[abcd]. Adjustable Wrench[d]. Vanada[d]. Rust[e].

55' DDD 12/90

This début disc provides an excellent opportunity to explore the music of this talented young American composer. Michael Torke's unique blend of minimalist techniques and popular styles (that range from hip-hop to jazz) have created some of the most successful cross-over music in recent years. The upbeat pieces such as *Adjustable Wrench* and *The Yellow Pages* are the most obvious examples of his pop-inspired works; though the subtle influence of composers like Copland and Stravinsky can also be heard in the rhythmic drive and fastidious scorings. *Vanada* and *Slate* reveal greater complexities at work, though with no loss of immediacy or attractiveness. *Rust* (the title alludes to both a pitted texture and the colour) is a concerto for piano, winds and electric bass and displays the energy and rhythmic drive of this young composer at its most compelling; raunchy brass interjections, sleazy saxophone breaks and a funky off-beat electric bass line are led by the seemingly boundless energy of the solo piano. The performances, by members of the London Sinfonietta under the direction of Kent Nagano and David Miller, match the energy and vitality of the music, and one senses a genuine feeling of enjoyment and involvement in their playing. A well balanced recording, with clear and natural sound.

Eduard Tubin

Tubin. Symphony No. 3 (1940-42); Symphony No. 8 (1966). **Swedish Radio Symphony Orchestra/Neeme Järvi.** BIS CD342. Recorded in association with the Estonian Church Foundation, Vancouver.

> 63' DDD 9/88

Tubin's Third Symphony comes from 1940, six months after Stalin had "incorporated" Estonia into the Soviet Union. Not surprisingly, it is strongly nationalist in feeling, reflecting the mood of a nation that had just lost its independence. The first two movements are full of imaginative and individual touches, the listener borne along on a current of movement. The finale is not wholly free from rhetoric and bombast, but all the same it is a strong piece and those who have the Second and Fourth Symphonies will find familiar resonances. The Eighth Symphony, however, is possibly his masterpiece: it is the darkest in colouring and most intense in feeling of all his symphonies. It comes from 1966 and the opening movement has a sense of vision and mystery whose atmosphere stays with you long afterwards. There is an astringency and a sense of the tragic that leaves a strong impression. Järvi's tireless championship of Tubin puts us much in his debt and the playing of the Swedish Radio Symphony Orchestra displays real commitment. The recording has quite exceptional body, clarity and definition.

Tubin. Symphonies—No. 4 (1943)[a], "Sinfonia lirica"; No. 9 (1969)[b]. Toccata (1937)[b]. [a]**Bergen Symphony Orchestra,** [b]**Gothenburg Symphony Orchestra/Neeme Järvi.** BIS CD227. Item marked [a] from LP227 (12/83), [b] LP264 (3/85).

> 64' AAD 10/86

The atmosphere of the Fourth Symphony is predominantly pastoral, a mixture of the Slavonic and the Nordic, with a strongly Sibelian feel to much of it. It is immediately accessible music, with real imaginative vitality and a strong feeling for structure. A quarter of a century separates it from the Ninth Symphony, where the mood is elegiac and the gently restrained melancholy of the slower sections makes a strong emotional impact. The fluid harmonies are quite haunting but as always Tubin's musical language is direct, tonal and, in its way, quite personal. Though there is an overriding sadness and resignation about this music, there is not a trace of self-pity. The exuberant and inventive *Toccata* for orchestra is also an enjoyable piece. The orchestral playing is first-class and the recorded sound splendidly firm and rich.

Joaquin Turína *Refer to Index*

Edgard Varèse

French-American 1883-1965

Varèse. VARIOUS WORKS. [a]**Rachel Yakar** (sop); [b]**Lawrence Beauregard** (fl); [c]**New York Philharmonic Orchestra**; [d]**Ensemble Intercontemporain** /[e]**Pierre Boulez.** Sony Classical CD45844. Texts and translations included.
Ionisation (1929-31)[ce]. Amériques (1921)[ce]. Arcana (1925-7. All from CBS 76520, 6/78)[ce]. Density 21·5 (1936)[b]. Offrandes (1921)[ade]. Octandre (1923)[de]. Intégrales (1924-5. All from IM39053, 3/85)[de].

77' ADD/DDD 10/90

These classic recordings make a welcome return to the catalogue, especially since the music of Varèse has been so poorly represented on disc and in the concert hall in recent years. Quite why so important a figure in twentieth-century music should be neglected like this is hard to say, and even more difficult to comprehend when one samples the quality of the music presented here. Varèse was a pioneer, a quester and above all a liberator. Music for him was a form of twentieth century alchemy— the transmutation of the ordinary into the extraordinary, an alchemical wedding of intellectual thought with intuitive imagination. Indeed, it was the writings of the fourteenth century cosmologist and alchemist Paracelsus that formed the inspiration behind his orchestral work *Arcana*, a vast canvas of sound built entirely out of one melodic motive. Discernible are echoes of Stravinsky and others, but the totality of *Arcana* is pure Varèse. The same is true of *Amériques*, a title that Varèse emphasized was not to be taken as "purely geographical but as symbolic of discoveries—new worlds on earth, in the sky or in the minds of men". Here romanticism and modernism seem to coexist side by side, where allusions from works such as *La mer* and *The Firebird* seem like racial memories carried into his brave new world. The remaining items consist of smaller chamber works which display Varèse's most radical, though equally rewarding, styles. Boulez and his players give committed, virtuosic performances of these challenging and intriguing works. Well worth exploring.

Ralph Vaughan Williams

British 1872-1958

Vaughan Williams. WORKS FOR STRING ORCHESTRA. [a]**Maurice Bourgue** (ob); **English String Orchestra/William Boughton.** Nimbus NI5019.
Fantasia on a Theme by Thomas Tallis (1910). Oboe Concerto in A minor (1944)[a]. Concerto grosso (1950). Fantasia on Greensleeves (1934). Five Variants of "Dives and Lazarus" (1939).

64' DDD 6/85

The Oboe Concerto consists of a *Rondo pastorale* in the composer's most fresh, open-air manner; a very short, high stepping *Minuet and Musette*, and a finale in the form of a scherzo with two trios, the second of which is grave and reflective. It is an immediately enjoyable piece, and Maurice Bourgue gives a good, idiomatic account and is well accompanied by the orchestra. Boughton's account of the *Tallis* Fantasia is good, though it lacks the spirituality and eloquence of the readings of Boult and Marriner. If the *Concerto grosso* is not a major work its five short movements are characteristically warm and vivacious. In the *Dives and Lazarus* Variants a harp adds piquancy to the rich string texture, and the variations are on a tune most will know as *The star of the County Down*. The *Greensleeves* Fantasia is a simple but poignant arrangement of the folk-tune and a second tune called *Lovely Joan*. All these works receive good performances by Boughton and his orchestra and the sound calls for no reservation.

Vaughan Williams. Job—a masque for dancing. **David Nolan** (vn); **London Philharmonic Orchestra/Vernon Handley.** EMI Eminence CD-EMX9506. From EMX412056-1 (8/84).

| 48' DDD 10/87 |

The work of William Blake was close to the heart of Vaughan Williams, and from Blake's *21 Illustrations to the Book of Job*, he produced a ballet score that came to represent a watershed in his career, looking backwards to the pastoral, folk-song idiom of his Third Symphony and forwards to the violence and vigour of the Fourth. *Job* requires an orchestra that is particularly flexible, with full and poignantly-toned soloists and a string body that can produced a rounded, consistent timbre with great depth. The London Philharmonic display all those qualities here, and a good deal more besides, and all is captured in a spacious, characterful acoustic and in a full-bodied recording that can handle equally well the hushed opening of the work and the enormities of Scene 6. This highly persuasive performance proves particularly good value at bargain price.

Vaughan Williams. A London Symphony. Fantasia on a Theme by Thomas Tallis (1910). **London Philharmonic Orchestra/Bernard Haitink.** EMI CDC7 49394-2.

| 66' DDD 7/88 | |

Vaughan Williams. A London Symphony. Concerto Grosso. **London Symphony Orchestra/Bryden Thomson.** Chandos CHAN8629.

| 65' DDD 10/89 |

Bernard Haitink   [photo: EMI/MacDomnic]

A London Symphony presents a vision of the capital far removed from the busy cosmopolitan metropolis it has become today. The London Vaughan Williams knew then was more elegant and less hectic, though alas its Edwardian charm would soon be changed for ever by the First World War. At the beginning of the work slow, Westminster chimes signal the beginning of the day; the main section of the first movement then evokes London's bustle and busyness. In the second *Lento* movement we explore some quieter byways, while the *Scherzo-Nocturne* third movement depicts the city at night. The finale looks at several city scenes and its epilogue portrays the River Thames at day's end. Bernard Haitink obtains excellent playing from the LPO, and he is particularly successful in bringing out the Symphony's contrasts and colour. Some details emerge more clearly than ever before in a very fine recording and there is an impressively powerful quality in Haitink's conducting. His sense of structure and line also bring powerful dividends in the *Tallis* Fantasia.

Whilst the LSO are not quite on best form on the Chandos issue, with some moments of suspect intonation, the clear layout of this performance, so finely aimed at the climax of the final movement and then sustained into the magical Epilogue, carries all before it. The succulent recording admirably reflects

Thomson's delight in the sheer beauty of sound that Vaughan Williams can summon, and it is agreeably wide-ranging for the coupled *Concerto Grosso* of 1950, performed with an equal empathy for its idiom.

Vaughan Williams. A Sea Symphony. **Felicity Lott** (sop); **Jonathan Summers** (bar); **Cantilena; London Philharmonic Choir and Orchestra/ Bernard Haitink.** EMI CDC7 49911-2. Text included.

♩♪ **71' DDD 1/90**

A firm hand on the tiller is needed to steer a safe course through this, Vaughan Williams's first and most formally diffuse symphony, completed in 1909. Haitink is clearly an ideal choice of helmsman and he is helped by a remarkably lucid recording that resolves details that would rarely be revealed in live performance. What might be more unexpected here is the obvious affinity he shows for this music: whilst never transgressing the bounds of Vaughan Williams's characteristically English idiom, he manages to place the work in the European mainstream, revealing a whole range of resonances, from Bruckner and Mahler to the Impressionists. Not all the glory should go to the conductor, of course. Both soloists are particularly fine, the vulnerability behind the spine-tingling power of Felicity Lott's voice providing excellent contrast to the staunch solidity of Jonathan Summers. The LPO Chorus, aided by Cantilena, are on top form and the whole enterprise is underpinned by the London Philharmonic's total commitment and expertise. Here is the recording of this glorious work for which many were waiting.

Vaughan Williams. Sinfonia antartica. **Sheila Armstrong** (sop); **London Philharmonic Choir and Orchestra/Bernard Haitink.** EMI CDC7 47516-2. From EL270318-1 (10/85).

♩♪ **42' DDD 1/87**

Scored for wordless soprano solo and chorus plus a large orchestra, this Seventh Symphony was based on the composer's music for the film *Scott of the Antarctic.* It comprises five movements; the Prelude, which conveys mankind's struggle in overcoming hostile natural forces; a *Scherzo*, which depicts the whales and penguins in their natural habitat; "Landscape", which portrays vast frozen wastes; Intermezzo, a reflection of the actions and thoughts of two members of the party; and "Epilogue", describing the final tragic assault on the South Pole. Bernard Haitink's conducting is highly imaginative, very concentrated and very committed and the LPO respond to him with some wonderfully atmospheric playing, full of personality and colour. Sheila Armstrong's eerie disembodied soprano voice and the remote chorus heighten the atmosphere, so that the score emerges as a powerful, coherent essay in symphonic form. Every detail has been captured by a magnificently sonorous and spacious recording.

Vaughan Williams. A Pastoral Symphony[a]. Symphony No. 4 in F minor[b]. [a]**Heather Harper** (sop); **London Symphony Orchestra/André Previn.** RCA Gold Seal GD90503. Item marked [a] from GL89691 (1/86), [b] GL89692 (1/86).

♩♪ **73' ADD 11/86**

Previn's view of these symphonies is very sharp and clear with the LSO giving incisive, vital performances. It was an interesting idea to couple *A Pastoral Symphony*, where the composer is at his most inward and poetic, with the abrasive, angry Fourth Symphony. Previn's way with the *Pastoral* detracts in no way from the work's stature and his is a most persuasive performance. In the Fourth Symphony he does not tear into the work as some (including the composer) have done; he has an eye for its structure. The energy is very much there, with buoyant rhythms and sharp accents, but it is more controlled. The transfers are most successful and only a very slight lack of fullness in the sound indicates that the recordings are at least 15 years old.

Vaughan Williams. Symphony No. 5 in D major. Flos campi—suite[a]. [a]**Christopher Balmer** (va); [a]**Liverpool Philharmonic Choir; Royal Liverpool Philharmonic Orchestra/Vernon Handley.** EMI Eminence CD-EMX9512. From EMX2112 (8/87).

• 62' DDD 3/88 £ Ⓑ

At mid-price, this is a bargain disc artistically and economically. The recording is full-toned and carefully balanced, preserving the luminous qualities of two of Vaughan Williams's most visionary and subtly devised scores; and the RLPO's playing under Vernon Handley is totally in sympathy with the music. The performance of *Flos campi* is outstandingly good. This work is deeply influenced by Ravel and has marvellous use of a wordless choir to intensify the erotic and sensuous longing of the music inspired by the *Song of Solomon*. The viola's impassioned and lyrical outpouring is beautifully played by Christopher Balmer, with excellent woodwind soloists in support, and the Liverpool Philharmonic Choir sings with secure intonation and flexible dynamic range. Handley's interpretation of the Fifth Symphony emphasizes the strength and passion in this music. His control of the architectural splendour of the first movement is masterly and he allows the ecstasy of the slow movement to unfold most naturally.

Vaughan Williams. Symphony No. 6 in E minor. Fantasia on a Theme by Thomas Tallis. The Lark Ascending[a]. [a]**Tasmin Little** (vn); **BBC Symphony Orchestra/Andrew Davis.** Teldec British Line 9031-73127-2.

• 62' DDD 8/91

Andrew Davis has clearly thought long and hard before committing this enigmatic and tragic symphony to disc, and the result is one of the most spontaneous and electrifying accounts of the Sixth Symphony available. The urgency and vigour of the first and third movements is astonishing, leaving one with the impression that the work might have been recorded in one take. His

treatment of the second subject's reprise in the closing pages of the first movement is more underplayed and remote than the beautifully sheened approach of some recordings, but is arguably more nostalgic for being so. The feverish, nightmare world of the *Scherzo* is a real *tour de force* in the hands of an inspired BBC Symphony Orchestra, and the desolate wasteland of the eerie final movement has rarely achieved such quiescence and nadir as here. Davis's *Tallis Fantasia* has the same searching intensity as Barbirolli's famous 1962 recording for EMI, and is finely poised with a beautifully spacious acoustic. The disc concludes on a quietly elevated note with Tasmin

Little's serene and gently introspective reading of *The Lark Ascending*. Recording is excellent.

Vaughan Williams. String Quartets—No. 1 in G minor; No. 2 in A minor. Phantasy Quintet[a]. **English Quartet** (Diana Cummings, Colin Callow, vns; Luciano Iorio, va; Geoffrey Thomas, vc) with [a]**Norbert Blume** (va). Unicorn-Kanchana DKPCD9076.

61' DDD 9/89

See the word 'Phantasy' or its like in the title of some British chamber work of the early years of this century, and you would rarely lose money betting that it was produced for the wealthy patron, Walter W. Cobbett, who was fascinated by the Elizabethan form. He commissioned Vaughan Williams's Quintet through the Worshipful Company of Musicians in 1912, and received a short piece in four sections, played without break. The scoring is highly effective and the players here lose no opportunity to bring out the music's richly evocative atmosphere, perceptively varying tone-colour and vibrato to add an extra dimension to the notes of the score. They capture the contrasting moods of the First and Second String Quartets, of 1908 and 1944 respectively, with a very keen awareness of the different backgrounds to these pieces. Quartet No. 1, with its overtones of Ravel (with whom Vaughan Williams had been studying), is the most lighthearted of these three works, whilst No. 2 has a flavour of wartime darkness, emphasized by the dominance of the viola—it was dedicated to the violist of the Menges Quartet, Jean Stewart. These front-ranking performances are set in a pleasing, resonant acoustic that lends a genial ease to the proceedings.

Vaughan Williams. VOCAL WORKS. [a]**Elizabeth Connell**, [a]**Linda Kitchen**, [a]**Anne Dawson**, [a]**Amanda Roocroft** (sops); [a]**Sarah Walker**, [a]**Jean Rigby**, [a]**Diana Montague** (mezs); [a]**Catherine Wyn-Rogers** (contr); [a]**John Mark Ainsley**, [a]**Martyn Hill**, [a]**Arthur Davies**, [a]**Maldwyn Davies** (tens); [acd]**Thomas Allen**, [a]**Alan Opie** (bars); [a]**Gwynne Howell**, [a]**John Connell** (basses); [b]**Nobuko Imai** (va); [bcd]**Corydon Singers; English Chamber Orchestra/Matthew Best.** Hyperion CDA66420. Texts included. Serenade to Music[a]. Flos campi[b]. Five mystical songs[c]. Fantasia on Christmas carols[d].

68' DDD 9/90

In 1938 Sir Henry Wood celebrated his 50 years as a professional conductor with a concert. Vaughan Williams composed a work for the occasion, the *Serenade to Music*, in which he set words by Shakespeare from Act 5 of *The Merchant of Venice*. Sixteen star vocalists of the age were gathered together for the performance and Vaughan Williams customized the vocal parts to show off the best qualities of the singers. The work turned out to be one of the composer's most sybaritic creations, turning each of its subsequent performances into a special event. Hyperion have gathered stars of our own age for this outstanding issue and Matthew Best has perceptively managed to give each their head whilst melding them into a cohesive ensemble. A mellow, spacious recording from Mark Brown and Antony Howell has allowed the work to emerge on disc with a veracity not achieved before. The coupled vocal pieces are given to equal effect and the disc is substantially completed by Nobuko Imai's tautly poignant account of *Flos campi*, in which the disturbing tension between viola solo and wordless chorus heighten the work's crypticism. Altogether, an imaginative issue that is a must for any collection.

Giuseppe Verdi

Italian 1813-1901

Verdi. OVERTURES AND PRELUDES. **Berlin Philharmonic Orchestra/ Herbert von Karajan.** DG 419 622-2GH. From 413 544-1GX2 (2/86). NABUCCO; ERNANI; I MASNADIERI; MACBETH; IL CORSARO; LA BATTAGLIA DI LEGNANO; LUISA MILLER; RIGOLETTO; LA TRAVIATA; I VESPRI SICILIANI; UN BALLO IN MASCHERA; LA FORZA DEL DESTINO; AIDA.

♪ 73' ADD 10/87

Karajan was one of the most adaptable and sensitive of dramatic conductors and in this sensible selection from his celebrated 1976 collection of all of Verdi's overtures, he gives us some fine insights into the composer's skill as an orchestrator, dramatist and poet. Even the lesser known Preludes are enhanced by Karajan's dramatic instincts. Good recordings.

Verdi. Messa da Requiem[a]. OPERA CHORUSES. [a]**Susan Dunn** (sop); [a]**Diane Curry** (mez); [a]**Jerry Hadley** (ten); [a]**Paul Plishka** (bass); **Atlanta Symphony Chorus and Orchestra/Robert Shaw.** Telarc CD80152. Texts and translations included.
Opera choruses: DON CARLOS—Spuntato ecco il dì. MACBETH—Patria oppressa. OTELLO—Fuoco di gioia. NABUCCO— Va pensiero, sull'ali dorate. AIDA—Gloria all'Egitto.

♪ ② 1h 53' DDD 3/88 **B**

Verdi. Messa da Requiem[a]. Quattro pezzi sacri[b]. [a]**Maria Stader** (sop); [a]**Oralia Dominguez** (mez); [a]**Gabor Carelli** (ten); [a]**Iván Sardi** (bass); [b]**Berlin RIAS Chamber Choir; St Hedwig's Cathedral Choir, Berlin; Berlin Radio Symphony Orchestra/Ferenc Fricsay.** DG Dokumente mono 429 076-2GDO2. Texts and translations included. Item marked [a] recorded at a performance in Berlin on October 23rd, 1960, [b] January 14th, 1952.

♪ ② 2h 12' ADD 11/89 **B**

Of all nineteenth-century choral works, Verdi's setting of the Requiem Mass seems to be the most approachable. The choral writing is of the utmost splendour and conviction, that for the soloists is a very personal statement of belief although written by an unbeliever. In many sections soloists and chorus are intermingled in a masterly fashion, and the writing for the orchestra is always appropriate to the text. Robert Shaw directs a performance that avoids histrionics and display and impresses by sheer musicianship. Tempos are well judged and for once rarely depart from the composer's markings. The team of soloists are well blended. The chorus are well drilled and full bodied and contribute lustily to the operatic choruses included as a bonus. The recording is very fine, spacious yet clear.

In his performance, recorded live like Toscanini's, Ferenc Fricsay came very close to equalling the former's achievement in a performance that matches lyrical intensity with tragic force (the conductor *must* have been influenced by the fact that he knew he hadn't long to live). The discipline

Robert Shaw *[photo: Telarc/Carter*

here on all sides also matches Toscanini's and the choral singing, better recorded, is marginally superior. Fricsay's account of the *Four Sacred Pieces* is more than a filler: it's an arresting and moving interpretation of Verdi's last work for chorus.

Verdi. OPERA CHORUSES. **Chicago Symphony Chorus and Orchestra/ Sir Georg Solti.** Decca 430 226-2DH. Texts and translations included. NABUCCO—Gli arredi festivi giù cadano infranti; Va, pensiero, sull'ali dorate. I LOMBARDI—Gerusalem!; O Signore, dal tetto natio. MACBETH—Tre volte miagola; Patria oppressa. I MASNADIERI—Le rube, gli stupri. RIGOLETTO—Zitti zitti. IL TROVATORE—Vedi! le fosche notturne spoglie; Squilli, echeggi la tromba guerriera. LA TRAVIATA—Noi siamo zingarelle … Di Madride nio siam mattadori (with Marsha Waxman, mez; David Huneryager, Richard Cohn, basses). UN BALLO IN MASCHERA—Posa in pace. DON CARLOS—Spuntato ecco il di d'esultanza. AIDA—Gloria all'Egitto. OTELLO—Fuoco di gioia. REQUIEM—Sanctus.

70' DDD 4/91

Verdi. OPERA CHORUSES. **Slovak Philharmonic Choir; Slovak Radio Symphony Orchestra/Oliver Dohnányi.** Naxos 8 550241. NABUCCO—Gli arredi festivi giù cadano infranti; Va, pensiero, sull'ali dorate. MACBETH—Patria oppressa. IL TROVATORE—Vedi! le fosche notturne spoglie; Ora co'dadi, ma fra poco. LA TRAVIATA—Noi siamo zingarelle; Si ridesta in ciel (with Alena Cokova, mez; Stanislav Vrabel, bass). DON CARLOS—Spuntato ecco il dì d'esultanza. AIDA—Gloria all'Egitto. OTELLO— Fuoco di gioia. LA BATTAGLIA DI LEGNANO— Deus meus, pone illos ut rotam (Eva Jenisova, sop; Cokova); Giuramento (L'udovit Ludha, ten). ERNANI—Si rideste il Leon di Castiglia. LA FORZA DEL DESTINO—Rataplan! rataplan! (Ida Kirilová, mez).

56' DDD 4/91

Verdi's choruses occupy a special place in his operas. They are invariably red-blooded and usually make a simple dramatic statement with great impact. Such is their immediacy and communicative force that they have sometimes produced an influence on listeners, over and above that pertinent to the plot, especially where the audience has already been primed with patriotic nationalistic feeling by local events outside the theatre. The arresting "Chorus of the Hebrew Slaves" ("Va pensiero") from *Nabucco* is a prime example. Probably the best-known and most popular chorus in the entire operatic repertoire, it immediately tugs at the heart-strings with its gentle opening cantilena, soon swelling out to a great climax. Solti, in his splendidly vibrant Decca collection, with the Chicago Symphony Chorus, shows just how to shape the noble melodic line which soars with firm control, yet retaining the urgency and electricity in every bar. He is equally good in "Gli arredi festivi", from the same opera, not only in the bold opening statement, shared between singers and the resplendent sonority of the Chicago brass, but also later when the mood lightens, and women's voices are heard floating over seductive harp roulades. The dramatic contrasts at the opening of "Gerusalem!" from *I Lombardi* are equally powerfully projected, and the brass again makes a riveting effect in "Patria oppressa" from *Macbeth*. But, of course, not all Verdi choruses offer blood and thunder: the volatile "Fire chorus" from *Otello* flickers with an almost visual fantasy, while the wicked robbers in *I Masnadieri* celebrate their excesses (plunder, rape, arson and murder) gleefully, and with such rhythmic jauntiness that one cannot quite take them seriously. The "Gypsies chorus" from *La Traviata* has a nice touch of elegance, and the scherzo-like "Sanctus", from the *Requiem*, which ends the concert, is full of joy. But it is the impact of the dramatic moments which is most memorable, not least the big triumphal scene from *Aida*, complete with the ballet music, to provide a diverse interlude in the middle. Throughout we have demonstration-worthy sound from the Decca engineers in the suitably resonant acoustic of Chicago's Orchestra Hall, and the back-up documentation includes full translations.

It might be thought that after such a degree of spectacle the alternative super-bargain collection by the Slovak forces under Oliver Dohnányi might sound a little flat. Not so! Even though this is such a modestly priced CD, costing about a third as much as the Decca disc, the digital sound is first class and the singing of the Slovak chorus has plenty of Verdian fervour. The singers are placed rather more backwardly in the overall Naxos sound picture, but the effect is in some ways more natural, with no lack of vocal splendour. Indeed in the "Grand March" scene from *Aida* (which omits the ballet sequence) the direct impact is most telling, with the fanfare trumpets blazing out on either side of the chorus with great presence. Dohnányi, too, finds a light touch to pick up the fantasy of the "Fire Chorus", while the Slovak brass are splendid in "Patria oppressa". This collection is shorter than Solti's, but it includes some attractive items not in the Decca programme from *Ernani*, *La Forza del destino*, and two vintage choruses from *La battaglia de Legnano*. The documentation is good, but omits translations, but this seems reasonable for a disc that costs so little.

Verdi. ATTILA. **Samuel Ramey** (bass) Attila; **Cheryl Studer** (sop) Odabella; **Giorgio Zancanaro** (bar) Ezio; **Neil Shicoff** (ten) Foresto; **Ernesto Gavazzi** (ten) Uldino; **Giorgio Surian** (bass) Leone; **Chorus and Orchestra of La Scala, Milan/Riccardo Muti.** EMI CDS7 49952-2. Notes, text and translation included.

② 1h 49' DDD 5/90

This is one of the most successful of the collaborations between Muti and the La Scala forces. The raw vigour of Verdi's early triumph is splendidly captured by Muti's fiery yet sensitive direction, with his forces fired to great things. Tenor excepted, this cast couldn't be bettered anywhere today. Samuel Ramey is an incisive, dark-hued Attila, singing with accuracy and confidence. His main adversary is the indomitable Odabella, here taken with spirit, vital attack and well-fashioned phrasing by Cheryl Studer, who might now give us the Norma for which we have all been waiting. Giorgio Zancanaro can be rough as Ezio but he is dramatically well in the picture, and Neil Shicoff is never less than honourable in tone and line. The recording, though not ideal in every respect, gives the voices their rightful prominence.

Verdi. I DUE FOSCARI. **Piero Cappuccilli** (bar) Francesco Foscari; **José Carreras** (ten) Jacopo Foscari; **Katia Ricciarelli** (sop) Lucrezia; **Samuel Ramey** (bass) Jacopo Loredano; **Vincenzo Bello** (ten) Barbarigo; **Elizabeth Connell** (sop) Pisana; **Mieczyslaw Antoniak** (ten) Officer; **Franz Handlos** (bass) Doge's servant; **Austrian Radio Chorus and Symphony Orchestra/ Lamberto Gardelli.** Philips 422 426-2PM2. Notes, text and translation included. From 6700 105 (4/78).

② 1h 44' ADD 12/89

This is one of the most impressive of Verdi's early scores, a dark, dour drama of a dynastic and family drama played out on a historic plane. The performance is worthy of the piece. Gardelli has always been a loving exponent of Verdi's 'galley-years' opera and here his conducting brings out the colour and character of the piece unfussily yet with innate eloquence. Tempos, dynamics and rhythmic emphasis are all ideally adumbrated; so is the depth of feeling in the score. He is blessed with a near-ideal cast, all three principals being at the peak of their achievement in 1978 when the set was made. Cappuccilli is absolutely in his element as the gloomy old Doge and father, a portrait to set alongside his superb Boccanegra. His breath control and line in his first aria, "O vecchio cor", is a classic of Verdian singing. Carreras, as the condemned Jacopo, sings with the right feeling of sincerity and desperation in his Prison scene. Ricciarelli offers the role of Lucrezia with lustrous tone and unflinching attack, one of her best performances on disc. She and Cappuccilli make the most of their wonderful duet in the last act. The recording is true and well balanced.

Verdi. LA FORZA DEL DESTINO. **Maria Callas** (sop) Leonora; **Richard Tucker** (ten) Don Alvaro; **Carlo Tagliabue** (bar) Don Carlos; **Elena Nicolai** (mez) Preziosilla; **Nicola Rossi-Lemeni** (bass) Il Padre Guardiano; **Renato Capecchi** (bass) Fra Melitone; **Gino del Signore** (ten) Trabuco; **Rina Cavallari** (sop) Curra; **Chorus and Orchestra of La Scala, Milan/Tullio Serafin**. EMI mono CDS7 47581-8. Notes, text and translation included. From Columbia 33CX1258/60 (6/55).

③ 2h 44' ADD 10/87

Maria Callas is more than unusually well-suited to this Verdi heroine. Leonora's ardour, sincerity and, above all, vulnerability are recreated as she threads sadness through a line like "troppo, troppo sventurata", as she exalts in "Tua grazia, O Dio", or gives a heart-rending cry for peace in "Pace, pace". No one, though, should be deceived into thinking that this recording is a mere showcase for Callas, for Richard Tucker's Alvaro is a performance of what one can only call charisma: light and youthful, there is a smile and a sob in the voice as appropriate—and it works. Renato Capecchi offers a sharp vignette of Fra Melitone, Elena Nicolai a thrilling Preziosilla, and Tullio Serafin directs his La Scala forces with a keen ear to both the overt heartbeat and the emotional subtext of Verdi's most potent score.

Verdi. FALSTAFF. **Tito Gobbi** (bar) Falstaff; **Rolando Panerai** (bar) Ford; **Luigi Alva** (ten) Fenton; **Elisabeth Schwarzkopf** (sop) Alice Ford; **Anna Moffo** (sop) Nannetta; **Fedora Barbieri** (mez) Quickly; **Renato Ercolani** (ten) Bardolfo; **Nicola Zaccaria** (bass) Pistola; **Tomaso Spatoro** (ten) Dr Caius; **Nan Merriman** (mez) Meg Page; **Philharmonia Chorus and Orchestra/Herbert von Karajan**. EMI CDS7 49668-2. Notes, text and translation included. From SAX2254/6 (7/61).

② 2h ADD 9/88 **B**

Verdi's *Falstaff* is one of those works that sum up a career with perfection, yet though it was his last opera it was also his first comic opera. This classic

recording enshrines one of the finest Falstaffs to have graced the stage in post-war years, Tito Gobbi. His assumption of the role is magnificent, and the completeness with which he embraces the part tends to overshadow his many successors. Assembled around this larger-than-life character is a near ideal cast, sprightly of gait, sparklingly comic and above all, beautifully sung. Karajan's conducting is always deeply cherishable as he leads the Philharmonia Orchestra surefootedly through the score and the recording has come up sounding as fresh as the day it was set down.

Tito Gobbi [*painting: Leonard Boden*

Verdi. FALSTAFF. **Giuseppe Valdengo** (bar) Falstaff; **Frank Guarrera** (bar) Ford; **Herva Nelli** (sop) Alice; **Teresa Stich-Randall** (sop) Nannetta; **Antonio Madasi** (ten) Fenton; **Cloe Elmo** (contr) Mistress Quickly; **Nan Merriman** (mez) Meg Page; **Gabor Carelli** (ten) Doctor Caius; **John Carmen Rossi** (ten) Bardolph; **Norman Scott** (bass) Pistol; **Robert Shaw Chorale; NBC Symphony Orchestra / Arturo Toscanini.** Notes, text and translation included. Recorded at NBC broadcasts on April 1st and 8th, 1950. From HMV ALP1229/31 (3/55).

AIDA. **Herva Nelli** (sop) Aida; **Eva Gustavson** (mez) Amneris; **Richard Tucker** (ten) Radames; **Giuseppe Valdengo** (bar) Amonasro; **Norman Scott** (bass) Ramfis; **Dennis Harbour** (bass) King; **Virginio Assandri** (ten) Messenger; **Teresa Stich-Randall** (sop) Priestess; **Robert Shaw Chorale; NBC Symphony Orchestra / Arturo Toscanini.** Notes, text and translation included. Recorded at NBC broadcasts on March 26th and April 2nd, 1949. From RB16021/3 (6/57).

CHORAL WORKS AND OPERA EXCERPTS. **NBC Symphony Orchestra / Arturo Toscanini.** RCA Gold Seal mono GD60326. Texts and translations included.

Quattro pezzi sacri—Te Deum (with Robert Shaw Chorale. Recorded at an NBC broadcast on March 14th 1954. From HMV ALP1363, 6/56). Requiem (Herva Nelli, sop; Fedora Barbieri, mez; Giuseppe di Stefano, ten; Cesare Siepi, bass; Robert Shaw Chorale. NBC Broadcast, January 27th, 1951. ALP1380/81, 12/56). NABUCCO—Va, pensiero (Westminster Choir. NBC broadcast, January 31st, 1943). LUISA MILLER—Quando le sere al placido (Jan Peerce, ten. NBC broadcast, July 25th, 1943. Both ALP1452, 4/57). Inno delle Nazioni (Peerce; Westminster Choir. NBC broadcasts, December 8th and 20th, 1943. ALP1453, 4/57).

⑦ 6h 13' ADD 5/90

At last one of the most enjoyable of all opera recordings is once again available. Nobody knew better than Toscanini how to bring *Falstaff* to life, how to extract from it all the fun and sentiment it contains. Toscanini loved Verdi's great comic masterpiece and he strained every sinew, in matters of tempos, alert detail in the orchestra, control of dynamics, to fulfil his dedicated mission of interpretation. Yet everything seems natural, inevitable, unforced and spontaneous—and the fact that this was a live performance only adds to its feeling of a unique occasion. With this feast laid before it, the audience remained remarkably quiet throughout. The manner in which Toscanini accommodates his singers puts to flight forever his reputation as a martinet, allowing no leeway for personal readings on the part of the singers. The main vocal glory of the set is Giuseppe Valdengo's wonderful reading of the title role, full of subtle inflections, beautifully sung, ripe in characterization, fruit of long hours of preparation with the maestro. Herva Nelli is a delightful Alice Ford, Cloe Elmo a fruity Mistress Quickly, Stich-Randall an ethereal Nannetta, Frank Guarrera an imposing Ford. The remainder of the cast is almost up to this level of achievement. The transfer to CD has been well managed. This is a must for any Verdi lover.

With the *Aida* some caveats have to be entered. In spite of the conductor's contribution, this set suffers both from an indifferent cast and a less successful recording and, in this case, the transfer to digital sound seems to have added an unwanted edge to voices and instruments. Even so, here is further evidence of Toscanini's complete understanding of a composer with whom he had worked and whom he understood better than any of his successors. Although those who must have the Requiem in a modern stereo recording will want to own the Telarc recording, those who are prepared to tolerate mono will have their efforts rewarded by Toscanini's superb interpretation. His has been the classic version by which all its successors have been judged. In its newly-mastered CD version it sounds even more electrifying than in the past.

By turns incandescent and beseeching, the interpretation is never self-indulgent, almost at all times faithful to Verdi's ideas about tempo and dynamics, adding up to a spiritual and emotional experience seldom repeated. Also on offer is a selection of choral pieces of which the patriotic *Hymn to the Nations* is an idiosyncratic rarity, ecstatically performed. There is insufficient space to dwell further on the sheer pleasures to be found in these sets. They are representative of the very best in Verdi conducting, and should be a source of revelation to a new generation of collectors who may have an unclear view of what Toscanini was about.

Verdi. MACBETH. **Sherrill Milnes** (bar) Macbeth; **Fiorenza Cossotto** (mez) Lady Macbeth; **Ruggero Raimondi** (bass) Banquo; **José Carreras** (ten) Macduff; **Giuliano Bernardi** (ten) Malcolm; **Carlo del Bosco** (bass) Doctor; **Leslie Fyson** (bar) Servant; **Neilson Taylor** (bar) Herald; **John Noble** (bass) Assassin; **Ambrosian Opera Chorus; New Philharmonia Orchestra/ Riccardo Muti.** EMI CDS7 47954-8. Notes, text and translation included. From SLS992 (12/76).

③ 2h 41' ADD 5/89

With its jovial assassins and witches Verdi's *Macbeth* used to be something of a joke. That time is long past, and now the score is duly revered for its psychological penetration as well as the powerful surge of its melodies. Of the principal contenders on CD, this version under Muti is the most satisfying. Muti maintains the tension most effectively and has a striking superiority in many passages where the rhythmic element is of special importance. He also benefits from the excellence of the Ambrosian chorus both in the cleanness of their singing and their expertise in creating the illusion of a visual, acted performance. To their respective roles Carreras brings intensity and Raimondi a massive sonority. But the decisive factor is the strength of Milnes as Macbeth and Cossotto as his Lady. Cossotto has ample range and apparently unlimited power to meet the purely vocal demands brilliantly; she also has an apt ruthlessness in her tone, as well as the variety of coloration to express the changes of mood in the Sleepwalking scene. For the complex, troubled character of Macbeth, Milnes presents a finely judged balance of hardness and sympathy: a performance worthy of Shakespeare as well as Verdi.

Verdi. LA TRAVIATA. **Maria Callas** (sop) Violetta Valéry; **Alfredo Kraus** (ten) Alfredo Germont; **Mario Sereni** (bar) Giorgio Germont; **Laura Zanini** (mez) Flora Bervoix; **Maria Cristina de Castro** (sop) Annina; **Piero De Palma** (ten) Gaston; **Alvero Malta** (bar) Baron Douphol; **Alessandro Maddalena** (bass) Doctor Grenvil; **Vito Susca** (bass) Marquis D'Obigny; **Manuel Leitao** (ten) Messenger; **Chorus and Orchestra of the Teatro Nacional de San Carlos, Lisbon/Franco Ghione.** EMI mono CDS7 49187-8. Notes, text and translation included. Recorded at a performance in the Teatro Nacional de San Carlos, Lisbon on March 27th, 1958. From RLS757 (10/80).

② 2h 3' ADD 11/87 **P** Ⓑ

Verdi. LA TRAVIATA. **Renata Scotto** (sop) Violetta Valéry; **Alfredo Kraus** (ten) Alfredo Germont; **Renato Bruson** (bar) Giorgio Germont; **Sarah Walker** (mez) Flora Bervoix; **Cynthia Buchan** (mez) Annina; **Suso Mariategui** (ten) Gaston; **Henry Newman** (bar) Baron Douphol; **Richard Van Allan** (bass) Marquis d'Obigny; **Roderick Kennedy** (bass) Doctor Grenvil; **Max-René Cosotti** (ten) Giuseppe; **Christopher Keyte** (bass)

Messenger; **Ambrosian Opera Chorus; Band of HM Royal Marines; Philharmonia Orchestra/Riccardo Muti.** EMI CDS7 47538-8. Notes, text and translation included. From SLS5240 (5/82).

(2) 2h 9' DDD 11/87   B

Verdi. LA TRAVIATA (sung in English). **Valerie Masterson** (sop) Violetta; **John Brecknock** (ten) Alfredo; **Christian du Plessis** (bar) Germont; **Della Jones** (mez) Flora; **Shelagh Squires** (mez) Annina; **Geoffrey Pogson** (ten) Gaston; **John Gibbs** (bar) Baron; **Denis Dowling** (bar) Marquis; **Roderick Earle** (bass) Doctor; **Edward Byles** (ten) Giuseppe; **John Kitchiner** (bar) Messenger; **English National Opera Chorus and Orchestra/Sir Charles Mackerras.** EMI CMS7 63072-2. Notes and text included. From SLS5216 (10/81).

(2) 1h 58' ADD 10/89   P B

Most sopranos in the part of Violetta (forced to give up her true love for the sake of convention) make you cry in the last act; Callas also made you cry in the second. A fullness of heart and voice informs everything she does in the long colloquy with the elder Germont. The sorrow and emptiness that enters her tone when she realizes she will have to give up her beloved Alfredo is overwhelmingly eloquent. Then the final scene is almost unbearable in its poignancy of expression: the reading of the letter so natural in its suggestion of emptiness. However, the sense of sheer hollowness at "Ma se tornando ..." proves the most moving moment of all as Violetta knows nothing can save her life. All that and so much else suggests that Callas more than anyone understood what the role is about.

To add to one's pleasure the young Kraus is as appealing as any tenor on disc as Alfredo. His Schipa-like tone, his refinement of phrase, especially in his duets with Callas, and his elegant yet ardent manner are exactly right for the part. Mario Sereni may not be in his colleagues' class, but his elder Germont is securely, sincerely and often perceptively sung. Franco Ghione is a prompt and alert conductor and the mono recording has plenty of theatrical presence.

Renata Scotto, also, was always an affecting Violetta on stage and her portrayal on Muti's disc displays utmost understanding for its deep emotions. She is aptly partnered by Renato Bruson and Alfredo Kraus, who once again shows

an innate feeling for Verdian line and phraseology and blends his voice cleanly with Scotto's. Riccardo Muti gives us the score complete (the Callas recording is cut) and ensures faithfulness to Verdi's tempos and dynamic markings. The recording, too, has great theatrical feeling. "ENO at its very best" was the verdict when their recording first appeared in 1981. This *Traviata* provided eloquent testimony to the standards of their more workaday occasions, with a popular opera at the very heart of the Italian repertoire and a representative cast, the strength of which lay not simply in the three main roles but in having such excellent artists as Della Jones and the veteran Denis Dowling in secondary parts. Mackerras, a former Musical Director of the company and always closely associated with it, brings to the performance his customary care for detail and feeling for overall cohesion, and both orchestra and chorus are admirably responsive. Views on opera in translation will always vary, and such encouragement from the chorus as "That's how to take it! Splendid!" may suggest the ethos of Lords rather than that of the Palais-Royal; still, the advantages of immediate intelligibility are undeniable and the enunciation is remarkably clear. Similarly, the English style of singing has the merits of clean, well-placed tone and scrupulous attention to the score, even if some of the richness and emotional fervour of Italian tradition is lacking. Valerie Masterson's assured technique is matched by the vividness of her characterization; she gives a touching and accomplished performance.

Verdi. OTELLO. **Jon Vickers** (ten) Otello; **Leonie Rysanek** (sop) Desdemona; **Tito Gobbi** (bar) Iago; **Florindo Andreolli** (ten) Cassio; **Mario Carlin** (ten) Roderigo; **Miriam Pirazzini** (mez) Emilia; **Ferrucio Mazzoli** (bass) Lodovico; **Franco Calabrese** (bass) Montano; **Robert Kerns** (bar) Herald; **Rome Opera Chorus and Orchestra/Tullio Serafin.** RCA Victor GD81969. Text and translation included. From LDS6155 (1/61).

② 2h 24' ADD 11/88 £ Ⓑ

The role of Otello is notoriously demanding and there are few voices that one would say were 'made for it'. Jon Vickers's is certainly one of them. Simply as singing it is a magnificent performance: the voice is at its most beautiful and the breadth of his tone in the upper notes is astonishing. Stylistically, too, he is quite remarkably scrupulous, allowing himself no effect that is not authorized in the score, and always exact in his observations of *piano* markings. Giving this recording a unique distinction is Tito Gobbi as Iago, justly the most famous singer of the role in post-war years and the Desdemona too is clearly a great artist. Serafin conducts in a way that allows everything to be clearly heard, forfeiting some excitement but never cheapening by exaggeration or sentimentality. He secures clean, spirited playing from the Rome orchestra and keeps a control that is firm without being inflexible. This is a well-produced set that has scarcely aged over the years.

Verdi. IL TROVATORE. **Maria Callas** (sop) Leonora; **Giuseppe di Stefano** (ten) Manrico; **Rolando Panerai** (bar) Count di Luna; **Fedora Barbieri** (mez) Azucena; **Nicola Zaccaria** (bass) Ferrando; **Luisa Villa** (mez) Ines; **Renato Ercolani** (ten) Ruiz, Messenger; **Giulio Mauri** (bass) Old Gipsy; **Chorus and Orchestra of La Scala, Milan/Herbert von Karajan.** EMI mono CDS7 49347-2. Notes, text and translation included. From Columbia 33CXS1483, 33CX1484/5 (11/57).

② 2h 9' ADD 12/87 Ⓑ

Written in between *Rigoletto* and *La traviata, Il trovatore* has its own distinct identity. Pictorially, the nightscape of its action is penetrated by the watchman's torch, the gipsy's campfire and the cruel flame of the witch's stake. Dramatically, the passions of the present flare up among the shadows of a death-ridden past. Musically, the melodies surge to the background of an uneasy chromaticism, with taut rhythms and a predominantly minor tonality. A great performance can be exhilarating, but an indifferent one will often appear depressingly shabby. This recording finds Callas in fine voice and liable at any moment to bring a special thrill of conviction and individuality. As so often when one returns to reissues of her recordings, it is to find her quite remarkably restrained for most of the time: then a moment of rapt lyricism or fierce declamation produces a tingling effect with its feeling of spontaneous intensity and personal involvement. Her collaboration with Karajan is also among the most distinguished on record, and it often seems that his more calculated procedure with its care for the dignity of the score acts as both a foil and a balance to her impulsively emotional approach. Among the other singers, the most impressive is Fedora Barbieri, giving here her most inspired performance on record and Rolando Panerai, whose dark vibrancy suits the character of the Count di Luna. If di Stefano has neither the requisite steel in his voice nor the nobility of style, he is best in the full-voiced passion of the final scene.

Verdi. AIDA. **Maria Callas** (sop) Aida; **Richard Tucker** (ten) Radames; **Fedora Barbieri** (mez) Amneris; **Tito Gobbi** (bar) Amonasro; **Giuseppe Modesti** (bass) Ramphis; **Nicola Zaccaria** (bass) King of Egypt; **Elvira Galassi** (sop) Priestess; **Franco Ricciardi** (ten) Messenger; **Chorus and Orchestra of La Scala, Milan/Tullio Serafin.** EMI mono CDS7 49030-8. Notes, text and translation included. From Columbia 33CX1318/20 (1/56).

③ 2h 24' AAD 11/87 ⓟ Ⓑ

Aida, the daughter of the Ethiopian king, is a prisoner at the Egyptian court where she falls in love with Radames, an Egyptian captain of the guard; Amneris, the Egyptian princess, also loves him. The tensions between these characters are rivetingly portrayed and explored and the gradual build-up to Aida's and Radames's union in death is paced with the sureness of a master composer. Callas's Aida is an assumption of total understanding and conviction; the growth from a slave-girl torn between love for her homeland and Radames, to a woman whose feelings transcend life itself represents one of the greatest operatic undertakings ever committed to disc. Alongside her is Fedora Barbieri, an Amneris palpable in her agonized mixture of love and jealousy—proud yet human. Tucker's Radames is powerful and Gobbi's Amonasro quite superb—a portrayal of comparable understanding to stand alongside Callas's Aida. Tullio Serafin is quite simply ideal and though the recording may not be perfect by current standards, nowhere can it dim the brilliance of the creations conjured up by this classic cast.

Verdi. RIGOLETTO. **Tito Gobbi** (bar) Rigoletto; **Giuseppe di Stefano** (ten) Duke; **Maria Callas** (sop) Gilda; **Nicola Zaccaria** (bass) Sparafucile; **Adriana Lazzarini** (mez) Maddalena; **Giuse Gerbino** (mez) Giovanna; **Plinio Clabassi** (bass) Monterone; **William Dickie** (bar) Marullo; **Renato Ercolani** (ten) Borsa; **Carlo Forti** (bar) Count Ceprano; **Elvira Galassi** (sop) Countess Ceprano; **Chorus and Orchestra of La Scala, Milan/Tullio Serafin.** EMI mono CDS7 47469-8. Notes, text and translation included. From Columbia 33CXS1324, 33CX1325/6 (2/56).

② 1h 58' ADD 2/87 Ⓑ

The story of the hunchbacked jester Rigoletto at the court of a licentious Duke who seduces the Fool's daughter Gilda by masquerading as a poor student, and the consequent attempts at revenge on the part of Rigoletto, produced from Verdi one of the most telling of his mid-period triumphs. His identification with each of the characters and the sheer energy and sensuous ardour of the score is quite remarkable. Nowhere else on record have these characterizations been delineated with such intelligence and commitment as by Gobbi, Callas and di Stefano on this 30-year-old set. Over all Serafin presides with an unerring grasp of Verdian timing.

Verdi. UN BALLO IN MASCHERA. **Giuseppi di Stefano** (ten) Riccardo;
Tito Gobbi (bar) Renato; **Maria Callas** (sop) Amelia; **Fedora Barbieri** (mez)
Ulrica; **Eugenia Ratti** (sop) Oscar; **Ezio Giordano** (bass) Silvano; **Silvio
Maionica** (bass) Samuel; **Nicola Zaccaria** (bass) Tom; **Renato Ercolani**
(bar) Judge; **Chorus and Orchestra of La Scala, Milan/Antonino Votto.**
EMI mono CDS7 47498-8. Notes, text and translation included. From Columbia
33CX1472/4 (10/57).

② 2h 10' ADD 9/87

Ballo manages to encompass a vein of lighthearted frivolity (represented by the
page, Oscar) within the confines of a serious drama of love, infidelity, noble and
ignoble sentiments. No more modern recording has quite caught the opera's true
spirit so truly as this one under Votto's unerring direction. Callas has not been
surpassed in delineating Amelia's conflict of feelings and loyalties, nor has di
Stefano been equalled in the sheer ardour of his singing as Riccardo. Add to that
no less a singer than Tito Gobbi as Renato, at first eloquent in his friendship to
his ruler, then implacable in his revenge when he thinks Riccardo has stolen his
wife. Fedora Barbieri is full of character as the soothsayer Ulrica, Eugenia Ratti a
sparky Oscar. It is an unbeatable line-up.

Verdi. SIMON BOCCANEGRA. **Piero Cappuccilli** (bar) Simon Boccanegra;
Katia Ricciarelli (sop) Maria Boccanegra/Amelia; **Plácido Domingo** (ten)
Gabriele Adorno; **Ruggero Raimondi** (bass) Jacopo Fiesco; **Gian Piero
Mastromei** (bar) Paolo Albiani; **RCA Chorus and Orchestra/Gianandrea
Gavazzeni.** RCA Red Seal RD70729. Notes, text and translation included.
From SER5696 (2/74).

② 2h 5' ADD 9/87

Verdi. SIMON BOCCANEGRA. **Tito Gobbi** (bar) Simon Boccanegra;
Victoria de los Angeles (sop) Amelia; **Giuseppe Campora** (ten) Gabriele;
Boris Christoff (bass) Fiesco; **Walter Monachesi** (bar) Paolo; **Paolo Dari**
(bar) Pietro; **Paolo Caroli** (bar) Captain; **Silvia Bertona** (mez) Maid; **Chorus
and Orchestra of the Rome Opera House/Gabriele Santini.** EMI mono
CMS7 63513-2. Notes, text and translations included. From HMV ALPS1634,
ALP1635/6 (12/58).

② 1h 59' ADD 9/90

This opera has the most complex of plots, difficult to unravel in the opera house
but more easily understood with the libretto in front of you at home. It mainly
concerns the struggle between the nobility and the populace, represented
respectively by Fiesco and Boccanegra and complicated by the fact that the
seafaring Simon has seduced the noble's daughter Maria, who has borne his
daughter, Amelia. The RCA set is lovingly conducted by Gavazzeni with that
easy yet unassuming command of Verdian structure which is not always achieved
by his successors. His cast is an excellent one headed by the warm, sympathetic
Boccanegra of Cappuccilli and the youthful, attractive Amelia of Ricciarelli. The
recording is spacious and clear in detail.

The EMI issue is an apt alternative to modern versions, a kind of classic
because of the unsurpassed performances of its principals. Gobbi did much to
bring this previously neglected work back into the repertory. He shows a deep
sympathy with the public and private dilemmas of the Doge and expresses them
in plangently accented tones, a true Verdian line, and—in the Council Chamber
scene—supreme authority. As his implacable adversary Fiesco, Christoff gives
one of his most imposing portrayals on disc, inflecting the text superbly with an
exuding authority. Victoria de los Angeles is a pure-voiced, properly intense
Amelia, Giuseppe Campora a vibrant Gabriele. Santini's conducting is admirable.
With a passing regret at one or two small cuts, this set can be warmly

recommended and will show anyone how much can be achieved by acting with the voice. The mono recording is adequate.

Verdi. DON CARLOS. **Plácido Domingo** (ten) Don Carlos; **Montserrat Caballé** (sop) Elisabetta; **Shirley Verrett** (mez) Princess Eboli; **Sherrill Milnes** (bar) Rodrigo; **Ruggero Raimondi** (bass) Philip II; **Giovanni Foiani** (bass) Grand Inquisitor; **Delia Wallis** (mez) Thibault; **Ryland Davies** (ten) Count of Lerma; **Simon Estes** (bass) A Monk; **John Noble** (bar) Herald; **Ambrosian Opera Chorus; Royal Opera House Orchestra, Covent Garden/Carlo Maria Giulini.** EMI CDS7 47701-8. Notes, text and translation included. From SLS956 (7/71).

③ 3h 28' ADD 7/87

In no other Verdi opera, except perhaps *Aida*, are public and private matters so closely intermingled, so searchingly described as in this large-scale, panoramic work, in which the political intrigues and troubles of Philip II's Spain are counterpointed with his personal agony and the lives and loves of those at his court. This vast canvas inspired Verdi to one of his most varied and glorious scores. Giulini, more than any other conductor, searches out the inner soul of the piece and his cast is admirable. The young Plácido Domingo makes a vivid and exciting Carlos, whilst Montserrat Caballé spins glorious tone and phrases in encompassing Elisabeth's difficult music. Shirley Verrett is a vital, suitably tense Eboli, Sherrill Milnes an upright, warm Rodrigo and Ruggero Raimondi a sombre Philip. Throughout, the Covent Garden forces sing and play with fervour and understanding for their distinguished conductor.

Verdi. I VESPRI SICILIANI. **Cheryl Studer** (sop) Elena; **Chris Merritt** (ten) Arrigo; **Giorgio Zancanaro** (bar) Montforte; **Ferruccio Furlanetto** (bass) Procida; **Gloria Banditelli** (contr) Ninetta; **Enzo Capuano** (bass) De Béthune; **Francesco Musinu** (bass) Vaudemont; **Ernesto Gavazzi** (ten) Danieli; **Paolo Barbacini** (ten) Tebaldo; **Marco Chingari** (bass) Roberto; **Ferrero Poggi** (ten) Manfredo; **Chorus and Orchestra of La Scala, Milan/Riccardo Muti.** EMI CDS7 54043-2. Notes, text and translation included. Recorded at performances in La Scala, Milan during December 1989 and January 1990.

③ 3h 19' DDD 1/91

Verdi's French opera, here given in its more familiar Italian guise, is a difficult work to bring off. Verdi felt he had to try to accommodate Parisian taste for the grand and theatrically exciting while at the same time showing his own preferences for the interplay of characters. It's to the credit of this performance,

taken live from La Scala, that both aspects are thrillingly encompassed by virtue of Muti's vivid and acute conducting that never allows the score to sag yet allows for its many and varied moods. Although he plays it at full length, EMI have nonetheless managed to contain it on three discs. The singers, with one serious exception, are equal to their roles, none more than Studer as an Elena of positive character and vocal security. Chris Merritt turns in his best performance on disc to date as the hero Arrigo. Even better is Zancanaro as the tyrant Montforte, who yet has an anguished soul. Furlanetto is frankly overparted by the demands of the role of Procida, leader of the Sicilian rebellion, but that drawback shouldn't prevent anyone from enjoying the *frisson* of hearing La Scala, on a good night, performing comparatively rare Verdi with such zest.

Tomas Luis de Victoria
Spanish 1548-1611

Victoria (ed. Turner). Responsories for Tenebrae. **Westminster Cathedral Choir/David Hill.** Hyperion CDA66304. Texts and translations included.

• 75' DDD 7/89

Westminster Cathedral is probably one of the few places where compositions of such noble inspiration may still be heard during the last three days of Holy Week. Such a living link with tradition goes to explain the inner understanding, the tremendous pathos of a superbly tragic and musically satisfying performance. The carefully chosen texts tell of the betrayal and arrest of Jesus, his passion and burial. The music expresses with anguish the suffering and sorrow of those days. Certain passages in the recording are particularly memorable: a gentle treble lead at the opening of "Una hora", the dramatic juxtaposition of the evil vigil of Judas and the naïvety of the disciples' sleep. Variations of tempo, especially that for the plotting of Jeremiah's enemies and the exact dovetailing, as in "Seniores", combine to heighten the dramatic effect. These pieces, of tragic magnificence, are performed with intensity and integrity, so that a great recording will now ensure that an incomparable treasure of Christian music will be safely preserved for future generations.

Victoria. Missa O quam gloriosum. Motet—O quam gloriosum. Missa Ave maris stella. **Westminster Cathedral Choir/David Hill.** Hyperion CDA66114. Texts and translations included. From A66114 (10/84).

• 57' DDD 6/86

The *Missa O quam gloriosum* is not a work of enormous technical complexity but rather seeks for its effect in measure and poise. The long soaring treble lines have a serenity and restrained intensity that have made it Victoria's most often performed Mass. The Westminster Cathedral Choir sing with a fervour and passion that puts their Anglican colleagues in the shade in this repertoire. The *Missa Ave maris stella* is a more elaborate work with a plainchant melody and the highlight of this rarely performed work must be the beautiful second *Agnus dei*, with divided tenors—gloriously performed by the choir. Recording is first rate.

Heitor Villa-Lobos
Brazilian 1887-1959

Villa-Lobos. Guitar Concerto[a]. Five Preludes[b]. 12 Etudes[c]. **Julian Bream** (gtr); **London Symphony Orchestra/André Previn.** RCA Red Seal RD89813. Items marked [a] and [b] from SB6852 (2/72), [c] RL12499 (12/78).

• 69' ADD 2/87

This disc illustrates Villa-Lobos's interest in writing for the guitar. Two sets of solo works flank the concerto, a brief (18 minute) and attractive work of spiky syncopation and fleet-fingered solo writing. The piece retains a 'chamber' feel and Villa-Lobos never unleashes the full might of the orchestra, so one rarely feels the naturalness of the balance to be strenuously or artificially achieved. Bream's warm tone is nicely caught by the recording. The 12 *Etudes* employ a technical range of quite remarkable variety; the *glissandos* are striking and perfectly executed by Julian Bream. The Preludes are bigger works and seek to portray the variety of Brazilian life in a number of moods.

Villa-Lobos. PIANO WORKS. **Cristina Ortiz.** Decca 417 650-2DH. Bachianas brasileiras No. 4 (pf version). Guia prático. Poema singélo. Caixinha de música quebrada. Saudades das selvas brasileiras No. 2. As tres Marias. Valsa da dor. Cirandas—No. 4, O cravo brigou com a rosa; No. 14, A canôa virou. Ciclo brasileiro.

· **67' DDD 12/87**

Cristina Ortiz has chosen a programme which sensitively evokes Brazilian life—children's songs, folk-songs, affectionate pictures in music of favourite places, all add up to a rounded musical portrait. The *Bachianas brasileiras* No. 4 is performed complete and Ortiz reveals her Brazilian nationality in the vivid depiction of the araponga, a bird with a call like a hammer on an anvil. The charming *Caixinha de música quebrada* ("The broken little musical box") has a "Ravelian" flavour, and Ortiz plays it with corresponding attention to detail and delicacy of touch. The recording is very fine indeed and provides an excellent introduction to an all too-rarely heard repertoire.

Villa-Lobos. WORKS FOR STRINGS AND VOICE. [a]**Pleeth Cello Octet;** [b]**Jill Gomez** (sop); [c]**Peter Manning** (vn). Hyperion CDA66257. Texts and translations included where appropriate.
Bachianas brasileiras—No. 1[a]; No. 5[ab]. Suite for voice and violin (1923)[bc]. **Bach** (trans. Villa-Lobos); The Well-tempered Clavier[a]—Prelude in D minor (BWV853); Fugue in B flat major (BWV846); Prelude in G minor (BWV867); Fugue in D major (BWV874).

· **54' DDD 12/87**

Sandwiched between two of the composer's best-known works, the First and Fifth of the *Bachianas brasileiras*, are the Suite for voice and violin and four pieces arranged from Bach's *48*. In the Suite Villa-Lobos allows soprano voice and violin to chase, cavort and imitate with great fluidity and freedom. It is just the sort of piece at which Jill Gomez excels, her feeling for mood and rhythm are ideal and Peter Manning is a spirited partner. The other pieces on the disc employ massed cellos and the Pleeth Cello Octet play with uncommon sympathy. The two *Bachianas* capture a real sense of the music's flavour and the Bach arrangements are fascinating studies in the fusion of identities—a fusion developed and perfected in the *Bachianas* where the forms and ideals of Bach are melded with the wholly Brazilian idioms of Villa-Lobos. A well recorded and most intelligently constructed programme.

Villa-Lobos. CHAMBER WORKS. **William Bennett** (fl); [ae]**Neil Black** (ob); [a]**Janice Knight** (cor ang); [aef]**Thea King** (cl); [acf]**Robin O'Neill** (bn); [d]**Charles Tunnell** (vc); [b]**Simon Weinberg** (gtr). Hyperion CDA66295. Quinteto em forma de chôros[a]. Modinha[b]. Bachianas brasileiras No. 6[c]. Distribuçião de flôres[b]. Assobio a jato[d]. Chôros No. 2[e]. Canção do amor[b]. Trio for oboe, clarinet and bassoon[f].

· **61' DDD 9/89**   ⁹ₚ

If there is one consistent feature in Villa-Lobos's enormous and diverse output, it is his unpredictability. His restless, supercharged mind never tired of experimenting with new sonorities, and he never felt inhibited, in the course of a work, from following unrelated new impulses. This has the effect of making his music at the same time attractive and disconcerting. The multi-sectional Quintet, the most significant item here, is highly complex but extremely entertaining in its quirky way; and it is played with marvellous neatness, finely judged tonal nuances and high spirits. The rarely heard Trio, the earliest work here, is a particularly spiky atonal piece, typical of its period (1921), depending almost entirely on exuberantly thrusting and counter-thrusting rhythm: it calls for virtuosity, and gets it. The sixth of the *Bachianas brasileiras* (easily the best available recorded performance) is most sensitively shaped, and the second *Chôros*, which makes great demands on the two players both individually and in mutual responsiveness, is outstandingly polished. A disc of outstanding artistry.

Antonio Vivaldi
Italian 1678-1741

Vivaldi. 12 Concertos, Op. 9, "La cetra". **Monica Huggett** (vn); **Raglan Baroque Players/Nicholas Kraemer** (hpd). EMI CDS7 47829-8. From EX270557-3 (4/87).

② Ih 56' DDD II/87

These concertos are not of uniform quality but the best are very fine indeed. The opening *Allegro* of No. 2 has more than a momentary glance at the sparkling bow-work of *The Four Seasons*, and the double concerto writing of No. 9 is work of great finesse. The vigorous *Presto* of No. 5, unusually prefaced by a slow introduction, is a splendid example of virtuoso violin writing. Monica Huggett plays all the concertos with enormous excitement, relishing the *scordatura* (retuning a string) writing and allowing the music to languish when the occasion arises. The Raglan Baroque Players accompany attentively and Nicholas Kraemer provides some inventive harpsichord playing. This is refreshing music, undemanding but full of charm, and the recording is comparably good.

Vivaldi. 12 Violin Concertos, Op. 4, "La stravaganza". **Monica Huggett** (vn); **Academy of Ancient Music/Christopher Hogwood.** L'Oiseau-Lyre Florilegium 417 502-2OH2.

② Ih 4I' DDD 3/87

In *La stravaganza* Vivaldi makes a further decisive step towards the virtuoso solo violin concerto and though the quality of the music is a little uneven, the set nevertheless contains several movements of outstanding beauty. From among them we might single out the *Grave* of the Concerto No. 4 in A minor whose suspensions, chromaticisms and lyrical solo violin part cast a spell of almost fairy-tale enchantment, and the *Largo* of the Concerto No. 12 in G major with its ostinato bass above which a simple but haunting melody is treated to a series of variations. Monica Huggett gives a lively, inspired account of the music. Her warm tone, well-nigh impeccable intonation, sensitive dynamic shading and sheer virtuosity lead us to the heart of these pieces in a seemingly effortless fashion. There is a rich vein of fantasy coursing through *La stravaganza* and this is vividly realized in her communicative playing. The small string forces provide sympathetic support and Christopher Hogwood generates an enthusiastic atmosphere with well-judged tempos and tautly sustained rhythms.

Vivaldi. FLUTE CONCERTOS. **Orchestra of the Eighteenth Century/ Frans Brüggen** (fl/rec). RCA Red Seal Seon RD70951. From RL30392 (4/82).
Concertos—G major, RV435; F major, RV442. *Chamber Concertos*—F major, RV98, "La tempesta di mare"; G minor, RV104, "La notte"; D major, RV90, "Il gardellino"; G major, RV101.

♪ 53' DDD 2/87

Frans Brüggen is well known as a virtuoso recorder player and appears as both soloist and director in these notably imaginative performances of Vivaldi's music.

He listens to every nuance of inflexion and unfailingly capitalizes on the rich sonorities provided by Vivaldi's carefully chosen instrumental combinations. What too often sounds routine in the composer's tuttis is here transformed into elegant and bold gestures, with a lively feeling for caricature. Brüggen's own playing reaches a pinnacle in the set of variations which conclude the Sixth Concerto and which he dispatches with dazzling virtuosity. The recording is admirably clear, picking up every detail of baroque bassoon mechanism!

Frans Brüggen [*photo: Philips/van Teylingen*]

Vivaldi. FLUTE CONCERTOS. **Lóránt Kovács** (fl); **Franz Liszt Chamber Orchestra/János Rolla.** Hungaroton White Label HRC127.
F major, RV433, "La tempesta di mare"; G minor, RV439, "La notte"; D major, RV428, "Il gardellino"; G major, RV435; F major, RV434; G major, RV437.

♪ 53' ADD 10/89 £

It was not until the late 1720s that the flute began to gain a foothold in Italy. Vivaldi's six Concertos for Flute and Strings were published in about 1728 though all but one of them were adaptations of earlier concertos in which the treble recorder played a prominent role. These performances are lively and sympathetic and capture much of the impressionist programmatic content implied in the first three concertos of the set. Lóránt Kovács is an accomplished player—he uses a modern flute—and he is sympathetically supported by the strings of the Franz Liszt Chamber Orchestra under their director, János Rolla. Vivaldi requires imagination and at times considerable technical skill from his soloists and Kovács rises to the occasion with panache and stylistic awareness. The performances are not for purists but they will disappoint few who readily respond to Vivaldi's lively rhythmic sense and his feeling for melody. Modestly packaged but effectively recorded and very keenly priced.

Vivaldi. The Four Seasons. **Drottningholm Baroque Ensemble/Nils-Erik Sparf** (vn). BIS CD275.

♪ 40' DDD 8/86 Ⓑ

These concertos are not Vivaldi's most advanced works in concerto form but they contain the essence of his genius: fertile invention, rhythmic vigour and inspired melodies. The performances here are imaginative and refreshingly unbuttoned in their exuberant spirit. They respond to the music with an earthy robustness which forcefully emphasizes Vivaldi's gifts at caricature; the portrayal of bucolic, peasant merriment in the "Autumn" concerto has all the colourful immediacy of a Brueghel painting, whilst the harmonies and figurations of "Winter" are chillingly abrasive; but it is in the thunderstorm finale of "Summer" that the vivid imagination and sense of fun, which characterize these performances, are given full rein. The recording is notable for its clarity and for the contrast it affords between solo and ripieno strands. The acoustic is an ideal one and the accompanying notes include the four anonymous sonnets which appeared in Vivaldi's printed edition.

Vivaldi. L'estro Armonico, Op. 3. **Academy of Ancient Music/ Christopher Hogwood.** L'Oiseau-Lyre Florilegium 414 554-2OH2. From D245D2 (12/81).

② 96' DDD 1/86

This set of Concertos is arranged as a display of variety, and ordered in a kaleidoscopic way that would maintain interest were it to be played entire. These works are often played with an inflated body of *ripieno* (orchestral) strings, but in this recording they are played as Vivaldi intended them; only four violins are used. The contrast does not come from antiphony or weight of numbers but is provided through the *tutti* versus episodic passages. One could not assemble a more distinguished 'cast' than that of the AAM in this recording, showing clearly just why this music is best played on period instruments, and by specialists in baroque style—who are not afraid to add a little embellishment here and there. Neither the enchanting performances nor the quality of their recording could be better; this is required listening.

Vivaldi. CONCERTOS—ALLA RUSTICA. **The English Concert/Trevor Pinnock.** Archiv Produktion 415 674-2AH.
G major, RV151, "Alla rustica"; B flat major for violin and oboe, RV548 (with Simon Standage, vn; David Reichenberg, ob); G major for two violins, RV516 (Standage, Elizabeth Wilcock, vns); A minor for oboe, RV461 (Reichenberg); G major for two mandolins, RV532 (James Tyler, Robin Jeffrey, mndls); C major, RV558 (Standage, Micaela Comberti, vns "in tromba"; Philip Pickett, Rachel Beckett, recs; Colin Lawson, Carlos Reoira, chalumeaux; Tyler, Jeffrey, mndls; Nigel North, Jakob Lindberg, theorbos; Anthony Pleeth, vc).

53' DDD 9/86

The *Concerto con molti stromenti*, RV558, calls for a plethora of exotic instruments and Vivaldi's inventiveness, everywhere apparent, seems to know no bounds. The vigorous melodies have splendid verve whilst the slow movements are no less exciting. The concertos, which employ plucked instruments, are particularly entrancing to the ear—here is virtuosity indeed, with Pinnock sensibly opting for an organ continuo to emphasize the difference between the plucked strings and the bowed. The Double Mandolin Concerto, RV532, is beautifully played with a real build-up of tension in the tuttis. The playing of The English Concert is affectionate and rhythmically precise and the recording is good with the gentler sounding instruments well brought out of the fuller textures.

Vivaldi. MAESTRO DE'CONCERTI. **Taverner Players/Andrew Parrott.**
EMI Reflexe CDC7 47700-2.
Multiple Concertos—G minor, RV577, "per l'orchestra di Dresda"; G major,
RV575; C major, RV556, "per la Solennita di S Lorenzio". Concerto in C major,
RV114. Chamber Concerto in D major, RV95, "La pastorella". Flute Concerto
in G minor, RV439, "La notte" (with Janet See, fl).

> 58' DDD 5/88

This anthology serves to emphasize the great variety of colour and texture that
exists in Vivaldi's Concertos and it contains both large- and small-scale orchestral
concertos. It is a delightful programme and the playing brings to life Vivaldi's
music in an effective manner. There are many fine obbligato contributions and
Janet See, the solo flautist in a well-known Concerto from Opus 10, is
pleasingly inventive in her embellishments. One of the features which brings
additional charm to the performances is the care with which the basso continuo
has been 'realized'. As well as the obligatory organ or harpsichord, archlute,
theorbo and guitar contribute to the texture, adding a vivid if optional dash of
colour. Other instruments which make appearances of varying prominence
include treble recorders, oboes, clarinets and bassoons; but it is the smaller-scale
works and notably *La pastorella* (RV95) which in the end have the greater appeal.
Recorded sound is clear and pleasantly reverberant.

Vivaldi. STRING CONCERTOS. **I Musici.** Philips 422 212-2PH.
Concerto in D major for two violins and two cellos, RV564. Concerto in G
minor for two cellos, RV531. Concerto in C major for violin and two cellos,
RV561. Concerto in F major for three violins, RV551. Concerto in F major for
violin and cello, RV544. Concerto in F major for violin and organ, RV542.

> 61' DDD 5/89

Many of Vivaldi's concertos deploy two or more string soloists and there are
some very attractive examples of them in this recording. To his endlessly
resourceful treatment of *ritornello* form in the quicker movements, Vivaldi adds
further variety by ringing the changes on his solo forces—the number of violins
and/or cellos, which may converse with one another or play in concert. In
RV542 the solo honours are shared between violin and organ and some
delightful sonorities result, whilst RV531, the only two-cello concerto in
Vivaldi's *oeuvre*, contains a lovely *Adagio* in which the soloists speak to one
another tenderly. I Musici are renowned for their enthusiasm and love of tonal
opulence and this recording is also a fine example of the proper use of modern
instruments. Clarity of texture is a *sine qua non* and it is provided by both
players and recordists in this very fine issue.

Vivaldi. CELLO SONATAS. **Anner Bylsma** (vc); **Jacques Ogg** (hpd);
Hideimi Suzuki (cont). Deutsche Harmonia Mundi RD77909.
E flat major, RV39; E minor, RV40; F major, RV41; G minor, RV42; A minor,
RV43; A minor, RV44.

> 62' DDD 6/90

Nine cello sonatas by Vivaldi have survived and in this virtuoso recital Anner
Bylsma plays six of them. Vivaldi wrote as expressively for the cello as for his
own instrument, the violin, and Bylsma's interpretations are variously endowed
with fire and melancholy. He brings gesture to the music, sometimes in the
manner of a caricaturist, at others with nobler, grander statements. Tempos are
occasionally a little hard driven and technically demanding passages consquently
accident prone, but at all times Bylsma sounds passionately involved in the
music, giving performances which seem refreshingly far away from the

specialized disciplines of the recording studio. Bylsma's choice of sonatas is attractive, though, since none of the nine works are in any sense of the word dull, sacrifices have had to be made. It is regrettable perhaps that neither of the B flat Sonatas is included, but the best known and perhaps finest of all, in E minor, is played with lyricism and a fine sense of poetry. Here and in the G minor Sonata Vivaldi reached considerable expressive heights and if only for these two works Bylsma's performances are to be treasured. Fine recorded sound but the documentation, especially where catalogue numbers are concerned, is slipshod and unhelpful.

Vivaldi. SACRED CHORAL WORKS, Volume 1. [abcd]**Margaret Marshall,** [d]**Felicity Lott** (sops); [bc]**Anne Collins** (mez); [b]**Birgit Finnilä** (contr); **John Alldis Choir; English Chamber Orchestra/Vittorio Negri.** Philips 420 648-2PH. Texts and translations included. Items marked [a], [b] and [e] from 6769 032 (12/79), [c] 6768 016 (12/78), [d] 6768 149 (9/80).
Introduzione al Gloria—Ostro picta in D major, RV642[a] (ed. Giegling). Gloria in D major, RV589[b] (ed. Negri). Lauda Jerusalem in E minor, RV609[c]. Laudate pueri Dominum in A major, RV602[d] (ed. Giegling). Laudate Dominum in D minor, RV606[e] (ed. Giegling).

66' ADD 5/88

Vivaldi. SACRED CHORAL WORKS, Volume 2. **Margaret Marshall,** [cd]**Felicity Lott,** [c]**Sally Burgess** (sops); [b]**Ann Murray,** [d]**Susan Daniel** (mezs); [c]**Linda Finnie,** [bc]**Anne Collins** (contrs); [b]**Anthony Rolfe Johnson** (ten); [b]**Robert Holl** (bass); [bcd]**John Alldis Choir; English Chamber Orchestra/Vittorio Negri.** Philips 420 649-2PM. Texts and translations included. Items marked [a] and [b] from 6768 016 (12/78), [c] and [d] 6769 046 (12/80).

67' ADD 2/89

A lively performance of the better-known of Vivaldi's two settings of the *Gloria* as well as several other less familiar items are included in these two volumes. One of the most captivating works is a setting for double choir and soloist of the psalm, *Laudate pueri*, RV602. No lover of Vivaldi's music should overlook this radiant piece which is beautifully sung and vividly recorded. Negri's direction is lively and his evident affection for Vivaldi's music seems to have fired the enthusiasm of all concerned, prompting firm and responsive support from both choir and orchestra. Margaret Marshall, who is outstanding in her solos, and Felicity Lott are well matched in their duets and the timbre of their voices is suited both to the repertoire and to the style of the performances. Recorded sound is excellent and full Latin texts with translations are included in the booklet.

Vivaldi. VOCAL AND ORCHESTRAL WORKS. [a]**Emma Kirkby,** [b]**Suzette Leblanc, Danièle Forget** (sops); [b]**Richard Cunningham** (alto); [a]**Henry Ingram** (ten); **Tafelmusik** [a]**Chamber Choir and Baroque Orchestra/ Jean Lamon** ([c]vn). Hyperion CDA66247. Texts and translations included where appropriate.
In turbato mare irato, RV627[a]. Concertos—D minor, "Concerto madrigalesco", RV129; G minor, RV157; G major, "Concerto alla rustica", RV151. Lungi dal vago volto, RV680[ac]. Magnificat, RV610[a][ab].

57' DDD 12/87

This thoughtfully and effectively chosen programme deserves the attention of all baroque music enthusiasts. The approach of the Tafelmusik Baroque Orchestra, playing period instruments, is both stylish and sympathetic. They are joined by

Emma Kirkby who sings two of Vivaldi's little-known chamber cantatas with precision, warmth of sentiment and dazzling virtuosity. These performances are the high spots of the programme but few listeners will be disappointed with the lively account of three of Vivaldi's little concertos for strings; one of them, the *Concerto alla rustica*, is particularly enchanting. The remaining item, the Magnificat, is an effective work scored for divided choir with an orchestra of strings and oboes, although sadly the oboes have been omitted. The choral singing is firm and the disc as a whole is appealing and well recorded.

Richard Wagner *German 1813-1883*

Wagner. OPERA CHORUSES. **Bayreuth Festival Chorus and Orchestra/Wilhelm Pitz.** DG Privilege 429 169-2GR. From SLPM136006 (5/59).
Opera Choruses: Der fliegende Holländer; Tannhäuser; Lohengrin; Die Meistersinger von Nürnberg; Götterdämmerung; Parsifal.

53' ADD 4/90 £

Most of the favourites are here: Spinning Chorus, Wedding Chorus, pilgrims, sailors, vassals, the good folk of Nuremberg, knights of the Grail and boys up in the cupola. There is nothing from *Tristan und Isolde*, and indeed not much to choose from, but one might have expected the hearty Communion chorus from *Parsifal*. As it is, there is much to enjoy as a way of renewing appetite for the operas themselves, and perhaps in some instances serving as an introduction. If the operas are new to any intending purchaser it is as well to note that beyond the German text of the first line no information is supplied. Moreover some of the other printed material is wrong (the mezzo sings in *Der fliegende Holländer* not *Tannhäuser*, and Josef Greindl is in the *Götterdämmerung* excerpt not *Parsifal*). Tracks 5 and 6 (*Tannhäuser*) and 10 and 11 (*Meistersinger*) run without a break, so that the list of items could prove misleading. As to the performances, the choral work is excellent when the men are singing, somewhat tremulous when the sopranos are involved. Recording varies from vivid (as in *Lohengrin* and *Götterdämmerung*) to misty (*Meistersinger*). The bargain price and fond memories of Wilhelm Pitz are the principal incentives here.

Wagner. TANNHAUSER. **Wolfgang Windgassen** (ten) Tannhäuser; **Anja Silja** (sop) Elisabeth; **Eberhard Waechter** (bar) Wolfram; **Grace Bumbry** (mez) Venus; **Josef Greindl** (bass) Hermann; **Gerhard Stolze** (ten) Walther; **Franz Crass** (bass) Biterolf; **Georg Paskuda** (ten) Heinrich; **Gerd Nienstedt** (bass) Reinmar; **Else-Margrete Gardelli** (sop) Shepherd; **Bayreuth Festival Chorus and Orchestra/Wolfgang Sawallisch.** Philips 420 122-2PH3. Notes, text and translation included. Recorded at a performance in the Festspielhaus, Bayreuth in June 1962. From SAL3445/7 (6/64).

③ 2h 50' ADD 8/87

Wagner's opera about the medieval minstrel-knight of the title who wavers between the erotic charms of Venus and the pure love of Elisabeth is hard to bring off in the opera house and in the recording studio. Its structure is diffuse and its demands on the singers, Tannhäuser in particular, inordinate. The opera calls for a dedication and dramatic intensity such as it received in Wieland Wagner's staging at Bayreuth in 1962. Sawallisch directs an account that catches the fervour of the protagonist from the start and goes on to relate the torture in his soul as he is cast out from society and refused forgiveness by the Pope. The title part itself is sung with tense feeling, keen tone and immaculate diction by

Wolfgang Windgassen—the famous Rome Narration has seldom sounded so anguished. Anja Silja's clear, evocative voice and youthful eagerness inform all aspects of Elisabeth's role and as Venus, Grace Bumbry caused something of a sensation through her glamorous appearance and rich tones. Eberhard Waechter sings the part of the sympathetic Wolfram with glowing tone and sensitive phrasing. Together, cast and conductor make the inspired Third Act a fitting conclusion to this inspired reading.

Wagner. TANNHAUSER—Overture. Siegfried idyll. TRISTAN UND ISOLDE—Prelude and Liebestod[a]. [a]**Jessye Norman** (sop); **Vienna Philharmonic Orchestra/Herbert von Karajan.** DG 423 613-2GH. Text and translation included. Recorded at a performance in the Grosse Festspielhaus during the 1987 Salzburg Festival.

54' DDD 8/88   **(B)**

For the Wagner specialist who has a complete *Tannhäuser* and *Tristan* on the shelves, this disc involves some duplication. Even so, it is not hard to make room for such performances as are heard here. For the non-specialist, the programme provides a good opportunity for a meeting halfway, the common ground between Master and general music-lover being the *Siegfried Idyll*. This offers 20 minutes of delight in the play of musical ideas, structured and yet impulsive, within a sustained mood of gentle affection. The orchestration is something of a miracle, and it can rarely have been heard to better advantage than in this recording, where the ever-changing textures are so clearly displayed and where from every section of the orchestra the sound is of such great loveliness. It comes as a welcome contrast to the *Tannhäuser* Overture, with its big tunes and *fortissimos*, the whole orchestra surging in a frank simulation of physical passion. A further contrast is to follow in the *Tristan* Prelude, where again Karajan and his players are at their best in their feeling for texture and their control of pulse. Jessye Norman, singing the *Liebestod* with tenderness and vibrant opulence, of tone brings the recital to an end, with scarcely a single reminder that it was recorded live.

Wagner. DER FLIEGENDE HOLLANDER. **Simon Estes** (bass-bar) Holländer; **Lisbeth Balslev** (sop) Senta; **Matti Salminen** (bass) Daland; **Robert Schunk** (ten) Erik; **Anny Schlemm** (mez) Mary; **Graham Clark** (ten) Steersman; **Bayreuth Festival Chorus and Orchestra/Woldemar Nelsson.** Philips 416 300-2PH2. Notes, text and translation included. Recorded at a performance in the Festspielhaus, Bayreuth in June 1985.

② 2h 14' DDD 8/86

Wagner. DER FLIEGENDE HOLLANDER. **Theo Adam** (bar) Holländer; **Anja Silja** (sop) Senta; **Martti Talvela** (bass) Daland; **Ernst Kozub** (ten) Erik; **Annelies Burmeister** (mez) Mary; **Gerhard Unger** (ten) Steersman; **BBC Chorus; New Philharmonia Orchestra/Otto Klemperer.** EMI Studio CMS7 63344-2. Notes, text and translation included. From SAN207/9 (12/68).

③ 2h 32' ADD 2/90

The young Wagner, sailing across the North Sea for the first time to England, went through a violent storm, and the experience left so vivid an impression that it prompted him to go ahead with a project he had already conceived, to turn the legend of the Flying Dutchman, condemned to sail the seas for ever till absolved by love, into an opera. The very opening of the Overture recaptures the violence of that storm at sea, and it leads to a work in which for the first time the full individuality of the would-be revolutionary can be appreciated. The Philips's version, warmly and vigorously conducted by Woldemar Nelsson,

Otto Klemperer   [photo: EMI/Meitner-Graf]

vividly captures the excitement and tensions of a stage performance, together—it has to be admitted—with a fair amount of stage noise from the milling choruses of seamen. The cast is a strong one, headed by Simon Estes in the title-role and the nobility and confidence of his performance are most compelling, conveying total involvement. Lisbeth Balslev sings tenderly and movingly and Matti Salminen is outstanding in the role of Senta's father. But it is the chorus which are responsible as much as any soloist in this opera for dramatic excitement, and the finely drilled singers of the Bayreuth chorus crown an electrically intense experience.

Klemperer's magisterial interpretation treats the opera symphonically, which is all gain. As ever he justifies moderate speeds by virtue of the way he sustains line and emphasizes detail. At the same time the reading has a blazing intensity quite surprising from an older conductor. The storm and sea music in the Overture and thereafter has a stunning power and the Dutchman's torture and unrequited passion is graphically evoked in the orchestra. Indeed, the playing of the Philharmonia is a bonus throughout. As well as anyone Klemperer catches the elemental power of the work, its adumbration of surging emotions against a sea-saturated background. Theo Adam conveys all the anguish of the Dutchman's character contained within a secure line. His is a profoundly moving interpretation, most intelligently sung. As Senta, Anja Silja is the very epitome of trust and love unto death, the performance of a great singing-actress, sung in an all-in, occasionally piercing manner. Talvela is a bluff, burly Daland, Ernst Kozub a sympathetic Erik and Unger offers a clearly articulated, ardent Steersman.

Wagner. DIE MEISTERSINGER VON NURNBERG. **Theo Adam** (bass-bar) Hans Sachs; **Helen Donath** (sop) Eva; **René Kollo** (ten) Walther von Stolzing; **Sir Geraint Evans** (bass-bar) Beckmesser; **Peter Schreier** (ten) David; **Karl Ridderbusch** (bass) Veit Pogner; **Eberhard Büchner** (ten) Vogelgesang; **Ruth Hesse** (mez) Magdalene; **Horst Lunow** (bass) Nachtigall; **Zoltán Kélémen** (bass) Kothner; **Hans-Joachim Rotzsch** (ten) Zorn; **Peter Bindszus** (ten) Eisslinger; **Horst Hiestermann** (ten) Moser; **Hermann Christian Polster** (bass) Ortel; **Heinz Reeh** (bass) Schwarz; **Siegfried Vogel** (bass) Foltz; **Kurt Moll** (bass) Nightwatchman; **Leipzig Radio Chorus; Dresden State Opera Chorus; Staatskapelle, Dresden/Herbert von Karajan.** EMI CDS7 49683-2. Notes, text and translation included. From SLS957 (10/71).

④ 4h 26' ADD 7/88

Joyfully celebrating youth and midsummer, altruism and civic pride, Wagner is here the unstinting giver. It's a cornucopia of an opera, generous with the tunes, the colour, the sheer glory of sound as well as the desires and disappointments of the normal human heart. It is also essentially a company-opera, a vast collaborative enterprise which certainly benefits from the presence of a few great singers in the leading roles. In this recording, greatness is found not so much in the cast as in the man at the centre. Karajan directs an inspired, expansive performance, catching all the splendour and lyrical warmth of the writing. The singers are excellent in ensemble, and the whole company is alert in the disciplined chaos at the end of Act 2. Kollo's tone has power and clarity, Helen Donath's Eva is fresh and pretty and Theo Adam's Sachs is genial and authoritative. But the best singing comes from the two basses, Karl Ridderbusch (an unusually warm-hearted Pogner) and Kurt Moll. In a class of its own is Sir Geraint Evans's Beckmesser, his sly, nervously-calculating absurdity wonderfully preserved in this vivid recording.

Wagner. LOHENGRIN. **Jess Thomas** (ten) Lohengrin; **Elisabeth Grümmer** (sop) Elsa of Brabant; **Christa Ludwig** (mez) Ortrud; **Dietrich Fischer-Dieskau** (bar) Telramund; **Gottlob Frick** (bass) King Henry; **Otto Wiener** (bass) Herald; **Vienna State Opera Chorus; Vienna Philharmonic Orchestra/Rudolf Kempe.** EMI CDS7 49017-8. Notes, text and translation included. From SAN121/5 (2/64).

③ 3h 29' ADD 2/88

This is a *Lohengrin* of considerable historical interest, a finely judged studio recording with a superb cast under a conductor whose ability to shape and control the music's long paragraphs, in the most natural and unobtrusive way, will not be underestimated by listeners who have endured more mannered, less well-integrated performances. To find so much restraint and understatement in Wagner is no mean feat. Among the singers, pride of place must go to Jess Thomas and his persuasive account of the title role. Fischer-Dieskau's Telramund is the perfect adversary; there's a genuine anguish in this interpretation that gives the character rare substance. A comparable contrast exists between Elizabeth Grümmer's Else and Christa Ludwig's Ortrud: Grümmer moving from somnambulistic naïvety to uncomprehending despair, Ludwig from bitterness to malevolent triumph. With Gottlob Frick and Otto Weiner providing strong support, this is a cast with no weak links. Nor should the fine contribution of the Vienna chorus and orchestra be overlooked. Kempe was a musician's conductor, as the uniformly excellent response of all involved in this enterprise amply confirms.

Wagner. TRISTAN UND ISOLDE. **Ludwig Suthaus** (ten) Tristan; **Kirsten Flagstad** (sop) Isolde; **Blanche Thebom** (mez) Brangäne; **Dietrich Fischer-Dieskau** (bar) Kurwenal; **Josef Greindl** (bass) King Marke; **Edgar Evans** (ten) Melot; **Rudolf Schock** (ten) Shepherd; **Rhoderick Davies** (ten) Sailor; **Chorus of the Royal Opera House, Covent Garden; Philharmonia Orchestra/Wilhelm Furtwängler.** EMI mono CDS7 47322-8. Notes, text and translation included. From ALP1030/5 (3/53).

④ 3h 56' ADD 5/86

Wagner. TRISTAN UND ISOLDE. **Wolfgang Windgassen** (ten) Tristan; **Birgit Nilsson** (sop) Isolde; **Christa Ludwig** (mez) Brangäne; **Eberhard Waechter** (bar) Kurwenal; **Martti Talvela** (bass) King Marke; **Claude Heater** (ten) Melot; **Peter Schreier** (ten) Sailor; **Erwin Wohlfahrt** (ten) Shepherd; **Gerd Nienstedt** (bass) Helmsman; **Bayreuth Festival Chorus and Orchestra/Karl Böhm.** DG 419 889-2GH3. Notes, text and translation included. Recorded during the 1966 Bayreuth Festival. From SKL912/16 (1/67).

③ 3h 39' ADD 7/88

Furtwängler was a supreme interpreter of Wagner and his classic set also features one of the greatest Wagnerian singers of all time, Kirsten Flagstad. Furtwängler's view is spacious, as the relentless crescendo of the opening Prelude makes plain, yet such is the tension and the incandescence of the

Philharmonia Orchestra that the whole performance holds together with a compulsion rarely achieved on record. Kirsten Flagstad may be a noble Isolde rather than a sensuously feminine one, but her performance too has never been transcended in its richness, sureness and command, while Ludwig Suthaus sings the role of Tristan with clarity and precision, helped by the finely balanced recording. Notable among the others is the young Fischer-Dieskau as the old retainer, Kurwenal.

The balances are almost always undistractingly right and on CD, with intrusive background eliminated, the mono recording is more involving than the modern stereo of more recent versions. One historical oddity is that the top Cs which Isolde has to sing in the opening section of the love duet were taken not by Flagstad but—on her insistence—by the young Elisabeth Schwarzkopf. There was no jiggery-pokery with tape, just a finely placed note or two from Flagstad's chosen deputy, recorded at the same time in the studio. It is a deception one can readily accept for the sake of a supreme recording of a transcendental opera.

However, Böhm's recording is a live Bayreuth performance of some distinction, for on stage are the most admired Tristan and Isolde of their time, and in the pit the 72-year-old conductor directs a performance which is unflagging in its passion and energy. Böhm has a striking way in the Prelude and *Liebestod* of making the swell of passion seem like the movement of a great sea, sometimes with gentle motion, sometimes with the breaking of the mightiest of waves. Nilsson characterizes strongly and her voice with its marvellous cleaving-power can also soften quite beautifully. Windgassen's heroic performance in the Third Act is in some ways the crown of his achievements on record, even though the voice has dried and aged a little. Christa Ludwig is the ideal Brangäene, Waechter a suitably-forthright Kurwenal, and Talvela an expressive, noble-voiced Marke. Orchestra and chorus are at their finest.

Wagner. PARSIFAL. **Jess Thomas** (ten) Parsifal; **George London** (bass-bar) Amfortas; **Martti Talvela** (bass) Titurel; **Hans Hotter** (bass-bar) Gurnemanz; **Gustav Neidlinger** (bass) Klingsor; **Irene Dalis** (mez) Kundry; **Niels Möller** (ten) First Grail Knight; **Gerd Neinstedt** (bass) Second Grail Knight; **Sona Cervená** (mez) First Squire; **Ursula Boese** (contr) Second Squire; **Gerhard Stolze** (ten) Third Squire; **Georg Paskuda** (ten) Fourth Squire; **Gundula Janowitz, Anja Silja, Else-Margrete Gardelli, Dorothea Siebert, Rita Bartos** (sops), **Sona Cervená** (mez) Flower Maidens; **Bayreuth Festival Chorus and Orchestra/Hans Knappertsbusch.** Philips 416 390-2PH4. Notes, text and translation included. Recorded at the 1962 Bayreuth Festival. From SAL3475/9 (11/64).

④ 4h 10' ADD 6/86

Wagner. PARSIFAL. **Peter Hofmann** (ten) Parsifal; **José van Dam** (bass-bar) Amfortas; **Victor von Halem** (bass) Titurel; **Kurt Moll** (bass) Gurnemanz; **Siegmund Nimsgern** (bass) Klingsor; **Dunja Vejzovic** (mez) Kundry; **Claes H. Ahnsjöh** (ten), **Kurt Rydl** (bass) Knights of the Grail; **Marjon Lambriks, Anne Gjevang** (mezs), **Heiner Hopfner** (ten), **Georg Tichy** (bass) Squires; **Barbara Hendricks, Janet Perry, Inga Nielsen** (sops), **Audrey Michael** (mez), **Doris Soffel, Rohângiz Yachmi** (contrs) Flower Maidens; **Hanna Schwarz** (mez) Voice from above; **German Opera Chorus; Berlin Philharmonic Orchestra/Herbert von Karajan.** DG 413 347-2GH4. Notes, text and translation included. From 2741 002 (4/81).

④ 4h 16' DDD 10/84

There have been many fine recordings of this great Eastertide opera, but none have so magnificently captured the power, the spiritual grandeur, the human frailty and the almost unbearable beauty of the work as Hans Knappertsbusch.

This live recording has a cast that has few equals. Hotter is superb, fleshing out Gurnemanz with a depth of insight that has never been surpassed since. London's Amfortas captures the frightening sense of impotence and anguish with painful directness whilst Thomas's Parsifal grows as the performance progresses and is no mean achievement. Dalis may lack that final degree of sensuousness but gives a fine interpretation. Throughout Knappertsbusch exercises a quite unequalled control over the proceedings; it is a fine testament to a great conductor. The Bayreuth acoustic is well reproduced and all in all it is a profound and moving experience.

Nevertheless, Karajan's is also is a haunting performance. Beginning in an almost leisurely fashion, it grows in intensity, expansive in the first Act, fiercely concentrated in the second, inspired in the third. Its Gurnemanz and Kundry are excellent and José van Dam's Amfortas is extraordinarily beautiful. Peter Hofmann is rather the reverse, expressive with words but uneven in voice-production. The recording has a few quirks of balance and sound-level, but in general it is something of a technical triumph: historically notable too, for it was the first operatic recording to be both digital and multi-track.

Wagner. DER RING DES NIBELUNGEN.
DAS RHEINGOLD. **Theo Adam** (bass-bar) Wotan; **Gerd Nienstedt** (bass) Donner; Hermin **Esser** (ten) Froh; **Wolfgang Windgassen** (ten) Loge; **Gustav Neidlinger** (bass) Alberich; **Erwin Wohlfahrt** (ten) Mime; **Martti Talvela** (bass) Fasolt; **Kurt Boehme** (bass) Fafner; **Annelies Burmeister** (mez) Fricka; **Anja Silja** (sop) Freia; **Vera Soukupova** (mez) Erda; **Dorothea Siebert** (sop) Woglinde; **Helga Dernesch** (sop) Wellgunde; **Ruth Hesse** (mez) Flosshilde; **Bayreuth Festival Chorus and Orchestra/Karl Böhm.** Philips 412 475-2PH2. Notes, text and translation included. Recorded at a performance in the Festspielhaus, Bayreuth in 1967. From 6747 037 (9/73).

② 2h 17' ADD 7/85 Ⓑ

DIE WALKURE. **James King** (ten) Siegmund; **Leonie Rysanek** (sop) Sieglinde; **Gerd Nienstedt** (bass) Hunding; **Birgit Nilsson** (sop) Brünnhilde; **Theo Adam** (bass) Wotan; **Annelies Burmeister** (mez) Fricka, Siegrune; **Danica Mastilovic** (sop) Gerthilde; **Helga Dernesch** (sop) Ortlinde; **Gertraud Hopf** (mez) Waltraute; **Sieglinde Wagner** (contr) Schwertleite; **Liane Synek** (sop) Helmwige; **Elisabeth Schärtel** (contr) Grimgerde; **Sona Cervená** (mez) Rossweisse; **Bayreuth Festival Chorus and Orchestra/Karl Böhm.** Philips 412 478-2PH4. Notes, text and translation included. Recorded at a performance in the Festspielhaus, Bayreuth in 1967. From 6747 037 (9/73).

④ 3h 30' ADD 2/85 Ⓑ

SIEGFRIED. **Wolfgang Windgassen** (ten) Siegfried; **Erwin Wohlfahrt** (ten) Mime; **Theo Adam** (bass) Wanderer; **Gustav Neidlinger** (bass) Alberich; **Birgit Nilsson** (sop) Brünnhilde; **Vera Soukupova** (mez) Erda; **Kurt Boehme** (bass) Fafner; **Erika Köth** (sop) Waldvogel; **Bayreuth Festival Orchestra/Karl Böhm.** Philips 412 483-2PH4. Notes, text and translation included. Recorded at a performance in the Festspielhaus, Bayreuth in 1967. From 6747 037 (9/73).

④ 3h 43' ADD 8/85 Ⓑ

GOTTERDAMMERUNG. **Wolfgang Windgassen** (ten) Siegfried; **Birgit Nilsson** (sop) Brünnhilde; **Josef Greindl** (bass) Hagen; **Martha Mödl** (mez) Waltraute; **Thomas Stewart** (bar) Gunther; **Gustav Neidlinger** (bass-bar) Alberich; **Ludmila Dvořáková** (sop) Gutrune; **Marga Höffgen** (contr) First Norn; **Annelies Burmeister** (mez) Second Norn; **Anja Silja** (sop) Third Norn; **Dorothea Siebert** (sop) Woglinde; **Helga Dernesch** (sop) Wellgunde; **Sieglinde Wagner** (contr) Flosshilde; **Bayreuth Festival Chorus and**

Orchestra/Karl Böhm. Philips 412 488-2PH4. Notes, text and translation included. Recorded at a performance in the Festspielhaus, Bayreuth in 1967. From 6747 037 (9/73).

④ 4h 9' ADD 5/85 **B**

DAS RHEINGOLD[a]. **George London** (bass-bar) Wotan; **Kirsten Flagstad** (sop) Fricka; **Set Svanholm** (ten) Loge; **Paul Kuen** (ten) Mime; **Gustav Neidlinger** (bass) Alberich; **Claire Watson** (sop) Freia; **Waldemar Kmentt** (ten) Froh; **Eberhard Waechter** (bar) Donner; **Jean Madeira** (contr) Erda; **Walter Kreppel** (bass) Fasolt; **Kurt Böhme** (bass) Fafner; **Ode Balsborg** (sop) Woglinde; **Hetty Plümacher** (sop) Wellgunde; **Ira Malaniuk** (mez) Flosshilde.
DIE WALKURE[b]. **James King** (ten) Siegmund; **Régine Crespin** (sop) Sieglinde; **Birgit Nilsson** (sop) Brünnhilde; **Hans Hotter** (bass-bar) Wotan; **Christa Ludwig** (mez) Fricka; **Gottlob Frick** (bass) Hunding; **Vera Schlosser** (sop) Gerhilde; **Berit Lindholm** (sop) Helmwige; **Helga Dernesch** (sop) Ortlinde; **Brigitte Fassbaender** (mez) Waltraute; **Claudia Hellmann** (sop) Rossweisse; **Vera Little** (contr) Siegrune; **Marilyn Tyler** (sop) Grimgerde; **Helen Watts** (contr) Schwertleite.
SIEGFRIED[c]. **Wolfgang Windgassen** (ten) Siegfried; **Hans Hotter** (bass-bar) Wanderer; **Birgit Nilsson** (sop) Brünnhilde; **Gerhard Stolze** (ten) Mime; **Gustav Neidlinger** (bass) Alberich; **Marga Höffgen** (contr) Erda; **Kurt Boehme** (bass) Fafner; **Dame Joan Sutherland** (sop) Woodbird.
GOTTERDAMMERUNG[d]. **Birgit Nilsson** (sop) Brünnhilde; **Wolfgang Windgassen** (ten) Siegfried; **Gottlob Frick** (bass) Hagen; **Gustav Neidlinger** (bass) Alberich; **Dietrich Fischer-Dieskau** (bar) Gunther; **Claire Watson** (sop) Gutrune; **Christa Ludwig** (mez) Waltraute; **Lucia Popp** (sop) Woglinde; **Dame Gwyneth Jones** (sop) Wellgunde; **Maureen Guy** (mez) Flosshilde; **Helen Watts** (contr) First Norn; **Grace Hoffman** (mez) Second Norn; **Anita Välkki** (sop) Third Norn; **Vienna State Opera Chorus; Vienna Philharmonic Orchestra/Sir Georg Solti.** Decca 414 100-2DM15. Notes, texts and translations included. Item marked [a] from SXL2101/3 (3/59), [b] SET312/6 (9/66), [c] SET242/6 (4/63), [d] SET292/7 (5/65).

⑮ 14h 37' ADD 3/89 £ **B**

Wagner's *Der Ring des Nibelungen* is the greatest music-drama ever penned. It deals with the eternal questions of power, love, personal responsibility and moral behaviour, and has always been open to numerous interpretations, both dramatic and musical. For every generation, it presents a new challenge, yet certain

musical performances have undoubtedly stood the test of time. One would recommend the recording made at Bayreuth in 1967 because, above all others, it represents a true and living account of a huge work as it was performed in the opera house for which it was largely conceived. Every artist who appears at Bayreuth seems to find an extra dedication in their comportment there, and on this occasion many of the singers and the conductor surpassed what they achieved elsewhere. Böhm's reading is notable for its dramatic drive and inner tension. For the most part he also encompasses the metaphysical aspects of the score as well, and he procures playing of warmth and depth from the Bayreuth orchestra. Birgit Nilsson heads the cast as an unsurpassed Brünnhilde, wonderfully vivid in her characterization and enunciation, tireless and gleaming in voice. Wolfgang Windgassen is equally committed and alert as her Siegfried and Theo Adam is an experienced, worldly-wise Wotan. No *Ring* recording is perfect or could possibly tell the whole story but this faithfully recorded, straightforward version conveys the strength and force of the epic's meaning.

So many words have been written about the Decca recordings that to read all of them would undoubtedly take a good deal longer than a complete performance of the *Ring*. What should still be said is that although Solti's interpretation was not captured over a week or so in a single theatrical presentation of the cycle, it remains not only a remarkably consistent but a consistently exciting experience. John Culshaw's production has provoked much comment over the years, usually concerning his use of sound effects, and also debating the vexed question of whether the generally backward placing of the singers makes it difficult or impossible for them to command the full, riveted attention that Wagner's heroes and heroines demand. So it must be emphasized again that for the most part the singers do not sound as if they are drowning in a turbulent orchestral sea; and it is one of the great virtues of these discs that the quality of the singing equals the splendour of the Vienna Philharmonic's playing. Hans Hotter's Wotan is an immensely accomplished, powerful and moving performance and though some collectors may regret that a different singer was used for the *Rheingold* Wotan, George London is excellent in his own right. As Siegfried, Wolfgang Windgassen can seem almost too dignified and decorous in comparison with his more impetuous rivals, but he is always secure and steadfast in face of the role's tremendous challenges, and a worthy partner to Nilsson's mercurial Brünnhilde. One could go on. There really are no weak links, and although at medium price the documentation is not as complete as it might be, Solti's *Ring* is now an irresistible bargain.

Wagner. SIEGFRIED (sung in English). **Alberto Remedios** (ten) Siegfried; **Norman Bailey** (bar) Wanderer; **Rita Hunter** (sop) Brünnhilde; **Gregory Dempsey** (ten) Mime; **Derek Hammond-Stroud** (bar) Alberich; **Anne Collins** (contr) Erda; **Clifford Grant** (bass) Fafner; **Maurine London** (sop) Woodbird; **Sadler's Wells Opera Orchestra/Sir Reginald Goodall.** EMI CMS7 63595-2. Notes and English text included. Recorded at performances in the Coliseum, London on August 2nd, 8th and 21st, 1973. From HMV SLS875 (4/74).

④ 4h 38' ADD 3/91   £ 9 P Ⓑ

The Goodall recording of the *Ring* has over the years gained an almost legendary reputation. Now that the first work that was committed to disc has appeared on CD, that reputation proves to have been well justified. The breadth and cogency of Goodall's reading, its epic quality, once more stand out as a magnificent achievement. Even more remarkable is Goodall's unerring sense of transition, as important in this opera as it is in any of the cycle's components. For this cycle Goodall had assembled a group of specially prepared singers; every part was carefully cast and sung with a sense of characterization and articulacy of enunciation (in Andrew Porter's excellent translation) that will surely gain the performance new friends. The team is headed by Alberto Remedios's youthful-sounding and forthright Siegfried, a performance that nicely combines lyrical ardour with heroic timbre. Around him in the various colloquia of which this work is largely comprised are Gregory Dempsey's characterful but seldom exaggerated Mime, Norman Bailey's authoritative, worldly-wise Wanderer and eventually, on the mountain-top, Rita Hunter's gleaming Brünnhilde. To these fine performances can be added Derek Hammond-Stroud's menacing Alberich and Anne Collins's grave, imposing Erda. The live recording has stood the test of time. This is a performance worthy to be placed among any in the original language.

Wagner. GOTTERDAMMERUNG. **Hildegard Behrens** (sop) Brünnhilde; **Reiner Goldberg** (ten) Siegfried; **Matti Salminen** (bass) Hagen; **Ekkehard Wlaschiha** (bar) Alberich; **Bernd Weikl** (bar) Gunther; **Cheryl Studer** (sop) Gutrune; **Hanna Schwarz** (mez) Waltraute; **Hei-Kyung Hong** (sop) Woglinde; **Diane Kesling** (mez) Wellgunde; **Meredith Parsons** (contr) Flosshilde; **Helga Dernesch** (mez) First Norn; **Tatiana Troyanos** (mez) Second Norn; **Andrea Gruber** (sop) Third Norn; **Metropolitan Opera Chorus and Orchestra/James Levine**. DG 429 385-2GH4. Notes, text and translation included.

④ 4h 30' DDD 8/91

This performance of the climax of the *Ring* cycle is of a stature to match the inspired nature of the opera. Levine encompasses every aspect, heroic and tragic, of the vast work, finding the right tempos for each section and welding them

James Levine   [photo: DG]

together as imperceptibly as the composer into a consistent and inspired whole. He is magnificently supported by his own Metropolitan Opera Orchestra who play and are recorded with remarkable fidelity and virtuosity. Levine's cast, the one with whom he has performed the work at the Met and on television, is as about as excellent as could be assembled today, headed by Hildegard Behrens's all-consuming Brünnhilde, responsive to every aspect of the role's many-faceted character. Reiner Goldberg isn't quite her equal as an interpreter but, as Siegfried, he sings with unfailing

musicality and with a firm line. Evil is convincingly represented by Salminen's implacable, black-voiced Hagen. Hanna Schwarz is a deeply eloquent Waltraute, who makes the very most of her long narration. Cheryl Studer's lyrical Gutrune and Bernd Weikl's sound Gunther are further assets, as are the splendid Norns and Rhinemaidens.

William Walton
British 1902-1983

Walton. Violin Concerto (1939). Viola Concerto (1929). **Nigel Kennedy** (vn, va); **Royal Philharmonic Orchestra/André Previn**. EMI CDC7 49628-2. From EL749628-1 (1/88).

57' DDD 4/88

These Concertos are among the most beautiful written this century. Walton was in his late twenties when he composed the viola work and in it he achieved a depth of emotion, a range of ideas and a technical assurance beyond anything he had so far written. Lacking in the brilliance of the violin, the viola has an inherently contemplative tonal quality and Walton matches this to perfection in his score, complementing it rather than trying to compensate as other composers have done. There is a larger element of virtuosity in the Violin Concerto, but it is never allowed to dominate the musical argument. Sir Yehudi Menuhin recorded both works and now Nigel Kennedy has equalled, and in some respects surpassed his achievement, giving wonderfully warm and characterful performances which are likely to stand unchallenged as a coupling for a long time. He produces a beautiful tone quality on both of his instruments, which penetrates to the heart of the aching melancholy of Walton's slow music, and he combines it with an innate, highly developed and spontaneous-sounding sense of rhythmic drive and bounce which propels the quick movements forward with great panache. Previn has long been a persuasive Waltonian and the RPO respond marvellously, with crisp and alert playing throughout. The recordings are very clear and naturally balanced with the solo instrument set in a believable perspective.

Walton. The Quest—ballet (ed. Palmer). The Wise Virgins—ballet suite. **London Philharmonic Orchestra/Bryden Thomson.** Chandos CHAN8871.

62' DDD 4/91

These two strongly-coloured Walton ballets make an especially effective coupling in such brilliantly played, attractively recorded performances. And one, *The Quest*, based on Spenser's *Faerie Queen*, is recorded here in its entirety for the first time. The work was a rushed, wartime enterprise, "written more or less as one writes for the films", as the composer commented in a letter to John Warrack. It was first performed in April 1943 by the Sadler's Wells Ballet company and was not afterwards revived; the score was lost until 1958 and even then only a four-movement suite—arranged by Vilem Tausky, and approved and later recorded by Walton—saw the light of day. In reviving the work, Christopher Palmer has added the extra instruments used in the suite, knowing that Walton had been inhibited by the small size of the band available to him for the work's première. *The Wise Virgins*, based on music by J.S. Bach, is perennially popular and, like *The Quest*, receives a typically full-blooded, totally committed reading from Bryden Thomson, who stirs the London Philharmonic to great heights of power and dexterity. The recording venue's liberal acoustic has not prevented Chandos from letting us hear all that Walton intended.

Walton. Symphonies—No. 1 in B flat minor[a]; No. 2[b]. [a]**London Philharmonic Orchestra,** [b]**London Symphony Orchestra/Sir Charles Mackerras.** EMI Eminence CD-EMX2151.

74' DDD 12/89 £ 9ₚ

Vaughan Williams. The Wasps—Overture[a]. **Walton.** Symphony No. 1 in B flat minor[b]. **London Symphony Orchestra/ André Previn.** RCA Victor Gold Seal GD87830. Item marked [a] from SB6856 (3/72), [b] SB6691 (1/67).

52' ADD 2/89 £

Walton's First Symphony has yet to receive the ideal recording but Mackerras's version has a weighty vigour that does not give much to any version currently available. Where this issue really scores is in coupling a particularly fine account of the more elusive and rather less popular Second Symphony. This is a much misunderstood and, thereby, underrated work. With its brief span and costly instrumentation it is not its own best advocate for concert programming, yet it provides the ideal complement to the First Symphony on CD. The LPO summon here both brittle incisiveness and luxuriant rapture to capture the quixotic moods of this distracted piece, and Mackerras tailors the balance to the acoustic in order to allow evocative inner lines to emerge. This performance would be very recommendable at full-price: on Eminence, it's essential.

Although Previn's version of the First Symphony is still easily the finest on disc, there were always doubts over the quality of the recording which, even when new, sounded dull-edged and lacking in inner detail. Now, even though the sound is still not first-rate, digital processing has done so much to clean up the textures that the recording quality is no longer an inhibition. From the very opening, Previn maintains enormous tension by keeping the rhythmic vigour at full stretch and, even in the slow third movement, he allows the emotional bite no real relaxation. This singularity of purpose, the great brilliance of orchestral sonority and empathetic balance are the key features in the success of this performance, compounding the intensity as the work progresses.

Vaughan Williams's music for Aristophanes's play *The Wasps* was written for a 1909 Cambridge production and its finest features are embodied in the Overture. Previn's dazzling performance has been a long-time favourite, with the LSO at its best and pulling out all the stops. The recording is exemplary, spacious and detailed, marvellously balanced and yet unobtrusive. Coupled, these two performances remain a wonderful reminder of the Previn/LSO partnership at its finest.

Walton. FILM MUSIC, Volume 2. **Academy of St Martin in the Fields/ Sir Neville Marriner.** Chandos CHAN8870.
Spitfire Prelude and Fugue. A Wartime Sketchbook (arr. Palmer). Escape Me Never—suite (arr. Palmer). The Three Sisters (ed. Palmer). The Battle of Britain—suite.

65' DDD 12/90

Walton's film work reveals a remarkably fluent appreciation of the important role music plays in the medium and his magnificent scores for Olivier's Shakespeare trilogy (*Henry V*, *Hamlet* and *Richard III*) have quite rightly crossed over into the concert repertoire. But it is a little unfortunate that their popularity has somewhat overshadowed Walton's other achievements in this area for, as this collection proves, much more of his film music merits similar recognition. The emphasis here is on the composer's music for the war film and the familiar *Spitfire Prelude and Fugue*, with its stirring and characteristically solid march theme, provides a strong opening. *A Wartime Sketchbook* is an adroit arrangement by Christopher Palmer of contrasting segments from *Went the Day Well?*, *Next of Kin*, *The Foreman went to France* and *Battle of Britain* which lives up to its title most successfully (Walton's own authentic foxtrots, put over with delightful ease by the Academy, are particularly evocative), whilst the 11-minute selection from *Battle of Britain* serves to emphasize once again the idiocy of the nameless studio executive who decreed that the entire score should be scrapped (the stunning "Battle in the air" did remain in the film, however). Away from the battlefield, the programme also includes *Escape Me Never*, a heady and warmly romantic score complete with a strikingly rhythmic ballet, and *The Three Sisters*, Walton's final film score which perhaps overplays its references to the Russian national anthem but compensates with a lovely waltz in the "Dream Sequence". Sir Neville has just the right approach to this music and the orchestra's sturdy performances have been captured in a bright and well-detailed recording.

Walton. Façade[a]. Overtures—Portsmouth Point; Scapino[b]. Siesta[b].
Arnold. English Dances, Op. 33[c]. [a]**Dame Edith Sitwell;** [a]**Sir Peter Pears** (spkrs); [a]**English Opera Group Ensemble/Anthony Collins;** [bc]**London Philharmonic Orchestra/Sir Adrian Boult.** Decca London mono 425 661-2LM. Items marked [a] from LXT2977 (11/54), [b] LXT5028 (6/55), [c] LW5166 (6/55).

> 74' DDD

Walton. Façade—an entertainment[a].
Sitwell. Poems. **Prunella Scales, Timothy West** (spkrs); [a]members of **London Mozart Players/Jane Glover.** ASV CDDCA679. Texts included.
Poems: Two Kitchen Songs. Five Songs—Daphne; The Peach Tree; The Strawberry; The Greengage Tree; The Nectarine Tree. On the Vanity of Human Aspirations. Two Poems from "Facade"—The Drum; Clowns' Houses. The Wind's Bastinado. The Dark Song. Colonel Fantock. Most Lovely Shade. Heart and Mind.

> 64' DDD/ADD 4/90

Both these issues deserve to be considered for a well-stocked collection. The Decca is the classic and authoritative reading of the fully approved selection of *Façade* settings. Dame Edith herself reads two-thirds of the numbers, Sir Peter the remaining third. The poetess herself reads them with such *joie de vivre*, such a natural feeling for her own verses and inflections that nobody could be expected to rival her. Her timing is perfect, her delivery deliciously idiosyncratic, the intonations obviously what she and presumably Walton wanted. Sir Peter isn't far behind her in ability to relish the writing and the instrumental ensemble plays with refinement allied to virtuosity. The 1950s mono recording stands the test of time remarkably well. The new performance offers something rather different. Scales and West often divide poems between them, which is a modern and not untoward fashion. They also employ accents where the texts suggest them. That gives the famous pieces a different aspect, but one that is in itself quite valid when executed with such flair as here and the speakers are well supported by artists from the London Mozart Players. They also include some re-discovered numbers. Here the fillers are more appropriate than on the Decca/London reissue: more poems by Sitwell, lambent, florid, wordy verse, read with all the character and feeling one would expect from these actors. The recording is faultlessly managed.

Carl Maria von Weber

German 1786-1826

Weber. Clarinet Concertos—No. 1 in F minor, J114; No. 2 in E flat major, J118. Clarinet Concertino in E flat major, J109. **Orchestra of the Age of Enlightenment/Antony Pay** (cl). Virgin Classics VC7 90720-2.

> 52' DDD 10/88

Among the major composers, it was Weber who most of all enriched the solo repertory of the clarinet. He was inspired by his acquaintance with a fine player, in this case Heinrich Bärmann, and for this recording Antony Pay has used a modern copy of a seven-keyed instrument of around 1800, to which two extra keys have been added to come nearer to the ten-keyed instrument that Bärmann played. The orchestra also uses period instruments and in several passages, such as the hymnlike one with horns in the slow movement of the F minor Concerto, one hears this in their subtly different tone. The music itself is consistently fluent and elegant, witty and attractive and is stylishly played, with lovely clarinet tone in all registers.

Weber. ORCHESTRAL WORKS. **Berlin Philharmonic Orchestra/ Herbert von Karajan.** DG Galleria 419 070-2GGA.
Invitation to the Dance. *Overtures*—Der Beherrscher der Geister; Euryanthe; Oberon; Abu Hassan; Der Freischütz; Peter Schmoll.

56' ADD 6/88

Often rich in atmosphere and melodically inspired, Weber's operas invariably have an overture at which, as this mid-price disc illustrates, he excelled. The distillation of the mood and thematic significance achieved in these brief introductions invariably reached great concentration. A slow prelude, often mystical and veiled in character, leads into a faster *Vivace* section which presents the primary thematic material for the forthcoming opera. The overtures to *Oberon*, *Der Freischütz* and *Peter Schmoll* work in this way, whilst *Abu Hassan*, *Euryanthe* and *Der Beherrscher der Geister* literally burst in with unchecked verve and excitement—the first having a Turkish flavour with its use of percussion, the last having a tremendous timpani call set at its centre. Karajan and the Berlin Philharmonic Orchestra play these skilful works for all they are worth and they sound even better for it.

Weber. DER FREISCHUTZ. **Peter Schreier** (ten) Max (Hans Jörn Weber); **Gundula Janowitz** (sop) Agathe (Regina Jeske); **Edith Mathis** (sop) Aennchen (Ingrid Hille); **Theo Adam** (bass) Caspar (Gerhard Paul); **Bernd Weikl** (bar) Ottokar (Otto Mellies); **Siegfried Vogel** (bass) Cuno (Gerd Biewer); **Franz Crass** (bass) Hermit; **Gerhard Paul** (spkr) Samiel; **Günther Leib** (bar) Kilian (Peter Hölzel); **Leipzig Radio Chorus; Staatskapelle Dresden/Carlos Kleiber.** DG 415 432-2GH2. Notes, text and translation included. From 2720 071 (11/73).

② 130' ADD 11/86

This opera tells of a forester Max and his pact with the forces of darkness to give him the ability to shoot without missing. Carlos Kleiber's recordings are always fascinating and for this one he went back to the manuscript seeking out details rarely heard in the standard opera house text. His direction is imaginative and where controversial (his tempos do tend to extremes) one feels he presents a strong case. His cast is very fine too: Schreier's Max is more thoughtful than some, though always ready to spring back after his hellish encounters. Janowitz is a lovely Agathe and Mathis a perky Aennchen, whilst Adam's Caspar is suitably diabolic. The use of actors to speak the dialogue does take a little getting used to, but the recording is good and the Dresden orchestra play magnificently.

Anton Webern

Austrian 1883-1945

Webern. COMPLETE WORKS, Opp. 1-31. **Various artists.** Sony Classical CD45845. Notes, texts and translations included. From 79204 (12/78).
Passacaglia, Op. 1 (London Symphony Orchestra/Pierre Boulez). Entflieht auf leichten Kähnen, Op. 2 (John Alldis Choir/Boulez). Five Songs from "Der siebente Ring", Op. 3. Five Songs, Op. 4 (Heather Harper, sop; Charles Rosen, pf). Five Movements, Op. 5 (Juilliard Quartet). Six Pieces, Op. 6 (LSO/ Boulez). Four Pieces, Op. 7 (Isaac Stern, vn; Rosen, pf). Two Songs, Op. 8 (Harper, sop; chamber ensemble/Boulez). Six Bagatelles, Op. 9 (Juilliard Qt). Five Pieces, Op. 10 (LSO/Boulez). Three Little Pieces, Op. 11 (Gregor Piatigorsky, vc; Rosen, pf). Four Songs, Op. 12 (Harper, sop; Rosen, pf). Four Songs, Op. 13. Six Songs, Op. 14 (Harper, sop; chbr ens/Boulez). Five Sacred Songs, Op. 15. Five Canons on Latin Texts, Op. 16 (Halina Lukomska, sop;

chbr ens/Boulez). Three Songs, Op. 18 (Lukomska, sop; John Williams, gtr; Colin Bradbury, cl/Boulez). Two Songs, Op. 19 (John Alldis Ch, mbrs LSO/ Boulez). String Trio, Op. 20 (mbrs Juilliard Qt). Symphony, Op. 21 (LSO/ Boulez). Quartet, Op. 22 (Robert Marcellus, cl; Abraham Weinstein, sax; Daniel Majeske, vn; Rosen, pf/Boulez). Three Songs from "Viae inviae", Op. 23 (Lukomska, sop; Rosen, pf). Concerto, Op. 24 (mbrs LSO/Boulez). Three Songs, Op. 25 (Lukomska, sop; Rosen, pf). Das Augenlicht, Op. 26 (John Alldis Ch, LSO/Boulez). Piano Variations, Op. 27 (Rosen, pf). String Quartet, Op. 28 (Juilliard Qt). Cantata No. 1, Op. 29 (Lukomska, sop; John Alldis Ch; LSO/ Boulez). Variations, Op. 30 (LSO/Boulez). Cantata No. 2, Op. 31 (Lukomska, sop; Barry McDaniel, bar; John Alldis Ch; LSO/Boulez). Five Movements, Op. 5—orchestral version (LSO/Boulez). **Bach** (orch. Webern): Musikalischen Opfer, BWV1079—Fuga (Ricercata) No. 2 (LSO/Boulez). **Schubert** (orch. Webern): Deutsche Tänze, D820 (Frankfurt Radio Orchestra/Anton Webern. Recorded at a performance in the studios of Radio Frankfurt on December 29th, 1932).

③ 3h 43' ADD 6/91

Webern is as 'classic' to Pierre Boulez as Mozart or Brahms are to most other conductors, and when he is able to persuade performers to share his view the results can be remarkable—lucid in texture, responsive in expression. Despite his well-nigh exclusive concern with miniature forms, there are many sides to Webern, and although this set is not equally successful in realizing all of them, it leaves the listener in no doubt about the music's sheer variety, as well as its emotional power, whether the piece in question is an ingenious canon-by-inversion or a simple, folk-like *Lied*. From a long list of performers I would single out Heather Harper and the Juilliard Quartet for special commendation; and the smooth confidence of the John Alldis Choir is also notable. The recordings were made over a five-year period (1968-72) and have the typical CBS dryness of that time. Even so, in the finest performances which Boulez himself directs—the *Orchestral Variations*, Op. 30 is perhaps the high point—that remarkable radiance of spirit so special to Webern is vividly conveyed. It is a fascinating bonus to hear Webern himself conducting his Schubert arrangements—music from another world, yet with an economy and emotional poise that Webern in his own way sought to emulate.

Webern. ORCHESTRAL WORKS. **Berlin Philharmonic Orchestra/ Herbert von Karajan.** DG 20th Century Classics 423 254-2GC. From 2711 014 (3/75).
Passacaglia, Op. 1. Five Movements, Op. 5. Six Pieces, Op. 6. Symphony, Op. 21.

46' ADD 7/88

This mid-price disc, with good, digitally remastered sound, provides an excellent introduction to one of modern music's most important and influential masters. All three phases of Webern's development are represented. In the *Passacaglia* the youthful late-romantic is ready to shake off the shackles of Brahms and Strauss, and Karajan brings particular intensity to the work's moments of crisis and upheaval. In Op. 5 and Op. 6 the process of miniaturization is well under way, and together they provide powerful evidence of the fact that concentration and economy brought no loss of emotional power. Even in the less extravagant orchestration of the 1928 version, the funeral march movement from Op. 6 is as stark and volcanic an experience of raw grief and despair as any Mahler Adagio. After this the ten-minute, two-movement Symphony, with its coolly symmetrical serial canons, may sound like a retreat from reality. It is certainly more classical in concept than the earlier works, but that means a more equal balance of restraint and expressiveness, not a rejection of either. As an outstanding exponent of late-romantic symphonies, Karajan is especially sensitive to the lyricism, as well as the refinement, of the music.

Webern. COMPLETE MUSIC FOR STRING QUARTET. **Quartetto Italiano** (Paolo Borciani, Elisa Pegreffi, vns; Piero Farulli, va; Franco Rossi, vc). Philips 420 796-2PH. From 6500 105 (7/71).
Slow Movement for string quartet (1905). String Quartet (1905). Five Movements for string quartet, Op. 5. Six Bagatelles for string quartet, Op. 9. String Quartet, Op. 28.

| 53' ADD 4/88 |

Webern's embracing of the 12-tone compositional technique was nothing if not absolute. Unlike Berg he sought the logical conclusion of this technique with a single-mindedness that admitted nothing of Berg's romanticism. One result of his desire to hone his music down to the purity of utterance dictated by the 12-tone technique is its extreme brevity—his entire *oeuvre* fits on to three LPs. This disc contains his string quartet music and makes a fascinating survey of his development as a composer. About half the works are immediately accessible, eloquent and expressive in turns, and beautifully performed by the sadly missed Quartetto Italiano. Opp. 5 and 9 show Webern's powers as a composer dealing with miniature forms and the String Quartet, Op. 28 of 1938 shows him at his most compressed, relying on special string techniques and that extreme intensity only silence can express. One can only speculate where Webern's musical quest might have led had he not met such a tragic end.

Kurt Weill

German/American 1900-1950

Weill. SONGS. **Ute Lemper** (sop); **Berlin Radio Ensemble/John Mauceri.** Decca New Line 425 204-2DNL. Texts and translations included.
Der Silbersee—Ich bin eine arme Verwandte (Fennimores-Lied); Rom war eine Stadt (Cäsars Tod); Lied des Lotterieagenten. Die Dreigroschenoper—Die Moritat von Mackie Messer; Salomon-Song; Die Ballade von der sexuellen Hörigkeit. Das Berliner Requiem—Zu Potsdam unter den Eichen (arr. Hazell). Nannas-Lied. Aufstieg und Fall der Stadt Mahagonny—Alabama Song; Wie man sich bettet. Je ne t'aime pas. One Touch of Venus—I'm a stranger here myself; Westwind; Speak low.

| 50' DDD 3/89 |

The songs in this collection are mostly from the major works Weill composed between 1928 and 1933, but also included are one from his years in France and three items from the 1943 Broadway musical *One Touch of Venus*. The collection introduces a most exciting talent in the person of Ute Lemper. By comparison with the husky, growling delivery often accorded Weill's songs in the manner of his widow Lotte Lenya, we here have a voice of appealing clarity and warmth. What distinguishes her singing, though, is the way in which these attributes of vocal purity are allied to a quite irresistible dramatic intensity. Her "Song of the Lottery Agent" is an absolute *tour de force*, apt to leave the listener emotionally drained, and her *Je ne t'aime pas* is almost equally overwhelming. Not least in the three numbers from *One Touch of Venus*, sung in perfect English, she displays a commanding musical theatre presence. With John Mauceri on hand to provide authentic musical accompaniments, this is, one feels, how Weill's songs were meant to be heard.

Weill. Die sieben Todsünden[a]. Kleine Dreigroschenmusik. [a]**Julia Migenes** (sop); [a]**Robert Tear,** [a]**Stuart Kale** (tens); [a]**Alan Opie** (bar); [a]**Roderick Kennedy** (bass); **London Symphony Orchestra/Michael Tilson Thomas.** CBS Masterworks CD44529. Text and translation included.

55' DDD 3/89

The 'ballet with song', *Die sieben Todsünden* ("The Seven Deadly Sins") was the last of Kurt Weill's collaborations with the dramatist Bertolt Brecht. It consists of moments devoted to each of the seven sins, the whole bound together with a prologue and epilogue. Though

Julia Migenes   [photo: Erato/Sarratt]

less widely known than *The Threepenny Opera*, some consider it Weill's masterpiece, and certainly there is writing of a symphonic passion that one does not always find elsewhere in the Brecht/Weill output. Unfortunately this recording uses a version of the score produced after the composer's death, incorporating much downward transposition of the vocal line and some reorchestration. Still, the work is brilliantly done, with Julia Migenes bringing out the bitterness and irony of the text whilst combining it with a seductive, even erotic soprano. In support Michael Tilson

Thomas weaves a dazzling sound, bringing out the jazz elements of the score and unifying the movements quite superbly. The same virtues are also to be found in Weill's dance-band suite from the *Dreigroschenoper*, which makes a compelling fill-up. Recorded sound is first-class.

Weill. DIE DREIGROSCHENOPER. **Lotte Lenya,** Jenny; **Erich Schellow,** Macheath; **Willy Trenk-Trebitsch,** Mr Peachum; **Trude Hesterburg,** Mrs Peachum; **Johanna von Kóczián,** Polly Peachum; **Wolfgang Grunert,** Tiger Brown; **Inge Wolffberg,** Lucy; **Wolfgang Neuss,** Streetsinger; **Günther-Arndt Choir;** members of the Dance Orchestra of **Radio Free Berlin/ Wilhelm Brückner-Rüggeberg.** CBS Masterworks CD42637. Notes, text and translation included. From 77268 (12/72).

68' ADD 3/89

In *Die Dreigroschenoper* ("The Threepenny Opera") Kurt Weill sought to match the satire of Bertolt Brecht's updating of John Gay's *The Beggar's Opera* with numbers in the dance rhythms and jazz-tinged orchestrations of the time. The number that later became famous as "Mack the Knife" is merely the best known of the many catchy numbers in a score that none the less bears the hallmark of a cultivated musician. This 1958 reading has eclipsed all others. It has the distinction of featuring the composer's widow, Lotte Lenya, in the role of Jenny that she had created back in 1928. The recording carries about it an undeniable feeling of authenticity in the pungency of its satire and the catchiness of its score. Johanna von Kóczian is a charming Polly, Erich Schellow a winning Macheath, and Trude Hesterberg a formidable Frau Peachum, while Wilhelm Brückner-Rüggeberg has just the right feel for Weill's dance rhythms. This is an absolutely complete recording of the score, including the once expurgated

"Ballad of Sexual Dependency" and the usually omitted "Jealousy Song". Despite its age, the recorded sound remains good, and the whole is a compelling experience.

Weill. DER SILBERSEE. **Wolfgang Schmidt** (ten) Severin; **Hildegard Heichele** (sop) Fennimore; **Hans Korte** (bar) Olim; **Eva Tamassy** (mez) Frau von Luber; **Udo Holdorf** (ten) Baron Laur; **Frederic Mayer** (ten) Lottery Agent; **Cologne Pro Musica; Cologne Radio Symphony Orchestra / Jan Latham-König.** Capriccio 60 011-2. Notes, text and translation included.

② 1h 47' DDD 8/90

The sub-title of *Der Silbersee*, "A winter's tale", is to be interpreted both literally and metaphorically, for this is a remarkable parable of the dark night of the soul of a Germany about to be plunged into Nazi oppression: the infamous Reichstag fire took place only a matter of days after its première. The symbolism is patent in this tale of poverty, famine, avarice, unscrupulous trickery and turbulent emotions, and a final escape over a bleak lake to an uncharted future: cultured theatre-goers at the time would in any case have remembered that the same sub-title was affixed to Heine's satirical verse epic *Deutschland*. Apart, however, from the punch of Georg Kaiser's social and political message, Weill's music is impressively powerful and moving, both in his 'serious' vein (as in the voices of the policeman Olim's conscience after he has shot Severin, escaping after raiding a food store, or the lovely orchestral passage while snow is falling on the lake) and in his 'popular' (the lottery agent's tango or the foxtrot at a celebratory meal). It should perhaps be emphasized that this is a play with music rather than a 'proper opera'; but the skilful reduction here of the spoken dialogue (very well handled by the actors) throws the music into greater relief. It includes several big set-pieces, such as the girl Fennimore's ballad about Caesar's death (small wonder the Nazis banned the work!), Severin's savage cry for revenge, and the "Fools' paradise" song of the wicked schemers Frau von Lubin and Baron Laub. It is vital however that these should be heard in their rightful context; and the strength of this performance—something of a triumph for Jan Latham-König, his producer and the cast—lies in its tremendous dramatic grip.

Jaromir Weinberger *Refer to Index* Czech 1896-1967

Hugo Wolf Austrian 1860-1903

Wolf. ORCHESTRAL WORKS. **Orchestre de Paris / Daniel Barenboim.** Erato 2292-45416-2. Items marked [a] recorded at performances in the Salle Pleyel, Paris during February 1988.
Penthesilea[a]. DER CORREGIDOR—Prelude; Intermezzo. Italian Serenade[a]. Scherzo and Finale.

57' DDD 4/90

Daniel Barenboim has done Wolf's admirers a great service by not only giving *Penthesilea* its first recording for many years, but by adding all of Wolf's other purely orchestral music. We can now speculate about what manner of symphonist he might have become: an assured and masterly one if the so-called scherzo and finale are anything to go by. They date from his teens, and the scherzo in particular is both finely made and ingeniously imagined. The joyously exuberant finale is almost light music, and good company for the two little operatic entr'actes and the already popular *Italian* Serenade. *Penthesilea* prompts similar questions about how Wolf might have developed as an operatic composer if he had followed up the wayward but entrancing *Der Corregidor* with something on a mythic subject and a grander scale. It is gorgeously coloured music, wildly inventive and hugely urgent; a bit undisciplined at times, and occasionally over-scored (Wolf knew that; he was struggling to revise the piece in the last months before his mind broke down) but with unobtrusively firm control from the conductor and superfine playing (both provided here) it becomes possible to suspect that the next stage of Wolf's creativity might have been to rival Strauss as Wagner's operatic successor. The recording, made at a public concert, has a moment or two of congestion but is otherwise both rich and brilliant.

Wolf. Intermezzo. Italian Serenade. String Quartet in D minor. **Artis Quartet** (Peter Schumayer, Johannes Meissl, vns; Herbert Kefer, va; Othmar Muller, vc). Accord 22080-2.

57' DDD 6/90

Wolf's astonishing String Quartet suggests that his early death and the discouragingly contemptuous treatment his larger works received during his lifetime, robbed us of a great composer of chamber music, possibly also a great symphonist. The Quartet is without the slightest shadow of doubt a masterpiece. For a composer not yet 20 to have had such a mastery of large-scale structure, such skilled command of complex thematic working and such confidence in handling big and dramatic ideas is nothing short of breathtaking. But these profoundly serious qualities are combined with a youthful prodigality of invention and an exuberance of spirit that are winning as well as awesome. Only the work's huge difficulty in performance can have kept it on the furthest fringes of the repertory for so long. How fortunate that for its first recording in many years it should have been taken up by such an urgently communicative as well as such a virtuoso group as the Artis Quartet. The popular *Italian* Serenade, charmingly done, is a welcome supplement; the *Intermezzo*, still more neglected than the String Quartet, shares its qualities and adds to them a measure of enchanting humour. Excellent recorded sound, too: unreservedly recommended.

Wolf. Italienisches Liederbuch. **Elisabeth Schwarzkopf** (sop); **Dietrich Fischer-Dieskau** (bar); **Gerald Moore** (pf). EMI CDM7 63732-2. Text and translation included. From SAN210/1 (2/69).

79' ADD 12/90

Even today the songs of Hugo Wolf are underrated, and do not always draw an audience or sell on disc. If anything can change that situation it ought to be this reissue of a classic account of Wolf's most delightful Songbook, in which the blessings and cares and amusements of love are charmingly retailed. Walter Legge, the century's greatest Wolf advocate after Ernest Newman, was the knowledgeable producer behind this offering, which was joyfully greeted in its LP form some 20 years ago. Its transfer to CD is greatly to be welcomed. Between them Schwarzkopf and Fischer-Dieskau have just about every attribute, vocal and interpretative, to sing these pieces with total devotion and understanding. The many characters portrayed within so subtly and unerringly by the composer are all brought to life by the wit and wisdom of his interpreters without whom the songs would lie forgotten on the page. As their partner the veteran Gerald Moore plays with all his old skill and perception. All one needs to add is that the recording is unforced and natural. This is a 'must' for all lovers of Lieder.

Wolf. LIEDER. **Olaf Bär** (bar); **Geoffrey Parsons** (pf). EMI CDC7 49054-2. Texts and translations included.

Gebet. Neue Liebe. Auf ein altes Bild. Schlafendes Jesuskind. Er ist's. Im Frühling. Auf einer Wanderung. Der Gärtner. Lied eines Verliebten. Auftrag. Storchenbotschaft. Bei einer Trauung. Selbstgeständnis. Begegnung. Nimmersatte Liebe. Peregrina I. Peregrina II. Der Jäger. Jägerlied. An die Geliebte. Verborgenheit. Auf eine Christblume I. Auf eine Christblume II. Zum neuen Jahr.

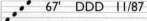

67' DDD 11/87

Geoffrey Parsons   *[photo: Virgin Classics/Copland]*

Hugo Wolf is one of those composers whose reputation rests on just one genre—song. He was not a composer who approached his craft with the same melodic fluidity as Schubert; his songs are more sinuous, more harmonically intense and more demanding of the performer on a purely expressive level—they can't simply be sung. For Olaf Bär, the Mörike Lieder present the greatest challenge to date. His warm, pliable baritone voice is ideal at capturing the yearning, heartfelt mood of a song such as *Im Frühling* or the lighter more outgoing mood of *Auftrag*. For anyone wanting to explore Wolf's powerful and unique art or follow the highly promising career of a fine baritone, this disc is ideal. The accompaniments are sensitively handled by Geoffrey Parsons whose experience perfectly complements a fertile talent. The recording is good.

Maurice Wright   *Refer to Index*   *American 1949-*

Robert Wright and George Forrest   *American 1914- and 1915-*

KISMET (Wright/Forrest, after Borodin). Cast includes **Valerie Masterson, Donald Maxwell, David Rendall, Richard Van Allan, Judy Kaye; Ambrosian Chorus; Philharmonia Orchestra/John Owen Edwards.** TER Classics CDTER2 1170. Includes five songs from "Timbuktu".

② 97' DDD 7/90

There have been a number of expensively mounted star-led studio recordings of the big musicals in recent years, most of them flawed somewhere along the line in their casting of the principal roles. How good then to be able to welcome a faultlessly performed, superbly played and thrillingly recorded account of Wright and Forrest's musical extravaganza which was subtitled in the original programme *A Musical Arabian Night*. This venerable team would probably be the first to acknowledge their debt to Borodin whose music, from the opera *Prince Igor* to a Little Serenade for Piano, they've reworked so convincingly in their tale of a poet (Donald Maxwell) in ancient Baghdad whose daughter Marsinah (Valerie Masterson) he plans to marry to a handsome

Caliph (David Rendall) after drowning her husband, the wicked Wazir (Richard Van Allan) in a fountain! The score reads like a hit parade of the 1950s, "Stranger in Paradise", "Night of My Nights", "And This is my Beloved" and "Baubles, Bangles and Beads" which has become a favourite with jazzers over the years. Even those readers who might shy away from operetta or thumb their noses at the reworking of the classics will acknowledge the wholehearted conviction with which *Kismet* is executed by this nearly all British cast, under John Owen Edwards's idiomatic direction. The one import in this line-up is Broadway's Judy Kaye who delivers a gutsy rendition of "Not Since Ninevah", the score's one homage to syncopation and the glitter of neon light. Several years after *Kismet*, Wright and Forrest rewrote their old favourite for Eartha Kitt and an all black cast as *Timbuktu* and it is with several songs from that score that this pair of CDs is filled out.

Jan Dismas Zelenka
Bohemian 1679-1745

Zelenka. ORCHESTRAL WORKS. **Berne Camerata/Alexander van Wijnkoop.** Archiv Produktion 423 703-2AX3. From 2710 026 (11/78). Capriccios—No. 1 in D major; No. 2 in G major; No. 3 in F major; No. 4 in A major; No. 5 in G major. Concerto a 8 in G major. Sinfonia a 8 in A minor. Hipocondrie a 7 in A major. Overture a 7 in F major.

·/ ③ 164' ADD 1/89

This three-CD album contains all Zelenka's surviving orchestral music. Most of it is anything but commonplace and some of it has a quirky individuality which Baroque enthusiasts will find intriguing if nothing more. The most readily conspicuous feature of the five *Capriccios* is that of the horn writing whose virtuosity exceeds that of almost all his contemporaries; but he shares with Telemann a predilection for rhythms and melodies deriving from central European folk tradition. Barry Tuckwell and Robert Routch turn in dazzling performances on modern horns and are effectively matched by the crisp and invigorating playing of the Berne Camerata. The remaining pieces are formally varied and though sometimes Zelenka just fails to maintain a high level of interest, for the most part his music is full of charm and, at its best, is quite irresistible. The Berne Camerata present a colourful picture of Zelenka's music in this fascinating anthology and their performances are well recorded and thoroughly documented.

Alexander Zemlinsky
Austrian 1871-1942

Zemlinsky. EINE FLORENTINISCHE TRAGODIE, Op. 16. **Doris Soffel** (mez) Bianca; **Kenneth Riegel** (ten) Guido Bardi; **Guilermo Sarabia** (bass) Simone. **Berlin Radio Symphony Orchestra/Gerd Albrecht.** Schwann CD11625. From VMS1625 (9/85).

·/ 53' DDD 12/85

Zemlinsky's *A Florentine Tragedy* is an opulent work entwining adultery, murder and sexual desire in a powerful union. Bianca, the wife of a wealthy Florentine merchant Simone, is having an adulterous liaison with Guido. Simone returns to find the two lovers together; he gradually grasps the situation and after a cat-and-mouse game with Guido challenges him to a duel and kills him. The story is based on a play by Oscar Wilde and, typically, has a verbal lushness powerfully matched by Zemlinsky's potent score. The cast of three is strong with some electric moments as the tension increases. Gerd Albrecht directs sympathetically and the orchestra play this rich score well. Nicely recorded.

Zemlinsky. Lyrische Symphonie, Op. 18. **Julia Varady** (sop); **Dietrich Fischer-Dieskau** (bar); **Berlin Philharmonic Orchestra/Lorin Maazel.** DG 419 261-2GH. Texts and translations included. From 2532 021 (3/82).

44' DDD 6/87

Zemlinsky's powerful symphonic song cycle for soprano and baritone employs the vast forces of the late-romantic orchestra at its most opulent. The poems by the composer gradually build up, if not to a narrative, then to a series of symbolist portrayals of the spirit of love. The male singer contributes a more abstract, more idealized yearning after the "dweller in my endless dreams", the soprano a more down-to-earth evocation of emotional longing. Dietrich Fischer-Dieskau and his wife Julia Varady cope well with the tormented legato phrasing and tortured harmonies as the vision of an idealized love shimmers before their eyes just beyond their reach. The Berlin Philharmonic play this unfamiliar score with great virtuosity, strongly conducted by Lorin Maazel and have been recorded in a wonderfully mellow acoustic.

Collections

THE ALDEBURGH RECITAL. Murray Perahia (pf). Sony Classical CD46437.
Beethoven: 32 Variations in C minor on an Original Theme, WoO80.
Schumann: Faschingsschwank aus Wien, Op. 26. **Liszt:** Hungarian Rhapsody No. 12, S244. Consolation No. 3 in D flat major, S172. **Rachmaninov:** Etudes-tableaux, Op. 33—No. 2 in C major. Etudes-tableaux, Op. 39—No. 5 in E flat minor; No. 6 in A minor; No. 9 in D major.

59' DDD 4/91 **Ⓑ**

Murray Perahia's attachment to Beethoven and Schubert has always been close. What may surprise some of his followers is to find the second half of this recital given over to such overtly demonstrative romantics as Liszt and Rachmaninov. It was a programme he had recently played at London's Festival Hall before recording it in 1989 at the Maltings in Snape—though not as part of that year's Aldeburgh Festival, as the title might suggest. Collectors can rest assured that no extraneous audience noise disturbs these 59 minutes. The piano is faithfully and sympathetically reproduced, with only an occasional touch of edginess in some of Rachmaninov's bigger climaxes. The playing itself is a joy. Potent contrasts of character allied with an inevitable-sounding continuity give Beethoven's C minor Variations (allegedly disowned by their composer) a maturity commensurate with his 36 years of age. Schumann's *Faschingsschwank aus Wien* in its turn gains a new youthful spontaneity and sparkle from his delectable lightness of touch and rhythmic *élan*. Even if rubato could have been more teasing in Liszt's twelfth *Rhapsody*, its virtuoso demands are brilliantly met, and surely not even Liszt himself could have floated the melody of the D flat *Consolation* with more assuaging beauty of tone and line. In the concluding Rachmaninov group Perahia throws his cap to the winds with the best of them while at the same time preserving his own unmistakably crystalline sound-world.

AMERICAN CONCERT SONGS. Thomas Hampson (bar); **Armen Guzelimian** (pf). EMI CDC7 54051-2.
Griffes: An Old Song Re-sung. **Giannini:** Tell me, oh blue sky! **Sacco:** Brother Will, Brother John. **Hanby:** Darling Nelly Gray. **Foster** (trans. Riegger): Ah! May the red rose live always (with Kenneth Sillito, vn). **Romberg:** MAYTIME—Will you remember? **Damrosch:** Danny Deever, Op. 2 No. 7. **Harrison:** In the Gloaming. **Speaks:** On the Road to Mandalay. **Hageman:** Do not go, my love. **J. Duke:** Luke Havergal. **Charles:** When I have sung my songs. **Cadman:** At Dawning, Op. 29 No. 1 (Sillito, vn). **Korngold:** Tomorrow. **Haydn Wood:** Roses of Picardy. **Messager:** MIRETTE—Long ago in Alcala. **Traditional:** Shenandoah. The Erie Canal (both arr. Ames). The nightingale (arr. C. Shaw). The lass from the Low Countree (arr. Niles).

66' DDD 3/91 **❓**

"Why should the beautiful die?" asks Thomas Hampson in Stephen Foster's song *Ah! May the red rose live always* and, by applying this notion to neglected songs, he and Armen Guzelimian (with Kenneth Sillito riding violin obbligato in a couple of the numbers) take a journey down Memory Lane. "American Concert Songs" refers here to those popular numbers that might have been included in a typical American concert of the earlier years of this century, rather than ones specifically written by American composers—in fact, a few on this disc are of British origin. Hampson has a rare feel for the idiom and a powerful, solid-toned voice that he can turn to delicate and touching effect in the more sentimental items. However, his musicality and good taste never let sentimentality take hold of these performances, and in this, and every other aspect, he is admirably supported by the subtle accompaniment of Guzelimian. The recording engineers have reflected and enhanced the variety of timbre the performers bring to the different songs so that the recital retains interest throughout and each item attains maximum individual impact. Altogether a delight.

AMERICAN PIANO SONATAS, Volume 1. **Peter Lawson.** Virgin Classics VC7 91163-2.
Copland: Piano Sonata (1939-41). *Ives* (ed. Cowell): Three-page Sonata. *Carter:* Piano Sonata (1945-6 rev. 1982). *Barber:* Piano Sonata, Op. 26.

76' DDD 5/91

This disc offers four relatively unfamiliar but highly characterful American piano works in authoritative performances by a Manchester-born pianist who clearly has their idiom at his fingertips—as well as their pretty challenging notes. As played here, the Copland Piano Sonata of 1941 has softness as well as strength, and for all its powerful utterance there is a strangely compelling lyricism at work too; one can see why the young Leonard Bernstein adored the work and played it. The recording matches the music, being on the close side but extremely lifelike as piano sound. Ives's *Three-page Sonata*, which at over seven minutes is longer than the miniature that its title suggests, is a gnomic utterance, but as always with this composer we feel that he has something to say that could be said in no other way. Carter's Piano Sonata is an early work of 1946, which the composer revised much later in 1982; its debt to Copland is evident, but there is also a personal voice and the scope and sweep of the music is deeply impressive. Barber's Sonata (1949), which was written for Horowitz, is less radical in idiom than the other works played and thus more immediately approachable if by no means conventional, being a work of considerable power and eloquence, very well written for the piano. The booklet note by Professor Wilfrid Mellers is valuable if wordy—at one point in the Copland Sonata he invites us to hear "disembodied boogie-woogie, remotely echoing the world's bustle … suspended above empty harmonies that pulse as unobtrusively as a heart-beat … the city's contrarieties dissolve into space and eternity".

THE ART OF THE PRIMA DONNA. Dame Joan Sutherland (sop); **Chorus and Orchestra of the Royal Opera House, Covent Garden/ Francesco Molinari-Pradelli.** Decca 425 493-2DM2. Texts and translations included. From SXL2556/7 (12/60).
Arne: ARTAXERXES—The soldier tir'd. *Bellini:* LA SONNAMBULA—Care compagne … Come per me sereno … Sopra il sen. NORMA—Sediziose voci … Casta diva … Ah! bello a me ritorna. PURITANI—Son vergin vezzosa; O rendetemi la speme … Qui la voce … Vien, diletto. *Delibes:* LAKME—Ah! Où va la jeune Indoue. *Gounod:* FAUST—O Dieu! que de bijoux … Ah! je ris. ROMEO ET JULIETTE—Je veux vivre. *Handel:* SAMSON—Let the bright Seraphim. *Meyerbeer:* LES HUGUENOTS—O beau pays de la Touraine! *Mozart:* DIE ENTFUHRUNG AUS DEM SERAIL—Martern aller Arten. *Rossini:* SEMIRAMIDE—Bel raggio lusinghier. *Thomas:* HAMLET—A vos jeux, mes amis. *Verdi:* OTELLO—Mia madre aveva una povera ancella … Piangea cantando. LA TRAVIATA—E strano … Ah fors' è lui … Sempre libera. RIGOLETTO—Gualtier Maldè … Caro nome.

② 1h 49' ADD 1/90

Those who have not heard Dame Joan until recent times can only speculate on
the full beauty of her voice in its prime. This album, from 1960, preserves

Dame Joan Sutherland   *[photo: Decca/Barda*

the real Sutherland quality as well as any of her records have done and it is a delight from start to finish. Sutherland and her husband, Richard Bonynge, have long been interested in the history of opera and particularly of its singers, so *The Art of the Prima Donna* was arranged to relate each of the solos to a famous soprano of the past. Arne's *Artaxerxes* recalls Mrs Billington, and the final items are associated with more recent artists such as Tetrazzini and Galli-Curci. It presents a brilliant conspectus, with Sutherland mastering the most fearsome of technical demands and showing a wonderfully complete command of the required skills. She was then fresh from the triumph at Covent Garden in *Lucia di Lammermoor* which brought her international fame in 1959. Her voice was at its purest, and her style had not developed the characteristics which later partly limited the pleasure of her singing. What the record may not quite convey is the sheer house-filling volume of her voice. Even so, nobody who hears these recordings can be in any doubt about her mastery or about the aptness of the title, bestowed on her by the Italians, of "la stupenda".

BALLET GALA. English Concert Orchestra/Richard Bonynge. Decca 421 818-2DH2.
Minkus (arr. March): Paquita. Don Quixote. *Pugni* (arr. March): Pas de quatre. *Offenbach*: Le papillon. *Drigo* (arr. Lanchbery): Le corsaire. *Auber*: Pas classique. Les rendez-vous (arr. Lambert). *Drigo* (arr. March): Diane et Actéon. *D. Scarlatti* (arr. Tommasini): The good-humoured Ladies. *Thomas*: Françoise de Rimini.

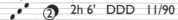 ② 2h 6' DDD 11/90

This is a delightful selection of largely unfamiliar ballet music from the nineteenth century, which makes a pleasant change from the usual collection of oft-recorded Tchaikovsky favourites. Although many of the excerpts here are heard in arrangements by more recent hands, the essential flavour of the original works has been retained. Little of the music is particularly striking but it is all nonetheless wonderfully tuneful, animated and very easy on the ear. However, the two sprightly Minkus excerpts, Drigo's exciting *Pas de deux* from *Le corsaire* and highlights from Offenbach's only full-length ballet *Le papillon* are probably the pieces most likely to afford prolonged enjoyment. Richard Bonynge is a trusty interpreter of this sort of repertoire and with the help of equally dedicated playing from the ECO he makes each work shine to its best advantage. The excellent recording is a further bonus, bringing out all the colourful orchestral details with notable clarity. This set is a treat not only for ballet lovers but anyone who appreciates attractive, well-crafted melodies.

BAROQUE CLASSICS. Taverner Players/Andrew Parrott. EMI Reflexe CDM7 69853-2.
Handel: Solomon—Arrival of the Queen of Sheba. Harp Concerto in B flat major, Op. 4 No. 6 (with Andrew Lawrence-King, hp). *Purcell:* Three Parts upon a Ground. A Suite of Theatre Music: The Indian Queen—Trumpet Overture, Symphony, Dance; Abdelazer—Rondeau; The Gordion Knot Unty'd—Chaconne. *Pachelbel:* Canon and Gigue. *Bach:* Sinfonias—Cantata No. 29; Cantata No. 156; Cantata No. 31; Cantata No. 174; Christmas Oratorio, BWV248. Cantata No. 106—Sonatina. Cantata No. 147—Jesus bleibet meine Freude (with Taverner Consort).

> 60' DDD 12/88

If you have ever felt the desire to hear 'baroque classics' as the composer might have heard them, but have been deterred by the unfriendly sounds and deadpan renditions offered by some early-instrument groups, you may do the former without suffering the latter by adding this disc to your collection. Though the performances have every benefit of stylistic scholarship and early-instrumental mastery they are in no way 'dry', nor are there any chalk-on-blackboard sounds to set the teeth on edge; on the contrary, the late David Reichenberg's oboe playing is likely to be a delightful revelation. Like other baroque composers, Bach was wont to rework some of his music for other media: thus you may recognize the Sinfonias from Cantatas 29, 156 and 31 as being related to the *Preludium* of the Third Violin Partita (BWV1006), the *Largo* of the F minor Harpsichord Concerto (BWV1056) and the first movement of the Third Brandenburg Concerto (BWV1048). This represents a doorway to the appreciation of baroque music in authentic performance, through which you may enter with as much enthusiasm as do the Taverner Players.

BAROQUE FAVOURITES. [a]Academy of St Martin in the Fields/Sir Neville Marriner; [b]Bath Festival (Chamber) Orchestra/Sir Yehudi Menuhin. Classics for Pleasure CD-CFP4557.
Pachelbel: Canon in D major[a]. *Purcell:* Chacony in G minor, Z730[a]. *Vivaldi:* Concerto in B minor, Op. 10 No. 3[b] (with Sir Yehudi Menuhin, Robert Masters, Eli Goren and Sydney Humphreys, vns). *Corelli:* Concerto Grosso in F major, Op. 6 No. 2[b] (Menuhin, Masters, vns; Derek Simpson, vc). *Gluck:* ORFEO ED EURIDICE—Dance of the Blessed Spirits[a]. *Monteverdi* (ed. Leppard): Se vittorie si belle. O sia tranquillo (Gerald English, Hugues Cuenod, tens; Bath Festival Ensemble/Raymond Leppard). *Handel:* Concerto grosso in A major, Op. 6 No. 11[b].

> 66' ADD 11/89 £ Ⓑ

What qualifications are required, I wonder, for a piece of music to be eligible for consideration as a "baroque favourite"? The exclusion of Albinoni's *Adagio*—a sickly confection with which Albinoni had nothing whatsoever to do—merits a strong recommendation for this anthology. Some of the pieces, such as Gluck's *Dance of the Blessed Spirits* and Pachelbel's *Canon* are indeed standard favourites but others like the Monteverdi madrigals and the Corelli Concerto Grosso may strike listeners as much less familiar. The performances are lively though somewhat variable in their degree of finesse. The programme is somewhat arbitrarily chosen and the absence of Bach from the menu a surprising omission. Never mind, the disc offers variety and entertainment and if it leads the curious to explore further the rich legacy of these and other baroque composers, then its arbitrariness will not have been in vain.

BAROQUE ORGAN MUSIC. Peter Hurford (org). Argo 414 496-2ZH.
Played on the Blank organ of the Bethlehemkerk, Papendrecht, The Netherlands.
G. Böhm: Prelude and Fugue in C major. Vater unser im Himmelreich. Auf
meinen lieben Gott. Von Himmel hoch da komm'ich her. *L. Couperin:* Branle
de basque. Fantaisie in G minor. *J. K. Kerll:* Capriccio sopra il cucu.
Buxtehude: Mensch, willt du leben seliglich. Wir danken dir, Herr Jesu
Christ. Vater, unser im Himmelreich. *Walond:* Voluntary No. 5 in G major.
G. B. Pescetti: Sonata in C minor. *Pachelbel:* Ciaccona in D minor.
Sweelinck: Unter der Linden grüne. *Stanley:* Voluntary in C major, Op. 5
No. 1.

71' DDD 10/87

At first glance we may be a little dismayed to find an anthology called "Baroque
Organ Music" which omits a single note of Bach. More careful scrutiny of the
contents, however, may well persuade us that it is for our own good since Peter
Hurford has chosen a programme of all too seldom-heard music by composers
who were also noted organists of their day. The outstanding figures here are Jan
Pieterszoon Sweelinck, Georg Böhm, Dietrich Buxtehude, Johann Pachelbel and
Louis Couperin and although these works form the main body of the recital,
listeners are unlikely to be disappointed by the several smaller, lighter-textured
pieces with which Hurford makes discerning contrast, as well as showing off the
appealing character of the organ.

BLACK ANGELS. Kronos Quartet (David Harrington, John Sherba, vns;
Hank Dutt, va; Joan Jeanrenaud, vc). Elektra-Nonesuch 7559-79242-2.
Crumb: Black Angels. *Tallis* (arr. Kronos Qt): Spem in alium. *Marta:*
Doom. A sigh. *Ives* (arr. Kronos Qt/Geist): They are there! *Shostakovich:*
String Quartet No. 8 in C minor, Op. 110.

62' DDD 4/91

This is very much the sort of imaginative programming we've come to expect
from this talented young American quartet. With an overall theme of war
and persecution the disc opens with George Crumb's *Black Angels*, for electric
string quartet. This work was inspired by the Vietnam War and bears two
inscriptions to that effect—*in tempore belli* (in time of war) and "Finished on
Friday the Thirteenth of March, 1970", and it's described by Crumb as "a
kind of parable on our troubled contemporary world". The work is divided
into three sections which represent the three stages of the voyage of the
soul—fall from grace, spiritual annihilation and redemption. As with most
of his works he calls on his instrumentalists to perform on a variety of
instruments other than their own—here that ranges from gongs, maracas
and crystal glasses to vocal sounds such as whistling, chanting and whispering.
Doom. A sigh is the young Hungarian composer István Marta's disturbing
portrait of a Rumanian village as they desperately fight to retain their sense of
identity in the face of dictatorship and persecution. Marta's atmospheric blend
of electronic sound, string quartet and recorded folk-songs leave one with a
powerful and moving impression. At first sight Tallis's *Spem in alium* may seem
oddly out of place considering the overall theme of this disc, but as the sleeve-
notes point out the text was probably taken from the story of Judith, in which
King Nebuchadnezzar's general Holofernes besieged the Jewish fortress of
Bethulia. Kronos's own arrangement of this 40-part motet (involving some
multi-tracking) certainly makes a fascinating alternative to the original. A
particularly fine account of Shostakovich's Eighth String Quartet (dedicated
to the victims of fascism and war) brings this thought-provoking and imaginative
recital to a close. Performances throughout are outstanding, and the recording
first class.

CABARET CLASSICS. Jill Gomez (sop); **John Constable** (pf). Unicorn-Kanchana DKPCD9055. Texts and translations included.
Weill: Marie Galante—Les filles de Bordeaux; Le grand Lustucru; Le Roi d'Aquitaine; J'attends un navire. Lady in the Dark—My ship. Street scene—Lonely house. Knickerbocker Holiday—It never was you. *Zemlinsky:* Songs, Op. 27—Harlem Tänzerin; Elend; Afrikanischer Tanz. *Schoenberg:* Arie aus dem Spiegel von Arcadien. Gigerlette. Der genügsame Liebhaber. Mahnung. *Satie:* La diva de l'Empire. Allons-y, Chochotte. Je te veux.

57' DDD 6/88

Jill Gomez [photo: Virgin Classics

Schoenberg writing cabaret songs with a popular touch? Yes, and quite catchy ones too, as can be heard particularly in *Gigerlette*—prompting the intriguing speculation of what might have been had he not concentrated on *Gurrelieder*. On the other hand, his *Der genügsame Liebhaber* and Zemlinsky's three songs would have been most unlikely to go down with cabaret audiences, however intellectual. At the other end of the spectrum are Satie's café-concert songs (the sentimental waltz *Je te veux* is languidly attractive) and the Weill items, which were not written for cabaret but are drawn from a 1934 Paris play and post-war Broadway musicals. That all these songs do not require a gin-sodden voice or raucous delivery is demonstrated with the utmost artistry by Jill Gomez, in turn seductive, pathetic, sly, sweet, swaggering, passionate, salacious—or simply singing beautifully. Her performance of Weill's *Lonely house* (one of his best) remains hauntingly in the mind.

CONCERTANTE CELLO WORKS. Steven Isserlis (vc); **Chamber Orchestra of Europe/John Eliot Gardiner.** Virgin Classics VC7 91134-2.
Tchaikovsky: Variations on a Rococo Theme, Op. 33. Pezzo capriccioso, Op. 62. Nocturne, Op. 19 No. 4. Andante cantabile, Op. 11. *Glazunov:* Two Pieces, Op. 20. Chant du menestrel, Op. 71. *Rimsky-Korsakov:* Serenade, Op. 37. *Cui:* Deux morceaux, Op. 36—Scherzando; Cantabile.

64' DDD 10/90

This delicious collection of Russian concertante works for cello offers the immediate advantage of a version of Tchaikovsky's *Rococo* Variations that aligns closely with the composer's original intentions for the work—many other recordings use heavily edited and reordered versions. Its second advantage is the considered, clean-toned playing of Steven Isserlis, one of a mighty handful of first-rate cello soloists that the UK can now boast. His style is not as demonstrative as that of some, though he is quite capable of opening the emotional floodgates when it is appropriate, and his delicacy and stylish phrasing bring out the best in this programme. Whether the music is lyrical, introspective, or playful, his restraint lends it another level of meaning that illuminates its inner life. Praise must also go to John Eliot Gardiner and the Chamber Orchestra of Europe. Accompanying of this sort is never easy, as expert control is demanded for long periods with few attendant moments in the spotlight. Gardiner and the engineers have attained an ideal balance between soloist and orchestra and the players demonstrate an intuitive feel for the late

nineteenth-century idiom of the music.

CONTEMPORARY WORKS FOR STRING QUARTET. Kronos Quartet

(David Harringon, John Sherba, vns; Hank Dutt, va; Joan Jeanrenaud, vc).
Elektra-Nonesuch 7559-79111-2. From 979 111-1 (7/87).
P. Sculthorpe: String Quartet No. 8 (1969). *Sallinen:* String Quartet
No. 3. *Glass:* Company (1983). *C. Nancarrow:* String Quartet (1942).
J. Hendrix (arr. Rifkin): Purple Haze.

49' DDD 2/89

The Kronos Quartet   *[photo: Warner Classics/McKenzie*

Of all string quartets currently active none has done more than the Kronos to change the image of the medium. Snappy dressing and theatrical presentation are part of it, so are rock arrangements like the Jimi Hendrix *Purple Haze* on this CD. But there is nothing trendy about their choice of repertoire and the technical finish of their playing can stand the closest scrutiny—it's just that they have an added rhythmic bounce and colouristic flair which are the envy of many another ensemble. The stylistic and geographical spread of this programme is impressive. There is Sculthorpe, an Australian responding to the music of Bali, Sallinen, a Finn responding hauntingly to his own country's folk music and Nancarrow, an American now resident in Mexico and best known for his zany series of Studies for pianola. This selection should win over any listener wary of anything more modern than Bartók. And you could not wish for more full-blooded advocacy or more vivid recording quality.

DRAW ON SWEET NIGHT. Hilliard Ensemble/Paul Hillier. EMI Reflexe

CDC7 49197-2. Texts included.
Morley: O greefe even on the bud. When loe, by breake of morning. Aprill is in my mistris face. Sweet nimphe, come to thy lover. Miraculous love's wounding. Fyer and lightning. In nets of golden wyers. *Weelkes:* Thule, the period of cosmographie. O care thou wilt dispatch mee. Since Robin Hood. Strike it up tabor. *Wilbye:* Sweet hony sucking bees. Adew, sweet Amarillis. Draw on sweet night. *J. Bennet:* Weepe O mine eyes. *Gibbons:* The silver swanne. *Tomkins:* See, see, the shepheard's Queene. *Ward:* Come sable night. *Vautor:* Sweet Suffolke owle.

55' DDD 2/89

This refreshingly attractive and well-presented anthology of English madrigals promises to be a delight for the specialist and non-specialist alike. The programme is nicely balanced: the more richly textured, *Sweet hony sucking bees*, are interspersed with a number of the little two- and three-part Morley canzonets, either charmingly phrased and dovetailed by two well-matched sopranos (*Sweet nimphe, come to thy lover*), or sung with boundless energy by two tenors, or two tenors and a bass (the tautly drummed *Strike it up tabor*). The order in which the pieces occur is planned to reflect the changing moods of a single day and variety of mood and emotion is perhaps the chief characteristic of this choice collection. Another unusual feature is the adoption of what is claimed to have been Elizabethan pronunciation of English. This gives the sound of the music a rather special flavour, with the style, the tuning, the lively diction and the wit all contributing to the general excellence and immediacy of this performance.

EARLY ITALIAN MUSIC. Cologne Musica Antiqua/Reinhard Goebel.
Archiv Produktion 415 296-2AH. Texts and translations included. Items marked
[a] from 2533 460 (12/81), [b] 2533 420 (1/80).
Monteverdi: Il combattimento di Tancredi e Clorinda[a] (Patrizia Kwella, sop; Nigel Rogers, ten; David Thomas, bass). Lamento d'Arianna[a] (Carolyn Watkinson, contr). *C. Farina:* Sonata in G minor, "La desperata"[a] (Watkinson). *Fontana:* Sonata a tre violini[b]. *Rossi:* Sonata sopra l'aria di Ruggiero[b]. *Marini:* Passcaglia a 4[b]. Sonata sopra la Monica[b]. Eco a tre violini[b]. *Buonamente:* Sonate a tre violini[b].

· 68' ADD 5/86   P S

Of Monteverdi's second opera, *Arianna*, written in 1608 to celebrate a royal wedding, only its eponym's "Lament" has survived—in two arrangements (by Monteverdi); that on this recording is in the form of a solo aria. *Il combattimento di Tancredi e Clorinda* (1624) is a stage work in which a narrator tells the story of the crusader Tancredi, who fights and mortally wounds the Moslem Clorinda (both have their own arias), only to find to his dismay that beneath the armour is a woman; she forgives him and embraces Christianity. The writing is powerful in its effect. The early seventeenth century was a time of feverish experiment and development in Italy, that of the birth of new musical forms, the growth of instrumental virtuosity and the search for greater expressiveness. The juxtaposition of these vocal works of Monteverdi with the virtuoso violin music of some of his contemporaries emphasizes the point: common to both are, *inter alia*, the frequent changes of tempo and mood, and the *mesa di voce*, the 'hairpinned' dynamics on long notes. What Marini's *Eco a tre violini* lacks in musical substance it makes up for in the imaginativeness of its concept. These are truly magnificent performances, superbly recorded and quite irresistible.

THE ENGLISH CONNECTION. Academy of St Martin in the Fields/Sir Neville Marriner. ASV CDDCA518. From DCA518 (5/83).
Vaughan Williams: The Lark Ascending (Iona Brown, vn). Fantasia on a Theme by Thomas Tallis. *Elgar:* Serenade in E minor, Op. 20. *Tippett:* Fantasia concertante on a Theme of Corelli.

· 62' DDD 2/85   Ⓑ

It is difficult to imagine a more 'English' work than *The Lark Ascending*. Written in the last days of pre-First World War peace, it evokes the tranquillity of a rural England which would never be quite the same again. Iona Brown's solo violin soars effortlessly above the orchestra: she and Marriner contrive a performance which is admirable in every way. This is coupled with the *Tallis* Fantasia, written for the spacious acoustic of Gloucester Cathedral, and Elgar's *Serenade*, an early work but entirely characteristic of the great composer's skill in writing music which pretends no great profundity yet charms and moves the spirit. Tippett's *Fantasia concertante* is a slightly harder piece to assimilate: its busy counterpoint again has a very English quality despite an aura of the Italian *concerto grosso*. There is a slight edge to the string sound on this disc, but it is not enough to affect enjoyment of a very attractive programme.

ENGLISH MUSIC FOR STRINGS. Guildhall String Ensemble/Robert Salter. RCA Red Seal RD87846.
Britten: Simple Symphony, Op. 4. *Tippett:* Little Music. *Walton:* Sonata. *Oldham/Tippett/L. Berkeley/Britten/Searle/Walton:* Variations on an Elizabethan theme, "Sellinger's Round".

69' DDD 5/89

ENGLISH MUSIC FOR STRINGS. Guildhall String Ensemble/Robert Salter (vn). RCA Victor Red Seal RD87761.
Holst: St Paul's Suite, H118. *Delius* (orch. Fenby): Two Aquarelles. *Ireland:* A Downland Suite—Minuet. *Finzi:* Prelude, Op. 25. Romance, Op. 11. *Walton:* Henry V—Passacaglia (Death of Falstaff); Touch her soft lips and part. *Elgar* (ed. Young): The Spanish Lady—suite. *Warlock:* Capriol Suite.

61' DDD 9/88

The Guildhall String Ensemble are a most skilful, professional band and these enterprising collections show them off to great advantage. Britten's early *Simple Symphony*, a slight but accomplished work, is given a suitably playful reading as is Tippett's charming *Little Music*, though here they nicely capture the slightly mysterious quality of the piece. The two substantial works on the disc are also authoritatively despatched. The *Variations on an Elizabethan theme* was composed by five different composers for the 1953 Aldeburgh Festival and these undemanding variations on an old English dance tune make enjoyable listening, especially when performed so well. The Walton Sonata is a 1972 reworking on his 1947 String Quartet. The transformation from solo strings to a more substantial body works well and takes on a new, and for some, more accessible nature.

The unusual item in the second collection is the group of five short pieces rescued from a late, unfinished opera by Elgar—not vintage Elgar by any means but attractive nevertheless. Holst's much better-known suite has a simple but robust cheerfulness. Ireland's elegant little *Minuet* began life as a test piece for military band and the two Delius pieces are effective transcriptions by Eric Fenby of two wordless part-songs. Warlock used old French dance tunes in a suite which also conveys his own lively personality; Finzi's two pieces have a typical, wistful nostalgia, and Walton's grave little fragments from his music for Olivier's film are effective in their own right. The recordings are beautifully spacious and capture well the ensemble's fine string tone.

THE ESSENTIAL HARPSICHORD. Virginia Black. Collins Classics 5024-2.
Arne: Keyboard Sonata No. 3 in G major. *D. Scarlatti:* Keyboard Sonatas—C major, Kk159; G major, Kk337; E major, Kk380. *Bach:* Italian Concerto, BWV971. *Balbastre:* Pièces de clavecin I—La Suzanne. *Daquin:* Pièces de clavecin I—Le coucou. *Duphly:* Pièces de clavecin III—Le Forqueray. *F. Couperin:* Livre de clavecin II—Les baricades mistérieuses. Livre de clavecin III—Le dodo; Le tic-toc-choc. *Handel:* Keyboard Suites—No. 5 in E major, "Harmonious Blacksmith"; No. 7 in G minor—Passacaille. *Mozart:* Piano Sonata in A major, K331/300*i*—Rondo alla turca. *Paradies:* Toccata in A major. *Rameau:* Les cyclopes. *W.F. Bach:* Polonaise in E minor.

74' DDD 5/91

Virginia Black has assembled a delightful programme of music which should conquer all ears not yet won over by the sound of a harpsichord. She is a communicative player, spontaneous in transferring her thoughts to the keyboard and with a lively sense of poetry. These qualities and others too may be sensed in her interpretation of Bach's *Italian Concerto*. This is the most substantial piece in her recital and it comes over well with clearly articulated phrases, rhythmic elasticity and well-chosen tempos. There are occasions when Miss Black pushes the music along just a little harder than is good for it—listeners may sense that in the concluding Variations of Handel's famous so-called *Harmonious Blacksmith* theme—but her liveliness of temperament ensures her performances against any accusations of stuffy convention or dullness. Only the W.F. Bach Polonaise seems perhaps not to speak from the heart. A recital, in short, which deserves to win friends. Few are likely to be disappointed either by her choice of music or her colourfully imaginative treatment of it.

A EUROPEAN ORGAN TOUR. Priory PRCD903.
Reger: Symphonic Fantasia and Fugue, Op. 57, "Inferno" (Graham Barber/St Mary Magdalene, Bonn). *Bowen:* Fantasia, Op. 136 (Marc Rochester/St David's Hall, Cardiff). *Dupré:* Variations sur un Nöel, Op. 20 (Kimberly Marshall/St Sernin, Toulouse). *Karg-Elert:* Cathedral Windows (John Scott Whiteley/York Minster). *Bach:* Fantasia in C major, BWV573 (Scott Whiteley/St Bavo, Haarlem).

70' DDD

From the comfort of your armchair, you can enjoy a real taste of Europe. Here on a single, generously-filled disc are the authentic voices of some of the finest organ builders (Muller, Cavaillé-Coll, Klais, Walker and Peter Collins) from Europe's leading organ building nations (Holland, France, Germany and Britain). There is also an interesting programme of music, with only one of the pieces available elsewhere. That is Dupré's Op. 20 Variations. He wrote it with a Cavaillé-Coll organ in mind, and the example in St Sernin, Toulouse is certainly one of the best-preserved. Not only that, in Kimberly Marshall this music finds a most sensitive and eloquent advocate. It is good to hear Bach played on an instrument built in his lifetime too. But this Fantasia in C is unusual: only the first page exists in Bach's manuscript and the version played here was completed this century by Wolfgang Stockmeier. John Scott Whiteley gives it a compelling performance as he does Karg-Elert's beautifully evocative and richly colourful suite. York Bowen's only published organ work is the Fantasia written for the Festival of Britain in 1951. That was a time of radical thinking and fundamental changes in British organ design and it is entirely appropriate that it should be played on the brand new Peter Collins instrument in Cardiff's magnificent concert hall.

EVGENI KISSIN IN TOKYO. Evgeni Kissin (pf). Sony Classical CD45931. Recorded at a performance in Suntory Hall, Tokyo on May 12th, 1987. *Rachmaninov:* Lilacs, Op. 21 No. 5. Etudes tableaux, Op. 39—No. 1 in C minor; No. 5 in E flat minor. *Prokofiev:* Piano Sonata No. 6 in A major, Op. 82. *Liszt:* Concert Studies, S144—La leggierezza; Waldestauschen. *Chopin:* Nocturne in A flat major, Op. 32 No. 2. Polonaise in F sharp minor, Op. 44. *Scriabin:* Mazurka in E minor, Op. 25 No. 3. Etude in C sharp minor, Op. 42 No. 5. *Anon* (arr. Saegusa): Natu—Wa Kinu. Todai—Mori. Usagi.

73' DDD 11/90

One reason for buying this CD is that it contains dazzling piano playing by a 15-year-old Russian set fair for a career of the highest distinction. A better reason is that the recital contains as full a revelation of the genius of Prokofiev as any recording ever made in any medium. The Sixth Sonata is the first of a trilogy which sums up the appalling sufferings of Russia under Stalin in a way only otherwise found in Shostakovich's 'middle' symphonies. Kissin plays it with all the colour and force of a full orchestra and all the drama and structural integrity of a symphony, plus a kind of daredevilry that even he may find difficult to recapture. As for the rest of the recital only the Rachmaninov pieces are as memorable as the Prokofiev, though everything else is immensely impressive (the Japanese encore-pieces are trivial in the extreme, however). Microphone placing is very close, presumably in order to minimize audience noise; but the playing can take it, indeed it may even be said to benefit from it.

FETE A LA FRANCAISE. Montreal Symphony Orchestra/Charles Dutoit. Decca 421 527-2DH.
Chabrier: Joyeuse marche. España. *Dukas:* L'apprenti sorcier. *Satie* (orch. Debussy): Gymnopédies—Nos. 1 and 3. *Saint-Saëns:* SAMSON ET DALILA—Bacchanale. *Bizet:* Jeux d'enfants. *Thomas:* RAYMOND—Overture. *Ibert:* Divertissement.

70' DDD 6/89

With great style and huge amounts of panache Charles Dutoit presides over a highly enjoyable collection of French 'lollipops'. Moving forward from Chabrier's *Joyeuse Marche*, this *fête* includes such favourites as *The sorcerer's apprentice*, deliciously pointed and coloured, Chabrier's tribute to Spain, *España*, and Saint-Saëns's steamy Bacchanale from *Samson et Dalila*. A cool, limpid interlude is provided by two Satie *Gymnopédies*, here in orchestrations by Debussy. The whole programme is rounded off with tremendous fun by Ibert's outrageous *Divertissement* in a truly winning performance. The Montreal Symphony Orchestra are, without doubt, a first-rate orchestra and their grasp of French repertoire is certainly not equalled by any native band. Add to that a recording of quite breathtaking brilliance and you have a disc to treasure and delight.

FRENCH CHAMBER MUSIC. [a]Catherine Cantin (fl); [b]Maurice Bourgue (ob); [c]Michel Portal (cl); [d]Amaury Wallez (bn); [e]André Cazalet (hn); Pascal Rogé (pf). Decca 425 861-2DH.
Saint-Saëns: Caprice sur des airs danois et russes, Op. 79[abc]. *D'Indy:* Sarabande et menuet, Op. 72[abcde]. *Roussel:* Divertissement, Op. 6[abcde]. *Tansman:* Le Jardin du Paradis—Danse de la sorcière[abcde]. *Françaix:* L'heure du berger[abce]. *Poulenc:* Elégie[e]. *Milhaud:* Sonata for flute, oboe, clarinet and piano, Op. 47[abc].

67' DDD 5/91

French composers are noted for their special fondness for writing for wind instruments, but their wide diversity of styles is illustrated by this attractive disc, which is notable for superbly clean and sensitive playing by musicians in complete accord with each other and in instinctive sympathy with the music. Of the three works here for wind quintet and piano, the Roussel *Divertissement* is a particular delight, in turn sprightly and seductive; the d'Indy movements (transcribed from an earlier suite for the curious combination of trumpet, two flutes and string quartet) are an expressively contrapuntal sarabande and an oddly chirpy minuet; and the pungent Tansman dance is from an unfinished ballet. Jean Françaix's habitual spirit of *gaminerie* reigns in his three portraits for wind quartet and piano, written with his usual consummate craftsmanship. The works for wind trio and piano could scarcely be more unlike: Saint-Saëns's suave confection on (reputedly bogus) Danish and Russian airs, with a brilliant piano part, and Milhaud's often abrasive sonata (despite a pastoral opening), which ends with a dirge for victims of a Spanish influenza epidemic. And there's Poulenc's elegy for Dennis Brain, its broad lament tinged with just a touch of the humour that Dennis himself would have enjoyed.

**FRENCH ORCHESTRAL WORKS. [a]French Radio National Orchestra;
[b]Royal Philharmonic Orchestra/Sir Thomas Beecham.** EMI Beecham
Edition CDM7 63379-2.
Bizet: Carmen—Suite No. 1 (from HMV HQS1108, 12/67)[a]. *Fauré:* Pavane,
Op. 50 (HMV ASD518, 4/63)[a]. Dolly Suite, Op. 56 (orch. Rabaud. HQS1136,
5/68)[a]. *Debussy:* Prélude à l'après-midi d'un faune (ASD259, 6/59)[b]. *Saint-
Saëns:* Le rouet d'Omphale, Op. 31 (ASD259)[b]. *Delibes:* Le Roi s'amuse—
ballet music (HQS1136)[b].

68' ADD 7/90   £

Even to those who never heard him in the flesh there is no mistaking Beecham's
relish in, and flair for, the French repertoire. His combination of mischievous
high spirits, almost dandyish elegance, cool outer classicism masking passionate
emotion, swagger, refined nuance and delicate charm was perhaps unique—not
matched even by such committed Francophiles as Constant Lambert. *Elan* is at
once in evidence here in the *Carmen* prelude, and subtle dynamic gradations in
the entr'actes to Acts 2 and 4; there is lightness, vivacity and tenderness in
Fauré's *Dolly* suite and a true Gallic reserve in his *Pavane*; and he enters with
prim finesse into Delibes's pastiche dances. Debussy's erotic study, on repeated
hearings of this performance, becomes the more Grecian and effective for its
conscious understatement; and only the Saint-Saëns symphonic poem, for all the
RPO's delicacy, seems to hang fire. But four or five bull's-eyes out of six is a
pretty good score, and at medium price not to be missed.

FRENCH ORGAN WORKS. Jennifer Bate (org). Unicorn-Kanchana
DKPCD9041. From DKP9041 (1/86). Played on the organ of St Peter's
Cathedral, Beauvais, France.
Boëllman: Suite gothique, Op. 25. *Guilmant:* Cantilène pastorale. March on
Handel's "Lift up your heads", Op. 15. *Saint-Saëns:* Sept improvisations, Op.
150—No. 7 in A minor. *Gigout:* Dix pièces d'orgue—Scherzo; Toccata in B
minor. Grand choeur dialogué.

44' DDD 10/87

Jennifer Bate reminds us in this recital that the French tradition of organ music
was already strong in the nineteenth and early twentieth centuries. Boëllman's
Suite gothique is richly written and culminates in the brilliant Toccata which is
often played on its own in recitals, whilst Guilmant's *Pastoral Cantilena* is a gently
flowing piece. Saint-Saëns's *Seven Improvisations* were composed when he was 82,
but the durability of his craftsmanship is evident in the brisk and elegant scherzo
of the Seventh. The Gigout Toccata is appropriately fiery, while the Scherzo
which follows is gentler and the *Grand choeur dialogué* provides a vivid dialogue
between two manuals with contrasting registration. Bate plays all this music with
both affection and panache, and the quality of the recording is first rate, the
reverberant acoustic never blurring textures.

FRENCH SONGS. Rachel Yakar (sop); **Claude Lavoix** (pf). Virgin Classics
VC7 91089-2. Texts and translations included.
Hahn: Quand je fus pris au pavillon. Je me metz en vostre mercy. Le rossignol
des lilas. Si mes vers avaient des ailes. L'Air. La Nuit. L'Enamourée. Seule. Les
Fontaines. Le souvenir d'avoir chanté. L'Incrédule. D'une prison. Chansons
grises. *Bizet:* Sonnet. Rose d'amour. Pastorale. *Chabrier:* Chanson pour
Jeanne. Lied. L'lle heureuse.

62' DDD 3/90

Reynaldo Hahn was too much of a conductor to be rated very highly as a
composer, too much of a pianist and singer to be thought of primarily as a

conductor, and too witty a writer and talker to be taken quite seriously in any capacity. His talent was prodigious, and it was as a child prodigy that he wrote his best-known song, *Si mes vers avaient des ailes*. It was composed at the age of 13, its melody a little more obvious, its accompaniment more simple than in the songs of his later years, yet having qualities of grace and lightness that were to remain typical. He never wrote with weighty pretensions, and when sadness tinges a song, as in *D'une prison*, it is never taken to justify harshness in the music. Other feelings enter, just as a nostalgia for the courtly graces of time past, and this is found in *Quand je fus pris au pavillon* and *Je me metz en vostre mercy*. There is also the more impressionistic style of the *Chansons grises*, the title suggesting their delicacy of colouring and emotion. All of these find suitable companions in the songs of Bizet and Chabrier, and sensitive interpreters in Rachel Yakar and Claude Lavoix, the singer keenly attentive to the word-setting, the pianist subtle in his appreciation of the underlying mood of each song.

FRENCH SONGS AND DUETS. [a]**Ann Murray** (mez); [b]**Philip Langridge** (ten); **Roger Vignoles** (pf). Virgin Classics VC7 91179-2. Texts and translations included.
Chausson: La caravane, Op. 14[b]. Sept mélodies, Op. 2—No. 3, Les papillons[a]; No. 5, Sérénade italienne[b]; No. 7, Le colibri[a]; Two duos, Op. 11—No. 2, Le réveil. *Fauré:* Arpège, Op. 76 No. 2[b]. Pleurs d'or, Op. 72. Puisqu'ici bas, Op. 10 No. 1. Soir, Op. 83 No. 2[a]. *Gounod:* Barcarola. Boire à l'ombre[b]. Ce que je suis sans toi[a]. Le premier jour de mai[a]. Sérénade[b]. *Messiaen:* La mort du nombre (with Andrew Watkinson, vn). *Saint-Saëns:* Aimons-nous[b]. L'attente[a]. La cloche[a]. Danse macabre. Viens!

67' DDD 6/91

This enterprising collection includes some little-known works, for rescuing which thanks are due to this intelligent husband-and-wife team, backed by an excellent and sympathetic pianist. Chausson's sombre *La caravane*, for example (admirably sung by Langridge), can fairly be

Ann Murray & Philip Langridge   [photo: Virgin Classics/Crowthers

called an unjustly neglected masterpiece. The most substantial work here, of particular interest in view of the composer's later development, is the 22-year-old Messiaen's *La mort du nombre*, a dialogue between a soul in purgatory and his beloved who has attained spiritual peace: it calls forth feelings of intense torment by Langridge and rapt serenity from Murray, with a first-class contribution from Vignoles (plus a small but significant violin obbligato). Fauré's warmly sensuous *Pleurs d'or* is perhaps the most outstanding other duet here, but there is charm, also, in Gounod's *Barcarola* (sung in the French translation of the Italian original) and satiric humour in Saint-Saëns's *Danse macabre* (later expanded into the popular symphonic poem). In the solos, *La cloche* (with Murray at her best) belies its composer's reputation for only superficial facility, and Langridge shows a striking range from the easy lyricism of Gounod's *Sérénade* to the passion of Saint-Saëns's *Aimons-nous*.

THE GARDEN OF ZEPHIRUS. FIFTEENTH-CENTURY COURTLY SONGS. **Gothic Voices/Christopher Page** with **Imogen Barford** (medieval hp). Hyperion CDA66144. Texts and translations included. From A66144.
Dufay: J'attendray tant qu'il vous playra. Adieu ces bons vins de Lannoys. Mon cuer me fait tous dis penser. *Briquet:* Ma seul amour et ma belle maistresse. *Anthonello de Caserta:* Amour m'a le cuer mis. *Landini:* Neesun ponga speranza. Giunta vaga biltà. *Reyneau:* Va t'en, mon cuer, avent mes yeux. *Matheus de Sancto Johanne:* Fortune, faulce, parverse. *Francus de Insula:* Amours n'ont cure de tristesse. *Brollo:* Qui le sien vuelt bien maintenir. *Anonymous:* N'a pas long temps que trouvay Zephirus. Je la remire, la belle.

50' DAD 12/86

Christopher Page   [photo: Hyperion

Springtime, as Chaucer and almost all medieval poets remind us, stirs the gentle heart from sleep. But it was Zephyr, the West Wind who inspired the humble lover to seek his lady. As often as not she was unattainable but it was an ennobling aspiration, nonetheless. This aspect of refined or courtly society is engagingly captured by Gothic Voices under its Director, Christopher Page in a selection of French and Italian chansons, ballades and rondeaux dating from the early to mid fifteenth century. The wealth of vivid images, warm sentiments and formal variety contained in the poems is highlighted both by the musical settings themselves and by polished, communicative performances. The rondeaux of Dufay are perhaps especially affecting—ardent lovers of France and followers of Bacchus will be refreshed by a fragrant tribute to the wines of the Laon district in his *Adieu ces bons vins de Lannoys*—but Landini's ballate, sounding a more objective note, are hardly less so. Full texts with translations are provided and the recorded sound is excellent.

GERMAN CHAMBER MUSIC. Barthold Kuijken (fl); **Sigiswald Kuijken** (vn, va da gamba); **Wieland Kuijken** (vc, va da gamba); **Robert Kohnen** (hpd). Accent ACC58019D. From ACC8019 (8/81).
J.S. Bach: Trio Sonata in E flat major, BWV525 (trans. for flute, violin and continuo in G major). *C. P. E. Bach:* Trio Sonata in A major for flute, violin and continuo, Wq146. *Telemann:* Sonata in G major for flute, two violas da gamba and harpsichord. Suite in D minor for flute, violin and continuo.

57' DDD 3/86

A recital of carefully chosen pieces, sensitively played and extremely well recorded, makes this one of the most appealing baroque chamber-music anthologies presently on the market. The interpretative skills of these musicians are impressive, both on account of their thoughtfulness and for their unerring sense of an appropriate style. The repertoire consists mainly of rarely performed pieces of more than passing interest. The J.S. Bach 'Sonata in G major' is an arrangement for transverse flute, violin and continuo of the E flat Sonata for two manuals and pedal, whilst the two Telemann pieces show off the composer's chamber style at its most original and engaging. The C.P.E. Bach Trio Sonata, though marginally less interesting, perhaps, is a long way off being either dull or routine. Documentation is sketchy but is hardly required when the music speaks for itself as eloquently as this.

GERMAN CHURCH MUSIC. Exon Singers/Christopher Tolley. Priory PRCD243.
H. L. Hassler: Motets—Deus noster refugium; Verbum caro factum est; O admirabile commercium; Cantate Domino Jubilate Deo; O Domine Jesu Christe; O sacrum convivium. **Bruckner:** Tantum ergo in A flat major. **Liszt:** O salutaris hostia, S43. **Cornelius:** Three Choral Songs, Op. 18.

53' DDD 7/89

The Exon Singers began as a group of students from Exeter University who gathered during vacations to sing the services in various cathedrals. Here they explore an unjustifiably neglected area of the repertoire. Hassler studied with Gabrieli in Venice and became a master of the Venetian Polyphonic style. The motet, "O admirabile commercium", is one of his best examples, bearing comparison with anything by Palestrina. Bruckner was a devout Catholic and composed some of his most personal and deeply-felt music for liturgical use. This is one of no less than eight settings he made of the *Tantum ergo* and its simple, direct style will come as a surprise to those who know Bruckner only through the symphonies. Peter Cornelius's songs for unaccompanied eight part choir are richly colourful and the Exon Singers produce some sumptuous singing here. Christopher Tolley is a thorough and sympathetic musician who inspires his singers to some magnificent performances. Their beautifully blended and perfectly balanced tone, caught in a splendidly warm and full-bodied recording, is a model of unaccompanied choral singing. This is a disc to treasure.

GUITAR RECITAL. Eleftheria Kotzia (gt). Pearl SHECD9609.
Tippett: The blue guitar. **Pujol:** Tristango en vos. Preludio tristón. Candombe en mi. **Villa-Lobos:** Five Preludes. **Delerue:** Mosaïque. **Giorginakis:** Four Greek images. **Fampas:** Greek Dances Nos. 1 and 3.

67' DAD 6/89

Many guitar recitals have a familiar appearance, but Ms Kotzia is not given to stale cloning in her choice of repertory; she assembles a nicely varied programme of music by six composers, none of whom is Spanish. The Five Preludes of Villa-Lobos, vignettes of Brazil and its life, have been recorded many times but this clear and firm account is, if not the best, good enough to live with. None of the other items has any other current recording; the most substantial is Tippett's only solo-guitar work, *The blue guitar*. Georges Delerue is briefer but no less purposeful in putting together his 'mosaic' of textures. The rest speak with distinctly regional accents: Pujol's Preludes celebrate Argentinian folk idioms in present-day popular terms, whilst Giorginakis's *Images* and Fampas's arrangements of traditional dances are as Greek as Ms Kotzia herself. Her freshness, spontaneity and positiveness are mirrored in this squeaky-clean and admirable recording. She clearly enjoys herself and transmits her pleasure to the listener.

IN NOMINE. Fretwork (Richard Campbell, treb viols; Julia Hodgson, Richard Boothby, ten and bass viols; Elizabeth Liddle, treb and ten viols; William Hunt, treb, ten and great bass viols) with [a]**Christopher Wilson** (lte). Amon Ra CDSAR29.

Tallis: In Nomines—à 4, No. 1; à 4, No. 2. *Tallis* (attrib.): Solfaing Song à 5ª. Fantasia à 5 (reconstr. Milsom). Libera nos, salva nos à 5. *Tye:* In Nomines—à 5, "Crye"; à 5, "Trust". *Cornyshe:* Fa la sol à 3. *Baldwin:* In Nomine à 4. *Bull:* In Nomine à 5ª. *Byrd:* In Nomine à 4, No. 2. Fantasia à 3, No. 3ª. *Taverner:* In Nomines—for luteª; à 4. *Preston:* O lux beata Trinitas à 3ª. *R. Johnson* (c.1490-c.1565): In Nomine à 4. *Parsons:* In Nomine à 5. Ut re mi fa sol la à 4. *Ferrabosco I:* In Nomine à 5ª. Lute Fantasia No. 5ª. Fantasia à 4ª.

60' DDD 3/88

For the wary, *In Nomines* are instrumental chamber works popular in England during the sixteenth and seventeenth centuries, in which counterpoints are woven around a pre-existing tune from the Sarum antiphon *Gloria tibi Trinitas*. Fretwork is an ensemble of young viol players who are rapidly revitalizing the English repertory. Many of the composers will be familiar; others—such as Tye, Cornyshe, Baldwin, Preston, Johnson and Parsons—will be known only to the initiated. Nevertheless, together they represent the core of a rich tradition of music for accomplished amateurs, music which kings and commoners alike enjoyed playing up until the Restoration. This is a very attractive and well recorded programme of undemanding music.

ITALIAN BAROQUE MUSIC. English Chamber Orchestra/Raymond Leppard. Classics for Pleasure CD-CFP4371. From HQS1232 (10/70). *Albinoni:* Sonatas a cinque, Op. 2—No. 3 in A major; No. 6 in G minor. *Corelli:* Concerto Grosso in F major, Op. 6 No. 9. *Vivaldi:* Concertos—D major, RV121; E flat major, RV130, "Al Santo Sepolcro"; G minor, RV156.

44' ADD 11/89 £

This well-chosen anthology of late baroque Italian concertos was recorded in 1970. Ideas about how to perform eighteenth-century music have changed considerably since then but in no way does that diminish interpretations as tasteful and animated as these. A disc such as this contains much that was most stylish in baroque performance 20 years ago and many a supposedly 'authentic' approach to the same repertory has subsequently fallen far short of what Raymond Leppard and the English Chamber Orchestra achieve here. The two Albinoni works are, perhaps, especially appealing for their tender slow movements which Leppard treats with affecting warmth; but there is little or nothing here to disappoint listeners. The programme is pleasingly contrasted, well played and well recorded.

JACQUELINE DU PRE—HER EARLY BBC RECORDINGS. Jacqueline du Pré, [f]William Pleeth (vcs); **[deg]Ernest Lush, [c]Stephen Kovacevich** (pfs). EMI Studio mono CDM7 63165/6-2. Recorded at broadcast performances on [a]January 7th, 1962, [b]January 26th, 1962, [c]February 25th, 1965, [dg]March 22nd, 1961, [e]September 3rd, 1962, [f]March 17th, 1963.
CDM7 63165-2—Bach: Solo Cello Suites—No. 1 in G major, BWV1007[a]; No. 2 in D minor, BWV1008[b]. *Britten:* Cello Sonata in C major, Op. 65—Scherzo and March[c]. *Falla* (arr. Maréchal): Suite populaire espagnole[d]. *CDM7 63166-2—Brahms:* Cello Sonata No. 2 in F major, Op. 99[e]. *F. Couperin:* Nouveaux Concerts—Treizième Concert[f]. *Handel* (arr. Slatter): Oboe Concerto in G minor, HWV287[g].

② 60' 52' ADD 9/89 £ [9]P

We owe the BBC and EMI a debt of gratitude for making these valuable
recordings available on disc. The performances date from her mid- to late-

teens, and reveal a maturity and passion that is rare in so young a performer. This, together with her wonderful gift of communication, make these performances very special indeed. The two Bach Cello Suites have a magical, intimate poetry that transfixes the attention from the very first note and her beautifully phrased and lyrical readings more than compensate for any slight imperfections of articulation. Sadly we have only the Scherzo and March movements from the Britten Cello Sonata, and judging by the quality of these, a complete performance would surely have been a recording to treasure. These are sparkling performances, full of wit and good humour, reflecting the obvious rapport between the two young artists. The recording of Falla's *Suite populaire espagnole* dates from 1961 when du Pré was only 16 but is no less assured or technically accomplished. The performance is full of life and rhythmic vitality, with some very tender and expressive playing, as in the cantabile melodies of the "Nana" and "Cancion" movements. The mono recordings are not of the highest quality (the Bach Suites are taken from transcription discs, so there are traces of surface noise and clicks) but this is of little relevance when we are presented with playing as beautiful and captivating as this.

LAMENTO D'ARIANNA. VARIOUS SETTINGS. The Consort of Musicke/Anthony Rooley. Deutsche Harmonia Mundi Editio Classica GD77115. Texts and translations included. From 1C 165 169504-3 (2/85). *Monteverdi:* Lamento d'Arianna a voce sola. Lamento d'Arianna a 5. Pianto della Madonna voce sola. *Bonini:* Lamento d'Arianna in stile recitavo. *Pari:* Il lamento d'Arianna. *Costa:* Pianto d'Arianna a voce sola. *Il Verso:* Lasciatemi morire a 5. *Roscarini:* Reciproco amore a 3.

(2)   1h 48'   ADD   12/90   £ ✒

This is an historic recording and it recalls a moment of particular significance in the history of music. Monteverdi's *Arianna* first saw the light of day in Mantua in 1608. None of it survives except for Arianna's great dramatic lament after she has been abandoned by Teseo. The lament, which had apparently moved the Mantuan audience to tears, was central to the whole opera and it became extremely popular in its own right. Other composers imitated it and a new style of dramatic composition for solo voice was born as a result. In 1984 Anthony Rooley had the splendid idea of searching out some of these other seventeenth- century compositions and bringing them all together in a single programme. The two resulting LPs are now reissued as CDs and we can enjoy, first and foremost, Monteverdi's own original version, ably sung with profound understanding by Emma Kirkby, with accompaniment for chitarrone; and also the composer's well-known five-part madrigal using the same material (1614), as well as his much later (1640) reworking of this music, transformed into a somewhat sentimental meditation, for solo voice and organ, a religious lament placed in the mouth of the Madonna at the foot of the Cross. The five lesser-known compositions have each something new to offer: Bonini's dramatic setting may well come closest to the action of the original opera; Pari's contribution is a series of 12 madrigals analysing the successive emotions of the heroine. Costa's solo lament (Emma Kirkby again) is totally restrained and dignified. Antonio il Verso's madrigalian version, for all its extravagance, is clearly derived from Monteverdi's model. Roscarini, the latest of the six (1695), pushes extravagance to its limits. All of this is delightfully performed. This is a recording that throws much fascinating light on the way music changed course during the seventeenth century, but it is no less enjoyable for fulfilling such a useful purpose.

LIEDER. Dietrich Fischer-Dieskau (bar); **Gerald Moore** (pf). EMI CMS7 63167-2. Items marked [a] recorded at a performance in the Mozarteum, Salzburg on July 30th, 1962, [b] August 1st, 1963, [c] August 17th, 1964.
Busoni[a]: Lied des Unmuts. Zigeunerlied. Schlechter Trost. Lied des Mephistopheles. **Pfitzner**[a]: Sie haben heut abend Gesellschaft, Op. 4 No. 2. In Danzig, Op. 22 No. 1. Zum Abschied meiner Tochter, Op. 10 No. 3. Nachts, Op. 26 No. 2. **R. Strauss**[a]: Wozu noch, Mädchen, soll es frommen, Op. 19 No. 1. Ach weh, mir unglückhaften Mann, Op. 21 No. 4. Herr Lenz, Op. 37 No. 5. Traum durch die Dämmerung, Op. 29 No. 1. Ruhe, meine Seele, Op. 27 No. 1. Morgen, Op. 27 No. 4. Freundliche Vision, Op. 48 No. 1. Die Nacht, Op. 10 No. 3. Zueignung, Op. 10 No. 1. **Mahler**[a]: Rückert Lieder—Ich bin der Welt abhanden gekommen; Um Mitternacht. Lieder und Gesänge—Zu Strassburg auf der Schanz; Selbstgefühl. Des Knaben Wunderhorn— Des Antonius von Padua Fischpredigt. **Schubert**[b]: Erlkönig, D328. Der Wanderer, D493. Gruppe aus dem Tartarus, D583. Memnon, D541. An die Freunde, D654. Freiwilliges Versinken, D700. An die Leier, D737. Heliopolis II, D754. Der Musensohn, D764. Du bist die Ruh, D776. Der Einsame, D800. Im Abendrot, D799. Auf der Bruck, D853. Die Sterne, D939. Nachtviolen, D752. Geheimes, D719. Der Wanderer an den Mond, D870. Der Kreuzzug, D932. Nacht und Träume, D827. Schwanengesang, D957—Das Fischermädchen; Abschied. **Brahms**[c]: Die schöne Magelone, Op. 33. Feldeinsamkeit, Op. 86 No. 2. Auf dem See, Op. 59 No. 2. Komm bald, Op. 97 No. 5. Wie bist du, meine Königin, Op. 32 No. 9.

③ 3h 29' ADD 11/89 £ 9 P

A warm tribute is paid here to one of the great singers of our time. EMI have made splendid digital transfers of these 30-year-old recordings of Fischer-Dieskau singing the kind of repertoire in which he has always been supreme. He is at the very height of his powers (when he was in his late thirties) and at each of these 'live' recitals he was joined by that great doyen of accompanists, Gerald Moore. Between them they make music of the most supreme artistry. Rarely has such a perfect partnership between singer and accompanist been caught on record and there is certainly that added *frisson* of a 'live' performance. In truth, though, the audience hardly impinges on this recording and only the most hard-hearted of hi-fi fanatics could begrudge sharing such a sublime musical experience with the odd cough, click or clap. Collectors of more unusual repertoire will find much food for thought in the Busoni and Pfitzner songs. Busoni places quite severe demands on the pianist, and it is an object lesson in how to make the extremely difficult sound as easy as breathing that Gerald Moore gives us here. Mahler and Strauss provide some memorable music, with Strauss's *Traum durch die Dämmerung* one of the real highlights of the set. But it is, of course, with Schubert and Brahms that Fischer-Dieskau displays his consummate skill in performances of matchless technique and musical insight.

LIEDER AND SONG RECITAL. Peter Schreier (ten); **Wolfgang Sawallisch** (pf). Philips 426 237-2PH. Texts and translations included.
Brahms: Deutsche Volkslieder—No. 1, Sagt mire, o schönste Schäf'rin; No. 4, Guten Abend, mein tausiger Schatz; No. 15, Schwesterlein, Schwesterlein; No. 34, Wie komm'ich denn zur Tür herein? Wiegenlied, Op. 49 No. 4.
Prokofiev: Three Children's Songs, Op. 68. The Ugly Duckling, Op. 18 (all sung in German). **Schumann:** Dichterliebe, Op. 48. Der Nussbaum, Op. 25 No. 3.

72' DDD 4/90

This recital, a live recording made in Munich in 1984, caught Schreier and his pianist, Sawallisch, at the top of their form as a partnership. Their account of *Dichterliebe* encompasses every facet of the cycle, holding the attention from start to finish through the intensity of its utterance and flights of imagination. The grief, so poetically and movingly expressed by Heine and Schumann, is here delineated with raw immediacy yet no sense of exaggeration. The troubled, abandoned lover sings, in Schreier's plangent tones, with a poignant, tearful feeling that goes to the heart of things and Sawallisch's playing is fully supportive of the tenor's reading. As compared with Bär, Schreier sings in the original keys throughout: his is a more overtly emotional reading, but both deserve recommendation. In the Brahms, Schreier and Sawallisch rightly adopt a lighter, yet equally pointed style. The Prokofiev group shows Schreier equally adept in a very different idiom. Here, instead of attempting phonetic Russian, he very sensibly uses his own German translations and thus makes the most of the text. The audience noises, applause apart, are minimal and the recording conveys the sense of a real occasion.

MELODIES FRANCAISES. José van Dam (bar); **Jean-Philippe Collard** (pf). EMI CDC7 49288-2. Texts and translations included.
Berlioz: Les nuits d'été, Op. 7. *Ibert:* Chansons de Don Quichotte. *Fauré:* Claire de lune, Op. 46 No. 2. Les berceaux, Op. 23 No. 1. En prière. *Poulenc:* Chansons gaillardes. *Ropartz:* Quatre poèmes d'après l'intermezzo.

77' DDD 1/90

Berlioz's cycle *Les nuits d'été* dates from 1841 and though these six songs are more often heard in their later orchestral version this original one with piano is more intimate and helps us to appreciate Theophile Gautier's texts. Fauré is represented by three characteristically gentle songs; but otherwise the recital invites us to explore less familiar territory. The songs that Ibert wrote for a 1932 film about Don Quixote are less well known than Ravel's on the same subject, but they offer both tenderness and wit, and although Guy Ropartz's *Four Poems* have less obvious charm they too are beautifully imagined. For many people, though, a special delight in this collection will be Poulenc's *Chansons gaillardes*, whose title might perhaps be translated as "Saucy Songs"; these are vivid settings of eight anonymous and uninhibited seventeenth-century texts about such pleasures as love and drinking. The Belgian baritone José van Dam has a vocal maturity and keen intelligence that together allow him to do justice to all this music, and his deft and sensitive piano partner Jean-Philippe Collard could not be bettered. The recording is clear and atmospheric.

MELODIES SUR DES POEMES DE BAUDELAIRE. Felicity Lott (sop); **Graham Johnson** (pf). Harmonia Mundi Musique d'abord HMA90 1219. Texts included.
Duparc: L'invitation au voyage. La vie antérieure. *Faureé:* Chant d'automne. La rançon. Hymne. *Bréville:* Harmonie du soir. *Sauguet:* Le chat. *Capdevielle:* Je n'ai pas oublié, voisine de la ville. *Chabrier:* L'invitation au voyage. *Debussy:* La balcon. Harmonie du soir. Le jet d'eau. Recueillement. La mort des amants. *Séverac:* Les hiboux.

65' DDD 4/88   £

This is an outstandingly creative and ingenious piece of programme-planning. The recital begins with Duparc's two masterly Baudelaire songs, demonstrating that with the right temperament and approach the writer is by no means unsettable. The Fauré, Chabrier and Debussy settings are in a sense uncharacteristic. In another sense, though, how very characteristic of Fauré that the most successful of his three songs (the charming *Hymne*) should set a poem that is hardly characteristic of Baudelaire, and how thoroughly typical that Chabrier should have lavished on *L'invitation au voyage* a virtual prospectus of his later musical style, and that he should then have withdrawn the song in modest acknowledgement of Duparc's supremacy. It is a striking piece, sung here with all the panache that its bold gestures need. The Debussy here is the enraptured young Wagnerite, matching Baudelaire's imagery with his own rich, saturated colours and brocaded textures: heady, sumptuous and impulsive. The four 'minor' composers each contribute a more than minor song that makes one eager to hear more of their work: a finely spun line rising to genuine passion from de Bréville, a delicately pretty miniature from de Séverac, Capdevielle's amply curving melody and, best of all, Sauguet's haunting evocation of a cat. Felicity Lott has the subtlety and the intelligence for these pieces and her pianist is no less resourceful. The recording is good and though texts are provided, translations are not.

MUSIC OF THE GOTHIC ERA. Early Music Consort of London/David Munrow. Archiv Produktion 415 292-2AH. From 2723 045 (11/76). **Léonin:** Viderunt omnes. **Pérotin:** Viderunt omnes. **Anonymous 13th-century French** (Montpelier Codex): Alle, psallite cum luya. Amor potes. S'on me regarde. In mari miserie. O mitissima. **Petrus de Cruce:** Aucun ont trouvé. **Adam de la Halle:** De ma dame vient. J'os bien a m'amie parler. **Anonymous 14th-century French** (Roman de Fauvel): La mesnie fauveline. **Philippe de Vitry:** Impudentur circumivi. Cum statua. **Anonymous 13th/14th-centuries French** (Ivrea Codex): Clap, clap, par un matin. Febus mundo oriens. **Machaut:** Qui es promesses. Lasse! comment oublieray. Hoquetus David. **Anonymous 14th-century French** (Chantilly Codex): Inter densas deserti meditans.

61' ADD 8/85

There is still no better all-round introduction to the marvels of medieval music than this exquisite anthology, a selection from the last and arguably the most enduring project undertaken by the late David Munrow. Much of this music had never been performed in modern times before and the singing and playing exude unusual freshness and vitality, inspired no doubt by the sheer excitement of discovery. The most indispensable performances here are without question those of music by Léonin and Pérotin, the earliest named European composers of polyphony. Their audacious and ambitious settings of *Viderunt omnes*, written for the newly-built Cathedral of Notre Dame in Paris during the second half of the twelfth century, rank among the most thrilling and taxing music ever devised for the human voice, and Munrow's interpretations remain unsurpassed. Following them comes a survey of the early history of the motet which in its chronological layout and comprehensiveness is no less an education than an entertainment. The only real regret is that the contents of the original three-LP boxed set have been pared down to an hour's worth of highlights.

MUSIC FOR THE LION-HEARTED KING. Gothic Voices/Christopher Page. Hyperion CDA66336. Texts and translations included. **Anonymous Twelfth Century:** Mundus vergens. Novus miles sequitur. Sol sub nube latuit. Hac in anni ianua. Anglia, planctus itera. Etras auri reditur. Vetus abit littera. In occasu sideris. Purgator criminum. Pange melos lacrimosum. Ver pacis apperit. Latex silice. **Gace Brulé:** A la doucour de la bele seson. **Blondel de Nesle:** L'amours dont sui espris. Ma joie me semont. **Gui IV, "Li chastelain de Couci":** Li nouviauz tanz.

60' DDD 10/89

Christopher Page has a remarkable gift for creating enthralling programmes of early music bound together by a brilliantly-chosen central theme, or appellation. This new collection is no less distinguished and every bit as fascinating, musically and historically. Whether or not Richard himself ever actually listened to any of these pieces is beside the question: they are all representative of the period of his lifetime and are gathered together here in his name for the 800th anniversary of his coronation (1189). Two types of twelfth-century vocal music are represented: the *conductus*—which can be written for one, two, three or even four voices and the *chanson*, or noble, courtly love song. The singers cannot be applauded too highly for performances marked by an extraordinary insight into how this music should be tackled, that is, with a fair degree of restraint as well as know-how, given the sort of audience it might have had in Richard's day: the royal court or the household of some high-ranking ecclesiastic.

NEW YEAR'S DAY CONCERT IN VIENNA, 1987. [a]**Kathleen Battle** (sop); **Vienna Philharmonic Orchestra/Herbert von Karajan.** DG 419 616-2GH. Recorded at a performance in the Grosser Musikvereinsaal, Vienna on January 1st, 1987.
J. Strauss II: DIE FLEDERMAUS—Overture. Annen-Polka, Op. 117. Vergnügszug, Op. 281. Unter Donner und Blitz, Op. 324. Frühlingsstimmen, Op. 410[a]. An der schönen, blauen Donau, Op. 314. *Josef Strauss:* Sphärenklänge, Op. 235. Delirien, Op. 212. Ohne Sorgen, Op. 271. *J. Strauss II/Josef Strauss:* Pizzicato Polka. *J. Strauss I:* Beliebte Annen-Polka, Op. 137. Radetzky-Marsch, Op. 228.

69' DDD 11/87

This is not only the finest collection of music by the Strauss family in the present CD catalogue, it has claims to being the finest Johann Strauss compilation ever recorded. It was the first time Karajan had conducted a New Year concert in Vienna and before he did so he prepared himself by returning to the scores for a

Kathleen Battle [photo: DG/Steiner]

period of intensive study. In the famous *Radetzky March* the audience was allowed to join in with the traditional hand-claps, but Karajan had only to glance over his shoulder and the sound was almost instantaneously quelled, so that the lyrical strains of the piece were not drowned. Throughout, the performances have the spontaneity of the most memorable live occasion. The Waltzes, *Delirien* and *Sphärenklänge*, are superb and in *Frühlingsstimmen* Kathleen Battle's deliciously radiant roulades are wonderfully scintillating, yet lyrically relaxed. The polkas, too, have irrepressible flair and high spirits. But it is at the arrival of the great *Blue Danube* that the magic of magic arrives. The horns steal out of the silence with their famous arpeggio theme and the strings take it up with an almost voluptuous richness. The rhythmic lilt has a special feeling unique to the VPO and at the end one is left quite overwhelmed by the experience, as if hearing the piece for the very first time. The recording is quite superb, with the acoustic of the Musikverein adding bloom and richness without robbing the definition of its natural clarity; few live occasions have been caught on the wing like this. An indispensable disc.

NEW YEAR'S DAY CONCERT, 1989. Vienna Philharmonic Orchestra/ Carlos Kleiber. Sony Classical CD45938. Recorded at performances in the Grosser Saal, Musikverein, Vienna on December 31st 1988 and January 1st, 1989. From CBS CD45564 (7/89).
J. Strauss II: Accelerationen—Walzer, Op. 234. Bauern-Polka, Op. 276. DIE FLEDERMAUS— Overture. Künstlerleben—Walzer, Op. 316. Eljen a Magyar!—Ungarische Polka schnell, Op. 322. Im Krapfenwaldl—Französiche Polka, Op. 336. Frühlingsstimmen—Walzer, Op. 410. RITTER PASMAN— Csárdás. An der schönen, blauen Donau—Walzer, Op. 314. *Josef Strauss:* Die Libelle—Polka Mazur, Op. 204. Moulinet—Polka, Op. 57. Plappermäulchen—Polka schnell, Op. 245. Jockey—Polka schnell, Op. 278. *Johann II/Josef Strauss:* Pizzicato-Polka. *Johann Strauss I:* Radetzky March, Op. 228.

♪♪ 76' DDD 2/91	£

The special ingredient added in 1989 to Vienna's usual New Year's Day confection of waltzes and polkas from the Strauss family was Carlos Kleiber. He brought a depth of flavour to the expected spice and froth without making the mixture too heavy, and the result delighted even the most particular gourmets. Captured on disc, the concert retains much of the sparkle of the occasion and some of Kleiber's individual contribution to Strauss interpretation, but the issue as a whole is perhaps best heard as a record of a special event that incidentally meets a demand that most of the standard, run-of-the-mill collections of Strauss waltzes only half-heartedly fulfil. The Sony recording is surprisingly good considering the problems of recording live in this venue and whilst the sound does not equal the best of some studio recordings of this repertoire, it does sizzle with authenticity.

OPERA CHORUSES. Chorus and Orchestra of the Royal Opera House, Covent Garden/Bernard Haitink. EMI CDC7 49849-2. Texts and translations included.
Beethoven: FIDELIO—O welche Lust (with John Mark Ainsley, ten; Alistair Miles, bar). *Berlioz:* LES TROYENS—Royal Hunt and Storm. *Bizet:* CARMEN—Les voici! voici la quadrille! (Haberdashers' Aske's School Boys' Choir). *Donizetti:* LUCIA DI LAMMERMOOR—Per te d'immenso giubilo; D'immenso giubilo. *Giordano:* ANDREA CHENIER—O pastorelle, addio. *Mascagni:* CAVALLERIA RUSTICANA—Easter Hymn (Helen Field, sop). *Verdi:* AIDA—Gloria all'Egitto. NABUCCO—Va, pensiero. OTELLO—Fuoco di gioia. IL TROVATORE—Vedi! le fosche notturne spoglie. *Wagner:* LOHENGRIN—Treulich geführt. *Weber:* DER FREISCHUTZ—Was gleicht wohl auf Erden dem Jägervergnügen.

♪♪ 61' DDD 12/89	Ⓑ

After an evening at the opera it is usually the arias and soloists that come in for remark and discussion, but quite often what actually brings the greatest enjoyment and remains in the memory as most vivid and colourful is a chorus or a passage of ensemble. Composers tend to reserve their broadest tunes for the chorus, and in this selection we have the Easter Hymn, Anvil Chorus, Wedding March and Chorus of Hebrews, all among the world's best. Less obvious, and a delight in context (both here and in the opera), is the Pastoral from *Andrea Chenier*. Altogether deeper in feeling, and most moving of all, is the Prisoners' Chorus from *Fidelio*. In each of the excerpts, the Covent Garden Chorus (so often overlooked in reviews) show themselves fully worthy of the attention bestowed on them. Haitink, never insensitive, sometimes misses the full effect of a climax, but the Orchestra are in fine form and give a particularly good account of the Royal Hunt and Storm from *The Trojans*. For the general listener it is a record that will give pleasure in itself and in stirring up a determination to go and see the operas again; for the Covent Garden *habitué* it will bring back memories, almost as if one were turning the pages of a picture-book, as the scenes and evenings return vividly to mind.

OPERA FINALES. Josephine Barstow (sop); **Scottish Opera** [a]**Chorus and Orchestra/John Mauceri.** Decca 430 203-2DH. Texts and translations included.
R. Strauss: SALOME—Es ist kein Laut zu vernehmen ... Ah! Du wolltest mich nicht deinen Mund küssen lasses, Jokanaan! (with Claire Livingston, mez; Graham Clark, ten). **Cherubini:** MEDEE—Eh quoi je suis Médée![a] (Clare Shearer, mez; John Treleaven, ten). **Janáček:** THE MAKROPULOS AFFAIR—She's on the whisky! (Anne Williams-King, mez; Graham Clark, Alasdair Elliott, tens; Jason Howard, Steven Page, bars). **Puccini** (comp. Alfano): TURANDOT—Principessa di morte![a] (Lando Bartolini, ten).

77' DDD 9/90

At the world première of *Turandot* in 1926 Toscanini turned to the audience and said "This is where the master laid down his pen." In fact Puccini had written sketches for the last scene, and Franco Alfano had worked on them very ably, producing a version which was played on the second night and has been adopted ever since. What was not generally known until as late as 1982 is that Alfano's reconstruction had been reduced by about a third. This is the first recording of the complete score, and after hearing it the listener is very unlikely to be satisfied with the finale as usually given, for this has far more colour, imagination and splendour. The disc is a valuable addition to the catalogue if on this account only. But its appeal does not end there. The closing scene in *Salome* has rarely leapt out from the disc to make as vivid a dramatic effect as here, and the ending of *The Makropulos Affair* loses surprisingly little of its inspired effectiveness by being heard as an excerpt. It is here that Josephine Barstow is at her best: elsewhere one feels a need for firmer production and more opulent tone, but this is her music, and she sings with touching beauty as well as the intelligence and spirit that so regularly distinguish her work. It is a pity that the printed notes do not put the scenes into dramatic context, but all else is fine, including the orchestral playing and contributions of the other singers.

ORGAN MUSIC FROM KING'S. Philip Ledger. EMI Eminence CD-EMX 2137. Played on the organ of King's College Chapel, Cambridge.
Bach: Toccata and Fugue in D minor, BWV565. **Brahms:** Chorale Prelude on "Es ist ein Ros' entsprungen". **Liszt:** Prelude and Fugue on BACH. **Vaughan Williams:** Prelude on "Rhosymedre". **Franck:** Chorale No. 3 in A minor. **Vierne:** Berceuse, Op. 31 No. 19. **Widor:** Toccata from Symphony No. 5 in F major, Op. 42.

54' ADD 3/89

Here are some of the most popular organ pieces of all. Widor's *Toccata* has never lost its immense popular appeal, while Bach's Toccata and Fugue in D minor has the distinction of being the most recorded piece of organ music on CD. Liszt's work based on the four-note figure derived from spelling Bach's name in German notation is one of the most exciting of romantic virtuoso organ works, with notes piling in one on top of the other and the organ compelled to produce an immense array of colours. The three quieter pieces (Brahms, Vaughan Williams and Vierne) are among the most beautiful of all organ miniatures. Only the most pernickety of enthusiasts would find anything to complain about in these splendid performances. Philip Ledger combines an academic thoroughness with a secure technique and just the right element of showmanship to bring the extrovert pieces off effectively and to avoid over-sentimentality in the reflective ones. The recordings capture splendidly both the unique flavour of this organ and the wonderfully resonant acoustic of this world-famous chapel.

PIANO RECITAL. Sviatoslav Richter. DG Dokumente 423 573-2GDO. *Scriabin:* Piano Sonata No. 5 in F sharp major, Op. 53. *Debussy:* Estampes (both from SLPM138849, 4/63. Recorded at performances in Italy during November 1963). Préludes, Book 1—Voiles; Le vent dans la plaine; Les collines d'Anacapri. *Prokofiev:* Piano Sonata No. 7 in B flat major, Op. 84. Visions fugitives, Op. 22—Nos. 3, 6 and 9 (all from SLPM138950, 8/65).

67' ADD 9/88

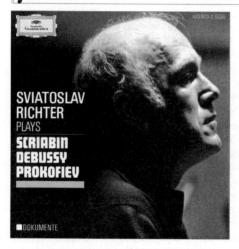

SVIATOSLAV RICHTER PLAYS SCRIABIN DEBUSSY PROKOFIEV

■DOKUMENTE

Richter has long been acclaimed as one of the most dedicated champions of Prokofiev's keyboard music, with the Eighth Sonata always particularly close to his heart. It would certainly be hard to imagine a more profoundly and intensely experienced performance than the one we get here, or one of greater keyboard mastery. After the yearning introspection of the temperamental opening movement and the *Andante*'s evocation of a more gracious past, the rhythmic tension and sheer might of sonority he conjures in the finale make it easy to understand why the composer's biographer, I.V. Nestyev, suspected some underlying programme culminating in "heroic troops resolutely marching ahead, ready to crush anything in their path". In the uniquely Prokofievian fantasy of the three brief *Visions fugitives* he is wholly bewitching. As for the Fifth Sonata of Scriabin, his impetuous start at once reveals his understanding of its manic extremities of mood. For just these Russian performances alone, this excellently refurbished disc can be hailed as a collector's piece. And as a bonus there is Debussy too, with infinite subtleties of tonal shading to heighten atmospheric evocation.

PIANO WORKS. Maurizio Pollini. DG 419 202-2GH. Items marked [a] from 2530 225 (6/72), [b] 2530 893 (7/78).
Stravinsky: Three movements from "Petrushka"[a]. *Prokofiev:* Piano Sonata No. 7 in B flat major[a]. *Webern:* Variations for piano, Op. 27[b]. *Boulez:* Piano Sonata No. 2 (1948)[b].

69' ADD 11/86

The capacity to stupefy is not the only measure of greatness in a performer; but it is an important factor, and in very few piano recordings is it embodied to the extent of this one. It is there from the very first bar of the first *Petrushka* movement—few pianists have ever attempted the tempo Pollini takes. Similarly, the Boulez Second Sonata has never been recorded with anything approaching this accuracy, glinting articulation and incandescent vigour. The bitterness at the heart of Prokofiev's slow movement with its remorseless tolling of bells is starkly revealed, and Pollini responds no less acutely to the distilled poetry behind the apparently arid surface of Webern's *Variations*. Clearly the Russian works are the more likely to grab the first-time listener; the Webern and Boulez may leave you utterly cold, or else touch regions of your psyche you did not know you had. With Pollini as exponent and with exemplary DG recording, the second possibility should not be ruled out. Intellectually, dramatically, lyrically, virtuosically, whichever way you look at it, this is a superlative disc.

PIANO TRANSCRIPTIONS. Louis Lortie. Chandos CHAN8733. Items marked [a] from CHAN8620 (5/89), remainder new to UK.
Stravinsky: Three movements from "Petrushka"[a]. **Prokofiev:** Ten pieces from "Romeo and Juliet", Op. 75—Juliet as a young girl; Montagues and Capulets; Romeo and Juliet before parting. **Ravel:** La valse[a]. **Gershwin:** Rhapsody in Blue.

57' DDD 9/89

In Liszt's day the piano transcription could be a valuable means for the wider dissemination of orchestral music, as well as a vehicle for dazzling individual virtuosity. Since the advent of the recording the educational function has ceased to apply, but the potential for audience-dazzlement remains. With all four composers in Louis Lortie's recital it is also true to say that orchestral inventiveness draws an important part of its inspiration from pianistic idioms and *vice versa*. The three *Petrushka* movements are notorious for their pyrotechnic demands—none of which floor Lortie, whose playing is quite breathtaking in its finesse. His Prokofiev and Ravel are no less outstanding, with an almost uncanny ear for atmospheric texture (beautifully captured by Chandos in as fine a piano recording as you are likely to hear). The Gershwin *Rhapsody* is less happy—its individual touches seem more forced than idiomatic. But that's a minor blemish on an otherwise magnificent recital.

POPULAR ORCHESTRAL MUSIC. Dallas Symphony Orchestra/ Eduardo Mata. RCA VD87727. From RCD14439 (6/83).
Dukas: The Sorcerer's Apprentice. **Enescu:** Roumanian Rhapsody No. 1 in A major, Op. 11. **Mussorgsky:** A Night on the Bare Mountain. **Tchaikovsky:** Capriccio Italien, Op. 45.

51' DDD 9/89   £ qp

This disc is something of a showcase for Eduardo Mata and the Dallas Symphony Orchestra, with a recorded sound that is in the demonstration bracket. All four works receive excellent performances, but the Tchaikovsky and Enescu items are in a class of their own, and can be counted as amongst the finest in the catalogue. The *Capriccio Italien* is a truly riveting performance, with the opening brass fanfares sounding so realistic that you are transported to the best seat in the concert hall. This is a very Italianate reading, which glows with a sumptuous and full-bodied string sound, and the coda has a marvellous feeling of joy and abandonment, whilst still maintaining an air of elegance. Mussorgsky's *A Night on the Bare Mountain* is given a very fine performance technically, with excellent articulation in the strings and powerful playing from the brass section, but somehow misses the terror of the piece. Much the same can be said of their account of Dukas's ever popular *The Sorcerer's Apprentice*, which is a very smooth and polished reading, but lacking perhaps that last ounce of malfeasance required to really make the spine tingle in the climax. Enescu's kaleidoscopic *Roumanian* Rhapsody No. 1 provides the perfect ending to this superb disc (a real encore item if ever there was one). The Dallas Symphony Orchestra play with unflagging energy here, with the woodwind section positively sparkling. At mid-price this disc is an absolute must.

POPULAR VIOLIN REPERTOIRE. Itzhak Perlman; [a]**The English Chamber Orchestra/Daniel Barenboim.** Classics for Pleasure CD-CFP4492. From SEOM22 (1/76).
Sarasate: Carmen Fantasy, Op. 25 (with The Royal Philharmonic Orchestra/Lawrence Foster). *Tartini* (arr. Kreisler): Variations on a Theme by Corelli (with Samuel Sanders, pf). *Nováček:* Perpetuum mobile (with Sanders). *Scott Joplin* (arr. Perlman): The Entertainer (with André Previn, pf). *J.S. Bach:* Violin Concerto in E major, BWV1042[a]. *Paganini:* Caprices—No. 9 in E major, Op. 1; No. 24 in A minor, Op. 1.

49' ADD 1/91 £

This ebullient little compilation of violin virtuosity was first issued in 1975 but, digitally remastered, it sounds as fresh now as it did then. No attempt is made to disguise its composite nature: three pieces with piano are interpolated between the two major works with orchestra—Sarasate's delicious *Carmen Fantasy* and the Bach Concerto—and they are rounded off with solo pieces, two of the great Paganini *Caprices*. Nevertheless, the whole hangs together admirably, with plenty of contrast, yet balanced by stylistic links between the Sarasate and Paganini, the Tartini and Bach. Perlman tackles the Herculean demands of the *Carmen Fantasy* with relish and, although even he does not always bring off the razzle-dazzle to perfection, the vigour and self-awareness of the music are splendidly caught. In the Bach, the ECO dig deep for Barenboim, and the close spread of the soundstage contributes to the impression of a classic recording of yesteryear, minus its attendant limitations. It is this performance that is the meat of the disc, and Perlman's pyrotechnics in the following Caprices provide the frothy desert. At less than 50 minutes we are left asking for more, but perhaps, at bargain price, that would be greed?

THE ROMANTIC CLARINET. Emma Johnson (cl); **English Chamber Orchestra/Gerard Schwarz.** ASV CDDCA659.
Weber: Clarinet Concerto No. 2 in E flat major, Op. 64. *Spohr:* Clarinet Concerto No. 1 in C minor, Op. 26. *Crusell:* Clarinet Concerto No. 3 in B flat major, Op. 11.

70' DDD

This nicely balanced and beautifully played recital couples three concertos of great charm from around the turn of the last century. All three works were written with specific clarinet virtuosos in mind. Weber's prowess as an operatic composer finds an exciting outlet in his charming Concerto which treats the clarinet very much in the role of soloistic diva. The Spohr Concerto is gentler in texture, searching out the more plangent qualities of the solo instrument. Crusell's three concertos are works of great charm and melodiousness and are rightly enjoying a just revival in recent years—no doubt to due to Emma Johnson's characterful advocacy. She plays beautifully and with great taste throughout this disc. The English Chamber Orchestra accompany with great panache and Gerard Schwarz presides sympathetically. The recording is good with a pleasantly immediate presentation of the soloist.

RUSSIAN MUSIC. [a]**London Symphony Chorus; London Symphony Orchestra/Sir Georg Solti.** Decca Weekend Classics 417 689-2DC. From LXT6263 (2/67).
Borodin: Prince Igor—Overture; Polovtsian Dances[a]. *Glinka:* Russlan and Ludmilla—Overture. *Mussorgsky:* Khovanshchina—Prelude. A Night on the Bare Mountain.

76' ADD 1/90 £ 9p Ⓑ

This excellent collection of Russian orchestral favourites, recorded in 1966, has lost none of its brilliance, warmth or clarity of detail in this CD transfer. The recorded balance is superb and sharply focuses the scintillating playing of the LSO under Solti's baton. This is nowhere more noticeable than in the Overture to *Russlan and Ludmilla.* Solti takes this at breathtaking speed, and one wonders if it is possible to maintain this without coming to grief; doubts, however, are soon dispelled as we are treated to a continuous stream of dazzling virtuosity and meticulous articulation, without losing any warmth of tone. Mussorgsky's gentle and folk-song inspired *Khovanshchina* Prelude provides a perfect foil to the Overture, before we launch once more into the orchestral fireworks with Solti's powerfully evocative account of Mussorgsky's *Night on the Bare Mountain*: a spine-chilling depiction of a witches' sabbath on St John's Eve, whose orgiastic revels are finally exorcized by the tolling of church bells. The two Borodin items that complete the disc come from his opera *Prince Igor*—the twelfth-century Russian warrior hero who was captured by the Polovtsians. The Overture is beautifully played, with a rich and sumptuous tone and equal amounts of élan, and the "Polovtsian Dances" are heard here in the complete version, with its percussion accompanied first dance and chorus (both sometimes omitted), and is the finest available version on disc. An ideal encapsulation of splendid Russian music and a bargain not to be missed.

SACRED CHORAL WORKS. Westminster Abbey Choir/Simon Preston. Archiv Produktion 415 517-2AH. Texts and translations included.
Palestrina: Missa Papae Marcelli. Tu es Petrus. *Allegri:* Miserere. *Anerio:* Venite ad me omnes. *Nanino:* Haec dies. *Giovannelli:* Jubilate Deo.

59' DDD 5/86

To listen to this disc is to enjoy a feast of sacred choral music composed by members of the well-known school of eminent Roman musicians of the

Simon Preston   [photo: DG/Bayat]

sixteenth and early seventeenth centuries. Palestrina heads the list with his *Missa Papae Marcelli*, but no less famous is the Allegri Miserere, which is performed here with a musical understanding and penetration that is comparatively rare. The alternating *falsobordone* verses excel in richness, and those of the semi-chorus, admirably distanced from the main choir, float across and upwards with an ethereal quality of amazing beauty and magic. The Choir of Westminster Abbey find plenty of scope to display their varied musical skills in the Mass itself, the psalm, and the four motets, and particularly enjoyable is the precision and crispness of the rhythm in Giovannelli's *Jubilate*, and also the careful balance and fullness of the sound in Anerio's *Venite ad me*. The unlikely venue of All Saints, Tooting has proved to be a particularly rewarding one.

SACRED CHORAL WORKS. Various artists. Classics for Pleasure CD-CFP4532. From EMI recordings made between 1957-81.
Arias from Sacred Choral Works by: ***Bach, Handel, Mozart, Haydn, Rossini, Mendelssohn, Fauré*** and ***Verdi.***

65' ADD 8/89 £

Here is a good collection of popular arias, which includes some interesting contributions from singers of the recent past. Elsie Morison's clear soprano tone and unfussy musicianship can be admired in "I know that my Redeemer liveth" from Handel's *Messiah*, from which oratorio Richard Lewis also sings "Comfort ye" and "Ev'ry valley" in fine style. Lewis's acount of "Sound an alarm" from Handel's *Judas Maccabeus* is also very accomplished, as is the young Kiri Te Kanawa's rendering of "Laudamus te" from Mozart's Mass in C minor, K427. Janet Baker's "O rest in the Lord" from Mendelssohn's *Elijah* was also recorded at a fairly early stage in her career, when her gorgeous voice still had a contralto characteristic and Lucia Popp's singing of the "Alleluja" from Mozart's *Exsultate, jubilate*, K165, also has an appealing freshness. Victoria de los Angeles is not quite at her best in the "Pie Jesu" from Fauré's Requiem and Robert Gambill's comparatively recent recording of "Cujus animan" from Rossini's *Stabat mater* is fairly ordinary, but items from Joan Sutherland, John Shirley-Quirk, Dietrich Fischer-Dieskau and Nicolai Gedda all have some distinction. The recordings are mostly over 20 years old, but all bear their years lightly.

SCHERZI FROM SEVENTEENTH CENTURY GERMANY. Cologne Musica Antiqua/Reinhard Goebel. Archiv Produktion 429 230-2AH. ***J.H. Schmelzer:*** Balletto in G major, "Fechtschule". Polonische Sackpfeiffen in G major. ***Biber:*** Sonata in B flat major, "Die Bauern-Kirchfartt genannt". Battalia in D major. Serenade in C major, "Nightwatchman's Call". Sonata in A major, "La Pastorella". Sonata jucunda in D major (attrib). Sonata in G major, "Campanarum" (attrib). ***J.J. Walther:*** Sonata in G major, "Imitatione del Cuccu".

66' DDD 1/91

This entertaining disc is not without its zany moments; do not, for instance, be unduly deterred at the outset by hearing the band cross a spacious hallway or saloon before tuning up, for what follows is a highly imaginative sequence of largely unfamiliar pieces of a mildly programmatic character. Most of the music hails from the Austrian south of Germany and contains that rewarding blend of fantasy and virtuosity which Reinhard Goebel and his Musica Antiqua Köln understand so well. They play with rhythmic clarity and a feeling for gesture and Goebel, furthermore, overlooks neither the humour nor the charming eccentricities present in some of these fascinating pieces. His own solo violin playing in Sonatas by Biber (*La Pastorella*) and Walther (*Imitatione del Cuccu*) is detailed, incisive and passionate and both these and other estimable qualities he furthermore demands from his ensemble. Unusual sonorities and startling harmonies are inherent in this music and Goebel savours every one of them. Biber's *Battalia* is vividly interpreted, at times with ferocious but entirely appropriate zeal and the delightful *Nightwatchman's Call* is played with warmth and sensibility. Goebel's accompanying essay and Arcimboldo's illustration provide a pleasing complement to an entertaining programme.

THE SERVICE OF VENUS AND MARS. [a]**Andrew Lawrence-King** (medieval hp); **Gothic Voices/Christopher Page.** Hyperion CDA66238. Texts and translations included where appropriate.
P. de Vitry: Gratissima virginis/Vos qui admiramini/Gaude gloriosa/ Contratenor. *P. des Molins:* De ce que fol pense. *Pycard:* Gloria. *L. Power:* Sanctus. *F. Lebertoul:* Las, que me demanderoye. *J. Pyamour:* Quam pulchra es. *Dunstable:* Speciosa facta es. *Soursby:* Sanctus. *R. Loqueville:* Je vous pri que j'aye un baysier[a]. *Anonymous fourteenth century:* Singularis laudis digna. De ce fol pense (after des Molins)[a]. Lullay, lullay. *Anonymous fourteenth or fifteenth centuries:* There is no rose of swych virtu. Le gay playsir[a]. Le grant pleyser[a]. The Agincourt Carol.

50' DDD 11/87

This collection is of music loosely associated with the Order of the Garter, founded by Edward III in the middle years of the fourteenth century. It includes some wonderful English works of the years 1340-1440, including the motet *Singularis laudis digna*, a wonderful canonic Gloria by Pycard, works by composers of the school of Dunstable (who influenced continental composers as no English composer has done since), and finally the famous carol celebrating Henry V's victory at Agincourt. Gothic Voices have in the last few years set new standards in the performance of this kind of music their attention to inner detail produces some beautiful results. Hyperion's characteristically informative and persuasive notes are also considerably helpful in bringing this music to life.

SIXTEENTH- AND SEVENTEENTH-CENTURY CHORAL WORKS. **King's College Choir, Cambridge/Stephen Cleobury** with [a]**David Briggs** (org). EMI CDC7 47065-2. From EL270095-1 (12/84).
Allegri: Miserere mei, Deus (with Timothy Beasley-Murray, treb). *Nanino:* Adoramus te Christe a 5. *Marenzio:* Magnificat a 8[a]. *Frescobaldi:* Messa sopra l'aria della Moniça. *Ugolini:* Beata es Virgo Maria a 12[a].

45' DDD 5/85

The central work on this disc, Allegri's setting of the penitential Psalm 51, *Have mercy upon me, O God*, is by far the simplest in construction, alternating a single strand of plainsong with straightforward harmonic passages for five-part choir and verses for a quartet of solo voices. Yet it speaks to the heart nowadays as clearly as it did in the early seventeenth century when it was written. There is a special frisson each time the treble soloist soars effortlessly to his top C. All the composers represented here worked in Rome, and this anthology seeks to illustrate the variety of musical styles current in Roman church music at this time. The choir sing all this ageless music with that understated confidence for which they are famous. Their voices are as cool as the spreading fan vault high above their heads. The recording embraces the stillness of this great space but with a balance which loses no detail.

SONGS OF LOVE AND WAR. **Julianne Baird** (sop); **Myron Lutzke** (vc); **Colin Tilney** (hpd). Dorian DOR90104. Texts and translations included.
Caccini: Amor, ch'attendi, amor, che fait. Amarilli mia bella (two versions). Caduca fiamma. *Sances:* Usurpator tiranno—cantata a voce sopra la Passacaglia.

Accenti queruli—cantata a voce sopra la Ciaconna. *Monteverdi:* Lasciatemi morire—Lamento d'Arianna a 1. *Handel:* O numi eterni, "La Lucrezia", HWV145. *Frescobaldi:* Il secondo libro di Toccate …—Toccata VIII (harpsichord solo). *Hasse:* Pastorelle che piangete.

64' DDD 1/91

The time has passed when early music performance was governed by the Rule Book without benefit of emotional response, an approach that did more harm to vocal than to instrumental music. Julianne Baird is prominent amongst those devoted to restoring common humanity to early music, aware and mindful of what the 'bible' says but reacting to her texts in ways she feels to be comfortable and natural. The songs and cantatas in this recording centre on the more sombre aspects of love—longed-for, one-sided or lost, and the war *per se* which features in the album title appears only peripherally in part of the programme. Another unifying feature is that the style of all the music is Italian, even when the composers are not. Two juxtapositions are particularly interesting: the two 'ground-based' cantatas by Sances, and the two versions of *Amarilli*, the second a floridly decorated one, despatched with consummate ease. Ms Baird's voice is clear (but warm) and flexible, and her portrayals of emotion never step out of proper stylistic line. Colin Tilney's solo contribution allows Baird (and us) to breathe in mid-programme. The admirable quality of the recording and of the annotation (texts given in four languages) helps to make this an irresistible disc.

SPANISH GUITAR WORKS. Eduardo Fernández (gtr). Decca 417 618-2DH.
Albéniz: Suite española—Sevilla (arr. Llobet); Asturias (arr. Segovia). España: Seis hojas de album—Tango (arr. Segovia). *Llobet:* Six Catalan folk-songs. *Granados* (arr. Fernández): Danzas españolas—Andaluza; Danza triste. *Alard* (arr. Tárrega): Estudio brillante. *Tárrega:* Five Preludes. Minuetto. Five Mazurkas. Recuerdos de la Alhambra. *Segovia:* Estudio sin luz. Estudio. *Turina:* Fandanguillo. Ráfaga.

64' DDD 2/88

When the classic guitar came to life around the turn of this century it was carried on a wave of Spanish romanticism and this area of the repertory remains central to an understanding of it. The virtuoso/composer Francisco Tárrega was the 'father of the modern guitar', Miguel Llobet was his student, and it was Andrés Segovia who carried their 'gospel' around the world; they thus represent a kind of 'dynasty'. This programme, including both arrangements and original guitar works, is a document of the guitar's renaissance and it is cleanly played by the Uruguayan virtuoso Eduardo Fernández, with clear tone and with an expressiveness that never overflows into sentimentality. The recording is utterly lifelike.

SPIRIT OF THE GUITAR. MUSIC OF THE AMERICAS. **John Williams** (gtr). CBS Masterworks CD44898.
York: Sunburst. Lullaby. *Mangoré:* Aconquija. La ultima canción. *Piazzolla:* Verano porteño. Cueca. *Ponce:* Scherzino mexicano. *Lauro:* Natalia. El niño. Maria Luisa. *Brouwer:* Berceuse. Danza caraterística. *C. Byrd:* Three blues (for classic guitar). *Villa-Lobos:* Chôros No. 1. *Sagreras:* El colibri. *Crespo:* Norteña.

54' ADD 8/89

Early forms of the classic guitar were among the instruments introduced into South America by the Spanish *conquistadores* in the sixteenth century; there they survived and prospered. Together with various other related plucked-string instruments, the present-day 'classic' guitar now flourishes in the multi-racial climate of that continent and its music has acquired a concomitant diversity of styles, characterized by tunefulness and rhythmic vitality. John Williams has assembled an immediately attractive programme of pieces by composers (some of whom play or played the guitar) from Paraguay, Argentina, Mexico, Venezuela, Brazil and Cuba. In time, the guitar spread through North America and, in this century, learned to speak jazz; items in Williams's programme by two guitarist-composers from the USA mark this further spread, those by Charlie Byrd are benignly jazz-based. The disc as a whole, played with Williams's precision-engineered perfection and finely recorded, celebrates the guitar's transatlantic transposition of a wholly light-musical level.

SWEET POWER OF SONG. Felicity Lott (sop); **Ann Murray** (mez); **Graham Johnson** (pf) with [a]**Galina Solodchin** (vn) and [a]**Jonathan Williams** (va). EMI CDC7 49930-2. Texts and translations included.
Beethoven[a]: 25 Irish Songs, WoO152—Sweet power of song; English Bulls. 12 Irish Songs, WoO154—The Elfin Fairies; Oh! would I were but that sweet linnet. **Berlioz:** Pleure, pauvre Colette. Le trébuchet, Op. 13 No. 3. **Brahms:** Vier Duette, Op. 61. **Chausson:** Two duos, Op. 11. **Fauré:** Pleurs d'or, Op. 72. Tarantelle, Op. 10 No. 2. **Gounod:** D'un coeur qui t'aime. L'Arithmétique. **Saint-Saëns:** Pastorale. El desdichado. **Schumann:** Liederalbum für die Jugend, Op. 79—No. 15, Das Glück; No. 19, Frühlings Ankunft; No. 23, Er ist's; No. 26, Schneeglöckchen.

> 62' DDD 11/90

This is a delightful presentation of an entertaining programme. The singers' careers have run concurrently with growing success on the international scene yet faithful to Graham Johnson as founding members of the Songmakers' Almanac. Here they recall many evenings of happy duetting at that group's recitals. They sing together with an instinctive rapport that is most gratifying. Johnson has devised a programme for them that provides an ingenious variety of mood and style. Beethoven's Irish Songs may not be great music but they are given vivid advocacy here. So are the more attractive and deeper duets by Schumann and Brahms. The Berlioz pieces, nicely contrasted, are well done; so are the Gounod, Fauré and Chausson items, even if a shade more accenting of words would have been welcome here. The real winner among the French items—surely a collector's item of the future—is Gounod's *L'Arithmétique*, an amusing lesson in Victorian thrift delivered in both French and English. Johnson supplies appropriate accompaniments and interesting notes. The recording naturally balances voices and piano.

SYMPHONIC SPECTACULAR. Cincinnati Pops Orchestra/Erich Kunzel. Telarc CD80170.
Shostakovich: Festival Overture, Op. 96. **Wagner:** DIE WALKURE—Ride of the Valkyries. **Falla:** El amor brujo—Ritual fire dance. **Bizet:** L'Arlésienne—Suite No. 2: Farandole. **Järnefelt:** Praeludium. **Chabrier:** España. **Tchaikovsky:** Marche slave, Op. 31. **Halvorsen:** Entry of the Boyars. **Enescu:** Roumanian Rhapsody No. 1 in A major, Op. 11. **Khachaturian:** Gayaneh—Sabre dance.

> 54' DDD 10/89

From this disc's title you might suppose that it provides a diet of music that is loud, fast, and luridly orchestrated—and you wouldn't be far wrong in that assessment. Yet there must be some leavening to make this palatable and the Cincinnati Pops provide this in those unguarded moments that most of these works contain, when more reposeful ideas allow the players to bring gentle solos and quiet dialogues to the fore. The opening of the first of Enescu's *Roumanian Rhapsodies*, some episodes in Chabrier's *España*, and much of Järnefelt's *Praeludium* are such instances, and the playing here is particularly refined and atmospheric. When the heat is on, the orchestra reveals its familiarity with this music and lets rip with invigorating zest. The recording copes unobtrusively with all this, without complaint or artificial highlighting, and the orchestra is genially set in its moderately resonant acoustic. Tchaikovsky's *Marche slave* is ideally treated by this ambience and Erich Kunzel can maintain a fair pace throughout without the chords producing too lengthy a delay. If a collection of lollipops is what you are looking for, you could do a lot worse than opting for this nicely balanced selection.

TRUMPET CONCERTOS. Håkan Hardenberger (tpt); **Academy of St Martin in the Fields/Sir Neville Marriner.** Philips 420 203-2PH.
Hummel: Trumpet Concerto in E major. *Hertel:* Trumpet Concerto in D major. *J. Stamitz* (realized Boustead): Trumpet Concerto in D major. *Haydn:* Trumpet Concerto in E flat major, HobVII*e*/1.

59' 12/87

This recording made such a remarkable impression when it first appeared in 1987 that it created overnight a new star in the firmament of trumpeters. The two finest concertos for the trumpet are undoubtedly those of Haydn and Hummel and Hardenberger plays them here with a combination of sparkling bravura and stylish elegance that are altogether irresistible. Marriner and his Academy accompany with characteristic finesse and warmth, with the lilting dotted rhythms of the first movement of the Hummel, seductively jaunty. The lovely *Andante* of the Haydn is no less beguiling and both finales display a high spirited exuberance and an easy bravura which make the listener smile with pleasure. He is no less distinctive in the lesser concerto of Johann Hertel and the other D major work attributed to Johann Stamitz but probably written by someone with the unlikely name of J.B. Holzbogen. This takes the soloist up into the stratosphere of his range and provides him also with some awkward leaps. The Hertel work also taxes the soloist's technique to the extremities but Hardenberger essays all these difficulties with an enviably easy aplomb and remains fluently entertaining throughout. The recording gives him the most vivid realism and presence but it is a pity that the orchestral backcloth is so reverberant; otherwise the sound is very natural.

TWENTIETH-CENTURY CHAMBER WORKS. Jascha Heifetz (vn); [a]**Gregor Piatigorsky** (vc); [b]**Emanuel Bay**, [c]**Artur Rubinstein** (pfs). RCA Victor Gold Seal GD87871.
Debussy[b]:Violin Sonata in G minor. Préludes— Book 1, No. 8, La fille aux cheveux de lin (arr. Hartmann. Both mono and new to UK). *Respighi:* Violin Sonata in B minor[b] (new to UK). *Ravel* (arr. Roques): Sonatine in F sharp minor—Menüet[b] (from RB16243, 6/61). Piano Trio in A minor[ac] (HMV mono DB9620/22, 6/51). *Martinů:* Duo[a] (SB6661, 7/66).

73' ADD 9/90

Though the twentieth century has produced many fine violinists, the name of Jascha Heifetz still inspires a special awe, not least among fellow musicians, for his playing had exceptional eloquence and personality alongside a technical command that he displayed not only in dexterity but more often than not by imparting a subtle, inimitable colour to his tone when shaping a phrase. The works here are of the violinist's own time, for he had already made his début

aged five a decade before Debussy wrote his Violin Sonata towards the end of the First World War. He recorded that Sonata with Emanuel Bay in 1950, but we would not know it when hearing the sound as successfully remastered here, and this is playing of real distinction, even if the elusive middle movement is arguably over-forceful. Heifetz and his celebrated colleagues are also impressive in the Ravel Trio recorded in the same year, also a wartime work but of a different kind, having great power and feeling, though the gentle little Minuet from the piano Sonatine is taken too briskly. The Respighi and Martinů pieces are perhaps less striking at first, but here too we are fully held by the authority of the playing. As already suggested, little apology need be made for the sound in the major works despite the age of the recordings, though there is 78-type needle hiss in *La fille aux cheveux de lin* and one misses really quiet tone in the Ravel Trio. This disc is not only one for connoisseurs of fine violin playing.

TWENTIETH-CENTURY FLUTE CONCERTOS. Jennifer Stinton (fl); [a]Geoffrey Browne (cor ang); Scottish Chamber Orchestra/Steuart Bedford. Collins Classics 1210-2.

Honegger: Concerto da camera[a]. **Ibert:** Flute Concerto (1934). **Nielsen:** Flute Concerto, FS119. **Poulenc** (orch. L. Berkeley): Flute Sonata.

66' DDD 8/91

This is basically a vehicle for the artistry of the flautist Jennifer Stinton who presents two flute concertos (by Nielsen and Ibert) plus a transcription of the Poulenc Flute Sonata and a duo concertante by Honegger for flute, cor anglais and strings dating from the period of the Fourth Symphony. The Honegger in which Jennifer Stinton is joined by Geoffrey Browne will come as a surprise to those music-lovers who have not encountered it before; it is pastoral in character and has enormous charm and these artists play with great sympathy for the idiom. Gallic charm is a feature of the Ibert Concerto which also comes off very well. She gives thoroughly expert performances both of this lollipop and Sir Lennox Berkeley's arrangement of the no-less delightful Poulenc. The note reminds us that Honegger was present at the first performance of the Nielsen Concerto (which took place in Paris in 1926), which as the only Scandinavian piece is the 'odd-man-out' here. Though it is less brilliant than the Gallois performance, it is well played and the recording is very good in respect to balance, naturalness and presence.

TWENTIETH CENTURY OBOE MUSIC. Robin Williams (ob); [a]Julian Kelly (pf). Factory Classical FACD236.

Poulenc: Oboe Sonata[a]. **Britten:** Six Metamorphoses after Ovid, Op. 49. **Hindemith:** Oboe Sonata[a]. **Lalliet:** Prelude and Variations[a].

49' DDD 1/90

A very enjoyable recital of twentieth-century oboe music. The Poulenc Sonata was written in 1962, and was one of his last compositions. It is largely elegiac in character and this is finely captured in this elegant and sensitive performance. The gently flowing tempo in the opening Elegie is just right, and Williams's carefully shaped phrasing has much beauty and symmetry. The spirit of Prokofiev (whose memory the work is dedicated to) seems to hover over the energetic Scherzo with its spiky rhythms and angular melodic line, and the sadness of the "Deploration" has great plangency. The highlight of the disc is Williams's performance of Britten's *Six Metamorphoses after Ovid*; this highly inventive piece for solo oboe is a set of six character studies after Greek mythological beings: Pan, Bacchus, Phaeton etc. Williams's musicality really shines through, coupling subtle dynamic shading (Pan and Niobe) with great dexterity (Arethusa). Rhythmic vitality is strongly projected by both players in the jaunty opening movement of Hindemith's two movement Sonata (1938), and this is well contrasted with the more introspective *Sehr langsam* movement. A first-rate performance of Lalliet's *Prelude and Variations* rounds off the disc nicely. The recorded sound is fine, if a little close.

TWENTIETH CENTURY PIANO WORKS. Rolf Hind. Factory Classical FACD256.
Ligeti: Six Etudes, Book 1. *Martland:* Kgakala. *Messiaen:* Catalogue d'oiseaux—Le courlis cendré. *Carter:* Piano Sonata.

66' DDD 1/90

Even if you would need a lot of persuading to attend an all-twentieth century piano recital in the concert hall, you might well find Rolf Hind's programme well-chosen and well-balanced enough to listen to as if it were a short, continuous concert. Hind is a powerful player who needs good reason (that is, unambiguous instructions in the score) before he takes refuge in restraint. This means that his reading of Ligeti's second study is less gentle that it might be, but this is a rare miscalculation, and he crowns the set with an overwhelming realization of the complex textures of the sixth study, which seems to express a very direct and intense anguish. Martland's *Kgakala*—an African word meaning 'distance'—is the shortest item, but earns its place alongside Carter and Messiaen at their grandest. Carter's Sonata, from the days before he set tonality aside, and Messiaen's hypnotic evocation of the curlew's piercing melancholy are both, in their utterly different ways, major works, as well as intensely personal statements. Rolf Hind penetrates to the personalities behind the structures, and a close but undistorted recording helps to make sure that the listener is involved from first note to last.

A VENETIAN CORONATION, 1595. Gabrieli [a]Consort and Players/Paul McCreesh. Virgin Classics Veritas VC7 97110-2. Texts and translations included.
G. Gabrieli: Intonazioni—ottavo tono; terzo e quarto toni; quinto tono alla quarta bassa (James O'Donnell, org solo). Canzonas—XIII a 12; XVI a 15; IX a 10. Sonata VI a 8 pian e forte. Deus qui beatum Marcum a 10[a]. Omnes gentes a 16[a]. *A. Gabrieli:* Intonazioni—primo tono (O'Donnell); settimo tono (Timothy Roberts, org). Mass Movements[a]—Kyrie a 5-12; Gloria a 16; Sanctus a 12; Benedictus a 12. O sacrum convivium a 5[a]. Benedictus Dominus Deus sabbaoth (arr. Roberts. O'Donnell, Roberts). *Bendinelli:* Sonata CCC-XXXIII. Sarasinetta. *M. Thomsen:* Toccata I.

71' DDD 5/90

The coronation of a new Doge of Venice was always a special occasion, and never more than when Marino Grimani (1532-1605) was elected to that office. We do not know what music was played then, but the whole ceremony is notionally and credibly reconstructed in this recording by Paul McCreesh and his cohorts. The recording was made in Brinkburn Priory, a church whose acoustic (aided by some deft manipulation of the recording controls) is spacious enough to evoke that of the Basilica of St Mark, the site of the original event. Space *per se* is vital to the music of the Gabrielis, who excelled in using it by placing instrumental and vocal groups in different parts of the building—which thereby became an integral part of the music. A fine selection of music that *could* have been played then is enhanced by the opening tolling of a bell, a crescendo marking the leisurely approach of the ducal procession, and the impression of architectural space created by changing stereo focus. It would be difficult to speak too highly of the performances, supplemented by first-class annotation, in this memorable recording. A trip to Venice would cost a lot more than this disc but, though you could visit the real St Mark's, it would not buy you this superb musical experience.

VARIATIONS ON AMERICA. Simon Preston (org). Argo 421 731-2ZH. Recorded on the organ of the Methuen Memorial Music Hall, Massachusetts, USA.
Sousa (arr. anon): Stars and Stripes Forever! *Saint-Saëns* (arr. Lemare): Danse macabre, Op. 40. *Ives:* Variations on "America". *Buck:* Variations on "The Last Rose of Summer", Op. 59. *Bossi:* Etudes symphonique, Op. 78. *Lemare:* Andantino in D flat major. *Guilmant:* Sonata No. 1 in D minor, Op. 42.

66' DDD 11/90

There is more outrageous fun and brilliant showmanship on this CD than anyone has a right to expect. Argo have certainly made their comeback to the catalogue with a bang! The large organ in the Methuen Memorial Music Hall, Massachusetts actually began life in the Boston Music Hall, but was moved to its new home in 1899 in order to give more platform space to the newly-created Boston Symphony Orchestra. Boston's loss (albeit generously compensated by the new orchestra) was certainly Massachusetts's gain for here is an instrument capable of providing thrills and excitement in ample measure. It does demand, though, a player of exceptional virtuosity and music of suitable flamboyance. Both these criteria are more than met with Simon Preston and his programme of American or American-inspired music. All of these pieces would have been used at some time to entertain the huge audience which would flock to recitals in the days of the great travelling virtuosos such as France's Alexandre Guilmant and England's Edwin Lemare, whose *Andantino* in D flat became so popular that it was turned into an immensely successful 'pop' song—*Moonlight and Roses*. The home-grown composers, Messrs Sousa, Buck and Ives (the 'America' of the *Variations* actually being the same tune as the English National Anthem), vie with the Europeans in providing truly outrageous pieces. Here is organ music of the most extrovert kind. While Simon Preston's playing of these pieces is undeniably brilliant, for sheer technical audacity nothing outdoes his spectacular performance of Bossi's *Etudes symphonique*—a piece requiring from the player footwork which would be the envy of the most accomplished breakdancer on the Manhattan sidewalks.

VIHUELA MUSIC OF THE SPANISH RENAISSANCE. Christopher Wilson. Virgin Classics Veritas VC7 91136-2.
Milán: Libro de musica de vihuela de mano, "El Maestro", Book 1—Fantasias I, VIII, XI and XII; Pavanas IV and VI. *Narváez:* Los seys libros del Delfin—Guardame las vacas (two versions); Milles regres; Fantasia; Baxa de contrapunto. *Mudarra:* Tres libros de música en cifra para vihuela—Romanesca: o guardame las vacas; Pavana de Alexandre; Gallarda; conde claros; Fantasia que contrahaze la harpa en la manera de Ludovico. *Valderrábano:* Silva de Sirenas—Fantasia; Soneto lombardo a manera de dança; Soneto. *Fuenllana:* Orphenica Lyra—Duo de Fuenllana; Tant que vivray; Fantasia de redobles; De Antequera sale el moro. *López:* Fantasia. *Pisador:* Libro de Musica de Vihuela—Dezilde al cavallero que; Madona mala vostra; Pavana muy llana para tañer. *Mendoza:* Diferencias de folías. *Daza:* El Parnasso—Quien te hizo Juan pastor; Fantasia. *Anonymous 16th Century:* La morda.

59' DDD 4/91

This generously filled disc reflects virtually the entire vihuela repertory from Luis Milán (1536) to the much less familiar Esteban Daza (1572). The vihuela is a member of the viol family but whose strings, typically arranged in six or seven courses, each paired in unison, are plucked rather than bowed. Christopher Wilson, better known to us as a lutenist, has chosen his programme well though the quality of the music is, almost inevitably, uneven. The most impressive pieces belong to the earliest of the composers represented here—Milán, Mudarra and Narváez. Between them they produced music rich in fantasy and varied both in colour and form. Wilson brings their compositions to life imaginatively, rhythmically and with a fluent technique that should win many friends. The recording itself is admirable, capturing the wide range of colours of which both instrument and performer are capable.

VIRTUOSO ITALIAN VOCAL MUSIC. Catherine Bott (sop); **New London Consort/Philip Pickett.** L'Oiseau-Lyre Florilegium 417 260-2OH. Texts and translations included.
Rore/Casa: Beato me direi. *Cavalieri:* Godi turba mortal. *Cavalieri/ Archilei* (attrib.): Dalle più alte sfere. *Luzzaschi:* O primavera. *G. Caccini:* Sfogava con le stelle. Filli, Mirando il cielo. Al fonte, al prato. *F. Caccini:* O che nuovo stupor. *Rasi:* Ahi, fuggitivo, ben. *Gagliano:* Pastor levate sù. *Marini:* Con le stelle in ciel che mai. Ite hormai, "Invito all'allegrezza". *Frescobaldi:* Dunque dovrò—Aria di Romanesca. A piè della gran croce—Sonnetto spirituale, "Maddalena alla Croce". Se l'aura spira. *Monteverdi:* Exulta, filia Sion. Laudate Dominum in sanctis eius. *Bernardi:* O dulcissima dilecta mea. *Rossi:* La gelosia. *Carissimi:* Ferma, lascia ch'io parli—Il lamento in morte di Maria Stuarda.

69' DDD 11/88

To perform Italian early Baroque virtuoso pieces convincingly requires not only technical mastery and a certain elegance of vocal delivery, but also an intimate understanding of that bond between words and music that lies at the heart of the style. On this recording Catherine Bott displays a rich emotional range which projects the music to great dramatic effect. Part of her success is to do with the power and tonal flexibility of her voice, clear and bright at the upper end of the range and warm and evocative in its lower register. As to the ornamentation itself, this is negotiated almost effortlessly and to literally breathtaking effect in a piece such as Monteverdi's *Exulta, filia Sion*. The New London Consort accompany with great sensitivity, exploring in the process extremes of timbre and effect ranging from a simple organ accompaniment in Luzzaschi's *O primavera* to the excitingly full and percussive qualities of *Dalle più alte sfere*. This is a remarkable disc, not least for its brave exploration of unfamiliar repertory; no one with an interest in Italian music of the early Baroque can afford to miss it.

VLADIMIR HOROWITZ. THE LAST RECORDING. **Vladimir Horowitz** (pf). Sony Classical CD45818.
Haydn: Keyboard Sonata in E flat major, HobXVI/49. *Chopin:* Mazurka in C minor, Op. 56 No. 3. Nocturnes—E flat, Op. 55 No. 2; B major, Op. 62 No. 1. Fantaisie-impromptu in C sharp minor, Op. 66. Etudes—A flat major, Op. 25 No. 1; E minor, Op. 25 No. 5. *Liszt:* "Weinen, Klagen, Sorgen, Zagen", Präludium, S179. *Wagner/Liszt:* Paraphrase on Isolden's Liebestod from "Tristan und Isolde", S447.

58' DDD 8/90

More than any other pianist of his generation, Vladimir Horowitz was a legend
in his lifetime, not only for his staggering technique but also for the personality

and authority of his playing. Other pianists such as Rubinstein and Arrau may have been finer all-rounders (there were gaps in his repertory even in the classical and romantic field), but none has left so many performances distinguished by a special individuality that is covered, though hardly explained, by the word magic. As Murray Perahia has written, from the point of view of a pianist over 40 years his junior, "he was a man who gave himself completely through his music and who confided his deepest emotions through his playing". The performances in this last of his recordings, made in New York in 1989 and with superlative piano sound, are wonderfully crystalline and beautifully articulated, yet there is warmth too in the Haydn sonata that begins his programme and nothing whatever to suggest that octogenarian fingers were feeling their age or that his fine ear had lost its judgement. The rest of the disc is devoted to Chopin and Liszt, two great romantic composers with whom he was always associated, the last piece being Liszt's mighty transcription of Wagner's *Liebestod*, in which the piano becomes a whole operatic orchestra topped by a soprano voice singing out her love for the last time. Apparently this was the last music Horowitz ever played, and no more suitable ending can be imagined for a great pianistic career informed by a consuming love of music that was expressed in playing of genius. A uniquely valuable record.

Vladimir Horowitz [photo: DG/Steiner]

VOCAL RECITAL. Régine Crespin (sop); [b]**John Wustman** (pf); [a]**Suisse Romande Orchestra/Ernest Ansermet.** Decca 417 813-2DH. Texts and translations included. Items marked [a] from SXL6081 (3/64), [b]SXL6333 (6/68). **Berlioz:** Les nuits d'été. **Ravel:** Shéhérazade[a]. **Debussy:** Trois chansons de Bilitis[b]. **Poulenc:** Banalities[b]—Chansons d'Orkenise; Hôtel. La courte paille[b]—Le carafon; La reine de coeur. Chansons villageoises[b]—Les gars qui vont à la fête. Deux poèmes de Louis Aragon[b].

68' ADD 11/88

Some recordings withstand the test of time and become acknowledged classics. This is one of them. Crespin's voluptuous tone, her naturally accented French and her feeling for the inner meaning of the songs in both these cycles are everywhere evident. Better than most single interpreters of the Berlioz, she manages to fulfil the demands of the very different songs, always alive to verbal nuances. In the Ravel, she is gorgeously sensuous, not to say sensual, with the right timbre for Ravel's enigmatic writing. The other songs on this CD enhance its worth. Crespin offers a highly evocative, perfumed account of the Debussy pieces and is ideally suited to her choice of Poulenc, of which her interpretation of "Hôtel" is a classic. Ansermet and his orchestra, though not quite note perfect, are—like the singer—right in timbre and colour for both these rewarding cycles. The sound is reasonable given the age of the recording. This is a most desirable acquisition.

WIEN MODERN. [a]**Vienna Jeunesse Choir; Vienna Philharmonic Orchestra/Claudio Abbado.** DG 429 260-2GH. Texts and translations included. Recorded at performances in the Musikverein, Vienna in October 1988. *Boulez:* Notations I-IV (1945/78). *Ligeti:* Atmosphères (1961). Lontano (1967). *Nono:* Liebeslied (1954)[a]. *Rihm:* Départ (1988)[a].

46' DDD 4/90

'Live' recordings of contemporary music concerts are, understandably, rare. Too much can go wrong: in particular, the playing, however well-rehearsed, can develop the rough edges of anxiety and even hostility which make for dispiriting listening, especially when repeated. All the more reason, then, to celebrate the fact that *Wien Modern* is something of a triumph. Even without the crowning glory heard at the actual event, Berg's great set of *Three Orchestral Pieces*, Op. 6, the programme has the strong central focus of two of Ligeti's hypnotic orchestral soundscapes, played with brilliant precision under Abbado's strong yet never over-bearing control. The Boulez miniatures—reworkings of early piano pieces—are no less riveting. The rarity, Nono's early exercise in 12-note lyricism, and the novelty, Wolfgang Rihm's specially-composed Rimbaud setting, are not on the same high level of inspiration, but in these secure, confident performances, with an electric, live concert atmosphere conveyed in a first-class recording, they contribute substantially to what was, unmistakably, a very special musical occasion.

WORKS FOR CLARINET AND PIANO. Sabine Meyer (cl); **Alfons Kontarsky** (pf). EMI CDC7 49711-2.
Martinů. Sonatina (1956). *Penderecki:* Three Miniatures (1956). *Milhaud:* Sonatine, Op. 100. *Lutoslawski:* Dance Preludes (1953). *Hindemith:* Sonata in B flat (1939).

50' DDD 4/90

The Hindemith is the obvious classic among twentieth-century clarinet sonatas; most clarinettists play it, though few with Sabine Meyer's combination of all its qualities: thoughtful sobriety, even grandeur of utterance as well as smooth cantabile and agile friskiness. The Martinů is rather less familiar, but Meyer is so fond of its hauntingly lyrical slow movement and its hints elsewhere of quiet pastoral (and its obvious memories of Martinů's happy years in Paris) that she will win it many friends: it, too, is a classic. So is Lutoslawski's sequence of epigrammatic miniatures: tiny but very concentrated pieces, each demanding precise and subtly intense characterization, but allowing perilously little time for it. Meyer's range of colour and expression are invaluable here and they enable her to make the most of two non-classics: the amiable grace of the Milhaud rises above its new-kid-on-the-block assertiveness, the brisk toccatas and lyrical centre-piece of the Penderecki reminding us that he was a composer once. Kontarsky is a sympathetic but very positive partner; a pity that the recording subdues him somewhat. No complaints otherwise. This is an entertaining as well as an enterprising collection.

WORKS FOR VIOLA AND PIANO. Yuri Bashmet (va); **Mikhail Muntian** (pf). RCA Victor Red Seal RD60112.
Schubert: Sonata in A minor, D821, "Arpeggione". *Schumann:* Märchenbilder, Op. 113. Adagio and Allegro, Op. 70. *Bruch:* Kol nidrei, Op. 47. *Enescu:* Konzertstück.

73' DDD 12/90

The booklet tells us that Yuri Bashmet, still only 38, has already had 30 new works for the viola dedicated to him. And on the strength of this recital, excellently recorded last year in a Bristol church, one is tempted to predict that the number will very soon be doubled—not least because of this Russian artist's glorious tone. Perhaps first thanks should go to him and his closely attuned pianist, Mikhail Muntian, for enriching the CD catalogue with Georges Enescu's rarely heard *Konzertstück*, written in Paris in the composer's impressionable early twenties, and played here with intuitive understanding of its fantasy and lyrical rapture. Like that work, the four miniatures of Schumann's *Märchenbilder* of 1851 were also inspired by the viola itself, whereas Schumann's *Adagio and Allegro*, Bruch's *Kol nidrei* (based on one of the oldest and best-known synagogue melodies) and Schubert's A minor Sonata were originally written for valve-horn, cello and the now obsolete arpeggione respectively. But with his wide range of colour and his "speaking" phrasing Bashmet makes them all entirely his own, only causing the occasional raised eyebrow with slower tempo for slow numbers (such as Schumann's lullaby-like Op. 113, No. 4 and the *Adagio* of Schubert's Sonata) than could be enjoyed from players without his own fine-spun, intimately nuanced line. Strongly recommended.

WORKS FOR VIOLIN. Cho-Liang Lin (vn); [a]**Sandra Rivers** (pf); [b]**Philharmonia Orchestra/Michael Tilson Thomas;** [c]**Chicago Symphony Orchestra/Leonard Slatkin.** CBS Masterworks CD44902. Items marked [a] from IM39133 (2/85); [b] 39007 (6/84), [c] 42315 (3/87).
Mendelssohn: Violin Concerto in E minor, Op. 64[b]. *Bruch:* Violin Concerto No. 1 in G minor, Op. 26[c]. *Sarasate:* Introduction et Tarantelle, Op. 43. *Kreisler:* Liebesfreud[a].

61' DDD 3/91   £

The current catalogue is not short of good recordings of the Mendelssohn Violin Concerto and Bruch's First Concerto, and the two certainly make a good pair on a CD, particularly when the 50 odd minutes that they take are complemented, as here, with two short pieces (though only with piano) by virtuoso violinists who not surprisingly wrote superbly for their instrument. At medium price, this is a desirable disc, for Cho-Liang Lin plays with passion and tenderness, bringing out the various, but always romantic, moods of the two main works and the graceful *salon* charm of the others. He has an unfailingly expressive tone quality, and can shape an individual phrase with elegance while keeping in perspective the longer term issues of paragraphs and indeed whole movements. Maybe some other players have found a more sensuous beauty in the melody of the slow movement in the Mendelssohn, and let themselves go more as regards tempo in the finale, but Lin's slight restraint pays dividends with its own kind of aristocratic eloquence and his refinement is also a positive feature in the Bruch. The recordings are not especially new and come from different locations, which in three cases are American ones: the oldest is that of the Mendelssohn, which was recorded in London and dates from 1982. But the sound is well enough matched and fully digital as well as offering both clarity and atmosphere.

Information

Compact Disc Outlets-UK

AVON
†BATH COMPACT DISCS, 11 Broad Street, Bath
 BA1 5LJ
THE GRAMOPHONE RECORD, 65 Westbury Hill,
 Westbury-on-Trym, Bristol BS9 3AD
MILSOM & SON LTD, Northgate, Bath BA1 5AS
†PASTORAL MUSIC, 11 Christmas Steps, Bristol
 BS1 5BS
RAYNER'S RECORD CENTRE, 84 Park Street, Bristol
 BS1 5LA
PAUL ROBERTS HI-FI & VIDEO, 203 Milton Road,
 Weston-Super-Mare, BS22 8EF (branches elsewhere)

BEDFORDSHIRE
BEDFORD AUDIO-COMM, 29 Bedford Road, Kempston
 MK43 0EU

BERKSHIRE
HICKIE & HICKIE, 153 Friar Street, Reading RG1 lHG

BUCKINGHAMSHIRE
CHAPPELL'S OF BOND STREET, 21 Silbury Arcade,
 Central Milton Keynes MK9 3AG
RECORD HOUSE, 36 High Street, Aylesbury HP20 lSF

CAMBRIDGESHIRE
CMS RECORDS, la All Saint's Passage, Cambridge
 CB2 3LT
HEFFER'S BOOKSELLERS, 20 Trinity Street, Cambridge
 CB2 3ET
MILLER'S MUSIC CENTRE, 12 Sussex Street,Cambridge
 CB1 lPW

CHESHIRE
ASTON AUDIO, 4 West Street, Alderley Edge, Cheshire
 SK9 7EF
CHESTER CD CENTRE, 14 Godstall Lane, Chester
 CH1 lLN
CIRCLE RECORDS, 33-35 Victoria Street, Liverpool
 L1 6BG
CONCERT CORNER, 9 Union Street, Southport,
 PR9 0QF
RUSHWORTH'S MUSIC HOUSE, Rushworth's Corner,
 42/6 Whitechapel, Liverpool L1 6EE (branches
 elsewhere)

CLEVELAND
PLAYBACK, 122 Linthorne Road, Middlesborough
 TS1 2JR

CORNWALL
MUSIC MASTERS, 28 Fore Street, Lostwithiel PL22 0BL

DERBYSHIRE
COLLECTOR'S RECORD CENTRE, 6 Duckworth
 Square, Derby DE1 lJZ
MDT CLASSICS, 6 Old Blacksmith's Yard, Sadler Gate,
 Derby DE1 3PD
OASIS RECORDS, 314 Strand Arcade, Sadler Gate,
 Derby DE1 1BQ

DEVON
ACORN MUSIC (inc PETER RUSSELL'S HOT RECORD
 STORE), Grove Hill,Victoria Road, Barnstable,
 EX32 8DS
AMADEUS CLASSICS, 7 Frankfort Gate, Plymouth
 PL1 lQA
THE MUSIC DISC, 3 Cross Street, Barnstaple EX31 1BA
OPUS RECORDS, 14a Guildhall Centre, Exeter
 EX4 3HW

DORSET
BEALES, RECORD DEPT, 36 Old Christchurch Road,
 Bournemouth BH1 1LJ
COMPACT CLASSICS, 17 Quadrant Centre, St Peter's
 Road, Bournemouth BH1 2AB
COMPACT SOUNDS, 238 Ashley Road, Parkstone,
 Poole BH14 9BZ
THE MUSIC HOUSE, The Green, Sherborne DT9 3HX

ESSEX
BILLERICAY RECORD SUPPLIES, 7 Radford Way,
 Billericay CM1Z 0AA
BRENTWOOD MUSIC CENTRE, 2 Ingrave Road,
 Brentwood CM15 8AT
CHEW & OSBORNE LTD, 148 High Street, Epping,
 CM16 4AG
THE COMPACT DISCOUNT CENTRE,
 5 Headgate Buildings, Sir Isaacs Walk, Colchester
 CO1 lJJ
JAMES DACE & SON LTD, 33 Moulsham Street,
 Chelmsford CM2 0HX
HOWARD LEACH CLASSICAL, 49 Crouch Street,
 Colchester CO3 3EN

GLOUCESTERSHIRE
†AUDIOSONIC (GLOUCESTER) LTD
 6 The Promenade, Eastgate Shopping Centre,Gloucester
 GL1 lXJ
GOODMUSIC, 16 Cheltenham Trade Park, Arle Road,
 Cheltenham GL51 8LX

HAMPSHIRE
CARUSOS, Unit 4, Bargate Centre, Southampton
COUNTY MUSIC, 14 St George's Street, Winchester
 SO23 8BG
ORPHEUS RECORDS, 27 Marmion Road, Southsea
 PO5 2AT
VENUS, 8 Downing Street, Farnham GU9 7PB
WHITWAMS, 70 High Street, Winchester SO23 9DE

HEREFORDSHIRE
KING'S RADIO (HEREFORD) LTD,
 35 Widemarsh Street, Hereford HR4 9EA

KENT
†CAMDEN CLASSICS, 16 Camden Road,
 Tunbridge Wells TN4 ODS
THE CLASSICAL LONGPLAYER, 6 St Peters Street,
 Canterbury CT1 2AT
†EDEN COMPACT DISCS, PO Box 29, Edenbridge,
 TN8 5AW
THE MUSIC CENTRE, 3 Vale Road, Tunbridge Wells
 TN1 lBS

LANCASHIRE
†CLASSICAL CDs, Repeat House, Bright Road, Eccles,
 Manchester M30 0WR
FORSYTHS, 126-8 Deansgate, Manchester M3 2GR
GIBBS BOOKSHOP, 10 Charlotte Street, Manchester
 M1 4FL
REIDY'S, 11-13 Penny Street, Blackburn BB1 6HJ
SMITH'S, 41 Mesnes Street, Wigan WN1 lQY
†SQUIRES GATE MUSIC CENTRE, Squires Gate,
 Station Approach, Blackpool FY8 2SP

LEICESTERSHIRE
CLASSIC TRACKS, 21 East Bond Street, Leicester
 LE1 4SX
ST MARTIN'S RECORDS, 23 Hotel Street, Leicester
 LE1 5EW

LONDON

LES ALDRICH MUSIC SALON, 98 Fortis Green Road, Muswell Hill, London N10 3HN

BARBICAN MUSIC SHOP, Cromwell Tower, Whitecross Street, Barbican, London EC2Y 8DD

BARGAIN RECORDS, 9 The Arcade, High Street Eltham, London SE9 lBE

BUSH RECORDS, 113 Shepherd's Bush Centre, London W12 8PP

CHIMES MUSIC SHOP, 44 Marylebone High Street, London W1M 4AD

COLISEUM SHOP, St Martin's Lane, London WC2N 4ES

COVENT GARDEN RECORDS, 84 Charing Cross Road, London WC2H 0JA

DILLON'S UNIVERSITY BOOKSHOPS, 3 Malet Street, London WClE 7JN (branches elsewhere)

†FARRINGDON RECORDS, 52-54 High Holborn, London WClV 6RL (Branches elsewhere in London)

HARRODS LTD, Knightsbridge, London SWlX 7XL

THOMAS HEINITZ LTD, 35 Moscow Road, London W2 4AH

HMV RECORD SHOPS, 363 Oxford Street, London WlR lFD (branches elsewhere)

HAROLD MOORES RECORDS, 2 Great Marlborough Street, London WlV lDE

†MUSIC DISCOUNT CENTRE, 437 The Strand, London WC2R 0QU (branches elsewhere in London)

MUSIC & VIDEO EXCHANGE, 38 & 56 Notting Hill Gate, London Wll 3JS

ORCHESOGRAPHY, 15 Cecil Court, St Martin's Lane, London WC2N 4EZ

SOUND EXCHANGE, 50 Spencer Court, Spencer Road, London SW20 0QW

†TEMPLAR RECORDS, 9a Irving Street, London WC2H 7AT

TOWER RECORDS, 1 Piccadilly, London WlV 9LA (branches elsewhere in London)

TURNTABLE, 40 Station Road, Chingford, London E4 7BQ

VIRGIN MEGASTORE, 14-16 Oxford Street, London WlN 9FL (branches elsewhere)

MIDDLESEX

THE CD SHOP, 206 Field End Road, Eastcote, Pinner HA5 1RD

MUSIQUE, l Market House, High Street, Uxbridge UB8 lAQ

NORFOLK

†CD SEND, 105b Dereham Road, Norwich NR2 4HT

JARROLD & SONS LTD, 1-7 London Street, Norwich NR2 lJF

PRELUDE RECORDS, 9 St Giles Street, Norwich NR1 2JL

NORTHAMPTONSHIRE

CLASSICAL SOUNDS, Watling Court, 84E Watling Street, Towcester NN12 7BS

POLYHYMNIA, 3 Derngate, Northampton NN1 lTU

SPINADISC RECORDS, 75a Abington Street, Northampton NN1 2BH (branches elsewhere)

NOTTINGHAMSHIRE

CLASSICAL CDs, 27 Heathcote Street, Nottingham NG1 3AA

†WINGS MAIL ORDER, 52 Laverick Road, Jacksdale NG16 5LQ

OXFORDSHIRE

BLACKWELL'S MUSIC SHOP, 38 Holywell Street, Oxford OX1 3SW

RMR RECORDS, 3 Wilcote View, North Leigh, Witney OX8 6SF

SHROPSHIRE

CROTCHET & Co, Church Stretton SY6 6DR

DURRANT RECORDS, 84 Wyle Cop, Shrewsbury, SY1 lUT

SUFFOLK

†MAILDISC & Co, Linstead Road, Huntingfield, Halesworth IP19 0QP

GALLEON MUSIC, High Street, Aldeburgh, IP15 5AX

SURREY

H & R CLOAKE LTD, 29 High Street, Croydon CRO 1QB

COMPACT DISC INTERNATIONAL, 24 Tunsgate, Guildford GU1 3QS

MINIM, 916 London Road, Thornton Heath CR4 7PE

RECORD CORNER, Pound Lane, Godalming GU7 1BX

†RICHMOND RECORDS, 19 Paradise Road, Richmond TW9 lSA

TRANSITIONS, 19 The Centre, Walton-on-Thames KT12 1QJ

SUSSEX

BASTOW CLASSICS, 50 North Street, Chichester PO19 lNQ

THE CLASSICAL LONGPLAYER, 31 Duke Street, Brighton BN1 1AG

THE COMPACT DISC CLUB, The Woods, 14 The Arcade, Bognor Regis PO21 lLH

FINE RECORDS, 32 George Street, Hove BN3 3YB

MICHAEL'S CLASSICAL RECORD SHOP, 183 Montague Street, Worthing BN11 3DA

OTTAKERS PLC, 34 Duke Street, Brighton BN1 lAG (branches eleswhere)

†CG ROBSON IMPORTS LTD, 39 Winchcombe Road, Eastbourne BN22 8DE

SEAFORD MUSIC, 24 Pevensey Road, Eastbourne BN21 3HP

SOUNDS, 2 New Road, Brighton BN1 1UF

TYNE & WEAR

CLASSICAL CHOICE, 71 North Road, Durham DH1 4SQ

†JG WINDOWS LTD, 1-7 Central Arcade, Newcastle-upon-Tyne NE1 5BP

WARWICKSHIRE

SOUNDS EXPENSIVE, 12 Regent Street, Rugby CV21 2QF

WEST MIDLANDS

CD SHOP LTD, City Plaza, Cannon Street, Birmingham B2 5EF

EASY LISTENING, 1135 Warwick Road, Acocks Green, Birmingham B27 6RA

FIVE WAYS HIGH FIDELITY, 12 Islington Row, Edgbaston, Birmingham B15 lLD

HUDSONS BOOKSHOP, 116 New Street, Birmingham B2 4JJ (branches elsewhere)

†TANDY'S RECORDS LTD, 24 Islington Row, Edgbaston, Birmingham B15 lLJ

WILTSHIRE

MITCHELL MUSIC, 15 Cross Keys Corner, Salisbury

THE COLLECTOR'S ROOM AT SUTTON'S, 3 Endless Street, Salisbury SP1 lDH

YORKSHIRE

ADAGIO CLASSICAL RECORDS, 6 Westminster Arcade, Parliament Street, Harrogate HG1 2RN

BANKS & SON (MUSIC) LTD, 18 Lendal, York YO1 2AY

CALM & CLASSICAL, 144 West Street, Sheffield S1 4ES

CLASSICAL RECORD SHOP, 2 The Merrion Centre, Leeds LS2 8NG

FORSYTHS, 40 Great George Street, Leeds LS1 3DL
GOUGH & DAVY, 13-16 Savile Street, Hull HU1 3EH
†MAXJON RECORDS, 32 Elmfield Road, Huddersfield
  HD2 2XH
RIVERSIDE RECORDS, 2 Low Ousegate, York
  YO1 1QU
J WOOD & SONS, 11 Market Street, Huddersfield
  HD1 2EH (branches elsewhere)
WILSON PECK, 13 Rockingham Gate, Sheffield S1 4JD

CHANNEL ISLANDS
BASE HI-FI, 35 Hilgrove Street, St Helier, Jersey
COMPACT DISC CENTRE, 25 Halkett Street, St Helier,
  Jersey
DISC CENTRE, 13 Don Street, St Helier, Jersey
LES RICHES STORES LTD, St Brelade's Bay,
  St Brelade's, Jersey
NO 19 RECORDS & TAPES, 19 Le Pollet, Guernsey
SOUNDTRACK, Church Square, St Peter Port, Guernsey
TELESKILL LTD, 3-4 Market Street, St Peter Port,
  Guernsey

ISLE OF MAN
ISLAND COMPACT DISC CENTRE,
  Parliament Square, Ramsey

N IRELAND
CLASSICAL TRACKS, 15 Castle Arcade, Belfast
  BT1 5DG
KOINONIA, 6 Pottinger's Entry, High Street, Belfast
  BT1 2JZ

SCOTLAND
BAUERMEISTER BOOKSELLERS,
  15-16 George IV Bridge, Edinburgh EH1 lEH

DEVOY, 1099 Argyle Street, Glasgow G3 8ND
JAMES KERR & Co, 98-110 Woodlands Road, Glasgow
  G3 6HB
RAE MACINTOSH (MUSIC) LTD,
  6-8 Queensferry Street, Edinburgh EH2 4PA
†SILVER SERVICE CD, 24 Touch Wards, Dunfirmline,
  Fife KY12 7TG
JOHN SMITH & SON, 69 Kent Road, Glasgow G3 7EG
JAMES THIN LTD, 53-59 South Bridge, Edinburgh
  EH1 lYS

WALES
ABERGAVENNY MUSIC, 23 Cross Street, Abergavenny
  WP7 5EW
†CITY RADIO, 24 Charles Street, Newport, Gwent
  NP9 lJT (branches elsewhere)
PALACE BOOKS LTD, 78 High Street, Porthmadog,
  Gwynedd LL49 9NW (branches elsewhere)

MULTIPLES
The following outlets have branches throughout the
  country:
ALTO
BOOTS
DILLONS
HMV
OUR PRICE
WH SMITH
TOWER
VIRGIN

Many shops listed offer a mail order service. At the
time this list was compiled those marked † were known
to be specialists

Record Company Names and Addresses

ALBANY RECORDS (UK)—PO Box 12, Carnforth, Lancashire LA5 9PD (0524 735873)

ARCHIV PRODUCKTION—1 Sussex Place, Hammersmith, London W6 9XS (081-846 8515)

ARGO—1 Sussex Place, Hammersmith, London W6 9XS (081-846 8515)

ASV—Martin House, 179-181 North End Road, London W14 9NL (071-381 8747)

BMG ENTERPRISES (BMG CLASSICS)—Cavendish House, 423 New King's Road, London SW6 4RN (071-973 0011)

BMG ENTERPRISES—Lyng Lane, West Bromwich, West Midlands B70 7ST (061-525 3000)

SCOTT BUTLER DISC AND TAPE FACTORS—Unit 2, Lansdowne Mews, Charlton Lane, London SE7 (081-293 5258)

CBS RECORDS—*see* SONY MUSIC ENTERTAINMENT

CHANDOS RECORDS—Chandos House, Commerce Way, Colchester, Essex CO2 8HQ (0206 577300)

CLASSICS FOR PLEASURE—1-3 Uxbridge Road, Hayes, Middlesex UB4 0SY (081-561 8722)

COLLINS CLASSICS—77-85 Fulham Palace Road, Hammersmith, London W6 8JB (081-741 7070)

THE COMPLETE RECORD CO—2 Hepburn Mews, 63a Webbs Road, London SW11 6SE (071-924 3174)

CONIFER RECORDS—Horton Road, West Drayton, Middlesex UB7 8JL (0895 447707)

CRD—PO Box 26, Stanmore, Middlesex HA7 4XB (081-958 7695)

DECCA CLASSICS—1 Sussex Place, Hammersmith, London W6 9XS (081-846 8515)

DEUTSCHE GRAMMOPHON CLASSICS—1 Sussex Place, Hammersmith, London W6 9XS (081-846 8515)

DISCOVERY RECORDS—The Old Church Mission Room, King's Corner, Pewsey, Wilts SN9 5BS (0672 63931)

ELEKTRA-NONESUCH—46 Kensington Court, London W8 5DP (071-938 5542)

EMI RECORDS—20 Manchester Square, London W1A 1ES (071-486 4488)

EMI CLASSICS—30 Gloucester Place, London W1A 1ES (071-486 6022)

EMI—Sales & Distribution Centre, 1-3 Uxbridge Road, Hayes, Middlesex UB4 0SY (081-848 9811)

ERATO—46 Kensington Court, London W8 5DP (071-938 5542)

FACTORY CLASSICAL—322 Uxbridge Road, London W3 9QP

GAMUT DISTRIBUTION—1B Lancaster Way, Ely, Cambridgeshire CB6 3NP (0353 662366)

GIMELL RECORDS—4 Newtec Place, Magdalen Road, Oxford OX4 1RE (0865 244557)

HARMONIA MUNDI (UK)—19-21 Nile Street, London N1 7LR (071-253 0863)

HYPERION RECORDS—PO Box 25, Eltham, London SE9 1AX (081-294 1166)

KEYBOARD RECORDS—418 Brockley Road, London, SE4 2DH (081-699 2549)

KINGDOM RECORDS—Crown House, 119 The Broadway, London NW2 3JG (081-208 4448)

KOCH INTERNATIONAL—23 Warple Way, London W3 0RX (081-749 7177)

L'OISEAU-LYRE—1 Sussex Place, Hammersmith, London W6 9XS (081-846 8515)

LYRITA—99 Green Lane, Burnham, Slough, Bucks SL1 8EG (0628 604208)

MERIDIAN RECORDS—PO Box 317, Eltham, London SE9 4SF (081-857 3213)

MUSIC FOR PLEASURE—1-3 Uxbridge Road, Hayes, Middlesex UB4 0SY (081-561 8722)

MUSIDISC (UK)—32 Queensdale Road, London W11 4SB (071-602 1124)

NEW NOTE DISTRIBUTION—Unit 2, Orpington Trading Estate, Sevenoaks Way, St Mary Cray, Orpington, Kent BR5 3SR (06898 77884)

NIMBUS RECORDS— Wyastone Leys, Monmouth, Gwent NP5 3SR (0600 890682)

OLYMPIA COMPACT DISCS—4th Floor North, Glenthorne House, Hammersmith Grove, London W6 0LG (081-741 9192)

PAVILION RECORDS—Sparrows Green, Wadhurst, East Sussex TN5 6SJ (0892 883591)

PHILIPS CLASSICS—1 Sussex Place, Hammersmith, London W6 9XS (081-846 8515)

PICKWICK GROUP—The Hyde Industrial Estate, The Hyde, London NW9 6JU (081-200 7000)

PINNACLE—Electron House, Cray Avenue, St Mary Cray, Orpington, Kent BR5 3PN (06898 70622)

POLYGRAM CLASSICS—1 Sussex Place, Hammersmith, London W6 9XS (081-846 8515)

POLYGRAM RECORD OPERATIONS—PO Box 36, Clyde Works, Grove Road, Romford, Essex RM6 4QR (081-590 6044)

PRIORY RECORDS—Unit 25, Airfield Estate, Long Marston, Tring, Herts, HP23 4QR (0296 662793)

SAYDISC—Chipping Manor, The Chipping, Wotton-under-Edge, Glos GL12 7AD (0453 845036)

SELECT MUSIC AND VIDEO DISTRIBUTORS—34a Holmethorpe Avenue, Holmethorpe Estate, Redhill, Surrey (0737 248950)

SONY MUSIC ENTERTAINMENT—1 Red Place, London W1Y 3RE (071-629 5555)

TARGET RECORDS—Target House, Cornwall Road, Croydon, Surrey CR9 2TG (081-686 3322)

H R TAYLOR—139 Bromsgrove Street, Birmingham B5 6RG (021-622 2377)

TELDEC CLASSICS—46 Kensington Court, London W8 5DP (071-938 5542)

TER CLASSICS—107 Kentish Town Road, London NW1 8PB (071-485 9593)

TRIM RECORDS—10 Dane Lane, Wilstead, Bedford MK45 3HT (0234 741152)

UNICORN-KANCHANA RECORDS—PO Box 339, London W8 7TJ (071-727 3881)

VIRGIN CLASSICS—474 Harrow Road, London W9 3RU (071-266 2060)

VIRGIN RECORDS—Kensal House, 553-579 Harrow Road, London W10 4RH (081-968 6688)

Manufacturers and Distributors

Entries are listed thus: MANUFACTURER or LABEL. UK Distributor *(Series)*

ACCENT. Gamut

ACCORD. (Musidisc). Gamut

AMON RA (Saydisc). Gamut/Harmonia Mundi/H R Taylor

ARABESQUE. Albany

ARCHIV PRODUKTION. PolyGram Record Operations. *(Archiv Produktion, Archiv Produktion Galleria)*

ARGO. PolyGram Record Operations

ARION. Discovery

AUVIDIS. Koch International. *(Astrée, Valois)*

ASV. ASV/Koch International. *(ASV, Gaudeamus)*

BIS. Conifer

CALLIOPE. Harmonia Mundi

CAPRICCIO. Target

CBS. Sony Music Entertainment. *(CBS, Masterworks, Digital Masters, Maestro)*

CHANDOS. Chandos. *(Chandos, Chaconne, Collect)*

CHESKY. New Note/Trim

CLASSICS FOR PLEASURE. Music for Pleasure

CLAVES. Albany

COLLINS CLASSICS. Harmonia Mundi

CONIFER. Conifer

CONTINUUM. Gamut

CPO. Priory

CRD. Chandos

DECCA. PolyGram Record Operations. *(Decca, New Line, London, Ovation, Enterprise, Grand Opera, Historic, Serenata, Weekend)*

DELOS. Pinnacle

DENON. Conifer

DEUTSCHE HARMONIA MUNDI. BMG Enterprises. *(Deutsche Harmonia Mundi, Editio Classica)*

DG. PolyGram Record Operations. *(DG, DG Galleria, 3-D Classics, 20th Century Classics, Dokumente, Karajan Symphony Edition, Privilege)*

DORIAN. Conifer

ECM New Series. New Note

ELEKTRA-NONESUCH. Warner Classics

EMI. EMI. *(EMI, Reflexe, Studio, Beecham Edition, Great Recordings of the Century, Melodiya, Phoenixa, Références)*

EMI Eminence. Music for Pleasure

EMI Laser. Music for Pleasure

ERATO. Warner Classics. *(Erato, MusiFrance)*

ETCETERA. Harmonia Mundi

FACTORY CLASSICAL. Koch International

FINLANDIA. Conifer

GAMUT CLASSICS. Gamut

GIMELL. Gamut/H R Taylor/Target

GLOBE. New Note

HANSSLER. Koch International

HARMONIA MUNDI. Harmonia Mundi.

HUNGAROTON. Conifer. *(Hungaroton, Antiqua, White Label)*

HYPERION. Gamut/Complete Record Co. *(Hyperion, Helios)*

JECKLIN DISCO. Pinnacle

KEYBOARD. Keyboard Records/Butler

KINGDOM. KINGDOM

KOCH INTERNATIONAL CLASSICS. Koch International

LASERLIGHT (Capriccio). Target

LYRITA. Conifer

L'OISEAU-LYRE. PolyGram Record Operations

MARCO POLO. Select

MERIDIAN. Gamut

MUSICA SVECIAE. Gamut

NAXOS. Select

NEW WORLD. Koch International

NIMBUS. Nimbus

NOVALIS. ASV/Koch International

NUOVA ERA. New Note

OLYMPIA. Complete Record Co. *(Olympia, Explorer)*

OMEGA. Target

ORFEO. Harmonia Mundi

OTTAVO. Priory

PEARL (Pavilion). Harmonia Mundi/H R Taylor

PHILIPS. PolyGram Record Operations. *(Philips, Silver Line, Legendary Classics, Musica da Camera, Concert Classics)*

PICKWICK. Pickwick/Gamut/H R Taylor. *(IMP Classics, IMP Red Label)*

POLSKIE NAGRANIA (Muza). Complete Record Co

PRIORY. Priory

RCA. BMG Enterprises. *(RCA Victor, Red Seal, Gold Seal, Papillon, Seon, Victrola)*

RICERCAR. Gamut

ROYAL OPERA HOUSE RECORDS. Conifer

RPO. Pickwick/Gamut/ASV/Koch International

SALABERT ACTUELS. Harmonia Mundi

SCHWANN. Koch International

SIMAX. Target

SONY CLASSICAL. Sony Music Entertainment

SUPRAPHON. Koch International

SUPRAPHON GEMS. Target

TELARC. Conifer

TELDEC. Warner Classics. *(Teldec Classics, British Line, Das Alte Werk, Das Alte Werk Reference)*

TER Classics. Conifer/Pinnacle

UNICORN-KANCHANA. Harmonia Mundi. *(Unicorn-Kanchana, Souvenir)*

VIRGIN CLASSICS. PolyGram Record Operations. *(Virgin Classics, Veritas)*

VIRGIN VENTURE (Virgin Records). PolyGram Record Operations

WERGO. Harmonia Mundi

Indexes

Names and Nicknames

A

A wandering minstrel
Sullivan: (The) Mikado-operetta

Abegg Variations
Schumann: Theme and Variations on the name "Abegg"—piano, Op 1

Abraham and Isaac
Stravinsky: Abraham and Isaac

Academic Festival Overture
Brahms: Academic Festival Overture, Op 80

Accademico
Vaughan Williams: Concerto for Violin and Strings in D minor

Accursed Huntsman
Franck: (Le) Chasseur maudit—symphonic poem

Adelaide
Beethoven: Adelaide—Lied, Op 46

Adelaide Concerto
Mozart (attrib): Concerto for Violin and Orchestra in D, K294a

Adieu
Mendelssohn: Songs without Words—Op 85/2, A minor

Adieu a Varsovie
Chopin: Rondo in C minor, Op 1

Aeolian Harp
Chopin: Etudes, Op 25—No 13 in A flat

Africa
Saint-Saëns: Fantasie for piano and orchestra in G minor, Op 89

Age of Anxiety Symphony
Bernstein: Symphony No 2

Age of Gold
Shostakovich: (The) Age of Gold—suite from the ballet, Op 21a

Agon
Stravinsky: Agon—ballet

Air de ballet
Gretry: Zemire et Azor—Air de ballet

Air on a G string
Bach: Suite No 3 in D, BWV1068—Air

Alassio
Elgar: In the South, Op 50

Alexander Nevsky
Prokofiev: Alexander Nevsky—cantata

Alla francesca
Vivaldi: RV117—Concerto for Violin and Strings in A minor

Alla Rustica
Vivaldi: RV151—Concerto for Strings in G

Alleluja
Haydn: Symphony No 30 in C

All'Inglese
Vivaldi: RV546—Concerto for Violin and Strings in A

Alpine Symphony
Strauss, R: (Eine) Alpensinfonie, Op 64

Also sprach Zarathustra
Strauss, R: Also sprach Zarathustra—tone poem after Nietzsche

American Quartet
Dvořák: String Quartet in F, Op 96

Amico Fritz
Mascagni: (L')Amico Fritz—opera

Amoroso
Vivaldi: RV271—Concerto for Violin and Strings in E

Ancient Airs and Dances
Respighi: Antiche arie e danze per liuto—orchestra

Andante cantabile
Tchaikovsky: String Quartet No 1 in D, Op 11—movt 2

Antar
Rimsky-Korsakov: Symphony No 2, Op 9

Antartica
Vaughan Williams: Symphony No 7

Anvil Chorus
Verdi: (Il) Trovatore—No 4a

Appassionata
Mendelssohn: Songs without Words—Op 38/5, A minor

Appassionata Sonata
Beethoven: Piano Sonata No 23 in F minor, Op 57

Aranjuez
Rodrigo: Concierto de Aranjuez—guitar and orchestra

Archduke Trio
Beethoven: Piano Trios—No 7 in B flat, Op 97

Arioso
Bach: Cantata No 156—Ich steht mit einem Fuss im Grabe—Sinfonia

Arrival of the Queen of Sheba
Handel: Solomon—No 8c

Art of Fugue
Bach: Art of Fugue, BWV1080

Art thou troubled
Handel: Rodelinda—Dove sei

Arte del Violino
Locatelli: Concerti and Caprices, Op 3

As Vesta was from Latmos Hill
Weelkes: As Vesta was, from Latmos Hill descending—madrigal

Au fond du temple saint
Bizet: (Les) Pêcheurs de perles—No 2b

Autumn
Chaminade: Automne—piano, Op. 35

Autumn
Vivaldi: (12) Concerti, Op 8—No 3, F, RV293

Awake, thou wintry earth
Bach: Cantata No 129—Gelobet sei der Herr, mein Gott

B

Babar the Elephant
Poulenc: Babar the Elephant—narrator and piano

Babiy Yar Symphony
Shostakovich: Symphony No 13 in B flat minor

Bach goes to Town
Templeton: Topsy-Turvy Suite—harpsichord

Bachianas Brasileiras No 5
Villa-Lobos: Bachianas Brasileiras No 5—voice and cellos

Ballet of the Sylphes
Berlioz: (La) damnation de Faust—No 12a

Balm Study
Chopin: Etudes, Op 25—No 14 in F minor

Barber of Bagdad
Cornelius: (Der) Barbier von Bagdad—opera

Barcarolle
Mendelssohn: Songs without Words—Op 85/6, B flat major

Barcarolle
Offenbach: (Les) Contes d'Hoffmann—No 16

Battle of Kerzhents
Rimsky-Korsakov: (The) Legend of the Invisible City of Kitezh—No 3

Battle of Prague
Kotzwara: (The) Battle of Prague

Desérts
Varèse: Desérts

Devil and Kate
Dvořák: (The) Devil and Kate—opera

Devil's Trill Sonata
Tartini: (12) Sonatas—violin and continuo,
Op 2—No 12

Di Ballo
Sullivan: Overture di Ballo—overture

Di tre re
Honegger: Symphony No 5

Diabelli Variations
Beethoven: 33 Variations on a waltz by Diabelli,
Op 120

Didione Abbandonata
Tartini: Sonatas for Violin and Continuo,
Op 6—No 10 in G minor

Dido's Lament
Purcell: Dido and Aeneas—No 2

Dissonance Quartet
Mozart: String Quartet No 19 in C, K465

Distratto
Haydn: Symphony No 60 in C

Divine Poem
Scriabin: Symphony No 3 in C, Op 43

Doctor Gradus ad Parnassum
Debussy: Children's Corner—No 1

Doctor Miracle
Bizet: (Le) Docteur Miracle

Doktor Faust
Busoni: Doktor Faust—poem for music

Domestica
Strauss, R: Sinfonia domestica, Op 53

Don Quichotte
Telemann: Overture-Suite for Strings in G
(Burlesque de Don Quichotte)

Don Quixote
Minkus: Don Quixote—ballet

Don Quixote
Strauss, R: Don Quixote—fantastic variations for
cello and orchestra

Donnerwetter
Mozart: (6) German Dances, K605—No 3

Don't be cross
Zeller: (Der) Obersteiger Sei nicht bös

Dorian Fugue
Bach: Toccata and Fugue in D minor, BWV538

Dove sei
Handel: Rodelinda—Dove sei

Dream of Gerontius
Elgar: (The) Dream of Gerontius—oratorio

Dream Quartet
Haydn: String Quartets, Op 50—No 5, F

Drum Mass
Haydn: Mass No 10 in C

Drum-roll Symphony
Haydn: Symphony No 103 in E flat

Duetto
Mendelssohn: Songs without Words—Op 38/6,
A flat

Dumbarton Oaks
Stravinsky: Concerto in E flat

Dumky
Dvořák: Piano Trio in E minor, Op 90

Dusk
Armstrong Gibbs: Fancy Dress—Dance Suite,
Op 82/1—No 3

E

E lucevan le stelle
Puccini: Tosca—No 16

Easter Hymn
Mascagni: Cavalleria Rusticana—No 6a

Easter Symphony
Foerster: Symphony No 4 in C minor

Ebony Concerto
Stravinsky: Ebony Concerto—clarinet and jazz
ensemble

Eco in Lontano
Vivaldi: RV552—Concerto for two Violins and
Strings in A

Edward
Brahms: (4) Ballades—No 1 in D minor

EC Anthem
Beethoven: Symphony No 9 in D minor,
Op 125—mvt 4 (finale)

Egdon Heath
Holst: Egdon Heath (Homage to
Hardy)—orchestra, H127

Egyptian Concerto
Saint-Saëns: Concerto for Piano and Orchestra
No. 5 in F, Op 103

Eine kleine Nachtmusik
Mozart: Serenade in G, K525

Elegy
Bax: Trio for flute, viola and harp

Elevamini
Williamson: Symphony No 1

Elizabeth of Glamis
Coates: (The) Three Elizabeths—Suite

Elvira Madigan
Mozart: Piano Concerto No 21 in C, K467—movt 2

Emerald Isle
Sullivan: (The) Emerald Isle—operetta

Emperor Concerto
Beethoven: Piano Concerto No 5 in E flat, Op 73

Emperor Quartet
Haydn: String Quartets, Op 76—No 3, C—Theme
and Variations

En bateau
Debussy: Petite Suite—No 1

En blanc et noir
Debussy: En blanc et noir—two pianos

English Folk Song Suite
Vaughan Williams: English Folk Song Suite

Enimga Variations
Elgar: Variations on an Original Theme, Op 36

Entry of the Gladiators
Fučík: Entry of the Gladiators—triumph march,
Op 68

Eroica Symphony
Beethoven: Symphony No 3 in E flat, Op 55

Eroica Variations
Beethoven: (15) Variations and Fugue in F flat,
Op 35

España
Chabrier: España—Rapsodie

Espansiva
Nielsen: Symphony No 3

España Waltz
Waldteufel: España—waltz

Estro armonico
Vivaldi: (12) Concerti, Op 3

Eyeglass Duet
Beethoven: Duo in E flat for viola and cello

F

FAE Sonata
Brahms: Scherzo in C minor (FAE Sonata), Op 5

Fair Maid of Perth
Bizet: (La) Jolie fille de Perth—opera

Fairest Isle
Purcell: King Arthur—Fairest Isle

Fairy Queen
Purcell: (The) Fairy Queen—semi-opera

Fairy's kiss
Stravinsky: (La) Baiser de le fée—ballet

Fall of Warsaw
Chopin: Etudes, Op 10—No 12 in C minor
(Revolutionary)

Fancy
Stanley: (10) Voluntaries, Op 7—No 6 in F

Fantasia on Christmas Carols
Vaughan Williams: Fantasia on Christmas Carols

Fantasia Quartet
Haydn: String Quartets, Op 76—No 6, E flat

Fantasy Sonata
Tippett: Piano Sonata No 1

Fantasía para un gentilhombre
Rodrigo: Fantasía para un gentilhombre—guitar
and orchestra

Farewell Symphony
Haydn: Symphony No 45 in F sharp minor

Faust Symphony
Liszt: (A) Faust Symphony—tenor, chorus and
orchestra, S108

Favorito
Vivaldi: RV277—Concerto for Violin and Strings
in E minor

Façade
Walton: Façade—reciter(s) and chamber ensemble

Feast of Saint Lawrence
Vivaldi: RV556—Concerto in C

Feste Romane
Respighi: Roman Festivals—symphonic poem

Festin de l'araignée
Roussel: (Le) Festin de l'Araignée

Festive
Smetana: Triumph Symphony in E, Op 6

Fifths Quartet
Haydn: String Quartets, Op 76—No 2, D minor

Fille aux cheveux
Debussy: Préludes—Book 1—No 8

Fille de Madame Angot
Lecocq: (La) Fille de Madame Angot

Fingal's Cave
Mendelssohn: (The) Hebrides Overture, Op 26

Finlandia
Sibelius: Finlandia, Op 26

Fire Symphony
Haydn: Symphony No 59 in A

Fireworks
Stravinsky: Fireworks—fantasy for orchestra, Op 4

Fireworks Music
Handel: Music for the Royal Fireworks

First cuckoo
Delius: On hearing the first cuckoo in Spring

Flight of the Bumble Bee
Rimsky-Korsakov: (The) Tale of Tsar Saltan—No 3

Flocks in pastures green abiding
Bach: Cantata No 208—Schlafe können sicher
weiden

Flower Duet
Delibes: Lakmé—No 4b

Flower Song
Bizet: Carmen—No 15c

Flower Song
Puccini: Madama Butterfly—No 13c

Foggy Dew
Britten: The Foggy, Foggy Dew—folksong
arrangement

Forelle (Trout)
Schubert: (Die) Forelle—Lied, D550

Forest Murmurs
Wagner: Siegfried—No 25

Fountains of Rome
Respighi: Fountains of Rome—symphonic poem

Four Ages
Alkan: Grande Sonate, Op 33

Four Last Songs
Strauss, R: Vier Letze Lieder

Four Saints in Three Acts
Thomson: Four Saints in Three Acts—opera

Four Sea Interludes
Britten: Peter Grimes—Nos 2, 11, 16 and 25

Four Seasons
Vivaldi: (12) Concerti, Op 8—Nos 1-4

Four Serious Songs
Brahms: (4) Erste Gesänge—song collection, Op
121

Four Temperaments
Nielsen: Symphony No 2

Four Temperaments
Hindemith: (The) Four Temperaments

Fourth of July
Ives: Holidays—Symphony—No 3

Frank Bridge Variations
Britten: Variations on a theme of Frank Bridge,
Op 10

Frauenliebe und -leben
Schumann: Frauenliebe und -leben—song cycle,
Op 42

Frei aber Einsam
Brahms: Scherzo in C minor (FAE Sonata), Op 5

Frog Quartet
Haydn: String Quartets, Op 50—No 6, D

From Bohemia's woods and fields
Smetana: Má Vlast—No 4

From My Life
Smetana: String Quartet No 1 in E minor

From Old Note Books
Prokofiev: Piano Sonata No 4 in C minor, Op 29

From the Home Country
Smetana: Duos for violin and piano

From the New World
Dvořák: Symphony No 9 in E minor, Op 95

Funeral March
Beethoven: Piano Sonata No 12 in A flat, Op. 26

Funeral March
Chopin: Piano Sonata No 2 in B flat minor,
Op 35—mvt 2

Funeral March
Beethoven: Symphony No 3 in E flat, Op 55—mvt
2

Funeral Ode
Bach: Cantata No 198—Lass Furstin, lass noch
einen Strahl

Funeral Symphony
Haydn: Symphony No 44 in E minor

Fur Elise
Beethoven: (25) Bagatelles—No 25 in A minor

Fêtes
Debussy: Nocturnes—No 2

G

Gardellino
Vivaldi: RV90—Concerto in D

Garden of Fand
Bax: Garden of Fand—tone poem

Gaîté Parisienne
Offenbach: Gaîté Parisienne—ballet

Geist Trio
Beethoven: Piano Trios—No 5 in D, Op 70/1

Gesängszene
Spohr: Concerto for Violin and Orchestra No 8 in
A minor, Op 47

Ghost Trio
Beethoven: Piano Trios—No 5 in D, Op 70/1

Gianni Schicchi
Puccini: Gianni Schicchi—opera

Gipsy and the Nightingale
Benedict: Gipsy and the Nightingale—Song

Gipsy Princess
Kálmán: Zirkusprinzessin—operetta

Gipsy Songs
Dvořák: Gypsy Melodies

Girl with the flaxen hair
Debussy: Préludes—Book 1—No 8

Glagolitic Mass
Janáček: Glagolitic Mass

Goin' home
Dvořák: Symphony No 9 in E minor, Op 95
Golden Age
Shostakovich: (The) Age of Gold—suite from the
ballet, Op 21a
Golden Cockerel
Rimsky-Korsakov: (Le) Coq d'Or—opera
Golden Legend
Sullivan: (The) Golden Legend—cantata
Golden Sonata
Purcell: Sonatas in four parts—No 9 in F
Goldfinch Concerto
Vivaldi: (12) Concerto, Op 10—No 3, G, RV248
Goldfish
Debussy: Images—No 6
Golliwog's cakewalk
Debussy: Children's Corner—No 6
Good Friday Music
Wagner: Parsifal—No 32
Gothic Symphony
Brian, H: Symphony No 1 in D minor
Gothique Symphony
Widor: Symphony No 9 in C minor, Op 70
Goyescas
Granados: Goyescas—suite for piano
Graduation Ball
Strauss II, J: Graduation Ball—ballet arrangement
Grand Canyon
Grofé: Grand Canyon Suite
Grand March
Verdi: Aida—No 10b
Great C major
Schubert: Symphony No 9 in C, D944
Great Mass
Mozart: Mass No 18 in C minor, K427
Great Mass
Bruckner: Mass No 3 in F minor
Great Organ Mass
Haydn: Mass No 5 in E flat
Grosse Fuge
Beethoven: Grosse Fuge in B flat, Op 133
Gum-suckers March
Grainger: In a Nutshell—mvt 4
Gypsy Baron
Strauss II, J: (Der) Zigeunerbaron—operetta
Gypsy Rondo
Haydn: Piano Trio No 25 in G, HobXV/25—movt 3

H

Habanera
Bizet: Carmen—No 5
Haffner Serenade
Mozart: Serenade in D, K250
Haffner Symphony
Mozart: Symphony No 35 in D, K385
Hail bright Cecilia
Purcell: Ode for St Cecilia's Day
Hallelujah Chorus
Handel: Messiah—No 44
Hallelujah Concerto
Handel: Concerti for Organ and Strings II,
Op 7—No 7, B flat, HWV306
Hamlet
Tchaikovsky: Hamlet—Fantasy Overture
Hamlet
Thomas: Hamlet—opera
Hammerklavier Sonata
Beethoven: Piano Sonata No 29 in B flat, Op 106
Handel Variations
Brahms: Variations and Fugue on a theme by
Handel, Op 24
Handel's Largo
Handel: Serse—No 1b
Harmonie Messe
Haydn: Mass No 14 in B flat

Harmonies poétiques et réligieuses
Liszt: Harmonies poétiques et réligieuses—piano,
S173
Harmonious Blacksmith
Handel: (8) Suites, Set I, HWV426-33—No 5a
Harold in Italy
Berlioz: Harold in Italy—symphony for viola and
orchestra, Op 16
Harp Quartet
Beethoven: String Quartet No 10 in E flat, Op 74
Harp Study
Chopin: Etudes, Op 25—No 13 in A flat
Hassan
Delius: Hassan—incidental music
Haunted Ballroom
Toye: (The) Haunted Ballroom—Waltz
Haydn Quartets
Mozart: String Quartets Nos 14-19
Haydn Variations
Brahms: Variations on a theme of Haydn, Op 56
Haydn's Toy Symphony
Mozart, L: Cassation in G (Toy Symphony)
Heavens are telling
Haydn: (Die) Schöpfung—No 13
Hebrews' Chorus
Verdi: Nabucco—No 18
Heiligmesse
Haydn: Mass No 9 in B flat
Heldenleben
Strauss, R: (Ein) Heldenleben—tone poem, Op 40
Hen Symphony
Haydn: Symphony No 83 in G minor
Henry VIII
Saint-Saëns: Henry VIII—opera
Heroic Polonaise
Chopin: Polonaises—No 6 in A flat, Op 53
Hero's Life
Strauss, R: (Ein) Heldenleben—tone poem, Op 40
Hiawatha
Coleridge-Taylor: Hiawatha's Wedding Feast
Historical Symphony
Spohr: Symphony No 6 in G, Op 116
Hodie
Vaughan Williams: Hodie—Christmas cantata
Hoe Down
Copland: Rodeo
Hoffmeister Quartet
Mozart: String Quartet No 22 in D, K499
Holberg Suite
Grieg: Holberg Suite, Op 40
Holidays Symphony
Ives: Holidays—Symphony
Hommage pour le tombeau de Debussy
Falla: Homenaje "Le tombeau de Claude
Debussy"—guitar
Horn Signal Symphony
Haydn: Symphony No 31 in D
Humming Chorus
Puccini: Madama Butterfly—No 14
Hungarian Fantasia
Liszt: Fantasia in Hungarian Folk Themes—piano
and orchestra, S123
Hungarian March
Berlioz: (La) damnation de Faust—No 3b
Hungarian Rhapsodies
Liszt: (19) Hungarian Rhapsodies—piano, S244
Hunnenschlacht
Liszt: Hunnenschlacht—symphonic poem
Hunt Quartet
Mozart: String Quartet No 17 in B flat, K458
Hunt Symphony
Haydn: Symphony No 73 in D
Hunting Song
Mendelssohn: Songs without Words—Op 19/3, A
Hymn of Praise
Mendelssohn: Symphony No 2 in B flat, Op 52

I

I dreamt I dwelt in marble halls
  Balfe: Bohemian Girl—I dreamt I dwelt in marble halls

I know that my Redeemer liveth
  Handel: Messiah—No 45

I vow to thee, my country
  Holst: (The) Planets, H125—mvt 4

I will lay me down in peace
  Greene: O God of my righteousness—anthem

If I were king
  Adam: Si j'étais Roi—opera

Il Distratto Symphony
  Haydn: Symphony No 60 in C

Ilya Murometz
  Glière: Symphony No 3

Im chambre separée
  Heuberger: (Der) Opernball—operetta

Im Walde
  Raff: Symphony No 3, Op 153

Imperial Mass
  Haydn: Mass No 11 in D minor

Imperial Symphony
  Haydn: Symphony No 53 in D

In a Monastery Garden
  Ketèlbey: In a Monastery Garden—characteristic intermezzo

In a Persian Market
  Ketèlbey: In a Persian Market—intermezzo music

In a Summer Garden
  Delius: In a Summer Garden

In an Eighteenth-century drawing room
  Mozart: Piano Sonata No 15 in C, K545

In an English country garden
  Grainger: Country Gardens

In London Town
  Elgar: Cockaigne Overture, Op 40

In the steppes of Central Asia
  Borodin: In the steppes of Central Asia

Incantation
  Martinů: Piano Concerto No 4

Indian Queen
  Purcell: (The) Indian Queen—semi-opera

Indian Suite
  MacDowell: Suite No 2, Op 48

Inextinguishable
  Nielsen: Symphony No 4

Intimate letters
  Janáček: String Quartet No 2

Invitation to the Dance
  Weber: Invitation to the Dance—Rondo brillant in D flat, J260 (orch Berlioz)

Irene
  Holbrooke: Nonet for woodwind and strings

Irish Symphony
  Sullivan: Symphony in E

Irish Symphony
  Stanford: Symphony No 3 in F minor, Op 28

Isle of the Dead
  Rachmaninov: Isle of the Dead—symphonic poem

It was a lover and his lass
  Morley: It was a lover and his lass—ayre

Italian caprice
  Tchaikovsky: Capriccio italien, Op 45

Italian Concerto
  Bach: Concerto in the Italian style (Italian Concerto, BWV971)

Italian impressions
  Charpentier, G: Impressions d'Italie

Italian Serenade
  Wolf: Italian Serenade—string quartet

Italian Symphony
  Mendelssohn: Symphony No 4 in A, Op 90

Ivan IV
  Bizet: Ivan IV—opera

Ivanhoe
  Sullivan: Ivanhoe—opera

J

Jardins sous la Pluie
  Debussy: Estampes—No 3

Jena Symphony
  Witt: Symphony in C

Jeremiah Symphony
  Bernstein: Symphony No 1

Jesu, joy of man's desiring
  Bach: Cantata No 147—Herz und Mund und Tat und Leben—No 10

Jeunehomme Concerto
  Mozart: Piano Concerto No 9 in E flat, K271

Jeux d'enfants
  Bizet: Jeux d'enfants—petite suite

Jewel Song
  Gounod: Faust—No 13

Jewels of the Madonna
  Wolf-Ferrari: (I) Gioielli della Madonna—opera

Jig Fugue
  Bach: Fugue in G, BWV577

Job
  Vaughan Williams: Job—masque for dancing

Joke Quartet
  Haydn: String Quartets, Op 33—No 2, E flat

Josephslegende
  Strauss, R: Josephslegende—ballet

Jota Aragonesa
  Glinka: Jota aragonesa—Spanish Overture No 1

Joyeuse marche
  Chabrier: Joyeuse marche—marche française

Jupiter Symphony
  Haydn: Symphony No 13 in D

Jupiter Symphony
  Mozart: Symphony No 41 in C, K551

K

Kaddisch Symphony
  Bernstein: Symphony No 3

Kaiser Quartet
  Haydn: String Quartets, Op 76—No 3, C—Theme and Variations

Katharinentanze
  Haydn: (12) Minuetti da ballo, HobIX/4

Kegelstadt Trio
  Mozart: Trio in E flat, K498

Kindertotenlieder
  Mahler: Kindertotenlieder—song cycle

King Arthur
  Elgar: King Arthur—incidental music

King Arthur
  Purcell: King Arthur—semi-opera

King of the stars
  Stravinsky: (Le) Roi des étoiles—cantata

King's Hunt
  Byrd: (The) Hunt's up—keyboard

Kreutzer Sonata
  Beethoven: Sonata for Violin and Piano No 9 in A, Op 47

Kreutzer Sonata
  Janáček: String Quartet No 1

Kullervo
  Sibelius: Kullervo Symphony, Op 7

L

La donna è mobile
  Verdi: Rigoletto—No 17

Lady and the Fool
  Verdi: (The) Lady and the Fool—ballet

Lamentatione Symphony
  Haydn: Symphony No 26 in D minor

Mediterranean
Bax: Mediterranean

Mefistofele
Boito: Mefistofele—opera

Melody in F
Rubinstein: (2) Pieces—No 2

Menuets des follets
Berlioz: (La) Damnation de Faust—No 18

Mercury Symphony
Haydn: Symphony No 43 in E flat

Merry Widow
Lehár: (Die) Lustige Witwe

Midi, Le
Field: Nocturnes—No 18, E, H13K

Midi Symphony
Haydn: Symphony No 7 in C

Midsummer Vigil
Alfvén: Swedish Rhapsody No 1, Op 19

Mikrokosmos
Bartók: Mikrokosmos

Military Polonaise
Chopin: Polonaises—No 3 in A, Op 40/1

Military Symphony
Haydn: Symphony No 100 in G

Mimi's farewell
Puccini: (La) Bohème—No 11

Minute Waltz
Chopin: Waltz in D flat, Op 64/1

Miracle Symphony
Haydn: Symphony No 96 in D

Missa Papae Marcelli
Palestrina: Missa Papae Marcelli—6vv

Missa Solemnis
Beethoven: Mass in D minor, Op 123

Mládí
Janáček: Mládí (Youth)—septet for wind ensemble

Moldau
Smetana: Má Vlast—No 2

Moonlight Sonata
Beethoven: Piano Sonata No 14 in C sharp minor, Op 27/2

Morning, Noon and Night
Suppé: (Ein) Morgen, ein Mittag, ein Abend in Wien—local play with songs

Morning papers
Strauss II, J: Morgenblätter—waltz, Op 279

Morning song
Mendelssohn: Songs without words—Op 62/4, G

Mortify us by Thy goodness
Bach: Cantata No 22—Jesus nahm zu sich die Zwölfe

Moses and Aaron
Schoenberg: Moses und Aron—opera

Mozartiana
Tchaikovsky: Suite No 4 in G, Op 61

Musetta's Waltz Song
Puccini: (La) Bohème—No 7b

Musica Notturna della strade di Madrid
Boccherini: String Quartet in C, G324

Musical Joke
Mozart: (Ein) Musikalischer Spass, K522

My heart ever faithful
Bach: Cantata No 68—Ach Gott, wie manches Herzlied—No 2

N

Naïla
Delibes: Naïla—waltz (Pas de fleurs)

Nelson Mass
Haydn: Mass No 11 in D minor

Nessun dorma
Puccini: Turandot—No 17

New Lambach Symphony
Mozart: Symphony in G

New World Symphony
Dvořák: Symphony No 9 in E minor, Op 95

Night in Venice
Strauss II, J: (Ein) Nacht in Venedig—operetta

Night music in the streets of Madrid
Boccherini: String Quartet in C, G324

Night on a bare mountain
Mussorgsky: (A) Night on a bare mountain

Nightingale Song
Zeller: (Der) Vogelhändler—No 12b

Nights in the gardens of Spain
Falla: Noches en los jardines de España—symphonic impressions

Nightwatchman
Biber: Serenade in C

Nimrod
Elgar: Variations on an Original theme, Op 36, 'Enigma'

None shall sleep
Puccini: Turandot—No 17, Nessun dorma

Noonday Witch
Dvořák: (The) Noonday Witch—symphonic poem

Norse
MacDowell: Piano Sonata No 3 in D minor

Norwegian Moods
Stravinsky: (4) Norwegian Moods—orchestra

Norwegian rhapsody
Lalo: Rapsodie norvégienne

Notte
Vivaldi: RV439—Concerto for Flute, Bassoon and Strings in F

Notte
Vivaldi: RV501—Concerto for Bassoon and Strings in B flat

Novelletten
Schumann: (8) Novelletten—piano, Op 21

November steps
Takemitsu: November Steps—orchestra

Nuages
Debussy: Nocturnes—No 1

Nuits d'été
Berlioz: Nuits d'été—solo voices and orchestra

Nullte Symphony
Bruckner: Symphony No 0 in D minor

Nuns' Chorus
Strauss II, J: Casanova—Nuns' Chorus and Laura's Song

Nursery Suite
Elgar: Nursery Suite—orchestra

O

O my beloved father
Puccini: Gianni Schicchi—O mio babbino caro

O praise the Lord
Greene: Praise the Lord, o my Soul—anthem

O Star of Eve
Wagner: Tannhäuser—No 25b

Ocean Symphony
Rubinstein: Symphony No 2 in C, Op 42

Oceanides
Sibelius: (The) Oceanides—tone poem

October
Shostakovich: Symphony No 2 in C

Ode for St Cecilia
Handel: Ode for St Cecilia's Day

Ode to Joy
Beethoven: Symphony No 9 in D minor, Op 125—mvt 4

Ode to Queen Mary
Purcell: Welcome to all the pleasures

Oedipus Rex
Stravinsky: Oedipus Rex—opera

Offrandes
Varèse: Offrandes—soprano and chamber ensemble

Prometheus
Liszt: Prometheus—symphonic poem

Prometheus Unbound
Bantock: Prometheus Unbound—brass band

Prometheus Unbound
Parry: Scenes from Shelley's Prometheus Unbound

Prometheus—Poem of Fire
Scriabin: Prometheus—piano, chorus and orchestra, Op 60

Prussian Quartets
Mozart: String Quartets, K575; K589; K590

Prussian Quartets
Haydn: (6) String Quartets, Op 50

Prussian Sonatas
Bach, C P E: Keyboard Sonatas, Wq48

Prélude à l'après-midi d'un faune
Debussy: Prélude à l'après-midi d'un faune

Purcell's Trumpet Voluntary
Clarke, J: Suite for Trumpet and Strings in D—No 4

Q

Quartet for the end of time
Messaien: Quatuor pour le fin de temps

R

Rage over a lost penny
Beethoven: Rondo a Capriccioso in G, Op 129

Ragtime
Stravinsky: Rag-time—chamber ensemble

Raindrop Prelude
Chopin: Preludes, Op 28—No 15 in D flat

Razor Quartet
Haydn: (3) String Quartets, Op 55—No 2, F minor

Razumovsky Quartets
Beethoven: String Quartets Nos 7-9, Op 59

Recondita armonia
Puccini: Tosca—No 2

Red Pony
Copland: (The) Red Pony—orchestral suite from the film score

Red Poppy
Glière: (The) Red Poppy—ballet

Rediffusion March
Coates: Music Everywhere—march

Reflets dans l'eau
Debussy: Images—No 1

Reformation Symphony
Mendelssohn: Symphony No 5 in D

Reine de France Symphony
Haydn: Symphony No 85 in B flat

Relique Sonata
Schubert: Piano Sonata No 15 in C, D840

Renard
Stravinsky: Renard—burlesque in song and dance

Resurrection Symphony
Mahler: Symphony No 2

Revolutionary Study
Chopin: Etudes, Op 10—No 12 in C minor

Rhenish Symphony
Schumann: Symphony No 3 in E flat, Op 97

Ride of the Valkyries
Wagner: (Die) Walküre—No 31

Rider Quartet
Haydn: (3) String Quartets, Op 74—No 3, G minor

Rio Grande
Lambert: (The) Rio Grande—alto, chorus and orchestra

Riposo
Vivaldi: RV270—Concerto for Violin and Orchestra in E

Ritorna vincitor!
Verdi: Aida—No 6a

Ritual Fire Dance
Falla: El amor brujo—No 8

Rococo Variations
Tchaikovsky: Variations on a Rococo Theme—cello and orchestra

Roi des étoiles
Stravinsky: (Le) Roi des étoiles—cantata

Roman Festival
Respighi: Roman Festival—symphonic poem

Romantic Symphony
Bruckner: Symphony No 4 in E flat

Romeo and Juliet
Prokofiev: Romeo and Juliet—ballet

Romeo and Juliet
Tchaikovsky: Romeo and Juliet—Fantasy Overture

Roméo et Juliette
Berlioz: Roméo et Juliette—dramatic symphony

Roméo et Juliette
Gounod: Roméo et Juliette—opera

Rondo alla turca
Mozart: Piano Sonata in A, K331—mvt 3

Rosary Sonatas
Biber: (16) Sonatas for Violin and Continuo

Rouet d'Omphale
Saint-Saëns: (Le) Rouet d'Omphale in A—orchestra

Roxelane Symphony
Haydn: Symphony No 63 in C

Rugby
Honegger: (3) Symphonic Movements—No 2

Rule, Britannia
Arne: Rule Britannia

Russian Quartets
Haydn: (6) String Quartets, Op 33

Rustic Scenes
Brian: English Suite No 5

Rustic Wedding Symphony
Goldmark: Symphony, Op 26

Rustle of Spring
Sinding: Rustle of Spring—piano, Op 32/3

S

Sabre Dance
Khachaturian: Gayaneh—ballet—No 1

Sailors' Chorus
Wagner: (Der) Fliegende Holländer—No 20

Salomon Symphonies
Haydn: Symphonies Nos 93-104

Salut d'amour
Elgar: Salut d'amour (Liebesgrüss), Op 12

Salzburg Symphonies
Mozart: Divertimenti, K136-8

Santa Lucia
Cottrau: Santa Lucia—song

Sardana
Casals: (La) Sardana—cello ensemble

Scapino
Walton: Scapino—Comedy Overture

Schelomo
Bloch: Schelomo—cello and orchestra

Schoolmaster Symphony
Haydn: Symphony No 55 in E flat

Schubert's Serenade
Schubert: Schwanengesang, D957—song collection—No 4, Ständchen

Schulmeister Symphony
Haydn: Symphony No 55 in E flat

Scottish Symphony
Mendelssohn: Symphony No 3 in A minor

Sea Drift
Delius: Sea Drift—baritone, chorus and orchestra

Sea fever
Ireland: Sea Fever—song

Sea Pictures
Elgar: Sea Pictures—contralto and orch, Op 37

Sea Symphony
  Vaughan Williams: Symphony No 1
Seasons
  Spohr: Symphony No 9 in B flat, Op 143
Seasons
  Haydn: (Die) Jahreszeiten—oratorio
Seasons
  Glazunov: (The) Seasons—ballet
Seasons
  Tchaikovsky: (The) Seasons—piano, Op 37b
Seguidille
  Bizet: Carmen—No 10a
Sei nicht bös
  Zeller: (Der) Obersteiger—Sei nicht bös
Semplice Symphony
  Nielsen: Symphony No 6
Senta's Ballad
  Wagner: (Der) Fliegende Holländer—No 13
Serenade for the doll
  Debussy: Children's Corner—Suite—No 3
Serenata notturna
  Mozart: Serenade in D, D239
Serieuse Symphony
  Berwald: Symphony No 1 in G minor
Seven Deadly Sins
  Weill: (Die) Seiben Todsünden—spectacle
Seven Last Words of Christ
  Haydn: Seven Last Words—string quartet, Op 51
Seven Stars Symphony
  Koechlin: Seven Stars Symphony
Sheep may safely graze
  Bach: Cantata No 208—Was mir behagt, ist die
    muntre Jagd
Shepherds' Farewell
  Berlioz: (L')Enfance du Christ—trilogie sacrée
Shepherds' Thanksgiving
  Beethoven: Symphony No 6 in F, Op 68 (Pastoral)
Show Boat
  Kern: Show Boat—musical comedy
Shropshire Lad
  Butterworth: (A) Shropshire Lad—Rhapsody
Shropshire Lad
  Butterworth: (A) Shropshire Lad—song cycle
Si tra i ceppi
  Handel: Berenice—opera—Si tra i ceppi
Siegfried Idyll
  Wagner: Siegfried Idyll
Siegfried's Journey to the Rhine
  Wagner: Götterdämmerung—No 5
Siegfried's Funeral March
  Wagner: Götterdämmerung—No 37
Silent Night
  Gruber: Stille Nacht—carol
Silver swan
  Gibbons: (The) Silver swan—madrigal (5vv)
Simple Symphony
  Britten: Simple Symphony, Op 4
Sinfonia Antartica
  Vaughan Williams: Symphony No 7
Sinfonia da Requiem
  Britten: Sinfonia da Requiem, Op 20
Sinfonia tragica
  Brian: Symphony No 6
Singuliere Symphony
  Berwald: Symphony No 3 in C
Sirènes
  Debussy: Nocturnes—No 3
Skaters' Waltz
  Waldteufel: (Les) Patineurs—Waltz
Skazka
  Rimsky-Korsakov: Skazka—orchestra, Op 29
Slavonic March
  Tchaikovsky: Marche slave, Op 31
Sleepers, awake
  Bach: Cantata No 140—Wachet auf, ruft uns die
    Stimme

Snow is dancing
  Debussy: Children's Corner—Suite—No 4
Softly awakes my heart
  Saint-Saëns: Samson et Dalila—No 13b
Soir Symphony
  Haydn: Symphony No 8 in G
Soirée dans Grenade
  Debussy: Estampes—No 2
Soldiers' Chorus
  Gounod: Faust—No 18a
Song of the birds
  Casals: (El) Cant dels ocells—cello and piano
Song of the Earth
  Mahler: (Das) Lied von der Erde—symphony for
    contralto, tenor and orchestra
Song of the Flea
  Mussorsgky: Mephistopheles' song of the flea
Song of the Night
  Szymanowski: Symphony No 3, Op 27
Song of the Night
  Mahler: Symphony No 7
Song of the Volga Boatmen
  Traditional: (The) Song of the Volga
    Boatmen—Russian folksong
Sorcerer's Apprentice
  Dukas: (L')Apprenti sorcier—Scherzo on a ballad
    by Goethe
Sortie in E flat
  Léfebure-Wély: Sortie in E flat—organ
Sospetto
  Vivaldi: RV199—Concerto for Violin and Strings
    in C minor
Sound the trumpet
  Purcell: Come ye sons of art away
Source, La
  Delibes: (La) Source—ballet
Souvenir de Florence
  Tchaikovsky: Souvenir de Florence—string sextet,
    Op 70
Spanish caprice
  Rimsky-Korsakov: Capriccio espagnol, Op 34
Spanish Lady
  Elgar: (The) Spanish Lady—opera
Sparrows Mass
  Mozart: Mass No 6 in F, K192
Spartacus
  Khachaturian: Spartacus—ballet
Spem in alium
  Tallis: Spem in alium—motet (40vv)
Spider's web
  Roussel: (Le) Festin de l'araignée—symphonic
    fragments
Spinning Chorus
  Wagner: (Der) Fliegende Holländer—No 11
Spinning Song
  Mendelssohn: Songs without Words—Op 67/4, C
Spring
  Vivaldi: (12) Concerti, Op 8—No 1, E (RV269)
Spring is coming
  Handel: Ottone—La speranza è giunta
Spring Sonata
  Beethoven: Sonata for Violin and Piano No 5 in F,
    Op 24
Spring Song
  Mendelssohn: Songs without Words—Op 62 No 6
Spring Symphony
  Britten: Spring Symphony—soloists, chorus and
    orchestra, Op 44
Spring Symphony
  Schumann: Symphony No 1 in B flat, Op 38
St Anne's Fugue
  Bach: Prelude and Fugue in E flat, BWV552
St Anthony
  Haydn (attrib): Divertimento in B flat
St Anthony Chorale
  Brahms: Variations on a theme by Haydn, Op 56a

Index to Reviews

Artist Index

A

C

663

E

I

L

N

T